TREVANIAN
FOUR COMPLETE NOVELS

TREVANIAN

FOUR COMPLETE NOVELS

The Eiger Sanction

The Loo Sanction

The Main

Shibumi

AVENEL BOOKS · NEW YORK

This edition is published by Avenel Books,
distributed by Crown Publishers, Inc.,
by arrangement with Trevanian.
h g f e d c b a
AVENEL 1981 EDITION

Manufactured in the United States of America

Lines from the following songs are used in *The Main* by permission: "The Best Things in Life Are Free"–Copyright © 1927 by DeSylva, Brown & Henderson, Inc. Copyright renewed. Assigned to Chappell & Co., Inc. All Rights Reserved. Used by permission of Chappell & Co., Inc. "Keep Your Sunny Side Up"–Copyright © 1929 by DeSylva, Brown & Henderson, Inc. Copyright renewed. Assigned to Chappell & Co., Inc. All Rights Reserved. Used by permission of Chappell & Co., Inc. "Rainbow on the River" by Paul Francis Webster and Louis Alter–Copyright © 1936, renewed 1963, Leo Feist, Inc., New York, N.Y. "My Heart Is a Hobo" by Johnny Burke and James Van Heusen–Copyright © 1947 by Burke and Van Heusen, Inc. Copyright renewed and assigned to Bourne Co. and Dorsey Brothers Music, Inc.

Library of Congress Cataloging in Publication Data

Trevanian.
    Four complete novels.

    Contents: The Eiger sanction—The Loo sanction— The Main—Shibumi.
    I. Title.
PS3570.R44A6   1981   813'.54   81-3564
ISBN 0-517-34796-2   AACR2

CONTENTS

TREVANIAN

FOUR COMPLETE NOVELS

The Eiger Sanction

Montreal: *May 16*

EARLIER THAT NIGHT rain had fallen on Boulevard St. Laurent, and there were still triangular pools on the uneven sidewalk. The rain had passed, but it remained cool enough to justify CII operative Wormwood's light tan raincoat. His taste ran more to trench coats, but he dared not wear one, knowing his fellow agents would scoff. Wormwood compromised by turning the collar of his raincoat up and plunging his hands deep into his pockets. One of these hands was clenched around a piece of bubble gum he had received only twenty minutes before from an evil-smelling gnome on the forbidding grounds of Ste. Justine hospital. The gnome had stepped out suddenly from the bushes, giving Wormwood a dreadful start, which he had tried to convert into a gesture of Oriental defense. The image of feline alertness might have been more effective if he had not had the misfortune to back into a rosebush.

Wormwood's step was crisp along the emptying street. He felt uplifted by a sense—not of greatness, to be sure—but of *adequacy*. For once he had not muddled the job. His reflection rippled along a dark shopwindow, and he was not displeased with what he saw. The confident glance and determined stride more than compensated for the sloping shoulders and balding head. Wormwood twisted his palms outward to correct his shoulder slump because someone once told him that the best way to achieve manly posture was to walk with the palms forward. It was most uncomfortable, and it made him walk rather like a penguin, but he did it whenever he thought of it.

He was painfully reminded of his recent encounter with the rosebush, but he discovered that he could relieve his discomfort by nipping the seam of his pants between thumb and forefinger and tugging it away from his buttocks. And this he did from time to time, ignoring the open curiosity of passersby.

He was content. "It's got to be a matter of confidence," he told himself. "I knew I could pull this off, and I pulled it off!" He treasured a theory that one attracted bad luck by anticipating it, and the results of his last several assignments seemed to lend support to the concept. In general, theories did not hold up for Wormwood. To his problem of balding, he had applied the principle of Keep It Short and You'll Keep It Long, and he always wore a crew cut that made him appear less significant than necessary, but his hair continued to fall. For a while, he had clung to the theory that early balding indicated uncommon virility, but personal experience eventually forced him to abandon this hypothesis.

"This time I'm home free, and no screw-up. Six o'clock tomorrow morning I'll be back in the States!"

His fist tightened down on the bubble gum. He could not afford another failure. The men at home base were already referring to him as the "one-man Bay of Pigs."

As he turned left into Lessage Lane, the street seemed empty of sound and people. He took note of this. By the time he had turned south again on St. Dominique, it was so silent that the sound of his footfalls seemed to clip back at him from the facades of unlit, dreary brick buildings. The silence did not disturb him; he whistled as a matter of choice.

"This think-positive bit really scores," he thought jazzily. "Winners win, and that's a fact." Then his round boyish face contracted into concern as he wondered if it was also true that losers lose. He tried to remember his college logic course. "No," he decided at length, "that doesn't necessarily follow. Losers don't always lose. But winners always win!" He felt better for having thought it out.

He was only one block from his third-rate hotel. He could see the damaged sign H TEL in vertical red neon down the street.

"Almost home free."

He recalled CII Training Center instructions always to approach your destination from the opposite side of the street, so he crossed over. He had never fully understood the reason for this rule, beyond simple sneakiness, but it would no more occur to him to demand an explanation than it would to disobey.

St. Dominique's wrought iron streetlamps had not yet fallen prey to urban uglification in the form of lip-blacking mercury lamps, so Wormwood was able to amuse himself by watching his shadow slip out from beneath his feet and grow long before him, until the next lamp assumed domination and projected his shadow, ever shortening, behind him. He was looking over his shoulder, admiring this photic phenomenon, when he ran into the lamppost. Upon recovery, he glanced angrily up and down the street, mentally daring anyone to have seen.

Someone had seen, but Wormwood did not know this, so he glared at the offending lamppost, straightened his shoulders by twisting his palms forward, and crossed to his hotel.

The hall was reassuringly redolent of that medley of mildew, Lysol, and urine characteristic of run-down hotels. According to subsequent reports, Wormwood must have entered the hotel between 11:55 and 11:57. Whatever the exact time, we may be sure he checked it, delighting as always in the luminosity of his watch's dial. He had heard that the phosphorescent material used on watch dials could cause skin cancer, but he felt that he made up for the risk by not smoking. He had developed the habit of checking the time whenever he found himself in a dark place. Otherwise, what was the use of having a watch with a luminous dial? It was probably the time he spent considering this that made the difference between 11:55 and 11:57.

As he climbed the dimly lit staircase with its damp, scrofulous carpet, he reminded himself that "winners win." His spirits sank, however, when he heard the sound of coughing from the room next to his. It was a racking, gagging, disease-laden cough that went on in spasms throughout the night. He had never seen the old man next door, but he hated the cough that kept him awake.

Standing outside his door, he took the bubble gum from his pocket and examined it. "Probably microfilm. And it's probably between the gum and the paper. Where the funnies usually are."

His key turned the slack lock. As he closed the door behind himself, he breathed with relief. "There's no getting around it," he admitted. "Winners—"

But the thought choked in mid-conception. He was not alone in the room.

With a reaction the Training Center would have applauded, he popped the bubble gum, wrapper and all, into his mouth and swallowed it just as the back of his skull was crushed in. The pain was very sharp indeed, but the sound was more terrible. It was akin to biting into crisp celery with your hands over your ears—but more intimate.

He heard the sound of the second blow quite clearly—a liquid crunch—but oddly it did not hurt.

Then something did hurt. He could not see, but he knew they were cutting open his throat. The image of it made him shudder, and he hoped he wouldn't be sick. Then they began on his stomach. Something cold rippled in and out of his stomach. The old man next door coughed and gagged. Wormwood's mind chased the thought that had been arrested by his first fright.

"Winners win," he thought, then he died.

New York: *June 2*

". . . AND, IF NOTHING else, this semester should have taught you that there is no significant relationship between art and society—despite the ambitious pronunciamentos of the popular mass-culturists and mass-psychologists who are driven to spiteful inclusions when faced by important fields beyond their ken. The very concepts of 'society' and 'art' are mutually foreign, even antagonistic. The regulations and limitations of . . ."

Dr. Jonathan Hemlock, Professor of Art, spun out his closing lecture to the mass class in Art and Society—a course he abhorred to teach, but one which was the bread and butter of his department. His lecture style was broadly ironic, even insulting, but he was vastly popular with the students, each of whom imagined his neighbor was writhing under Dr. Hemlock's superior disdain. They interpreted his cold acidity as an attractive bitterness in the face of the unfeeling bourgeois world, an epitome of that *Weltschmerz* so precious to the melodramatic soul of the undergraduate.

Hemlock's popularity with students had several unrelated bases. For one, at thirty-seven he was the youngest full professor in the Art faculty. The students assumed therefore that he was a liberal. He was not a liberal, nor was he a conservative, a Tory, a wet, an isolationist, or a Fabian. He was interested only in art, and he was indifferent to and bored by such things as politics, student freedom, the war on poverty, the plight of the Negro, war in Indochina, and ecology. But he could not escape his reputation as a "student's professor." For example, when he met classes after an interruption caused by a student revolt, he openly ridiculed the administration for lacking the ability and courage to crush so petty a demonstration. The students read this as a criticism of the establishment, and they admired him more than ever.

". . . after all, there are only Art and non-Art. There are no such things as Black Art, Social Art, Young Art, Pop Art, Mass Art. These are merely fictional rubrics designed to grace, through classification, the crap of inferior daubers who . . ."

Male students who had read of Hemlock's international exploits as a mountain climber were impressed by the image of scholar/athlete, despite the fact that he had not climbed for several years. And young ladies were attracted by his arctic aloofness, which they assumed concealed a passionate and mysterious nature. But he was far from the physical idiom of the romantic type. Slim and of average height, only his precise and wiry movements and his veiled green-gray eyes recommended him to their sexual fantasies.

As one might suspect, Hemlock's popularity did not extend to the faculty.

They resented his academic reputation, his refusal to serve on committees, his indifference to their projects and proposals, and his much-publicized student charisma, which term they always inflected so as to make it sound like the opposite of scholarly integrity. His major protection against their snide bile was the rumor that he was independently wealthy and lived in a mansion on Long Island. Typical academic liberals, the faculty were stunned and awkward in the face of wealth, even rumored wealth. There was no way for them to disprove or substantiate these rumors because none of them had ever been invited to his home, nor were they likely to be.

". . . the appreciation of art cannot be learned. It requires special gifts—gifts which you naturally assume you possess because you have been brought up on the belief that you were created equal. What you don't realize is that this only means you are equal to one another . . ."

Speaking automatically, Hemlock allowed his eye to wander over the front row of his amphitheatre classroom. As usual, it was filled with smiling, nodding, mindless girls, their skirts hitched too high and their knees unconsciously apart. It occurred to him that, with their up-turned little smiles and round, empty eyes, they looked like a row of umlaut U's. He never had anything to do with the female students: students, virgins, and drunks he held to be off limits. Opportunities were rife, and he was not enfeebled by free-floating morality; but he was a sporting man, and he ranked the making of these dazzled imbeciles with shining deer and dynamiting fish at the base of the dam.

As always, the bell coincided with the last word of his lecture, so he wrapped up the course by wishing the students a peaceful summer unsullied by creative thought. They applauded, as they always did on last day, and he left quickly.

As he turned the corner of the hall, he encountered a miniskirted co-ed with long black hair and eyes made up like a ballerina's. With excited catches of breath, she told him how much she had enjoyed the course and how she felt closer to Art than ever before.

"How nice."

"The problem I have, Dr. Hemlock, is that I have to keep a B average, or I lose my scholarship."

He fished in his pocket for his office keys.

"And I'm afraid I'm not going to do well enough in your final. I mean—I have gained a great *feeling* for Art—but you can't always put feelings down on paper." She looked up at him, gathered her courage, and tried hard to make her eyes terribly meaningful. "So, if there's anything I can do to get a better grade—I mean, I'd be willing to do anything at all. Really."

Hemlock spoke gravely. "You've considered all the implications of that offer?"

She nodded and swallowed, her eyes shining with anticipation.

He lowered his voice confidentially. "Do you have anything planned for tonight?"

She cleared her throat and said no, she didn't.

Hemlock nodded. "Do you live alone?"

"My roommate's gone for the week."

"Good. Then I suggest you break out the books and study your ass off. That's the surest way I know to ensure your grade."

"But . . ."

"Yes?"

She crumpled. "Thank you."

"A pleasure."

She walked slowly down the hall as Hemlock entered his office, humming to himself. He liked the way he had done that. But his euphoria was transient. On his desk he found notes he had written to himself, reminders of bills soon due and past due. University rumors of private wealth were baseless; the truth was that Hemlock spent each year a little more than three times his income from teaching, books, and commissions for appraisal and evaluation. Most of his money—about forty thousand a year—he earned by moonlighting. Jonathan Hemlock worked for the Search and Sanction Division of CII. He was an assassin.

The telephone buzzed, and he pressed down the flashing button and lifted the receiver. "Yes?"

"Hemlock? Can you talk?" The voice belonged to Clement Pope, Mr. Dragon's first assistant. It was impossible to miss the strained, hushed tone. Pope loved playing spy.

"What can I do for you, Pope?"

"Mr. Dragon wants to see you."

"I assumed as much."

"Can you get over here in twenty minutes?"

"No." Actually, twenty minutes was ample time, but Jonathan loathed the personnel of Search and Sanction. "What about tomorrow?"

"This is top drawer. He wants to see you *now.*"

"In an hour, then."

"Look, pal, if I were you I'd get my ass over here as soon as—" but Jonathan had hung up.

For the next half hour Jonathan puttered around his office. When he was sure he would arrive at Dragon's in something over the predicted hour, he called a taxi and left the campus.

As the grimy, ancient elevator tugged him to the top floor of a nondescript Third Avenue office building, Jonathan automatically noted the familiar details: the scaly gray paint on the walls, the annual inspection stamps slapped haphazardly over one another, the Otis recommendation for load limit, twice scratched out and reduced in deference to the aging machinery. He anticipated everything he would see for the next hour, and the anticipation made him uneasy.

The elevator stopped and swayed slackly while the doors clattered open. He stepped out on the top floor of offices, turned left, and pushed open the heavy NO ADMITTANCE fire door leading to a stairwell. Sitting on the dank cement stairs, his toolbox beside him, was a huge Negro workman in coveralls. Jonathan nodded and stepped past him up the steps. One flight up, the stairs came to an end, and he pressed out through another fire door to what had been the loft of the building before CII had installed a suite of offices there. The smell of hospital, so sharply remembered, filled the hallway where an overblown cleaning woman slowly swung a mop back and forth over the same spot. On a bench to one side of a door bearing: "Yurasis Dragon: Consulting Service," sat a beefy man in a business suit, his briefcase in his lap. The man rose to face Jonathan, who resented being touched by these people. All of them, the Negro worker, the cleaning woman, the businessman, were CII guards; and the toolbox, the mop handle, and the briefcase all contained weapons.

Jonathan stood with his legs apart, his hands against the wall, embarrassed and annoyed with himself for being embarrassed, while the businessman's professional hands frisked part of his body and clothing.

"This is new," the businessman said, taking a pen from Jonathan's pocket. "You usually carry one of French make—dark green and gold."

"I lost it."

"I see. Does this have ink in it?"

"It's a pen."

"I'm sorry. I'll either have to keep it for you until you come out, or I can check it out. If I check it out, you'll lose the ink."

"Why don't you just keep it for me."

The businessman stepped aside and allowed Jonathan to enter the office.

"You are eighteen minutes late, Hemlock," Mrs. Cerberus accused as soon as he had closed the door behind him.

"Thereabouts." Jonathan was assailed by the overwhelming hospital smell of the glistening outer office. Mrs. Cerberus was squat and muscular in her starched white nurse's uniform, her coarse gray hair cropped short, her cold eyes pinched into slits by pouches of fat, her sandpaper skin appearing to have been scrubbed daily with sal soda and a currycomb, her thin upper lip aggressively mustachioed.

"You're looking inviting today, Mrs. Cerberus."

"Mr. Dragon does not like to be kept waiting," she snarled.

"Who among us really does?"

"Are you healthy?" she asked without solicitude.

"Reasonably."

"No cold? No known contact with infection?"

"Just the usual lot: pellagra, syphilis, elephantiasis."

She glared at him. "All right, go in." She pressed a button that unlocked the door behind her, then returned to the papers on her desk, not dealing with Jonathan further.

He stepped into the interlock chamber; the door clanged shut behind him; and he stood in the dim red light Mr. Dragon provided as a mezzo-phase from the glittering white of the outer office to the total dark of his own. Jonathan knew he would adapt to the dark more quickly if he closed his eyes. At the same time, he slipped out of his suit coat. The temperature in the interlock and in Mr. Dragon's office was maintained at a constant 87°. The slightest chill, the briefest contact with cold or flu virus would incapacitate Mr. Dragon for months. He had almost no natural resistance to disease.

The door to Mr. Dragon's office clicked and swung open automatically when the cooler air Jonathan had introduced into the interlock had been heated to 87°.

"Come in, Hemlock," Mr. Dragon's metallic voice invited from the darkness beyond.

Jonathan put out his hands and felt his way forward toward a large leather chair he knew to be opposite Mr. Dragon's desk.

"A little to the left, Hemlock."

As he sat, he could dimly make out the sleeve of his white shirt. His eyes were slowly becoming accustomed to the dark.

"Now then. How have you been these past months?"

"Rhetorical."

Dragon laughed his three dry, precise ha's. "True enough. We have been keeping a protective eye on you. I am informed that there is a painting on the black market that has taken your fancy."

"Yes. A Pissarro."

"And so you need money. Ten thousand dollars, if I am not misinformed. A bit dear for personal titillation."

"The painting is priceless."

"Nothing is priceless, Hemlock. The price of this painting will be the life of a man in Montreal. I have never understood your fascination with canvas and crusted pigment. You must instruct me one day."

"It's not a thing you can learn."

"Either you have it or you haven't, eh?"

"You either got it or you ain't."

Dragon sighed. "I guess one has to be born to the idiom." No accent, only a certain exactitude of diction betrayed Dragon's foreign birth. "Still, I must not deride your passion for collecting paintings. Without it, you would need money less often, and we would be deprived of your services." Very slowly, like a photograph in the bottom of a developing tray, the image of Mr. Dragon began to emerge through the dark as Jonathan's eyes dilated. He anticipated the revulsion he would experience.

"Don't let me waste too much of your time, Mr. Dragon."

"Meaning: let's get to the matter at hand." There was disappointment in Dragon's voice. He had taken a perverse liking to Jonathan and would have enjoyed chatting with someone from outside the closed world of international assassination. "Very well, then. One of our men—code call: Wormwood—was killed in Montreal. There were two assailants. Search Division has located one of them. You will sanction this man."

Jonathan smiled at the cryptic jargon of CII, in which "demote maximally" meant purge by killing, "biographic leverage" meant blackmail, "wet work" meant killing, and "sanction" meant counterassassination. His eyes adjusted to the dark, and Dragon's face became dimly visible. The hair was white as silk thread, and kinky, like a sheep's. The features, floating in the retreating gloom, were arid alabaster. Dragon was one of nature's rarest genealogical phenomena: a total albino. This accounted for his sensitivity to light; his eyes and eyelids lacked protective pigment. He had also been born without the ability to produce white corpuscles in sufficient quantity. As a result, he had to be insulated from contact with people who might carry disease. It was also necessary that his blood be totally replaced by massive transfusions each six months. For the half century of his life, Dragon had lived in the dark, without people, and on the blood of others. This existence had not failed to affect his personality.

Jonathan looked at the face, awaiting the emergence of the most disgusting feature. "You say Search has located only *one* of the targets?"

"They are working on the second one. It is my hope that they will have identified him by the time you arrive in Montreal."

"I won't take them both. You know that." Jonathan had made a moral bargain with himself to work for CII only when it was fiscally necessary. He had to be on his guard against sanction assignments being forced on him at other times.

"It may be necessary that you take both assignments, Hemlock."

"Forget it." Jonathan felt his hands grip the arms of his chair. Dragon's eyes were becoming visible. Totally without coloration, they were rabbit pink in the iris and blood red in the pupil. Jonathan glanced away in involuntary disgust.

Dragon was hurt. "Well, well, we shall talk about the second sanction when the time comes."

"Forget it. And I have some bad news for you."

Dragon smiled thinly. "People seldom come to me with good news."

"This sanction is going to cost you twenty thousand."

"Twice your usual fee? Really, Hemlock!"

"I need ten thousand for the Pissarro. And ten for my house."

"I am not interested in your domestic economy. You need twenty thousand dollars. We normally pay you ten thousand for a sanction. There are two sanctions involved here. It seems to work out well."

"I told you I don't intend to do both jobs. I want twenty thousand for one."

"And I am telling you that twenty thousand is more than the job is worth."

"Send someone else then!" For an instant, Jonathan's voice lost its flat calm.

Dragon was instantly uneasy. Sanction personnel were particularly prone to emotional pressures from their work and dangers, and he was always alert for signs of what he called "tension rot." In the past year, there had been some indications in Jonathan. "Be reasonable, Hemlock. We have no one else available just now. There has been some . . . attrition . . . in the Division."

Jonathan smiled. "I see." After a short silence, "But if you have no one else, you really have no choice. Twenty thousand."

"You are completely without conscience, Hemlock."

"But then, we always knew that." He was alluding to the results of psychological tests taken while serving with Army Intelligence during the Korean War. After re-testing to confirm the unique pattern of response, the chief army psychologist had summarized his findings in singularly unscientific prose:

> . . . Considering that his childhood was marked by extreme poverty and violence (three juvenile convictions for assault, each precipitated by his being tormented by other youngsters who resented his extraordinary intelligence and the praise it received from his teachers), and considering the humiliations he underwent at the hands of indifferent relatives after the death of his mother (there is no father of record), certain of his antisocial, antagonistic, annoyingly superior behaviors are understandable, even predictable.
>
> One pattern stands out saliently. The subject has extremely rigid views on the subject of friendship. There is, for him, no greater morality than loyalty, no greater sin than disloyalty. No punishment would be adequate to the task of repaying the person who took advantage of his friendship. And he holds that others are equally bound to his personal code. An educated guess would suggest that his pattern emerges as an overcompensation for feelings of having been abandoned by his parents.
>
> There is a personality warp, unique to my experience and to that of my associates, that impels us to caution those responsible for the subject. The man lacks normal guilt feelings. He is totally without the nerve of conscience. We have failed to discover any vestige of negative response to sin, crime, sex, or violence. This is not to imply that he is unstable. On the contrary he is, if anything, too stable—too controlled. Abnormally so.
>
> Perhaps he will be viewed as ideal for the purposes of Army Intelligence, but I must report that the subject is, in my view, a personality somehow incomplete. And socially very dangerous.

"So you refuse to take the two sanctions, Hemlock, and you insist on twenty thousand for just one."

"Correct."

For a moment the pink-and-red eyes rested thoughtfully on Jonathan as Dragon rolled a pencil between his palms. Then he laughed his three dry, precise ha's. "All right. You win for now."

Jonathan rose. "I assume I make contact with Search in Montreal?"

"Yes. Search Section Mapleleaf is headed by a Miss Felicity Arce—I assume that is how it is pronounced. She will give you all instructions."

Jonathan slipped on his coat.

"About this second assassin, Hemlock.When Search has located him—"

"I won't need money for another six months."

"But what if *we* should need *you?*"

Jonathan did not answer. He opened the door to the interlock, and Dragon winced at the dim red light.

Blinking back the brilliance of the outer office, Jonathan asked Mrs. Cerberus for the address of Search Section Mapleleaf.

"Here." She thrust a small white card before his eyes and gave him only five seconds to memorize it before replacing it in her file. "Your contact will be Miss Felicity Arce."

"So that really is how it's pronounced. My, my."

Long Island: *June 2*

Now on CII expense account, Jonathan took a cab all the way from Dragon's office to his home on the north shore of Long Island.

A sense of peace and protection descended on him as he closed behind him the heavy oaken door to the vestibule, which he had left unaltered when he converted the church into a dwelling. He passed up through a winding, Gothic-arched stair to the choir loft, now partitioned into a vast bedroom overlooking the body of the house, and a bathroom twenty feet square, in the center of which was a deep Roman pool he used as a bath. While four faucets roared hot water into the pool, filling the room with steam, he undressed, carefully brushed and folded his clothes, and packed his suitcase for Montreal. Then he lowered himself gingerly into the very hot water. He floated about, never allowing himself to think about Montreal. He was without conscience, but he was not without fear. These sanction assignments were accomplished, as difficult mountain climbs once had been, on the highhoned edge of nerve. The luxury of this Roman bath—which had absorbed the profits from a sanction—was more than a sybaritic reaction to the privations of his childhood, it was a necessary adjunct to his uncommon trade.

Dressed in a Japanese robe, he descended from the choir loft and entered through heavy double doors the body of his house. The church had been laid out in classic cruciform, and he had left all the nave as open living space. One arm of the transept had been converted to a greenhouse garden, its stained glass replaced by clear, and a stone pool with a fountain set in the midst of tropical foliage. The other arm of the cross was lined with bookshelves and did service as a library.

He padded barefoot through the stone-floored, high-vaulted nave. The light from clerestories above was adequate to his taste for dim cool interiors and vast unseen space. At night, a switch could be thrown to illuminate the stained glass from without, sketching collages of color on the walls. He was particularly fond of the effect when it rained and the colored light danced and rippled along the walls.

He opened the gate and mounted two steps to his bar, where he made himself a martini and sipped with relish as he rested his elbows back on the bar and surveyed his house with contented pride.

After a time, he had an urge to be with his paintings, so he descended a curving stone stairwell to the basement chamber where he kept them. He had labored evenings for half a year putting in the floor and walling the room with panels from a Renaissance Italian palace that had served interim duty in the grand hall of an oil baron's North Shore mansion. He locked the door behind him and turned on the lights. Along the walls leaped out the color of Monet, Cézanne, Utrillo, Van Gogh, Manet, Seurat, Degas, Renoir, and Cassatt. He moved around the room slowly, greeting each of his beloved Impressionists, loving each for its particular charm and power, and remembering in each instance the difficulty—often danger—he had encountered in acquiring it.

The room contained little furniture for its size: a comfortable divan of no period, a leather pouf with strap handles so he could drag it along to sit before one picture or another, an open Franklin stove with a supply of dry cedar logs in an Italian chest beside it, and a Bartolomeo Cristofore pianoforte which he had had renovated and on which he played with great precision, if little soul. On the floor was a 1914 Kashan—the only truly perfect oriental. And in a corner, not far from the Franklin stove, was a small desk where he did most of his work. Above the desk and oddly out of keeping with the decor were a dozen photographs attached haphazardly to the wall. They were candid shots of mountain episodes capturing climbers with awkward or boyishly clowning expressions—brave men who could not face a lens without embarrassment which they hid by ludicrous antics. Most of the photographs were of Jonathan and his lifelong climbing companion, Big Ben Bowman, who, before his accident, had bagged most of the major peaks of the world with characteristic lack of finesse. Ben simply battered them down with brute strength and unconquerable will. They had made an odd but effective team: Jonathan the wily tactician, and Big Ben the mountain-busting animal.

Only one of the photographs was of a lowland man. In memory of his sole friendship with a member of the international espionage clique, Jonathan kept a photo in which the late Henri Baq grinned wryly at the camera. Henri Baq, whose death Jonathan would one day avenge.

He sat at his desk and finished the martini. Then he took a small packet from the drawer and filled the bowl of an ornate hookah which he set up on the rug before his Cassatt. He hunched on the leather pouf and smoked, stroking the surface of the canvas with liberated eyes. Then, from nowhere, as it did from time to time, the thought strayed into his mind that he owed his whole style of life—academics, art, his house—to poor Miss Ophel.

Poor Miss Ophel. Sere, fluttering, fragile spinster. Miss Ophel of the sand-paper crotch. He had always thought of her that way, although he had had the good sense to play it shy and grateful when she had visited him in the juvenile home. Miss Ophel lived alone in a monument to Victorian poor taste on the outskirts of Albany. She was the last of the family that had founded its fortune on fertilizer brought down the Erie Canal. But there would be no more Ophels. Such modest maternity as she possessed was squandered on cats and birds and puppies with saccharine nicknames. One day it occurred to her that social work might be diverting—as well as being *useful.* But she lacked the temperament for visiting slums that stank of urine and for patting children's heads that well might have had nits, so she asked her lawyer to keep an eye out for a needy case that had some refinement about it. And the lawyer found Jonathan.

Jonathan was in a detention home at the time, paying for attempting to decrease the surplus population of North Pearl Street by two bantering Irish boys who had assumed that, because Jonathan astounded the teachers of P.S. 5 with his knowledge and celerity of mind, he must be a queer. Jonathan was the smaller boy, but he struck while the others were still saying "Oh, yeah?" and he had not overlooked the ballistic advantage of an eighteen-inch lead pipe he had spied lying in the alley. Bystanders had intervened and saved the Irish boys to banter again, but they would never be handsome men.

When Miss Ophel visited Jonathan she found him to be mild and polite, well informed, and oddly attractive with his gentle eyes and delicate face, and definitely *worthy.* And when she discovered that he was as homeless as her puppies and birds, the thing was settled. Just after his fourteenth birthday, Jonathan took up residence in the Ophel home and, after a series of intelligence and aptitude tests, he faced a parade of tutors who groomed him for university.

Each summer, to broaden his education, she took him to Europe where he discovered a natural aptitude for languages and, most importantly to him, a love for the Alps and for climbing. On the evening of his sixteenth birthday there was a little party, just the two of them and champagne and petits fours. Miss Ophel got a little tipsy, and a little tearful over her empty life, and very affectionate toward Jonathan. She hugged him and kissed him with her dusty lips. Then she hugged him tighter.

By the next morning, she had made up a cute little nickname for it, and almost every evening thereafter she would coyly ask him to do it to her.

The next year, after a battery of tests, Jonathan entered Harvard at the age of seventeen. Shortly before his graduation at nineteen, Miss Ophel died peacefully in her sleep. On the surprisingly small residue of her estate, Jonathan continued his education and took occasional summer trips to Switzerland, where he began to establish his reputation as a climber.

He had taken his undergraduate degree in comparative linguistics, cashing in on his logical bent and native gift for language. He might have gone on in that field, but for one of those coincidences that form our lives in spite of our plans.

As a caprice, he took a summer job assisting a professor of Art in the cataloging of artistic orts left over from the confiscation of Nazi troves after the war. The *gratin* of these rethefts had gone to an American newspaper baron, and the leavings had been given to the university as a sop to the national conscience—a healthy organ that had recently rebounded from the rape of Hiroshima with no apparent damage.

In the course of the cataloging, Jonathan listed one small oil as "unknown," although the packing slip had assigned it to a minor Italian Renaissance painter. The professor had chided him for the mistake, but Jonathan said it was no error.

"How can you be so sure?" the professor asked, amused.

Jonathan was surprised at the question. He was young and still assumed that teachers knew their fields. "Well, it's obvious. We saw a painting by the same man last week. And this was not painted by the same hand. Just look at it."

The professor was uncomfortable. "How do you know that?"

"Just look at it! Of course, it's possible that the other one was mislabeled. I have no way to know."

An investigation was undertaken, and it developed that Jonathan was correct. One of the paintings had been done by a student of the minor master. The fact had been recorded and had been general knowledge for three hundred years, but it had slipped through the sieve of Art History's memory.

The authorship of a relatively unimportant painting was of less interest to the professor than Jonathan's uncanny ability to detect it. Not even Jonathan could explain the process by which, once he had studied the work of a man, he could recognize any other painting by the same hand. The steps were instant and instinctive, but absolutely sure. He always had trouble with Rubens and his painting factory, and he had to treat Van Gogh as two separate personalities—one before the breakdown and stay at St. Rémy, one after—but in the main his judgments were irrefutable, and before long he became indispensable to major museums and serious collectors.

After schooling, he took a post teaching in New York, and he began publishing. The articles rolled off, and the women rolled through his Twelfth Street apartment, and the months rolled by in a pleasant and pointless existence. Then, one week after his first book came off the press, his friends and fellow citizens decided he was particularly well suited to blocking bullets in Korea.

As it turned out, he was not often called upon to block bullets, and the few that came his way were dispatched by fellow Americans. Because he was intelligent, he was put into Army Intelligence: Sphinx Division. For four wasted years, he defended his nation from the aggressions of the leftist imperialism by uncovering attempts of enterprising American soldiers to flesh out their incomes by sharing Army wealth with the black markets of Japan and Germany. His work required that he travel, and he managed to squander a laudable amount of government time and money on climbing mountains and on collecting data to keep his academic reputation shiny with articles.

After the nation had handily taught the North Koreans their lesson, Jonathan was released to civilian activities, and he took up more or less where he had left off. His life was pleasant and directionless. Teaching was easy and automatic; articles seldom needed and never received the benefit of a second draft; and his social life consisted of lazing about his apartment and making the women he happened to meet, if the seduction could be accomplished with limited effort, as usually it could. But this good life was slowly undermined by the growth of his passion for collecting paintings. His Sphinx work in Europe had brought into his hands a half dozen stolen Impressionists. These first acquisitions kindled in him the unquenchable fire of the collector. Viewing and appreciating were not enough—he had to possess. Channels to underground and black market paintings were open to him through Sphinx contacts, and his unequaled eye prevented him from being cheated. But his income was insufficient to his needs.

For the first time in his life, money became important to him. And at that very juncture, another major need for money appeared. He discovered a magnificent abandoned church on Long Island that he instantly recognized as the ideal home for himself and his paintings.

His pressing need for money, his Sphinx training, and his peculiar psychological makeup, devoid of any sense of guilt—these things combined to make him ripe for Mr. Dragon.

Jonathan sat for a while, deciding where he would hang his Pissarro when he purchased it from the pay for the Montreal sanction. Then he rose lazily, cleaned and put away the hookah, sat at his pianoforte and played a little Handel, then he went to bed.

Montreal: *June 5*

THE HIGH RISE apartment complex was typical of middle-class democratic architecture. All of the dwellers could get a glimpse of La Fontaine Park, but none could see it well, and some only after acrobatic excesses from their cramped, cantilevered balconies. The lobby door was a heavy glass panel that hinged eight inches from the edge; there was red commercial wall-to-wall carpet, plastic ferns, a padded self-service elevator, and meaningless escutcheons scattered along the walls.

Jonathan stood in a sterile hallway, awaiting response to the buzzer and glancing with distaste at an embossed Swiss print of a Cézanne designed to lend luxury to the corridor. The door opened and he turned around.

She was physically competent, even lush; but she was hardly gift wrapped. In her tailored suit of tweed, she seemed wrapped for mailing. Thick blond bangs, cheekbones wide, lips full, bust resisting the constriction of the suit jacket, flat stomach, narrow waist, full hips, long legs, tapered ankles. She wore shoes, but he assumed her toes were adequate as well.

"Miss . . . ?" he raised his eyebrows to force her to fill in the name because he was still unwilling to rely on the pronunciation.

"Felicity Arce," she said, holding out her hand hospitably. "Do come in. I've looked forward to meeting you, Hemlock. You're well thought of in the trade, you know."

She stepped aside and he entered. The apartment was consonant with the building: expensive anticlass. When they shook hands, he noticed that her forearm glistened with an abundance of soft golden hair. He knew that to be a good sign.

"Sherry?" she offered.

"Not at this time of night."

"Whiskey?"

"Please."

"Scotch or bourbon."

"Do you have Laphroaig?"

"I'm afraid not."

"Then it doesn't matter."

"Why don't you sit down while I pour it." She walked away to a built-in bar of antiqued white under which lurked a suspicion of pine. Her movements were strong, but sufficiently liquid about the waist. He sat at one end of a sectional divan and turned toward the other, so that it would be downright impolite of her to sit anywhere else. "You know," he commented, "this apartment is monumentally ugly. But my guess is that you are going to be very good."

"Very good?" she asked over her shoulder, pouring whiskey generously.

"When we make love. A little more water, please."

"Like so?"

"Close enough."

She smiled and shook her head as she returned with the drink. "We have other things to do than make love, Hemlock." But she sat on the divan as he directed her to with a wave of his hand.

He sipped. "We have time for both. But of course it's up to you. Think about it for a while. And meanwhile, tell me what I have to know about this sanction."

Miss Arce looked up at the ceiling and closed her eyes for a second, collecting her thoughts. "The man they killed was code call: Wormwood—not much of a record."

"What was he doing in Canada?"

"I have no idea. Something for CII home base. It's really none of our business anyway."

"No, I suppose not." Jonathan held out his hand and she took it with a slight greeting pressure of the fingers. "Go on."

"Well, Wormwood was hit in a small hotel on Casgrain Avenue—hm-m-m, that's nice. Do you know that part of town?"

"No." He continued stroking the inside of her wrist.

"Fortunately, CII home base was covering him with a backup man. He was in the next room, and he overheard the hit. As soon as the two assassins left, he went into Wormwood's room and made a standard strip of the body. Then he contacted Search and Sanction immediately. Mr. Dragon got me right on it."

Jonathan kissed her gently. "You're telling me that this backup man just sat next door and let this Wormwood get it?"

"Another whiskey?"

"No, thank you." He stood up and drew her after him. "Where is it? Through there?"

"The bedroom? Yes." She followed. "You must know how they work, Hemlock. The backup man's assignment is to observe and report, not to interfere. Anyway, it seems they were testing a new device."

"Oh? What kind of device? I'm sorry, dear. These little hooks always confuse me."

"Here, I'll do it. They've always had a problem covering the movements and sound of the backup man when they stake him out in the next room. Now they've hit on the idea of having him *make* noise, rather than trying to keep him quiet—"

"Good God! Do you keep these sheets in the refrigerator?"

"That's silk for you. What they're experimenting with is a tape recording of the sound of an old man's coughing—playing it day and night, advertising the presence of someone in the next room, but someone no one would imagine is an agent. Oh! I'm very sensitive there. It tickles now, but it won't later. Isn't that clever?"

"The coughing old man? Oh, yes, clever."

"Well, as soon as Mr. Dragon sent me the B-3611 form I got to work. It was pretty easy. The outside is particularly good for me."

"Yes, I sensed that."

"It seems this Wormwood wasn't a total incompetent. He wounded one of the two men. The backup agent saw them leave the hotel, and even from the window he could tell that one of them was limping. The other one—the one who wasn't hurt—must have been panicked. He ran—Oh, that is beautiful!—He ran into a lamppost across from the hotel. When he stopped to recover, the backup man recognized him. The rest was—agh! Agha!—the rest was easy."

"What's the mark's name?"

"Kruger. Garcia Kruger. A very bad type."

"You're kidding about the name."

"I never kid about names. Oh-a-ar! Graggah!"

"What do you mean, he's a bad type?"

"The way he got Wormwood. He—Oh, God! He . . . He . . ."

"Press down with the soles of your feet!"

"All right. Wormwood swallowed a pellet he was carrying. Kruger went after it with a knife. Throat and stomach. Oh! Adagrah! Oh, yes . . . yes . . . yes . . ."

"Read much Joyce?"

She forced words out through a tight jaw, small squeaks of air escaping from her contracted throat. "No, Agh! Why do you ask?"

"Nothing important. What about the other man?"

"The one who limped? Don't know yet. Not a professional, we're sure of that."

"How do you know he's not a professional?"

"He got sick while Kruger was working on Wormwood. Threw up on the floor. Ogha? Ogah? Arah-ah-agh-ga-gahg!" She arched her strong back and lifted him off the bed. He joined her in release.

For a time there were soft caresses and gentle pelvic adjustments.

"You know, Hemlock," her voice was soft, relaxed, and a little graveled from effort. "You really have magnificent eyes. They're rather tragicomic eyes."

He expected this. They always talked about his eyes afterwards.

Some time later, he sat on the edge of the tub, holding up a rubber sac in an unsuccessful attempt to allow water to seek its own level. Part of his charm lay in these little attentions.

"I've been thinking about your gun, Hemlock."

"What about it?"

"The information sent up by Mr. Dragon indicated you used a large caliber."

"True. I have to. I'm not much of a shot. Finished?"

"Uh-huh."

They dressed and had another whiskey in the sterile living room. In detail, Miss Arce went over the daily habits and routine of Garcia Kruger, answering questions raised by Jonathan. She ended with: "It's all in the tout we amassed. You should study it, then destroy it. And here's your gun." She gave him a bulky brown package. "Will I see you again?"

"Would that be wise?"

"I suppose not. May I tell you something? Just as I—well, at the top—can you imagine what ran through my mind?"

"No."

"I remembered that you were a killer."

"And that bothered you?"

"Oh, no! Quite the contrary. Isn't that odd?"

"It's rather common, actually." He collected the tout and the gun and walked to the door. She followed him, anticipating a final kiss, insensitive to his postcoitus frost.

"Thank you," she said softly, "for the advice about pushing down with the feet. It certainly helps."

"I like to leave people a little richer for having known me."

She held out her hand and he took it. "You really have magnificent eyes, Hemlock. I'm very glad you came."

"Good of you to have me."

In the hall, as he waited for the elevator, he felt pleased about the evening. It had been simple, uncomplicated, and temporarily satisfying: like urination. And that was the way he preferred his lovemaking to be.

In general, his sex life was no more heroic than, say, the daydreams of the average bachelor. But romantic activity tended to peak when he was on sanction assignments. For one thing, opportunities abounded at such times. For another, his sexual appetite was whetted by the danger he faced, perhaps a microcosmic instance of that perverse force of nature that inflates birthrates during wartime.

Once in bed, he was really very good. His mechanical competence was not a matter of plumbing, in which respect he differed little from the mass of men. Nor, as we have seen, was it a result of wooing and careful preparation. It was, instead, a function of his remarkable staying powers and his rich experience.

Of the experience, it suffices to say that his control was seldom betrayed by the tickle of curiosity. After Ankara, and Osaka, and Naples, there were no postures, no ballistic nuances foreign to him. And there were only two kinds of women with whom he had never had experience: Australian Abos and Eskimos. And neither of these ethnic gaps was he eager to fill, for reasons of olfactory sensitivity.

But the more significant contribution to his epic endurance was tactile. Jonathan felt nothing when he made love. That is to say, he had never experienced that local physical ecstasy we associate with climax. To be sure, his biological factory produced semen regularly, and an overabundance disturbed him, interfered with his sleep, distracted him from work. So he knew great relief at the moment of discharge. But his relief was a termination of discomfort, not an achievement of pleasure.

So he was more to be pitied for the basis of his remarkable control than he was to be envied for the competence it granted him.

Montreal: *June 9*

HE FINISHED HIS smoke then flushed the contents of his ashtray down the toilet. He sat fully clothed on his bed and did a calming unit, breathing deeply and regularly, softening in turn every muscle in his body, his fingertips pressed lightly together and his concentration focused on his crossed thumbs. The dim of his hotel room was lacerated by lances of sunlight through the partially closed blinds. Motes of dust hovered in the shafts of light.

He passed the morning rehearsing Garcia Kruger's daily routine for a final time before he destroyed the Search tout. Then he had visited two art galleries, strolling with deliberate step, pressing his metabolic rate down to prepare himself for the task before him.

When his body and mind were completely ready, he rose slowly from bed and opened the top drawer of a chest to take out a brown bag folded over the top like a lunch bag, but containing the silenced revolver Miss Arce had given him. He slipped an identical bag, empty and folded flat, into his coat pocket, then he left his room.

Kruger's office was on a narrow, dirty street just off St. Jacques, near the Bonaventure Freight Station. "Cuban Import and Export—Garcia Kruger." An ostentatious name for a company that received and sent no shipments, and a ludicrous name for the man, the product of some random sperm a German sailor had left for safekeeping in the womb of a Latin lady. Just in front of the building some children were playing, *cache-cache* among the stoops. In fleeing from a pursuer, a ragged gamin with a hungry face and aerodynamic ears bumped into Jonathan, who held onto him to keep him from falling. The boy was surprised and embarrassed, so he scowled to conceal his discomfort.

"I'm afraid you've had it, kid," Jonathan said in French. "Running into a Protestant citizen is an act of FLQ terrorism. What's your name?"

The boy read game-playing in Jonathan's mock-tough voice, and he went along with it. "Jacques," he said, with the broad *au* diphthong of Quebec horsetalk.

Jonathan mimed a notebook in the palm of his hand. "J-a-c-q-u-e-s. Right! If it happens again, I'll turn you over to Elliot."

After an instant of indecision, the boy grinned at Jonathan and ran off to continue his play.

Garcia Kruger shared a second floor with a dentist and a dance instructor. The lower halves of their windows were painted over with advertisements. Just inside the entrance, Jonathan found the cardboard box he had instructed Miss Arce to have left for him. He carried it up the worn wooden stairs, the loose strips of cross-hatched metal squeaking under his foot. The corridor was cool and silent after the brilliant, cacophonous street. Both the dentist and the dance instructor had gone home for the day, but Jonathan knew from the tout that he would find Kruger in.

His knock was answered by, "Who's there?" from an irritated voice within.

"I'm looking for Dr. Fouchet," Jonathan said in a valid imitation of the smiling/stupid voice of a salesman.

The door opened a few inches and Kruger looked out over a latch chain. He was tall, cadaverous and balding, with a day's growth on his cheeks and dots of white mucus in the corners of his eyes. His shirt was crumpled blue and white stripe, wet in irregular crescents under the arms. And on his forehead there was a scabbed-over bruise, doubtless from his contact with the lamppost.

Jonathan looked awkward and incompetent with the cardboard box in his arms and the brown paper bag balanced on top and held under his chin. "Hi. I'm Ed Benson? Arlington Supplies?"

Kruger told him the dentist was gone for the day, and started to close the door. Jonathan quickly explained that he had promised to bring Dr. Fouchet a sample of their new dental floss, but he had been delayed ". . . and not by business either," he added, winking.

Kruger leered knowingly, and from his teeth it was evident that he was only casually acquainted with the dentist. But his tone was not civil. "I told you he was out."

Jonathan shrugged. "Well, if he's out, he's out." He started to turn away. Then, as though an idea had struck him, "Say! I could leave the sample with you, sir. And you could give it to Dr. Fouchet in the morning." He produced his most disarming smile. "It would sure get my ass out of the sling."

Grudgingly, Kruger said he would take it. Jonathan started to hand him the box, but the latch chain was in the way. Kruger closed the door with an angry snap, undid the chain, and opened it again. As Jonathan entered, he babbled about how hot it was on the street, but how it wasn't so much the heat as the humidity that got you down. Kruger grunted and turned away to look out the window, leaving Jonathan to put the box down wherever he could in the littered office.

Thunt! The sound of a silenced thirty-eight firing through a paper bag.

Kruger was spun around and slammed into the corner between the windows on which "Cuban Imports" was written backward. He stared at Jonathan with total astonishment.

Jonathan watched him narrowly, expecting a movement toward him.

Kruger lifted his hands, palm up, with a touching gesture of "Why?"

Jonathan considering firing again.

For two terribly long seconds, Kruger remained there, as though nailed to the wall.

Jonathan began to smart with discomfort. "Oh, come, on!"

And Kruger slid slowly down the wall as death dimmed his eyes and set them in an infinity focus, the repulsive white dots of mucus still visible. Never having met Kruger before today, and not having any apparent motive, Jonathan had no fear of identification. He folded up the ruptured bag and placed it and the gun inside the fresh bag he had brought along.

People never carry guns in brown paper bags.

Outside in the glare of the street, the children still played around the stoops. Little Jacques saw Jonathan emerge from Kruger's building, and he waved from across the street. Jonathan made a gun with his fingers and shot at the boy, who threw up his hands and fell to the pavement in a histrionic facsimile of anguish. They both laughed.

Montreal/New York/
Long Island: *June 10*

WHILE HE WAITED for the plane to taxi off, Jonathan laid out his briefcase and papers on the seat beside him and began taking notes for the long overdue article on "Toulouse-Lautrec: A Social Conscience." He had promised it to the editors of an art journal with a liberal bent. He could spread out in comfort because it was his practice, when on CII expense account, to purchase two adjacent seats to insulate himself against unwanted conversation. On this occasion, the extravagance may have been unnecessary, as the first-class compartment was nearly empty.

His line of thought was severed by the paternal and plebeian voice of the pilot assuring him that he knew where they were going and at what altitude they would fly. His interest in the Lautrec article was too fragile to survive the interruption, so he began glancing through a book he had promised to review. It was a study of *Tilman-Reimanschneider: The Man and His Times*. Jonathan was acquainted with the author and he knew the book would be a compromise between academic and general readerships—an alternation between the turgid and the cute. Nevertheless, he intended to give it a handsome review in obedience to his theory that the surest way to maintain position at the top of the field was to advance and support men of clearly inferior capacities.

He sensed the brush of her perfume, a spicy but light fragrance that he recalls to this day, suddenly and when he least wants to.

"Both of these seats are yours?" she asked.

He nodded without looking up from his work. To his great disappointment, he had caught a glimpse of a uniform out of the tail of his eye, and he rejected her, realizing that stewardesses, like nurses, were something a man made do with in strange towns when there was not time to seek women.

"Veblen had a phrase for that." Her voice was like a flow of warm honey.

Surprised by erudition in a stewardess, he closed the book on his lap and looked up into the calm, amused eyes. Soft brown with harlequin flecks of gold. "The phrase would apply equally to Mimi in the last act."

She laughed lightly: strong white teeth and slightly petulant lips. Then she checked his name off a list on a clipboard, and walked aft to deal with other passengers. With unabashed curiosity, he examined her taut bottom with its characteristic African shape that lifts black women to so convenient an angle. Then he sighed and shook his head. He returned to the Riemanschneider study, but his eyes moved over the pages without the words getting to his brain. Later he took notes; then he dozed.

"Shit?" she asked, her lips close to his ear.

He woke and turned his head to look up at her. "Pardon me?" The movement brought her bust to within three inches of his nose, but he kept his eyes on hers.

She laughed—again the harlequin flecks of gold in the brown eyes—and sat back on the armrest.

"You *did* begin this conversation by saying 'shit,' didn't you?" he asked.

"No. I didn't say it. I asked it."

"Does that go along with coffee, tea, and milk?"

"Only on our competitors' lines. I was reading over your shoulder, and I saw the word 'shit' with two exclamation points on your notepad. So I asked."

"Ah. It was a comment on the content of this book I'm reviewing."

"A study of scatology?"

"No. A shoddy piece of research obfuscated by crepuscular logic and involute style."

She grinned. "I can stand crepuscular logic, but involute style really makes my ass tired."

Jonathan enjoyed the raised oriental corners of her eyes in which a hint of derision lurked. "I refuse to believe you're a stewardess."

"As in: What's a girl like you doing in . . . ? Actually, I'm not a stewardess at all. I'm a highjacker in drag."

"That's reassuring. What's your name?"

"Jemima."

"Stop it."

"I'm not putting you on. That's my real name. Jemima Brown. My mother was hooked on ethnic lore."

"Have it your way. So long as we both admit that it's clearly too much for a black girl to have a name like that."

"I don't know. People don't forget you if your name is Jemima." She adjusted her perch on the armrest, and the skirt slipped up.

Jonathan concentrated on not noticing. "I doubt that men would forget you easily if your name was Fred."

"Goodness me, Dr. Hemlock! Are you the kind of man who tries to pick up stewardesses?"

"Not normally but I'm coming around to it. How did you know my name?"

She became serious and confidential. "It's this mystic thing I have with names. A gift of sorts. I look at a person carefully. Then I concentrate. Then I check the passenger list. And *voilà!* The name just comes to me."

"All right. What do people call you when they're not hooked on ethnic lore?"

"Jem. Only they spell it like the jewel kind of gem." A soft gong caused her to look up. "We're coming in. You'll have to fasten your safety belt." Then she moved aft to deal with the less interesting passengers.

He would have liked to ask her out to dinner or something. But the moment had been lost, and there is no social sin like poor timing. So he sighed and turned his attention to the tilted and toylike picture of New York beyond the window.

He saw Jemima briefly in JFK terminal. While he was hailing a taxi, she passed with two other stewardesses, the three walking quickly and in step, and he remembered his general dislike of the ilk. It would not be accurate to say that he put her out of his mind during the long drive home to the North Shore, but he was able to tuck her away into a defocused corner of his consciousness. It was oddly comforting to know she existed out there—like having a little something keeping warm on the back of the stove.

Jonathan soaked in the steaming water of his Roman bath, the tension of the past few days slowly dissolving, the cords of his neck unknotting, the tightness behind his eyes and in his jaw muscles melting reluctantly. But the knot of fear remained in his stomach.

A martini at his bar; a pipe in the basement gallery; and he found himself rummaging around in the kitchen for something to eat. His search was rewarded with some Danish biscuits, a jar of peanut butter, a small tin of kimchee, and a split of champagne. This gastronomic holocaust he carried to the wing of the transept he had converted into a greenhouse garden, and there he sat beside the plashing pool, lulled by the sound of the water and the brush of warm sunlight.

Little drops of perspiration tingled on his back as he began to doze, the vast peace of his house flowing over him.

Then suddenly he snapped up—an image of suprised eyes with white dots of mucus had chased him out of a dream. He was nauseated.

Getting too old for this, he complained. How did I ever get into it?

Three weeks after the discovery of the abandoned church had added to his need for money, he had found himself in Brussels attending a convention and squandering Ford Foundation money. Late one wet and blustery night, a CII agent dropped into his hotel room and, after beating about the bush, asked him to do a service for his country. Recovering from a good laugh, Jonathan asked for a fuller explanation. The task was fairly simple for a man with Sphinx training: they wanted him to slip an envelope into the briefcase of an Italian delegate to the convention. It is difficult to say why he agreed to the thing. He was bored, to be sure, and the hint of fiscal return came at a time when he had just located his first Monet. But there was also the fact that the Italian had recently had the effrontery to suggest that he knew almost as much about the Impressionists as Jonathan.

At all events, he did the thing. He never knew what was in the envelope, but he later heard that the Italian had been picked up by agents of his own government and imprisoned for conspiracy.

When he returned to New York, he found an envelope waiting for him with two thousand dollars in it. For expenses, the note had said.

In the ensuing months, he performed three similar messenger jobs for CII and received the same liberal pay. He was able to buy one painting and several sketches, but the church was still beyond his means. He feared that someone else would buy his home—he already thought of it as his. The danger of this was really rather remote. Most of the Long Island religious groups were abandoning traditional churches in favor of A-frame redwood boxes more suited to their use of God.

The climax of this work—a testing period, he discovered later—came in Paris where he was passing the Christmas vacation advising a Texas museum on purchases—attempting to convince them that small paintings could be as valuable as big ones. CII set up an assignment, a simple matter of introducing damaging material into the notebooks of a French government official. Unfortunately, the mark walked in while Jonathan was at work. The ensuing battle went badly at first. As the pair grappled and wrestled around the room, Jonathan was distracted by his attempt to protect a Limoges shepherdess of rare beauty which was in constant danger of being knocked from its fragile table. Twice he released his hold on the Frenchman to catch it as it toppled, and twice his adversary took the opportunity to belabor his back and shoulders with his walking stick. For many minutes the struggle continued. Then suddenly the Frenchman had the statuette in his hand and he hurled it at Jonathan. With shock and fury at the wanton destruction of a thing of beauty, Jonathan saw it shatter against a marble fireplace. He roared with rage and drove the heel of his hand into the rib cage just below the heart. Death was instantaneous.

Later that night Jonathan sat near the window of a café on the Place St.

Georges, watching snow swirl around scuttling passersby. He was surprised to recognize that the only thing he felt about the episode—other than the bruises—was a deep regret over the Limoges shepherdess. But one thing he decided irrevocably: he would never again work for CII.

Late one afternoon, shortly after the beginning of the second semester, he was interrupted in his office work by a visit from Clement Pope. His dislike for this officious flunkey was immediate and enduring.

After Pope had cautiously closed the office door, checked into the cubicle reserved for Jonathan's assistants, and glanced out the windows to the snow-dappled campus, he said meaningfully, "I'm from CII. SS Division."

Jonathan scarcely glanced up from his papers. "I'm sorry, Mr. Pope. Working for you people no longer amuses me."

"SS stands for Search and Sanction. You've heard of us?"

"No."

Pope was pleased. "Our security is the tightest. That's why nobody has heard of us."

"I'm sure your reputation is deserved. Now, I'm busy."

"You don't have to worry about that Frog, buddy-boy. Our people in Paris covered it up." He sat on the edge of the desk and paged through the first papers he found there.

Jonathan's stomach tightened. "Get out of here."

Pope laughed. "You really expect me to walk out that door, pal?"

Jonathan judged the distance between them. "Either the door or the window. And we're four stories up." His gentle, disarming smile came on automatically.

"Listen, pal—"

"And get your ass off my desk."

"Look, buddy—"

"And don't call me 'buddy' or 'pal.'"

"Man, if I weren't under orders . . ." Pope flexed his shoulders and considered the situation for a second, then he rose from the desk. "Mr. Dragon wants to talk to you." Then, to save face, he added, "And right now!"

Jonathan walked to the corner of his office and drew himself a cup of coffee from the urn. "Who is this Mr. Dragon?"

"My superior."

"That doesn't narrow the field much, does it."

"He wants to talk to you."

"So you said." Jonathan set the cup down. "All right. I'll make an appointment for him."

"To come here? That's funny!"

"Is it?"

"Yeah." Pope frowned and made a decision. "Here, read this, pal." He drew an envelope from his coat pocket and handed it to Jonathan.

Dear Dr. Hemlock:

If you are reading this, my man has already failed to persuade you by sheer force of personality. And I am not surprised. Naturally, I should have come to see you in person, but I don't get about well, and I am most pressed for time.

I have a proposition for you that will demand very little of your time and which can net you upwards of thirty thousand dollars per annum, tax free. I believe a stipend like this would allow you to purchase the church on Long Island you have been yearning for, and it might even permit you to add to your illegal collection of paintings.

Obviously, I am attempting to impress you with my knowledge of your life and secrets, and I do hope I have succeeded.

If you are interested, please accompany Mr. Pope to my office where you shall meet . . .

Your Obedient Servant,
Yurasis Dragon

Jonathan finished the letter and replaced it thoughtfully in its envelope.

"Well?" Pope asked. "What do you say, pal?"

Jonathan smiled at him as he rose and crossed the room. Pope was smiling in return when the backhand slap knocked him off balance.

"I told you not to call me 'pal.' Dr. Hemlock will do just fine."

Tears of anger and smart stood in Pope's eyes, but he controlled himself. "Are you coming with me?"

Jonathan tossed the letter onto his desk. "Yes, I think I shall."

Before they left, Pope took the letter and put it in his pocket. "Mr. Dragon's name appears on paper nowhere in the United States." he explained. "Matter of fact, I don't remember him writing a letter to anyone before."

"So?"

"That ought to impress you."

"Evidently I impress Mr. Dragon."

Jonathan groaned and woke up. The sunlight had gone, and the greenhouse garden was filled with a gray, inhospitable light. He rose and stretched the stiffness out of his back. Evening was bringing leaden skies from the ocean. Outside, the chartreuse undersides of leaves glowed dimly in the still air. The forevoice of thunder predicted a heavy rain.

He padded into the kitchen. He always looked forward to rain, and he prepared to receive it. When, some minutes later, the storm rolled over the church, he was enthroned in a huge padded chair, a heavy book in his lap and a pot of chocolate on the table beside him. Beyond the pool of light in which he read, dim patterns of yellow, red, and green rippled over the walls as the rain coursed down the stained glass windows. Occasionally, the forms within the room brightened and danced to flashes of lightning. Hard-bodied rain rattled on the lead roof; and wind screamed around corners.

For the first time, he went through the ritual of the ancient elevator in the Third Avenue office building, of the disguised guards outside Dragon's office, of the ugly and hygienic Miss Cerberus, of the dim red light and superheated interlock chamber.

His eyes slowly irised open, discovering misty forms. And for the first time Dragon's bloodred eyes emerged to shock and sicken him.

"You find my appearance disturbing, Hemlock?" Dragon asked in his atonic, cupric voice. "Personally, I've come to terms with it. The affliction is most rare—something of a distinction. Genetic indispositions like these indicate some rather special circumstances of breeding. I fancy the Hapsburgs took a similar pride in their hemophilia." The dry skin around Dragon's eyes crinkled up in a smile, and he laughed his three arid ha's.

The parched, metallic voice, the unreal surroundings, and the steady gaze of those scarlet eyes made Jonathan want this interview to end. "Do you have anything against coming to the point?"

"I don't mean to draw this chat out unduly, but I have so little opportunity to chat with men of intelligence."

"Yes, I met your Mr. Pope."

"He is loyal and obedient."

"What else can he be?"

Dragon was silent for a moment. "Well, to work. We have made a bid on an abandoned Gothic church on Long Island. You know the one I mean. It is our intention to have it torn down and to convert the grounds into a training area for our personnel. How do you feel about that, Hemlock?"

"Go on."

"If you join us, we shall withdraw our bid, and you will receive a sufficient advance in salary to make a down payment. But before I go on, tell me something. What was your reaction to killing that French fellow who broke the statuette?"

In truth, Jonathan had not even thought about the affair since the morning after it happened. He told Dragon this.

"Grand. Just grand. That confirms the Sphinx psychological report on you. No feelings of guilt whatsoever! You are to be envied."

"How did you know about the statuette?"

"We took telephoto motion pictures from the top of a nearby building."

"Your cameraman just happened to be up there."

Dragon laughed his three dry ha's. "Surely you don't imagine the Frenchman walked in on you by coincidence?"

"I could have been killed."

"True. And that would have been regrettable. But we had to know how you reacted under pressure before we felt free to make this handsome offer."

"What exactly do you want me to do?"

"We call it 'sanctioning.' "

"What do other people call it?"

"Assassination." Dragon was disappointed when the word dropped without rippling Jonathan's exterior. "Actually, Hemlock, it's not so vicious as it sounds to the virgin ear. We kill only those who have killed CII agents in the performance of their duties. Our retribution is the only defense the poor fellows have. Allow me to give you some background on our organization while you are making up your mind to join us. Search and Sanction . . ."

CII came into being after the Second World War as an anode organization for collecting the many bureaus, agencies, divisions and cells engaged in intelligence and espionage during that conflict. There is no evidence that these groups contributed to the outcome of the war, but it has been claimed that they interfered less than did their German counterparts, principally because they were less efficient and their errors were, therefore, less telling.

The government realized the inadvisability of dumping onto the civilian population the social misfits and psychological mutants that collect in the paramilitary slime of spy and counterspy, but something had to be done with the one hundred and two organizations that had flourished like fungus. The Communists were clearly devoted to the game of steal-the-papers-and-photograph-something; so, with a kind of ambitious me-too-ism, our elected representatives brought into being the bulky administrative golem of the CII.

The news media refer to CII as "Central Intelligence Institute." This is a result of creative back-thinking. Actually, CII is not a set of initials; it is a number, the Roman reading of the 102 smaller organizations out of which the department was formed.

Within two years, CII had bedcome a political fact of alarming proportions. Their networks spread within and without the nation, and the information they collected concerning the sexual peculiarities and financial machinations of many of our major political figures made the organization totally untouchable and autonomous. It became the practice of CII to inform the President after the fact.

Within four years, CII had made our espionage system the laughingstock of

Europe, had aggravated the image of the American abroad, had brought us to the brink of war on three occasions, and had amassed so vast a collection of trivial and private information that two computer systems had to be housed in their underground headquarters in Washington—one to retrieve fragments of data, the second to operate the first.

A bureaucratic malignancy out of control, the organization continued to grow in power and personnel. Then the expansion unexpectedly tapered off and stopped. CII computers informed its leaders of a remarkable fact: its losses of personnel abroad were just breaking even with its ambitious recruiting operations at home. A team of analysts from Information Limited was brought in to study the astonishing attrition. They discovered that 36 percent of the losses were due to defection; 27 percent were caused by mishandling of punched computer cards (which losses they advised CII to accept because it was easier to write the men off than to reorganize Payroll and Personnel Division); 4 percent of the losses were attributed to inadequate training in the handling of explosives; and 2 percent were simply "lost"—victims of European railroad schedules.

The remaining 31 percent had been assassinated. Loss through assassination presented very special problems. Because CII men worked in foreign countries without invitation, and often to the detriment of the established governments, they had no recourse to official protection. Organization men to the core, the CII heads decided that another Division must be established to combat the problem. They relied on their computers to find the ideal man to head the new arm, and the card that survived the final sorting bore the name: Yurasis Dragon. In order to bring Mr. Dragon to the United States, it was necessary to absolve him of accusations lodged at the War Crimes Tribunal concerning certain genocidal peccadillos, but CII considered him worth the effort.

The new division was called Search and Sanction—or the SS. The in-house slang name, Sweat Shop, is based on the initials and a back formation corruption of "wet shop," in which "wet work"—killing—is the primary function. The Search Division handled the task of discovering those responsible for the assassination of a CII agent. Sanction Division punished the offenders with death.

It was typical of Dragon's sense of the dramatic that the personnel of Sanction all carried code names based on poisons. "Wormwood" had been a Sanction courier. And there was a beautiful Eurasian woman who always made love to the target (of either sex) before killing. Her code name was Belladonna. Dragon never assigned Jonathan a code name. He considered it providential that he already bore a name appropriate to a scholar: Hemlock, the poison of Socrates.

Dragon gave a glossed and romantic version of these facts to Jonathan. "Are you with us, Hemlock?"

"If I refuse?"

"I wouldn't have brought you here had I considered that likely. If you refuse, the church you have set your heart on will be demolished, and your personal freedom will be in jeopardy."

"How so?"

"We know about the paintings you have collected. And duty would demand that we report their existence, unless, of course, doing so would deprive us of a trusted and useful associate." The carmine eyes flickered under cotton puff eyebrows. "Are you with us?"

Jonathan experienced a plunging vertigo as he nodded over the book in his lap. He caught his breath and blinked down at the unremembered page. The chocolate had cooled and a tan skin had formed over it. The thunder and wind had passed over, leaving only the regular, soporific rattle of rain against the stained glass windows. He rose, turned off the reading light, and walked with the certainty of custom through the dark nave. Still weary after a day of lazing, he rested for a time in his vast sixteenth-century bed, looking out past the rail of the choir loft to the dimly rippling colored windows, letting his aural attention stray, tuning in and out the sound of the rain.

The Montreal tension was still a knot in his stomach. The first layers of sleep closed over him gently, only to be harshly dissipated when he jolted upright in fear. He tried to hold any image before his mind to cover the white dots of mucus. And he found himself concentrating on harlequin flecks in warm brown eyes.

Suddenly he was awake and sick. He had passively fought it all day, but he could no longer. After vomiting, he lay quite nude on the cold tiles of his bathroom floor for more than an hour, putting his mind back together.

Then he returned to bed, and to the image of the harlequin flecks.

Long Island: *June 11*

JONATHAN'S RISE TO consciousness was neither crisp nor lucid. He came up through turgid layers of discomfort. Dream remnants were mixed with intruding reality. In either the reality or the dream, someone was trying to take his jewels from him—family jewels, they were. No. No, Gems.

His groin tingled. He brought the room into focus through defensive slits. "Oh, no!" He croaked. "What the hell are you doing, Cherry?"

"Good morning, Jonathan," she said cheerily. "Did that tickle?"

He groaned and turned over on his stomach.

Cherry, dressed only in her tennis shorts, slipped under the sheet with him, her lips touching his ear. "Nibble, nibble, nibble," she said, and did.

"Go away," he muffled into his pillow. "If you don't leave me alone, I'll . . ." He could think of no appropriate punishment, so he groaned.

"What will you do?" she asked brightly. "Rape me? You know, I've been thinking about rape a lot lately. It's not a good thing because it doesn't give the couple a chance to communicate on an interhuman level. But it has one advantage over masturbation. It isn't so lonely. You know what I mean? Well, if you're bent on raping me, I guess I'll have to take it like a woman.'" And she spun over and threw her arms and legs out, like St. Andrew crucified.

"Oh, for Christ's sake, Cherry! I ought to spank your ass."

She was instantly up on one elbow, speaking with serious concern. "I never suspected you were a sadist, Jonathan. But I guess it's the duty of a woman in love to satisfy the sexual peculiarities of her man."

"You're not a woman in love. You're a woman in heat. But all right! You win! I'm getting up. Why don't you go down and make me a cup of coffee."

"It's right there beside you, impetuous lover. I made it before I came up." There was a tray with a coffee pot and two cups on the bedside table. She arranged his pillows as he pulled himself to a sitting position, then she poured out his coffee and passed him the cup, which he had to struggle to balance when she climbed back into bed and sat beside him, their shoulders and hips touching, her leg over his. Jonathan sensed that the major league sex play was over for the moment, but she was still nude to the navel and her bikini tan gave her white breasts the advantage of contrast against the soft copper of the rest of her.

"Hey, Jonathan?" she said earnestly, as she looked into the bottom of her coffee cup, "let me ask you something. It's true, isn't it, that the early morning would be about the best time for me to get at you. It's true, isn't it, that men often wake up with erections."

"That usually means they have to piss," he growled into his cup.

She digested this bit of information in silence. "Nature is wasteful," she commented sadly. Then her spirits bounced back. "But never mind! Sooner or later, I'll catch you at an unguarded moment. Then *bam!*"

"Bam?"

"Not very onomatopoetic, I guess."

"Let's hope not."

She was withdrawn for a moment, then she turned to him and asked, "It isn't *me*, is it? I mean, if I weren't a virgin you'd take me, wouldn't you?"

He locked his fingers behind his head and stretched all the way to his pointed toes. "Certainly. In an instant. Bam."

"Because," she pursued, "I'm really fairly pretty, and I'm filthy rich, and my bod's not bad." She paused for a complimentary comment. "Hey! We were talking about my bod!" Again she paused. "Well, at least my breasts are nice, aren't they?"

He did not look over. "Certainly. They're great."

"Now cut it out! *Look* at them. They're a little small by current standards, but they're firm and cute, don't you think?"

He cradled one in his palm and inspected it with professional myopia. "Very fine," he vouched. "And two in number, which is especially reassuring."

"Then why don't you break down and make love to me?"

"Because you are self-consciously cute. Furthermore, you are a virgin. I could forgive the cuteness on the assumption that you'll outgrow it. But the virginity— never. Now why don't you put your blouse back on."

"No-o. I don't think so. Who knows? You might suddenly get a normal impulse and—ta-da!"

"Ta-da?"

"It's better than bam. Here, let me give you more coffee." She refilled his cup then carried her own to the edge of the loft, where she leaned against the railing, looking out over the nave musingly.

Cherry was Jonathan's nearest neighbor, occupying with her domestic staff a rambling mansion a quarter of a mile down the road. They shared the cost of maintaining the artificial sand beach that connected their properties. Her late father, the corporation lawyer James Mathew Pitt, had bought the estate shortly before his death, and Cherry enjoyed managing the property. During trips, Jonathan entrusted her with the care of his home and the payment of his local bills. Of necessity, she had a key, and she drifted in and out to use his library and to borrow champagne for her parties. He never attended these parties, not caring to meet the liberated young people of her circle. Needless to say, Cherry knew nothing about him, save that he was a teacher and art critic and that, so far as she knew, he was independently well off. She had never been invited to descend into the private gallery in the basement.

Little by little, their sex play had developed into a pattern of epic enticements and stoic refusals, the whole thing based on their mutual understanding that it was Jonathan's role to fend her off. She would have been at a loss, had he ever failed to do so. The battle was never totally without charm because it was fought with humor on both sides. And there was the spice of distant possibility to keep a tang in their relationship.

After a longish silence, Cherry spoke without turning to him. "Do you realize that I am the only twenty-four-year-old virgin on Long Island—discounting paraplegics and some nuns? And it's all your fault. You owe it to mankind to get me started."

Jonathan swung out of bed. "Avoiding virgins is not only a matter of ethics with me. It's also a matter of mechanics. Virgins are hard on older men."

"O.K. Punish yourself. Deny yourself the delights of the flesh. See if I care." She followed him into the bathroom where she had to raise her voice to be heard over the roar of water into his Roman pool. "I really do care, you know. After all, *someone's* got to get me started."

He called from the toilet beyond. "Someone's got to collect the garbage too. But not me." He punctuated with a flush.

"Nice analogy!"

He returned to the bathroom and lowered himself into the hot water. "Why don't you get dressed and go make us a little breakfast."

"I want to be your lover, not your wife." But she returned reluctantly to the bedroom.

"And put your shirt on before you go down," he called after her. "You might meet Mr. Monk down there." Mr. Monk was the groundsman.

"I wonder if *he'd* be willing to relieve me of this disgraceful chastity?"

"Not on what I pay him," Jonathan mumbled to himself.

"I assume you want your eggs raw," she called as she left.

After breakfast, she wandered about in the greenhouse garden while he brought the morning mail into the library, where he intended to do a touch of work. He was surprised and disturbed not to find the usual blue envelope from CII containing his cash payment. By routine, it was always placed by hand in his mailbox during the night after his return from a sanction. He was sure this was no oversight. Dragon was up to something. But there was nothing he could do but wait, so he went over his accounts and discovered that, after he had spent the ten thousand for the new Pissarro and paid his groundsman in advance for the summer, he would have very little left. There would be no lavish living this season, but he would get by. His major concern was that he had promised the underground art dealer in Brooklyn that he would have the money today. He decided to telephone and persuade him to hold the painting for an extra day.

". . . so when *can* you pick it up, Jonathan?" the dealer asked, his voice crisp with the overarticulated consonants of the Near East.

"Tomorrow, I imagine. Or the next day."

"Make it the next day. Tomorrow I take the family to Jones Beach. And you will have the twelve thousand we agreed on?"

"I will have the *ten* thousand we agreed on."

"It was only ten?" the dealer asked, his voice laden with grief.

"It was only ten."

"Jonathan, what am I doing? I am allowing my friendship for you to threaten the future of my children. But—a deal is a deal. I am philosophic. I can lose with grace. But make sure you bring the money before noon. It is dangerous for me to keep the item here. And also, I have another prospective buyer."

"You're lying, of course."

"I don't lie. I steal. There is another buyer. For twelve thousand. He contacted me today. So, if you don't want to lose the painting, be prompt. You understand?"

"I understand."

"Good. So! How is the family?"

"I'm not married. We go through this every time. You always ask me how the family is, and I always remind you that I am not married."

"Well, I an a forgetful man. Remember how I forgot it was only ten thousand? But seriously, you should get a family. Without children to work for, what is life? Answer me that."

"I'll see you in two days."

"I look forward to it. Be punctual, Jonathan. There is another buyer."

"So you told me."

For several minutes after he hung up, Jonathan sat gloomily at his desk, his spirits dampened by fear of losing the Pissarro. He wondered uneasily what was in Dragon's oblique mind.

"Feel like banging balls?" Cherry called from across the nave.

There was nothing to be gained by moping, so he agreed. The storm had rinsed the sky clear of clouds and the day was brilliant with sunlight. They played tennis for an hour, then they cut their thirsts with splits of champagne. She imitated his sacrilegious habit of drinking the wine from the bottle, like beer. Later they cooled off with a short swim. Cherry swam in her tennis togs, and when she came out, her shorts were nearly transparent.

"I feel like an Italian starlet," she remarked, looking down at the dark écu outline through her wet shorts.

"So do I," he said, dropping down on the hot sand.

They small-talked while she let handfuls of sand seep from her fist onto his back. She mentioned that she was going to spend the weekend on the Point with some of her friends. She invited him to come along. He refused; her too-young and too-liberal friends bored him with their nomadic affections and catatonic minds.

A cool wind scudded down the beach, an omen that there would be rain again before evening, and Cherry, after proposing without much hope that Jonathan take her into the warmth of his bed, went home.

On his way back to the church, Jonathan caught sight of Mr. Monk, his groundsman. For a moment he considered backtracking to avoid encounter, but embarrassed at being cowed by an employee, he walked bravely onward. Mr. Monk was the best gardener on the Island, but he was not much sought after. Thoroughly paranoiac, he had developed a theory that grass, flowers, and shrubs were his personal enemies, out to get him by means as diabolic as they were devious. It was his practice to rip up weeds, trim hedges, or cut grass with sadistic glee and retributive energy, all the while heaping scatological abuse on the offending flora. As though to spite him, gardens and grounds flourished under his hand, and this he viewed as a calculated insult, and his hatred flowed the more freely.

He was growling to himself as he punished the edge of a flower bed with a spade when Jonathan approached diffidently. "How are things going, Mr. Monk?" he asked tentatively.

"What! Oh, it's you, Dr. Hemlock. Rotten! That's how things are going! These shitty flowers want nothing but water! Water, water, water! A bunch of turd-eating lushes, they are. Water heads! Say, what kind of swimming suit was that neighbor lady wearing? I could see right through to her boobs. A little cross-eyed, they were. You take a look at this spade! Near bent in half! That's how they make them these days! Not worth a tiny pinch of coon shit! I remember the time a spade . . ."

Jonathan mumbled apologetically that everything looked fine, and he sneaked off toward his house.

Once under the cool and reassuring expanse of the vaulted nave, he discovered he was hungry. He compiled a lunch of macadamia nuts, Polish sausage, an apple, and a split of champagne. Then he smoked a pipe and relaxed, purposely not harkening for the ring of his telephone. Dragon would contact him when he was ready. Best just to wait for him.

To distract his thoughts, he went down to the gallery and passed some time with his paintings. When he had taken as much from them as he could just then, he sat at his desk and worked desultorily on the overdue Lautrec article, but it was no good. His mind returned to Dragon's intentions, and to the threatened Pissarro. Without putting it into words, he had known for some time that he could not continue working for CII. Conscience, of course, played no part in his growing disaffection. The only pangs he ever felt over killing a member of the scabby subculture of espionage were resentments at being brought into contact with them. Perhaps it was weariness. Tension, maybe. If only there were a way to support his life-style, his home, and his paintings without association with the Dragons and the Popes and the Melloughs . . .

Miles Mellough. His jaw set at the thought of the name. For nearly two years he had been waiting patiently for fate to give him a chance at Miles. He must not leave the cover of CII until that debt was attended to.

He had permitted very few people to penetrate his armor of cool distance. To those who had, he was fiercely loyal, and he insisted that his friends participate in his rigid views of friendship and loyalty. But in the course of his life, only four men had gotten close enough to merit his friendship, and to run the concomitant risk of his wrath. There was Big Ben Bowman, whom he had not seen for three years, but with whom he used to climb mountains and drink beer. And there was Henri Baq, a French espionage agent who had had the gift of finding laughter in everything, and whose gut had been cut open two years ago. And there was Miles Mellough, who had been responsible for Baq's death after having been Henri and Jonathan's closest friend.

The fourth had been The Greek, who had betrayed Jonathan during a sanction job. Only luck, and a desperate four-mile swim through a night sea had saved Jonathan's life. Of course, Jonathan should have been worldly enough to realize that any man who trusts a Cyprian Greek deserves a Trojan fate, but this did not prevent him from biding his time until he ran across him in Ankara. The Greek was not aware that Jonathan knew who had sold him out—perhaps, being Greek, he had even forgotten the incident—so he accepted the gift of his favorite arrack without hesitation. The bottle had been doctored with Datura. The old Turk who did the job used the ancient method of burning the Datura seeds and catching the smoke in an earthen jar into which the arrack was then poured.

The Greek is now, and will always be, in an asylum, where he sits huddled in a corner, rocking back and forth, humming a single note endlessly.

The score with The Greek settled, only Miles Mellough's debt was still outstanding. Jonathan was sure that one day he would happen upon Miles.

The jangle of the telephone jarred him from his morbid stream of free association.

"Hemlock? Reports are in from Montreal. Good job, pal." Clement Pope's brassy insurance salesman voice was enough to make Jonathan testy.

"My money wasn't in the mailbox this morning, Pope."

"Well, how about that?"

Jonathan took a deep breath to control himself. "Let me talk to Dragon."

"Talk to me. I can handle it."

"I'm not going to waste time with a flunkey. Get Dragon to the phone."

"Maybe if I came out there and we had a good chat . . . ?" Pope was taunting. He knew that Jonathan could not afford to be seen in his company. With Dragon's necessary seclusion, Pope had become the public face of SS Division. Being seen with him was tantamount to having a "Support CII" sticker on your automobile.

"If you want the money, pal, you'd better cooperate. Dragon won't talk to you over the phone, but he will see you."

"When?"

"Right now. He wants you to take the train in as soon as possible."

"All right. But remind him that I am depending on that money."

"I'm just sure he knows that, buddy-o." Pope hung up.

Someday, Jonathan promised himself, I'll be alone in a room with that bastard for just ten minutes . . .

Upon reconsideration, he settled for five.

New York: *June 11*

"YOU'RE LOOKING ESPECIALLY attractive this afternoon, Mrs. Cerberus."

She did not bother to look up. "Scrub your hands in the sink over there. Use the green soap."

"This is new." Jonathan crossed to the hospital sink with its surgeon's elbow lever instead of the conventional twist tap.

"That elevator is filthy," she said, her voice as scaly as her complexion. "And Mr. Dragon is in a weakened condition. He's near the end of a phase." This meant that he would soon receive his semiannual total replacement transfusion.

"Do you intend to donate?" Jonathan asked, rubbing his hands dry under a jet of hot air.

"We are not the same blood type."

"Do I detect a note of regret?"

"Mr. Dragon's blood type is very rare," she said with evident pride.

"In humans at any rate. May I go in now?"

She fixed a diagnostic glare on him. "Any colds? Flu? Digestive disorder?"

"Only a mild pain in the ass, and that's a recent development."

Mrs. Cerberus pressed the buzzer on her desk, and she waved him into the interlock without further comment.

The usual dim red light was not on, but the rising heat was as stifling as ever. The door to Dragon's office clicked open. "Come in, Hemlock." Dragon's metallic voice had a weak flutter in it. "Please forgive the absence of the red light. I am more than usually fragile, and even that dim light is painful to me."

Jonathan groped forward for the back of the leather chair. "Where is my money?"

"That's my Hemlock. Directly to the point. No time wasted with the conventional amenities. The slums have left their mark."

"I need the money."

"True. Without it you will be unable to meet your house payments—to say nothing of purchasing that Pissarro you covet. By the way, I hear there is another bidder on the painting. Pity if you lost it."

"You intend to hold out on me?"

"Permit me an academic question, Hemlock. What would you do if I were to withhold payment?"

"Light these." Jonathan slipped his fingers into his shirt pocket.

"What have you there?" There was no worry in Dragon's voice. He knew how thoroughly his men searched everyone who entered.

"A book of matches. Do you have some idea of the pain it's going to cause you when I strike them one by one?"

Dragon's thin fingers flew automatically to his eyes, but he knew that his colorless skin would afford little protection. With forced bravado he said, "Very good, Hemlock. You confirm my confidence in you. In future, my men will have to search for matches as well."

"My payment?"

"There. On the desk. Actually, I intended to give you the money all the time. I kept it only to assure your coming here to listen to my proposition." He laughed his three arid ha's. "That was a good one with the matches!" The laugh changed into a weak, wheezing cough, and for a time he could not speak. "Sorry. I'm not really well."

"To put you at ease," Jonathan said, slipping the chubby envelope of bills into his coat pocket, "I should tell you that I don't have any matches. I never smoke in public."

"Of course! I had forgotten." There was real praise in his voice. "Very good indeed. Forgive me if I have seemed overly aggressive. I am ill just now, and that makes me tetchy."

Jonathan smiled at the uncommon word. Occasionally Dragon's alien English was betrayed by just such sounds: odd word choices, overpronunciations, mishandlings of idiom. "What's this all about, Dragon?"

"I have an assignment you must take."

"I thought we talked about that. You know I never take jobs unless I need the money. Why don't you use one of your other Sanction people?"

The pink-and-red eyes emerged. "I would if it were possible. Your reluctance is a nuisance. But this assignment requires an experienced mountain climber and, as you might imagine, men of such talents do not abound within our department."

"I haven't climbed for more than three years."

"We have considered that. There is time to bring you back into condition."

"Why do you need a climber?"

"I could discuss details only if you were willing to cooperate on the assignment."

"In which case, forget it."

"I have a further inducement for you, Hemlock."

"Oh?"

"One of our former employees—an erstwhile friend of yours, I believe—is involved in the affair." Dragon paused for effect. "Miles Mellough."

After a moment, Jonathan said, "Miles is none of your business. I'll take care of him in my own way."

"You are a rigid man, Hemlock. I hope you don't break when you are forced to bend."

"Forced how."

"Oh, something will occur to me." There was a heavy flutter in his voice and he pressed his hand against his chest to relieve the pain. "On your way out, would you ask Mrs. Cerberus to come to me, there's a good fellow?"

Jonathan pressed back into the shallow entrance to Dragon's office building, trying to avoid the rain which fell in plump drops that exploded into a haze on the sidewalk. The liquid roar eclipsed the city's babble. An empty taxi came slowly up the street, and Jonathan jumped out to take his place in a line of supplicants who waved and shouted as the cab cruised majestically by, the driver whistling contentedly to himself, doubtless contemplating some intriguing problem of Russian grammar. Jonathan returned to the shelter of his meager cave and looked out glumly on the scene. Streetlights came on, their automatized devices duped into believing it was evening by the darkening storm. Another taxi appeared and Jonathan, knowing better, nevertheless stepped forward to the curb on the outside chance that this driver was not independently wealthy and had some mild interest in profit. Then he saw that the taxi was occupied. As he turned back, the driver sounded his horn. Jonathan stood still, puzzled and getting wetter. The driver beckoned him over. Jonathan pointed at his chest with a foolish "me?" expression on his face. The back door opened and Jemima called out, "Are you going to get in, or do you like it out there?"

Jonathan jumped in, and the cab turned out into traffic, disdainfully ignoring trumpeted protests from the car abreast that was forced into the oncoming stream.

"I don't mean to drip on you," Jonathan said, "but you really do look lovely. Where did you come from? Did I mention you look lovely?" He was boyishly glad to see her again. It seemed that he had thought of her often. But probably not, he decided. Why should he?

"I saw you step out," she explained, "and you looked so funny that I took pity on you."

"Ah. You fell for an ancient ploy. I always try to look funny when I'm drowning in the rain. You never know when some passing stewardess will take pity on you."

The cabby turned and looked over the back of the seat with classic indifference in competing traffic. "That'll be double fare you know, buddy."

Jonathan told him that was just fine.

"Because we ain't supposed to pick up two fares in the rain like that." He deigned to glance briefly at the oncoming traffic.

Jonathan said he would take care of it.

"Hell, everybody and his brother would be picking up the whole damned city if we didn't charge double fare. You know that for yourself."

Jonathan leaned forward and smiled at the driver politely in the rearview mirror. "Why don't we divide up the labor here? You drive, and we'll talk." Then he asked Jemima, "How do you manage to look so calm and lovely when you're starving to death?"

"Am I starving to death?" The harlequin flecks of gold danced with amusement in her warm brown eyes.

"Certainly, you are. It's a wonder you haven't noticed it."

"I take it you're inviting me out to dinner."

"I am that. Yes."

She looked at him quizzically. "Now, you know that when I picked you up in the rain, I didn't pick you up in all the possible senses of that phrase, don't you?"

"Good Lord, we hardly know each other! What are you suggesting? How about dinner?"

She considered it a moment, tempted. Then, "No-o, I think not."

"If you hadn't said no, what would your second choice have been?"

"Steak, red wine, and a small tangy salad."

"Done." Jonathan leaned forward and told the driver to turn south to an address on Fourteenth Street.

"How about making up your mind, buddy?"

"Drive."

When the taxi pulled up in front of the restaurant, Jemima touched Jonathan's sleeve. "I saved you from melting. You are going to buy me a dinner. And that's it, right? After dinner everybody goes home. Each to his own home. OK?"

He took her hand and looked earnestly into her eyes. "Gem, you have very fragile faith in your fellowman." He squeezed the hand. "Tell me about it? Who was he—the man who hurt you so?"

She laughed, and the cab driver asked if they were going to get out or not. As Jemima dashed into the restaurant, Jonathan paid the cabby and told him he had been a real brick. Rain and traffic obscured the last word, so the driver stared at Jonathan for a moment, but he decided it was wiser to drive off in a wheel-squealing miff.

The restaurant was simple and expensive, designed for eating, not for gazing at the decor. Partly because he felt festive, and partly to impress Jemima, Jonathan ordered a bottle of Lafite.

"May I suggest 1959?" the wine steward asked, with the rhetorical assumption that his guidance was impeccable.

"We're not French," Jonathan said, not taking his eyes from Jemima.

"Sir?" The arch of the eyebrow had that blend of huff and martyrdom characteristic of upper echelon servants.

"We're not French. Prenubile wines hold no fascination for us. Bring a '53 if you have it, or a '55 if not."

As the steward departed, Jemima asked, "Is this Lafite something special?"

"You don't know?"

"No."

Jonathan signaled the steward to return. "Forget the Lafite. Bring us an Haut-Brion instead."

Assuming the change was a fiscal reconsideration, the steward made an elaborate production of scratching the Lafite off his pad and scribbling down the Haut-Brion.

"Why did you do that?" Jemima asked.

"Thrift, Miss Brown. Lafite is too expensive to waste."

"How do you know, I might have enjoyed it."

"Oh, you'd have enjoyed it all right. But you wouldn't have appreciated it."

Jemima looked at him narrowly. "You know? I have this feeling you're not a nice person."

"Niceness is an overrated quality. Being nice is how a man pays his way into the party if he hasn't the guts to be tough or the class to be brilliant."

"May I quote you?"

"Oh, you probably will."

"Ah-h—Johnson to Boswell?"

"James Abbott McNeill Whistler to Wilde. But not a bad guess."

"A gentleman would have pretended I was right. I was right about your not being a nice person."

"I'll try to make up for it by being other things. Witty, or poetic perhaps. Or even terribly interested in you, which, by the way, I am." His eyes twinkled.

"You're putting me on."

"I admit it. It's all a facade. I just pretend to be urbane as an armor for my vulnerable hypersensitivity."

"Now I'm getting a put-on within the put-on."

"How do you like being on Flugle Street?"

"Help."

Jonathan laughed and let the con lie where it was.

Jemima sighed and shook her head. "Man, you're really a social buzz saw, aren't you. I like to put people on myself by skipping logical steps in the conversation until they're dizzy. But that sort of thing isn't even in your league, is it."

"I don't know that you could call it a league. After all, there's only one team and one player."

"Here we go again."

"Let's take time out for dinner."

The salad was crisp, the steaks huge and perfect, and they washed them down with the Haut-Brion. Throughout the meal they chatted lightly, allowing the topic to pivot on a word or a sudden thought, ranging from art to politics to childhood embarrassments to social issues, clinging to a subject only so long as

there was amusement in it. They shared a sense of the ridiculous and took
neither themselves nor the great names in art and politics too seriously. Often it
was unnecessary to finish a sentence—the other predicting the thrust and nodding agreement or laughing. And sometimes they shared brief, relaxed silences,
neither feeling a need to keep up conversation as a defense against communication. They sat next to a window. The rain alternately rattled and relented. They
made ludicrous guesses about the professions and destinations of the passersby.
Without recognizing it, Jonathan was dealing with Gem as though she were a
man—an old friend. He drifted with the stream of conversation honestly, forgetting the pre-bed banter that usually constituted the basis of his small talk with
women.

"A college teacher?" Gem asked incredulously. "Don't tell me that, Jonathan.
You're undermining my stereotypes."

"How about you as a stewardess? How did that ever happen?"

"Oh, I don't know. Came out of college after changing majors every year and
tried to find a job as a Renaissance Woman, but there wasn't a heading like that
in the want ads. And traveling around seemed like a possible thing to do. It also
struck me as kind of fun to be the first black stewardess on the line—I was their
public relations *Negress.*" She pronounced the word prissily, ridiculing those
who would use it. "How about you? How did you happen to become a college
teacher?"

"Oh, I came out of college and tried to find a job as a Renaissance Man,
but . . ."

"All right. Forget it."

In the course of the chat, Jonathan discovered that she would be in New York
for a three-day layover, and that pleased him. They drifted into another easy
silence.

"What's funny?" she asked in response to his slight smile.

"Nothing," he said. "Me."

"Synonyms?"

"I just . . ." He smiled gently at her over the table. "It just occurred to me
that I am not bothering to be clever with you. I usually make it a point to be
clever."

"How about all that Flugle Street business?"

"Hustler talk. Dazzle talk. But I don't think I'd care to dazzle you."

She nodded and looked out the window, giving her attention to the random
scatter of light where the rain danced on the puddles. After a while, she said,
"That's nice."

He knew what she meant. "Yes, it's nice. But it's a little disconcerting."

She nodded again. And they both knew she meant that it was a little disconcerting for her, too.

A series of non-sequitur pivots brought them to the subject of houses, and
Jonathan waxed enthusiastic about his own. For half an hour he described
details to her, trying hard to make her see them. She listened actively, letting
him know through small movements of her eyes and head that she understood
and shared. When he stopped suddenly, realizing that he had been talking
steadily and probably boorishly, she said, "It must be nice to feel that way
about a house. And it's safe too, of course."

"Safe?"

"A house can't lean on you emotionally. Can't burden you by loving you
back. You know what I mean."

He knew exactly, and he experienced a negative twinge at her emotional
acumen. It occurred to him that he would enjoy having her at his home—passing
a day sitting around and chatting. He told her so.

"It sounds like fun. But we couldn't go now. That wouldn't be good. I pick you up in a cab, we have dinner, then we run off to your house. Technically speaking, that would constitute a 'quicky.' It doesn't sound like our sort of thing."

He agreed that it was not their sort of thing. "We could make some sort of pact. I imagine we're capable of not making love for a day or two."

"You'd cheat."

"Probably."

"And if you didn't, I would."

"I'm glad to hear that."

The restaurant was closing, and their waiter had already made many polite intrusions with offers of unwanted service. Jonathan tipped rather too much, paying for the splendid time he had had, rather than for the service, which he had not noticed.

They decided to walk back to her hotel because it was not too far, and because the streets were empty and cool after the rain. They strolled, sharing swatches of talk and longer periods of silence. Her hand was in the bend of his arm, and she drew his attention to little things she noticed with a slight press of her fingers, which he acknowledged with a gentle return flex.

Surprisingly quickly they found themselves at her hotel. In the lobby they shook hands, then she said, "Is it all right if I come out on the train tomorrow morning? You can meet me at the station, and we'll take a look at this church of yours."

"I think that would be . . . just fine."

"Good night, Jonathan."

"Good night."

He walked to the train station, noticing along the way that the city seemed less ugly than usual. Probably the rain.

Long Island: *June 12*

HE PADDED ACROSS the expanse of his choir loft bedroom, concentrating on his coffee cup, but spilling some into the saucer anyway. It was a large, two-handled *café au lait* mug, and for several minutes he leaned against the rail, taking long resuscitating draughts and looking down with pride and pleasure upon the nave where low-angle morning sun pierced the dim space with lances of variegated light. He was only at peace when he had his home around him, like armor. His thoughts strayed back and forth between pleasant anticipation of Jemima and vague discomfort over the tone of his last meeting with Dragon.

Later, down in the gallery, he screwed up his courage and tried again to work on the Lautrec article. He penciled a few notes, then the lead broke. That was it. Fate. He might have plowed on, wading through uninspired, mealy prose—but not if it entailed resharpening his pencil. It wasn't his fault that the pencil had broken.

On his desk top lay the blue pay envelope from Dragon, chubby with tenscore one-hundred-dollar bills. He picked it up and looked around for a safe place to put it. His eye caught none, so he dropped it back on the desk. For a man who went to such extremes to make money, Jonathan had none of the instincts of the miser. Money had no attraction for him. Goods, comforts, and possessions were another matter. It delighted him to remember that by tomorrow afternoon he would own the pointillist Pissarro. He looked around the walls, deciding where to hang it, and his eye fell on the Cézanne that Henri Baq had stolen for him in Budapest as a birthday present. Memories of Henri came to him: the curiously warped Basque wit . . . their laughter when they described close calls to each other . . . that staggering drunk in Arles when they had played at bullfighting with their jackets and the angry traffic. And he recalled the day Henri died, trying to hold his guts in with his hands, seeking a witty punch line to go out on, and not being able to come up with one.

Jonathan snapped his head to clear the images out, but no good. He sat at the pianoforte and chorded aimlessly. They had been a team—he and Henri and Miles Mellough. Miles worked for Search, Jonathan for Sanction, and Henri for the French counterpart of CII. They had performed assignments competently and quickly, and they always found time to sit around in bars, talking about art and sex and . . . whatever.

Then Miles set up Henri's death.

Jonathan slipped into a bit of Handel. Dragon had said that Miles was involved somehow in this sanction he was trying to force on Jonathan. For almost two years, Jonathan had anticipated the day when he could face Miles again.

Don't think about it. Jemima is coming.

He left the chamber, locking the door behind him, and strolled over the grounds to while away the slow-moving time before her arrival. The breeze was fresh, and the leaves of the plane trees lining the drive scintillated in the sun. Overhead, the sky was taut blue, but on the northern horizon over the water hovered a tight bundle of cloud that promised a fresh storm that night. Jonathan loved storms.

He wandered through the formal English garden with its newly clipped box hedges enclosing an involute maze. From the depths of the labyrinth he could hear the angry click! click! click! of Mr. Monk's trimming shears.

"Argh! There!" Click! "That'll teach you, you simple-minded shrub!" Click! Click! "OK, wise ass twig! Stick it out, and I'll cut it off for you! Like that!" Click!

Jonathan tried to locate the sound within the maze so he might avoid an encounter with Mr. Monk. Stealthily, he moved down the alley, rolling the pressure underfoot to reduce the sound.

"You got something against them other branches?" Mr. Monk's voice was honey sweet. "Oh-h-h, you don't like their company. Well, I understand. You're just some kind of loner, keepin' away from the bunch like that." Then suddenly he roared, "Pride! That's your trouble! And I got a cure for pride!" Click! "There!"

Jonathan squatted beside the wall of hedge, not daring to move, uncertain of the direction of Mr. Monk's voice. There was a long silence. Then he began to picture himself, cringing at the thought of meeting his groundsman. He smiled, shook his head, and stood up.

"What you doin', Dr. Hemlock?" Mr. Monk asked from directly behind him.

"Oh! Well! Hello." Jonathan frowned and dug his toe into the turf. "This—ah—this grass here, Mr. Monk. I've been examining it. Looks funny to me. Don't you think so?"

Mr. Monk had not noticed, but he was always willing to believe the worst of growing things. "Funny in what way, Dr. Hemlock?"

"Well, it's . . . greener than usual. Greener than it ought to be. You know what I mean."

Mr. Monk examined the area near the shrubbery, then compared it with nearby grass. "Is that right?" His eyes grew round with rage as he turned on the offending patch.

Jonathan walked down the alley with determined casualness and turned at the first corner. As he paced more quickly to the house, he heard Mr. Monk's voice from within the labyrinth.

"You stupid weeds! Always screwing up! If you ain't brown and scruffy, you're too green! Well, this'll fix you!" Snip!

Jonathan drove along the tree-lined road to the station. The train would probably be late, in the Long Island tradition, but he could not run the risk of keeping Jemima waiting. His automobile was a vintage Avanti—a car consonant with his hedonistic life-style. It was in poor condition because he drove it hard and gave it little attention, but its line and grace appealed to him. When it finally broke down for good, he intended to use it as a planter on his front lawn.

He parked close to the platform, his bumper touching the gray, weathered planking. The warming sun liberated a smell of creosote from the wood. Because it was Sunday, the platform and the parking area were deserted. He leaned back in the seat and waited drowsily. He would never consider standing on a train platform to wait because . . .

. . . Henri Baq had bought his on the cement arrival dock of the Gare St. Lazare. Jonathan often thought of the steamy clangor of that vast steel-domed station. And of the monstrous grinning clown.

Henri had been off guard. An assignment had just ended, and he was going on his first vacation without his wife and children. Jonathan had promised to see him off, but he had been delayed in the tangle of traffic in the Place de L'Europe.

He caught sight of Henri, and they waved over the heads of the crowd. It must have been just then that the assailant slipped the knife into Henri's stomach. The dispatcher's voice boomed its undecipherable drone into the hiss of steam and rattle of baggage wagons. By the time Jonathan pushed his way through the throng, Henri was leaning against a huge poster for the Winter Circus.

"*Qu'as-tu?*" Jonathan asked.

Henri's drooping Basque eyes were infinitely sad. He clutched the front of his jacket with one hand, the fist pressed against his stomach. He smiled foolishly and shook his head with an I-don't-believe-it expression, then the smile contorted into a grin of pain, and he slid to a sitting posture, his feet straight out before him like a child's.

When Jonathan stood up after feeling Henri's throat for pulse, he came face to face with the insane grin of the clown on the poster.

Marie Baq had not wept. She thanked Jonathan for coming to tell her, and she gathered the children together in another room for a talk. When they came back, their eyes were red and puffy, but none of them was still crying. The eldest boy—also Henri—assumed his role and asked Jonathan if he would care for an apéritif. He accepted, and later he took them across the street to a café for supper. The youngest, who did not really understand what had happened, ate with excellent appetite, but no one else did. And once the eldest girl made a snorting noise as the dike of her control broke, and she ran to the ladies' room.

Jonathan sat up that night over coffee with Marie. They talked of practical and fiscal matters across the kitchen table covered with oilcloth from which daydreaming children had picked flecks of plastic. Then for a long time there was nothing to talk about. Close to dawn she pushed herself out of the chair with a sigh so deep it whimpered. "One must continue to live, Jonathan. For the little ones. Come. Come to bed with me."

There is nothing so life-embracing as lovemaking. Potential suicides almost never do. Jonathan lived with the Baqs for two weeks, and each night Marie used him like medicine. One evening she said calmly, "You should go now, Jonathan. I don't think I need you anymore. And if we continued after I ceased to need you, that would be a different thing."

He nodded.

When the youngest son heard that Jonathan was going away he was disappointed. He had intended to ask Jonathan to take him to the Winter Circus.

Several weeks later, Jonathan learned that Miles Mellough had set up the assassination. Because Miles left CII at the same time, Jonathan had never been sure which side had ordered the sanction.

"Nice job of meeting the train," Jemima said looking in the window from the off-driver side.

He started. "I'm sorry. I didn't notice it come in." He realized how thin that sounded, considering the desolate platform.

As they drove toward his place, she trailed her hand out the window, cupping the wind aerodynamically, as children do. He thought she looked smart and fresh in her white linen dress with its high mandarin collar. She sat deep in the seat, either completely relaxed or totally indifferent.

"Are those the only clothes you brought?" he asked, turning his head toward her, but keeping his eyes on the road.

"Yes, sure. I'll bet you were expecting some night things discreetly carried in a brown paper bag."

"The bag could have been any color. I wouldn't have cared." He braked and turned into a side road, then backed onto the highway again.

"You forgot something?"

"No. We're going back to the village. To buy you some clothes."

"You don't like these?"

"They're fine. But they're not much for working in."

"Working?"

"Certainly. You thought this was a vacation?"

"What kind of work?" she asked warily.

"I thought you might enjoy helping me paint a boat."

"I'm being had."

Jonathan nodded thoughtfully.

They stopped at the only shop in the village open on Sundays, a spurious Cape Cod structure decorated with fishing nets and glass balls calculated to delight weekend tourists from the city. The proprietor was no taciturn Down Easter; he was an intense man in his mid-forties, tending slightly to weight, wearing a tight-fitting Edwardian suit and a flowing pearl gray ascot. When he spoke, he thrust his lower jaw forward and relished the nasal vowels with deliberate sincerity.

While Jemima was in the back of the store picking out some shorts, a shirt, and a pair of canvas shoes, Jonathan selected other things, accepting the proprietors' estimate of size. The advice was not given graciously; there was a tone of peevish disappointment. "Oh, about a ten, I guess," the proprietor said, then compressed his lips and averted his eyes. "Of course, it will change when she's had a few children. Her kind always does." His eyebrows were in constant motion, each independent of the other.

Jonathan and Gem had driven a distance when she said, "That's the first time I've been a victim of prejudice on those grounds."

"I've known and admired a lot of women," Jonathan said in an accurate imitation of the proprietor's voice. "Some of my best friends are women . . ."

"But you wouldn't want your brother to marry one, right?"

"Well, you know what happens to land values if a woman moves into the neighborhood."

The shadows of trees lining the road rippled in regular cadence over the hood, and sunlight flickered stroboscopically in the corners of their eyes.

She squeezed one of the packages. "Hey, what's this?"

"I'm sorry, but they didn't have any brown paper bags."

She paused a second. "I see."

The car turned into the drive and came around a line of plane trees screening the church from view. He opened the door and let her precede him into the house. She stopped in the midst of the nave and turned around, taking the total in. "This isn't a house, Jonathan. It's a movie set."

He stepped around from his side of the boat to see how she was coming along. With her nose only ten inches from the wood and her tongue between her teeth with concentration, she was daubing at an area about a foot square that constituted the extent of her progress.

"You got the spot," he said, "but you've missed the boat."

"Hush up. Get around and paint your own side."

"All done."

She humphed. "Slapdash careless work, I imagine."

"Any chance of your finishing before winter sets in?"

"Don't worry about me, man. I'm the goal-oriented type. I'll keep at this until it's done. Nothing could lure me away from the dignity of honest labor."

"I was going to suggest lunch."

"Sold." She dropped the brush into the can of thinner and wiped her hands with a rag.

After bathing and changing clothes, she joined him at the bar for a prelunch martini.

"That's some bathtub you've got."

"It pleases me."

They drove across the island to take lunch at The Better 'Ole: seafood and champagne. The place was nearly empty, and it was cool with shadow. They chatted about how it was when they were children, and about Chicago jazz versus San Francisco, and Underground films, and how they both liked chilled melon balls for dessert.

They lay side by side on the warm sand under a sky no longer brittle blue, but bleaching steadily with a high haze that preceded the wall of heavy gray cloud pressing inevitably from the north. They had changed back into work clothes, but had not returned to work.

"That's enough sun and sand for me, sir," Jemima said eventually, and she pushed herself to a sitting position. "And I don't feel much like getting stormed on, so I'm going up and stroll around in the house. OK?"

He hummed drowsy acquiescence.

"Is it all right if I make a phone call? I have to tell the airline where I am."

He did not open his eyes, fearful of damaging the half-doze he was treasuring. "Don't talk more than three minutes," he said, barely moving his mouth.

She kissed him gently on his relaxed lips.

"OK," he said. "But no more than four minutes."

When he returned to the house it was late afternoon and the cloud pack was unbroken from horizon to horizon. He found Jemima lounging in the library, looking through a portfolio of Hokusai prints. He looked over her shoulder for a time, then drifted up to his bar. "It's getting cold. Care for some sherry?" His voice bounced through the nave.

"Sounds fine. I don't like your bar, though."

"Oh?"

She followed him as far as the altar rail. "It's too much nose-thumbing, if you know what I mean."

"As in, 'Oh, grow up'?"

"Yes. As in that." She accepted the chalice of wine and sat on the rail sipping it. He watched her with proprietary pleasure.

"Oh, by the way!" She stopped drinking suddenly. "Do you know that there's a madman on your grounds?"

"Is that so?"

"Yes. I met him on my way up here. He was snarling and digging a hole that looked terribly like a grave."

Jonathan frowned. "I can't imagine who that could be."

"And he was mumbling to himself."

"Was he?"

"Yes. Real vulgar stuff."

He shook his head. "I'll have to look into it."

She did the salad while he broiled steaks. The fruit had been chilling since they got home, and the purple grapes mauved over with a haze of frost when they met the humid air of the garden where places had been set at a wrought iron table, despite the probability of rain. He opened a bottle of Pichon-Longueville-Baron, and they ate while the onset of night smoothly transferred the source of light from the treetops to the flickering hurricane lamps on the table. The flicker stopped, the air grew dense and unmoving, and occasional flashes along the storm line glittered to the north. They watched the scudding sky grow darker while little breaths of cool wind leading the storm reanimated the lamps and fluttered the black-and-silver foliage around them. For long afterwards, Jonathan was to remember the meteor trail of Jemima's glowing cigarette when she lifted it to smoke.

He spoke out of a longish silence. "Come with me. I want to show you something."

She followed him back into the house. "There's a certain spookiness about this, you know," she said as he got the key from the back of the kitchen drawer and led her down the half-turn stone steps. "Into the catacombs? Probably a lime pit in the cellar. What do I really know about you? Maybe I should drop bits of bread so I can find my way back out."

Jonathan turned on the lights and stepped aside. She walked past him, drawn in by the paintings that radiated from the walls. "Oh, my! Oh, Jonathan!"

He sat at his desk chair, watching her as she moved from canvas to canvas with an uneven pulsing flow, attracted by the next painting, unwilling to leave the last. She made little humming sounds of pleasure and admiration, rather as a contented child does when eating breakfast alone.

Her eyes full, she sat on the carved piano bench and looked down at the Kashan for some time. "You're a singular man, Jonathan Hemlock."

He nodded.

"All this just for you. This megalomaniac house; these . . ." she made a sweeping gesture with her hand and eyes. "You keep all this to yourself."

"I'm a singularly selfish man. Like some champagne?"

"No."

She looked down and shook her head sadly. "All this matters to you a great deal. Even more than Mr. Dragon led me to believe."

"Yes, it matters, but . . ."

. . . For some minutes they said nothing. She did not look up, and he, after the first shocked glance, tried to calm his confusion and anger by forcing his eye to roam over the paintings.

Finally he sighed and pushed himself out of the chair. "Well, lady, I'd better be getting you to the depot. Last train for the city . . ." His voice trailed off.

She followed him obediently up the stone steps. While they had been in the gallery, the storm had broken violently above without their hearing it. Now they climbed up through layers of quickening, muffled sound—the metallic rattle of rain on glass, the fluting and flap of wind, the thick, distant rumblings of thunder.

In the kitchen she asked, "Do we have time for that glass of champagne you offered me?"

He protected his hurt by the dry freeze of politeness. "Certainly. In the library?"

He knew she was distressed, and he wielded his artificial social charm like a bludgeon, chatting lightly about the paucity of transportation to his corner of Long Island, and of the particular difficulties the rain imposed. They sat facing each other in heavy leather chairs while the rain rattled horizontally against the stained glass, and the walls and floor rippled with reds and greens and blues. Jemima cut into the flow of anticommunicative chat.

"I guess I shouldn't have just dropped it on you like that, Jonathan."

"Oh? How should you have dropped it, Jemima?"

"I couldn't let it go on—I mean, I couldn't let *us* go on without your knowing. And I couldn't think of a more gentle way to tell you."

"You might have hit me with a brick," he suggested. Then he laughed. "I must have been dazzled. You're a real dazzler. I should have recognized the anti-chance of coincidence. You on the plane from Montreal. You just happened to pass by Dragon's office in that taxi. How was it supposed to work, Jemima? Were you supposed to bring me to a white heat of desire, then deny your body unless I agreed to do this sanction for Dragon? Or were you going to whisper insidious persuasions into my ear as I lay in the euphoria of postcoitus vulnerability."

"Nothing so cool. I was told to steal your payment for the last assignment."

"That's certainly direct."

"I saw it lying on your desk downstairs. Mr. Dragon says you need the money badly."

"He's right. Why you? Why not one of his other flunkeys?"

"He thought I would be able to get close to you quickly."

"I see. How long have you worked for Dragon?"

"I don't really work for him. I'm CII, but I'm not Search and Sanction. They chose someone out of your department to avoid recognition."

"Very sensible. What do you do?"

"I'm a courier. The stewardess front is good for that."

He nodded. "Have you had many assignments like this? Using your body to get at someone?"

She considered, then rejected the easy lie. "A couple."

He was silent for a moment. Then he laughed. "Aren't we the pair? A selfish killer and a patriotic whore. We should mate just to see what the offspring would be. I have nothing against selfish whores, but patriotic killers are the worst kind."

"Jonathan." She leaned forward, suddenly angry. "Do you have any idea how important this assignment Mr. Dragon wants you to take is?"

He regarded her with bland silence; he had no intention of making anything easier.

"I know he didn't give you the details. He couldn't unless he was sure you would take the job. But if you knew what is at stake, you would cooperate."

"I doubt that."

"I wish I could tell you. But my instructions—"

"I understand."

After a pause, she said, "I tried to get out of it."

"Oh? Did you?"

"This afternoon, while we were lying on the beach, I realized what a rotten thing it would be to do, now that we were . . ."

"Now that we were what?" He arched his eyebrows in cool curiosity.

Her eyes winced. "Anyway, I left you and came up here to call Dragon and ask him to let me out."

"I assume he refused."

"He couldn't speak to me. He was undergoing a transfusion or something. But his man refused—whatshisname."

"Pope." He finished his wine and placed the glass on a table deliberately. "It's a little hard for me to buy, you know. You've been on this thing for some time—since Montreal. And you seem convinced that I ought to take this assignment—"

"You *must*, Jonathan!"

". . . and despite all that, you expect me to believe that one gentle afternoon has changed your mind. I can't help feeling you're making the mistake of trying to con a con."

"I haven't changed my mind. It's only that I didn't want to do the thing myself. And you know perfectly well that this has been more than just a gentle afternoon."

He looked at her, his eyes moving from one of hers to the other. Then he nodded, "Yes, it's been more than that."

"For me, it wasn't just this afternoon. I've spent days going over your records—which, by the way, are embarrassingly complete. I know what your boyhood was like. I know how CII roped you into your job in the first place. I know about the killing of your friend in France. And even before this assignment, I'd seen you on educational television." She grinned, "Lecturing about art in your superior, sassy way. Oh, I was ninety percent hooked before I met you. Then, down in your room—I was really pleased when you invited me down there. I couldn't help babbling. I knew from the files that you never bring anyone there. Anyway, down in the room, with you sitting there so happy, and all those beautiful paintings, and that blue envelope with your money sitting so unprotected on your desk . . . I had to tell you, that's all."

"You have anything else to say?"

"No."

"You don't want to talk about shoes, or ships, or sealing wax?"

"No."

"In that case," he crossed to her and drew her out of the chair by her hands. "I'll race you up the stairs."

"You're on."

A rain-shimmered shaft of light lay across her eyes, revealing at surprising moments the harlequin flecks of gold. He lowered his forehead to hers, closed his eyes, and hummed a raspy note of satisfaction and pleasure. Then he drew back so he could see her better. "I'm going to tell you something," he said, "and you mustn't laugh."

"Tell me."

"You have the most beautiful eyes."

She looked up at him with eternal feminine calm. "That's very sweet. Why should I laugh?"

"Someday I'll tell you." He kissed her gently. "On second thought, I probably won't tell you. But that warning about laughing still goes."

"Why?"

"Because if you laugh, you'll lose me."

The image amused her, so she laughed, and she lost him.

"I warned you, right? Although it really doesn't matter, for all the good I was doing you."

"Don't talk about it."

He laughed in his turn. "You know something? This is going to come at you as a big surprise. Endurance is my forte. I'm not conning. That's normally what I have to recommend me. Endurance. How's that for yaks?"

"We have all kinds of time. At least you didn't reach for a cigarette."

He rolled over onto his back and spoke quietly into the common dark above them. "All things taken into consideration, Nature's really a capricious bitch. I've never cared much about the women I was with—I usually don't feel much of anything. And so I'm a paragon of control. And they do very well indeed. But with you—when I cared and it mattered, and *because* I cared and it mattered—I suddenly become the fastest gun in the east. Like I said, Nature's a bitch."

Gem turned to him. "Hey, what is all this? You're talking like it was afterwards. And here all the time I've been hoping it was between times."

He swung out of bed. "You're right! It's between times. You just wait there while I get us a resuscitating split of champagne."

"No, wait." She sat up in bed, her body outlined with silver backlight and splendid. "Come back here and let me talk to you."

He lay across the bottom of the bed and put his cheek against her feet. "You sound serious and portentous and all."

"I am. It's about this job for Mr. Dragon—"

"Please, Gem."

"No. No, now just keep quiet for a second. It has to do with a biological device that the other side is working on. It's a very ugly thing. If they come up with it before we do . . . That could be terrible, Jonathan."

He hugged her feet to him. "Gem, it doesn't matter who's ahead in this kind of race. It's like two frightened boys dueling with hand grenades at three feet. It really doesn't matter who pulls the pin first."

"What does matter is that we aren't so likely to pull the pin!"

"If you're saying that the average shopkeeper in Seattle is a humane guy, that's perfectly true. But so is the average shopkeeper in Petropavlovsk. The fact is that the pin is in the hands of men like Dragon or, even worse, at the mercy of a short circuit in some underground computer."

"But, Jonathan—"

"I'm not going to take the job, Gem. I never do sanctions when I have enough money to get along. And I don't want to talk about it anymore. All right?"

She was silent. Then she made her decision. "All right."

Jonathan kissed her feet and stood up. "Now how about that champagne?"

Her voice arrested him at the top of the loft stairs. "Jonathan?"

"Madam?"

"Am I your first black?"

He turned back. "Does that matter?"

"Of course it matters. I know you're a collector of paintings, and I wondered . . ."

He sat on the edge of the bed. "I ought to smack your bottom."

"I'm sorry."

"You still want some champagne?"

She opened her arms and beckoned with her fingers. "Afterwards."

Long Island: *June 13*

JONATHAN SIMPLY OPENED his eyes, and he was awake. Calm and happy. For the first time in years there was no blurred and viscous interphase between sleeping and waking. He stretched luxuriously, arching his back and extending his limbs until every muscle danced with strain. He felt like shouting, like making a living noise. His leg touched a damp place on the sheet, and he smiled. Jemima was not in bed, but her place was still warm and her pillow was scented lightly with her perfume, and with the perfume of her.

Nude, he swung out of bed and leaned over the choir loft rail. The steep angle of the tinted shafts of sunlight across the nave indicated late morning. He called for Jemima, his voice booming back satisfactorily from the arches.

She appeared at the door to the vestry-kitchen. "You roared, sir?"

"Good morning!"

"Good morning." She wore the trim linen suit she had arrived in, and she seemed to glow white in the shadow. "I'll have coffee ready by the time you've bathed." And she disappeared through the vestry door.

He splashed about in the Roman bath and sang, loudly but not well. What would they do today? Go into the city? Or just loaf around? It did not matter. He toweled himself down and put on a robe. It had been years since he had slept so late. It must be nearly—Jesus Christ! The Pissarro! He had promised the dealer he would pick it up by noon!

He sat on the edge of the bed, waiting impatiently for the phone on the other end of the line to be picked up.

"Hello? Yes?" The dealer's voice had the curving note of artificial interest.

"Jonathan Hemlock."

"Oh, yes. Where are you? Why are you calling?"

"I'm at my home."

"I don't understand, Jonathan. It is after eleven. How can you be here by noon?"

"I can't. Look, I want you to hold the painting for me a couple of hours. I'm on my way now."

"There is no need to rush. I cannot hold the painting. I told you I had another buyer. He is with me at this moment. It is tragic, but I warned you to be here on time. A deal is a deal."

"Give me one hour."

"My hands are tied."

"You said the other buyer had offered twelve thousand. I'll match it."

"If only I could, my good friend. But a deal is—"

"Name a price."

"I am sorry, Jonathan. The other buyer says he will top any price you make. But, since you have offered fifteen thousand, I will ask him." There was a mumble off-phone. "He says sixteen, Jonathan. What can I do?"

"Who is the other bidder?"

"Jonathan!" The voice was filled with righteous shock.

"I'll pay an extra thousand just to know."

"How can I tell you, Jonathan? I am bound by my ethics. And furthermore, he is right here in the same room with me."

"I see. All right, I'll give you a description. Just say yes if it fits. That's a thousand dollars for one syllable."

"At that rate, think what the Megilloth would bring."

"He's blond, crew-cut, chunky, small eyes—close set, face heavy and flat, probably wearing a sport jacket, his tie and socks will be in bad taste, he is probably wearing his hat in your home—"

"To a T, Jonathan. T as in thousand."

It was Clement Pope. "I know the man. He must have a top price. His employer would never trust him with unlimited funds. I offer eighteen thousand."

The dealer's voice was filled with respect. "You have that much in cash, Jonathan?"

"I have."

There was another prolonged and angry mumble off-phone. "Jonathan! I have wonderful news for you. He says he can top your offer, but he does not have the cash with him. It will be several hours before he can get it. Therefore, my good friend, if you are here by one o'clock with the nineteen thousand, the painting is yours along with my blessing."

"Nineteen thousand?"

"You have forgotten the fee for information?"

The painting would cost almost everything Jonathan had, and he would have to find some way to face his debts and Mr. Monk's wages. But at least he would have the Pissarro. "All right. I'll be there by one."

"Wonderful, Jonathan. My wife will have a glass of tea for you. So now tell me, how are you feeling? And how are the children?"

Jonathan repeated the terms of the arrangement so there would be no mistake, then he hung up.

For several minutes he sat on the edge of the bed, his eyes fixed in space, his hatred for Dragon and Pope collecting into an adamantine lump. Then he caught the smell of coffee and remembered Jemima.

She was gone. And the blue envelope, chubby with its hundred-dollar bills, was gone with her.

In a brace of rapid telephone calls designed to salvage at least the painting, Jonathan discovered that Dragon, weak after his semiannual transfusion, would not speak to him, and that the art dealer, although sympathetic to his problem and solicitous of his family's health, was firm in his intent to sell the Pissarro to Pope as soon as the money was produced.

Jonathan sat alone down in the gallery, his gaze fixed on the space he had reserved for the Pissarro. Beside him on the desk was an untouched *café au lait* cup. And next to the cup was a note from Jemima:

Jonathan:

~~I tried to make you understand last night how important this assignment~~

~~Darling, I would give anything if—~~

~~Yesterday and last night meant more to me than I can ever tell you, but there are things that~~

I had to guess. I hope you take sugar in your coffee.

Love (really)
Jemima

She had taken nothing but the money. He found the clothes he had bought neatly folded on the kitchen table. Even their dishes from last night's supper were washed and put away.

He sat. Hours passed. Above him, unseen in the empty nave, shafts of colored light and blocks of shadow swung imperceptibly on silent hinges, and evening came.

The bitterest part of his anger was turned inward. He was ashamed at being so gullible. Her warmth and radiance had blinded him, a self-inflicted abacination.

In his mental list of those who had used friendship as a weapon against him, he inscribed Jemima's name under Miles Mellough's.

"The moving finger writes," he mused to himself, "and having writ, gestures."

He closed the door to the gallery and locked it—for the last time that summer.

New York: *June 14*

". . . THE BURDENS OF the flesh, eh, Hemlock?" Dragon's voice quivered fragilely. His body was thin and weightless under the black silk sheets; his brittle-boned head scarcely dented the ebony pillow upon which his ovine hair crumpled damply. Jonathan watched the long albescent hands flutter weakly at the hems of the turned-back bedding. A certain dim light was necessary to those who attended to his medical needs, and against the pain of this light, his eyes were covered with a thick, padded black mask.

Mrs. Cerberus bent over him, her lepidote face creased with concern as she withdrew a large needle from his hip. Dragon winced, but quickly converted the expression into a thin smile.

It was the first time Jonathan had been in the bedroom behind Dragon's office. The chamber was small and draped entirely in black, and the hospital stench was overpowering. Jonathan sat unmoving on a wooden bedside chair.

"They feed me intravenously for a few days after each transfusion. Sugar and salt solution. Not a gourmet's menu, you will agree." Dragon turned his head on the pillow, directing the black eyepads toward Jonathan. "I take it by your arctic silence that you are not overwhelmed by my stoicism and brave good humor?"

Jonathan did not respond.

With a wave so feeble that gravity tugged the hand down, Dragon dismissed Mrs. Cerberus, who brushed past Jonathan with a swish of starched clothes.

"I normally enjoy our chats, Hemlock. They have an exhilarating spice of dislike about them." He spoke in aspirate breaths, stopping midphrase when necessary, allowing his labored exhalation to group the words arbitrarily. "But in this condition I am not an adequate intellectual rival. So forgive me for coming directly to the point. Where is Miss Brown?"

"Oh? Is that really her name?"

"As it happens, yes. Where is she?"

"You're telling me you don't know?"

"She turned the money over to Mr. Pope yesterday. After which she quite disappeared. You'll forgive me if I suspect you."

"I don't know where she is. But I'm interested. If you find out, please tell me."

"I see. Remember, Hemlock, she is one of ours. And you are in an ideal position to know what happens to those who harm our people."

"Let's talk about the assignment."

"Nothing must happen to Miss Brown, Hemlock."

"Let's talk about the assignment."

"Very well." Dragon sighed, shuddering with the effort. "But I regret your loss of sportsmanship. How does the Americanism go? Win a few . . . ?"

"Did you used to pull the wings off flies when you were young, Dragon?"

"Certainly not! Not flies."

Jonathan chose not to pursue the subject. "I assume the sanction has to do with the second man in Montreal. The one who was wounded in the struggle with whoeveritwas?"

"Agent Wormwood. Yes. At the time we sent you to Montreal, Search knew almost nothing about this second man. Since that time, they have been piecing together fragments of information—rumors, second sheets from note pads, statements from informers, swatches of taped telephone conversations—all the usual bits from which guilt is constructed. To be truthful, we still have less information than we have ever worked with before. But it is absolutely vital that the man be sanctioned. And quickly."

"Why? It wouldn't be the first time your people pulled a blank. What's so important about this man?"

Dragon's phosphorescent brow wrinkled as he balanced a problem for a moment, then he said, "Very well, I'll tell you. Perhaps then you will understand why we have behaved so harshly with you. And perhaps you will share our anxiety over this man." He paused, seeking a place to begin. "Tell me, Hemlock. From your Army Intelligence experience, how would you describe the ideal biological weapon?"

"Is this small talk?"

"Most pertinent."

Jonathan's voice took on the pendulum rhythm of recitation. "The disease should kill, but not quickly. The infected should require hospitalization and care, so that each case pulls one or two attendants out of action along with the victim. It should spread of itself by contact and contagion so that it will expand beyond the perimeters of the attack zone, carrying panic with it. And it must be something against which our own forces can be protected."

"Exactly. In short, Hemlock, certain virulent forms of bubonic would be ideal. Now, for years the other side has been working to develop a biological weapon based on bubonic. They have come a long way. They have perfected the delivery device; they have isolated a strain of virus with ideal characteristics; and they have injections that render their forces immune."

"I guess we'd better not piss them off."

Dragon winced with semantic pain. "Ah, the slums. Never far from the surface with you, are they? Fortunately, our own people have not been idle. We have made considerable strides in similar directions."

"Defensively, of course."

"A retaliatory weapon."

"Certainly. After all, we wear the white hats."

"I'm afraid I do not understand."

"An Americanism."

"I see. Now, both sides have reached impasses. Our people lack the ability to immunize against the virus. The other side lacks a satisfactory culture medium that will keep the virus alive through the extremes of temperature and shock involved in intercontinental missile delivery. We are working on discovering their process of immunization, and they would like very much to know the composition of our culture medium."

"Have you considered direct barter?"

"Please don't feel called upon to lighten my illness with little jokes, Hemlock."

"How does all this fascinating business affect me?"

"CII was given the assignment of delaying the other side's progress."

"The task was entrusted to CII? The CII of the Cuban Invasion? The CII of the Gaza incident? The CII of the Spy Ships? It would seem our government enjoys playing Russian roulette with an automatic."

Dragon's voice was crisp. "In point of fact, Dr. Hemlock, we have gone a long way toward effectively negating their entire biological warfare program."

"And how was this wonder accomplished?"

"By allowing them to intercept our formula for the culture medium." There was a certain pride in Dragon's tone.

"But not the real one," Jonathan assumed.

"But not the real one."

"And they are so stupid that they will not discover this."

"It is not a matter of stupidity. The medium passes every laboratory test. When our people stumbled upon it—"

"Sounds like our people."

". . . *when our people* came upon the medium, they believed they had the answer to keeping the virus alive under all conditions. We gave it exhaustive tests. If we had not chanced to test it under combat conditions, we would never have discovered its flaw."

"Under combat conditions?"

"That is none of your affair." Dragon was angry at himself for the slip.

"It's about those white hats."

Dragon seemed to slump with fatigue, although he made no movement. He appeared to collapse from within, to become smaller in the chest and thinner in the face. He drew several shallow breaths, blowing each out through slack lips and puffing cheeks.

"So then, Hemlock," he continued after recovery, "you can understand our urgency."

"Frankly, I don't. If we're so far out ahead in this criminal competition . . ." he shrugged.

"We recently suffered a great setback. Three of our most important scientists have died within the last month."

"Assassination?"

"No-o." Dragon was palpably uncomfortable. "I told you that we had not yet developed an effective immunization, and . . . This is not a laughing matter, Hemlock!"

"I'm sorry." Jonathan wiped the tears from his eyes and attempted to control himself. "But the poetic justice . . ." He laughed afresh.

"You are easily moved to risibility." Dragon's voice was icy. "May I go on?"

Jonathan waved a permissive hand and chuckled again to himself.

"The method we used to allow the medium to fall into enemy hands was not without brilliance. We had it transferred to one of our agents, this Wormwood, in Montreal."

"And you let the fact of the transfer leak to the other side."

"More subtle than that, Hemlock. We did everything in our power to prevent them from intercepting—with one exception. We used an incompetent agent for the job."

"You just pushed this ass out in the traffic and let them run over him?"

"Wormwood was a man of dangerously limited abilities. Sooner or later . . ." He made a gesture of inevitability. "At this point, you enter the picture. For our little ploy to be successful, the assassination of Wormwood had to be avenged just as though we were seriously chagrined at his loss. Indeed, considering the importance of the information, the other side would expect us to sanction with more than usual vigor. And we must not disappoint them. CII considers it vital to the national defense that we pursue and liquidate *both* of the men involved in the assassination. And—for certain reasons—you are the only man who can accomplish the second sanction." Dragon paused, his mathematical mind scanning over the conversation to judge if he had left any vital matter out. He decided he had not. "Do you understand now why we brought such uncommon pressure to bear on you?"

"Why am I the only man who can accomplish the sanction?"

"First. Do you accept the assignment?"

"I accept."

The cotton tuft eyebrows raised a fraction of an inch. "Just like that? No further aggression?"

"You'll pay for it."

"I expect to. But not too much, of course."

"We'll see. Tell me about the target."

Dragon paused to collect his strength. "Allow me to begin with the details of Wormwood's murder. There were two men involved. The active role was played by Garcia Kruger, now no longer with us. It was probably he who delivered the first blow; it was almost certainly he who cut open Wormwood's throat and stomach with a pocket knife to retrieve the pellet he had swallowed. The second man was evidently not prepared for violence on this level. He was sickened by the operation; he vomited on the floor. I tell you this to acquaint you with the kind of man you will be dealing with. From his actions in the room and after, Search estimates that he is not a professional from the other side. The chances are that he was involved in the business for the money—a motive you must be sympathetic with."

"What's my target's name?"

"We don't know."

"Where is he now?"

"We don't know."

With growing doubt, Jonathan asked, "You have a description, haven't you?"

"Only the vaguest, I'm afraid. The target is male, not a Canadian citizen, and he is evidently an accomplished mountain climber. We were able to put that much together from one letter delivered to his hotel several days after his departure."

"That's lovely. You want me to kill every climber who hasn't the good fortune to be Canadian."

"Not quite. Our man will be involved in a climb in the Alps this summer."

"That narrows it to maybe three or four thousand men."

"Fewer than that, Hemlock. We know which mountain he will attempt."

"Well?"

"The Eiger." Dragon waited for the effect.

After a pause filled with images of the most terrifying moments in his climbing career, Jonathan asked with fatalistic assurance, "North Face, of course."

"That is correct." Dragon enjoyed the concern evident in Jonathan's voice. He knew of the two disastrous attempts Jonathan had made on that treacherous face, each of which had failed to claim his life by only the narrowest margin.

"If this man is taking a shot at the Eigerwand, the chances are good that my work will be done for me." Jonathan admired the target, whoever he was.

"I am not a pantheist, Hemlock. God is acknowledgedly on our side, but we are less sure of Nature. After all, you twice attempted the face, and yet you are alive." Dragon took pleasure in reminding him that: "Of course, both of your attempts were unsuccessful."

"I got back off the face alive both times. For Eigerwand, that's a kind of success." Jonathan turned back to business. "Tell me, how many teams are now training for a go at the North Face?"

"Two. One is an Italian team—"

"Forget that one. After the '57 affair, no sane man would go on the hill with an Italian team."

"So my researchers have informed me. The other attempt is scheduled for six weeks from now. The International Alpine Association is sponsoring a goodwill climb to be made by representative climbers from Germany, Austria, France, and the United States."

"I've read about it."

"The American representative was to have been a Mr. Lawrence Scott."

Jonathan laughed. "I know Scotty well; we've climbed together. You're insane if you imagine he had anything to do with the Montreal business."

"I am not insane. My disability is acroma, not acromania. We share your belief in Mr. Scott's innocence. Recall that I said he *was* to have been the American representative. Unfortunately, he had an automotive accident yesterday, and he will not climb for many years, if ever."

Jonathan recalled Scotty's free-swinging, ballet-cum-mathematics style. "You really are a shit, you know."

"Be that as it may, the American Alpine Association will contact you soon to replace Mr. Scott. There will be no objection from the international association. Your fame as a climber precedes you."

"The AAA wouldn't contact me. I haven't climbed for years. They know that. They know I'm not up to a go at the Eiger."

"Nevertheless, they will contact you. The State Department has brought certain pressure to bear on them. So, Hemlock," Dragon said with a tone of wrapping the business up, "your target is either the Frenchman, the German, or the Austrian. We have worked out a way to discover which one before the climb starts. But, to lend verisimilitude to your cover, you will train as though you were actually going to make the climb. And there is always the possibility that the sanction will be made on the face itself. By the way, an old friend of yours will be in Switzerland with you: Mr. Benjamin Bowman."

"Big Ben?" Despite the circumstances, the thought of drinking beer and joking with Big Ben again pleased Jonathan. "But Ben can't make that climb. He's too old for Eiger. So, for that matter, am I."

"The Alpine Association did not select him as a climber. He will be arranging equipment and transportation for the team and managing things. There's a term for it."

"Ground man."

"Ground man, then. We were rather hoping that Mr. Bowman knew about your work with us. Does he?"

"Certainly not."

"Pity. It might be useful to have a devoted associate with you, should it turn out that we cannot nominate the target for you before the climb begins. It might be wise for you to take him into your confidence."

Jonathan rejected the idea out of hand. With his simple and robust sense of ethics, Big Ben would never understand killing for profit. Risking one's life for sport was a different matter. That made excellent sense to Ben.

Dragon's mention that Jonathan would meet a former acquaintance flashed the image of Miles Mellough through his mind. He recalled Dragon's allusion to him during their last conversation. "What part does Mellough play in all this?"

"I assumed you would ask. Frankly, we are not sure. He arrived in Montreal two days before Wormwood's assassination, and he departed the day after. We both know Mr. Mellough too well to imagine a coincidence. It is my assumption that he acted as courier for the culture formula. Naturally, we did not interfere with him until he had passed on the information. Now that that's done, I have no objection to his falling victim to your epic sense of loyalty and honor—like that Greek fellow did. Indeed, we offer you Mr. Mellough as a kind of fringe benefit."

"Six weeks," Jonathan mused. "I'll have to work very hard at conditioning."

"That is your affair."

"Big Ben runs a training school in Arizona. I want to go there for a month."

"If you wish."

"At your expense."

Dragon's voice was heavy with the sarcasm he reserved for the mercenary instincts of his agents. "Naturally, Hemlock." He groped above him for a buzzer to summon Mrs. Cerberus. For his part, the conversation was ended. Jonathan observed his fumbling efforts without offering assistance. "Now that you know the background, Hemlock, you can appreciate why we need you—and only you—to undertake this sanction. You used to climb mountains, and there seem to be so many people of your acquaintance somehow involved in this matter. You appear to be tangled in the skein of fate."

Mrs. Cerberus entered with an officious rustle of crisp clothing. She brushed past Jonathan, knocking against his chair with her formidable hip. He wondered if this ghastly pair copulated. Who else would be available for Dragon? He looked at them and decided that, if they had offspring, they would produce something that could model for Hieronymus Bosch.

In dismissal Dragon said, "I will keep you informed to whatever extent I consider necessary."

"Doesn't it strike you that we have passed over the matter of payment?"

"Oh, of course. We intend to be particularly generous, considering the rigors of the assignment and the emotional difficulties concomitant to our little combat of wills. You will receive thirty thousand dollars upon completion of the sanction. Of course, the stolen twenty thousand dollars is on its way back to you. And as for the Pissarro, Miss Brown made it clear on the telephone the other day that she would not perform her task unless we promised to present it to you as a gift. And that we do. I am sure that is more than you expected."

"Frankly, it is more than I expected you to offer. But it's much less than I shall receive."

"Oh?" Mrs. Cerberus placed a restraining hand on Dragon's arm, solicitous of his blood pressure.

"Yes," Jonathan continued easily. "I shall receive the Pissarro right now, and a hundred thousand dollars when I finish the job. Plus expenses, of course."

"You recognize that this is outrageous."

"Yes. But I view it as retirement pay. This is the last assignment I am going to take for your people."

"That, of course, is your own decision. Unlike those on the other side, we have no desire to keep you after your affection for us has fled. But we do not intend to support you for life."

"A hundred thousand will only support me for four years."

"After which?"

"I'll think of something by then."

"I have no doubt of it. But a hundred thousand dollars is out of the question."

"Oh, no, it isn't. I have listened patiently while you described the pressing need for the sanction, and your need for me—and no one else—to handle it. You have no choice but to pay what I ask."

Dragon was pensive. "You are punishing us for Miss Brown. Is that it?"

Jonathan flashed angrily. "Just pay the money."

"I have been expecting your withdrawal from our organization for some time, Hemlock. Mr. Pope and I were discussing the possibility just this morning."

"That's another thing. If you want to keep Pope intact, keep him out of my way."

"You are striking to the right and left in your rage, aren't you." Dragon considered for a moment. "You have something more on your mind. You know perfectly well that I could promise the money now, then either fail to pay or get it back from you by some means."

"That will never happen again," Jonathan said coldly. "I shall receive the money now—a cashier's check sent to my bank with instructions that it will be paid to me on my appearance or your further instructions, not before seven weeks from now. If I fail to make the sanction, I'll probably be dead, and the check will go uncashed. If I make it, I take the money and retire. If I don't, you can instruct the bank to pay the money to you, on proof of my death."

Dragon pressed the thick pads against his eyes and searched the blackness for a flaw in Jonathan's case. Then his hands dropped to the black sheets. He laughed his three ha's. "Do you know, Hemlock? I think you have us." There was a mixture of wonder and admiration in his voice. "The check will be sent to your bank as you have directed; the painting will be in your home when you return."

"Good."

"I imagine this is the last time I shall have the pleasure of your company. I shall miss you, Hemlock."

"You always have Mrs. Cerberus here."

There was a flat sadness in the response. "True."

Jonathan rose to leave, but he was restrained by Dragon's last question. "You are quite sure that you had nothing to do with the disappearance of Miss Brown?"

"Quite sure. But I suspect she'll turn up sooner or later."

Long Island: *That Evening*

MAUVE AND PEWTER skies at sunset; the leaden skin of the ocean undulated in low furrows, alive only at the thin froth edge that the tide had languidly carried up close to his feet.

He had sat on the hard sand of the lower beach for hours, since his return from the city. Feeling heavy and tired, he rose with a grunt and batted the sand from his trousers. He had not yet been in the house, having chosen instead, after a moment of indecision at the door, to roam the grounds.

In the vestibule he discovered a large rectangle wrapped in brown paper and tied with string. He assumed it was the Pissarro, but he did not bother to examine it; indeed, he did not even touch it. As a matter of principle, he had insisted on its return from Dragon, but he no longer had a taste for it.

The nave was cool and thick with shadow. He walked its length and mounted the steps to his bar. He splashed half a glass of Laphroaig into a tumbler and drank it off, then he refilled his glass and turned to face the nave, leaning his elbows on the bar.

A dim arc of light caught the tail of his eye—the firefly trail of a cigarette.

"Gem?"

Jonathan crossed rapidly to the dim female figure sitting in the greenhouse garden.

"What are you doing here?"

"Making myself available, as usual," Cherry answered. "Is that for me?" She indicated the glass of Scotch.

"No. Go home." Jonathan sat in a wicker chair opposite her, not so displeased with the idea of company as he seemed, but feeling the sick adrenalin collapse of vast disappointment.

"I don't know what I'm going to do with you, Dr. Hemlock." Cherry rose to get the drink he had refused her. "You're always trying to butter me up," she said over her shoulder as she walked up to the bar. "I know what you're after with all that sweet talk about 'No! Go home.' You're just trying to get into my pants. Maybe the only way to get rid of you is to finally give in." She paused to allow him to respond. He did not. "Yeah, yeah, yeah," she continued, still covering her initial sting with a balm of words, "I guess that's the only way I'll get any peace. Hey! Is there such a thing as a Freudian pun?" Her next pause drew no response either. By now she had returned with her drink, and she slumped petulantly into her chair. "All right. How do you feel about the films of Marcel Carné? Do you believe the advantages of nonstick cooking with Teflon justify the expense of the space program? Or, what are your views on the tactical problems of mass retreat should there ever be a war between the Italians and the Arabs?" Then she paused. "Who's Gem?"

"Go home."

"By which I infer she is a woman. She must be something else, considering how fast you got over here, from the bar just now."

Jonathan's voice was paternal. "Look, dear. I'm not up to it tonight."

"The evening sparkles with puns. Can I get you another drink?"

"Please."

"You don't want me to go home really," she said as she went again to the bar. "You're feeling bad, and you want to talk about it."

"You couldn't be more wrong."

"About your feeling bad?"

"About my wanting to talk about it."

"This Gem person must really have come at you. I hate her without even knowing her. Here." She gave him the tumbler. "I'm going to get you all liquored up, and I'm going to make you on the rebound." She produced her best imitation of a witch's cackle.

Jonathan was angry, therefore embarrassed. "For Christ's sake, I'm not on the rebound!"

"Liar, liar, your pants are on fire. Say, I'll bet they really are."

"Go home."

"Was she pretty good in bed?"

Jonathan's voice chilled instantly. "Now you'd better really go home."

Cherry was cowed. "I'm sorry, Jonathan. That was a stupid thing to say. But gee-golly, pal, how do you think it affects a girl's ego when she's been trying to make a man for ever and ever, then some other woman with an unlikely name just takes him—like that." She tried several times to snap her fingers, but produced no sound. "I never could do that."

Jonathan smiled in spite of himself. "Listen, dear. I'll be leaving tomorrow morning."

"For how long?"

"Most of the summer."

"Because of this girl?"

"No! I'm going to do a little climbing."

"You just happen to suddenly decide on that after you meet this woman, right?"

"She has nothing to do with it."

"I really have to doubt that. All right. When are you leaving?"

"Dawnish."

"Well, great! We have the whole night. What do you say, mister. Huh? Huh? What do you say? You going to set me loose before you go? Remember, it's going to be a long summer for us virgins."

"Will you look after the place while I'm away?"

"Gladly. Now, let's talk about return favors."

"Drink up and go home. I have to get some sleep."

Cherry nodded resignedly. "OK. That woman must really have come at you. I hate her."

"Me too," he said quietly.

"Oh, bullshit, Jonathan!"

"There's a new facet of your vocabulary."

"I think I'd better go home."

He walked her to the door and kissed her on the forehead. "I'll see you when I get back."

"Hey, what do you say to a mountain climber? You tell an actor to break a leg, but that sounds kind of ominous for a mountain climber."

"You say you hope it's a go."

"I hope it's a go."

"Thank you. Good night."

"Great. Thanks a lot for that 'good night.' I'll just cling to that all night long."

Arizona: *June 15*

STANDING BETWEEN HIS suitcases at the grassy edge of a modest airfield, Jonathan watched the CII cabin jet from which he had just deplaned turn and, with a majestic conversion of power into pollution, taxi to the leeward end of the strip. The wave of heat behind its engine rippled the landscape; its atonic roar was painful.

From across the strip, a new but battered Land-Rover darted out between two corrugated metal hangars, skidded in a right-angle turn that sprayed dust over complaining mechanics, bounced with all four wheels off the ground over a mound of gravel, narrowly missed a Piper that was warming up, triggering a vigorous exchange of abuse between driver and pilot, then bore down on Jonathan with a maximum acceleration until, at the last possible moment, the four-wheel brakes were locked and the Rover screeched to a side-slipping stop, its bumper only inches from Jonathan's knee.

Big Ben Bowman was out before the Land-Rover stopped rocking. "Jon! Goddam my eyes, how are you?" He ripped one suitcase from Jonathan's grasp and tossed it into the back of the vehicle with scant concern for the contents. "I'll tell you one thing, ol' buddy. We're going to drink a bunch of beer before you get out of here. Hey!" His broad hairy paws closed down on Jonathan's upper arms, and after an awkward crushing hug, Jonathan was held out at arm's length for inspection. "You're looking good, ol' buddy. A little soft, maybe. But goddam my ass if it ain't good to see you! Wait till you see the ol' place. It's got . . ." The scream of the CII jet taxiing to take off eclipsed all sound, but Big Ben talked on insouciantly as he loaded Jonathan's second bag and grappled its owner into the Rover. Ben hopped around to jump in behind the wheel, slapped into gear, and they jumped off, bouncing over the drain ditch beside the field as they described a wide skidding turn. Jonathan gripped the seat and shouted as he caught sight of the CII jet roaring down on them from the left. Big Ben laughed and made a sharp cut to the right, and for a moment they raced parallel to the jet, under the shadow of its wing. "No chance!" Ben shouted over the combined din, and he turned left, passing so close behind the jet that Jonathan felt the hot, gritty blast of its engine.

"For Christ's sake, Ben!"

"Can't help it! Can't beat a jet!" Then he roared with laughter and jammed down on the gas pedal. They cut around the random scatter of airport buildings without using the designed roads, leaped the curbing to the main highway, and knifed through traffic with a U-turn that made brakes squeal and horns bleat angrily. Ben gestured classically to the offended drivers.

About a mile out of town they skidded off the highway onto a dirt road. "Just a piece down this way, ol' buddy," Ben shouted. "You remember?"

"About twenty miles, isn't it?"

"Yeah, about. Takes eighteen minutes, unless I'm in a hurry."

Jonathan gripped the "chicken bar" and said as casually as he could, "I don't see any special reason to hurry, Ben."

"You won't recognize the old place!"

"I hope I get a chance to see it."

"What?"

"Nothing!"

As they raced along, bouncing over chuckholes, Ben described some of the improvements he had made. Evidently the whole character of his climbing school had changed to some kind of resort ranch. He looked at Jonathan while he talked, only glancing at the road to make corrections when he felt the wheels go into the soft shoulder. Jonathan had forgotten Ben's crisis-style of driving. On a sheer face with nothing but rotten rock to cling to, there was no man he would rather have beside him, but in the driver's seat . . .

"Oh-oh! Hang on!"

They were suddenly in a cut-back turn and going too fast to make it. The Rover bounced over the shoulder, and the wheels on Jonathan's side dug into the soft sand. For an interminable moment they balanced on those wheels, then Ben whipped to the right, slamming the wheels back to the sand and beginning a fishtail skid. He steered into the skid and pressed down on the gas, converting the skid into a power slide that spun them back up onto the road. "Goddam my ass if I don't forget that turn every time!"

"Ben, I think I'd rather walk."

"OK, OK." He laughed and slowed down for a time, but by inevitable degrees their speed increased, and it was not long before Jonathan's hands were white-knuckled on the chicken bar again. He decided there was nothing to be gained by wearing himself out trying to guide the Land Rover by positive concentration, so he relaxed fatalistically and tried to empty his mind of thought.

Big Ben chuckled.

"What is it?" Jonathan asked.

"I was thinking about the Aconcagua. Remember what I did to that old bitch?"

"I remember."

They had met in the Alps. The gulf between their temperaments suggested that they would be an unlikely team, and neither had been pleased when they were thrown together because their partners were unavailable for climbs they had set their hearts on. So with formidable misgivings they decided to make the climbs together, and they treated each other with that politeness that substitutes for friendship. Slowly and reluctantly they discovered that their polar talents as climbers meshed to create a powerful team. Jonathan attacked a mountain like a mathematical problem, picking routes, evaluating supplies against energy, against time; Big Ben pounded the face into submission with his uncommon strength and indomitable will. Fanciful fellow climbers came to refer to them as The Rapier and The Mace, which nicknames caught the fancy of writers who contributed articles on their achievements to Alpine journals. Jonathan was particularly suited to rock work where the minute tactics of leverage and purchase fitted his intellectual style. Big Ben took over when they were on ice and snow where he would pant and bull through the drifts, breasting an upward path like an inevitable machine of fate.

In bivouac, their differences of personality again operated as a lubricant for the social friction these cramped and sometimes dangerous quarters induce. Ben was older by ten years, loquacious, loudly appreciative of humor. So divergent were their backgrounds and values that they were never in social competition. Even in the lodge after a victory they celebrated in their different ways with different people, and they rewarded themselves that night with different kinds of girls.

For six years they passed the climbing seasons together, bagging peaks: Walker, Dru, the Canadian Rockies. And their international reputations were in no way diminished by Jonathan's contributions to mountaineering publications in which their accomplishments were recorded with calculated phlegmatic understatement that eventually became the stylistic standard for such journals.

It was quite natural, therefore, that when a team of young Germans determined to assail Aconcagua, the highest peak in the Western Hemisphere, they contacted Jonathan and Ben to accompany them. Ben was particularly enthusiastic; it was his kind of climb, a grinding, man-eroding ascent requiring little in the way of surface tactics, but much in the way of endurance and supply strategy.

Jonathan's response was cooler. As was just, considering that they had conceived the plan, the Germans were to be the primary assault pair, Jonathan and Ben working in support and going after the peak only if something untoward happened to the Germans. It was fair that it should be so, but it was not Jonathan's way. Unlike Ben, who loved each step of a climb, Jonathan climbed for the victory. The great expense involved also dampened Jonathan's exuberance, as did the fact that his particular talents would be of secondary importance on a climb like this.

But Ben was not to be denied. Their financial problems he solved by selling the small ranch that was his livelihood; and in a long telephone call he persuaded Jonathan by admitting that, considering his age, this would probably be the last major climb he would ever make.

As it turned out, he was right.

From the sea, Aconcagua seems to rise up just behind Valparaiso, a regular and, from that distance, gentle cone. But getting there is half the hell. Its base is tucked in among a tangle of lower mountains, and the team spent a week alternating between the antithetical torments of miasmic jungle and dusty ravines as they followed the old Fitz-Gerald route to the foot.

There is in this world no more demoralizing climb than that vast heap of rotten rock and ice. It destroys men, not with the noble counterstrokes of an Eigerwand or a Nanga Parbat, but by eroding a man's nerve and body until he is a staggering, whimpering maniac. No single stretch of the hill is particularly difficult, or even interesting in the Alpine sense. It is no exaggeration to say that any athletic layman could handle any given thousand feet of it, if properly equipped and conditioned to the thin air. But Aconcagua rises thousands upon thousands of feet, and one climbs hour after hour up through shale and ragged rock, through moraine and crevassed glacier, day upon day, with no sense of accomplishment, with no feeling that the summit is nearing. And time and again, the flash storms that twist around the peaks pin the climbers down for who knows how long. Maybe forever. And still that pile of garbage left from the Creation goes on and upward.

Within three thousand feet of the summit, one of the Germans gave in, demoralized with mountain sickness and the bone-deep cold. "What's the use?" he asked. "It really doesn't matter." They all knew what he meant. So slight is the technical challenge of the Aconcagua that it is less a cachet to a climber's career than an avowal of the latent death wish that drives so many of them up.

But no bitch-kitty of a hill was going to stop Big Ben! And it was unthinkable that Jonathan could let him go it alone. It was decided that the Germans would stay where they were and try to improve the camp to receive the new summit team when they staggered back.

The next fifteen hundred feet cost Ben and Jonathan an entire day, and they lost half of their provisions in a near fall.

The next day they were pinned down by a flash storm. Saint Elmo's fire sparkled from the tips of their ice axes. With wooden fingers they clung to the edges of the strip of canvas that was their only protection from the screaming wind. The fabric bellied and flapped with pistol-shot reports; it twisted and contorted in their numb hands like a maddened wounded thing seeking vengeance.

With the coming of night, the storm passed, and they had to kick the canvas from hands that had lost the power to relax. Jonathan had had it. He told Ben they must go back the next morning.

Ben's teeth were clenched and tears of frustration flowed from the corners of his eyes and froze on the stubble of his beard. "Goddam it!" he sobbed. "Goddam this frigging hill!" Then his temper ruptured and he went after the mountain with his ice axe, beating it and tearing at it until the thin air and fatigue left him panting on the snow. Jonathan pulled him up and helped him back to their scant cover. By full dark they were dug in as comfortably as possible. The wind moaned, but the storm remained lurking in ambuscade, so they were able to get a little rest.

"You know what it is, ol' buddy?" Ben asked in the close dark. He was calm again, but his teeth were chattering with the cold, and that lent a frighteningly unstable sound to his voice. "I'm getting old, Jon. This has got to be my last hill. And goddam my ass if this old bitch is going to bust me. You know what I mean?"

Jonathan reached out in the dark and gripped his hand.

A quarter of an hour later Ben's voice was calm and flat. "We'll try tomorrow, right?"

"All right," Jonathan said. But he did not believe it.

The dawn brought ugly weather with it, and Jonathan surrendered his last feeble hope of making the summit. His concern now was getting down alive.

About noon, the weather healed up and they dug themselves out. Before Jonathan could phrase his reasons for turning back, Ben had started determinedly upward. There was nothing to do but follow.

Six hours later they were on the summit. Jonathan's memory of the last *étape* is foggy. Step after step, breaking through the wind crust and sinking up to the crotch in the unstable snow, they pressed blindly on, stumbling, slipping, reason reduced to concentration on the task of one more step.

But they were on the summit. They could not see a rope's length out into the swirling spindrift.

"Not even a goddamned view!" Ben complained. Then he fumbled with the drawstring of his plastic outer pants and dropped them away. After a struggle with his wool ski pants, he stood up free and expressed his contempt for the Aconcagua in ancient and eloquent style.

As they plunged and picked their way back down, eager to make time, but fearful of setting off an avalanche, Jonathan noticed that Ben was clumsy and unsteady.

"What's wrong?"

"Ain't got no feet down there, ol' buddy."

"How long since you felt them?"

"Couple of hours, I guess."

Jonathan dug a shallow shelter in the snow and fumbled Ben's boots off. The toes were white and hard as ivory. For a quarter of an hour Jonathan held the frigid feet against his bare chest inside his coat. Ben howled with vituperation as feeling returned to one foot, replacing numbness with surges of pain. But the other foot remained rigid and white, and Jonathan knew there was nothing to be gained by continuing first aid. But there was great danger of a fresh storm catching them in the open. They pushed on.

The Germans were magnificent. When the two came staggering into camp, they took Ben from Jonathan and all but carried him down. It was all Jonathan could do to stumble along behind, broken-winded and half snow-blind.

Ben looked uncomfortable and out of place sitting up against a pile of pillows in the Valparaiso hospital. By way of small talk, Jonathan accused him of malingering there because he was making the nurses every night.

"I wouldn't touch them with a barge pole, ol' buddy. Anybody who would take a man's toes when he ain't looking would take just about anything."

That was the last mention of the amputated toes. They both knew Big Ben would never make a major climb again.

They felt neither elation nor accomplishment as they watched the mountain slip into the sea beyond the stern of their ship. They did not feel proud of having made it, nor did the Germans feel shame for having failed. That is the way it is with that pile of fossilized shit.

Back in the States, Ben set about establishing his little school for climbing in a corner of Arizona where many kinds of natural face problems abound. So few people wanted the kind of advanced training he offered that Jonathan wondered how he kept his head above water. To be sure, he and twenty or so other skilled climbers made it a practice to patronize Ben's school, but that is just what it was—patronizing. The repeated struggles to force Ben to accept payment for lodging and training embarrassed Jonathan, and he stopped coming. Soon after, he stopped climbing altogether as his new home and his collection of paintings absorbed all his interest.

"Yeah," Ben shouted as they landed back in the seat after a bad bump, "I sure paid that old bitch back, didn't I?"

"You ever consider what would have happened if you had gotten local frostbite?"

Ben laughed. "Oh, my! There'd have been wailing and moaning on the reservation, and lots of Indian girls dripping tears, ol' buddy."

They broke over a little rise and started winding down into Ben's valley, leaving a rising trail of dust in their wake. Jonathan was surprised as he looked down on Ben's spread. It certainly had changed. Gone was the modest grouping of cabins around a cookhouse. There was a large swimming pool flashing emerald and surrounded on three sides by the body and wings of a pseudo-

Indian lodge, and what appeared to be a patio lounge was dotted with the white blobs of people in swimming suits who looked nothing at all like climbers. There was no comparison between this and the Spartan training school he remembered.

"How long has all this been here?" he asked as they slithered down the steep road.

"About two years. Like it?"

"Impressive."

They sped across the gravel parking area and banged into a retaining log before rocking to a stop. Jonathan climbed out slowly and stretched his back to regroup his bones. The unmoving earth underfoot was a pleasure.

It was not until they were sitting in the shadowy cool of the bar, concentrating on much appreciated glasses of beer, that Jonathan had leisure to look at his host. Robust virility was projected through every detail of Ben's face, from the thick, close-cropped silver hair to the broad leathery face that looked as though it had been designed by Hormel and shaped with a dull saber. Two deep creases folded in his heavily tanned cheeks, and the corners of his eyes crinkled into patterns like aerial photographs of the Nile Delta.

The first beers drained off, Ben signaled the Indian bartender for two more. Jonathan recalled Ben's epic fondness for beer that had been an object of comment and admiration among the climbing community.

"Very posh," Jonathan complimented, scanning his surroundings.

"Yeah, it begins to look like I'll make it through the winter."

The bar was separated by a low wall of local stone from the lounge, through which an artificial stream wound its way among the tables, each of which was on a little rock island connected to the walkways by an arched stone bridge. A few couples in sports clothes talked quietly over ice-and-foliage drinks, enjoying the air conditioning and ignoring the insipid music from ubiquitous but discreet speakers. One end of the lounge had a glass wall through which could be seen the pool and bathers. There was a scattering of prosperous-looking men with horizontal suntans who sat in drinking groups around white iron tables, or sat on the edges of gaudy padded sun chairs, concentrating on stock journals, their stomachs depending between their legs. Some waddled aimlessly along the sides of the pool.

Young ladies lolled hopefully on beach chairs, most of them with one knee up, revealing a beacon of inner thigh. Sunglasses were directed at books and magazines, but eyes above them scouted the action.

Ben regarded Jonathan for a moment, his drooping blue eyes crinkled up at the sides. He nodded. "Yeah, it's really good to see you, ol' buddy. My phony guests really make my ass weary. How you been doing? Keeping the world at arm's length?"

"I'm staying alive."

"How's that screwy church of yours?"

"It keeps the rain off my head."

"Good." He was pensive for a moment. "What's this all about, Jon? I got this telegram telling me to take care of you and get you into condition for a climb. They said they would pay all expenses. What does that mean, ol' buddy? 'All expenses' can cover a lot of ground. Are these people friends? Want me to take it easy on them?"

"By no means. They're not friends. Soak them. Give me the best accommodations you have, and put all your meals and drinks on my bill."

"Well now! Ain't that nice! Goddam my eyes if we don't have some kind of ball at their expense. Hey! Talking about climbing. I've been invited to be ground man for a bunch taking a shot at the Eiger. How about that?"

"It's great." Jonathan knew his next statement would cause comment, so he tried to drop it off-handedly. "Matter of fact, that's the climb I'm here to train for." He waited for the reaction.

Ben's smile faded frankly, and he stared at Jonathan for a second. "You're kidding."

"No."

"What happened to Scotty?"

"He had an auto accident."

"Poor bastard. He was really looking forward to it." Ben communicated with his beer for a moment. "How come they picked you?"

"I don't know. Wanted to add class to an altogether undistinguished team, I guess."

"Come on. Don't bullshit me, ol' buddy."

"I honestly don't know why they picked me."

"But you are going?"

"That's right."

A girl in an abbreviated bikini came up to the bar and squeaked her still-damp bottom onto a stool one away from Jonathan, who did not respond to her automatic smile of greeting.

"Beat it, Buns," Ben said, slapping her ass with a moist smack. She giggled and went back to the poolside.

"Getting much climbing in?" Jonathan asked.

"Oh, I gimp up some small stuff, just for the hell of it. Matter of fact, that part of the business is long gone. As you can see, my patrons come here to hunt, not climb." He reached over the bar and took an extra bottle of beer. "Come on, Jon. Let's go talk."

They threaded their way along the lounge walkway and over a bridge to the most secluded island.

After waving the waiter away, Ben sipped his beer slowly, trying to collect his thoughts. Then he carefully dusted the top of the table with his hand. "You're—ah—what now? Thirty-five?"

"Thirty-seven."

"Yeah." Ben looked out across his lounge toward the pool, feeling he had made his point.

"I know what you're thinking, Ben. But I have to go."

"You've been on the Eiger before. Twice, as I recall."

"Right."

"Then you know."

"Yes."

Ben sighed with resignation, then he changed the tone of his comments, as befitted a friend. "All right, it's your thing. The climb starts in six weeks. You'll want to get to Switzerland for some practice runs, and you'll need a little rest after I'm done with you. How long do you want to spend conditioning here?"

"Three, four weeks."

Ben nodded. "Well, at least you don't have any fat on you. But you're going to have to sweat, ol' buddy. How are the legs?"

"They reach from the crotch to the ground. That's about all you can say for them."

"Uh-huh. Enjoy that beer, Jon. It's your last for a week at least."

Jonathan finished it slowly.

Arizona: *June 16-27*

THE INSISTENT GRIND of the door buzzer insinuated itself into the narrative structure of Jonathan's dream, then it shattered his heavy sleep, and local reality flowed in through the cracks. He stumbled to the door and clawed it open without ever getting both eyes open at the same time. As he leaned against the frame, his head hanging down, the Indian bellboy wished him a good morning cheerily and told him that Mr. Bowman had left instructions to be sure Dr. Hemlock was wide awake.

"Whadymizid?" Jonathan asked.

"Pardon me, sir?"

"What . . . time . . . is . . . it?"

"Three-thirty, sir."

Jonathan turned back into the room and fell across the bed, muttering to himself, "This can't be happening."

No sooner had he slipped into a vertiginous sleep than the phone rang. "Go away," he mumbled without picking up the receiver, but it rang on without mercy. He pulled it onto the bed and pawed around with his eyes clamped shut until he had located the receiver.

"Rise and shine, ol' buddy!"

"Ben—argh—" He cleared his throat. "Why are you doing this to me?"

"Breakfast in ten minutes."

"No."

"You want me to send someone up there with a bucket of ice water?"

"He better be someone you're tired of having around."

Ben laughed and hung up. Jonathan rolled out and groped his way around until he lucked into the bathroom where he let a cold shower drum consciousness into him until he felt the danger of accident by falling was remote.

Ben pushed two more eggs onto Jonathan's plate. "Put them down, ol' buddy. And finish the steak."

They were alone in the lodge kitchen, surrounded by glowing, impersonal, stainless steel. Their voices had a cellblock bounce.

Jonathan looked at the eggs with nausea constricting his throat. "Ben, I've never lied to you, have I? Honest to God, I believe I'm dying. And I've always wanted to die in bed."

"Sit back down and get at that chow!"

It was one thing to push food into his mouth, but another to swallow it.

Ben chatted on, impervious to the stares of hate. "I've been up half the night working out details of the Eiger climb. I'm buying the heavy equipment for the team and bringing it over with me. I'll order your climbing kit with the rest. You can go with jeans and soft shoes for the first few days here. We ain't going to do anything hard right at first. Come on! Drink the milk!" Ben finished his beer and opened another can. The beer for breakfast was more than Jonathan could stand to look at. "You still get your climbing boots in Spain?"

Jonathan nodded heavily and found the lower part of the motion so appealing that he let his head hang there and tried to return to sleep.

"All right. Leave me their name and your account number and I'll get a cable off today. Come on! Time's a-wasting! Eat!"

The one-mile, two-minute drive across open grassland in inky predawn dark brought Jonathan fully awake.

For three hours without a rest they climbed a rough, switch-back trail up one of the faces that ringed around the flat-bottomed depression in which Ben had established his lodge. Morning came while they were trudging upward, but Jonathan took no joy in the russet mantle. When the path was wide enough, Ben walked alongside and chatted. The slight limp from the missing toes was all but imperceptible, save that he pushed off more strongly from one foot. Jonathan spoke little; he puffed along concentrating on the pains in his thighs and calves. He was carrying a thirty-five-pound training pack because Ben did not want him to get used to going light. That would not be the way of things on the Eiger.

About eight, Ben looked up the trail and waved. There was a figure sitting in the deep shadow of a rock, obviously waiting for them.

"Well, I'm going to turn back, ol' buddy."

"Thank God."

"No, not you. You need the work. George Hotfort yonder will take you on up."

The figure was coming down to meet them.

Jonathan protested, "Hey, she's a girl!"

"Yeah, there's been a lot of people notice that. Now, George," Ben said to the young Indian girl who had joined them, "this here's Jonathan Hemlock, my old climbing buddy. Jon, meet George Hotfort. Now listen, George, you bring him up another couple of hours, then get him back to the place in time for dinner." The girl nodded and leveled a scornful and superior look at Jonathan.

"I'll see you, ol' buddy." And Ben turned back down the trail.

Jonathan watched him go with genuine hate in his soul, then he turned to the girl. "You don't have to do everything he tells you, you know. Here's your chance to strike back at the white man."

The girl gazed on him without the trace of an expression on her wide-cheekboned, oriental face.

"Georgette?" he ventured.

She made a curt motion with her head and started up the hill, her long strong legs effortlessly pulling the trail under her swinging bottom.

"How about Georgianna?" He huffed along after her.

Each time she got a distance ahead, she waited, her back against a rock, watching his exertions calmly. But as soon as he came close enough to appreciate the filled denim shirt, she would push off the rock and move on, her hips swinging metrically with the long regular strides. Even at the steep angle of the rise, her ankles were supple enough to allow her heels to touch the ground, as the heels of Alpine guides do. Jonathan's calves were tight and inelastic; he was walking mostly on his toes, and feeling every step.

The trail steepened, and his legs started to wobble, causing him to lose his footing occasionally. Whenever this happened, he would look up and find her gazing at him with distant disgust.

The sweat ran from his hair into his eyes, and he could feel the thump of his pulse against his eardrums. The web straps of his pack chafed his shoulders. He was breathing orally by now, and his lips were thick and coated.

He wiped the sweat out of his eyes and looked up after her. Directly in front of him was a vertical bank about thirty feet high with only little dents in the baked earth for foot and hand holds. She stood on top looking down at him. He shook his head definitely and sat down on the trail. "Oh, no. No-o, no, no."

But after a couple of minutes of silence broken only by the distant whip of a lark, he turned to discover that she had not moved and was still regarding him placidly. Her face was smooth and powdery, not a trace of perspiration on it, and he hated her for that.

"All right, George. You win."

With a catalogue of pain, he clawed his way up the bank. When he had scrambled to the top he grinned at her, expecting some kind of praise. Instead, she archly walked around him, getting no nearer than three feet, and started on the return trip to the lodge. He watched her glissade easily down the bank and take the downward trail.

"You are a savage, George Hotfort. I'm glad we took your land!"

Back in the rock garden lounge, he consumed an enormous dinner with the concentration of a Zen neophyte. He had showered and changed clothes, and he felt a little more human, although his legs and shoulders still protested with dull, persistent aches. Ben sat across from him, eating with his usual vigor and drawing off great gulps of beer to wash the food down. Jonathan envied him the beer. George had left him a few hundred yards from the lodge and had returned up the trail without a word.

"What do you think of George?" Ben asked, stabbing at his face with a napkin.

"Lovely person. Warm and human. And a conversationalist of considerable accomplishment."

"Yeah, but she's a climbing fool, ain't she?" Ben spoke with paternal pride.

Jonathan admitted that she was that.

"I use her to help break in the handful of climbers who still come for conditioning and training."

"No wonder your trade has fallen off. What's her real name, anyway?"

"George *is* her real name."

"How did that happen?"

"She was named after her mother."

"I see."

Ben studied Jonathan's face for a moment, hoping to discover the discouragement that would make him give up the idea of climbing the Eiger. "Feeling a little bashed?"

"A little. I'll remember that workout the rest of my life. But I'll be ready to get back to work tomorrow."

"Tomorrow's balls! That was just an appetizer. You go back in an hour."

Jonathan started to object.

"Hush up and listen to your ol' buddy." Ben's broad face bunched up in folds around his eyes as he became serious for a moment. "Jon, you're no kid anymore. And the Eiger's one bitch-kitty of a face. Now, if I had my druthers, I'd have you give up this whole idea."

"Can't."

"Why not?"

"Just take my word for it."

"All right. I think you're out of your head, but if you're set on going, then goddam my eyes if I don't make sure you're in top condition. Because if you ain't, you're pretty like to end up a grease spot on those rocks. And it's not just for you either. I'm ground man for the team. I'm responsible for all of them. And I'm not going to let them be dragged off by a headstrong old man, you, who ain't ready for the climb." Ben punctuated his uncommonly long tirade with a deep pull of beer. "Now you just take yourself a swim in the pool yonder and then lay around the sun eye-balling the skin. I'll have them call you when it's time."

Jonathan did as he was told. He had begun to enjoy the game of estimating the ballistic competence of the various young ladies around the pool when a waiter came to tell him his rest period was over.

Once again Ben took him partway up the trail, then he was turned over to George, who paced him even farther and faster than in the morning. Jonathan spoke to her several times, but he could not dent the expressionless facade, much less get a word from her. It was twilight when she left him as before, and he limped back to his suite. He showered and fell on the bed with a lust for sleep. But Ben arrived just in time to prevent him from finding that refuge.

"No you don't, ol' buddy. You still got a big meal to put away."

Although he nodded off repeatedly over his plate, Jonathan consumed a big plank steak and a salad. And that night he found sleep without the usual soporific assistance of the Lautrec article.

The next morning (if three-thirty has any right to that title) found his joints filled with cement and pain. But he and Ben were on the trail by four-thirty. It was a different path and noticeably steeper, and again he was turned over to George Hotfort about halfway up. Again the easily swinging hips drew him upward as he muttered curses against his pain, the heat, his trembling legs, and all Indians. Again at each pause George's mocking, disdainful eyes observed his struggles without comment.

Dinner and a swim, and up again in the afternoon.

And the next day; and the next; and the next.

His climbing trim came back faster than he had dared to hope, and faster than Ben cared to admit. By the sixth day he was enjoying the training and keeping up with George all the way. They moved higher and steeper each day, always making more distance in the same amount of time, and sometimes now Jonathan led and George followed. On the seventh day he was scrambling up a shale drift when he looked back to see (oh, rewarding sight!) perspiration on George's brow. When she got to him she sat down and rested, breathing hard.

"Oh, come on George!" Jonathan pleaded. "We can't spend our lives sitting here. Upward, upward. Get thine swinging ass in gear." Because she never spoke, he had fallen into the habit of talking to her as though she could not understand. George evaluated the hang of scruffy rock above them and shook her head. Her denim shirt was dark with sweat under the arms and at each pocket where her breasts pressed against the cloth. She smiled at him for the first time, then she started back down the trail.

Never before had she accompanied him all the way back to the lodge, but this time, while Jonathan showered, she and Ben had a long talk. That evening a champagne cooler with half a dozen bottles of beer buried in ice appeared with dinner, and Ben told Jonathan that the first phase of his conditioning was over. They were through with the soft shoe work. His kit had been assembled, and the next morning they would go to work on the stone faces.

A second six-pack was consumed in Ben's rooms where he outlined the next few days. They would begin on easy faces, no more than ten or fifteen feet above the scree, where Jonathan would get the feel of the rock again. Once Ben was satisfied with his progress, they would move up and put a little void under themselves.

Their plans made, the two men chatted and drank beer for an hour. Ben took vicarious pleasure in watching his comrade's delight in the cold brew he had been denied throughout the first phase of conditioning, although he admitted mistrusting any man who could go without beer for that many days.

For some time Jonathan had been aware that his hardening body was growing eager to make love, not as affectionate expression, but as a biological eruption. It was for this reason that he asked Ben, more or less offhand, "Do you have anything going with George?"

"What? Oh! No." He actually blushed. "For Christ's sake, I'm twenty-five years older than her. Why do you want to know?"

"Nothing really. I'm just feeling tough and full of sperm. She happens to be around and she looks capable."

"Well, she's a grown-up girl. I guess she can go with whoever she wants."

"That might present a difficulty. I can't say she's been pestering me with her attentions."

"Oh, she likes you all right. I can tell from the way she talks about you."

"Does she ever speak to anyone but you, Ben?"

"Not as I know of." Ben finished his bottle at one long pull and opened another. "Kind of funny," he commented.

"What is?"

"You wanting George. Considering the way she's been grinding you down, a body would think you'd have some kind of hate going for her."

"Who knows the devious working of the id? In the back of my mind I may be carrying the image of impaling her—stabbing her to death, or something."

Ben glanced at Jonathan with a hint of a wince in his eyes. "You know what, ol' buddy. Way down deep you've got the makings of a real bad ass. I don't know that I'd like to be alone on a desert island with you if there was a limited food supply."

"No worry. You're a friend."

"Ever have any enemies?"

"A few."

"Any of them still around and kicking?"

"One." Jonathan considered for a moment. "No, two."

There had been rather a lot of beer, and Jonathan was asleep quickly. The Jemima dream began, as it had each night, with deceptive gentleness—a real rehearsal in sequence of their relations from the first meeting on the plane. The sudden images of Dragon's derisive face, like quick intercuts in a motion picture, never lasted long enough to force Jonathan awake. The flickering hurricane lamps dissolved into harlequin flecks. The arc of her cigarette glowed in the dark. He reached out for her, and she was so real he experienced a tactile tingle as he slid the flat of his hand over her hard-under-soft stomach. He felt it press up against his palm—and he was fully awake! Before he could sit up, George drew him tightly against her, gripping him with strong arms and wrapping supple legs around his. Her eyes too had a Mongol cast, and it was impossible to make the substitution.

He did not wake until after five. Because of recent habit, the late hour seemed to accuse. But then he recalled that they would be working faces today, and you cannot work a face before light. George had gone. She had left as silently as she had come. A stiffness in his lower back, a feeling of tender empty in his groin, and a slightly alkaline smell from beneath the sheets reminded him of the night. He had been awake when she left, but he feigned sleep, fearful of being called on to perform again.

As she showered, he promised himself to use the girl sparingly. She would send a man to a sanatorium in a fortnight, if he let her. She climaxed quickly and often, but was never satisfied. Sex for her was not a gentle sequence of objectives and achievements; it was an unending chase from one exploding bubble of thrill to the next—a plateau of sensation to be maintained, not a series of crests to be climbed. And if the partner seemed to flag, she introduced a variation calculated to renew his interest and vigor.

Like those of swimming, the techniques of climbing are never forgotten, once properly learned. But Jonathan knew he would have to discover what new limitations the past few years of age and inactivity had placed on his skill and nerve.

The experienced climber can move up a face he cannot cling to. A regular, predicted set of moves from one point of imbalance to its counterpoise will keep him on the face, so long as he continues moving, rather in the way a bicycle rider has little trouble with balance, unless he goes too slowly. It is necessary to read the pitch accurately, to plot out and rehearse the moves kinesodically, then to make them with smooth conviction from hold to hold, ending in a predicted and reliable purchase. In the past, this constellation of abilities had been Jonathan's forte, but during his first day of free climbing he made several misjudgments that sent him slithering down ten or fifteen feet to the scree, banging a little skin off elbows and knees and doing greater damage to his self-esteem. It was some time before he diagnosed his problem. The intervening years since his last climb had had no effect on his analytical powers, but they had eroded the fine edge of his physical dexterity. This erosion was beyond repair, so it was necessary that he train himself to think within the limits of his new, inferior body.

At first, for safety, Ben insisted that they use many pitons, making the face look as though lady climbers or Germans had been there. But it was not long before they were making short grade five and six pitches with a more Anglo-Saxon economy of ironmongery. One problem, however, continued to plague Jonathan, making him furious with himself. In the midst of a skillful and businesslike series of moves, he would suddenly find himself fighting the rock, succumbing to the natural, but lethal, desire to press his body against it. This not only deprived him of leverage for tension footholds, but it made it difficult to scan the face above for cracks. Once a climber presses the face, a fearful cycle begins. It is an unnoticed welling up of animal fear that first makes him hug the rock; hugging weakens his footholds and blinds him to purchases that might be within grasp; and this, now real, danger feeds the original fear.

On one occasion, after Jonathan thought he had overcome this amateurish impulse, he suddenly found himself caught up in the cycle. His cleated boots could find no grab, and suddenly he was off.

He fell only three of the forty meters between him and the rock below before his line snapped up short and he was dangling and twisting from the rope. It was a sound piton.

"Hey!" Ben shouted from above. "What the fuck you doin'?"

"I'm just hanging from this piton, wise ass! What are you doing?"

"I'm just holding your weight in my powerful and experienced hands and watching you hang from that piton. You look real graceful. A little stupid, but real graceful."

Jonathan kicked angrily off the rock and swung out and back, but he missed his grab.

"For Christ's sake, ol' buddy! Wait a minute! Now, don't do anything. Just rest there for a minute."

Jonathan dangled from the line, feeling foolish.

"Now think about it." Ben gave it a moment. "You know what's wrong?"

"Yes!" Jonathan was impatient, both with himself and with Ben's condescending treatment.

"Tell me."

With the singsong of rote Jonathan said, "I'm crowding the rock."

"Right. Now get back on the face and we'll go down."

Jonathan took a mind-clearing breath, kicked out and swung back, and he was on the face. During the whole of the retreat he moved glibly and precisely, forgetting the vertical gravity of the valley and responding naturally to the diagonal gravity of weight-versus-rope that kept him leaning well away from the face.

On the valley floor they sat on a pile of scree, Jonathan coiling rope while Ben drank the bottle of beer he had stashed in the shade of a rock. They were dwarfed by the nine "needles" towering around them. It was on one of these that they had been working, a column of striated, reddish rock that rose from the earth like a decapitated trunk of a giant fossil tree.

"How would you like to climb Big Ben tomorrow," Ben asked out of a lengthy silence. He was referring to the tallest of the columns, a four-hundred-foot shaft that eons of wind had eroded until it was wider at the top than at the base. It was the proximity of these peculiar formations that had caused Ben to select this spot for his climbing school, and he had promptly named the grandest after himself.

Jonathan squinted at the needle, his eyes locating half a dozen dicey areas before it had swept halfway up. "You think I'm ready?"

"More than ready, ol' buddy. Matter of fact, I figure that's your problem. You're overtrained, or trained too fast. You're getting a little skitterish." Ben went on to say that he had noticed Jonathan pushing off too hard when he was in a tension stance, taking little open moves without being sure of the terminal purchase, and letting his mind wander from the rock when it seemed too easy. It was during these moments of inattention that Jonathan suddenly found himself hugging the face. The best cure for all this might be an endurance run—something to break down the overcoiled legs and to humble the dangerously confident animal in Jonathan.

His eyes picking their way up from possible stance to stance, Jonathan played with the climb for twenty minutes before he accomplished the optical ascent. "Looks hard, Ben. Especially the top flange."

"It ain't no bedpost." Ben stood up. "Goddam my eyes if I don't think I'll come along with you!"

Jonathan glanced at Ben's foot before he could help it. "You really want to go?"

"No sweat. I've stumped up it once before. What do you say?"

"I say we walk up it tomorrow."

"Great. Now why don't you take the rest of the day off, ol' buddy."

As they walked back to the lodge, Jonathan experienced a lightness of spirit and eagerness for the morrow that had, in the old days, been the core of his love for climbing. His whole being was focused on matters of rock, strength and tactic, and the outside world with its Dragons and Jemimas could not force its way into the consciousness.

He had been eating well, sleeping perfectly, training hard, drinking much beer, and using George with gingerly discretion. This kind of elemental life would bore him beyond standing in a couple of weeks, but just then it was grand.

He leaned against the lodge's main desk, reading an effervescent postcard from Cherry sprinkled with *underlinings,* and ___, and !!!!, and . . . . . . , and (parenthesis), and ha! ha! ha! No one, evidently, had burned down his home. Mr. Monk was as angry and scatological as ever. And Cherry wanted to know if he could suggest some reading on the preparation of aphrodisiacs for a friend of hers (someone he had never met) for use on a man (whom he had also never met) and whom he would probably not like, inasmuch as this nameless party was such a heartless *turd!!!* as to allow lusty girls to go untapped.

Jonathan felt something touch his foot and looked down to see a nervous little Pomeranian with a rhinestone collar sniffing around. He ignored it and returned to his postcard, but the next moment the dog was mounting an amorous attack on his leg. He kicked it aside, but the dog interpreted this rejection as maidenly coyness and returned to the attack.

"Leave Dr. Hemlock alone, Faggot. I am sorry, Jonathan, but Faggot has not learned to recognize the straight, and he hasn't the patience to wait for an invitation."

Without looking up, Jonathan recognized the chocolate baritone of Miles Mellough.

Arizona: *June 27*

JONATHAN WATCHED THE lace-cuffed and perfectly manicured hands descend to pick up the Pomeranian. He followed the dog up to Miles's face, tanned and handsome as ever, the large blue eyes gazing languidly from beneath long black lashes, the broad, lineless forehead supporting a cluster of trained soft waves that swept around to the sides in a seemingly artless pattern that was the pride of Miles's hairdresser. The dog kissed at Miles's cheek, which affection he accepted without taking his eyes from Jonathan.

"How have you been, Jonathan?" There was a gentle mocking smile in his eyes, but their movements were quick, ready to read and avoid a thrust.

"Miles." The word was not a greeting, it was a nomination. Jonathan put his postcard into his pocket and waited for Miles to get on with it.

"How long has it been?" Miles dropped his eyes and shook his head. "A long time. Come to think of it, the last time we met was in Arles. We had just finished that Spanish thing—you and I and Henri."

Jonathan's eyes flickered at the mention of Henri Baq.

"No, Jonathan." Miles laid his hand on Jonathan's sleeve. "Don't imagine I have made a verbal blunder. It's about Henri that I want to chat. Do you have a moment?" Feeling the forearm muscles tense, Miles patted Jonathan's arm and withdrew his hand.

"There's only one possibility, Miles. You have an incurable disease and lack the guts to kill yourself."

Miles smiled. "That's very good, Jonathan. But wrong. Shall we have a drink?"

"All right."

"Rather like old times."

"Not at all like old times."

The eyes of all the young ladies in the lounge followed Miles as he preceded Jonathan along the walkway and over an arched stone bridge to an isolated table. His uncommon good looks, the grace and strength of his dancer's walk, and the extreme styling of his clothes would have eclipsed a man of less panache, but Miles moved slowly among the girls, granting them the benediction of his easy smile, honestly pitying them because he was ultimately unavailable.

As soon as they were seated, Miles released the dog which vibrated with tense energy until its toenails clicked on the rock, scrambled in circles of frenzy, then scampered along to a nearby table where he was captured, whimpering, by three young ladies in bikinis who were clearly delighted to possess this entree to the handsomest man they had ever seen. One of them approached the table carrying the shivering, clawing animal in her arms.

Miles rested his eyes on her breast languidly, and she produced a nervous laugh. "What do you call him?" she asked.

"Faggot, my dear."

"Oh, that's cute! Why do you call him that?"

"Because he's a bundle of nerves."

She did not understand, so she said, "That's cute!"

Miles beckoned the girl to his side and placed his hand lightly on her buttock. "Would you do me a great favor, dear?"

She giggled at the unexpected contact, but did not withdraw. "Surely. Glad to."

"Take Faggot and go play with him for a while."

"All right," she said. Then, "Thank you."

"There's a good girl." He patted the buttock in dismissal and the girl left the lounge, followed by her companions who were just dying to know what had transpired.

"They're cute little tricks, aren't they, Jonathan. And not completely without their uses. Bees are attracted to the honey."

"And drones," Jonathan added.

A young Indian waiter stood by the table.

"A double Laphroaig for my friend, and a brandy Alexander for me," Miles ordered, looking deeply into the waiter's eyes.

Miles's gaze followed the waiter as he made his way along the walkway and over the artificial streams of bubbling water. "Good-looking boy, that." Then he turned his attention to Jonathan, touching his palms together and resting his forefingers against his lips, his thumbs under his chin. Over the tips of his fingers, his still eyes smiled with gentle frost, and Jonathan reminded himself how dangerous this ruthless man could be, despite appearances. For a minute neither of them spoke. Then Miles broke it with a rich laugh. "Oh Jonathan. No one can best you at the game of cold silence. I should have known better than to try. Was my memory accurate about the Laphroaig?"

"Yes."

"A whole monosyllable! How gracious."

Jonathan supposed Miles would come to the subject in his own time, and he had no intention of helping him. Until the drinks came, Miles scanned the men and girls around the pool. He sat poised in his black velvet suit, high-rolled linen collar with a dropping velvet cravat, slim and expensive Italian boots. Obviously, he was doing well. It was rumored that, after leaving CII, Mellough had set himself up in San Francisco where he dealt in all kinds of merchandise, chiefly drugs.

In essential ways, Miles had not changed. Tall, brilliant in his physical trim, he pulled off his epic homosexuality with such style that plebeian men did not recognize it, and worldly men did not mind it. As always, girls were attracted to him in gaggles, and he treated them with the amused condescension of a glamorous Parisian aunt visiting relatives in Nebraska. Jonathan had seen Miles in tight and dangerous spots during their time together in CII, but he had never seen a hair out of place or a rumpled cuff. Henri had frequently mentioned that he knew no equal to Miles for cold physical courage.

Neither Jonathan nor Henri had objected to their comrade's sexual preference; indeed, they had benefited upon occasion from the clusters of women he attracted but did not satisfy. Miles's divergence had been one of his most valuable assets to CII. It had put him in contact with people and sources not open to the straight, and had given him the power of blackmail over several highly placed American political figures.

As the waiter placed the drinks on the table, Miles spoke to him. "You're a very attractive young man. It's God's gift to you, and you should be grateful for it. I hope you are. Now run along and attend to your duties."

The waiter smiled and left. Once he was out of earshot, Miles sighed and said, "I would say he's made, wouldn't you?"

"If you have time."

Miles laughed and raised his glass. "Cheers." He sipped the frothy mixture thoughtfully. "You know, Jonathan, you and I have similar approaches to love, or to balling, if you prefer. Both of us have discovered that the confident cold turkey technique drops more of them than all the romantic mooning around our sexual inferiors bait their little traps with. After all, the targets *want* to be made. They simply ask to be protected from guilt by feeling they've been swept off their feet. And it is refreshing for them to have their paths to evil lubricated with urbanity. Don't you agree?"

"I assume you're covered?"

"Of course."

"Where is he?"

"Behind you. At the bar."

Jonathan turned and glanced along the bar until, at the end, he sighted a blond primate who must have weighed two hundred twenty pounds. Jonathan guessed him to be in his mid-forties, despite the heavy purplish sun lamp tan and the long bleached hair that fell over his collar. He was typical of the ex-wrestlers and beachboys Miles carried along, half as bodyguards, half as lovers, should nothing better turn up.

"And that's all the cover you have?" Jonathan asked, returning to his drink.

"Dewayne is very strong, Jonathan. He used to be a world's champion."

"Didn't they all."

"I'll send Dewayne away, if he makes you nervous."

"He doesn't look like much of a threat."

"Don't depend on that. He's very well paid, and he's totally devoted to me." Miles's movie smile displayed his perfect teeth as he pushed the mash of ice around in his glass with a swizzle stick. Then he began rather tentatively, "It must seem odd to you that I have sought you out, instead of waiting for you to step up to me someday and relieve me of the burden of existence."

"Your phrasing answered any questions I might have had."

"Yes, I've grown weary of ice in my stomach every time I see a man who resembles you." He smiled. "You have no idea how damaging it's been to my cool."

"It will soon be over."

"One way or another. And I think I'm in a good bargaining position."

"Forget it."

"Not even curious?"

"About one thing. How did you know I was here?"

"Oh, you remember what we used to say: CII secrets and common knowledge differ only in that common knowledge . . ."

". . . is harder to come by. Yes, I remember."

Miles rested his large, soft eyes on Jonathan. "I didn't actually kill Henri, you know."

"You set him up. You were his friend and you set him up."

"But I didn't actually kill him."

"I probably won't actually kill you."

"But I'd rather be dead than like the Greek you gave Datura to."

Jonathan smiled with the bland, gentle look he donned before combat. "I didn't actually prepare the Datura. I paid someone else to do it."

Miles sighed and looked down, his long lashes covering his eyes. "I see your point." Then he looked up and tried a new tack. "Did you know that Henri was a double agent?"

In fact, Jonathan had discovered this several months after Henri's death. But it did not matter. "He was your friend. And mine."

"It was only a matter of time, for God's sake, Jonathan! Both sides wanted him dead."

"You were his friend."

Miles's voice became crisp. "I hope you'll understand if I find this harping on ethics a little presumptuous in a paid killer!"

"I was holding him when he died."

Mile's tone softened instantly. "I know. And I'm truly sorry about that."

"You remember how he always joked about going out with a clever line? At the last minute he couldn't think of one, and he died feeling foolish." Jonathan's control was flaking off.

"I'm sorry, Jonathan."

"Oh, that's fine. You are really and truly sorry! That fixes everything!"

"I did what I could! I arranged a small income for Marie and the children. What did you do? You rammed your rod up her that very night!"

Jonathan's hand flashed over the table, and Miles was snapped sideways in his chair with a backhand across the face. Instantly, the blond wrestler left his barstool and started toward the table. Miles stared hate at Jonathan, tears smarting in his eyes, then, after a struggle with his self-control, he raised his hand, and the wrestler stopped where he was. Miles smiled sadly at Jonathan and gestured the bodyguard away with the backs of his fingers. Angry at being denied his prey, the wrestler glared for a moment before returning to the bar.

Jonathan realized at that moment the first thing he would have to do would be to discourage the blond bodyguard.

"My fault probably, Jonathan. Shouldn't have baited you. I imagine my cheek is red and unsightly?"

Jonathan was angry with himself for allowing Miles to taunt him into premature action. He finished his Laphroaig and gestured to the waiter.

Until the waiter left the table neither Jonathan nor Miles spoke, nor did they look at each other until the cerebral toxic of adrenalin had drained off. Miles had turned away, not wanting the Indian waiter to see his glowing cheek.

Miles smiled forgiveness at Jonathan. He had not wiped the tears from his eyes, imagining they might help his case. "I tender you a bit of information as a propitiatory offering."

Jonathan did not respond.

"The man who made the fiscal arrangements with me for Henri's death was Clement Pope—Dragon's boy."

"That's good to know."

"Jonathan—tell me. What if Henri had set *me* up?"

"He would never have done that to a friend."

"But if he had. Would you have gone after him like you've come after me?"

"Yes."

Miles nodded. "I thought so." He smiled wanly. "And that vitiates my case considerably. But I still don't intend to allow myself to die, a sacrifice to your peculiar reverence for the epic traditions of friendship. Neither heaven nor reincarnation attracts me. The one seems dull, the other undesirable. So I feel bound to protect this fleeting life of mine with all my energies. Even if it means killing you, dear Jonathan."

"What are your other choices?"

"I would hardly have come to the marketplace if I were not in a position to bargain."

Big Ben entered the lounge. With his habitual broad smile, he started to join Jonathan, then he saw Miles, and sat at the bar instead, eyeing the blond wrestler with flagrant disdain.

"You might at least give me your attention, Jonathan."

"A friend just walked in."

"Does he realize the possible cost of that privilege?"

"You're wasting my time, Miles."

"I may be saving your life."

Jonathan retreated into his gentle combat smile.

"When I left CII, Jonathan, I went into business in San Francisco. I'm in transportation. I move things from one point to another point and distribute them. All sorts of things. It's amazingly profitable. But life has not been comfortable for me, with the specter of you lurking in every shadow."

"Distressing."

"Then, early this month, I received an assignment to transport a bit of information from Montreal to . . . somewhere else. Gaining the information necessitated the killing of an agent. I didn't participate in the assassination because, unlike you, I am not a predator." He glanced to see the reaction. There was none. "But I know who did the killing. You got one of them shortly later. And now you're after the other. Dragon has told you that he will have the identity of this other person by the time of the sanction. Maybe. Maybe not. I know who it is, Jonathan. And until you have that information, you're in great danger."

"How so?"

"If I tell this person who and what you are, the hunted will become the hunter."

"But you're willing to sell this man out to me?"

"In return for your promise to stop stalking me. Don't let this bargain pass you by."

Jonathan looked out the window at a circle of girls near the pool laughing and screeching as they playfully teased the neurotic Pomeranian, which danced frantically in one spot, its claws clicking on the tile, urine dribbling from beneath it. Jonathan turned and looked at the wrestler still sitting at the bar, keeping him under observation. "I'll think about it, Miles."

Miles smiled with patient fatigue. "Please don't play me like an amateur. I can't remain inactive and unprotected while you 'think about it.' I believe it was you who first advised me never to con a con."

"You'll know my decision within five minutes. How's that?" Then Jonathan's voice mellowed. "Whichever way it goes, Miles. We were once friends . . . so . . ." He held out his hand. Miles was surprised, but pleased. They shook hands firmly before Jonathan left for the bar where only Ben and the blond bodyguard sat. The latter leaned back on two legs of his stool, his back to the bar and his elbow hooked over it, eyeing Jonathan with a snide superior expression. Jonathan approached him, his whole bearing diffident and apologetic. "Well, as you saw, Miles and I have made up," Jonathan said with a weak, uncertain smile. "May I buy you a drink?"

The wrestler scratched his ear in disdainful silence and leaned further back on his stool to create more distance between himself and this fawning nobody who had dared to slap Mr. Mellough.

Jonathan ignored this rejection. "Boy, I'm glad it worked out all right. No man of my size looks forward to tangling with a guy built like you."

The wrestler nodded understandingly and pressed his shoulders down to set the pectorals.

"Well, just so you know," Jonathan said. He converted his motion of departure into a skimming kick that swept the tilted barstool from beneath the wrestler. First the edge of the bar, then the brass rail cracked the blond head as it thudded down. Dazed and hurt, his long hair tumbled into his face, the wrestler had no time to move before Jonathan had stepped on his face with his heel and pivoted. The nose crunched and flattened underfoot. The sound brought gall to the back of Jonathan's throat, and his cheeks drew back with nausea. But he knew what was necessary in situations like these: they must remember the hurt.

Jonathan knelt over the wrestler and snatched the face up by the hair until it was only inches from his own.

"Hear me. I don't want you out on my flank like that. It scares me. I don't like being scared. So hear this. Come near me ever, and you're dead. Hey! Listen to me! Don't pass out while I'm talking to you!"

The wrestler's eyes were dulled by pain and confusion, and he did not respond.

Jonathan shook him by the hair until several strands came out between his fingers. "Did you understand what I said?"

"Yes." The reply was faint.

"Good boy." Jonathan set the head back gently on the floor. He stood up and faced Ben, who had watched the whole thing without moving. "Will you take care of him, Ben?"

"All right, ol' buddy. But goddam my ass if I understand what's going on."

"Talk about it later."

Two Indian busboys grunted under the task of conducting the toppling giant to his room, as Jonathan walked back to the entrance of the lounge. He stood there, looking across at Miles who, alone of the patrons, had been aware that a conflict had occurred. Their eyes, so similar in color and frost, intersected for a moment. Then Miles nodded slowly and turned his attention away, gracefully flicking a particle of dust from the sleeve of his velvet jacket. He had his answer.

Arizona: *That Evening*

HIS BACK AGAINST a vertical pillow, his feet straight out before him, Jonathan sat up in his bed. He rolled and licked his second smoke, then forgot to light it as he stared, eyes defocused, into the deepening gloom.

He was working out, in rough, how he would put Miles away. There was no chance of getting to him before he could alert the sanction target to his identity. Everything in Switzerland would hinge on Search identifying the man early.

Jonathan's attention suddenly narrowed to the present as he heard a faint metallic click outside his door. He slowly rose from bed, keeping a rolling downward pressure with his hands to reduce the sound of the springs. There was a soft knock, one calculated not to awaken him if he were sleeping. He had not expected Miles to make his move this quickly. He regretted the absence of a gun. The tapping was repeated, and again he heard the clink of metal. He crept to the wall on the hinge side of the door. A key turned in the lock, and the door opened a crack, a shaft of light bisecting the room. He tensed and waited. The door swung open deliberately, and someone without whispered. Two shadows spilled across the rug, one of a man, the other of a monstrous figure with a huge disk poised over its head. As the shadows advanced, Jonathan kicked the door shut and threw his weight against it. There was a crash and clatter of metal and shattering glass, and he realized instantly what it must have been.

Sheepishly he opened the door and looked out. Big Ben was leaning against the wall across the corridor, and an Indian waiter sat stunned on the floor in the midst of a wreckage of dishes and silver, his white uniform jacket a visual menu.

"Now you wouldn't believe this, ol' buddy, but there are folks who just say so when they ain't hungry."

"I thought you were someone else."

"Yeah. Well, I hope!"

"Come on in."

"What you got up your sleeve this time? Going to clout me with a chest of drawers?" Ben gave orders for the mess to be cleaned up and another dinner to be served, then he went into Jonathan's room, making much of leaping through the doorway in a bound and turning on the lights before something else befell him.

Jonathan assumed a businesslike tone, partially because he wanted to work on a plan he had made while sitting in the dark, partially because he did not want to dwell on his recent *faux pas.*

"Ben, what information do you have on the three men I'll be climbing the Eiger with?"

"Not much. We've exchanged a few letters, all about the climb."

"Could I read them over?"

"Sure."

"Good. Now, another thing. Do you have a detailed map of the area around here?"

"Sure."

"Can I have it?"

"Sure."

"What lies to the west of us?"

"Nothing."

"That's what it looked like from the high country. What kind of nothing is it?"

"Real bad-ass country. Rock and sand and nothing else. Goes on forever. Makes Death Valley look like an oasis. You don't have to go out there, ol' buddy. A man can die out there in two days. This time of year it gets up to a hundred fifteen in the shade, and you'd play hell finding any shade."

Ben picked up the phone and asked that a map and a packet of correspondence be brought from his office, along with a six-pack of beer. Then he called out to Jonathan who had gone into the bathroom to empty his ashtray, "Goddam my eyes if I know what's going on around here! 'Course, you don't have to tell me, if you don't want to."

Jonathan took him at his word.

"No. You don't have to tell me about it. What the hell? Slap guys around the lounge. Break heads at my bar. Bust up my dishes. None of my business."

Jonathan came into the room. "You keep a few guns around, don't you, Ben?"

"Oh-oh."

"Do you have a shotgun?"

"Now, wait a minute, ol' buddy."

Jonathan sat in a chair across from Ben. "I'm in a tight spot. I need help." His tone suggested that he expected it from a friend.

"You know you got all the help I can give, Jon. But if people are going to get killed around here, maybe I should know something about what's going on."

There was a knock at the door. Ben opened it, and the waiter stood there with the beer, the file, and the map. He entered only after looking carefully around the door, and he left as quickly as he decently could.

"Want a beer?" Ben asked, tearing the top from a can.

"No thanks."

"Just as good. There's only six."

"What do you know about this Miles Mellough, Ben?"

"The one you were talking to? Nothing much. He looks like he could give you change for a nine-dollar bill, all in threes. That's about all I know. He just checked in this morning. You want me to throw him out?"

"Oh, no. I want him right here."

Ben chuckled. "Boy, he's sure tickling the imaginations of a lot of girls. They're flocking around him as though he held the patent on the penis. I even saw George eyeing him."

"She'd be in for a letdown."

"Yeah, I figured."

"How about the other one? The big blond?"

"He checked in at the same time. They got adjoining rooms. I got the doctor up from town, and he fixed some on his nose, but I don't believe he's ever going to be a real close friend of yours." Ben crushed the empty beer can in his hands and opened another thoughtfully. "You know, Jon? That fight really bothered me some. You came at the man pretty slick for an aging college professor."

"You've gotten me into top shape."

"Uh-uhn. No, that ain't it at all. You set him up like you were used to setting people up. He was so faked out, he never had a chance. You remember I told you how I'd hate to be with you on a desert island with no food? Well, that's the kind of thing I mean. Like stepping on that big guy's nose. You'd already made your point. A body could get the feeling you got a real mean streak in you somewheres."

It was obvious that Ben needed at least a limited explanation. "Ben, these people killed a friend of mine."

"Oh?" Ben considered that. "Does the law know about it?"

"There's nothing the law can do."

"How come?"

Jonathan shook his head. He did not intend to pursue the matter.

"Hey, wait a minute! I just got a real scary flash. I suddenly got the feeling that all this has something to do with the Eiger climb. Else why would they know you were here?"

"Stay out of it, Ben."

"Now listen to me. You don't need any more trouble than that mountain's going to give you. I haven't told you this, but I better. You're training real good, and you're still a crafty climber. But I've been watching you close, Jon. And to be honest, you don't have more than a fifty-fifty chance on the Eiger at best. And that doesn't count your fooling around trying to kill people and them trying to kill you. I don't mean to dent your confidence, ol' buddy, but it's something you ought to know."

"Thanks, Ben."

A waiter knocked at the door and brought in a tray with a training meal for two, which they consumed in silence while Jonathan pored over the terrain map and Ben finished the cans of beer.

By the time the meal was a clutter of dirty dishes, Jonathan had folded up the map and put it into his pocket. He began questioning Ben about his forthcoming climbing partners. "How close has your correspondence with them been?"

"Nothing special. Just the usual stuff—hotel, rations, team rope and iron, how to handle the reporters—that sort of stuff. The German guy does most of the writing. He kind of thought the whole thing up in the first place, and he makes noise like a leader. That reminds me. Are you and I going to fly over together?"

"I don't think so. I'll meet you there. Listen, Ben, have any of them . . . ? Are they all in good physical shape?"

"At least as good as you."

"Have any of them been hurt lately? Or wounded?"

"*Wounded?* Not as I know of. One of them—the German—wrote that he had a fall early this month. But nothing serious."

"What kind of fall?"

"I don't know. Roughed up his leg some."

"Enough to make him limp?"

"Well, that's pretty hard to tell from a guy's handwriting. Hey, why you asking me all this shit?"

"Never mind. Will you leave this file of correspondence with me? I want to read it over—get to know these men a little better."

"No skin off my ass." Ben stretched and groaned like a sated bear. "You still planning to make that climb on the needle in the morning?"

"Of course. Why wouldn't I?"

"Well, it might be a little tough, climbing with a shotgun cradled over your arm."

Jonathan laughed. "Don't worry about it."

"Well, in that case, we better get some sleep. That needle ain't no tent pole, you know."

"You mean it ain't no bedpost."

"It ain't neither one."

Shortly after Big Ben had gone, Jonathan was propped up in bed studying the letters from the other climbers. In each case, the first letter was rather stiff and polite. Evidently, Ben's answers had been robust and earthy, because all succeeding letters cleaved to hard technical matters of climbing: weather reports, observations about conditions on the face, descriptions of recent training climbs, suggestions for equipment. It was in one of these letters that the German mentioned a short fall he had taken resulting in a gashed leg which, he assured Ben, would be in fine shape by the Eiger ascent.

Jonathan was deep in this correspondence, trying to read personality between the arid lines, when he recognized the scratching knock of George Hotfort wanting to be let in.

His recent encounter with Mellough made him cautious. He turned off his reading light before crossing to unlatch the door. George entered into the darkness uncertainly, but Jonathan latched the door behind her and conducted her to the bed. He was eager to use her as sexual aspirin, to relieve the tensions of the afternoon, although he knew he would only experience discharge and release without local sensation.

Throughout the event, George's eyes locked on his, expressionless in their Oriental mold, totally severed from her aggressive and demanding body.

Sometime later, while he slept, she slipped away without a word.

Arizona: *June 28*

HE SENSED THAT he was going to be magnificent.

Immediately upon waking, he was eager for the climb on Big Ben Needle. Once or twice in his climbing career he had experienced this scent of victory—this visceral hunch. He had it just before he set a time record on Grand Teton, and again when he introduced a new route up the Dru into the mountaineering handbooks. His hands felt strong enough to punch holds into the rock, if need be, and his legs carried him with more than vigor and ease, with a sensation of moon gravity. He was so finely tuned to this climb that his hands, when he rubbed the palms together, felt like rough chamois gloves capable of adhering to flat, slimy rock.

After his shower, he neither shaved nor combed his hair. He preferred to be rough and burry when he met the rock.

When Ben knocked at his door, he was already tying off his boots and admiring their feel: broken in from his recent training climbs, but the cleats in excellent condition.

"You look mighty ready." Ben had just gotten out of bed and was still in his pajamas and robe, grizzled and carrying with him his first can of beer.

"I feel great, Ben. That needle of yours has had it."

"Oh, I wouldn't be surprised if it took some of the shine off you before it's all over. It's near four hundred feet, mostly grade 6."

"Tell your cooks we'll be back in time for lunch."

"I doubt that. Especially considering you got to drag a tired old man along behind you. Come to my room and I'll get dressed."

He followed Ben down the hall and into his rooms where he declined the offer of a beer and sat watching dawn quicken, while Ben slowly found and donned the various elements of his climbing gear. The finding was not easy, and Ben grumbled and swore steadily as he shoveled clothes out of drawers onto the floor and emptied boxes of random paraphernalia onto his rumpled bed.

"You say I'm going to pull you along behind, Ben? I had imagined you would lead. After all, you know the route. You've been up before."

"Yeah, but I ain't one to hog all the fun. Goddam my eyes if I can find that other sock. Can't stand wearing socks that don't match. Puts me off balance. Hey! Maybe if I worked it out just right I could make up for these missing toes by wearing a lighter sock on that foot! 'Course I'd run the risk of ending up with the opposite of a limp. I might find myself up an inch or two off the ground, and that'd play hell with my traction. Hey, get off your ass and kick around in this stuff and see if you can find my climbing sweater. You know, the old green one."

"You're wearing it."

"Oh, yeah. So I am. But lookee here! I ain't got no shirt on under it!"

"Not my fault."

"Well, you ain't helping much."

"I'm afraid if I got out into the middle of the room they'd never find me again."

"Oh, George would come across you when she put all this mess away."

"George cleans up your room?"

"She's on my payroll, and she's got to do more to earn her keep than just be a spittoon for your sperm."

"You have a delicate sense of imagery, Ben."

"No shit? All right, I give up. Goddam my eyes if I can find them boots. Why don't you let me use yours?"

"And I go up barefoot?"

"Considering how sassy-assed and prime you're feeling, I didn't figure you'd notice the difference."

Jonathan leaned back in the chair and relaxed with the dawn view. "I really do feel good, Ben. I haven't felt like this for a long time."

Ben's characteristic gruffness fled for a moment. "That's good. I'm glad. I remember how it used to be for me."

"Do you miss climbing much, Ben?"

Ben sat on the edge of his bed. "Would you miss it if someone ran off with your pecker? Sure, I miss it. I'd been climbing since I was eighteen. At first, I didn't know what to do with myself. But then . . ." He slapped his knees and stood up. "Then, I got this place. And I'm living high on the hog now. Still . . ." Ben wandered over to the closet. "Here's my boots! I'll be goddamned!"

"Where were they?"

"In my shoe rack. George must have put them there, goddam her."

Over breakfast in the glittering, empty restaurant kitchen, Jonathan asked if Miles Mellough had done anything of interest after the fight.

"He worry you, Jon?"

"Right now I'm only worried about the climb. But I'll have to deal with him after I get back."

"If he don't deal with you first."

"Say it out."

"Well, one of my help heard this Mellough and his friend having a set-to in their rooms."

"Your help spends a lot of time with their ears to doors?"

"Not usually. But I figured you might want me to keep an eye on these guys. Anyway, the fancy one was some kind of pissed off at the way the other guy let you set him up. And the big fellow said that it would be different next time. Then later on they ordered a rental car from town. It's parked out front now."

"Maybe they want to take in the countryside."

"What's wrong with our guest cars? No, I figure they want to get somewhere in a hurry. Maybe after they've done something to be ashamed of. Like killing somebody."

"What makes you think they're going to kill somebody?"

Ben paused, hoping to make an effect, "The waiter told me the big fellow carries a gun." Jonathan concentrated on sipping his coffee and denied Ben the expected reaction. Ben tore off the top of a can of beer. "You don't seem much bothered about that guy carrying a gun."

"I knew he did, Ben. I saw it under his coat. That's why I stepped on his nose. So he wouldn't be able to see clearly. I needed walking away time."

"Here I was thinking you had a mean streak, and all the time you was just doing what you had to do."

"You should be ashamed of yourself."

"I could cut out the tongue that spoke evil of you, ol' buddy."

"I was just trying to stay alive."

"And that's why you want the shotgun?"

"No, not for protection. I need it for attack. Come on! That hill's eroding out there. There won't be much left of it by the time you get ready."

Jonathan's boots crunched over the loose fall rock around the base of the needle which beetled out overhead, still black on its western face in the early morning. A rock drill, a hammer, and fifteen pounds of pitons, snap rings, and expansion bolts clanged and dangled from the web belt around his waist.

"Right about here," he judged, guessing the position of a long vertical crack he had observed the day before. The crack, averaging four inches in width and running up from the base for a hundred feet, seemed to him to be the highway up the first quarter of the face. It was after the fissure petered out that the mushroom top began its outward lean, and then the going would be more challenging.

"Is this the way you started up, Ben?"

"It's one way, I guess," Ben said noncommittally.

They roped up. "You don't intend to be very helpful, do you?" Jonathan said, passing the loose coils of line to his partner.

"Hell, I don't need the practice. I'm just along for the ride."

Jonathan adjusted the straps on the light pack Ben had insisted he carry for training. Just before taking to the rock, they urinated into the arid ground, pressing out the last drops. Numberless beginners have overlooked, in their eagerness to start, this propitiatory libation to the gods of gravity, and have rued the oversight when they were later faced with the natural problem while on the face, both hands engaged in the more pressing matter of survival. The only solution available under such circumstances is not calculated to make the climber a social success during the press of congratulations following the climb.

"OK, let's go."

The move up the crack went quickly and uneventfully, save in places where the fissure was too wide for a snug foot jam. Jonathan drove no pitons for climbing, only one each thirty feet or so to shorten the fall, if there was one.

He enjoyed the feel of the rock. It had character. It was well-toothed and abrasive to the grip. There were very few good piton cracks, however. Most of them tended to be too wide, requiring one or two additional pitons as wedges, and they did not drive home with the hard ring of the well-seated peg. This would matter more once they began the three hundred feet of outward-leaning climb. Jonathan realized he would have to use the drill and expansion bolt more than he cared to. He had always drawn a fine, but significant line between piton and expansion bolt. The conquest of a face by means of the piton had elements of seduction about it; the use of the drill and bolt smacked of rape.

They moved smoothly and with high coordination. Ben tied off and belayed from below, while Jonathan inched up as far as his rope would allow before finding an acceptable purchase from which to belay Ben up to him. Ben's passage was always faster. He had the psychological advantage of the line; he used the holds and grips Jonathan had worked out.

Even after the crack petered out and progress slowed, Jonathan's feeling of indomitability persisted. Each square meter of face was a gameboard of tactics, a combat against the unrelenting, mindless opposition of gravity in which the rock was a Turkish ally, ready to change sides if the going got rough.

They inched up. Ben's experienced and sympathetic pressure on the line lending it cooperative life, always slack when Jonathan was moving, always snug when it alone held him on the face. For some time there had not been a free purchase where either man could hold to the rock without rope or piton.

Jonathan began to tire; the drag of his pack and the knotting pressure on thighs and calves were constant mortal reminders. But his hands were still strong, and he felt fine. Particularly did he enjoy the touch of the rock, warm where the sun was upon it, cool and refreshing in the shade. The air was so clean it had a green flavor, and even the salt taste of his sweat was good. Nevertheless, he did not object when, after three hours and with two-thirds of the face under them, Ben called for a rest.

It was another quarter of an hour before they found a slim lip of rock into which they could plant their heels. Jonathan tapped in extra pitons, and they hung there side by side against the ropes, facing outward, squatting on their haunches to rest their legs. Their bodies leaned some twenty degrees away from the face, which itself inclined ten degrees from the vertical. Ben struggled with his pack and produced a loaf of hard-crusted bread and a thick disc of cheese which he had carried along out of Alpine tradition. They ate with slow satisfaction, leaning out against their ropes and looking down at the small knot of thrill-seekers who had gathered near the base of the needle once someone at the lodge had seen men on the face of this seemingly impossible pillar.

"How you feeling, ol' buddy?"

"Just . . . really great, Ben."

"You're climbing fine. Best I ever seen you climb."

"Yes. I know I am." Jonathan's admiration was frank, as though he stood outside himself. "It might just be a fluke—a coincidence of conditioning and temperament—but if I were on the Eigerwand right now . . ." His voice trailed off as his imagination overcame each of the Eiger's notorious obstacles.

Ben returned to an old theme. "Why go at all, Jon? What do you want to prove? This is a great climb. Let it go at this."

Jonathan laughed. "You certainly have it in for the Eiger."

"I just have this feeling. That isn't your mountain, ol' buddy. She's knocked you off twice before. Hell's bells! This whole thing is screwy-assed! That fairy down there waiting to shoot you up. Or you waiting to shoot him up. Whichever it is. And all this about checking up on the men you're going to climb with. I don't know what's going on, and I don't think I want to know. But I got a feeling that if you try to take the Eiger while your mind's on these other things, that hill's going to flick you off onto the rocks. And you *know* that's going to smart some!"

Jonathan leaned out, not caring to talk about these matters. "Look at them down there, Ben. Miniature people. Miniaturized by the Japanese technique of slowly decreasing their intake of courage and individuality until they're only fit to serve on committees and protest air pollution."

"Yeah, they ain't much, are they? They'd sure get their cookies if one of us was to fall off. Give them something to talk about for the better part of the afternoon." Ben waved his arm. "Hi, turds!"

Those below could not hear, and they waved back vigorously and grinned.

"How'd you like a beer, ol' buddy?"

"I'd love one. Why don't you shout down for room service. Of course, the boy would deserve a considerable tip."

"We got beer."

"I hope you're kidding."

"Never. I kid about love and life and overpopulation and atomic bombs and such shit, but I don't ever kid about beer."

Jonathan stared at him with disbelief. "You carried a six-pack of beer up this rock? You're insane, you know that."

"Maybe insane, but not stupid. I didn't carry it. You did. I put it in your pack."

Jonathan contorted his body and grappled a six-pack out of his backpack.

"I'll be goddamned! I think I'm going to throw you down on those rubbernecks."

"Wait until I finish this beer."

Jonathan ripped the top off a can and sucked at the foam. "It's warm."

"Sorry about that. But I thought you'd balk at carrying ice."

They ate and drank in silence, Jonathan occasionally feeling a ripple of butterflies in his stomach as he looked into the space below him. In all his years of climbing, he had never completely lost the fluttering in the stomach and the tingle in the groin that came over him when he was not concentrating on problems of the face. It was not an unpleasant sensation and one that he associated with the natural way of things on a mountain.

"How far up would you say we are, Ben?"

"About two-thirds in distance. About halfway in time."

Jonathan nodded agreement. They had observed the day before that the last quarter of the climb, where the mushroom top began its outward flange, would be the most difficult. Jonathan was eager to get at it. "Let's push on."

"I haven't finished my beer!" Ben said with genuine offense.

"You've had two."

"I was talking about this third one." He tugged the top of the can and tipped it up until it was empty, swallowing with great gulps, some beer trickling from the corners of his mouth.

The next three hours involved a sequence of tactical problems, one after the other, the last forgotten as the next was met. For Jonathan there was nothing in Creation but himself and the rock—the next move, the quality of the piton, the sweat in his hair. Total freedom purchased at the risk of a fall. The only way to fly, if you happen to be a wingless animal.

The last five feet were rather special.

The weather had worked its erosive will on the fragile flange around the flat top of the needle. The outward angle was thirty degrees, and the rock was rotten and crumbling. Jonathan moved laterally as far as he could, but the rock did not improve and he could find no valid seat for a piton. He traversed back to just above Ben.

"What's going on?" Ben called up.

"Can't find a way up! How did you make it?"

"Oh, guts, skill, determination, talent. That sort of stuff."

"Screw you."

"Hey, look, ol' buddy. Don't do nothing hasty. This piton is mostly for show."

"If I go, the beer goes."

"Oh, my."

There was no safe way to make the curling lip. Jonathan swore under his breath as he clung to the face, considering the problem. An improbable solution presented itself.

"Give me some slack," he shouted down.

"Don't do nothing foolish, Jon. We've had a nice climb like it is."

"Ninety-nine percent of the way is called a failure. Give me the goddam slack!"

Crouched under the overhang, facing outward, Jonathan flattened his palms against the rock shelf above him. By maintaining constant pressure between his legs and the heels of his hands, he could ease out, one hand after the other. As the angle of his body increased, the force required to wedge himself in became greater until he could no longer lift a palm from the rock above lest he shoot out into space. He had to skid his hands along, inch by inch, grinding the skin off his palms and moistening the rock with blood. At last, his legs trembling with fatigue, his fingers found the edge of the flange and curled over it. He could not judge the soundness of the lip, and he knew that when he pulled up his knees his body might swing so far out that his hold would be lost. But he was no longer facing a decision. He could neither return nor hold the stance much longer. His strength was almost gone.

He squeezed until the finger bones were in contact with the rock through the pads of his fingertips. Then he released and tuck-rolled up.

For an instant, only his legs from the hips down were over the flange; the heavier part of his body and his pack began to drag him, head downward, into the void. He scrambled and fought back, slithering on his stomach, without finesse or technique, in a desperate animal battle against gravity.

He lay face down, panting, his mouth ajar and saliva dripping onto the flat hot rock of the top. His heart thudded in his ears painfully, and the palms of his hands stung with the bits of grit embedded in the raw flesh. A slight breeze cooled his hair, matted and thick with sweat. When he could, he sat up and looked around at the barren slab of stone that had been the goal of all this effort. But he felt just fine. He grinned to himself with the elation of victory.

"Hey? Jon?" Ben's voice came from under the lip. "Anytime you're through admiring yourself, you might bring me up with you."

Jonathan passed the line around a small outcropping of rock and held it in a sitting belay as Ben scrambled up over the edge.

They did not talk for ten minutes, weary with their climb and awed by the prospect around them. They were the highest things in the basin. To the west the desert stretched out forever, shimmering and featureless. From one edge of the tabletop they could look down on Ben's lodge, compressed by distance, its swimming pool a fragment of broken mirror glinting in the sun. Occasional gusts of wind swept the heavy heat off the rock and chilled their sweat-dampened shirts.

They opened the two remaining beers.

"Congratulations, ol' buddy. You bagged yourself another first."

"What do you mean?" Jonathan sipped the tepid froth gratefully.

"I never thought anybody'd climb this needle."

"But you've climbed it yourself."

"Who told you a thing like that?"

"You did."

"You ain't going to get very far in life, listening to known liars like that."

Jonathan was silent for a time.

"All right. Tell me about it, Ben."

"Oh, just this plot of mine that backfired. Some pretty fair country climbers have taken shots at this needle. But it stayed cherry. It's that last little bit that stopped them all. You got to admit that it was a mite hairy. Matter of fact, no sane man would have tried it. Especially with a friend tied on to the other end of the rope."

"I'm sorry, Ben. I didn't think about that."

"You're not the type likely to. Anyway, I figured that if you couldn't make a climb you thought I had made, even with my game foot, you'd think twice about going after the Eiger."

"You're all that set against my going?"

"I am, and that's a fact. I'm scared of it, ol' buddy." Ben sighed and crushed his beer can. "But, like I said, my plot kind of backfired. Now that you've made this climb, I guess nothing in the world's going to keep you away from the Eiger."

"I have no choice, Ben. Everything's tied to the climb. My house. My paintings."

"From what I hear, dead people don't get much kick out of houses and paintings."

"Look. Maybe this will make you feel better about it. If everything goes well,

I may not have to make the climb after all. There's a chance that I can finish my business before the climb starts."

Ben shook his head as though he felt something loose inside. "I don't get all this at all. It's too screwy-assed."

Jonathan touched his palms together to test for pain. They were tacky with the thick clear liquid of coagulation, but they did not hurt much. "Let's go back down."

Leaving their pitons for future climbers, and rappelling in great descending swoops, they reached the flat land in forty minutes, which seemed somehow unfair after the grueling six hours of the climb.

Immediately, they were surrounded by a throng of backslappers and congratulators who offered to buy drinks and gave suggestions on how they would have made the climb, if they had been climbers. Ben, one arm around each of two cute young things, led the crowd back to the lodge; and Jonathan, suddenly drained and leaden, now that nervous energy no longer sustained him, trudged along behind the convivial parade. He had been surprised to see Miles Mellough standing apart from the welcoming group, aloof and cool in a sky blue suit of raw silk, his well-combed Pomeranian squirming and whining in his arms. Miles fell in step with him.

"An impressive display. Do you know, Jonathan, that in all the time we were friends, I never saw you climb? It's rather graceful, in its way."

Jonathan walked on without answering.

"That last little part there was particularly tingling. It sent little thrills down my spine. But you made it after all. What's the matter? You seem rather done in."

"Don't count on it."

"Oh, I don't underrate you." He shifted the jittery dog from one arm to the other, and Jonathan noticed that it wore around its neck a ribbon of the same blue silk as Miles's suit. "It is you who insists on underrating me."

"Where's your boy?"

"Back in his room. Moping, I suspect. And looking forward to his next encounter with you."

"There better not be one. He's dog meat if I see him again on my side of the street."

Miles snuggled his nose into Faggot's fur and purred, "You mustn't take offense, little boy. Dr. Hemlock wasn't talking about you. He was using one of the little vulgarisms of his profession."

The dog whimpered and licked vigorously at Miles's nostrils.

"I hope you've reconsidered, Jonathan." The flat professionalism of Miles's tone contrasted sharply with the cooing purr he had used to the dog. Jonathan wondered how many men had been lulled into a lethal sense of security by Miles's feminine facade.

He stopped and turned to face Miles. "I don't think we have anything to talk about."

Miles adjusted his stance, putting the weight on one foot and pointing the toe of the other out in a relaxed variant of the fourth position in ballet, the better to show the line of his suit. "As a climber, Jonathan, your sense of brinksmanship is well developed. You're telling me now that you're willing to face an unknown target, rather than make your peace with me. All right. Allow me to raise the ante a little. Suppose I contact the target and identify *you*. That would put him in the shadow and you in the light. How would that feel? An interesting reversal of the normal pattern, isn't it?"

Jonathan had considered this uncomfortable possibility. "You don't have as good a bet as you think, Miles. Search is working on the identity of the man."

Mellough laughed richly. The sound startled Faggot. "That is lovely, Jonathan! You're willing to bet your life on the efficiency of CII? Does your barber perform operations on you?"

"How do I know you haven't already contacted the target?"

"And played away my last trump? Really, Jonathan!" He burrowed his nose into Faggot's fur and playfully nipped at his back.

Jonathan walked away toward the lodge.

Miles called after him. "You don't leave me much choice, Jonathan!" Then he nuzzled against Faggot's ear. "Your daddy doesn't have any choice, does he. He'll just have to tell on Dr. Hemlock." He looked after the retreating figure. "Or kill him."

Ben was grumpy and incommunicative throughout supper, but he manfully put away quantities of food and beer. Jonathan made no attempts at conversation, and often his attention strayed from the food and focused on an indeterminate point in space. At length he spoke without breaking his vacant stare. "Anything from your switchboard operator?"

Ben shook his head. "Neither of them has tried to call out, if that's what you mean. No telegrams. Nothing."

Jonathan nodded. "Good. Whatever you do, Ben, don't let them make contact with the outside."

"I'd sure give my front seat in hell to know what's going on around here."

Jonathan looked at him for a long moment, then asked, "Can I borrow your Land-Rover tomorrow?"

"Sure. Where you going?"

Jonathan ignored the question. "Do me a favor, will you? Have one of your people fill it up and put two extra jerry cans of gas and one of water in the back."

"This has something to do with this Mellough character?"

"Yes."

Ben was moodily silent for a time. "All right, Jon. Whatever you need."

"Thanks."

"You don't have to thank me for helping you put your ass in a sling."

"You know that shotgun we talked about yesterday? Will you load it and have it put in the Rover too?"

"Whatever you say." Ben's voice was grim.

Unable to sleep, Jonathan sat up in bed late into the night, working turgidly on the Lautrec article that had been the sponge of his free time for almost a month. George's scratching knock presented an excuse to abandon the arid labor. As usual, she was wearing jeans and a denim shirt, its collar turned up under her long black hair, the three top buttons undone, and her unbound breasts tugging the shirt up from the jeans in taut folds.

"How are you this evening. George?"

She sat on the edge of his bed and regarded him blandly with her large, dark eyes.

"Did you watch Ben and me make that climb today? Wasn't that something?" He paused, then responded for her. "Yes, that was something."

She slipped off her shoes then stood to unbutton and unzip her jeans with the brisk movements of a person with business to attend to.

"It looks as though I'll be leaving tomorrow or the day after. In some ways, George, I'll miss you."

With a clapper action of her bottom, she forced the jeans over her hips.

"No one can say that you've cluttered up our relationship with sticky sentiment or unnecessary chatter, and I appreciate that."

She stood for a second, the tails of her shirt brushing her olive thighs, then she began unbuttoning it, her placid eyes never leaving his.

"I have an idea, George. Why don't we give up this banal chatter and make love?" He barely had time to get his notes off the bed and turn off the light before she was tangled up amongst his limbs.

He lay on his stomach, his arms thrown limply across the bed, every muscle liquid with relaxation as George trickled her fingers from the small of his back to the nape of his neck. He hovered on the rim of sleep as long as he could, trying not to anticipate the eddies of thrill her fingernails churned up as they slid with barely perceptible contact around his waist, up his sides, and outward along his upper arms. By way of thanks, he hummed a couple of times with contentment, although he would rather not have put forth the effort.

She stopped stroking him, and he began to slip over the edge of consciousness.

"Ouch!"

He felt something like a wasp sting in his shoulder. George leaped out of bed and cowered in the darkest corner of the room. He fumbled the light on and looked around, squinting against the sudden glare. Quite nude, George pressed into her corner, the hypodermic needle still in her hands, both thumbs against the plunger and the point directed at him, as though it were a gun she could protect herself with.

"You little bitch." Jonathan, also nude, advanced on her.

Fear and hate flickering in her eyes, she made a lunge at him with the needle, and with one broad backhand blow he reeled her along the wall and into the opposite corner, where she crouched like a treed cougar, blood trickling from the corner of her mouth and one nostril, her lips drawn back in a frozen snarl that revealed her lower teeth. He was moving in to expand on her punishment when the buzzing in his ears settled toward his stomach and made him stagger. He turned back toward the door, now an undulating trapezoid, but he realized he would never make it. He stumbled toward the phone. His knees buckled under him, and he went down, knocking over the bedside table and plunging the room into darkness as the lamp burst with a loud implosion. The buzzing pulsed louder and in tempo with the dancing bursts of light behind his eyes.

"Desk," answered a thin, bored voice near him on the floor, somewhere in the rubble of broken glass. He pawed about blindly, trying to find the receiver. "Desk." He felt a volley of pains in the small of his back, and he knew the little bitch was kicking him with the relentless rhythm of frightened fury. "Desk." The voice was impatient. He could not ward off the kicks; all he could do was curl up around the receiver and take it. The pains became duller and duller until they were only pressures. "Desk." Jonathan's tongue was thick and alien. With his disobedient lips pressing against the mouthpiece, he struggled to form a word.

"Ben!" he blurted with a treble whimper, and the word chased him down into warm black water.

Arizona: *June 29*

A LIGHT FLUTTERED on the black water, and Jonathan, disembodied, rushed through miles of space toward it. He gained on the spark, and it grew larger, until it developed into a window with stripes of daylight glaring through a venetian blind. He was in his room. A great flesh-colored glob hung over him.

"How's it going, ol' buddy?"

He tried to sit up, but a thud of pain nailed him to the pillow.

"Relax. Doctor said you're going to be just fine. He says it may hurt for a few days when you piss. George sure gave your kidneys a going over."

"Give me something to drink."

"Beer?"

"Anything." Jonathan inched his way to a sitting position, moving up through strata of thickening headache.

Ben made a clumsy attempt to feed him the beer, but Jonathan relieved him of his heavy solicitude by snatching the can away after a third of it had spilled on his chest. "Where is she?" he asked once his thirst was slaked.

"I got her locked up, and a couple of my staff are watching her. Want me to call into town for the sheriff?"

"No, not yet. Tell me, Ben . . ."

"No, he hasn't. I figured you'd be wondering if this Mellough had checked out. The desk will call me if he tries."

"So it was Miles?"

"That's what George says."

"All right. He's had it. Let's get me into the shower."

"But the doctor said—"

Jonathan's suggestion as to what the doctor could do with his advice was beyond the routine of physiotherapy and, moreover, beyond ballistic probability.

Ben half carried him into the shower where Jonathan turned on the cold water and let it beat on him, clearing the moss from his mind. "Why, Ben? I'm really not that bad."

"The oldest reason in the world, ol' buddy," he shouted over the noise of the shower.

"Love?"

"Money."

The water was doing its work, but with the return of feeling came a pounding headache and pains in his kidneys. "Toss me in a bottle of aspirin. What did she shoot into me?"

"Here." Ben's big paw thrust the bottle through the shower curtain. "Doctor says it was some relative of morphine. He had a name for it. But it wasn't a lethal dose."

"So it would appear." The aspirin disintegrated in his hand with the splatter of water, so he tipped the bottle up to his mouth then washed the tablets down by gulping under the shower head. He gagged as bits of aspirin caught in his throat. "Morphine figures. Miles is in the drug business."

"Is that right? But how come he went that far and didn't put you away for good? George said he had promised her nothing serious would happen to you. Just wanted to scare you off."

"Her concern is touching."

"Maybe she just didn't want to die for murder."

"That sounds more like it." Jonathan turned off the water and began to towel himself down, but not too vigorously, because every sharp motion slopped pain around in his head. "My guess is that Miles intended to come in after George put me under and shoot me full of junk. The death would be attributed to an overdose. It's typical Mellough. Safe and oblique."

"He's a bad ass all right. What are you going to do about him?"

"Something massive."

After Jonathan dressed, they went down the hall to the room in which George was being kept. He felt a twinge of regret when he saw her swollen eye and the split lip he had given her, but this quickly faded when the bruises along his spine reminded him of how she had tried to help the morphine put him away.

She looked more Indian than ever, clutching a blanket around her shoulders, under which she was as naked as she had been when Ben broke in to save him.

"How much did he pay you, George?" he asked.

She almost spat back her response. "Goddam your eyes, you shit!"

These were the only words he ever heard her speak.

Ben could not help chuckling as they returned to Jonathan's room. "I guess she's been around me too much."

"It's not that, Ben. They always talk about my eyes afterwards. Look, I'm going to get a couple hours' sleep. Will you have your people at the desk make up my bill?"

"You leaving right away?"

"Soon. Is the Land-Rover ready?"

"Yeah."

"And the shotgun?"

"It'll be on the floorboards. I imagine you don't want Mellough to know you're checking out."

"On the contrary. But don't do anything special about it. He'll find out. Miles is a specialist in information."

He awoke refreshed three hours later. The effects of the morphine had worn off and his headache was gone, but his kidneys still felt a little soggy. He dressed with special care in one of his better suits, packed his suitcases, and telephoned to the desk to have them put in the Land-Rover.

As he entered the lounge he saw the blond wrestler sitting at the bar, a broad strip of tape over his swollen nose.

"Good afternoon, Dewayne." Ignoring the bodyguard's glare of hate, he passed through the lounge, along a walkway, and over a bridge to the table at which Miles sat, poised and impeccable in a suit of metallic gold.

"Join me, Jonathan?"

"I owe you a drink."

"So you do. And we all know what a stickler you are for old debts. You're looking very nice. Your tailor is accurate, if uninspired."

"I'm not feeling too well. I had a bad night."

"Oh? I'm sorry to hear that."

The young Indian waiter who had served them the first day approached the table, his glances at Miles filled with tender remembrance. Jonathan ordered, and the two of them watched the bathers around the pool until the drinks arrived and the waiter departed.

"Cheers, Jonathan?"

Jonathan drank off the Laphroaig and put the glass on the table. "I've decided to forget about you for now, Miles."

"Have you? Just like that?"

"I'm going to be staying here in training for a couple more weeks, and I won't be able to concentrate on it with you on my mind. I have a big climb in front of me." Jonathan was sure that Miles knew he had checked out. The obvious lie was calculated to make Miles think he had him on the run, and Miles was the kind to press such an advantage.

"I sympathize with your problem, Jonathan. Truly I do. But unless this means you are crossing me off your list for good . . ." He lifted his shoulders in helpless regret.

"I might do just that. Let's have dinner together tonight and talk about it."

"A delightful idea."

Jonathan had to admire Miles's silky control.

Jonathan rose. "See you this evening."

"I'm looking forward to it." Miles raised his glass in salute.

The Land-Rover was parked in the loading zone in front of the lodge. As Jonathan climbed in, he noticed on the floorboards next to the shotgun a thoughtful gift from Ben: a six-pack of cold beer. He opened a can and sipped at it while he glanced over the area map on his lap. He had earlier located a long dirt road running in thin broken lines deep into the desert. Ben had told him it was a little-used rut track that only government rangers drove on. For more than a hundred fifty miles, the road pierced into the core of the western desert, then it stopped abruptly.

Tracing back with his finger, he found the place where the dirt track began, branching west from a north-south gravel access road. This gravel road joined the main highway about a mile west of the turnoff to Ben's place. Considering the difference in speed between the Rover and the rental car at Miles's disposal, that mile of good highway promised to be the most dangerous stretch.

Fixing the map in his mind, Jonathan folded it away and drove off, slowly winding up from the basin. On one of the cutbacks he glanced down to find that Miles's car was already in pursuit. He pressed down on the gas.

Seated beside Dewayne, Faggot in his arms, Miles saw Jonathan's sudden increase in speed. "He knows we're following him. Go get him, Dewayne. Here's your chance to reinstate yourself in my good graces." And he fondly scratched behind Faggot's ears as the car sprayed dust in a skidding turn.

The Rover's superior traction and suspension made up for its disadvantage in speed, and the distance between the two did not much alter throughout the race until the last flat hundred yards before the highway, during which Miles gained perceptibly on the Rover. Dewayne pulled an automatic from his shoulder holster.

"Don't," Miles ordered. "We'll pull alongside on the highway where we can be sure of it." Miles knew the Rover had no chance of outdistancing him along the five miles of good road to town.

Jonathan approached the highway at full speed and quickly turned west, away from town.

For an instant Miles was troubled by the unexpected move. Then he decided that Jonathan realized the hopelessness of an open race and was seeking some back road on which the qualities of the Rover would give him a chance.

"I think this would be a good time to get him, Dewayne."

The car torqued low on its springs as it bounced onto the highway and screamed around the corner in pursuit.

Jonathan held the accelerator to the floor, but at seventy the Rover was flat out, and the automobile gained on him steadily. The gravel cutoff was only half a mile away, but the car behind was so close that he could distinguish Miles through the rearview mirror. In a moment they would swing out and pull up beside him. He saw Miles roll down his window and lean back to give Dewayne a clear field of fire.

When they were almost on his bumper, Jonathan reached down and switched on his lights.

Seeing the taillights flash, and imagining Jonathan had hit his brakes, Dewayne jammed down on his own, and the wheels squealed and smoked, while the Rover roared on at its best speed.

By the time Dewayne had fumbled his foot back onto the gas, Jonathan had gained sufficient distance to reach the gravel road with fifty yards lead. Miles swore to himself. It had been Henri who had told them about the headlight ploy.

Several times on the gravel road, when his lead was threatened, Jonathan wagged the wheel and caused the Rover to zigzag slightly, raising clouds of blinding dust which forced the car to fall back. In this way he held his advantage until he came to the ranger trail that led out into the desert. Once he was on this meandering track of potholes, and unbanked turns, and ruts so deep the automobile repeatedly bottomed, he had no difficulty maintaining his lead. He was even able to open another can of beer, although it splashed over him when he bounced into an unexpected hole.

"Just keep him in sight, Dewayne." At the turnoff onto the dirt road Miles had seen a weathered sign warning drivers that there was no outlet. Sooner or later, Jonathan would have to turn back. The road, often winding between giant outcroppings of sandstone, was not wide enough for two cars to pass. He had Jonathan in a box.

For nearly an hour the vehicles sped over the flat, gray-tan country where nothing grew in the powdery, baked earth. Dewayne had returned his gun to its holster where its pressure made him sweat freely. Faggot whimpered and pranced with sharp claws in Miles's lap. Sliding from side to side with each abrupt turn, Miles braced himself with pressure between feet and back. His lips were tight with chagrin at being unable to sit with poise. Even Faggot's frantic and moist gestures of affection irritated him.

The vehicles raced and jolted over the desert, lofting two high plumes of fine dust behind them.

Despite the stream of air gushing in through the open side of the Rover, Jonathan's back adhered with perspiration to the plastic seat. As he bounced over a rut, the jerry cans behind him clanged together, reminding him that it would not do for those chasing him to run out of fuel. He began to search for a site appropriate to his needs.

Dewayne hunched over the wheel and squinted into the dust rising before him. His jaw muscles flexed in anticipation of revenge.

About two miles farther on, Jonathan caught sight of an outcropping of rock, a single ragged sandstone boulder around which the track made an S-turn. It was ideal. He slowly eased off on the gas, allowing those behind to close to within a hundred yards. The instant he made the first turn, he hit his brakes, skidding to a stop and raising dense clouds of choking dust. He snatched the shotgun off the seat, leaped out of the Rover, and dashed for the boulder, knowing he had only seconds in which to scramble around the rock and come out from behind.

As Dewayne steered into the first turn, he was blinded by the swirl of dust. The Land-Rover loomed in front of him, and he jammed down on the brakes. Before the car had slid to a stop, Miles had his door open and had rolled out onto the ground. Dewayne twisted the window handle, grappling desperately at his automatic. Hemlock! The barrels of the shotgun jabbed painfully into his left side. He never heard the shot.

Jonathan snapped back the hammers of the shotgun as he raced desperately around the boulder. He heard the squeal of brakes, and plunged through the dust at a full run. Dewayne's face emerged out of the billowing white fog. He was trying to get his window down. Jonathan rammed the gun in through the half-opened window and snapped off both triggers.

The blast was deafening.

Dewayne snorted like a hammered steer as the force of the impact slid him across the seat and halfway out the open door, where he dangled and twitched until his nerves discovered they were dead.

Jonathan stepped around in front of the car and reached in under the hanging arms to extract the automatic. He wiped his sticky fingers off on a fragment of Dewayne's jacket he found several feet away from the car.

Miles stood in the settling dust, straightening his cuffs and slapping dirt from his gold suit. The Pomeranian danced epileptically about his legs.

"Really, Jonathan! This suit cost me three hundred dollars and, what's more, five fittings."

"Get into my car."

Miles picked up the squirming dog and walked in front of Jonathan to the Rover, his casual dancer's stride betraying no effect of recent events.

They drove on westward, deeper into the desert. Their lips began to crack with the salt that prevented the most meager vegetation from growing. Jonathan held the automatic high in his left hand so he could fend off any attempt Miles might make for it.

For an hour and a half they pressed on through the shimmering heat of the desert. Jonathan knew that Miles was ready to make his try for the gun. Slight contractions of his hand on his lap, and minute tensings of his shoulders predicted Miles's move. Just as he threw himself after the gun, Jonathan hit the brakes, and Miles went face first into the steering wheel. Jonathan snapped back the emergency brake and jumped out, dragging Miles after him by the collar. He dumped him onto the crackled ground and sprang back into the Rover. By the time Miles had staggered to his feet, a rivulet of blood caked with dirt running from his nose, Jonathan had backed the Rover in a sharp arc. Miles stood in the road, blocking the path with his body.

"You're not going to leave me out here!" The recognition of Jonathan's plan for him grew and filled him with horror as no bullet in the head could have.

Jonathan tried to steer around him, but before he could get up any speed Miles jumped onto the hood. He lay over it, his face pressed against the glass.

"For Christ's sake, Jonathan," he screamed. "Shoot me!"

Jonathan raced forward, then hit the brakes, dumping Miles off the hood. He roared in reverse away from the crumpled body, then sped on, making a wide curve to avoid him.

By the time Jonathan could see his dancing image in the rearview mirror, Miles had reclaimed his characteristic composure and was standing, the dog in his arms, looking after the diminishing Land-Rover.

Jonathan never forgot his last image of Miles, the gold suit glinting in the sunlight. Miles had set the dog down and had taken a comb from his pocket. He ran it through his hair and patted the sides into place.

Kleine Scheidegg: *July 5*

JONATHAN SAT AT a round metal table on the terrace of the Kleine Scheidegg Hotel, sipping a glass of grassy Vaudois, enjoying the slight snap of its latent effervescence. He looked across the up-tilted meadow to the gloomy north face of the Eiger. The unstable warmth of the weightless mountain sunlight was puffed away time and again by wisps of crisp highland air.

Touched only once a day and briefly by the sun, the dark concave face hovered malignantly above him, looking as though it had been scooped out of the body of the mountain by some Olympian shovel, its brittle gray-black crescent rim cutting into the glittering blue of the sky.

A breeze stirred, and he shivered involuntarily. He remembered his two previous attempts at the face, both beaten back by those brutal storms that roll in from the north and are collected and amplified in the natural amphitheatre of the Eigerwand. So common are these rages of wind and snow that the dour Bernese Oberland guides speak of them as "Eiger Weather." After the last nine-hour dicey retreat from the high ice field called the White Spider—that salient epitome of the mountain's treachery—he had promised himself never to try again.

And yet . . . It would be a fine mountain to take.

He adjusted his sunglasses and gazed with reluctant fascination at the awful sublimity of the Eiger. The view was uncommon; normally, heavy shrouds of mist hang from the crest, obscuring the storms that lash it, and muffling the crack and roar of avalanches that constitute the mountain's most potent defensive weapon. His eye snagged on each of those features associated with the defeat and death of some mountaineer.

He was afraid of the mountain; his groin tingled with the fear. But at the same time, his hands itched for the touch of its cold rock, and he was exhilarated at the thought of trying that fine savage again. This perverse dialogue between the flinching mind and the boisterous body is one every climber has experienced at one time or another. It was a pity that his sanction target would be nominated before the climb started. Maybe after it was over . . .

A long-limbed blond with a mountain tan squeezed between the close-set tables (although there was no one else on the terrace) and nudged Jonathan with her hip, causing some wine to spill from his glass.

"I *am* sorry," she said, willing to allow this accident to open a conversation.

Jonathan nodded a curt acceptance of her apology, and she passed on to use the coin-operated telescope that was in a direct line between him and the mountain (although there were six others available to her). She bent over the instrument, directing her excellent bottom toward him, and he could not help noting that her suntan must have been acquired in those very shorts. Her accent had been British, and she had the general look of the horsey type, the long taut legs developed from gripping the animal between her knees. He noticed that her shoes, however, were not British. Since the advent of mini, English women had gotten away from those remarkable clogs that once identified them on sight. It used to be said that British women's shoes were made by excellent craftsmen who had had shoes carefully described to them, but who had never actually seen a pair at first hand. They were, however, comfortable, and they wore well. And those were also the principal virtues of the women who wore them.

He followed the line of her telescope and rested his eyes again on the Eiger.

The Eiger. Appropriate name. When the early Christians came into these high meadows, they bestowed benign labels on the two higher mountains of the massif: Jungfrau, the Virgin; and Monch, the Monk. But this most malicious promontory was named for an evil pagan spirit. Eiger: the Ogre.

Before the turn of the century, all the faces of the Eiger had been climbed, except one, the north Eigerwand: the Ogre's Wall. Experienced mountaineers had listed it among the "impossible" faces, and so it was in the days of pure climbing, before sportsmen armed themselves with piton and snap ring.

Later, under the ring of the hammer, the "impossible" faces fell to the record books one by one, but the north face of the Eiger remained virgin. Then, in the mid-thirties, the Nazi cult of mountain and cloud sent wave after wave of young German boys, filled with a lust to accrue glory to their dishonored Fatherland, against the Eiger's defenses. Hitler offered a gold medal to whoever made the first ascent; and in neatly regimented sequence the flaxen-haired romantics died. But the mountain retained its hymen.

In mid-August of 1935 came Max Sedlmayer and Karl Mehringer, two lads with considerable experience in the more difficult climbs and a searing desire to chalk up the Eiger on the German scoreboard. Tourists watched their ascent through telescopes from this very terrace. These voyeurs of death were the ancestors of the modern "Eiger Birds," those carrion crows of the jet set who flock to the Kleine Scheidegg Hotel and pay exorbitant sums to titillate to the vicarious thrill of the climbers facing death, then return to their lives of musical beds refreshed and reinspired.

Sedlmayer and Mehringer moved up the first 800 feet which is not especially difficult, but totally exposed to falling rocks. To observers below it seemed that the climb was going well. Rope length after rope length, they skillfully belayed each other up. At the end of the first day they bivouacked at 9,500 feet, well above the windows of the Eigerwand tunnel of the Jungfrau Railway, a remarkable bit of engineering that cuts right through the massif, bringing trainfuls of tourists to the Bernese highlands. These windows were originally designed to jettison rubble and to ventilate the tunnel, but they have figured dramatically in attempts to rescue climbers.

Throughout the next day, Sedlmayer and Mehringer enjoyed uncommonly benevolent weather, and they made the upper rim of the First Ice Field, but they were moving very slowly. The vultures at the telescopes could see that the climbers had to hold their knapsacks over their heads to get some protection from the falling rocks and ice with which the Ogre greeted them. Time and again they were forced to stop and take refuge under some scanty overhang to avoid the more determined salvoes from above. Just as they got to the rim of the Second Ice Field, a curtain of mist descended, and for a day and a half they were obscured from the view of the grumbling tourists. During that night a storm raged around the Eiger, crashing such huge boulders down the face that several of the hotel guests complained that their sleep had been interrupted. It is possible that Sedlmayer and Mehringer slept poorly too. The temperature in the valley sank to −8°. Who can guess how cold it was up there on the face? The fine weather with which the White Spider had lured the boys into its web was over. Eiger Weather had begun.

When the clouds lifted on Sunday, the climbers were sighted, still moving up. The hotel guests cheered and toasted one another, and bets were placed against the time the young Germans would reach the top. But experienced climbers and guides glanced embarrassedly at one another and walked away from the crowds. They knew the lads had no chance and climbed only because avalanches had cut off their retreat, and anything was better than simply hanging from their pitons awaiting death.

They moved up slowly toward the Flatiron (the highest point Jonathan's party had reached during his first attempt at the Ogre). The clouds descended again, and the tourists were cheated of the thrill of watching them die.

That night a gale lashed the face.

There was a half-hearted attempt to organize a rescue team, but more in response to the desire to do something than to any hope of reaching them alive. In manifestation of typical Swiss compassion, the Bernese Oberland guides haggled over wages until it was too late to bother with the rescue. An intrepid German flyer dared the treacherous air currents to fly close to the face and search. He spotted the boys, frozen to death, still hanging from their harnesses.

With this, the Eiger began its nomenclature of human tragedy. To this day that spot on the point of the Flatiron above the Third Ice Field is called Death Bivouac. The game between the Eiger and Man was begun.

Score: Ogre—2; Man—0

Early in 1936 two Germans came to reclaim the bodies of their countrymen from where they had stood frozen against the wall for a year, a target for the prying telescopes on clear days. If possible, they were also going to attempt the summit. They decided to take a training climb first. An avalanche caught one up and broke his neck against a rock.

Ogre—3; Man—0

In July of that same year German Youth challenged the Ogre again. This time it was a team of four: Rainer, Angerer, Kurz, and Hinterstoisser. Again the tourists watched and placed bets. The young men, suffused with the *Zeitgeist* of Hitler's early days, made such melodramatic statements to the press as: "We must have the Wall, or it must have us!"

It had them.

The most experienced of the party, Hinterstoisser, discovered a tricky traverse across the face that turned out to be the key to subsequent climbs. But so confident were they of victory that they pulled in the rope after the last of the party had crossed. This gesture of cocky confidence killed them.

The party climbed well, although Angerer appeared to be injured, probably by falling rock, and the others had to slow down to help him along. Their first bivouac was just above the Rote Fluh, that red rock crag that is one of the more salient landmarks of the face. In one day they had gone more than halfway up the Eiger!

The next day, with the injured man becoming steadily weaker, they gained the Third Ice Field and tied off to camp just below Death Bivouac. When dawn allowed the rubbernecks at the coin-operated telescopes to enjoy the drama, the party had begun a descent. Obviously the condition of the injured man prevented them from continuing.

Smoothly and with remarkable speed, considering the incapacitated climber, they descended the first two ice fields. But night caught them, and they were forced to make a third bivouac. That night, with Eiger Weather freezing their soaked clothes into clanging armor of ice, must have been brutal. Their reserves of strength were sapped by the cold, and through all of the next day they only managed, 1,000 feet.

For a fourth time, and now out of food, they had to bivouac on the inhospitable face.

Some novices at the hotel opined that the team had a good chance. After all, they had only the Hinterstoisser Traverse and the Difficult Crack before them, then the going would be relatively easy.

But the team had overconfidently retrieved their rope from the traverse.

And the next morning it was completely iced over. Again and again, with a growing desperation that never overwhelmed his skill, the gifted Hinterstoisser attempted to make the verglas and slime of the traverse, and each time he was stopped by the hungry Ogre.

The mists descended, and the tourists could hear the roar of avalanches all through the night. Another name was attached to the Eiger: The Hinterstoisser Traverse.

Ogre—7; Man—0

Throughout 1937 team after team attacked the Eiger, only to be driven back. The mountain came close to claiming more victims during the remarkable retreat of Vorg and Rebitsch from Death Bivouac.

But the score remained the same.

In June of 1938 two Italians (there were national movements afoot in Italy too) fell to their deaths near Difficult Crack.

But rope and piton techniques were steadily perfected, while the natural defenses of the mountain remained as they had been since the memory of man, so in July of that year a German team finally removed the north face of the Eiger from the list of "impossibles."

Ogre—9; Man—1

Throughout the war years, the Eiger was free from incursions into its privacy. Governments provided young men with other ways to inscribe their names on the roles of glory—ways that converted suicide into murder, and soothed all with the balm of patriotism.

But directly these avenues to danger were sealed off by peace, the vertical snare of the Eiger beckoned again. In recent years, more than thirty men have slogged up the last snow slope, panting and crying and promising never to touch the stone of the Ogre again. But most of the attempts are still driven back by weather and avalanche, and the death toll continues to rise regularly. The critical ice field of the White Spider has played the antagonist role in most of the recent tragedies, like the one in 1957 in which three men died and a fourth was rescued only after hunger and thirst had driven him to splinter his teeth on glacier ice in an attempt to get something into his stomach.

Jonathan stared ahead, his mind unrolling the death record of the Eiger.

"Is there something wrong?" the English girl at the telescope asked.

He had forgotten her.

"Why are you staring at me like that?" She smiled, anticipating the reason.

"I wasn't staring at you, dear. I was staring through you."

"How disappointing. May I join you?" She interpreted his silence as invitation. "You've been looking at that mountain with such concentration that I couldn't help noticing you. I do hope you're not thinking of climbing it."

"Oh, no. Never again."

"You've climbed it before?"

"I've tried."

"Is it awfully fierce?"

"Awfully."

"I have a theory about mountain climbers. By the way, my name's Randie— Randie Nickers."

"Jonathan Hemlock. What's your theory, Randie?"

"Well . . . may I have some wine? That's all right. I'll just use your glass, if you don't mind. Well, my theory is that men climb mountains out of some kind of frustration. I think it's a kind of sublimation of other desires."

"Sexual, of course."

Randie nodded earnestly as she swallowed a sip of wine. "Yes, probably. This wine's half fizzy, isn't it."

He put his feet upon an empty chair and leaned back to receive the sun. "It has the giggling sparkle of Swiss maidens, blushed but pleased by the attention of rural swains, but these high spirits do not eclipse the underlying tartness of the petulant Oberland peasant that resides largely in the wine's malolactic fermentation."

Randie was silent for a moment. "I do hope you're teasing."

"Of course I am, Randie. Don't people usually tease you?"

"Not men. They typically try to make love to me."

"How do they do? Typically."

"Well, of late they've been doing very well indeed. I'm in Switzerland for a sort of holiday before I go home and settle down to a most proper married life."

"And you're spreading the blessings of your body around while there's still time."

"Something like that. Not that I don't love Rodney. He's the dearest person, really. But he *is* Rodney."

"And he's rich."

"Oh, I imagine so." Her brow clouded over for an instant. "I certainly *hope* he is. Oh, of course he is! What a fright you gave me. But the nicest thing about him is his name."

"Which is?"

"Smith. Rodney Smith."

"And that's the nicest thing about him?"

"It's not that Smith is all that grand of itself. I believe it's actually a fairly common name. But it will mean that I shall finally be rid of my name. It's been a plague to me all my life."

"Randie Nickers sounds all right to me."

"That's because you're an American. I could tell that from your accent. But 'knickers' is British slang for panties. And you can imagine what the girls at school did with that."

"I see." He took his glass back and poured himself some wine. He wondered what it was about him that attracted the nutty ones.

"You see what I mean?" Randie asked, forgetting that she had been thinking, rather than speaking.

"Not exactly."

"Oh, I have this theory that strangers gravitate immediately to the topics of their greatest mutual interest. And here we are talking about panties. It rather tells on us, doesn't it."

"You ride horses, don't you," he said, succumbing to the rule of non sequitur Randie's mind demanded.

"Yes, as a matter of fact! I show for my uncle. How on earth did you know?"

"I didn't know, really. I more hoped. Do you have a theory about women who delight in having strong beasts between their legs?"

She frowned. "I hadn't really thought about it. But I imagine you're right. It's something like your mountain climbing, isn't it? It's always delightful to have something in common." She looked at him narrowly. "Don't I know you from somewhere. The name's familiar." She mused, "Jonathan Hemlock . . . Ah! Aren't you an author?"

"Only a writer."

"Yes! I have it! You write books about art and everything. They're very keen on you at Slade."

"Yes, it's a good school. What would you rather we did, Randie? Take a walk through the village? Or shall we rush directly to bed."

"A stroll through the village would be grand. Romantic, actually. I'm glad we're going to make love. I have a theory about lovemaking. I view it as a first-rate icebreaker. You make love with a man, and the first thing you know you're holding hands and calling each other by first names. I prefer first names. Probably because of my own family name. Did I tell you what knickers are in England?"

"Yes."

"Well then, you can appreciate my attitude toward names. I have this theory about attitudes . . ."

Jonathan was not disconsolate when he discovered that Randie would be returning to London the following morning.

Kleine Scheidegg: *July 6-7*

IT HAD BEEN necessary to dress twice that morning, and they nearly missed the train. The last Jonathan saw of Miss Nickers as the train began to move away from the platform, she tugged down her compartment window and called, "You really have smashing eyes, you know, Jonathan!" Then she settled into her seat next to a homeward-bound skier and began animatedly explaining one of her theories to him.

Jonathan smiled as he remembered her tactic of self-excitation which consisted of calling parts, places, and postures by their most earthy names.

He turned up the steep cobblestone road that connects the village to the hotel. He had arranged to take a training climb with a local guide up the west flank of the Eiger. Although a far cry from the North Face, this west route had been blooded often enough to demand respect.

Beyond the training and acclimatization, there was another reason prompting him to stay away from the hotel as much as possible. Somehow, as always, despite the greatest precautions, the management of the hotel had sensed there was an attempt at the Eigerwand pending. Discreet telegrams had been sent out; the best suites were being held vacant for rich "Eiger Birds" who would soon begin to descend on the hotel. Like all climbers, Jonathan resented and detested these excitement-hungry jet setters who seek to titillate their callused nerve ends by vicarious thrill. He was glad that Ben and the other members of the climbing team had not yet arrived, because with them the carrion would descend in force.

Halfway up the cobblestone road, Jonathan stopped off at an outdoor café for a glass of Vaudois. The fragile mountain sun was pleasant on his cheek.

"Do you ever buy wine for girls you meet in bars?"

She had approached from behind, from the dark interior of the café. Her voice hit him like a palpable thing. Without turning around, and with fine command of his feelings, he reached over and pushed out a chair for her. She sat looking at him for a time, sadness balanced in her eyes.

The waiter came, received the order, returned with the wine, and departed. She slid her glass back and forth over a small puddle of water on the table, concentrating on it, rather than on his cool, uninviting eyes. "I had this whole speech worked out, you know. It was a good one. I could say it quickly, before you interrupted me or walked away."

"How did it go?"

She glanced up at him, then away. "I forget."

"No, come on. Let's hear it. I'm easily conned, as you know."

She shook her head and smiled faintly. "I surrender. I can't handle it on this level. I can't sit here and swap cool, mature words with you. I'm . . ." She looked up, desperate at the paucity of words in the face of human emotions. "I'm sorry. Really."

"Why did you do it?" He was not going to melt.

"Try to be a little fair, Jonathan. I did it because I believed—I *still* believe—you have to take this assignment."

"I've taken the assignment, Jemima. Things worked out just fine."

"Stop it! Don't you know what it would mean if the other side had a major biological weapon before we did?"

"Oh, of course. We have to keep it out of their hands at all costs! They're the kind of heartless shits who might drop it on some unsuspecting Japanese city!"

She glanced down. "I know you don't think it makes any difference. We talked about it that night. Remember."

"Remember? You're not a bad in-fighter."

She sipped her wine, the silence heavy on her. "At least they promised me that you wouldn't lose your painting."

"They kept their promise. Your conscience is clear."

"Yes." She sighed. "But there's still this problem I have."

"What's that?"

She said it matter-of-factly. "I love you."

After a pause, he smiled to himself and shook his head. "I've underrated you. You're a great in-fighter."

The silence grew denser, and she realized that she must abandon this heavy line of talk lest he simply walk away. "Say, I saw you walking around yesterday with a most un-Jemima type—blond and Anglo and all. Was she good?"

"Adequate."

"As good as—"

"No."

"I'm glad!"

Jonathan could not help smiling at her frankness. "How did you know I was here?"

"I studied your file in Mr. Dragon's office, remember? This assignment was detailed in it."

"I see." So Dragon had been so sure of him that he had included this sanction. Jonathan despised being predictable.

"Will I see you tonight, Jonathan?" There was bravery in her voice. She was willing to be hurt.

"I have a date to climb a hill today. We'll be up there overnight."

"What about tomorrow?"

"Please go away. I have no intention of punishing you. I don't want to hate you, or love you, or anything. I just want you to go away."

She folded her gloves in her lap. She had made up her mind. "I'll be here when you come down from the mountain."

Jonathan rose and dropped a bill on the table. "Please don't."

Her eyes brimmed suddenly with tears. "Why are you doing this, Jonathan? I know this isn't a one-way thing. I know you love me too."

"I'll get over it." He left the café and walked to the hotel with vigorous strides.

True to type, the Swiss guide grumbled and complained that they should have started with the first light of dawn. As it was, they would have to pass the night on the mountain. Jonathan explained that he had all along intended to pass the night there, for the conditioning. The guide classified himself: At first he did not understand (genus, Teutonic), then he refused to budge (species, Helvetic). But when Jonathan offered to double the fee, there was a sudden comprehension coupled with the assurance that the idea of spending a night on the mountain was a splendid one.

Jonathan had always found the Swiss to be a money-loving, dour, religious, money-loving, independent, well-organized, money-loving people. These men of the Bernese Oberland are fine mountaineers, always willing to face the rigors and risks of rescuing a climber trapped on the face of a mountain. But they never fail to send a carefully itemized bill to the man they have saved or, that failing, to his next of kin.

The climb was rigorous enough, but relatively uneventful. Jonathan would have resented the guide's interminable complaining about the cold during the overnight bivouac, had it not served to keep his mind away from Jemima.

Back at the hotel the next day, he received his bill. It seemed that, despite the double fee there were many little items still to be paid for. Among these were medical supplies they had not used, food for the bivouac (Jonathan had brought his own to test the freeze-dried rations), and a charge for "1/4 pair of boots." This last was too much. He called the guide to his room and questioned him. The guide assumed an attitude of cooperation and weary patience as he explained the obvious. "Shoes wear out; you would not deny that. Surely one cannot climb a mountain barefooted. Agreed? For Matterhorn I usually charge half a pair of shoes. Eiger is more than half the altitude of Matterhorn, and yet I only charged you for a quarter pair. I did this because you were a pleasant companion."

"I'm surprised you didn't charge me for wear on the rope."

The guide's eyebrows lofted. "Oh?" He took up the bill and scanned it minutely. "You are perfectly right, sir. There has been an omission." He drew a pencil from his pocket, licked the point, and painstakingly wrote in the neglected item, then corrected and checked the total. "Can I be of further service?" he asked.

Jonathan pointed to the door, and with a curt bow the guide left.

Jonathan's undefined sense of tension and anticipation was exacerbated by the depression Switzerland always brought upon him. He considered the placement of the magnificent Alps in this soulless country to be one of nature's more malevolent caprices. As he wandered around the hotel aimlessly, he came upon a group of lower-class Eiger Birds playing the fondue-kirsch-kiss game and giggling stupidly. He turned back toward his room with disgust. No one really likes Switzerland, except those who prefer cleanliness to life, he thought. And anyone who would live in Switzerland would live in Scandinavia. And anyone who would live in Scandinavia would eat lutefisk. And anyone who would eat lutefisk would . . .

He paced up and down in his room. Ben would not arrive until the next day, and Jonathan would be damned if he would spend an unnecessary day in this hotel, among these people, an object of curiosity for the early-arrived Eiger Birds.

His telephone rang.

"What!" he snapped into the receiver.

"How did you know it was me?" Jemima asked.

"What do you have planned for tonight?"

"Making love with you," she answered without hesitation.

"Dinner first at your café?"

"Great. Does this mean everything is all right between us?"

"No." He was surprised at her assumption.

"Oh." The line was silent for a moment. "See you in twenty minutes."

"Fifteen?"

Night had fallen quickly around the café terrace, as it does in the mountains, and they sipped in silence the last of their brandy. Jemima had been careful to make no allusions to their time together in Long Island. His mind was far away, and he failed to notice the inset of cool air slipping down from the flanks of Eiger.

"Jonathan?"

"Hm-m?"

"Am I forgiven?"

He shook his head slowly. "That isn't the point. I would never again be able to trust you."

"And you would want to?"

"Sure."

"Then you're really saying we might have made something of it."

"I'm pretty sure we could have."

"And now no chance? Ever?"

He did not answer.

"You're a warped man. And you know something else? You haven't kissed me yet."

He corrected the oversight. As their faces drew slowly apart, Jemima sighed, "Corn in Egypt, man. I didn't know lips had a memory of their own."

They watched the last yellow light desert the ragged crests surrounding them.

"Jonathan? About that business at your home . . ."

"I don't want to talk about it."

"It wasn't really the money that hurt you, was it? I mean—we were so good together. All day long, I mean. Not just in bed. Hey, you want to know something?"

"Tell me."

She laughed at herself. "Even after taking your money, I had to overcome an impulse to go back and make love to you again before I left. That would really have made you angry when you found out, wouldn't it?"

"Yes. Really."

"Say, how's the crazy one? What's his name?"

"Mr. Monk? I don't know. I haven't been back for some time."

"Oh?" She knew that bode poorly for her.

"No." Jonathan stood up. "I assume your room has a bed."

"It's pretty narrow."

"We'll work it out."

She knew better than bring up the past again that night.

Kleine Scheidegg: *July 8*

HE TOOK A late supper in the hotel dining room at a table somewhat apart from the thin scattering of patrons.

He was not pleased with himself. He felt he had handled the Jemima business badly. They had risen early, taken a walk through the tilted meadows, watched the dew make the tips of their shoes glisten, taken coffee on the terrace of her café, chatted nonsense, made jokes at the expense of passersby.

Then they shook hands, and he left for his hotel. The whole thing was unclean. Particles of emotion clung to their relationship. She was a presence down there in the village, waiting, and he was annoyed with himself for not making a clean break. He knew now that he would not punish her for her perfidy, but he also knew that he would never forgive her for it. He could not remember ever having forgiven anyone.

Several of the guests had dressed for dinner—early-arrived Eiger Birds. Jonathan noticed that half of the terrace telescopes had been roped off for the private—and costly—use of people nominated by the hotel management.

He pushed food around his plate without appetite. There were too many unsettled things churning at the back of his mind. There was Jemima, and the sanction assignment, and the knowledge that Mellough might have alerted his target, and the despised Eiger Birds. Twice he had noticed himself being pointed out by men in tuxedos to their young/pretty/dumb companions. One middle-aged ogler had waved him a tentative semaphore of greeting with her napkin.

It was with relief that he heard a familiar voice booming through the dining room from the lobby beyond.

"Goddam my ass if this ain't something! What the hell you mean you ain't got a room for me?"

Jonathan abandoned his coffee and brandy and crossed the dining room to the desk. The hotel manager, a tight little Swiss with the nervous propriety of his class, was attempting to calm Big Ben down.

"My dear Herr Bowman—"

"Dear Herr's ass! Just stick your nose back in that book and come up with my reservations. Hey, ol' buddy! You're looking good!"

Jonathan gripped Ben's paw. "What's the trouble?"

"Oh, this rinky-dink's screwed up my reservations. Says he can't find my telegram. From the looks of him, he couldn't find his tallywhacker with a six-man scouting party."

Jonathan realized what was going on. "The Eiger Birds are starting to fly in," he explained.

"Oh, I see."

"And our friend here is doing everything he can to create vacancies he can sell to them at inflated prices." Jonathan turned to the listening manager. "Isn't that it?"

"I didn't know this person was a friend of yours, Dr. Hemlock."

"He's in charge of the climb."

"Oh?" the manager asked with extravagant innocence. "Is someone going to climb our mountain?"

"Stop it."

"Perhaps Herr Bowman could find a place in the village? There are cafés that—"

"He's going to stay here."

"I am afraid that is impossible, Herr Doctor." The manager's lips pursed tightly.

"All right." Jonathan drew out his wallet. "Make up my bill."

"But, if you leave . . ."

"There will be no climb. That's correct. And your incoming guests will be very angry."

The manager was the essence of agonized indecision.

"Do you know what I think?" Jonathan said. "I think I saw one of your clerks sorting a batch of telegrams in your inner office. It's possible that Mr. Bowman's was among them. Why don't you go back and look them over."

The manager grasped at the offer to save face and left them with a perfunctory bow.

"You met the others yet?" Ben asked, looking around the lobby with the undisguised distaste of a competitor.

"They haven't arrived."

"No shit? Well, they'll be in tomorrow then. Personally, I can use the rest. My hoof's been acting up the last couple of days. Gave it too much workout while you were at the place."

"How's George Hotfort?"

"Quiet."

"Is she grateful that I didn't turn her over to the authorities?"

"I guess. She ain't the kind to burn candles."

The manager returned and performed a masque of surprised delight. He had found Ben's telegram after all, and everything was in order.

"You want to go directly to your room?" Jonathan asked as the uniformed bellhops collected Ben's luggage.

"No. Guide me to the bar and buy me some beer."

They talked late into the night, mostly about the technical problems of the Eigerwand. Twice Ben brought up the Mellough incident, but both times Jonathan turned him back, saying they could talk about it later, maybe after the climb. Since he had arrived in Switzerland, Jonathan had come more and more to believe that he would make the climb. For long periods of time, he forgot what his real mission was. But this fascination was too expensive a luxury, so before turning in for the night he asked to borrow again all the correspondence between Ben and the climbers who would arrive the next morning.

Jonathan sat up in his bed, the letters arranged in three stacks on the blankets, one for each man. His concentration circumscribed by the tight pool of his bedside lamp, sipping at a glass of Laphroaig, he tried to fashion personalities from the scant evidence of the correspondence.

Jean-Paul Bidet. Forty-two years old. A wealthy manufacturer who had by dint of unsparing work expanded his father's modest shop into France's foremost producer of aerosol containers. He had married rather late, and had discovered the sport of mountain climbing while on his honeymoon in the Alps. He had no climbing experience outside Europe, but his list of Alpine conquests was formidable. He had made most of his major climbs in the company of famous and expensive guides, and to a degree it was possible to accuse him of "buying" the peaks.

From the tone of his letters, written in a businessman's English, Bidet seemed congenial, energetic, and earthy. Jonathan was surprised to discover that he intended to bring his wife along to witness his attempt at the meanest mountain of them all.

Karl Freytag. Twenty-six years old. Sole heir to the Freytag industrial complex specializing in commercial chemicals, particularly insecticides and herbicides. He had begun climbing during college holidays, and before he was twenty he had formed an organization of German climbers over which he presided and which published a most respectable quarterly review of mountaineering. He was its editor-in-chief. There was a packet of offset reprints from the review that described his climbs (in the third person) and accented his capacities as a leader and route-finder.

His letters were written in a brittle, perfect English that did not admit of contractions. The underlying timbre suggested that Freytag was willing to cooperate with Herr Bowman and with the international committee that had sponsored the climb, but the reader was often reminded that he, Freytag, had conceived of the climb, and that it was his intention to lead the team on the face.

Anderl Meyer. Twenty-five years old. He had lacked the means to finish his medical studies in Vienna and had returned to earning his living as a carpenter with his father. During the climbing season he guided parties up his native Tyrolean Alps. This made him the only professional in the team. Immediately upon being forced to leave school, Meyer had become obsessed with climbing. By every means from scrimping to begging, he had managed to include himself in most of the major climbs of the last three years. Jonathan had read references to his activities in the Alps, New Zealand, the Himalayas, South America, and most recently in the Atlas Range. Every article had contained unreserved praise for his skill and strength (he was even referred to as a "young Hermann Buhl") but several writers had alluded to his tendency to be a loner and a poor team man, treating the less gifted members of his parties as anchors against his progress. He was what in gambling would be called a plunger. Turning back was, for him, the ultimate disgrace; and he would make moves on the face that would be suicide for men of more limited physical and psychic dispositions. Similar aspersions had been cast on Jonathan, during his years of active climbing.

Jonathan could form only the vaguest image of Meyer's personality from the letters. The veil of translation obscured the man; his English was stilted and imperfect, often comically obtuse because he translated directly from the German syntax, dictionary obviously in hand, and there were occasional medleys of compounded nouns that strung meaninglessly along until a sudden terminal verb tamped them into a kind of order. One quality, however, did emerge through the static of translation: a shy confidence.

Jonathan sat in bed, looking at the piles of letters and sipping his Scotch. Bidet, Freytag, Meyer. And whoever it was might have been alerted by Mellough.

Kleine Scheidegg: *July 9*

HE SLEPT LATE. By the time he had dressed and shaved, the sun was high and the dew was off the meadow that tilts up toward the north face of Eiger. In the lobby he passed a chatting group of young people, their eyes cleansed, their faces tightened by the crisp thin air. They had been out frolicking in the hills, and their heavy sweaters still exuded a chill.

The hotel manager stepped around the desk and spoke confidentially. "They are here, Herr Doctor. They await you."

Jonathan nodded and continued to the dining room entrance. He scanned the room and discovered the group immediately. They sat near the floor-to-ceiling windows that gave onto the mountain; their table was flooded with brilliant sunlight, and their colorful pullovers were the only relief from the dim and sparsely populated room. It looked as though Ben had assumed, as the natural privilege of his experience and age, social command of the gathering.

The men rose as Jonathan approached. Ben made introductions.

"Jonathan Hemlock, this here's Gene-Paul Bidette." He clearly was not going to have anything to do with these phony foreign pronunciations.

Jonathan offered his hand. "Monsieur Bidet."

"I have looked forward to meeting you, Monsieur Hemlock." Bidet's slanted peasant eyes were frankly evaluative.

"And this is Karl Freytag."

Amused, Jonathan matched the unnecessary force of Freytag's grip. "Herr Freytag?"

"Herr Doctor." He nodded curtly and sat down.

"And this here's Anderil Mayor."

Jonathan smiled professional approval into Meyer's wry, clear blue eyes. "I've read about you, Anderl," he said in German.

"I've read about you," Anderl answered in his soft Austrian accent.

"In which case," Jonathan said, "we have read about each other."

Anderl grinned.

"And this lady here is Missus Bidette." Ben sat down immediately his uncomfortable social duty was discharged.

Jonathan pressed the offered fingers and saw his reflection in her dark sunglasses. "Madame Bidet?"

She dipped her head slightly in a gesture that was, at one time, a greeting, a shrug at being Madame Bidet, and a favorable evaluation of Jonathan—a gesture altogether Parisienne.

"We just been small-talking and eyeballing the hill," Ben explained after Jonathan had sent the waiter after a fresh pot of coffee.

"I had no idea this mountain Jean-Paul has been talking about for a year now would be so beautiful," Madame Bidet said, taking off her sunglasses for the first time that morning and letting her calm eyes rest on Jonathan.

He glanced up at the Eiger's cold, shadowed face and the long wisps of captured cloud at the summit.

"I would not say beautiful," Bidet offered. "Sublime, perhaps. But not beautiful."

"It is the possibility of conflict and conquest that is beautiful," Freytag clarified for all time and for all people.

Anderl peered at the mountain and shrugged. Obviously he had never thought of a mountain as beautiful or ugly: only as difficult or easy.

"Is that all you are having for breakfast, Herr Doctor?" Freytag asked as Jonathan's coffee was served.

"Yes."

"Food is an important part of conditioning," Freytag admonished.

"I'll bear that in mind."

"Meyer here shares your peculiar eating habits."

"Oh? I didn't know you were acquainted."

"Oh, yes," the German said. "I contacted him shortly after I organized this climb, and we have made several short climbs together to attune him to my rhythms."

"And you to his, I assume."

Bidet reacted to the cool tone of the exchange by inserting a hasty note of warmth and camaraderie. "We must all use first names. Don't you agree?"

"I'm afraid I don't know your wife's first name," Jonathan said.

"Anna," she offered.

Jonathan said the full name to himself and repressed a smile that only a native English speaker would understand.

"How are the weather reports?" Karl asked Ben officially.

"Not real good. Clear today; maybe tomorrow. But there's a bunch of weak fronts moving in on us that makes it pretty dicey after that."

"Well, that settles it," Karl announced.

"What does that settle?" Jonathan asked between sips of coffee.

"We must go now."

"Have I time to finish my coffee?"

"I mean, we must go as soon as possible."

Ben squinted at Karl incredulously. "With the possibility of a storm in three days?"

"It has been climbed in two." Karl was crisp and on the defensive.

"And if you don't make it in two? If you're pinned down up there in heavy weather?"

"Benjamin has a point there," Jean-Paul interposed. "We must not take childish risks."

The word "childish" rankled Karl. "One cannot climb without some risk. Perhaps the young face these risks more easily."

Jonathan glanced from the mountain to Ben, who turned down the corners of his mouth, closed his eyes, and shook his head heavily.

Anderl had not been a part of this discussion. Indeed, his attention was fixed on a group of attractive young girls out on the terrace. Jonathan asked his opinion on the advisability of climbing with a two-day weather limit. Anderl thrust out his lower lip and shrugged. He did not care whether they climbed in good weather or bad. Either would be interesting. But if they were not going to climb today or tomorrow, he had other things he might give his attention to.

Jonathan liked him.

"So we reach an impasse," Karl said. "Two in favor of climbing right now, and two opposed. The dilemma of the democratic process. What compromise do you suggest? That we climb halfway up?" His voice was heavy with Teutonic wit.

"It's *three* opposed," Jonathan corrected. "Ben has a vote."

"But he will not be climbing with us."

"He's our ground man. Until we touch rock, he has more than a vote; he has complete control."

"Oh? Has that been decided upon?"

Anderl spoke without taking his eyes from the girls on the terrace. "It is always like that," he said with authority. "The ground man has the last word now, and the leader once we are on the face."

"Very well," Karl said to cut off discussion on a point he was losing. "That brings us to another issue. Who is to be leader?" Karl glanced around the table, ready to defend himself against any opposition.

Jonathan poured himself another cup and gestured with the pot; his offer of coffee was declined by Karl with a brusque shake of the head, by Jean-Paul who put his hand over his cup, by Anna with a movement of her fingertips, by Anderl who was paying no attention, and by Ben with a grimace, his beer mug still a quarter full. "I thought it was pretty much set that you would lead, Karl," Jonathan said quietly.

"And so it was. But that decision was reached before the American member of the team had his unfortunate accident and was replaced by a man of such international repute—up until a few years ago, at least."

Jonathan could not repress a smile.

"So that we start off with a firm understanding," Karl continued, "I want to make sure everyone is in agreement about who shall lead."

"You make a good point," Jean-Paul said. "It is true that Jonathan has climbed the mountain twice before."

Gallic reasonableness was countered with Teutonic exactitude. "A correction, if I may. The good doctor has *failed* to climb the mountain twice. I don't mean to offend you, Herr Doctor, but I am forced to say that I do not consider a record of failure automatically grants you the right to lead."

"I'm not offended. Is it all that important to you that you lead?"

"It is important to our group. I have spent months designing a new route that departs in significant ways from the classic ascent. I am sure that once I have gone over it with you, you will all agree it is well thought out and quite feasible. And taking the face by a new route will put us in the record books."

"And *that's* important to you?"

Karl glanced at him with surprise. "Of course."

Anderl had pushed his chair away from the table and was watching the power struggle with amusement in the folds of his thin, heavily tanned face.

Anna relieved her boredom by shifting her glance from Jonathan to Karl, the two natural leaders of the group. Jonathan sensed she was making a choice.

"Why don't we leave it at this," Jean-Paul said, moderating. "This afternoon we shall all go over the route you have planned, Karl. If it looks good to us, then you will be leader on the mountain. But until we are on the face, Benjamin will be in command."

Karl agreed, certain the appeal of his new route would convince them. Ben concurred with a glum glance at Karl. Jonathan agreed. And Anderl didn't care one way or the other.

"So!" Jean-Paul clapped his hands together to punctuate the end of what had been, for him, an unpleasant encounter. "Now we will take our coffee and become better acquainted with one another. Right?"

"Oh?" said Jonathan. "I had assumed that you and Karl were already acquainted."

"How so?" Jean-Paul asked, smiling.

"In a business way, I had imagined. Your company makes aerosol containers, his produces pesticides. It would seem natural that . . ." Jonathan shrugged.

Karl frowned at the mention of pesticides.

"Ah! I see," Jean-Paul said. "Yes, I can see that it would be a natural error. As a matter of fact, our meeting here is the first. It is sheerest coincidence that we are in related industries."

Anna glanced out the window and spoke to no one in particular. "In fact, I had assumed that every manufacturer of liquids in Europe had been to our house at one time or another."

Jean-Paul laughed and winked at Jonathan. "She finds some of my colleagues a little dull."

"Oh?" Jonathan asked, wide-eyed.

The conversation turned to social trivialities, and after fifteen minutes of this Ben rose and excused himself, saying he wanted to check over the equipment. Anderl decided to help him, and the two of them went off.

Jonathan watched Ben depart with his characteristic hyperenergetic hopping gait with which he compensated for his limp. A thought crossed his mind.

"I hear you were injured last month," he said conversationally to Karl.

"Yes. A fall. Nothing really."

"It was your leg, I believe."

"Yes. I cut it against a rock. I assure you it will not hamper my climbing in the least."

"Good."

Karl and Jean-Paul fell to chatting about mountains they had both climbed, comparing routes and events. Jonathan had an opportunity to sit back with his cup and examine the three of them at his leisure. There had been nothing in the behavior of any member of the team to suggest he knew what Jonathan was and why he was there.

Anna Bidet's thoughts had turned inward, hidden behind the long lashes which veiled her quick, intelligent eyes. For some time she had been withdrawn, quite content with the company of her own mind. From time to time she would focus out on the men around her and listen for a moment before deciding there was nothing to interest her in the conversation, then she would dissolve back into herself. Jonathan let his eyes rest on her. Her clothes, her rare comments, her glances occasionally flashing in question or amusement, then eclipsing with a sudden drop of the lashes—everything was studied and effective. She was at one time dignified and provocative, a combination that is the exclusive property of Parisian women of a certain class and age.

She emerged from her reverie with the feel of Jonathan's gaze upon her. She returned it frankly and with amusement.

"An interesting combination," she said quietly.

"What is?"

"Art critic, scholar and mountain climber. And I'm sure there's more to you than that."

"What do you make of it?"

"Nothing."

Jonathan nodded and turned his attention to Jean-Paul, who obviously did not come from her world. His recent wealth fit him like his clothes, a little imperfectly because he lacked the panache to dominate them. He was over age for a major climb, but there was no fat on his sturdy agricultural body. One eye dropped down like a tragic clown's, but his expression was alive with intelligence and conviviality. His nose made a long, thin line starting rather too far up above the eyes and taking a capricious jog to one side about halfway down. The mouth was crooked and mobile enough to grant him that facial plasticity so intrinsic to a French peasant's communication. All in all, the face looked as though Nature had designed a perfectly nondescript mold, then had laid its palm against the muzzle while the clay was fresh and had given a slight twist to the left.

Jonathan appreciated his qualities. His dislike of conflict and his logical moderation made him the ideal lubricant among the dynamic and aggressive personalities common to climbing. It was a pity that he was a cuckold—at least an emotional cuckold. Jonathan pictured him with a nightcap, a candlestick in one hand, and a *pispot* in the other.

It was an unkind image, so he shifted his attention to Karl Freytag who at that moment was carefully and significantly advancing an argument proving that the route Jean-Paul had taken up the Dru the season before had been poorly chosen. When Jean-Paul laughed and said, "All I know is that it got me to the summit and back!" Karl shrugged, unwilling to continue reasoning with a man who took the matter so lightly.

Karl's face was broad and regular, but too immobile to be interesting; he was handsome without being attractive. His blond—really colorless—hair was fine and lank, and he combed it back in a flat pompadour from his wide, aggressively intelligent forehead. He was the tallest man in the party by two inches, and his excellent body tone enabled him to maintain his rigid sitting posture without appearing foolish.

"Well!" Jean-Paul said, breaking off his chat with Karl and turning to Jonathan and Anna. "You two don't seem to have been chatting."

"We were comparing silences," Jonathan said, "and hers turned out more interesting than mine."

"She's a remarkable woman." Jean-Paul looked at his wife with undisguised pride.

"I believe that."

"She was in ballet before her unfortunate marriage, you know." Jean-Paul was in the habit of protecting himself by beating others to the assumption that the union had been socially and emotionally morganatic. It was not only that he was a manufacturer; his company made a comically common household article.

Anna laughed softly. "Jean-Paul likes to think he snatched me from the stage at the height of my career. Actually, age and declining popularity were working toward the same goal."

"Nonsense!" Jean-Paul asserted. "No one could ever guess your age. How old do you think she is, Jonathan?"

Jonathan was embarrassed for both of them.

"My husband admires frankness, Doctor Hemlock. He considers tact to be a kind of deviousness."

"No but. Come on, Jonathan. How old would you say Anna is?"

Jonathan lifted his hands palms up in a gesture of helplessness. "I—ah—imagine a man would only consider her age if he were trying to decide whether the praise should go to Nature or to the lady herself."

It had not been very good, but Anna applauded mockingly, soundlessly tapping the tips of three fingers into her palm.

Sensing that nothing of consequence was going to be talked about here, Karl rose and excused himself. Jean-Paul moved down one chair to tighten the party.

"It is certainly magnificent," he said, looking dreamily out to the Eiger. "It's a perfect choice for my last mountain."

"Your last?"

"I am no longer young, Jonathan. Think of it! At forty-two, I shall be the oldest man to climb it. These two young men are fantastic climbers. We shall have our work cut out, you and I. You are—forgive me but—you are . . . ?"

"Thirty-seven."

"Ah! Just my wife's age!"

She closed her eyes and opened them tiredly.

To change the subject, Jonathan asked, "Are you interested in climbing, Anna?"

"Not especially."

"But she will be proud of me when I return, won't you, dearest?"

"Very proud."

"I don't know when I've felt so good," Jean-Paul said, stretching his arms athletically and allowing one to drop across Anna's shoulders. "I feel I have achieved the best conditioning possible at my age. Each night for the past six months I have performed a complicated set of calisthenics. And I have been religious about them. I work so late that my poor wife is usually asleep when I join her." He laughed and patted her.

"By now she must be very eager," Jonathan said, "to see you make the climb."

Anna glanced at him, then looked away to the windows which were beginning to dapple with a light rain.

From habit Jean-Paul cursed the break in the weather, but his experience in these Bernese Alps told him that the preceding sunshine, not this rain, was the exception.

"This will bring fresh snow to the upper reaches," he said matter-of-factly.

"Yes, some," Jonathan agreed. He refilled his cup and excused himself to step out onto the terrace where he stood under an overhanging eave and enjoyed the smell of the rain.

The sky was zinc, and the color of the few gnarled evergreens that clung to the rocky soil of Kleine Scheidegg had been subtracted to olive drab by the loss of sunlight. There was no wind, and he sipped his coffee and listened to the rustle of rain in the meadow grass.

They were a cool lot. One of them, at least, was cool. He had met the possible sanction targets, but no gesture, no nervousness, no glance had given him a hint. Jonathan would be on dicey ground until Search contacted him with the target's identity.

Gray and listless mists concealed the upper third of the North Face. He recalled the ghoulish pun German sports writers resurrected each time a team attempted the Eiger. Instead of Nordwand, North Wall, they called it the Mordwand, Murder Wall. The days were past when German and Austrian youths threw their lives against the Eigerwand with reckless Wagnerian *Todeslieb;* great names had mastered the face: Hermann Buhl, Lionel Terray, Gaston Rébuffat; and dozens of lesser men had climbed it, each eroding, with his success, a fragment of the glory accruing to the task; but nonetheless, as he stood in the half-shelter sipping his coffee and looking across the meadow, Jonathan experienced an expanding desire to try again the face that had twice driven him back.

On his way up to Ben's room, he passed Anderl in the corridor, and they exchanged nods of greeting. He had taken an instant liking to this short, sinewy lad with his mop of dark hair so obviously unused to the comb, and his long strong fingers designed by nature for finding and clinging to the smallest indentations in the rock. It would be too bad if Anderl turned out to be the sanction target.

His knock at Ben's door was answered by booming, "Fuck off!"

Jonathan opened the door and peeked in.

"Oh, it's you, ol' buddy. Come on in. And lock the door behind you."

Jonathan moved a coil of nylon line off the spare bed and stretched out. "Why the fierce greeting?"

Ben had been packing the haversacks, evenly distributing the weight, but making sure each pair of kits contained every necessity for a good bivouac, should the team break into two climbing ropes. "Oh, I thought you were one of those reporters." He grumbled something to himself as he snatched tight a strap. Then, "Goddam my eyes if they ain't been pecking at my door every five minutes. There's even a newsreel team here. Did you know that?"

"No. But I'm not surprised. The Eiger Birds are here in force now. The hotel's filled up and they're spilling over into Alpiglen and Grindelwald."

"Fucking ghouls."

"But the fattest cats of all are right here in the hotel."

Ben tied off one of the haversacks with a grunt. "Like who?"

Jonathan mentioned the names of a Greek merchant and his recently-acquired American society wife. The management of the hotel had erected a large rectangular oriental tent that gave onto one of the telescopes on the terrace. The tent was hung in silk and equipped with heaters and a small refrigerator, and the telescope had been reserved for their personal use, after being scrubbed down carefully with disinfectant. Every social precaution had been taken to insulate them from the company of the lesser Eiger Birds, but the Greek's penchant for lavish waste and gross practical jokes had instantly attracted the attention of the press.

Jonathan noticed a powerful brass telescope in the corner of the room. "You bring that with you?"

"Sure. You figure I'm going to line up with a pocketful of coins to watch you on the face?"

"I'm afraid you're going to have to make your peace with the newsmen."

"Why?"

"It would be best if you kept them informed, once we're on the hill. Just basic statistics: how high we are, the weather, our route—things like that."

"Tell 'em nothing, that's my motto. Fuck 'em."

"No. I think you should cooperate a little. If you don't, they'll make copy out of their imaginations."

Ben tied off the last of the kits and opened a bottle of beer from his supply on the dresser. "Whew! I've been busier than a one-legged man in an ass-kicking contest. But I got you people ready to move out at a minute's notice. There's a report of a cone of high pressure moving in, and you *know* that bitch-kitty of a hill ain't going to give you more than two or three days of weather." He tossed a ring of ice pitons off his bed and stretched out.

Jonathan asked for his evaluation of the climbers, and Ben screwed up his face. "I don't know. Too much of a mixed bag for my taste. That German kid's too cocky-assed."

"I have a feeling he's a good climber, though."

"Could be. But he ain't many grins in a bivouac. He's got all the makings of a first-class snot. Doesn't seem to realize that we were making major climbs when he was still shitting yellow. Now that Austrian boy—"

"Anderl."

"Yeah, Anderl. Now, he's a climber. He's got the right look. Kinda looks like you did." Ben leaned up on one elbow and added pointedly. "Thirteen years ago."

"All right. All right."

"Hey, ol' buddy? Toss your poor crippled friend another can of beer?"

Jonathan grunted up and did so, noticing for the first time that Ben was drinking American beer, an extravagance in Switzerland. But like most big American beer drinkers, Ben had no taste for the relatively thick German product. Jonathan leaned against the window and watched the rain. He saw

Anderl out on the meadow, his arm around a girl who had his jacket over her head. They were returning to the hotel. "What do you think about Jean-Paul, Ben?"

"Not so good. The way I peg it, you are just a gnat's ass inside the age limit for this kind of go. And he's on the other side of the line."

Jonathan did not agree. "He looks to me like he has a lot of staying power. There's generations of peasant endurance in the man."

"If you say so, ol' buddy." Ben swung his legs down and sat up, his tone changing suddenly, like a man who is finally getting to the point. "Back at my place you said that maybe you wouldn't be making this climb after all. Is that still the way it is?"

Jonathan sat on the windowsill. "I don't know. There's a job I have to do here. The climbing's really only side action."

"Pretty big league, for side action."

"True."

"What kind of job?"

Jonathan looked into Ben's laugh-lined face. There was no way to tell him. Out beyond the window there were islets of snow on the meadow being grayed and decayed by the rain. "The skiers must be cursing this rain," he said for something to say.

"What kind of job?" Ben persisted. "Does it have something to do with that Mellough guy?"

"Only obliquely. Forget it, Ben."

"Kinda hard to forget. After you left, all hell broke loose at the lodge. There were government men all over the place, talking tough and generally making asses of themselves. They were scouting out in the desert and getting themselves lost and organizing patrols and cutting around with helicopters. They had the whole county in an uproar before they were through."

Jonathan smiled to himself at the image of a CII operation of this type: all the coordination of a joint Arab/Italian invasion. "They call it undercover work, Ben."

"Is that what they call it? What happened out there anyway? When you brought back the shotgun, it had been fired. And no one ever saw Mellough and his boyfriend again."

"I don't want to talk about it. I have to do what I do, Ben. Without it, I would lose my house and things I have spent years collecting."

"So? You lose your house. You could still teach. You like teaching, don't you?"

Jonathan looked at Ben. He had never really thought about whether or not he liked teaching. "No, I don't think so. I like being around good heads that appreciate my mind and taste, but as for simple teaching—no. It's just a job."

Ben was silent for a time. He finished the beer and crushed the can in his hand. "Let's call off the climb," he said firmly. "We'll tell 'em you're sick or something. Trouble with hemorrhoids, maybe."

"My Achilles anus? No way, Ben. Forget it." Jonathan wiped the haze from the window with the back of his hand and peered out at the misted mountain. "You know what's weird, Ben?"

"You."

"No. What's really weird is that I want another shot at the hill. Even forgetting the thing I have to do here, it's something I really want to do. You understand the feeling?"

Ben fiddled for a moment with a coil of nylon line. "Of course I understand it. But I'll tell you something, ol' buddy. The sweet smell of decay is heavy in the air."

Jonathan nodded.

Conversation among the team at luncheon centered on the weather, which had settled to a steady, plump rain which occasional gusts of wind rattled against the windows. They knew it would bring fresh snow to the Third Ice Field and, higher, to the White Spider. Much depended on the temperature on the face. If it was cold, and the snow dry and powdery, it would slip off in regular hissing slides, leaving the glaciated perennial ice and névé clean enough for a climb. If, on the other hand, the temperature should rise and make the snow moist and cohesive, it would build up, poising on the 60° inclines of the ice fields, ready to avalanche at the slightest disturbance.

Ben knew Jonathan had studied the surface of the North Face during his conditioning climb up the west flank two days before.

"Could you see much?"

"Yes. The weather was clear."

"Well?" asked Karl.

"It looked fine, for Eiger. The snow was old and crusted. And the whole face was dryer than I've ever seen it." Jonathan was referring to the inexplicable "drying up" of the North Wall that had been in progress over the past thirty years. Pitches that had been expansive snowfields in the late thirties were wet and icy rock by the end of the fifties. "One good thing. The Hinterstoisser Traverse was almost clear of ice."

"That does not affect us," Karl announced. "My route does not include the Hinterstoisser Traverse."

Even the phlegmatic Anderl shared the general silence this statement generated. Jonathan's cup of chocolate hovered for an instant in its rise to his lips, but he recovered quickly and sipped without comment, denying Karl the pleasure of shocking him. That Traverse, to which a young German had given his name in death, had been the key to all successful ascents of the mountain. No team had ever bypassed that critical bridge and made the summit, and only one team that had dared returned alive.

"I shall detail my route after luncheon," Karl said, shunting away the negative silence.

With a gentle smile concealing his thoughts, Jonathan watched Karl over his cup for a moment, then he shifted his attention to the meadow and the mountain beyond.

The climbing team had reserved a table overlooking the meadow, and they generally sat with their backs to the restaurant, trying to ignore the presence of the Eiger Birds who, by now, had arrived en masse.

Several times during each meal, waiters had arrived with notes from the more affluent or aggressive Eiger Birds inviting the climbers to supper or to some evening entertainment which, if accepted, would have elevated the host in the eyes of his peers. These notes were always passed to Ben who took pleasure in slowly tearing them up unread in full view of the smiling, waving sender.

The discerning ornithologist would have distinguished three species of Eiger Bird among the flittering gathering that babbled in half a dozen languages.

The *gratin* of the Eiger Bird society were internationally famous idlers who had flown in from midsummer *étapes* on their annual pleasure migrations to have their sensation-drained nerves tickled by the sexual stimulant of death. They had gathered from all parts of the world, but not one had come from those once-popular refuges that have been contaminated by middle-class imitators: the Riviera, Acapulco, the Bahamas, the Azores, and, most recently lost to upward social mobility, the Morocco coast. Their pecking order was rigid, and each new arrival stepped obediently into his place, more defined by who belonged beneath him than by who belonged above. The Greek merchant and his wife assumed as their fiscal right the apex of the social pyramid; fragile-blooded and thin-faced Italian nobility with limited means were at the bottom.

A lower subspecies of leisure necrophiles were much more numerous. They were easily distinguishable by the garishness of their plumage and the tense and temporary nature of their mating habits. There were paunchy men with purplish tans, cigars, thinning hair, and loud, awkward gestures designed to communicate youthful energy. They were to be seen during feeding time fumbling after their teatty, sponsored companions who giggled and went vacant in the face when touched.

The female of this subspecies were women of uncertain age, crisp of feature, monotonically dyed hair, skin tight at the temples from cosmetic surgery. Their alert and mistrusting eyes darted to follow the dark Greek and Sicilian boys they carried with them and used.

And on the fringes, virile lesbians protected and dominated their fluttering lace-and-mauve possessions. And male homosexuals bickered and made up.

The lowest order of Eiger Bird was the newspaper and television men who fed on the orts and droppings of the others. They were conspicuous by their clannishness and their inexpensive clothes, often rumpled as a badge of their romantic migratory lives. For the most part they were a glib and overdrinking lot who took cynical advantage of the reduced rates offered them by the hotel in return for the advertisement value of the Kleine Scheidegg dateline.

Film actors formed an interconnecting subculture of their own. Lacking the fiscal credentials to associate with the elite, they carried with them a communicable visibility that made them valuable to all who would be seen and read about. Actors were not treated as people, but as social possessions. In this way, they resembled Grand Prix drivers.

One exception to this general status of film personalities was a husband and wife team who, because of their accumulated wealth and personal brass, were a kind of *gratin* in their own right. Since their arrival at the hotel that morning, an arrival attended by great flutter and flap, loud greetings of casual acquaintances, and histrionic overtipping, they had made two overtures to the climbers, both of which had been parried. The actor had responded to the rejection with heroic resignation; the actress had been loudly miffed, but had recovered her aplomb when she heard that the Greek merchant's wife had done no better.

Different from the Eiger Birds, and alien to them, were a small group of young men who had been attracted to Kleine Scheidegg by the rumor of the ascent. These were the only people with whom the team had intercourse or sympathy. In shy twos and threes, young climbers had arrived by train and motorcycle from Austria, Germany, and Chamonix to set up their red or yellow tents on the meadow, or to rent rooms in the cheaper cafés of Alpiglen and Grindelwald. Feeling out of place among the rich hotel guests, they quietly sought out Ben to mumble good wishes and shake hands. Many of them slipped bits of paper into Ben's palm containing their addresses or the locations of their tents, then they departed quickly, always refusing offered refreshment. The scribbled notes were for Ben's use if it became necessary to form a rescue party. All these climbers knew the reputation of the Bernese guides, and they knew that a man on the face could freeze to death before necessary financial arrangements could be worked out. The more forward of these young men ventured to shake hands with Jonathan or Anderl, the two members of the party of whom they had read in mountain journals. This did not please Karl.

Throughout the meal, Anderl amused himself by eye-fencing with two little twits who had arrived with a merchant type with a loud voice and a penchant for prehensile attention. The merchant made clear his annoyance at the flirtation, and this amused Anderl the more.

Ben's eyes twinkled with paternal teasing as he said to Anderl, "Now you watch it, boy. You're going to need all your energy on the hill."

Anderl answered without looking away from the girls. "I climb only with my hands and feet."

Jonathan finished his coffee and rose, promising to meet the others in Ben's room in half an hour to go over Karl's proposed route. Anna got up too; she had no intention of boring herself with the forthcoming planning session. Together they walked to the lobby where Jonathan picked up his mail. One envelope had neither stamp nor postmark, so he tore it open first and glanced at the note. It was an invitation to an intimate supper with the Greek merchant and his American wife. Mentioned also (in the wife's round, plump hand) was the fact that they had recently purchased a lot of paintings through Sotheby's. She would be delighted to have Jonathan glance them over and make an evaluation. She reminded him that he had once performed a similar service for her first husband.

Jonathan stepped to the desk and hastily wrote a note. He mentioned that evaluation was a professional, not social, activity for him. He added that he had to decline the offer of supper as he would be involved in preparations for the climb and, anyway, he was suffering from a debilitating hangnail.

Anna looked at him quizzically from the other side of the elevator car, her habitual expression of defensive amusement crinkling her eyes.

"That must have given you pleasure."

"You read over my shoulder?"

"Of course. You're very like my husband, you know."

"Would he have declined an invitation from those people?"

"Never! His self-image would have driven him to accept."

"Then how am I similar?"

"You also acted without choice. Your self-image forced you to decline." She paused at the door to her suite. "Would you care to come in for a moment?"

"I think not, thank you."

She shrugged. "As you wish. Opportunities to decline seem to abound for you today."

"If I read the signs correctly, I am not the one you've selected anyway."

She arched her eyebrows, but did not respond.

"I assume it's Karl," he continued.

"And you also assume it is any concern of yours?"

"I have to climb with both of them. Be discreet."

"I thought you were usually paid for your evaluations." She entered her room and closed the door behind her.

Jonathan sat in a deep chair beside the window. He had just finished a smoke and was in full relax. On his lap was a small bundle of mail that had, from the evidence of superimposed postal hieroglyphics, been chasing him for some time. The rain, mixed now with dancing pebbles of hail, drilled against the window in treble timpani, and the light filling the room was greenish-gray and chill.

He went through his mail listlessly.

From the chairman of his department: ". . . and I'm pleased to be able to announce a considerable salary increase for the next academic year. Of course, it is impossible to reflect in dollars the value . . ."

Yeah, Yeah. Flip. Into the wastepaper basket.

A bill on the house. Flip.

"The administration has granted a mandate to form a special committee on student unrest, with particular emphasis on the task of channeling this social energy into productive and. . . ."

Flip. He missed the basket. It was his practice never to serve on committees. A bill on the house. Flip.

The journal was in dire need of his article on Lautrec. Flip.

The last was a postage-free official envelope from the American Embassy in Bern. It contained a photocopy of a cryptogram from Dragon.

"Message starts . . . Hemlock . . . break . . . Search has had no success in designating your objective . . . break . . . Alternate plan now in operation . . . break . . . Have placed details in the hands of Clement Pope . . . break . . . Plan will crystalize for you tomorrow . . . break . . . Can anything be done to decrease the attention the news media have given to your proposed climb . . . question mark . . . break . . . Miss Brown remains outside our cognizance . . . break . . . best regards . . . break, break . . . Message ends."

Flip.

Jonathan relaxed into the depths of his chair and watched the hail pebbles ricochet up from the windowsill. Two basso rolls of thunder caused his attention to strain through the clatter of rain and hail. He wanted very much to hear the heavy rumble of an avalanche on the face, because if avalanches did not scrub the face clean of amassed snow and poised rubble . . .

He would have to do something definite about Jemima.

It was all piling up on him.

He rolled another smoke.

What was Dragon's purpose in putting Pope in charge of designating the target? Despite his mannerisms of the B-movie detective, Pope had had no very distinguished record with Search before Dragon had elevated him to number two position in SS Division.

This sudden infliction of Pope upon the scene was disturbing, but there was no unraveling the serpentine patterns of check and double check, of distrust and redundancy that substituted for security in CII, so Jonathan put it out of his mind for the moment.

He slumped down in his chair and closed his eyes while the smoke loosened him up. It was the first time he had had to himself since meeting the other climbers, and he took the opportunity to recall how each had reacted. Nothing had indicated the least suspicion or fear. Good. He was fairly sure that Miles Mellough had not had a chance to contact the target before the affair in the desert, but he was relieved to have the added evidence of their behavior.

The jangle of his telephone intersected his thoughts.

"Guess where I'm calling from?"

"I don't know, Gem." He was surprised at the fatigued sound of his own voice.

"From Bern. How about that?"

"What are you doing in Bern?" He was both relieved and oddly distressed.

"I'm not in Bern. That's just it. I'm in my café, just a pleasant fifteen-minute walk from your hotel. Which you may take as an invitation, if you have a mind to."

Jonathan waited, assuming she would explain.

"They routed my call through Bern. Isn't that weird?"

"Not really." Jonathan had experience with Swiss telephone systems, which rival only the French for efficiency. "The whole thing is based on the assumption that the shortest distance between two points is a cube."

"Well, *I* thought it was weird."

He suspected she had no real reason for calling him, and he could sense a tone of helpless embarrassment in her voice.

"I'll try to see you tomorrow, Gem."

"OK. But if you feel an irresistible urge to drop in on me tonight, I'll try to arrange my schedule to make . . ." She gave up on it. Then, after a pause, "I love you, Jonathan." The ensuing silence begged for a response. When none came, she laughed without foundation. "I don't mean to drip all over you."

"I know you don't."

Her pickup was artificially gay. "Right then! Until tomorrow?"

"Until then." He held the line for a moment, hoping she would hang up first. When she did not, he placed the receiver gently onto its cradle, as though to soften the end of the conversation.

The sun glinted through a rift in the clouds, and hail and rain fell in silver diagonals through shafts of sunlight.

Two hours later the five men sat around a table in the middle of Ben's room. They leaned over a large photographic blowup of the Eigerwand, the corners of which were held down by rings of pitons. Karl traced with his finger a white line he had inked on the glossy surface.

Jonathan saw at a glance that the proposed route was a blend of the Sedl-mayer/Mehringer approach and the classic path. It constituted a direct climb of the face, a linear attack that met the obstacles as they came with a minimum of traversing. It was almost the line a rock would take if it fell from the summit.

"We take the face here," Karl said, pointing to a spot three hundred meters left of the First Pillar, "and we go straight up to the Eigerwand Station. The climb is difficult—grade five, occasionally grade six—but it is possible."

"That first eight hundred feet will be wide open," Ben said in objection. And it was true that the first pitch offered no protection from the rock and ice that rattle down the face each morning when the touch of the sun melts the frost that has glued the loose rubble to the mountain through the night.

"I am aware of that," Karl responded. "I have weighed all the dangers. It will be vital that we cover that pitch in the early morning."

"Continue," Jean-Paul urged, already seduced by the prospect of being one of the first to take the face on a direct line.

"If all goes well, our first bivouac should be here." Karl's finger brushed a dark spot on the snow-crusted face just above the Eigerwand Station. There was a long gallery cut through the mountain during the building of the Jungfrau railroad tunnel. The gallery had been drilled through for ventilation and for jettisoning rubble from the main tunnel, and it was a favorite stopping-off place for tourists who walked to its well-protected edge and gaped down over the breath-catching void.

"In fact, we might get as high as Death Bivouac on the first day." Karl's finger traced a rippled shadow of mixed ice and rock. "And from then on, it's a matter of following the classic route." Freytag was aware that he had elided past the hitherto unclimbed part of the face, so he looked around the circle of men, ready to face objections.

Anderl leaned over the enlarged photograph and squinted for several minutes at a narrow diagonal band below the Eigerwand Station window. He nodded very slowly. "That might go. But we would have to stay out of the ice—hold to the rock as much as possible. It's a chute, Karl. I'll bet water rushes through it all day long. And it's a natural alley for avalanche. I would not care to be standing in it directing traffic like a policeman when the avalanche comes roaring through."

The laughter that greeted the image petered out hollowly. Jonathan turned from the table and looked down at the hazy meadow beyond the window.

Ben spoke slowly. "No one's ever been on that part of the face. We have no idea what it's like. What if the rock doesn't go? What if you're forced down into the gut of the chute?"

"I have no interest in suicide, Herr Bowman. If the edges are not a go, we shall retreat and follow the Sedlmayer/Mehringer route."

"The route that brought them to the Death Bivouac," Ben clarified.

"The weather killed them, Herr Bowman! Not the route!"

"You got some deal with God on weather?"

"Please, please," Jean-Paul interposed. "When Benjamin questions your route, Karl, he is not attacking you personally. For myself, I find the route intriguing." He turned to Jonathan at the window. "You have said nothing, Jonathan. What do you think?"

The mist had lifted from the face, and Jonathan was able to address his statements to the mountain. "Let me make sure of a couple of things, Karl. Assuming we make the Third Ice Field as you plan, the rest of the ascent will be classic, am I right? Up the Ramp, across the Traverse of the Gods, into the Spider, and up the Exit Cracks to the Summit Ice Field?"

"Exactly."

Jonathan nodded and ticked off each of the salient features on the face with his eyes. Then his glance returned to Karl's diagonal chute. "Certainly you realize that your route would not do for a retreat, if we were blocked higher up."

"I consider it self-defeating to plan in terms of retreat."

"I consider it stupid not to."

"Stupid!" Karl struggled with his control. Then he shrugged in peevish accord. "Very well. I shall leave the planning of a retreat route to Doctor Hemlock. After all, he has had more experience in retreating than I."

Ben glanced at Jonathan, surprised that he allowed this to pass with only a smile.

"I may take it then that my plan is accepted?" Karl asked.

Jonathan nodded. "Under the condition that the weather clears and freezes the new snow on. Without that, no route would go for a few days."

Jean Paul was pleased with the agreement and went back over the route step by step with Karl, while Jonathan drew Anderl aside and asked him how he felt about the climb.

"It will be fun to try that diagonal pitch," was Anderl's only comment.

Ben was clearly unhappy with the route, with the team, with the whole idea of the climb. Jonathan crossed to him.

"Buy you a beer?"

"No thanks."

"What?"

"I don't feel like a beer. I feel like getting out of this whole business."

"We need you."

"I don't like it."

"What's the weather report like?"

Ben admitted reluctantly that the three-day prediction looked very good indeed: a strong high and a drop in temperature. Jonathan shared this good news with the party, and in a general mood of confidence they broke up, promising to take supper together.

By supper the weather in the valley had healed up with a palpable drop in temperature and a sudden clearing of the air. There was moonlight on the snow, and the stars could be counted. This fortuitous change and certain orthographic errors in the menu constituted the common small talk at the beginning of dinner, but before long the six of them had divided into four islands of concentration.

Jean-Paul and Karl chatted in French, limiting themselves to the climb and its problems. Karl enjoyed displaying the thoroughness with which he had considered every facet of the problem, and Jean-Paul enjoyed understanding.

Anna focused her attention on Anderl, converting his native wry humor into wit, as women of experience can, by minute gestures of appreciation and attention, until he was performing at his social maximum. Jonathan recognized that she was using Anderl as an extramarital red herring, but he was pleased that the normally reticent Austrian was enjoying himself, whatever the reason.

Ben was in an undisguised funk. He pushed food around on his plate with neither hunger nor interest. Emotionally, he was through with the climb; he was no longer a part of the team, although he would perform his duties responsibly.

For a time, Jonathan was tangent to the rims of the two conversations, making comments only when a pause or a glance seemed to call for it. But soon he was able to withdraw into himself, unheeded and unlamented. He had been troubled by the tone of Dragon's communication. Search had not yet settled on the name of his target. What if they failed to nominate him until immediately before the climb? Could he do it on the face?

And which one? It would be hardest to kill Anderl, easiest to kill Karl. But not really easy. Always before, the sanction had been a name, a catalogue of habits and routines described in the arid Search tout. He had never seen the man's face until minutes before the sanction.

". . . disinterest you so much?" Anna was speaking to him, amusement in her eyes.

"I beg your pardon," Jonathan focused out of his reverie.

"You have not said twenty words all night. Do we disinterest you so much?"

"Not at all. I simply haven't had anything pertinent or amusing to say.'

"And that prevented you from speaking?" Karl laughed heartily. "How un-American!"

Jonathan smiled at him, thinking how terribly in need of a spanking he was. A trait of the Germans—a nation in need of a spanking.

Ben rose and mumbled his excuses. If the weather held—and they wouldn't know for sure until tomorrow—the climb would begin in twenty-nine hours, so he suggested that everyone get as much sleep as possible and run a final check of personal equipment. He left the table brusquely, and in his handling of the newsmen who spoke to him in the lobby he was especially curt and scatological.

Karl rose. "What Herr Bowman says is true. If the weather holds, we shall have to be away from here by three in the morning, day after tomorrow."

"So tonight is our last night?" Anna looked calmly at him, then bestowed her eyes on each of the company in turn for exactly equal time.

"Not necessarily our last night," Jonathan said. "We may get down again, you know."

"Bad joke," Karl pronounced.

Jonathan bade the departing party good-night, then sat down again to his coffee and brandy alone. He slipped again into umber thoughts. Dragon had only twenty-four hours in which to designate the target.

The mountain, and the target, and Jemima. And behind it all, his house and paintings—they were what mattered.

He found himself tightening up, so he sent little calming messages along his nerve system to sap and control the tension. But still his shoulders were stiff and it required muscular contraction to flatten the frown from his forehead.

"May I join you?" The phrasing was interrogative, but not the tone. Karl sat before Jonathan responded.

There was a short silence during which Jonathan sipped off the last of his brandy. Freytag was ill at ease, his normally rigid posture tightened to brittle. "I came to have a word with you."

"I assumed that, yes."

"I want to thank you for this afternoon."

"Thank me?"

"I had expected that you would oppose my route—my leadership. If you had, the others would have joined you. Herr Bowman is really your man, after all. And Bidet blows with the wind." Karl glanced down without altering his angular posture. "It is important to me, you know. Leading this party is important to me."

"So it would seem."

Freytag picked up a spoon and carefully replaced it where it belonged. "Herr Doctor?" he said without looking up. "You don't like me very much, do you?"

"No. Not much."

Karl nodded. "I thought not. You find me—unpleasant?" He looked at Jonathan, a faint smile bravely in place.

"Unpleasant, yes. Also socially inept and terribly unsure of yourself."

Karl laughed hoarsely. "Me? Unsure of myself?"

"Uh-huh. With the usual overcompensation for altogether justified feelings of inferiority that marks the typical German."

"Do you always find people to be typically this or that?"

"Only the typical ones."

"How simple life must be for you."

"No, life isn't simple. Most of the people I meet are."

Freytag adjusted the position of the spoon slightly with his forefinger. "You have been good enough to be frank with me, Herr Doctor. Now I shall be frank with you. I want you to understand why it is so important to me to lead this climb."

"That isn't necessary."

"My father—"

"Really, Karl. I don't care."

"My father is not sympathetic with my interest in climbing. I am the last of the family line, and it is his wish that I follow him in the business. Do you know what our corporation makes?"

Jonathan did not answer; he was surprised and uncomfortable at the fragile tone of Karl's voice, and he did not want to be a receptacle for this boy's troubles.

"We make insecticides, our family." Karl looked out the window toward patches of snow fluorescent with moonlight. "And that is rather amusing when you realize that during the war we made . . . we made . . ." Karl pressed his upper lip against his teeth and blinked the shine from his eyes.

"You were only five years old when the war ended, Karl."

"Meaning it wasn't my fault?"

"Meaning you have no right to the artificial tragedy you enjoy playing."

Karl looked at him bitterly, then turned aside. "My father thinks I am incapable—not serious-minded enough to assume my responsibilities. But he will have to admire me soon. You said that you find me unpleasant—socially inept. Well, let me tell you something. I do not have to depend on social niceties to achieve—what I want to achieve. I am a great climber. Both by natural gift and intensive training, I am a great climber. Better than you. Better than Anderl. When you are behind me on the rope, you will see." His eyes were intense. "Someday everyone will say that I am a great climber. Yes." He nodded curtly. "Yes. And my father will boast to his business friends about me."

Jonathan was angry with the boy at that moment. Now the sanction would be difficult, no matter which one it was. "Is that all you wanted to say to me, Karl?"

"Yes."

"Then you'd better get along. I assume Madame Bidet is awaiting you."

"She told you . . ."

"No." Jonathan turned away and looked out through the window to where the mountain's presence was a bulky starlessness in the night sky.

After a minute, he heard the young man rise and walk out of the dining room.

Kleine Scheidegg: *July 10*

JONATHAN AWOKE LATE, the sun already flaring through his window and pooling warmly on his blankets. He was not eager to face the day. He had sat up late in the dining room, staring at the black rectangle of the window beyond which was the invisible Eiger. His thoughts had wandered from the climb, to the sanction, to Jemima. When at last he had forced himself to go up to his room for sleep, he had met Anna in the hall; she was just closing the door to Karl's room.

Not a hair out of place, not a wrinkle in her dress, she stood looking at him calmly, almost contemptuously, sure of his discretion.

"May I offer you a nightcap?" he asked, pushing open his door.

"That would be nice." She passed before him into his room.

They sipped Laphroaig in silence, an odd bond of comradeship between them based on their mutual realization that they constituted no threat to each other. They would never make love; the qualities of emotional reserve and human exploitation they shared and admired insulated them from each other.

"Blessed are the meek," Anna mused, "for we shall inherit them."

Jonathan was smiling in agreement when suddenly he stopped and listened attentively to a distant rumbling.

"Thunder?" Anna asked.

Jonathan shook his head. "Avalanche."

The sound pulsed twice to higher volumes, then subsided. Jonathan finished his Scotch.

"They must be very frightening when you are up there," Anna said.

"They are."

"I cannot understand why Jean-Paul insists on making this climb at his age."

"Can't you?"

She looked at him dubiously. "For *me?*"

"As you well know."

She dropped her lavish lashes and looked into her whiskey glass. "*Pauvre être,*" she said quietly.

There were noticeable changes in emotional disposition around the breakfast table. Ben's funk had worn away and his more typical hardy humor had returned. The crisp weather and a strong high pressure cone that had moved in from the north inflated his hopes for the success of the climb. The recent snow on the higher ice fields had not had time to glaciate and bind to the perennial névé, but so long as the weather held, a major avalanche was not likely.

"Unless a foehn comes in," Karl corrected morosely.

The possibility of a foehn had been in the back of each climber's mind, but there was nothing to be gained by mentioning it. One could neither predict nor protect himself from these vagrant eddies of warm air that slip into the Bernese

Oberland infrequently. A foehn would bring raging storms to the face, and the warmer air would make the snow unreliable and avalanche-prone.

Karl's mood had changed also since the evening before. A kind of self-indulgent petulance had replaced the typical nervous aggression. This was due partly, Jonathan imagined, to regret over having spilled his emotional garbage at Jonathan's feet. It was also due in part to his having made love to Anna, a burden his sin-sodden Protestant morality could not face glibly the next morning in the presence of the husband.

And indeed Jean-Paul was dour that morning. He was tense and irritable and their waiter—never a model of skill and intelligence—received the brunt of his displeasure. It was Jonathan's belief that Jean-Paul was struggling with inner doubts about age and ability now that the moment of the climb was approaching inexorably.

Anderl, with his face creased in a bland smile, was in an almost yoga calm. His eyes were defocused and his attention turned inward. Jonathan could tell that he was tuning himself emotionally for the climb, now only eighteen hours away.

So it was by social default that Jonathan and Anna carried the burden of small talk. Anna suddenly stopped midphrase, her eye caught by something at the entrance to the dining room. "Good God," she said softly, laying her hand on Jonathan's arm.

He turned to see the internationally known husband and wife team of film actors who had arrived the day before to join the Eiger Birds. They stood at the entrance, slowly scanning about for a free table in the half-empty room until they were satisfied that no one of importance had missed their presence. A waiter, a-quiver with servility, hastened to their side and conducted them to a table near the climbers. The actor was dressed in a white Nehru jacket and beads that conflicted with his puffy, pock-marked, middle-aged face. His hair was tousled to a precise degree of tonsorial insouciance. The wife was aggressively visible in floppy pants of oriental print with a gathered blouse of bravely clashing color, the looseness of which did much to mute her bread-and-butter dumpiness, the plunging neckline designed to direct the eye to more acceptable amplitudes. Banging about between the breasts was a diamond of vulgar size. Her eyes, however, were still good.

After the woman had been seated with a flurry of small adjustments and sounds, the man stepped to Jonathan's table and leaned over it, one hand on Anderl's shoulder, the other on Ben's.

"I want to wish you fellows the best kind of luck in the whole wide world," he said with ultimate sincerity and careful attention to the music of his vowels. "In many ways, I envy you." His clear blue eyes clouded with unspoken personal grief. "It's the kind of thing I might have done . . . once." Then a brave smile pressed back the sadness. "Ah, well." He squeezed the shoulders in his hands. "Once again, good luck." He returned to his wife, who had been waving an unlit cigarette in a holder impatiently, and who accepted her husband's tardy light without thanks.

"What happened?" Ben asked the company in a hushed voice.

"Benediction, I believe," Jonathan said.

"At all events," Karl said, "they will keep the reporters' attention away from us for a while."

"Where the devil is that waiter!" Jean-Paul demanded grumpily. "This coffee was cold when it arrived!"

Karl winked broadly to the company. "Anderl. Threaten the waiter with your knife. That will make him come hopping."

Anderl blushed and looked away, and Jonathan recognized that Freytag, in his attempt at humor, had blundered into an awkward subject. Embarrassed at the instant chill his *faux pas* had brought to the table, Karl pressed on with a German instinct for making things right by making them bigger. "Didn't you know, Herr Doctor? Meyer always carries a knife. I'll bet it's there under his jacket right now. Let us see it, Anderl."

Anderl shook his head and looked away. Jean-Paul attempted to soften Freytag's brutishness by explaining quickly to Jonathan and Ben. "The fact is, Anderl climbs in many parts of the world. Usually alone. And the village folk he uses as porters are not the most reliable men you could want, especially in South America, as your own experience has doubtless taught you. Well, in a word, last year poor Anderl was climbing alone in the Andes, and something happened with a porter who was stealing food and—anyway—the porter died."

"Self-defense isn't really killing," Ben said, for something to say.

"He wasn't attacking me," Anderl admitted. "He was stealing supplies."

Freytag entered the conversation again. "And you consider the death penalty appropriate for theft?"

Anderl looked at him with innocent confusion. "You don't understand. We were six days into the hills. Without the supplies, I would not have been able to make the climb. It was not pleasant. It made me ill, in fact. But I would have lost my chance at the mountain otherwise." Clearly, he considered this to be a satisfactory justification.

Jonathan found himself wondering about how Anderl, poor as he was, had collected the money for his share in the Eiger climb.

"Well, Jonathan," Jean-Paul said, evidently to change the subject, "did you have a good night?"

"I slept very well, thank you. And you?"

"Not at all well."

"I'm sorry. Perhaps you should get some rest this afternoon. I have sleeping pills, if you want them."

"I never use them," Bidet said curtly.

Karl spoke. "Do you use pills to sleep in bivouac, Herr Doctor?"

"Usually."

"Why? Discomfort? Fear?"

"Both."

Karl laughed. "An interesting tactic! By quietly admitting to fear, you give the impression of being a very wise and brave man. I shall have to remember that one."

"Oh. Are you going to need it?"

"Probably not. I also never sleep well in bivouac. But with me it is not a matter of fear. I am too charged with the excitement of the climb. Now Anderl here! He is amazing. He tacks himself to a sheer face and falls asleep as though he were bundled up in a feather bed at home."

"Why not?" Anderl asked. "Supposing the worst, what is the value in being awake during a fall? A last glimpse at the scenery?"

"Ah!" Jean-Paul ejaculated. "At last our waiter finds a moment for us in his busy schedule!"

But the waiter was coming with a note for Jonathan on a small silver tray.

"It is from the gentleman over there," the waiter said.

Jonathan glanced in the indicated direction, and he experienced a stomach shock.

It was Clement Pope. He sat at a nearby table, wearing a checked sport coat and a yellow ascot. He waved sassily at Jonathan, fully realizing that he was blowing Jonathan's cover. The defensive, gentle smile came slowly to Jonathan's eyes as he controlled the flutter in his stomach. He glanced at the other members of the party, trying to read the smallest trace of recognition or apprehension in their faces. He could distinguish none. He opened the note, scanned it, then nodded and thanked the waiter. "You might also bring M. Bidet a fresh pot of coffee."

"No, never mind," Jean-Paul said. "I no longer have a taste for it. I think I shall return to my room and rest, if you will excuse me." With this he left, his stride strong and angry.

"What's wrong with Jean-Paul?" Jonathan asked Anna quietly.

She shrugged, not caring particularly at that moment. "Do you know that man who sent you the note?" she asked.

"I may have met him somewhere. I don't recognize him. Why?"

"If you ever see him again, you really should drop a hint about his clothing. Unless, of course, he wants to be taken for a music hall singer or an American."

"I'll do that. If I ever see him again."

Anderl's attention was snagged by the two young twits of the day before who passed the window and waved at him. With a shrug of fatalistic inevitability, he excused himself and stepped out to join them.

Immediately afterward, Karl invited Anna to join him in a stroll to the village.

And within three minutes of Pope's appearance, the company was reduced to Jonathan and Ben. For a time they sat sipping their cool coffee in silence. When he looked casually around, Jonathan saw that Pope had left.

"Hey, ol' buddy? What's got into Jean-Paul?" Ben had changed from the mispronunciation based on print to one based on ear.

"Just jumpy, I guess."

"Now, jumpy's a fine quality in a climber. But he's more than jumpy. He's pissed off about something. You been drilling his wife?"

Jonathan had to laugh at the directness of the question. "No, Ben. I haven't."

"You're sure?"

"It's a thing I'd know."

"Yeah, I guess. About the last thing you guys need is bad blood. I can just see you on the face, thumping on each other with ice axes."

The image was not alien to Jonathan's imagination.

Ben was pensive for a while before he said, "You know, if I was going up that hill with anybody—excepting you, of course—I'd want to be roped to Anderl."

"Makes sense. But you better keep your hands out of the larder."

"Yeah! How about that? When he decides to climb a mountain, he don't fool around none."

"Evidently not." Jonathan rose. "I'm going to my room. See you at supper."

"What about lunch?"

"No. I'll be down in the village."

"Got a little something waiting for you down there?"

"Yes."

Jonathan sat by the window in his room, staring out toward the mountain and bringing his thoughts into order. The bold appearance of Pope had been a surprise; for an instant he had been off balance. There had been no time to consider Dragon's reasons for so blatantly rupturing his cover. Because Dragon was chained immobile to his dark, antiseptic cell in New York, it was the face and person of Clement Pope that were universally recognized as SS Division leadership. There could be only one reason for his making so flagrantly open a contact. Jonathan became tight with anger at the recognition of it.

The anticipated knock came, and Jonathan crossed to the door and opened it.

"How's it been going, Hemlock?" Pope extended his broad businessman's hand which Jonathan ignored, closing the door behind them. Pope lowered himself with a grunt into the chair Jonathan had been occupying. "Nice place you got here. Going to offer me a drink?"

"Get on with it, Pope."

Pope's laugh lacked joy. "OK, pal, if that's the game you want to play, we'll use your ball park. Dismiss formalities and get to the nitty and the gritty. Right?"

As Pope tugged a small packet of note cards from his inside coat pocket, Jonathan noticed he was starting to run to fat. An athlete in his college days, Pope was still strong in a slow, massive way, but Jonathan estimated that he could be put away fairly easily. And he had every intention of putting him away—but not until he had drained him of useful information.

"Let's get the little fish out of the pond first, Hemlock, so we can clear the field of fire."

Jonathan crossed his arms and leaned against the wall by the door. "Let's mix any metaphors you want."

Pope glanced at his first note card. "You wouldn't have any news about the whereabouts of active 365/55—a certain Jemima Brown, would you?"

"I would not."

"You better be telling it like it is, pal. Mr. Dragon would be mucho pissed off to discover that you'd harmed her. She was just following our orders. And now she's disappeared."

Jonathan reflected on the fact that Jemima was in the village and that he would be meeting her within the hour. "I doubt that you'll ever find her."

"Don't make book on it, baby. SS has a long arm."

"Next card?"

Pope slipped the top card to the bottom of the pack and glanced at the next. "Oh, yeah. You really left us with a mess, baby."

Jonathan smiled, a gentle calm in his eyes. "That's twice you've called me 'baby.'"

"That's kind of a burr under your blanket, isn't it?"

"Yes. Yes, it is," Jonathan admitted with quiet honesty.

"Well, that's just tough titty, pal. The days are long gone when we had to worry about your feelings."

Jonathan took a long breath to contain his feelings, and he asked, "You were saying something about a mess?"

"Yeah. We had teams all over the desert trying to find out what happened."

"And did you?"

"The second day we came across the car and that guy you blew out of it."

"What about the other one?"

"Miles Mellough? I had to leave before we found him. But I got word just before I left New York that one of our teams had located him."

"Dead, I presume."

"Plenty dead. Exposure, hunger, thirst. They don't know which he died of first. But he was beaucoup dead. They buried him out on the desert." Pope snickered. "Weird thing."

"Weird?"

"He must have been real hard up for chow there toward the last."

"Oh?"

"Yeah. He ate a dog."

Jonathan glanced down.

Pope went on. "You know how much it cost us? That search? And keeping the whole thing quiet?"

"No. But I assume you'll tell me."

"No, I won't. That information's classified. But we get a little tired of the way you irregulars burn money like it was going out of style."

"That's always been a burr under your blanket, hasn't it, Pope? The fact that men like me earn more for one job than you get in three years."

Pope sneered, an expression his face seemed particularly designed for.

"I admit that it would be more economical," Jonathan said, "if you SS regulars did your own sanctioning. But the work requires skill and some physical courage. And those qualities are not available on government requisition forms."

"I'm not pissed about the money you're making on this particular job. This time you're going to earn it, baby."

"I was hoping you'd get around to that."

"You've already guessed—a big university professor like you must have guessed by now."

"I'd enjoy hearing it from you."

"Whatever turns you on. It's different strokes for different folks, I guess." He flicked to the next card. "Search has drawn a blank on your target. We know he's here. And he's on this climb with you. But we don't know which one for sure."

"Miles Mellough knew."

"Did he tell you?"

"He offered to. The price was too high."

"What did he want?"

"To live."

Pope looked up from the note card. He did his best to appear coldly professional as he nodded in sober understanding. But the cards fell from his knee, and he had to paw around to collect them.

Jonathan watched him with distaste. "So you've set me up to make the target commit himself, right?"

"No other way, buddy-boy. We figured the target would recognize me on sight. And now he has you spotted as a Sanction man. He's got to take a crack at you before you get him. And when he does, I have him identified."

"And who would do the sanction, if he got me?" Jonathan looked Pope over leisurely. "You?"

"You don't think I could handle it?"

Jonathan smiled. "In a locked closet, maybe. With a grenade."

"Don't bet on that, buddy. As it happens, we're going to bring in another Sanction man to do the job."

"I assume this was your idea?"

"Dragon OK'd it, but it came from me."

Jonathan's face was set in his gentle combat smile. "And it really doesn't matter that you've blown my cover, now that I have decided to stop working for you."

"That is exactly the way it crumbles." Pope was enjoying his moment of victory after so many years of smarting under Jonathan's open disdain.

"What if I just walk away and forget the whole thing?"

"No way, pal. You wouldn't get your hundred thousand; you'd lose your house; we'd confiscate your paintings; and you'd probably do a little time for smuggling them into the country. How does it feel to be in a box, pal?"

Jonathan crossed to pour himself a Laphroaig. Then he laughed aloud. "You've done well, Pope. Really very well! Want a drink?"

Pope was not sure how to handle this sudden cordiality. "Well, that's mighty white of you, Hemlock." He laughed as he received his glass. "Hey! I just said that was mighty white of you. I'll bet this Jemima Brown never said that to you. Right?"

Jonathan smiled beatifically. "No. As a matter of fact, she never did."

"Hey, tell me. How is that black stuff? Good, eh?"

Jonathan drank off half his glass and sat in a chair opposite Pope's, leaning toward him confidentially. "You know, Pope, I really ought to tell you in advance that I intend to waste you a little." He winked playfully. "You would understand that, in a case like this, wouldn't you?"

"Waste me? What do you mean?"

"Oh, just West Side slang. Look, if Dragon would rather I did the sanction myself—and I assume he would—I'm going to need a little information. Go over the Montreal thing with me. There were two men involved in the hit on whatshisname, right?"

"His name was Wormwood. He was a good man. A regular." Pope flipped through several cards and scanned one rapidly. "That's right. Two men."

"Now, you're sure of that? Not a man and a woman?"

"It says two men."

"All right. Are you sure Wormwood wounded one of the men?"

"That's what the report said. One of the two men was limping when he left the hotel."

"But are you sure he was wounded? Could he have been hurt earlier? Maybe in a mountain accident?"

"The report said he limped. Why are you asking? Was one of your people hurt in some kind of accident?"

"Karl Freytag says he hurt his leg in a short fall last month."

"Then Freytag could be your man."

"Possibly. What else have the Search people dragged up about our man?"

"Almost nothing. Couldn't have been a professional. We'd have gotten a line on him by now, if he were a professional."

"Could he have been the one who cut Wormwood open?"

"Maybe. We always assumed Kruger did the actual cutting. It's his kind of thing. But it could have been the other way, I suppose. Why?"

"One of the climbers had the capacity to kill a man with a knife. Very few people can do that."

"Maybe he's your man. Whoever it was, he has a weak stomach."

"The vomit on the floor?"

"Right."

"A woman might do that."

"There's a woman in this?"

"Bidet's wife. She could have worn male clothing. And that limp might have been anything—a twisted ankle coming down the stairs."

"You got yourself quite a can of worms there, baby."

For some perverse reason, Jonathan enjoyed drawing Pope along the mental maze he had wandered through for the last two nights. "Oh, it's more a can of worms than you think. Considering that this whole affair centers on a formula for germ warfare, it's kind of interesting that one of these men owns a company that makes aerosol containers."

"Which one?"

"Bidet."

Pope leaned forward, his eyes squeezed up in concentration. "You might be onto something there."

Jonathan smiled to himself. "I might be. But then, another of them is in the business of making insecticides—and there is reason to believe that they made nastier things during the war."

"One of the two of them, right? Is that the way you figure it?" Pope looked up suddenly, the light of an idea in his eyes. "or maybe *both* of them!"

"That's a possibility, Pope. But then—why? Neither of them needs the money. They could have hired the thing done. Now the third climber—Meyer—he's poor. And he needed money to make this climb."

Pope nodded significantly. "Meyer could be your man." Then he looked into Jonathan's eyes and blushed with the angry realization that he was being put on. He tossed off the rest of his drink. "When are you going to make your hit?"

"Oh, I thought I would wait until I knew which one was the target."

"I'll hang around the hotel until it's done."

"No, you won't. You're going to go right back to the States."

"No way, pal."

"We'll see. One more thing before you go. Mellough told me that you were the one who paid him for Henri Baq's sanction. Is that right?"

"We found out he was playing switchy-changey with the other side."

"But it was you who set him up?"

"That's my job, pal."

Jonathan nodded, a distant look in his eyes. "Well, I guess that's about it." He rose to see Pope to the door. "You should be pleased with yourself, you know. Even though I'm the man in the box, I can't help admiring the skill with which you've set me up."

Pope stopped in the middle of the room and looked at Jonathan narrowly, trying to decide whether he was being put on again. He decided he was not. "You know, pal? Maybe if we had given each other a chance, we might have become friends."

"Who knows, Pope?"

"Oh. About your gun. I've got one waiting for you at the desk. A CII standard with no serial number and a silencer. It's gift wrapped in a candy box."

Jonathan opened the door for Pope, who stepped out then turned back, bracing his weight against the frame, one hand on either side of the opening. "What was all that about 'wasting' me?"

Jonathan noticed that Pope's fingers had curled into the crack of the door. That was going to hurt. "You really want to know?"

Sensing a put-on again, Pope set his face into its toughest expression. "One thing you'd better keep in mind, baby. So far as I'm concerned, you irregulars are the most expendable things since paper contraceptives."

"Right."

Two of Pope's fingers broke as Jonathan slammed the door on them. When he jerked it open again, the scream of pain was in Pope's eyes, but it did not have time to get to his throat. Jonathan grabbed him by his belt and snatched him forward into an ascending knee. It was a luck shot. Jonathan felt the squish of the testicles. Pope doubled over with a nasal grunt that spurted snot onto his chin. Jonathan grasped the collar of his coat and propelled him into the room, driving his head against the wall. Pope's knees crumpled, but Jonathan dragged him to his feet and snapped the checked sports coat down over his arms before he could pass out. Jonathan guided Pope's fall so that he toppled face down across the bed, where he lay with his face in the mattress and his arms pinned to his sides by the jacket. Jonathan's thumbs stiffened as he sighted the spot just below the ribs where the kidneys could be devastated.

But he did not drive the thumbs in.

He paused, confused and suddenly empty. He was going to let Pope go. He knew he was going to, although he could hardly believe it. Pope had arranged Henri Baq's death! Pope had set him up as a decoy! Pope had even said something about Jemima.

And he was going to let Pope go. He looked down at the crumpled form, at the silly sports coat, at the toed-in flop of the unconscious legs, but he felt none of the cold hate that usually sustained him in combat. For the moment, something was missing in him.

He rolled Pope over and went into the bathroom, where he dipped a towel into the toilet, holding it by one end until it was sodden. Back in the room, he dropped the towel over Pope's face, the shock of the cold water producing an automatic convulsion in the unconscious body. Then Jonathan poured himself a small Laphroaig and sat in the chair again, waiting for Pope to come around.

With an unmanly amount of strangled groaning, Pope eventually regained consciousness. He tried twice to sit up before succeeding. The total of his pain—the fingers, the groin, the throbbing head—was so great that he could not tug his jacket back up. He slid off the bed and sat on the floor, bewildered.

Jonathan spoke quietly. "You're going to be all right, Pope. For a few days, you may walk a little oddly, but with proper medical attention you'll be just fine. But you won't be of any use here. So you're going to go back to the States as soon as possible. Do you understand that?"

Pope stared at him with bulbous, confused eyes. He still did not know what had happened to him.

Jonathan enunciated slowly. "You are going back to the States. Right now. And I am never going to see you again. That's right, isn't it?"

Pope nodded heavily.

Jonathan helped him to his feet and, bearing most of his weight, to the door. Pope clung to the frame for support. The teacher in Jonathan exerted itself. "To waste: to tear up, to harm, to inflict or cause to be inflicted physical punishment upon."

Pope clawed his way out, and Jonathan closed the door.

Jonathan opened the back of his portable typewriter and got out makings for a smoke. He sat deep in the chair, holding the smoke as long as he could on the top of his lungs before letting it out. Henri Baq had been a friend. And he had let Pope go.

Jemima had sat across from him in the dim interior of the café for a silent quarter of an hour, her eyes investigating his face and its distant, involute expression. "It's not the silence that bothers me," she said at last. "It's the politeness."

Jonathan tugged his mind back to the present. "Pardon me?"

She smiled sadly. "That's what I mean."

Jonathan drew a deep breath and focused himself on her. "I'm sorry. My mind is on tomorrow."

"You keep saying things like that—I'm sorry, and pardon me, and please pass the salt. And you know what really bothers me?"

"What?"

"I don't even have the salt."

Jonathan laughed. "You're fantastic, madame."

"Yeah, but what does it get me? Excuses. Pardons. Sorrys."

He smiled. "You're right. I've been miserable company. I'm—"

"Say it and I'll kick the shin!"

He touched her fingers. The tone of banter evaporated instantly.

Under the table, she squeezed his foot between hers. "What are you going to do about me, Jonathan?"

"What do you mean?"

"I'm yours to do with, man. You could kiss me, or press my hand, or make love to me, or marry me, or talk to me, or hit me, or . . . you are shaking your head slowly from side to side, which means that you do not intend to hit me, or make love to me, or anything at all, right?"

"I want you to go home, Gem."

She stared at him, her eyes shining with hurt and pride. "Goddam you, Jonathan Hemlock. Are you God or something? You make up your set of rules, and if somebody hurts you or tricks you, then you come down on him like a machine of fate!" She was angry because unwanted tears were standing in her eyes. She pushed them away with the back of her hand. "You don't make any distinction between a person like Miles Mellough and somebody like me—somebody who loves you." She had not raised her voice, but there was anger in the crisp consonants.

Jonathan counterpunched with the same hard tone. "Come on now! I wouldn't be in this thing if you hadn't stolen from me. I brought you to my house. I showed you my paintings. And briefly I loved you. And you know what you did? You gave Dragon the leverage to force me into this situation. A situation I have goddamned little chance of surviving. Tell me about love!"

"But—I had never met you when I took on the assignment!"

"You took the money in the morning. *Afterwards.*"

Her silence admitted the significance of the sequence. After a time, she tried to explain, but gave it up after a few words.

The waiter arrived with a carafe of coffee, and his presence froze them in an awkward hiatus. They cooled during the pause. When the waiter left, Jemima settled her emotions with a deep breath and smiled. "I'm sorry, Jonathan."

"Say 'I'm sorry' again and I'll kick your shin."

The sting of the conflict was gone.

She sipped her coffee. "Is it going to be bad? This thing on the mountain?"

"I hope it doesn't get to the mountain."

"But it's going to be bad?"

"It's going to be wet."

She shuddered. "I've always hated that phrase: wet work. Is there anything I can do?"

"Nothing at all, Jemima. Just keep out of it. Go home."

When next she spoke, her voice was dry, and she was examining the situation fairly and with distance. "I think we're going to blow it, Jonathan. People like us hardly ever fall in love. It's even funny to think of people like us in *luv*. But it happened, and we did. And it would be a shame . . . it would be a goddam shame . . ." She shrugged and looked down.

"Gem, some things are happening to me, I, ah—" He was almost ashamed to say it. "I let Pope go today. I don't know why. I just . . . didn't care."

"What do you mean? You let Pope go?"

"The particulars don't matter. But something funny . . . uncomfortable . . . is happening. Maybe in a few years—"

"No!"

The immediate rejection surprised him.

"No, Jonathan. I am a grown-up, desirable woman. And I don't see myself sitting around waiting for you to get mature enough, or tired enough to come knocking at my door."

He thought about it before answering. "That makes good sense, Gem."

They sipped their coffee without speaking. Then she looked up at him with growing realization in her harlequin eyes. "Jesus Christ," she whispered in wonder. "It's really happening. We're going to blow it. We're going to say goodbye. And that will be that."

Jonathan spoke gently. "Can you get a flight to the States today?"

She concentrated on the napkin in her lap, pressing it flat again and again with her hands. "I don't know. I guess so."

Jonathan rose, touched her cheek with the backs of his fingers, and left the café.

The climbers' last meal together was strained; no one ate much except Anderl, who lacked the nerve of fear, and Ben, who after all did not have to make the climb. Jonathan watched each of his companions in turn for signs of reaction to Clement Pope's arrival, but, although there were ample manifestations of perturbation, the natural pressures of the impending climb made it impossible to disentangle causes. Bidet's ill humor of the morning had ripened into cool formality; and Anna did not choose to emerge from behind her habitual defense of amused poise. Karl took his self-imposed responsibilities too seriously to indulge in social trivia. Despite the bottle of champagne sent to the table by the Greek merchant, the meal was charged with silences that descended unnoticed, until their weight became suddenly apparent to all, and they would drive them away with overly gay small talk that deteriorated into flotsam of half sentences and meaningless verbal involutions.

Although the room was crowded with Eiger Birds in garish informal plumage, there was a palpable change in the sound of their conversation. It lacked real energy. There was a sprinkling of girlish laughter allegro vivace sforzando over the usual drone of middle-aged male ponderoso. But underlying all was a basso ostinato of impatience. When was this climb going to start? They had been there two days. There was business to conclude and pleasure to pursue. When could one expect these falls—God forbid they should happen?

The actor and his florid mate entered the dining room late, as was their practice, and waved broadly to the climbers, hoping to create the impression that they were privileged with acceptance.

The meal closed on a businesslike note with Karl's unnecessary instructions that everyone get to sleep as soon as possible. He told the climbers that he himself would make the rounds of the rooms two hours before dawn, waking each man so that they could steal out before the guests and reporters knew they were gone.

The lights were off in Jonathan's room. Filtered moonlight from the snow beyond the window made the starched linen of the bed glow with its own phosphorescence. He sat in the dark; in his lap lay the gun Pope had left for him, heavy and clumsy with the silencer that gave it the look of an ironmonger's mutant. When he had picked it up at the desk (the gift of candy from one man to another arching the desk clerk's eyebrows) he had learned that Pope had departed for the States after receiving first aid for what he creatively described as a series of slips in his bathtub.

Despite his need for sleep before the climb, Jonathan dared not take a pill. That night was the target's last chance to make his defensive move, unless he had decided to wait until they were on the face. Although a hit on the precarious mountain would endanger the whole rope, it would certainly leave no evidence. Jonathan wondered how desperate the target was; and how smart.

But no use sitting there worrying about it! He pushed himself out of the armchair and unrolled his sleeping bag on the floor opposite the door where anyone entering would be silhouetted against the hall light. After sliding into the sleeping bag, he clicked the revolver off safety and cocked the hammer—two sounds he would not have to make later when sound might count. He placed the gun on the floor beside him, then he tried to sleep.

He had no great faith in these kinds of preparations. They were the kinds his sanction targets made, and to no avail. His mistrust was well founded. In the course of turning and adjusting his body in search of a little sleep, he rolled over on the gun, making it quite inaccessible under his sleeping bag.

He must have slept, because he experienced a plunging sensation when, without opening his eyes, he became aware of light and motion within the room.

He opened his eyes. The door was swinging ajar and a man—Bidet—was framed in the yellow rectangle. The gun in his hand was outlined in silver against the edge of the black door as he stealthily pressed it closed behind him. Jonathan did not move. He felt the pressure of his own gun under the small of his back, and he cursed the malignant fate that had put it there. The shaded bulk of Bidet approached his bed.

Although he spoke softly, Jonathan's voice seemed to fill the dark room. "Do not move, Jean-Paul."

Bidet froze, confused by the direction of the sound.

Jonathan realized how he had to play this. He must maintain the soft, authoritative drone of his voice. "I can see you perfectly, Jean-Paul. I shall certainly kill you if you make the slightest undirected movement. Do you understand?"

"Yes." Bidet's voice was husky with fright and long silence.

"Just to your right there is a bedside lamp. Reach out for it, but don't turn it on until I tell you."

There was a rustle of movement, then Jean-Paul said, "I am touching it."

Jonathan did not alter the mesmeric monotone of his voice, but he felt instinctively that the bluff was not going to hold up. "Turn on the lamp. But don't face me. Keep your eyes on the light. Do you understand?" Jonathan did not dare the excessive motion required to get his arms out of the sleeping bag and scramble about under it for his gun. "Do you understand, Jean-Paul?"

"Yes."

"Then do it slowly. Now." Jonathan knew it was not going to work!

He was right. Bidet did it, but not slowly. The instant the room flooded with eye-blinking light, he whirled toward Jonathan and brought his gun to bear on him where he lay incongruously in the eiderdown cocoon. But he did not fire. He stared at Jonathan with fear and anger balanced in his eyes.

Very slowly, Jonathan lifted his hand within the sleeping bag and pointed his finger at Bidet, who realized with a dry swallow that the protuberance within the bag was directed at the pit of his stomach. Neither moved for several seconds. Jonathan resented the painful lump of his gun under his shouder. But he smiled. "In my country, this is called a Mexican standoff. No matter which of us shoots first, we both die."

Jonathan admired Bidet's control. "How does one normally resolve the situation? In your country."

"Convention has it that both men put their guns away and talk the thing out. Any number of sleeping bags have been preserved from damage that way."

Bidet laughed. "I had no intention of shooting you, Jonathan."

"I guess it's your gun that confused me, Jean-Paul."

"I only wanted to impress you. Frighten you, perhaps. I don't know. It was a stupid gesture. The gun isn't even loaded."

"In which case, you would have no objection to tossing it onto the bed."

Bidet did not move for a moment, then his shoulders slumped and he dropped the gun onto the bed. Jonathan rose slowly to one elbow, keeping his finger pointed at Jean-Paul, as he slipped his other hand under the sleeping bag and retrieved his gun. When Bidet saw it emerge from beneath the waterproof fabric, he shrugged with a Gallic gesture of fatalistic acceptance.

"You are very brave, Jonathan."

"I really had no other choice."

"At all events, you are most resourceful. But it wasn't necessary. As I told you, I did not even load the gun."

Jonathan struggled out of the bag and crossed to his armchair where he sat without taking his gun off Bidet. "It's a good thing you decided not to shoot. I'd have felt silly wiggling my thumb and saying bang, bang."

"Aren't *both* men supposed to put their guns away after a Mexican—whatever?"

"Never trust a Gringo." Jonathan was relaxed and confident. One thing was certain: Jean-Paul was an amateur. "You had some purpose in coming here, I imagine."

Jean-Paul examined the palm of one hand, rubbing over the lines with his thumb. "I think I shall return to my room, if you don't mind. I have made an ass of myself in your eyes already. Nothing can be gained by deepening that impression."

"I think I have a right to some kind of explanation. Your entrance into my room was—irregular?"

Bidet sat heavily on the bed, his body slumping, his eyes averted, and there was something so deflated in his manner that Jonathan had no qualms about the fact that his gun was now within reach. "There is no more ridiculous image in the world, Jonathan, than the outraged cuckold." He smiled sadly. "I never thought I would find myself playing the Pantaloon."

Jonathan experienced that uncomfortable combination of pity and disgust he always felt toward the emotionally soft, particularly those who lacked control over their romantic lives.

"But I cannot become much more ludicrous in your eyes," Bidet continued. "I imagine you already know about my physical limitations. Anna usually tells her studs. For some reason, it inspires them to greater effort on her behalf."

"You are putting me in the awkward position of having to declare my innocence, Jean-Paul."

Jean-Paul looked at Jonathan with hollow nausea in his eyes. "You needn't bother."

"I'd rather. We have to climb together. Let me say it simply: I have not slept with Anna, nor have I any reason to believe that advances would be greeted with anything but scorn."

"But last night . . ."

"What about last night?"

"She was here."

"How do you know that?"

"I missed her . . . I looked for her . . . I listened at your door." He looked away. "That is despicable, isn't it."

"Yes, it is. Anna was here last night. I met her in the hall, and I offered her a drink. We did not make love."

Jean-Paul picked up his gun absently and toyed with it as he spoke. Jonathan felt no danger; he had dismissed Bidet as a potential killer. "No. She made love last night. I touched her later. I could tell from—"

"I don't want to hear about it. I have no clinical curiosity, and this is not a confessional."

Jean-Paul toyed with the small Italian automatic. "I shouldn't have come here. I have behaved in poor taste; and that is worse than Anna who had only behaved immorally. Let me ascribe it to the stress of the climb. I had had great hopes for this climb. I thought if Anna were here to see me climb a mountain that very few men would dare to even touch—that might—somehow. I don't know. Whatever it was, it was a senseless hope." He looked over at Jonathan with beaten eyes. "Do you despise me?"

"My admiration for you has found new limits."

"You phrase well. But then, you have the intellectual advantage of being emotionless."

"Do you believe me about Anna?"

Jean-Paul smiled sadly. "No, Jonathan. I don't believe you. I am a cuckold, but not a fool. If you had nothing to fear from me, why were you lying there on the floor, anticipating my revenge?"

Jonathan could not explain and did not try.

Jean-Paul sighed. "Well, I shall return to my room to blush in private, and you will be freed from the duty of having to pity and detest me." In a gesture of dramatic finality, he snapped back the slide of the automatic, and a cartridge arced from the chamber, struck against the wall, and bounced onto the rug. Both men looked at the shiny brass with surprise. Jean-Paul laughed without mirth. "I guess I am deceived more easily than I thought. I could have sworn the gun was empty."

He left without saying good-night.

Jonathan smoked and took a sleeping pill before attempting sleep again, this time in his bed, considering it now safe with the same kind of superstitious faith in antichance that prompts bomber pilots to fly into ack-ack puffs, or woodsmen to seek shelter from storms under lightning-cleft trees.

Eiger: *July 11*

THE ONLY SOUNDS they made as they walked singlefile toward the base of the mountain were the soft trudge of their footfalls and the hiss of Alpiglen grass against their gaitered boots, wet and glistening with dew. Bringing up the rear, Jonathan looked up at the mountain stars, still crisp and cold despite the threat of dawn to mute their brilliance. The climbers walked without the burden of pack, rope, and climbing iron. Ben and three of the young climbers who camped on the meadow had preceded them carrying the heavy gear as far as the foot of the scree slope.

The team responded to the silence, the earliness of the hour, and the weight of their objective with that sense of unreality and emotional imbalance common to the verge of a major climb. As he always did just before a climb, Jonathan attended hungrily to all physical stimuli. Within his body he followed the tingle and ripple of anticipation. His legs, tuned high for hard climbing, pulled the flat land under him with giddying ease. The chill brush of predawn wind on the nape of his neck, the smell of the grass, the organic viscosity of the dark around him—Jonathan focused on each of these in turn, savoring the sensations, gripping them with his tactile, rather than mental, memory. He had always wondered at this odd significance of common experiences just before a hard climb. He realized that this particularization of the mundane was a product of the sudden mutability of the world of the senses. And he knew that it was not the wind, the grass, the night that was threatened with mortality; it was the sensing animal. But he never dwelt on that.

Jean-Paul slackened his pace and dropped back to Jonathan, who resented this intrusion on his sacramental relations with simple sensation.

"About last night, Jonathan—"

"Forget it."

"Will you?"

"Certainly."

"I doubt it."

Jonathan lengthened his stride and let Jean-Paul fall behind.

They approached the fireflies of light that had directed them across the lea and came upon Ben and his group of volunteers laying out and checking the gear with the aid of flashlights. Karl considered it necessary to his posture as leader to issue a couple of superfluous instructions while the team quickly geared up. Ben groused heavily about the cold and the earliness of the hour, but his words were designed only to combat the silence. He felt empty and useless. His part in the climb was over, and he would return to Kleine Scheidegg to handle the reporters and watch the progress of the climbers through the telescope he had brought for the purpose. He would become an active member again only if something happened and he had to organize a rescue.

Standing next to Jonathan, but looking away up toward the mountain that was a deeper black within a blackness, Ben pulled his ample nose and sniffed, "Now you listen to me, ol' buddy. You come off that hill in one piece, or I'm going to kick your ass."

"You're a sloppy sentimentalist, Ben."

"Yeah, I guess." Ben walked away and gruffly ordered his young volunteers to accompany him back to the hotel. When they were younger and more dramatic, he might have shaken hands with Jonathan.

The climbers moved out in the dark, scrambling up the scree and onto the rock rubble at the base. By the time they touched the face proper, the first light had begun to press form into the black mass. In that cringing light, the rock and the snow patches appeared to a common, dirty gray. But Eiger rock is an organic tonic gray, produced by the fusion of color complements in balance, not the muddy gray that is a mixture of black and white. And the snow was in reality crisp white, unsooted and unpitted by thaw. It was the light that was dirty and that soiled the objects it illuminated.

They roped up, following their plan to make the lower portion of the face in two separate, parallel lines of attack. Freytag and Bidet constituted one rope, and Karl had most of their pitons clanging about his middle. He intended to lead all the way, with Bidet retrieving such iron as had to be planted. Jonathan and Anderl had shared their iron because, by common unspoken assent, they preferred to leapfrog, alternating the sport of route-finding and leading. Naturally, they moved much faster this way.

It was nine in the morning, and the sun was touching, as it did briefly twice each day, the concave face of the Eigerwand. The principal topic of conversation among the Eiger Birds in the dining room was a prank the Greek merchant had played on his guests during a party the night before. He had soaked all the rolls of toilet paper in water. His American society wife had considered the prank to be in poor taste and, what is more, unnecessarily wasteful of money.

Ben's breakfast was interrupted by a shout from the terrace followed by an excited rush of Eiger Birds toward the telescopes. The climbers had been spotted. The economic machinery of the hotel went into operation with the lubrication of careful preparation. Uniformed attendants appeared at each telescope (except the one that had been reserved at great cost by the Greek merchant). With typical Swiss efficiency and monetary foresight, the attendants were equipped with tickets—a different color for each instrument—on which three-minute time allocations were printed. These were sold to the Eiger Birds at ten times the normal cost of the coin-operated machines, and milling queues immediately began to form around each telescope. The tickets were sold with the understanding that the management would not return money in the case of heavy weather or clouds obscuring the climbers.

Ben felt the bitter gorge of disgust rise in the back of his throat at the sight of these chattering necrophiles, but he was also relieved that the climbers had been discovered. Now he could set up his own telescope in the open meadow away from the hotel and keep a guardian eye on the team.

He was just rising from his coffee when a half dozen reporters breasted upstream against the current of the excited exodus and pushed into the dining room to surround Ben and ask him questions about the climb and the climbers. Following earlier plans, Ben distributed brief typewritten biographies of each man. These had been prepared to prevent the newspeople from resorting to their florid imaginations. But the personal accounts, containing only the birthplaces and dates, occupations, and mountaineering careers of the team members, were barren resources for those newsmen who sought human interest and sensationalism, so they continued to assail Ben with a babble of aggressive questions. Taking his breakfast beer along with him, his jaw set in grim silence, Ben pushed through them, but one American reporter grasped his sleeve to stop him.

"Now, you're real sure you have no further use for that hand?" Ben asked, and he was instantly released.

They followed him tenaciously as he crossed the lobby with his energetic, hopping stride, but before he could get to the elevator door a tweeded English woman columnist—tough, stringy, and sexless, with precise clipped diction—interposed herself between him and the elevator door.

"Tell me, Mr. Bowman, in your opinion do these men climb out of a need to prove their manhood, or is it more a matter of compensating for inferiority feelings?" Her pencil poised over her notebook as Ben responded.

"Why don't you go get yourself screwed? Do you a lot of good."

She had copied down the first words before the gist of the message arrested her pencil, and Ben escaped into the elevator.

Jonathan and Anderl found a shallow shelf just to the west of the mouth of the chute that Karl had estimated would be the key to the new route. They banged in a piton and tied themselves on while they awaited the arrival of Karl and Jean-Paul. Although the beetling cliff above them flowed with icy melt water, it protected them from the rock fall that had been plaguing their climb for the past half hour. Even as they arranged coils of rope under them to keep out the wet, chunks of rock and ice broke over the crest of the cliff and whined past, three or four feet out in front of them, to burst on the rocks below with loud reports and a spray of mountain shrapnel.

Their ledge was so narrow that they had to sit hip to hip, their legs dangling out over the void. The climb had been fast and magnificent, and the view was breathtaking, so, when Anderl produced a bar of hard chocolate from his coat pocket and shared it with Jonathan, they felt exhilarated and contented, munching away wordlessly.

Jonathan could not ignore the sound that surrounded them as totally as silence. For the last hour, as they approached the mouth of the chute on a line a little to the right of it, the roar of rushing water had increased in volume. He imagined, although he could not see from his perch, that the chute was a cataract of melt water. He had climbed up through waterfalls like this before (the Ice Hose over on the normal route was no mean example) but his experience had not decreased his respect for the objective danger.

He glanced over at Anderl to see if his worry was shared, but the blissful, almost vacant smile on the Austrian's face was evidence that he was in his element, full of contentment. Some men are native to the mountain and, while they are on rock, the valley does not exist, save as the focus point for that patient and persistent gravity against which they hold out. Jonathan did not share Anderl's contented insouciance. So long as he had been climbing, the world had narrowed to the rope, the rock, the purchase, and body rhythms. But now, with a safe stance and time to reflect, lowland troubles returned to him.

For instance, it could be Anderl. Anderl could be the target. And a hunter in his own right now. At least half a dozen times in the past three hours, Anderl had only to cut the rope and give a slight tug, and Jonathan would no longer be a threat. The fact that he had not done so in no way excluded him as a possibility. They were too close to the base; there would be evidence, and a cut rope looks very different from a frayed rope. And too, they were probably being watched at every moment. From far down there, from the toy terrace of the miniature hotel there were probably half a score of eyes empowered by convex glass to observe them.

Jonathan decided he could rest easy. If it happened, it would be higher up, up where the distance made them little dots, barely distinguishable to the most powerful glass. Perhaps when cloud and mist descended to conceal them altogether. Up where the body and the severed rope would not be found for months, even years.

"What are you frowning about?" Anderl asked.

Jonathan laughed. "Morbid thoughts. About falling."

"I never think about falling. What's the use? If a fall wants to happen, it will happen without my thinking about it. I think about climbing. That requires thinking." He punctuated this simple philosophy by pushing the last of the chocolate into his mouth.

This was the longest speech Jonathan had ever heard Anderl make. Clearly, here was a man who came to full life only on the mountain.

First Karl's hand, then his head came into view over the outcropping of rock below, and soon he was in a stance just under theirs, steadily taking in the line that led down to Jean-Paul until he too had hoisted himself over the ridge, red-faced but triumphant. The new arrivals found a slim ledge for themselves, banged in protecting iron, and rested.

"What do you think of my route now, Herr Doctor?" Karl shouted.

"So far so good." Jonathan thought of the roaring melt water above them.

"I knew it would be!"

Jean-Paul drew lustily at his water bottle, then rested out against the rope that was connected to his piton by a snap ring. "I had no idea that you gentlemen intended to *run* up the hill! Have pity on my age!" He laughed hastily, least anyone imagine he was not joking.

"You will have time to rest now," Karl said. "We shall be here for at least an hour."

"An hour!" Jean-Paul protested. "We have to sit here for an hour?"

"We shall rest and have a little breakfast. It's too early to climb up through the chute."

Jonathan agreed with Karl. Although a climber on the Eiger must expect to be the target for fairly regular sniping by rock and ice fall, there is no sense in facing the veritable fusillade with which the mountain covers its flanks in mid-morning. Stones and mountain rubble that are frozen into place through the night are released by the melting touch of morning sun and come arcing, bouncing, and crashing down from the vast collection trough of the White Spider, directly, although distantly, above them. The normal line of ascent is well to the west of this natural line of fire.

"We shall allow the mountain to dump out her morning garbage before we try the chute," Karl announced. "Meanwhile, let us enjoy the scenery and have a bite to eat. Yes?"

Jonathan read in Karl's artificial cheer that he, too, was affected by the roar of water rushing down the chute, but it was equally obvious that he would not be receptive to criticism or advice.

Nevertheless: "Sounds like we have a wet time ahead of us, Karl."

"Surely, Herr Doctor, you have no objection to a morning shower."

"It's going to take a lot out of us, even if it is a go."

"Yes. Mountain climbing is demanding."

"Snot."

"What?"

"Nothing."

Jean-Paul took another drink of water then passed the plastic canteen over to

Karl, who returned it, declining to drink. After he had struggled the bottle into his pack, Jean-Paul looked out over the valley with awe and appreciation. "Beautiful, isn't it. Really beautiful. Anna is probably watching us through a telescope at this very moment."

"Probably," Jonathan said, doubting it.

"We'll take the chute in a rope of four," Karl said. "I shall lead: Anderl will bring up the rear."

Jonathan attended again to the sound of the water. "This route would be easier in winter when there is less melt."

Anderl laughed. "Do you suggest we wait?"

Ben heard a bustle of excited talk on the terrace beneath his window, and a distinctly Texan voice epitomized the multilingual dirge of complaint.

"Shee-it! How about that? I use my tickets up watching them sit on the rock, then as soon as my time's over, they start doing something. Hey, Floyd? How much was that in real money?"

Ben ran down from his room and into the meadow, well away from the hotel and the Eiger Birds. It took him ten minutes to set up his telescope. From the first, this long diagonal chute of Karl's had worried him more than any other pitch on the climb. The distant face sharpened into focus, then blurred past it, then emerged clear in the eyepiece again. He began at the bottom of the chute and panned up and right, following the dark scar up the face. There was a fuzz of spray at the outlet of the chute that told him it must be a veritable river of rushing melt water, and he knew the climbers would have to fight their way upstream through it, the flow tugging them away from their holds, all the while exposed to the hazards of rock fall that rattled through this natual channel. His palms were clammy by the time he picked up the lowest climber. Yellow jacket: that would be Anderl. And up the thin spider thread of rope to a white jacket: Jean-Paul. Above him was the pale blue windbreaker of Jonathan. Karl was out of sight behind a fold of rock. They were moving erratically and very slowly. That gush of water and ice fragments must be hell, Ben thought. Why don't they break off? Then he realized that they could not retreat. Once committed in a string of four to pressing up through the weight of rushing water, they had to go on. The slightest easing off, the slightest cooperation with the downward flow, and they stood a good chance of tumbling down through the channel and arcing out through the fuzz of spray into the void.

At least they were moving up; that was something. They climbed one at a time, while the others found what purchase they could to protect the vulnerable climber. Perhaps Karl had found a secure stance up there out of sight, Ben told himself. Perhaps they were safer than they seemed.

There was a sudden tension in the string of colored dots.

They were no longer moving. Ben's experience told him something had happened.

He cursed at not being able to see better. A slight, impatient movement of the telescope, and he lost them. He swore aloud and located them again in the eyepiece. The thread above Anderl was slack. White jacket—Bidet—was hanging upside down. He had fallen. The rope above him was taut and led up to blue jacket—Jonathan, who was stretched out spread-eagle on the rock. That meant he had been pulled off his stance and was holding his own weight and Bidet's with his hands.

"Where the hell's Karl!" Ben shouted. "Goddam his ass!"

Jonathan clenched his teeth and concentrated his whole being on keeping his fingers curled into the crack above him. He was alone in an agony of effort, isolated by the deafening roar of water just to his left. A steady, numbing stream flowed down his sleeves and froze his armpits and chest. He did not waste breath shouting. He knew that Anderl below would do what he could, and he hoped Karl above and out of sight had found a crack for a piton and was holding them in a strong stance. The dead weight of Jean-Paul on the rope around his waist was squeezing the air out of him, and he did not know how long he could hold on. A quick look over his shoulder revealed that Anderl was already scrambling, open and unprotected, up through the roaring trough toward Bidet, who had not stirred since the rock that had sung past Jonathan's ear had struck him on the shoulder and knocked him out of his stance. Jean-Paul lay head downward in the middle of the torrent, and the thought flashed through Jonathan's mind that it would be ridiculous to die of drowning on a mountain.

His hands no longer ached; there was no feeling at all. He could not tell if he was gripping hard enough to hold, so he squeezed until the muscles in his forearms throbbed. If water or rock knocked Anderl off, he would never be able to hold them both. What in hell was Karl up to!

Then the rope slackened around his middle, and a surge of expanding pain replaced the pressure. Anderl had reached Jean-Paul and had jammed his body crosswise in the chute, holding Bidet in his lap to give Jonathan the slack he needed to recover his stance.

Jonathan pulled upward until his arms vibrated with the effort, and after interminable seconds, one boot found a toehold and the weight was off his hands. They were cut, but not too deeply, and the flow of icy water prevented them from throbbing. As quickly as he dared, he uncoiled enough rope to allow him to climb up, and he followed the arcing line of rope up and around a fold of rock where he found Karl.

"Help me!"

"What's the matter?" Karl had found a niche and was braced in it to belay the climbers below. He had been totally unaware of the crisis beneath him.

"Pull!" Jonathan shouted, and by main strength they dragged Bidet up away from Anderl's wedged body. Not a moment too soon. The strong Austrian's legs had begun to quiver with the task of holding Bidet up.

Anderl bypassed Jean-Paul's inert body and climbed up to the stance recently occupied by Jonathan. Bidet was safe now, held from two points of purchase. From their position, neither Jonathan nor Karl could see what was occurring below, but Anderl told them later that Jean-Paul had a comically quizzical expression on his face as he returned to consciousness and found himself dangling in a vertical river. The falling rock had done him no real damage, but he had struck his head hard against the face when he fell. With the automatic responses of the climber prevailing over his dizziness, he began to scramble up. And before long the four of them were crowded into Karl's small, secure niche.

When the last jacket disappeared behind the fold of rock at the top of the chute, Ben stood up from his telescope and drew the first full breath he had taken in ten minutes. He looked around for deep grass, and he vomited.

Two of the young climbers who had been standing by, concerned and helpless, turned away to give Ben privacy. They grinned at each other out of embarrassment.

"Wet and cold, but not much the worse for wear," Karl diagnosed. "And the worst of it is behind us. You really needn't be so glum, Herr Doctor."

"We can't get back through that chute," Jonathan said with finality.

"Fortunately, we shall not have to."

"If it comes to a retreat—"

"You have a Maginot mentality, Herr Doctor. We shall not retreat. We shall simply climb up out of this face."

Jonathan felt a hot resentment at Karl's bravado, but he said nothing more. Instead, he turned to Anderl who shivered on the ledge beside him. "Thank you, Anderl. You were fine."

Anderl nodded, not egotistically, but in genuine appreciation of the sureness and correctness of his actions. He received his own critical approval. Then he looked up at Karl. "You didn't know we were in trouble?"

"No."

"You didn't feel it on the line?"

"No."

"That is not good."

Anderl's simple evaluation stung Karl more than recriminations could have.

Jonathan envied Anderl his composure, sitting there on the lip of rock, looking out over the abyss, musing into space. Jonathan was in no way composed. He shivered, wet through and cold, and he was still nauseated with the sudden spurt of adrenalin.

Bidet, for his part, sat next to Jonathan, gingerly touching the bump on the side of his head. He suddenly laughed aloud. "It's strange, isn't it? I remember nothing after the stone knocked me off my stance. It must have been quite an event. Pity I slept through it."

"That's the spirit!" Karl said, slightly accenting the first word to differentiate between Jean-Paul's attitude and Jonathan's. "Now, we shall rest here for a moment and collect our senses, then up we go! From my study of the route, the next four hundred meters should be child's play."

Every fiber of Ben's body was weary, drained by the sympathetic tensions and physical stresses with which he had tried to help the climbers, conducting their movements, as it were, by kinesthetic telepathy. His eyes burned with strain, and the muscles of his face were set in grooves of concern. He had to give a grudging credit to Karl who, once the torrent of the chute was behind, had led the party up in a clean, rapid ascent of the virgin rock; up past the windows of the Eigerwand Station and through a long gully packed with snow and ice that brought them to a prominent pillar standing out from the rock pitch separating the First and Second Ice Fields. Making that pillar had consumed two hours of desperate climbing. After two unsuccessful attempts, Karl had disemburdened himself of his pack and had attacked it with such acrobatic abandon that he had received an unheard flutter of applause from the hotel terrace when he topped it. Belayed from above, the other climbers had made the pillar with relative ease.

Following its diurnal custom, Eiger's cloudcap descended and concealed the climbers for two hours in the afternoon, during which time Ben relaxed his cramped back and responded to insistent reporters with grunts and monosyllabic profanity. Those Eiger Birds who had been cheated of their turns to ogle and thrill complained bitterly, but the hotel management was adamant in its refusal to refund money, explaining with uncharacteristic humility that it could not control acts of God.

Moving rapidly to conserve what daylight they had, the team climbed up through the mist, ascending the ice couloir that bridges the Second and Third Ice Fields. When the clouds lifted, Ben could see them making what appeared to be a safe, if uncomfortable bivouac a little to the left of the Flatiron and below Death Bivouac. Sure the day's climbing was done, Ben allowed himself to break the invisible thread of observation that had bound him to the climbers. He was satisfied with the day's work. More than half the face was beneath them. Others had climbed higher the first day (indeed, Waschak and Forstenlachner had climbed the face in a single stretch of eighteen hours through ideal weather conditions), but none had done better over an unexplored path. From this point on, they would be following the classic route, and Ben felt more confident of their chances—providing the weather held.

Drained of energy and a little sick with the acid lump in his stomach, Ben folded up the legs of his telescope and walked heavily across the terrace. He had not eaten since breakfast, although he had fortified himself with six bottles of German beer. He paid no attention to the Eiger Birds still clustered around the telescopes. And indeed, the Birds' attention was wandering away from the climbers who, it seemed, would be running no further risks that day and providing no further excitement.

"Isn't that precious!" one of the rigorously made-up older women gushed to her paid companion, who dutifully squeezed her hand and pointed his Italian profile in the required direction. "Those little flecks of cloud!" the woman rhapsodized, "all pink and golden in the last light of day! They're really very, very pretty."

Ben looked up and froze. Ripples of buttermilk cloud were scudding in rapidly from the southeast. A *foehn*.

Attacking the reluctant Swiss telephone system with desperate tenacity, and crippled by his lack of German, Ben finally contacted the meteorological center. He discovered that the foehn had run into the Bernese Oberland without warning. It would hold through the night, bringing fierce storms to the Eiger face and melting out much of the snow and ice with its eerie press of warm air, but they assured Ben that a strong high descending from the north would drive the foehn out by midday. With the high, however, was expected record cold.

Ben replaced the phone in its cradle and stared sightlessly at the mnemonic graffiti on the wall of the telephone *cabine*.

A storm and a melt, followed by record cold. The entire face would be glazed with a crust of ice. Ascent would be impossible; retreat would be extremely difficult, and, if the Hinterstossier Traverse were heavily iced over, equally impossible. He wondered if the climbers in their precarious bivouac knew what Eiger Weather had done for them.

The two slight lips of rock they had found were scarcely adequate for bivouac, but they had decided against climbing on through the last half hour of light and running the risk of night finding them with no shelter at all. They had perched in their order on the rope; Karl and Jonathan occupying the higher ledge, Anderl and Jean-Paul taking the lower, slightly wider site. Scooping out snow with their ice axes and driving in a pattern of pitons on which to secure themselves and their gear, they nested as well as the stingy face would allow. By the time bivouac was made, the first bold stars had penetrated the darkening sky. Night descended quickly, and the sky was seeded with bright, cold, indifferent stars. From that north face, they had no hint of the foehn storm closing in on them from the southeast.

A collapsible spirit burner balanced tentatively on the slim ledge between him and Jean-Paul, Anderl brewed cup after cup of tepid tea made from water that boiled before it was really hot. They were close enough to pass the cups around, and they drank with silent relish. Although each man forced himself to swallow a few morsels of solid food, glutinous and tasteless in their desiccated mouths, it was the tea that satisfied their cold and thirst. The brewing went on for an hour, the tea relieved occasionally by a cup of bouillon.

Jonathan struggled into his eider-filled sleeping bag and found that, by forcing himself to relax, he could control the chattering of his teeth. Save when he had actually been climbing, the cold that followed their drenching in the frigid water of the chute had made him shudder convulsively, wasting his energy and eroding his nerves. The ledge was so narrow that he had to sit astride his pack to cling without continuous effort, and even then his position was almost vertical. His rope harness was connected to the pitons behind by two separate ropes, just in case Karl should attempt to cut one while he dozed. Although Jonathan took this sensible precaution, he considered himself to be fairly safe. The men below could not reach him easily, and his position directly above them meant that if Karl knocked or cut him off, his fall would carry the other two with him, and he doubted that Karl would care to be on the face alone.

After his own safety, Jonathan was most concerned about Jean-Paul, who had made only the most minimal arrangements for comfort. Now he slumped his weight against the restraining pitons and stared down into the black valley, receiving the proffered cups of tea dumbly. Jonathan knew there was something very wrong.

The rope connecting two men on a mountain is more than nylon protection; it is an organic thing that transmits subtle messages of intent and disposition from man to man; it is an extension of the tactile senses, a psychological bond, a wire along which currents of communication flow. Jonathan had felt the energy and desperate determination of Karl above him, and he had sensed the vague and desultory movements of Jean-Paul below—odd manic pulses of strength alternating with the almost subliminal drag of uncertainty and confusion.

As the fall of night combined with their physical inactivity to give the cold a penetrating edge, Anderl shook Jean-Paul out of his funk and helped him struggle into his sleeping bag. Jonathan recognized from Anderl's solicitude that he, too, had sensed something defocused and queer through the rope that had connected his nervous system to Jean-Paul's

Jonathan broke the silence by calling down, "How's it going, Jean-Paul?"

Jean-Paul twisted in his harness and looked up with an optimistic grin. Blood was oozing from his nostrils and ears, and the irises of his eyes were contracted. Major concussion.

"I feel wonderful, Jonathan. But it's strange, isn't it? I remember nothing after the stone knocked me off my stance. It must have been quite an event. Pity I slept through it."

Karl and Jonathan exchanged glances. Karl was going to say something when he was interrupted by Anderl.

"Look! The stars!"

Wisps of cloud were racing between them and the stars, alternately revealing and concealing their twinkle in a strange undulating pattern. Then, suddenly, the stars were gone.

The eeriness of the effect was compounded by the fact that there was no wind on the face. For the first time in Jonathan's memory, the air on Eiger was still. And, more ominous yet, it was warm.

No one spoke to break the hush. The thick plasticity of the night reminded Jonathan of typhoons in the South China Sea.

Then, low at first but increasing in volume, came a hum like the sound of a large dynamo. The drone seemed to come from the depths of the rock itself. There was the bitter-sweet smell of ozone. And Jonathan found himself staring at the head of his ice axe, only two feet from him. It was surrounded by a greenish halo of St. Elmo's fire that flickered and pulsed before it arced with a cracking flash into the rock.

Faithful to the last to his Teutonic penchant for underlining the obvious, Karl's lips formed the word, *"foehn!"* just as the first rock-shaking explosion of thunder obliterated the sound of the word.

Eiger: *July 12*

BEN SNAPPED UP from a shallow doze with the gasp of a man drowning in his own unconsciousness. The distant roar of avalanche bridged between his chaotic sleep and the bright, unreal hotel lobby. He blinked and looked around, trying to set himself in time and space. Three in the morning. Two rumpled reporters slept in chairs, sprawled loose-hinged like discarded mannikins. The night clerk transferred information from a list to file cards, his movements somnolent and automatic. The scratch of his pen carried across the room. When Ben rose from his chair, sweat adhered his buttocks and back to the plastic uphostery. The room was cool enough; it was the dreams that had sweated him.

He stretched the kinks out of his back. Thunder rumbled distantly, and the noise was trebled by the crisper sound of snowslide. He crossed the lobby and looked onto the deserted terrace, lifeless in the slanting light through the window, like a stage setting stored in the wings. It was no longer raining in the valley. All the storm had collected up in the concave amphitheatre of the Eigerwand. And even there it was losing its crescendo as a frigid high from the north drove it out. It would be clear by dawn and the face would be visible—if there were anything to be seen.

The elevator doors clattered open, the noise uncommonly loud because it was not buried in the ambient sound of the day. Ben turned and watched Anna walk toward him, her poise and posture betrayed by makeup that was thirty hours old.

She stood close to him, looking out the window. There had been no greetings. "The weather is clearing a little, it seems," she said.

"Yes." Ben did not feel like talking.

"I just heard that Jean-Paul had an accident."

"You *just* heard?"

She turned toward him and spoke with odd angry intensity. "Yes, I just heard it. From a young man I was with. Does that shock you?" She was bitter and punishing herself.

Ben continued to stare dully into the night. "I don't care who you fuck, lady."

She lowered her lashes and sighed on a tired intake of breath that fluttered. "Was Jean-Paul hurt badly?"

Ben inadvertently paused half a beat before answering. "No."

Anna examined his broad, heavily lined face. "You are lying, of course."

Another, more distant roll of thunder echoed from the mountain. Ben slapped the back of his neck and turned away from the window to cross the lobby. Anna followed.

Ben asked the desk clerk if he could get him a couple of bottles of beer. The clerk was effusive in his regrets, but at that hour there was no way within the rigid boundaries of his printed instructions that he could accommodate.

"I have brandy in my room," Anna offered.

"No thanks." Ben cocked his head and looked at her. "All right. Fine.'

In the elevator Anna said, "You didn't answer when I said you were lying. Does that mean Jean-Paul's fall was serious?"

Fatigue from his long watch was seeping in and saturating his body. "I don't know," he admitted. "He moved funny after his fall. Not like something was broken, but—funny. I got the feeling he was hurt."

Anna unlocked the door to her room and walked in ahead of Ben, turning on the lights as she passed through. Ben paused for a moment before entering. "Come in, Mr. Bowman. What is wrong?" She laughed dryly. "Oh, I see. You half expected to see the young man I mentioned." She poured out a liberal portion of brandy and returned to him with it. "No, Mr. Bowman. Never in the bed I share with my husband."

"You draw the line in funny places. Thanks." He downed the drink.

"I love Jean-Paul."

"Uh-huh."

"I did not say I was true to him physically; I said I love him. Some women have needs beyond the capacities of their men. Like alcoholics, they are to be pitied."

"I'm tired, lady."

"Do you think I am trying to seduce you?"

"I have testicles. There don't seem to be any other requirements."

Anna retreated into laughter. Then instantly she was serious. "They will get down alive, won't they?"

The brandy worked quickly up the dry wick of Ben's worn body. He had to struggle against relaxation. "I don't know. They may be. . . ." He set down the glass. "Thanks. I'll see you around." He started for the door.

She finished the thought with atonic calm. "They may be dead already."

"It's possible."

After Ben left, Anna sat at her dressing table, idly lifting and dropping the cut glass stopper of a perfume bottle. She was at least forty.

The four figures were as motionless as the mountain they huddled against. Their clothing was stiff with a brittle crust of ice, just as the rock was glazed over with a shell of frozen rain and melt water. It was not yet dawn, but the saturation of night was diluting in the east. Jonathan could dimly make out the ice-scabbed folds of his waterproof trousers. He had been crouched over for hours, staring sightlessly into his lap, ever since the force of the storm had abated sufficiently to allow him to open his eyes. Despite the penetrating cold that followed the storm, he had not moved a muscle. His cringing posture was exactly what it had been when the foehn struck, tucked up in as tight a ball as his stance permitted, offering the elements the smallest possible target.

It had broken upon them without warning, and it was not possible to reckon the time it had lasted—one interminable moment of terror and chaos compounded of driving rain and stinging hail, of tearing wind that lashed around them and wedged itself between man and rock, trying to drive them apart. There were blinding flashes and blind darkness, pain from clinging and numbness from the cold. But most of all there had been sound: the deafening crack of thunder close at hand, the persistent scream of the wind, the roar and clatter of the avalanche spilling to the right and left and bouncing in eccentric patterns over the outcropping of rock that protected them.

It was quiet now. The storm was gone.

The torrent of sensation had washed Jonathan's mind clean, and thought returned slowly and in rudimentary forms. He told himself in simple words that he was looking at his pants. Then he reasoned that they were covered with a crust of ice. Eventually, he interpreted the pain as cold. And only then, with doubt and wonder, but no excitement, he knew that he was alive. He must be.

The storm was over, but the dark and the cold only slowly retreated from his consciousness, and the transition from pain and storm to calm and cold was an imperceptible blend. His body and nerves remembered the fury, and his senses told him it had passed, but he could recall neither the end of the storm nor the beginning of the calm.

He moved his arm, and there was a noise, a tinkling clatter as his movement broke the crust of ice on his sleeve. He clenched and unclenched his fists and pressed his toes against the soles of his boots, forcing his thickened blood out to his extremities. The numbness phased into electric tingle, then into throbbing pain, but these were not unpleasant sensations because they were proofs of life. The dark had retreated enough for him to make out Karl's bowed and unmoving back a few feet from him, but he wasted no thought on Karl's condition; all his attention was focused on the returning sense of life within himself.

There was a sound just beneath him.

"Anderl?" Jonathan's voice was clogged and dry.

Anderl stirred tentatively, like a man checking to see if things were still working. His coating of ice shattered with his movement and tinkled down the face. "There was a storm last night." His voice was gruffly gay. "I imagine you noticed."

With the advance of dawn came a wind, persistent, dry, and very cold. Anderl squinted at his wrist altimeter. "It reads forty meters low," he announced matter-of-factly. Jonathan nodded. Forty meters low. That meant the barometric pressure was two points higher than normal. They were in a strong, cold high that might last any amount of time.

He saw Anderl move cautiously along his ledge to attend to Jean-Paul, who had not yet stirred. A little later Anderl set to the task of brewing tea on the spirit stove, which he placed for balance against Jean-Paul's leg.

Jonathan looked around. The warmth of the foehn had melted the surface snow, and it had frozen again with the arrival of the cold front. An inch of ice crusted the snow, slippery and sharp, but not strong enough to bear a man's weight. The rocks were glazed with a coat of frozen melt water, impossible to cling to, but the crust was too thin to take an ice piton. In the growing light, he assessed the surface conditions. They were the most treacherous possible.

Karl moved. He had not slept, but like Anderl and Jonathan he had been deep in a protective cocoon of semiconsciousness. Pulling himself out of it, he went smoothly and professionally through the task of checking the pitons that supported him and Jonathan, then he exercised isometrically to return circulation to his hands and feet, after which he began the simple but laborious job of getting food from his kit—frozen chocolate and dried meat. All through this, he did not speak. He was humbled and visibly shaken by the experiences of the night. He was no longer a leader.

Anderl twisted against the rope holding him into his nook and stretched up to offer Jonathan a cup of tepid tea. "Jean-Paul . . ."

Jonathan drank it down in one avaricious draught. "What about him?" He passed the metal cup back down and licked the place where his lip had adhered to it and torn.

"He is dead." Anderl refilled the cup and offered it up to Karl. "Must have gone during the storm," he added quietly.

Karl received the tea and held it between his palms as he stared down at the rumpled and ice-caked form that had been Jean-Paul.

"Drink it," Jonathan ordered but Karl did not move. He breathed orally in short, shallow breaths over the top of the cup, and the puffs of vapor mixed with the steam rising off the tea.

"How do you know he is dead?" Karl asked in an unnaturally loud, monotonic voice.

"I looked at him," Anderl said as he refilled the small pot with ice chips.

"You saw he was dead! And you set about making a cup of tea!"

Anderl shrugged. He did not bother to look up from his work.

"Drink the tea," Jonathan repeated. "Or pass it over here and let me have it before it gets cold."

Karl gave him a look saturated with disgust, but he drank the tea.

"He had a concussion," Anderl said. "The storm was too much. The man inside could not keep the man outside from dying."

For the next hour, they swallowed what food they could, exercised isometrically to fight the cold, and placated their endless thirsts with cup after cup of tea and bouillon. It was impossible to drink enough to satisfy themselves, but there came a time when they must move on, so Anderl drank off the last of the melted ice and replaced the pot and collapsible stove in his pack.

When Jonathan outlined his proposal for action, Karl did not resist the change in leadership. He had lost the desire to make decisions. Again and again his attention strayed and his eyes fixed on the dead man beneath him. His mountain experience had not included death.

Jonathan surveyed their situation in a few words. Both the rock and the snow were coated over with a crust of ice that made climbing up out of the question. A frigid high, such as the one then punishing them with cold could last for days, even weeks. They could not hole up where they were. They must retreat.

To return down Karl's chute was out of the question. It would be iced over. Jonathan proposed that they try to get down to a point just above the Eigerwand Station Window. It was just possible that they might be able to rope down from there, despite the beetling overhang. Ben, waiting and watching them from the ground, would realize their intention, and he would be waiting with help at the Window.

As he spoke, Jonathan read in Anderl's face that he had no great faith in their chances of roping down from above the Station Window, but he did not object, realizing that for reasons of morale, if nothing else, they had to move out. They must not stay there and face the risk of freezing to death in bivouac as, years before, Sedlmayer and Mehringer had done not a hundred meters above them.

Jonathan organized the rope. He would lead, slowly cutting big, tublike steps in the crusted snow. Karl would be next on the rope. A second, independent line would suspend Jean-Paul's body between them. In this way Karl could belay and protect Jonathan without the additional drag of Jean-Paul, then, when they were both in established stances, they could maneuver the load down, Jonathan guiding it away from snags, Karl holding back against gravity. As the strongest in the party, Anderl would be last on the rope, always seeking a protected stance in case a slip suddenly gave him the weight of all three.

Although the dangers of the descent were multiplied by bringing Jean-Paul with them, no one thought of leaving him behind. It was mountain tradition to bring your dead with you. And no one wanted to please the Eiger Birds by leaving a grisly memento on the face that would tingle and delight them at their telescopes for weeks or months until a rescue team could retrieve it.

As they packed up and tied Jean-Paul into the sleeping bag that would act as a canvas sled, Karl grumbled half-heartedly against the bad luck that had kept them from bagging the mountain. Anderl did not mind retreating. With surface conditions like these, it was equally difficult to move in either direction, and for him the challenge of climbing was the point of it all.

Watching the two men at their preparations, Jonathan knew he had nothing to fear from his sanction target, whoever it was. If they were to get down alive, they would have to cooperate with every fiber of their combined skill and strength. The matter would be settled in the valley, if they reached the flat land intact. In fact, the whole matter of his SS assignment had the unreal qualities of a fantastic operetta, viewed in terms of the grim presence of the mountain.

The descent was torturously slow. The frozen crust of the snow was such that at one step the surface was so hard the crampons would take no bite, but at the next the leg would break through to the softer snow below and balance would be lost. The snowfield clung to the face at an angle of 50°, and Jonathan had to lean out and down from the edge of each big step to chop out the next with his ice axe. He could not be content with those stylish toe steps that can be formed with two skillful swings of the axe; he had to hack out vast tubs, big enough to hold him as he leaned out for the next, and big enough to allow Anderl to take a belaying stance at each step.

The routine was complicated and expensive of energy. Jonathan moved down alone for one rope length, belayed from above by Karl who, in turn, was held by Anderl. Then he cut out an especially broad stance from the protection of which he carefully guided Jean-Paul's body down to him as Karl let the burden slip bit by bit, always fighting its tendency to tear itself from his grip and fly down the face carrying all of them with it. When the canvas bundle reached Jonathan, he secured it as best he could, driving Jean-Paul's ice axe into the crust and using it as a tie-off. Then Karl came down to join him, moving much more quickly down the big steps. The third phase of the pattern was the most dangerous. Anderl had to move down half the distance to them, where he could jam himself into one of the better steps and set his body to protect them through the next repetition of the cycle. Anderl moved essentially without protection, save for the "psychological rope" that regularly slackened between him and Karl. Any slip might knock his fellow climbers out of their step or, even should his line of fall miss them, they would have very little chance of withstanding the shock of a fall twice the length of the rope. Anderl knew his responsibility and moved with great care, although he continually called down to them cheerfully, grousing about the pace or the weather or any other trivial matter that came to mind.

Slow though their progress was, for Jonathan, who had to cut each of the steps and who could rest only while the others closed up from above, it was desperately tiring.

Three hours; two hundred and fifty meters.

He panted with exertion; the cold air seared his lungs; his arm was leaden with swinging the axe. And when he stopped to receive Jean-Paul and let the others close up, one torture was exchanged for another. At each rest, the frigid wind attacked him, freezing the perspiration to his body and racking him with convulsions of shivering. He wept with the pain of fatigue and cold, and the tears froze on his stubbled cheeks.

The goal of the cliffs above the Eigerwand Station was too demoralizingly distant to consider. He concentrated on objectives within human scope: one more swing of the axe, one more step to hack out. Then move on.

Five hours; three hundred twenty-five meters.

Progress diminishing. Must rest.

Jonathan conned his body, lured it into action. One more step then you can rest. It's all right. It's all right. Now, just one more step.

The jagged edges of the ice crust around each deep step cut through his waterproof pants as he leaned out. It cut through his ski pants. It cut into his flesh, but the cold dulled the hurt.

One more step, then you can rest.

Since the first light of dawn Ben had been in the meadow, scanning the face with his telescope. The young climbers who had volunteered for the rescue grouped themselves around him, their faces tight with concern. No one could recall weather this cold so late in the season, and they estimated in low voices what it must be like up on the face.

Ben had prepared himself psychologically to find nothing on the face. In his mind he had rehearsed the calm way he would stroll back to the hotel and send off telegrams to the Alpine Clubs sponsoring the climbers. Then he would wait in his room, perhaps for days, until the weather softened and he could organize a team to recover the bodies. He promised himself one petcock for his emotions. He was going to hit somebody: a reporter, or better yet an Eiger Bird.

He swept the telescope back and forth over the dark crease beside the Flatiron where, just before nightfall, he had seen them making bivouac. Nothing. Their clothing iced over, the climbers blended invisibly into the glazed rock.

On the hotel terrace Eiger Birds were already queued up at the telescopes, stamping about to warm themselves, and receiving great bowls of steaming coffee from scuttling waiters. The first rumors that there was nothing to be seen on the face had galvanized the tourists. Hungry for sensation and eager to display depths of human sympathy, Eiger Hens told one another how terrible it all was, and how they had had premonitions during the night. One of the twits Anderl had used burst suddenly into tears and ran back into the hotel, refusing to be consoled by her friends. When they took her at her word and left her alone in the empty lobby for twenty full minutes, she found the inner resources to return to the terrace, red-eyed but brave.

The Eiger Cocks nodded to one another significantly and said that they had known it all along. If anyone had had the sense to ask their advice, they would have told them that the weather looked ugly and changeable.

Muffled up securely against the cold, and convoyed by a solicitous entourage, the Greek merchant and his American wife walked through the crowd which grew silent and pressed back to make way for them. Nodding to the left and right, they assumed their roles as major mourners, and everyone said how especially hard this must be on them. Their tent had been kept warm through the night by two portable gas stoves, but still they had to endure the rigors of chill wind as they took turns rising from breakfast to scan the mountain with the telescope that had been reserved for their private use.

Ben stood in the meadow, sipping absently at the tin cup of coffee one of the young climbers had pressed anonymously into his hand. A murmur, then a squealing cheer came from the terrace. Someone had spied a trace of movement.

He dropped the cup on the rimed grass and was at the eyepiece in an instant. There were three of them moving slowly downward. Three—and something else. A bundle. Once they were well out onto the snow, Ben could make out the colors of their windbreakers. Blue (Jonathan) was in the lead. He was moving down very slowly, evidently cutting out wide steps of the kind that cost time and energy. He inched down almost a rope's length before the second man—red (Karl)—began to lower a gray-green something—lump—down to him. Then Karl descended relatively quickly to join Jonathan. The last—yellow (Anderl)—climbed carefully down, stopping halfway and setting a deep belay. There was no one behind Anderl.

The bundle must be Jean-Paul. Injured . . . or dead.

Ben could imagine what that surface must be like after the melting foehn and the hard freeze. A treacherous scab of ice that might pull away from the under snow at any time.

For twenty minutes Ben remained at the telescope, his tightly reined body aching to do something helpful, but uncertain of the intentions of the climbers. Finally, he forced himself to straighten up and stop the torment of guessing and hoping. At their terribly slow pace, it would be hours before he could be certain of how they would try to execute their retreat. He preferred to wait in his room where no one could observe his vicarious fear. They might attempt the long traverse over the classic route. Or they might retrace their line of ascent, forgetting that Karl's chute was iced over now. There was a third possibility, one Ben prayed Jonathan would have vision enough to elect. They might try for the cliffs above the Eigerwand Station Window. It was remotely possible that a man might rope down to the safety of that lateral gallery. No one had ever attempted it, but it seemed the best of a bad lot of alternatives.

"Morning! Are you going to be using your telescope?"

Ben turned to see the confident, boyish smile of the actor beaming at him. The stiffly made-up actress wife stood beside her husband, her sagging throat bound up in a bright silk neckerchief, shivering in the stylish ski clothes that had been specifically designed to make her appear taller and less dumpy.

The actor modulated richly, "The lady would hate to go home without having seen anything, but we really can't have her standing around in line with those other people. I know you understand that."

"You want to use *my* telescope?" Ben asked, unbelieving.

"Tell him we'll pay for it, love," the wife inserted, then she blessed the young climbers with her handsome eyes.

The actor smiled and used his most chocolate voice. "Of course we'll pay for it." He reached out for the instrument, smiling all the while his effective, disarming grin.

Contrary to subsequent news reports, Ben never really hit him.

The actor reacted to the flash of Ben's hand and winced away with surprising celerity. The movement cost him his balance, and he fell on his back on the frozen ground. Instantly, the wife screamed and threw herself over her fallen mate to protect him from further brutality. Ben snatched her up by the hair and bent over them, speaking in rapid, hushed tones. "I'm going up to my room, and I'm leaving this telescope right where it is. If either of you fucking ghouls touches it, your doctor's going to have one hell of a time getting it out."

He walked away to the sound of laughter from the young climbers and a spate of scatological vitriol from the actress that revealed her familiarity with most of the sexual variants.

Ben bore across the terrace with his energetic, hopping stride, not swerving an inch from his course through the milling crowd, and taking a retributive pleasure in each jolting impact that left one of the Eiger Birds dazed and startled in his wake. In the deserted bar he ordered three bottles of beer and a sandwich. While he waited, Anna approached, pressing through the terrace throng to join him. He did not want to talk to her, but the barman was slow.

"Is Jean-Paul all right?" She asked as she neared him.

"No!" He took up the clinking bottles between the fingers of one hand and the sandwich in the other, and he left the bar for his room.

He ate and drank sitting morosely on the edge of his bed. Then he lay down, his fingers locked behind his head, staring at the ceiling. Then he got up and walked around the room, pausing at the window at each circuit. Then he lay down again. And got up again. Two hours dragged on in this way before he gave up the attempt to rest.

At the telescope in the meadow again, Ben was nearly certain that the climbers were making for the cliffs above the station window. They were near the edge of a rock pitch that separates the ice field from the small shelf of snow above the window. The distance between them and safety could be covered by a thumb at arm's length, but Ben knew there were hours of labor and risk in that stretch. And the sun was slipping down. He had made arrangements for a special train to carry the rescue team up the cogwheel railroad that bore through the heart of the mountain. They would depart when the time was right and be at the window to receive the climbers.

He hunched over his telescope, pouring sympathetic energy up the line of visual contact.

His whole body jolted convulsively when he saw Anderl slip.

There was a grating sound, and Anderl realized the surface was moving beneath him. A vast scab of crusted snow had loosened from the face and was slipping down, slowly at first, and he was in the middle of the doomed island. It was no use digging in; that would be like clinging to a falling boulder. Reacting automatically, he scrambled upward, seeking firm snow. Then he was tumbling sideward. He spread his limbs to stop the deadly roll and plunged his axe into the surface, covering it with his body. And still he slipped down and sideward, a deep furrow above him from the dig of his axe.

Jonathan had been huddled with Karl and Jean-Paul in the deep step he had just cut out. His eyes were fixed on the snow before him, his mind empty, and he shivered convulsively as he had at each *étape*. At Karl's shout, a sudden squirt of adrenalin stopped the shivering instantly and, his eyes glazed with fatigue, he watched with a stupid calm the snowslide come at him.

Karl pushed Jonathan down upon the encased corpse and covered both with his body, locking his fingers around the ice axe that was their belay point. The avalanche roared over them, deafening and suffocating, clutching at them, piling up under them and trying to tug them away from their step.

And with a sudden ringing silence, it was over.

Jonathan clawed his way up past Karl's limp body and scooped the fresh snow out of the step. Then Karl scrambled up, panting, his hands bleeding, skin still stuck to the cold axe. Jean-Paul was half covered with snow, but he was still there.

"I can't move!" The voice was not far from them.

Anderl was spread-eagled on the surface of the snow, his feet not three meters from the edge of the rock cliff. The snowslide had carried him down, then had capriciously veered aside, over the others, and left him face down, his body still covering the axe that had broken his slide. He was unhurt, but each attempt to move caused him to slip downward a few inches. He tried twice, then had the good judgment to remain still.

He was just out of reach, and the freshly uncovered snow was too unstable to be crossed. The rope from Karl to Anderl lay in a hairpin loop up toward his earlier stance and back sharply, but only the two ends of it emerged from the snow that had buried it.

Anderl slipped down several inches, this time without attempting to move.

Jonathan and Karl tugged and whipped the rope, trying desperately to un-bury it. They dared not pull with all their strength lest it suddenly come free and precipitate them off the face.

"I feel foolish," Anderl called. And he slipped farther down.

"Shut up!" Jonathan croaked. There was nothing for an ice piton to hold onto, so he hurriedly slapped his axe and Karl's deep into the soft snow, then he laced the slack they had tugged in from Anderl's line back and forth between the two axe handles. "Lie down on that," he ordered, and Karl mutely obeyed.

Jonathan unroped himself and started up Anderl's buried line, alternately clinging to it and ripping it out of the snow. Each time he gained a little slack he lay still on the steeply inclined surface as Karl whipped the loose rope around the axes. It was all-important that there be as little slack as possible when the line came free. Once he reached the point at which the rope began to curve down toward Anderl, he had to move quickly, knowing that he must be very close to Anderl when the line came free. Movement now was most awkward, and the adrenalin that had fed Jonathan's body was burning off, leaving heavy-limbed nausea in its stead. He wrapped his legs around the rope and tugged it loose with one hand, expecting at any moment to come sliding down on top of Anderl as they both snapped to the end of their slack.

It happened when they were only ten feet apart, and fate was in a humorous mood. The line slipped slowly out of the snow and they skidded gently sideward, Jonathan atop Anderl, until they were directly below Karl and the protection of the big step, their feet overhanging the lip of the rock cliff. They scrambled up with little difficulty.

The instant he fell into the almost vertical snow cave, Jonathan collapsed from within. He crouched near Jean-Paul's body, shivering uncontrollably, limp with fatigue.

Anderl was cheerful and talkative, and Karl was obedient. Between them they widened the step, and Anderl set about making tea. The first cup he gave to Jonathan with two small red pills, heart stimulants.

"I certainly felt ridiculous out there. I wanted to laugh, but I knew that the motion would make me slip, so I bit my lip. It was wonderful the way you came out to get me, Jonathan. But in the future I wish you would not use me to ride around on like a sled. I know what you were doing. Showing off for the people down on the terrace. Right?" He babbled on, brewing tea and passing it around like a solicitous Austrian aunt.

The heart stimulant and the tea began to make inroads on Jonathan's fatigue. He practiced controlling his shivering as he stared at the maroon ooze of blood around the rips in his pants. He knew he would not be able to stand another night in open bivouac. They had to move on. His exhalations were whimpers: for him, the last stages of fatigue. He was not certain how long he could continue to wield the ice axe. The muscles of his forearms were knotted and stiff, and his grip was a thing of rusted metal. He could clamp his fist shut or release it totally, but he had no control over the middle pressures.

He knew perfectly well that, in this condition, he should not be leading. But he did not dare turn the rope over to either of the younger men. Karl had retreated into automaton depression, and Anderl's brassy chatter had a disturbing note of hysteria about it.

They collected themselves to move out. As he took the metal cup back, Anderl examined Jonathan's gray-green eyes as though seeing him for the first time. "You're very good, you know, Jonathan. I've enjoyed climbing with you."

Jonathan forced a smile. "We'll make it."

Anderl grinned and shook his head. "No, I don't think so. But we shall continue with style."

They took the cliff quickly, rappelling on a doubled rope. That which looked most daring to Eiger Birds below was in reality much less demanding than slogging down through the snowfields. Evening was setting in, so they did not waste time retrieving Anderl's rope.

Months later it could still be seen dangling there, half rotten.

One more snowfield to cross and they would be perched above the station windows. The brutal cycle began again. It was colder now with the sun going. Jonathan set his jaw and turned off his mind. He cut step after step, the shocks against the axe head traveling up his throbbing arm directly to the nape of his neck. Chop. Step down. Lean out. Chop. And shiver convulsively as the others close up. The minutes were painfully long, the hours beyond the compass of human time.

Time had been viscous for Ben too; there would have been consolation in action, but he controlled his impulse to move until he was sure of their line of descent. When he had seen the last man rappel from the cliff and move out onto the final, relatively narrow snowfield, he stood up from the telescope. "All right," he said quietly, "let's go."

The rescue team trudged to the train depot, making a wide arc around the hotel to avoid arousing the interest of reporters and rubbernecks. However, several newsmen had received reports from the PR-minded railroad authorities and were waiting at the platform. Ben was sick of dealing with them, so he did not argue about taking them along, but he made it most clear what would happen to the first man who got in the way.

Despite the arrangements made earlier, time was wasted convincing the Swiss officials that the costs of the special train would indeed be met by the organizations sponsoring the climb, but at last they were on their way, the young men sitting silently side by side in the car as it jolted and swayed up to plunge into the black of the tunnel. They reached their destination within thirty minutes.

The clatter of climbing gear and the scrape of boots echoed down the artificially lit tunnel as they walked from the Eigerwand Station platform along the slightly down-sloping lateral gallery that gave onto the observation windows. The mood of the group was such that even the reporters gave up asking stupid questions and offered to carry extra coils of rope.

With great economy of communication, the team went to work. The wooden partitions at the end of the gallery were wrenched out with ice axes (while railroad officials reminded Ben that this would have to paid for) and the first young man stepped out onto the face to plant an anchoring set of pitons. The blast of freezing air they encountered humbled them all. They knew how that cold must be sapping the strength of the men on the face.

Ben would have given anything to lead the group making the rescue, but his experience told him that these young men with all their toes intact and youthful reserves of energy could do the job better than he. Still, he had to fight the desire to make many small corrective suggestions because it seemed to him that they were doing everything just a little bit wrongly.

When the young leader had reconnoitered the face, he crawled back into the gallery. His report was not reassuring. The rock was plastered with a coating of ice half an inch thick—too thin and friable to take an ice piton, but thick enough to cover and hide such viable piton cracks as the rock beneath might have. They would have to peck away at the ice with their axes to bare the rock for each piton. And that would be slow.

But the most disturbing information was that they would not be able to move upward toward the climbers more than ten meters. Above that, the rock face beetled out in an impassable overhang. It looked as though a skillful man could move out as much as a hundred feet to the right or left from the window ledge, but not up.

As the young man gave his report, he slapped his hands against his knees to restore circulation. He had been out on the face for only twenty minutes, but the cold had stiffened and numbed his fingers. With the setting of the sun, the gallery tunnel seemed to grow palpably colder. Low-temperature records would be set that night.

Having established an anchoring base just outside the window, there was nothing to do but wait. The likelihood of the climbers chancing to rope down directly above the window was remote. Even assuming the direct line would go, they had no way to know from above exactly where the window was. Because of the overhang, the first man would be dangling out several yards from the face. They would have to inch over to him, somehow get a line out to him, and pull him in. Once that line was tied down, the retrieval of the others would be easier . . . if they had the strength left to make it down . . . if they had enough rope to pass the overhang . . . if the cold had not stupefied them . . . if their running line did not jam . . . if their anchor point above on the lip of the cliff held.

Every few minutes, one of the young men went out on the face and yodeled up. But there was no answer. Ben paced up and down the gallery, the newsmen sagely pressing against the rock walls to stay out of his way. On one return walk, he cursed and stepped out on the face himself, unroped, holding one of the anchoring pitons with one hand and leaning out with something of his former insouciant daring. "Come on, Jon!" he shouted up. "Get your ass off that hill!" No answer.

But something else struck Ben as odd. His voice had carried with abnormal crisp resonance. There was no wind on the Eiger. It was strangely still, and the cold was settling down like a silent, malignant presence. He listened to the eerie silence, broken only occasionally by the artillery crack of a random chunk of rock arcing off from somewhere above and exploding against the base far below.

When he scrambled back in through the gallery window, he slid his back down the tunnel wall and sat crouching among the waiting rescuers, hugging his knees until the shivering stopped, and licking his hand where he had left palm skin on the steel piton.

Someone lit a portable stove, and the inevitable, life-giving tea began to be passed around.

The temperature fell as the daylight at the end of the gallery grew dimmer and bluer.

One of the young men at the mouth of the tunnel yodeled, paused, and yodeled again.

And an answering call came from above!

There was a mumble of excitement in the gallery, then a sudden hush as the young climber yodeled again. And again he received a clear response. A newsman glanced at his watch and scribbled in a notepad, as Ben stepped out on the lip of the window with the three men selected to make contact with the climbers. An exchange of calls was made again. In the windless hush, it was impossible to tell how far from above the calls were coming. The yodeler tried again, and Anderl's voice replied with peculiar clarity. "What is this? A contest?"

A young Austrian in the rescue team grinned and nudged the man next to him. That was Anderl Meyer for you! But Ben detected in the sound of Anderl's voice the last desperate gesture of a proud, spent man. He lifted his hand, and those on the ledge with him were silent. There was a scuffling sound above and to the left. Someone was being lowered over the bulge of rock, far to the left, a hundred and twenty feet from safety. From the clink of snap rings. Ben knew he was coming down in an improvised harness. Then the boots appeared, and Jonathan slipped down slowly, twisting under his line, dangling some ten feet away from the face. Twilight was setting in quickly. While Jonathan continued his slow, twirling descent, the three rescuers began to traverse toward him, chipping away at the treacherous coating of ice, and rapping in pitons each time they uncovered a possible crack. Ben stayed on the ledge by the window, directing the activities of the three. There was no room out there for others who were eager to help.

Ben did not call out encouragement to Jonathan. He knew from the slump of the body in the harness that he was at the very rim of endurance after having broken the way for all three since dawn, and he had no breath to waste on talk. Ben prayed that Jonathan would not succumb to that emotional collapse so common to climbers once the end was almost within grasp.

The three young men could not move quickly. The face was almost vertical with only an iced-over ledge three inches wide for toehold. If they had not been experienced at executing tension traverses against the line, they would not have been able to move at all.

Then Jonathan stopped in mid-descent. He looked up, but could not see over the lip of the overhang.

"What's wrong up there?" Ben called.

"Rope . . . !" Anderl's voice had the gritting of teeth in it. ". . . Jammed!"

"Can you handle it?"

"No! Can Jonathan get on the face and give us a little slack?"

"No!"

There was nothing Jonathan could do to help himself. He turned slowly around on the line, six hundred feet of void below him. What he wanted most of all was to sleep.

Although he was far below them, Ben could hear the voices of Karl and Anderl through the still frigid air. He could not make out the words, but they had the sound of an angry conference.

The three young men continued to move out, now halfway to Jonathan and starting to take chances, knocking in fewer pitons to increase their speed.

"All right!" Anderl's voice called down. "I'll do what I can."

"No!" Karl screamed. "Don't move!"

"Just hold me!"

"I can't!" There was a whimper in the sound. "Anderl, I can't!"

Ben saw the snow come first, shooting over the edge of the overhang, a beautiful golden spray in the last beam of the setting sun. Automatically, he pressed back against the face. In a flash, like one alien frame cut into a movie, he saw the two dark figures rush past him, veiled in a mist of falling snow and ice. One of them struck the lip of the window with an ugly splat. And they were gone.

Snow continued to hiss past; then it stopped.

And it was silent on the face.

The three young men were safe, but frozen in their stances by what they had witnessed.

"Keep moving!" Ben barked, and they collected their emotions and obeyed.

The first shock knocked Jonathan over in his harness, and he hung upside down, swinging violently, his mind swirling in an eddy of semiconsciousness. The thing hit him again, and blood gushed from his nose. He wanted to sleep, and he did not want the thing to hit him again. That was the extent of his demands on life. But for the third time they collided. It was a glancing blow, and their ropes intertwined. Instinctively, Jonathan grasped at it and held it to him. It was Jean-Paul hanging half out of his bedroll shroud, stiff with death and cold. Jonathan clung to it.

When Anderl and Karl fell, their weight snapped the line between them and the corpse, and it tumbled over the edge and crashed down on Jonathan. It saved him from falling, counterbalancing his weight on the line that connected them and passed through a snap link and piton high above. They swung side by side in the silent cold.

"Sit up!"

Jonathan heard Ben's voice from a distance, soft and unreal.

"Sit up!"

Jonathan did not mind hanging upside down. He was through. He had had it. *Let me sleep. Why sit up.*

"Pull yourself up, goddamit!"

They won't leave me alone unless I do what they want. What does it matter? He tried to haul himself on Jean-Paul's line, but his fingers would not close. They had no feeling. *What does it matter?*

"Jon! For Christ's sake!"

"Leave me alone," he muttered. "Go away." The valley below was dark, and he did not feel cold any longer. He felt nothing at all. He was going to sleep.

No, that isn't sleep. It's something else. All right, try to sit up. Maybe then they'll leave me alone. Can't breathe. Nose stopped up with blood. Sleep.

Jonathan tried again, but his fingers throbbed., fat and useless. He reached high and wound his arm around the rope. He struggled halfway up, but his grip was slipping. Wildly, he kicked at Jean-Paul's body until he got his legs around it and managed to press himself up until his rope hit him in the forehead.

There. Sitting upright. Now leave me alone. Stupid game. Doesn't matter.

"Try to catch this!"

Jonathan squeezed his eyes shut to break the film from them. There were three men out there. Quite close. Tacked on the wall. *What the hell do they want now? Why don't they leave me alone?*

"Catch this and slip it around you!"

"Go away," he mumbled.

Ben's voice roared from the distance. "Put it around you, goddamit!"

Mustn't piss Ben off. He's mean when he's pissed off. Groggily, Jonathan struggled into the noose of the lasso. *Now that's it. Don't ask any more. Let me sleep. Stop squeezing the goddamned breath out of me!*

Jonathan heard the young men call anxiously back to Ben. "We can't pull him in! Not enough slack!"

Good. Leave me alone, then.

"Jon?" Ben's voice was not angry. He was coaxing some child. "Jon, your axe is still around your wrist."

So what?

"Cut the line above you, Jon."

Ben's gone crazy. He must need sleep.

"Cut the line, ol' buddy. It'll only be a short fall. We've got you."

Go ahead, do it. They'll keep at you until you do. He hacked blindly at the nylon line above him. Again and again with mushy strokes that seldom struck the same place twice. Then a thought slipped into his numb mind, and he stopped.

"What did he say?" Ben called to the rescuers.

"He said that Jean-Paul will fall if he cuts the line."

"Jon? Listen to me. It's all right. Jean-Paul's dead."

Dead? Oh, I remember. He's here and he's dead. Where's Anderl? Where's Karl? They're somewhere else, because they're not dead like Jean-Paul. Is that right? I don't understand it. It doesn't matter anyway. What was I doing? Oh, yes. Cut the fucking rope.

He hacked again and again.

And suddenly it snapped. For an instant the two bodies fell together, then Jean-Paul dropped away alone. Jonathan passed out with the pain of his ribs cracking as the lasso jerked tight. And that was merciful, because he did not feel the impact of his collision with the rock.

Zurich: *August 6*

JONATHAN LAY IN bed in his sterile cubicle within the labyrinthine complex of Zurich's ultramodern hospital. He was terribly bored.

". . . Seventeen, eighteen, nineteen down; by one, two, three, four, five . . ."

With patience and application, he discovered the mean number of holes in each square of acoustic tile in the ceiling. Balancing this figure on his memory, he undertook to count the tiles. This total he intended to multiply by the number of holes in each tile to arrive at the grand total of holes in his entire ceiling!

He was terribly bored. But his boredom had lasted only a few days. For the greater part of his hospitalization, his attention had been occupied with fear, pain, and gratitude at being alive. Once during the trip down the Gallery Window he had risen foggily to the surface of consciousness and experienced the Dantesque confusion of light and motion as the train swayed and clattered through the tunnel. Ben's face rippled into focus, and Jonathan complained thickly, "I can't feel anything from the waist down."

Ben mumbled some reassuring sounds and dissolved.

When Jonathan next contacted the world, Dante had given way to Kafka. A brilliant ceiling was flying past above him, and a mechanized voice was paging doctors by name. A starched white upside-down female torso bent over him and shook its dumpling head, and they wheeled him on more quickly. The ceiling stopped its giddy rush, and male voices somewhere nearby spoke with grave rapidity. He wanted to tell them that he could feel nothing from the waist down, but no one seemed interested. They had cut away the laces of his boots and were taking off his pants. A nurse clicked her tongue and said with a mixture of sympathy and eagerness, "That may have to be amputated."

No! The word rushed to Jonathan's mind, but he passed out before he could tell them that he would rather die.

Ultimately, they saved the toe in question, but not before Jonathan had endured days of pain, strapped to his bed under a plastic tent that bathed his exposure-burnt extremities in a pure oxygen atmosphere. The only relief he got from the bone-eroding immobility was a daily sponging down with alcohol and cotton. Even this respite carried its calculated indignities, for the mannish nurse who did the job always handled his genitals like cheap bric-a-brac that had to be dusted under.

His injuries were widespread, but not serious. In addition to the exposure and frostbite, his nose had been broken by the impact of Jean-Paul's corpse; two of his ribs had cracked when the lasso snapped tight; and his collision with the face had resulted in a mild concussion. Of all of these, the nose bothered him longest. Even after the physical restrictions of the oxygen atmosphere tent had been lifted and the ribs had mended sufficiently to make the adhesive tape more troublesome than the pain, the broad bandage across the bridge of his nose continued to torment him. He could not even read, because the visual distraction of the white pad tempted him to stare strabismically.

But boredom was the greatest plague of all. He received no visitors. Ben had not accompanied him to Zurich. He stayed at the hotel, paying off bills and attending to the retrieval and transportation of the dead. Anna remained too, and they made love a few times.

So great was the boredom that Jonathan was driven to finishing the Lautrec article. But when he read it over the next morning, he growled and tossed it into the wastebasket beside his bed.

The climb was over. The Eiger Birds flew south to their padded nests, sated with sensation for the moment. Newsmen waited around for a couple of days, but when it became apparent that Jonathan would survive, they left the city in a noisy flutter, like carrion disturbed at their cadaver.

By the end of the week the climb was no longer news, and soon the attention of the press was siphoned off to the most publicized event of the decade. The United States had deposited two grinning farm boys on the moon, by which achievement the nation aspired to infuse into the community of man a New Humility in the face of cosmic distance and American technology.

The only letter he received was a postcard from Cherry, one side of which was covered with stamps and postal marks that showed it had gone from Long Island to Arizona to Long Island to Kleine Scheidegg to Sicily to Kleine Scheidegg to Zurich. Sicily? The handwriting was oval and large at first, then regularly smaller and more cramped as she had run out of space.

"Wonderful news!!! I have been released from that burden (hem, hem) I carried for so long! Released and released! Fantastic man! Quiet, gentle, calm, witty—and a lover of *me*. Happened like that (imagine snap of fingers)! Met. Married. Mated. And in that order, too! What's this world coming to? You've lost your chance. Cry your eyes out. God, he's wonderful, Jonathan! We're living at my place. Come and see us when you get home. Which reminds me, I drop over to your place once in a while to make sure no one's stolen it. No one has. But some bad news. Mr. Monk quit. Got a steady job working for the National Park Service. How's Arizona? Released, I say! Tell you all about it when you get back.

"All right, how's Switzerland?"

Flip.

Jonathan lay looking up at the ceiling.

The first day after restrictions against visitors were lifted, he had the company of a man from the American Consulate. Short, plump, with long hair criss-crossed over the naked pate, ranine eyes blinking behind steel-rimmed glasses, he was of that undramatic type CII recruits specifically because they do not fit the popular image of the spy. So consistently does CII use such men that they have long ago become stereotypes that any foreign agent can pick from a crowd at a glance.

The visitor left a small tape recorder of a new CII design that had the "play" and "erase" heads reversed, both operative in the "play" mode, so that the message was destroyed as it was played. The model was considered a marked improvement over its more secretive predecessor, which erased before playing.

As soon as he was alone, Jonathan opened the lid of the recorder and found an envelope taped to the underside. It was a confirmation from his bank of the deposit of one hundred thousand dollars to his account. Confused, he pushed the "play" button, and Dragon's voice spoke to him, even thinner and more metallic than usual through the small speaker. He had only to close his eyes to see the iridescent ivory face emerging through the gloom, and the pink eyes under tufted cotton eyebrows.

My dear Hemlock . . . You have by now opened the envelope and have discovered—with surprise and pleasure, I hope—that we have decided to pay the full sum, despite our earlier threat to deduct your more outrageous extravagances . . . I consider this only fair in the light of the discomfort and expense your injuries have cost you. . . . It seems obvious to us that you were unable to make the sanction target reveal himself, and so you took the sure, if grimly uneconomical, path of sanctioning all three men. . . . But you always were extravagant. . . . We assume the killing of M. Bidet was accomplished during your first night on the mountain, under the cover of dark. . . . How you contrived to precipitate the other two men to their deaths is not clear to us, nor does it interest us particularly. . . . Results concern us more than methods, as you may recall.

Now, Hemlock, I really ought to rebuke you for the shopworn condition in which you returned Clement Pope. . . . You escape my wrath only because I had all along planned to bestow some deserved punishment on him. . . . And why not at your hands? . . . Pope had been assigned to the Search task of locating your target, and he failed to identify his man. . . . As an eleventh-hour expedient, he came up with the notion of setting you up as a decoy. . . . It was certainly second-rate thinking and the product of a frightened and incompetent man, but there were no viable alternatives open to us. . . . I had faith that you would survive the admittedly tense situation, and, as you see, I was correct. . . . Pope has been removed from SS and has been assigned to the less demanding task of writing vice-presidential addresses. . . . After the beating you gave him, he is quite useless to us. . . . He suffers from what in a good hunting dog would be called gun-shyness.

It is with great reluctance that I place your file among the "inactives," although I will confide in you that Mrs. Cerberus does not share my melancholy. . . . To tell the truth, I suspect in my heart of hearts that we shall be working together before long. . . . Considering your tastes, this money will last no more than four years, after which—who can say?

Congratulations on your ingenious solution to the crisis, and good luck to you in your Long Island shrine to your self-image.

The end of the tape flap-flap-flapped as the take-up reel spun. Jonathan turned the machine off and set it aside. He shook his head slowly and said to himself helplessly. "Oh, God."

"Let me see now. It was forty-two down by—one, two, three, four . . ."

Ben had difficulty getting in the door. He swore and kicked at it viciously as he stumbled in, a huge cellophane-wrapped basket of fruit in his arms.

"Here!" he said gruffly, and he thrust the crinkling burden toward Jonathan, who had been laughing uncontrollably since first Ben burst in.

"What is this wonderful thing you bring me?" Jonathan asked between racks of laughter.

"I don't know. Fruit and such shit. They hustle them down in the lobby. What's so goddam funny?"

"Nothing." Jonathan was limp with laughing. "It's just about the sweetest thing anyone's ever done for me, Ben."

"Oh, fuck off."

The bed shook with a fresh attack of laughter. While it was true that Ben looked silly grasping a beribbonned basket in his ample paw, Jonathan's laughter carried notes of hysteria born of boredom and cabin fever.

Ben set the basket on the floor and slouched down in a bedside chair, his arms folded across his chest, the image of grumpy patience. "I'm real glad I cheer you up like this."

"I'm sorry. Look. All right." He sniffed back the last dry, silent laugh. "I got your postcard. You and Anna?"

Ben waved his hand. "Funny things happen."

Jonathan nodded. "Did you find . . . ?

"Yeah, we found them at the base. Anderl's father decided to have him buried in the meadow within sight of the face."

"Good."

"Yes. Good."

And there was nothing more to say. This was the first time Ben had visited Jonathan in the hospital, but Jonathan understood. There is nothing to say to a sick man.

After a pause, Ben asked if they were treating him all right. And Jonathan said yes. And Ben said good.

Ben mentioned the Valparaiso hospital after Aconcagua where their roles had been reversed while Ben recuperated from toe amputations. Jonathan remembered and even managed to dredge up a couple of names and places that they could both nod over energetically, then let slip away.

Ben walked around the room and looked out the window.

"How are the nurses?"

"Starched."

"Have you invited any aboard?"

"No. They're a pretty rank lot."

"That's too bad."

"Yes, it is."

Ben sat down again and flicked lint off his pants for a while. Then he told Jonathan that he intended to catch a plane back to the States that afternoon. "I should be in Arizona by tomorrow morning."

"Give my love to George."

"I'll do that."

Ben sighed, then stretched vigorously, then said something about taking care of yourself, then rose to go. When he picked up the fruit basket and put it near the bed, Jonathan began to laugh afresh. This time Ben stood there taking it. It was better than the long silences. But after a while he began to feel stupid, so he put the basket down and made for the door.

"Oh, Ben?"

"What?"

Jonathan brushed away the tears of laughter. "How did you get mixed up in the Montreal business in the first place?"

. . . Ben had stood for many minutes at the window, his forehead resting against the frame, looking down on the traffic that crawled along the colorless street lined with optimistic saplings. When at last he spoke, his voice was husky and subdued. "You really took me off balance."

"That's the way I had rehearsed it while I lay here counting holes in the ceiling."

"Well, it worked just fine, ol' buddy. How long have you known?"

"Just a couple of days. At first it was just bits and pieces. I kept trying to picture the man with the limp in Montreal, and none of the men on the mountain quite fit. You were the only other person coming for the climb. Then all sorts of things fell into place. Like the coincidence of meeting Mellough at your lodge. And why would George Hotfort stick me with a half dose? Miles wouldn't do that. He already had my answer. And why would George do that for Miles? So far as I know, there was only one thing that really interested her, and Miles couldn't offer that. But she might do something like that for you. And you might want her to do it because you wanted me to kill Miles quickly, before he could tell me who the man in Montreal was."

Ben nodded fatalistically. "I used to wake up in a sweat, imagining that Mellough had told you out there on the desert, and you were playing cat and mouse with me."

"I never gave Miles a chance to tell me anything."

It was Jonathan who broke the ensuing silence. "How did you get mixed up with him?"

Ben continued to stare out the window at the traffic. Evening was setting in, and the first streetlamps had come on. "You know how I tried to make a go of it with that little climbing school after I couldn't climb anymore. Well, it never did pay for itself. Not many people came, and those who did—like you—were mostly old climbing buddies what I hated to charge. There's not a whole lot of ads in the help-wanted pages for gimpy ex-climbers. I suppose I could have found some nine-to-five sort of thing, but that isn't my style. I guess you know what I mean, considering what you do to make your money."

"I don't do it anymore. I've quit."

Ben looked at him seriously. "That's good, Jon." Then he returned to watching the traffic crawl through the darkening streets. His voice was dry when he spoke. "One day this Miles Mellough shows up out of nowhere and says he has a proposition for me. He'd set me up with a posh resort and a little climbing school on the side, and all I have to do is let his people come and go with no questions. I knew it was some kind of illegal. Matter of fact, Mellough never pretended it wasn't. But I was pretty far in debt and . . ." His voice trailed off.

Jonathan broke through the nicotine-colored cellophane and took an apple out of the basket. "Miles was big-leaguing dope. I imagine your place doubled as a rest camp for his wholesale hustlers and a depot for east-west traffic."

"That's about it. It went on for a couple of years. And all that time I never knew that you and Mellough were enemies. I didn't even know you knew each other."

"All right, that ties you to Mellough. It doesn't explain why you went to Montreal."

"I don't get much kick out of talking about it."

"I think you owe me an explanation. I would never have gone on the mountain if you'd told me before."

Ben snorted. "No! You'd have shot me and collected your pay."

"I don't think so."

"You're telling me you'd have given up your house and paintings and everything?"

Jonathan was silent.

"You're not sure, are you, Jon."

"No. I'm not sure."

"Honest isn't enough, Jon. Anyway, for what it's worth I tried many times to talk you out of going on the hill. I didn't want to die, but I didn't want you to die on the mountain because of me."

Jonathan was not going to be side-tracked. "Tell me how you got to Montreal."

Ben sighed stertorously. "Oh, I did some stupid things, ol' buddy. Things an experienced hand like you would never do. I signed for some shipments—things like that. Then, my . . ." He squeezed his eyes closed and pressed his thumb and forefinger into the sockets. "Then, my daughter got messed up with drugs and . . . Mellough took care of her. He brought her to a place where they cleaned her up. After that, he had me. And I owed him."

Jonathan frowned. "Your daughter, Ben?"

Ben's eyes chilled over. "Yes. Something you didn't know, Doctor. George Hotfort is my little girl."

Jonathan remembered making love to her and later slapping her around. He lowered his eyes to the unbitten apple and began polishing it slowly on the sheet. "You're right. It's something I didn't know."

Ben did not choose to linger on the subject of George. "All this time, Mellough knew, of course, that you and I were friends. He was angling for a way to set me up in big trouble so he could swap me in return for your taking him off your list and letting him breathe easy for a change."

"It's his kind of con. He always did things obliquely."

"And this Montreal business gave him the chance to set me up. He told me I had to come along. I had to go with some turd named Kruger while he received a paper or something. I didn't know anyone was going to get killed. Even if I had, I didn't have a whole lot of choice."

"But you didn't have anything to do with the killing, did you?"

"I guess you can't say that. I didn't stop it, did I? I just stood there and watched it happen." His voice was bitter with self-disgust. "And when Kruger started to cut him open, I . . ."

"You threw up."

"Yeah, that's right! I guess I'm not the killer type." He turned back to the window. "Not like you, ol' buddy."

"Spare me that crap. You don't have anything against killing in the abstract. You were perfectly willing to have me kill Mellough for you. It's just that you can't do it yourself."

"I suppose."

Jonathan dropped the apple back into the basket. It had been a gift from Ben. "Tell me. Why did you come up and get me off the face? If I had died with the others, you would have been home free."

Ben smiled and shook his head. "Don't imagine for a minute I didn't consider it, ol' buddy."

"But you're not the killer type?"

"That, and I owed you one for the time you walked me down off the Aconcagua." Ben turned squarely to Jonathan. "What happens now?"

"Nothing."

"You wouldn't bullshit an old buddy, would you?"

"The CII people are satisfied that they have their man. And I don't see any reason to disabuse them. Especially since I've already been paid."

"What about you? I know how you are about friends who let you down."

"I don't have any friends who have let me down."

Ben thought that over. "I see. Tell me, ol' buddy. Do you have any friends at all?"

"Your solicitude is touching, Ben. When do you catch your plane?"

"I've got to get going right now."

"Fine."

Ben paused at the door. "Take care of yourself, ol' buddy."

"Thanks for the fruit."

Jonathan stared at the door for several minutes after it closed behind Ben. He felt hollow inside. For several days he had known that he would never climb again. He had lost his nerve. And Ben was gone. And Jemima was gone. And he was tired of counting holes in the ceiling.

He turned the light off and the blue of late evening filled the room. He closed his eyes and tried to sleep.

What the hell. He didn't need them. He didn't need any of it. When he got back to the States, he was going to sell the goddam church.

But not the paintings!

The Loo Sanction

St. Martin's-In-The-Fields

HIS PAIN WAS vast. But at least it was finite. Sharp-edged waves of agony climaxed in intensity until his body convulsed and his mind was awash. Then, just before madness, the crests broke and swirled over his limen of consciousness, and he escaped into oblivion.

But always he emerged again from the delirum, cold and perspiring, weaker than before, and more frightened.

A crisp wind fluted through the arches of the belfry in which he was prisoner and drove his tears horizontally back to his temples. During troughs of awareness between crises of pain, his mind cleared, and he was bewildered by his reactions to impending death. Matthew Parnell-Greene ("Uranus" in the planet-code of the counterespionage agency that employed him) had always known that violent death was a very real alternative to retirement in his line of work. He was not physically brave—his imagination was too active for that—so he had sought to mute his fear by callusing that imagination. He had forced himself to rehearse being shot, being knifed, taking a faceful of cyanide gas from a tube concealed in a folded newspaper, being poisoned—his urbane flair always insisting upon the poison being in exotic foods consumed at really good restaurants. And he had attempted to toughen his tender imagination by abrading it with anticipations of the more disgusting alternatives. He had been drowned in a bathtub; he had been suffocated, his face blue and his eyes bulging within a polyethylene bag; air had been injected into his heart. Always he had died well, with a certain dignity, not struggling dumbly against impossible odds. He had imagined pain, but the end had always come quickly. He had long ago realized that he could not withstand torture and had decided he would cooperate fully with his questioners, should it come to that.

Fear, pain, anger, even self-pity had been anticipated so often that they held no more dread than he could stand. But his anxious fantasies had not prepared him for the emotion that now overwhelmed his mind: disgust. Disgust was bitter in the back of his throat. Disgust curled the corners of his mouth and dilated his nostrils. When they found him, he would be unsightly, revolting. The thought of it embarrassed him intensely.

In the two hours since a watery dawn had made London visible below him, Parnell-Greene's eyes had dimmed many times, with each fresh crisis of pain that carried him over the brink of unconsciousness as some membrane inside him ripped through, sending waves of shock through his body.

How long had he been there? Six hours? Half his life? His existence seemed divided into two parts, one containing forty-seven active, colorful years; the other, six hours of pain. And it was the second half that really mattered.

He remembered them bringing him to St. Martin's. Although he had been heavily drugged, it was all perfectly lucid. The drugs had been pleasant, euphoric; they had sapped his will, but he remembered everything. Two of them had brought him. They had stood on either side of him because he was unsteady on his feet. He had sat for a time with one of them—The Mute—in a back pew, while the other went up to the belfry to see that the apparatus was in place. He remembered the oaken contribution box with its notice:

> Contributions to keep
> this church always open
> and to maintain its services

They had led him up the winding metal staircase and out onto the dark windy platform of the belfry. And then they had . . . and then they . . . Parnell-Greene wept at the sadness of it.

He sobbed, and that was a mistake. The convulsion ruptured something inside, pain clawed through his body and throbbed in his head. He fainted.

The streets below the church streamed with people. Hundreds gushed up Villiers Street and poured from Charing Cross Station, all hurrying toward work or standing with turgid obedience in queues, waiting to crowd into red double-decker buses, bodies touching, eyes assiduously averted. Escalators spewed anonymities from the undergrounds: young office men, bareheaded and red-eyed; cloth-capped laborers, sullen and stunned with lives of monotony; shopgirls and secretaries, miniskirted despite the season, their hands, faces, and legs ruddy and chapped; older women on the prowl for bargains, waddling through the press, heavy objects in their dangling string bags a threat to passing shins.

Any one of them might have seen Parnell-Greene's huddled silhouette in the arch of the belfry, but no one looked up. In the automaton way of British workers, their chins were sunk in their collars, their minds involute.

Perspiration was cold on his forehead when he returned to consciousness. He breathed carefully, his mouth wide open so as not to make a movement. At last, his tightly bound arms were numb, and that was a blessing. For the first hour or so, the loss of circulation had caused a regular dull ache that was somehow more wearing than the irregular ecstasies of agony when something tore within him.

He did not shout for help. He had tried that at first, but no one could hear his feeble voice from the height of the belfry, and each attempt had been rewarded with a bursting sac of liquid pain.

Slowly, the numbing of his overloaded nerves came into balance with this new level of agony, and neutralized it. He knew that more exquisite levels of pain would come, but it was no longer an animate enemy he might get by the throat and crush, and crush! His pain and his life had welded into one. They would always be together now. When there was no longer pain, there would no longer be life.

He felt very cold, and very sad.

He looked out, across the river, over the bulk of the Charing Cross Hotel. There were the elements of new London. The inarticulate, utilitarian bulk of the Royal Festival Hall. The addled architecture of Queen Elizabeth Hall, a compromise between a penal institution and a space station. New London. Economical and unmerciful architecture. And beyond, cubes of aluminum and glass persuaded the skyline of London to imitate Chicago. Some of the bloodless hulks stood unfinished, victims of continual strikes. Above these ugly heaps, giant construction cranes lurked, dinosaur skeletons poised to feed on huge blocks of salt.

Distressed, he turned his eyes away. So much of it was going! Even the façades temporarily spared from Progress were masked by scaffolding and canvas as they were being steamed and scrubbed to rid them of the character of patina.

It was all going.

He felt liquid dripping down his legs. And not only blood, he realized with despair. Revolting. Disgusting.

A bit of sun broke through the low layers of zinc cloud. He began to feel warm. Light. As though he were floating. It would be good to be weightless. Merciful numbness began to spread upward. His throat thickened. He was so tired.

The whir and clatter of machinery tugged him back to consciousness. The clapper of the great bell was grinding back against its spring, and it hovered for a second before it shot forward. The belfry roared and vibrated! The apparatus shook violently. The pain was pyrotechnic as everything within him burst!

Now Parnell-Greene screamed.

Unheard.

That evening the facts were carried by the London newspapers, each reflecting the taste of its readership:

MAN IMPALED IN ST. MARTIN'S-IN-THE-FIELDS

OPPOSITION QUESTIONS SECURITY OF NATIONAL BELFRIES

BELL RINGER INVESTIGATES THUD!

EARLY CHURCHGOER GETS THE POINT!

BBC 2 interrupted its year-long series on the development of the viola da gamba for a special broadcast in which three university dons outlined the uses of torture in general and impalement in particular in the Western world. Then a panel of experts discussed the implications of this latest impalement on the eve of Britain's entry into the Common Market. Finally, a woman Labour MP made the point that this literal impalement had shocked and sickened the nation, while it remained perfectly indifferent to the figurative impalement of womanhood on the phallus of male chauvinism over the years, which, after all, was . . .

Bloomsbury

YOU!" THE SINGER accused, pointing over the heads of the crowd with an arched forefinger, the other fist on his hip, his eyes wild and round in their pits of green mascara, his gold-tinsel wig glittering under the spotlight. "You! . . .*

. . . you're driving me crazy.
What can I do? What can I do?
My love for you makes everything hazy . . ."

---

* from the song "You're Driving me Crazy" by Walter Donaldson copyright 1930, 1957 by Donaldson Publishing Co. Used by permission of Mrs. Walter Donaldson.

His thin metallic alto blended with the muted instruments as his stiff torso dipped in tempo to the song, his knees flexing mechanically. He stood on a raised platform, and his eyebrowless, clown-white face bobbed rhythmically over the heads of the chitchatting crowd. The showrooms of Tomlinson's Galleries buzzed with conversation: intimate talk, meaningful and intense; significant talk about art and life; witty talk designed to be overhead and repeated.

". . . so I simply put myself into his hands. He designs all my clothes and even selects the shirts and ties. In effect, he does me as he sees me . . ."

". . . for God's sake, Midge, he's not only your husband, he's my friend. Do you think I want to hurt him? . . ."

". . . it would be a challenge to paint you. I would like to try and capture your—ah—depth and to expressed it in—well, frankly—in sexual terms . . ."

". . . well, if you ask me, it was a blatant act of defiance—a challenge to the police. To impale a man on a wooden stake right in the belfry of St. Martin's-In-The-Fields! Have you had your martini, love?"

The minute Jonathan Hemlock stepped into the crowded reception room, he was sorry he had come. He looked over heads, but he didn't find the woman he was supposed to meet, so he began slowly to ease toward the door, juggling his glass adroitly and nodding to the empty-eyed models who hung impatiently on the arms of older men, and who smiled at him as he passed. But just as he made the door, David Tomlinson caught him by the arm, directed him to the center of the room, and jumped up on a pouf.

"Listen, everybody! Everybody?" (Silence rippled reluctantly from the center outward.) "I have the very great honor to introduce you to Dr. Jonathan Hemlock who's come all the way from America to set us all straight on art and all that." (Titters and one "hear-hear.") "All sorts of people have consorted to get him over here: the Guggenheim, the Arts Council—all that benevolent lot. And we must make good use of him. No comments from you, Andrew!" (Titters.) "Now you'll have to watch yourselves because Dr. Hemlock actually *knows* something about art." (Groans and one giggle.) "I'm sure you've all read his books, and now he's here in the flesh, as it were. And remember this! You saw him first at Tomlinson's." (Laughter and light applause.)

Tomlinson stepped down from the pouf and spoke with such sincerity that he appeared to be in pain. "I am truly delighted that Van was able to persuade you to come. You've *made* the evening. May I call you Jonathan?"

"No. Look, you haven't seen Van, have you?"

"In point of fact, I haven't."

Jonathan grunted and slipped away to the bar where he ordered a double Laphroaig. He didn't notice fforbes-Ffitch's approach in time to avoid it.

"Heard you were going to be here, Jon. Thought I'd drop around for the event." fforbes-Ffitch spoke with the crisp, busier-than-thou accents of the academic hustler. He had taken his doctorate in the United States, where apparently he had majored in grantsmanship, which training he applied with such industry that he became the youngest head of department at the Royal College of Art and had recently been made a trustee of the National Gallery.

"Say, Jon. Tell me, did you receive my memo?"

Jonathan never used fforbes-Ffitch's first name. He didn't even know what it was. "What memo?"

fforbes-Ffitch preened his drooping moustache by pressing it down with his thumb and cleared his throat to speak importantly. "That one about your doing a lecture series for us in Scandinavia."

Jonathan had received it weeks before and had dismissed it as an attempt by f-F to brighten his reputation as a man who knows important people and gets things done. "No, I never received it."

"How does the idea sound to you?"

"Terrible."

"Oh? Oh? I see. Well, that is too bad. Ah—quite a gathering here this evening, don't you think?"

"No."

"Well, yes. I agree with you. Not real scholars, of course. But . . . important people. Well! I have to be going. Desk piled with work crying out to be done."

"You'd better get to it."

"Right. Cheers."

Jonathan felt great social fatigue as he watched f-F depart through the crowd, shaking hands with all the "names," studiously ignoring the others. No doubting it, f-F was a man on his way to a knighthood.

Jonathan had just finished his whiskey and was ready to get out when Vanessa Dyke appeared at his side.

"Having fun, love?" she asked evilly.

He smiled blandly out onto the throng and spoke to her out of the side of his mouth. "Where have you been? You told me it wouldn't be another of these."

She waved at someone across the room. "The truth is, I lied. Simple as that."

"One of these days, Van . . ."

"I look forward to it." She tapped out a Gauloise on her thumbnail and lit it, cupping the match like a sailor on a windy deck, then she squinted through the curling acrid smoke to find a handy ashtray, failing which, she tossed the match onto the thick carpeting. One fist on her hip, she looked disdainfully over the party, the pungent French cigarette dangling from the side of her mouth, the hard, intelligent eyes examining and dismissing the guests. An expatriate American, Vanessa wrote the leanest, most penetrating art criticism current in England under the name Van Dyke, which the uninitiated took to be an alias. Jonathan had known her for years and had always admired and liked her, even during the flamboyant stage of her life when she had turned up at parties with a young whore on either arm, flaunting her homosexuality with defensive vigor. They disagreed totally about art, and had great battles in private, but should someone less informed join in, they united to destroy him.

Jonathan looked at her profile and noticed with surprise that age was making rapid inroads on her. Still thin as a reed under the black slacks and turtlenecked sweater that were her trademark, she had short tousled hair shot with gray, and the alert, nervous movements of her expressive hands revealed nails bitten to the quick.

"Have you met the Struggling Young Person?" she asked, leaning against the bar with her elbows and surveying the gathering without sympathy.

"No. Why did you ask me to come here?"

Vanessa avoided the question. "Have you seen his shit?"

"I glanced around when I came in."

"That's him over there." She gestured with her pointed chin.

Jonathan looked through the milling bodies to a dour young man with a shaggy beard and a corduroy hunting jacket, flaunting his nonclass by drinking beer. He was surrounded by people so eager to be seen in his company that they were willing to pay the price of listening to him. Hovering in the background was a sere, uncertain girl in a long dress of madras, her nose sharp between falls of long oily hair. She had the intense look of a graduate student's wife concerned with social injustice, and Jonathan took her to be the painter's mistress.

Christ, they all look alike!

Knowing that the tenor of his thoughts would be identical to her own, Vanessa shrugged, saying, "Well, at least he's fairly unassuming."

Jonathan looked again over the modern daubs on the carpeted walls. "What are his options?"

A couple were pushing their way through the crowd toward Jonathan. "Oh, Christ," he said from between teeth clenched in a smile.

"Come on," Vanessa said, drawing her arm through his and guiding him away, leaning against him in a masque of romantic conversation. But as they turned the first corner they ran smack into a conversational group of three that blocked their passage.

"Van, you harlot!" greeted a young man in a pale blue suede jacket with metal-tipped fringe. "You've just taken our much-touted art expert here all for yourself and you're gobbling him all up!" He looked at Jonathan, his eyebrows arched in anticipation of an introduction.

Vanessa ignored him, turning to a middle-aged man wearing heavy clothes and an open, eager expression that had a canine flavor. "Sir Wilfred Pyles, Jonathan Hemlock. I believe your commission had something to do with getting him here."

"Good to see you here, Jon."

"You mean at this party, Fred?"

"Well, no. I meant in the country actually."

"Ah-ha!" Vanessa said. "I had no idea you two knew one another."

"Yes indeed," Sir Wilfred explained. "I've been an admirer of Jon's for years. But not as an art critic. I'm afraid I'm only one of those chaps who know what they like. No, my acquaintance with Jonathan Hemlock was under rather a different heading. I used to be an enthusiastic amateur mountaineer, don't you know. Just puffing about and hill bashing, really. But I read all the journals and became familiar with this fellow's exploits. And, when I had a chance to meet him, I grabbed it. That was—how long ago was it, Jon?"

Jonathan smiled, uncomfortable as he always was when talking about climbing. "I haven't climbed for years."

"Well, I shouldn't wonder. I mean—that must have been a nasty business on the Eiger. Three men, was it?"

Jonathan cleared his throat. "I don't climb seriously anymore."

"Not only that," Vanessa said, squeezing his arm, realizing that he wanted to change the subject, "he's given up serious criticism as well. Or haven't you read his latest bag of garbage?" She turned to the crisp, beautiful woman of uncertain years who stood beside Sir Wilfred. "And you are . . . ?"

"Oh, yes. Sorry," Sir Wilfred said. "Mrs. Amelia Farquahar. A friend of mine, actually."

"No one's introduced me yet," the suede jacket said.

Vanessa patted his cheek. "That's because no one's noticed you yet, darling boy."

"Oh, I doubt that. I doubt that." But his peeve lasted only a second. "Actually, we were having a lively conversation when you broke in. Lively and a little naughty."

"Oh?" Vanessa asked Mrs. Farquahar.

"Yes. We were, in fact, discussing the myth of vaginal climax." Mrs. Farquahar turned to Jonathan. "What are your opinions on that, Dr. Hemlock?"

"As an art critic?"

"As a mountain climber, if you'd rather."

Sir Wilfred grunted. "All part of women's liberation, I shouldn't wonder. I hear you've been having quite a lot of that in your country."

"Mostly among the losers," Jonathan said, smiling.

Vanessa smiled back. "You turd."

"And you, Miss Dyke?" Mrs. Farquahar asked. "Do you have an opinion on that?"

Vanessa dropped her cigarette butt in suede jacket's wineglass. "I don't think it's a myth at all. The misconception is that it takes a penis to achieve it."

"How interesting," said Mrs. Farquahar.

"I say!" injected suede jacket, feeling somehow he had been left out of the conversation. "Did you read about that man found impaled in St. Martin's-In-The-Fields?"

"Oh, ghastly business," Sir Wilfred said.

"Oh, I don't know. If you have to go . . ." He wriggled a shoulder and took a sip of wine.

While he was coping with the mouthful of tobacco, Vanessa said to Mrs. Farquahar, "Come, let me introduce you to the young man who has drawn this sparkling company together."

"Yes. I'd like that."

They pushed off through the crowd, Vanessa leading the way and prowing through the congested sea of people. Suede jacket stood on tiptoe and waved extravagantly to someone who had just entered, then struggled off after a word of apology.

Jonathan and Sir Wilfred stood side by side against the wall. "What's all this about climbing, Fred?" Jonathan asked without looking at him. "You get a nosebleed from standing on a thick carpet."

"Just the first thing that came to my mind, Jon." The flappy tones of the bungling British civil servant dropped away from his speech.

"I see. Are you still in the Service?"

"No, no. I've been on the shelf for several years now. The extent of my counterespionage activities now is trying to find out how much my chauffeur tells my wife."

"When I saw your name on my appointment to come over here, I assumed MI-5 had found you an elastic cover."

"I'm afraid not. I am well and truly out to pasture. The electronic age has caught up with me. One has to be a damned engineer these days to stay in the game. No, I serve my country by chairing committees devoted to the task of bring cultural enrichment to our shores. You constitute a cultural enrichment." He laughed. "Who would have thought in the old days when we were flogging about Europe, now on the same team, now in opposition, that we would be brought so low."

"You *do* know that I'm out of it totally now?" Jonathan wanted to sure.

"Oh, certainly. First thing I checked upon when your name came up. The chaps at the old office said you were—to use their uncomplimentary compliment—politically subpotent. By which I take it that you and CII have parted company."

"That we have. By the way, congratulations on your knighthood."

"Not so much of an achievement as you might imagine. These days few people escape that distinction. When you leave the Service they automatically lumber you with a K.B.E. They've found it's cheaper than a gold watch, I suspect. Ah, the ladies return."

As she approached, Vanessa said to Jonathan, "I didn't lure you here just to punish you with my acquaintances. There's something I want to show you." She turned to Mrs. Farquahar. "Jon and I have to run off for a moment."

Mrs. Farquahar smiled and inclined her head.

In the hall where it was relatively quiet Jonathan asked, "What's this all about, Van?"

"You'll see. A chance for you to pick up some pocket money. But look, don't get uptight, and for God's sake, don't cause any trouble. That could be very bad for me." She led the way down a corridor, past the table at which the maids and caterer's assistants were flirting, to the door of a small private display room. "Come on."

Jonathan entered, then stopped short. A bronze Horse and Rider by Marino Marini stood in the center of a darkened room, its ragged modeling accented by the acute angle of a shaft of dramatically placed light. About forty inches high, a sand-colored forced patina, the modeling seemed to combine those primitive, lumpy Etrurian characteristics typical of Marini with an almost oriental twist of the heads of both horse and rider that was most uncharacteristic. But the fat rider's stubbed cigar of a penis was a Marini signature. Jonathan walked slowly around the casting, pausing occasionally to take in some detail, his concentration totally committed. So absorbed was he that it was a while before he noticed a man leaning against the far wall, posed under a dim light that had been arranged with almost as much care as that given to the Horse. He wore an extremely trendy suit of dusty gold velvet, and a ruffle of starched lace stood at his throat. His arms were folded across his chest, his stance poised and practiced, but an inner tension prevented his posture from appearing relaxed. He watched Jonathan steadily, following him with gray eyes so pale they seemed colorless.

Jonathan examined the man with frank curiosity. It was the most beautiful male bust he had ever seen—an unearthly, bloodless beauty such as masters of the Early Renaissance sometimes touched upon. Intuitively, he knew the man was aware of the effect of his cold beauty, and he had stationed himself in that particular light to heighten it.

"Well, Jonathan?" Vanessa had been standing back out of the light. Her voice was hushed most uncharacteristically.

Jonathan glanced again at the Renaissance man. Something in his demeanor made it clear that he did not intend to speak and did not wish to be spoken to. Jonathan decided to let him play out his silly game.

"Well what?" he asked Van.

"Is it genuine?"

Jonathan was surprised at the question, forgetting as often he did that his gift was quite unique. As some people have perfect pitch, Jonathan had a perfect eye. Once he had seen a man's work, he never mistook it. It was, in fact, upon that gift that his reputation had been founded and not, as he preferred others to believe, on his scholarship. "Of course it's genuine. Marini cast three of these and later broke one. No one knows why. Some defect probably. But only two now exist. This is the Dallas Horse. I didn't know it was in England."

"Ah—" Vanessa fumbled for a Gauloise to cover her tension, then she asked offhandedly, "What price do you think it would bring?"

Jonathan looked at her, startled. "It's for sale?"

She took a deep drag and blew smoke up at the ceiling. "Yes."

Jonathan looked across at the Renaissance man who had not moved a muscle and who still watched him, the colorless eyes picked out by a shaft of light just under the dark eyebrows.

"Stolen?" Jonathan asked.

"No," Vanessa answered.

"Doesn't he talk?"

"Please, Jonathan." She touched his arm.

"What the hell's going on? Is he selling this?"

"Yes. But he wanted you to have a look at it first."

"Why? You don't need me to authenticate it. Its provenances are impeccable. Even a British expert could have certified it." He addressed this to the man standing on the opposite side of the bar of light illuminating the Horse. When the man spoke, his tessitura was just as one would have predicted: precise, carefully modulated, colorless.

"How did you know it was the Dallas Horse, Dr. Hemlock?"

"Ah, you speak. I thought you just posed."

"How did you know it was the Dallas Horse?"

As curtly as possible, Jonathan explained that everyone who knew anything at all about the Marini Horses knew the story of the one purchased by the young Dallas millionaire who subsequently picked it up at the plane himself, loaded it into the back of his pickup, then brought it to his ranch. In unloading, it was dropped and broken. Subsequently it was brazed together by an auto mechanic and, because it was imperfect, it was relegated to adorning the barbecue pit. "Any novice would recognize it," he said, pointing to the rough brazing.

The Renaissance man nodded. "I knew the story, of course."

"Then why did you ask?"

"Testing. Tell me. What do you suppose it will bring in an open sale?"

"I'm a professional. I get paid for making evaluations."

Vanessa cleared her throat. "Ah, Jon, he gave me an envelope for you. I'm sure it will be all right."

Neither the voice nor the words were in character for the gruff, hard-drinking Vanessa Dyke, and Jonathan's distaste for this whole theatrical setup grew. He answered crisply. "Impossible to say. Whatever the buyer can afford. It depends on how much he wants it, or how much he wants others to know he owns it. If my memory serves me, the Texan you got it from gave something in the neighborhood of a quarter of a million of it."

"What would it bring now?" Vanessa asked.

Jonathan shrugged. "I told you. I can't say."

The Renaissance man spoke without moving even a fold in the fabric of his suit. "Let me ask you an easier question. Something you *can* answer."

Jonathan's slum boyhood toned his response. "Listen, art lover. Keep your fee. Or better yet, shove it up your ass." He turned to leave, but Vanessa stood in his way.

"Please, Jon? A favor to me?"

"What's this yahoo to you?"

She frowned and shook her head, not wanting to go into it now. He didn't understand, and he was angry, but Vanessa was a friend. He turned back. "What do you want to know?"

The Renaissance man nodded, accepting Jonathan's capitulation. "The Horse will be offered for sale soon. It will bring a very high price. At what point would people in the art world find the price unbelievable? At what point would the newspapers make something of it?"

Jonathan assumed there was a tax dodge on. "There would be talk, but no one would be unduly astonished at, say, half a million. If it came from the right sources."

"Half a million? Dollars?"

"Yes, dollars."

"I paid more than that for it myself. What if the price were well beyond that?"

"How much beyond?"

"Say . . . five million . . . *pounds.*"

Jonathan laughed. "Never. The other privately held one could be loosened for a tenth of that. And that one's never been broken."

"Perhaps the buyer wouldn't want the other one. Perhaps he has a fondness for flawed statues."

"Five million pounds is a lot to pay for a perverted taste for things flawed."

"Such a price, then, would cause talk."

"It would cause talk, yes."

"I see." The Renaissance man looked down to the floor. "Thank you for your opinion, Dr. Hemlock."

"I think we'd better get back now, Jon," Vanessa said, touching his arm.

Jonathan stopped in the hall and collected his coat from the porter. "Well? Are you going to tell me what that was all about?"

"What's to tell? A mutual friend asked me to arrange a contact between you two. I was paid for it. Oh, here." She gave him a broad envelope, which contained a thick padding of bills.

"But who is that guy?"

She shrugged. "Never saw him before in my life, lover. Come on. I'll buy you a drink."

"I'm not going back in there. Anyway, I have an appointment tonight."

Vanessa looked over his shoulder in the direction of Mrs. Farquahar. "I think I have too."

As he slipped into his overcoat, he looked back toward the door to the private showroom. "You have some weird friends, lady."

"Do you really think so?" She laughed and butted her cigarette in the salver meant to receive tips, then she walked into the crowded reception room where the singer with the gold-tinsel wig and the green mascara was bobbing over the heads of the company, chanting in thin falsetto something about a cup of coffee, a sandwich, and you.

The Renaissance man settled into the passenger seat of his Jensen Interceptor and adjusted his suit coat to prevent its wrinkling. "Has he left?"

The Mute nodded.

"And he's being followed?"

The Mute nodded again.

The Renaissance man clicked on the tape deck and settled to listen to a little Bach as the car crunched along the driveway, its lights out.

A young man with a checked sports coat and a camera depended from his neck stood in a red telephone kiosk beneath a corner streetlamp. While the phone on the other end of the line double-buzzed, he clamped the receiver under his chin awkwardly as he scrawled in a notebook. He had been holding the license number on the rim of his memory by chanting it over and over to himself. Hearing an answering click and hum, he pressed in his twopence piece and said in a hard "r" American accent, "Hi, there."

A cultured voice responded, "Yes? What is it, Yank?"

"How did you know it was me?"

"That hermaphroditic accent of yours."

"Oh. I see." Crestfallen, the young man abandoned his phony American sound and continued with the nasal drawl of public school. "He has left the party, sir. Took a cab."

"Yes?"

"Well, I thought you would like to know. He was followed."

"Good. Good."

"Shall I tag along?"

"No, that wouldn't be wise." The cultured voice was silent for a moment. "Very well. I suppose you have the Baker Street ploy set up?"

"Right, sir. By the way, just in case you want to know, I took note of the time of his departure. He left at exactly . . . Good Lord."

"What is it?"

"My watch has stopped."

The man on the other end of the line sighed heavily. "Good night, Yank."

"Good night, sir."

Covent Garden

JONATHAN SAT DEEP in the back of the taxi, attending only vaguely to the hissing pass of traffic over wet streets. He experienced his usual social nausea after public gatherings of reviewers, teachers, gallery owners, patrons—the paracreative slugs who burden art with their attention—the parasites who pretend to be symbionts and who support, with their groveling leadership, the teratogenetic license of democratic art.

"Fucking grex venalium," he muttered to himself, displaying both aspects of his background—the slums and the university halls.

Forget it, he told himself. Don't let them get to you. He looked forward this evening to a pleasant hour or two with MacTaint, his favorite person in London. A thief, a rogue, and a con with a fine sense of scatology and a haughty disdain for such social imperatives as cleanliness, MacTaint seemed to be visiting modern London from the pages of Dickens or the chorus of *Threepenny Opera*. But he knew painting as did few people in Europe, and he was England's most active dealer in the gray market of stolen art. Although Jonathan had never before been to MacTaint's home, they had often met in little pubs around Covent Garden to drink and joke and talk about painting.

He smiled to himself as he recalled their first meeting three months earlier. He had returned to his flat after a day marred by lectures to serious, ungifted students; meetings with committees whose keen senses of parliamentary procedure obscured their purposes; and gatherings of academic people and art critics, all fencing for position in their miniature arena. He was fed up, and he needed to pass some resuscitating time with his paintings, the eleven Impressionists that were all that remained from the four years he had worked for the Search and Sanction Division of CII. These paintings were the most important things in his life. After all, he had killed for them. Under the protection and blessing of the government, he had performed a half-dozen counterassassinations ("sanctions," in the crepuscular bureaucratese of CII).

Tired and depressed, he had pushed open the door to his flat, and walked in on a party in progress. Every light was on, his whiskey had been broken out, Haydn played on the phonograph, and the furniture had been moved about to facilitate examination of the eleven Impressionists lining the walls.

But it was a party for only one person. An old man sat alone in a deep wing chair, glass in hand, his tattered overcoat still on, its collar up to his ears revealing only tousled gray hair and a bulbous, new-potato nose.

"Come in. Come in," the old man invited.

"Thank you," Jonathan said, hoping the irony had not been too heavy.

"Have some whiskey?"

"Yes, I think I will." Jonathan poured out a good tot of Laphroaig. "Could I freshen up yours?"

"Oh, that's good of you, son. But I've had sufficient."

Jonathan tugged off his raincoat. "In that case, get the hell out of here."

"In a while. In a while. Relax, lad. I'm feasting my tired eyes on that bit of crusted pigment there. Manet. Good for the soul."

Jonathan smiled, intrigued by this old leprechaun who looked like a cross between a provincial professor emeritus and a dirty dustman. "Yes, it's a first-quality copy."

"Pig shit."

"Sir?"

The visitor leaned forward, dandruff falling from his matted hair, and enunciated carefully. "Pig shit. If that's a copy, I'm a glob of whore's spit."

"Have it your own way. Now get out." As he approached the gnomish housebreaker, Jonathan was deterred by a barrier of odor: ancient sweat, body dirt, mildewed clothing.

The old man raised his hand. "Before you set to bashing me about, I'd best introduce myself. I'm MacTaint."

After a stunned moment, Jonathan laughed and shook MacTaint's hand. Then, for several hours, they drank and talked about painting. At no time did MacTaint take off the tattered, heel-length overcoat, and Jonathan was to learn that he never did.

MacTaint downed the last of the whiskey, set the bottle on the floor beside his chair, and regarded Jonathan with an evaluative squint from beneath shaggy white eyebrows, the salient characteristic of which was maverick hairs that hooked out like antennae over the glittering eyes. "So! You are Jonathan Hemlock." He chuckled. "I can tell you, lad, that your appearance on the scene scared the piss out of a lot of us. You could have been a vast nuisance, you know, with that phenomenal eye of yours. My colleagues in the business of reproducing masters might have found it difficult to pursue their vocations with you about. There was even talk of relieving you of the burden of your bleeding life. But then! Then came the happy news that you, like all worthy men, were at heart a larcenous and acquisitive son of a bitch."

"I'm not very acquisitive anymore."

"That's true, come to think of it. You haven't made a purchase for—how long is it?"

"Four years."

"And why is that?"

"I parted company with my source of money."

"Oh, yes. There was rumor of some kind of government association. As I recall, it was the kind of thing no one wanted to know about. Still. You haven't done half badly. You own these grand paintings, two of which, if I may remind you, came through my own good offices."

"I've never been sure, Mac. What are you? A thief or a handler."

"A thief, by preference. But I'll flog another man's work when times are hard. And you? What are you—other than a frigging enigma?"

"Frigging enigma?"

MacTaint scratched the scruff on his scalp. "You know perfectly well what I mean. My comrades on the continent shared my curiosity about you at first, and we pooled our fragments of information. Bits and pieces that never seemed to form a whole picture. You had this gift, this eye that made it possible for you to spot a fake at a glance. But the rest didn't make much sense. University professor. Critic and writer. Collector of black market paintings. Mountain climber. Employed in some kind of nasty government business. Frigging enigma, that's what you are . . ."

The taxi driver swore under his breath and jerked back the hand brake. They were frozen in a tangle of traffic around Trafalgar Square. Jonathan decided to walk the rest of the way. His eagerness to be away from the people at Tomlinson's had made him an hour early for his appointment with MacTaint anyway, and he could use the exercise.

To get away from the crowds and the noise for a second, he turned down Craven Street, past the Monk's Tavern, to Craven Passage and The Arches where destitute old women were settling in to pass the night on the paving stones, scraps of cardboard beneath them to absorb the damp, their backs against the brick walls, bits of fabric tugged about them for warmth. They drowsed with the help of gin, but never so deep into sleep that they missed the odd passerby whom they begged for coins or fags with droning, liturgical voices.

Swinging London.

He held to the back streets as long as possible. His mind kept returning to the Renaissance man he had met at Tomlinson's. Five million pounds for a Marini Horse? Impossible. And yet the man had seemed so confident. The event had made Jonathan uncomfortable. It had those qualities of the deadly absurd, of melodramatic hokum and very real threat that he associated with the lethal game players of international espionage, that group of social mutants he had despised when he worked for CII, and whom he had driven from his memory.

He turned back up into the lights and noise of center city. The rain had developed into a dirty, hanging mist that blurred and blended the stew of neon and noise through which crowds of fun-seekers jostled their way.

Modern young girls took long steps with bony legs under ankle-length skirts, their thin shoulders stooped with poor posture, some with frizzly hair, others with lank. They were the kind who abjured cosmetic artifice and insisted upon being accepted for what they were—antiwar, socially committed, sexually liberated, dull, dull, dull.

Working-class girls clopped along in the thick-soled plastic shoes Picasso's kid had inflicted on mass fashion, their stride already displaying hints of the characteristic gait of adult British women: feet splayed, knees bent, backs rigid—seeming to suffer from some chronic rectal ailment. Substantial legs revealed to the crotch by miniskirts, vast liquid breasts sloshing about within stiff brassieres, chattering voices ravaged by the North London glottal gasp, complexions the victims of the Anglo-Saxon penchant for vitamin-free diets. Doughy bodies, doughy minds. Gastronomic anomalies. Dumpling tarts.

Swinging London.

Jonathan walked close to the buildings where passage was clearest.

"Penny for the Guy, mister?"

The voice had come from behind. He turned to find three leering hooligans in their early twenties, jeans and thick steel-toed boots. One of them pushed a wheelchair in which reclined a Guy Fawkes effigy composed of stuffed old clothes and a comic mask beneath a bowler.

"What do you say, mister?" The biggest hooligan held his sleeve. "A penny for the Guy?"

"Sorry." Jonathan pulled away. He walked on with the sense of their presence etching his spine, but they didn't follow.

He turned into New Row with its gaslights, shuttered greengrocers, and bakeries. His pace carried him slowly away from the Mazurka Clubs, Nosh Bars, and Continuous Continental Revues of Piccadilly, and deeper into Covent Garden with its odd mélange of market and theatrical activities. Italian wholesale fruit companies, seedy talent agencies, imported olive oil, and a school of modern dance and ballet—tap a specialty.

Near a streetlamp, a solitary hustler carnivorously watched him approach. She was plump and fortyish, her legs chubby above thick white knee socks. She wore a short dress and a school blazer with emblem, and her stiff platinum hair was done in two long braids that fell on either side of her full cheeks. Obedient to recent police regulations, she did not solicit verbally, but she put one thumb into her mouth and rocked her thick body from side to side, making her eyes round and little girllike. As he passed, Jonathan noticed the scaly cake of her makeup, patched over, but not redone each time she sweated some off in the course of her work.

As he got deeper into the market, the acrid smell of traffic gave way to the high sweet smell of spoiled fruit, and the litter of paper was replaced by a litter of lettuce leaves, slimy and dangerous underfoot.

Down a dark side street, an out-of-tune piano thumped ragged chords as the silhouettes of tired dancers leapt over drawn window shades. Young girls sweating and panting in their damp exercise costumes. Stars in the making.

"Penny for the Guy, mister?"

He spun around, his back against the brick wall, both hands open before his chest.

The two children yelped and ran down the street, abandoning the old pram and its pitiful, floppy effigy wearing a Sneezy the Dwarf mask.

Jonathan called after them, but his shout served only to speed them on. When the street was quiet again, he laughed at himself and tucked a pound note into the Guy's pocket, hoping the children might sneak back later to retrieve it.

He walked on through the gaggle of lanes, then turned off into a cul-de-sac where there were no streetlamps. The end of a dilapidated court was blocked off by heavy double doors of weathered, splintery wood that swung silently on oiled hinges. The black within was absolute, but he knew he had found his way because of the rancid, cumin smell of ancient sweat.

"Ah, there you are, lad. I'd just decided to come looking for you. It's easy enough to get lost if you've never been here before. Here, follow me."

Jonathan stood still until MacTaint had opened the inner door, flooding the inky court with pale yellow light. They entered a large open space that had once been a fruit merchant's warehouse. Odd litter was piled in the corners, and two potbellied coal stoves radiated cheerful heat, their long chimney pipes stretching up into the shadows of the corrugated steel roof some twenty-five feet overhead. Well spaced from one another, three painters stood in pools of light created by bulbs with flat steel shades suspended on long wires from above. Two of them continued working at their easels, oblivious to the intrusion; the third, a tall cadaverous man with an unkempt beard and wild eyes, turned and stared with fury at the source of the draft.

Jonathan followed MacTaint through the warehouse to a door at the far end, and they passed into a totally different cosmos. The inner room was done in lush Victoriana: crystal chandeliers hung from an ornate ceiling; blue-flocked wallpaper stood above eggshell wainscoting; a good wood fire flickered in a wide marble fireplace; mirrors and sconces on all the walls made an even distribution of low intensity light; and comfortable deep divans and wing chairs in soft blue damask were in cozy constellations around carved and inlaid tables. A full-blown woman in her mid-fifties sat on one of the divans, her flabby arm dangling over the back. The bright orange of her hair contested with the blood red of her pasty lipstick, and festoons of bold jewelry clattered as she screwed a cigarette into a rhinestone holder.

"Here we are," MacTaint said as he shuffled in his ragged greatcoat over to the crystal bar. "He wasn't lost after all. This, good my love, is Jonathan Hemlock, about whom you have heard me say nothing. And this vast cow, Jon, is Lilla—my personal purgatory. Laphroaig, I suppose?"

Lilla twirled her cigarette holder into the air in greeting. "How good of you to pay us a visit. Mr. MacTaint has never mentioned you. While you're at it, my dear, you might bring me a little drop of gin."

"Friggin' lush," MacTaint muttered under his breath.

"Come. Sit here, Dr. Hemlock." Lilla thumped dust out of the divan seat beside her. "I take it you're connected with the theatre?"

Jonathan smiled politely into the drooping, overly made-up eyes. "No. No, I'm not."

"Ah. A pity. I was for many years associated with the entertainment world. And I must admit that I sometimes miss it. The laughter. The happy times."

MacTaint shambled over with the drinks. "Her only dealings with theatre were that she used to stand outside and try to hustle blokes too drunk to care what they got into. Here you go, love. Bottoms up, as they used to say in your trade."

"Don't be crude, love." She tossed back the glass of gin and smacked her lips, a motion that jiggled her pendulous cheeks. Then she clapped a ham-sized hand onto Jonathan's forearm and said, "Of course, I suppose it's all changed now. The old artists have gone, it's all youngsters with long hair and loud songs." She relieved herself of a shuddering sigh.

"It's worse than you think," MacTaint said, drooping into a damask chair and hooking another over with his toe so he could put his feet up on it. "The law doesn't allow you to carry sandwich boards advertising the positions you specialize in. And curb service on rubber mattresses is definitely not in."

"Fuck you, MacTaint!" Lilla said in a new accent that carried the snarl of the streets in it.

MacTaint instantly responded in kind. "Hop it, you ha'-penny cunt! I'd kick your arse proper for you, if I wasn't afraid of losing me boot!"

Lilla rose with tottering dignity and offered her hand to Jonathan. "I must leave you gentlemen. I have letters to do before retiring."

Jonathan rose and bowed slightly. "Good night, Lilla."

She made her way to the door at the far end of the room, sweeping up a bottle of gin as she passed the bar. She had to tack twice to gain the center of the door, which then gave her some difficulty in opening. In the end she gave it a hinge-loosening kick that knocked it ajar. She turned and waved her cigarette holder at Jonathan before disappearing.

Jonathan looked questioningly at MacTaint, who bared his lower teeth in a grimace of pleasure as he dug his fingernails into the ingrown stubble under his chin. "She drinks, you know," he said.

"Does she?"

"Oh, yes. I found her out there in the yard fifteen years ago," he explained, shifting the scratching to under an arm. "Somebody'd beat her up pretty badly."

"So you took her in?"

"To my eternal regret. Still! An occasional spat is good for the glands. She's a good old hole, really."

"What was this number she was doing for me?"

MacTaint shrugged. "Bits of old roles she's done, I suppose. She's more than a little mental, you know."

"She's not the only one. Cheers." Jonathan drank off half his whiskey and looked around the room with genuine appreciation. "You live well."

MacTaint nodded agreement. "I don't move many paintings anymore. Only one or two a year. But what with no income tax, I do well enough."

"Who are those painters outside?"

"Damned if I know. They come and they go. I keep the place warm and light, and there's always tea and bread and cheese about for them. Sometimes there's only one or two of them, sometimes half a dozen. That tall one who gave you the evil eye, he's been around for years and years. Still working on the same canvas. Feels he owns the place—by squatter's right, I shouldn't wonder. Complains sometimes if the cheese isn't to his liking. The others come and go. I suppose they hear about the place from one another."

"You're a good man, MacTaint."

"Ain't that the bleeding truth. Did I ever tell you that I was once a painter myself?"

"No, never."

"Oh, yes! More than forty years ago I came down to The Smoke to study art. Full of theories I was, about art and socialism. You didn't look at my paintings, you read them. Essays, they were. Hungry children, strikers being bashed up by the police, that sort of business. Trash. Then finally I discovered that my calling lay in stealing and flogging paintings. It's fun to do what you're good at."

They fell silent for a time, watching the fire loop yellow and blue in the hearth. It settled with a hiss of sparks, and the sound pulled MacTaint from his musings. "John? I asked you to drop over this evening for a reason."

"Not just to drink up your whiskey?"

"No. I've got something I want you to see." He grunted out of his chair and crossed to a painting that had been standing in an ornate old frame, its face to the wall. He carried it back tenderly and set it up on a chair. "What do you think of that?"

Jonathan scanned it and nodded. Then he leaned forward to examine it in detail. After five minutes, he sat back and finished off his Laphroaig. "You're not thinking of selling it, are you?"

MacTaint's eyes twinkled beneath his shaggy eyebrows. "And why not?"

"I was thinking of your reputation. You've never peddled a fake before."

"Goddamn your eye!" MacTaint cackled and scratched his scruffy head. "That would pass muster anywhere in the world."

"I'm not saying it's not a good copy—in fact it's extraordinary. But it is a forgery, and you don't flog fakes."

"Don't bother your head about that. I've never sold a piece of shoddy goods before, and I never shall. But slake my curiosity, lad. How can you tell it's phony?"

Jonathan shrugged. It was difficult to explain the almost automatic processes of mind and eye that constituted his gift. "Oh, a thousand things," he said.

"For instance?"

He sat back and closed his eyes, dredging up the original of J.-B.-S. Chardin's *House of Cards* from the lagan of his memory and holding it in focus as he studied the mental image. Then he opened his eyes slowly and examined the painting before him. "All right. This was done in Holland. At least, the Van M. technique was used. A relatively valueless painting of the proper age and size was sanded down, and the surface crackle was brought up by successive bakings of layers of paint."

MacTaint nodded.

"But the crackle was not perfect here." He touched the white areas around the face of the young man in a three-cornered hat. "And when the crackle didn't bake through perfectly, your forger rolled the canvas to force it. Basically a good job, too. But in these areas it ought to be deeper and more widely spaced. Your man seems to have forgotten that white dries more slowly than other pigments."

"And that's the only flaw? Crackle?"

"No, no. Dozens of other errors. Most of them are excessive precision. Forgers tend to be more exact in their draftsmanship than the artist was. Look here, for instance, at the perspective on the boy's left eye."

"Looks all right to me."

"Precisely. On the original, Chardin made a slight error—probably caused by two sittings during the drawing. And look here at the coin. It's as carefully drawn as the marker there. In the genuine painting, the coin has blurred outlines, as though it were in a different field of focus from the marker."

MacTaint shook his head in admiration, and a fall of dandruff floated to his lap. "Goddamn those eyes of yours."

"Even forgetting my eyes, this thing would bounce the minute it hit the market. The original hangs in the National Gallery."

"Oh, get along with you!"

They laughed, knowing that many forgeries hang bravely and unchallenged in the major galleries of the world, while the originals hang in clandestine splendor in private collections. This was, in fact, the case with all but one of Jonathan's own Impressionists.

"Would this pass inspection, Jon?"

They both knew that the real skills of major curators were limited to the documentation of ownership patterns, despite their tendencies to report in terms of a genuine knowledge. "With what provenance?" Jonathan asked.

"Oh . . . let's say it was hanging in the National Gallery in place of the real one."

Jonathan raised his eyebrows, his turn to feel admiration. "No question at all," he pronounced with confidence. "But how would you get at the real Chardin, Mac? Since the '57 thing, they've stiffened their security and there hasn't been a successful theft."

"What makes you think that?" MacTaint's eyes were round with feigned surprise, and he looked more than ever like a mischievous leprechaun.

"But there's a weight alarm system. You couldn't possibly get one off the wall without being detected."

"Of course it would be detected. It's always detected."

"Always? Tell me, Mac. How many paintings have you nicked from the National Gallery?"

"All told?" MacTaint squinted sideways in concentration. "Over the years? Ah-h, let's see . . . seven."

"Seven!" Jonathan stared at the old man. "I'll take that drink now," he said quietly.

"Here you go."

"Ta."

"Cheers."

They drank in silence. Jonathan shook his head. "I'm trying to see this in my mind, Mac. First, you walk to the gallery."

"I do that. Yes. In I walk."

"Then you take the painting from the wall. The alarms go off."

"Dreadful noise."

"You hang up a reasonably good forgery in its place, and you stroll out. Is that it?"

"Well, I don't stroll, exactly. More like running arse over teakettle. But in broad terms, yes, that's it."

"Now the alarm system tells them which picture has been tampered with, right?"

"Correct."

"And yet it never occurs to them to give the painting a professional scrutiny."

"They give it a great deal of attention. But not scrutiny." MacTaint was enjoying Jonathan's confusion immensely. "You're dying to know how I do it, aren't you?"

"I am."

"Well, I'm not going to tell you. Give that mind of yours something to chew on. You'll figure it out easily enough when you read about it in the newspapers."

"When will that be?"

"Exactly one week from tonight."

"You're a crafty and secretive son of a bitch."

"Part of my charm."

"MacTaint . . ." Jonathan didn't pursue it. He had no doubt at all but that the old fox would get the painting.

"All right," MacTaint relented, "I'll give you a little hint." He fished up a penknife from the depths of his overcoat pocket and pulled open one of the blades with a broken crusty thumbnail. Then he leaned over the painting for a second before slashing it twice, making a broad X through the face of the boy. "There. How's that?"

"You are a nut, MacTaint. I'm getting out of here."

MacTaint chuckled to himself as he showed Jonathan to the door. "Haven't you ever wanted to do something like that, lad? Slash a painting? Or break a raw egg in your hand? Or kiss a strange lady in an elevator?"

"You're a nut. Give my love to Lilla."

"I have enough trouble trying to give her my own."

"Good night."

"Yes."

The warehouse-cum-studio was in darkness, save for a single light hanging from the corrugated roof and the reddish glow of banked coal fires through the mica windows of the potbellied stoves. Only one painter was still at work, alone in absorbed concentration within the single circle of light. Jonathan walked silently across the cement floor and stood at the edge of the light, watching. His attention was so taken by the alert, feline motions of the painter attacking the canvas, then drawing back to judge effect, that it was some moments before he realized she was a woman. Seemingly oblivious of his presence, she squeezed off the excess paint from her brush between her thumb and forefinger and wiped them on the seat of her jeans, then she put the brush between her teeth sideways and took up a finer one to correct some detail. Her cavalier method of cleaning brushes was evidently habitual, because her bottom was a chaos of pigment, and Jonathan found this more interesting than the modernistic daub on the easel.

"What do you think of it?" she asked between her teeth, without turning around.

"It's certainly colorful. And attractively taut. But I think its potential for motion is its most appealing feature."

She stepped back and scrutinized the canvas critically. "Taut?"

"Well, I don't mean rigid. More lean and compact."

"And *interesting?*"

"Most interesting."

"That's the kiss of death. When people don't like what you've done, but they don't want to hurt your feelings, they always fall back on 'interesting.'"

Jonathan laughed. "Yes, I suppose that's true." He was delighted by her voice. It had the curling vowels of Irish, and the range was a dry contralto.

"No, now tell me true. What do you honestly think of it?"

"You really want to know?"

"Probably not." With a quick movement she brushed a wisp of amber hair away with the back of her hand. "But go ahead."

"Like most modern painting, I think it's undisciplined, self-indulgent crap."

She took the brush from her mouth and stood for a moment, her arms crossed over her chest. "Well now. No one could accuse you of trying to chat a girl up just to get into her knickers."

"But I am chatting you up," he protested, "and probably for that reason."

She looked at him for the first time, her eyes narrowed appraisingly. "Does that work very often—just saying it out boldly like that?"

"No, not very often. But it saves me a hell of a lot of wasted energy."

She laughed. "Do you really know anything about art?"

"I'm afraid so."

"I see." She thoughtfully replaced her brushes in a soup tin filled with turpentine. "Well. That's it, I guess." She turned to him and smiled. "Are you in a mood to celebrate?"

"Celebrate what?"

"The end of my career."

"Oh, come now!"

"No, no. Don't flatter yourself that it's just your opinion, informed though you assure me it is. As it happens, I agree with you totally. I suppose I'm a better critic than painter. Still, I've made one great contribution to Art. I've taken myself out of it."

He smiled. "All right. How would you like to celebrate?"

"I think dinner might be a good idea for starts. I haven't eaten since morning."

"You're broke?"

"Stoney."

"The only thing open this time of night woould be one of the more fashionable restaurants." He glanced involuntarily at her clothes.

"Don't worry. I shan't embarrass you. I'll just clean up and change before we go."

"You have your clothes here?"

She nodded her head toward two suitcases standing against the wall. "My rent came due this morning, you see. And the landlady never cared for the stink of turps in the halls anyway." She began scrubbing the paint from her hands with a cloth dipped in turpentine.

"You intended to sleep here?"

"Just for the night. The old geezer wouldn't mind. Other painters have done it from time to time. I used the last of my money to send an SOS telegram to relatives in Ireland. They'll be sending something down in the morning, I suspect. You can turn your back if the female nude disturbs you—not that I'll be all that nude."

"No, no. Go ahead. I've passed some of my happiest moments in the presence of the nude figure."

She wriggled out of her close-fitting jeans and kicked them up into her hands. "Of course, as a nude, I wouldn't have been much to Rubens's taste. I'm quite the opposite of ample, as you can see. In fact, I'm damned near two-dimensional."

"They're two of my favorite dimensions."

She was just pulling her jumper over her head, and she stopped in mid-motion, looking out through the head opening. "You've a glib and shallow way of talking. I suppose the girls find that dishy."

"But you do not."

"No, not especially. But I don't hold it against you, for I suppose it's just a habit. Will this do, do you think?" She drew up from the open suitcase a long green paisley gown that set off the cupric tones of her hair.

"That will do perfectly."

She tossed it on over her head, then patted down her short fine hair. "I'm ready."

He gave her her choice of restaurants, and she selected an expensive French one near Regent's Park on the basis that she had never had the money to go there and it was fun to be both beggar and chooser. Nothing about the meal was right. The butter in the scampi meunière tasted of char, the salade niçoise was more acid than bracing, and the only wine available at temperature was a Pouilly-Fuissé, that atonic white that occupies so large a sector of British taste. But Jonathan enjoyed the evening immensely. She was a charmer, this one, and the quality of the food did not matter, save as another subject for laughter. The lilt and color of her accent was contagious, and he had to prevent himself from slipping into an imitation of it.

She ate with healthy appetite, both her portions and his, while he watched her with pleasure. Her face intrigued him. The mouth was too wide. The jawline was too square. The nose undistinguished. The amber hair so fine that it seemed constantly stirred by unfelt breezes. It was a boyish face with the mischievous flexibility of a street gamine. Her most arresting feature was her eyes, bottle green and too large for the face, and thick lashes like sable brushes. Their special quality came from the rapid eddies of expression of which they were capable. Laughter could squeeze them from below; another moment they would flatten to a look of vulnerable surprise; then instantly they were narrow with incredulity; then intense and shining with intelligence; but at rest, they were nothing special. In fact, no single element of her face was remarkable, but the total he found fascinating.

"Do you find me pretty?" she asked, glancing up and finding his eyes on her.

"Not pretty."

"I know what you mean. But it's a good old face. I enjoy doing self-portraits. But I have to suppress this mad desire I have to add to my measuring thumb. Your face is not so bad, you know."

"I'm glad."

She turned to her salad. "Yes, it's an interesting face. Bony and craggy and all that. But the eyes are a bother."

"Oh?"

"Are you sure you're not hungry?"

"Positive."

"Actually, they're smashing. But they're not very comfortable eyes." She glanced up and looked at them professionally. "It's difficult to say if they're green or gray. And even though you smile and laugh and all that, they never change. You know what I mean?"

"No." Of course he knew, but he liked having her talk about him.

"Well, most people's eyes seem to be connected to their thoughts. Windows to the soul and all. But not yours. You can't read a thing by looking into them."

"And that's bad?"

"No. Just uncomfortable. If you're not going to eat that salad, I'll just keep it from going to waste."

Over coffee, over cognac, over more coffee, they talked without design.

"Do you know what I've always wished?"

"No. What?"

"I've always wished I was a tall, terribly handsome black woman. With long legs and a chilling, disdainful sideways glance."

He laughed. "Why have you wished that?"

"Oh, I don't know really. But think of the clothes I could get away with wearing!"

". . . oh, it was a typical middle-class Irish childhood, I suspect. Cooed over and spoiled as a baby; ignored as a child. Taught how to pass tests and how to stand with good posture. My father was a rabid Irish nationalist, but like most he had suspicions of inferiority. He sent me off to university in London—to get a *really good* education. And they were delighted when I came back with an English accent. I hated school as a girl. Sports and gymnastics particularly. I remember that we had a very, very modern physical culture teacher. A great bony woman, she was, with a prissy voice and a faint moustache. She tried to introduce the girls to the joys of eurythmics. You should have seen us! A gaggle of awkward girls—some with stick legs and knobby knees, others placid and fat—all trying to follow instructions 'to writhe with an inner passion and reach up expressively for the Sun God and let him penetrate your body.' We'd giggle about inner passions and penetrations, and the teacher would call us shallow, silly girls and dirty-minded. Then she'd writhe for us to show how it should be done. And we'd giggle some more. Cigarette?"

"I don't smoke."

She didn't seem to realize that she had stopped her story midway and had turned her thoughts inward.

He allowed the silence to run its course, and when she focused again on him with a slight start, he said, "So you won't be going back to Ireland?"

She butted her cigarette out deliberately. "No. Not ever." She lit another and stared at the gold lighter as though she were seeing it for the first time. "I should never have gone to the North. But I did and . . . too much happened there. Too much hatred. And death." She sighed and shook her head briskly. "No. I'll never go back to Ireland."

"So, do you like Sterne?" she said.

"Ah . . . funny you should mention him."

"Why?"

"I haven't the slightest idea who you're talking about."

"Sterne," she said, "the writer."

"Oh. That Sterne."

"I've always had this deep intuition that I would get on well with any man who had a fondness for Sterne, Trollope, and Galsworthy."

"Have it worked out like that?"

"I don't know. I've never met anyone who liked Sterne."

"More coffee?"

"Please."

". . . and you took up painting?"

"Oh, little by little. Not with much courage at first. Then I took the plunge and decided I would do nothing but paint until my money ran out. The family was dead against it, especially as they had wasted so much money sending me over here to school. I suppose they would have been happier if I had gone into prostitution. At least they would have understood the profit motive. Well, I painted and painted, and nobody at all noticed. Then I ran out of money and sold everything I had of any value. But the first thing I knew, I was stoney broke and didn't even have rent money."

"And that was that."

"And that was that." She looked up and smiled. "And here I am."

"I have a confession to make," he said seriously.

"You're a typhoid carrier?"

"No."

"You're designed to self-destruct in seven minutes?"

"No."

"You're a boy."

"No. You'll never guess."

"In which case, I give up."

"I have never liked the films of Eisenstein. They bore me to screaming."

"That is serious. What do you do for espresso talk?"

"Oh, I'm not excusing myself. I recognize it to be a great flaw in my character."

". . . oh, I love to drive! Fast, at night, in back lanes, with the lights off. Don't you?"

"No."

"Most men do, I think. British men especially. They use fast cars sexually, if you know what I mean."

"Like Italians."

"I suppose."

"Maybe that's why both countries produce so many competent grand prix drivers. They get practice on public roads."

"But you don't like to drive fast?"

"I don't need it."

She smiled. "Good." The vowel was drawn out and had an Irish curl.

". . . Philosophy of life?" he asked, smiling to himself at the idea. "No, I've never had one. When I was a kid, we were too poor to afford them, and later on they had gone out of fashion."

"No, now, don't send me up. I know the words sound pompous, but everyone has some kind of philosophy of life—some way of sorting out the good things from the bad . . . or the potentially dangerous."

"Perhaps. The closest I've come to that is my rigid adherence to the principle of leave-a-little."

"Leave a little what?"

"Leave-a-little everything. Leave a party before it becomes dull. Leave a meal before you're cloyed. Leave a city before you feel that you know it."

"And I suppose that includes human relationships?"

"Most especially human relationships. Get out while they're still on the upswing. Leave before they become predictable or, what is worse, *meaningful*. Be willing to lose a few events to protect the memory."

"I think that's a terrible philosophy."

"I'm sorry. It's the only one I've got."

"It's a coward's philosophy."

"It's a survivor's philosophy. Shall we have the cheese board?"

He half stood in greeting as she returned to the table. "A last brandy?" he asked.

"Yes, please." She was pensive for a second. "You know, it just now occurred to me that one might make a useful barometer of national traits by studying national toilet tissues."

"Toilet tissues?"

"Yes. Has that ever occurred to you?"

"Ah . . . no. Never."

"Well, for instance. I was just noticing that some English papers are medicated. You'd never find that in Ireland."

"The English are a careful race."

"I suppose. But I've heard that American papers are soft and scented and are advertised on telly by being caressed and squeezed—right along with adverts for suppository preparations and foods that are finger-licking good. That says something about decadence and soft living in a nation with affluence beyond its inner resources, doesn't it?"

"What do you make of the waxed paper the French are devoted to?"

"I don't know. More interest in speed and flourish than efficiency?"

"And the crisp Italian papers with the tensile strength of a communion wafer?"

She shrugged. It was obvious that one could make something of that too, but she was tired of the game.

She took his arm as they walked along the wet street to a corner more likely to produce taxis.

"I'll drop you off at Mac's. It's more or less on my way."

"Where *do* you live?"

"Right here." They were indeed passing the entrance to the hotel in which he had a penthouse apartment.

"But you said—"

"I thought I'd give you a way out."

She walked along in silence for a while, then she squeezed his arm. "That was a nice gesture. Truly gentle."

"I'm like that," he said, and laughed.

"But it *is* a bit odd that you just happen to live two doors from the restaurant."

"Now wait a minute, madam. *You* picked the restaurant."

She frowned. "That's true, isn't it. Still, it's a troubling coincidence."

He stopped and placed his hands on her shoulders, searching her face with mock sincerity. "Could it be . . . fate?"

"I think it's more likely a coincidence."

He agreed and they started off again, but back toward the hotel.

The phone double-buzzed several times before an angry voice answered. "Yes? Yes?"

"Good evening, sir."

"Good Lord! Do you know what time it is?"

"Yes, sir. Sorry. I just thought you'd like to know that they just went into his hotel on Baker Street."

"Is there any trouble? Is everything prepared?"

"No trouble, sir."

"Then why are you calling?"

"Well, I just thought you would want to be kept in the picture. They entered the hotel at exactly . . . oh, my. I must get this watch seen to."

There was a silence on the other end of the line.

Then, "Good night, Yank."

"Good night, sir."

Baker Street

LORD LOVE US!" she said. "This is ghastly!"

Jonathan laughed as he passed on ahead, turning on lights as he went. She followed him through two rooms.

"Is there no end to it?" she asked.

"There are eleven rooms. Including six bedrooms, but only one bath."

"That must cause some awkward traffic problems."

"No. I live here alone."

She dropped into the spongy pink velvet upholstery of an oversized chaise longue carved with conchs, serpentine sea dragons, and bosomy mermaids painted in antique white enamel and picked out in metallic gold. "I'm afraid to touch this rubbish. Afraid I'll catch something."

"Not an unfounded fear. Nothing is more communicable than bad taste, as

Ortega y Gasset has warned us. Look at pop art or the novels of Robbe-Grillet."

She looked at him quizzically. "You really are an academic, aren't you?" She scanned the pink marble fireplace, the harlequin wallpaper, the Danish modern furniture, the yellow shag rug, the burgundy-tinted glass sconces, the wrought-iron wall plaques. The saccharine profusion caused her nostrils to dilate and her throat to constrict. "How can you stand to live here?"

He shrugged. "It's free. And I have a little flat in Mayfair. I only stay here when I'm in this end of town."

"Goodness me. Impressive, sir. *Two* flats in the midst of a housing shortage. And he reads Ortega y . . . whoever. What more could a beggar girl ask?"

"She could ask for a drink." He poured from a hammered aluminum decanter in the form of a wading bird. "The single advantage of this place is that it makes going out into the street a pleasure. And you need something like that in London. Cheers."

"Cheers. You don't find London attractive?"

"Well, it's made me reevaluate my aesthetic ranking of Gary, Indiana."

She took her drink and wandered into the next room, which was less taste-fully appointed. "How did you come by this place? Do you have enemies in real estate?"

"No. It belongs to a film producer who took a twenty-year lease on it years ago to soak up some of the 'funny money' he had made in England, but couldn't take out of the country. He uses it as a *pied-à-terre* when in London, and he gives keys to friends who might be passing through. When I told him I'd be spending a year in England, he offered to lend it to me."

"Did he decorate it himself?"

"He used furniture and props from his films. The Doris Day/Rock Hudson sort of things."

"I see. Where do you stay to get away from the noise?"

"Come along." He led her through two rooms to one that had been left unfurnished. He had dragged in some of the quieter pieces and had hung his collection of Impressionists around the slate gray walls. It was in this room that he had first found MacTaint drinking his wiskey and admiring his paintings.

The canvases arrested her. She set down her glass and stood before a pointil-list Pissarro in silence.

"I have a hobby of collecting the best copies I can find," he told her.

"Beautiful."

"Oh, yes. Even copies, they're capable of putting modern painting in its place."

"All right, sir," she said in heavy brogue, "that will be enough of that altogether." She crossed to the tall windows and looked out on the pattern of lamplights in the park below. "Six bedrooms, is it? Choice of room must be an interesting cachet for the women you bring up here."

"Don't fish."

"Sorry. You're quite right."

"In point of fact, it occurs to me that I have never invited a woman up here."

She looked at him over the top of her glass, her green eyes round with a masque of ingenuousness. "And I am the very, very first one?"

"You're the first one I've *invited.*" He told her about waking one morning to find a woman staggering about in his bathroom. Despite her sunken eyes and greenish look of recent dissipation, he had recognized her as a film actress whom cosmetic surgery and breast injections kept employed past her time. She had evidently gotten a key from the producer years before, and had come there drunk after a night on the town with a brace of Greek boys. They had dropped her off after taking what money she had in her purse. She hadn't remembered anything of the night and after Jonathan had given her a breakfast bland enough to keep down, she had tucked a straying breast back into her gown, bestowed a snickering leer upon him through bloodshot eyes, and asked him how they had done.

"And what did you tell her?"

Jonathan shrugged. "What could I tell her? I said she had been fantastic and it had been a night I would never forget. Then I got her a cab."

"And she left?"

"After giving me her autograph. It's over there."

She went to the mantel and unfolded a sheet of paper. "But it's blank."

"Yes. The pen was out of ink, but she didn't notice."

She folded the paper carefully and replaced it. "Poor old dear."

"She doesn't know that. She thinks she's having a ball."

"Still, it makes me want to cry."

"If she ever found that out, she'd leave blank autographs behind her everywhere."

She returned to the window and looked out in silence, her cheek against the drapery. After a time she said, "It was nice of you."

"Just the easiest way out."

"I suppose so." She turned and looked at him thoughtfully. "What's your name?"

"Jonathan Hemlock. And yours?"

"Maggie. Maggie Coyne."

"Shall we go to bed, Maggie?"

She nodded and hummed. "Yes, I'd like that. But . . ." Her eyes crinkled impishly. "But I'm afraid I have some rather bad news for you."

He was silent for several seconds.

"You're kidding. This doesn't happen to good guys."

"I wish I were kidding. I really didn't mean to cheat you. But I didn't have a place to stay, don't you see?"

"I'll be goddamned."

"Pity we didn't meet a day or two later."

"Only a day or two?"

"Yes."

Jonathan rose. "Madam! It has always been my contention that the more subtle pleasures of lovemaking are reserved for those with daring and abandon. How do you feel about that?"

She grinned. "I have always felt the same way, sir."

"Then we're of a mind."

"We are that."

"En route."

At the first light of morning he woke hazily and turned to her, fitting her bottom into his lap. She snuggled against him slightly in response, and he wrapped her up in his arms.

"Good morning." His voice was husky as a result of little sleep and much exercise.

"Good morning," she whispered.

He rested his forehead against the back of her head and buried his face in her hair. "Maggie."

"What?"

"Nothing. Saying your name."

"Oh. That's nice. It isn't much of a name, though. Not romantic. No vowels to sing. Like Diane, or Alexandra, or Thomasyn. Maggie is a substantial name. Beefy. You may not waste away dreaming of a Maggie, but you can always trust a good old Maggie."

He smiled at the curling sound of her vowels. Proximity and body heat began to work their effect, apparent almost at once to her because of their postures. "I think I'll just make a little trip to your WC first, if you can stand the wait."

He released her. "Don't come back cold."

She slipped out of bed, and he slipped back toward sleep.

"Jonathan?"

He was fully awake immediately. She had spoken softly, but there was a brittle tension in her voice that set off alarms in him. He sat up.

"What is it?"

She stood in the doorway, an unlit cigarette dangling between her fingers. With only her brief panties on, she looked frail and vulnerable.

"What is it, Maggie?"

"The bathroom." Her voice was thin.

"Yes?"

"Jonathan?" Tight terror in her voice.

As he swung out of bed, he took up his robe and handed it to her, then he went quickly down the hall to the open door of the bathroom.

A man sat on the toilet seat, huddled over with his arms wrapped around his stomach. He was dressed in a black suit, and his graying hair was perfectly combed. The scene was denied dark humor by the terrible stench that filled the room and by the thick amoeba of blood that spread over the tile floor, fed by drips from his saturated trousers.

Jonathan's experience with CII told him exactly what had happened. The man had been gut shot, and as always in such cases, a convulsion of the sphincter had caused him to defecate. The mixed smells of blood and excrement were potent.

Jonathan stepped to him, carefully avoiding the thickening blood on the floor. He placed his fingertips against the throat. The man was not dead, but the pulse was faint and fluttery. The man lifted his head and looked blearily at Jonathan. There was no chance for him. The eyes had that wall-eyed spread that attends death. The pupils were contracted. There was dope in him.

Jonathan's attention was attracted to a slight pulsing motion in the man's lap. He was holding his guts in with his hands. He tried to speak, but only a glottal whisper came out. Jonathan put his ear close to the mouth, resisting the revulsion caused by the stink of human feces.

"I . . . I'm awfully . . . sorry. Disgraceful thing . . . I . . ."

"Who are you?"

"Shameful . . ."

"Who are you?"

Out of the tail of his eye, Jonathan saw Maggie standing at the bathroom door. Her face was a plane of disgust and horror. She was trying to calm herself by lighting her cigarette, but in her nervousness she couldn't operate the lighter.

"Get out."

"What?" She was confused.

"Get out. He's ashamed."

She disappeared.

"Oh, God . . . Oh, good God . . ." The man's body tensed. He stared up at Jonathan with anguish and disbelief, his teeth clenched, his head shuddering with his vein-bursting effort to cling to life. "Oh! God!"

Then he let it go. He slumped and let life go.

He made one last sound. A name.

Then he slipped off the toilet seat almost gracefully, and his cheek came to rest in his own blood. His hands fell away, and the gray green guts protruded. The seat of his trousers was wet and stained with excrement.

Jonathan stood up and stepped back. For the first time he noticed something crammed in behind the toilet bowl. It was a Halloween mask—Casper the ghost. He stepped out of the bathroom and closed the door quietly behind him.

Maggie was standing down the hall, her back pressed against the wall defensively, her face pale with terror. He put his arm around her for support and conducted her to the bedroom.

"Here. Lie down. Put your feet up."

"I think I'm going to be sick," she said faintly.

"It's shock. Go ahead, be sick. Put your finger down your throat."

She tried, and gagged. "I can't!"

"Listen to me, Maggie! I don't mean to be cruel or unfeeling, but you've got to pull yourself together. We've got to get out of here. That man in there . . . This is a setup. I've seen them before. For your own good, do exactly what I tell you. If you're going to be sick, do it. If not, get dressed. Then lie down and rest until I've done a couple of things. OK?"

She stared at him, confused and frightened by his cool efficiency. "What is this? What's happening?"

"Just do what I told you. Here. Give me that. I'll light it for you."

"Thank you."

"There. Now, move over."

"What are you doing to do?"

"Nothing." Jonathan lay full length on his back beside her and closed her eyes. He put his palms together in a prayerlike gesture and brought them to his face, the thumbs under his chin and the forefingers touching his lips. Then he regulated his breathing, taking very shallow breaths deep in the stomach. He focused his mind on the image of an unrippled pond, calm in a chill dawn light. Tension drained from him; the adrenaline seeped away; his mind grew peaceful and clear.

In three minutes he opened his eyes slowly and brought the room back into focus. He was all right.

He rose and moved around the room quickly, getting dressed and emptying pockets and drawers in search of money.

Maggie finished her cigarette, her eyes never leaving him; something in his adroit, professional movements fascinated her. And frightened her.

He looked over the room to see that everything was done, then he knelt on the bed and brushed the hair away from her forehead. "Come on, now. Get dressed, dear." He nuzzled into the closure of her dressing gown and kissed each of her breasts lightly. Then he left to collect money from the other bedrooms.

Typical of poor boys who have finally become financially comfortable, he was ostentatiously careless with money and kept a fair amount around in cash. By the time he had come back to their bedroom, combed and shaved, he had gathered almost three hundred pounds, largely in crumpled, forgotten notes.

She was sitting on the edge of the bed, dressed, but still dazed.

He sipped his third café crème. Maggie had desultorily stirred hers when it arrived, but had not drunk it; a tan scum had formed on its surface. She stared into the glass unseeing, her thoughts focused within her. From their table deep within a coffee shop across the street, Jonathan watched the entrance of his Baker Street residence carefully. They had not spoken since ordering.

She broke the silence without looking up from her glass. "Are we safe here? Right across the street?"

He nodded, his eyes not leaving the hotel's revolving door. "Fairly safe, yes. They'll expect us to try to make distance."

"They? Who are they?"

"I don't know."

"But you have some idea?"

"It could be CII. An American intelligence organization I used to work for. Years ago."

"Doing what?"

He glanced at her. How could he tell her he had been an assassin? Or even, to split moral hairs, a counterassassin? He returned to watching the doorway across the street.

"But why would they want to implicate you in . . . in that terrible business back there?"

"They have devious, perverted minds. Impossible to know what they're up to. Chances are they want me to work for them again."

"I don't understand."

"Drink your coffee."

"I don't want it."

They returned to silence and to their own thoughts. And after a time the impulse to speak came to both at once.

"Do you know what was the worst . . . Pardon? You were saying?"

"Look, Maggie, I'm very sorry . . . Excuse me . . . The worst what?"

"Sorry . . . No, you go ahead."

"Sorry . . . I was just going to say the obvious, love. I'm terribly sorry you're implicated in this."

"Am I? Really implicated, Jonathan?"

He shook his head. "No, no. Not really. I'll get you clear of it. Don't worry."

"And what about you?"

"I can take care of myself."

"True." She searched his eyes. "Too well, really."

"What is that supposed to mean?"

"Well, that's what I was going to say before. When I think about it, the worst part of the whole thing was your reaction. So brisk. Professional. As though you were used to this sort of business. You were terribly calm."

"Not really. I was scared and confused. That's why I had to take that unit of light meditation."

"On the bed?"

"Yes."

"And you can sort yourself out just like that? In a few minutes?"

"I can now. After years of practice."

She considered that for a moment. "There must have been some terrible things in your life, for you to have to develop—"

"There! There they are!"

She followed his eyes to the hotel entrance. Through gaps in the traffic, she saw two men emerge and stand on the pavement, looking up and down the street. One of them was dressed oddly in flared trendy trousers, cowboy boots, and a longish, tight plaid sports jacket. The collar of his aloha shirt was folded over the jacket collar in the style of twenty-five years ago, and a bulky camera dangled from around his neck. The other man was tall and powerfully built. His bullet-shaped head was shaved, and there were deep folds of skin halfway up the back of his neck. He wore a thick turtleneck sweater under a tweed jacket, and gave the impression of a prizefighter, save for his large, mirror-faced sunglasses.

Aloha Shirt said something to Bullet Head. From his expression, he was angry. Bullet Head barked back, clearly not willing to take the blame. They looked again up and down the street, then Aloha made a signal with his hand, and a dark Bentley pulled up to the curb. They got in, Bullet in front, Aloha alone in back. The Bentley pulled into the traffic, bullying its way into the flow on the strength of its prestige.

Maggie looked at Jonathan, who was studying the faces of the other passersby in front of the hotel. "That's all," he said to himself. "Just the two."

"How do you know—"

He held up his hand. "Just a moment." He watched the street narrowly until, in about three minutes, the Bentley passed again, slowing down as it went by the hotel entrance, the men within leaning forward to examine it carefully. Then the car sought the center lane and drove off.

"Ok. They won't be back. Not for a few hours, anyway. But they've undoubtedly left someone inside."

"How do you know they were the ones?"

"Instinct. They have the look of the weird types you find in espionage. And their subsequent behavior nailed it."

"Espionage? What on earth is going on, Jonathan?"

He shook his head slowly. "I honestly don't know."

"Have you done something?"

"No." He felt anger and bitterness rise inside him. "I think it's something they want me to do."

"What sort of thing?"

He changed the subject curtly. "Tell me, how would you describe the boss one. The one with the camera and the gaudy shirt?"

She shrugged. "I don't know. An American, I suppose. A tourist?"

"Not a tourist. Even in his excitement, he checked the traffic from right to left. As though he were used to driving on the left. Americans check it from left to right."

"But the cowboy boots?"

"Yes. But the trousers were of British cut."

"He did look odd, come to think of it. Like an American. But like an American in old movies."

"Exactly my impression."

"What does that tell you?" She leaned forward conspiratorially.

Jonathan smiled at her, suddenly amused by the tone of their conversation. "Nothing, really. Drink your coffee."

She shook her head.

He withdrew into himself for several minutes, his brow furrowed, his eyes focused through the patterned wall he was staring at. Unit by unit he put together the flow of his necessary actions for the rest of the day. Then he took a deep breath and resettled his attention on Maggie. "OK, listen." He drew his wallet from his jacket pocket. Folded in it were his checkbook, several sheets of writing paper, stamps, and envelopes, all of which he had collected in his tour of the penthouse flat. "I'll be damned!" He had also drawn out the envelope containing money the Renaissance man had given him for his ad hoc appraisal of the Marini Horse. He had completely forgotten about it. So he wasn't working all that lucidly after all. His reactions had rusted in the years since he had quit this kind of business forever. He opened the envelope and counted the money: ten fifty-pound notes. Good. He wouldn't have to use a check after all. "Here," he said, passing two hundred pounds over the table, "take this."

She moved her hand away from the notes, as though to avoid contaminating contact. "I don't need it."

"Of course you need it. You don't have a room. You don't have any money. And you can't go back to MacTaint's."

"Why not?"

"They'll have someone watching it. This thing is pretty carefully put together.

They must have been on me most of the night. I don't too often sleep up there. I usually stay in my Mayfair flat."

"If you hadn't met me . . ."

"Nonsense. If they really wanted to get to me, they'd have done it sooner or later."

"Something occurs to me, Jonathan. How did they get in?"

"Oh, any number of ways. Picked the lock. Used a key. And there are a lot of keys around. I told you about that drunk actress."

"Still, it must have been difficult. Carrying that poor man."

"He was alive when they brought him in. They shot him there in the bathroom. No blood in the hall. He was heavily doped up."

"But still, how did they get him up to your flat."

He shook his head. While they had waited for the elevator to bring them down from his apartment, he had noticed a folding wheelchair against the wall. That, together with the Casper mask stuffed behind his toilet, told him that they'd brought the poor son of a bitch here as a Guy Fawkes dummy. Jonathan saw no reason to share this grisly detail with Maggie.

"Here, take the money."

"No, really . . ."

"Take it."

Her hand shook as she accepted the folded notes.

"I know, dear. And I'm sorry. It's really a piece of bad luck that you got mixed up in this. But you'll be all right. They're not after you."

Tears appeared in her eyes, as much in reaction to the stress and fear as anything else. She didn't apologize for them, nor did she try to blink them away. "But they are after *you*. And I'm afraid for you." She pulled herself together by the technique of assuming a broad Irish accent. "I've grown rather fond of you, don't you know?"

"I've grown fond of you too, madam. Maybe after I've sorted this thing out . . ."

"Yes. Let's do try."

"Will you have some coffee now?"

She nodded and sniffed back the last of the tears.

He ordered more coffee and some croissants, and they didn't speak until after the waiter had brought them and departed. She drank her coffee and broke up a croissant, but she didn't eat it. She pushed her plate aside and asked, "Will you be able to let me know how you're getting on?"

"That wouldn't be wise. For you, Maggie. Anyway, I won't know where you're staying. And I don't want to."

"Oh, but I'd feel dreadful not knowing if you were all right."

"All right. Look, tomorrow afternoon I will be giving a lecture at the Royal Institute of Art. You can attend. That way you'll be able to see me and you'll know I'm all right. If it looks as though we can meet afterward, I'll end the discussion by saying that I hope to have an opportunity to pursue some of these matters with interested individuals in private. And about an hour later, I'll meet you right here. OK?"

She frowned, confused. "You intend to go ahead with this lecture?"

"Oh yes. With all my social engagements. In this sort of game, they win if they can completely disrupt my life. That would force me either to come to terms with them, or to go on hiding forever. I'm reasonably safe in the open, in public places. You notice that they didn't bring the police with them just now. The big trick will be getting to and from the lecture, and keeping out of sight in the meanwhile. But I've been trained in this sort of game. So don't worry."

"What kind of advice is that?"

He smiled. "Well, don't worry too much anyway."

"Do you really think you can avoid them forever?"

"No. Not forever. But I'll get a chance to think. And I'll try to pick my own ground for meeting them."

"What are you going to do now? After I leave you?"

"I have to arrange some mechanical things. I don't have clothes. I don't have a place to stay. Once I've settled that, I suppose I'll go to the movies."

"Go to the movies?"

"Best place to lose yourself for a few hours. One of those porno houses where you can rent a raincoat."

"Rent a raincoat?"

"Never mind."

"What are you doing to do about that man . . . we found? You can't just leave him there."

"I can't do anything else. Anyway, unless I miss my guess, he won't be there in an hour. They don't want the police in on this if they can help it. I wouldn't be much use to them in prison. No, they were supposed to walk in on me and get hard evidence. A photograph or something. They they'd have the leverage to force me to work for them. But something went wrong—what, I don't know. Maybe we woke up too early and got out too fast. They'll have to drop back and think up something else. And I'm hoping that will take them a little while."

She shuddered. "I'm sorry. I try not to think of him . . . the man in your loo . . . but every once in a while the image of him—"

Jonathan looked up at her suddenly. "In my loo?"

"Yes. In your bathroom. What is it?"

"The man said a word just before he died. A name, I thought. I thought he said Lew, as in Lewis. Or Lou as in Louise. But he could have meant loo as in bathroom."

"What would that mean?"

Jonathan shook his head. "I haven't the slightest idea."

Just before they parted, after they had gone back over the arrangements for meeting after the Royal Institute lecture, Maggie made an observation that had occurred to Jonathan as well. "It's an odd feeling. The change of tone between this morning and the bantering in the restaurant last night. I can't help this curious sensation that we have known one another for years and years. In just a few hours we've been through laughter, and love, and all this trouble. It's an odd feeling."

"I admire the way you've braced up under this."

"Ah, well, you see, I've had practice. The troubles in Belfast got very close to me. The soul develops calluses very quickly. That's the real terror of violence: a body gets used to it."

"True." Indeed, he had surprised himself with the speed with which he had swung into the patterns and routines of a kind of existence he had thought was far behind him. "I'll see you soon, Maggie."

"Yes. Soon."

He stood in the red public telephone box and memorized the numbers of two railroad hotels.

"Great Eastern Hotel?" The operator's voice had the sing-song of rote.

He pushed the twopence in. "Reservations, please."

At the Great Eastern, he reserved a room under the name Greg Eastman. Then he called the Charing Cross Hotel and reserved a room under the name Charles Corsley. Railroad hotels were the kind he needed. Quiet, middle class, very large, and used to transients. He would actually stay at the Great Eastern where a lift could bring him directly from the Underground station into the

lobby, making it unnecessary to go onto the open street. His reservation at the
Charing Cross was only for a pickup of clothes.

Next he called his tailor on Conduit Street.

"Ah, yes. Dr. Hemlock. May we be of service?"

"I need two suits, Matthew."

"Of course, sir. Shall we make an apointment for a fitting?"

"I haven't time for that. You have my paper there."

"Quite so, sir."

"I need the suits this evening."

"*This* evening? Impossible, Dr. Hemlock."

"No, it isn't. You carry Bruno Piattellis, don't you? Pull a couple off the racks,
and have one of your tailors alter them to my paper. Conservative in color, not
too trendy in cut. You could do it in three or four hours, if you put two men on
it."

"We *do* have other commitments, sir."

"Double the price of the suit. And twenty quid for you."

The clerk sighed histrionically. "Very well, sir. I'll see what can be done."

"Good man. Have them delivered to the Charing Cross Hotel, to Mr. (he had
to think for a second of the mnemonic device he had used for names) Mr.
Charles Crosley."

The next call was to his shirtmaker in Jermyn Street. A little more pot-
sweetening was necessary there because he despised ready-made shirts, and they
would have to be cut from his patterns on file. But eventually he received their
commitment to have six shirts delivered by five o'clock, together with stockings
and linen.

Jonathan's last call was to MacTaint.

"Ah, is that you, lad? Just a minute." (The hiss of a phone being cupped over
with a hand.) "Lilla? I'm on the phone. Shut your bleeding cob!" (An angry
babble from off phone.) "Put a sock in it! . . . now, what can I do for you,
Jonathan?"

"I'm going to mail off three hundred quid to you this afternoon."

"That's nice. Why?"

"I'm in a little trouble. I want a source of money that's not on my person."

"Police?"

"No."

"Ah. I see. *Real* trouble. What do I do with the money?"

"Keep two fifty handy to send to me if I contact you. I'll probably be at the
Great Eastern. My name will be Greg Eastman."

"And the remaining fifty's for my trouble?"

"Right."

"Done. Keep well, lad."

Jonathan ran off. He appreciated MacTaint's professionalism. It was right that
he accept the fee without whimpering protestations of friendship, and it was
right that he ask no questions.

The telephone box was near an Underground entrance, and Jonathan took
the long escalator into the tube. Until this trouble was sorted out, he would
travel primarily through the anonymous means of the Underground.

He reemerged into the sunlight near Soho, and he made his way to a double-
feature skin flick: *Working Her Way through the Turkish Army* and *Au Pair
Girls in the Vatican*. For four hours he was invisible in the company of the lost,
the lonely, the ill, and the warped, who pass their afternoons in torn seats that
smell of mildew, candy-wrapper litter under their feet, staring with frozen pupils
at Swedish "starlets" moaning in bored mock ecstasy as they make coy orificial
use of members and gadgets.

London

JONATHAN STAYED IN the cover of the crowds around Charing Cross Monument, keeping the façade of the Charing Cross Hotel under observation. It was nearly five, and the go-home traffic had thickened. Queues for buses coiled and re-coiled: in a few minutes vehicular and human traffic would nearly coagulate. He was relying on that, in case the people who were after him had had the experience or intelligence to think of checking with his tailor.

He looked up to the belfry clock of St. Martin's-In-The-Fields for the time, and he recalled the newspaper reports of the unfortunate fellow who had been found impaled there. A delivery van bearing the name of his shirtmaker had already arrived at the front entrance of the hotel, but he had seen nothing of the bullet-headed boxer in sunglasses or of the 1950 vintage American tourist. Still the suits hadn't arrived from his tailor; that was disconcerting because every-thing depended on his being able to pick up his clothes during the rush hours.

At five o'clock straight up, a taxi pulled into the bustle of the rank outside the hotel, and a young man alighted. He breasted his way through the press of people, a large white box carried high. That would be the suits. Jonathan strolled across the street and stood against the façade of the hotel. No sun-glasses, no Aloha Shirt, no Bentley. He waited until a taxi stopped to discharge passengers, then approached the driver.

"Wait for me here, will you? Five minutes."

"Can't do that, mate. Rush hour, you know."

Jonathan took a ten pound note from his pocket and ripped it in half. "Here. The other half when I get back in five minutes."

The driver was undecided for a second. "Right." He glanced through the rearview mirror at the growing queue of taxis behind. "Make it quick."

Jonathan entered the lobby through the restaurant and glanced around before picking up a house phone.

"This is Charles Crosley in 536. There will be some parcels for me. Would you ask the porter to have them sent up?"

Through the glass of the telephone cabinet he watched the receptionist, hoping she would not check to see if his key had been picked up. In the rush of guests and inquiries at this hour, she did not. A bellboy responded to a sum-mons and went to the parcels room where he collected a small and a large box. As he carried them toward the lifts, Jonathan stepped out from the telephone booth and fell in behind him. Just as the lift doors closed, Jonathan caught the bustle of two men entering the main lobby hurriedly. Aloha Shirt and Bullet Head.

So they had thought to check with his tailor after all. But just a little too late, if everything worked out well.

"You must be bringing those to me."

"Sir?"

"Crosley? Room 536?"

"Oh, yes, sir."

Jonathan pushed the fourth-floor button. "Here, I'll take them." He passed the bellboy a pound note.

"But you're on five, sir."

"That's true. But my secretary is on four." He winked, and the lad winked back.

Waiting for the elevator car to bring him back to the lobby, he watched the indicator for the next car count its way to five, then stop. He had a minute on them. Time enough, provided his taxi driver had been able to resist the anger and impatience of men behind him in the rank.

The Bently was parked at the entrance, and the driver, a beefy lad with longish hair, recognized Jonathan as he passed. He clambered out of the car and took a step or two toward Jonathan, changed his mind and turned toward the hotel entrance to alert his comrades, then thought better of it and decided that he must not lose sight of Jonathan. He ran back to the Bentley and, not knowing what to do, leaned in the driver's window and pressed his horn. Startled taxi drivers in the rank sounded their horns in retribution. Confused by the blare of horns, a car stopped at the intersection, and a lorry behind him slammed on its brakes and barked irritation with its two-toned air horn. Passing cars swerved aside and blasted their horns angrily. Bus drivers slammed their fists onto their horn buttons. Traffic around the Circus joined in.

Jonathan shouted to his taxi driver over the din, "Charing Cross Underground!"

"But that's only a block away, mate!"

Jonathan passed forward the other half of the torn note. "Then you've made out, haven't you?"

The driver added his horn to the cacophony and pulled away from the curb. "Bleeding Americans," he muttered. "Bloody well mental they are."

Just as the taxi turned the corner, Aloha Shirt and Bullet Head burst through the revolving doors, flinging out before them a bewildered old woman who spun around twice before sitting on the steps, dizzy. The Bentley was only half a block behind as Jonathan jumped out at the Underground entrance. Holding his bulky packages over his head, he ran down the long double escalator, passing those who obediently kept to the right. The passageways were crowded with commuters, and the parcels were both a burden and a weapon. Instantly he came out on the waiting platform, he walked along to the "Way Out" end, so he had an avenue of escape should the train not come in time.

And he waited. No train. Girls babbled to one another, and old men stared ahead sightlessly, in the coma of routine. The train did not come. An advertising placard requested readers to attend a benefit concert for Bangladesh, and a scrawled message beside it enjoined them to "Fuck the Irish" and another said "Super Spurs." No train.

There was a flutter in the crowd at the far end of the tunnel, and Bullet Head and Aloha Shirt rushed out to the platform. The former's head was glistening with sweat as he looked up and down, scanning the faces of the throng. Jonathan pressed against the wall, but no good. They spotted him, and the two of them were breasting through protesting commuters in his direction.

Jonathan slipped out the exit and up a tiled passageway toward the double escalators. A train had pulled in at another dock, and just behind him came a flood of people, rushing to make connections. At the head of this mob, he was able to trot up the long escalator two steps at a time. At the top he looked back. Aloha Shirt and Bullet Head were crowded into the center of the human ice jam, slowly oozing up the escalator. Jonathan U-turned and stepped onto the nearby empty down escalator. His pursuers watched with helpless rage as he passed them, not five yards away. They struggled to push ahead, but sharp words and threats of physical retribution from men in cloth caps forced them to accept the inevitable, if not philosophically. As they drew abreast, Jonathan nodded in sassy greeting and slipped his middle finger along the side of the box in his arms. The did not react to the taunting gesture, and Jonathan realized he had used the one-finger American version, rather than the two-finger British orthography for the universal symbol.

No sooner had he stepped back out onto the platform than he felt the rush of stale air that signaled the arrival of a train. It stopped with a clatter of opening doors, there was a gush and countergush of people, the doors slammed shut, and it pulled out with a squeal. Bullet Head, outstripping his panting companion, ran along just outside the window, shouting his rage and frustration. Jonathan leaned over and communicated with him in sign language, this time in British. As they plunged into the black tunnel, Jonathan glanced up to see a look of frozen indignation on the face of a prim old lady on the seat opposite. He had inadvertently made the gesture within inches of her nose.

"Well, tipped up this way, it *could* mean Victory, you know. Or Peace? I'll bet you don't want to talk about it, right?"

Jonathan took breakfast in the Victorian abundance of the grand dining room of the Great Eastern. The railroad hotel was a perfect cover. With his native panache, he would have been conspicuous in a bed and breakfast place, and they—whoever they were—would already have checked the ranking hotels.

The night before, he had taken a long, very hot bath in a bathroom so cool that it rapidly filled with thick swirling steam. He had lain soaking in the deep tub, the open hot tap keeping the temperature of the water high, until the stresses and fatigues of the day had seeped out of his body. His skin glowing from the bath, he had gotten into bed naked between stiffly starched sheets. He would need rest when the business began again tomorrow, so he emptied his mind and set his breathing pace low as he folded his hands together and brought on sleep through shallow meditation. Each stray thought that eddied into his mind he pushed aside, gently, so as not to disturb the unrippled surface of the pond in his imagination. The last conscious image—Maggie's imperfect but pleasing face—he allowed to linger before his eyes before easing it aside.

Whatever happened, he had to keep her to the lee of trouble.

Luncheon at the Embassy was, as always, both vigorously animated and abysmally dull. Jonathan considered his attendance at such functions the price he had to pay for their lavish support of his stay in England, but he made it a practice to be dull company, talking to as few people as possible. It was in this mood that he carried his glass of American champagne away toward the social paregoric of an untrafficked corner. But it was not sufficiently insulated.

"Ah! There you are, Jonathan!"

It was fforbes-Ffitch, whom Jonathan seemed fated to encounter at every function.

"Listen, Jonathan. I've just been in a corner with the Cultural Attaché, and he gives his support to this idea of mine to send you off for a few lectures in Sweden. The American image isn't particularly bright there just now, what with the Southeast Asia business and all. Could be an excellent thing, jointly sponsored by the USIS and the Royal College. Sound enticing?"

"No."

"Oh. Oh, I see."

"I told you the other evening I wasn't interested."

"Well, I thought you might just be playing hard to get."

Jonathan looked at him with fatigue in his eyes. "Don't rush at it, f-F. You'll make it. With your hustle and ambition, I have no doubt you'll be Minister of Education before you're through. But don't climb on my back."

fforbes-Ffitch smiled wanly. "Always straight from the shoulder, aren't you? Well, you can't blame a fellow for trying."

Jonathan looked at him with heavy-lidded silence.

"Quite," f-F said perkily. "Bot you will honor your commitment to lecture for us at the Royal College this afternoon, I hope."

"Certainly. But your people have been remiss in their communications."

"Oh? How so?"

"No one has told me the topic of my lecture. But don't rush. It's still an hour away."

fforbes-Ffitch frowned heavily and importantly. "I am sorry, Jonathan. My staff has been undergoing a shake-up. Heads rolling left and right. But I've not put together a trim ship yet. In any department I run, this kind of incompetence is simply not on." He touched Jonathan's shoulder with a finger. "I'll make a call and sort it out. Right now."

Jonathan nodded and winked. "Good show."

fforbes-Ffitch turned and left the reception room with an efficient bustle, and Jonathan was in the act of retreating into another low traffic corner when he was intercepted by the host, the Senior Man Present. He was typical of American Embassy leadership—a central casting type with wavy gray hair, a hearty hand-shake, and an ability to say the obvious with a tone of trembling sincerity. Like most of his ilk, his qualifications for statesmanship were based upon an ability to get the vote out of some Spokane or other, or to contribute lavishly to campaign funds.

"Well, how's it been going, Dr. Hemlock?" The Senior Man Present asked, pulling Jonathan's hand. "We don't see enough of you at these affairs."

"That's odd. I have quite the opposite impression."

"Yes," the Senior Man Present laughed, not quite understanding, "yes, I imagine that's true. It's always like that though, really. Even when it doesn't appear to be. That's one of the things you learn in my line of work."

Jonathan agreed that it probably was.

"Say," the SMP asked with a show of offhandedness, "you're out in the wind of public opinion. What kind of ground swells do you get concerning the American elections?"

"None. People don't talk to me about it because they know I wouldn't be interested."

"Yes." The SMP nodded with profound understanding. "No—ah—no comments about the Watergate bugging business?"

"None."

"Good. Good. Nothing to it, really. Just an attempt to implicate the President in some kind of messy affair. Between you and me, I think the whole thing was cooked up either by the other party or by the Communists. I imagine it will blow over. This sort of thing always does. That's one thing you learn in my line of work."

"Good Lord, Jonathan, there's been a ballup." fforbes-Ffitch was back. "Ah!" He smiled profuse greetings to the SMP. "Did I catch you two chatting about my plans for a lecture series in Sweden?"

"Yes, you did," the SMP lied with practiced insouciance. "And I'm all for it. If there's anything my office can do to move things ahead . . ."

"That's awfully good of you, sir."

After shaking hands with warm cordiality, both his hands cupped around Jonathan's, the SMP returned to his hostly duty of pressing a drink on a visiting Moslem.

"You say there's been a ballup?" Jonathan asked.

"Yes. I am sorry. Our fault entirely. I'll cancel, if you want."

Jonathan had been looking forward to seeing Maggie in the audience during this lecture, perhaps even meeting her in the cafe afterward.

"What's the trouble?" he asked.

"They've advertised that you're going to lecture on *cinema*. I've got the title here: 'Criticism in Cinema: Use and Abuse.' "

Jonathan laughed. "No problem. Not to worry. I'll vamp it."

"But . . . cinema? You're in painting, aren't you?"

"I'm in just about everything. And, despite Godard, cinema is still essentially a visual art. Do you have a car here?"

"Why, yes." fforbes-Ffitch was surprised and pleased. "Could I run you over to the college?"

"If you would." f-F's lickspittle conversation would be fair pay for the cover of traveling with him, in case Aloha Shirt and Bullet Head should be hanging about outside the post office bulk of the Embassy.

". . . which rhythms are established by cutting rate and cutting tone. While the intensity of the visual beat is a function of what Whitaker, in his lean description of film linguistics, has called 'cutting volume.' Does that answer your question?"

Jonathan scanned the packed audience for a glimpse of Maggie while he responded automatically to the questions. The hall was filled, and a few people were standing at the back of the house. Because of the overcrowding, a policeman was present. In his tall hat and stiff uniform, he was in sharp contrast to the earthy-arty appearance of the audience.

Someone with a thin nasal voice in the back of the hall was proposing a question when Jonathan caught sight of Maggie against the back wall. She stood under one of the conical light fixtures set in the ceiling of the overhanging balcony, and the soft narrow beam isolated her from the mass and mixed with the amber of her soft hair. He was pleased she was there.

". . . and therefore ineluctably interrelated with it?"

He had not caught the whole of the question, but he recognized the style of inquiry: another involute question asked by a bright young person, not to learn, but to demonstrate the level of his recent reading.

Jonathan faked his way out. "That's a sinewy and complicated question with ramifications that would take more time than we have to explore adequately. Suppose you break off the fragment that most puzzles you and phrase that concisely."

The thin voice hemmed and hawed, then restated his question in full, adding additional fragments of erudition that occurred to him.

But Jonathan's attention was even slighter than it had been before. At the back of the hall, leaning against the wall, was Bullet Head. Jonathan scanned around. Aloha Shirt was making his way down the right aisle. Jonathan looked for Maggie. She still stood in her beam of light, evidently unaware of them.

A pause and a cough. The question had been posed, and they awaited an answer. A couple of remembered key words in the question gave Jonathan adequate cue to form an answer: "That shifts us from the discussion of film qua film to a look at the state of film study and criticism in the world. But I'm willing to make the shift if you are. In broad, it is safe to say that current film study and criticism are both a chaos and a desert. First, we must acknowledge that, with the exception of Mitry and perhaps Bazin, there are no film critics of substance."

Where the hell was that bobby?

"All we really have are reviewers on varying altitudes of diction. The French school—if one can call that colloidal suspension of spatting personalities a school—works from the principle that cinema is a Gallic invention, the subtleties of which can never properly be mastered by peoples of less fortunate nativity."

Bullet Head was making his way down the left aisle. Maggie still stood alone in the cone of light.

"Their most insidious export since the French pox has been their capricious insistence that American cinema is greatest at its most common denominator. They have seduced spineless American and British scholars into giving the benediction of serious study to such thin beer as the films of Capra, Hawks, and Jerry Lewis."

The young driver of the Bentley was moving across the back of the hall toward Maggie! Where in hell was that policeman?

"The situation is no healthier in the United States, where the ranking reviewers operate as petulant social starlets. Snide infighting, phrasemaking, and pantheon building are the symptoms of their critical affliction. Then, of course, you have the Village Blat types pandering to their young readers' assumption that befuddlement is Obscurantism and that technical incompetence denotes social concern. But the greatest burden to American film criticism is that it is resident in the universities and therefore blighted by the do-nots."

Aloha Shirt stood at the foot of the stage steps on one side, Bullet Head on the other. The young driver had slipped to Maggie's side.

"The East Coast universities devote their attention to obscure films, sequences, and film makers that require the beacon of critical analysis to rescue them from the limbo of deserved obscurity. This symbiotic affair between film maker and critic has entangled them in studies of Vertov and Antonioni that delight small coteries of wide-eyed apostles, but contribute nothing to the mainstream of cinema. The West Coast schools are little better. All hardware and hustle, they produce students in whom the technical proficiency of Greenwich Village is blended with the sensitivity of 'I Love Lucy.' "

The driver leaned over and said something to Maggie. She looked at Jonathan, her eyes wide. He shook his head in answer. The driver took her arm and guided her out the back door. Where the fuck was that bobby?

"And in the center of the continent, insulated by landmass and disposition from contradictory thought, is what might be called the Chicago School of Criticism. Here we find bitter, envious young men who, lacking the spark of creativity, attempt to deny its existence in others by focusing their attention on filmic *genres*. As though films made themselves, and the men who direct them are no more artists than are they, the leveling critics."

A question came from the hall. Jonathan glanced into the wings and was relieved to see the dependable bulk of the policeman, his hands behind his back, his eyes on the lights in the grid, stoic and bored. A rock in the storm.

"As a guest in your country, I should say nothing about the state of British film study other than it's well financed and the government seems particularly patient with the several institutions who have been sorting themselves out for years now. I feel sure they will get around to making a contribution to film study by the end of the century."

Ignoring the applause, Jonathan made quickly for the wings, where he addressed the police officer, who appeared to be surprised at being approached by him. "There are three men out there, officer."

"Is that a fact, sir?"

"They've got a girl with them."

"Have they, sir?"

"I haven't time to explain. Come with me."

"Right you go, sir."

A quick glance over his shoulder told Jonathan that Aloha Shirt and Bullet

Head had not come onto the stage. The bobby following along, he pushed through the exit doors from the wings and ran down a deserted outer corridor. Echoing footfalls advanced toward them from around the far corner. Jonathan stopped, the policeman beside him. The footsteps continued to near. Then the four of them came around the corner, Bullet Head and Aloha Shirt in front, the driver with Maggie behind. They stopped at their end of the hall.

Jonathan and the bobby walked slowly toward them. "Let her go," Jonathan said, his voice unexpectedly loud in the empty corridor.

The policeman spoke. "Is this the man, sir?"

"Yes."

"Yes."

Jonathan and Aloha Shirt had spoken at the same time.

"Right you are then!" The big bobby took Jonathan by the arm with a grip like metal.

"What the hell is going on?" Jonathan protested.

"Our car is just outside, officer," Aloha Shirt said. "Bring him along, won't you?"

"Come on now, sir." The officer spoke with condescending paternalism. "Let's not have any trouble."

Bullet Head closed the distance between them with a menacing swagger. "Maybe *I* should take him. He wouldn't give me no trouble." He brought his porcine face close to Jonathan's. "*Would* you, mate?"

Jonathan looked past the ape to Aloha Shirt, who seemed to be in charge. "The girl isn't in this thing."

"Isn't she?"

"Let her go."

"Can it, buddy," Aloha Shirt said. The sound was odd: American words with a British accent.

"If you let her go, I'll come with you without trouble."

Bullet Head sucked his teeth and thrust out his head. "You're coming along with us no matter what, mate."

Jonathan smiled at him. "You'd love me to make a run for it, wouldn't you?"

"You got it right there, chum. I'm sick of chasing your arse around London."

"But you're not carrying a gun. Fat though you are, I can see you're not carrying a gun."

"Here, none of that," the policeman warned.

"I got *these*, mate." Bullet Head held out his hands, blunt and vast.

Jonathan turned to the bobby. "Officer?"

The policeman's politeness was automatic. "Sir?"

That was it! At that instant Jonathan had it!

For a fraction of a second everything was right—the position of Jonathan's body relative to Bullet Head's, the slight relaxing of the policeman's grip as he answered—at that instant Jonathan could have made it. The heel of his hand into the tip of Bullet Head's nose would have disabled him, possibly killed him if a bone splinter were driven into the brain. He could have been away from the officer with one jerk, and he'd have had Aloha Shirt by the larynx before the driver could react. That would have given him the life of one man between his thumb and forefinger as hostage. Once on the street, he knew he would be an odds-on-favorite in any game of hide-and-seek.

But he let it go. Maggie was three strides too far away. The driver would have had her before Jonathan had Aloha Shirt.

Damn it!

"Sir?" the bobby asked again.

Jonathan's shoulders slumped. "Ah . . . did you enjoy my lecture?"

"Oh yes, sir. Not that I followed all of it. It's your accent, you know."

"Come on!" Bullet Head growled, "let's get it moving!"

The Bentley was parked outside, and behind it was another dark sedan with a driver. As they descended the long sweep of shallow granite steps, Jonathan felt the Kafkaesque anomaly of the situation. They were being abducted with the help of a policeman, in the middle of the afternoon, with people all around.

Maggie was deposited in the back seat of the sedan with a young man who had seemed to be loitering against a postbox, while Jonathan was conducted into the back of the Bentley. Aloha Shirt got in back with him; Bullet Head and the driver in front; and they pulled away from the curb, the two cars staying close together until they got onto a motorway. They picked up speed and started off toward Wessex.

"Care for a coffin nail?" Aloha Shirt asked, producing a pack of American cigarettes.

"No, thanks."

Aloha Shirt smiled affably. "No need to get uptight, Dr. Hemlock. You struck out, but everything's going to be A-okay."

"What about the girl?"

"She's fine and dandy. No sweat." Aloha Shirt smiled again. "I should make introductions. The driver there is Henry."

The driver stretched to seek Jonathan's reflection in the rearview mirror and grinned in greeting. "Good to meet you, sir."

"Hello, Henry."

"And my burly sidekick there is The Sergeant."

"Not 'Bullet Head'?"

The Sergeant scowled and turned to stare out the windscreen, his jaw set tight.

"And I'm called Yank." He grinned. "It's kind of a weird moniker, but they call me that because I dig American things. Clothes. Slang. Everything. For my money, you guys are where it's at."

In the space of a few minutes, Yank had used slang sampling a thirty-year span of American argot, and Jonathan assumed he got it from late night movies. "Where are we going, Yank?"

"You'll see when we get there. But don't worry. Everything's cool. We're from Loo." He said this last with some pride.

"From where?"

"Loo."

The Olde Worlde Inn

As THEY RUSHED along the motorway, Yank sketched in the history and function of the Loo organization. Though his instructions allowed him to impart no information beyond this, he said they would meet a man at their destination who would clarify everything.

Following the typical pattern of development for espionage organizations in democratic countries, England's earliest felt need was for a domestic agency to ferret out and control enemy espionage and sabotage within its borders. Building up its information files on real and imagined enemies, and occasionally stumbling onto a genuine spy cell while groping about for a fictive one, this bureaucratic organism grew steadily in size and power, justifying each new expansion on the basis of the last. From a single cluttered desk in the Military Intelligence building, it swelled to occupy an entire office: Room #5. And by the simplistic codes of the service, it became known as MI-5.

It eventually occurred to the intelligence specialists that they might do well to assume an active as well as passive role in the game of spy-spy, so they set up a sister organization to control British agents operating abroad. The traditional British penchant for independence dictated that these two agencies be fully autonomous, and the rivalry between them extended to refusal to admit of the existence of the other. But this resulted in a certain erosion of manpower, inasmuch as the agents of each organization spent much of their time spying on, thwarting, and occasionally killing the agents of the other. In a master stroke of organizational insight, it was decided to open communications between the two agencies, and the international branch was installed in the next office down the corridor, becoming known in official circles as MI-6.

In harness, they muddled their way through the Second World War, relying largely on the French organizational concept, "système D." Their agents earned reputations for bravery and enterprise, which qualities were vital to survival, considering the blunderers who insisted on parachuting French-speaking agents into Yugoslavia. No energy was spared in the rounding up of Irish nationalists on the basis of the rumor that Ireland was a secret signatory of the Axis Pact.

At home, their operatives uncovered spy rings that were passing information by means of cryptic keys in the knitting patterns of balaclavas that women's institutes were supplying to troops in Africa. And they captured no fewer than seven hundred German parachute spies, nearly all of whom had been trained with such insidious thoroughness that they spoke no German at all and pretended to be innocently pushing their bicycles to work in munitions plants. It was obvious that these were agents of the highest importance, because their controls had gone to the trouble of giving them covers that included homes hit by the blitz and county clerk records supplying them with generations of British ancestors.

In Europe, MI-6 agents blew up bridges in the path of the advancing Allied armies, thus preventing hasty and ill-considered thrusts. It was they who uncovered Switzerland's intention to declare war on Sweden as a last resort. And on three separate occasions only bad luck prevented them from capturing General Patton and his entire staff.

When the war was over, each agent was required to write a book on his adventures, then he was permitted to enter trade. But the romance surrounding MI-5 and MI-6 was tarnished somewhat by a pattern of defections and information leaks that embarrassed British Intelligence almost as much as the existence of that agency was an embarrassment to British intelligence. Clearly, something had to be done to prevent these defections and leakages and to maintain the honor and reputation of the organization. Following the fashion of the day, the government turned to the United States for its model.

At about the same time in America, the 102 splinter spy groups that had sprung up in the Army, Navy, State Department, Treasury, and Bureau of Indian Affairs were merged into a vast bureaucratic malignancy, the CII. This organization, like its British opposite number, was having its share of defections and its share of witch-hunting self-examination spawned by the McCarthy panic. In reaction, it organized an internal cell designed to police and control its own personnel and to protect them from assassination abroad. This last was achieved by the sanction threat of counterassassination, and the cell that performed these internal and external sanctions was known as the Search and Sanction Division—popularly known as the SS Squad. It was for SS that Jonathan had worked, before he managed to release himself rom their coils.

Emulating the American structure, the British developed an elite inner cell which they installed in the next room up the corridor, which room happened to be a toilet. Despite the fact that they refurbished the space to accommodate its new function, wags immediately gave the assassination group the nickname: The Loo.

". . . and that ought pretty much put you into the big picture," Yank concluded. "At least you know who we are. Any questions?"

Jonathan had been listening with only half an ear as he watched the countryside flow past his window, a grimy twilight beginning to soften the line of the background hills. They had left the motorway and were threading through country lanes. When they passed through a village, Jonathan noticed the arms over a public house: vert, three blades of grass proper, a bend of the first. Obviously they were still in Wessex and had been weaving through back roads without making much linear progress. He glanced out the back window to make sure the car carrying Maggie was still following close behind.

"No sweat," said Yank, "they know where they're going. Everything's real George."

"That's wonderful. Now, why don't you tell me what this is all about?"

"No can do. The Guv will lay it on you when we get there. You'll like the Guv. He's old school and all that, but he's no square from Delaware. He's hip to the scene."

The Bentley turned in at a roadside inn called the Olde Worlde and crunched over a gravel drive to the back where it stopped against a retaining log. The car carrying Maggie followed and parked twenty yards away. Two young men conducted her to the back door of the inn.

"Well, what do you think of it?" Yank asked as Jonathan stepped out and was flanked by The Sergeant and Henry. "Nice pad, eh?"

Jonathan scanned the sprawling warren. It was phony Tudor, built at the end of the last century by the look of it, and certainly not originally designed to be an inn. Dozens of details had that inorganic appliqué quality of a style imitated. But where taste and constraint had been lacking, funds had not, for the glass, the wood, the brick were of the best quality available in the 1880s—that last moment before craftsmanship fell victim to the machine and the union.

"This way, sir." Henry's accent had the chewed diphthongs of the working class. They conducted Jonathan around to the front of the inn where, at the reception desk, they were greeted by a healthy, overly made-up young lady wearing a tight sweater and a mini so short that the double stitching of her panty hose showed. Her accent, clothes, and makeup clubbed her with Henry's class, and by the looks they exchanged, it was evident that Henry and she had something going.

"Is this the 'special' you've got with you?" she asked, giving Jonathan a head-to-toe look meant to be sultry.

"That's right," Yank said. "He's to see the Guv straight off."

"The Guv's down to the church. Evening service. Will he be staying long?"

Jonathan resented being spoken of in the third person. "No, I won't be staying long, duck."

"A few days," Yank said.

"Then I'll put him in 14," the bird said. "You and The Sergeant can have the rooms on either side. How's that?"

Yank took the key and led the way as they climbed a narrow, ornately carved staircase to the second floor where, after passing through a maze of dark broken corridors with irregular floors that squeaked under carpeting, they stopped before a door. The Sergeant opened it and gestured Jonathan in with a flick of the thumb.

The room was large, uncomfortable, and cold, as befitted its period. The first thing that caught Jonathan's eyes was the open wardrobe in which the clothes he had had brought to the hotel were hung.

"We were expecting you," Yank said, openly proud of his organization's efficency.

Jonathan crossed the room and looked out over the vista. Beneath his window was a neat garden, scruffy now with autumn brownness, in the center of which was a formal quatrefoil pond, the water green with algae and rippling in the brisk wind. Beyond the garden rolled the gentle hills of Wessex, sucked empty of color by the metallic overcast. The prospect was marred by the thick bars on the window.

"The bars help to keep out the draft," The Sergeant said with a heavy chuckle.

Jonathan glanced at him wearily, then spoke to Yank. "They're all your people, I suppose. Hotel personnel and all?"

"That's right. Loo owns the whole shooting match. By the way," he said with a knowing ogle, "what did you think of the girl at the desk? Slick chick, eh? Lucky bugger!"

Jonathan wasn't sure, but he assumed the bird did tricks for the special guests. "When do I meet the head crapper?"

"Who?"

"Mr. Loo. The *Guv.*"

"Soon," Yank said, obviously annoyed at Jonathan's irreverence. "I think you'll be comfortable here. There'll be one inconvenience, though. You'll be locked in until the Guv says otherwise, and the WC's down the hall, so . . ." Yank shrugged, embarrassed that British inns lacked the convenience of American ones.

The Sergeant broke in. "So if you have to go potty, mate, just rap on the wall, and I'll take you down by the hand. Got it?"

Jonathan regarded The Sergeant languidly as he asked Yank, "Does he have to stay around? Don't you have a kennel?"

The Sergeant rankled. "I hope I'm not going to have any trouble from you, mate!"

"Hope's cheap, anus. Indulge yourself." He turned to Yank. "What about Miss Coyne, the young lady you picked up with me? There's no reason to hold her. She's nothing to me."

"Don't worry about her. She'll be all right. Now why don't you wash up and grab a few Zs before your chat with the Guv."

Left alone in the room, Jonathan stood by the window, feeling off-balance and angry. His sense of déjà vu was total. These people with their ornately staged machinations, this feeling of the ring closing in on him, the vulgar Sergeant for whom murder and mayhem would be an exercise, the veneered Americanism of Yank—everything here was a British analogue of the CII. And if this "Guv" was true to form, he would be urbane, hale, friendly, and ruthless.

He lay back on the bed, his fingers pressed lightly together and his eyes set in infinity focus on the wall before him, and he began deliberately to empty his mind, image by image, until he had achieved a state of neutrality and balance. The muscles of his body softened and relaxed, last of all his stomach and forehead.

When they knocked at his door twenty minutes later, he was ready. The machinery of his mind and body was running calmly and smoothly. He had reviewed the events of the past two days and had come to one distasteful realization: it was possible, it was likely even, that Maggie had set him up for the Loo people.

With the threatening presence of The Sergeant close behind them, Yank and Jonathan walked some two hundred yards down the road from the Olde Worlde Inn before turning off into a yew-lined lane that led through an arched gateway to a curious church.

As they stepped into the vestibule, the teetering tonal imbalance of amateur singers making a joyful noise unto the Lord announced that evening service was in progress. The Sergeant remained outside, while Yank and Jonathan advanced into the church. It amused Jonathan to see Yank tiptoe across to a back pew and kneel briefly in rushed and mumbled prayer before sitting up and staring at the serving priest with an expression of bland and dour piety. Jonathan glanced around at the decor of the church and was surprised to find it was Art Nouveau: a style unique in his experience for religious architecture. He examined it with open curiosity as the vicar began his sermon to the handful of faithful scattered sparsely among the pews.

"No doubt you will recall," the voice was a rumbling bass with the nasal and lazy vowels of the well-educated Englishman, "we have begun to examine the meaning of the sacraments. And this evening I should like to take a look at baptism—the one sacrament that, for most of us, is an involuntary act."

The decor of the church fascinated Jonathan without pleasing him. Mother-of-pearl and pewter were inlaid into the ornate floral carving; tubercular angels, their long-waisted bodies curved in limp S-forms, their fragile-fingered hands pressed lightly together in prayer, looked down on the congregation with large, heavy-lidded eyes; exotic, short-lived flowers drooped from slender stems up the stained glass windows; and above the altar a glistening effeminate Christ in polished pewter trampled the head of a snake with ruby eyes.

The service continued through communion, and everyone but Jonathan went up to receive the Host. Jonathan watched Yank return from the rail, his palms pressed together, his eyes lowered, Christ melting in his mouth.

At a signal from Yank, Jonathan remained seated as the rest of the faithful filed out after a last vigorous attack on Song. Then Yank conducted him to the vestry where the Vicar was finishing off the last of the communion bread.

"Sir?" Yank's voice was diffident. "May I introduce Dr. Hemlock?"

The Vicar turned and with an open gracious smile of greeting took Jonathan's hand between his large hirsute paws. "This *is* a pleasure," he said, winking. "So good of you to come." His mellow basso warmed with practiced civility. "Just allow me to finish and we'll have a good natter." He drank off the last of the communion wine and wiped out the chalice carefully, while Jonathan studied his full puffy face with its tracery of red capillaries over the cheekbones and in ruddy abundance on the substantial amorphic nose. His hair had retreated beyond the horizon line of his broad forehead, but was long on the sides and blended with his full muttonchop sideburns.

"Odd ritual, this," the Vicar said, replacing the utensils. "The last morsels of consecrated bread and wine must be consumed by the priest. I suppose it arose out of some fear of contamination and sacrilege, should the body and blood of Christ find its way into the alimentary canal of an unbeliever." He winked.

"What is missionary work but the effort to introduce Christ to the uninitiated?" Jonathan commented.

The Vicar laughed robustly. "Precisely! Precisely! You, I dare to assume, do not avail yourself of the sacrament often."

"No form of cannibalism appeals to me."

"Oh. I see. Yes." The Vicar folded the last of his vestments carefully and set them aside. From behind, his formidable bulk seemed to fill the black flowing garment. "Shall we take a turn around the churchyard, Dr. Hemlock. It's quite lovely in the last light. We shall not be needing you, Yank. I'm sure you can find something to amuse yourself with for a few minutes."

Yank made a gesture akin to a salute and left the vestry. The Vicar looked after him with paternal warmth. "There's a very bright young man for you, Dr. Hemlock. Energetic. Zealous. We pulled him away from another project and made him your liaison with our organization because we thought you might be more comfortable working with someone who was au courant with things American." He put his heavy arm around Jonathan's shoulders and conducted him on a leisurely stroll down the nave of the Art Nouveau church. "Beautiful, isn't it? Quite unique."

"Is it yours?"

"God's, actually. But if you are asking if I am the regular vicar, the answer is no. I am standing in for him for a fortnight while he is on honeymoon in Spain. But the less said of that the better." He made a wide gesture with his arm. "When would you guess this church was built?"

Jonathan stepped away from the encircling arm and glanced around. "About 1905."

The Vicar stopped short, his bushy salt-and-pepper eyebrows arched high. "Amazing! Within a year!" Then he laughed. "Ah, but of course! Art is your province, isn't it." He glanced quickly at Jonathan. "That is, it is *one* of your occupations."

"It is my only occupation," Jonathan said with mild stress.

The Vicar clasped his hands behind his back and studied the parquet floor. "Yes, yes. Your Mr. Dragon informed me that you had left CII in some disgust after that nasty business in the Alps." He winked.

Jonathan leaned against the side of a pew and folded his arms. This vicar evidently knew a great deal about him. He even knew the name of Yurasis Dragon, head of Search and Sanction Division of CII: a name known to fewer than a dozen people in the States. Obviously, the Vicar would prefer to approach whatever dirty business he had in mind through the gentle back alleys of trivial polite conversation, but Jonathan decided not to cooperate.

"Yes," the Vicar continued after an uncomfortable pause, "that must have been a nasty affair for you. As I recall the details, you had to kill all three of the men you were climbing with, because your SS Division had been unable to specify which one was your target."

Jonathan watched him steadily, but did not respond.

"I suppose it takes a rather special kind of man to do that sort of thing," the Vicar said, winking. "After all, a certain camaraderie must grow up amongst men making so dangerous a climb as the Eiger. Isn't that so?"

No answer.

The Vicar broke the ensuing silence with artificial heartiness. "Well, well! At all events, the little project we have in mind for you will not be so grisly as that. At least, it need not be. You have that much to be grateful for, eh?"

Nothing.

"Yes. Well. Mr. Dragon warned me that you could be recalcitrant." The tone of robust friendliness dropped from his voice, and he continued speaking with the mechanical crispness of a man accustomed to giving orders. "All right then, let's get to it. How much did Yank tell you about us?"

"Only as much as you instructed him to. I take it that your Loo organization is a rough analogue of our Search and Sanction, and is occupied with matters of counterassassination."

"That is correct. However, what we have on for you is a little out of that line. What else do you know?"

Jonathan began walking down the nave toward the vestibule. "Nothing, really. But I have made certain assumptions."

The Vicar followed. "May I hear them?"

"Well, you, of course, are Mister Loo. But I haven't decided whether this church business is simply a front."

"No, no. Not at all. I am first and always a man of the Church. I served as chaplain during the Hitlerian War and afterward found myself still involved in government affairs. We are, after all, a state church." He winked.

"I see." Jonathan passed out through the vestibule and turned up a path that led through the churchyard, cool and iridescent in the gloaming. Yank and The Sergeant were standing at some distance, watching them as the Vicar fell into step alongside.

"It is not uncommon, Dr. Hemlock, for C. of E. churchmen to have some hobby to occupy their minds. Particularly if their livings are of the more modest sort. Nature study claims a great number; and some of the younger men toy about with social reform and that sort of thing. Circumstance and personal inclination directed me along other paths."

"Killing, to be specific."

The Vicar's response was measured and cool. "I have certain organization talents that I have place at the service of my country, if that's what you mean."

"Yes, that's what I meant."

"And, tell me, what else have you assumed?"

"That this young lady—Maggie Coyne, if that is her real name—"

"As it happens, it is."

". . . that this Miss Coyne is one of your operatives. That she set me up in that little affair of the man in my bathroom."

"My, my. You *are* perceptive. Whar brought you to this conclusion?"

Jonathan sat on a headstone. "In retrospect, the thing was too neat, too circumstantial. I seldom use the Baker Street penthouse. But your men knew I would be there that particular night. And it was Miss Coyne who proposed the restaurant a half block away."

"Ah, yes."

"And along with a rack of trumped-up circumstantial evidence linking me with the poor bastard, there must be some hard evidence—probably photographic. Right?"

"I blush at our being so transparent."

Jonathan rose and they continued their stroll.

"How did you get the photographs?"

"The young woman took them."

"When? With what?"

"The cigarette—"

". . . The cigarette lighter!" Jonathan shook his head at his stupidity. A gold cigarette lighter in the possession of a girl who didn't know where her next meal was coming from. A camera, of course. And she had fumbled with it, unable to light her cigarette, as she stood there at the bathroom door.

He snatched a twig from a shrub, stripped the leaves with an angry gesture, and crushed them in his hand. "And the gun, of course, would be found in my apartment."

"Very well hidden. It would be found only after an extensive search. But it *would* be found." The Vicar winked.

Jonathan walked on slowly, rolling the leaf pulp between his palms. "I'm curious, padre . . ."

"The sign of a healthy intellect."

"After hitting that man in my john, your men left. They didn't try to put the hand on me then, presumably because they didn't yet have the photographs."

"Just so."

"Why did they come back later?"

"To pick up the cigarette lighter and develop the film. Miss Coyne was supposed to leave it behind."

"But she didn't."

"No, she did not. And that threw my chaps into some confusion."

"Why do you suppose she broke the plan?"

"Ah." The Vicar lifted his hands and let them fall in a gesture of helplessness.

"Who can probe the human heart with only the brutish tools of logic, eh, Dr. Hemlock? She was shocked perhaps by the sight of that poor fellow in your bathroom? It is even possible that some affection for you misdirected her loyalties."

"In that case, why didn't she destroy the films?"

"Ah, there you go. Asking for sequential logic in the workings of emotion. Man is nothing if not labyrinthine. And when I say 'man' I include, of course, woman. For in this context, as in the romantic one, man embraces woman. I shall never understand why Americans doubt the Briton's sense of humor."

Jonathan could. "So your men were running around London looking for both Miss Coyne and me."

"You gave us a few difficult hours. But all that is behind us now. But come now! Let's not look on the gloomy side. Provided you lend your skills to our little project, the police will be allowed to remain in that state of blissful ignorance so characteristic of them." The Vicar stopped beside a fresh grave that did not yet have a headstone. "That's poor Parnell-Greene," he said, sighing deeply, "unfortunate fellow."

"Who's Parnell-Greene?"

"Our most recent casualty. You'll learn more about him later." He made a sweeping gesture with his arm. "All of them here," he said, his voice resonant and wavering, "they're all ours. All Loo people."

Jonathan glanced at the inscriptions on nearby stones, just legible in the fading light. *Passed into the greater life. Went to sleep. Returned home. Found everlasting glory.*

"Didn't any of them die?" he asked.

"Pardon me?"

"Nothing."

"The name and dates on the stones are false, of course. But they're all our brave lads." He sighed stentoriously. "Good youngsters, every one."

"No shit?"

The Vicar stared at him with reproof, then he laughed. "Ah, yes! Mr. Dragon warned me of your tendency to revert to the social atavism of your boyhood. It used to pain him, or so he said."

"You seem to be on good terms with Dragon."

"We correspond regularly, share information and personnel, that sort of thing. Does that surprise you? We also have arrangements with our Russian and French counterparts. After all, every game must be played by certain rules. But I must admit that Mr. Dragon was not of much help in the matter now before us, occupied as he is with dire events on his own doorstep. No doubt you have heard about this Watergate business?"

"Oddly enough, it was mentioned just today at the Embassy. It seems to me to be a lot of fuss over a trivial and incompetent bit of spy-spy."

"One would think so, but it can't be all that trivial if CII has been brought in on it. The affair evidently requires fairly heavy hushing up, and Mr. Dragon is involved in that side of it. I shouldn't be surprised if the statistics on death by accident showed an unaccountable rise over the next month or so. But I take it from your distant expression that you are not overly concerned with this election."

"It's difficult to get excited when the choice is between a fool and a villain."

"Personally, I prefer villains. They are more predictable." The Vicar winked vigorously.

"So it was Dragon who put you onto me?"

"Yes. We knew, of course, that you were in the country, but we had been informed that you had retired from our line of work, so we did not interfere with your visit. At that time we had no intention of using you. There is nothing more dangerous than an unwilling and uncooperative active. But. This business came along and . . ." The Vicar blew out his broad cheeks and shrugged fatalistically. ". . . we had no other option, really."

"But why me? Why not one of your own people?"

"You will learn that in due course. Lovely evening, isn't it? The precious moment when day and night are in delicate balance."

Jonathan knew he was hooked. If he refused to cooperate, Loo would certainly hang him for the murder of that poor bastard on the toilet, even though it would make his services unavilable. Like CII, Loo realized that threats and blackmail were effective only if the mark was sure that the threat would be carried out at all cost.

"All right," Jonathan said, sitting on a grave marker, "let's talk about it."

"Not just now. I'm awaiting some last odd bits of information from London. Once I have them, I shall be able to put you totally into the picture. Shall I see you at the rectory tomorrow? Say, midmorning?"

The Vicar made a simple gesture with his fingertips and Yank, who had been keeping them under close surveillance, straining his eyes in the gloom, came trotting over. Literally trotting.

As he ascended the narrow stairs to the second floor of the inn, Jonathan stepped aside to allow Maggie to pass on her way down. She paused and looked at him with troubled eyes. "I suppose it would sound a little foolish to say I'm sorry?"

"Foolish certainly. And inadequate."

She brushed back a wisp of amber hair and forced herself to maintain eye contact with him. "I'll run the risk, then, of being foolish."

"Come on," The Sergeant growled from behind, "I don't have all night to stand about!"

Jonathan turned to him and smiled his gentle combat smile. He beckoned him closer and spoke softly into the bland moon face with its shaved head and crisp military moustache. "You know something? I am becoming very annoyed with everything that's happening here. And I have this conviction that my annoyance is eventually going to purge itself on you. And when it does . . ." Jonathan grinned and nodded. ". . . and when it does . . ." He patted The Sergeant's cheek. Then he turned away and went up to his room.

The Sergeant, not sure what had just happened, scratched the patted cheek angrily and mumbled after the retreating figure, "Anytime, yank. Anytime!"

Yank had come to fetch him down to supper in the low-ceilinged, pseudo-Tudor dining room, a recent addition featuring stucco with capricious finger-swirl patterns and pressed plastic wooden beams placed in positions that could not possbily bear weight. There were fewer than a dozen diners served by a Portuguese waiter in an ill-fitting tuxedo who went about his task with great style and flourish that interfered with his efficiency.

Jonathan and Yank occupied a corner table, while The Sergeant sat alone three tables away and occupied himself, when he was not pushing great fork-loads of food into his mouth, by glowering at Jonathan with a menacing intensity that was almost comic. Henry, the driver, sat in close conversation with the bird from the reception desk, who often giggled and pressed her knee against his. The rest of the guests were young men stamped from Henry's mold: longish hair, beefy faces, dark suits with flared jackets, and belled trousers.

"I see that Miss Coyne hasn't come down to supper," Jonathan said.

"No," Yank said. "She's eating in her room. Not feeling too well."

"A girl of delicate sensitivities."

"I reckon so."

It was a classically English meal: meat boiled until it was stringy, waterlogged potatoes, and the ubiquitous peas and carrots, tasteless and mushy. Directly the edge of his hunger was dulled, Jonathan pushed his plate away.

Although he had been eating with great appetite, Yank imitated Jonathan's gesture. "This English chow's a crime, isn't it?" he said. "Give me hamburgers and French fries any old time."

"Who are all these young men?" Jonathan asked.

"Guards, mostly," Yank said. "Shall I order some Java?"

"Please. All these guards for me? I'm flattered."

"No, they don't work here. They work . . ." He was visibly uncomfortable. ". . . up the road."

"At the church?"

Yank shook his head. "No-o. We have another establishment. Back in the fields."

"What kind of establishment?"

"Ah! I think I caught the waiter's eye." Yank held his coffee cup in the air and pointed to it. The Portuguese waiter was at first confused, then with a dawn of understanding, he held up a cup from an empty table and pointed to it, raising his eyebrows high in question. Yank nodded and mouthed the word: C-o-f-f-e-e, with exaggerated lip movement.

When the tea arrived, Jonathan's curiosity made him ask, "This other establishment you mentioned. What goes on there?"

Yank's discomfort returned. "Oh. It's nothing. Say!" He changed the subject without subtlety. "I really envy you, you know."

"Oh? Always had a secret desire to be kidnapped?"

"No, not that. I guess I envy every American. Can't understand why you came to live among us limeys. If I ever get to the old forty-eight, you can bet your bottom dollar I'll hang in there. And I'm going to do it some day. I'm going to the States and get a ranch in Nebraska or somewhere and settle down."

"That's just wonderful, Yank."

"It's not just a dream, either. I'm going to do it. As soon as I get the loot together."

Back in his room Jonathan lay in the dark and stared up toward the ceiling. His deep anger at being used, boxed in, manifested itself as pressure behind his eyes that built up and began to throb. He was rubbing his temples to relieve the pressure when he heard the sound of a key turning in his lock. He opened his eyes and, without moving his head, watched the bird from the reception desk enter and approach his bed.

"You asleep?"

"No."

She sat on the edge of his bed and put her hand on him. "Feel like having a go?"

He smiled to himself and examined her face in the gloom. She was pretty enough in the plastic way of English girls of her class and age. "I had the impression that you had something going with the young man who drove me here."

"Who, Henry? Well, I do, of course. We're thinking about getting married one of these days. But that's my private life, and this is my work. The blokes who come here are always tensed up, and I help them to relax. It's all part of the service, you might say."

"A civil service trollop."

"It's a job. Good pension. Henry and me have decided that I should go on working after we're married. Until we have kids, that is. We're saving our money, and we got fifteen books of green stamps. One of these days, we're going to get a little off license in Dagenham. He's got a level head on him, Henry has. Well, then. If you won't be wanting me, I'll get back to the telly. Wouldn't want to miss 'It's a Knockout' if I could help it."

"No, I won't be needing you. You're a cute little girl, but this is a bit clinical for me."

She shrugged and left. There was no understanding some men.

He was in a deep layer of sleep when the visceral throb of the discotheque snapped him into consciousness—sticky-minded and stiff-boned. He could not believe it! The volume was so high that the thump of the back-beat bass was a physical thing vibrating the floor and rattling the drinking glass on the washstand. The singsong, hyperthyroid patter of the disc jockey introduced the next selection in a rapid, garbled East End imitation of American fast patter deejays, and the room began to vibrate again. He swung out of bed and pounded on the wall to be let out. The was no response, so he rattled the door, and it opened in his hand. So. He was no longer locked in. The Vicar must have told them that he was firmly hooked and would not try to escape.

After splashing his face and changing shirts, he went down to the foyer to find it and the adjacent pub packed with young people, shouting at each other, pushing through, beer mugs held high, and brandishing cigarettes. He pressed through the crowd in the saloon bar, trying to find a way out of the din, and instead found himself in a discotheque, surrounded by youngsters who hopped and sweated to the deafening throb of amplifiers in a murky darkness broken occasionally by a flash of color from a jury-rigged strobe light. The noise was brutal, particularly the amplified bass, which vibrated in his sinuses.

A form approached him through the smoky dark. "Did the noise wake you up?" Yank asked.

"What?"

"Did the noise wake you up?"

Jonathan shouted into Yank's ear. "Let's not do that number. Show me how to get out of here."

"Follow me!"

They threaded through bodies gyrating in a miasma of smoke and stale beer, and out a back door to the parking area, now filled with cars and small knots of young men, talking together and erupting into jolts of forced laughter whenever one of them said something bawdy.

Well beyond the car park, in the garden Jonathan could look down on from his window, the noise was low enough to permit speaking. They stopped and Yank lit up a cigarette.

"What is going on here?" Jonathan asked.

"We have discotheque five nights a week. Kids come all the way from London. It's the Guv's idea. It provides cover for our operation here, and a little extra income."

Jonathan shook his head in disbelief. "When does it come to an end?"

"Closing time. About ten thirty."

"And what am I supposed to do in the meantime?"

"Don't you dig music?"

Jonathan glanced at him. "My door is no longer locked. I take it I'm free to wander about now?"

"Within limits. Perhaps it would be better if I came along."

They strolled through the garden and up a footpath that led away from the inn. Yank babbled on about the virtues of America, things American, places he was going to go and things he was going to do when he saved up enough money to emigrate. "I guess it sounds as though I had it in for old Blighty. Not true, really. There are a lot of British things—ways of life, traditions—that I admire and that I'll miss. But they're really gone anyway. Gone, or on their way out. England has become a sort of low-budget United States. And if you have to live in the United States, you might as well live in the real one. Right?"

Jonathan, who had not been listening, indicated a fork in the path. "What's up this way?"

"Oh . . . nothing really." Yank started to take the lower fork.

"No. Let's go on along here."

"Well . . . you can't go very far up that way anyway. Fenced off, you know."

"What's up there?"

"Another branch of our operation. The guards you saw come from there. I don't have anything to do with it."

"What is it?"

"It's . . . ah . . . it's called the Feeding Station."

"A farm?"

"Sort of. Let's be getting back."

"You go back. I can't take the noise."

"OK. But don't go too far up this path. The dogs are loose at night."

"Dogs? To keep people out of the Feeding Station?"

"No." Yank took a long drag on his cigarette. "To keep people in."

Jonathan sat in the darkness on a stone bench beside the quatrefoil pool. A light mist was settling in the windless air, and his skin tingled with cold. There was a crimson smear in the northern sky, the last burning off of the stubble fields; and the air carried the autumn smell of leaf smoke. The discotheque had closed down, and the crowds had poured out to their cars, laughing and hooting, in the car park. Horns had sounded and gravel had been sprayed, and one last drunk, alone and stumbling in the dark, had called for "Alf" several times with growing desperation before staggering onto the road to hitchhike.

There was a period of deep silence before the night creatures felt safe; then began the chirp of insects, the rustle of field mice, the plop of frogs.

Jonathan sat alone and depressed. He had been so sure his break with CII was permanent. He had repressed all the nasty memories. And here he was. They had him again. But what bothered him most was not the irony of it, or the loss of freedom of choice. It was the discovery that he had not left this business as far behind as he had thought. Already, the high-honed, aggressive mental set necessary to survive in this class of action had returned to him, quite naturally, as though it had always been there buried under a thin cover of distaste.

He heard her approach from fifty yards away. He didn't bother to turn his head. There was no stealth in the footfalls, no urgent energy, no danger signals.

"Do you have a light?" she asked, after she had stood beside him for some time without attracting the least recognition of her existence.

"What happened? Your cigarette lighter run out of film?"

She made a pass at laughter. "It doesn't matter really. I don't have a cigarette anyway."

"Just this deep desire to communicate. I know the feeling."

"Jonathan, I hope you don't feel too badly toward me, because—"

"Yes, this lack of communication is the major problem in the world as we know and love it around us in everyday life. All people are essentially good and loving and peace-seeking, but they have trouble communicating that fact to one another. Right? Perhaps it's because they raise barriers of mistrust. People ought to learn to trust one another more. The only people you can really trust are women named Maggie. Someone once told me that the name Maggie, while not melodious, was at least substantial. You could always trust good old Maggie."

"All right. I give up."

"Good." He rose and started back toward the inn.

She followed. "There is one thing, though."

"Let me guess. You'd give anything in the world if you hadn't had to set me up. You could almost weep when you think of me, lying there in the deep sleep of the sexually exercised and satisfied—probably a boyish smile on my face—while you slipped out of bed and opened the door to let the Loo men in and gutshoot that poor bastard on my crapper."

"Really, I didn't know—"

"Certainly! After all, I was just a cipher to you at first. But later, it was different. Right? After we'd exchanged trivial confidences and fucked a bit, you discovered deeper feelings. But by then it was too late to back out. Maggie! . . ." He reined his anger and lowered his voice. "Maggie, your actions lack even the charm of new experience for me. I was nailed once before by a lady. The only difference is that she was in the major leagues."

Her eyes had not left his, and she had not flinched through his tirade. "I know, Jonathan."

He realized that he had reached out and was grasping her upper arms tightly. He released her, snapping his hands open. "How do you know?"

"Your records. CII sent up your entire file, and I was required to study it carefully before . . ."

"Before setting me up."

"All right! Before setting you up!"

He believe the shame in her sudden rush of anger. Suddenly he felt very tired. And he regretted his loss of control. He looked away from her and forced his breathing to assume a lower rhythm.

She spoke without temper and without pleading. "I want to tell you this."

"I don't need it."

"*I* need it. I didn't know what they had in mind. I thought they were going to set you up with a drug plant or something. When they appeared at the door with that poor man, I . . . I . . ."

"He was alive at that time."

She swallowed and looked past him, down the road gleaming faintly in the ghost light of moon above fog. Talking about it required that she pick at the painful scab of memory. "Yes. He was badly doped up. He couldn't even stand without help. And he was wearing that horrid grinning mask. They had to carry him in and put him onto the . . . But he was aware of what was happening. I could see it in his eyes—just the eyes behind the cutouts in the mask. He looked at me with such . . ." She blinked back the tears. "There was such sadness in his eyes! He was begging me to help him. I felt that. But I . . . Lord God above, it's a terrible business we're in, Jonathan."

He drew her head against his chest. It seemed the only reasonable thing to do. "Why didn't they kill him cleanly?"

She couldn't speak for a while, and he heard the squeaking sound of tears being swallowed. "They were supposed to. The Vicar was very angry with them for bungling it. They went into the bathroom while I waited outside. Then you turned over in your sleep and made a sound. I was frightened you might wake up, so I tapped at the door, and at the same moment I heard a popping sound."

"A silencer."

"Yes, I suppose. They rushed out immediately, but one of them was swearing under his breath. My knock had startled him and spoiled his aim."

He rocked her gently.

"I crept back into bed, trying not to wake you. I didn't know what to do. I just lay there, staring into the dark, concentrating as hard as possible, trying to keep dawn from coming."

"But no luck."

"No luck at all. Morning came. You woke up. Then . . . I just couldn't make love when you wanted."

He nodded. That was to her credit. "Come on. Let's take a walk around the inn before turning in."

She sniffed and pulled herself together. "Yes, I'd like that."

They strolled slowly, arm about and arm about, each accommodating for their difference in stride. "Tell me," he said, "why didn't you throw the cigarette case away?"

"You know about that? Well, I suppose the real question is why didn't I leave it behind in your room, as I was supposed to do. I don't know. At the moment, I thought I might be protecting you by denying them the films. But directly I had time to think it out, I realized that they were determined to get you. There was no point in denying them the films. They'd only have set something else up, and you would have had to go through that."

"I see." He looked down, watching their shoes step out in rhythm. "Who were the men who came to my flat?"

"The two you rode here with in the Bentley. Not Yank, the other two."

"And who did the shooting?"

"The Sergeant."

"Figures." He added another line to the bill The Sergeant was running up with him. The payoff became inevitable.

They walked without speaking for a time, breathing in the moist freshness of the night air.

"It may be silly," she said at last, "but I'm glad you didn't take Sylvia up on it."

"Who is Sylvia?"

"The girl who works here. You know, Henry's friend."

"Oh, her. Well, she isn't my type."

They were at the door again. She turned and asked, "Am I your type?"

He looked at her for several seconds. "I'm afraid so."

They went in.

"I'm sorry about that," she said out of a long silence. She was sitting up, braced against the carved oaken headboard, and she had just lit another cigarette.

He hugged her around the hips and put his cheek into the curve of her waist. They had made love, and slept, and made love again, and now his voice was ragged with sleepiness. "Sorry about what?"

"About that last bit—those internal contractions when I climax. I can't help them. They're beyond my control."

He growled and mumbled, "By all means, do let's talk about it."

She laughed at him. "Don't you like to talk about it afterward? It's supposed to be very healthy and modern and all."

"I suppose. But I'm old-fashioned enough to be sentimental about the operation. For the first few minutes anyway."

"Hm-m." She took a drag on her cigarette, her face briefly illuminated in the glow. "Your kind of people are like that."

He turned over. "My kind of people?"

"The violent ones. They tend to be sentimental. I guess sentiment is their substitute for compassion. Kind of a surrogate for genuine feelings. I read somewhere that ranking Nazis used to weep over Wagner."

"Wagner makes me weep too. But not from sentiment. Go to sleep."

"All right." But after a moment of silence: "Still, I am sorry if my little spasms ruined any plans you had for epic control."

"Sorry for me? Or sorry for yourself?"

"Oh, you *are* feeling a bit bristly, aren't you? Do you always suffer from postcoitus aggression?"

He rose to one elbow. "Listen, madam. It doesn't seem to me that I started any of this. The only thing I'm feeling at this moment is postcoitus fatigue. Now good night." He dropped back on his pillow.

"Good night." But he could tell from the tension of her body that she was not prepared to sleep. "Do you know what I wish you suffered from?" she asked after a short silence.

He didn't answer.

"Introcoitus camaraderie, that's what," she said, and laughed.

"OK. You win." He pulled himself up and rested against the headboard. "Let's talk."

She scooted down under the covers. "Oh, I don't know. I'm kind of tired."

"You're going to get popped right in the eye."

"I'm sorry. But you are fun to tease. You rise to the bait so eagerly. What do you want to talk about, now that you've got me wide awake?"

"Let's talk about you, for lack of more interesting things. Tell me, how did a nice girl like you, et cetera . . ."

"Why am I working for Loo?"

"Yes. We both know why *I* am."

She knew that taunt was not completely in jest, but she decided he had a right to some bitterness. Perhaps the best thing to do would be to share the truth with him. After all, the truth did mitigate her complicity. "Well, most of what I told you about myself the other night was true. I was born in Ireland. Went to university over here, then returned. I was young and silly and politically committed—looking for a cause, I suppose. Or bored maybe. I used to meet my brother and some of his friends at a coffee shop, and we would talk about a united Ireland. Angry speeches. Plans and plots. You know the sort of thing. Then one day my brother was gone. I discovered that he had gotten into Ulster. He had always said he wanted to take an active part in the thing, but I had written that off as romantic game-playing. He was a poet, you see. Flashing eyes and floating hair and all that. I don't imagine you would have liked him."

"He died?"

He felt her nod. "Yes. He was found in his car." Her voice became very soft. "They shot him through the ear. And I . . . I . . ."

He hugged her head to his side. "Don't talk about it."

"No, I want to. It's good for me. For months the image of him being shot in that car haunted me. I used to have nightmares. And do you know what image used to shock me awake, all sweating and panting?"

He patted her.

"The noise of it! Can you imagine the terrible noise of it?"

Jonathan felt helpless and stupid. He was sorry for her, but he knew the emptiness of saying so. "Who did it?" he asked. "UDA? IRA?"

She shrugged. "It doesn't really matter, does it? They're all the same."

"I'm surprised you realize that. Good for you."

"Oh, I didn't know it then, of course. I wanted revenge. More for myself than for my brother, I suppose. I went to Belfast and joined a cell of activists. And . . ."

"You got your revenge?"

"I don't know. We set bombs. People got hurt—probably the wrong people. After a while, I came to my senses and realized how stupid the whole business was, and I decided to return to Dublin. And that's when I was picked up and arrested. Things always happen that way."

"You were sentenced?"

"No. They were taking me from one prison to another in an army vehicle, when they were run off the road by armed hijackers. The soldiers were all shot. The hijackers took me with them. Only me. They left the other prisoners."

"I assume the hijackers were Loo people."

"Yes."

"How long ago was this?"

"Only a month. They brought me here for a week of briefing on your background file from CII. Then they placed me at Mr. MacTaint's where we met. And that's it."

Jonathan slid down beside her, and they lay for a time staring into the dark above them. "Why *you*, I wonder," he said at length. "Not that I'm complaining."

She took a deep breath. "I don't know. I could paint—well, in a way. And there was no question about my being cooperative. All the Vicar has to do is lift a telephone, and I'm back in Belfast facing charges. And this time I'll have to answer for those dead soldiers as well."

Jonathan's fists clenched and unclenched. "He's quite a number, that vicar. No messing around with fluctuating loyalties for him. When he wants you, he ties you up properly."

"True. He's got both of us. And he does the whole thing with a hearty handshake and polite small talk."

"And a wink."

"Oh, yes. And a wink. I suppose that winking is just a nervous tic, but it's a nuisance. It's infectious when you're talking to him. You have this urge to wink back, and that wouldn't do at all."

Jonathan was relieved that the talk was taking this lighter tone. The last thing in the world he needed was the burden of this girl's problems or, worse yet, her affection. Lovemaking was no threat to his precious insulation. Two people meet on the neutral ground of lust, they scratch their itches, then they go back into themselves. Nothing shared, nothing lost. But this sort of thing—this sharing of ideas and problems, this quiet talk into the common dark—this could be dangerous. Sapping.

Maggie leaned across him and butted her cigarette out in the bedside ashtray. Then she resettled herself against him and ran her fingers over his stomach idly. "This is kind of old hat for you, isn't it? I read in your file about that Eiger affair—about that girl who roped you into it." She felt his stomach tighten, but she plunged ahead with that well-intentioned instinct for the emotional jugular that characterizes good women grimly determined to understand and help. "Her name was Jemima Brown, wasn't it?"

There was no inflection in Jonathan's voice when he said, "Yes."

"Was she at all like me?"

"No. Not at all."

"Oh." She removed her hand from him. "Did you love her?"

Jonathan got up and sat on the edge of the bed. Beyond the window, the night horizon was still smudged by a reddish glow of burning stubble out in the fields, but this false dawn was not so distant from the real one, for the birds were beginning to sound the odd chirp in expectation.

Maggie sat up and patted the bed beside her. "I'll make you a bargain," she said in comic broad brogue. "Bring your fine body back here, and I'll not plague you with me queries into your emotional life. Which is not to say that I won't be making any demands upon you at all, at all."

He rejoined her, stretching out flat on his back and feeling that he had been childishly touchy. She scooted down beside him and pressed her forehead against his. He looked into her impish green eye—one only and large at this distance. "You have a way of coming out one up, haven't you?" he said.

"Instinct for emotional survival. Do you realize that we've made sexual pigs of ourselves in the little time we've had together?"

"Shameful."

"Isn't it just. Physically prodigal, I'd call it."

"I think it's only fair to warn you that I'm an aging man. I may not be up to it."

"Lord, I hate double entendre."

Breakfast, the only meal English cooks feel comfortable with, was interrupted by The Sergeant bursting into the dining room, his face flushed and streaming with sweat. "Where the 'ell 'ave you been!" he shouted at Jonathan, who was finishing a last cup of tea with Yank and Maggie at a corner table somewhat out of the draft. "I've been runnin' me arse off around these bleedin' 'ills!"

Jonathan set down his napkin and looked out the window on the countryside, where the corn stubble was pastel under the lowering gray sky.

The Sergeant crossed to their table in three angry strides, and his bulk hovered over Jonathan.

"More tea?" Jonathan asked Maggie.

"No, thank you."

"I'm talking to you, mate!" The Sergeant put his heavy hand on Jonathan's shoulder. Jonathan glanced down at the thick fingers as though they had dropped from a passing bird, then he looked across at Yank with raised eyebrows.

Yank intervened nervously. "Come on, now. No need to get your dander up. He's just been sitting here having breakfast with us. Cool it, man."

"When I went into his room this morning, the bleedin' bed 'adn't been slept in. Looked like he's scarpered. The lads and me's been all over the grounds lookin' for 'im!"

"You must have worked up quite an appetite," Jonathan commented softly. "And it's obvious that you needed the exercise."

"I'm fitter than you'll ever be, mate."

"In which case you don't need my support to stand up." Jonathan glanced again at the hand, which was removed from his shoulder with an angry snap.

"Let's drop it," Yank told The Sergeant. "After all, the Guv has given Dr. Hemlock the run of the place."

"You know he don't want 'im up . . . there." The Sergeant jerked his head in the direction of the path leading to the Feeding Station. "And anyway, nobody told me nothin' about 'im having the run of the place."

"I am telling you now," Yank said distinctly, clarifying for Jonathan the chain of command from the Vicar. "Now be a good lad and sit down to your breakfast."

The Sergeant glowered at Jonathan, then left, grumbling.

Yank leaned forward and spoke confidentially to Jonathan. "I wouldn't put him on, If I were you. He's no quiz kid, but he's got a temper, and he's a master of hand-to-hand combat."

"I am forewarned."

"By the way. Just out of curiosity, where *did* you pass the night?"

Maggie smiled into her plate.

Jonathan answered offhandedly, timing his response to catch Yank with a forkful of eggs on the way to his mouth. "At the Feeding Station."

The fork hovered, then returned to the plate still laden. The color had drained from Yank's face. "That's a good deal less funny than you fancy, Dr. Hemlock."

It amused Jonathan to note that all traces of American accent fled from Yank's voice under pressure, just as multilingual people always return to their native language when they swear, count, or pray.

Unable to eat, Yank excused himself and left.

"That was cruel," Maggie said.

"Uh-huh. What do you know about this Feeding Station?"

"Nothing really. It's up the path there. Guards and dogs and all. Sometimes the guards come down here to the bar or to take lunch, but they never talk about it."

"Can you find out about it for me?"

"I can try."

"Do that."

It had turned wet and blustery by the time Jonathan was allowed to walk to the vicarage with only the light guard of Yank, who kept up a running conversation of trivia, quite recovered from his crisis of distrust over the mention of the Feeding Station. When they reached the gate, Yank joined two other young men dressed in the flared dark suits and wide bright ties that were almost a Loo uniform. Jonathan could not help noticing how much like East End hoods they looked.

He found the Vicar in his garden, dressed in a stout hunting jacket and twill breeches tucked into thick stockings. His shoes were heavy, boat-toed brogans. The costume contrasted sharply with Jonathan's close-fitting city clothes and custom-made light shoes. The Vicar did not seem to be aware of Jonathan's presence as he muttered angrily to himself while scattering fish food to the carp in his pond. Then he looked up. "Ah, Dr. Hemlock! Good of you to come."

"You seem distressed."

"What? Oh. Well, I am a bit. Nothing to do with your affair. It's that damned Boggs! Will you take something? Coffee, perhaps, or tea?"

"Thank you, no."

"Just as good. I was hoping we might take a little walk through the fields as we chatted. No place like the open country for privacy. There are insects in the hedgerows, but no bugs—if you have my meaning there."

Jonathan looked up at the threatening, gusting sky.

"No worry about the weather," the Vicar assured him. "Forecast predicts only occasional rain." He winked.

Jonathan shrugged and followed him to the bottom of the garden where the path became a narrow foot trail through a tangled coppice. "How did this Boggs get damned?" he asked the back of the figure trudging out briskly before him.

"Pardon? Oh, I see. Well, Boggs owns the land next to the church. A farmer, you know. Been ripping out hedgerows again. Do you know that more than five thousand miles of hedgerows are ripped up annually in England?"

"Pity they didn't get this one." Jonathan mumbled after stumbling over a root.

"What?"

"Nothing."

"Five thousand miles of homes for small creatures and nestings for birds torn out every year! And some of our hedgerows were planted in Saxon times! But the farmers say they get in the way of modern machinery. They are sacrificing the inheritance of centuries for a few pounds profit. No sense of responsibility to nature. No sense of history. Oh, I *am* sorry! Did that branch catch you as I let it go? And do you know what Boggs has done now?"

Jonathan didn't care.

"He sold off the tract next to the church to construction speculators. Think of it! In a year's time there may be an estate of retirement homes abutting the churchyard. Thin-shelled boxes with names like 'End O' The Line,' and 'Dunroam Inn'!"

"Does all this really matter to you? Or is this a little show for my benefit?"

The Vicar stopped and turned. "Dr. Hemlock, the Church is my life. And I take a special interest in preserving the living monuments of its architecture. Every penny I make from my avocation with the government goes to that end." He winked.

"And is that how you justify the ugly things your organization does?"

"It might be. If patriotism required justification."

"I see. You picture yourself as a kind of whore for Christ. Presumably Magdalen was your college."

The Vicar's expression frosted over, his face seemed to flatten, and he spoke with crisper tones. "It occurs to me that we might do better to confine our communication to the problem before us." He turned and continued his walk, pushing through the brush to a field of stubble.

"Let's do that."

"It does without saying," the Vicar spoke over his shoulder, "that everything you learn in the course of your work with us is absolutely confidential. My young assistant—the man you know as Yank—has told you in outline the function of the Loo organization. Rather like the Search and Sanction Division of your CII, Loo is assigned the thankless task of providing protection for MI-5 and MI-6 operatives by technique of counterassassination. For good or for ill, our position as most secret of the secret and most efficient of the efficient brings extraordinary tasks to my doorstep. The affair at hand is one such. It is not in essence what your people would call a sanction. There is no specific assignment to kill a given person. To state it better: The affair does not absolutely require assassination. But the chances are you will be pressed to that extreme in an effort to remain alive yourself. Oh, my goodness! I should have warned you about that boggy spot. Here, give me your hand. There! Ah, you seem to have left a shoe behind. Never mind, I'll fetch it out for you. There. Good as new!"

The Vicar pressed on, inhaling deeply the brisk breeze that carried needles of rain with it. "I think it would be clearer if I presented the situation to you in terms of morals, for modern trends in turpitude lie at the core of the issue. Sexual license, to be specific. The New Morality—which is neither true morality nor particularly new, as a casual reference to the social lives of the Claudian emperors will affirm—has infected every stratum of society, from the universities to the coal pits—not that that is such a great gulf fixed, what with the democratization of the schools. Perhaps it is only natural that a generation that has passed the greater part of its life under the covert threat of atomic annihilation, that has seen the traditional bulwarks of family and class crumble under the pressures of enforced egalitarianism and liberalism gone to seed, that has experienced the decline of formal literature and art and the rise of television, pop art, folk masses, thriller novels, happenings, and the rest of it—all of which appeal to the nerve ends rather than to the mind, and to immediate reaction rather than to tranquil contemplation—perhaps it is only natural that such a generation would seek the sexual narcotic. Although as a churchman I cannot condone such activities, as a humanitarian I can grant the existence of powerful stimuli prompting people toward burying their minds in the mire of flesh and orgasm. Wish we had a flask of tea with us. That would warm you up. Come, let's press on and get the blood circulating.

"It suffices to say that a general retreat into sexual excess has become a fact of life in all circles, save the working class, which has been protected from infection by virtue of its want of imagination. And it would seem that unnatural sexuality is a habit-forming vice. Once he embarks on its use, the thrill-seeker develops a tolerance for the more . . . ah . . . commonplace activities, and finds they no longer serve to relax him and to dim his mind. The nerves seem to develop calluses, as it were. And so the sybarite is pressed toward more . . . ah . . . unconventional . . . ah . . ."

"I see."

"I thought you might. For some years now this grass fire of the senses, if I may avail myself of metaphor, has been spreading amongst persons in the government and civil service. At first it was limited to the relatively safe and pallid practice of exchanging wives while on holiday. But in time, the fire demanded more occult fuels. And, as one might expect, certain organizations sprang up to supply these demands. Most of them are smutty little operations offering simple varieties of number, race, and posture, together with the dubious advantage of becoming famous through the efforts of spying newspaper photographers. A little higher on the scale were places that offered variants long popular on the Continent—particularly in France, of course. Girls dressed as nuns, girls in caskets—that sort of thing. Look there! Did you see them? Two hares bounded across that bit of meadow. The autumn hare! Memories of boyhood, eh?"

Jonathan turned up the collar of his jacket and stared ahead miserably.

"At the apex of this pyramid of vice—Oh, my, I *do* wax Victorian. At the apex is a small and terribly expensive operation that offers to elite clientele what might be described as sexual maxima. I shall not abuse you with the details of these events. Suffice it to say that the organization in question is also involved in the importation of Pakistanis—illegal immigrants who cannot find gainful employment and who are driven to extremes to stay alive. This organization finds particular use for Pakistani children of both sexes between the ages of nine and fifteen. And I must confess that it is not only men in government that frequent this establishment, but often their wives and daughters as well. And all this nastiness goes on to the accompaniment of excellent wines and lobster—in season."

"I assume the clientele is not limited to clerks and middle-management personnel."

"Sadly, it is not. I blush to admit that among the clients are certain Very Highly Placed Persons." He winked.

"Do the bed linens bear the stamp 'by appointment'?"

The Vicar flushed, angry. "Certainly not, sir!"

Jonathan held up one hand in a gesture of peace. "Just wanted to know what league I was playing in."

"I see." The Vicar was not mollified. He turned and continued trudging on, entering an overgrown wood, anger making him increase his stride and breast his way through the tangle. When his anger had burned out, he continued. "For a year or two, this activity went on. A deplorable business, but not one that endangered the security of the country, so far as we knew. But then something happened that required me to review my evaluation of The Cloisters—for that is the ironic name of the resort in which these excesses take place."

"It's in the country somewhere?"

"No. London. Hampstead, in fact. Look there! A rhododendron! Like you, a visitor to our shores."

"What happened with The Cloisters? Blackmail?"

"No. Not really. And that's the uncomfortable part of it. But I'll get to that in a moment.

"One afternoon—just after tea, as I recall—I received a confusing call from my opposite number in MI-5. He had a report, the content of which had galvanized that normally lethargic branch of the service into activity. As one might suspect, they had no idea what to do with the information, but they had the good sense to push it over onto my plate. A man had stopped by at their office, a civil servant in the middle ranks with the Defense Ministry, and had boldly revealed to them a number of astonishing facts. Getting a bit above himself, he had participated in the leisure activities offered at The Cloisters. I don't know whether his money ran out or his conscience prevailed, but after a time he discontinued his visits. Then one afternoon he was visited by a caller who, with all the trappings of civility, demanded that he come later that evening to the Cloisters. The poor wretch dared not refuse. When he arrived, he was taken to a private salon where he was treated to a private showing of motion pictures."

"And he was surprised to find himself the star of the film. Argh-ga!"

"You anticipate correctly. Good Lord! I knew it! I told Boggs a dozen times that stile was rotten and wanted mending. I *knew* it would give way just when someone was straddling the fence. You didn't by any chance—"

"No! I'm all right!"

"Could I give you a hand down?"

"I'll make it!"

"You're quite sure you're all right? You're walking a bit oddly."

Jonathan crashed angrily on through the pathless thicket.

"The strange thing," the Vicar continued, "was that there was no threat of blackmail. Indeed, no pressure was brought to bear on the official to continue frequenting The Cloisters. But it was made perfectly clear to him that any mention of their activities would be met by an immediate publication of the film. As you might suspect, he was distressed beyond telling, but he was assured that he was not alone in this uncomfortable position. They evidently had a large number of films implicating a wide spectrum of government personalities."

"Why do you assume they are collecting this evidence, if not blackmail?"

"We don't know. But it doesn't really matter in any substantive way. The very existence of this information constitutes a time bomb planted in the seat of government—ah, there's the kind of maladroit metaphor that used to set us to laughing in school—and we have no idea when it will go off, or who will be harmed in the explosion. One thing is certain: a revelation of this caliber would damage Her Majesty's government beyond repair."

For a time the Vicar seemed to be lost in gloomy contemplation of so terrible a fate. They walked along a footpath that had been pulverized by horses into a ribbon of gummy slime.

To get on with the thing, Jonathan asked, "Why did this man come to MI-5 with information that would certainly end his career?"

"I wouldn't know, of course. Shame, one might conjecture. Or a sense of patriotism. As I said, he was of a *middle* rank in the civil service. Mere clerks are seldom affected by patriotism, and the leadership is immune to shame. The entire question is academic, however, inasmuch as our first move had to be to assure ourselves of this chap's silence. Inner pressures had driven him to divulge all to us. Who could know what his next action might be? The popular newspapers? At all costs, this scandal had to be kept from public view. And *that,* you had better know, remains our primary concern."

"So you had him sanctioned?"

The Vicar did not respond at once. "Not exactly," he said in a distant voice.

The truth dawned on Jonathan. "Oh, I see. That is lovely. The poor bastard showed up on my toilet, having failed to pull his trousers down."

"Just so. And I must tell you how much I regret the bungling of that matter. There was no call to burden you with the poor fellow's last words, to say nothing of the disgusting olfactory effect of the misplaced bullet. I can assure you the man responsible has been reprimanded." He winked.

"I have a feeling he will be punished further."

"Oh? Then you know who it was?" The Vicar's voice carried genuine admiration. "You certainly have a flair for getting information quickly. I feel vindicated in my choice of you for this somewhat delicate mission."

"Which is? . . ."

The Vicar refused to abandon his sequential progression through events. "Directly we received this information, we began our investigation. One of our best men was set to the task—a man who, because of his Grecian penchant in matters sexual, would have a subtle entrée into the goings-on at The Cloisters. That man's name was Parnell-Greene."

"The fresh grave I saw yesterday evening?"

"I'm afraid so. But before they got onto him, he was able to pass on some valuable fragments of information. We know, for instance, the identity of the man in charge of The Cloisters. He is best known to us as Maximilian Strange. German, by birth. Born as Max Werde in October of 1922 in Munich. The Werde family had been in the business of flesh-selling for three generations. Posh dens of vice catering to the upper classes—well, to the rich, at least. Young Max seems to have taken to the family line with rare energy, for we find him in 1943 at the tender age of twenty-one catering to the rather vigorous sexual appetites of ranking German officers. In Berlin and in at least two provincial cities, he managed sumptuous pleasure establishments stocked with girls and boys he had hand-picked from the concentration camps. The activity was . . . ah . . . irregular. Indeed, there was one small house on the outskirts of Berlin that was called the Vivisectory because . . ."

"I get the picture."

"Good. Recounting it is painful."

"You're a man of delicate sensibilities," Jonathan said.

"Irony, if it is to be effective, should lightly etch a phrase. Not drip from each word. But rhetoric is not our study here. When next our researches catch sight of Werde—or Strange, as he calls himself now—the war is over and he is purveying rather Roman entertainments in such places as Morocco, the Antibes, Samos—all the haunts of what you call the jet set. These amusements involve young people painted with gilt, participants from the audience daubed with grease, and activities between animals and humans—the favored beast being, for some obscure reason, the camel," He winked.

"It is at this time that we got our first description of the man. There are no photographs in existence. He is described as a handsome man in his early twenties. This is odd, because you realize that, by then, he was just over forty years old. We also discover that he has an inordinate interest in health, diet, exercise, and the general maintenance of his uncommonly youthful appearance. His linguistic attainments include a faultless command of English and French, along with Arabic, of course, as any man trafficking in his line of goods must have. Not much to go on by way of description, I fear."

"Not much."

"Again Mr. Strange disappears from sight. And two years ago, The Cloisters is launched in London, with Maximilian Strange at the helm of this fire ship. There you have him, Dr. Hemlock. Your adversary. Certainly a worthy opponent."

"His worthiness doesn't interest me. I'd much rather he was a fool. I'm neither a sportsman nor a hunter."

"Yes, I suppose there is a subtle difference between being a hunter and being a killer."

Jonathan let it pass. "Knowing what you do about Strange, you could certainly put a stop to his operation. I assume he is in the country illegally."

"I have tried to impress upon you the scope of the disaster that would derive from the slightest leakage of these films, or the activities they record. Neither the police nor any other agency of law enforcement must be brought in on this. Our police—like your own—are not distinguished by competence and disretion. And you may wonder why we just don't buy these films back, ransom them, so to speak. Well, Loo frankly doesn't have that kind of money in its war chest, and we must get the film back without alerting persons in the government who must not become involved in this delicate matter—that's part of why MI-5 comissioned us to act for them. We could, of course, dispatch some of our Loo actives to visit The Cloisters and leave no living beings behind them. But what if they failed to locate the films? What if Maxililian Strange has protected himself by leaving the films with someone who would publish them the moment something happened to him? No. No. This must be done delicately. And finally. And that is where you come in."

"Why me?"

"The late Parnell-Greene was able to pass on one further bit of information before his cover fell and he made his unfortunate visit to St. Martin's-In-The-Fields. He heard your name mentioned by Mr. Strange."

"My name?" Jonathan leapt over a ditch and scambled up a muddy bank. "You certainly don't think I'm implicated in The Cloisters."

"Certainly not." The Vicar braced himself against the wind and pressed on, shouting over his shoulder, "If we thought that for an instant, we would be entertaining you at another of our facilities."

"The Feeding Station?" The wind tore the words from Jonathan's mouth and flung them at the Vicar, who stopped in his tracks, astonished at Jonathan's knowledge of their operation. But again he was pleased with his ability to secure information quickly.

He nodded to himself and strode on. "We ran a thorough check on you, including communication with our colleagues in Moscow, Paris, and Washington. After assuring ourselves that The Cloisters was not a front from your Mr. Dragon and CII mucking about in our affairs, as that aggressive organization is wont to do, we counted it a stroke of rare good luck that a trained professional such as yourself was somehow involved in all this. Oh, goodness! I *am* sorry! But you really should be more careful where you tread in a cow pasture. Rather like Paris streets, in that respect. May I give you a hand up?" He winked uncontrollably.

"No!"

"Oh my, oh my. What a pity."

"Forget it. I'm not particularly fond of this jacket anyway."

"It does seem odd, if I may say so, that a man who was once a ranking mountain climber should find a little walk in the country so fraught with difficulty."

"Eagles don't become members of the Audubon Society."

"I beg your pardon?"

Jonathan was becoming angry with himself for allowing the droning civility of this vicar to erode his cool. "Listen. Exactly how did I get implicated in all this?"

"I haven't the foggiest. We only know what Parnell-Greene was able to pass on before his death. There are two threads connecting you to The Cloisters. We know that Maximilian Strange is very interested in you indeed."

"But—"

"We don't know why. Indeed, I had rather hoped you would be able to tell us. You have not, by chance, dealt with him at one time or another?"

"No idea."

"Pity. It might have been a starting point. The other thread linking you to The Cloisters is more direct. What you might call a friend-of-a-friend relationship. On two occasions Parnell-Greene met Miss Vanessa Dyke on the premises."

That stopped Jonathan.

"This might have been totally coincidental," the Vicar continued, "but it does constitute an intertangency between you and Mr. Strange. At all events, it is clear that your best path into The Cloisters is through Miss Dyke. Permit me to hold this barbed wire up for you. Oh, well. You said you were not particularly fond of that jacket. Let's take the shortcut back through the fields. Yes, Dr. Hemlock, I cannot adequately express my regret at having to ring you in on this business. We had no original intention to, you know, even after Parnell-Greene first reported that The Cloister people were interested in you. He was doing an admirable job of penetrating their organization, and we had no immediate use for you, although we took the precaution of planting our Miss Coyne with your rather seedy friend, MacTaint. Just in case."

"And when they hit this Parnell-Greene, you decided to bring me in as his replacement."

"Precisely. Their manner of disposing of poor Parnell-Greene will give you some idea of the kind of men you are up against. He was found impaled on a wooden stake in the belfry of St. Martin's-In-The-Fields."

"Baroque."

"Baroque, yes. But very modern at the same time. A bit of advertising that any public-relations man would approve. When one considers the extra danger involved in setting up so spectacular an assassination, one must come to the view that they were doing more than simply removing a potential danger. They were giving public notice to any who might attempt to interfere with their affairs, notice that was both efficient and darkly creative."

"Creative?"

"Just so. And with a diabolic sense of irony. I have alluded to Parnell-Greene's sexual deviation. He was a pederast; specifically his tastes ran to the passive role. Ergo, a certain grisly flair involved in the choice of anal impalement as a method of execution, don't you think, Dr. Hemlock?"

Jonathan trudged on in heavy silence for several minutes until, breaking through a thorn hedge, they were once again in the Vicar's garden.

"You'll want some brisk hot tea to ward off the cold. Let's go into the den, and I'll have it brought."

The rain swept in over the vicarage with full vigor. After the tea tray had been delivered by one of the young men with flared suit and broad bright tie, Jonathan said, "Why don't you just tell what you want me to do?"

"That must be obvious. We want the films. And we want them quickly, before they can do whatever they have in mind with them." He winked twice.

"And what about this Maximilian Strange and his people?"

"I assume their number will be reduced by those who have the misfortune of standing between you and the films."

"And that will be the end of The Cloisters?"

The Vicar pursed his lips. "Not really. After consideration, I have decided that closing The Cloisters would have no effect on the appetites that maintain it. They would simply seek elsewhere. So, when all this is over, The Cloisters will continue its services. But under new management."

"It will become a Loo operation?"

"I think that would be best, don't you? The possession of the films together with data we collect in the operation of the establishment will bring effective control of the government under an organization that has the best interests of the nation at heart, together with the background and education to know what those best interests are. More tea?"

"That would make Loo totally autonomous, wouldn't it?"

"Why yes." The Vicar's eyes opened wide with ingenuous frankness. "I believe it will. Just as the information your CII has collected concerning the fiscal and sexual irregularities of your political leaders has long rendered it independent. But I can assure you *we* shall never use our autonomy to undertake ill-conceived invasions of neighboring islands, or to cover up bungling attempts to spy on political headquarters. However . . ." His eyes softened as he envisioned the future. ". . . Such power might enable us to effect a final solution to the Irish Problem."

"You'll understand if I find little real difference between the Loo and The Cloisters."

"Ah, but so far as you are concerned, there is one most salient difference. *We* can put you into prison for thirty years for murder."

"*They* can kill me."

The Vicar shrugged. "Well, if it comes to that . . . but really! Our chat has taken an unnecessarily nasty turn." He winked.

"All right. For nuts and bolts, what kind of support can I expect in getting the films?"

"From the police, none. We cannot run the smallest risk of this affair becoming public. Loo will continue its researches, and you will be advised of any new developments through Yank, who will operate as your contact with us. We are also pursuing another line of entry into The Cloisters, partially in support of you, partially as a second line of defense, should some misfortune befall you. Do not be surprised if you meet Miss Coyne within the walls of that evil establishment. For the rest, you are on your own. You will, of course, have my earnest prayers to support you. And you must never underestimate the power of prayer, Dr. Hemlock."

Rain rattled against the windows of the snug little den with its damp wood fire releasing bluish flames that lapped lambently at the wrought-iron grate. The rainwater had stopped dripping from Jonathan's hair down his collar, and the room was becoming close and steamy with the drying of their clothes. Jonathan cleared his throat. "Listen. I want you to let Miss Coyne out of this. She's done her bit by ringing me in on it."

"Oh? Do I hear the sound of affection? A romance perhaps? How charming!"

"Never mind the crap. Just let her out of it."

"But, my dear man, where would she go? I have no doubt she told you her distressing story. Were it not for us, she would this moment be sitting in a Belfast prison. And were it not for our continuing protection, she might be picked up in the streets at any time. Where is she to go? Do you intend to become responsible for her?" He winked.

"No. I don't."

"Well, there you have it. In point of fact, she came to me this morning and asked to be allowed to help you. Perhaps she's feeling a little guilty, eh? May I offer you one of these biscuits? They've digestives, and I can particulary recommend them."

Jonathan shivered and drew his wet jacket around him. "I'd better be getting back to the inn."

"I do hope you haven't caught a cold. Nasty things at this time of the year." He rose and accompanied Jonathan to the door. "You can work out particulars with Yank, who has been instructed to assist you in every way. This afternoon you will receive a little training from The Sergeant."

"Training? From The Sergeant?"

"Yes. You are with Loo now. Drawing the Queen's shilling, as it were. And there are certain regulations to which you will have to conform. From your CII records it appears you are a bit short of formal training in hand-to-hand combat. And The Sergeant—an expert in such matters—has offered to brush you up. In fact, he leaped at the opportunity."

"I'll bet."

"I shall not have a chance to see you again before you go, so let me leave this with you: Be very careful in your dealings with Maximilian Strange. He is a clever man. And be particularly wary of the man called 'The Mute.'"

"Who is that?"

"He works for Strange, he undertakes such physical punishments as Strange considers necessary. We're quite sure he was the one who did for Parnell-Greene. Evidently he does such things for pleasure. So do be careful, there's a good fellow."

"What on earth happened to you?" Maggie's surprise converted into laughter, which she suppressed as soon as Jonathan's eyes told her he had no intention of being a good sport about his condition. "Do leave your shoes outside. I'll ask one of the boys to clean them." The corners of her mouth curled. "If he can find them, that is."

Jonathan stopped cold in the act of prying his shoes off while trying to avoid the cakes of mud and grass. He drew a very deep sigh of self-control, then continued. His fingers slipped, and he came up with a handful of mud.

Maggie did not laugh. Pointedly. "Come along up. I'll draw you a nice hot bath."

He growled.

His eyes closed, his elbows floating loose, he soaked in the large old-fashioned tub, only his mouth and nose out of the steaming water. But it was some time before the heat penetrated to his frozen marrow. Maggie perched on the edge of the tub, attending to him with a blend of maternity and laughter in her gamin face.

"What shall we do with these trousers?" she asked, holding them at arm's length between thumb and forefinger before letting them drop to the floor with a squishing sound.

He heard the reverberating rumble of her speech from under the water, but he could not make out the words. "What?" he asked, lifting his ears above surface.

"I was just asking . . . oh, never mind."

"You seem to be taking my condition rather lightheartedly."

"No. No."

"People die of exposure, you know."

"I'll fetch you a towel."

"Exposure to the elements. Do you still think this is funny?"

She shook her head.

"Why have you turned your back to me? Can't you look me in the face and tell me you don't think this is funny?"

She shook her head again.

"All right, lady. You have a count of five, at the end of which in you come to join me."

"I'm all dressed!"

"Two."

"What happened to one?"

"Four."

"You wouldn't . . . !"

The sere, middle-aged cleaning woman looked up from her sweeping and gasped. Approaching her down the hall were Jonathan and Maggie wrapped in towels, she with her dripping clothes over her arm, and he his torn and muddy ones. For the benefit of their round-eyed spectator, he shook Maggie's hand and thanked her for a delightful time. She asked if he would care to drop into her room for a while before lunch, and he said yes, he thought that might be fun. Then he turned to the chambermaid. "Would you care to join us?"

Horrified, speechless, she backed against the wall and held the broom handle protectively before her chest. It was perfectly adequate coverage. He shrugged, said something about ships passing in the night, and followed Maggie to her room.

"How are you going to dress?" Maggie asked as soon as the door was closed.

"I'll go to my own room as soon as I think the maid has left. I wouldn't want to spoil her orgy of outrage." He lay on her bed and stretched his body to get the kinks out. "Were you able to find out anything about the Feeding Station?"

"Hm-m, yes. Rather more than I'd care to know, really. It's a ghastly business."

"Tell me."

"Well . . . that man—the one in your bathroom the other night? He was a product of the Feeding Station. Yank told me all about it. He didn't want to at first, but once he started, it came gushing out, like something he needed to be rid of."

He leaned up on one elbow. Her tone told him she was finding it difficult to talk about it.

She slipped into a bathrobe and sat on the bed beside him. "Evidently the concept of the Feeding Station is a result of two problems faced by MI-5 and 6 and Loo. The first is the problem of defection and treachery within their ranks. These aren't very common, but they are dealt with vigorously. In fact, the defectors are assassinated. You do the same in the United States, I believe."

"Yes. The assassinations are called 'sanctions' if the target is someone outside the CII, and 'maximum demotes' if the target is one of their own men."

"Well, it seems that these assassinations were often difficult and awkward. There were bodies to dispose of; the police nosing about; and the Loo man who performed the assassination had to surface to award the punishment, maybe thereby stripping his cover for some more important task. So this was the first problem: the difficulty of performing assassinations."

"The second problem?"

"Corpses. Recently dead bodies are at a premium. They are used by the various branches of intelligence for setups, like the one you were victim of. And it seems they also use them as the ultimate deep cover for an active who has to go underground. Rather than simply disappear, the agent dies, or seems to. And there is no better cover than being dead and buried. They also use corpses to leak misguiding information to the other side—whoever that may be at the moment."

"How do they do that?"

"Evidently, a man is found in his hotel room dead of a heart attack, or perhaps he dies in a fatal traffic accident. And he has certain information on him that identifies him as a courier, together with some false data Loo wants implanted. In Lisbon or Athens—wherever the police are for sale—the other side ends up with the false information. They never imagine that a man would give his life just to fob off a bit of rot on them, so they always take it at face value."

"I see. So the Vicar put one and one together and decided to use the bodies of men written off for assassination to fulfill the Loo's need for fresh corpses. I assume they kidnap them and bring them to the Feeding Station to hold until they're needed."

"I don't know. I suppose so. I do know that bodies from the Feeding Station are always in short supply in relation to the needs of the services. The fact that the Vicar used one to rope you in gives you some idea of the importance of this affair, and of your importance to its success."

"I'm flattered. But why is the establishment called the 'Feeding Station'?"

"Well . . ." She rose and lit a cigarette. "That's the really grisly part of the matter—the part that upsets Yank so. It seems they are kept all doped up at a small farm back in the country near here. And they are fed . . . oh, lord."

"Go on."

". . . and they are fed on special diets. You see, Loo discovered that the first thing the Russians do when they have a corpse in want of identification is to pump its stomach and check the contents. And it wouldn't do for a supposed

Greek to produce the remnants of steak-and-kidney pie. So, along with matters of proper clothing, the right dust in the trouser cuffs, and all that sort of business, they have to be sure the right food is . . ." She shrugged.

"Thus: the Feeding Station. They're quite a bunch, these Loo people."

"I feel sorry for Yank, though. His reaction to the whole thing is so violent, you forget for a moment that he's part of it."

"Yeah, he's an odd one to find in this business. Of course, they're all odd ones in this business, come to think of it."

"But we're involved in this. We're not odd."

"No! Christ, no. Come over here."

Jonathan was resting in his room after lunch when Yank knocked and entered. "Greetings, Gate. I've just come from the Guv. He laid everything out for me. How do you feel about our working together on this gig?" He sat in the overstuffed chair and put his feet up on the dresser.

Jonathan had been shielding his eyes from the light, his arm thrown across his face, and Yank's potpourri of slang gleaned from a span of thirty years evoked the image of a bearded and sandaled man wearing a zoot suit and a porkpie hat. Jonathan lifted his arm and squinted at Yank. "I can dig it," he said, getting into the spirit of the thing.

"First thing, of course, you'll need a gun." Yank's tone was heavily serious. He'd been around. He knew about these things.

Jonathan dropped his arm back over his eyes and sighed. It was just like working again for CII. A kind of inefficient, rural CII. Each event had a lived-in feeling. "Right. Of course. The gun. I didn't want to carry it. But it should be in my flat when I return."

"Gotcha. The Mayfair flat, or the one on Baker Street?"

"Baker Street. And I'll need *two* guns. One in the bottom of my shirt drawer, covered by three or four shirts and surrounded by rolled-up socks. The second above it, covered by only one shirt."

"Whatever you say, man. You snap the whip; we'll make the trip. But why two guns hidden in the same place?" Then it dawned. "Oh, I get it! If they search the room, they'll find the top gun and not look further for the other one. Now *that* is what cool is all about!"

Jonathan lifted his arm and looked at Yank to ascertain if he was real.

"What kind of guns will you be wanting? Our MI–6 lads run to Italian automatics."

"I know they do. They're deadly as far as you can throw them. I want American-made .45 revolvers—five cartridges in, and the hammer down on an empty."

"Not an automatic?"

"No. If there's a misfire, I want something coming up."

"They're awfully bulky you know." Yank blushed involuntarily. "But then, of course, you know."

Jonathan sighed and sat up. "Listen, when I bring the guns along, I won't be going to a party. And I won't care if the handles match my cummerbund. I am not MI–6."

"Yes. Of course. Sorry." The American accent had diappeared again.

Jonathan lay back and rubbed his temples. "Another thing. Have someone who knows his business dumdum the bullets."

Yank's sporting sense was offended.

"Tell whoever does it that I want to be able to spin a man around if I only hit him in the hand. Lead slugs without jackets. Points both scooped out and crosshatched."

"Yes," Yank said coldly. "I quite understand."

Jonathan smiled to himself. Yank really had no stomach for his job. The romance and peekaboo of being a government agent doubtless appealed to him, but, as his reaction to the Feeding Station had shown, the grisly "wet work" of the business upset him.

But he recovered quickly. "When you get back to your pad, you'll find everything A-okay. I suppose you'll want a box of cartridges? Taped under the toilet top, maybe," he added helpfully.

Jonathan laughed aloud. If he couldn't do it with ten shots, it would be because he was too dead.

"OK. So much for the gun. After tea, you'll be having a little brushup with The Sergeant. He's a top man in both judo and karate. Marine champion in his day. You could learn a lot from him."

Jonathan nodded absently.

Yank swung his feet down from the dresser. "Right. See you later, alligator."

As he left, Jonathan returned to rubbing his temples. "After a while . . . ," he mumbled.

Jonathan and Maggie took tea together in a corner of the phony Tudor dining room beneath a window. She was quiet and distant, and he assumed she was thinking about her role as an inside person at The Cloisters. He was willing to let the silence lie over them. They no longer needed to touch or to talk.

Briefly, a warm sun penetrated the hanging clouds and touched her cupric hair. The light was vagrant and indirect, seeming to come from within the hair, as gloamings seem to rise from the ground. She was looking down, and her eyes were half hidden by her soft lashes.

"You're a beautiful woman, Maggie Coyne," he said matter-of-factly.

She looked up at him, the bottle green eyes caught in a triangle of sunlight. The light dimmed out as the sun disappeared into a wrap of misty clouds.

Then Yank arrived. "We gotta get to gettin'," he said brightly. "The Sergeant's waiting on you in the exercise room."

Jonathan smiled good-bye to Maggie and followed Yank out of the dining room. As they passed through the lounge, he picked up a back copy of *Punch* and started thumbing through it idly as they mounted the stairs.

From within the exercise room came the sound of guttural grunts, a shouted open vowel, then, as they entered, the splatting thud of a man being slammed down on the mats.

The room was a converted library with its paneled walls incongruously covered with hanging tumbling mats, as was the parqueted floor. It was directly above the pub, and there was a faint odor of stale beer rising from the floor and mixing with the saline smell of sweat. Henry was just rising from the mats slowly and painfully while another Loo man was kicking at a mat-wrapped beam, his toes curled to take the impact on the balls of his feet. He shouted with each blow as he shifted his practice from a front attack to a lateral one.

In the center of the room, large and hulking in his loosely bound judo jacket, was The Sergeant, his heavy frame oddly graceful as he shuffled toward Henry who was crouched in a defensive posture. Jonathan knew that The Sergeant had seen them enter and would do something to impress him, and he mildly pitied Henry.

Yank leaned against the padded wall and watched in silent admiration as The Sergeant stalked his prey, not bothering to feint and grunt. He carried his hands a bit too high. Bait for the trap, Jonathan thought. Henry feinted at The Sergeant, then went in to take advantage of the high guard. A clutch at the jacket, a sweeping kick, and Henry was in the air. He was not able to lay out fully and achieve the flat, wide distribution fall that would absorb most of the impact, and he came down on one shoulder with a liquid nasal grunt.

Stepping over Henry, and pretending to see them for the first time, The Sergeant said, "Well, bless me if it isn't the American doctor." He was confident and at his ease, for this was *his* ground.

Jonathan's face was bland. "That was amazing," he said, and The Sergeant thought he detected a hint of nervousness in the way he fingered the magazine.

"Just training, mate. Well, let's get to it. What's your pleasure? Judo? Karate?"

Jonathan looked around helplessly at the other men in the room, who were watching him with must interest and some amusement. The Sergeant had been talking about this encounter all day. "Well, actually, neither one. I suppose you've read my records from CII." He laughed hollowly. "Everyone else seems to have."

The Sergeant closed the distance between them and stood looking down at Jonathan from a three-inch-height advantage, his thumbs hooked in his loosely tied black belt. "I looked over the part the Guv give me. But I couldn't make no sense of it. Where it should read 'level of competence,' it said something odd."

"Yes." Jonathan walked past The Sergeant and sat down at a little library table in a protected alcove, set back out of the way of the combatants. The chair he selected left the only vacant one in the corner of the room. "I believe the records said 'not qualified, but passed.' "

"Right. That was it. Now, what the bloody hell is that supposed to mean?"

Jonathan shrugged and looked up at him with diffident, wide eyes. "Well, it's a peculiar thing. It means that I've never qualified myself in any hand-to-hand sport. Boxing, judo, karate—none of them. But the instructors—men like you—saw fit to pass me anyway."

The Sergeant crossed and stood over him. "Well, you'll not find anything slipshod like that in Loo. If I pass you, you're damned right qualified."

"I suppose you know what's best. But I'd like to explain something to you." Jonathan searched hard for the right words, and as he did so, he stared absentmindedly at The Sergeant's crotch. Growing uncomfortable, The Sergeant shuffled for a moment, then sat down in the corner chair opposite Jonathan.

Jonathan's demeanor was uncertain. "Well, if I explain this weird thing to you, perhaps you can give me some pointers that will help me improve my tactics."

"That's what I'm here for, mate."

"You see. Although I have never learned much about formal methods of fighting, I almost always win. Isn't that odd?"

The Sergeant regarded the slim body across from him. "I'd say you were bloody jammy."

"Perhaps," Jonathan admitted openly. "But there's more to it than that. You see, when I was a boy, I knocked around on the streets. And I was fairly lightweight then too. But I had to find some way to stay in one piece when it came to Fist City." He smiled wanly. "As it did from time to time."

Yank made mental note of the the term "Fist City." He would use it someday.

"And how did you manage that?" The Sergeant asked, obviously bored with this talk and eager to get on with it.

"Well, for one thing, I seemed to be able to lull the other man into a sense of security. Then, too, I learned that no fight has to last more than five seconds, and the man who lands the first two blows inevitably wins, if he is not bound to conventions of sportsmanship, or to the effete nonsense of any given technique."

The Sergeant wasn't sure, but he felt that there was a knock at his trade in that somewhere. His shoulders squared perceptibly.

Jonathan treated him to the gentle clouded smile that other men had recalled in retrospect. "You see, there's a period of warming up in any fight. The bowing and shuffling of judo; the angry words before a barroom brawl. And I learned that I could do best by attacking with whatever weapon was handy while the other fellow was still pumping himself up for the fight."

The Sergeant snorted, "That's all very good, *if* there's a weapon handy."

Jonathan shrugged. "Oh, there's always a weapon handy. A brick, a belt, a pencil—"

"A pencil!" The Sergeant roared with laughter, then addressed the small audience. "You 'ear this? The yank here toughs up his opponents by tappin' em on the head with a pencil! Must take a while!"

Jonathan recalled an incident in Yokohama in which his assailant had ended with a Ticonderoga #3 driven in four inches between his ribs. But he grinned sheepishly at The Sergeant's derision.

For his part The Sergeant no longer felt anger toward Jonathan. It was now scorn. He had seen this kind before. All lip and sass until it came down to the mats.

"No, now really, Sergeant. There must be a dozen useful weapons in this room," Jonathan protested through the light laughter of the lookers-on.

"Like *what*, for instance?"

Jonathan looked around almost helplessly. "Well, like . . . I don't know . . . like this magazine, for instance."

The Sergeant looked disdainfully at the *Punch* on the table between them. "And what would you do with that? Read him the jokes and make him laugh himself to death?" He was pleased with himself for getting off a good one.

"Well, you could . . . well, look. If I rolled it up tight, like this. See? Now, wait. You have to get it tight. And when it's compact it weighs more than a stick of wood of the same size. And you know how sharp the edges of paper are. The end here could really cut a fellow up."

"Could it just? Well—"

Eight seconds later he was on his back in a litter of tables and chairs, and the back of an inverted chair crushing hard against his larynx. Jonathan stood over him, and blood oozed from The Sergeant's eye socket, where the end of the magazine had been jabbed home with a cutting, twisting motion. The thrust into his stomach had brought The Sergeant's hands down and had left his nose undefended for the crunching upward smash of the magazine that broke it with pain that eddied to his gut and the back of his throat. The flat-handed cymbals slap on his ears had punctured the eardrums with air implosion, so he could barely hear what Jonathan growled at him from between clenched teeth.

"What are you going to do now, Sergeant?"

The Sergeant couldn't answer. He was gagging under the pressure of the chair in his throat, and his temples throbbed with the pulse of blocked blood.

"What are you going to do now?" Jonathan's voice was guttural and subhuman. He was in the white fury necessary to key himself to put bigger men away so totally that they never thought of coming back after him.

The Sergeant managed a strangled sound. He couldn't see well through the blood, but he caught a terrifying glimpse of Jonathan's glassy, gray green eyes.

Jonathan closed his eyes for a second and breathed deeply, calming himself within. The adrenaline rush was still a lump in his stomach.

He spoke quietly. "I could have done that with half the punishment. But I figured the apologetic little man in my bathroom owed you something."

He released the pressure and set the chair aside. As he pulled down his cuffs so that the proper one-half inch protruded from his jacket, he said, "I'll bet I know the words you're looking for, Sergeant: not qualified, but passed. Right?"

Jonathan was sitting alone in the hotel bar, sipping a double Laphroaig when Yank joined him.

"Oh, brother! You really whipped his pudding for him. Had it coming, I reckon."

Jonathan finished his drink. "You reckon that, do you?"

Yank slid into the barstool next to him. "I guess you'll be going back to London in the morning. When you get to your flat, you'll find a list of telephone numbers there—one for each day. You can use them to keep me informed of your progress, and I'll pass the good word on to the Guv. Any questions?"

None small enough for Yank to handle.

"Oh, yeah," Yank said. "About this Vanessa Dyke. I suppose you'll be getting in contact with her to get an angle on entrée into The Cloisters. Do you want me to have her watched until you get there?"

"Christ, no."

"But the Guv said that she—"

"She probably met your Parnell-Greene by coincidence."

"Maybe. But she was the last person he reported having met before we found him dead. Of course, you could be right. Maybe it was just a case of two queers getting together to compare notes. Right?"

Jonathan tilted his head back and looked at him coldly. "Miss Dyke is an old friend."

"Sure, but—"

"Get out of here."

"Now wait a minute. I have—"

"Out. Out."

Yank shuffled nervously for a moment, then he cleared his throat and tried to make an exit without loss of face. "OK, then. I'll be getting back to the city." He made a slow fanning gesture with the fingers on one hand. "Later, sweet patater."

Yank had gone back to London, and Henry had taken The Sergeant to a doctor in the village to attend to his nose and eye, and to see if anything could be done about his hearing, so Jonathan and Maggie had the dining room to themselves. A heavy rain had descended with the evening, enveloping the inn in the white noise of frying bacon. A draft fluttered the candle between them, and she rubbed her upper arms as though she were cold. She wore the muted green paisley gown she had worn on their first evening together—only three nights ago, was it?

Despite moments of laughter and animation, their contact was uncertain and frail, and several times he realized that they had been silent for rather a long time, each in his own thoughts. With a little effort he would pick it up again, but the chat invariably thinned into silence again.

". . . they tend to be blue this time of the year, don't they?"

He had been staring at the rain streaks on the window. "What? Pardon me?"

"Tangerines."

"Oh. Yes." He looked out the window again, then he frowned and looked back to her. "Blue?"

She laughed. "You were miles away."

"True. I'm sorry."

"You're leaving in the morning?"

"Hm-m."

"Going to take up this line of contact through your friend . . . ah?"

"Vanessa Dyke. Yes, I suppose so. It seems the only angle we've got on getting me into The Cloisters. I can't believe she really has anything to do with all this, though."

"I hope not. I mean, if she's a friend of yours, I hope not."

"Me too." He tilted back his head and looked at her for a moment. "The Vicar told me you were to be placed inside The Cloisters."

She nodded, then she examined the cheese board with sudden discretionary interest. He realized that she was trying to pass over the thing, make it seem less important than it was. "Yes," she said. "They've found a way to locate me inside by tomorrow night. Would you like a little of this Brie? It's Brie de Meaux, I think."

"Brie de Melun, actually. It'll be dangerous inside there, you know."

"You know, I'm as bad at cheese as I am at wine."

"The Vicar said you volunteered to work inside."

"Did he?" Her arched eyebrows and playful green eyes slowly dissolved to a calmer less protected gaze, then she lowered her lashes and looked at the cheese knife, which she aimlessly pushed back and forth with her finger. "I guess I lack great moral strength. I can't carry such burdens as guilt and shame very far. By helping you now, I hope I'll be able to convince myself that I've made up for getting you into this thing. Because . . ." She looked up at him and smiled. "Because . . . I've grown a little fond of you, sir." The saccharinity of this last was diluted by her broad comic brogue.

Her hand was available for pressing, but that was hardly the kind of thing Jonathan would do.

They got through coffee and cognac without any need for conversation. The rain had stopped, and the enveloping sound that had gone unnoticed was palpable in its absence. The new, denser silence contributed to the emptiness of the drafty dining room and the dimming of candle flames drowning in melted wax to produce a voided, autumnal ambience.

"They've put a car at my disposal," Jonathan said, voicing the last step of a thought pattern. "I suppose I could go into London tonight. Get my mind sorted out against tomorrow."

"Yes. You could."

"Then I'd be able to call on Vanessa first thing in the morning."

"Shall I come help you pack?"

"Do you think that's wise?"

"No."

"Come help me pack."

It was early dawn when he loaded his suitcase into the yellow Lotus, pressing the boot closed so as not to disturb the misty silence. His hands came up wet from the coating of dew that smoked the car. A bird sounded a tentative note, as though seeking avian support for his suspicion that this grudging gray might be morning. No confirmation was forthcoming. There was no sky.

"Yes," he muttered to himself, "but what about the early worm?"

The interior of the car was coldly humid, and it smelled new. He turned on the wipers to clear the windscreen of condensation, then he looked up toward the window of her room before pressing the stiff gearbox into reverse and easing back over the crunching gravel.

He had untangled himself from her carefully and eased out of bed so as not to disturb her. Her position had not changed when he returned from the bathroom, dressed and shaven. He had looked up at her with a wince when the locks of his suitcase snapped too loudly, but she didn't move. As he eased the door open, she said in a voice so clear he knew she had been awake for some time:

"Keep well."

"You too, Maggie."

Putney

THE LOTUS WAS tight and the roads were clear that early in the morning, so Jonathan pulled into the parking area of the Baker Street Hotel far too early to telephone Vanessa, who was a constitutionally nocturnal animal. He bought a few newspapers in the lobby and ordered breakfast sent up to his penthouse flat, and an hour later he was sitting before an untidy tray, newspapers littered around him. Time passed torpidly, and he found himself staring through the page of print, his mind on the unknown persona of Maximilian Strange. With sudden decision, he rose and located Sir Wilfred Pyles's number in his rotary file. After a sequence of guardian secretaries at the U.K. Cultural Commission, Sir Wilfred's hearty and gruffly civil voice said, "Jon! How good of you to call so early in the morning."

"Yes, I'm sorry about that."

"Quite all right. Coincidentally, I just opened a letter from that academic wallah—whatshisname, the Welshman?"

"fforbes-Ffitch?"

"That's the one. Seems he has a plot to send you off to Sweden on some kind of lecture series. Asked me to use my good offices to persuade you to go."

"He doesn't give up easily."

"Hm-m. National trait of the Welsh. They call it laudable determination; others see it as obtuse bullheadedness. Still, one becomes used to it. Teachers and baritones constitute the major exports of Wales, and one can't blame them for trying to be rid of both. But look here, if you are determined to scatter gems of insight on the saline soil of the Vikings, you can count on the commission's support."

"That's not what I called you about."

"Ah-ha."

"I need a bit of information."

"If it's within my power."

"How are your contacts at MI-5?"

"Oh." There was a prolonged pause at the other end of the line. "*That* kind of information, is it? As I told you, I've been on the beach for several years."

"But surely your contacts haven't dried up."

"Oh, I suppose I still have some of that influence that accompanies the loss of power. But before we go further, Jon . . . you're not up to any nastiness, are you?"

"Fred!"

"Hm-m. I warn you, Jon—"

"Just a background check—maybe with an Interpol input."

"I see." Sir Wilfred was capable of subarctic tones.

"I want you to run down a name for me. Will you do it?"

"You are absolutely sure you're not engaged in anything that will bring discomfort to the government."

"I could mention times when we were working together and *you* were strung out."

"Please spare me. All right. The name?"

"Maximilian Strange. Any bells?"

"A faint tinkle. But it's been years since I've been involved in all that. Very well. I'll call you later this afternoon."

"I'd better call you. I can't be sure of my schedule."

"I'll need a little time. About five?"

"About five."

"Now I have your word, haven't I, that you're not up to anything detrimental to our side? Because if you are, Jon, I shall be actively against you."

"Don't worry. I'm working for the White Hats. And if anything were to blow, you could rely on 'maximum deniability.' "

Sir Wilfred laughed. They had always made fun of the advertising agency argot that riddled CII communications.

"If any questions come up, Fred, just pass the buck to me."

"Precisely what I had intended to do, old man."

"You're a good person."

"I've always felt that. Ciao, Jon."

"Tchüss."

After waiting another long half hour, Jonathan dialed Vanessa Dyke's number. He arranged to drop over for a cup of tea and a chat. She seemed a little reluctant to meet him, but their friendship of years turned the trick. After he hung up, he spent a few minutes looking out his window over Regent's Park, sorting himself out. Two things had bothered him about the conversation with Van. Her speech had been blurred, as though she had been drinking. And the first question she had asked was: "Are you all right, Jon?"

He had never visited Vanessa in London, and the minute he stepped from the Underground station, he felt that this part of Putney was an odd setting for her vivacious, pungent personality. The high street was typical of the urban concentrations south of the river, its modest Victorian charm scabbed over by false fronts of enameled aluminum and glass brick; short rows of derelict town houses stared blind through uncurtained and broken windows, awaiting destruction and replacement by shopping centers; the visual richness of decay was diluted here and there by the mute cube of a modern bank; and there were several cheap cafes featuring yawning waitresses and permanent table decorations of crumbs and spills.

Clouds and smoke hung in umber compound close above the housetops, and a dirty drizzle made the pavements oily. Every woman pushed a pram containing a shopping bag, a laundry bag, and, presumably, a baby; and every man shuffled along with his head down.

Monserrat Street was a double row of shabby brick row houses, built with a certain architectural nostalgia for Victorian comfort and permanence, but with the cheaper materials and sloppier craftsmanship of the 1920s. The shallow gardens were tarnished and scruffy, the occasional autumn flower dulled by soot, and all looking as though they were maintained by the aged and the indifferent. An abnormal number of houses were vacant and placarded for sale, an indication that West Indians were approaching the neighborhood.

The garden at #46 was a pleasant contrast to the rest. Even this late in the season, and even in this color-sucking weather, there was an arresting balance and control that used the limited space comfortably. The hydrangeas were particularly consonant with the district and the mood of the climate; moist and subtle in mauve, blue, and tarnished white.

"Tragedy struck the life of noted art critic and scholar when his swinging, ballsy image was abruptly shattered yesterday afternoon." Van stood at her door, leaning against the bright green frame, a glass of whiskey and a cigarette in the same hand.

"Hello, Van."

". . . Bystanders report having observed this internationally notorious purveyor of manly charm engaged in the mundane and middle-class activity of admiring hydrangeas."

"OK. OK."

". . . Reports differ as to the exact hue of the flowers under question. Dr. Hemlock refuses comment, but his reticence is taken by many to be a tacit admission that he is becoming older, mellower, and—so far as this reporter can see—wetter with each minute he stands out there. Why don't you come in?"

He followed her into a dark overfurnished parlor, its Victorian fittings, beaded lampshades, antimacassars, and velvet drapes the antithesis of the black-and-white enamel, ultramodern apartment that had been hers when first they met in New York fifteen years earlier. Only the Swiss typewriter on a spool table by the window and a tousled stack of notes on the sill gave evidence of her profession. It was difficult to imagine that her regular flow of journalistic art criticism, with its insight and acid, had its source in this quaint and comfortable room.

"Want a drink, Jon?"

"No, thank you."

"Why not? Somewhere on the high seas at this moment, the sun is over the yardarm."

"No, thanks."

She dropped into a wing chair. "So? To what do I owe the honor?"

Jonathan toyed with a vase of cut hydrangeas on the court cupboard. "Why are you trying to make me feel uncomfortable, Van?"

She ignored his question. "I hate hydrangeas. You know that? They smell like women's swimming caps. Similarly, I hate flowery oriental teas. They smell like actresses' handbags. You'll notice I didn't say 'purses.' That's because I abhore sexual imagery. It's also because I eschew olfactory inaccuracy." She leaned back against the wing of the chair and looked at him for a second. "You're right. I'm feeling nasty, and I'm sorry if I'm making you uncomfortable. 'Cause we're old friends, pal-buddy-pal. You know what? You are the only straight in the world with soul."

Jonathan sat opposite her in a floral armchair, not because he felt like sitting, but because it seemed unfair to stand over her when she was so obviously distressed and off-balance. He had never heard her throw up so thick a haze of words to hide in. Her back was to the window, and its wet, diffused light illuminated her face with unkind surgical accuracy. The short black hair, semé with gray, looked lifeless, and the lines etched in her thin face constituted a hieroglyphic biography of wit and bitterness, laughter and intelligence—accomplishment without fulfillment.

"How are the Christians treating you, madam?" he asked, recalling the opening cue of a habitual pattern of banter from the old days.

She didn't pick up the cue. "Oh, Jon, Jon. We grow old, Father Jonathan, lude sing goddamn. Well, to hell with them all, darling. A pestilence on their shanties—wattles, clay, and all. And the lues take their virgin daughters." She lit a cigarette from the stub of the last. "Let's get to your business. I suppose it's about that guy I introduced you to at Tomlinson's? The guy with the Marini Horse?"

"No. Matter of fact, I'd forgotten all about him."

"He hasn't contacted you again since that evening?"

"No."

He could see the tension drain from her face. "I'm glad, Jon. He's a good person to avoid. A real bad actor."

"He pays well, though."

"Faust could have said that. Well then! If it's not the Marini Horse, what impels you to break in on my matronly solitude?"

He paused and collected himself before launching into what was sure to be an imposition on an old friendship. "I'm in some trouble, Van."

She laughed. "Don't worry about it. These days, it's no worse than a bad cold."

"I have to get into The Cloisters."

For a moment, she was suspended in mid-gesture, reaching for her glass. Then she looked him flat in the eyes, shifting her glance from one pupil to the other, her eyes narrowed in her attempt to analyze his intent. She sat back deep in her chair and sipped her drink in cold silence.

After a time she said, "Why The Cloisters? That isn't your kind of action. Too baroque."

"We grow old, Mother Vanessa. We need help."

"Oh, bullshit!"

"OK. I told you I was in trouble. Explaining will deepen my trouble. And it might give you some. I'm mixed up with some nasty people, and they'll do old Jonathan in, unless he can get into The Cloisters and accomplish something for them."

"And you came here to cash in old debts of friendship."

"Yes."

"Dirty bastard."

"Yes."

She stood up and wiped the haze off a pane of the window, and for a while she stared out past the garden and rain to the dull brick façades across the street. She ran her fingers through her cropped hair and tugged hard at a handful. Then she turned to him. "Now I *insist* you have a drink with me."

"Done."

She poured out a good tot of Laphroaig and passed him the glass. Then she perched herself up on the wide windowsill and spoke while looking out on the rain, squinting one eye against the smoke that curled up from the cigarette in the corner of her mouth. "I'd better tell you first off that you're in more trouble than you know. I mean . . . Jon, I don't know how much pressure these people can bring to bear on you to force you to try to get into The Cloisters, but it better be pretty big league. Because The Cloisters people are maximal bad asses. They could kill you, Jon. Honest to God."

"I know."

"Do you? I wonder. You remember reading about this Parnell-Greene? The one in the tower of St. Martin's? The Cloisters people did that. And think of *how* they did it, Jon. That wasn't just a killing. That was an advertisement. A warning in good ol' Chicago gangland style."

"I've been filled in on Maximilian Strange's response to intruders."

She drew a very long oral breath. "Maximilian Strange. Jon, you're in worse trouble than I thought. I wish I could tell you. But if I did, I'd run a fair risk of being killed. I know that I've often described my life as a pile of shit." She smiled wanly. "But it's the only pile of shit I've got."

Jonathan leaned forward and took her hand. "Van, I'm very sorry you're in this thing at all. I'm not asking you to get me into The Cloisters yourself, because I know they could trace it back to you. Just put me onto someone who can. You know it's important, or I wouldn't ask."

She stood and set her glass aside. "Let me think about it while I make us a pot of tea. We'll drink tea and watch the rain."

"Sounds fine. I'd like that."

As he glanced over the titles of some of her books, she made tea in the kitchen, talking to him all the while in a heightened voice. "You know, scruffy and middle class though it is, I really love this house, Jonathan. I bought it, and fixed it up, and painted it, and swore at the plumbing—all by myself. And I love it. Especially at night when I'm working by the window and I can watch nameless people shuffle by in the rain. Or on days like this, drinking tea."

"It's a great place, Van."

"Yeah. You're about the only person from the old New York bunch who would understand that. The little row house, the antimacassars, the mauve hydrangeas—all pretty far from the image I used to cut."

"True. Even the other evening at Tomlinson's you were still playing it for superbutch."

"I know it's silly. I just feel impelled to be the first to say it. You know what I mean?"

"I know."

"What?"

"I know!"

"Still. This is the real me. Little lady peeking through lace curtains. Cup of tea in hand. Brilliant statement taking form on my typewriter. Gas fire hissing in hearth. Christ, I'll be glad when I get so old I'm never horny. Being on the hunt makes you act such a fool." She came in with a small pot under a cozy and two Spode cups, and pulled her chair up close to his and poured. "I used to fear the thought of becoming an ugly old woman. But now that I'm there, I can tell you this: It beats hell out of being an ugly young girl."

Jonathan raised his cup. "Cheers."

"Cheers, Jon."

They drank in silence as the rain stiffened against the window.

"Grace," she said at last.

"Madam?"

"The person who can get you into The Cloisters. A really beautiful black woman who owns a club in Chelsea. She's very close to Strange."

"Her name is Grace?"

"Yes. Amazing Grace. Kind of a stage name, I suppose. A nom de guerre. Her club is superposh with expensive drinks and cute little black hookers with tiny waists and fine wide asses. But she's the real attraction herself."

"Beautiful?"

"Oh Christ yes!"

"Amazing Grace. Great name."

"Great chick. Her place is called the Cellar d'Or. It doesn't open until midnight."

Jonathan finished his tea and put down the cup. "I better get a lot of sleep before I go over there. It may be a long night."

Vanessa walked him to the door. "Listen, old friend and aging stud, you'll take real care of yourself, won't you?"

"I will. Now, let's think about you. Is there somewhere you could go for a few days? Somewhere well away from here?"

"I see your point. There's a woman I know in Devon. She writes mysteries."

". . . and she lives in a cottage, keeps a Siamese cat, and drinks red wine."

Her eyebrows lifted.

"No, I don't know her, Van. It's just that people love to play out their stereotypes."

"Even you?"

"Probably. But it's hard to recognize. I'm a typical example of a species of which there is only one living specimen."

"Blowhard bastard."

"Right family, but what's the genus?"

"Wiseass?"

"I didn't know you were up on animal taxonomy. But seriously, Van. You will get out of town, won't you?"

"Yes, I will."

"This afternoon?"

"I have a little work to do. I'll get through it as soon as I can."

"Make sure you do."

She smiled. "For a cold-blooded bastard, you're not a bad guy. Come, give us a big hug."

They embraced firmly.

Halfway down the walk, he stopped to smell the wet hydrangeas again. "I've got a problem," he told Vanessa who was leaning against the bright green door, the Gauloise dangling from her lips. "I can't remember what bathing caps smell like."

"Like hydrangeas," Van said.

Back in the gaudy Baker Street flat, he stretched full length on the bed he and Maggie had used a few days before. Beyond the windows, a cold wet evening had already descended, and he lay in the growing gloom, alone and unmoving, putting himself together for whatever lay ahead at the Cellar d'Or.

Amazing Grace. Outlandish name, but somehow consonant with this whole bizarre business. This was not at all like his sanction experiences with CII. Those had been simple mechanical affairs. He had taken an assignment only when he really needed the money, and had gone to Berne or Montreal or Rome, met a Search agent who had already done all the background work, and received the complete tout on the target: his habits, the layout of his home or office, his daily routine. And after working it out, he had walked in, performed the sanction, and walked away. They were never real people; only faceless beings, most of them examples of the humanoid fungus that populates the world of espionage—scabs and pus pots the world was better rid of.

And there had been very little personal danger for him. He traveled freely under his professional role of art historian. He had no motive, no personal relation to the target. He didn't even have fingerprints. CII had seen to that. When he became a sanction active, his fingerprints disappeared from all government, police, and army files.

But this Loo business was different. He hated this job, and he was afraid of it. He had quit working for Search and Sanction because his nerves had become frayed, and because his tolerance for working with well-meaning patriotic monsters had worn thin. And now he was older, and the task was more complicated. And there was Maggie to look after. The ingredients of disaster.

Shit!

But they had him. Loo and that damned vicar had him against the wall. And he wasn't going to prison for murder, even if it meant killing a dozen Maximilian Stranges.

He ran a shallow meditation unit and got some rest that way, slightly under the surface of the still pond he projected on the back of his eyelids.

He snapped out of it. It was time to call Sir Wilfred Pyles.

"Don't speak," Sir Wilfred said directly they were connected. "Fifteen minutes. This number." He gave Jonathan a number, then hung up.

During the fifteen minutes before he dialed, Jonathan sat hunched over the instrument, realizing that something had tumbled. Sir Wilfred obviously couldn't use his own phone for fear of a tap and he doubtless moved to a public phone to await the call.

The phone was picked up on the first ring. "Jon?"

"Yes."

"I assume you have the picture?"

"Yes."

"Rather like old times, eh?"

"I'm afraid so. I take it something tumbled."

"Indeed it did! You're into something very hot, Jon. I rang up an old chum in MI-5 and asked him to run a little check for me. They often do it for old boys who want to sort out a business acquaintance, or a call girl. He said he'd be delighted to. It seemed a piece of cake. But when I mentioned the name of your Maximilian Strange, he froze up and asked me to hold the line. Next thing you know, one of those intense young spy wallahs was talking to me, demanding to know details. Well, I fobbed him off as best I could, but I'm sure he saw right through me."

"So you weren't able to find out anything."

"Well, nothing directly. But their reactions speak volumes. If that constitutionally lethargic lot in MI-5 were stirred to action by the mere mention of your fellow's name, he must be top drawer. You haven't gotten to Bormann by any chance?"

"No, nothing like that."

"I'm afraid I've done you a disservice, Jon. MI-5 is on to you."

"You told them my name?"

"Of course. Surely you haven't forgotten the code of our line of work: every man for himself."

". . . and fuck the hindmost."

"You must be thinking of the Greek secret service. Well, tchüss, Jon."

"Ciao, buddy."

Jonathan raked his fingers through his hair, and took several deep oral breaths before lying back on the bed.

Shit. Shit. Shit!

He lay there for hours, forcing himself to doze occasionally. Eventually, he swung out of bed and prowled around the house for something to eat. He was not really hungry; he had taken care of that before coming up to his flat, eating a large meal of slow-burning protein; treating his body, as he used to in his mountain-climbing days, as a machine requiring the right fuel, the proper amount of rest, the correct exercise. He had eaten correctly. If there was any action tonight, it would come between midnight and three o'clock. The protein would be in mid-burn by then, and he would have consumed two or three drinks—just the right amount of fast-burning alcohol.

A goddamn machine!

It was only to fill the time and distract his mind that he looked around for food. As usual, wherever he lived, the only food in the place was a chaotic tesserae of exotic bits. He had always had a fascination for rare foods, and he enjoyed wandering about in the gourmet sections of large department stores, picking up whatever struck his fancy. His search of the kitchen produced a small jar of macadamia nuts, a tin of truffles in brine, preserved ginger, and a half bottle of Greek raisin wine. He ate the lot.

As he wandered through his flat, turning off lights behind him, it occurred to him to check the guns he had asked Yank to stash for him. His directions for concealment had been followed exactly. He took one out and examined it. The bulky blue steel .45 revolver felt heavy and cold in his hand as he snapped out the cylinder and checked the load. The slugs were scooped and a deep cross had been cut into the head of each. No range. No accuracy to speak of. The bullet would begin to tumble five yards from the barrel. But when it hit, it would splat as wide and thin as a piece of tinfoil, and a nick in the forearm would slam the victim down as though he had been struck by a train. Good professional job of dumdumming.

He considered taking one of the guns with him to Chelsea. Then he decided against it. It was impossible to conceal a howitzer like this, and a pat down would tip him before he had come within striking distance of The Cloisters and Maximilian Strange. He'd just have to be careful.

He flicked the cylinder back and replaced the gun.

The phone rang.

"What's up, Doc?"

"Why are you calling, Yank?"

"Oh, I got a couple of things up my sleeve. My arm, for one. No laugh? Oh, well. Then tell me this: How did things go with Miss Dyke?"

"I had a pleasant visit."

"And?"

"And I got a possible lead to The Cloisters."

"Oh? What was it?"

"I'll tell you about it if it works out."

"No, you'd better tell me about it now. The Vicar wants to know what you're up to at every moment. He wouldn't want to have to start back at square one if something were to happen to you. Or if you were to do something foolish."

"Like?"

"Like try to run off. Or sell out. Or something like that. Not that I really think you would. Having met the Vicar, I think you have a pretty good idea of what he would do to anyone who tried to do the dirty on him."

"Ship me off to the Feeding Station?" Jonathan brought that up on purpose.

After a swallow: "Something like that. So tell me. What is your lead to The Cloisters?"

"A woman named Grace. Amazing Grace. She runs a place called the Cellar d'Or. Mean anything to you?"

"Are you sure it's a woman?"

"What do you mean?"

"Amazing Grace is a hymn, after all. Get it?"

"Oh, for Christ's sake!"

"Sorry. No, I never heard of the woman. But I'll check through the Loo files for you. Anything else?"

"Yes. Do you have a tail on me?"

"Pardon?"

"A man's been following me all day. Out to Vanessa's and back. Is he one of yours?"

"I don't know what you mean."

"Medium build, blue raincoat, one hundred and sixty pounds, glasses, left-handed, rubbers over his shoes. He's probably standing down in the street right now, wondering how to appear to be reading his newspaper in the dark. If he's not yours, he's MI–5's. Too fucking amateur to be anything else."

"How could he be MI–5? They're not in on this."

"They are now. I made a mistake."

"The Vicar's not going to like that."

"Hard shit. Can you get in contact with MI-5 and pull this guy off? There are probably three of them, the other two out on the flanks. That's normal shadow procedure for your people."

"It could be they're only trying to help."

"Help from MI-5 is like military advice from the Egyptian army. If you don't get rid of them, I'll do it myself, and that will hurt them. I don't want them blowing my scant cover. Remember, I'm the only man you've got in the game."

"Not quite. We've managed to situate Miss Coyne."

"Oh?"

Yank was instantly aware that he had breached security. "More about that later, when we get together with the Vicar for a final briefing. Meanwhile, good hunting tonight. See you in the funny papers."

Jonathan hung up and crossed to the window to look down on the man who had followed him from Vanessa's. Christ, he was getting sick of British espionage. Sick of this whole thing. He indulged his anger for a while, then brought it under control by taking shallow breaths. Calm. Calm. You make mistakes when you're angry. Calm.

Chelsea

AS JONATHAN STEPPED from the Underground train at Sloane Square, he was still being followed by the fool in the blue raincoat who had been with him since Vanessa's. Presumably, Yank had not been able to get through to MI-5 and give them the word to discontinue surveillance. Jonathan decided to let him hover out there on his flank. At least he could keep an eye on him until the time came to shake him off, should the shadowing seem to endanger his cover.

Halfway up the tiled exit tunnel he passed an American girl sitting on a parka. Flotsam of the flower tide. She abused a cheap guitar and whined a Guthrie lament, having chosen a spot where the echo would enrich her thin voice with bathroom resonances and allow her to slide off miscalculated notes under the cover of reverberation. She was barefoot, and there was a large rip in the stomach of her tugged and shapeless khaki sweater. The surface of the parka was salted with small coins to invite passersby to contribute to maintenance.

Jonathan dropped no coin, nor did the man following in the blue raincoat.

Once away from the square, he closed into himself as he walked along seeking the address Vanessa had given him. He had no desire to come into contact with the jostling crowds of street people. It had been fifteen years since last he had been in Chelsea. In those days, a few of the young people who chatted in pubs or made single cups of cappuccino last two hours eventually went home to paint or write. But not these youngsters. They neither produced nor supported. Chelsea had always been self-consciously artsy, but now it had become younger, less attractive, more American. Head shops crowded up against the Safeway, and jeans were to be had in a thousand varieties. Discotheques. Whiskey a go-gos. Boutiques with scented candles and merchandise of green stamp quality. Shops vied for obscure names. Tall girls with hunched shoulders clopped along the pavement, and peacock boys swaggered in flared suits of plum velvet, cuffs flapping with dysfunctional bells. Rancorous music bled from doorways. People in satchel-assed jeans stared sullenly at him, an obvious representative of "the establishment," that despised class that oppressed them and paid their doles.

He had hoped the young would spare Chelsea the humiliation they had inflicted on San Francisco, Greenwich Village, the Left Bank. And he was angry that they had not.

But after all, he mused, one had to be fair-minded. These youngsters had their virtues. They were doubtless more content than his generation, hooked as it was on the compulsion to achieve. And these young people were more at peace with life; more alert to ecological dangers; more disgusted by war; more socially conscious.

Useless snots.

He turned off into a side street, past a couple of antique shops, and continued along a row of private houses behind black iron fences. Each had a steep stone stairway leading down to a basement. And one of these descending caves was illuminated by a dim red light. This was the Cellar d'Or.

He sat watching the action from his nook at the back of one of the artificial plaster grottoes that constituted the Cellar d'Or's decor. The light was dim and the carpets jet black, and the uninitiated had to be careful of their footing. The fake stone grottoes were inset with chunks of fool's gold, and all the other surfaces, the tables, the bar, were clear plastic in which bits of sequins and gold metal were entrapped. The glow lighting came from within these plastic surfaces, illuminating faces from beneath. And the air between objects was black.

He sipped at his second, very wet Laphroaig served, as were all the drinks in the club, in a small gold metal chalice. The most insistent feature of the club's bizarre interior was a large photographic transparency that revolved in the center of the room. It was lit from within, and every eye was drawn frequently to the woman who smiled from the full-length photograph. She stood beside what appeared to be a very high marble fireplace, her steady, mildly mischievous gaze directed at the camera and, therefore, at each man in the room, no matter where he sat. She was nude, and her body was extraordinary. A mulatto with café au lait skin, her breasts were conical and impertinent, her waist slight, her hips wide, and perfectly molded legs drew the eye to small, well-formed feet, the toes of which were slightly splayed, like those of a yawning cat. The black triangle of her écu appeared cotton soft, but it was something about the muscles and those splayed toes that held Jonathan's attention. Stomach, arm, leg, and hip, there was a look of lean, hard muscle under the powdery brown skin—steel cable under silk.

That would be Amazing Grace.

The Cellar d'Or was essentially a whorehouse. And a rather good one. All the help—the chippies, the barmen, the waiters—were West Indian, and the music, its volume so low it seemed to fade when one's attention strayed from it, was also West Indian. Despite the general air of ease and rest, the place was moving a fair amount of traffic. Men would arrive, and during their first drink they would be joined by one of the girls who sat in twos and threes at the most distant tables. Another drink or two and some light chat, and the couple would disappear. The girl would return, usually alone, within a half hour. And all this action was presided over by a smiling giant of a majordomo who stood by the door or at the end of the bar and watched over the patrons and the whores with a broad benevolent smile, his jet black head shaved and glistening with reflections of gold. Nothing in his manner, save the feline control of his walk, gave him the look of the professional bouncer, but Jonathan could imagine the cooling effect he would have on the occasional troublemaker, descending on him like a smiling machine of fate and disposing of him with a single rapid gesture that most insouciant lookers-on would mistake for a friendly pat on the shoulder. The giant wore a close-fitting white turtlenecked jersey that displayed a pattern of muscles so marked that, even at rest, he appeared to be wearing a Roman breastplate under his shirt. In age, he could have been anywhere from thirty to fifty.

One of the girls detached herself from a co-worker and approached Jonathan's table. She was the second to do so, and she looked very nice indeed as she crossed the floor: full-busted, long-legged, and an ass that moved hydraulically.

"You would care to buy me a drink?" she asked, her accent and phrasing revealing that she was a recent immigrant.

Jonathan smiled good-naturedly. "I'd be delighted to buy you a drink. But I'd rather you drank it back at your own table."

"You don't like me?"

"Of course I like you. I've liked you ever since we first met. It's just that . . ." He took her hand and assumed his most tragic expression. "It's just . . . you see, I had this nasty accident while I was driving golf balls in my shower and . . ." He turned his head aside and looked down.

"You are joking me," she said, not completely sure.

"In fact, I am. But I do have some serious advice for you. Did you see that fellow who came in here after I did? The one with the blue raincoat?"

She looked over toward the far corner, then wrinkled her nose.

"Oh, I know," Jonathan said, "he's not as pretty as I am. But he's loaded with money, and he came here because he's shy with women. When you first approach him, he'll pretend he doesn't want anything to do with you. But that's just a front. Just a game he plays. You keep at him, and by morning, you'll have enough money to buy your man a suit."

She gave him a sidelong glance of doubt.

"Why would I lie to you?" Jonathan said, offering his palms.

"You sure?"

He closed his eyes and nodded his head, tucking down the corners of his mouth.

She left him and, after a compulsory pause at the bar so as not to seem to be flitting from one fish to another, she patted her hair down and made her way to the far corner. Jonathan smiled to himself in congratulation, sipped at his Laphroaig, and let his eyes wander over the photograph of Amazing Grace. Lovely girl. But time was passing, and he would have to make some kind of move soon if he was going to meet her.

Oh-oh. Maybe not. Here he comes.

Like everything else about the giant, his smile was large. "May I buy you a drink sir?" Quiet though it was, his voice had a basso rumble you could feel through the table.

"That's very good of you," Jonathan said.

The giant made a gesture to the waiter, then sat down, not across from Jonathan as though to engage him in conversation, but beside him, so they were looking out on the scene together, like old friends. "This is the first time you have visited us, is it not, sir?"

"Yes. Nice place you've got here."

"It is pleasant. I am called P'tit Noel." The giant offered a hand so large that Jonathan felt like a child shaking it.

"Jonathan Hemlock. But you're not West Indian."

P'tit Noel laughed, a warm chocolate sound. "What am I then?"

"Haitian, from your accent. Although your education has spoiled some of that."

"Very good, sir! You are observant. Actually, my mother was Haitian; my father Jamaican. She was a whore, and he a thief. Later, he went into politics and she into the hotel business."

"You might say they swapped professions."

He laughed again. "You might at that, sir. Although I was schooled in this country, I suppose something of the patois will always be with me. Now, you know everything about me. Tell me everything about yourself."

Jonathan had to smile at the disregard for subtlety. "Ah, here come the drinks."

The waiter had not needed an order. He knew what Jonathan was drinking, and evidently P'tit Noel always drank the same thing, a chalice of neat rum.

Jonathan raised his glass to the large transparency of Amazing Grace. "To the lady."

"Oh, yes. I am always glad to drink to her." He drew off the rum in two swallows and set the goblet down on the gold table.

"Beautiful woman," Jonathan said.

P'tit Noel nodded. "I am happy to know you are interested in women, sir. I was beginning to doubt. But if you are holding out for her, you waste your time. She does not go with patrons." He looked again at the photograph. "But yes. She is a beautiful woman. Actually, she is the most beautiful woman in the world." He said this last with the hint of a shrug, as though it were obvious to anyone.

"I'd like to meet her," Jonathan said as casually as possible.

"Oh, sir?" There was an almost imperceptible tensing of the pectoral muscles.

"Yes, I would. Does she ever come in?"

"Two or three times each evening. Her apartments are above."

"And when she comes, is she dressed like that?" he indicated the transparency.

"Exactly like that, sir. She is proud of her body."

"As she should be."

P'tit Noel's smile returned. "It is very good for business, of course. She comes. She takes a drink at the bar. She wanders among the tables and greets the patrons. And you would be surprised how business picks up for the girls the moment she leaves."

"I wouldn't be surprised at all, P'tit Noel."

"Ah. You pronounce my name correctly. It is obvious you are not English."

"I'm an American. I'm surprised you couldn't tell from my accent."

P'tit Noel shrugged. "All pinks sound alike."

They both laughed. But Jonathan only shallowly. "I want to meet her," he said while P'tit Noel's laugh was still playing itself out.

It stopped instantly.

"You have the eyes of a sage man, sir. Why seek pain?" He smiled, and with a sense of comradeship Jonathan noticed that the smile did not come from within. It was a coiled, defensive crinkle in the corners of the eyes. Precisely the gentle combat smile that Jonathan assumed to put the victim off pace.

"Why are you so tight?" Jonathan asked. "Surely many men come in here and express interest in the lady there."

"True, sir. But such men have only love on their minds."

"How do you know *I'm* not sperm-blind?"

P'tit Noel shook his head. "I feel it. We Haitians have a sense for these things. We are a superstitious people, sir. The moment you came in, I sensed that you were trouble for Mam'selle Grace."

"And you intend to protect her."

"Oh yes, sir. With my life, if need be. Or with yours, should it sadly come to that."

"No doubt about how it would go, is there?" Jonathan said, skipping unnecessary steps in the conversation.

"Actually, none at all, sir."

"There's an expression in the hill country of the United States."

"How does it go, sir?"

"While you're gettin' dinner, I'll get a sandwich."

"Ah! The idiom is clear. And I believe you, sir. But the fact remains that you would lose any battle between us."

"Probably. But you would not escape pain."

"Probably."

"I'll make you a deal."

"Ah! *Now* I recognize you to be an American."

"Just tell the lady that I want to talk to her."

"She knows you then?"

"No. Tell her I want to talk about The Cloisters and Maximilian Strange." Jonathan looked for the effect of the words upon P'tit Noel. There was none.

"And if she will not see you?"

"Then I'll leave."

"Oh, I *know* that, sir. I am asking if you will leave without disturbance." Jonathan had to smile. "Without disturbance."

P'tit Noel nodded and left the table.

Five minutes later he returned. "Mam'selle Grace will see you. But not now. In one hour. You may sit and drink if you wish. I shall tell the girls that you are not a fish." His formal and clipped tone revealed that he was not pleased that Amazing Grace had deigned to receive the visitor.

Jonathan decided not to wait in the club. He told P'tit Noel that he would take a walk and return in an hour.

"As you wish, sir. But be careful on the streets. It is late, and there are *apache* about." There was as much threat in this as warning.

Jonathan walked through the tangle of back streets slowly, his hands plunged deep into his pockets. Fog churned lazily around the streetlamps of the deserted lanes. He had made a pawn gambit, and it had been passed. He had lost nothing, but his position had become passive. They now made the moves and he reacted. An hour was a long time. Time enough for Amazing Grace to contact The Cloisters. Time enough for Strange to decide. Time enough to send men. Perhaps he had made an error in not bringing a gun.

On the other hand, the Vicar had said The Cloisters people were seeking him out for some reason, and they had been doing so even before Loo had involved him in this thing. If Strange needed him, why would he seek to harm him? Unless they knew he was working for Loo. And how would they know that?

It was a goddamn merry-go-round.

Near a corner, he found a telephone kiosk. His primary reason for leaving the Cellar d'Or had been to phone Vanessa and make sure she was off in Devon and out of the line of fire. As the unanswered phone double-buzzed, his eyes wandered over hastily penned and scratched messages: doodles, telephone numbers, an announcement that one Betty Kerney was devoted to an exotic protein diet. There was a sad graffito penned in a precise, cramped hand: "Mature person seeks company of young man. Strolls in the country and fishing. Mostly friendship." No meeting time; no telephone number. Just a need shared with a wall. After the phone had rung many times, Jonathan hung up. He was relieved to know that Vanessa was out of it.

It was nearly time to return to the Cellar d'Or, and he had seen nothing of the man in the blue raincoat since he had left him trying to disentangle himself from the coyly persistent Jamaican whore, pay for his drink, and collect his raincoat. All this without arousing undue attention. They were an incompetent bunch. Just like the CII.

During his quiet stroll through the fog, he had decided how he would play this thing with Amazing Grace. There were two possibilities. On the one hand, Strange might only have her try to sound him out—discover his reason for seeking him. In that case Jonathan would let Grace know that he was aware of the activities at The Cloisters and of the fact that Maximilian Strange wanted to contact him for some reason. He would tell her he was interested in anything that might prove profitable, if it was safe enough. On the other hand, Strange might have decided to send men to pick Jonathan up and bring him to The Cloisters. In this case it would be important not to seem eager to get inside. He would have to put up some resistance, enough to make it look good. He would have to hurt some of them, while he tried to avoid hurt to himself. Once inside The Cloisters, he would have to play it by ear. It would be a narrow thing.

Damn. If only he knew why Strange was trying to contact him.

He paused for a second beneath a streetlight to get his bearings back to the Cellar d'Or. The blind alley leading to the side entrance was only a block or two from here. There was a shuffling sound down the street, and he turned in time to see a figure jump from the pool of light two streetlamps away.

The blue raincoat. The last thing he needed was this MI-5 ass tagging along. It would make him appear to be bait, and he'd never talk his way out of that.

There was a second of elastic silence, then Jonathan heard another sound, borne on the fog from across the street. There were two more of them.

He ran.

He had only twenty-five yards on them as he broke into the blind mews behind the club and banged loudly at the back door. The noise echoed through the brick cavern, but there was no response. From the dustbins and garbage cans that littered the alley, he found a champagne bottle, which he clutched by the neck, thankful for the weight of the dimpled bottom as he pressed back into a shadowy niche behind a projecting corner of damp brick. The three figures appeared, strung out across the entrance of the alley. Backlit by a streetlight, their long shadows falling before them on the wet cobblestones, they looked like extras from a Carol Reed film. Jonathan could see their featureless silhouettes, mat black in a nimbus of silver phosphorescent fog. He remained motionless, his heart beating in his temples from the effort of his run and from anger at being endangered by these bungling government serfs.

They stopped halfway down the alley and exchanged some muttered words. One seemed to want to go away, another thought they should enter the Cellar d'Or and investigate. After a moment of vacillation, they decided to enter the club. Jonathan pressed back against the wall as they neared. Getting all three was going to be difficult. As they came abreast him, he brought the bottle down on the head of one with a satisfyingly solid crack. The other two jumped away, then rushed at him with well-schooled reactions. Hands clutched at him, a fist hit him on the shoulder; a shoe cracked into his shin. He jerked away with a broad backhand sweep with the bottle that made them dodge back for an instant. One grabbed up a bottle from a dustbin and hurled it. He ducked as it exploded into fragments behind him.

A shaft of light fell upon the scene as the door behind Jonathan opened and the dominating bulk of P'tit Noel filled the frame.

"Thank God," Jonathan said.

Together they waded into the hooligans, and it was over in five seconds. Jonathan used his bottle on one; P'tit Noel struck the other with the flat palms of his open hands, loud concussing blows that splatted against his head and slammed him against the wall.

One of the men was still conscious, sitting against the brick wall, blood streaming from his nose and mouth where P'tit Noel's palm had flattened them. Another was moaning in semiconsciousness. The last was a silent heap among the garbage cans.

P'tit Noel dragged each up in turn by his lapels and held him against the wall with one hand while he opened the man's eyelids with his fingers, professionally checking the set and dilation of the pupils. "They'll live," he said, as a matter of information.

"Pity."

P'tit Noel wiped his palms on the shirt of one of the downed men. "Why don't you step in and brush yourself off, sir," he said over his shoulder. "Mam'selle Grace will see you now."

"What about these yahoos?"

"Oh, I think they will be gone by morning."

P'tit Noel conducted Jonathan to his small living quarters behind the club and offered him the use of his bathroom to clean up. He wasn't really hurt. There was some stiffness in one shoulder, his trousers stuck to his shin where the kick had brought blood, and he was experiencing the mild nausea of adrenaline recession, but he would be fine. As he stepped from the bathroom, P'tit Noel greeted him with a glass of rum, hot and soothing going down.

"You took your time answering the door."

"Actually, I did not hear you knock, sir."

"Then how come you turned up? For which, by the way, much thanks."

"Intuition. Premonition. As I told you, I am Haitian."

"Voodoo and all?"

"You know voodoo, sir?"

"Not really. No."

P'tit Noel smiled. "It exists. I passed some time studying the legal implications of crime committed under its influence. Because of the limits of my British education, I was prone to scoff at first."

"Which limitations are those?"

"The limitations of logic and evidence. Of European sequential thought."

"You were a student in Jamaica?"

"No, I was a lawyer, sir."

Jonathan admired the cool way he laid that on him. "You know, P'tit Noel, you've developed a magnificent way of saying 'sir.' When you use the word, it sounds like an arrogant insult."

"Yes, I know, sir."

P'tit Noel led him up a narrow staircase to the first floor where the ambience was that of the well-appointed town house—totally alien to the gaudy glitter of the club. They passed down a hallway and stopped before a double door of dark oak. P'tit Noel tapped lightly.

"I shall leave you now, sir. You may go in."

Jonathan thanked him again for his intervention, opened the door, and stepped into a lavishly furnished room of crimson damask and Italian marble.

Grace was indeed amazing.

She stood in the middle of the room, wearing a transparent peignoir of a white diaphanous material. Poised, her fine body was even more seductive when covered with a mist of fabric through which the circles of her brown nipples and the triangle of her écu were a dim freehand geometry. But it was her stature that gave Jonathan pause. Little wonder the marble mantel in the photograph had seemed uncommonly high. Amazing Grace was only four feet six inches tall.

"Good evening, Grace," he said, settling his smiling gaze on her large oriental eyes.

Her nose wrinkled up and she laughed hoarsely. "Well, you handled that just fine, Dr. Hemlock."

"I'm unflappable. Particularly when I'm stunned."

"Is that so." She turned away and walked over the thick red carpet toward a little grouping of furniture before the fireplace. The splayed toes of her bare feet seemed to grip the rug. "Don't just stand there, boy. Come on over here and have a drink with me." She lifted a decanter of clear liquid and filled two sherry glasses, then she arranged herself on a small chaise longue, taking up all the space in an unprovocative way that denied the possibility of his joining her on it.

He took his glass and sat across from her and near the crackling wood fire.

"Happy times," she said, lifting her glass and draining it.

"Cheers." He swallowed—then he swallowed again several times to get it down. His eyes were damp and his voice thin when he spoke. "You drink neat Everclear?"

"Honey bun, I don't drink for flavor."

"I see." Jonathan had been surprised by her accent from the first. He had assumed that she, like her staff, was West Indian. But she was American.

"Omaha," she explained.

"You're kidding."

"Sweety, people don't kid about coming from Omaha. That's like bragging about having syphilis. Pour yourself another."

"No. No—thank you. It's *good.* But no thank you."

She laughed again, a rich brawling sound that was infectious. "Hey, tell me. No shit now. How can a swinging type like you be a doctor? You don't look like you'd waste time jamming nurses behind screens."

"I'm not that kind of doctor. What about yourself? How did you end up in the flesh trade?"

"Oh, just answered an advertisement. 'Positions wanted.'" She hooted a laugh. "But seriously, I did a couple years in Vegas working at a joint that specialized in uncommon meat. My being tiny makes tiny men feel big. Then I decided that management was more fun than labor, so I saved up my money and . . ." She made an inclusive sweep of her hand.

"It looks like you're doing very well."

"I'll probably make it through the winter." Instantly the shine in her eyes dimmed. "Is that enough?"

"Enough?"

"Small talk, honey bun."

Jonathan smiled. "Almost. One more question. P'tit Noel. Is he your lover? I only ask out of a sense of self-preservation."

"Are you kidding, man? I mean, he's nuts about me and all, that goes without saying. I imagine he'd eat half a mile of my shit just to see where it came from. But we don't fuck. I'm a little girl, and he is a big man. He'd puncture my lungs."

The flood of earthy imagery made Jonathan laugh.

"Besides," she continued, refilling her glass, "I don't use men anymore. When I need it, I have a girl in. Women know where the bits are and what they want. They're more efficient."

"Like the Everclear."

"Right."

He shook his head. "You're amazing, Grace."

She drank off half the glass. "So? What did you want to see me about?"

"I want to see Maximilian Strange."

"Why?"

"I believe he wants to see me."

"Why?"

"I'll ask him when I see him."

"What brought you here?"

Jonathan sighed. "Please, lady. That will slow us down a lot."

"All right. No peekaboo. Tell me why you want to see Max. We're partners. Or didn't you know that?"

Jonathan's eyebrows raised. "Partners? *Equal* partners?"

She finished her drink and poured another. "No, Max doesn't have any equals. He's one of a kind. The most beautiful man; the most cruel man. He holds all the patents on excitement."

"It sounds like you feel about Strange the way P'tit Noel feels about you."

"That's not far wrong."

Jonathan rose and looked around. "Grace? There's something I want to do. And you can help me."

"Yeah?"

"I've got this problem. How can I tell you this without offending you? Honey, I've got to piss."

"Nut!" She laughed. "It's back there. Through the bedroom."

When he returned she had taken off her peignoir and was standing with her back to the fire, rubbing her bare buttocks and stretching to her tiptoes in the warmth.

"Do you know that you're nude, madam?"

"I like to walk around bare-assed. I feel free. And it turns men on, and I get a kick out of that. 'Cause they ain't going to get nothin.' " She said this last in a low-down Ras accent.

"Well, you keep flashing that fine body around, you'll get yourself raped one of these days."

"By you?" she asked with taunting scorn.

"No, I've given up rape. The pillow talk is too limited."

She frowned seriously. "You know, if some stud decided to rape me, I think I'd fight it. I'd let him in. Then I'd tighten up the old sphincter and cut it right off."

"What a lesson that would be for him." But her taut, cabled muscles under smooth skin gave the image credibility, and he couldn't help a quick local wince.

His trip to the bathroom had been profitable. There was a window giving out onto a flat metal roof. He had left it open. If they came for him, he'd be able to give them a chase that would prevent anyone from thinking he was overeager to get into The Cloisters.

"Tell me, Grace. When you talked to Strange on the phone, did he give you any idea when he'd like to meet me?"

"What makes you think I called him?"

"You called me Dr. Hemlock. P'tit Noel didn't know my title."

Her feline composure faded perceptibly. "I guess I screwed up, right?"

"A little. But I won't mention it to Strange."

She was relieved, and he realized that Maximilian Strange did not tolerate error—even from partners. "When does he want to meet me?"

"They'll be here any minute now to pick you up."

"Uh-huh. Well, I don't think I can make it tonight. Let's set something up for tomorrow."

She smiled at the thought of anyone thinking about changing Max's plans. "No. He said tonight. He'll be pissed if you're not here."

"He may have to live with that."

At that moment there was the sound of footfalls outside the door. Several men.

She smiled at him and lifted her arms in an exaggerated shrug. "Too late, honey bun."

"Maybe not. You just stand there warming your ass, and don't try to stop me.

I'm a real terror against girls of your size." He ran to the bathroom and scrambled out the window onto the metal roof. As he did, he could hear her opening the door and talking rapidly to the men. There were barked orders, and one of the men rushed through the flat toward the bathroom, as the others ran back down the stairs.

Jonathan flattened out against the brick wall beside the bathroom window. A big head came poking out, and he hit it with his fist just behind the ear. The face slapped down against the stone sill with the click of breaking teeth, and the head slid back inside with a moan and a sigh.

His eyes not yet accustomed to the dark, Jonathan crept along the top of the roof on all fours. He came blank up against a brick wall and felt his way along it to a corner. By then his eyes had dilated and he could see dimly. Below him was a narrow gap, a cut of black between two windowless brick buildings. It didn't seem to lead anywhere, so he decided to climb upward, toward the dirty, city-glow smear of fog. The gap was only about four feet wide. He slipped off his shoes and, falling back on his mountain experience, eased out over the void and jammed himself between the two brick walls, his back against one, his feet flat against the other. He executed a scrambling chimney climb, holding himself into the fissure by the pressure of his feet against the opposite wall and inching up at the expense of his suit jacket and a quantity of palm skin. The building before him went up beyond his vision, but the one at his back was only three stories tall. When he got to the lip of the flat roof, he shot himself over with a final thrust with his legs, and he lay panting on the wet seamed metal. He crawled across the roof and looked down. Below was a cobblestone alley strewn with garbage cans, and it appeared to give out onto the street. There was a light from a distant streetlamp, and he could see to negotiate a heavy, cast-iron drainpipe that led from the roof to the floor of the alley. From afar, he could hear a call and an answering shout, but he couldn't make out the direction. The descent was fairly easy, but when he landed a piece of broken glass went through his sock into the sole of his foot.

Jesus Christ! The same fucking alley!

He pulled the triangle of glass out and gingerly made his way through the shattered bottles.

It occured to him how ironic it would be if, in attempting to avoid appearing anxious to get into The Cloisters, he had evaded them altogether.

But no worry on that score. There was a shout. Footfalls. And there they were, two of them in the gap, blocking his exit, their forms punctuating the glowing nimbus of fog. They moved toward him slowly.

"All right, gentlemen. I give up. You win."

But they didn't answer, and by their slow inexorable advance he took it that they wanted some revenge for their toughed-up mate above.

Just then a door opened behind him and he was caught in a shaft of light. It was P'tit Noel.

"Thank God," Jonathan said. He heard the explosive sound of P'tit Noel's openhanded slap to the back of his head, but he didn't feel it. He seemed to float away horizontally, and later he remembered hoping he wouldn't land in the broken glass.

Hampstead

BEFORE OPENING HIS eyes or moving, he waited until full consciousness had gradually replaced the spinning nightmare vertigo. He was aware of the rocking motion of the automobile and the harsh drag of the floor carpeting against his cheek each time they turned a corner. He was cramped and stiff, but there was no pain in his head, as there ought to have been. The sick dream of it all was intensified by the dark, so he opened his eyes, and he found himself looking strabismally at the glossy tips of a pair of patent leather shoes not four inches from his nose. Light came and went in raking flashes as they passed by lights.

It was as he tried to sit up that the pain came—a vast swooning lump of it, as though someone were forcing a sharp fragment of ice through the arteries of his brain. His eyes teared involuntarily with the pain, but when it passed, it passed completely, not even leaving behind the throb of a headache. He struggled to a sitting position. They were in a taxi. The three men with him watched his efforts dully, without speaking or offering help. He got to his knees, pulled down the jump seat, and sat on it heavily. There were two men across from him on the back seat, and a third beside him on the other jump seat. The streaked drops of rain on the windows glittered with each passing streetlamp.

He looked down. There was no registration number for the cab in the usual frame between the jump seats. They had evidently taken a leaf from the Chicago gangs, using a private taxi for basic transportation because its vehicular anonymity allowed it to prowl the streets at any hour of the night without arousing undue attention.

The driver, unmoving on his side of the glass partition, was undoubtedly one of them. There were neither door nor window handles on the inside of the passenger compartment. Very professional. Unaided, the driver could deliver a man without additional guard.

Jonathan took stock of the men with him. He could forget the driver. Drivers are never leaders. The man on the jump seat lifted his hand to his swollen, discolored mouth from time to time, gingerly touching the split upper lip. That must be the one who had the misfortune to stick his head out the bathroom window. He inadvertently inhaled orally, and winced with pain as the cold air touched the exposed nerves of his broken front teeth. Jonathan was glad he wasn't alone with this one. The owner of the patent leather shoes who sat facing him was a furtive little man with nervous eyes and a tentative moustache. A diagonal scar, more like a brand than a cut, ran in a glairy groove from the right cheek to the left point of his chin, intersecting his lips and moustache, and giving him the appearance of having two mouths. He sat well over against his armrest to make room for the third man, whose great bulk was arranged in an expansive sprawl. That would be the leader of this little squad. Jonathan addressed him.

"I assume we're going to The Cloisters?"

Viscously, the big man brought his heavy-lidded eyes to rest on Jonathan's face where they settled without recognition, not even shifting from eye to eye. The broad face was dominated by an overhanging brow, and his slab cheeks flanked an oval mouth, the thick, kidney-colored lips of which were always moist. So extreme was the droop of his eyelids that he tilted back his head to see, exposing only the bottom half of his pupils. Jonathan recognized the psychological type. He had met them occasionally when working for CII. They were used in low priority sanctions because they were effective, cheap, and expendable. Often they would do "wet work" without pay. Violence was a pleasurable outlet for them.

Attempts at conversation were not going to be fruitful, so Jonathan set to examining his condition. He explored the base of his skull with his fingers and found it only a little tender. The nose was clear, and he could focus his eyes rapidly, so there hadn't been any concussion. The openhanded slap to the back of the neck with which P'tit Noel had put him away is one of the premiere blows in the repertory of violence. It can kill without a bruise and is undetectable without an autopsy to reveal blood clots and ruptured capillaries in the brain. But to use the blow in its middle ranges requires a fine touch. Jonathan had to admire P'tit Noel's skill. Not bad . . . for a lawyer.

Despite the Haitian's professional art, Jonathan was a mess. His trousers were torn and filthy, his jacket was scuffed from the chimney climb up the brick wall, and he had no shoes. For his meeting with Maximilian Strange, he would lack the social poise and sartorial one-upmanship he usually enjoyed. Even among these goons, he felt awkward.

"Sorry about those teeth of yours, pal," he said unkindly. "You're really going to make a haul when the Tooth Fairy comes around."

The man on the jump seat produced a compound of growl and sneer, which he instantly regretted as the in-suck of air made him twist his head in pain.

The taxi was easing down a steep cobble street, past what appeared through the streaked windows to be large villas of the late eighteenth century. But then they passed an anachronous modern shopping plaza that looked like a project by a first-year design student in a polytechnic. It seemed carved in soap, and the dissonance it obtruded into the fashionable district spoke eloquently of the truism that the modern Englishman deserves his architectural heritage as much as the modern Italian merits the Roman heritage of efficiency and military prowess. Then they turned and reentered an area of fine old houses. Jonathan recognized the district as Hampstead: Tory homes amid Labour inconveniences.

The taxi turned up through open iron gates and into a driveway that curved past the front entrance. They continued around and to the back of the sprawling stone house and pulled up at the rear. The driver stepped out and opened the door for them.

Directed by small unnecessary nudges from behind, Jonathan was conducted into a dimly lit waiting room where two of them stood guard over him while the kidney-lipped hulk passed on upstairs, ostensibly to announce their arrival. Jonathan used this time to sort himself out. Alone, unarmed, rumpled, and off pace, he had to ready himself for whatever turns and twists this evening might take. He stood with his back against a wall and his knees locked to support his weight. Closing his eyes, he ignored his guards as he touched his palms together, the thumbs beneath his chin, the forefingers pressed against his lips. He exhaled completely and breathed very shallowly, using only the bottom of his lungs, sharply reducing his intake of exygen. Holding the image of the still pool in his mind, he brought his face ever closer to its surface, until he was under.

"All right! You! Let's go!" The dapper little man with two mouths touched Jonathan's shoulder. "Let's go!"

Jonathan opened his eyes slowly. Ten or fifteen minutes had passed, but he was refreshed and his mind was quiet and controlled.

They led him up a narrow staircase and through a door.

He winced and held up his hand to screen away the painfully bright light.

"Here," Two-mouths said, "put these on." He passed Jonathan a pair of round dark green glasses that cupped into the eye sockets and had an elastic cord to go around the head.

Six sunlamps on stands were the source of the painful ultraviolet light, and on one of the low exercise tables between the banks of lamps was a man, nude save for a scanty posing pouch, doing sit-ups as a flabby masseur held his ankles for leverage.

Everyone in the room wore the dark green eyecups. Looking around, Jonathan was put in mind of photographs he had seen of Biafran victims with their eyes shot out.

"Welcome . . ." The exerciser grunted with his sit-up, and he swung forward to touch his forehead to his knees, then lay back again. "Welcome to the Emerald City, Dr. Hemlock. How many is that, Claudio?"

"Seventy-two, sir."

Jonathan recognized the voice just an instant before he recalled the face behind the green eyecups. It was the classically beautiful Renaissance man he had met with Vanessa Dyke at Tomlinson's Galleries. The man with the Marini Horse.

"I assume you're Maximilian Strange?" Jonathan said.

"All right, Claudio. That will be enough." Strange sat on the edge of the padded exercise table and pulled off the eye guards as the ultraviolet lamps were turned off. Taking his glasses off, Jonathan found the normal light in the room oddly cold and feeble in contrast to the glare of the lamps in the hotter end of the spectrum. "I regret your having to wait downstairs while I finished my exercise, Dr. Hemlock. But routine is routine." Strange lay down on the table, and Claudio started to cover him with a thick, cream-colored grease, beginning with the face and neck and working downward. "There is a popular myth, Dr. Hemlock, that exposure to the sun ages one's skin and causes wrinkles. Actually, it's the loss of skin oils that sins against the complexion. An immediate treatment with pure lanolin will replace them adequately. You said you *assumed* I was Maximilian Strange. Didn't you really *know?*"

"No. How could I?"

"How indeed? Do you take good care of your body?"

"No particular care. I try to keep it from being stabbed and clubbed and suchlike. But that's all."

"You make a common mistake there. Men tend to consider indifference to their appearance to be a mark of rugged virility. Personally, I celebrate beauty, and therefore, of course, I celebrate artifice. Growing old is neither attractive nor inevitable. The mind is always young. The challenge resides in keeping the body also young." There it was again: that slight jamming of sentence structure that hinted of Strange's German origins. The only other clue was his pronunciation, neither exactly British nor exactly American. A kind of midatlantic sound that one found only on the American stage. "Exercise, sun, diet, and taking one's excesses in moderation," he continued. "That is all that is required to keep the face and body. How old do you think I am?"

"I can only guess. I'd say you were about . . . fifty-one."

Strange stopped the masseur's hand and turned to look at Jonathan closely for the first time. "Well, now. That is remarkable. For a guess."

"I'd go on to guess that you were born in Munich in 1922." It was showing off, but it was the right thing to do. Jonathan was pleased with the way it was going so far. He was giving the appearance of holding nothing back, not even the fact that he had background knowledge about Strange.

Strange looked at him flatly for a moment. "Very good. I see you intend to be frank." Then he broke into a deep laugh. "Good God, man! What happened to your clothes?"

"I fell down the side of a brick wall."

"How exhibitionistic. Did you have trouble with Leonard?"

"Is Leonard this droopy-eyed ass here?"

"The very man. But your taunts will go unanswered. Poor Leonard is incapable of banter. He is a mute."

Leonard watched Jonathan glassily from beneath heavy-lidded eyes. His meaty face seemed incapable of subtle expression, its heavy-hanging muscles responding only to broad, basic emotions.

Strange climbed from the exercise table and picked up a thick towel. "Will you join me in a steam bath, Dr. Hemlock?"

"Do I have a choice?"

"No, of course not. And you could use a wash anyway." He led the way. "Few people know the proper way to use lanolin, Dr. Hemlock. It must be applied thickly just after your sunbath. Then you allow the steam to melt off the excess. The pores of the skin retain what is necessary for moisture." He stopped and turned to make his next point. "Soap should never be used on the face."

"You'll forgive me, Mr. Strange, if I find this concern for beauty and youth a little grotesque in a man of your age."

"Certainly not. Why should I forgive you?"

Leonard accompanied the two of them to the tiled dressing room that separated the steam bath from the exercise area. As Jonathan stripped down and wrapped a towel around his waist, Strange informed him that his stay at The Cloisters might be a prolonged one, so they had taken the precaution of having his rooms broken into and some of his clothes brought back.

"And while you were searching for my clothes, you had a chance to take a more general look around."

"Just so."

"And you found?"

"Just clothes. You use a very good tailor, Dr. Hemlock. How do you manage that on a professor's salary?"

"I take bag lunches."

"I see. Ah, but of course, you are doing well on your books—popular art criticism for the masses. How dreary that must be for you."

The three men passed into the steam room, Leonard looking grotesquely comic with only a towel to hide his powerful but inelegant primate body. Not once, not even while undressing, had his hooded eyes left Jonathan, and when they sat on the scrubbed pine benches of the steam room, he positioned himself in the corner, protectively between Jonathan and Strange.

The jets had been open for some time, and now the room was filled with swirling steam that eddied and echoed their movements; the temperature was in the mid-nineties. But Jonathan found no relaxation in the heat and steam. During the introductory badinage, he had recovered from his surprise at discovering that Strange and the Renaissance man were one, and now he had begun to model a cover story for himself. It covered the ground thinly, but he had no time to test it for fissures.

Strange closed his eyes and rested back, soaking up the steam, his confidence in Leonard's protection absolute. "You realize, of course, that this Dantesque room may be your last living memory."

Jonathan did in fact realize this.

Strange continued, his voice a lazy drone. "You sought to impress me just now by dropping information concerning my past. What more do you know?"

"Not much. I've been trying to track you down, and in the course of it I discovered that you were in the whorehouse business—if I may simplify."

Strange waved an indifferent hand.

"I also discovered you are in the country illegally, and that you have been in one aspect or another of the flesh trade as far back as my sources go."

"What are these sources?"

"That's my affair."

"I think I can guess at them. You were in CII. You were an assassin—or, to be polite, a counterassassin. It is my opinion that you found out what you wanted to know about me from old contacts in that service."

"I'm impressed you know that much about me."

"I'm an impressive man, Dr. Hemlock. So tell me. Why were you seeking me out?"

"The Marini Horse."

"What is that to you? I know something of your financial condition. Surely you don't expect to be able to buy the Horse."

"I don't even particularly care for Marini, nor for any of the moderns for that matter."

"Then what is your interest?"

"I need money. And I thought I might turn a buck out of it."

"How?"

"You have to admit there were some bizarre aspects to our meeting at Tomlinson's. You intend to sell the Horse, and evidently for more money than one would have considered possible. I naturally began to think about that and wonder what I might do to turn it to my fiscal advantage."

"Go on." Strange did not open his eyes.

"Well, my public evaluation of the statue could increase its value by a great deal. Just at this barren moment in art criticism, things tend to be worth whatever I say they're worth."

"Yes, I'm aware of your singular position. A one-eyed man among the blind, if you ask me."

"I thought you might be willing to share some of the excess profit with me."

"Not an unreasonable thought." Strange rose and crossed through the thickening stream to a large earthenware jar of cold water. He poured several dippersful over his head and rubbed his chest vigorously. "Good for toning the skin. Care for some?"

"No, thanks. I don't want to be refreshed. I want to relax and get some sleep."

"Later perhaps. If all goes well, we shall take supper together, after which you may wish to sample our amenities here, the most modest of which is a comfortable bed. What would you say if I told you that, while you were seeking to contact me about the Marini Horse, I was bending every effort to contact you?"

"Frankly, I would doubt you. Coincidences make me uncomfortable."

"Hm-m. They make me uncomfortable too, Dr. Hemlock. It seems we have that in common. And yet there are coincidences here. And discomfort. Could it be that it is not particularly coincidental for two such men as we to see profit in the same thing?"

"That could be." This was the narrow bit. The only story Jonathan had been able to put together quickly was Strange's own. He knew he'd be driving up the same street Strange was driving down, and he knew the coincidence of it would loom large, but at least he been able to mention it first. He rose to get some cold water after all, and with his first movement, Leonard srang to his feet with surprising alacrity for a man of his bulk and interposed his body between Jonathan and Strange. "Oh, relax, dummy!"

"Sit down, Leonard. I think Dr. Hemlock is aware of the impossibility of his getting out of here without my permission. And I think he realizes how quickly and vigorously an attempt to do me harm would be punished. You must forgive Leonard his passion for duty, Dr. Hemlock. He has been at my side for—oh, fifteen years now, it must be. I'm really very fond of him. His canine devotion and extraordinary strength make him useful. And he has other gifts. For instance, he has an enormous tolerance for pain. Not his own, of course. When it is necessary to discipline one of the young people working for me here, I simply award him or her to Leonard for a night of pleasure. For a few days afterward, the poor thing is of little use in my business, and occasionally he requires medical attention for hemorrhage or some such, but it is amazing how sincerely he regrets his misdeeds and how rigidly he subsequently conforms to our rules of performance." Strange looked at Jonathan, his pale eyes without expression. "I tell you this, of course, by way of threat. But it is perfectly true, I assure you."

"I don't doubt it for a moment. Does he also do your killing for you?"

Strange returned to the pine bench, sat down, and closed his eyes. "When that is necessary. And only when he's been especially good and deserving of reward. When did you leave CII? And why?"

"Four years ago," Jonathan said, as immediately as possible. So that was to be Strange's interrogation style, was it? The rapid question following non sequitur upon less direct chat. Jonathan would have to field the balls quickly and offhandedly. It was a most one-down way to play the game.

"And why?"

"I'd had enough. I had grown up. At least, I'd gotten older." That would be the best way to stay even. Tell trivial truths.

"Four years ago, you say. Good. Good. That tallies with the information I have concerning you. When first it occurred to me that you might be of use in my little project for selling the Marini Horse, I took the trouble to look into your affairs. I have friends . . . debtors, really . . . at Interpol/Vienna, and they did a bit of research on you. I cannot tell you how my confidence increased when I discovered that you had been a thief, or at least a receiver, of stolen paintings. But my friends in Vienna said that you had not purchased a painting for four years. That would seem to coincide with the time you left the lucrative company of CII. Why did you work for them?"

"Money."

"No slight tug of patriotism?"

"My sin was greed, not stupidity."

"Good. Good. I approve of that."

Jonathan noticed that Strange never raised an eyebrow, or smiled, or frowned. He had trained his face to remain an expressionless mask. Doubtless to prevent the development of wrinkles.

"I think that is enough steam, don't you?" Strange said, rising and leading the way back to the exercise room where the man with two mouths was waiting with a glass of cold goat's milk, which Strange drank down before he and Jonathan lay out on exercise tables to be rubbed down. The masseur scrubbed Jonathan with a rough warm towel before beginning to knead his shoulders and back, while Leonard performed the same service for Strange.

Strange turned his head toward Jonathan, his cheek on the back of his hands, and looked at him casually when he asked, "Who is it you visit in Covent Garden?"

Jonathan laughed while he thought quickly. "How long have I been under surveillance?"

"From the evening we met at Tomlinson's. My man lost track of you for a while there. Traffic jam. He waited for you at your apartment."

"Which apartment?"

"Ah, precisely. At that time we didn't know about the Baker Street residence. You use it very seldom. My people waited for some time at your Mayfair flat before further inquiry revealed the existence of the Baker Street penthouse. By the time we arrived there, you had left, but the flat was not empty. There was a man in your bathroom. A dead man. But you had disappeared."

"Hey! Watch it!" Jonathan shouted.

"What's wrong?"

"This steel-clawed son of a bitch is pulling my tendons out."

"Be gentle with the doctor, Claudio. He's a guest. Yes, we quite lost sight of you until, a couple of hours ago, I received a call from Grace. Dear Grace is a colleague of mine. A close and honored friend."

"So?"

"So I would like some explanation that puts these odd bits together. And I do hope it's convincing. I would enjoy an evening of civilized chat."

"Well, I told you I was trying to gain entrée to your place here. I had no idea you were also looking for me, so I tried through Amazing Grace."

"Yes, but how did you know about Grace?"

"You said it yourself. I still have some CII connections. Hey! Take it easy, you ham-handed bastard!" Jonathan sat up and pushed the masseur away.

"Oh, very well," Strange said with some irritation. "I'd rather cut my massage short than listen to you complain about yours. But you should really establish a routine for keeping fit. Look at me. I'm ten years older than you, and I look ten years younger."

"We have different life priorities."

Strange led the way into a lavish dressing room, the walls of which were covered with mirrors set in bronze. The reflections of the three men echoed in infinite redundancy, and Jonathan found himself a principal in a finely synchronized sartorial ballet performed by scores of Hemlocks and scores of Stranges, while scores of droopy-lidded Leonards looked on, their faces impassive, their heads tilted back on thick necks.

When he saw his clothes laid out, Jonathan felt a pulse of relief. He had wondered why Strange had not mentioned finding at least one of the revolvers when his men had picked up his clothes. But these came from his Mayfair flat, not the Baker Street one. Luck was with him. But still he was walking a razor's edge, reactive and imbalanced from the start, never sure how much truth he had to surrender to neutralize the facts already in Strange's possession. He had done well enough so far, but he had had to turn the flow of inquisition away from time to time, with inconsequential small talk or complaining about the masseur, to give himself time to collect his balance and pick a direction. So far, he had been plausible, if not overwhelmingly convincing. But there were big holes—like the dead man on his toilet—that Strange would surely probe. And one link was still open. To close it might expose Vanessa Dyke.

". . . but it is a terrible mistake not to give the body the work and diet necessary to keep it young and attractive," Strange was saying. "I know the routines are strenuous and the restrictions irritating, but nothing worth having is ever cheap."

"That's funny. I clearly remember being assured by a song of the Depression that the best things in life were free."

"Opiate hogwash. Self-delusions with which the congenital have-nots seek to excuse their life failures and make less of the accomplishments of others. As I recall, that insipid song suggests that Love, in particular, is free. My dear sir, my life's work is founded on the knowledge that love—technically competent and interesting love—is extraordinarily expensive."

"Perhaps the song was using the word differently."

"Oh, I know the kind of love it meant. Fictions of the fourteenth-century jongleur. Friendship run riot. Pointless nestlings; sharings of tacky dreams and tawdry aspirations; promises of emotional dependency that pass for constancy; fumbling manipulations in the backs of cars; the sweat of the connubial bed. *That* kind of love may be thought free, and considered dear at the price. But in fact it is not free at all. One pays endlessly for the shabby amateurism of romantic love. One enters into eternal contractual obligations under the terms of which the partners pledge to erode one another forever with their infinite dullness. Still, I suppose they lack the merit to deserve more, and probably the imagination to desire more. Should I open the doors of The Cloisters to one of this ilk for a night, he would blunder about, *asinus ad lyram*, until he found, down in the kitchens, some sweating cook or stringy scullery maid who could be a soul mate and who would understand and care for him for all time. There we are! Dressed and civilized. Shall we take a little refreshment?"

"If you wish."

"Good. There are one or two points that want clarifying."

"Personally, I'd like to get around to the topic of the sale of the Marini Horse. Focusing our attention particularly on what profit I can expect from it."

Strange laughed. "In due course. After all, we're still not absolutely sure that you are going to survive this interrogation, are we? Come along."

The center mirror hinged open like a door, swilling the scores of reflected images around the room in a blurred rush. They passed into a small sitting room about the size and shape of a projection booth, dimly lit, its walls made of glass. Three sides looked out onto the principal salon of The Cloisters: a large, brilliantly illuminated room in the Art Deco style. Glass beads, mechanical foliage, repetitious angular motifs, rainbow and sunrise patterns pressed into buffed aluminum wall panels.

The patrons were dressed in extravagant costumes provided by the management; and shepherdesses, devils, inquisitors, cavaliers, and Mickey Mouses lounged about, chatting, drinking, laughing. But all this panoply was in pantomime; the glass walls were soundproof.

Moving among the patrons were half a dozen hostesses dressed in flapper style: long loops of beads, cloche-bobbed hair, bound breasts under silk frocks, rolled-down hose exposing rouged and dimpled knees. With their artificial lashes of the stiff "surprise" style, their beauty spots, and their bee-stung lips, they looked like mannequins in back issues of high fashion magazines as they served drinks and exotic canapés, or bent over patrons in teasing, flirtatious conversation.

One of the patrons, a Catherine de' Medici of uncertain years, with face skin tight from cosmetic surgery that had not included her wattle, approached the glass wall and stared in unabashedly. She moistened the tip of her little finger with the tip of her tongue and made a minute adjustment in her eye liner, then she patted the back of her hair, turned and took a long appreciative sideways glance into the room before pivoting away to greet an approaching highwayman with the boneless face, whimpering smile, and lank hair of his class.

"One-way mirrors," Strange said unnecessarily as he settled into a deep leather chair after carefully hitching up the crease of his trousers. "The decor was Grace's idea. There is something fundamentally evil about the New People of the 1920s that seems to liberate our customers."

Jonathan stood near the one-way glass wall and looked out, his arms folded on his chest. "Art Deco was a monstrous moment in art. When the flamboyant decay of Art Nouveau percolated down to the masses, through the intermediary of machine reproduction, it was unavoidable that the half-trained, ungifted, self-indulgent artists would proclaim the resultant hodgepodge a new art form. After all, here was something even *they* could do. In my view, the recent revival of interest in Art Deco indicts the modern artist and the modern critic—people who communicate and communicate, yet remain inarticulate."

"Oh, I am terribly sorry that our taste doesn't please you. But, *de gustibus . . .*"

"Nonsense. It's the only thing really worth disputing."

Strange laughed shallowly. Laughter was his substitute for smiling, preferred because it did not necessitate creasing the cheeks. And there were as many tones to his laughter as there are nuances in other people's smiles. "At all events, I enjoy this little chamber here. We call it the Aquarium. But it's an aquarium in reverse. The fish are out there in the salon, and the amused observers here in the bowl. And it is charming to realize that that room out there contains a good fifty percent of the real governmental power in Britain."

"All gathered here to find respite from the heavy burdens of leadership by losing themselves in the ecstasy of your contrived orgies?"

"You shouldn't sneer at the exoticism of our offerings. Quite naturally, our patrons expect something out of the ordinary: prenubile girls, catamites, fellatio—that sort of thing. One can not blame them. Coming here for common garden variety sex would be like ordering sausage, chips, and two veg at Maxim's. But what is really amusing is that half the silly asses out there don't even know what goes on in our splendid cloaca. They believe The Cloisters is only a fashionable, bizarre, and exclusive club with excellent food and wine and charming hostesses."

"Oh? The flapper types aren't hookers?"

"Oh, no. Young models, aspiring actresses, university girls—just window dressing. The costuming goes with the decor. The more enterprising and promising graduate to the more lucrative activities upstairs, but most of them stay with us only a month or so, then pass on to duller activities: careers, marriages, such like. We're constantly replacing hostesses. But I am forgetting my duties as host. I have promised you refreshment. May I suggest brewer's yeast in fresh tangerine juice?"

"It's tempting. But I think I'll have scotch. Do you have Laphroaig?"

Strange turned the question to the dapper, two-mouthed minion who stood behind them, having accompanied them into the Aquarium while Leonard was dressing.

"I'll see, sir." But he did not depart until Leonard came in to relieve him.

"I'm afraid I'm not up to the finer points of scotch," Stange said. "I never drink alcohol. By the way, tell me about the man we found dead in your bathroom. Who was he?"

"I don't know," Jonathan said as smoothly as possible. He had been anticipating this tactic of the sudden question.

"Who killed him?"

"I did."

Strange looked at Jonathan with frank admiration at the immediacy of the answer. "Go on," he said, after a nod of approval.

"It was because of that man that I came looking for you. You've discovered that I used to work for CII in counterassassination. The work was not so dangerous as one might think. Since my targets were men who had assassinated CII agents, they typically came from a level of society neither lamented nor avenged—not by the various law enforcement agencies, at any rate. And, because I took random assignments, I could never be tied to the death by motive. Typically, I never met the mark before the moment of the hit. But . . . but because society is not yet prepared to counter the problem of overpopulation by sterilizing and terminating rotten and unproductive genetic stock, my targets were not without relatives.

"From the few babbled words he got out before I shot him, it appears that he was the brother of some forgotten mark. He had come to retrieve the family honor, such as it was."

"But you shot him first."

"Just so."

"And left him in your *bathroom?*"

"I didn't pick the meeting ground. Bathrooms have tile floors that are easily cleaned up."

Strange nodded appreciatively. "I see."

Leonard entered from behind and replaced Two-mouths, who went off to fetch the drinks.

"You certainly got rid of the body quickly. Our men returned to your rooms a few hours after first discovering the corpse, and it was gone. How did you manage that?"

"I'll make you a deal. I won't ask you how to run a whorehouse, and you don't ask me about assassination."

"That seems fair enough. You mentioned that this business in your bathroom was linked in some way to your desire to penetrate The Cloisters. Would you amplify that a bit?"

"While the poor ass was babbling about how he had been on my trail for years, he let slip the name of the person who had fingered me. He was waving a gun in my face, and I suppose he imagined I would not live to benefit from the information."

"By the way, how did you kill this man?"

"With his own gun."

"How did you get it from him?"

"How do you keep your girls from getting clap?"

Strange laughed. "All right, all right. Go on."

"The informant was a man highly placed in CII. A man who never liked me because I could not pass up opportunities to point out the more blatant stupidities of that asinine and bungling organization. I have every reason to believe that he will continue putting the finger on me. And someday, someone may get lucky."

"Why don't you kill this man?"

"He knows me. I'd never get close enough to him. So I have to hire the job done. And for that, I need a lot of money. And that is why the deal with the Marini Horse attracted me."

"And so you began to seek me out?"

"And so I began to seek you out." That was it. His story was improvised and thin, just covering the major events with little of that extraneous fabric that fills out the good lie. There was nothing to do now but sit and see how it went down.

Strange was silent for a time, his pale eyes looking phlegmatically out onto the salon scene playing mutely before him. Then he nodded slowly. "It is possible. Both your recent actions and my research into your past would seem to bear your story out. The only thing that disturbs me is the coincidence of it all. But then . . . I suppose coincidence exists." He turned to Jonathan and rested his pale eyes on him. "Why don't you take supper with Grace and me this evening. We can talk over the details of the Marini sale. Assuming all goes well, you might care to sample our exotic entertainments later. By way of a nightcap."

"I've had a hard day."

Strange laughed. "If it weren't so late and the streets weren't empty, I would tempt your fatigued appetite by sending a couple of my men out in a van to pick up something from the streets for you—fresh from the garden, you might say. A schoolgirl on her way home, perhaps, or a nun just back from confessional?"

"Don't you have some trouble with cooperation from those you abduct?"

"Oh . . . not if they're properly prepared. We use a concoction of halluci-nogens and cantharis that seems to be effective—Oh, my dear Dr. Hemlock! I wish you could have seen the cloud of disgust that just swept over your face! I would have thought you had a more leathery conscience than that."

"It's not conscience. Just taste."

"In this business only the bizarre is profitable. The basic components of sex are so mundane: a little heat, a little friction, a little lubrication. One must dress up such cheap raw materials considerably if he hopes to vend them at high profit. Packaging is everything. But, ah . . . here we are at last."

Two-mouths entered through the mirror door bearing a tray with two glasses. Jonathan could not repress a surge of repulsion when he looked at Strange's glass, the gray-tan yeast powder already settling in the tangerine juice and collecting at the bottom. Strange sipped off some of the liquid, then swirled the remainder to carry the yeast back into temporary suspension while he drank it.

"Looks ghastly," Jonathan commented.

"You get used to it. In fact, one comes to rather like it."

Jonathan turned away in gastronomic self-defense. Out in the salon, one of the flapper hostesses caught his eye. As she chatted with a costumed customer, she brushed aside a vagrant wisp of amber hair with the back of her hand. She was only a few feet from the wall of one-way mirrors, and he could see the bottle green of her eyes.

"What interests you so much out there?" Strange asked, joining him at the glass wall.

"Your clients," Jonathan said, indicating a group of men chatting with super-cilious gravity, blithely ignorant of the risible effect of their outlandish costumes.

"Hm-m. Silly asses. Look at them, playing out their dumb show of authority and power. Pompously going through the motions of statecraft. They are finished as a people, the English, but they haven't sense to know it. There was a time when Darwinian laws applied to nations as well as to individuals—when the weak and incapable disappeared. If it hadn't been for the sentiment of other nations—yours particularly, Dr. Hemlock—1950 would have marked the end of this effete social organism. I enjoy making them dress up like that, and they take great delight in doing it. It's a national trait—pageantry, make-believe. A nation of people who thirst to be what they are not. That probably accounts for their production of so many gifted actors."

"You despise the British, then?"

"More scorn, I should say."

"But I thought the Germans rather admired and imitated them."

"Oh, we have much in common. Our weaknesses, to be specific. Our army organizations were modeled after theirs. It was the British, you know, who first experimented with the concentration camp as a vehicle for the final solution to genetic problems."

"No, I didn't know that."

"Oh, yes. In the Boer War. Twenty-six thousand women and children died of disease, malnutrition, and neglect. Vitriol in their sugar; small metal hooks implanted in their meat—that sort of business. Oh yes, the British have been world leaders in many things. But no longer. Now they inflict themselves on the Common Market and become the economic sick man of Europe. In fifteen years only Spain and Portugal will boast a lower standard of living. And it's their own fault. With myopic management and the laziest, least competent workmen in Europe, they suffer from congenital inefficiency. Not the placid, happy ineffi-ciency of the Latins, with their mañana mentalities and hedonistic lassitude. No, the British brand of incompetence is involute and labored. It's a bustling, nervous inefficiency that fails to make up in charm and quality of life what it sacrifices in productivity. The Briton has become a compromise between the Continental, whom he used to despise out of contempt, and the American, whom he now despises out of envy. His is a land of Old World technology and New World beauty. And that's all there is to say about the British."

Jonathan was going to protest against this gratuitous attack on their hosts when Strange continued, "You know, during the war there used to be a riddle in contempt of the Belgian army. One used to ask, 'What would you do if a Belgian soldier threw a hand grenade at you?' And the answer was, 'Pull out the pin, and throw it back.' If the question were asked of the British soldier, it would be totally academic because the hand grenades would arrive six months after the promised date of delivery, the workmanship would be faulty, and the army would be on strike anyway."

"If they disgust you so, why are you here?"

"The police, old man! It is a popular myth that British criminals are Europe's most clever, just barely kept in rein by the brain-children of Conan Doyle and Ian Fleming. These people glory in their train robbers and confidence men, their Robin Hoods from Stepney Green. It is typical of their blinkered Weltanschauung that it never occurs to them that it is not the dash and cleverness of their petty hoodlums that win the day, it is the monumental incompetence of their police. For a man in my profession, the British police are the most comfortable in Europe, just as the Dutch are the least. Of course, if you were interested in civil liberties, it would be quite the other way around. Surely the table is laid for supper by now. You must be looking forward to meeting Amazing Grace again."

Conversation in the small paneled dining room was light and oblique, never touching on the matter of the Marini Horse, nor indeed on the events that had led to this peculiar early morning supper. Amazing Grace conducted the chat with the skill of a geisha, giving both men opportunities to display wit, and leavening all with her personal touch of ribald earthiness. As was her preference in social moments, she was nude, and so the room was kept warm and cozy by a gas fire set in a fireplace of curiously wrought iron. While she and Jonathan dined on rack of lamb, Strange went through a series of dishes featuring pallid substances with mealy aromas. In place of the wine they enjoyed, he drank goat's milk. It was only with the fruit and cheese that his diet and theirs converged. The cheese board bore many cheeses, yet only one. There was Danish blue, Roquefort, Gorgonzola, and Stilton. Strange explained that, next to yogurt, the blue-veined cheeses were best for digestion. The fruits were all organically grown and free from insecticides, and there were no bananas which, it seemed, were eatable only in the tropics where they were allowed to ripen naturally.

Jonathan admired the way in which Amazing Grace excelled as hostess, enthroned on her special elevated chair, and he remarked in passing that she had all the social graces of a parson's daughter, together with some of the traditionally suspected appetites.

"But I *was* a parson's daughter," she said with a rich laugh. "Not that all that many people have heard of The First Evangelical Synagogue of the Blessed Lord and All His Works."

Two-mouths brought in the brandy and coffee on a tray, then joined Leonard against the wall in silent vigil.

"There's a certain social advantage to eating in the destructive way you two seem to enjoy," Strange said. "The arrival of brandy is the accepted signal for talk of business. And, as I have none of my own, may I use yours for that purpose?"

"Well, if things are going to get serious," Grace said, "I'll slip into a robe. I wouldn't want my bobbing little boobies distracting anyone."

Jonathan said that was a thoughtful gesture.

"All right," Strange began, flicking an imaginary bit of lint from his sleeve. "As you know, I intend to turn the Marini Horse into liquid money. The other evening, when I broached that possibility to you, you said that the five million pounds I was expecting to get would cause some comment in art circles."

"More like a riot, I'd say."

"Even if the figure were arrived at in public auction at Sotheby's?"

"Particularly then. Marini is still alive; his work lacks the fiscal kudos of his death. And after all, the man is a Modern."

"Yes, I am aware of your reactionary preferences in art. I've read a couple of your books by way of trying to understand your personality. But the abstract artistic value of the casting is not to the point here. What I am interested in is getting the price I want without undue public notice. More specifically, Dr. Hemlock, I want forty-eight hours from the time of the sale before there is any official reaction. Can you arrange that?"

"At a price."

"That's my kind of man!" Grace interjected.

"What price?" Strange asked.

"Well, naturally, I would like to get whatever the market will bear. But I'm afraid my native greed will have to give way to a very real interest in survival. I told you that I have to hire a man to put that CII official away before he fingers me again. I estimate that that will cost me about fifty thousand dollars."

"So much?"

"He's a deep man, hard to get at."

"Very well, fifty thousand then."

"A little more, I'm afraid. To pull this off, I shall need baksheesh to spread around among the local critics and newspaper people—mostly indirect baksheesh, of course."

"Give me a total," Strange said curtly.

"Thirty thousand pounds."

Strange and Grace exchanged glances. "Your services are dear," Strange said.

"Oh, please. If you're pulling in five million, then—"

"Yes. All right. Thirty thousand then. But let me impress on you, as a gesture of friendship, how foolish it would be for you to try to double-cross me on this."

"You would sic the dummy there on me, right?"

"Indeed I would. And I have a feeling that Leonard is none too fond of you as it is, after the dental damage you inflicted on his mate."

"If you're through flexing your muscles, there are some things I have to know if I'm to do this business for you."

"Such as?"

"Is the Marini legally yours?"

"Oh yes. Bill of sale and all."

"I assume you will deliver it to Sotheby's for the auction?"

"The morning of that day, yes."

"Where is it now?"

Strange turned to him slowly, like a casemate gun swinging onto a target. "That is none of your business. It is perfectly safe, and it can be produced quite quickly, at my volition. Anything more?"

"One thing. How much time do I have to prepare the way?"

"The auction is Wednesday morning."

"Four days? I only have four days?"

"That will have to be enough. Grace and I cannot afford to linger about. And, anyway, my affection for the British is not without limits. I shall be glad to see the last of this narrow little island."

Grace stood and stretched, her fingers stiff and reflexed in the air, her abbreviated peignoir rising above the taut buttocks, her splayed toes gripping the carpet. "I think I'll go into the Aquarium for a nightcap. Maybe a look at the customers will turn me on." She smiled and left the room, the purling of her tense body under its gossamer gown arresting conversation until she had disappeared.

"Nice little bonbon there," Jonathan commented.

"Oh, yes. I enjoy bringing her pleasure. I arrange complicated little events for her. She's so daring and inventive, it's great fun to plan for her."

"You're a selfless man."

Strange laughed. "My dear man! I never indulge in sexual activity myself."

"Never?"

"Not since I was a boy. I passed my youth in establishments of this kind. As you may know, it is the practice of candy manufacturers to allow their workers to eat to their heart's content when first they are employed. Within a few months, the workers become so cloyed that they make no further inroads on the merchandise."

"And you never—"

"Never. Too draining. Too hard on the body. But I have my own vice. Unfortunately, it's the most expensive vice in the world."

Jonathan pictured Amazing Grace's body. "Wasteful," he couldn't help commenting.

"I have other uses for Grace. A devoted ally, and a decoration without equal. I delight in the effect we create together. She, petite, proud, beautiful, sensuous. And I . . ." He paused and shrugged. "And I am graceful and classically handsome. There is not a jaw that does not tighten with envy when we make an entrance."

He had admitted being handsome so matter-of-factly as to make it almost acceptable. And indeed, he was classically handsome, the most handsome man Jonathan had ever seen outside Greek sculpture.

But he was not attractive. His features were so regular, so smooth, so anticipated that the eye slipped over them, finding nothing to engage it. The face lacked the arresting traction of biographic imprint: there were no creases of concern, no grooves of concentration, no crinkles of laughter. Even the pallid, round eyes kept clear and sparkling with tinted eyedrops were devoid of narrative. The fall of light and shadow over his smoothly tanned features had the uninspired, geometric quality of the novice artist's solution to a problem of chiaroscuro—very accurate, very dull.

"Shall we join Grace for a nightcap?" Jonathan asked, eager to end this evening while he was still ahead.

"By all means. Oh, there *is* one more thing, come to think of it. How did you get on to Grace and the Cellar d'Or establishment?"

For the first time, Jonathan was taken off balance by Strange's technique of the sudden question dropped non sequitur.

Strange laughed. "Miss Dyke must be very fond of you indeed to impart such delicate information."

"I put a little pressure on her," Jonathan said simply. Since they already knew, he confessed offhandedly to glean what advantage seeming honesty had. He was glad she was off with her writer friend with the cats and red wine.

Strange nodded. "It's comforting to know where your loyalties lie."

"With myself, as always."

"The trademark of the successful man." Strange rose. "Do let's join Grace."

When they arrived in the Aquarium, Grace was curled up in the deep leather chair, sipping at a tumbler of Everclear. "May I offer you some?"

"No," Jonathan said quickly. He crossed over and looked out onto the salon, as Strange took up a perch on the arm of Grace's chair and, with an absent-minded proprietorial gesture, began to roll the nipple of one breast between thumb and forefinger.

"Is everything settled?" she asked.

"I think so. Dr. Hemlock and I share qualities of selfishness and greed that augur well for a profitable cooperation."

In the salon outside, a handful of rather spent clients sat about. Two portly old gentlemen in caps and bells descended the wide Art Deco stairs, looking drained and fragile. They collected their waiting mates and left. Only two hostesses were still on duty, and one of these was leaning against the aluminum wall, her face lax and puffy. "You say the hostesses aren't hookers?" Jonathan asked.

"Do I detect a tone of carnal interest?" Strange said.

"Yes, you do. Tired though I am, I feel a bit like celebrating our agreement."

"Which one turns you on?" Grace asked.

"Looks like there's only two to pick from. I really don't care. You're the licensed meat inspector here. Which one would you suggest? The blonde?"

Grace sat up and looked over the choices. "I wouldn't say so. That other one—she's got the right muscle arrangement for it. She's an Irish girl. Our model agency sent her over this morning and I interviewed her. She's not really cute, with that ragamuffin face of hers, but there's something about those big green eyes and that hair that I felt was perfect for the flapper look." Grace's professional eye scanned the girl's legs and buttocks. "Yeah," she said sitting back, "she'll give you the better ride."

"If she is willing," Jonathan said.

"Don't worry about that," Strange said. "I'll arrange it for you—a gift to seal our bargain in the Arabic way. A little shot of dream juice, and she will be yours—moist and panting. But you're sure you wouldn't prefer something a bit more—occult?"

"No. She'll do fine. But no cantharis."

"Why not?"

"I'm tired. If I can't make it, I don't want her groaning about and groping at me all night."

Strange laughed. "As you wish. We have a little something that will render her perfectly pliable. She will know what is going on, but she will be without will. But I'm afraid she may babble a bit."

"Better a babbler than a groper."

"Pity the options are so limited." Strange rose. "I'll bid you good night, if I may. It's already seventeen minutes after my bedtime, and, as you may have noted, I am a man of routine. I'll attend to the Irish bit on my way. We'll take breakfast together and discuss details. Is noon too early for you?"

He left without awaiting an answer to this rhetorical question.

Amazing Grace poured herself another drink and sat again in the deep chair, her knees drawn up and her feet on the seat, her furry écu revealed between her heels. "Well, what do you think of Max? Isn't he a beautiful person?"

"I suppose," he said, pressing his eyes with his thumb and forefinger in an effort to relax the tension in his temples. "But there's something hokey and childish in the way he plays it for Mephistopheles. A kind of campish eviler-than-thou."

Out in the salon, Jonathan saw Two-mouths approach Maggie and speak to her. She frowned and followed him toward a back door. Jonathan hoped she wouldn't put up too much of a fight when they put the needle in her.

"You're not trying to tell me that Max didn't impress you, are you, honey bun?"

"Oh, no. He impressed me all right. In fact, he scares the shit out of me."

She laughed. "I really like you, Hemlock. You must have been some kind of bad actor in your day. Only really tough men admit to being scared. Cheers." She emptied her glass, and he could not help swallowing twice sympathetically in a vicarious effort to help her get it down. "But," she continued, "he's a rare and beautiful animal. He's really evil, you know. Black mass sort of thing. Not just nasty or naughty or crotch-happy, like most men who think they're bad. But really *evil.* And there's nothing sexier than that. You have to get past sin, past sacrilege before things get really delicious."

"What does P'tit Noel think about all this?"

"He doesn't even know about The Cloisters. And if he did, it wouldn't matter. He'd do anything in the world for me. Like a puppy dog—like a real big, real fierce puppy dog, that is."

"Hey, would you mind not pointing that thing at me? It makes me nervous." She laughed and pulled down her peignoir.

"And you don't feel sorry for P'tit Noel?"

"Hell no. I know his type. He likes getting hurt. Big gesture; romantic crash. Like winos who drink because it's so goddamn tragic and attractive to be a wino. You know what I mean?"

"Yes, madam, I do." He ran his fingers through his hair, tugging at the back of it to suppress his fatigue. "May I ask you something, Grace?"

"Shoot."

"I can't understand how Van Dyke got mixed up with you people. I've known her for years, and I can't imagine what Strange could have paid her that would bring her into this."

"He didn't pay her," she said, tickling her lips with the rim of her empty glass and smiling at him. "*I* did."

Jonathan looked down. "I see."

Two-mouths conducted him through the exercise room into the now empty salon, its Art Deco sconces still ablaze. Jonathan looked toward the wall of mirrors behind which he assumed Amazing Grace was sitting, finishing a last Everclear. He waved good night to her, feeling a little foolish as he saw only his reflection wave back.

Up the wide staircase with its aluminum walls buffed in patterns of swirls, and down the long corridor, Two-mouths kept up a patter of talk to which Jonathan attended only vaguely.

"You could of knocked me over with a feather, you could, sir, when Mr. Strange told me to fix up that hostess for you. I thought you'd be done for sure, what with how you give such a beating to Lolly—he's the one what's teeth you cracked off, Lolly is. She didn't half put up a fight, that little Mick. Took two of us to get the needle in. Good thing for her Leonard wasn't there. He'd have done it right enough, and no fuss either. She wouldn't of been able to walk for a week, if Leonard had done it. He doesn't half rip 'em when he gets a chance. Well, here we are, sir. Pleasant dreams."

Jonathan entered the dark bedroom, and the door clicked locked behind him. The city glow beyond the window gave dim illumination, and he could see a bundled figure on the bed. She turned in her delirium and moaned softly, then she laughed to herself.

It was in rooms like this that the compromising films of government officials had been taken, and possibly some of them had been taken in the dark. Jonathan removed his jacket and checked his shirt sleeve. The starch gave off none of the phosphorescent glow that would indicate infrared light, so at least this room was not equipped with cameras and sniper scope lenses. But it was doubtless bugged and, under the drugs, she might say something that would give him away. He had to keep that in mind.

He undressed quickly and approached the bed. Maggie had been tossed onto it, still dressed in her flapper frock. One shoe was off and the other dangled from a toe, and a rope of beads had fallen across her face. In the dim light she opened her eyes and stared up at him, frowning. She was confused, trying hard to understand what was happening to her. As the needle had entered her, she had reminded herself that she must do nothing to endanger Jonathan's cover, and that thought had gone swirling down with her into the churn and chaos of distorted reality. She had clung to it for a time, then she had forgotten what it was she was clinging to. But it was important. She remembered that much.

"What? . . . What . . ." She looked at him, her eyes pleading for help. Then she laughed again.

"My name is Jonathan Hemlock," he told her immediately, really speaking for the microphones. It would not do for her to name him out of the blue.

"Jonathan? Jonathan?"

"That's right. But you can call me 'honey.' Come on, let's get your clothes off."

"Are my clothes still on?" She spoke with the clumsy diction of someone whose lip is rubbery from dentist's Novocain. "Isn't that funny?"

"A knee-slapper. Come on. Turn over."

He undressed her as quickly as possible, but with her limp and uncooperative body, it was not easy. Indeed, some bits would have been comic under less dangerous circumstances. She, at least, found it funny.

"Say," she said with the sudden seriousness of a drunk. "Do you really think we should be doing this?"

"Why not? We live in a permissive society."

"But . . . here? Isn't it . . . isn't it dangerous?"

"I'll be careful."

"What? What? I don't understand, Jonathan."

"You see? You remember my name."

"Yes, of course. Of course I know your name. You're—"

He kissed her. She hummed and drew him down to her.

He was painfully tired, but sleep was evasive. The open microphone was like a living thing in the dark, straining to catch their words, and the presence of it was palpable and uncomfortable. Maggie slept. The drugs had been good for her in one way. They had liberated her even beyond her usual abandoned and inventive lovemaking, and climax had been a total and body-shuddering thing for her, as though the sensation had begun in the small of her back and gushed outward. She had worked hard at it, and then she had slept, curled up on her side, sitting in his lap, his arms around her, completely and safely wrapped up by him.

He did not know she had awakened when she spoke softly. "Jonathan?"

He instantly thought of the bug—probably in the headboard to catch guests' quietest words. "Go to sleep, honey," he said rather harshly.

"I love you, Jonathan." It was a declarative sentence. A matter of fact. She might have said it was Tuesday, or raining.

"Well, that's just great, honey. You're a warm, wonderful, loving person. Now please let me get some sleep, will you?" But the microphone could not transmit the message in the way he hugged her in and buried his cheek in her hair.

He wondered if he would ever get to sleep, get the rest his body demanded. He was still wondering this when he awoke to find it was full day and there was a brilliant bar of sunlight across the bed. He opened his eyes and looked up. Maggie was there, sitting on the edge of the bed. She had been awake for some time, looking at his sleeping face, occasionally touching his hair gently, fearful of disturbing him, but desiring the possessive contact.

"Good morning," he said feebly, and he took her hand, only to find that his grip was too weak to squeeze it. The efforts of the past two days had caught up with him, and he had slept at coma depth.

"Good morning," she said, the brogue dealing carelessly with the vowels. She put her finger to her lips and pointed to the headboard, where a small core of metal shone dully in the center of a carved decoration.

He nodded and brought her with him as he turned around in the bed, lying with their heads at the footboard. They kissed good morning, and he brought his lips into contact with her ear and whispered to her soundlessly. "Play it out. Good girl wakes up in bed with strange man."

"Don't!" she said aloud. "Please don't."

He made a wry face at her histrionics. She shrugged; she had never pretended to be an actress.

"Do you remember last night?" he asked aloud. Then whispering he added, "You were fantastic." The danger of this double-talk was mischievously exciting, and they were in a docilely playful mood.

"Yes, I remember," she said aloud, as though ashamed. "I remember your name and . . . what we did. But how did I get here?"

"You don't recall that?"

"Something . . . a needle. I can't remember all of it." She whispered, "The Vicar wants to see you this evening at his place. Something important has come up."

"Well, don't worry about it, honey," he told the microphone. "I'm sure they'll pay you for your trouble. And it really wasn't all that bad, was it?"

"Was I . . . was I good?" Her voice carried that tone of nuzzling coyness Jonathan associated with sticky mornings after, once the phase of self-recrimination had been passed. He was sorry she knew it.

"Don't worry about it," he said aloud. "You're probably a fine cook."

By way of punishment, she ran the tip of her tongue into his ear.

"Hey!"

"What is it?" she asked aloud, all innocence.

"I just remembered the time. It's late and I have worlds to conquer." He rose from bed and went into the bathroom to bathe and shave.

"Will I see you again?" she asked, enjoying the game of acting for the microphone.

"What?" he shouted from the next room over the rush of water.

"Will I see you again?"

"Certainly. Certainly. I'll look you up!"

"You don't even know my name!"

"That's all right. I'm not nosy!"

"Bastard," she muttered quietly, feeling clever about introducing just the right note of the girl whose innocence has been around.

He arrived for breakfast in the paneled dining room to find that Strange and Grace had finished and were having a last cup of tea—Earl Grey for her, rose hip for him.

"Good morning," Jonathan said cheerily. "Sorry I'm late. Slept like a hammered steer."

"Doubtless the effect of a clear conscience," Strange observed, as he broke off a bit of dry toast and put it into his mouth, rubbing his fingers together lightly to flick off crumbs that might otherwise have dropped onto his spotless white flannels.

Jonathan lifted the covers of serving dishes on the sideboard and found some eggs with chives. "And how are you this morning—or early afternoon?" He addressed Amazing Grace, who was sitting nude in a broad shaft of sunlight, her body stretched out to receive the warmth, her eyes almost closed with feline pleasure. Her tea saucer was balanced on her écu, and from Jonathan's angle it seemed that her crotch was steaming into the sunlight. He crossed to her and cupped one of her conical breasts in his palm. "I'm going to get you one of these days," he warned.

She opened her eyes. "God, you're a horny one. Didn't that Irish bit drain you off a little?"

"She's an hors d'oeuvre type; you, on the other hand, are meat and potatoes."

"You sure got a sweet way with words, honey bun."

Jonathan sat across from Strange and began to eat his eggs with appetite.

"You are in high spirits today, Dr. Hemlock."

"There's been a big load lifted from me."

"You speak of the official in Washington you intend to silence?"

"What else?" He poured himself some coffee. "Say, that girl was an odd one. Do you know what she said to me, right off the bat?"

"That she loved you?" Strange asked, unable to pass up the opportunity to show off.

Jonathan set his cup down and looked up in surprise. "Yes. How did you . . . ?" Then he laughed. "The room was bugged. Of course."

"They all are. I listened to your tapes this morning as I went over my accounts. A kind of Muzak to lighten my labors."

"I'll be damned. That should have occurred to me. How do you think the girl will take being jabbed full of junk, then drilled by a stranger?"

"The process differs from romantic love only in degree and efficiency. She's a modern young lady. I judge she'll be satisfied with a handsome bonus. By the way, she called you a bastard while you were in the shower."

"Is that right? And I thought I had her by the heart. Just goes to show how vulnerable the congenital romantic can be. Would you pass the toast?"

Breakfast progressed with small talk of the kind designed to cover meaning. It was not until Grace left to dress and return to the Cellar d'Or that Strange got down to business.

"I assume you have thought about the task before you, Dr. Hemlock?"

"I have some ideas. If things work out just right, we should be able to get your asking price for the Horse without government inquiry. But I'll have to play it largely by ear, and I'll need your permission to use a free hand in making the arrangements."

Strange glanced at him. "What kind of arrangements?"

"I'm not sure yet. But I'll have to do something bold—some grand gesture that will blind them with its obviousness. By the way, I'll need some of that money for grease and baksheesh."

"How much?"

"All of it?"

Strange laughed. "Really, Dr. Hemlock!"

"Just thought I'd try. I suppose ten thousand pounds would do it."

Strange's pale eyes evaluated Jonathan for a long moment. "Very well. The money will be ready for you when you leave."

"Good."

"Ah-h, Dr. Hemlock . . . Don't think of doing anything foolhardy. Please remember that unfortunate fellow who was found impaled in the belfry of St. Martin's-In-The-Fields."

"I get the picture. Is there more coffee?"

"Certainly. Leonard did that business at my request, not that the impulsive devil didn't get pleasure from it on his own. The informer was drugged and brought to the church, where the stake had earlier been set in place. They lifted the fellow to just above it, the point lightly touching his anus. Then Leonard jumped down and swung his weight from his ankles, driving him well on. Gravity did the rest. But with that unhurried pace characteristic of natural forces." Strange laid his hand on Jonathan's arm and squeezed it paternally. "I hope you understand why I am burdening you with the lurid details."

"Yes, I understand."

"Good. Good." He patted the arm and withdrew his hand.

Jonathan's eyes were clouded with his gentle combat smile when he said, "Tell me. Would you mind passing the marmalade?"

Covent Garden/Brook Street
The Vicarage

THE LONE PAINTER who worked with tunnel concentration before a vast canvas in MacTaint's converted fruit warehouse was the ragged, furious man with long skinny arms who had come to assume over the years that the space, the stove, and the tea were his by squatter's right. He snapped his head around angrily as Jonathan pushed open the corrugated metal door, allowing a gust of wind to enter with him. The painter continued to fix Jonathan with a wild stare until the door had been slid to, guillotining the offending shaft of blue daylight that had intruded on the yellow pool of tungsten light from the naked bulb hanging from a long frayed cord.

Jonathan's light greeting was parried by a rasping growl as the painter used the interruption as an opportunity to heap another shovelful of coal into the large potbellied stove. As a final gesture of impatience, he kicked the stove door closed violently, almost immediately regretting that he was not wearing shoes.

Receiving no answer to his light knock on the inner door, but hearing a voice from within, Jonathan pushed the door open and looked in. Lilla was sprawled in a deep wing chair before the television, a half-empty glass of gin dangling from her pudgy hand and the crumbs of some earlier feast decorating the front of her feathered dressing gown. In a self-satisfied drone of BBC English, a commentator was summing up the industrial situation which, it appeared, was not so bad as it might be. True, the gas workers were on strike, as were the train drivers, the teachers, the hospital workers, the automotive workers, and the truckers; but the dockers might soon return to work, and there was a chance that the threatened strikes of the civil servants, the electricians, the printers, the construction workers, and the miners might be delayed if the government conceded to their demands.

"Hello?"

She turned her head and peered in his general direction, her eyes watery and uncertain. "Now, don't tell me, young man. I never forget a face."

"Is MacTaint around?"

"He's gone beyond. To relieve his bladder, as we used to say in the theatre. Come in. Entrez. I was just havin' my mid-afternoon pick-me-up. Care to join me?" She gestured toward the bar with her half-full glass of gin, slopping the contents in a discrete arc.

"No, thank you, Lilla. I just wanted to see—"

"You know my name! So we *have* met before. I told you I never forget a face. It was in the theatre, of course. Now, let me see . . ."

Just then MacTaint came shuffling in, wearing his long overcoat and mumbling to himself. "Ah, Jonathan! Good to see you!"

"The gentleman and I was just havin' a chat about the old days in the business, if you don't mind."

"What business was that?"

"The theatre, as you know perfectly well."

"Oh yes, I remember now. You used to sell chocolates in the aisle and your ass in the alley out back. The chocolates went better, as I recall."

"Here! That will be enough of that, you stinking old fart." She turned her wobbling head to Jonathan. "Do excuse the diction."

"Right, now get along with you. We have business to talk over."

"Don't exercise that tone of voice in my presence, you dinky-cocked son of a bitch!"

"Slam a bung in it, you ha'penny flop, and get your dripping hole upstairs!"

"Really!" Lilla drew herself up, fixed MacTaint's general area with a stare of quivering disdain, and swept to her exit.

MacTaint scratched at his scruffy beard, his lower teeth bared in painful pleasure. "Sorry about her, lad. Of late she's been nervy as a cat shitting razor blades. But she's a good old bitch, even if she does take a sip now and then."

"I could use a drink, if there's any left."

"Done." Eddies of ancient sweat were almost overcoming as MacTaint brushed past on his way to the bar, moving with his characteristic shambling half trot. He returned with two glasses of Scotch and handed one to Jonathan, then he sprawled heavily in a fainting couch of rosewood, one ragged boot up on the damask upholstery, his chin buried in the collar of his amorphic overcoat. "Well, here's to sin." He swilled it off with a great smacking of lips. "Now! I suppose you're needing your two hundred quid."

"No. You keep it. For your trouble."

"That's very good of you. But holding it's been no trouble."

"I'm talking about future trouble."

"I was afraid you might be." The old man's eyes glittered beneath his antennal eyebrows. "What future trouble?"

"I'm still not in the clear, Mac."

"Sorry to hear that."

"I need help."

MacTaint pursued an itch from his cheek to his shoulder, then down his back inside the greatcoat, but it seemed just out of reach to his fingertips. "What kind of help?" he asked after scratching his back against the chair.

Jonathan sipped his whiskey. "The theft of the Chardin. Is it still on?"

Instantly Mac's voice was flat and tentative, and the leprechaun façade fell away. "It is, yes."

"And it's still scheduled for Tuesday night?"

"Yes. Why do you ask?"

"I want to go with you." Jonathan placed his glass carefully on the parqueted side table.

MacTaint examined a new tear in his canvas trousers with close interest. "Why?"

"Can't tell you, Mac. But it's tied up with the trouble I'm in."

"I see. Why didn't you lie and make up some convincing story?"

"I would never do that, Mac."

"Because we're such great friends?"

"No. Because you'd see through it."

MacTaint enjoyed a good laugh, then a short choke, then a long racking cough that ended with his spitting on the carpet. "You're a proper villain, Jonathan Hemlock. That's why I like you. You con a man by admitting you're conning a man. That's very fine." He wiped his eyes with his fist and changed tone. "Tell me this. Will taking you along screw up my work?"

"I don't see why. You only need a couple of minutes, using your technique."

"Ah, then you know what my technique is?"

"I've had a couple of days to figure it out. Only one possibility. You get a good fake. You mutilate it, break in, and swap it for the original. Everyone assumes there's been an act of vandalism—not a theft. The fake is repaired with care, and if anyone ever notices a blemish, it's put down to the repair job."

"Precisely, my son! And, though I say it who shouldn't, there's a touch of genius in it. I nicked my share of paintings in the past ten years this way."

"And that accounts for the rash of vandalism in British museums."

"Not quite. In one case a real vandal broke in and damaged a painting, the heartless son of a bitch!"

Jonathan waited a moment before asking, "Well? Can I go with you?"

MacTaint clawed meditatively at the scruff on his scalp. "I suppose so. But mind you, if there's trouble, it's devil take the hindmost. I love you like a son, Jon. But I wouldn't do porridge even for a son."

"Great. What time do I meet you on Tuesday night?"

"About ten, I suppose. That will give us time for a few short ones before we go."

"You're a good man, MacTaint."

"True enough. True enough."

Because it was handier, Jonathan went to his Mayfair flat to make a pattern of calls to selected art reviews and critics who create British taste. His approach differed slightly, but only slightly, as he covered the range from *The Guardian* to *Time and Tide*. In each case he introduced himself, and there was the inevitable catch in the conversation as the person on the other end of the line realized to whom he was speaking. Jonathan began by assuming the critic had heard that a Marini Horse was in the country and was going up for auction within a week. He smiled as the critic inevitably responded that he had indeed heard something of this. What he was seeking, Jonathan said, was reliable verification of the rumor that the Horse would bring between three and five million in the bidding. After a pause, the critic said he wouldn't be surprised—not a bit surprised. Their initial flush of pleasure at being consulted by Jonathan Hemlock inevitably gave way to the public school whine of superior knowledge. Jonathan knew the type and expected their self-esteem to expand to fill any space he left for it.

He made a point of mentioning each time that the mossbacks of the National Gallery had pulled off quite a coup in securing the Marini Horse for a one-day exhibition just before it went off to the auction room, but he assumed the critic already knew all about that. The critic knew all about that, and several of them intimated that they had had some modest part in the arrangements. Each conversation ended with pleasantries and regrets for not having got together for lunch—a social hiatus Jonathan intended to fill in at the first opportunity.

As he dialed each new number, Jonathan pictured the last man hastily thumbing through reference volumes, taking rapid notes and frowning importantly.

In his mind Jonathan could see the prototypical article, some version of which would appear in a score of major and minor papers the day after tomorrow. "It has long been the opinion of this writer that the innovative work of Marini has suffered from a lack of study and recognition in England. But it is to be hoped that this gap will be closed by a forthcoming landmark event that I have been following closely: the public auction of one of Marini's characteristic bronze

Horses. Unless I miss my guess, the Horse will bring something in the neighborhood of five million, and although this figure may surprise the reader (and some of my colleagues, I am sorry to say), it is no surprise at all to the few who have followed the work of this modern sculptor whose genius is only now coming into full recognition.

"It is particularly telling that the National Gallery, not distinguished by its innovative imagination, has arranged to place the Marini Horse on display for one day before it is sold and—who knows—possibly lost to England forever. Etc. Etc."

Jonathan's finger was tender with dialing by the time he had finished his list of two-step opinion leaders. But he made one further call, this one to fforbes-Ffitch at the Royal College of Art.

"Jonathan! How good of you to call! Just a moment. Let me clear the decks here, so I can talk to you." fforbes-Ffitch held the telephone away from his mouth to tell his secretary that he would continue his dictation later.

"Now then, Jonathan! Good Lord! I'm up to my ears. No rest for the wicked, eh?"

"Nor for the poorly organized."

"What? Oh. Oh, yes." He laughed heavily at the jest, to prove he had gotten it. "One thing is certain: The men higher up certainly cleave to the adage that the only way to get a job done is to give it to a busy man. My desk's awash with things that have to be done yesterday. Oh, say! So sorry I didn't see you after that lecture here the other day. A smashing success. Sorry about the mix-up in topics. But I think you landed on your feet. And I have to admit that it was a bit of a feather in the cap to get you there. Never hurts to know who to know, right?"

"It was about feathers and caps that I wanted to talk."

"Oh?"

"You've been after me to do that series of lectures in Stockholm."

"I have indeed! Don't tell me you're weakening?"

"Yes. That is the quid. And there's a quo. You're a trustee of the National Gallery, aren't you?"

"Yes. Youngest ever. Something to do with the government attempting to project a 'with-it' image. Does what you want have something to do with the Gallery?"

"Let's get together and talk about it this afternoon."

"Lord, Jonathan. Don't know that I can. Calendar bulging, you know. Here, let's see what I can do." Holding the phone only a little away from his mouth, fforbes-Ffitch clicked on his intercom. "Miss Plimsol? What do I look like for this afternoon? Over."

A voice told him he had a conference coming up in ten minutes, then he had arranged to take a business drink with Sir Wilfred Pyles at the club.

"A drink with Sir Wilfred?" fforbes-Ffitch repeated, in case Jonathan had not heard. "What time is that? Over."

"Four o'clock, sir."

"Sixteen hundred hours, eh? Right. Over and out. Jonathan? What do you say to a drink at my club at sixteen forty-five hours?"

"Fine."

"You know the club, don't you?"

"Yes, I know it."

"Right, then. See you there. Been grand chatting with you. Let's hope everyone benefits. Ta-ta."

Just as Jonathan set the phone back on its cradle, it rang under his hand, and the effect of the coincidence was a little rattling.

"Jonathan Hemlock."

"Hey, long time no see, man. Until Miss Coyne checked in with me a couple of hours ago, we didn't know what had happened to you."

"I'm fine, Yank. Why are you calling?"

"I've been trying to get you for two hours. But your line was always busy. What's up, doc?"

"You can tell the Vicar that things are moving along."

"Great. But you can tell him yourself. Tonight. Things are coming to a head. He wants to have a little confab with you. Can do?"

"Miss Coyne mentioned that to me. Where?"

"At the Vicarage."

"All right. I'll drive out. Probably get there six or seven in the evening."

"Roger-dodger. Oh, by the way. Sorry I wasn't able to get through to those MI-5 guys in time."

"That's all right. I took care of them."

"Yes, I know. The man at MI-5 had me on the carpet. Two of the guys are still in hospital."

"They probably need the rest."

"I thought it would be best if we didn't mention this to the Vicar. No use getting his bowels in an uproar. You dig?"

"Whatever."

"Okeydoke. Hang in there."

Jonathan hung up. Talking to Yank always filled him with bone-deep fatigue—like the prospect of going shopping with a woman.

Then one oblique consolation to all this occurred to him. Whatever happened, he had ten thousand pounds from Strange—about twenty-five thousand dollars made at the cost of a few hours of telephoning. The trick was, living to spend it.

fforbes-Ffitch's club was only a short walk up from Claridge's, not far from Jonathan's Mayfair flat. It was typically clubby: a good address for taking lunch; a large and comfortable dining room with stiff linen and conversation, where one was served by nanny waitresses with skins the color and texture of the Yorkshire puddings they foisted upon you; the carafe wine was decent; and there were heavy comfortable leather chairs in the lounge for taking coffee and brandy, and for being seen chatting with people who wanted to be seen chatting with you. As an institution, it shared the catholic British problem of not being what it used to be. There simply wasn't the money floating about to support such monuments to gentle leisure since British socialism, failing in its efforts to share the wealth, had devoted itself to sharing the poverty.

The ostensible criteria for club membership were relations with the world of art and letters, but there were more critics than painters, more publishers than writers, more teachers than practitioners. Typically correct in bulk and shoddy in detail, it was the kind of place that prided itself on an excellent Stilton soaked in port, but served white pepper. The members wore suits, the fine material and careless fitting of which bespoke London's better tailors, but they wore short socks that displayed rather a lot of shiny, pallid shin as they sat sprawled in the lounge.

fforbes-Ffitch was just saying good-bye to Sir Wilfred when the part-French hostess conducted Jonathan into their company.

"Ah! There you are, Jonathan. Sir Wilfred, may I present Jonathan Hemlock? He's the man I was just mentioning—"

"Hello, Jon."

"Fred."

"Damned if it doesn't seem that everybody in London is devoted to the task of introducing us. Makes me wonder if there was something faulty in our first acquaintance."

"Oh." fforbes-Ffitch was crestfallen. "You've met, then."

"Rather often, really," Sir Wilfred said. "We've just been chatting, fforbes-Ffitch and I, about your going to Stockholm to do that series of lectures for him. You will have my commission's fiscal support. Delighted you have decided to do it, Jon."

"It isn't settled yet."

"Oh?" Sir Wilfred raised his eyebrows at fforbes-Ffitch. "I'd rather got the impression it was."

"I'm sure we'll be able to work it out," f-F said quickly, with an offhand gesture.

"Say, may I have a word with you, Jon? You wouldn't mind, would you?"

"Not at all," fforbes-Ffitch said. He stood smiling politely at the silent men, then with a sudden catch he said, "Oh! Oh, I see. Yes. Well, I'll order a couple of drinks then." He departed for the bar.

Sir Wilfred drew Jonathan toward the deep-set windows that overlooked the street. "Tell me, Jon. Are you quite all right? I am speaking of this Maximilian Strange business, of course."

"Don't worry, Fred. There's nothing going on. It was a false alarm."

Sir Wilfred examined Jonathan's eyes closely. "Well, let's hope so." Then his manner relaxed and brightened. "Well, now I must be off."

"The demands of business?"

"What? Oh. No. The demands of dalliance, actually. Take care."

Jonathan found fforbes-Ffitch sitting rigidly on the front edge of a deep lounge chair in a quiet corner. He was making much of being a busy man kept waiting, frowning and checking his watch. "You might have told me you knew Sir Wilfred," he complained, as Jonathan sat across from him. "Saved me a touch of embarrassment."

"Nonsense. Embarrassment becomes you."

"Oh? Really? No, you're having me on."

"Look, I don't want to take too much of your valuable time."

fforbes-Ffitch appreciated that. "Right. Got another appointment at seventeen thirty hours."

"Roger. Then let's get to it." Jonathan made his case quickly. ff-F was obviously committed to gaining credit by persuading Jonathan to undertake the lecture series in Sweden. In fact, he had rather overstated Jonathan's willingness to Sir Wilfred. OK. Jonathan would do the lectures if in return ff-F would use his influence as a trustee of the National Gallery to persuade them to display the Marini Horse publicly the day before it was auctioned off.

"Oh, I don't know, Jonathan. A privately owned object in the Nat? Never been done before. Has all the characteristics of a publicity trick. I just don't know if they'll go along with it."

"Oh, I was hoping your influence would be sufficient to swing it." Jonathan's instinct for the jugular proved correct.

"I may be able to, Jonathan. Certainly give it a bash."

"You might mention in your argument that half the art reviewers in England will be mentioning in their papers that the piece will be on display at the Gallery. Your fellow trustees wouldn't want to disappoint the taxpaying public, to say nothing of making fools of the critics, none of whom are too friendly with what they describe as the reactionary practices of that elite group."

"How on earth could the newspapers be saying such a thing?"

Jonathan lifted his palms in an exaggerated shrug. "Who knows where they get their wild ideas?"

fforbes-Ffitch looked long and very slyly at Jonathan. "This is your doing, isn't it?" he accused, shaking a finger.

"You see right through me, don't you? No use trying to con a con."

fforbes-Ffitch nodded conspiratorially. "All right, Jonathan. I think I can
assure you that the other trustees will listen to reason. But not without a battle.
And in return, you owe me one lecture tour. I know you'll love Stockholm."
True to club routine, the drinks arrived just as they had risen to leave.

Maggie sat on the edge of an oaken bench beside the hearth, unmindful of
the glass of port beside her. The focus of her soft unblinking attention was the
languets of flame that flickered deep within the log fire, but the attitude of her
body and her half-closed eyes indicated that she was looking through the fire
into something else. Daydreams, perhaps.
Leaning against a bookcase in the Vicar's study, Jonathan watched the play of
light in her fine autumnal hair. The unlit side of her face was toward him, and
her profile was modeled by an undulating band of firelight along the forehead
and nose. Subtle shifts of color from the flames were amplified in her hair, now
accenting the amber, now the copper.
A gust in the stormy night drafted through the chimney, flaring the embers
with a bassoon moan, and breaking her fragile concentration. She blinked and
inhaled like someone awakening, then she turned and greeted him with a slight
smile.
"Boyoboy, it's sure raining cats and dogs," Yank said from across the room
where he had been nursing a funk and dealing heavy blows to the Vicar's port
supply. He had been set off his feed earlier that evening while they were dining
at the Olde Worlde Inn. They had been served lamb couscous, and someone
had jokingly mentioned that they owed the feast to governmental indecision.
The Feeding Station had been preparing a victim to be found dead in Algiers,
but there had been a change in plans. Yank had blanched and left the room.
Until this banal meteorological observation, he had been uniquely silent, and
the forced energy in his voice indicated that he was not completely over the
crisis of disgust.
"Sorry to keep you waiting." The Vicar entered with a drawn and preoccu-
pied air. His gray face and the lifeless hang of his jowls and wattle over his
ingrown celluloid dog collar attested to days of tension and strain, as did the
intensification of his nervous wink. "At least I see you have found the port.
Good." He lowered himself heavily into his reading chair beside the fire. As a
passing gust of wind stiffened the tongues of flame and sucked them up the fire
step, Jonathan recognized the ironically Dickensian quality of their little
grouping.
"Let me say at the outset that I am not very pleased with you, Dr. Hemlock,"
the Vicar said, winking.
"Oh?"
"No. Not pleased. You have not kept in regular contact with us as you were
instructed to do. Indeed, were it not for Miss Coyne's report of this afternoon,
we shouldn't even have known that you had gained entrée into The Cloisters."
"I've been busy."
"No doubt. You have also been disobedient. But I shall not dwell on your
insubordination."
"That's wonderful of you."
The Vicar stared at Jonathan with heavy reproof. Then he winked. "The
situation is grave. Much graver than I could have guessed. As you will recall, we
were puzzled over the fact that Maximilian Strange did not seem to be making
use of the damaging film for blackmail. Doubts concerning his ultimate motive
for collecting the filthy evidence have plagued us almost as much as have the
films themselves. And the Loo organization overseas has concentrated all its
energies on solving the enigma. Bits and pieces of information have been
collected, and they fit together to make a frightening picture. Not to put too fine

a point on it, the situation is this: England is for sale." He paused dramatically to allow the significance of this to sink in. "In point of fact, effective control of the British government is to be auctioned off. The power holding those re-criminating films will be able to bleed us dry—trade concessions, NATO secrets, North Sea oil—all this will go to the highest bidder."

Jonathan found himself wondering whether it was the fact of the sale or the democratic nature of the bidding that pained him the more deeply.

"At this very moment," the Vicar continued, "representatives of every major power are congregating in London; gold transfers are being arranged in Switzer-land; and secret talks are being conducted in embassies. Not excluding your own embassy, Dr. Hemlock," he added with stern emphasis.

"Who knows? You may enjoy working for Yurasis Dragon when CII takes you over."

"Don't be flip, Hemlock!" He winked angrily. "I promise you that long before such a thing is realized, you will be in the dock facing irrefutable charges of murder. Is that clear?"

"Get off my ass, padre."

"Sir?" He winked three times in rapid succession.

"Your threats are empty. You say the entire Loo organization has been working on this?"

"They have."

"Do they know when the sale is to take place?"

"No, not precisely."

"Do they know where?"

"No, they don't."

"Do they know where the films are now?"

"No!"

"I know all three. So get off my ass, and stop making empty threats."

Maggie smiled into her glass, as the Vicar brought his indignation under professional control. He rose heavily and crossed to his desk, where he shuffled some papers around pointlessly, making thinking time. "Dr. Hemlock, you represent everything I detest in the aggressive American personality."

Jonathan checked his watch.

The Vicar's hands closed into fists. Then they relaxed slowly, and he turned back. "But . . . I have learned in my business to admire efficiency, whatever its source. So!" He pressed his eyes closed and took a deep breath. "I assume you have worked out a way to intercept the films and deliver them to me?"

"I have."

"You realize, of course, that you must accomplish this quite on your own. I won't have the police in on this, or the Secret Service. No one must have the slightest hint of the awkward predicament our leaders have gotten themselves into."

"You've made that abundantly clear."

"Good. Good. Now tell me—where are the films?"

"They're inside a bronze casting by Marini."

"How do you know this?"

"Fairly obvious deduction. Maximilian Strange has engaged me to help him sell a Marini Horse at auction for five million pounds—more than a hundred times its market value. It's obvious that the Marini is not the item for sale. The Horse is only the envelope."

"I see. Yes. Where does this auction take place?"

"At Sotheby's, three days from now. The Horse will be on display at the National Gallery the day before the auction, and that's when I get the films."

"You are going to steal them from the National Gallery?"

"Yes. I have a friend who is a regular nocturnal visitor there."

"And you are quite sure you can manage this?"

"I have great faith in my friend's ability to get in and out of the National Gallery at will. I shall be going with him on this occasion."

"He knows about the films?"

"No."

"Good. Good." The Vicar mulled over the information for a time, winking to himself. "Tell me. How did the films get inside the statue in the first place?"

"This particular Marini is known as the Dallas Horse. It was broken by a careless Texan, then brazed together. The story is widely known in art circles. It was a simple matter to cut it open along the braze, deposit the films, then braze it over again."

"I see. And you are absolutely sure the films are there?"

"I'm satisfied they are. Maximilian Strange detests England. It's his only passion. If he were only selling a bronze statue, there would be no reason to do so from London. In fact, the statue was brought over here from the States. Clearly it's the films that are the homegrown product."

The Vicar returned to his reading chair and mused for several minutes, slight noddings of his head accompanying his location of each piece in its place. "Yes, I'm sure you're right," he said at last. "It's so like Strange. An open auction at Sotheby's!" He chuckled. "Brazen and amazing man. A worthy foe."

"You told me earlier that you considered Strange to be the cleverest man in Britain . . . which might be considered damning with faint praise."

The Vicar looked up. "Did I? Well, now I am sure I was right." He turned to Yank, who had been looking on without participating, still heavy with the wine he had been drinking to excess. "Fill the doctor's glass. It appears we have reason to celebrate."

"I'll take the wine, but you shouldn't delude yourself that we're home and dry. I still have to go back into The Cloisters and deal with Strange. You see, he doesn't know that his Horse is going on display in the National Gallery. He won't know that until he reads the newspapers. And I'm not sure how he will react. He's been keeping the Horse somewhere deep, and he won't be pleased to have it in the open, its gut full of films, for twenty-four hours before the auction."

"What might he do?"

"He might smell a rat. If he does, he'll probably go to ground with the films."

"What then?"

"We lose."

"I shouldn't say that so fliply, if I were you, Dr. Hemlock. Remember the dire consequences to your freedom should you fail at this."

Jonathan closed his eyes wearily and shook his head. "I don't think you see the picture. If Strange doesn't buy my story about putting the Horse on display to allay governmental curiosity over the selling price, then his response to me will be vigorous, probably total. And your threat of trial for murder won't matter much."

"You seem to take that rather calmly."

"Cite my alternatives!"

"Yes, I see. My, you *are* in a tight spot, aren't you?"

Jonathan's desire to punch that fat face was great, but he tightened his jaw and held on. "I am going to make one demand of you," he said.

"What would that be?" the Vicar asked civilly.

"Miss Coyne's out of this from here on. In fact, she is out of your organization altogether."

The Vicar looked from him to Maggie. "I see. I had been given to understand that you two were romantically involved—well, physically involved at least. So I suppose this request is to be expected. Are you sure this is what the young lady wants? Perhaps she would prefer to see you through this. Lend some support, if need be. Eh?"

"It's not her choice. I want her out."

The Vicar blew out an oral breath, his heavy cheeks fluttering. "Why not? She has served her purpose. Certainly, my dear. You are free to go. And have no fears about your little flap in Belfast. It will all be taken care of." He enjoyed playing Lord Bountiful; it was the churchman in him. "However," he continued, turning to Jonathan, "I do think you would do well to take advantage of the Loo organization and bring a couple of our men along with you to the National Gallery."

Jonathan laughed. "The very last thing I need is the burden of your pack of bunglers. Those men from MI–5 who tailed me to the Cellar d'Or almost blew my cover."

"Yes, Yank told me about that. I was most disturbed. I assure you it won't happen again."

"I wasn't able to contact the guys in time to call them off," Yank explained from his corner.

"I don't care about that. Just keep any Loo people away from me."

"I'm afraid our Loo organization doesn't impress you much, Dr. Hemlock. Indeed, I have a feeling that you share with Strange a certain disdain for things British."

"Don't take it to heart. I arrived during an awkward period for your country. The twentieth century."

The Vicar tapped the desk with his fingertips. "You had better succeed, Hemlock," he said, winking furiously.

The split-reed cry of the wind around the corners of the Olde Worlde Inn slid with the force of the storm from a basso hum to a contralto quiver. Jonathan listened to it in the dark, his eyes wandering over the dim features of the ceiling.

They had not spoken for a long time, but he knew from the character of the current between them that she was awake.

"I have to give the papers time to carry the story about the Marini Horse. There's nothing for me to do tomorrow but keep out of sight."

She turned to him and placed her hand on his stomach in response.

"Do you want to spend the day with me?" he asked.

"Here?"

"Christ, no. We could run down to Brighton."

"Brighton?"

"That's not as mad as it seems. Brighton's interesting in the middle of winter. Desolate piers. Storm swept. The Lanes are empty, and the wind flutes through them. Amusement areas boarded up. There's a melancholy charm to resort areas in the off-season. Strumpets all dressed up with no place to go. Circus clowns standing in the snow."

"You're a perverse man."

"Sure. Do you want to come with me?"

"I don't know."

A metallic tympany of sleet rattled against the window, then the stiff wind backed around, and the room was silent.

"Last night, at The Cloisters . . ." She paused, then decided to press on. "Do you remember what I said?"

Of course he remembered, but he hoped she had been babbling and would forget it all later. "Oh, you were pretty much out of your head with the dope. You were just playing out fantasies."

"Is that what you want to believe?"

He didn't answer. Instead, he patted her arm.

"Don't do that! I'm not a puppy, or a child that's stubbed its toe."

"Sorry."

"I'm sorry too. Sorry the idea of being loved is such a burden to you. I think you're an emotional cripple, Jonathan Hemlock."

"Do you?"

"Yes, I do."

The downward curl of the last vowel made him smile to himself.

"I have a plan," he said after a silence. "When this thing is over, we'll get together and play it out. Gingerly. Week by week. See how it goes."

She had to laugh. "Lord love us, if you haven't found the tertium quid between proposal and proposition."

"Whichever it is, do you accept?"

"Of course I do."

"Good."

"But I don't think I'll go to Brighton with you."

He rose to one elbow and looked down at her face, just visible in the dark. "Why not?"

"There's no point to it. I'm not a masochist. If we went to Brighton together—with its sad piers and rain and . . . all of that—we'd end up closer together. We'd laugh and share confidences. Make memories. Then if something happened to you . . ."

"Nothing's going to happen to me! I'm a shooter, not a shootee."

"They're shooters too, darling. And worse. I'm frightened. Not only for you. I'm frightened selfishly for myself. I don't want to get all tangled up in you—my life so tangled up in your life that I can't tell which is which. Because if that were to happen, and then you were killed, I would take it very badly. I wouldn't be brave at all. I'd just roll myself into a ball and make sure I never got hurt again. I'd spend the rest of my life looking out through lace curtains and doing crossword puzzles. Or I might end up in a nunnery."

"You'd make a terrible nun."

"No. Now lie down and listen to me. Stop it. Now, here's what I'm going to do. Tomorrow morning I'm going back to my flat, and I'm going to get right into bed with a hot water bottle and a book. And every once in a while, I'll pad out and make myself some tea. And when night comes, I'll take a bunch of pills and sleep without dreaming. And the next day, I'll do the same. I hope it rains all the time, because Sterne goes best with rain. Then Tuesday night, I'll meet you here at the Vicarage. You'll give over the films, and we'll say good-bye to them, and away we'll go. And if you *don't* turn up at the Vicarage. If you . . . well then, maybe I'll go down to Brighton alone. Just to see if you're lying about the wind fluting through The Lanes."

"I'll be there, Maggie. And we'll go off to Stockholm together."

"Stockholm?"

"Yes. I didn't tell you. We've agreed to do a month in Sweden. I know a little hotel on the Gamla Stan that's . . ."

"Please don't."

"I'm sorry."

"And please don't telephone me before it's all over. I don't think I could stand waiting for the phone to ring every moment."

He felt very proud of her. She was handling this magnificently. He gave her a robust hug. "Oh, Maggie Coyne! If only you could cook!"

She turned over and looked into his eyes with mock seriousness. "I really can't, you know. I can't cook at all."

Jonathan was relieved. This was much easier on him. Play it out with banter and charm. "You . . . can't . . . cook!"

"Only cornflakes. Also, I hate Eisenstein, I can't type, and I'm not a virgin. Do you still want me?"

Joanthan gasped. "Not . . . not a virgin?"

"I suppose I should have told you earlier. Before you gave your heart away."

"No. No. You were right to conceal it until I had a chance to discover your redeeming qualities. It's just that . . . just give me a little time to get used to the idea. It hurts a little at first. And for God's sake, don't ever tell me his name!"

"*His* name?" she asked with innocent confusion. "Oh! Oh, you mean *their* names."

"Oh, God! How can you twist the knife like that?"

"Simple as pie. I just take it by the handle, and—"

"Ouch! You gormless twit!"

Eventually they kissed, then they nestled into what had become their habitual sleeping entwinement. The rain rattled on the window, and the wind exercised the Chinese tonic scale. At last, Jonathan slipped into a deep sleep.

"Jonathan?"

He gasped awake, sitting up, hands defensively before his face. "What?"

"Why do you think I'd make a terrible nun?"

"Good night, Maggie."

"Good night."

Putney

IT WAS MIDMORNING when Jonathan arrived back at the Baker Street penthouse, having driven rapidly up from Brighton with the windows of the Lotus down and the wet wind swirling his hair.

The day spent alone had been good for him. His nerves were settled, and he felt fit and fast. It had rained without letup—a drowning, drenching rain that gushed down drainpipes and frothed into the gutters. He had bought a cap and a scarf and had walked slowly through the deserted Lanes and out onto the blustery piers—his wide raincoat collar the outer boundary of his vision and caring.

It was best that Maggie had not come with him. She was a wise girl.

He had eaten in a cheap cafe, the only customer. The owner had stood by the rain-streaked front window, his hands tucked up under his stained apron, and lamented the high cost of living and the weather, which, he had reason to know, had been changed for the worse by Sputniks and atomic tests.

To keep a low profile, he had stayed at a cheap bed and breakfast place, the energetic, talkative landlady of which recognized his accent and asked if he had ever met Shirley Temple face to face—bless her soul with that good ship Lollypop and that blackie who used to dance up and down the stairs (they can all dance, you have to give them that). Too bad all the picture houses were being made into bingo parlors, but then they don't make movies like that anymore, so maybe it wasn't such a loss. Still . . . the landlady hummed a bit of "Rainbow on the River" to herself. No. He had never met Bobby Breen either. Pity.

That night he had jolted awake—stark awake so suddenly that ugly fragments of a nightmare were caught in the light of memory before they could scurry into the dark of the unconscious. The Cloisters. Strange had not bought his story and was going to kill him. Two-mouths rode on a bronze horse, both of them grinning. Leonard's drooping eyelids revealed only bloodshot whites. He was choking . . . gasping in a mute attempt at laughter. Amazing Grace was there—haughty, nude. He was strapped to an exercise table. An altar. Eccyclemic violence.

Then the images had faded, all sucked down into the vortex of the memory hole. He had smiled at himself, wiped the icy sweat off his face, and gone back to sleep.

As soon as he entered his penthouse flat, before unpacking or even removing his overcoat, he telephoned Vanessa Dyke. All morning he had been uneasy about her, fearing that she would return to London early for some reason. The phone double-buzzed again and again, and he felt a sense of relief. Then, just as he was going to hang up, there was a click and a male voice said, "Yes?"

Jonathan thought he recognized the voice. "May I speak to Miss Dyke?" he asked, apprehensively.

"No, you cannot. You certainly cannot do that." The voice was mushy with drink, but he now recognized it.

"What are you doing there, Yank?"

"Oh, yes. Dr. Hemlock, I believe. The man who makes jokes about the Feeding Station."

"Pull yourself together, shithead! What are you doing there? Has anything happened to Van?"

It was a different, an empty and weak Yank who responded. "You'd better come over here."

"What is it?"

"You'd better come over."

Goddamnit!

He angrily snapped open the drawer of his chest. Automatically he checked the load of the two .45 revolvers: five double dumdum bullets in each cylinder and the hammer over an empty. He put the guns in the bottom of an attaché case and covered them with the half-dozen newspapers he had purchased outside his hotel, each one carrying an article on the forthcoming auction of the Marini Horse, and the news that it would be on display at the National Gallery today. The papers would provide an excuse for the attaché case when he brought it to The Cloisters.

But first Vanessa.

He stepped from the cab and paid the driver, then he turned up through the open gate and the shallow garden with its tarnished hydrangeas.

Yank opened the door before he knocked, a vagueness of expression and a toppling rigidity of stance indicating that he had been drinking. "The bad guys beat you to it, Jonathan baby. Come on in and make yourself at home."

Jonathan pushed past him into the sitting room where he and Vanessa had taken tea a few days before. It was cold now, and damp. No one had thought to light the fire. The portable typewriter was still on the spool table by the window, and reference books were open upside down beside it. The Spode from which they had drunk was still laid out, the cozy slumped beside the pot, the evaporated lees of tea a dark stain in the bottom of the cups.

She had never left for Devon.

Jonathan glanced around at the quaintly old-womanish furniture, the lace curtains, the antimacassars. Everything accused him.

"Dead?" he asked perfunctorily.

Yank was standing in the doorway, supporting himself against the frame. "She struck out. Dead as a doornail—or was that Marley?"

"Where is she?"

"Yonder." He waved in the direction of the kitchen beyond a closed door. He picked up a bottle of Vanessa's whiskey and poured some into a glass.

"Cloisters?" Jonathan asked, taking the glass from him and setting it aside.

"Who else, amigo? Their modus operandi is a calling card. It was done in the style of the Parnell-Greene murder. I think I'd best sit down." He dropped into an easy chair and let his head rest on the antimacassar as he breathed orally in the short pants of nausea. "There must have been three or four of them. They . . ." He wet his lips and swallowed. "They raped her. Repeatedly. And not just with their . . . with themselves. They used . . . things. Kitchen utensils. She died of hemorrhage. She's in there. You can take a look if you want. I had to, so it's only just that you should." He stood up too quickly, his balance uncertain. "You know? You know what I was thinking. It was probably the only time she ever made love with a man."

Jonathan turned half away, then spun back, driving the heel of his hand into Yank's jaw. He went down in a boneless heap. It was unfair, but he had to hit somebody.

There was a half-filled suitcase on a chair. She must have been packing when they walked in on her. On the carpet was a long cigarette burn. The cigarette had probably been slapped from the corner of her mouth.

He steeled himself and stepped over Yank to enter the kitchen. She was on the kitchen table, covered from face to knees with a raincoat. Yank's. Only the torso was on the table. The bare, unshaven legs hung over the edge. The feet were long and bony, like the Christ of a Mexican crucifix, and their limp, toed-in dangle spoke death louder even than the sweet, thick stink. Needing to accept his share of the punishment, Jonathan pulled down the coat and looked at the face. It was contorted into a snarl that bared the teeth. He looked away.

There had been no bruises on her face. Apparently they had kept her conscious as long as possible. Two or three of them must have held her onto the table while Leonard raped her, before looking through the kitchen drawers to find things to . . .

Leonard! Jonathan said the name aloud to himself.

Yank was back on his feet by the time Jonathan returned to the sitting room, but he was unsteady. And he was weeping.

"I'm getting out of this," Yank said to the wall.

"Sit down. Pull yourself together. You're not all that drunk."

"How can people do this kind of thing? And not only The Cloisters people. How can something like the Feeding Station exist? I don't want any of this. I just want a ranch in Nebraska!"

"Sit down! I'm not impressed by your sudden delicacy in the face of violence. Just remember that I wouldn't be involved in this thing—and Vanessa wouldn't have been—if you people hadn't roped me in with that murder setup. So just shut up! Are the police in on this yet?"

"You're a cold-blooded bastard, aren't you? A real professional."

"How hurt do you want to get?"

"Go ahead! Beat me up!"

Jonathan wanted to. He really wanted to.

But he took a breath and asked, "Have the police been informed?"

Yank drooped his head and held it in his hands. "No," he said quietly. "They'll receive an anonymous call later. After we're out of here."

Jonathan looked around the room. He hadn't given her name to Strange, he had only confirmed it as a token of sincerity. So it wasn't really his fault. And immediately he felt contempt for himself for taking refuse in that thought.

Before leaving, he turned back to Yank. "Don't forget your raincoat."

Yank looked up at his with disbelief and disgust swimming in his bleary eyes. "She was your friend."

Jonathan left. For an hour he walked through the zinc-colored streets of Putney, through the gritty fog, past melancholy brick row houses, some of which had tarnished hydrangeas in their pitiful little front gardens.

Then he caught a cab for The Cloisters.

The Cloisters

". . . PHYSICAL BEAUTY IS a worthy goal in its own—unh—right, of course. But there are fringe benefits. The rituals—unh—it entails are almost—unh—as valuable as the ends—unh!" Max Strange rested for a moment at the top of a sit-up. "How many is that?" he asked his masseur.

"Sixty-eight, sir."

Strange blew out a puff of air and began again. "Sixty-nine—unh—seventy—unh. For instance, Dr. Hemlock, I do my best thinking—unh—when I am sunbathing or exercising, or taking steam." He dropped back on the exercise table with a grunt. "That's enough."

As the masseur spread creamy lanolin on Strange's body, Jonathan looked around the exercise room, green and dim through the round glasses that protected his eyes from the ultraviolet rays of the bank of sun lamps surrounding Strange. Leonard and Two-mouths stood near him, and three other of Strange's enforcers leaned against the walls with studied, sassy languor, among them the scowling fellow with yellowish temporary caps on his front teeth. The bulging green glasses made the group look like those man/insect mutants so popular with makers of low budget science fiction films.

Jonathan checked his hate, blanking out the image of Vanessa, closing out Leonard. He had to appear casual and loose.

Strange's face and throat were being massaged with heated lanolin, and his voice was rather constricted as he said, "While I've been taking a little sun and exercise, I've been thinking about you a great deal."

"That's nice," Jonathan said. "I brought along some copies of newspapers. Evidence that I have been busy. After these write-ups, no one will question the price the Horse will bring."

"Yes, I've already seen the papers."

"I suppose you're pleased."

"To a degree. But all this about putting the Horse on display at the National Gallery. I don't recall our agreeing on that."

"It was an inspiration of the moment. I told you I would need a certain freedom of movement. After my first couple of contacts, I realized that the critics weren't going to buy my story wholeheartedly without some kind of special kudos. And the idea of lending the authority of the National occurred to me. It cost me most of the ten thousand to arrange it."

"I see." Strange stayed the masseur's hand. "That's enough. You may turn off the lights." He sat up on the edge of the table and took off his protective glasses. "You have a subtle mind, Dr. Hemlock."

"Thank you."

Strange looked at him without expression. "Yes . . . a subtle mind. Come along. We'll take a little steam together. Do you a world of good."

"Not just now, thanks."

Strange glanced to the floor. "It's a pity, is it not, that most attempts to phrase politely run the risk of rhetorical ambiguity."

They were an unlikely assortment of form and flesh, the four of them sitting in the billowing steam, towels about their waists. Raw material for Daumier. There was the rotisserie-tanned, classically muscled body of Strange—youngest and oldest of them all; Jonathan's lean, sinewy mountain climber's physique; the thin and brittle frame of the two-mouthed weasel—fish-belly white and hairless, a dried chicken carcass, a xylophone of ribs, one mouth grinning from social discomfort, the other pouting for the same reason; and the primate hulk of Leonard with its thick, short neck and stanchion legs—tufts of hair bristling from the sloping shoulders, his head tilted back, his heavy-lidded eyes ever upon Jonathan.

Until Strange spoke, the silence had been accented by the monotonous hiss of entering steam. "I am displeased with you, Dr. Hemlock. You shouldn't have arranged to put the Horse on public display without my permission."

"Well, there's not much we can do about that now."

"True. Any change in your widely publicized plan would attract attention. I have no choice. And *that* is why I am displeased."

"Don't worry. The security system in the National is among the best in the world."

"That is not the point."

"What the hell *is* the point?"

Strange turned to the thin-chested man with two mouths. "Darling, go fetch that little leather box, there's a good man."

The weaselly serf rose and left the chamber, swirling eddies of vapor in his wake.

"Darling?" Jonathan couldn't help asking.

"His name. Kenneth Darling. I know, I know. Fate delights in her little ironies. But at this moment I am less interested in the deviousness of Fate than I am in yours."

"Any particular deviousness?" Might as well play it out.

Strange leaned his head back against the sweating tile wall and closed his eyes. "Where have you been for the past two days?"

"Arranging for the auction. Contacting critics and reviewers. Setting up the National Gallery display. Earning my money, really."

"Conscientious man."

"Greedy man. What's troubling you, Max?"

"I had you followed from the time you left here."

"Nu?"

"And again, as before, my man lost you in the maze of streets in Covent Garden."

Jonathan shrugged. "I'm sorry your people are incompetent. If I'd known the idiot was following me, I'd have left a trail of bread crumbs."

"For two days, you did not return to either your Baker Street flat or the one in Mayfair. Where were you?"

Jonathan sighed deeply, then spoke slowly and clearly, as though talking to a backward child or a travel agent. "After making the arrangements for the Horse, I went to ground down in Brighton. Why, you will now ask, did I go to ground? I'll tell you why I went to ground. It seemed wise to maintain as low a profile as possible until the thing was done. What did I do in Brighton? Well, I read a bit. And I took long walks through The Lanes. And one evening, I—"

"Very well!"

"Are you satisfied?"

"Don't talk like one of my employees."

"By the way, where are your employees? When I came in, the place seemed deserted."

"So it is, save for a small staff. The Cloisters is no longer in business."

"That will leave a great gap in the social lives of our betters."

Strange waved off this oblique line of conversation with the back of his hand. "When you returned to London this morning, you went to your Baker Street apartment. From there you took a taxi to Miss Vanessa Dyke's house in Putney."

"Right. Right. The fare was one pound six—one fifty with tip. The driver thought the government ought to ban private cars from the city. Particularly when there is fog—which, by the way, he ascribed to massive ice floes broken off the polar cap in result of recent Apollo moon shots—"

"Please!"

"I don't want you to think I'm holding any details back."

"While in Putney, you undoubtedly discovered the accident that had befallen Miss Dyke."

Jonathan glanced at Leonard. "Accident. Yes."

"It must seem to you," Strange said, stretching his legs over the pine bench until the muscles stood out, "that our treatment of Miss Dyke was overreactive. After all, she was guilty only of setting you on our path at a time when we were actively seeking you out ourselves. But the years have taught me that violence and terror, if they are to be effective deterrents, must be exercised systematically and inexorably. We propose certain rules of conduct, and we have to enforce them without reference to individual motives. In this we operate as governments do. It is our good fortune to have Leonard here to carry out the punishments. I loose him like an ineluctable Fury, and punishment becomes both automatic and profound. The effect of Miss Dyke's action is of no weight in this. She was punished for her intention."

Cold air entered the steam room, and the vapor undulated as Darling returned carrying a small black leather case.

"Ah!" said Strange. "Here we are. Leonard, will you give Darling a hand?"

Leonard rose and threw his thick arms around Jonathan's chest, locking his hands in front and pinning Jonathan's arms to his sides. After the first automatic reaction, resistance to that python grip was pointless. With fumbling haste, Darling opened the case, took out a syringe, and injected its contents into Jonathan's shoulder.

"You may let him go, Leonard. But if he makes the slightest gesture of aggression toward me, I want you to beat him, hurting him rather a lot." Strange looked obliquely at Jonathan. "It's not that I'm a physical coward, Dr. Hemlock. But it would be a great pity if you were to damage my face. Surely, as a lover of beauty, you understand."

Jonathan breathed as shallowly as possible, fighting to bring his pulse rate down and to clear his mind. "What's going on, Strange?"

Strange laughed. "Oh, do come on! The midnight bell has rung. Time to stop the dance and remove our masks. Don't worry about the hypodermic. It won't kill you. In fact, there will be no effect at all for five or ten minutes. And even then, you'll find it quite pleasant. The little girl you toyed with the other evening was under a similar drug. It relaxes you, calms your aggressive impulses, makes you docile and obedient."

Jonathan felt nothing as yet. "Why are you doing this?"

"Oh, I think you've served your purpose now, don't you? And you should be pleased to know that your plans will go ahead just as you wanted. In an hour the armored van will arrive to carry the Horse to the National Gallery, where it will be the object of attention by the ogling masses. And tomorrow it will be on the floor of Sotheby's. We've know about you all along, of course. About your friends in Loo. About the pompous old vicar."

Did he know about Maggie? That was Jonathan's primary worry.

"Tell me, Jonathan—I feel I may use your first name now—is your mind still clear enough to reason out why I have let you go so long?"

"It's fairly obvious. You had a real problem in arranging the open auction of the films without alerting the British authorities."

"Precisely. And the good Lord sent you along to do it for us—*and* with the benediction of the Loo organization, too! Obviously, you intended to intercept the Marini Horse while it was in the National Gallery. But now you won't have to trouble yourself about that. Tomorrow, a little after noon, the gavel falls. The British government, with all its trade concessions, defense secrets, wealth, and problems, becomes the property of the highest bidder. And Amazing Grace and I disappear."

"But if I don't show up with the films . . ." Jonathan stopped and frowned. That's odd, he thought. He had forgotten what he was going to say.

Strange laughed. "Naturally, I have considered that. Your vicar knows the films are in the Horse, and if you don't bring them, he will be constrained to make other arrangements—loathe though he is to bring the police in on this. I have taken that possibility into account, and I have neutralized it. And of course I'm neutralizing you. You won't be going anywhere near the National Gallery."

Jonathan somehow didn't care. The steam felt very good. Caressing. It penetrated his muscles and tingled them pleasantly. There was nothing to be afraid of. Maximilian Strange was a handsome man, a cultured man . . . what did that have to do with anything? "Do I, ah . . ." What was he going to say? "Oh, yes! Do I die?"

"Oh, I imagine so," Strange said with warm concern. "But not just now."

"I see," Jonathan said, recognizing the profound meaning in these words. "And if I don't die now," he reasoned, "then I die later. I mean, everyone dies sooner or later, you know." He felt he had them here. No one could deny that.

"We'll keep you around for a while, just in case something goes wrong. You may be of some bargaining value."

That was right, Jonathan thought. He should have thought of that himself. That was a very good idea.

"Help him up to his room," the steam said.

"No, that's all right," Jonathan's voice said. "Thank you, but that's all right. I can . . ." But he couldn't. He couldn't stand up. And that was amazingly funny. No, it was not funny. It was really very serious. And dangerous.

But funny.

A helpful man named Darling—that's funny too—helped Jonathan to his feet. Leonard looked on benevolently.

"Don't dress him," the steam said thoughtfully. "Nudity has a great psychological deterrent. No one is brave when he is nude."

That was wise, really. How could you be a hero with your ass hanging out? Poor Leonard. He couldn't talk. But he had killed Vanessa! Don't forget that. And these other goons, they had held her onto the table. Jonathan would teach them.

"Leonard," he said soapily, tapping his knuckle against the tree-trunk chest, "you're dumb. You know that? You are as dumb as a bullet. You are, in fact, a dumdum."

"Come along, mate." Darling led him out of the steam room.

"It's cold out here, Darling. I need my attaché case to keep me warm." Would they see through that?

"Just come along with me, mate. You're drunk with the dope." Darling's voice had an odd echo. Then Jonathan realized why. He had two mouths! Naturally, he echoed.

The stairs were very difficult to climb. It was the undulations, of course. The room they led him to was the one he had been in the other evening. With Maggie.

Mustn't mention her name!

Jonathan was guided to the bed, where he lay down slowly, very slowly, deeply.

"Wait a minute!"

Darling answered from everywhere. "What is it?"

"I don't seem to have my attaché case. I need it . . . for a pillow."

"Look, mate. Give over, won't you? I've already been through it and took out the guns. Mr. Strange give 'em to me as a present."

Jonathan was deeply disappointed. "That's too bad. I wanted to shoot you all. You know what I mean?"

Darling laughed dryly. "That's hard lines for you, mate. I guess you struck out. Now you just rest there. I'll be back in a couple of hours to shoot you."

"Oh?"

"With more dope. It only lasts four or five hours."

"Oh, I'm sorry about that. But then, all things are mutable. Except change, of course. I mean . . . change can't be mutable because . . . well, it's like all generalizations being false . . . and angels on the point of a pin. You know what I mean?"

But Darling had left, locking the door behind him.

Jonathan lay nude, spread-eagle on his back, watching with awe and admiration the permutations of the ceiling rectangle into parallelograms and trapezoids. Amazing that he had never noticed that before.

He was cold. Sweating and cold. There were no blankets on the bed. Only one sheet. And the chintzy bastards had taken his clothes!

He pulled the corner of the sheet over his chest and gripped it hard as he felt his body rise, up past the images and ideas above him. He tried to focus on those images and ideas, but they vanished under concentration, like the dim stars that can only be seen in peripheral vision.

It seemed that he had to get out of there. Go to a museum with MacTaint. For some reason . . . for some reason.

It was true what Darling had said. He had well and truly struck out. Struck out. Struck out.

Later—four minutes? four hours?—he tried to get up. Nausea. The floor rippled when he stood on it, so he knelt and put his forehead on the rug, and that was better.

Yes! He had to go with MacTaint to get the films from within the Marini Horse. Of course! But it was cold. His skin was clammy to the touch.

The window.

Then the pattern on the rug caught his attention. Beautiful, brilliant, and in constant subtle motion. Beautiful.

Forget the rug! The window!

He crawled over to it, repeating the word "window" again and again so he wouldn't forget what he was doing. He pulled himself up and looked out. Fog. Almost evening. He had been out for hours. They would be back soon to shoot him up again.

With both hands he lifted the latch and pushed the window open. He had to wrap his arms around the center post of the casement before he dared to put his head out and look down.

No way. Never. The room was on the top floor. Red tile eaves overhung the window, and below there was a deadfall of three stories to a flagstone terrace. The building was faced with flush-set stone. No cracks, no mortise, no ledges to the window casements.

No way. Even in his prime as a climber, he could not have descended that face without an abseil rope.

Abseil rope. He turned back into the room, almost fainting with the suddenness of the movement.

Nothing. Only the sheet. Too short. That was why they had taken away his bedding.

He was able to walk back to the bed. He reeled, and he had to catch himself on the bedpost, but he had not had to crawl. His mind was clearing. Another half hour, maybe. Then he would be able to move about. He would be able to think. But he didn't have a half hour. They would be back before that.

He lay flat on his back on the bed, shivering with the cold that seemed to come from within his bones. The euphoria had passed, and a dry nausea had replaced it. Now, try to think. How to get rid of the effect quickly when they came back and shot him up again? He had to think it out before they returned, and he again sank into the pleasant, deadly euphoria.

Yes. Burn the dope up! With exercise. As soon as they left next time, he would start exercising. Make the blood flow quickly. Precipitate the effects and burn them off. That might work! That might give him half an hour to move and think before they returned to give him the third dose.

Oh, but he would forget! Once the crap was in him, he would lie there and groove on the ceiling, forgetting to exercise. He would forget his plan.

He looked around the room desperately. There was a narrow mantelpiece over an ornate hearth that had been blocked up. That would do. He would have four or five clear minutes after they put the dope in him and before it got into his bloodstream. During that time, he would exercise furiously to force the onset of the effects. Then, before he started to trip out, he would climb up on the mantel, where he would do isometrics to keep the heart pumping, to get the crap through him and out. And if his mind wandered, if the dope started to float him away, he would fall from the mantel ledge. That would snap him out of it. And if he could, he would climb back and begin exercising again. Somehow he would force the effects to pass off more quickly. He would gain time before the third needle.

Now relax. Empty your head.

There was a sound down the hall. They were returning.

Relax. Make them think you're still out. He produced the image of a still pond on the backs of his eyelids. This time control mattered. He had to get under quickly.

Darling preceded Leonard into the room. He clicked on the lights, and they advanced on the bed with its still form stretched over a wrinkled puddle of sheet.

"Still out," Darling said, as he opened the black leather case. "Gor, what's this? Look at him! The sweat's fair pouring off him! He's cold! Here. Put your hand on his chest. Feel his heart thumping there. What do you think, Leonard? Maybe he's one of them low tolerance blokes. Another dose might do for him."

But Leonard took the syringe from Darling's hand and, snapping Jonathan over by his arm, drove the needle into the shoulder muscle and squirted home the contents, not caring if there was air in the ampul.

"He didn't even flinch," Darling said. "Took the fund out of it for you, didn't it? I told you he was out. If he dies before Mr. Strange wants, remember that I'm not taking the blame."

They left, turning out the lights and locking the door behind them.

Slowly, Jonathan opened his eyes. He allowed his body's demand for oxygen to take control of his breathing rate. He felt all right; weak but in control. But he knew that the delightful killer was in there, mixing with his blood. He rose from bed as hastily as his sketchy balance would allow and brought the small sheet with him to the open window. After some fumbling, he tied one end of it to the center post, allowing the seven feet of slack to dangle outside. Then he lay down on the floor and began exercising. Sit-ups until his stomach muscles quivered, then push-ups.

For more than a minute, he sensed no effect from the dope. Up. Down. Up. Down. Up—and up, and up. He seemed to rise so slowly, so effortlessly. That's it, he told himself. The exercise was working. He was bringing it on quickly. He decided it was time to get on the mantel. He stood up. But the room was telescoping on him—all the lines rushing into the corners in exaggerated foreshortening.

"God," he muttered. "I waited too long! It's coming too fast!"

The gas hearth was there, way over on the other side of the room. He put his arms out and leaned toward it, hoping he would reel and fall in that direction. But the crash came from behind. He had staggered backward and hit the wall behind him. The room seemed filled with the rasp of his breathing. He was afraid they would hear it.

Can't walk to it. Get down on the floor and crawl. Safer, Beautiful. Beautiful rug. Oh, No! He was alone in an endless sea of floor. He didn't know which direction to go. He could see the mantelpiece when he looked up, but it kept changing directions, and it didn't get any nearer.

He sat on the floor, one foot under him, the other leg stretched out before him, his head hanging down and his chin on his chest, his oral breathing shallow and rapid. He felt weightless. And contented. He was comfortable, and it was too funny—this trying to find a mantel.

No! He ground his teeth together and forced himself to think. Keep crawling. Find a wall. Then crawl along it. Must lead to the hearth eventually.

He crawled on. Once he rested with his face in a corner of the room, and the walls felt soft and comfortable against his cheeks. He wanted so much to sleep. But he snapped himself out of it and crawled on. Then his hand touched marble—beautifully grained, somehow luminescent marble. That was the mantelpiece.

Now climb up on the ledge!

Too high. Too hard.

Climb.

Twice he slipped and fell back to the floor, and it took all his mental strength to resist the desire to stay there and enjoy the ceiling.

At last he stood on the narrow ledge of the mantel, his back against the wall, his arms cruciform, fingers trying to hold onto the flowers in the wallpaper. He was frightened and his heart pounded. The floor, rippling and blurring, was so far down there.

Good. The fear was good. It made his pulse race. It would burn off the dope. Now exercise. Isometric tension . . . release. Tension . . . release.

He had the impression that he could see by means of darkness as other people saw by means of light. And so much darkness was coming in through the open window that he could see details in the room clearly. There were bursting sacs of light behind his eyes. The rug. Beautiful color. It floated up toward him slowly, seductively.

The pain and shock of the fall brought him briefly to his senses. He was lying face down on the rug. He couldn't breathe through his nose. Blood. It didn't hurt. It made him want to sleep.

The climb back up was cerebral. His sense of balance was gone, along with his sense of direction. He had to tell himself that tops tend to be above bottoms.

He had to think out the fact that leaning out would cause a fall. Eventually he was on the mantel ledge, on his knees. He could not stand. Kneeling, his chest now against the wall, he began the isometric exercises. Tension . . . release. Tension . . . release.

An infinity of timelessness passed. He needed to sleep. Right now. He rested back on the supporting air.

This time, he slept through the fall and crash.

The cold woke him up. He was sweating and cold. His mouth was dry from oral breathing, and his upper lip was stiff. He touched the stiff lip. It was flaky, gritty. The blood from his nose had congealed. He had been out for some time. But he knew from the nausea and the cold that the hallucinatory effects of the drug had passed. He was weak and dizzy, but he could think and he could move. He got to his hands and knees slowly and looked around the room. Dark shadows, a rectangle of gray city smear at the window. The window. He remembered.

With the help of the bedpost, he got to his feet and reeled to the window. The night air was freezing cold as it flowed over his sweating, naked body. He stood, supporting himself on the casement and sucking in great breaths of damp refreshing air. The sheet was still knotted about the center post.

Looking down, he could just make out the stone terrace three stories below. A mist of light from a room below spilled out over the wet flagstones. He climbed up onto the sill and stood in the frame. Then he gripped the underledge of the eaves and leaned out. And instantly he was overcome by vertigo, drowning in dizziness. Desperately, he scrambled back. Too soon. He would have to wait until the last moment. Just before they came in. Give his mind a chance to get as clear as it would ever be.

Leonard and Darling left their dart game with fellow employees and crossed the deserted Art Deco salon, their reflections following them along the wall of mirrors that hid the Aquarium. They took the long curving stairway two steps at a time because they were a little late for the next scheduled injection. Leonard unlocked the door, and Darling switched on the lights.

"Christ!" Darling ejaculated.

In a rush they checked the closet, the bathroom, and under the bed. Then Leonard noticed the open window and the sheet knotted around the center post. He slammed his fist against the casement in fury.

"The Guv won't half be browned off at this!" Darling said. "He'll have our arses for it!" He looked down to the terrace below. "Can't have got far. That sheet didn't help much. Must of broke both his legs. Come on!"

They ran from the room, Leonard charging down the staircase to examine the grounds, while Darling ran up the corridor to his room, where he snatched up the revolvers he had liberated from Jonathan's attaché case.

Head downward on the steep sloping roof, Jonathan lay tense and still. When he had heard them approaching the door, he had gripped the underedge of the eaves and swung out, tuck-rolling up and over. For a terrible moment, only the lower half of his body was on the slippery roof, his torso and head dangling over. The incline was greater than he had expected, and the sharp overlapping edges of the tiles prevented him from scrambling up. Only his fingertip hold on the underside of the edge prevented him from falling to the terrace below, but the pressure out against his reflexed wrists was agonizing and enervating. He clenched his teeth to keep from screaming with the pain as he pressed against his wrists with all his force, his jaw muscles roped and his head shuddering with the effort as he wriggled up against the sawtoothed set of the rough tile edges, gouging skin from his knees and rib cage and abrading his scrotum. His leverage was spent before he could get his chin past the eaves, and his angle on the roof was such that he could maintain his purchase only by keeping the throbbing wrists locked and by spreading his legs, increasing the area of traction to the maximum. Blood rushed to his head, and his racing pulse thrummed with dry lumps in his ears.

The lights came on in the room below, dimly illuminating the fog around him. He heard Darling say "Christ!," then there was the sound of a search through the room. Would the sheet mislead them? His lungs needed air, and he opened his mouth wide to breathe, so the intake would make less noise. Some of the dope was still in him, making thought slimy and vision uncertain. The strength was leaking out of him, draining from his wrists and shoulders.

He slipped . . . only a couple of inches, but he couldn't get it back. Now even more weight over the edge. Vertigo. The dim flagstone terrace so far below. No strength. Wrists winced with pain.

Leonard's head appeared just below him. The Mute snatched at the dangling sheet, then peered down. Jonathan squeezed his eyes shut and concentrated with all his force: Don't look up! Don't look up! The cold of the wet tiles against his nude body was numbing. Again he slipped two inches! But at that second Leonard banged his fist against the casement in fury, covering the sound. Darling said something from within.

They ran out of the room.

A strangled, whimpering groan escaped Jonathan. Getting down would be as dangerous as getting up had been. The pitch of the roof was sharp, and there was a thin coat of greasy dirt on the tiles lubricated by the moisture of the fog. Once he pulled in his legs and let the slip start, there would be no stopping it. With those limp and throbbing wrists, he would have to catch the underedge of the eaves as he slid past and swing back in through the window. If he was off by six inches to either side, he would crash against the building and fall to the flagstone below.

No use thinking about it. No time. No strength left.

He let go.

He was an inch or two off, and as he swung into the room backward, he clipped his head on the center post of the window casement. Dizziness and pain made him reel as he got to his feet, but he drove on, head down, running for the open door.

As Darling started back down the hall with the big revolvers, he heard the crash in Jonathan's room and ran toward it. They collided in the doorway, and went down in a jumble in the hall. Jonathan fought blindly and desperately, grappling for Darling's throat and getting it, both thumbs against the larynx. He could feel that there was little strength left in his grip, so he closed his eyes and bared his teeth, pressing desperately as Darling struggled to bring either revolver to bear on Jonathan's naked side. He wriggled like a beached fish as Jonathan squeezed for all he was worth, expecting at any moment to hear the roar of a gun and to have his guts blown out by a flattening dumdum. From nowhere, the thought came to Jonathan of Vanessa struggling on her kitchen table. Darling had probably held her down as Leonard had prodded at her. With a final surge of desperate fury, Jonathan drove his thumbs through, and the larynx crumpled like a papier-mâché pin box. Darling gargled and died.

For a second Jonathan lay there gasping, his forehead on Darling's silent chest. He got to his knees and picked up the revolvers. Keep moving, he ordered himself. He blinked away the large spots of blindness in the center of his eyes and stumbled on, down the wide curving staircase and across the sterile Art Deco salon. He burst into the exercise room, dropping to the floor with both guns up before him. It was empty. But he could hear them now, shouting outside the house. He cocked back both hammers with his thumbs and struggled to his feet. Dizzy. Nausea.

He reeled toward the door to the small paneled dining room and kicked it open with the ball of his foot.

The dope swam in his head, and the scene played out like a dream—a slow-motion ballet. Strange and Grace were dining. She turned toward the opening door, her naked breasts wobbling viscously with the motion. Strange floated to his feet and put out one hand, palm forward as though in a Hindu gesture of blessing. Jonathan raised one gun and fired. The roar reverberated in his head, and even the recoil kick seemed to lift his hand slowly. Like magic, the left side of Strange's face disappeared and in its place was a splash of red gelatin. Grace clutched the air, her face contorted into a scream of horror, but no sound came. Strange sank away under the table, and she fainted.

From too slow, things began to go too fast. Jonathan stumbled back into the exercise room, panting and unsteady. He needed to vomit. The sound of running men was closer. He turned on the bank of sun lamps and directed them toward the outer door. "I'm sick!" he whimpered aloud as he fumbled on the round green glasses haphazardly, one eye squeezed closed by the elastic band.

They burst into the room. Three of them. The broken-toothed one in the lead tried to shield his eyes from the blinding glare, holding his automatic before his face. Jonathan's first shot blew his arm off at the shoulder, and he spun and fell, spraying the other two with his blood. The next dumdum took the one closest to the door in the small of the back as he scrambled to retreat. His body was lifted into the air and slammed against the wall of exercise bars. He did not fall because his arm got tangled in the bars, but his body jerked convulsively.

The third man got off a wild shot in the direction of the lights, and one of them imploded above Jonathan's head, showering him with hot glass. Jonathan's return shot blew away the man's leg at the knee. He stood for a second, surprised. Then he fell to the unsupported side.

The silence rang with the absence of gun roars. The man tangled in the exercise rings slid to the floor, his forehead rattling on each rung. Then it was still.

"I'm sick!" Jonathan told them again, the words thick and muffled.

The tide of vertigo rose within him. The back of his throat was bitter with vomit. Mustn't pass out! Leonard is still out there somewhere! Hold on!

He tugged the green glasses off and staggered over to the door to the dressing room. Mirrors. An infinity of naked men with guns. Blood caked on their faces; their knees and chest scuffed and bleeding. He opened the center mirror and went into the Aquarium.

And there was Leonard. He had a Mauser machine pistol and was fitting on the wooden holster/stock, slowly and deliberately, his hooded eyes expressionless. He was on the other side of the one-way glass, standing alone in the empty Art Deco salon, pressed close to the mirrored wall, waiting for Jonathan to emerge through the exercise room door.

Jonathan's heart pulsed in his temples. He was so tired, so sick. He only wanted to sleep. The mist of dope in his brain cleared for a moment. Vanessa. Leonard and Vanessa—and kitchen utensils. He set his teeth and crept soundlessly to the mirrored panel before him. He raised both guns, their barrels almost touching the glass, and he waited as Leonard on his side inched forward, waited until Leonard's huge body had moved directly in front of the barrels. One gun was pointed at Leonard's neck, the other at his ear.

The mirror exploded and Leonard's headless body surfed over the parqueted floor on a hissing tide of shattered glass. It twitched violently, tinkling and grinding in the glass. Then it stopped.

And Jonathan threw up.

Covent Garden

THE DRIVER OF taxi #68204 threaded through the tangle of narrow lanes above
Hampstead High Street in search of a fare. He accepted philosophically the
improbability of making a pickup in that quiet district at that time of night, and
he decided to return to center city. As he stopped at a deserted intersection, he
began to sing "On the Road to Mandalay" under his breath, shifting keys with
liberal insouciance. The back door of his cab opened, and a passenger entered.
   "Where to, mate?" the driver asked over his shoulder without turning around.
   "Covent Garden."
   "Right you are." The driver pulled away, humming his inadvertent variations
on the theme of "Roses of Picardy." He vaguely wondered what a man with an
American accent wanted in Covent Garden at that time of night. "The market?"
he asked over his shoulder.
   "What? Oh. Yes. The market will do."
   The passenger's voice was faint and confused, and the driver feared that he
might have picked up a drunk who would soil the back of his cab. He pulled
over to the curb and turned around. "Now, listen, mate. If you're drunk . . . I'll
be buggered!" The passenger was nude. "'Ere! Wot's all this!"
   "Go to the market. I'll give you directions from there."
   The driver was prepared to put a stop to all this rubbish, when he noticed two
very large revolvers on the seat beside the passenger. "The market, is it?" He
released the hand brake and drove on. Not singing.
   They stopped at the entrance to a narrow, unlit alley in the heart of the
Garden district. "This it, mate?"
   "Yes." The passenger sounded as though he had dropped off during the ride.
"Listen, driver, I don't seem to have any money on me . . ."
   "Oh, that's all right, mate."
   "If you'll just come in with me, I'll—"
   "No! No, that's all right. Forget it."
   The passenger rubbed the back of his neck and his eyes, as though trying to
clear his mind. "I . . . ah . . . I know this must seem irregular to you, driver."
   "No, sir. Not at all."
   "You're sure you don't want to come in for your money?"
   "Oh yes, sir. I'm quite sure. Now, if this is the place you want . . ."
   "Right." Jonathan climbed painfully out of the cab, taking his revolvers with
him, and the taxi sped off.

   The outer workshop of MacTaint's place was empty, save for the gaunt, wild-
eyed painter who looked up crossly as Jonathan's entrance brought a gust of
cold air with it. He muttered angrily under his breath and returned to the
magnum opus he had been working on for eleven years: a huge pointillist

rendering of the London docks done with a three-hair brush.

Jonathan strode stiff-legged past him, still unsteady on his feet, and made for the entrance to the back apartment.

The painter returned to his work. Then, after a minute, he raised his emaciated, Christlike face and stared into the distance. There had been something odd about that intruder. Something about his dress.

He steeped sleepily in the deep hot water of the bath, a half-empty tumbler of whiskey dangling loosely from his hand over the edge of the tub. Although the water still stung and located all his abrasions—knees, chest, shoulder, the back of his head where he had cracked it swinging back in through the window—his mind was quite clear. The worst of it was over. All he had to do now was to get the films from within the Marini Horse.

MacTaint entered the bathroom, carrying towels, shuffling along in his shaggy greatcoat, despite the steamy atmosphere of the room. "You didn't half give Lilla a start, coming in like that with blood all over you and your shiny arse hanging out. I thought I was going to have to mop up the floor after her. Got her settled down with a bottle of gin now, though."

"Give her my apologies, as one theatre personage to another."

"I'll do that. Gor, look at you! They gave you a fair bit of stick, didn't they?"

"They got a little stick themselves."

"I'll bet they did." He ogled the bath water with mistrust. "That ain't good for you, Jon. Bathing saps the strength. Dilutes the inner fluids."

"Could I have another pint of milk?"

"Jesus, lad! Is there no end to the harm you're willing to do yourself?" But he went out to fetch the milk, and when he returned he swapped the bottle for the empty glass in Jonathan's hand.

Jonathan pulled off the metal lid and drank half the pint down without taking the bottle from his lips. "Good. I'm feeling a lot better."

"Maybe. But not good enough, my boy. There's no way in the world you could go along with me tonight. Not with your shoulder like that. Say! They got your beak too, did they?"

"No, I did that myself. Falling from a mantel."

". . . a mantel?"

"Yes. I climbed up there to keep awake."

"Oh, yes."

"But I fell off again."

". . . I see. I'll tell you one thing, Jon. I'm glad I'm not in academics. Too demanding by half."

"Look, Mac. You're sure you can get into the Gallery tonight?"

MacTaint looked at him narrowly. "You ain't in no condition to come along, I tell you. And I ain't having you put sand in my tank."

"I know. I recognize that." Jonathan reached over and poured milk into his tumbler, then he put in a good tot of whiskey. "Tell me how you're going to get the Chardin."

MacTaint looked around for a glass for himself and, not finding one, he dumped the toothbrushes out of a cup on the sink and used that. Then he made himself comfortable on the lid of the toilet seat. "I go right up the outside of the building. They got scaffolding up for steam cleaning the façade. All part of 'Keep London Tidy.' And no chance of being seen, what with the canvas flaps they got hung on the scaffolding to keep the dirt and water from getting on blokes below. The window latch is in position, but it doesn't do nothin'. I've had a lad working on it with a file, bit by bit, for the past two months. I just nip up the scaffolding, in through the window, and do the dirty to the national art treasures."

"Guards?"

"Lazy old arseholes waiting for their pensions to come through. It'll only take a couple of seconds to swap my Chardin for theirs."

Jonathan turned on the hot water with his toes and felt the warmth eddy up under his legs, stinging afresh his scuffs and cuts. "Tell me, Mac. How much do you expect to make from the Chardin?"

"Five, maybe seven thousand quid. Why?"

"There's something I want in there. Just one chamber away. I'll give you five thousand for it."

"You've got that much?"

"A man gave me ten thousand to do something for him. I'll split it with you."

"A painting?"

"No. Several reels of film. They're inside a hollow bronze horse by Marini that's on display in the next chamber."

MacTaint scratched at the top of his head, then studiously regarded a fleck of scruff on his fingernail. "And you were going to get it while you were along with me?"

"Right."

"Even though that might have fucked up my business?"

"That's right."

"You're a proper villain, Jonathan."

"True."

"A bronze horse, you say? How do I get away with it? I mean, I might attract a little attention running through the streets, dragging a bronze horse behind me."

"You'll have to break the horse with a hammer. One big blow will crack it."

"I can't help feeling the guards might hear that."

"I'm sure they will. You'll have to move like hell. That's why I'm offering you so much money."

MacTaint clawed at the flaky whiskers under his chin meditatively. "Five thousand, eh?"

"Five thousand."

"What's on the film?"

Jonathan shook his head.

"Well, I suppose that was a mug's question." He wiped the sweat from his face with the cuff of his overcoat. "It's hot in here."

"Yes, and close too." Jonathan had been trying to breathe only in shallow oral breaths since MacTaint had entered. "Well?"

MacTaint scratched his ear medtatively, then he squished his bulbous, carmine-veined nose about with the palm of his hand. "All right," he said finally. "I'll get your damned film for you."

"That's great, Mac."

"Yes, yes," he growled.

"When will you get back here with it?"

"About an hour and a half. Or, if they catch me, in about eleven years."

"Can you drop the film off at my place in Mayfair?"

"Why not?"

"I'll give you the address. You're a wonderful man, MacTaint."

"A bloody vast fool is what I am." He shuffled off to find some clothes as Jonathan rose to get out of the bath. He was temporarily arrested by a bolt of pain in his shoulder, but it passed off and he was able to dry himself one-handedly, with some stiff acrobatics.

"Here you go," MacTaint said, returning with a pile of rags. "They're me own. Of course, they ain't my best, and they may not fit so well, but beggars and choosers, you know. And take those frigging cannons with you. I don't want them laying about the place."

Getting into the clothes was an olfactory martyrdom, and Jonathan promised himself another shower directly he got to his apartment.

He got to his apartment later than he would have guessed, having to walk all the way, despite the five pounds MacTaint had given him. A few late-prowling taxis had come within sight, but they had not stopped at his signal; indeed they had accelerated. The clothes.

As he got his key from the ledge over the door, he heard his phone ring within. He fumbled at the lock in his haste because all the way home he had been thinking of calling Maggie to tell her it was all over and he was safe.

"Yes?"

Yank's phony American accent was a great disappointment. "I've been calling everywhere for you. Where have you been?"

"I've been busy."

"Yes, I know." There was a flabby sound to Yank's voice; he had not fully recovered from his booze-up on Vanessa's whiskey during his self-indulgent crisis of disgust. "I'm calling from The Cloisters."

"What are you doing there?"

"We just raided the place, figuring you might be in hot water. You left quite a mess behind you. The place is deserted—that is, there are no living people here."

"I assume Loo is going to cover all that up for me?"

"Oh, sure. Look, I'm on my way out to the Vicarage. Want me to drop by and pick you and the films up?"

"I don't have the films yet."

There was a pause. "You don't have them?"

"Don't panic. I'll have them in an hour, then I'll pick up Miss Coyne and meet you at the Vicarage."

"Miss Coyne's already on her way. I called her to find out if she knew where you were. She didn't, of course, so I told her we'd meet her there."

"I see. Well, don't bother to pick me up. If we drove out together, you'd talk to me. And I don't need that."

"You sure know how to hurt a guy. Okeydoke, I'll meet you at the Vicarage. Don't take any wooden—"

Jonathan hung up.

He had bathed and changed and was resting in the dark of his room when MacTaint banged on the door.

"You wouldn't have a drop of whiskey about the place?" were his first words. "Oh, by the way . . . here." He handed Jonathan a cylindrical package bound up in black plastic fabric. "You know what you can do with your friggin' films?"

"Trouble?" He passed the bottle.

"I'd say that. Yes. Never mind the glass." He took a long pull. "Tell me, lad. Do you have any idea how much noise is made by busting open a bronze statue in an empty gallery hall?"

"I assume it didn't go unnoticed."

"You'd have thought the buzz bombs were back. Sure you don't want any of this?" He took another long pull, then he tugged the bottle down suddenly, laughing and spilling a little over his lapels. "You should have seen me scarpering my aged arse down the scaffolding, the canvas under my arm, and balancing your damned bundle. All elbows and knees. No grace at all. Bells ringing and people shouting. Oh, it was an event, Jon."

"Let's see it."

MacTaint took the Chardin from where it rested facing the wall and set it up on a chair in good light, then he dropped down onto the sofa beside Jonathan, his motion puffing out eddies of stink from within his clothes. "Ain't it lovely, though."

Jonathan looked at it for several minutes. "You have a buyer yet?"

"No, but . . ."

"I have five thousand."

MacTaint turned and examined Jonathan, his eyes squinted under the antennal brows. "Welcome back, lad."

"You're an evil old bastard, MacTaint." Jonathan rose and gave him the five thousand pounds he had set aside for the films, then he found the other five Strange had given him for expenses and handed that over as well.

"Ta," Mac said, stuffing the wad of bills into the pocket of his tattered overcoat. "Not a bad night, taken all in all. But I'd best be off. Lilla gets nervy if I'm out too late."

The Vicarage

PATCHES OF MIST on the low-lying sections of the road into Wessex were silvered by the full moon that skimmed through a black tracery of treetops, keeping pace with the Lotus as it twisted through back lanes, deserted at this early hour. Jonathan's shoulder was still stiff, and driving one-handed was tiring, so he maintained a moderate speed. It had been a difficult week. His reflex time had been eroded, and to keep himself awake he reviewed the events that had brought him to here and this—driving out to meet Maggie, the black plastic cylinder of amateur sex movies jiggling on the seat beside him.

Because he was deeply tired, people and events, words and coincidences of the past five days rolled through his mind, the connections obeying subtler laws than simple chronology. One event passed through his mind, then as he came around the bend of another occasion . . . there it was. Obviously! The odd bits of tessera that hadn't fit in anywhere suddenly fell into place.

Maggie . . .

He pressed down on the accelerator and switched off his driving lights so the plunges into wispy ground mist did not blind him.

He pumped his brakes and broadsided into the rough lane that led from the road to the Vicarage. As the car rocked to a stop, the door of the Vicarage burst open, and Yank rushed toward the car. The broad form of the Vicar filled the yellow frame behind Yan, something bulky in his hand.

Just as Jonathan ducked down, his windscreen shattered into a milky crystal web. A second bullet blew out the wing window and slapped into the back of the bucket seat. He grappled the .45 out of the map compartment, clutched open the door, and rolled out onto the damp grass. On the other side of the steaming undercarriage, Yank's foot skidded to a stop. Jonathan shot it, and it became a knee. He shot that, and it became an unmoving head and shoulder, the face pressed into the gravel.

The roar of the gun reverberating beneath the car covered the stumbling run of the Vicar, who now stood over Yank's inert body, a log of firewood poised ready to strike.

"Are you all right, Dr. Hemlock?" he called, wheezing for breath.

Jonathan got to his knees and leaned his head against the car. "Yes. I'm all right." The cool of the metal dispersed his dizziness. "Is he dead?"

"No. But he's bleeding badly. Seems to be missing a leg."

Jonathan could hear a crisp, pulsing sound, as though someone were finishing up pissing into gravel. "We'd better get a tourniquet on him. I've got to ask him some questions."

"You do have the films with you, I hope."

"Jesus H. Christ, padre!"

They carried Yank into the cozy den with its smell of furniture polish and wood smoke, and the Vicar set about attending to Yank with an efficient display of first-aid knowledge. He applied a tourniquet just above the missing knee, and before long the spurting blood flow was reduced to a soppy ooze.

"Oh dear, oh dear," the Vicar mumbled each time he noticed the damage the blood was doing to the Axminster rug.

Jonathan helped himself to the Vicar's brandy as he stood beside the fireplace, watching the older man work with quick trained hands. "He's not coming around, is he?"

"I'm afraid not. Not much chance of regaining consciousness after a shock like that." The Vicar looked up and winked, and for the first time Jonathan noticed a purple contusion across his forehead.

"Yank hit you?"

The Vicar rose with effort and touched the spot gingerly. "Yes, I suppose so. I'd forgotten about it. We had a bit of a tussle. When he got here, he was the worse for drink. He said something offensive—I don't recall just what—and when I turned around, he was pointing a gun at me. He began babbling things about Max Strange, and needing the money to buy a ranch in Nebraska, and . . . oh, all sorts of things. He wasn't quite right in the head, you know. The violence and danger of his double game had been too much for him. He was never the right kind of personality for this business." He winked. "Then your car drove in suddenly and took his attention. I grappled with him. He struck me down with his gun, and out he went. I took up a stick of firewood, but by the time I could come to your aid, it was not necessary. I could do with a drop of that brandy myself."

"Did he say anything about Maggie Coyne? Give you any idea of where she is?"

"I'm afraid not. You feel she's in danger?"

"She's in danger . . . if she's alive at all. Yank must have told Strange about her. And Strange had a simple formula for dealing with spies and informers."

"You sound as though you *knew* Yank was in the pay of Strange."

"Only for the last fifteen minutes. The pileup of coincidences finally broke through my stupidity. Strange knew about your Parnell-Greene. He knew about me. He knew I had talked to Vanessa Dyke. Always a couple of steps ahead. He had too much information; there was too much coincidence. It had to come from inside. And Yank was at Van's house after she was murdered—no police, just Yank. He was pretending to be drunker than he was. Later, he wanted to pick me and the films up at my flat. It all fits in. But the coagulating agent was just a phrase—something one of Strange's men said after they had shot me full of dope. He told me I had struck out."

"Meaning what?"

"That's the point. The expression comes from American baseball. Only Yank would have used it."

"I see." The Vicar winked meditatively. "What shall we do about Miss Coyne?"

Jonathan pressed a finger into his temple and massaged it. "She could be anywhere. Her apartment, maybe."

"Oh, I doubt that. I've called several times in the past two days. Never an answer. I was seeking information about you, because Yank had stopped report-ing in—and now we know why. Finally, he did call this afternoon to tell me that events had altered your plans. He told me you had gotten the films, but the situation was such that you could not carry them on your person. He said you have mailed them. All of that, I see now, was Strange's plot to neutralize any action of mine. I was supposed to sit here awaiting the cheerful call of the postman, while they made the sale and got away. And, of course, I would have done just that."

Jonathan's concentration was still on Maggie. "I've got to do something. I guess I could start at her apartment, then—wait a minute! Why would Yank want the films?"

"That's obvious, isn't it? Strange will pay heavily for them."

"But Strange's dead. Yank knew that."

"I'm afraid you're mistaken there. Yank described to me the rather gaudy mayhem you wreaked on the staff of The Cloisters. He was proud of that, you see. The virile fury of a fellow American, and all that. And he mentioned that you had inflicted a ghastly facial wound on Strange. A certain Miss Amazing . . . or was it Miss Grace . . . well, whoever . . . she carried Strange away to a sanctuary."

"Did he mention a name? A place?"

From the floor Yank gasped shallowly, then moaned . . . like a child strug-gling to awake from a nightmare.

Jonathan knelt beside him. "Yank?" he said softly. Yank was under again. *"Hey!"* Jonathan slapped the chill cheek.

"That won't get you anywhere," the Vicar said.

But Yank's eyelids fluttered. His eyebrows arched in an attempt to tug open the eyes. But they remained closed.

"Where's Maggie Coyne?" Jonathan demanded.

A moan.

"Where's Strange?"

Yank's voice was distant and mucous. "I . . . wanted . . . I only wanted . . . ranch . . . Nebraska."

"Where is Strange?"

"Please? Not . . . Feeding Station." Yank's body stiffened and relaxed. He was unconscious again.

The Vicar stood up with a grunt. "Ironic. He's frightened of the Feeding Station. Ironic."

"What's ironic?"

"He doesn't realize that you have saved him from that grisly fate."

"I have?"

"Oh, yes. There is almost no call at all for one-legged bodies." The Vicar winked.

The Cellar d'Or

AFTER TURNING OVER the films, Jonathan retrieved the other .45 from the blinded Lotus. As Yank's car warmed up, he checked the load; there were only two bullets left. Enough.

A soft rain and low clouds blurred the limen between night and dawn as he drove through London streets that were desolate and gravid with despair. He pulled up before the Cellar d'Or. As he descended the narrow stone steps leading to the basement entrance, he could hear the whir of a vacuum cleaner within. The door was unlocked.

A black crone with a red bandanna pushed her vacuum cleaner desultorily back and forth over the black carpet and did not look up as he entered the bar. With the working lights on, the gold and black decor looked tawdry and cheap, and the air was stale with cigarette smoke and the smell of booze. Jonathan waited a moment for his eyes to adapt to the dimmer light.

"Close the door behind you, sir. It is cold this morning."

Jonathan recognized the basso rumble of P'tit Noel's voice. Then he saw him, sitting at the back of the lounge.

"I am sorry, sir, but we have closed. Like ghosts, our customers fade away with the *cocorico* of the morning rooster."

Jonathan raised the revolver in his hand and walked back slowly toward P'tit Noel.

"It is odd, is it not, sir, that roosters around the world do not speak the same language. In Haiti, they say *cocorico,* while in Britain they—"

"Where's Strange?"

"Sir?"

"Don't screw around, P'tit Noel. I'm tired."

The Haitian rose languidly and blocked the entrance to the internal stairway, his Roman breastplate muscles tense under the white knit pullover. Without taking his calm eyes from Jonathan's face he spoke in patois to the chairwoman. "Vas-toi en, tanta."

The cleaner was clicked off, its whir dying with a Doppler fade, and the crone departed noiselessly.

"The gun is for me?" P'tit Noel asked.

"Not really. But I don't intend to grapple with you."

"Actually, I am a strong man, sir. I could probably absorb the first bullet and still get a hand on your throat."

"Not a bullet from this gun."

P'tit Noel looked into the big bore.

"Are they upstairs?" Jonathan asked.

"They were expecting someone. Not you. Someone with a package."

"He won't be coming. Listen, I don't care about Grace. If she stands between me and Strange, I'll cut her in half. If she stands back, I'll let her go."

P'tit Noel considered this. He nodded slowly. "Mam'selle Grace has a gun. Give me a chance to get her out of the room. If you do not harm her, I shall leave you alone. The man is nothing to me."

He turned and led the way up the stairs and down a corridor. Raising a hand to gesture Jonathan back, he tapped at the door softly.

Amazing Grace's voice was strained. "Yes?"

"It is I, Mam'selle Grace. He is here, the one you await."

Jonathan pressed back against the wall as the lock clicked and the door opened. "Where the hell have you—Hey!"

P'tit Noel's hand snapped in with the speed of a mongoose and snatched Grace out into the hall by her arm. She screamed as her little automatic arched across the corridor and clattered to the floor. "Max!" Then she saw Jonathan, and fury glittered in her eyes. "It's Hemlock, Max!" She threw her diminutive naked body toward him, fingernails spread like talons, her lips drawn back revealing thin sharp teeth. "I'll kill you, you son of a bitch!" P'tit Noel swept her up as though she were weightless. It took all of his strength to hold her as she squirmed and snarled in his arms, her naked body oily with the sudden sweat of rage. "Let me go, you nigger bastard!" He began to walk clumsily toward the stairs, his awkward, savage burden screaming and kicking and clawing at him. But he could not bring himself to strike her, or even to protect himself from the punishment of her impotent, desperate anger. She dug her fingernails into his cheek and tore four deep furrows of red through the brown, but he only looked at her with resigned, unhappy eyes.

"Please, please!" She sobbed and panted promises. "I'll let you screw me if you let me go! Max! Max!"

He made consoling sounds as he continued down the stairs. She clung, pale-knuckled, to the railings, but the steady power of his momentum tore them slowly away.

Even after they disappeared down the stairs, Jonathan could hear her screams and invective. There was one last tormented wail, then the sound of sobbing.

A muffled voice spoke from within the apartment. Jonathan kicked open the door and dashed across the opening to draw fire. But no shot came. The muffled sound again. Incomprehensible words, as though someone were speaking through a gag. He pressed against the wall outside, the revolver before his face.

The words became distinguishable. The voice was a guttural whisper through clenched teeth. "Come . . . in, Dr. Hemlock."

Jonathan eased the door farther open with his toe and looked through the crack. Strange lay limp on the red velvet sofa, his shirt off and a wet towel covering half his face. He had both hands lifted to show that he had no gun.

Jonathan entered and locked the door behind him. He crossed to the bedroom, checked it out, then returned.

Strange's uncovered eye followed his every movement, hate and pain mixed in its expression. He spoke with great effort, his diction trammeled through clenched teeth. "Finish the job, Hemlock."

"I have."

"No. Not finished. I'm still alive."

"If you want to die, why don't you do it yourself?"

"Can't. No gun. Grace wouldn't help me. Too weak to get to window."

The eye glittered with sudden anger. "Do you know what you did to me?" With a convulsion of effort and a snort of pain, he tore the towel from the side of his face. The cheek was gone, and grinning molars were visible to just below where the ear would have been. The teeth were held in by tapered pink tubes of exposed root. And the eye, lacking support, dangled like a limp mollusk. The bleeding had been staunched, but the flesh oozed with a clear liquid and it had begun to fester.

Jonathan glanced away as Strange replaced the towel. When he looked back, the eye was crying. "Please kill me, Hemlock. Please? My whole life . . . devoted . . . beauty." The voice grew faint and the fingertips fluttered. The visible cheek had the subaqueous tint of somatic shock, and Jonathan was afraid he would pass out.

"What have you done with Maggie Coyne?"

The eye was dim and confused. "Who?"

He didn't even know her name. "The girl! The one Yank informed on. Where is she?"

"She . . . she's—" The eye pressed shut as he tried to clear his mind. "No. I have something to bargain with, haven't I?"

Jonathan considered for a moment. "All right. Tell me where she is, and I'll kill you."

"You give . . . word . . ." The head nodded as the tide of shock rose.

"Come on!"

The eye opened again, the lid fluttering with the effort. "Word as a gentleman?"

"Where is she?"

"Dead. She is dead."

Jonathan's insides chilled. He closed his eyes and sucked air in through his lower teeth. He had known it. He had felt it back at the Vicarage. And again as he drove through the sad, deserted city. It had seemed as though some energy out there—some warm force of metaphysical contact had been cut off. But he had conned himself with fragile fables. Maybe they held her hostage. Maybe she had escaped.

Strange's eye grew large with terror as Jonathan turned and walked aimless toward the door. "You promised!"

"Who killed her?" Jonathan asked, not really caring.

"I did!"

"You? Yourself?"

"Yes!" There was a flabby hiss to the word as air escaped through his cheekless teeth.

Jonathan looked down on him dully. "You're lying. You're trying to make me kill you in anger. But I'm not going to. I'm going to call for an ambulance. And I'll warn them you're suicidal. So they'll protect you from yourself. They'll fix you up—more or less. And it will be months before you find a way to kill yourself. All that time they'll be looking at you. Nurses. Doctors. Prison guards. Lawyers. They'll look at you. And remember your face."

Strange's swathed head vibrated with impotent rage. "You son of a bitch!"

Jonathan started toward the door, the revolver dangling in his hand. "See you in the newspapers, Strange."

Strange grasped the back of the sofa for support and pulled himself up. The effort caused the wet towel to fall from his mutilated face. "Leonard killed her!"

Jonathan turned back.

"I told you once, Hemlock, that I had a vice—expensive—subtler than sex. My vice is expensive because it costs lives. I like to watch the kinds of things Leonard does to women. Leonard was in particularly creative form with this girl of yours. And I watched! She didn't disappoint me, either. She had a strong will. It took a long, long time. We had to revive her often, but—"

Strange won.

He got his way after all.

Stockholm 28 Days Later

". . . IN FACT, THE word 'style' has been gutted of meaning. Overused. Misused. It's a critic's word. No painting has 'style.' Come to think of it, few critics do."

The audience tittered politely, and Jonathan bowed his head, losing his balance slightly and catching at the side of the podium. When he continued speaking, he was too close to the microphone, and he set up a feedback squeal. "Sorry about that. Where was I? Oh. Right! It is as meaningless to speak of the *style* of the Flemish School as it is to babble about the *style* of this or that painter."

"You miss my point, sir!" objected the young, terribly intelligent instructor who had introduced the subject.

"I don't miss your point at all, young man," Jonathan said, taking a sip from the glass of gin he fondly hoped passed for water. "I anticipate your obscure point, and I choose to ignore it."

At the back of the auditorium, the with-it young American who was responsible for USIS cultural lectures in Sweden cast an anxious glance toward fforbes-Ffitch, who had flown over from London to see how the lectures he had cosponsored were going.

"Is he always like this?" fforbes-Ffitch asked in a thin whisper.

"I don't think he's been sober since he came," the American said.

fforbes-Ffitch arched his eyebrows and shook his head disapprovingly.

". . . but you can't deny that the Flemish School and that of Art Nouveau are *stylistically* antithetical," the bright Swedish instructor insisted.

"Bullshit!" Jonathan made an angry gesture with his arm and struck the microphone, causing an amplified thunk to punctuate his statement. He shushed the mike with his forefinger across his lips. "Of course, one can cite broad differences between the two movements. The Flemish painters chose in bulk to deal with natural subjects in a vigorous, healthy, if somewhat bovine manner. While the Art Nouveau types dealt with organic, hypersophisticated, almost tropically malignant *things*. But no painter belongs to a school. Critics concoct schools after the fact. For instance, if you want to look at 'typically Art Nouveau' treatments of floral subjects, I refer you to the Flemish painter Jan van Hysum or, to a lesser degree, to Jacob van Walscappelle."

"I'm afraid I don't know the painters to whom you refer, sir," the young Swede said stiffly, giving up all hopes of having his thesis supported by this acrid American critic whose books and articles were just then holding the art world in uncomfortable thrall.

The great majority of the audience was composed of young, shaggy Americans, this USIS center operating, as most of them do, more as a sponsored social club for Americans on the drift than as an effective outlet for American information and propaganda. Jonathan's lectures had broken the usual pattern of boycotting and sparse attendance that resulted from strong feelings against America's failure to grant amnesty to the men who had fled to Sweden to avoid the Vietnam debacle.

"It's a wonder there's a soul here," fforbes-Ffitch whispered, "if he's been drunk and nasty like this every night."

The American diplomat-in-training shrugged. "But it's been the best houses we've ever had. I don't understand it. They eat it up."

"Odd lot, the Swedes. Masochists. National guilt over Nobel and his damned explosives, I shouldn't wonder."

Jonathan's voice boomed over the loudspeakers. "I shall end this last of my lectures, children, by allowing our joint hosts to say a few words to you. They are obviously bursting with a need to communicate, for they have been babbling together at the back of the hall. I have it on good authority that your USIS host will speak to you on the subject: Why has the nation failed to grant amnesty to young men who had the courage to fight war, rather than to fight people." Jonathan stepped from the stage, stumbling a little, and the audience turned expectant faces toward the back of the auditorium.

The young USIS man blushed and tried to fake his way through, raising his voice to the verge of falsetto. "What we really wanted to know was . . . ah . . . are there any more questions?"

"Yeah, I got a question!" shouted a black from the middle of the group. "How come all this Watergate shit didn't come out until after Nixon got his ass reelected?"

Another American stood up. "Tell him that if he grants us amnesty and lets us come home, we won't tell anyone about the garbage he's made of the American image abroad."

fforbes-Ffitch took this opportunity to say that none of this had anything to do with him. "I'm English," he told two nearby people who didn't care.

By then Jonathan had walked up the side aisle and had joined the flustered USIS man. He put his arm around the lad's shoulder and confided in a low voice, "Get in there, kid. You can handle them. After all, you're a government-trained communicator." He winked and walked on.

"Well," said the USIS man to the audience, "if there are no further questions for Dr. Hemlock, then I ask—"

The hoots and boos drowned him out, and the audience began to break up, chattering among themselves and laughing.

Jonathan made his way to a display room off the foyer. On exhibition were a lot of clumsy ceramics done by star students and faculty of a well-known California school of design, and brought there to show the Swedes what our young artists could do. One of the pieces had a title calculated to suggest creative angst and personal despair. It was called "The Pot I Broke," and that's what it was. Next to it was a particularly pungent social statement in the form of a beer mug featuring Uncle Sam with black features and bearing the cursive legend "Don't drink from me." But the star piece of the collection was a long cylinder of red tile that had drooped over during the baking, and had subsequently been titled "Reluctant Erection."

Jonathan took a deep breath and leaned his head against the burlap-covered wall. Too much. Too much hooch. He had been drinking for weeks. Weeks and weeks and weeks.

"Is it so bad as that?" asked one of the Swedish girls who had been looking around for him and was standing at the door.

Jonathan pushed himself off the wall and sucked in a big breath to steady the world. "No, it's great stuff. That's our subtle way to win you over. Dazzle you with our young art. A nation that can produce this stuff can't be all bad."

The girl laughed. "At least it shows your young people have a sense of humor."

"Don't I wish. Every time I see a piece of young crap, I try to forgive the artist by assuming it's a put-on—camp—but it won't wash. I'm afraid they're serious. Trivial, of course, and tedious . . . but serious. I assume there's a party somewhere?"

She laughed. "They're waiting for you."

"Wonderful." He went into the foyer and joined a group of young Swedes exuding energy and good spirits. They invited him to come along with them to dinner, then off on a crawl of bars and parties, as they had done every night. They were attractive youngsters: physically strong, clear-minded, healthy. He had often reflected on how life-embracing the Swedes were on average, forgetting the traveler's adage that the most attractive people in the world are those one first sees after leaving England.

Outside the cold was jagged and the wind penetrating. While the young people waited, blowing into their hands, Jonathan said a very formal good night to the green-coated Beräknings Aktiebolag guard who patrolled the American Culture Center in response to repeated bomb threats. He felt sorry for the poor devil, stiff-faced and tearing in the numbing cold. He even offered to stand his watch for him.

A bar. Then another bar. Then someone's house. There was a heated discussion and a fight. Another bar—which closed on them. Someone had a wonderful idea and telephoned someone who was not home. Jonathan crowded with the four remaining students into a little car, and they drove back to the Gamla Stan to return him to his hotel on Lilla Nygatan, for he had been drinking heavily and had become embarrassingly antisocial.

They dropped him off on the edge of the medieval island, which is closed to private vehicles. Someone asked if he was sure he could find his way, and he told them to drive on—in fact, go to hell. When the red taillights of the car had disappeared into the swirling snow, he turned to find that a Swedish girl had gotten out with him. So. The party was still on! He put his arm around her—girls feel good in thick fur coats, like teddy bears—and they trudged around looking for an open bar or a *cave*. They found one, an "inne stället for visor, jazz och folkmusik," and they sat drinking whiskey and shouting their conversation against blaring music until the place closed.

They walked unsteadily through deserted narrow streets, holding on to one another, the snow deep on the cobblestones and still falling in large indolent flakes that glittered and spiraled around the gas lamps. Jonathan said he didn't much care for Christmas cards. She didn't understand. So he repeated it, and she still didn't get it, so he said forget it.

A little later he fell.

They were passing through the narrow arched alley of Yxsmedsgränd when he slipped on the ice and fell into a bank of snow. He struggled to get up, and slipped again.

She laughed gaily and offered to help him.

"No! I'm all right. In fact, I'm very comfortable here. I think I'll stay the night. Say, what happened to my overcoat?"

"You must have left it at the party."

"No, that was my youth I left at the party. How do you like that for a bitterer-than-thou tragic romantic riposte? Don't be swayed, honey. It's all hokum designed to get you into bed. You're sure you don't have my overcoat?"

"Come on. We'll go to your hotel." She laughed good-naturedly and helped him up. "Does it embarrass you to do something like that? To slip and fall when you are with a girl?"

"Yes, it does. But that is because I am a male chauvinist swine."

"Pig."

"Pig, then. What are you?"

"I'm an art student. I've read all your books."

"Have you? And now you're going to hop into bed with me. Proof of the adage that success has balls. OK. Let's get to it. Dawn is coming with a red rag among its shoulder blades."

"Pardon?"

"Shakespeare. A modest paraphrase."

There was a great rectangular weight in his forehead, and he tried to bang it away with the back of his fist. "How old are you, honey?"

"Nineteen. How old are you?"

He looked up at her slowly as the drink drained from his head. He was not well; but he was cold sober. "What was that?"

She laughed. "I said, how old are *you?*" The last vowel had a curl to it—a Scandinavian curl, but not unlike an Irish curl.

He looked at her very closely, glancing from eye to eye. She was a pretty enough little girl, but they were the wrong eyes. Not bottle green.

"What's wrong?" she asked. "Are you sick?"

"I'm worse off than that. I'm sober. Say . . . look. Here's the key to my hotel. The address is on it. You stay there tonight. It's all right. It's comfortable."

"Don't you like me?"

He laughed dryly. "I think you're just great, honey. The hope of the future. Bye-bye."

"Where are you going?"

"For a walk."

The sun rose brilliant and cold over the placid water of Riddarfjärden, a crisp yellow sun that gave light without warmth. A single tugboat dragged a wake of glittering, eye-aching silver through the thick black green water, its chug-a-da the only sound in the windless chill. Jonathan's eyes, teared by the cold and squinting against the light, followed the tug's deliberate progress as he leaned against the fence near the Gamla Stan tube stop. His hands were fisted into his jacket pockets, his collar turned up, his shoulders tense to combat the shivering. The brilliant, crusted white of the snow that blanketed the quay was unmarked, save for a long single line of blue-shadowed footsteps that connected his still form to a narrow alley between the ancient buildings that clustered up the hill behind him.

Fatigue made him sigh, and two jets of vapor flowed over his shoulders.

A girl stepped out into the sunlight from the dank cavern of the Gamla Stan tube station where she had passed the night sheltered from the snow and wind. She looked around disconsolately and pulled her surplus army parka more closely around her. She was burdened with a knapsack and a cheap guitar, and the American flag sewn to the butt of her jeans had come loose and frayed at one corner. Her monumentally plain face was gaunt, and her red-rimmed eyes showed hunger and misery. She looked at Jonathan with mistrust. He examined her with distant indifference. A grinning yellow sun-face sticker on her guitar advised him to "have a nice day."

London and Essex, 1973

The Main

To Tony Godwin
on behalf of the writers he helped

One

EVENING ON THE Main, and the shops are closing. Display bins have been pulled back off the sidewalks; corrugated shutters clatter down over store windows. One or two lights are kept on as a deterrent to burglary; and empty cash registers are left ajar so that thieves won't smash them open pointlessly.

The bars remain open, and the cafés; and loudspeaker cones over narrow music stalls splash swatches of noise over sidewalks congested with people, their necks pulled into collars, their shoulders tight against the dank cold. The young and the busy lose patience with the crawling, faceless Wad. They push and shoulder their way through, confusing the old, irritating the idle. The mood of the crowd is harried and brusque; tempers have been frayed by weeks of pig weather, with its layers of zinc cloud, moist and icy, pressing down on the city, delaying the onset of winter with its clean snows and taut blue skies. Everyone complains about the weather. It isn't the cold that gets you, it's the damp.

The swarm coagulates at street corners and where garbage cans have been stacked on the curb. The crowd surges and tangles, tight-packed but lonely. Tense faces, worried faces, vacant faces, all lit on one side by the garish neon of nosh bars, saloons, cafés.

In the window of a fish shop there is a glass tank, its sides green with algae. A lone carp glides back and forth in narcotized despair.

Schoolboys in thick coats and short pants, bookbags strapped to their backs, snake through the crowd, their faces pinched with cold and their legs blotchy red. A big kid punches a smaller one and darts ahead. In his attempt to catch up and retaliate, the small boy steps on a man's foot. The man swears and cuffs him on the back of the head. The boy plunges on, tears of embarrassment and anger in his eyes.

Fed up with the jams and blockages, some people step out into the street and squeeze between illegally parked cars and the northbound traffic. Harassed truck drivers lean on their air horns and curse, and the braver offenders swear back and thrown them the fig. The swearing, the shouting, the grumbling, the swatches of conversation are in French, Yiddish, Portuguese, German, Chinese, Hungarian, Greek—but the lingua franca is English. The Main is a district of immigrants, and greenhorns in Canada quickly learn that English, not French, is the language of success. Signs in the window of a bank attest to the cosmopolitan quality of the street:

HABLAMOS ESPAÑOL

OMI OYMEN ΕΛΛΗΝΙΚΑ

PARLIAMO ITALIANO

WIR SPRECHEN DEUTSCH

FALAMOS PORTUGUES

And there is a worn street joke: "I wonder who in that bank can speak all those languages?"
"The customers."

Commerce is fluid on the Main, and friable. Again and again, shops open in a flurry of brave plans and hopes; frequently they fail, and a new man with different plans and the same hopes starts business in the same shop. There is not always time to change the sign. Retail and wholesale fabrics are featured in a store above which the metal placard reads: PAINTS.

Some shops never change their proprietors, but their lines of goods shift constantly, in search of a profitable coincidence between the wants of the customer and the availability of wholesale bargains. In time, the shopkeepers give up chasing phantom success, and the waves of change subside, leaving behind a random flotsam of wares marking high tides in wholesale deals and low tides in customer interest. Within four walls you can buy camping gear and berets, batteries and yard goods, postcards and layettes, some slightly damaged or soiled, all at amazing discounts. Such shops are known only by the names of their owners; there is no other way to describe them.

And there are stores that find the task of going out of business so complicated that they have been at it for years.

The newspaper seller stands beside his wooden kiosk, his hands kept warm under his canvas change belt. He rocks from foot to foot as he jiggles his coins rhythmically. He never looks up at the passers-by. He makes change to hands, not to faces. He mutters his half of an unending conversation, and he nods, agreeing with himself.

Two people press into a doorway and talk in low voices. She looks over his shoulder with quick worried glances. His voice has the singsong of persuasion through erosion.
"Come on, what do you say?"
"Gee, I don't know. I don't think I better."
"What you scared of? I'll be careful."
"Oh, I better be getting home."
"For crying out loud, you do it for the other guys!"
"Yeah, but . . ."
"Come on. My place is just around the corner."
"Well . . . no, I better not."
"Oh, for crying out loud! Go home then! Who wants you?"

An old Chasidic Jew with *peyiss, shtreimel* level on his head, long black coat scrupulously brushed, returns home from work, maintaining a dignified pace through the press of the crowd. Although others push and hurry, he does not. At the same time, he avoids seeming too humble, for, as the saying has it, "too humble is half proud." So he walks without rushing, but also without dawdling. A gentle and moderate man.

Always he checks the street sign before turning off toward his flat in a low brick building up a side street. This although he has lived on that street for twenty-two years. Prudence can't hurt.

"The Main" designates both a street and a district. In its narrowest definition, the Main is Boulevard St. Laurent, once the dividing line between French and

English Montreal, the street itself French in essence and articulation. An impoverished and noisy street of small shops and low rents, it naturally became the first stop for waves of immigrants entering Canada, with whose arrival "the Main" broadened its meaning to include dependent networks of back streets to the west and east of the St. Laurent spine. Each succeeding national tide entered the Main bewildered, frightened, hopeful. Each successive group clustered together for protection against suspicion and prejudice, concentrating in cultural ghettos of a few blocks' extent.

They found jobs, opened shops, had children; some succeeded, some failed; and they in turn regarded the next wave of immigrants with suspicion and prejudice.

The boundary between French and English Montreal thickened into a no man's land where neither language predominated, and eventually the Main became a third strand in the fiber of the city, a zone of its own consisting of mixed but unblended cultures. The immigrants who did well, and most of the children, moved away to English-speaking west Montreal. But the old stayed, those who had spent their toil and money on the education of children who are now a little embarrassed by them. The old stayed; and the losers; and the lost.

Two young men sit in a steamy café, looking out onto the street through a window cleared of mist by a quick palm swipe. One is Portuguese, the other Italian; they speak a mélange of Joual slang and mispronounced English. Both wear trendy suits of uncomfortable cut and unserviceable fabric. The Portuguese's suit is gaudy and cheap; the Italian's is gaudy and expensive.

"Hey, hey!" says the Portuguese. "What you think of that? Not bad, eh?"

The Italian leans over the table and catches a quick glimpse of a girl clopping past the café in a mini, platform boots, and a bunny jacket. "Not so bad! *Beau pétard, hein?*"

"And what you think of those *foufounes?*"

"I could make her cry. I take one of those in each hand, eh? Eh?" In robust mime, the Italian holds one in each hand and moves them on his lap. "She would really cry, I'm tell you that." He glances up at the clock above the counter. "Hey, I got to go."

"You got something hot waiting for you?"

"Ain't I *always* got something hot waiting?"

"Lucky son of a bitch."

The Italian grins and runs a comb through his hair, patting down the sides with his palm. Yeah, maybe he's lucky. He's lucky to have the looks. But it takes talent, too. Not everybody's got the talent.

In just over five hours, he will be kneeling in an alley off Rue Lozeau, his face pressed against the gravel. He will be dead.

There is a sudden block in the flow of pedestrians. Someone has vomited on the sidewalk. Chunks of white in a sauce of ochre. People veer to avoid it but there is a comma of smear where a heel skidded.

A cripple plunges down the Main against the flow of pedestrian traffic. Each foot slaps flat upon the pavement as he jerks his torso from side to side with excessive, erratic energy. He lurches forward, then plants a foot to prevent himself from falling. A lurch, a twist, the slack flap of a foot. He is young, his face abnormally bland, his head too large. A harelip contorts his mouth into something between a grin and a sneer. His eyes are huge behind thick iron-rimmed glasses which are twisted on his face so that one eye looks through the bottom of its lens, while the other pupil is bisected by the top of its lens. Coiled back against his chest is a withered, useless hand in a pale blue glove. An incongruous curved pipe is clenched between his teeth, and he sucks it moistly. Sweet aromatic smoke pours over his shoulder and disintegrates in the eddies of his lurching motion.

Pedestrians are startled out of their involute thoughts to see him barging toward them through the crowd. They move aside to make room, eager to avoid contact. Eyes are averted; there is something frightening and disgusting about the Gimp, who drives ahead in his determined, angry way. The human flood breaks at his prow, then blends back in his wake, and people forget him immediately he has passed. They have their own problems, their own plans; each is isolated in and insulated by the alien crowd.

Chez Pete's Place is a bar for the street *bommes;* it is the only place that admits them, and their presence precludes any other clientele. Painted plywood has replaced glass in the window, so it is always night inside. The fat proprietor sits slumped behind the bar, his watery eyes fixed on a skin magazine in his lap. Around a table in the back sit a knot of ragged old men, their hands so filthy that the skin shines and crinkles. They are sharing a half-gallon bottle of wine, and one of the *bommes,* Dirtyshirt Red, is spiking his wine with whisky from a pint bottle screwed up in a brown paper bag. He doesn't offer to share the whisky, and the others know better than to ask.

"Look at that stuck-up son of a bitch, won't ya?" Dirtyshirt Red says, lifting his chin toward a tall, gaunt tramp sitting alone at a small table in the corner, out of the light, his concentration on his glass of wine.

"Potlickin' bastard thinks he's too good to sit with the rest of us," Red pursues. "Thinks his shit don't stink, but his farts give him away!"

The other tramps laugh ritually. Ridiculing the Vet is an old pastime for all of them. No one feels sorry for the Vet; he brings it on himself by bragging about a nice snug kip he's got somewhere off the Main. No matter how cold it is, or how hard up a guy is, the Vet never offers to share his kip; he won't even let anybody know where it is.

"Hey, what you dreamin' about, Vet? Thinking about what a hero you was in the war?"

The Vet's broad-brimmed floppy hat tilts up as he raises his head slowly and looks toward the table of jeering *bommes.* His eyebrows arch and his nostrils dilate in a caricature of superiority, then his musings return to his wine glass.

"Oh, yeah! Big hero he was! Captured by the Germans, he was. Left by the Limeys at Dunkirk 'cause they didn't want him stinkin' up their boats. And you know what big hero thing he done when he was in prison camp? He lined his ass with ground glass so the Germans would get castrated when they cornholed him! Big hero! That's why he walks funny! He claims he was wounded in the war, but I heard different!"

There are snickers and nudgings around the table, but the Vet does not deign to respond. Perhaps he no longer hears.

Lieutenant Claude LaPointe crosses Sherbrooke, leaving the somber mass of the Monastère du Bon Pasteur behind. His pace slows to the measured rhythm of the beatwalker. The Main has been his patch for thirty-two years, since the Depression was at its nadir and frightened people treated one another with humanity, even in Montreal, the most impolite city in the world.

LaPointe presses his fists deep into the pockets of his shapeless overcoat to tug the collar tighter down onto his neck. Over the years, that rumpled overcoat has become something of a uniform for him, known by everybody who works on the Main, or who works the Main. Young detectives down at the Quartier Général make jokes about it, saying he sleeps in it at night, and in the summer uses it as a laundry bag. Feelings differ about the man in the overcoat; some recognize a friend and protector, others see a repressive enemy. It depends upon what you do for a living; and even more it depends on how LaPointe feels about you.

When he was young on the street, the Main was French and he its French cop. As the foreigners began to arrive in numbers, there was coolness and distance between them and LaPointe. He could not understand what they wanted, what they were saying, how they did things; and for their part they brought with them a deep distrust of authority and police. But with the wearing of time, the newcomers became a part of the street, and LaPointe became their cop: their protector, sometimes their punisher.

As he walks slowly up the street, LaPointe passes a bakery that is something of a symbol of the change the years have brought to the Main. Thirty-odd years ago, when the Main was French, the bakery was:

PATISSERIE ST. LAURENT

Ten years later, in response to the relentless pressure of English, one word was added to permit the French to use the first two-thirds of the sign and the Anglos the last two-thirds:

PATISSERIE ST. LAURENT *Bakery*

Now there are different breads in the window, breads with odd shapes and glazes. And the women waiting in line gossip in alien sounds. Now the sign reads:

PATISSERIE ST. LAURENT *Bakery*
APTOπΩΛEION

The throng is thinning out as people arrive at destinations, or give up trying. LaPointe continues north, uphill, his step heavy and slow, his professional glance wandering from detail to detail. The lock on that metal grating over the store window wants replacing. He'll remind Mr. Capeck about it tomorrow. The man standing in that doorway . . . it's all right. Only a *bomme*. The streetlight is out in the alley behind Le Kit-Kat, a porno theatre. He'll report that. Men who get overexcited in the porno house use that alley; and sometimes rollers use it too.

Deep in his pocket, LaPointe's left hand lies lightly over the butt of his stub .38. In summer he carries it in a holster behind his hip, so he can keep his jacket open. In winter he leaves it loose in his left overcoat pocket, so his right hand is free. The pistol is so much a part of him that he releases it automatically when he reaches for something, and takes it up again when his hand returns to his pocket. The weight of it wears out the lining, and at least once each winter he has to sew it up. He is clumsy with a needle, so the pocket becomes steadily shallower. Every few years he has to have the lining replaced.

In more than thirty years on this street of voluble and passionate people, a street on which poverty and greed and despair find expression in petty crime. La Pointe has fired his weapon only seven times. He is proud of that.

A harried child, her eyes down as she gnaws nervously at her lip, bumps into LaPointe and mutters "Excuse me" without looking up, her voice carrying a note of distress. She is late getting home. Her parents will be angry; they will scold her because they love her. The Lieutenant knows the girl and the parents. They want her to become a nurse, and they make her study long hours because she is not good at schoolwork. The girl tries, but she does not have the ability.

For her training, for her future, her parents have suffered years of scrimping and self-denial. She is everything to them: their future, their pride, their excuse.

The girl spends a lot of time wishing she were dead.

As he passes Rue Guilbault, LaPointe glances down and sees two young men idling by the stoop of a brownstone. They wear black plastic jackets, and one swings back and forth from the railing. They *chantent la pomme* to a girl of fourteen who sits on the stoop, her elbows resting on the step above, her meager breasts pressed against a thin sweater. She taunts and laughs, and they sniff around like pubescent puppies. LaPointe knows the house. That would be the youngest Da Costa girl. Like her sisters, she will probably be selling ass on the street within two years. Mama Da Costa's dream of the girls following their aunt into the convent is beginning to fade.

LaPointe is walking behind two men who speak a strained English. They are discussing business, and how it's easy for the rich to get richer. One maintains that it's a matter of percentages; if you know the percentages, you're set. The other agrees, but he complains that you've got to be rich to find out what the percentages *are*.

They step apart gingerly to avoid colliding with the cripple who lurches toward them, his pipe smoke trailing a smear in the red neon of a two-for-one-bar.

LaPointe stands in the middle of the sidewalk. The cripple stumbles to a stop and wavers before the policeman.

"Say-hey, Lieutenant. How's it going?" The Gimp's speech is blurred by the affliction that has damaged his centers of control. His mother was diseased at the time of his birth. He speaks with the alto, adenoidal whine of a boxer who has been hit on the windpipe too often.

LaPointe looks at the cripple with fatigued patience. "What are you doing at this end of the street, Gimp?"

"Nothing, Lieutenant. Say-hey, I'm just taking a walk, that's all. Boy you know, this pig weather is really hanging on, ain't it, Lieutenant? I never seen anything like . . ."

LaPointe is shaking his head, so the Gimp gives up his attempt to hide in small talk. Taking one hand from his overcoat pocket, the Lieutenant points toward a narrow passage between two buildings, out of the flow of the crowd. The cripple grimaces, but follows him.

"All right, Gimp. What are you carrying?"

"Hey, nothin', Lieutenant. Honest ! I promised you, didn't I?"

LaPointe reaches out; in his attempt to step back, the cripple stumbles against the brick wall. "Hey, please! We need the money! Mama's going to be pissed at me if I don't bring back any money!"

"Do you want to go back inside?"

"No! Hey, have a heart, Lieutenant!" the cripple whines. "Mama'll be pissed. We need the money. What kind of work can a guy like me get? Eh?"

"Where's it stashed?"

"I tol' you! I ain't carrying . . ." The Gimp's eyes moisten with tears. His body slumps in defeat. "It's in a tube," he admits sullenly.

LaPointe sighs. "Go up the alley and get it out. Put it inside your glove and give it to me." LaPointe has no intention of handling the tube.

The cripple moans and whimpers, but he turns and lurches up the alley a few steps until he is in the dark. LaPointe turns his back and watches the passing pedestrians. An old man steps toward the mouth of the recess to take a piss, then he sees LaPointe and changes his mind. The cripple comes back, clutching one glove in his withered hand. LaPointe takes it and puts it into his pocket. "All right, now where did this shit come from, and where were you bringing it?"

"Say-hey, I can't tell you that, Lieutenant! Mama'll beat me up for sure! And those guys she knows, they'll beat me up!" His eyes, bisected by the rims of his glasses, roll stupidly. LaPointe does not repeat his question. Following his habit in interrogation, he simply sighs and settles his melancholy eyes on the grotesque.

"Honest to God, Lieutenant, I can't tell you! I don't dare!"

"I'd better call for a car."

"Hey, no! Don't put me back inside. Those tough guys inside like to use me 'cause I'm a cripple."

LaPointe looks out over the crowd with weary patience. He gives the Gimp time to think it over.

". . . Okay, Lieutenant . . ."

In a self-pitying whimper, the cripple explains that the stuff came from people his mother knows, tough guys from somewhere out on the east end of town. It was to be delivered to a pimp named Scheer. The Lieutenant knows this Scheer and has been waiting for a chance to run him off the Main. He has not been able to put a real case together, so he has had to content himself with maintaining constant harassing pressure. For a moment he considers going after Scheer with the Gimp's testimony, then he abandons the thought, realizing what a glib defense lawyer would do to this half-wit in the witness box.

"All right," LaPointe says. "Now listen to me. And tell your mother what I say. I don't want you on my patch anymore. You have one month to find someplace to go. You understand?"

"But, say-hey, Lieutenant? Where'll we go? All my friends are here!"

LaPointe shrugs. "Just tell your mother. One month."

"Okay. I'll tell her. But I hate to piss her off. I mean, after all . . . she's my mother."

LaPointe sits at the counter of a café, his shoulders slumped, his eyes indifferently scanning the passersby beyond the window.

A small white radio on a shelf by the counterman's ear is insisting that

> *Everybody digs the Montreal Rock*
> *Oh, yes! Oh, yes!*
> *Oh, yes! O-o-h YES!*
> *Everybody digs the Montreal Rock!*

LaPointe sighs and digs into his pocket to pay for the coffee. As he rises he notices a sign above the counterman's head. "That's wrong," he says. "It's misspelled."

The counterman gives a sizzling hamburger a definitive slap with his spatula and turns to examine the sign.

APPL PIE—30¢

He shrugs. "Yeah, I know. I complained, and the painter cut his price."

"Samuel?" LaPointe asks, referring to the old man who does most of the sign painting on this part of the Main.

"Yes." The counterman uses the inhailed *oui* typical of Joual.

LaPointe smiles to himself. Old Samuel always makes fancy signs with underlinings and ornate swirls and exclamation points, all at no extra cost. He is given to setting things off with quotation marks, inadvertently raising doubt in the customer's mind, as in:

"FRESH" FISH DAILY

He is also an independent artist who spells words the way he pronounces them. The counterman is lucky the sign doesn't read: EPP'L PIE.

Not fifty paces off the Main, down Rue Napoléon, the bustle and press are gone and the noise is reduced to an ambient baritone rumble. The narrow old street is lit by widely spaced streetlamps and occasional dusty shopwindows. Children play around the stoops of three-story brick row houses. Above the roofline, defused city-light glows in the damp, sooty air. Each house depends on the others for support. They have not collapsed because each wants to fall in a different direction, and there isn't enough room.

It is after eight o'clock and cold, but the children will play until the fourth or fifth two-toned call of an exasperated mother brings them toe-dragging up the stoops and off to sleep, probably on a sofa in a front room, or in a cot blocking a hallway, covered with wool blankets that are gummy to the touch—bingo blankets that absorb body warmth without retaining it.

LaPointe leans against the railing of a deserted stoop, holding on tightly as the tingle rises in his chest. It is a familiar feeling by now, an oddly pleasant sensation in the middle of his chest and upper arms, as though there were carbonated water in his veins. Sometimes pain follows the tingling. His blood fizzes in his chest; he looks up at the light-smeared sky and breathes slowly, expecting to find a little flash of pain at the end of each breath, and relieved not to.

Little kids a few stoops away are playing *rond-rond,* and at the end of each minor-key chant they all fall giggling to the sidewalk. The English-speaking kids play the same game with different words—about a ring of roses. All the children of Europe preserve in their atavistic memory the scar of the Black Death. They reel to simulate the dizziness; they make sounds like the symptomatic sneezing; they sing of bouquets of posies to ward off the miasma of the Plague. Then, giggling, they all fall down.

When LaPointe was a kid in Trois Rivières, he used to play in the streets at night, too. In summer, all the grownups would sit out on the stoops because it was stifling indoors. The men wore only undershirts and drank ale from the bottle. And old lady Tarbieau . . . LaPointe remembers old lady Tarbieau, who lived across the street and who used to tend everybody's onions. She always pretended to care about people's problems in order to find out what they were. LaPointe's mother didn't like old lady Tarbieau. The only off-color thing he ever heard his mother say was in response to Mme. Tarbieau's nosiness. One night when all the block was out on the stoops, old lady Tarbieau called across the street, "Mme. LaPointe? Didn't I see the rent man coming out of your house today? It's only the middle of the month. I always thought you paid your rent the same way I do." And LaPointe's mother answered, "No, Mme. Tarbieau. I don't pay my rent the same way you do. I pay in money."

Poor Mme. Tarbieau, already aged when LaPointe was a boy. He hadn't thought of her for years. He pictures the old busybody in his mind, and realizes that this is probably the first time anybody has remembered her for a quarter of a century. And probably this will be the last time any human memory will hold her. In that case, she is gone . . . really gone.

The tingle in his arms and chest has passed, so he pushes his fists further into his pockets and walks on toward the liquor store, in and out of the cones of streetlight, where kids dart from stoop to stoop, like starlings on a summer evening.

One summer, the summer after his father left home never to come back, LaPointe discovered that playing with the other kids around the stoops had become dull and pointless. In the long evenings, he used to walk alone on the street, looking up at the moon through newly hung electric wires. The moon would follow him, sliding along over the weaving wires. He would turn quickly and go up the street, and the moon followed. He would stop suddenly, then go again, but the moon was never tricked. Once, when he had been running, then stopping, running and stopping, all the time looking up and getting a little dizzy, he was startled to find himself standing only inches from the Crazy Woman who lived down the block. She grinned, then laughed a wheezing note. She pointed a finger at him and said he was a *fou*, like her, and they would sizzle in hell side by side.

He ran away. But for the rest of the week he had nightmares. He was terrified at the thought of going crazy. Maybe he was already crazy. How do you know if you're crazy? If you're crazy, you're too crazy to know you're crazy. What does "crazy" mean? Say the word again and again, and the sense dries out, leaving only a husk of sound. And you hear yourself saying a meaningless noise over and over again.

That was the last summer he played on the streets. The following winter his mother died of influenza. Grandpapa and Grandmama were already dead. He went to St. Joseph's Home. And from the Home, he went into the police.

LaPointe squeezes his eyes closed and pulls himself out of it. He has found himself daydreaming like this a lot of late, remembering old lost things, unimportant things triggered by some little sound or sight on the Main.

He smiles at himself. Now, that *is* crazy.

The middle-aged Greek counterman looks up and smiles as LaPointe enters the deserted liquor store. He has been expecting the Lieutenant, and he reaches up for the bottle of red LaPointe always brings along to his twice-weekly games of pinochle.

"Everything going well?" LaPointe asks as he pays for the wine.

The counterman gulps air and growls, "Oh, fine, Lieutenant." He gulps again. "Theo wrote. Got the letter—" Another gulp. "—this morning."

"How's he doing?"

"Fine. He's up for parole soon."

It was too bad that LaPointe had to put the son inside for theft so shortly after the father had an operation for throat cancer. But that's the way it goes; that is his job. "That's good," He says. "I'm glad he's getting parole."

The counterman nods. For him, as for others in the quartier, LaPointe is the law; the good and the bad of it. He will never forget the evening seven years ago when the Lieutenant walked in to buy his usual Thursday night bottle of wine. A young man with slick hair had been loitering in the store, carefully looking over the labels of exotic aperitifs and liqueurs. LaPointe paid for his wine and, in the same movement of putting his change into his pocket, he drew out his gun.

"Put your hands on top of your head," LaPointe said quietly to the young man.

The boy's eyes darted toward the door, but LaPointe shook his head slowly. "Never," he said.

The young man put his hands on top of his head, and LaPointe snatched him by his collar and bent him over the counter. Two swift movements under the boy's jacket, and LaPointe came up with a cheap automatic. While they waited for the arrival of a police car, the boy sat on the floor in a corner, cowed and foolish, his hands still on top of his head. Customers came and went. They glanced uneasily towards the boy and LaPointe, and they carefully avoided coming near them, but not one question was asked, not one comment made. They ordered their wine in subdued voices, then they left.

There had been several hold-ups in the neighborhood that winter, and the old man who ran the cleaners down the street had been shot in the stomach.

It never occurred to anyone to wonder how LaPointe knew the boy was pumping up his courage for a hold-up. He was the law on the Main, and he knew everything. Actually, LaPointe had known nothing until the moment he stepped into the shop and passed by the boy. It was the tense nonchalance he instantly recognized. The Indian blood in LaPointe smelled fear.

The Greek counterman is comforted to know that LaPointe is always out there in the street somewhere. And yet . . . this is the same man who arrested his son Theo for auto theft and sent him to prison for three years. The good of the law, and the bad. But it could have been worse. LaPointe had put in a good word for Theo.

The Lieutenant continues north on the Main, the bottle of wine, twisted up in a brown paper bag, heavy in his overcoat pocket. He passes a closed shop and automatically checks the padlock on the accordion steel grid covering its window. Once a beat cop . . .

But LaPointe had better get moving along. He doesn't want to be late for his pinochle game.

Two

". . . SO ALL THE wise men and *pilpulniks* of Chelm get together to decide which is more important to their village, the sun or the moon. Finally they decide in favor of the moon. And why? Because the moon gives light during the night when, without it, they might fall into ditches and hurt themselves. While the sun, on the other hand, shines only during the day, when already it is light out. So who needs it!" David Mogolevski snorts with laughter at his own story, his thick body quaking, his growling basso filling the cramped little room behind the upholstery shop. His eyes sparkle as he looks from face to face, nodding and saying, "Eh? Eh?" soliciting appreciation.

Father Martin nods and grins. "Yes, that's a good one, David." He is eager to show that he likes the joke, but he has never known how to laugh. Whenever he tries out of politeness, he produces a bogus sound that embarrasses him.

David shakes his head and repeats, his eyes tearing with laughter, "The sun shines only during the day! So who needs it!"

Moishe Rappaport smiles over the top of his round glasses and nods support for his partner. He has heard each of David's jokes a hundred times, but he still enjoys them. Most of all, he enjoys the generous vigor of David's laughter; but sometimes he is tense when David starts off on one of his longer tales, because he knows the listener has probably already heard it, and may be unkind enough to say so. There is no danger of that with these pinochle friends; they always pretend never to have heard the stories before, although Moishe and David have been playing cards with the priest and the police lieutenant every Thursday and Monday night for thirteen years now.

The back room is cramped by stacks of old furniture, bolts of upholstery, and the loom on which Moishe makes fabrics for special customers. A space is cleared in the center under a naked light bulb, and a card table is set up. At some time during the night there will be a break, and they will eat sandwiches prepared by Moishe and drink the wine LaPointe brought.

Father Martin contributes only his presence and patience—and this last is no small offering, for he is always David's partner.

Throughout the evening there is conversation. Moishe and Father Martin look forward to these opportunities to examine and debate life and love; justice and the law; the role of Man; the nature of Truth. They are both scholarly men to whom the coincidences of life denied outlets. David injects his jokes and a leavening cynicism, without which the philosophical ramblings of the other two would inflate and leave the earth.

LaPointe's role is that of the listener.

For all four, these twice-weekly games have become oases in their routines, and they take them for granted. But if the games were to end, the vacuum would be profound.

Each would have to search his memory to recall how they got together in the first place; it seems they have always played cards on Thursdays and Mondays. In fact, Father Martin met David and Moishe while he was canvassing the Main for contributions toward the maintenance of his battered polyglot parish. But how that led to his playing cards with them he could not say. LaPointe entered the circle just as casually. One night on his way home after putting the street to bed, he saw a light in the back of the shop and tapped at the window to see if everything was all right. They were playing three-handed cutthroat. Maybe LaPointe was feeling lonely that night without knowing it. In any event, he accepted their invitation to join the game.

They were all in their forties when first they started playing. LaPointe is fifty-three now; and Moishe must be just over sixty.

David rubs his thick hands together and leers at his friends. "Come, deal the cards! The luck has been against me tonight, but now I feel strong. The good Father and I are going to *schneider* you poor babies. Well? Why doesn't somebody deal?"

"Because it's your deal, David," Moishe reminds him.

"Ah! That explains it. Okay, here we go!" David has a flashy way of dealing which often causes a card to turn over. Each time this occurs he says, "Oops! Sunny side up!" His own cards never happen to turn over. He sweeps in his hand with a grand gesture and begins arranging it, making little sounds of surprised appreciation designed to cow adversaries. "Hello, hello, hel-lo!" he says as he slips a good card into place and taps it home with his finger.

David's heritage is rural and Slavic; he is a big man, unsubtle of feature and personality; gregarious, gruff, kind. When he is angry, he roars; when he feels done in by man or fate, he complains bitterly and at length; when he is pleased, he beams. The robust, life-embracing *shtetl* tradition dominates his nature. In business he is a formidable bargainer, but scrupulously honest. A deal is a deal, whichever way it turns. Although it is Moishe's skill and craftsmanship that makes their little enterprise popular with decorators from Westmont, the business would have failed a hundred times over without the vigor and acumen of David. His personality is perfectly reflected in the way he plays cards. He tends to overbid slightly, because he finds the game dull when someone else has named trump. When he is taking a run of sure tricks, he snaps each card down with a triumphant snort. When he goes set, he groans and slaps his forehead. He gets bored when Moishe and Father Martin delay the game with their meandering philosophical talks; but if *he* thinks of a good story, he will reach across the table and place his hand upon the cards to stop play while he holds forth.

Moishe, too, is revealed in his cardplaying. He collects his hand and arranges it carefully. Behind the round glasses, his eyes take an interior focus as he evaluates the cards. He could be the best player by far, if he were to concentrate on the game. But winning isn't important to him. The gathering of friends, the talk, these are what matter. Occasionally, just occasionally, he takes a perverse delight in bearing down and applying his acute mind to the job of setting David, particularly if his friend has blustered a little too much that evening.

Slight, self-effacing, Moishe is the very opposite of his business partner.

During the days he is to be found in the back room, tacks in his mouth, driving each one precisely into place with three taps of his hammer. Tap . . . TAP . . . tap. The first rap setting the point, the second neatly driving the tack home, the third for good measure. Or he will be working at his small loom, his agile fingers flying with precision. If he is in a repeat pattern requiring little attention, his expression seems to fade as his mind ranges elsewhere, on scenes of his youth, on hypothetical ethical problems, on imagined conversations with young people seeking guidance.

As a young man he lived in Germany in the comfortable old ghetto house where his great-grandfather had been born, a home that always smelled of good cooking and beeswax polish. They were a family of craftsmen in wood and fabric, but they admired learning, and the most revered of their relatives were those who had the gifts and devotion for Talmudic scholarship. As a boy he showed a penchant for study and that mental habit of seeing things simultaneously in their narrowest details and their broadest implications that marks the Talmudic scholar—a gift Moishe calls "intellectual peripheral vision." His mother was proud of him and found frequent opportunities to mention to neighbor ladies that Moishe was up in his room studying again, instead of out playing and wasting his time. She would lift her hands helplessly and say that she didn't know what she would do with that boy—all the time studying, learning, saying brilliant things. Maybe in the long run it would be better if he were a common ordinary boy, like the neighbors' sons.

Moishe's adoring sister used to bring up little things for him to eat when he was studying late. His father also supported his intellectual inclination, but he insisted that Moishe learn the family craft. As he used to say, "It doesn't hurt a brilliant man to know a little something."

When the Nazi repression began, the Rappaports did not flee. After all, they were Germans; the father had fought in the 1914 war, the grandfather in the Franco-Prussian; they had German friends and business associates. Germany, after all, was not a nation of animals.

Moishe alone survived. His parents died of malnutrition and disease in the ever-narrowing ghetto; and his sister, delicate, shy, unworldly, died in the camp.

He came to Montreal after two years in the anonymous cauldron of a displaced persons camp. Occasionally, and then only in casual illustration of some point of discussion, Moishe mentioned the concentration camp and the loss of his family. LaPointe never understood the tone of shame and culpability that crept into Moishe's voice when he spoke of these experiences. He seemed ashamed of having undergone so dehumanizing a process; ashamed to have survived, when so many others did not.

Claude LaPointe sorts his cards into suits, taps the fan closed on the table, then spreads it again by pinching the cards between thumb and forefinger. He re-scans his hand, then closes it in front of him. He will not look at it again until after the bidding is over. He knows what he has, knows its value.

For the third time, Father Martin sorts his cards. The diamonds have a way of getting mixed up with the hearts. He pats the top of his thinning hair with his palm and looks at the cards mournfully; it is the kind of hand he dreads most. He doesn't mind having terrible cards that no one could play well, and he rather enjoys having so strong a hand that not even he can misplay it. But these cards of middle power! Martin admits to being the worse cardplayer in North America. Should he fail to admit it, David would remind him.

When first he came to the Main, an idealistic young priest, Martin had affection for his church, nestled in a tight row of houses, literally a part of the street, a part of everyone's life. But now he feels sorry for his church, and ashamed of it. Both sides have been denuded by the tearing down of row houses to make way for industrial expansion. Rubble fields flank it, exposing ugly surfaces never meant to be seen, revealing the outlines of houses that used to depend on the church for structural support, and used to defend it. And the projects he dreamed of never quite worked out; people kept changing before he could really get anything started. Now most of Father Martin's flock are old Portuguese women who visit the church at all times of day, bent women with black shawls who light candles to prolong their prayers, then creep down the aisle on painful legs, their gnarled fingers gripping pew ends for support. Father Martin can speak only a few words of Portuguese. He can shrive, but he cannot console.

When he was a young man in seminary, he dared to dream of being a scholar, of writing incisive and illuminating apologetics that applied the principles of the faith to modern life and problems. He would sometimes wake up at night with a lucid perception of some knotty issue—a perception that was always just beyond the stretch of his memory the next morning. Although his mind teemed with ideas, he lacked the knack of setting his thoughts down clearly. Prior considerations and subsequent ramifications would invade his thinking and carry him off to the left or right of his main thesis, so he did not shine in seminary and was never considered for that post he so desired in a small college where he could study and write and teach. There was a joke in seminary: publish or parish.

But Father Martin's mind still runs to ethics, to the nature of sin, to the proper uses of the gift of life; so, while being David's bungling partner is mortifying, the conversations with Moishe make it worthwhile. And there is something right about that, too. A payment in humiliation for the opportunity to learn and to express oneself.

"Come on! Come on!" David says. "It's your bid, Claude. Unless, of course, you and Moishe have decided to save face by throwing in your hands."

"All right," LaPointe says. "Fifteen."

"Sixteen." Father Martin says the word softly, then sucks air in through his teeth in an attempt to express the fact that he has a fair playing hand but no meld to speak of.

"Ah-ha!" David ejaculates.

Father Martin catches his breath. David is going to plunge after the bid, dragging the uncertain priest after him to a harrowingly narrow victory or a crushing defeat.

Moishe studies his cards, his gentle eyes seeming to pass over the number indifferently. He purses his lips and hums a soft ascending note. "Oh-h-h. Seventeen, I suppose."

"Eighteen!" is David's rapid reply.

Father Martin winces.

LaPointe taps the top of the face-down stack before him. "All right," he says, "nineteen, then."

"Pass," says Father Martin dolefully.

"Pass," says Moishe, looking at his partner slyly from behind his round glasses.

"Good!" David says. "Now let's sort out the men from the sheep. Twenty-two!"

LaPointe shrugs and passes.

"Prepare to suffer, fools," David says. He declares spades trump, but he has only a nine and a pinochle to meld.

Gingerly, apologetically, Father Martin produces a king and queen of hearts.

David stares at his partner, hurt and disbelief flooding his eyes. "That's all?" he asks. "This is what you meld? One marriage?"

"I . . . I was bidding a playing hand."

LaPointe objects. "Why don't you just show one another your hands and be done with it?"

Moishe sets down his cards and rises. "I'll start the sandwiches."

"Wait a minute!" David says. "Where are you going? The hand isn't over!"

"You are going to play it out?" Moishe asks incredulously.

"Of course! Sit down!"

Moishe looks at LaPointe with operatic surprise. He spreads his arms and lifts his palms toward the ceiling.

Roaring out his aces in an aggressive style that scorns the effeminate trickery of the finesse, David takes the first four tricks. But when he tries to cross to his partner, he is cut off by LaPointe, who manages to finesse a ten from Father Martin, then sends the lead to Moishe, who finishes the assassination.

At one point, Father Martin plays a low club onto a diamond trick.

"What?" cries David. "You're out of trump?"

"Aren't clubs trump?"

David slumps over and softly bangs his forehead against the table top. "Why me?" he asks the oilcloth. "Why *me?*"

Too late, the lead returns to David, who slams down his last five cards, collecting impoverished and inadequate tricks.

He stares heavily at the tabletop for a few seconds, then he speaks in a low and controlled voice. "My dear Father Martin. I ask the following, not in anger, but in a spirit of humble curiosity. Please tell me. Why did you bid when *you had nothing in your hand but SHIT!*"

Moishe removes his glasses and lightly rubs the red dents on the bridge of his nose. "There was nothing Martin could have done to save you. You overbid your hand and you went set. That's all there is to it."

"Don't tell me that! If he had come out with his ten earlier—"

"You would have won one more trick. Not enough to save you. You had two clubs left; I had the ace, Claude the ten. And if you had returned in diamonds— at that time you still had the queen—Martin would have had to trump it with his jack, and I would have overtrumped with the king." Moishe continues to rub his nose.

David glares at him in silence before saying, "That's wonderful. That is just wonderful!" The tension in David's voice causes Martin to look over at him, his breathing suspended. "Listen to the big scholar, will you? If my jack of hearts has its fly unbuttoned, he remembers! But when it comes to accounts, suddenly he's a *luftmensh*, too busy with philosophical problems to worry about business! Oh, yes! Taking care of the business is too commonplace for a man who spends all his time debating does an ant have a *pupik!* For your information, Moishe, I was talking to the priest! So butt out for once! Just butt out!"

David jumps up, knocking the table with his knees, and slams out of the room.

In the ensuing silence, Father Martin looks from Moishe to LaPointe, upset, confused. LaPointe draws a deep breath and begins desultorily to collect the cards. The moment David began his abuse, Moishe froze in mid-action; and now he replaces his glasses, threading each wire temple over its ear.

"Ah . . . listen," he says quietly. "You must forgive David. He is in pain. He is grieving. Yesterday was the anniversary of Hannah's death. He's been like a balled-up fist all day."

The others understand. David and Hannah had been children together, and they had married young. So close, so happy were they that they dared express their affection only through constant light bickering and quarreling, as if it were unlucky to be blatantly happy and in love in a world where others were sad and suffering. After they immigrated to Montreal, Hannah's world was focused almost totally on her husband. She never learned French or English and shopped only in Jewish markets.

During the pinochle games, David used to talk about Hannah constantly; complaining, of course. Bragging about her in his negative way. Saying that no woman in the world was so fussy about her cooking, such a nuisance about his health. She was driving him crazy! Why did he put up with it?

Then, six years ago, Hannah died of cancer. Sick less than a month, and she died.

For weeks afterward, the card games were quiet and uncomfortable; David was distant, uncharacteristically polite and withdrawn, and no one dared to console him. His eyes were hollow, his face scoured with grief. Sometimes they would have to remind him that it was his play, and he would snap out of his reverie and apologize for delaying the game. David apologizing! Then, one evening, he mentioned Hannah in the course of conversation, grumbling that she was a nag and a pest. And moreover she was fat. *Zaftig* young is fat old! I should have married a skinny woman. They're cheaper to feed.

That was how he would handle it. He would continue complaining about her. That way, she wouldn't be gone completely. He could go on loving her, and being exasperated beyond bearing by her. Occasionally the sour void of grief returned to make him desperate and mean for a day or two, but in general he could handle it now.

The complicated double way he thought of his wife was expressed precisely one night when he happened to say, "Should Hannah, *alshasholm,* suddenly return, *cholilleh,* she would have a fit!"

"So just pretend nothing happened when he comes back," Moishe says. "And whatever you do, don't try to cheer him up. A man must be allowed to grieve once in a while. If he avoids the pain of grieving, the sadness never gets purged. It lumps up inside of him, poisoning his life. Tears are solvent."

Father Martin shakes his head. "But a friend should offer consolation."

"No, Martin. That would be the easy, the comfortable thing to do. But not the kindest thing. Just as David is not grieving for Hannah—people only grieve for themselves, for *their* loss—so we wouldn't be consoling him for his own sake. We would be consoling him because his grief is awkward for *us.*"

LaPointe feels uncomfortable with all this talk of grief and consolation. Men shouldn't need that sort of thing. And he is about to say so, when David appears in the doorway.

"Hey!" he says gruffly. "I went out to make the sandwiches, and I can't find anything. What a mess!"

Moishe smiles as he rises. David has never made the sandwiches in his life. "You find some glasses for the wine. I'll make the sandwiches, for a change."

As David rummages about grumpily for the glasses, Moishe steps to a narrow table against the wall on which are arranged cold cuts and a loaf of rye bread. He cuts the bread rapidly, one stroke of the knife for each thin, perfect slice.

"It's amazing how you do that, Moishe," Father Martin says, eager to get the conversation rolling.

"Agh, that's nothing," David pronounces proudly. "Have you ever seen him cut fabric?" He spreads two fingers like scissors and makes a rapid gesture that narrowly misses Father Martin's ear. "Psh-sh-sht! It's a marvel to watch!"

Moishe chuckles to himself as he continues slicing. "I would call that a pretty modest accomplishment in life. I can just see my epitaph: 'Boy! Could he cut cloth!'"

"Yeah, yeah," David says, fanning his hand in dismissal of Moishe's modesty. "Still, think what a surgeon you would have made."

Father Martin has a funny idea. "Yes, he'd make a great surgeon, if my appendix were made of damask!"

David turns and looks at him with heavy eyes. "What? What's this about your appendix being damask?"

"No . . . I was just saying that . . . well, if Moishe were a surgeon . . ." Confused, Martin shrugs and drops it.

"I still don't get it," David says flatly. He is embarrassed about his recent loss of control, and Father Martin is going to feel the brunt of it.

"Well . . . it was just a joke," Martin explains, deflated.

"Father," David says, "let's make a deal. *You* listen to confessions from old ladies too feeble to make interesting sins. *I'll* tell the jokes. To each according to his needs; from each according to his abilities."

"Look who's the communist," Moishe says, trying to attract some of the fire away from Martin.

"Who said anything about being a communist?" David wants to know.

"Forget it. Did you manage to find the glasses?"

"What glasses? Oh. The glasses."

Moishe puts a plate of sandwiches on the table, while David brings three thick-bottomed water glasses and a handleless coffee mug, which he gives to Father Martin. The wine is poured, and they toast life.

David drains his glass and pours another. "Tell me, Father, do you know the meaning of *aroysgevorfeneh verter?*"

Father Martin shakes his head.

"That's Yiddish for 'advice given to a priest about how to play pinochle.' But that's all right. I forgive you. I understand why you overbid."

"I don't believe I overbid . . ."

"The *reason* you overbid was because you had a marriage of hearts. And who can expect a priest to know the value of a marriage? Eh?"

Father Martin sighs. David always delights in little digs at celibacy.

"Now *me!*" David gestures broadly with his sandwich. "I know the value of a marriage. My wife Hannah was Ukrainian. Take my advice, Father. Never marry a Ukrainian. *Nudzh, nudzh, nudzh!* When she was born, she complained about the midwife slapping her on the ass, and she never got out of the habit. There is an old saying about Ukrainian women. It is said that they never die. Their bodies get smaller and smaller through wind erosion until there is nothing left but a complaining voice by the side of the fireplace. Me, I know the value of a marriage. I would have bid nothing!"

LaPointe laughs. "I'd like to see the hand you wouldn't bid on."

David laughs too. "Maybe so. Maybe so. Hey, tell me, Claude. How come you never married, eh?"

Father Martin glances uneasily at LaPointe.

When Martin was a young priest on the Main, he had known LaPointe's wife. He was her confessor; he was with her when she died. And later, after the funeral, he happened upon LaPointe, standing in the empty church. It was after midnight, and the big uniformed cop stood alone in the middle of the center aisle. He was sobbing. Not from grief; from fury. God had taken from him the only thing he loved, and after only a year of marriage. More urbane men might have lost their faith in God; but not LaPointe. He was fresh from downriver, and his Trifluvian belief was too fundamental, too natural. God was a palpable being to him, the flesh-and-blood man on the cross. He still believed in God. And he hated His guts! In his agony he shouted out in the echoing church, "You son of a bitch! Rotten son of a bitch!"

Father Martin didn't dare approach the young policeman. It chilled him to realize that LaPointe wanted God to appear in the flesh so he could smash His face with his fists.

After that night, LaPointe never came to church again. And over the years that followed, the priest saw him only in passing on the Main, until they happened to come together in the card games with David and Moishe. Because LaPointe never mentioned his wife, Father Martin didn't dare to.

That was how LaPointe handled it. One great howl of sacrilegious rage; then silence and pain. He did not grieve for Lucille, because to grieve was to accept the fact of her death. There were a muddled, vertiginous few months after the funeral, then work began to absorb his energy, and the Main his ragged affection. Emotional scar tissue built up around the wound, preventing it from hurting. Preventing it, also, from healing.

"How come you never married, Claude?" David asks. "Maybe with all the *nafka* on the streets you never needed a woman of your own. Right?"

LaPointe shrugs and drinks down his wine.

"Not that there would be many working the street in this pig weather," David continues. "Have you ever seen the snow hold off so long? Have you even seen such ugly weather? Jesus Christ! Forgive me, Father, but I always swear in Catholic so if God overhears, he won't understand what I'm saying. Anyway, what's so bad about swearing? Is it a crime?"

"No," Father Martin says quietly. "It's a sin."

Moishe glances up. "Yes, Martin. I like that distinction." He presses his palms together and touches his lips with his forefingers. "I don't know how many times I have considered this difference between crime and sin. I am sure that sin is worse than crime. But I've never been able to put my finger exactly on the difference."

"Oh boy," David says, rising and looking under a shelf for the schnapps bottle. "*I* should have problems that trivial."

"For instance," Moishe continues, ignoring David, "to throw an old woman out of her apartment because she cannot pay her rent is not a crime. But surely it is a sin. On the other hand, to steal a loaf of bread from a rich baker to feed your starving family is obviously a crime. But is it a sin?"

David has returned with half a bottle of schnapps and is pouring it around into the empty wine glasses. "Let me pose the central question here," he insists. "*Who cares?*"

Father Martin flutters his fingers above his glass. "Just a little, thank you, David. Take this case, Moishe. Let us say your man with the starving family breaks into a grocery store and steals only the mushrooms, the caviar, the expensive delicacies. What do you have? Sin or crime?"

Moishe laughs. "What we have then is a priest with a subtle mind, my friend."

"Who ever heard of such a thing?" David demands. "Tell me, Claude. You're the expert on crime here. Who breaks into a grocery store and steals the mushrooms and the caviar only?"

"It happens," LaPointe says. "Not exactly that, maybe. But things like that."

"Who does it?" Moishe asks, pouring out more schnapps for himself. "And why?"

"Well . . ." LaPointe sniffs and rubs his cheek with his palm. He'd really rather be the listener, and this is a hard one to explain. "Well, let's say a man has gone hungry often. And let's say it doesn't look like things are going to change. He's hungry now, and he'll be hungry again tomorrow, or next week. That man might break into a grocery and steal the best foods to have a big gorge—even if he doesn't like the taste of mushrooms. Because . . . I can't explain . . . because it will be something to remember. You know what I mean? Like the way people who can't keep up with their debts go out and splurge for Christmas. What's the difference? They're going to be in debt all their lives. Why not have something to remember?"

Moishe nods reflectively. "I see exactly what you mean, Claude. And such a robbery is a crime." He turns to Father Martin. "But a sin?"

Father Martin frowns and looks down. He isn't sure. "Ye-e-s. Yes, I think it's a sin. It's perfectly understandable. You could sympathize with the man. But it's a sin. There is nothing remarkable about a sin being understandable, forgivable."

David is passing the bottle around again, but Martin puts his hand firmly over his glass. "No, thank you. I'm afraid it's time for me to go. I suppose the world will have to wait until next Monday for us to sort out the difference between sin and crime."

"No, wait. Wait." Moishe prevents him from rising with a gesture. He has drunk his schnapps quickly, and his eyes are shiny. "I think we should pursue this while it's on our minds. I have a way to approach the problem practically. Let's each of us say what he considers to be the greatest sin or the greatest crime."

"That's easy," David says. "The greatest crime in the world is for four *alter kockers* to talk philosophy when they could be playing cards. And the greatest sin is to bid when you have nothing in your hand but a lousy marriage."

"Come on, now. Be serious." Moishe takes up the almost empty schnapps bottle and shares it equally around, attempting to anchor his friends to the table with fresh drinks. He turns to the priest. "Martin? What in your view is the greatest sin?"

"Hm-m-m." Father Martin blinks as he considers this. "Despair, I suppose."

Moishe nods quickly. He is excited by the intellectual possibilities of the problem. "Despair. Yes. That's a good one. Clearly a sin, but no kind of crime at all. Despair. A seed sin. A sin that supports other sins. Yes. Very good."

David gulps down his drink and declares. "I'll tell you the greatest crime!"

"Are you going to be serious?" Moishe asks. "Your playing the *letz* nobody needs."

"But I am serious. Listen. The only crime is theft. Theft! Do you realize that a man spends more time in prison for grand larceny than for manslaughter? And what is murder to us but the theft of a man's life? We punish it seriously only because it's a theft that no one can make restitution for. And rape? Nothing but the theft of something a woman can use to make her living with, like prostitutes . . . and wives. It's all theft! All we really worry about is our possessions, and all our laws are devoted to protecting our property. When the thief is bold and obvious, we make a law against him and send someone like Claude here to arrest him. But when the thief is more cowardly and subtle—a landlord, maybe, or a used-car salesman—we can't make laws against him. After all, the men in Ottawa *are* the landlords and the used-car salesmen! We can't threaten them with the law, so we tell them that what they are doing is sinful. We say that God is watching and will punish them. The law is a club brandished in the fist. Religion is a club held behind the back. There! Now tell me, is that talking serious or what?"

"It's talking serious," Moishe admits. "But it's also talking shallow. However, for you it's not a bad try."

"Forget it, then!" David says, peeved. "What's the use of all this talk anyway? It helps the world *vi a toyten bankes.*"

Moishe turns to LaPointe. "Claude?"

LaPointe shakes his head. "Leave me out of this. I don't know anything about sin."

"Ah!" David says. "The man who has known no sin! Dull life."

"Well, crime then," Moishe pursues. "What's the greatest crime?"

LaPointe shrugs.

"Murder?" Father Martin suggests.

"No, not murder. Murder is seldom . . ." LaPointe searches for a word and ends up with a silly-sounding one. "Murder is seldom *criminal*. I mean . . . the murderer is not usually a criminal—not a professional. He's usually a scared kid pulling a holdup with a cheap gun. Or a drunk who comes home and finds his wife in bed with someone. Sometimes a maniac. But not often a real criminal, if you see what I mean. What about you, Moishe?" LaPointe asks, wanting to shunt the questions away from himself. "What do you think is the greatest sin?"

Moishe is feeling the effects of the schnapps. He fixes his eyes on the tabletop, and he speaks of something he very seldom mentions. "I thought a lot about crime, about sin, when I was in the camps. I saw great crimes—crimes so vast they lose all sense of human misery and can be expressed only in statistics. A man who has seen this finds it easy to shrug off a single beating outside a bar, or a theft, or one killing. The heart and the imagination, like the hands, can grow calluses, can become insensitive. That's what it means to be brutalized. They brutalized us, and by that I don't mean being beaten or tortured by brutes. No. I mean being beaten until you *become* a brute. Until, in fact, you become such an animal that you *deserve* to be beaten." Moishe looks up and sees expressions of concern and close attention in the faces of his friends. Even David does not offer a flip remark. It always happens, when they drink a little more than usual, that Moishe gets tipsy first. The priest is abstemious, and the other two have thick bodies to absorb the alcohol. He feels foolish. He smiles wanly and shrugs. The shrug says: I'm sorry; let's forget it.

But Father Martin wants to understand. "So you make the greatest sin the brutalizing of a fellow man? Is that it, Moishe?"

Moishe runs his fingers through his long, thin hair. "No, it is not that simple. Degree of sin is not based upon the act. It's more complicated than that." He is not sure he can say it neatly. Often Moishe brings the card talk around to some point he has rehearsed and rephrased again and again during his workday. But this evening it is not like that. When he speaks, he does so hesitantly, with pauses and searches for words. For once he is not sharing with his friends the results of thought; he is sharing the process.

"Yes, I suppose brutalizing could be one of the great sins. You see . . . how do I put this? . . . it isn't the *act* that determines the degree of sin. And it isn't the motive. It's the *effect*. To my mind, it is much worse to chop down the last tree in the forest than to chop down the first. I think it is much worse to kill a good husband and father than to kill a sexual maniac. In both cases the act and the motive could be identical, but the effect would be different."

"So, yes. Brutalizing a man could be a great sin, because a man who has become a brute can never love. And sins against love are the greatest sins, and deserve the greatest punishments. Theft is a crime, often a sin; but it only operates against money or goods. Murder is a crime, often a sin; but the degree of sin depends upon the value of the life, which might not be worth living, or which might have brought pain and misery to others. But love is always good. And sins against love are always the worst, because love is the only . . . the only especially *human* thing we have. So, rape is the greatest sin, greater than murder, because it is a sin against love. And I don't only mean violent rape. In fact, violent rape is perhaps the least sinful kind of rape because the perpetrator is not always responsible for his acts. But the subtler kinds of rape are great sins. The businessman who makes getting a job dependent on having sex with him, he is a rapist. The man who takes a plain girl out for dinner and an expensive evening because he knows she will feel obliged to make love with him, he is a rapist. The young man who finds a girl starving for affection and who talks of love in order to get sex, he is a rapist. All these crimes against love. And without love . . . my God, without love. . . !" Moishe looks around helplessly, knowing he is making a fool of himself. He is perfectly motionless for a moment, then he chuckles and shakes his head. "This is too ridiculous, my friends. Four old men sitting in a back room and talking of love!"

"*Three* men," David corrects, "and a priest. Come on! One last hand of cards! I feel the luck coming to me."

LaPointe fetches a cloth and wipes the table.

David deals quickly, then picks up his hand, making little sounds of appreciation as he slips each card into place. "Now, my friends, we shall see who can play pinochle!"

The bidding goes rather high, but David prevails and names trump.

He goes set by four points.

LaPointe, Moishe, and Father Martin are grouped around the door of the shop, buttoning their overcoats against the cold wet wind that moans down the almost empty street. David lives in the apartment above the shop, so did not accompany them to the door. He said good night and began clearing things away for the next day's business, all the while muttering about how nobody could win a game while schlepping a priest on his back.

As he shakes hands good night, Father Martin is shivering, and his eyes are damp with the cold. Moishe asks why he isn't wearing a scarf, and he says he lost it somewhere, making a joke of being absent-minded. He says good night again and walks up the street, bending against the wind to protect his chest. LaPointe and Moishe walk together in the other direction, the wind pushing them along. They always walk together the three blocks before Moishe's turnoff, sometimes chatting, sometimes in silence, depending upon their moods and the mood of the evening. Tonight they walk in silence because the mood of the evening has been uncommonly tense and . . . personal. It is just after eleven and, although their block is almost deserted, the action on the lower Main will be in full flow. LaPointe will make one last check, putting the street to bed before returning to his apartment. Once a beat cop . . .

Moishe chuckles to himself. "Agh, too much schnapps. I made a fool of myself, eh?"

LaPointe walks several steps before saying, "No."

"Maybe it's the weather," Moishe jokes. "This pig weather is enough to wear anyone down. You know, it's amazing how weather affects personalities. It'll be better when the snow comes."

LaPointe nods.

They cross the street and start down a block that is lit by saloon neon and animated by the sound of jukeboxes. A girl is walking on the other side of the street. She is young and unnaturally slim, her skinny legs bent as she teeters on ridiculous, fashionably thick clog soles. She wears no coat, and her short skirt reveals a parenthesis between her meager thighs. She is not more than seventeen, and very cold indeed.

"See that girl, Moishe?" LaPointe says. "Do you believe she is committing the greatest sin?"

Moishe glances at the girl as she passes a bar and looks in the window for prospects who don't seem too drunk. He turns his eyes away and shakes his head. "No, Claude. It's never the girls I blame. They are the victims. It would be like blaming the man who gets run over by a bus because, if he hadn't been there, there wouldn't have been an accident. No, I don't blame them. I feel sorry for them."

LaPointe nods. Prostitution is the least violent crime on the Main and, if it doesn't involve rolling the mark and isn't controlled by pimps protected by the heavies from the Italian Main, LaPointe habitually overlooks it. He feels particularly sorry for the whores who don't have the money to work out of apartments or hotels—the young ones fresh in from the country, broke and cold, or the old ónes who can only score drunks and who have to take it standing in a back alley, their skirts up, their asses pushed up against a cold brick wall. He feels pity for them, but disgust, too. Other crimes make him feel anger, fear, rage, helplessness; but this kind of scratch prostitution produces in him as much disgust as pity. Maybe that's what Moishe means by a sin against love.

They stop at the corner and shake hands. "See you Monday," Moishe says, turning and walking down his street.

LaPointe thrusts his hands deep into the pockets of his baggy overcoat and walks down the Main.

As he passes a deep-set doorway, a slight motion catches the tail of his eye. His hand closes down on the butt of his revolver.

"Step out here."

At first there is no movement. Then a grinning, ferret-thin face appears around the corner. "Just keeping out of the wind, Lieutenant."

LaPointe relaxes. "Got no kip tonight?" He speaks English because Dirtyshirt Red has no French.

"I'm okay, Lieutenant," the *bomme* says, reaching under his collar to adjust the thickness of newspaper stuffed beneath his shirt to keep out the cold. "I sleep here lots of times. Nobody cares. I don't bother nobody. I won't get too cold." Dirtyshirt Red grins slyly and shows LaPointe a bottle wrapped in a brown paper bag. "It's half full."

"What are you going to do when the snow comes, Red? You got something lined up?" There are seven *bommes* whom LaPointe recognizes as living on the Main and having rights based on long residence. He takes care of them on their level, just as he takes care of the prostitutes on theirs, and the shopkeepers on theirs. There used to be eight recognized tramps, but old Jacob died last year. He was found frozen to death between stacks of granite slabs behind the monument-maker's shop. He drank too much and crawled in to sleep it off. It snowed heavily that night.

"No, I don't have anything lined up, Lieutenant. But I ain't worried. Something will come along. That's one thing you can say: I've always been lucky."

LaPointe nods and walks on. He doesn't like Dirtyshirt Red, a sneak thief, bully, and liar. But the *bomme* has been on the Main for many years, and he has his rights.

It is past midnight, and the street is beginning to dim and grow quiet. Thursday is a slow night on the Main. LaPointe decides to leave St. Laurent and check out the tributary streets to the east. He passes through the darkened Carré St. Louis, with its forgotten statue of the dying Cremazie:

> *Pour Mon Drapeau*
> *Je Viens Ici Mourir*

The fountain no longer works, and on the side of the empty basin someone has written in black spray paint: LOVE. Next to that there is a peace sign, dried rivulets of paint dripping down from it, like the blood that used to drip from the swastikas in anti-Nazi posters. And under the peace sign there is: FUCK YO . . . then the spray can ran out.

That would be young Americans who have come to Montreal to avoid the Vietnam draft. They have a special flair for spray paint. LaPointe is not fond of the young, bearded boys from the States who hang around dimly lit coffee bars filled with eerie music and odd-smelling incense, brandishing their battered guitars, singing in nasal groans, cadging drinks from sympathetic college girls, or practicing their more-tragic-than-thou stares into space. Most of them live off federal dole, cutting into funds already inadequate for the needs of the poor of east Montreal.

But they will pass, and they are no real trouble, aside from the nuisance of marijuana and other kiddie shit. They bring yet another alient accent to the Main, with their hard "r's" and their odd pronunciation of "out" and "house" and "about," but LaPointe assumes he will get used to them, as he got used to all the others.

In general, his feelings toward Americans are benevolent, for no better reason than that when he went on his brief honeymoon—now thirty-one years ago—he found the thoughtfulness of road signs in French as far south as Lake George Village; while in his own country, the French signs stopped abruptly at the Ontario border.

At least these young draft avoiders are quiet. Not like the American business-men from the convention quarters of the Expo site on Ile Ste. Hélène. Those types are a real nuisance. They get drunk in their chrome-and-leatherette hotel bars, and small bands of them come up to the Main, seeking a little action, mistaking poverty for vice. They flash too much money and bargain childishly with the whores. As often as not they get rolled or punched up. Then LaPointe has to respond to complaints lodged with the Quartier Génèral, has to listen to diatribes about tourism and its value to Montreal's economy.

Always turning toward the darkest streets, LaPointe picks his way through the tangle of back lanes until he comes out again onto the Main, quiet now and nearly closed up.

As he passes the narrow alley that runs beside the Banque de Nova Scotia, he feels a slight rush of adrenalin in his stomach. Even after all these years, his nerves, quite independent of his conscious mind, take a systemic jolt whenever he passes that alley. It's become automatic, and he is used to it. It was in that alley that he got hit; it was there that he sat awaiting death, expecting it. And once a man loses his sense of immortality, he never regains it.

He had put the street to bed, like tonight; and he was on his way home. There was a tinkle of glass down the alley. A figure dropped down to the brick pavement from a window at the back of the bank. Three of them, running toward LaPointe. He fired into the air and called to them to stop. Two of them fired at once, two flashes of light, but he had no memory of the sound because a slug took him square in the chest and slammed him against the metal door of a garage. He slid down the door, sitting on one twisted foot, the other leg straight out in front of him. They fired again, and he *heard* the slug slap into the meat of his thigh. Holding his gun in both hands, he returned fire. One went down, Dead, he later learned. The other two ran.

After the shots, there was no sound in the alley, save for the sigh of wind around the corner of the garage. He sat there, slipping in and out of conscious-ness, staring at his own foot, and thinking how silly he would look when they found him, one foot under his butt, the other straight out in front of him. A long time passed. A minute, perhaps. A very long time. He opened his eyes and saw a yellow cat crossing before him. Its tail was kinked from an ancient break. It stopped and looked at him, one forepaw poised, not touching the ground. Its eyes were wary, but frigid. It tested the ground with its paw. Then it walked on, indifferent.

The wound in his chest felt cold. He put his hands over it to keep the wind out. His last conscious thought was a stupid, drunken one. Must keep the wind out. Mustn't catch cold. Catch cold at this time of year, and you don't get rid of it until spring.

He knew he was going to die. He was absolutely sure. The fact was more sad than terrifying.

He was four and a half weeks in the hospital. The leg wound was superficial, but the slug in his chest had grazed the aorta. The doctors said things about his being lucky to have the constitution of an *habitant* peasant. After leaving the hospital he had a period of recuperation, lounging around his apartment until he couldn't stand it any longer. Even though he wasn't technically back on active service yet, he began making rounds of the Main at night, putting the street to bed. Once a beat cop . . .

Soon he was back in his office, doing his regular duties. He received his third commendation for bravery and, a year later, his second Police Medal. Down at the Quartier Général, the myth of the indestructible LaPointe was even more firmly established.

Indestructible maybe, but altered. Something subtle but significant had shifted in his perception. He had accepted the fact of his death so totally, had surrendered to it with such calm, that when he did not die, he felt unfinished, open-ended, off balance.

For the first time since he had cauterized his emotions with hate after the death of his wife, he felt lonely, a loneliness expressed in a kind of melancholy gentleness toward the people of his patch, particularly toward the old, the children, the losers.

It was shortly after he was hit in the alley that he met and began to play pinochle with Moishe, David, and Martin—his friends.

Only one rectangle of dingy neon breaks the dark of Rue Lionais, a beer bar that is a hangout for loudmouths and toughs of the *quartier*. LaPointe mentally runs down a list of its usual clientele and decides to drop in. The barman greets him loudly and with a bogus grin. Knowing the loud greeting is a warning signal for the customers, LaPointe ignores the owner and looks about the dim, fuggy room. One man catches his eye, a dandy dresser with the thin, mobile face of a hustler. The dandy is sitting with a group of middle-aged toughs whose faces record a lot of cheap hooch and some battering. LaPointe stands in the arched entranceway and points at the dandy. When the man raises his eyebrows in a mask of surprise, LaPointe crooks his finger once.

As the dandy rises, one of the toughs, a penny-and-nickel arm known as Lollipop, gets to his feet as if to protect his mate. LaPointe looks at the tough, his eyes calm and infinitely bored; he shakes his head slowly. For a face-saving moment, the tough does not move. Then LaPointe points a stabbing finger toward their booth, and the tough sits down, grumbling to himself.

The dandy flashes a broad smile as he approaches LaPointe. "Good to see you, Lieutenant. Now isn't that coincidence? I was just telling—"

"Cut the shit, Scheer. I ran into the Gimp on the street."

"The Gimp?" Scheer frowns and blinks as he pretends to search his memory. "Gee, I don't think I know anybody by—"

"What day is this, Scheer?"

"Pardon me? What day?"

"I'm busy."

"It's Thursday, Lieutenant."

"Day of the month."

"Ah . . . the ninth?"

"All right, I want you to stay off the street until the ninth of next month. And I don't want to see any of your girls working."

"Now look, Lieutenant! You don't have any right! I'm not under arrest!"

LaPointe's eyes open with mock surprise. "Did I hear you say I don't have any right?"

"Well . . . what I meant was . . ."

"I'm not interested in what you meant, Scheer. LaPointe is giving you a punishment. One month off the street. And if I see you around before that, I'm going to hurt you."

"Now, just a minute—"

"Do you understand what I just said to you, asshole?" LaPointe reaches out with his broad stubby hand and pats the dandy's cheek firmly enough to make his teeth click. "Do you understand?"

The dandy's eyes shine with repressed fury. "Yes. I understand."

"How long?"

"A month."

"And who's giving you the punishment?"

Scheer's jaw muscles work before he says bitterly, "Lieutenant LaPointe."

LaPointe tilts his head toward the door. "Now, get out."

"I'll just tell the guys I'm going."

LaPointe closes his eyes and shakes his head slowly. "Out."

The dandy starts to say something, then thinks better of it and leaves the bar. LaPointe turns to follow him, but he stops and decides to visit the booth. By standing up aggressively, this Lollipop has challenged his control. That is dangerous, because if LaPointe ever lets these types build up enough courage, they could beat him to a pulp. His image must be kept high in the street because the shadow of his authority covers more ground than his actual presence can. He approaches the booth.

The three toughs pretend not to see him coming. They stare down at their bottles of ale.

"You. Lollipop," LaPointe says. "Why did you stand up when I called your friend over?"

The big man doesn't look up. He sets his mouth in determined silence.

"I think you were showing off, Lollipop," LaPointe says quietly.

The brute shrugs and looks away.

LaPointe picks up the tough's half-finished bottle of ale and pours it into his lap. "Now you sit there awhile. I wouldn't want you going out into the street like that. People would think you pissed your pants."

As LaPointe leaves the bar, he hears two of the toughs laughing while the third growls angrily.

That's just fine, LaPointe thinks. It's the kind of story that will get around.

He turns up Avenue Esplanade toward his second-floor apartment in a row of bow-windowed buildings facing Parc Mont Royal. Above the park, a luminous cross stands atop the black bulk of the Mont. The wind gusts and flaps the tails of his overcoat. His legs are heavy as he mounts the long wooden stoop of number 4240.

He closes the door of his apartment and flicks on the slack toggle switch. Two of the four bulbs are burnt out in the red-and-green imitation Tiffany lamp. He tugs off his overcoat and hangs it over the wooden umbrella stand. Then, by habit, he goes into the narrow kitchen and sets water to boil. The stove's pilot light is blocked with ancient grease and has to be lit with a match. The circle of blue flame pops on and singes his fingers, as always. He snaps his hand back and swears without passion, as usual.

While the water is heating, he goes into the bedroom and sits heavily on the bed. The only light is the upward-lancing beam of a streetlamp below his window, illuminating the ceiling and one wall but leaving the floor and the furniture in darkness. He grunts as he pulls off his shoes and wriggles his toes before stepping into his carpet slippers. He loosens his tie, pulls his shirt out from under his belt and scratches his stomach.

By now the water will be boiling, so back he goes into the unlit kitchen, his slippers slapping against his heels. His coffee-maker is an old-fashioned pressure type, with a handle to force the water through the grounds. His cup is always on the counter, its bottom always wet because he never wipes it, just rinses it out and turns it upside down on the drainboard.

Coffee cup in hand, he pads into the living room, where he settles into his overstuffed armchair by the bow window. Over the years, the springs and stuffing of the chair have shifted and bunched until it fits him perfectly. Holding the saucer under his chin in the way of workingclass men from Trois Rivières, he sips noisily. Four long sips and the cup is empty, save for the thick dregs. He believes that his routine cup of coffee before bed helps him to sleep. He sets the cup aside and turns to look out of the window. Beyond the limp curtain is the park, and above the dark hump of Mont Royal, the sky is a smudged gray-black, dim with cityglow. Within the park's iron fence, lampposts lay vague patterns of light along the footpath. The street is empty; the park is empty.

He scrubs his matted hair with the palm of his hand and sighs, comfortable and half anesthetized by the platitudes of routine that comprise his life in the apartment. Sitting slumped like this, wearing slippers, his shirt over his belly, he does not look like the tough cop who has become something of a folk hero to young French Canadian policemen because of his personal, only coincidentally legal style of handling the Main, and because of his notorious indifference to administrators, regulations, and paper work. Rather, he looks like a middle-aged man whose powerful peasant body is beginning to sag. A man who has come to prefer peace to happiness; silence to music.

He stares out the window, his mind almost empty, his face slack. He no longer really sees the apartment he and Lucille rented a week before their marriage. Since her death only a year later, he has changed nothing. The frumpy furniture in the catalogue styles of the thirties stands now where it ended up after a flurry of arrangement and rearrangement under Lucille's energetic, but vacillating, inspiration. When at last it was done and things had ended up pretty much where they began, they sat together on the bright flowered sofa, her head on his shoulder, until very late at night. They made love for the first time there on the sofa, the night before their marriage.

Of course, the apartment was to be only temporary. He would work hard and go to night school to learn English better. He would advance on the force, and they would save their money to buy a house, maybe up toward Laval, where there were other young couples from Trois Rivières.

Over the years, the gaudy flowers on the sofa had faded, more on the window end than the other, but it has happened so slowly that LaPointe has not noticed. The cushions are still plump, because no one ever sits on them.

He blinks his eyes, and presses his thumb and forefinger into the sockets. Tired. With a sigh, he pushes himself out of the deep chair and carries his cup back to the kitchen, where he rinses it out and puts it on the drainboard for morning.

Dressed only in his shorts, he shaves over the rust-stained washbasin in the small bathroom. He acquired the habit of shaving before going to bed during his year with Lucille. His thick, blue-black whiskers used to irritate her cheek. It was several months before she told him about it, and even then she made a joke of it. The fact that in the mornings he always appears at the Quartier Général with cheeks blue with eight hours of growth has given rise to another popular myth concerning the Lieutenant: LaPointe owns a magic razor; he always has a one-day growth of beard. Never two days of growth, never clean-shaven.

After scraping the whiskers off his flat cheeks, his straight razor making a dry rasping sound even with the grain, he rinses his mouth with water taken from the tap in cupped hands. He straightens up and leans, his elbows locked, on the basin, looking in the mirror. He finds himself staring at his thick chest with its heavy mat of graying hair. He can see the slight pulse of his heart under the ribs. He watches the little throb with uncertain fascination. It's in there. Right there.

That's where he's going to die. Right there.

The very efficient young Jewish doctor with a cultured voice and a tone of mechanical sincerity had told him that he was lucky, in a way.

Inoperable aneurism.

Something like a balloon, the doctor explained, and too close to the heart, too distended for surgery. It was a miracle that he had survived the bullet that had grazed the artery in the first place. He was lucky, really. That scar tissue had held up pretty well, it had given him no trouble for twelve years. Looked at that way, he was lucky.

As he sat listening to the young doctor's quiet, confident voice, LaPointe remembered the yellow cat with the kinked tail and one forepaw off the ground.

The doctor had handled many situations like this; he prided himself on being good at this sort of thing. Keep it factual, keep it upbeat. Once the doctor permits a little hole in the dike of emotion, he can end up twenty minutes—even half an hour—behind in his appointments. "In cases like this, when a man doesn't have any immediate family, I make it a habit to explain everything as clearly and truthfully as I can. To be frank, with a mature man, I don't think a doctor has the right to withhold anything that might delay the patient's attending to his personal affairs. You understand what I mean, M. Dupont?"

LaPointe had given him a false name and had said he was retired from the army, where he had received the wound in combat.

"Now, your first question, quite naturally, is what kind of time do I have? It's not possible to say, M. Dupont. You see, we doctors really don't know everything." He smiled at the admission. "It could come tomorrow. On the other hand, you could have six months. Even eight. Who knows? One thing is sure; it will happen like that." The doctor snapped his fingers softly. "No pain. No warning. Really just about the best way to go."

"Is that right?"

"Oh, yes. To be perfectly honest, M. Dupont, it's the way I would like to go, when my time comes. In that respect, you're really quite lucky."

There was a young receptionist with a fussy, cheerful manner and a modish uniform that swished when she moved. She made an appointment for the next week and gave LaPointe a printed reminder card. He never returned. What was the point?

He walked the streets, displaced. It was September, Montreal's beautiful month. Little girls chanted as they skipped rope; boys played tin-can hockey in the narrow streets, spending most of their energy arguing about who was cheating. He wanted to—expected to—feel something different, dramatic; but he did not, except that he kept getting tangled up in memories of his boyhood, memories so deep that he would look up and find that he had walked a long way without noticing it.

Evening came, and he was back on the Main. Automatically, he chatted with shopkeepers, took coffee in the cafés, reaffirmed his presence in the tougher bars. Night came, and he strolled through back streets, occasionally checking the locks on doors.

The next morning he woke, made coffee, carried down the garbage, and went to his office. Everything felt artificial; not because things were different, but because they were unchanged. He was stunned by the normalcy of it all; a little dazed by a significant absence, as a man going down a flight of stairs in the dark might be jolted by reaching the bottom when he thought there was another step to go.

And yet, he had guessed what was wrong before he went to the doctor. For a couple of months there had been that effervescence in his blood, that constriction in his upper arms and chest, those jagged little pains at the tops and bottoms of breaths.

In the middle of that first morning, there was one outburst of rage. He was pecking away at an overdue report, looking up the spelling of a word, when suddenly he ripped the page from his dictionary and threw the book against the wall. What the fucking use is a fucking dictionary! How can you look up the spelling of a fucking word when you don't know how to spell the fucking thing?

He sat behind his desk, stiff and silent, his fingers interlaced and the knuckles white with pressure. His eyes stung with the unfairness of it. But he couldn't push through to feeling sorry for himself. He could not grieve for himself. After all, he had not grieved for Lucille.

He insulated himself from his impending death by accepting it only as a fact. Not a real fact, like the coming of autumn; more like . . . the number of feet in a mile. You don't do anything about the number of feet in a mile. You don't complain about it. It's just a fact.

With great patience, he mended the torn page in his dictionary with transparent tape.

LaPointe pulls the string of the bathroom ceiling light and goes into the bedroom. The springs creak as he settles down on his back and looks up at the ceiling, glowing dimly from the streetlamp outside.

His breathing deepens and he finds himself vaguely considering the problem of worn-out water hosing. Last Sunday he spent a lazy morning sitting in his chair by the window, reading *La Presse*. There was a do-it-yourself article describing things you could make around the house with old water hosing. He has a house; a fantasy house in Laval, where he lives with Lucille and the two girls. Whenever he passes shops that have garden tools, he daydreams about working in his garden. Several years ago he put in a flagstone patio from the plans in a special section of the paper devoted to Fifteen Things You Can Do to Improve the Value of Your House. That patio figures often in his reveries just before sleep. He and Lucille are having lemonade under a sun umbrella he once saw in a hardware store window—Clearance!!! Up to ⅔ Off!!! The girls are off somewhere, and they have the house to themselves for a change. Sometimes, in his imaginings, his girls are kids, sometimes teen-agers, and sometimes already married with children of their own. During the first years after Lucille's death, the number and sex of their children shifted around, but it finally settled on two girls, three years apart. A pretty one, and a smart one. Not that the pretty one is what you would call a dummy, but . . .

He turns over in bed, ready to sleep now. The springs creak. Even when it was new, the bed had clacked and creaked. At first, the noise made Lucille tense and apprehensive. But later, she used to giggle silently at the thought of imagined neighbors listening beyond the wall, shocked at such carryings-on. . . .

Three

THE PHONE RINGS.

Half of the sound blends into the eddy of a dream; half is jagged and real, still echoing in the dark room.

The phone rings again.

He swings out of bed and gropes into the dark living room. The floor is icy. The phone ri—

"Yes! LaPointe."

"Sorry, Lieutenant." The voice is young. "I hate to wake you up, but—"

"Never mind that. What's wrong?"

"A man's been killed on your patch." The caller's French is accurate, but it has a continental accent. He is an Anglophone Canadian.

"Murdered?" LaPointe asks. Stupid question. Would they call him for an automobile accident? He still isn't fully awake.

"Yes, sir. Knifed."

"Where?"

"Little alley near the corner of Rue Lozeau and St. Dominique. That's just across from—"

"I know where it is. When?"

"Sir?"

"When did it happen?"

"I don't know. I just got here with Detective Sergeant Gaspard. We took an incoming from a patrol car. The Sergeant asked me to call you."

"All right. Ten minutes." LaPointe hangs up.

He dresses quickly, with fumbling hands. As he leaves he remembers to take the paper bag of garbage with him. He may not get back in time for the collection.

It is three-thirty, the coldest part of the night. Following the pattern of this pig weather, the overcast has lifted with the early hours of morning, taking with it the smell of city soot. The air is still and crystalline, and the exhaust from a patrol car parked halfway up the narrow alley shoots a long funnel of vapor out into the street. A revolving roof light skids shafts of red along the brick walls and over the chests and faces of the half-dozen policemen and detectives working around the corpse. Bursts of blue-white glare periodically fill the alley, freezing men in midgesture, as the forensic photographer takes shots from every angle. Two uniformed officers stand guard at the mouth of the alley, tears of cold in their eyes, their gloved fingers under their armpits for warmth.

Despite the cold and the hour, a small knot of rubbernecks has gathered at the mouth of the alley. They move about and stand on tiptoe to catch glimpses, and they talk to one another in hushed, confidential tones, instant friends by virtue of shared experience.

LaPointe crosses the street just as an ambulance pulls up. He stands for a time on the rim of the knot of onlookers, unobtrusively joining them. Some maniac killers, like some arsonists, like to blend with the crowd and experience the effects of their actions.

There is a street *bomme* in conversation with a small uncertain man whose chin is buried in a thick wrap of scarf. This latter looks out of place here, like a bank clerk, or an accountant. LaPointe lays his hands on the shoulder of the *bomme*.

"Oh, hi-ya, Lieutenant."

"What are you doing up at this end of the street, Red?"

"It got too cold in that doorway. The wind shifted. It was better walking around."

LaPointe looks into the tramp's eyes. He is not lying. "All the same, stay around. Got any *fric?*"

"None I can spend." Like most *clochards*, Dirtyshirt Red always keeps a dollar or two stashed back for really hard times.

"Here." LaPointe gives him a quarter. "Get some coffee." With a jerk of his head he indicates the all-night Roi des Frites joint across the street.

The clerk, or accountant, or pederast, moves away from the *bomme*. Anyone on talking terms with a policeman can't be perfectly trustworthy.

LaPointe looks up and down the street. The air is so cold and clear that

streetlights seem to glitter, and the corners of buildings a block away have
sharp, neat edges, like theatrical sets. Everyone's breath is vapor, twin jets when
they exhale through their noses. From somewhere there comes the homey,
yeasty smell of bread. The bakeries would be working at this hour, men stripped
to the waist in hot back rooms, sweating with the heat of ovens.

As LaPointe turns back toward the alley, it starts. A light, rather pleasant
tingle in his chest, as though his blood were carbonated. God damn it. A
rippling fatigue drains his body and loosens his knees. A constriction swells in
his chest, and little bands of pain arc across his upper arms. He leans against the
brick wall and breathes deeply and slowly, trying to appear as nonchalant as
possible. There are dark patches in his vision, and bright dots. The flashing red
light atop the police car begins to blur.

"Lieutenant LaPointe?"

The chest constrictions start to ebb, and the stabs of pain in his arms become
duller.

"Sir?"

Slowly, his body weight returns as the sense of floating deflates. He dares a
deep breath taken in little sucks to test for pain.

"Lieutenant LaPointe?"

"What, for Christ's sake!"

The young man recoils from the violence of the response. "My name's Guttmann, sir."

"That's *your* problem."

"I'm working with Detective Sergeant Gaspard."

"That's his problem."

"I was the one who telephoned you." The young officer-in-training's voice is
stiff with resentment at LaPointe's uncalled-for sarcasm. "Sergeant Gaspard is
down the alley. He asked me to keep an eye out for you."

LaPointe grunts. "Well?"

"Sir?"

LaPointe settles his heavy melancholy eyes on the OIT. "You say Gaspard is
waiting for me?"

"Yes, sir. Oh. Follow me, sir."

LaPointe shakes his head in general criticism of young policemen as he
follows Guttmann into the alley where a bare-headed photographer from the
forensic lab is packing up the last of his equipment.

"That you, LaPointe?" Gaspard asks from the dark. Like a handful of the
most senior men on the force, Gaspard *tutoyers* LaPointe, but he never uses his
first name. In fact, most of them would have to search their memories to come
up with his first name.

LaPointe lifts a hand in greeting, then drops the fist back into the pocket of
his rumpled overcoat.

The forensic photographer tells Gaspard that he is going back to the Quartier
Général with the film. He will get it into an early batch, and it will be developed
by mid-morning. He sniffs back draining sinuses and grumbles, "Colder than a
witch's *écu!*"

"*Titon,*" Gaspard corrects absent-mindedly, as he shakes hands with La-
Pointe.

"We haven't searched the body yet. We've been waiting for Flash Gordon
here to take the class pictures." Gaspard addresses the photographer. "Well? If
you're through, I'll let my men move the bundle."

The victim is a young male dressed in a trendy suit with belled trousers, a
shirt with a high rolled collar, and shoes of patent leather. He had dropped to
his knees when stabbed, then he had fallen forward. LaPointe has never seen a
corpse in that posture: on its knees, its buttocks on its heels, its face pressed into

the gravel, its arms stretched out with the palms down. It looks like a young priest serving High Mass, and showing off with excessive self-abasement.

LaPointe feels sorry for it. A corpse can look ugly, or peaceful, or tortured; but it's too bad to look silly. Unfair.

Guttmann and another detective turn the body over to examine the pockets for identification. A piece of gravel is embedded in the boy's smooth cheek. Guttmann flicks it off, but a pink triangular dent remains.

LaPointe mutters to himself, "Heart."

"What?" Gaspard asks, tapping out a cigarette.

"Must have been stabbed through the heart." Without touching each of the logical steps, LaPointe's experience told him that there were only two ways the body could have ended up in that comic posture. Either it had been stabbed in the heart and died instantly, or it had been stabbed in the stomach and had tried to cover up the cold hole. But there was no smell of excrement, and a man stabbed in the stomach almost always soils himself through sphincter convulsion. Therefore, heart.

To turn the body over, the detectives have to straighten it out first. They lift it from under its arms and pull it forward, unfolding it. When they lower it to the pavement, the young face touches the ground.

"Careful!" LaPointe says automatically.

Guttmann glances up, assuming he is being blamed for something. He already dislikes the bullying LaPointe. He doesn't have much use for the old-time image of the tough cop who uses fists and wisetalk, rather than brains and understanding. He has heard about LaPointe of the Main from admiring young French Canadian cops, and the Lieutenant is true to Guttmann's predicted stereotype.

Sergeant Gaspard pinches one of his ears to restore feeling to the lobe. "First time I've ever seen one kneeling like that. Looked like an altar boy."

For a moment, LaPointe finds it odd that they had similar images of the body's posture. But, after all, they share both age and cultural background. Neither of them is a confessing Catholic any longer, but they were brought up with a simple fundamentalist Catholicism that would define them forever, define them negatively, as a mold negatively defines a casting. They are non-Catholics, which is a very different thing from being a non-Protestant or a non-Jew.

The detectives go through the pockets routinely, one putting the findings into a clear plastic bag with a press seal, while Guttmann makes a list, tipping his note pad back awkwardly to catch the light from the street.

"That's it?" Gaspard asks as Guttmann closes his notebook and blows on his numb fingers.

"Yes, sir. Not much. No wallet. No identification. Some small change, keys, a comb—that sort of thing."

Gaspard nods and gestures to the ambulance attendants who are waiting with a wheeled stretcher. With professional adroitness and indifference, they turn the body onto the stretcher and roll it toward the back doors of the ambulance. The cart rattles over the uneven brick pavement, and one arm flops down, the dead hand palsied with the vibrations.

They will deliver it to the Forensic Medicine Department, where it will be fingerprinted and examined thoroughly, together with the clothes and articles found in the pockets. The prints will be telephotoed to Ottawa, and by morning Dr. Bouvier, the department pathologist, should have a full report, including a make on the victim's identity.

"Who found the body?" LaPointe asks Gaspard.

"Patrol car. Those two officers on guard."

"Have you talked to them?"

"No, not yet. Did you recognize the stiff?" It is generally assumed that LaPointe knows by sight everyone who lives around the Main.

"No. Never saw him before."

"Looked Portuguese."

LaPointe thrusts out his lower lip and shrugs. "Or Italian. The clothes were more Italian."

As they walk back to the mouth of the alley, the ambulance departs, squealing its tires unnecessarily. LaPointe stops before the uniformed men on guard. "Which of you found the body?"

"I did, Lieutenant LaPointe," says the nearest one quickly. He has the rectangular face of a peasant, and his accent is Chiac. It is a misfortune to speak Chiac, because there is a tradition of dour stupidity associated with the half-swallowed sound; it is a hillbilly accent used by comics to enhance tired jokes.

"Come with us," LaPointe says to the Chiac officer, and to his disappointed partner, "You can wait in the car. And turn that damned thing off." He indicates the revolving red light.

LaPointe, Gaspard, Guttmann, and the Chiac officer cross the street to the Roi des Frites. The policeman left behind is glad to get out of the cold, but he envies his partner's luck. He would give anything to take coffee with LaPointe. He could just see the faces of the guys in the locker room when he dropped casually, "Lieutenant LaPointe and I were having a coffee together, and he turns to me and says . . ." Someone would throw a towel at him and tell him he was full of shit up to his eyebrows.

Dirtyshirt Red rises when the policemen enter the bright interior of the all-night coffee place, but LaPointe motions him to sit down again. Quite automatically, he has already taken over the investigation, although Gaspard from homicide is technically in charge of it. It is an unspoken law in the department that what happens on the Main belongs to LaPointe. And who else would want it?

The four men sit at a back table, warming their palms on the thick earthenware cups. The Chiac officer is a little nervous—he wants to look good in front of Lieutenant LaPointe; even more, he doesn't want to seem a boob in relation to this Anglo tagging along with Sergeant Gaspard.

"By the way, have you met my Joan?" Gaspard asks LaPointe.

"I met him." LaPointe glances at the big-boned young man. Must be a bright lad. You only get into the OIT apprentice program if you are in the top 10 percent of your academy class, and then only after you have done a year of service and have the recommendation of your direct superior.

When LaPointe began on the force, there were almost no Anglo cops. The pay was too low; the job had too little prestige; and the French Canadians who made up the bulk of the department were not particularly kind to interlopers.

"He's not a bad type, for a Roundhead," Gaspard says, indicating his apprentice, and speaking as though he were not present. "And God knows it's not hard to teach him. There's nothing he already knows."

The Chiac officer grins, and Guttmann tries to laugh it off.

Gaspard drinks off the last of his coffee and taps on the window to get the attention of the counterman for a refill. "Robbery, eh?" he says to LaPointe.

"I suppose so. No wallet. Only change in the pockets. But . . ."

Gaspard is an old-timer too. "I know what you mean. No signs of a fight."

LaPointe nods. The victim was a big, strong-looking boy in his mid-twenties. Well built. Probably the kind who lifts weights while he looks darkly at himself in a mirror. If he had resisted the theft, there would have been signs of it. On the other hand, if he had simply handed over his wallet, why would the mugger knife him?

"Could be a nut case," Gaspard suggests.

LaPointe shrugs.

"Christ, we need that sort of thing like the Pope needs a Wassermann," Gaspard says. "Thank God there was a robbery."

The Chiac patrolman has been listening, maintaining a serious expression and making every effort to participate intelligently. That is, he has been keeping his mouth shut and nodding with each statement made by the older men. But now his cold-mottled forehead wrinkles into a frown. Why is it fortunate that there was a robbery? He lacks the experience to sense that there was something not quite right about the killing. . . . something about the position of the body that makes both LaPointe and Gaspard intuitively uncomfortable. If there had been no robbery, this might have been the start of something nasty. Like rape mutilations, motiveless stabbings are likely to erupt in patterns. You get a string of four or five before the maniac gets scared or, less often, caught. It's the kind of thing the newspapers love.

"I'll walk it around for a few days," LaPointe says. "See what Bouvier's report gives us. You don't mind if I take it on, do you?" The question is only pro forma. LaPointe feels that all crime on his patch belongs to him by right, but he is careful of the feelings of the other senior men.

"Be my guest," Gaspard says with a wave of his arm that indicates he is happy to be rid of the mess. "And if I ever get the clap, you can have that, too."

"I'll route the paper work through you, so we don't upset the Masters."

Gaspard nods. That is the way LaPointe usually works. It avoids direct run-ins with the administration. There is nothing official about LaPointe's assignment to the Main. In fact, there is no organizational rubric that covers him. The administration slices crime horizontally into categories: theft, bunco, vice, homicide. LaPointe's responsibility is a vertical one: all the crime on the Main. This assignment was never planned, never officially recognized, it just developed as a matter of chance and tradition; and there are those in authority who chafe at this rupture of the organizational chain. They consider it ridiculous that a full lieutenant spends his time crawling around the streets like a short timer. But they console themselves with the realization that LaPointe is an anachronism, a vestige of older, less efficient methods. He will be retiring before long; then they can repair the administrative breach.

LaPointe turns to the uniformed policeman. "You found the body?"

Caught off guard, and wanting to respond alertly, the Chiac cop gulps, "Yes, sir."

There is a brief silence. Then LaPointe lifts his palms and opens his eyes wide as if to say, "Well?"

The young officer glances across at Guttmann as he tugs out his notebook. The leather folder has a little loop to hold a pen. It's the kind of thing a parent or girlfriend might have given him when he graduated from the academy. He clears his throat. "We were cruising. My partner was driving slowly because I was checking license plates against the watch list of stolen cars—"

"What did you have for breakfast?" Gaspard asks.

"Pardon me, sir?" The Chiac officer's ears redden.

"Get on with it, for Christ's sake."

"Yes, sir. We passed the alley at . . . ah . . . well, let's see. I wrote the note about ten minutes later, so that would put us at the alley at two-forty or two-forty-five. I saw a movement down the alley, but we had passed it by the time I told my partner to stop. He backed up and I got a glance of a man hopping down the alley. I jumped out and started to chase him, then I came across the body."

"You gave pursuit?" LaPointe asks.

"Well . . . yes, sir. That is, after I discovered that the guy on the ground was dead, I ran to the end of the alley after the other one. But he had disappeared. The street was empty."

"Description?"

"Not much, sir. Just caught a glimpse as he hopped away. Tallish. Thin. Well, not fat. Hard to tell. He had on a big shabby overcoat, sort of like . . ." The officer quickly looks away from LaPointe's shapeless overcoat. ". . . you know. Just an old overcoat."

LaPointe seems to be concentrating on a rivulet of condensed water running down the steamy window beside him. "*Il a clopiné?*" he asks without looking at the officer. "That's twice you said the man 'hopped' off. Why do you choose that word?"

The young man shrugs. "I don't know sir. That's what he seemed to do . . . sort of hobble off. But quick, you know?"

"And he was dressed shabbily?"

"I had that impression, sir. But it was dark, you know."

LaPointe looks down at the tabletop as he taps his lips with his knuckle. Then he sniffs and sighs. "Tell me about his hat."

"His hat?" The young officer's eyebrows rise. "I don't remember any . . ." His expression seems to spread. "Yes! His hat! A big floppy hat. Dark color. I don't know how that could have slipped my mind. It was kind of like a cowboy hat, but the brim was floppy, you know?"

For the first time since they entered the Roi des Frites, Guttmann speaks up in his precise European French, the kind Canadians call "Parisian," but which is really modeled on the French of Tours. "You know who the man is, don't you, Lieutenant? The one who ran off?"

"Yes."

Gaspard yawns and rubs his legs. "Well, there it is! You see, kid? You're learning from me how to solve cases. Just talk people into committing their crimes on the Main, and turn them over to LaPointe. Nothing to it. It's all in the wrist." He speaks to LaPointe. "So it's routine after all. The guy was stabbed for his money, and you know who . . ."

But LaPointe is shaking his head. It's not that simple. "No. The man this officer saw running away is a street *bomme*. I know him. I don't think he would kill."

"How do you know that, sir?" Guttmann's young face is intense and intelligent. "What I mean is . . . anyone can kill, given the right circumstances. People who would never steal might kill."

With weary slowness, LaPointe turns his patient fatigued eyes on the Anglo.

"Ah . . ." Gaspard says, "did I mention that my Joan here had been to college?"

"No, you didn't."

"Oh, yeah! He's been through it all. Books, grades, long words, theories, raise your hand to go to the bathroom—one finger for pee-pee, two for ca-ca." Gaspard turns to Guttmann, who takes a long-suffering breath. "One thing I've always wondered, kid," Gaspard pursues. "Maybe you can tell me from all your education. How come a man grins when he's shitting a particularly hard turd? I mean, it isn't all that much fun, really."

Guttmann ignores Gaspard; he looks directly at LaPointe. "But what I said is true, isn't it? People who would never steal might kill, under the right circumstances?"

The kid's eyes are frank and vulnerable and they shine with suppressed embarrassment and anger. After a second, LaPointe answers, "Yes. That's true."

Gaspard grunts as he stands and stretches his settled spine. "Okay, it's your package, LaPointe. Me, I'm going home. I'll collect the reports in the morning and send them over to you." Then Gaspard gets an idea. "Hey! Want to do me a favor? How about taking my Joan here for a few days? Give him a chance to see how you do your dirty work. What do you say?"

The Chiac officer's mouth opens. These goddamned Roundheads get all the luck.

LaPointe frowns. They never assign Joans to him, just as they never give him committee work. They know better.

"Come on," Gaspard persists. "He can sort of be liaison between my shop and yours. Take him off my back for a few days. He cramps my style. How can I pick up a quick piece of ass with him hanging around all the time, taking notes?"

LaPointe shrugs. "All right. For a couple of days."

"Great," Gaspard says. As he buttons his overcoat up to the neck, he looks out the window. "Look at this goddamned weather, will you! It's already socking in again. By dawn the clouds will be back. Have you ever seen the snow hold off so long? And every night it gets cold as a witch's tit."

LaPointe's mind is elsewhere. He corrects Gaspard thoughtlessly. "*Écu.* Cold as a witch's *écu.*"

"You're sure it's not tit?"

"*Écu.*"

Gaspard looks down at Guttmann. "You see, kid? You're going to learn a lot with LaPointe. Okay, men, I'm off. Keep crime off the streets and in the home, where it belongs."

The Chiac officer follows Gaspard out into the windy night. They get into the patrol car and drive off, leaving the street totally empty.

"Thanks, Lieutenant," Guttmann says. "I hope you don't feel railroaded into taking me on."

But LaPointe has already crooked his finger at Dirtyshirt Red, who shuffles over to the table. "Sit down, Red." LaPointe shifts to English because it's Red's only language, the language of success. "Have you seen the Vet tonight?"

Dirtyshirt Red makes a face. Over the years he has fostered a fine hatred for his fellow *bomme,* with all his blowing off about being a war hero, and always bragging about his great kip—a snug sleeping place he has hidden away somewhere. A comforting idea strikes Dirtyshirt Red.

"Is he in trouble, Lieutenant? He's a badass, believe you me. I wouldn't put nothin' past him! What's he done, Lieutenant?"

LaPointe settles his melancholy eyes on the *bomme.*

"Okay," Red says quickly. "Sorry. Yeah, I seen him. Down Chez Pete's Place, maybe 'bout six, seven o'clock."

"And you haven't seen him since?"

"No. I left to go down to the Greek bakery and get some toppins promised me. I didn't want that potlickin' son of a bitch hanging around trying to horn in. He's harder to shake than a snot off a fingernail."

"Listen, Red. I want to talk to the Vet. You ask around. He could be holed up somewhere because he probably got a lot of drinking money tonight."

The thought of his fellow tramp coming into a bit of luck infuriates Dirtyshirt Red. "That wino son of a bitch, the potlickin' splat of birdshit! *Morviat!* Fartbubble! Him and his snug pad off somewheres! I wouldn't put nothin' past him. . . ."

Dirtyshirt Red continues his flow of bile, but it is lost on LaPointe, who is staring out the window where beads of condensation make double rubies of the taillights of predawn traffic. Trucks, mostly. Vegetables coming into market. He feels disconnected from events; a kind of generalized déjà vu. It's all happened before. Some different kid, killed in some different way, found in some different place; and LaPointe sorting it out in some other café, looking out some other window at some other predawn street. It really doesn't matter very much anymore. He's tired.

Without seeming to, Guttmann has been examining LaPointe's reflection in the window. He has, of course, heard tales about the Lieutenant, his control over the Main, his dry indifference to authorities within the department and to political influences without, improbable myths concerning his courage. Guttmann is intelligent enough to have discounted two-thirds of these epic fables as the confections of French officers seeking an ethnic hero against the Anglophonic authorities.

Physically, LaPointe satisfies Guttmann's preconceptions: the wide face with its deep-set eyes that is practically a map of French Canada; the mat of graying hair that appears to have been combed with the fingers; and of course the famous rumpled overcoat. But there are aspects that Guttmann had not anticipated, things that contradict his caricature of the tough cop. There is a quality that might be called "distance"; a tendency to stay on the outer rim of things, withdrawn and almost daydreaming. Then too, there is something disturbing in LaPointe's patient composure, in the softness of his husky voice, in the crinkling around his eyes that makes him seem . . . the only word that Guttmann can come up with is "paternal." He recalls that the young French policemen sometimes refer to him as "Papa LaPointe," not that anyone dares to call him that within his hearing.

". . . and that potlickin' cockroach—that gnat—tells everybody what a hero he was in the war! That pimple on a whore's ass—that wart—tells everybody what a nice private kip he's got! That son of a bitch gnat-wart tells—"

With the lift of a hand, LaPointe cuts short Dirtyshirt Red's flow of hate, just as he is getting up steam. "That's enough. You ask around for the Vet. If you locate him, call down to the QG. You know the number." With a tip of his head, LaPointe dismisses the *bomme*, who shuffles to the door and out into the night.

Guttmann leans forward. "This Vet is the man with the floppy hat?"

LaPointe frowns at the young policeman, as though he has just become aware of his presence. "Why don't you go home?"

"Sir?"

"There's nothing more we can do tonight. Go home and get some sleep. I'll see you at my office tomorrow."

Guttmann reacts to the Lieutenant's cool tone. "Listen, Lieutenant. I know that Gaspard sort of dumped me on you. If you'd rather not . . ." He shrugs.

"I'll see you tomorrow."

Guttmann looks down at the Formica tabletop. He sucks a slow breath between his teeth. Being with LaPointe isn't going to be much fun. "All right, sir. I'll be there at eight."

LaPointe yawns and scrubs his matted hair with his palm. "You're going to have a hell of a wait. I'm tired. I won't be in until ten or eleven."

After Guttmann leaves, LaPointe sits looking through the window with unfocused eyes. He feels too tired and heavy to push himself up and trudge back to the cold apartment. But . . . he can't sit here all night. He rises with a grunt.

Because the streets are otherwise empty, LaPointe notices a couple standing on a corner. They are embracing, and the man has enclosed her in his overcoat. They press together and sway. It's four-thirty in the morning and cold, and their only shelter is his overcoat. LaPointe glances away, unwilling to intrude on their privacy.

When he turns the corner of Avenue Esplanade, the wind flexes his collar. Litter and dust swirl in miniature whirlwinds beside iron-railed basement wells. LaPointe's body needs oxygen; each breath has the quality of a sigh.

A slight movement in the park catches his eye. A shadow on one of the benches at the twilight rim of a lamplight pool. Someone sitting there. At the foot of his long wooden stoop, he turns and looks again. The person has not moved. It is a woman, or a child. The shadow is so thin it doesn't seem that she is wearing a coat. LaPointe climbs a step or two, then he turns back, crosses the street, and enters the park through a creaking iron gate.

Though she should be able to hear the gravel crunching under his approaching feet, the young girl does not move. She sits with her knees up, her heels against her buttocks, arms wrapped around her legs, face pressed into her long paisley granny gown. Beside her, placed so as to block some of the wind, is a shopping bag with loop handles. It is not until LaPointe's shadow almost touches her that she looks up, startled. Her face is thin and pale, and her left eye is pinched into a squint by a bruise, the bluish stain of which spreads to her cheekbone.

"Are you all right?" he asks in English. The granny gown makes him assume she is Anglo; he associates the new, the modern, the trendy with the Anglo culture.

She does not answer. Her expression is a mixture of defiance and helplessness.

"Where do you live?" he asks.

Her chin still on her knees, she looks at him with steady, untrusting eyes. Her jaw takes on a hard line because she is clenching her teeth to keep them from chattering. Then she squints at him appraisingly. "You want to take me home with you?" she asks in Joual French, her voice flat; perhaps with fatigue, perhaps with indifference.

"No. I want to know where you live." He doesn't mean to sound hard and professional, but he is tired, and her direct, dispassionate proposition took him unawares.

"It's none of your business.'

Her sass is a little irritating, but she's right; it's no business of his. Kids like this drift onto the Main every day. Flotsam. Losers. They're no business of his, until they get into trouble. After all, he can't take care of them all. He shrugs and turns away.

"Hey?"

He turns back.

"Well? Are you doing to take me home with you, or not?" There is nothing coquettish in her tone. She is broke and has no place to sleep but she does have an *écu*. It's a matter of barter.

LaPointe sighs and scratches his hairline. She appears to be in her early twenties, younger than LaPointe's daydream children. It's late and he's tired, and this girl is nothing to him. A skinny kid with a gamine face spoiled by that silly-looking black eye, and anything but attractive in the oversized man's cardigan that is her only protection against the wind. The backs of her hands are mottled with cold and purple in the fluorescent streetlight.

Not attractive, probably dumb; a loser. But what if she turned up as a rape statistic in the Morning Report?

"All right," he says. "Come on." Even as he says it, he regrets it. The last thing he needs is a scruffy kid cluttering up his apartment.

She makes a movement as though to rise, then she looks at him sideways. He is an old man to her, and she knows all about men. "I don't do anything . . . special," she warns him matter-of-factly.

He feels a sudden flash of anger. She's younger than his daughters, for Christ's sake! "Are you coming?" he asks impatiently.

There is only a brief pause before she shrugs with protective indifference, rises, and takes up her shopping bag. They walk side by side toward the gate. At first he thinks she is stiff with the cold and with sitting all huddled up. Then he realizes that she has a limp; one leg is shorter than the other, and the shopping bag scrapes against her knee as she walks.

He opens his apartment door and reaches around to turn on the red-and-green overhead lamp, then he steps aside and she precedes him into the small living room. Because the putty has rotted out of the big bow windows, they rattle in the wind, and the apartment is colder than the hallway.

As soon as he closes the door, he feels awkward. The room seems cramped, too small for two people. Without taking off his overcoat, he bends down and lights the gas in the fireplace. He squats there, holding down the lever until the limp blue flames begin to make the porcelain nipples glow orange.

Oddly, she is more at ease than he. She crosses to the window and looks down at the park bench where she was sitting a few minutes ago. She rubs her upper arms, but she prefers not to join him near the fire. She doesn't want to seem to need anything that's his.

With a grunt, LaPointe stands up from the gas fire. "There. It'll be warm soon. You want some coffee?"

She turns down the corners of her mouth and shrugs.

"Does that mean you want coffee, or not?"

"It means I don't give a shit one way or the other. If you want to give me coffee, I'll drink it. If not . . ." Again she shrugs and squeaks a little air through tight lips.

He can't help smiling to himself. She thinks she's so goddamned tough. And that shrug of hers is so downriver.

The French Canadian's vocabulary of shrugs is infinite in nuance and paraverbal articulation. He can shrug by lifting his shoulders, or by depressing them. He shrugs by glancing aside, or by squinting. By turning over his hands, or simply lifting his thumbs. By sliding his lower lip forward, or by tucking down the corners of his mouth. By closing his eyes, or by spreading his face. By splaying his fingers; by pushing his tongue against his teeth; by tightening his neck muscles; by raising one eyebrow, or both; by widening his eyes; by cocking his head. And by all combinations and permutations of these. Each shrug means a different thing; each combination means more than two different things at the same time. But in all the shrugs, his fundamental attitude toward the role of fate and the feebleness of Man is revealed.

LaPointe smiles at her tough little shrug, a smile of recognition. While he is in the kitchen putting the kettle on, she moves over to the mantel, pretending to be interested in the photographs arranged in standing frames. In this way she can soak up warmth from the gas fire without appearing to need or want it. As soon as he returns, she steps away as nonchalantly as possible.

"Who's that?" she asks, indicating the photographs.

"My wife."

Her swollen eye almost closes as she squints at him in disbelief. The woman in the photos must be twenty-five or thirty years younger than this guy. And you only have to look around this dump to know no woman lives here. But if he wants to pretend he has a wife, it's no skin off her ass.

He realizes the room is still cold, and he feels awkward to be wearing a big warm overcoat while she has nothing but that oversized cardigan. He tugs off the coat and drops it over a chair. It occurs to him to give her his bathrobe, so he goes into the bedroom to find it, then he steps into the bathroom and starts running hot water in the deep tub with its claw feet. He notices how messy the bathroom is. He is swishing dried whiskers out of the basin when he realizes that the coffee water must have dripped through by now, so he starts back, forgetting the robe and having to go back for it.

Christ, it's complicated having a guest in your house! Who needs it?

"Here," he says grumpily. "Put this on." She regards the old wool robe with caution, then she shrugs and slips it on. Enveloped in it, she looks even smaller and thinner than before, and clownlike, with that frizzy dustmop of a hairstyle that the kids wear these days. A clown with a black eye. A child-whore with a street vocabulary in which *foutre* and *fourrer* do most of the work of *faire,* and with everything she owns in a shopping bag.

LaPointe is in the kitchen, pouring out the coffee and adding a little water from the kettle because it is strong and she is only a kid, when he hears her laugh. It's a vigorous laugh, lasting only six or eight notes, then stopping abruptly, still on the ascent, like the cry of a gamebird hit on the rise.

When he steps into the living room, carrying her cup, she is standing before the mirror that hangs on the back of the door; her face is neutral and bland; there is no trace of the laugh in her eyes. He asks, "What is it? What's wrong? Is it the robe?"

"No." She accepts the coffee. "It's my eye. It's the first time I've seen it."

"You find it funny, your eye?"

"Why not?" She brings her cup over to the sofa and sits, her short leg tucked up under her buttock. She has a habit of sitting that way. She finds it comfortable. It has nothing to do with her limp. Not really.

He sits in his overstuffed chair opposite as she sips the hot coffee, looking into the cup as a child does. That laugh of hers, so total and so brief, has made him feel more comfortable with her. Most girls would have expressed horror or self-pity to see their faces marred. "Who hit you?" he asks.

She shrugs and blows a puff of air in a typically Canadian gesture of indifference. "A man."

"Why?"

"He promised me I could spend the night, but afterward he changed his mind."

"And you raised hell?"

"Sure. Wouldn't you?"

He leans his head back and smiles. "It's a little hard to imagine being in the situation."

She stops in mid-sip and sets the cup down, looking at him levelly. "What the hell's that supposed to mean?"

"Nothing."

"Why'd you say it then?"

"Forget it. You're from out of town, aren't you?"

She is suddenly wary. "How'd you know that?"

"You have a downriver accent. I was born in Trois Rivières myself."

"So?" She picks up her cup again and sips, watching him closely, wondering if he's trying to get something for nothing with all this friendly talk.

He makes a sudden movement forward, remembering the bath he is running. Her cup rattles as she jerks back and lifts an arm to protect herself.

Then he realizes the tub won't be half full yet. Water runs slowly through the old pipes. He sits back in his chair. "I didn't mean to startle you."

"You didn't startle me! I'm not afraid of you!" She is angry to have cowered so automatically after her swaggering talk.

Is this the same kid who just now was laughing at herself in the mirror? *Pauvre gamine.* Tough; sassy; vulnerable; scared. "I thought the tub might be overflowing. That's why I jumped up. I'm drawing a bath for you."

"I don't want any goddamned bath!"

"It will warm you up."

"I'm not even sure I want to stay here."

"Then finish your coffee and go."

"I don't even want your fucking coffee!" She stares at him, her narrow chin jutting out in defiance. Nobody bosses her around.

He closes his eyes and sighs deeply. "Go on. Take your bath," he says quietly.

In fact, the thought of a deep hot bath . . . All right. She would take a bath. To spite him.

Steam billows out when she opens the bathroom door. The water is so hot that she has to get in bit by bit, dipping her butt tentatively before daring to lower herself down. Her arms seem to float in the water above her small breasts. The heat makes her sleepy.

When she comes back into the living room, dressed only in his robe, he is sitting in the armchair, his chin down and his eyes closed. Heat from the gas burner has built up in the room, and she feels heavy and very drowsy. Might as well get it over with and get some sleep.

"Are you ready?" she asks. "If you're not, I can help you." She lets the front of the robe hang open. That ought to get him started.

He blinks away the deep daydream about his daughters and the Laval house, and turns to look at her. She's so thin that there are hollows in her pelvis. The black tangle of hair at the *écu* has a wiry look. One knee is slightly bent to keep the weight on both feet. The breasts are so small that there is a flat of chestbone between them.

"Cover yourself up," he says. "You'll catch cold."

"Now just a minute," she says warily. "I told you in the park that I don't do anything special—"

"I know!"

She takes his anger as proof that he had hoped for some kind of old man's perversion.

He stands up. "Look, I'm tired. I'm going to bed. You sleep here." While she was in the bath, he had made up the sofa, taking one of the pillows from his bed and pulling down two Hudson Bay blankets from the shelf in the closet. They smelled a little of dust, but there is nothing as warm as a Hudson Bay. There is no sheet. He owns only four, and he hasn't picked up his laundry yet this week. He thought of giving her his, but they are not clean. Nothing in the apartment is prepared for visitors. Since Lucille's death, there have never been any.

She slowly closes the robe. So he really hadn't meant for them to sleep together at all. Maybe it's the leg. Maybe he doesn't like the thought of screwing a cripple. She's met others like that. Well, to hell with him. She doesn't care.

While he is rinsing out the cup and emptying the coffee-maker in the kitchen, she makes herself comfortable on the sofa and pulls the heavy blankets over her. Only when the delicious weight is pressing on her does she realize how tired she is. It almost hurts her bones to relax.

On his way to the bedroom, he turns off the gas. "You don't need it while you're sleeping. It's bad for the lungs."

Who the hell does he think he is? Her father?

When he turns off the overhead light, the windows that seemed black become gray with the first damp light of dawn. He pauses at the bedroom door. "What's your name, by the way?"

Sleepiness already rising in the dry wick of her fatigue, she mutters, "Marie-Louise."

"Well . . . good night then, Marie-Louise."

She hums, half annoyed by the fact that he keeps talking. It doesn't occur to her to ask his name.

Four

EVEN BEFORE HE opens his eyes, he knows it is late. Something in the quality of the sounds out in the street is wrong for getting-up time. He sits on the edge of his bed and groggily reaches for his bathrobe. It is not there. Only then does he remember the girl sleeping in his robe out in the living room.

He tiptoes through on his way to the kitchen, fully dressed, although he usually takes his coffee before dressing. He doesn't want her to see him padding around in his underwear.

She lies on her side, curled up, the blankets so high that only her mop of frizzed hair is visible. From the line of her body beneath the blankets, he can tell that her hands are between her legs, the palms touching the sides of her thighs. He remembers sleeping like that when he was a kid.

His cup is on the drainboard, where it always is, but he has to rummage about in the cupboard to find another. He puts too little water in the kettle, underestimating the amount needed for two cups, but he decides not bo boil more because the coffee already made will get cold. Pouring from one cup to another to make equal shares doesn't work out well, and he loses about a quarter of a cup. He grumbles *"Merde"* with each accident or miscalculation. It's really a nuisance having someone living with you. Staying with you, that is.

Because the cups are only half full, he has no difficulty balancing them as he carries them into the living room.

She is still asleep as he places the cups carefully on the table by the window. The worn springs of his chair clack; he grimaces and settles down more slowly. Maybe he shouldn't wake her; she is sleeping so peacefully. But what's the point of making coffee for two if you don't give it to her? But, no. It's best to let the poor kid sleep.

"Coffee?" he asks, his voice husky.

She doesn't move.

All right. Let her sleep, then.

"Coffee?" he asks louder.

She half hums, half groans, and her head turns under the blankets.

Poor kid's worn out. Let her sleep.

"Marie-Louise?"

A hand slips out and tugs the blanket from her cheek. Her eyelids flutter, then open. She blinks twice and frowns as she tries to remember the room. How did she get here?

"Your coffee will get cold," he explains.

She looks at him blearily, not recognizing him at first. "What?" she asks, her voice squeaky. "Oh . . . you." She presses her eyes shut before opening them again. The puffiness of her black eye has gone down, and the purplish stain has faded toward green.

"Your coffee's ready. But if you'd rather sleep, go ahead."

"What?"

"I said . . . you can go back to sleep, if you want."

She frowns dazedly. She can't believe he woke her up to tell her that. She puts her hand over her eyes to shade them from the cold light as she recollects, then turns and looks at him, wondering what he is up to. He didn't want it last night, so he's probably after a little now.

But he's just sitting there, sipping his coffee.

When she sits up, she notices that her robe is open to the nipples; she tugs it back around her. She accepts the cup he hands her and looks into it bleakly. "Do you have any milk?"

"No. Sorry."

She sips the thick dark brew. "How about sugar?"

"No. I don't keep sugar in the house. I don't use it, and it attracts ants."

She shrugs and drinks it anyway. At least it's hot.

They don't talk, and instead of looking at one another, they both look out the window at the park across the street. A woman is pushing a pram along the path while a spoiled child dangles from her free hand, twisting and whining. She gives it a good shake and a splat on the bottom that seems to improve its humor.

Marie-Louise can see the bench where he found her. It's going to be cold and damp again today, and she won't be able to make a score until dark, if then. Maybe he would let her stay. No, probably not. He'd be afraid she might steal something. Still, it's worth a try.

"You feel better this morning?" she asks.

"Better?"

"If you don't have to rush off, we could . . ." Palm up, her hand saws the air between them horizontally in an eloquent Joual gesture.

"Don't worry about it," he says.

"It won't cost you. Just let me stay until dark." She produces a childish imitation of a sexy leer that is something between the comic and the grotesque, with that black eye of hers. "I would be good to you." When he does not respond, another thought occurs to her. "I'm all right," she promises. "I mean . . . I'm healthy."

He looks at her calmly for several seconds. Then he rises. "I have to go to work. Would you like more coffee?"

"No. No, thank you."

"Don't you like coffee?"

"Not really. Not without milk and sugar."

"I'm sorry."

She lifts her shoulders. "It's not your fault."

He pulls out his wallet. "Look . . ." He doesn't know exactly how to say this. After all, it doesn't matter to him one way or the other if she stays or goes. "Look, there's a store around the corner. You can buy things for your breakfast. The . . . the stove works." What a stupid thing to say. Of course the stove works.

She reaches up and takes the offered ten-dollar bill. This must mean she can stay until night.

He takes up his overcoat. "Okay. Good, then." He goes to the door. "Oh, yes. You'll need a key to get back in after your shopping. There's one on the mantel." It occurs to him that it must seem stupid to leave the extra key on the mantel, because you would have to be in the apartment to get it. And if you're already in the apartment . . . But Lucille had always left it there, and he never misplaced his own key, so . . .

As he is leaving, she asks, "May I use your things?"

"My things?"

"Towel. Deodorant. Razor."

Razor? Oh, of course. He has forgotten that women shave under their arms. "Certainly. No, wait a minute, I use a straight razor."

"What's that?"

"You know . . . just a . . . straight razor."

"And you don't want me using it?"

"I don't think you can. Why don't you buy yourself a razor? There's enough money there." He closes the door behind him and gets halfway down the stairs before something occurs to him.

"Marie-Louise?" He has opened the door again.

She looks up. She has been pawing through her shopping bag of clothes, planning to take this chance to wash out a few things and dry them in front of the gas heater before he comes back. She acts as though she's been caught at something. "Yes?"

"The stove. The pilot light doesn't work. You have to use a match."

"Okay."

He nods. "Good."

When he arrives at the Quartier Général, the workday is in full swing. The halls outside the magistrates' courts are crowded with people standing around or waiting on benches of dark wood, worn light in places by the legs and buttocks of the bored, or the nervous. One harassed woman has three children with her, separated in age by only the minimal gestation period. She hasn't made up that day; perhaps she has given up making up. The youngest of her kids clings to her skirt and whimpers. Her tension suddenly cracking, she screams at it to shut up. For an instant the child freezes, its eyes round. Then its face crumples and it howls. The mother hugs and rocks it, sorry for both of them. Two young men lounge against a window frame, their slouching postures meant to convey that they are not impressed by this building, these courts, this law. But each time the door to the courtroom opens, they glance over with expectation and fear. There are a few whores, victims of a street sweep somewhere. One is telling a story animatedly; another is scratching under her bra with her thumb. A girl in her late teens, advanced pregnancy dominating her skinny body, chews nervously on a strand of hair. An old man rocks back and forth in misery, rubbing his palms against the tops of his legs. It's his last son; his last boy. Youngish lawyers in flowing, dusty black robes and starched dollars crossed at the throat, their smooth foreheads puckered into self-important frowns, stalk through the crowd with long strides calculated to give the impression that they are on important business and have no time to waste.

LaPointe scans automatically for faces he might recognize, then steps into one of the big, rickety elevators. Two young detectives mumble greetings; he nods and grunts. He gets out on the second floor and goes down the gray corridor, past old radiators that thud and hiss with steam, past identical doors with ripple-glass windows. His key doesn't seem to work in his lock. He mutters angrily, then the door opens in his hand. It wasn't locked in the first place.

"Good morning, sir."

Oh, shit, yes. Gaspard's Joan. LaPointe has forgotten all about him. What was his name? Guttmann? LaPointe notices that Guttmann has already moved in and made himself at home at a little table and a straight-backed chair in the corner. He hums a kind of greeting as he hangs his overcoat on the wooden coat tree. He sits heavily in his swivel chair and begins to paw around through his in-box.

"Sir?"

"Hm-m."

"Sergeant Gaspard's report is on your desk, along with the report he forwarded from the forensic lab."

"Have you read it?"

"No, sir. It's addressed to you."

LaPointe is following his habit of scanning the Morning Report first thing in his office. "Read it," he says without looking up.

It seems strange to Guttmann that the Lieutenant seems uninterested in the report. He opens the heavy brown interdepartmental envelope, unwinding the string around the plastic button fastener. "You'll have to initial for receipt, sir."

"*You* initial it."

"But, sir—"

"Initial it!" This initialing of routing envelopes is just another bit of the bureaucratic trash that trammels the ever-reorganizing department. LaPointe makes it a practice to ignore all such rules.

What's this? A blue memo card from the Commissioner's office. Look at this formal crap:

FROM: Commissioner Resnais
TO: Claude LaPointe, Lieutenant
SUBJECT: Morning of 21 November: appointment for
MESSAGE: I'd like to see you when you get in.

Resnais
(dictated, but not signed)

LaPointe knows what Resnais wants. It will be about the Dieudonné case. That weaselly little turd of a lawyer is threatening to lodge a 217 assault charge against LaPointe for slapping his client. We must protect the civil rights of the criminal! Oh, yes! And what about the old woman that Dieudonné shot through the throat? What about her, with her last breaths whistling and flapping moistly through the hole?

LaPointe pushes the memo card aside with a growl.

Guttmann glances up from the report on the kid they found in the alley. "Sir? Something wrong?"

"Just read the report." He must be tired this morning. Even this kid's careful continental French annoys him. And he seems to take up so goddamned much room in the office! LaPointe hadn't noticed last night how big the kid was. Six-two, six-three; weighs about 210. And his attempt to fit himself into as little space as possible behind that small table makes him seem even bigger and bulkier. This isn't going to work out. He'll have to turn him back over to Gaspard as soon as possible.

LaPointe shoves the routine papers and memos away and rises to look out his office window toward the Hôtel de Ville. There are scaffolds clinging to the sides of the Victorian hulk, and above the scaffolds the sandblasters have cleaned to a creamy white a façade that used to bear the comfortable patina of soot with water-run accents of dark gray. For months now, they have been sandblasting the building, and the roaring hiss has become a constant in LaPointe's office, replacing the rumble of traffic as a base line for silence. It is not the noise that bothers LaPointe, it is the change. He liked the Hôtel de Ville the way it was, with its stained and experienced exterior. They change everything. The law, rules of evidence, acceptable procedure in dealing with suspects. The world is getting more complicated. And younger. And all these new forms! This endless paper work that he has to peck out with two fingers, hunched over his ancient typewriter, growling and smashing at the keys when he makes an error . . .

. . . It's strange to think of her using his Mum. Putting his Mum under her arms. He supposes young girls don't use Mum. They probably prefer those fancy sprays. He shrugs. Well, that's just too bad. Mum is all he has. And if it's not good enough for her . . .

"No identification," Guttmann says, mostly to himself.

"What?"

"The forensic lab report, sir. No identification of that man in the alley. And no make on the fingerprints."

"They checked with Ottawa?"

"Yes, sir."

"Hm-m." The victim looked like the type who ought to have a record, if not for petty arrests, at least as an alien. No fingerprints. One possibility immediately occurs to LaPointe. The victim might have been an unregistered alien, one of those who slip into the country illegally. They are not uncommon on the Main; most of them are harmless enough, victims of the circular paradox of having no legal nationality, and therefore no passports and no means of legitimate immigration, therefore, no legal nationality. Several of the Jews who have been on the street for years are in this category, particularly those who came from camps in Europe just after the war. They cause no trouble; anyway, LaPointe knows about them, and that's what counts.

"What else is in the report?"

"Not much, sir. A technical description of the wound . . . angle of entry and that sort of thing. They're running down the clothing."

"I see."

"So what do we do now?"

"We?" LaPointe looks at the daunting pile of back work, of forms and memos and reports on his desk. "Tell me, Guttmann. When you were in college, did you learn to type?"

Guttmann is silent for fully five seconds before saying, "Ah . . . yes, sir?" The rising note says it all. "You know, sir," he adds quickly, "Sergeant Gaspard had me filling out reports for him when I was assigned as his Joan. It struck me that was a sort of perversion of the intention of the apprentice program."

"A *what?*"

"A perversion of the . . . That was one of the reasons I was glad when he let me work with you."

"It was?"

"Yes, sir."

"I see. Well, in that case, you start working on this junk on my desk. Whatever requires a signature, sign. Sign my name if you have to."

Guttmann's face is glum. "What about Commissioner Resnais?" he asks, glad to have a little something to pique back with. "There was a memo about him wanting to see you."

"I'll be down in Forensic Medicine, talking to Bouvier, if anyone calls."

"And what should I tell the Commissioner's office, if they call?"

"Tell them I'm perverting your intentions . . . that was it, wasn't it?"

As LaPointe steps out of the elevator on the basement level, he is met by a medley of odors that always brings the same incongruous image to his mind: a plaster statue of the Virgin, her bright blue eyes slightly strabismic through the fault of the artist, and a small chip out of her cheek. With this mental image always comes a leaden sensation in his arms and shoulders. The stale smells of the Forensic Medicine Department are linked to this odd sensation of weight in his arms by a long organic chain of association that he has never attempted to follow.

The odor in these halls is an olio of chemicals, floor wax, paint cooking on hot radiators, dusty air, the sum of which is very like the smells of St. Joseph's

Home, where he was sent after the pneumonia took his mother. (In Trois Rivières, it wasn't pneumonia; it was *the* pneumonia. And it didn't kill one's mother; it *took* her.)

The smells of St. Joseph's: floor wax, hot radiators, wet hair, wet wool, brown soap, dust, and the acrid smell of ink, dried and caked on the sides of the inkwell.

Inkwell. The splayed nib scrapes over the paper. You have to write it a hundred times, perfectly, without a blemish. That will teach you to daydream. Your mind slips away from the exercise for a second, and the point of the nib digs into the cheap paper on the upstroke. A splatter of ink makes you have to start all over again. It's a good thing for you that Brother Benedict didn't find the *moue* on you. You'd get something worse than a hundred lines for that. You'd get a *tranche*.

Moue. You make *moue* by pressing bread into a small tin box and moistening it with a little water and spit. In a day or two, it begins to taste sweet. It is the standard confection of the boys at St. Joseph's, and is munched surreptitiously during classes, or is traded for favors, or gambled in games of "fingers" in the dormitory after lights out, or given to the big boys to keep from being toughed up. Because the bread is stolen from the dinner line, *moue* is illegal in St. Joseph's, and if you're found with it on you, you get a *tranche*. You can pick up *tranches* for other sins too. For talking in line, for not knowing your lessons, for fighting, for sassing. If you haven't worked off all your *tranches* by the end of the week, you don't eat on Sunday.

A *tranche* is a fifteen-minute slice of time spent in the small chapel the boys call the Glory Hole, where you kneel before the plaster Mary, your arms held straight out in cruciform, under the supervision of old Brother Jean who seems to have no other duties than to sit in the second row of the Glory Hole and record the boys' punishments. You kneel there, arms straight out. And for five minutes it's easy. By the end of the first fifteen minutes, your arms are like lead, your hands feel huge, and the muscles of your shoulders are trembling with effort. Maybe you shouldn't try for your second *tranche*. Anything less than a full fifteen-minute slice doesn't count at all. You can do as much as fourteen minutes before your arms collapse, and it's as though you hadn't even tried. Oh, to hell with it! Go for a second one. Get the goddamned thing over with. Halfway through the second *tranche* you know you're not going to make it. You squeeze your eyes shut and grit your teeth. Everyone says that Brother Jean cheats, makes the second slice longer than the first. You ball up your fists and fight against the numbness in your shoulders. But inevitably the arms sag. "Up. Up," says Brother Jean gently. With a sneer of pain, you pull your arms back up. You take deep breaths. You try to think of something other than the pain. You stare at the face of the plaster Virgin, so calm, so pure, with her slightly crossed eyes and her goddamned stupid chipped cheek! The hands fall, clapping to the sides of the legs, and you grunt with the sudden change in the timbre of the pain. Brother Jean's voice is flat and soft. "LaPointe. One *tranche.*"

Every time he steps off the elevator into the basement and breathes these particular odors, LaPointe's arms feel heavy, for no reason he can think of.

For a second, he attributes the sensation to his heart, his aneurism. He awaits the rest of it—the bubbles in his blood, the constriction, the exploding lights behind the eyes. When these do not come, he smiles at himself and shakes his head.

The door to Dr. Bouvier's office is open, and he is talking to one of his assistants while he examines a list on a clipboard, holding the board close to his right eye, huge behind a thick lens. His left eye is hidden behind a lens the color of nicotine. It must be an ugly eye, for he takes pains to prevent anyone from seeing it. He tells his assistant to make sure something is done by this afternoon, and the young man leaves. Bouvier scratches his scalp with the back of his pencil, then cocks his head toward the door. "Who's that?" he demands.

"LaPointe."

"Ah! Come in. For God's sake, don't hover. How about some coffee?"

LaPointe sits in a scrofulous old leather chair beneath one of the high wire-screened windows that let a ghost of daylight into the basement rooms. Bouvier feels along the ledge behind him until he touches a cup. He puts his finger down into it and, finding it wet, deduces it is his. He feels for another, finds it, and brings it close to his right eye to be sure he has not butted cigarettes in it. His minimal standards of sanitation satisfied, he fills the cup and thrusts it in LaPointe's direction.

In his own way, Bouvier is as much an epic figure in the folklore of the department as LaPointe. He is famous, of course, for his coffee. Imaginations strain in efforts to account for the taste and testure of this ghastly brew. He is famous also for his desk, which is piled with letters, forms, memos, requisitions, and files to a height that is an offense to the law of gravity. Bouvier also possesses, both in legend and in fact, a remarkable memory for minute details of past cases, a memory that has developed proportionally as he descended toward blindness. By means of this memory, he is sometimes able to reveal a linking *modus operandi* between what appear to be unrelated events or cases. His "interesting little insights" have occasionally led to solutions, or to the discrediting of facile solutions already in hand. But these "interesting little insights" are not always welcome, because they sometimes reopen files everyone would rather leave closed.

Like LaPointe, Bouvier is a bachelor, and he puts in a prodigious amount of time down in the bowels of the QG, where his duties have spread far beyond those normally assigned to a staff pathologist. His authority has expended into each vacuum created by a departing man or a new reorganization, until, by his own admission, his domain is so wide that the department would collapse two days after he left.

Not that he's ever likely to leave. From medical school he went directly into the army, where he served through the Second World War. When he got out, money was tight and he took a temporary job with the police until he could set up in practice. Time passed, and his eyesight began to fail. He stayed on with the department because, as he used to say himself, a patient's confidence might be eroded a bit if, as a brain surgeon, Bouvier had to begin by saying: "Now, sir, if you would please direct my hands toward your head."

He sits in the straight-backed kitchen chair behind his heaped-up desk, sniffing as he pushes up the glasses that continually slip down his stubby nose. He broke them a few years ago, and they are patched at the bridge with dirty adhesive tape. He intends to get new ones one of these days. "Well?" he asks, as LaPointe presses his refilled cup into his hand, "I assume you're here on behalf of that kid who got reamed on your patch. Anything special about the case?"

LaPointe shrugs. "I doubt it."

"Good. Because I don't think you will close this one. If you took the time to read my report, writen in crisp but lucid professional language, you would know that there were no fingerprints on record with Ottawa. And we all appreciate the heavy significance of that."

Bouvier reveals his bitterness at ending up a police pathologist by his sarcasm and cynicism, and by a style of speech that mixes swatches of erudition with vulgarity and gallows humor. To this he adds a jerky, non sequitur conversational tactic that dazzles many and impresses some.

LaPointe long ago learned to handle the technique by simply waiting until Bouvier got around to the point.

"Can you tell me anything that is not in the report?" LaPointe asks.

"A great deal, of course. I could tell you things ranging through aesthetics, to thermodynamics, to conflicting theories concerning the functions of Stonehenge; but I suspect your interests are more restricted than that. Informational tunnel vision: an occupational hazard. All right, how about this? Your young man used hair spray, if that's any help."

"None at all. Is the press release out?"

"No, I've still got it here in my out-box." Bouvier waves vaguely toward the heaped tabletop. By departmental practice, information concerning murder, suicide, or rape cases is not released to the newspapers until Bouvier has finished his examination and the next of kin are informed. "You want me to hold it?"

"Yes. For a couple of days." When pressure from newspapers or family allows, LaPointe likes to start his inquiries before the press release is out. He prefers to make the first mention of the crime, to watch for qualities of surprise or anticipation.

"I could probably block it up here forever," Bouvier says. "I doubt that anyone will be around inquiring after this one. Except maybe a woman claiming breach of promise, or a pregnancy suit, or both. He made love shortly before his death."

"How do you know that?"

Bouvier sips his coffee, makes a face, and cocks his nicotine lens at the cup. "This is terrible. I think something's fallen into the pot. I'll have to empty it one of these days and take a look. On second thought, maybe I don't want to know. Say, I hear you've broken down and taken on a Joan."

Three-quarters blind and never out of his den in the bowels of the building, Dr. Bouvier knows everything that is going on in the Quartier Général. He makes a point of letting people know that he knows.

"Gaspard sent his Joan over to me for a few days."

"Hm-m. I can't help feeling sorry for the kid. He's an interesting boy, too. Have you read his file?"

"No. But I suppose you have."

"Of course. Did very well in college. Excellent grades. The offer of a scholarship to do graduate study in social work, but he chose instead to enter the force. Another instance of a strange demographic pattern I have observed. Year by year, the force is attracting a better class of young men. On the other hand, what with kids bungling their way through amateur holdups to get a fix, crime is attracting a lower class than it once did. It was simpler in our day, when the men on both sides were of the same sociological, intellectual, and ethical molds. But what you *really* wanted to know was how I divined that the young man in the alley made love shortly before he was killed. Simple really. He failed to wash up afterwards, in direct contradiction to the sound paternal advice given in army VD films. I wonder if they ever consider how carefully they're going to be examined after they get themselves gutted, or in some other way manage to shuffle their mortal coils off to Buffalo. I remember my mother always telling me to wear clean shorts, in case I got hit by a truck. For much of my youth I entertained the belief that clean shorts were a totemic protection against trucks— in much the same way that apples keep doctors away. When I think of the daring and dangerous things I used to do in the middle of heavy traffic to amuse my friends, all in the belief that I was invulnerable because I had just changed my shorts! So tell me, what are the gods up to these days? Is our anointed Commissioner Resnais still driving toward a brilliant future in politics, as he drives the rest of us toward dreams of regicide?"

"Every day they dream up a new form, a new bit of paper work. We've got paper work coming out of our ears."

"Hm! Have you talked to your doctor about that? I just read in a medical journal about a man who drank molten iron and pissed out telephone wire. Something of an exhibitionist, I suspect. Even more to the point, we haven't finished checking out your stiff's clothing. The analysis of dust and lint and crap in pockets and cuffs isn't quite done. I'll contact you if anything comes up. Matter of fact, I'll give the case a bit of thought. Might even come up with one of my 'interesting little insights.' "

"Don't do me any favors."

"Wouldn't dream of it. And to prove that, how about another cup of coffee?"

Guttmann is typing out an overdue report when LaPointe enters. He has taken the liberty of going through the Lieutenant's desk and clearing out every forgotten or overlooked report and memo he could find. He tried to organize them into some kind of sequence at first, but now he is taking them in random order and bungling through as best he can.

LaPointe sits at his desk and surveys the expanse of unlittered surface. "Now, that looks better," he says.

Guttmann looks over the piles of paper work on his little table. "Did you find out anything from Dr. Bouvier, sir?"

"Only that you're supposed to be a remarkable young man."

"Remarkable in what way, sir?"

"I don't remember."

"I see. Oh, by the way, the Commissioner's office called again. They're pretty upset about your not coming right up when you got in."

"Hm-m. Any call from Dirtyshirt Red?"

"Sir?"

"That *bomme* you met last night. The one who's looking for the Vet."

"No, sir. No call."

"I don't imagine the Vet will be out on the streets before dark anyway. He has drinking money. What time it it?"

"Just after one, sir."

"Have you had lunch?"

"No, sir. I've been doing paper work."

"Oh? Well, let's go have lunch."

"Sir? Do you realize that some of these reports are six months overdue?"

"What does that have to do with getting lunch?"

"Ah . . . nothing?"

They sit by the window of a small restaurant across Bonsecours Street from the Quartier Général, finishing their coffee. The decor is a little frilly for its police clientele, and Guttmann looks particularly out of place, his considerable bulk threatening his spindly-legged chair.

"Sir?" Guttmann says out of a long silence. "There's something I've been wondering about. Why do the older men on the force call us apprentices 'Joans'?"

"Oh, that comes from long ago, when most of the force was French. They weren't called 'Joans' really. They were called *'jaunes.'* Over the years it got pronounced in English."

"Jaunes? Yellows? Why yellows?"

"Because the apprentices are always kids, still wet behind the ears . . ."

Guttmann's expression says he still doesn't get it.

". . . and yellow is the color of baby shit," LaPointe explains.

Guttmann's face is blank.

LaPointe shrugs. "I suppose it doesn't really make much sense."

"No, sir. Not much. Just more of the wiseass ragging the junior men have to put up with."

"That bothers you, eh?"

"Sure. I mean . . . this isn't the army. We don't have to break a man's spirit to get him to conform."

"If you don't like the force, why don't you get out? Use that college education of yours."

Guttmann looks quickly at the Lieutenant. "That's another thing, sir. I guess I'm supposed to be sorry that I got a little education. But I'm afraid I just can't cut it." His ears are tingling with resentment.

LaPointe rubs his stubbly cheek with the palm of his hand. "You don't have to cut it, son. Just so long as you can type. Come on, finish your coffee and let's go."

Leaving Guttmann waiting on the sidewalk, LaPointe returns to the restaurant and places a call from the booth at the back. Five times . . . six . . . seven . . . the phone rings, unanswered. He shrugs philosophically and sets the receiver back into its cradle. But just as he hangs up, he thinks he hears an answering click on the other end. He dials again quickly. This time the phone is answered on the first ring.

"Yes?"

"Hello. It's me. Claude."

"Yes?" She does not place the name.

"LaPointe. The man who owns the apartment."

"Oh. Yeah." She has nothing more to say.

"Is everything all right?"

"All right?"

"I mean . . . did you buy enough for breakfast and lunch?"

"Yes."

"Good."

There is silence.

She volunteers, "Did you call just now?"

"Yes."

"I was in the bathroom. It stopped ringing just when I answered."

"Yes, I know."

"Oh. Well . . . why did you call?"

"I just wanted to know if you found everything you need."

"Like what?"

"Like . . . did you buy a razor?"

"Yes."

"That's good."

A short silence.

Then he says, "I won't be back until eight or nine tonight."

"And you want me out by then?"

"No. I mean, it's up to you. It doesn't matter."

A short silence.

"Well? Should I go or stay?"

A longer silence.

"I'll bring some groceries back with me. We can make supper there, if you want."

"Can you cook?" she asks.

"Yes. Can't you?"

"No. I can do eggs and mince and things like that."

"Well, then, I'll do the cooking."

"Okay."

"It'll be late. Can you hold out that long?"

"What do you mean?"

"You won't get too hungry?"

"No."

"Well then. I'll see you tonight."

"Okay."

LaPointe hangs up, feeling foolish. Why call when you have nothing to say? That's stupid. He wonders what he'll buy for supper.

The dumb twit can't even cook.

The secretary's skirt is so short that modesty makes her back up to file cabinets and squat to extract papers from the lower drawers.

LaPointe sits in a modern imitation-leather divan so deep and soft that it is difficult to rise from it. On a low coffee table are arranged a fine political balance of backdated *Punch* and *Paris Match* magazines, together with the latest issue of *Canada Now.* The walls of the Commissioner's reception room are adorned with paintings that have the crude draftsmanship and flat perspective of fashionable Hudson Bay Indian primitive; and there is a saccharine portrait of an Indian girl with pigtails and melting brown comic-sad eyes too large for her face, after the style of an American husband-and-wife team of kitsch painters. The size of the eyes, their sadness, and the Oriental upturn of the corners make it look as though the girl's mother plaited her braids too tightly.

Along with the popular Indian trash on the walls, there are several framed posters, examples of the newly established Public Relations Department. One shows a uniformed policeman and a middle-aged civilian male standing side by side, looking down at a happy child. The slogan reads: *Crime Is Everybody's Business.* LaPointe wonders what crime the men are contemplating.

The leggy secretary squats again, her back to the file cabinet, to replace a folder. Her tight skirt makes her lose her balance for a second, and her knees separate, revealing her panties.

LaPointe nods to himself. That's smart; to avoid showing your ass, you flash your crotch.

The door behind the secretary's desk opens and Commissioner Resnais appears, hand already out, broad smile in place. He makes it a habit to greet senior men personally. He brought that back with him from a seminar in the States on personnel management tactics.

Make the men who work FOR you think they work WITH you.

"Claude, good to see you. Come on in." Just the opposite of Sergeant Gaspard, Resnais uses LaPointe's first name, but does not *tutoyer* him. The Commissioner's alert black eyes reveal a tension that belies his facile camaraderie.

Resnais' office is spacious, its furniture relentlessly modern. There is a thick carpet, and two of the walls are lined with books—and not only lawbooks. There are titles dealing with social issues, psychology, the history of Canada, problems of modern youth, communications, and the arts and crafts of Hudson Bay Indians. No civilian visitor could avoid being impressed by the implication of social concern and modern attitudes toward the causes and prevention of crime. No ordinary cop, this Commissioner. A liberal intellectual working in the trenches of quotidian law enforcement.

Nor is it easy to dismiss Resnais as a bogus political man. He has in fact read each of the books in his office. He in fact does his best to understand and respond to modern community needs. He does in fact see himself as a liberal; as a policeman by vocation, and a politician by necessity. Resnais is not the man to attract devotion and affection from those under him, but the majority of the force respect him, and many of the younger men admire him.

Like LaPointe, Resnais began by patrolling a beat. Then he went to night school; perfected his English; married into one of the reigning Anglo families of Montreal; took leaves of absence, without pay, to finish his college education; made a career of delicate cases involving people and events that required protection from the light of newspaper exposure. Finally, he became the first career policeman to occupy the traditionally civilian post of commissioner. For this reason, he thinks of himself as a cop's cop. Few of the older men on the force share his view. True, he has been on the force for thirty years, but he was never a cop in the rough-and-tumble sense. He never shook information out of a pimp he despised. He never drank coffee at two in the morning out of a cracked mug, sleeplessness irritating his eyes, his overcoat stinking of wet wool. He never had to use the cover of a car door when returning fire.

LaPointe notices his personnel file on Resnais' desk, otherwise bare save for a neat stack of pale blue memo cards, an open note pad, and two perfectly sharpened pencils.

Men who look busy are often only disorganized.

Resnais stations himself in front of the floor-to-ceiling window, the glare of the overcast skies making it difficult to look in his direction without squinting.

"Well, how have you been, Claude?"

LaPointe smiles at the accent. Resnais is really trilingual. He speaks continental French; perfect English, although with the growled "r" of the Francophone who has finally located that difficult consonant; and he can revert to a Joual as twangy as the next man's when he is addressing a group from east Montreal, or speaking to senior French Canadian officers.

"I think I'll make it through the winter, Commissioner." LaPointe never uses his first name.

Resnais laughs. "I'm sure you will! Tough old son of a bitch like you? I'm sure you will!" There is something phony and condescending in his use of profanity, just like one of the guys. He clasps his hands behind his back and rocks up on his toes, a habit born of being rather short for a policeman. His body is thick, but he keeps in perfect trim by jogging with neighbors, swimming with members of his exclusive athletic club, and playing handball in the police league, for which he signs up just like any other cop, and where he accepts defeat at the hands of younger officers with laughing good grace. His expensive suits are closely cut, and he could pass for ten years younger than he is, despite the gleaming pate with its wreath of coal-black hair. Suntanning under lamps has given him a slightly purplish gleam. "Still living in the old place on Esplanade?" he asks offhandedly.

"Yes. Just like it says in my dossier," LaPointe responds.

Resnais laughs heartily. "I can't get away with anything with you, can I?" It is true that he makes a practice of looking over a man's file just before seeing him, for the purpose of refreshing himself on an intimate detail or two—number of children and their sexes, the wife's name, awards or medals. He drops these bits of information casually, as though he knows each man personally and holds in his memory details of his life. He once read somewhere that this was a trick used by a popular American general in the Second World War, and he adopted it as a good management tactic.

An employee gives of his TIME, a buddy gives of HIMSELF.

Unfortunately, there wasn't much in LaPointe's life to comment upon. No children, a wife long since dead, citations for merit and bravery all earned years ago. You're scraping the bottom of the barrel when you have to mention the street a man lives on.

"I don't want to waste too much of your time, Commissioner," LaPointe says, "So, if there's something . . ." He raises his eyebrows.

Resnais does not like that. He prefers to control the timing and flow of conversation when it involves delicate personnel problems like this one. To do so is an axiom of Small Group and One-to-One Communication Technique.

If you're not IN control, you're UNDER control.

"I was expecting you this morning, Claude."

"I was on a case."

"I see." The Commissioner again rocks onto his toes and squeezes his hands behind his back. Then he sits down in his high-backed desk chair and turns it so that he is looking not at LaPointe, but past him, out of the window. "Frankly, I'm afraid I have to give you what in the old days was called an ass-chewing."

"We still call it that."

"Right. Now look, Claude, we're both old-timers . . ."

LaPointe shrugs.

". . . and I don't feel I have to pull any punches with you. I've been forced to talk to you about your methods before. Now, I'm not saying they're inefficient. I know that sometimes going by the book means losing an arrest. But things have changed since we were young. Greater emphasis is placed today upon the protection of the individual than upon the protection of the society." There seem to be invisible quotation marks around this last sentence. "I'm not calling these changes good, and I'm not calling them bad. They are facts of life. And facts of life that you continue to ignore."

"You're talking about the Dieudonné case?"

Resnais frowns. He doesn't like being rushed. "That's the case in point right now. But I'm talking about more than this one instance. This isn't the first time you've gotten information by force. And it's not the first time I've told you that this is not the way things happen in my department." He instantly regrets having called it *his* department. Make every man feel a part of the organization. *He works best who works for himself.*

"I don't think you know the details of the case, Commissioner."

"I assure you that I know the case. I've had every bit of it rammed down my throat by the public prosecutor!"

"The old woman was shot for seven dollars and some change! Not even enough for the punk to get a fix!"

"That's not the point!" Resnais' jaw tightens, and he continues with exaggerated control. "The point is this. You got information against Dieudonné by means of force and threat of force."

"I knew he did it. But I couldn't prove it without a confession."

"How did you know he did it?"

"The word was out."

"What, *exactly,* does that mean?"

"It means the word was out. It means that he's a bragging son of a bitch who spills his guts when he takes on a load of shit."

"You're telling me he admitted to others that he killed the old woman . . . whatshername?"

"No. He bragged about having a gun and not being afraid to use it."

"That's hardly admission of murder."

"No, but I *know* Dieudonné. I've known him since he was a wiseassed kid. I know what he's capable of."

"Believe it or not, your intuition does not constitute evidence."

"The slugs from his gun matched up, didn't they?"

"The slugs matched up, all right. But how did you get the gun in the first place?"

"He told me where he had buried it."

"*After* you beat him up."

"I slapped him twice."

"*And* threatened to lock him up in a room and let him suffer a cold-turkey withdrawal! Christ, you didn't even have any hard evidence to connect him with the old woman . . . whatshername!"

"Her *name,* goddamn it, was Mrs. Czopec! She was seventy-two years old! She lived in the basement of a building that doesn't have plumbing. There's a bit of sooty dirt in front of that building, and in spring she used to get free seed packets on boxes of food, and plant them and water them, and sometimes a few came up. But her basement window was so low that she couldn't see them. She and her husband were the first Czechs on my patch. He died four years ago, but he wasn't a citizen, so she didn't have much in benefits coming in. She clung to her purse when that asshole junkie tried to snatch it because the seven dollars was all the money she had to last to the end of the month. When I checked out her apartment, it turned out that she lived on rice. And there was evidence that toward the end of the month, she ate paper. Paper, Commissioner."

"That's not the point!"

LaPointe jumps up from his chair. "You're right! That's not the point. The point is that she had a right to live out her miserable life, planting her stupid flowers, eating her rice, spending half of every day in church where she couldn't afford to light a candle! *That's* the point! And that hophead son of a bitch shot her through the throat! *That's the point!*"

Resnais lifts a denying palm. "Look, I'm not defending him, Claude. . . ."

"Oh? You mean you aren't going to tell me that he was underprivileged? Maybe his father never took him to a hockey game!"

Resnais is off balance. What's wrong with LaPointe? It isn't like him to get excited. He's supposed to be the big professional, so coldblooded. Resnais expected chilly insubordination, but this passion is . . . unfair. To regain control of the situation, Resnais speaks flatly. "Dieudonné is getting off."

LaPointe is stopped cold. He can't believe it. "What?"

"That's right. The public prosecutor met with his lawyers yesterday. They threatened to slap you with a two-seventeen assault, and the newspapers would love that! I have my—I have the department to think of, Claude."

LaPointe sits down. "So you made a deal?"

"I don't like that term. We did the best we could. The lawyers could probably have gotten the case thrown out, considering how you found the gun. Fortunately for us, they are responsible men who don't want to see Dieudonné out on the street any more than we do."

"What kind of deal?"

"The best we could get. Diedonné pleads guilty to manslaughter; they forget the two-seventeen against you. There it is."

"Manslaughter?"

"There it is." Resnais sits back in his high-backed desk chair and gives this time to sink in. "You see, Claude, even if I condoned your methods—and I don't—the bottom line is this: they don't work anymore. The charges don't stick."

LaPointe is lost and angry. "But there was no other way to get him. There was no hard evidence without the gun."

"You keep missing the point."

LaPointe stares straight ahead, his eyes unfocused. "You'd better get word to Dieudonné that if he ever sets foot on the Main after he gets out . . ."

"For Christ's sake! Don't you ever listen? Does a truck have to drive over you? You've embarrassed . . . the department long enough! I've worked like a son of a bitch to give this shop a good image in the city, and all it takes. . . ! Look, Claude. I don't like doing this, but I'd better lay it on the line for you. I know the reputation you have among the guys in the shop. You keep your patch cool, and I know that no other man, probably no team of men, could do what you do. But times have changed. And you haven't changed with them." Resnais fingers LaPointe's personnel file. "Three recognitions for merit. Twice awarded the Police Medal. Twice wounded in the line of duty—once very seriously, as I recall. When we heard about that bullet grazing your heart, we kept an open line to the hospital all night long. Did you know that?"

LaPointe is no longer looking at the Commissioner; his eyes are directed out the window. He speaks quietly. "Get on with it, Commissioner."

"All right. I'll get on with it. This is the last time you embarrass this shop. If it happens one more time . . . if I have to go to bat for you one more time . . ." There is no need to finish the sentence.

LaPointe draws his gaze back to the Commissioner's face. He sighs and rises. "Is that all you wanted to talk to me about?"

Resnais looks down at LaPointe's file, his jaw tight. "Yes. That's all."

The slam of the office door rattles the glass, and LaPointe brushes past Guttmann without a word. He sits heavily in his desk chair and stares vacantly at the Forensic Medicine report on that kid found in the alley. Instinct for self-preservation warns Guttmann to keep his head down over his typing and not say a word. For half an hour, the only sound in the room is the tapping of the typewriter and the hiss of the sandblasting across the street.

Then LaPointe takes a deep breath and rubs his mat of hair with his palm. "Did I get a call from Dirtyshirt Red?"

"No, sir. No calls at all."

"Hm-m." LaPointe rises and comes to Guttmann's little table, looking over his shoulder. "How's it going?"

"Oh, it's going fine, sir. It's lots of fun. I'd rather type out reports than anything I can think of."

LaPointe turns away, grunting his disgust for all paper work and all who bother with it. Outside the window, the city is already growing dark under the heavy layers of staionary cloud. He tugs down his overcoat from the wooden rack.

"I'm going up onto the Main. See what's happening."

Guttmann nods, not lifting his eyes from the form he is retyping, for fear of losing his place again.

"Well?"

The younger man puts his finger on his place and looks up. "Well what, sir?"

"Are you coming or not?"

A minute later, the door is locked, the lights off, and the unfinished report is still wound into the machine.

Five

BY THE TIME they cross Sherbrooke, the last greenish light is draining from sallow cloud layers over the city. Streetlights are already on, and the sidewalks are beginning to clog with pedestrians. A raw wind has come up, puffing in vagrant gusts around corners and carrying dust that is gritty between the teeth. The cold makes tears stand in Guttmann's eyes, and the skin of his face feels tight, but it doesn't seem to penetrate the Lieutenant's shaggy overcoat hanging to his mid-calves. Guttmann would like to pace along more quickly to heat up the blood, but LaPointe's step is measured, and his eyes scan the street from side to side, automatically searching out little evidences of trouble.

As they pass a shop, LaPointe takes his hand from his pocket and lifts it in greeting. A bald little man with a green eyeshade waves back.

Guttmann looks up at the sign overhead:

S. KLEIN—BUTTONHOLES

"Buttonholes?" Guttmann asks. "This guy makes buttonholes? What kind of business is that?"

LaPointe repeats one of the street's ancient jokes. "It would be a wonderful business, if Mr. Klein didn't have to provide the material."

Guttmann doesn't quite get it. He has no way of knowing that no one on the Main quite gets that joke either, but they always repeat it because it has the *sound* of something witty.

Each time they pass a bar, the smell of stale beer and cigarette smoke greets them for a second before it is blown away by the raw wind. Halfway up St. Laurent, LaPointe turns in at a run-down bar called Chez Pete's Place. It is fuggy and dark inside, and the proprietor doesn't bother to look up from the girlie magazine in his lap when the policemen enter.

Three men sit around a table in back, one a tall, boney tramp with a concave chest who has the shakes so badly that he is drinking his wine from a beer mug. The other two are arguing drunkenly across the table, pounding it sometimes, to the confused distress of the third.

"Floyd Patterson wasn't shit! He never . . . he couldn't . . . he wasn't shit, compared to Joe Louis."

"Ah, that's your story! Floyd Patterson had a great left. He had what you call one of your world's great lefts! He could hit . . . anything."

"Aw, he couldn't . . . he couldn't punch his way out of a wet paper bag! I used to know a guy who told me that he wasn't shit, compared to Joe Louis. You know . . . do you know what they used to call Joe Louis?"

"I don't care what they called him! I don't give a big rat's ass!"

"They used to call Joe Louis . . . Gentleman Joe. Gentleman Joe! What do you think of that?"

"Why?"

"What?"

"Why did they call him Gentleman Joe?"

"Why? Why? Because . . . because that Floyd Patterson couldn't punch worth shit, that's why. Ask anybody!"

LaPointe crosses to the group. "Has anyone seen Dirtyshirt Red today?"

They look at one another, each hoping the question is directed to someone else.

"You," LaPointe says to a little man with a narrow forehead and a large, stubbly Adam's apple.

"No, Lieutenant. I ain't seen him."

"He was in a couple hours ago," the other volunteers. "He asked around about the Vet." The name of this universally detested tramp brings grunts from several *bommes* at other tables. No one has any stomach for the Vet, with his uppity ways and his bragging.

"And what did he find out?"

"Not much, Lieutenant. We told him the Vet come in here late last night."

"How late?"

The proprietor lifts his head from the skin magazine and listens.

"Well?" LaPointe asks. "Was it after closing time?"

One of the tramps glances toward the owner. He doesn't want to get in trouble with the only bar that will let *bommes* come in. But nothing is as bad as getting in trouble with Lieutenant LaPointe. "Maybe a *little* after."

"Did he have money?"

"Yeah. He had a wad! His pension check must of come. He bought two bottles."

"Two bottles," another sneers. "And you know what that cheap bastard does? He gives one bottle to all of us to share, and he drinks the other all by hisself!"

"Potlickin' son of a bitch," says another without heat.

LaPointe crosses to the bar and speaks to the owner. "Did he seem to have money?"

"I don't sell on the cuff."

"Did he flash a roll?"

"He wasn't *that* drunk. Why? What did he do?"

LaPointe looks at the owner for a second. There is something disgusting about making your money off *bommes*. He reaches into his pocket and takes out some change. "Here. Give them a bottle."

The proprietor counts the change with his index finger. "Hey, this ain't enough."

"It's our treat. Yours and mine. We're going fifty-fifty."

The arrangement does not please the owner, but he reaches under the bar and grudgingly gets out a bottle of muscatel. By the time it touches the counter, one of the *bommes* has come over and picked it up.

"Hey, thanks, Lieutenant. I'll tell Red you're lookin' for him."

"He knows."

They have been wandering for an hour and a half, threading through the narrow streets that branch out from the Main, LaPointe stopping occasionally to go into a bar or café, or to exchange a word with someone on the street. Guttmann is beginning to think the Lieutenant has forgotten about the Vet and that young man stabbed in the alley last night. In fact, LaPointe is still on the lookout for Dirtyshirt Red and the Vet, but not to the exclusion of the rest of his duties. He never pursues only one thing at a time on his street, because if he did, all the other strings would get tangled, and he wouldn't know what everyone was up to, or hoping for, or worried about.

At this moment, LaPointe is talking with a fat woman with frizzy, bright orange hair. She leans out of a first-story window, her knobby elbows planted on the stone sill over which she has been shaking a dust mop in fine indifference to passers-by. From the tenor of their conversation, Guttmann takes it that she used to work the streets, and that she and LaPointe have a habit of exchanging bantering greetings on the basis of broad sexual baiting and suggestions on both sides that if they weren't so busy, they would each show the other what real lovemaking is. The woman seems well informed on events on the Main. No, she hasn't heard anything of the Vet, but she'll keep her ears open. As for Dirtyshirt Red, yes, that sniping bastard's been around, also looking for the Vet.

Guttmann can't believe she ever made a living selling herself. Her face is like an aged boxer's, a swollen, pulpy look that is more accented than masked by thick rouge, a lipstick mouth larger than her real one, and long false eyelashes, one of which has come unstuck at the corner. As they walk on, he asks LaPointe about her.

"Her pimp did that to her face with a Coke bottle," LaPointe says.

"What happened to him?"

"He got beat up and warned to stay off the Main."

"Who beat him up?"

LaPointe shrugs.

"So what did she do after that?"

"Continued to work the street for a couple of years, until she got fat."

"Looking like that?"

"She was still young. She had a good-looking body. She worked drunks mostly. Hooch and hard-ons blind a man. She's a good sort. She does cleaning and scrubbing up for people. She takes care of Martin's house."

"Martin?"

"Father Martin. Local priest."

"*She* is the priest's housekeeper?"

"She's a hard worker."

Guttmann shakes his head. "If you say so."

Back on St. Laurent, they are slowed by the last of the pedestrian tangle. Snakes of European children with bookbags on their backs chase one another to the discomfort of the crowd. Small knots of sober-faced Chinese kids walk quickly and without chatting. Workingmen in coveralls stand outside their shops, taking last deep drags from cigarettes before flicking them into the gutter and going back to put in their time. Young, loud-voiced girls from the dress factory walk three abreast, singing and enjoying making the crowd break for them. Old women waddle along, string bags of groceries banging against their ankles. Clerks and tailors, their fragile bodies padded by thick overcoats, thread diffidently through the crowd, attempting to avoid contact. Traffic snarls; voices accuse and complain. Neon, noise, loneliness.

"Now that is something," Guttmann says, looking up at a sign above a shop featuring women's clothes:

NORTH AMERICAN DISCOUNT SAMPLE DRESS COMPANY

The business is new, and it is located where a pizzeria used to be. The owners are greenhorns newly arrived on the Main. Older, established merchants refer to the shop as "the shmatteria."

"Shmatteria?" asks Guttmann.

"Yes. It's sort of a joke. You know . . . a pizzeria that sells *shmattes?*"

"I don't get it."

LaPointe frowns. That's the second time this kid hasn't gotten a street joke. You have to have affection for the street to get its jokes. "I thought you were Jewish," he says grumpily.

"Not in any real way. My grandfather was Jewish, but my father is a one-hundred-percent New World Canadian, complete with big handshake and a symbolic suntan he gets patched up twice a year in Florida. But what's this about . . . how do you say it?"

"Shmatteria. Forget it."

LaPointe does not remember that twenty-five years ago, when the now-established Jews first came to the Main, he did not know what a *shmatte* was either.

They climb up a dark flight of stairs with loose metal strips originally meant to provide grips for snow-caked shoes, but now a hazard in themselves. They enter one of the second-floor lounges that overlook St. Laurent. It is still early for trade, and the place is almost empty. An old woman mumbles to herself as she desultorily swings a mop into a dark corner by the jukebox. The only other people in the place are the bartender and one customer, a heavily rouged woman in white silk slacks.

LaPointe orders an Armagnac and sips it, looking down upon the street, where one-way northbound traffic is still heavy and the pedestrian flow is clogged. He has got off the street for a few minutes to give this most congested time of evening a change to thin out. Friday night is noisy in the Main; there is a lot of drinking and laughter, some fighting, and the whores do good business. But there will be a quieter time between six and eight, when everyone seems to go home to change before coming back to chase after fun. Most people eat at home because it's cheaper than restaurants, and they want to save their money to drink and dance.

Guttmann sips his beer and glances back at the customer in conversation with the bartender. She seems both young and middle-aged at the same time, in a way Guttmann could not describe. A dark wig falls in long curls to the middle of her back. He particularly notices her hands, strong and expressive, despite the big dinner rings on every finger. There is something oddly attractive about those hands—competent. Periodically, the customer glances away from her talk and looks directly at Guttmann, her eyes frankly inquisitive without being coy.

As they walk back down the long stairs to the street, Guttmann says, "Not really what you'd call a bird."

"What?" LaPointe asks, his mind elsewhere.

"That barfly back there. Not exactly the chick type."

"No, I guess not. Women never go to that bar."

"Oh," Guttmann says, as soon as he figures it out. He blushes slightly when he remembers the expressive, competent hands covered with dinner rings.

It is nearing eight o'clock, and the pedestrian traffic is thickening again. Blocking the mouth of a narrow alley is a knife sharpener who plies his trade with close devotion. The stone wheel is rigged to his bicycle in such a way that the pedals can drive either the bicycle or the grinding stone. Sitting on the seat, with the rear wheel up on a rectangular stand, he pedals away, spinning his stone. The noise of the grinding and the arc of damp sparks attract the attention of passers-by, who glance once at him, then hurry on. The knife sharpener is tall and gaunt, and his oily hair, combed back in a stony pompadour, gives him the look of a Tartar. His nose is thin and hooked, and his eyes under their brooding brows concentrate on the knife he is working on, on the spray of sparks he is making.

He pedals so hard that his face is wet with sweat, despite the cold. His thin back rounded over his work, his knees pumping up and down, his attention absorbed by the knife and the sparks, he does not seem to see LaPointe approaching.

"Well?" LaPointe says, knowing he has been noticed.

The Grinder does not lift his head, but his eyes roll to the side and he looks at LaPointe from beneath hooking eyebrows. "Hello, Lieutenant."

"How's it going?"

"All right. It's going all right." Suddenly the Grinder reaches out and stops the wheel by grabbing it with his long fingers. Guttmann winces as he sees the edge of the stone cut the web of skin between the Grinder's thumb and forefinger, but the old tramp doesn't seem to feel the pain or notice the blood. "It's coming, you know. It's coming."

"The snow?" LaPointe asks.

The Grinder nods gravely, his black eyes intense in their deep sockets. "And maybe sleet, Lieutenant. Maybe sleet! Nobody ever worries about it! Nobody thinks about it!" His eyebrows drop into a scowl of mistrust as he stares at Guttmann, his eyes burning. "You've never thought about it," he accuses.

"Ah . . . well, I . . ."

"Who knows," LaPointe says. "Maybe it won't snow this year. After all, it didn't snow last year, or the year before."

The Grinder's eyes flick back and forth in confusion. "Didn't it?"

"Not a flake. Don't you remember?"

The Grinder frowns in a painful bout of concentration. "I . . . think . . . I remember. Yes. Yes, that's right!" A sudden kick with his leg, and the wheel is spinning again. "That's right. Not a flake!" He presses the knife to the stone and sparks spray out and fall on Guttmann's shoes.

LaPointe drops a dollar into the Grinder's basket, and the two policemen turn back down the street.

Guttmann squeezes between two pedestrians and catches up with LaPointe. "Did you notice that knife, Lieutenant? Sharpened down to a sliver."

LaPointe guesses what the young man is thinking. He thrusts out his lower lip and shakes his head. "No. He's been on the Main for years. Used to be a roofer. Then one day when the slates were covered with snow, he took a bad fall. That's why he fears the snow. People on the street give him a little something now and then. He's too proud to beg like the other *bommes,* so they give him old knives to sharpen. They never get them back. He forgets who gave them to him, and he sharpens them until there's nothing left." LaPointe cuts across the street. "Come on. One more loop and we'll call it a night."

"Got a heavy date?" Guttmann asks.

LaPointe stops and turns to him. "Why do you ask that?"

"Ah . . . I don't know. I just thought . . . Friday night and all. I mean, I've got a date tonight myself."

"That's wonderful." LaPointe turns and continues his beat crawl, occasionally making little detours into the networks of side streets. He tests the locks on iron railings. He taps on the steamy window of a Portuguese grocery and waves at the old man. He stops to watch two men carrying a trunk down a long wooden stoop, until it becomes clear that they are helping a young couple move out, to the accompaniment of howls and profanity from a burly hag who seems to think the couple owe her money.

They are walking on an almost empty side street when a man half a block ahead turns and starts to cross the street quickly.

"Scheer!" LaPointe shouts. Several people stop and look, startled. Then they walk on hurriedly. The man has frozen in his tracks, but there is a kinesthetic energy in his posture, as though he would run . . . if he dared. LaPointe raises a hand and beckons with the forefinger. Reluctantly, Scheer crosses back and approaches the Lieutenant. In the forced swagger of his walk, and in his mod clothes, he is very much the dandy.

"What did I tell you when I saw you in that bar last night, Scheer?"

"Oh, come on, Lieutenant . . ." There is an oily purr to his voice.

"All right," LaPointe says with bored fatigue. "Get on that wall."

With a long-suffering sigh, Scheer turns to the tenement wall and spread-eagles against it. He knows how to do it; he's done it before. He tries to avoid letting his clothes touch the dirty brick.

Guttmann stands by, unsure what to do, as LaPointe kicks out one of Scheer's feet to broaden the spread, then runs a rapid pat down. "All right. Off the wall. Take off your overcoat."

"Listen, Lieutenant . . ."

"Off!"

Three children emerge from nowhere to watch, as Scheer tugs his overcoat off and folds it carefully before holding it out to LaPointe, each movement defiantly slow.

LaPointe chucks the coat onto the stoop. "Now empty your pockets."

Scheer does so and holds out the comb, change, wallet, and bits of paper to LaPointe.

"Drop all that trash down into the basement well there," LaPointe orders.

His mouth tight with hate, Scheer lets his belongings fall into the well fenced off by a wrought-iron railing. The wallet makes a splat because the bottom of the well is covered with an inch of sooty water.

"Now take out your shoelaces and give them to me."

By now the onlookers have grown to a dozen, two of them girls in their twenties who giggle as Scheer hops to maintain balance while tugging the laces out of the last pair of grommets. Petulantly, he hands them to LaPointe.

The Lieutenant puts them into his pocket. "All right, Scheer. After I leave, you can climb down and get your rubbish. I'll keep the shoelaces. It's for your own good. I wouldn't want you to get despondent over being embarrassed in public and try to hang yourself with them."

"Tell me! Tell me, Lieutenant! What have I ever done to you?"

"You're on the street. I told you to stay off it. I wasn't giving you a vacation, asshole. It was a punishment."

"I know my rights! Who are you, God or something? You don't *own* the fucking street!" He would never have gone that far if there hadn't been the pressure of the crowd and the need to save face.

LaPointe's eyes crinkle in a melancholy smile, and he nods slowly. Then his hand flashes out and his slap sends Scheer spinning along the railing. One of the loose shoes comes off.

LaPointe turns and strolls up the street, followed after a moment by the stunned and confused Guttmann.

"What was all that about, Lieutenant?" Guttmann asks. "Who is that guy?"

"No one. A pimp. I ordered him off the street."

"But . . . if he's done something, why don't you pick him up?"

"I have. Several times. But his lawyers always get him off."

"Yes, but . . ." Guttmann looks over his shoulder at the small knot of people around the pimp, who is just climbing out of the dirty basement well. The girls laugh as he tries to walk with his loose shoes flopping. He takes them off and carries them, walking tenderly in his stocking feet.

"But, sir . . . isn't that harassment?"

LaPointe stops and looks at the young officer appraisingly, his glance shifting from eye to eye. "Yes. It's harassment."

They walk on.

Guttmann sits alone in a small Greek café on Rue Cerat, cramped in a space that would be adequate for a man of average size. The place has only two oilcloth-covered tables crowded against the window, across from a glass-fronted display case containing cheese, oil, and olives for sale. A fly-speckled sign on the wall says:

7-UP—ÇA RAVIGOTE

While LaPointe is telephoning from a booth attached to the outside of the café, Guttmann is trying to work out a problem in his mind. He knows what he has to do, but he doesn't know how to do it. He has been withdrawn since the incident with Scheer half an hour before. Everything he believes in, everything he has learned, combine to make LaPointe's treatment of that pimp intolerable. Guttmann cannot accept the concept of the policeman as judge—much less as executioner—and he knows what he would have to do should Scheer bring a complaint against the Lieutenant. Further, his sense of fair play demands that he warn LaPointe of his decision, and that will not be easy.

When the Lieutenant returns from the telephone booth a girl of eighteen or nineteen comes from the back room to serve them little cups of strong coffee, her eyes always averted with a shyness that advertises her awareness of men and of her own sexual attractiveness. She has long black lashes and the comfortable beauty of a Madonna.

"How's your mother?" LaPointe asks.

"Fine. She's in back. Want me to call her?"

"No. I'll see her next time I drop by."

The girl lets her damp brown eyes settle briefly on Guttmann, who smiles and nods. She glances away sidewards, lowers her eyes, and returns to the back room.

"Pretty girl," Guttmann says. "Pity she's so shy."

LaPointe grunts noncommittally. Years ago, the mother was a streetwalker on the Main. She was a lusty, laughing woman always in good spirits, always with a coarse joke to tell, pushing her elbow into your ribs with the punch line. When, every month or two, LaPointe felt the need for a woman, she was usually the one he went with.

Then suddenly she was off the street. She had got pregnant; by a lover, of course, not a customer. With the birth of the child, she changed completely. She began to dress less flashily; she looked for work; she started attending church. She didn't often laugh, but she smiled a lot. And she devoted herself to her baby girl, like a child playing dolls. She borrowed a little money from LaPointe, who also countersigned her note, and she put a down payment on this back-street café. At five dollars a week, she paid LaPointe back, never missing a payment except around Christmas, when she was buying presents for her girl.

They never made love again, but he made it a habit to drop in occasionally during quiet times. They used to sit together by the window and talk while they drank cups of thick Greek coffee. He would listen as she went on about her daughter. It was amazing what that child could do. Talk. Run. And draw? An artist! The mother had plans. The girl would go to university and become a fashion designer. Have you ever seen her drawings? How can I tell you? Taste? You wouldn't believe it. Never pink and red together.

While in high school, this girl became pregnant. At first the mother couldn't understand . . . couldn't believe it. Then she was crazy with fury. She would kill that boy! She had an acrimonious shout-down with the boy and his parents. No, the boy would not marry her. And here's why . . .

The next time, LaPointe dropped in, the woman had changed. She was lifeless, dull, vacant. The took coffee together in the empty café, the woman looking out the window as she talked, her voice flat and tired. The girl had a reputation in high school for being a hot box. She made love with anybody, any time, anywhere—down in the boiler room, once in the boys' lavatory. Everybody knew about it. She was a slut. She wasn't even a whore! She gave it away!

LaPointe tried to comfort her. She'll get married one of these days. Everything will be all right.

No. It was a punishment from God. He's punishing me for being a whore.

"Good-looking girl," Guttmann says. "Pity she's so shy."

"Yes," LaPointe says. "A pity." He swirls his cup to suspend the thick coffee dust and finishes it off, sucking it through a cube of sugar pressed against the roof of his mouth. "Look, I just called in to the QG to have them pick up the Vet."

"Lieutenant. . . ?"

"We can't wait forever for Dirtyshirt Red. When they find him, they'll call you. When they do, get down there immediately. If he's not too drunk to talk, call me and I'll come down."

"You told them to call *me?*"

"Sure. You're here to get experience, aren't you?"

"Well, yes, but . . ."

"But what?"

"I have a date tonight. I told you."

"That's too bad."

Guttmann takes a deep breath. "Lieutenant?"

"Yes?"

"About that pimp back there?"

"Scheer? What about him?"

"Well, if I'm going to be working with you . . ."

"I wouldn't say you're working with me. It's more like you're following me around."

"Okay. Whatever. But I'm here, and I feel I have to be straight with you." Guttmann feels awkward looking into LaPointe's hooded, paternal eyes. He's sure he's going to end up making an ass of himself.

"If you have something to say, say it," LaPointe orders.

"All right. About the pimp. It's not right to harass a civilian like that. It's not legal. He has rights, whoever he is, whatever he's done. Harassment is the kind of stuff that gives the force a bad name."

"I'm sure the Commissioner would agree with you."

"That doesn't make me wrong."

"It goes a ways."

Guttmann nods and looks down. "You're not going to give me a chance to say what I want to say, are you? You're making it as hard as possible."

"I'll say it for you if you want. You're going to tell me that if this asshole brings charges against me, you feel that you would have to corroborate. Right?"

Guttmann forces himself not to look away from LaPointe's eyes with their expression of tired amusement. He knows what the Lieutenant is thinking: he's young. When he gets some experience under his belt, he'll come around. But Guttmann is sure he will never come around. He would quit the force before that happened. "That's right," he says, no quaver at all in his voice. "I'd have to corroborate."

LaPointe nods. "I told you he was a pimp, didn't I?"

"Yes, sir. But that's not the point."

That was what Resnais kept saying: that's not the point.

"Besides," Guttmann continues, "there are lots of women working the streets. You don't seem to hassle them."

"That's different. They're pros. And they're adults."

Guttmann's eyes flicker at this last. "You mean Scheer uses . . ."

"That's right. Kids. Junk-hungry kids. And if I deny him the use of the street, he can't run his kids."

"Why don't you take him in?"

"I *have* taken him in. I told you. It doesn't do any good. He walks back out again the same day. Pimping is hard to prove, unless the girls give evidence. And they're afraid to. He's promised that if they talk, they'll get their faces messed up."

Guttmann tips up his cup and looks into the dark sludge at the bottom. Still . . . even with a pimp who runs kids . . . a copy can't be a judge and executioner. Principles don't change, even when the case in hand makes it tough to maintain them.

LaPointe examines the young man's earnest, troubled face. "What do you think of the Main?" he asks, lifting the pressure by changing the subject.

Guttmann looks up. "Sir?"

"My patch. What do you think of it? You must realize that I've been dragging you around, giving you the grand tour."

"I don't know what I think of it. It's . . . interesting."

"Interesting?" LaPointe looks out the window, watching the passers-by. "Yes, I suppose so. Of course, you get a warped idea of the street when you walk it as a cop. You see mostly the hustlers, the *fous,* the toughs, the whores, the *bommes.* You get what Gaspard calls a turd's-eye view. Ninety percent of the people up here are no worse than anywhere else. Poorer, maybe. Dumber. Weaker. But not worse." LaPointe rubs his hair with his palm and sits back in his chair. "You know . . . a funny thing happened eight or ten years ago. I was doing the street, and I happened to be walking behind a man—must have been seventy years old—a man who moved in a funny way. It's hard to explain; I felt I knew him, but I didn't, of course. It wasn't *how* he looked at things; it was *what* he looked at. You know what I mean?"

"Yes, sir," lies Guttmann.

"Well, he stopped off for coffee, and I sat down next to him. We started talking, and it turned out that he was a retired cop from New York. *That* was what I had recognized without knowing it—his beatwalker's way of looking at things only an old cop would look at: door locks, shoes, telephone booths with broken panes, that sort of thing. He had come up here because his granddaughter was marrying a Canadian and the wedding was in Montreal. He got tired of sitting around making small talk with people he didn't know, so he wandered off, and he ended up on the Main. He told me that he felt a real pang, walking these streets. It reminded him of New York in the twenties—the different languages, the small shops, workers and hoods and chippies and housewives and kids all mixed up on the same street but not afraid of one another. He said it used to be like that in New York when the immigrants were still coming in. But it isn't like that anymore. It's a closed-up frightened city at night. Not even the cops walk around alone. We're about thirty years behind New York in that way. And as long as I'm on the Main, we are never going to catch up."

Guttmann imagines that all this has something to do with the harassment of that pimp, but he doesn't see just how.

"Okay," LaPointe says, stretching his back. "So if Scheer makes a complaint, you'll back him up."

"Yes, sir. I would have to."

LaPointe nods. "I suppose you would. Well, I have some grocery shopping to do. You'd better get home and get something to eat. Chances are they'll pick up the Vet tonight, and we may be up late."

LaPointe rises and tugs on his overcoat, while Guttmann sits there feeling— not defeated exactly in this business of Scheer, but undercut, bypassed.

"What's wrong?" LaPointe asks, looking down at him.

"Oh . . . I was just thinking about this date I've got for tonight. I hate to break it, because it's the first time we've been out together."

"Oh, she'll understand. Make up some lie. Tell her you're a cop."

LaPointe braces one of the grocery bags against the wall of the hall and gropes in his pocket for his key. Then it occurs to him that he ought to knock. There is no answer. He taps again. No response.

His first sensation is a sinking in his stomach, like a fast down elevator stopping. Almost immediately, the feeling retreats and something safer replaces it: ironic self-amusement. He smiles at himself—dumb old man—and shakes his head as he inserts his key in the slack lock and pushes the door open.

The lights are on. And she is there.

She is wearing Lucille's pink quilted dressing gown, which she must have gotten from the closet where Lucille's things still hang.

Lucille's dressing gown.

She is sitting on the sofa, one foot tucked up under her butt, sewing something, the threaded needle poised in the air. Her mouth is slightly open, her eyes alert.

"Oh, it's you," she says. "I didn't answer because I thought it might be the landlord. I mean . . . he might not like the idea of your having a girl in your apartment."

"I see." He carries the groceries into the narrow kitchen. She sets her sewing down and follows him.

"Here," he says. "Unwrap the cheese and let the air get to it."

"Okay. I've been walking around quietly so no one would hear me."

"You don't have to worry about that. Just set the cheese on a plate."

"Which plate?"

"Any one. It doesn't matter."

"Doesn't the landlord care if you have girls up here?"

LaPointe laughs. "I *am* the landlord." This is true, although he never thinks of himself as a landlord. Seven years after Lucille's death, he heard that the building was going to be sold. He was used to living there, and he could not quite grasp what it would mean to move away from their home, Lucille's and his—what that would imply. Because there was nothing to spend it on, he had saved a little money, so he arranged a long-term mortgage and bought the building. Just two years ago, he made the last payment. He had become so used to making out the mortgage check each month that he was surprised when it was returned to him with the notification that the mortgage was paid off. The other tenants—there are three—do not know he owns the building, because he arranged to have the bank receive their rents and credit them to his debt. He did this out of a kind of shame. His concept of "the landlord" was fashioned in the slums of Trois Rivières, and he doesn't care for the thought of being one himself.

Marie-Louise sits at the kitchen table, her elbow on the oilcloth, her chin in her hand, watching him tear up the lettuce for their salad. He has planned a simple meal: steak, salad, bread, wine. And cheese for dessert.

"It's funny seeing a man cook," she says. "Do you always cook for yourself?"

"I eat in restaurants, mostly. On Sundays I cook. I enjoy it for a change."

"Hm-m." She doesn't know what to make of it. She never met anybody who enjoyed cooking. God knows her mother didn't. It occurs to her that this old guy might be a queer. Maybe that's why he didn't make love to her last night. "What kind of work do you do?"

"I'm with the police." He says this with a shrug meant to shunt away any fear she might have of the police.

"Oh." She's not very interested in what he does.

He puts the salad bowl on the table before her. "Here. Make yourself useful. Mix this." The skillet is smoking, and the steaks hiss and sizzle as he drops them in. "What did you do today?" he asks, his voice strained because he is standing tiptoe, looking in the cupboard for an extra plate and glass.

"Nothing. I just sat around. Mended some things. And I took another bath. Is that all right?"

"Of course. No, you don't stir a salad. You toss it. Like this. See?"

"What difference does it make?" There is annoyance in her voice. She could never do anything right in her mother's kitchen either.

"It's the way it's done, that's all. Here, let's see." He lifts her chin with his palm. "Ah. That eye is looking better. Swelling's gone." She is not a pretty girl, but her face is alert and expressive. "Well." He takes his hand away and turns to cut the bread. "So you sat around and mended all day?"

"I went out shopping. Made breakfast. I borrowed that coat from your closet when I went out. It was cold. But I put it back again."

"Did it fit?"

"Not bad. You should have seen the man at the grocery look at me!" She laughs, remembering what she looked like in that coat. Her laughter is enthusiastic and vulgar. As before, it stops suddenly in mid-rise and is gone.

"Why did he look at you?" LaPointe asks, smiling along with her infectious laughter.

"I guess I looked funny in an old woman's coat."

He pauses and frowns, not understanding. She must mean an old-fashioned coat. It is not an old woman's coat; it was a young woman's coat. He attends to the steaks.

"There isn't much to do around here," she says frankly. "You don't have any magazines. You don't have TV."

"I have a radio."

"I tried it. It doesn't work."

"You have to jiggle the knob."

"Why don't you get it fixed?"

"Why bother? I know how to jiggle the knob. Okay, let's eat. I think everything's ready."

She eats rapidly, like a hungry child, but twice she remembers her manners and tells him it's good. And she drinks her wine too fast.

"I'll do the dishes," she offers afterwards. "That's something I know how to do."

"You don't have to." But the thought of her puttering around in the kitchen is pleasant. "All right, if you want to. I'll make the coffee while you're washing up."

There isn't really enough room for two in the narrow kitchen, and three times they touch shoulders. Each time, he says, "Excuse me."

". . . so I thought I might as well try Montreal. I mean, I had to go somewhere, so why not here? I was hoping I could get a job . . . maybe as a cocktail waitress. They make lots of money, you know. I had a girlfriend who wrote me about the tips."

"But you didn't find anything?"

She is curled up on the sofa, Lucille's pink quilted robe around her; he sits in his comfortable old chair. She shakes her head and looks away from him, toward the hissing gas fire. "No, I didn't. I tried everywhere for a couple of weeks, until I ran out of money. But the cocktail bars didn't want a cripple. And my boobs are small." She says this last matter-of-factly. She knows how it is in the world. Yet there is some wistfulness in it, or fatigue.

"So you started working the street."

She shrugs. "It was sort of an accident, really. I mean, I never thought of screwing for money. Of course, I had screwed men before. Back home. But just friends and guys who took me out on dates. Just for fun."

"Don't use that word." LaPointe knows that no daughter of his would ever use that word.

Marie-Louise cocks her head thoughtfully, trying to think back to the offending word. With her head cocked and her frizzy mop of hair, she has the look of a Raggedy Ann doll. "Screw?" she asks, uncertain. "What should I say?"

"I don't know. Making love. Something like that."

She grins, her elastic face impish. "That sounds funny. *Making love.* It sounds like the movies."

"But still . . ."

"Okay. Well, I never thought of . . . doing it . . . for money. I guess I didn't think anyone would pay for it."

LaPointe shakes his head. *Doing it* sounds worse yet.

"Well, I stayed with some people for a while. All people of my age, sort of living together in this big old house. But then I had a fight with the guy who sort of ran everything, and I moved to a room. Then I ran out of money and they kicked me out. They kept most of my clothes and my suitcase. That's why I don't have a coat. Anyway, I was kicked out, and I was just walking around. Scared, sort of, and trying to think of what to do . . . where I could go. See, it was cold. Well, I ended up at the bus station and I sat around most of the night, trying to look like I was waiting for a bus, so they wouldn't kick me out. But this guard kept eyeing me. I only had that shopping bag for my clothes, so I guess he knew I wasn't really waiting for a bus. And then this guy comes up to me and just straight out asks me. Just like that. He said he would give me ten dollars. He was sort of . . ." She decides not to say that.

"Sort of what?"

"Well . . . he wasn't young. Anyway, he brought me to his apartment. He came in his pants while he was feeling me up. But he paid anyway."

"That was good of him."

"Yeah," she agrees with a frankness that undercuts his irony. "It *was* sort of good of him, wasn't it? I didn't know that at the time, because I hadn't been around, and I thought everyone was like him. Nice, you know. He let me stay the night; and the next morning he bought me breakfast. Most of the others weren't like that. They try to cheat you out of your money. Or they say you can spend the night, but when they've had all they want, they kick you out. And if you make a fuss, sometimes they try to beat you up. Some of them really get a kick out of beating you up." She touches her eye with her fingertips. The swelling is gone, but a faint green stain remains. "You know what you have to do?" she confides seriously. "You have to get your money before he starts. A girl I went around with for a while told me that. And she was right."

"That was how long ago? When this old man picked you up?"

She thinks back. "Six weeks. Two months, maybe."

"And since then you've been getting along by selling yourself?"

She grins. That sounds even funnier than *making love.* "It's not so bad, you know? Guys take me to bars and I eat in restaurants. And I go dancing." She tucks her short leg up under her. "You might not think it, but I can dance real well. It's funny, but I can dance better than I can walk, you know what I mean? I like dancing more than anything. Do you dance?"

"No."

"Why not?"

"I don't know how."

She laughs. "Everyone knows how! There's nothing to know. You just sort of . . . you know . . . *move.*"

"It sounds like you had nothing but fun on the streets."

"You say that like you don't believe it. But it's true. Most of the time I had fun. Except when they got rough. Or when they wanted me to do . . . funny things. I don't know why, but I'm just not ready for that. The thought makes me gag, you know? Hey, what's wrong?"

He shakes his head. "Nothing."

"Does it bother you when I talk about it?"

"Nothing. Never mind."

"Some guys like it. I mean, they like you to talk about it. It gets them going."

"Forget it!"

She ducks involuntarily and lifts her arms as though to fend off a slap. Her father used to slap her. When the adrenalin of sudden fright drains off, it is followed by offense and anger. "What the hell's wrong with you?" she demands.

He takes a deep breath. "Nothing. I'm sorry. It's just . . ."

Her voice is stiff with petulance. "Well, Jesus Christ, you'd think a cop would be used to that sort of thing."

"Yes, of course, but . . ." He rolls his hand. "Tell me. How old are you?"

She readjusts herself on the sofa, but she doesn't relax. "Twenty-two. And you?"

"Fifty-two. No, three." He wants to return to the calm of their earlier conversation, so he explains unnecessarily, "I just had a birthday last month, but I always forget about it."

She cannot imagine anyone forgetting a birthday, but she supposes it's different when you're old. He is acting nice again. Her instinct tells her that he is genuinely sorry for frightening her. This would be the time to take advantage of his regret and make some arrangements.

"Can I stay here again tonight?"

"Of course. You can stay longer, if you want."

Push it now. "How much longer?"

He shrugs. "I don't know. How long do you want to stay?"

"Would we . . . make love?" She cannot help saying these last words with a comic, melodramatic tone.

He doesn't answer.

"Don't you like women?"

He smiles. "No, it isn't that."

"Well, why do you want me to stay, if you don't want to sleep with me?"

LaPointe looks down at the park, where a tracery of black branches intersects the yellow globes of the streetlamps. This Marie-Louise is the same age as Lucille—the Lucille of his memory—and she speaks with the same downriver accent. And she wears the same robe. But she is younger than the daughters he daydreams about, the daughters who are sometimes still little girls, but more often grown women with children of their own. Come to think of it, the daughters of his daydreams are sometimes older than Lucille. Lucille never ages, always looks the same. It never before occurred to him that the daughters are older than their mother. That's crazy.

"What's wrong?" she asks.

"I'll tell you what. I'll look around and see if I can find you a job."

"In a cocktail bar?"

"I can't promise that. Maybe as a waitress in a restaurant."

She wrinkles her nose. That doesn't appeal to her at all. She has seen lots of waitresses, running around and being shouted at during rush times, or standing, tired and bored, and staring out of windows when the place is empty. And the uniforms always look frumpy. If it weren't for this damned pig weather, and if the men never tried to beat you up, she'd rather go on like she is than be a waitress.

"I'll try to find you a job," he says. "Meanwhile you can stay here, if you want."

"And we'll sleep together?" She wants to get the conditions straight at the beginning. It is something like making sure you get your money in advance.

He turns from the window and settles his eyes on her. "Do you really want to?"

She shrugs a "why not?" Then she discovers a loose thread on the sleeve of the dressing gown. She tries to break it off.

He clears his throat and rubs his cheek with his knuckles. "I need a shave." He rises. "Would you like another coffee before we go to bed?"

She looks up at him through her mop of hair, the errant thread between her teeth. "Okay," she says, nipping off the thread and spitting out the bit.

He is shaving when the phone rings.

He has to wipe the lather from his cheek before putting the receiver to his ear. "LaPointe."

Guttmann's voice sounds tired. "I just got down here."

"Down where?"

"The Quartier Général. They called me at my apartment. They've picked up your Sinclair, and he's giving them one hell of a time."

"Sinclair?"

"Joseph Michael Sinclair. That's the real name of your bum, the Vet. He's in a bad way. Raving. Screaming. They're talking about giving him a sedative, but I told them to hold off in case you wanted to question him tonight."

"No, not tonight. Tomorrow will do."

"I don't know, sir . . ."

"Of course you don't know. That's part of being a Joan."

"What I was going to say was, this guy's a real case. It's taking two men to hold him down. He keeps screaming that he can't go into a cell. Something about being a claustrophobic."

"Oh, for Christ's sake!"

"Just thought you ought to know."

LaPointe's shoulders slump, and he lets out a long nasal sigh. "All right. You talk to the Vet. Tell him nobody's going to lock him up. Tell him I'll be down in a little while. He knows me."

"Yes, sir. Oh, and sir? Terribly sorry to disturb you at home."

What? Sarcasm from a Joan? LaPointe grunts and hangs up.

Marie-Louise is mending the paisley granny dress she was wearing when he found her in the park. She looks up questioningly when he enters the living room.

"I have to go downtown. What are you smiling at?"

"You've got soap on one side of your face."

"Oh." He wipes it off.

As he tugs on his overcoat, he remembers the coffee water steaming away on the stove. "Shall I make you a cup before I go?"

She shakes her head. "I don't really like coffee all that much."

"Why do you always drink it then?"

She shrugs. She doesn't know. She takes what's offered.

Six

BY THE THERMOMETER it is not so cold as last night, but that was a dry cold, crystallizing on surfaces, and this is a damp cold, the serrate edge of which penetrates to LaPointe's chest as he walks down the deserted Main. He does not find a cruising taxi until Sherbrooke.

LaPointe's footballs clip hollowly along the empty, half-lit halls outside the magistrates' courts. The sound is oddly loud and melancholy, without the covering envelope of noise that fills the building during the day.

The elevator doors open, and he walks down the brightly lit corridor of the Duty Office. There is sound and life here: the stuttering clack of a typewriter in clumsy hands; the hum of fluorescent lights; and somewhere a transistor radio plays popular music.

Guttmann steps into the hall at the sound of the elevator. He looks unkempt and haggard; more like a real cop, LaPointe thinks.

"Good morning, sir. He's in here." Guttmann's tone is flat and unfriendly.

"What the hell's wrong with you?" LaPointe asks.

"Sir?"

"Your attitude, tone of voice. What's wrong?"

"I didn't know it showed, sir."

"It shows. I warned you to cancel that date of yours."

"I did, sir. She went to a film with a friend. But she dropped by later for a drink. We live in the same apartment building."

"And the call got you out of bed?"

"Something like that."

"At an awkward time?"

"As awkward as it gets, sir."

LaPointe laughs. Guttmann recognizes the comic possibilities of the situation, but he doesn't find this particular case funny.

LaPointe enters the Duty Office, Guttmann following. Joseph Michael "the Vet" Sinclair is sitting on a wooden bench against the wall. His long arms are wrapped around his legs, his face is pressed against his knees, and he still wears his ridiculous floppy-brimmed hat. He rocks himself back and forth in misery, humming or moaning one note over and over again. His grip on reality seems fragile. Occasionally he looks around the room, bewildered and frightened, and his teeth begin to chatter, his breath comes in canine sniffs, and he struggles against screaming.

LaPointe's nostrils dilate with the stench of urine. Joseph Michael Sinclair has wet himself.

The symptoms resemble withdrawal. LaPointe has seen this once before. The Vet is a victim of claustrophobia. The Duty Office is a big room, so that isn't what is eroding his sanity. It was the trip down in a police car and, even more, the thought of being locked up in a cell. The Vet is trapped in the classic terrible cycle facing the claustrophobic: he is almost mad with the fear of being shut up, and if he gives way to his madness, they will lock him up.

"Where did you pick him up?" LaPointe asks one of the officers getting coffee at the dispensing machine, a tough Polish oldtimer who never bothered to take his sergeant's examinations because he doesn't want the hassle of responsibility. Although his French is thin and badly accented, he has always been accepted by the French Canadian cops as one of them, because he so obviously is not one of the others.

The coffee is hot, and the Polish cop winces as he changes the paper cup from hand to hand, looking for a place to set it down. His gestures are comically delicate, because the paper cup is fragile. He manages to balance it on a ledge and snaps his fingers violently. "Jesus H. Christ! We picked him up on St. Urbain, just south of Van Horne. Somebody named Red phoned in the tip. He gave us one hell of a chase. Took off across Van Horne, hopping like a gimpy rabbit! Right through the traffic! Cars and trucks hitting their brakes! Scared the shit out of the drivers. Their assholes must of bit chunks out of the car seats. And there I am, right after him, dancing and dodging through the traffic. Then your friend here climbs the fence and is halfway down the bank into the freight yard before I get to him. Look at that, will you?" He reaches around and tugs out the slack in the seat of his pants, showing a triangular rip. "Got that climbing the goddamned wire fence after the son of a bitch! Twenty-seven bucks shot in the ass!"

"Literally," Guttmann says.

"What?" the Polish cop demands.

"Did he give you any trouble?" LaPointe asks.

"Any trouble? Wild as a cat crapping razor blades, that's all! You wouldn't know it to see him now, but it took both of us to get him into the car. Kick? Wriggle? Scream? You'da thought we were gang-banging the Mother Superior."

LaPointe looks over at the miserable *bomme* whose eyes are now squeezed shut as he rocks back and forth, with each movement moaning a high, thin note that stops short in his throat. He is right on the limen of sanity.

"You didn't give him anything to calm him down, did you?"

"No, Lieutenant. Your Joan told us not to. Anyway, it wasn't necessary. As soon as we told him you were coming down, he settled right down. Just started moaning and rocking like that. A real nut case. Twenty-fucking-seven bucks! And not a month old!"

LaPointe crosses to the Vet and places his hand on his shoulder. "Hey?" He gives him a slight shake. "Hey, Vet?"

The tramp does not look up; he is lost in the treacherous animal comfort of his rocking and moaning. His own motion and his own sound surround and protect him. He doesn't want penetrations from the outside.

LaPointe has seen men go inside themselves like this before. He is afraid he'll lose the Vet if he doesn't bring him out right now. He takes off the wide-brimmed hat and lifts up the head by the hair. "Hey!"

The *bomme* tries to pull away, but LaPointe holds the hair tighter. "Vet? Vet!" The smell of urine is strong.

The Vet's vague humid eyes focus slowly on LaPointe's face. The slack, unshaven cheeks quiver. As he opens his mouth to speak, a bubble of thick spit forms between the lips and bursts with the first word.

"Lieutenant?" It is a pitiful, mendicant whine. "Don't let them lock me up. You know what I mean? I can't be locked up! I can't! I . . . I . . . I . . . I . . . I . . ." With each repetition, the voice rises a note as the Vet plunges toward panic.

LaPointe snatches the greasy hair. He mustn't lose him. "Vet! No one's going to lock you up!"

"No, you don't! I can't go inside! I can't!"

"Listen to me!"

"No! No! No!"

LaPointe slaps the tramp's cheek hard.

The Vet catches his breath and holds it, his cheeks bulging, his eyes wide open and staring up obliquely at the Lieutenant.

"Now, listen," LaPointe says more quietly. "Just listen," he says softly. "All right?"

The Vet lets his breath escape slowly and remains silent, but his eyes still stare, and there are rapid little pupillary contractions.

LaPointe speaks very slowly and clearly. "No one is going to lock you up. Do you understand that? No one is going to put you inside."

The *bomme's* squinting left eye twitches as he struggles to comprehend. As understanding comes, his body, so long rigid, droops with fatigue; his jaw slackens; his breathing slows; and the bloodshot eyes roll up as though in sleep.

LaPointe releases the hair, and the tramp's chin drops back into his chest. LaPointe lays his hand protectively on the nape of the Vet's neck as he turns to Guttmann. "Get some coffee down him."

Guttmann looks around for a coffeepot.

"The machine!" LaPointe says with exasperation, pointing to the coin-operated dispenser.

The two uniformed cops leave the Duty Office, the Polish old-timer fiddling with the back of his pants to see if he can hide the triangular rip, and his partner assuring him that nobody wants to look at his ass.

LaPointe leans against the wall and presses down his hair with his palm. "After you get a few cups of coffee down him," he tells Guttmann, "dunk his head in cold water and clean him up a little. Then bring him to my office."

Guttmann fumbles in his pocket as he looks with distaste at the heap of rags stinking of stale wine and urine. "I'm sorry, sir. I don't seem to have a dime."

"The machine takes quarters."

"I don't have any change at all."

With infinite patience, LaPointe produces a quarter from the depths of his overcoat pocket and holds it up between thumb and forefinger. "Here. This is called a quarter. It makes vending machines work. It also makes telephones work. What would you do if you had to make an emergency call from a public phone and you had no change on you?"

"I just threw on my clothes and came over when they called. I didn't even—"

"*Always* carry change for the phone. It could save somebody's life."

Guttmann takes the quarter. "All right, sir. Thanks for the advice."

"That wasn't advice."

Guttmann shoves the quarter into the slot brusquely. What the hell is bugging the Lieutenant? After all, *he* wasn't the one who was called away from a night with a bird to come down and wet-nurse a drunk who has pissed his pants!

As he starts to leave the Duty Office for his own floor above, LaPointe pauses at the door. He sniffs and rubs his cheek. He is shaven on only one side. "Look. I'm sorry, I . . . I'm tired, that's all."

"Yes, sir. We're probably all tired."

"Did you say it was your first time with that young lady of yours?"

"First for sure. And probably last." Guttmann is still angry and stung.

"Well, I hope not."

"Yes, sir. Me too."

It is fully half an hour before the door to LaPointe's office opens and Guttmann enters, bringing the Vet along by the arm. The old *bomme* looks pale and sick, but sober. Sober enough, at least. The shapeless old overcoat has been left behind, along with the wide-brimmed hat, and the collar and front of his shirt are wet from the dunking Guttmann has given him in a washbowl of the men's room. The hair is wet and dripping, and it has been raked back with fingers that left greasy black ropes. There is a small bruise over the eyebrow, half covered by a hank of hair plastered on the forehead.

"You hit him?" LaPointe asks.

"No, sir. He clipped his head on the edge of the washbowl."

"Do you have any idea what a lawyer would make of that? A lot more than harassment." LaPointe turns his attention to the *bomme*. "Okay, sit down, Vet."

The old tramp obeys sullenly. Now that his first panic is over, something of his haughty sassiness returns, and he attempts to appear indifferent and superior, despite the stink of urine that moves with him.

"Feeling better?" LaPointe asks.

The Vet does not answer. He lifts his head and looks unsteadily at LaPointe down his thin, bent nose. The intended disdain is diluted by an uncontrollable wobbling of the head.

LaPointe has never liked the Vet. He pities him, but the Vet is one of those men toward whom feelings of pity are always mixed with contempt, even disgust.

"Got a smoke?" The Vet asks.

"No." Once the Vet begins to feel safe, he'll be impossible to deal with. It's best to keep him from getting too confident. "I told you we weren't going to put you inside," LaPointe says, leaning back in his chair. "I'd better be straight with you. It's not really settled yet. You may be locked up, and you may not."

With almost comic abruptness, the tramp's composure shatters. His eyes flicker like a rodent's, and his breath starts to come in short gasps. "I can't go into a cell, Lieutenant. I thought you understood! I was wounded in the army."

"I'm not interested in that."

"No, wait! I was captured! A prisoner of war! For four years I was locked up! You know what I mean? I couldn't stand it. One day . . . one day, I began to scream. And I couldn't stop. You know what I mean? I knew I was screaming. I could hear myself. And I wanted to stop, but I didn't know how! You know what I mean? That's why I can't go to jail!"

"All right. Calm down."

The Vet is eager to obey, to put himself in LaPointe's good graces. He stops talking, shutting his teeth tight. But he cannot halt the humming moan. He begins to rock in his chair. Mustn't let the moan out. Mustn't start screaming.

Guttmann clears his throat. "Lieutenant?"

"Hm-m?"

"I think he may be a user. There's a fresh mark on his arm, and a couple of old tracks."

"No, he's not a user, are you, Vet? Between pension checks, he sells his blood illegally for wine money. That's right, isn't it, Vet?"

The *bomme* nods vigorously, still keeping his teeth clenched. He wants to be cooperative, but he doesn't dare speak. He's afraid to open his mouth. Afraid he'll start screaming, and they will put him into a room. Like the English army doctors did after he was liberated from prison camp. They put him into a room because he kept screaming. He was screaming because they locked him in a room!

The Vet breathes nasally, in short puffs, humming with each exhalation. The hum strokes his need to scream just enough to keep it within control, like lightly rubbing a mosquito bite that you mustn't scratch for fear of infection.

"Take it easy, Vet. Answer every question truthfully, and I'll make sure you get back on the street. All right?"

The tramp nods. With great effort, he forces his breathing to slow. Then he carefully unclenches his teeth. "I'll do . . . whatever . . . anything."

"Good. Now, last night you took a wallet from a man in an alley."

The Vet bobs his head once.

"I don't care about the money. You can keep it."

The Vet forces himself to speak. "Money . . . gone."

"You drank it up?"

He nods once.

"It's the wallet I want. If you can give me the wallet, you're free to go."

The Vet opens his mouth wide and takes three rapid, shallow breaths. "I have it! I have it!"

"But not on you."

"No."

"Where?"

"I can get it."

"Good. I'll come along with you."

The Vet doesn't want this. His eyes flick about the room. "No. I'll bring it to you. I promise."

"That's not good enough, Vet. You'd promise anything right now. I'll go with you."

The Vet's upper lip spreads flat over his teeth and his nostrils dilate. "I can't!" He begins to sob.

LaPointe scrubs his hair and sighs. "Is it your kip? You don't want me to find out where it is?"

The *bomme* nods vigorously.

"I'm sorry. But there's nothing for it. It's late, and I'm tired. Either we go right now to get the wallet, or you start ten days of a vag charge."

The tramp looks at Guttmann, his eyes pleading for intervention. The young man frowns and stares at the floor.

LaPointe stands up. "Okay, that's it. I don't have time to fool around with you."

"All right!" The Vet jumps to his feet and shouts into LaPointe's face. "All right! All right!"

LaPointe puts his hands on the tramp's shoulders and presses him back into his chair. "Take it easy." He turns to Guttmann. "Go down and check us out a car and driver."

Before leaving, Guttmann glances again at the Vet, who has retreated into the comfort of rocking and humming.

No sooner has the police car carried them three blocks from the Quartier Général and the threat of being locked up than the Vet's whimpering dread evaporates and he reverts to his cocky, egoistic self. He does not deign to talk to Guttmann, who sits beside him because LaPointe got in front to avoid the alkaline smell of urine. Instead, he leans forward and talks to the Lieutenant's back, explaining what happened in a loud voice because the windows of the car are open to avoid an onset of claustrophobia, and the bitter wind whistles through the car.

"I was just coming down the street, Lieutenant, when I happened to look up the alley and see this mark. He was kneeling down . . . low, you know? With his forehead on the bricks. I figures he's a drunk or maybe high on something. Maybe he's sick, I says to myself. I got first-aid training in the army. You can make a tourniquet with your belt. Did you know that? Sure. Easy as pie, if you know how. This riffraff on the street don't know anything. They never been in the army. They don't know shit from Shinola. Well, I walks up the alley. He don't move. There's nobody around. It's real cold and everybody's off the Main. Now, I wasn't thinking of rolling him or nothing. Honest to God, Lieutenant. I just thought he might be sick or something. Need a tourniquet, maybe. When I get close to him, I could see he was real well-dressed. He looks funny. I mean, you know, ridiculous. Kneeling there with his ass in the air. Then I notice his wallet's half out of his pocket. So . . . I just . . . took it. I mean, if I didn't take it, one of those street tramps was sure to. So why not? First come, first served; that's what we used to say in the army."

"You didn't know he was dead?"

"Honest to God, I didn't. There wasn't any blood or anything."

That is true. The bleeding was largely internal.

"So, anyway, it comes to me that I might as well lift his poke. Share the wealth, like we used to say in the army. So I reach over and pull it out. It comes out hard, what with him squatting over like that and the ass of his pants so tight, you know. And just as I got it, all of a sudden this cop car stops down to the end of the alley, and this cop shouts at me!" The Vet's breath begins to shorten as he relives his fear. "So I takes off! I was a-scared he might run me in! I can't be locked up, Lieutenant! If I'm in a closed place, I start to scream. You know what I mean? You know what I mean?"

"All right! Take it easy."

"Did I tell you that the army doctors kept me locked up after they liberated the camp?"

"You mentioned it. Where are we going?"

"Just straight up the Main. Up to Van Horne. I'll show you when we get there. Yeah, the army doctors kept me locked up in a hospital ward especially for fruitcakes. They didn't understand. I might have been there forever. But then this young doctor—Captain Ferguson, his name was—he says why don't they give me a chance on the outside. See how it would work. Well, I got out, and I stopped screaming just like that. They warned me not to get a job where I was cooped up, and I never did. I didn't have to. I'm a ninety percent disability. Ninety percent! That's a lot, ain't it? Hey, you got a cigarette?"

"No."

The driver twists to get a pack out of his pocket. "Give him one of mine, Lieutenant. We sure could use the smell of smoke in here."

As they near the intersection of Van Horne and St. Laurent, LaPointe becomes curious about this famous snug kip the Vet has always boasted about. It is generally known on the street that the Vet drinks up his pension check within two weeks and has to sell blood to keep alive after that. Like other tramps, winos, addicts, and hippie types *in extremis,* he lies about how long it has been since he gave blood, as he lies about diseases he has had. There is always a need for his uncommon type—another source of his endless bragging. Whenever he gets money, he buys a couple of bottles, but he never drinks much on the Main. He brings it off with him to his hideaway.

Following the Vet's directions, they turn left on Van Horne. The tramp's voice softens toward confidentiality as he speaks to LaPointe. "You can tell him to stop here at the corner. Just you come with me, Lieutenant. I don't want anyone else to come. Okay? Okay?"

"I'll leave the driver here. The young man is attached to me."

Guttmann glances over, uncertain whether or not LaPointe is sending him up.

The car pulls over to the curb, and LaPointe instructs the driver to wait for them.

An unlit side street of storage companies and warehouses ends abruptly at a woven wire fence that screens off a little-used freight shunt yard, the tracks of which glow dimly down in a black depression below and beyond the fence. LaPointe and Guttmann follow the Vet down the steep embankment, glissading dangerously over cinders, braking to prevent a headlong run that would precipitate them into the darkness below.

At the base of the slope, the Vet begins to cut across the tracks with the kind of familiarity that does not require light. LaPointe tells him to wait a minute, and he closes his eyes to speed up the dilation of his pupils. The smudgy dark gray cityglow has the effect of moonlight through mist, obscuring details, yet providing too much light to permit the eyes to adjust to the dark. Eventually, however, LaPointe can make out the parallel sets of rails and the glisten of tar on the ties. He tells the Vet to go on, but more slowly. He feels uncomfortable and out of his element, walking through this broken ground of cinder and weeds that is neither city terrain nor country, but a starved and sooty wasteland that the city has not occupied and the country cannot reclaim.

They cross over half a dozen sets of rails, then turn west, parallel to the tracks. Soon rust mutes the shine of the rails, and ragged black weeds indicate that they are in an unused wing of the shunt yard. One by one, the pairs of tracks end against heavy metal bumpers, until they are following the last along a wide curve close to a dark embankment. Without warning, the Vet turns aside and scrambles down a slope and along a faint trail through dead burrs, and stunted, hollow-stalked weeds brittle with the frost. Wind swirls in this declivity of the freight yard, one minute pushing LaPointe's overcoat from behind, and the next pressing against his chest and leaking in through the collar. The only sounds are the moan of the wind and the harsh rustle of their passage over frosted ground and through the weeds. They are isolated in this vast island of silence and dark in the midst of the city. All around them, but at a distance, the lights of traffic crawl in long double rows. A huge beer sign half a mile away at the far end of the freight yard flashes red-yellow-white, red-yellow-white. And from somewhere afar comes the wailing of an ambulance siren.

The Vet's pace slackens and he stops. "It's right over there, Lieutenant." He points toward the cliff, looming black against the dark gray of the cityglow sky. "I'll go get the wallet for you."

LaPointe peers through the gloom, but he can see no shelter, no shack.

"I'll go with you," he decides.

"I won't run off. Honest."

"Come on, come on! It's cold. Let's get it over with."

The Vet still hesitates. "All right. But he doesn't have to come, does he?"

Guttmann presses back his hair, which the wind is standing on end. "I'll wait here, Lieutenant."

LaPointe nods, then follows the Vet along the dim path.

Guttmann watches the vague figures blend into the dark, then disappear as they pass close to the embankment. He catches a bit of motion later, out of the corner of his eye where peripheral night vision is better. He strains to see, but he loses them. After several minutes, he hears the distant clank and scraping of metal—a heavy sheet of metal, from the sound of it. He hugs his coat around him and tucks his chin into his collar.

In about ten minutes he hears the crackle of dead, frozen stalks, then he sees them returning. The Vet's body is stooped and slack; he seems deflated. For the fourth time that night, the *bomme's* personality and manner have changed abruptly. The conditions of his life long ago ground away any pretensions of dignity, but there remains the husk of pride, and that has been damaged: the Lieutenant has seen his snug little kip. He passes Guttmann without a glance, and leads the policemen back through the field of frozen weeds, along the single unused track with its rusted rails, back over the pairs of glistening rails, to the base of the embankment, just below the wire fence and the light of the city.

"We can find our way from here," LaPointe tells the tramp.

Without a word, the Vet turns and starts back the way they came.

"Vet?" LaPointe calls.

The *bomme* stops in his tracks, but he doesn't turn to face them.

"You know I won't tell any of them about your kip, don't you?"

The Vet's voice is listless. "Yeah." He clutches the brim of his floppy hat against the wind and trudges back across the tracks.

LaPointe looks after him for a second. "Come on," he says. They scramble up the cinder embankment, over the wire fence, and soon they are back in the light, on the truncated street of warehouses. As Guttmann walks on, LaPointe stands for a moment and looks back over the shunt yard, a matte-black hole ripped out of the map of Montreal's streets and city lights. His sense of reality is upset. Somehow this street with its warehouses and the noise and light of passing traffic down at the corner seems artificial, temporary. That dark, desolate freight yard with its faint paths crowded in by black frozen burrs, with its silence in the midst of the city's noise, its dark in the midst of the city's light—that was real. It was not pleasant, but it was real . . . and inevitable. It is what the whole city would be six months after man was gone. It is the seed of urban ruin.

Oh, he's just tired; feeling a little *cafard*. There is vertigo in his sense of reality because he's been awake too long, because of the hard scramble up the cinder embankment, and because of the pleasant, terrifying tingle, this effervescence in his blood. . . .

Guttmann is cold, and he walks quickly toward the waiting police car with its dozing driver and its radio, against regulations, tuned to music. Then he realizes that LaPointe is not with him. He turns impatiently and sees the Lieutenant standing against the wire fence, his eyes closed. As Guttmann approaches, LaPointe opens his eyes and rubs his upper arms as though to restore circulation. Before Guttmann can ask what's wrong, the Lieutenant growls, "Come on! Let's not stand around here all night! It's cold, for Christ's sake!"

They sit in a back booth, the only customers of the A-One Café. When they came in, LaPointe greeted the old Chinese owner: "How's it going, Mr. A-One?"

The Chinese cackled and responded, "Yes, you bet. That's a good one!"

Guttmann assumed the greeting and response were ancient and automatic, a ritual joke they have shared for years.

Without asking what they wanted, the old man brought them two cups of coffee, thick and brackish, the lees from an afternoon pot. Then he returned to stand by the front window, motionless, his arms folded across his chest, his eyes focused on a mid-distance beyond his window.

The naked bulb above his head produces an oblique angle of light which deepens the furrows and rivulets of his face. His eyes do not blink.

LaPointe sits huddled in his coat, frowning meditatively as he slowly stirs his coffee, although he has not put sugar into it.

On the wall beside Guttmann's head is a gaudy embroidered hanging featuring a long-tailed bird resting on the branch of a tree bearing every kind of flower. And tacked up next to it is a picture of a very healthy girl in a swimsuit coyly considering the commitment involved in accepting the bottle of Coke thrust toward her by an aggressive male fist.

AVEC COKE Y A D'LA JOIE!

Guttmann stifles a yawn so deep that it brings tears. "Not much business," he says irrelevantly. "Wonder why he stays open all night."

LaPointe looks up as though he has forgotten the young man's presence. "Oh, you don't need much sleep when you're old. He has no wife. It helps to shorten the nights, I suppose."

For the first time, Guttmann wonders if LaPointe has a wife. He cannot imagine it; cannot picture him taking a Sunday afternoon walk in some park, a middle-aged matron on his arm. Then the image starts to form in Guttmann's mind of LaPointe in bed with a woman. . . .

"What is it?" LaPointe asks. "What are you smiling at?"

"Oh, nothing," Guttmann lies. "It's just that . . . I don't know what in hell I'm doing here. I don't know why I didn't take the car back to the Quartier Général." He pushes out a sigh and shakes his head at himself. "I must be getting dopey with lack of sleep."

LaPointe nods. "You've got what Gaspard calls 'the sits.' "

"What?" Guttmann is thrown off track by the unexpected shift to English.

"The sits. That's when you're so tired and numbheaded that you don't have the energy to get up and go home."

"That what I've got all right. The sits. That's a good name for it. I wish I were in bed right now."

LaPointe glances at him, a smile in his down-sloping eyes.

"No," Guttmann laughs. "She's back in her own apartment by now. But maybe all is not lost. We have a date for tomorrow."

"We're going to have to do some work tomorrow."

"But tomorrow's Saturday."

LaPointe put his elbow on the table and his forehead in his palm. "That's right. You see? Your college education wasn't a waste after all. You know the days of the week. After Friday, Saturday. Come to think of it, tomorrow's Sunday."

"What?"

"What time is it?"

"Ah, it's . . ." Guttmann tips his wrist toward the light. "Christ, it's almost two."

"Want some more coffee?"

"No, sir. After spending the day with you. I don't think I'll ever want another cup of coffee in my life." Guttmann glances toward the motionless Chinese. "Is that all he does? Just stand there looking inscrutable?"

"What does that mean? Inscrutable?"

"Inscrutable means . . . hell, sir, I don't know. My brain's gone to sleep. It means . . . ah . . . of or pertaining to the inability to scrute? Je scrute, tu scrutes, il scrute . . . shit, I don't know." He sits back, and his eyes settle on the Chinese again. "He must be lonely."

LaPointe shrugs. "I doubt it. He's past that."

This simple bit of human understanding from the Lieutenant disturbs Guttmann. He can't peg LaPointe in his mind. Like most liberals, he assumes that all thinking men are liberals. On the one hand, LaPointe is the classic old-timer who rags his juniors, pokes fun at education, harasses and bullies the civilians— the prototypical tough cop. On the other hand, he is a friend to ex-whores with bashed-up faces, a paternal watchdog who chats with people on the street, knows the bums, understands his patch . . . seems to have affection for it. Pride, even. Guttmann knows better than to think that people are black or white. But he expects to find them gray shades, not alternately black *then* white. Lieutenant LaPointe: Your Friendly Neighborhood Fascist.

"He should find some old duffers to play pinochle with," Guttmann says.

"Who?"

"The old Chinese who runs this place."

"Why pinochle?"

"I don't know. That's what old farts do when they don't know what else to do with themselves, isn't it? Play pinochle? I mean . . ." Guttmann stops and closes his eyes. He slowly shakes his head. "No, don't tell me. You play pinochle, don't you, sir?"

"Twice a week."

Guttmann hits his forehead with the heel of his hand. "I should have known. You know, sir, it just seems that fate doesn't want us to hit it off."

"Don't blame fate. It's your big mouth."

"Yes, sir."

"What have you got against pinochle?"

"Believe it or not, I don't have anything against pinochle. My grandfather used to play pinochle with his cronies late into the night sometimes."

"Your grandfather."

"Yes, sir. That's mostly what I remember him doing; sitting with his friends until all hours. Playing. Pretending it mattered who won and who lost. I just came to associate it with lonely old men, I guess."

"I see."

"I have nothing against the game. I'm a pinochle player myself, sir. My grandfather taught me."

"Are you any good?"

"Sir, excuse me. But doesn't it strike you as odd that we are sitting in a Chinese all-night coffee shop at two in the morning talking about pinochle?"

LaPointe laughs. The kid's okay. "Let's see what we've got here," he says, taking from his overcoat pocket the wallet the Vet gave him, and emptying the contents onto the table. There is a scrap of paper with two girls' names written in different hands, evidently by the girls themselves. First names only; not much help. There is a little booklet the size of a commemorative stamp, containing a dozen pictures of various sex positions and combinations: the kind of thing shown to objecting but giggling girls by a man who believes the myth that seeing the act automatically brings a woman to the point of panting necessity. In an accordion-pleated change pocket there are two contraceptives of the sort sold in vending machines in the toilets of cheap bars: guaranteed to afford maximum protection with minimum loss of sensation. Sold only for the prevention of disease. One of them features a "tickler"; the other is packed in a liquid lubricant. No money; the Vet got that. No driver's license. The wallet is cheap imitation alligator, quite new. There is a card in one of the plastic windows with places for the owner to provide particulars. Childishly, the dead man had felt impelled to fill it in. LaPointe passes the wallet over to Guttmann, who reads the round, infantile printing:

NAME	*Tony Green*
ADDRESS	*17 Mirabeau Street*
PHONE	*Apmt. 3B*
BLOOD TYPE	*Hot ! ! ! ! ! ! ! ! ! !*

"So the victim's name was Tony Green," Guttmann says.

"Probably not." There is a businesslike, mechanical quality to LaPointe's voice. "The printing is European. See the barred seven? The abbreviation for 'apartment' is wrong. That seems to give us a young alien. And the kid had a Latin look—probably Italian. But not a legal entrant, or his fingerprints would have been on file with Ottawa. He picked the name Tony Green for himself. If he runs true to form for Italian immigrants, his real name would be something like Antonio Verdi—something like that."

"Does the name mean anything to you? You know him?"

LaPointe shakes his head. "No. But I know the house. It's a run-down place near Marie-Anne and Clark. We'll check it out tomorrow morning."

"What do you expect to turn there?"

"Impossible to say. It's a start. It's all we have in hand."

"That, and the fact that the victim was a little hung up on sex. Oh, God!"

"Why 'Oh, God'?"

"You know that girl I had to leave tonight? Well, I promised her we'd go out tomorrow morning. Take coffee up on the Mount. Maybe drop in at a gallery or two. Have dinner maybe. Now I'll have to beg off again."

"Why do you do that? There's no real point in your coming along with me tomorrow, if you don't want to."

"Why do you say that, sir?"

"Well . . . you know. All this business of the apprentice Joans learning the ropes from the old-timers is a lot of crap. Things don't work that way. There's no way in the world that you're going to end up a street cop like me. You have education. You speak both languages well. You have ambition. No. You won't end up in this kind of work. You're the type who ends up in public relations, or handling 'delicate' cases. You're the type who gets ahead."

Guttmann is a little stung. No one likes to be a "type." "Is there anything wrong with that, sir? Anything wrong with wanting to get ahead?"

"No, I suppose not." LaPointe rubs his nose. "I'm just saying that what you might learn from me won't be of much use to you. You could never work the way I work. You wouldn't even want to. Look at how you got all steamed up about the way I handled that pimp, Scheer."

"I only mentioned that he has his rights."

"And the kids he bashes around? Their rights?"

"There are laws to protect them."

"What if they're too dumb to know about the laws? Or too scared to use them? A girl hits the city on a bus, coming from some farm or village, stupid and looking for a good time . . . excitement. And the first thing you know, she's broke and scared and willing to sell her ass." LaPointe isn't thinking of Scheer's girls at this moment.

"All right," Guttmann concedes. "So maybe something has to be done about men like Scheer. Stiffer laws, maybe. But not stopping him on the street and making an ass of him in front of people, for God's sake."

LaPointe shakes his head. "You've got to hit people where they're tender. Scheer is a strutting wiseass. Embarrass him in public and he'll keep off the street for a while. It varies with the man. Some you threaten, some you hurt, some you embarrass."

Guttmann lifts his palms and looks about with round eyes, as though calling upon God to listen to this shit. "I don't believe what I'm hearing, sir. Some you hurt, some you threaten, some you embarrass—what is that, a Nazi litany? Those are supposed to be tactics for keeping the peace?"

"They didn't tell you about that in college, I suppose."

"No, sir. They did not."

"And, of course, you'd play everything by the book."

"I'd try. Yes." This is simply said; it is the truth. "And if the book was wrong, I'd do what I could to change it. That's how it works in a democracy."

"I see. Well—by the book—the Vet was guilty of a crime, wasn't he? He took money from this wallet. Would you put him inside? Let him scream for the rest of his life?"

Guttmann is silent. He isn't sure. No, probably not.

"But that would be playing it by the book. And do you remember that *fou* who sharpens knives and worries about the snow? He'd make a great suspect for a knife murder. You almost sniffed him yourself. And do you know what would happen if you brought him in for questioning? He'd get confused and frightened, and in the end he would confess. Oh, yes. He'd confess to anything you wanted. And the Commissioner would be happy, and the newspapers would be happy, and you'd get promoted."

"Well . . . I didn't know about him. I didn't know he was . . ."

"That's the point, son! You don't know. The *book* doesn't know!"

Guttmann's ears are reddening. "But *you* know?"

"That's right! I know. After thirty years, I know! I know the difference between a harmless nut and a murderer. I know the difference between shit tracks on a man's arm and the marks left by selling blood to stay alive!" With a guttural sound and a wave of his hand LaPointe dismisses the use of explaining anything to Guttmann's type.

Guttmann sits, silently pushing his spoon back and forth between his fingers. He isn't cowed. He speaks quietly, without looking up. "It's fascism, sir."

"What?"

"It's fascism. The rule of a man, rather than the rule of law, is fascism. Even when the man has been around and thinks he knows what's best . . . even if the man is trying to do good things . . . to be fair. It's still fascism."

For a moment, LaPointe's melancholy eyes rest on the young man, then he looks over his head to the gaudy Chinese hanging and the Coke advertisement.

Guttmann expects a denial. Anger. An explanation.

That's not what comes. After a silence, LaPointe says, "Fascism, eh?" The tone indicates that he never thought of it that way. It indicates nothing more.

Once again, Guttmann feels undercut, bypassed.

LaPointe presses his eye sockets with his thumb and forefinger and sighs deeply. "Well, I think we'd better get some sleep. You can get the sits in your brain, as well as in your ass." He sniffs and rubs his cheek with his knuckles.

Guttmann delays their leaving. "Sir? May I ask you something?"

"About fascism?"

"No, sir. Back there in the freight yard. That *bomme* didn't want me to come with you and see his kip. And later you said something to him about not telling the others. What was that all about?"

LaPointe examines the young man's face. Could you explain something like this to a kid who learned about people in a sociology class? Where would it fit in with his ideas about society and democracy? There is something punitive in LaPointe's decision to tell him about it.

"You remember Dirtyshirt Red last night? You remember how he had nothing good to say about the Vet? All the *bommes* on the Main sleep where they can: in doorways, in alleys, behind the tombstones in the monument-maker's yard. And they all envy the nice snug private kip the Vet's always bragging about. They hate him for having it. And that's just the way the Vet wants it. He wants to be despised, hated, bad-mouthed. Because as long as the other tramps despise and reject him, he isn't one of them; he's something special. That make sense to you?"

Guttmann nods.

"Well—" LaPointe's voice is husky with fatigue, and he speaks quietly. "After we left you back there on the path, I followed him along a trail I could barely see. But there wasn't anything around. No shack, no hut, nothing. Then the Vet went behind a patch of bush and bent over. I could hear a scrape of metal. He was sliding back a sheet of corrugated roofing that covered a pit in the ground. I went over to the edge of it as he jumped down, sort of skidding on the muddy sides of the hole. It was about eight feet deep, and the bottom was covered with wads of rag and burlap sacking that squished with seep water when he walked around. He had a few boxes down there, to sit on, to use as a table, to stash stuff in. He fumbled around in one of these boxes and found the wallet. It was all he could do to get out of the pit again. The sides were slimy, and he slipped back twice and swore a lot. He finally got out and handed over the wallet. Then he slid the sheet of metal back over the hole. When he stood up and looked at me . . . I don't know how to explain it . . . there was sort of two things in his eyes at the same time. Shame and anger. He was ashamed to live in a slimy hole. And he was angry that somebody knew about it. We talked about it for a while. He was proud of himself. I know that sounds nuts, but it's how it was. He was ashamed of his hole, but proud of having figured it all out. I guess you could say he was proud of having made his hole, but ashamed of needing it. Something like that, anyway.

"One night a few years ago, he was drunk and looking for a place to hide, where the police wouldn't run him in for D and D. He found this cave-in hidden away among some bushes. Later on he thought about it, and he got a bright idea. He went back there at night with a spade he pinched somewhere, and he worked on the hole. He made it deeper and made the sides vertical. And whenever the sides crumble from him scrambling in and out, he works on it again. So his hole is always getting bigger. Rain gets in, and water seeps up from the slime, so he keeps adding rags and bags he picks up here and there. It's a clever little trap he's made for himself."

"Trap, sir?"

"That's what it is. That's how he uses it. He's afraid of being picked up drunk and put in a cell and left to scream. So every time he thinks he's got enough wine inside him to be dangerous, he buys another bottle and brings it back to his kip. Down there in the hole, he can drink until he's wild and raving. He's safe down there. Even when he's sober, it's hard for him to climb up those slimy sides. When he's drunk, it's impossible. He traps himself down there to save himself from being arrested and put inside. Of course, he's a claustrophobic, so sometimes he gets panicky down there. When his brain's soggy with wine, he thinks the walls are caving in on him. And he's terrified that a big rain might fill his pit with water when he's too drunk to get out. It's bad down there, you know. When he's drunk, he can't get out to shit or piss, so it's . . . bad down there."

"Jesus Christ," Guttmann says quietly.

"Yeah. He lives in a small hole in the ground *because* he's a claustrophobic."

"Jesus Christ."

LaPointe leans back in the booth and presses his mat of cropped hair hard with the palm of his hand. "And what do you do if you have to live in a slimey, stinking hole? You brag about it, of course. You make the other *bommes* despise you. And envy you."

Guttmann shakes his head slowly, his mouth agape, his eyes squeezed in pity and disgust. LaPointe's punitive intent in telling him about this has been effective.

"Tell you what," LaPointe says. "Don't come by to pick me up tomorrow until around noon. I need some sleep."

Without turning on the lights, he closes the door behind him and hangs his overcoat on the wooden rack. He flinches when the revolver in his pocket thuds against the wall; he doesn't want to wake her.

There is a crackling hiss in the room, and the crescent dial of the old Emerson glows dim orange. The station has gone off the air. Why didn't she turn the radio off? Ah. He forgot to tell her that you also have to jiggle the knob to turn it off. Then why didn't she pull out the plug? Dumb twit.

The ceiling of the bedroom is illuminated by the streetlamp beneath the window, and he can make out Marie-Louise's form in the bed, although she is below the shadow line. She sleeps on her side, her hands under her cheek, palms together, and her legs are in a kind of running position that takes up most of the bed.

He undresses noiselessly, teetering for a moment in precarious balance as he pulls off his pants. When he aligns the creases to fold the pants over the back of a chair, some change falls out of his pocket, and he grimaces at the sound and swears between his teeth. He tiptoes around to the other side of the bed and lifts the blankets, trying to slip in without waking her. If he curves his body just right, there is enough room to lie next to her without touching her. For five long minutes he remains there, feeling the warmth that radiates from her, but it is impossible to sleep when the slightest movement would either touch her or make him fall out of bed. Anyway, he feels ridiculous, sneaking into bed with her. He rises carefully, but the springs clack loudly in the silent room.

. . . at first the creaking bed had made Lucille tense. But later she used to giggle silently at the thought of imagined neighbors listening beyond the wall, shocked at such carryings-on.

At the noise, Marie-Louise moans in confused irritation. "What's the matter?" she asks in a blurred, muffled voice. "What do you want?"

He lays his hand lightly on her mop of frizzy hair. "Nothing."

Seven

"Hey?"

He does not move.

"Hey?"

"Ugh!" LaPointe wakes with a start, blinking his eyes against the watery light coming through the window. It is another gray day with low skies and diffused, shadowless brightness. He squeezes his eyes shut again before finally opening them. His back is stiff from sleeping on the narrow sofa, and his feet stick out from below the overcoat he has used as a blanket. "What time is it?" he asks.

"A little before eleven."

He nods heavily, still drugged with sleep. He sits up and scratches his head, grinning stupidly. These last two nights have taken their toll—his joints are stiff and his head cobwebby.

"I've got water boiling," she says. "I was going to make some coffee, but I don't know how to work your pot."

"Yes. It's an old-fashioned kind. Just a minute. Give me a chance to wake up. I'll do it." He yawns deeply. His overcoat covers him from the waist down, but his thick chest is exposed. He rubs the graying hair vigorously because it itches. *"Tabernouche!"* he grunts.

"Hard night?" she asks.

"Long, anyway."

She is wearing Lucille's pink quilted dressing gown again, but she has been up long enough to brush out her hair and put on eye make-up. There is a slight smell of gas in the room. She must have had some difficulty lighting the gas fire.

In his sleep, his penis has come out of the fly of his undershorts. He manages to tuck it back in with the same gesture as that with which he pulls up his overcoat and puts it on in place of a robe. Barefooted, he goes into the kitchen to make coffee.

She laughs half a dozen ascending notes, then stops short.

"What's wrong?"

"Oh, nothing. You look funny with your bare legs coming out of the bottom of your overcoat."

He looks down. "Yes, I suppose I do."

While he is pressing hot water through the fine grounds, it occurs to him that only one thing triggers her peculiar, interrupted laugh: people looking ridiculous. She laughed at her black eye, at him with soap on his cheek, at herself wearing Lucille's coat, and now at him again. It's a cruel sense of humor, one that doesn't even spare herself as a possible victim.

He gives her a cup of coffee and carries one with him to the bathroom, where he washes up and dresses.

Later, he fries eggs and toasts bread over the gas ring, and they take their breakfast in the living room, she coiled up on the sofa, her plate balanced on the arm, he in his chair.

"Why did you sleep out here?" she asks.

"Oh . . . I didn't want to disturb you," he explains, partially.

"Yeah, but why didn't you use the blankets I used last night?"

"I didn't really mean to sleep. I was just going to rest. But I dozed off."

"Yeah, but then why did you take your clothes off?"

"Why don't you just eat your eggs?"

"Okay." She spoons egg onto a bit of toast and eats it that way. "Where did you go last night?" she asks.

"Just work."

"You said you work with the police. You work in an office?"

"Sometimes. Mostly I work in the streets."

That seems to amuse her. "Yeah. Me too. You enjoy being a cop?"

He tucks down the corners of his mouth and shrugs. He never thought of it that way. When she changes the subject immediately, he assumes she isn't really interested anyway.

"Don't you get bored living here?" she asks. "No magazines. No television."

He looks around the frumpy room with its 1930's furniture. Yes, he imagines it would be dull for a young girl. True, there are no magazines, but he has some books, a full set of Zola, whom he discovered by chance twenty years ago, and whom he reads over and over, going down the row of novels by turn, then starting again. He finds the people and events surprisingly like those on his patch, despite the funny, florid language. But he doesn't imagine she would care to read his Zolas. She probably reads slowly, maybe even mouths the words.

Well, if she's bored, then she'll probably leave soon. No reason for her to stay, really.

"Ah . . . why don't we go out tonight?" he offers. "Have dinner."

"And go dancing?"

He smiles and shakes his head. "I told you I don't dance."

This disappoints her. But she is resourceful when it comes to getting her way with men. "I know! Why don't we go to a whisky à go-go after dinner. People can dance by themselves there."

He doesn't care much for the thought of sitting in one of those cramped, noisy places with youngsters hopping all around him. But, if it would please her . . .

She presses her tongue against her teeth and decides to gamble on pushing this thing to her advantage. "I . . . I really don't have the right clothes to go out," she says, not looking up from her cup. "I only have what I could sneak out in the shopping bag."

His eyes crinkle as he looks at her. He knows exactly what she's up to. He doesn't mind giving her money to buy clothes, if that's what she wants, but he doesn't like her thinking he's a dumb mark.

He sets down his cup and crosses to the large veneered chest. He has a habit of putting his housekeeping money into the top drawer every payday, and taking out what he needs through the month. He knows it's a bad habit, but it saves time. And who would dare to steal from Claude LaPointe? He is surprised at how many twenties have accumulated, crumpled up in the drawer; must be five or six hundred dollars' worth. Ever since the mortgage on the house was paid off, he has more money than he needs. He takes out seven twenties and flattens them with his hand. "Here. I'll be working today. You can go out and buy yourself a dress."

She takes the bills and counts them. Maybe he doesn't know how much a dress costs. So much the better for her.

"There's enough there to buy yourself a coat too," he says.

"Oh? All right." Before falling asleep last night, she thought about asking him for money, but she didn't know quite how to go about it. After all, they hadn't screwed. He didn't owe her.

While she sits looking out the window, thinking about the dress and coat, LaPointe examines her face. The green eye shadow she uses disguises what is left of her black eye. It's a nice pert face. Not pretty, but the kind you want to hold between your palms. It occurs to him that he has never kissed her.

"Marie-Louise?" he says quietly.

She turns to him, her eyebrows raised interrogatively.

He looks down at the park, colorless under yeasty skies. "Let's make a deal, Marie-Louise. For me, I like having you here, having you around. I suppose we'll make love eventually, and I'll enjoy that. I mean . . . well, naturally, I'll enjoy that. Okay. That's for me. For you, I suppose being here is better than sitting out your nights in some park or bus station. But . . . you find it dull here. And sooner or later you'll go off somewhere. Fine. I'll probably be tired of having you around by then. You can have money to buy some clothes. If you need other things, I don't mind giving you money.But I'm not a mark, and I wouldn't like you to think of me as one. So don't try to con me, and don't bullshit me. That wouldn't be fair, and it would make me angry. Is it a deal?"

Marie-Louise looks steadily at him, trying to understand what he's up to. She's not used to this kind of frankness, and she doesn't feel comfortable with it. She really wishes they had screwed and he had paid his money. That's neat. That's easy to understand. She feels as if she's being accused of something, or trapped into something.

"I knew there was money in that drawer," she says defensively. "I was looking around last night, and I found it."

"But you didn't take it and run off. Why not?"

She shrugs. She doesn't know why not. She's not a thief, that's all. Maybe she should have taken it. Maybe she will, someday. Anyway, she doesn't like this conversation. "Look, I better get going. Or did you want to come shopping with me?"

"No, I have to work—" LaPointe hears a car door slam down in the street. He half rises from his chair and peers down from the second-story window. Guttmann has just gotten out of a little yellow sports car and is looking along the row for the house number.

LaPointe tugs his overcoat on rapidly. He doesn't want Guttmann to see Marie-Louise and ask questions or, worse yet, pointedly avoid asking questions. The sleeve of his suit coat slips from his grasp, and he has to fish up through the arm of the overcoat to tug it down. "Okay," he says. "I'll see you this evening."

"Okay."

"What time will you be through shopping?"

"I don't know."

"Five? Five-thirty?"

"Okay."

As he clumps down the narrow stairs he grumbles to himself. She's too passive. There's nothing to her. Want some coffee? Okay. Even though she doesn't like coffee. Shall we eat at five? Okay. Do you want to say with me? Okay. Do you want to leave? Okay. Shall we make love? Okay. How about screwing out on the hall landing? Okay.

She doesn't care. Nothing matters to her.

Guttmann has his finger on the buzzer when the front door opens with a jerk and LaPointe steps out.

"Morning, sir."

LaPointe buttons up his overcoat against the damp chill. "Your car?" he asks, indicating with a thrust of his chin the new little yellow sports model.

"Yes, sir," Guttmann says with a touch of pride, turning to descend the steps.

"Hm-m!" Obviously the Lieutenant doesn't approve of sports cars.

But Guttmann is in too good a mood to care about LaPointe's prejudices. "That's to say, the car belongs to me and the bank. Mostly the bank. I think I own the ashtray and one of the headlights." His buoyancy is a result of a rare piece of good luck. When he called the girl this morning to tell her he would have to cancel their date, she beat him to it, telling him she had one hell of a head cold, and she wanted to sleep in to see if she could shake it off. He managed to sound disappointed, and he arranged to look in on her that evening.

LaPointe finds the tiny car difficult to get into, and he grunts as he slams the door on his coattail and has to open it again. In fact, he feels silly, riding around in a little yellow automobile. He would rather walk. Give him a chance to check on the street. Guttmann, for all that he is bigger than LaPointe, slips in quite easily. With a popping baritone roar, the car starts up and pulls away from the curb.

LaPointe cranes his neck to see if Marie-Louise is watching from the window. She is not.

They find a parking space on Clark, only half a block up from the rooming house. Opening the door, LaPointe scrapes it against the high curb; Guttmann closes his eyes and winces. LaPointe mutters something about stupid toy cars as he squeezes out and angrily slams the door behind him. Because it is Saturday, the street is full of kids, and one of them has paused in his game of "ledgey" to remark aloud that old men shouldn't ride around in little cars. LaPointe raises the back of his hand to him, but the boy just stares in sassy defiance as he wipes his nose gravely on the sleeve of a stretched-out sweater. LaPointe cannot repress a grin. A typical pugnacious French Canadian kid. A 'tit coq.

The rooming house is like others around the Main. Dull brick in need of paint; dirty windows with limp curtains of grayish fabric that hangs as though it is damp; a fly-specked card in the window of first floor front advertising rooms to let. This doesn't necessarily mean there is a vacancy. The concierge is probably too lazy to put the card in and take it out each time a short-time vagrant comes or goes. LaPointe climbs the wooden stoop and twists the old-fashioned bell, which rattles dully, broken. When there is no answer, he bangs on the door. Guttmann has joined him on the landing, looking back nervously at the small group of ragged kids that has gathered around his car. LaPointe bangs more violently, making the window rattle.

Almost immediately the door is snatched open by a slovenly woman who pushes back a lock of lank gray hair and snaps, "Hey! What the hell's wrong with you? You want to break down the door?" Her lower lip is swollen and cracked where someone hit her recently.

"Police," LaPointe says, not bothering to show identification.

She looks from LaPointe to Guttmann quickly, then stands back from the doorway. They enter a hall that smells of Lysol and boiled cabbage. The woman's attitude has changed from anger to tense uncertainty. "What do you want?" she asks, touching two fingers gingerly to the split lip.

The tentative tone of the question gives LaPointe his cue. She's frightened about something. He doesn't know what it is, and he doesn't care, but he'll push it a little to give her a scare and make her cooperative. "Routine questions," he says. "But not here in the hall."

She shrugs and enters her apartment, not inviting them to come in, but leaving the door open behind her. LaPointe follows and looks around as Guttmann, a little nervous, smiles politely and closes the door behind him. Without a warrant, you're supposed to await an invitation before entering a home.

The small room is crowded with junk furniture, and hot from an oversized electric heater she uses because it doesn't cost her anything. It just goes on the landlord's monthly bill. She keeps the place too hot because otherwise she'd feel she was losing money. LaPointe knows her type, knows how to handle her. He unbuttons his overcoat and turns to the woman just as she is glancing nervously out the window. She is expecting someone; someone she hopes will not come while the police are there. She adjusts the curtain, as though that is why she went to the window in the first place. "What do you want?" she asks sullenly.

For a moment, LaPointe does not answer. He looks levelly at her, draws a deep, bored breath and says, "You know perfectly well. I don't have time to play games with you."

Guttmann glances at him, confused.

"Look," the woman says. "Arnaud doesn't live here anymore. I don't know where he is. He moved out a month ago, the lazy son of a bitch."

"That's your story," LaPointe says, tossing a pillow out of the only comfortable chair and sitting down.

"It's the truth! Do you think I'd lie for him?" She touches her split lip. "The bastard gave me this!"

LaPointe glances at the fresh bruise. "A month ago?"

"Yes . . . no. I met him on the street yesterday."

"And he said good morning, and hit you in the mouth?"

The woman shrugs and turns away.

LaPointe watches her in silence.

She glances quickly toward the window, but does not dare to go and look out.

LaPointe sighs aloud. "Come on. I don't have all day."

For another minute, she remains tight-lipped. Then she gives in, shrugging, then letting her shoulders drop heavily. "Look, officer. The TV was a present. It doesn't even work good. He gave it to me, like he gave me this fat lip, and once the clap, the no-good bastard!"

So that's it. LaPointe turns to Guttmann, who is still hovering near the door. "Take down the serial number of the TV."

The young man squats behind the set and tries to find the number. He doesn't know why in hell he is doing this, and he feels like an ass.

"You know what it means if the set turns out to be stolen?" LaPointe asks the woman.

"If Arnaud stole it, that's his ass. I don't know anything about it."

LaPointe laughs. "Oh, the judge is sure to believe that." That's enough, LaPointe thinks. She's scared and ready to cooperate now. "Sit down. Let's forget the TV for now. I want to know about one of your roomers. Tony Green."

Confused by the change of topic, but relieved to have the questioning veer away from herself, the concierge instantly becomes confidential and friendly. "Tony Green? Honest, officer—"

"Lieutenant." It always surprises LaPointe to find people on the Main who don't know of him.

"Honest, Lieutenant, there's no one by that name staying here. Of course, they don't always give their right names."

"Good-looking kid. Young. Mid-twenties. Probably Italian. Stayed out all night last night."

"Oh! Verdini!" She makes a wide gesture and her lips flap with a puff of breath. "It's nothing when he stays out all night! It's women with him. He's all the time after it. Chases every *plotte* and *guidoune* on the street. Sometimes they even come here looking for him. Sometimes he has them in his room, even though it's against the rules. Once there were two of them up there at the same time! The neighbors complained about all the grunting and groaning." She laughs and winks. "His thing is always up. He wears those tight pants, and I can always see it bulging there. What's wrong? What's he done? Is he in trouble?"

"Give me the names of the women who came here."

She shrugs contemptuously and tucks down the corners of her mouth. The gesture opens the crack in her lip, and she licks it to keep it from stinging. "I couldn't be bothered trying to remember them. They were all sorts. Young, old, fat, skinny. A couple no more than kids. He's a real *sauteux de clôtures*. He puts it into all kinds."

"And you?"

"Oh, a couple of times we passed on the stairs and he ran his hand up under my dress. But it never went further. I think he was afraid of—"

"Afraid of this Arnaud you haven't seen in a month?"

She shrugs, annoyed with herself at her slip.

"All right. How long has this Verdini lived here?"

"Two months maybe. I can look at the rent book if you want."

"Not now. Give me the names of the women who came here."

"Like I told you, I don't know most of them. Just stuff dragged in off the street."

"But you recognized some of them."

She looks away uncomfortably. "I don't want to get anybody into trouble."

"I see." LaPointe sits back and makes himself comfortable. "You know, I have a feeling that if I wait here for half an hour, I may be lucky enough to meet your Arnaud. It'll be a touching scene, you two getting together after a month. He'll think I waited around because you told me about the TV. That will make him angry, but I'm sure he's the understanding type." LaPointe's expressionless eyes settle on the concierge.

For a time she is silent as she meditatively torments her cracked lip with the tip of her finger. At last she says, "I think I recognized three of them."

LaPointe nods to Guttmann, who opens his notebook.

The concierge gives the name of a French Canadian chippy whom LaPointe knows. She doesn't know the name of the second woman, but she gives the address of a Portuguese family that lives around the corner.

"And the third?" LaPointe asks.

"I don't know her name either. It's that woman who runs the cheap restaurant just past Rue de Bullion. The place that—"

"I know the place. You're telling me that *she* came here?"

"Once, yes. Not to get herself stuffed, of course. After all, she's a butch."

Yes, LaPointe knows that. That is why he was surprised.

"They had a fight," the concierge continues. "You could hear her bellowing all the way down here. Then she slammed out of the place."

"And you don't know any of the other people who visited this Verdini?"

"No, just *plottes*. Oh . . . and his cousin, of course."

"His cousin?"

"Yes. The guy who rented the room in the first place. Verdini didn't speak much English and almost no French at all. His cousin rented the room for him."

"Let's hear about this cousin."

"I don't remember his name. I think he mentioned it, but I don't remember. He gave me an address too, in case there were any problems. Like I said, this Verdini didn't speak much English." She is growing more tense. Time is running out against Arnaud's return.

"What was the address?"

"I didn't pay any attention. I got other things to do with my time than worry about the bums who live here."

"You didn't write it down?"

"I couldn't be bothered. I remember it was somewhere over the hill, if that's any help."

By "over the hill" she means the Italian stretch of the Main, between the drab little park in Carré Vallières at the top of the rise and the railroad bridge past Van Horne.

"How often did you see this cousin?"

"Only once. When he rented the room. Oh, and another time, about a week ago. They had a row and—hey! Chocolate!"

"What?"

"No . . . not chocolate. That's not it. For a second there I thought I remembered the cousin's name. It was right on the tip of my tongue. Something to do with chocolate."

"Chocolate?"

"No, not that. But something like it. Cocoa? No, that's not it. It's gone now. Something to do with chocolate." She cannot help drifting to the window and peeking through the curtains.

LaPointe rises. "All right. That's all for now. If that 'chocolate' name comes back to you, telephone me." He gives her his card. "And if I don't hear from you, I'll be back. And I'll talk to Arnaud about it."

She takes the card without looking at it. "What's the wop kid done? Some girl knocked up?"

"That's not your affair. You just worry about the TV set."

"Honest to God, Lieutenant—"

"I don't want to hear about it."

They sit in the yellow sports car. LaPointe appears to be deep in thought, and Guttmann doesn't know where to go first.

"Sir?"

"Hm-m?"

"What's a *plotte?*" Guttmann's school French does not cover Joual street terms.

"Sort of a whore."

"And a *guidoune?*"

"Same kind of thing. Only amateur. Goes for drinks."

Guttmann says the words over in his mind, to fix them. "And a . . . *sauteux de* . . . what was it?"

"A *sauteux de clôtures*. It's an old-fashioned term. The concierge probably comes from downriver. It means a . . . sort of a man who runs after women, but there's a sense that he chases young women more than others. Something like a cherry-picker. Hell, I don't know! It means what it means!"

"You know, sir? Joual seems to have more words for aspects of sex than either English or French-French."

LaPointe shrugs. "Naturally. People talk about what's important to them. Someone once told me that Eskimos have lots of words for snow. French-French has lots of words for 'talk.' And English has lots of—ah, there she goes!"

"What?"

"That's what I've been waiting for. The concierge just took the 'To Let' sign out of the window She was trying to get at it all the time we were there. It's a warning to her Arnaud to stay away. I'd bet anything it'll be put back as soon as we drive away."

Guttmann shakes his head. "Even though he bashes her in the mouth."

"That's love for you, son. The love that rhymes with 'forever' in all the songs. Come on, let's go."

They run down the two leads given them by the concierge. The first girl they catch coming out of her apartment as they drive up. LaPointe meets her at the bottom of the stoop and draws her aside to talk, while Guttmann stands by feeling useless. The girl doesn't know anything, not even his name. Just Tony. They met in a bar, had a couple of drinks, and went up to his room. No, she hadn't charged him for it. He was just a goodlooking guy, and they had a little fun together.

LaPointe gets back into the car. Not much there. But at least he learned that Tony Green's English was not all that bad. Obviously he had been taking lessons during the two months he stayed at the rooming house.

Guttmann is even more out of it at the second girl's house. Not a girl, really; a Portuguese woman in her thirties with two kids running around the place and a mother in a black dress who doesn't speak a word of French, but who hovers near the door of an adjoining bedroom, visible only to the standing Guttmann. From time to time, the mother smiles at Guttmann, and he smiles back out of politeness. The timing of the old woman's smiles is uncanny in conjunction with the daughter's confession. She seems to punctuate each sexual admission with a nod and a grin. Guttmann is put in mind of his deepest secret dread when he was a kid: that his mother could read his thoughts.

The young woman is scared, and she talks to LaPointe in a low, rapid voice, glancing frequently toward her mother's room, not wanting her to hear, even though she doesn't have two words of French. Just having her mother listen to the incomprehensible noise that carries this kind of confession is daunting. Her husband left her two years ago. A person has to have some fun in life. *The mother nods and grins.* Yes, she met Tony Green at a cabaret where she went with a girlfriend to dance. Yes, she did go to his room. *The mother nods.* No, not alone. She is embarrassed. Yes, the other woman, her friend, was with them. Yes, all three together in the same bed. *The mother grins and nods; Guttmann smiles back.* It wasn't her idea—all three in the same bed—but that's the way this Tony wanted it. And he was such a good-looking boy. After all, a person has to have some fun in life. It's rough, being left with two kids to bring up all by yourself, and a mother who is just about useless. *The mother nods.* It's rough, working eight hours a day, six days a week. The oldest girl goes to convent school. Uniforms. Books. It all costs money. So you have to work six days a week, eight hours a day. And nobody's getting any younger. It's a sin, sure, but a person has to have some fun. *The mother smiles and nods.*

LaPointe slides into the car beside Guttmann, and for a while sits in silence while he seems to sort through what the women have told him.

Guttmann can't help being impressed by LaPointe's manner as he talked to this woman and that girl in the street. At first they were afraid because he was a cop, but soon they seemed to be chatting away, almost enjoying unburdening themselves to someone who understood, like a priest. LaPointe asked very few questions, but he had a way of nodding and rolling his hand that requested them to go on . . . And what next? . . . And then? The Lieutenant's attitude was very different from his tough, bullying manner with the concierge. Guttmann remembers him saying something about using different tactics with different people: some you threaten, some you hit, some you embarrass.

And some you understand? Is understanding a tactic too?

"Let's go have a cup of coffee," LaPointe says.

"That's a wonderful idea, sir." Guttmann's stomach is still sour with all the coffee he drank yesterday. "I was hoping we'd have a chance to get some coffee."

The Le Shalom Restaurant is bustling with customers from the small garment shops of the district: young women with only half an hour off push and crowd to get carry-out orders; boisterous *forts* from the loading docks push sandwiches into their mouths and ogle the girls; intense young Jewish men in suits lean over their plates, talking business. There are few older Jews because most of them are first generation and still keep *Shabbes.*

Even though it's afternoon, most of the orders involve breakfast foods, because many of the people only had time for a quick cup of coffee that morning. And besides, eggs are the best food you can buy for the money. This area of Mount Royal Street is the center of the garment service industry, where labor from undereducated French Canadian girls is cheap. There are no big important companies in the district, but dozens of small, second-story operations that receive specialty orders from the bigger houses.

WORLDWIDE TUCKING & HEMSTITCHING
Nathan Z. Pearl, President

Two telephones behind the serving counter ring constantly. While three distraught girls hustle raggedly to clear and serve the tables, most of the real work is done by one middle-aged woman behind the counter. She does all the checks, serves the whole counter, answers all phone orders, keeps short orders rolling, argues and jokes with the customers, and wages a long-running feud with the harassed Greek cook.

To a customer: This your quarter? No? Must be for the coffee. Couldn't be a tip. Who around here would tip a quarter? *To the cook:* Two meat sandwiches. And lean for once! Where's my three orders of eggs? Like hell I didn't! What use are you? *To a customer:* Look, darling, keep your shirt on. I got only two hands, right? *To the phone:* Restaurant? Two Danish? Right. Coffee. One double cream. Right. One no sugar. What's the matter? Someone getting fat up there? Hold on one second, darling. . . . *To a customer:* What's your problem, honey? Here, give me that. Look, it's added up right. Nine, sixteen, twenty-five and carry the two makes fourteen, carry the one makes two. Check it yourself. And do me a favor, eh? If I ever ask you to help me with my income tax—refuse. *Back to the phone:* Okay, that was two-Danish-two-coffee-one-double-cream-one-no-sugar . . . and? One toast, right. One ginger ale? *C'est tout?* It'll be right up. What's that? Look, darling, if I took time to read back all the orders, I'd never get anything done. Trust me. *To a customer:* Here's your eggs, honey. Enjoy. *To a customer:* Just hold your horses, will you? Everyone's in a hurry. You're something special? *To the cook:* Well? You got those grilled cheese? *What* grilled cheese? Useless! Get out of my way! *To the phone:* Restaurant? Just give me your order, darling. We'll exchange cute talk some other time. Yes. Yes. I got it. You want that with the toast or instead of? Right. *To a customer:* Look, there's people standing. If you want to talk, go hire a hall. *To LaPointe:* Here we go, Lieutenant. Lean, like you like it. So who's the good-looking kid? Don't tell me he's a cop too! He looks too nice to be a cop. *To a customer:* I'm coming already! Take it easy; you'll live longer. *To herself:* Not that anybody cares how long you live.

The woman behind the counter is Chinese. She learned her English in Montreal.

The high level of noise and babble in the restaurant insulates any given conversation, so LaPointe and Guttmann are able to talk as they eat their plump hot meat sandwiches and drink their coffee.

"He's turning out to be a real nice kid," Guttmann says, "our poor helpless victim in the alley."

LaPointe shrugs. Whether or not this Tony Green was a type who deserved being stabbed is not the question. What's more important is that someone was sassy enough to do it on LaPointe's patch.

"Well, there's one thing we can rule out," Guttmann says, sipping his milky coffee after turning the cup so as to avoid the faint lipstick stain on the rim. "We can rule out the possibility of Antonio Verdini being a priest in civilian clothes."

LaPointe snorts in agreement. Although he remembered a case in which . . .

"Do you feel we're getting anywhere, sir?"

"It's hard to say. Most murders go unsolved, you know. Chances are we'll learn a lot about this Tony Green. Little by little, each door leading to another. We tipped the Vet because he has a funny hop to his walk. From him we got the wallet. The wallet brought us to the rooming house, where we learned a little about him, got a couple of short leads. From the girls we learned a little more. We'll keep pushing along, following the leads. Another door will lead us to another door. Then suddenly we'll probably come up against a wall. The last room will have no door. With a type like that—rubbers with ticklers, two women at a time, 'blood type: hot!'—anybody might have put him away. Maybe he got rough with some little *agace-pissette* who decided at the last moment that she didn't want to lose her *josepheté* after all, and maybe he slapped her around a little, and maybe her brother caught up with him in that alley, maybe . . . ah, it could be anybody."

"Yes, sir. There's also the possibility that we've already touched the killer. I mean, it could be the Vet. You don't seem to suspect him, but he did take the wallet, and he's not the most stable type in the world. Or, if Green was playing around with that concierge, her boyfriend Arnaud might have put him away. I mean, we have reason to suspect he's no confirmed pacifist." Guttmann finishes his sandwich and pushes aside the plate with its last few greasy *patates frites*.

"You know, you're right there," LaPointe says. "At some point or other in this business, the chances are we'll touch the killer. But we probably won't know it. We'll probably touch him, pass over him, maybe come back and touch him again. Or her. That doesn't mean we'll ever get evidence in hand. But you never know. If we keep pressing, we might get him, even blind. He might get jumpy and do something dumb. Or we might flush out an informer. That's why we have to go through the motions. Right up until we hit the blank wall."

"What do we do now?"

"Well, you go home and see if you can make up with that girl of yours. I'm going to have a talk with someone. I'll see you Monday at the office."

"You're going to question that woman who runs a restaurant? The lesbian the concierge mentioned?"

LaPointe nods.

"I'd like to come along. Who knows, I might learn something."

"You think that's possible? No. I know her. I've known her since she was a kid on the street. She'll talk to me."

"But not if I was around?"

"Not as openly."

"Because I'm a callow and inexperienced youth?"

"Probably. Whatever callow means."

As LaPointe turns off the Main, he passes a brownstone that has been converted into a *shul* by members of one of the more rigid Jewish sects—the ones with sidelocks—he can never remember its name. A voice calls to him, and he turns to see a familiar figure on the Main, walking slowly and with dignity, his *shtreimel* perfectly level on his head. LaPointe walks back and asks what the matter is. Their janitor is home sick with a cold, and they need a *Shabbes goy* to turn on the lights. LaPointe is glad to be of help, and the old Chasidic gentleman thanks him politely, but not excessively, because after all the Lieutenant is a public servant and everyone pays taxes. Too much thanks would give the appearance of artificial humility, and too humble is half proud.

He turns the corner of a side street to face a stream of damp wind as he walks toward La Jolie France Bar-B-Q, the café nearest the Italian boy's rooming house. It is the kind of place that does all its business at mealtimes, mostly from single workingmen who take their meals there at a weekly rate. So the place is empty when he enters, meeting a wall of pleasant heat after the penetrating cold. Almost immediately, the steamy windows and the thick smell of hot grease from *patates frites* make him open his overcoat and tug it off. He has his pick of tables, all of which are still littered with dishes and crumbs and slops. He sits instead at the counter, which is clean, if wet with recent wiping. Behind the counter a plump young girl with vacant eyes rinses out a glass in a sink of water that is not perfectly clear. She looks up and smiles, but her voice is vague, as though she is thinking of something else. "You want?" she asks absently.

Just then a short, sinewy woman with hair dyed orange-red and a Gauloise dangling from the corner of her mouth bursts through the back swinging door, hefting a ten-gallon can of milk on her hip. "I'll take care of the Lieutenant, honey. You get the dishes off the tables." With a grunt and a deft swing, she hoists the heavy can into place in the milk dispenser, then she threads its white umbilical cord down through the hole in the bottom. "What can I do for you, LaPointe?" she asks, not stopping her work, nor taking the cigarette from her mouth.

"Just a cup of coffee, Carrot."

"A cup of coffee it is." She takes up a butcher knife and with a quick slice cuts off the end of the white tube. It bleeds a few drops of milk onto the stainless-steel tray. "Aren't you glad that wasn't your *bizoune?*" she asks, tossing the knife into the oily water and taking down a coffee mug from the stack. "Not that you'd really miss it all that much at your age. Black with sugar, isn't it?"

"That's right."

"There you go." The mug slides easily over the wet counter. "Come to think of it, even if you don't chase the buns anymore, you were probably a pretty good *botte* in your day. God knows you're coldblooded enough." She leans against the counter as she speaks, one fist on a flat hip, the smoke of her fat French cigarette curling up into her eyes, which are habitually squinted against the sting of it. She is one of the few people who *tutoyer* LaPointe. She *tutoyers* all men.

"She's new, isn't she?" LaPointe asks, nodding toward the plump girl who is lymphatically stacking dishes while gazing out the window.

"No, she's used. Goddamned well used!" Carrot laughs, then a stream of raw smoke gets into her lungs and she coughs—a dry wheezing cough, but she does not take the cigarette from her lips. "New to you, maybe. She's been around for about a year. But then, I haven't seen you around here since I had that last bit of trouble. That makes a fellow wonder if your coming around means she's in trouble." She watches him, one eye squinted more than the other.

He stirs the unwanted coffee. "*Are* you in trouble, Carrot?"

"Trouble? Me? No-o-o. A middle-aged lesbian with rotten lungs, a bad business, a heavy mortgage, two shots in prison on her record, and the laziest bitch in North America working for her? In trouble? No way. I won't be in trouble until they stop making henna. *Then* I'm in trouble. That's the problem with being nothing but a pretty face!" She laughs hoarsely, then her dry cough breaks up the rising thread of gray cigarette smoke and puffs it toward LaPointe.

He doesn't look up from his coffee. "There was a good-looking Italian boy named Verdini, or Green. You went to his place."

"So?"

"You had a fight."

"Just words. I didn't hit him."

"No threats?"

She shrugs. "Who remembers, when you're mad. I probably told him I'd cut off his hose if he didn't stop sniffing around my girl. I don't remember exactly. You mean the son of a bitch reported me?"

"No. He didn't report you."

"Well, that's a good thing for him. Whatever I said, it must have scared him good. He hasn't been back here since. Do you know what that son of a bitch wanted? He used to come in here once in a while. He sized up the situation. I mean . . . just look at her. Look at me. You don't have to be a genius to size up the situation. So, while I'm waiting on the counter, this asshole is singing the apple to my girl. Well, he's a pretty boy, and she owns all the patents on stupid, so pretty soon she's ga-ga. But it isn't just her he wants. He thought it would be a kick to have us both at the same time! Sort of a round robin! He talked the dumb bitch into asking me if I'd be interested. Can you believe that? He gave her his address and told her we could drop in anytime. I dropped in, all right! I went over there and dropped on him like a ton of shit off a rooftop! Hey, what's all this about? If he didn't report me, why are you asking about him?"

"He's dead. Cut."

She reaches up slowly and takes the cigarette from the corner of her mouth. It sticks to the lower lip and tugs off a bit of skin. She touches the bleeding spot with the tip of her tongue, then daubs at it with the knuckle of her forefinger. Her eyes never leave LaPointe's. After a silence, she says simply, "Not me."

He shrugs. "It's happened before, Carrot. Twice. And both times because someone was after one of your girls."

"Yeah, but Jesus Christ, I only beat them up! I didn't kill them! And I did my time for it, didn't I?"

"Carrot, you have to realize that with your record . . ."

"Yeah. Yeah, I guess so. But I didn't do it. I wouldn't shit you, LaPointe. I didn't shit you either of those other times, did I?"

"But it wasn't a matter of murder then. And there were witnesses, so it wouldn't have done you any good to shit me."

Carrot nods. That's true.

The plump girl comes back to the counter carrying only four plates and a couple of spoons. She hasn't heard the conversation. She hasn't been paying attention. She has been humming a popular song, repeating certain passages until she thinks they sound right.

"That's good, honey," Carrot says maternally. "Now go get the rest of the dishes."

The girl stares at her vacantly, then, catching her breath as though she suddenly understands, she turns back and begins to clear the next table.

Carrot's face softens as she watches the girl, and LaPointe remembers her as a kid, a fresh-mouthed tomboy in knickers, flipping war cards against a wall—gory cards with pictures of the Sino-Japanese war. She was loud and impish, and she had the most vulgar tongue in her gang. The hair she tucked up into her cap used to be genuinely red. LaPointe recalls the time she smashed her toe when she and her gang were pushing a car off its jack for the hell of it. They brought her to the hospital in a police car. She didn't cry once. She dug her fingernails into LaPointe's hand, but she didn't cry. Any boy of her age would have wailed, but she didn't dare. She was never a girl; just the skinniest of the boys.

After a silence, LaPointe asks, "You figure she's worth it?"

"What do you mean?" Carrot lights another Gauloise and sucks in the first long, rasping drag, then she lets it dangle forgotten between her lips.

"A dummy like that? Is she worth the trouble you're in now?"

"Nobody says she's a genius. And talking to her is like talking to yourself . . . but with dumber answers."

"So?"

"What can I say? She's fantastic in the rack. The best *botte* I ever had. She just stares up at the ceiling, squeezing those big tits of hers, and she comes and comes and *comes*. There's no end to it. And all the time she's squirming all over the bed. You have to hang on and ride her, like fighting a crocodile. It makes you feel great, you know what I mean? Proud of yourself. Makes you feel you're the best lover in the world."

LaPointe looks over at the bovine, languid girl shuffling aimlessly to the third table. "And you would kill to keep her?"

Carrot is silent for a time. "I don't know, LaPointe. I really don't. Maybe. Depends on how mad I got. But I didn't kill that wop son of a bitch, and that's the good Lord's own truth. Don't you believe me?"

"Do you have an alibi?"

"I don't know. That depends on what time the bastard got himself cut."

That's a good answer, LaPointe thinks. Or a smart one. "He was killed night before last. A little after midnight."

Carrot thinks for only a second. "I was right here."

"With the girl?"

"Yeah. That is, I was watching television. She was up in bed."

"You were alone, then?"

"Sure."

"And the girl was asleep? That means she can't swear you didn't go out."

"But I was right here, I tell you! I was sitting right in that chair with my feet up on that other one. Last customer was out of here about eleven. I cleaned up a little. Then I switched on the TV. I wasn't sleepy. Too much coffee, I guess."

"Why didn't you go up to bed with her?"

Carrot shrugs. "She's flying the flag just now. She doesn't like it when she's flying the flag. She's just a kid, after all."

"What did you watch?"

"What?"

"On TV. What did you watch?"

"Ah . . . let's see. It's hard to remember. I mean, you don't really watch TV. Not like a movie. You just sort of stare at it. Let's see. Oh, yeah! There was a film on the English channel, so I changed over to the French channel."

"And?"

"And . . . shit, I don't remember. I'd been working all day. This place opens at seven in the morning, you know. I think I might have dropped off, sitting there with my feet up. Wait a minute. Yes, that's right. I did drop off. I remember because when I woke up it was cold. I'd turned off the stove to save fuel, and . . ." Her voice trails off, and she turns away to look out the window at the empty street, somber and cold in the zinc overcast. A little girl runs by, screeching with mock fright as a boy chases her. The girl lets herself be caught, and the boy hits her hard on the arm by way of caress. Carrot inhales a stream of blue smoke through her nose. "It doesn't sound too good, does it, LaPointe?"

Her voice is flat and tired. "First I tell you I was watching TV. Then when you ask me what was on, I tell you I fell asleep."

"Maybe it was all that coffee you drank."

She glances at him with a gray smile. "Yeah. Right. Coffee sure knocks you out." She shakes her head. Then she draws a deep breath. "What about *your* coffee, pal? Can I warm it up for you?"

LaPointe doesn't want more coffee, but he doesn't want to refuse her, He drinks the last of the tepid cup, then pushes it over to her.

While pouring the coffee, her back to him, she asks with the unconvincing bravado of a teen-age tough, "Am I your only suspect?"

"No. But you're the best."

She nods. "Well, that's what counts. Be best at whatever you do." She turns and grins at him, a faded imitation of the sassy grin she had when she was a kid on the street. "Where do we go from here?"

"Not downtown, if that's what you mean. Not now, anyway."

"You're saying you believe me?"

"I'm not saying that at all. I'm saying I don't know. You're capable of killing, with that temper of yours. On the other hand, I've known you for twenty-eight years, ever since I was a cop on the beat and you were a kid always getting into trouble. You were always wild and snotty, but you weren't stupid. With a day and a half to think up an alibi, I can't believe you'd come up with a silly story like that. Unless . . ."

"Unless what?"

"Unless a couple of things. Unless you thought we'd never trace the victim to here. Unless you're being doubly crafty. Unless you're covering for someone." LaPointe shrugs. He'll see. Little by little, he'll keep opening doors that lead into rooms that have doors that lead into rooms. And maybe, instead of running into that blank wall, one of the doors will lead him back to La Jolie France Bar-B-Q. "Tell me, Carrot. This Italian kid, did he have any friends among your customers?"

She gives him his coffee. "No, not friends. The only reason he ate here sometimes was because some of the guys talk Italian, and his English wasn't all that good. But he always had money, and a couple of my regulars went bar crawling with him once or twice. I heard them groaning about it the next morning, so sick they couldn't keep anything but coffee down."

"What bars?"

"Shit, I don't know."

"Talk to your customers tomorrow. Find out what you can about him."

"I'm closed on Sundays."

"Monday then. I want to know what bars he went to. Who he knew."

"Okay."

"By the way, does chocolate mean anything to you?"

"What kind of question is that? I can take it or leave it alone."

"Chocolate. As a name. Can you think of anybody with a name like chocolate or cocoa or anything like that?"

"Ah . . . wasn't there somebody who used to be on TV with Sid Caesar?"

"No, someone around here. Someone this Tony Green knew."

"Search me."

"Forget it, then." LaPointe swivels on his counter stool and looks at the plump girl. She has given up clearing the tables, or maybe she has forgotten what she was supposed to be doing, and she stands with her forehead against the far window, staring vacantly into the street and making a haze of vapor on the glass with her breath. She notices the haze and begins to draw X's in it with her little finger, totally involved in the activity. LaPointe cannot help picturing

her squirming all over the bed, kneading her own breasts. He stands up to leave.
"Okay, Carrot. You call me if you find out anything about this kid's bars or
friends. If I don't hear from you, I'll be back."

"And maybe you'll be back anyway, right?"

"Yes, maybe." He buttons up his overcoat and goes to the door.

"Hey, LaPointe?"

He turns back.

"The coffee? That's fifteen cents."

Eight

ON THE WAY to his apartment, LaPointe passes the headquarters of the First
Regiment of the Grenadier Guards of Canada. Two young soldiers with automatic rifles slung across their combat fatigues pace up and down before the
gate, their breath streaming from their nostrils in widening jets of vapor, and
their noses and ears red with the cold. They are watching a little group of
hippies across the street. Three boys and two girls are loading clothes and
cardboard boxes into a battered, flower-painted VW van, moving from a place
where they haven't paid their rent to a place where they won't. A meaty girl
who is above the social subterfuges of make-up and hair-washing is doing most
of the work, while another girl sits on a box, staring ahead and nodding in
tempo with some inner melody. The three boys stand about, their hands in their
pockets, their faces somber and pinched with the cold. They have fled from
establishment conformity, taking identical routes toward individuality. They
could have been stamped from the same mold, all long-legged and thin-chested,
their shoulders round and huddled against the cold.

By contrast, the guards keep their shoulders unnaturally square and their
chest boldly out. LaPointe assumes that once the hippies have driven away, the
guards will relax and round their shoulders against the wind. He smiles to
himself.

Before mounting the wooden stairs, LaPointe looks up at the windows of his
apartment. No lights. She must still be out shopping.

The static cold of the apartment is more chilling than the wind, so he
immediately lights the gas heater, then sets water to boil, thinking to have a nice
hot cup of coffee waiting for her when she comes back.

The water comes to a boil, and she has still not returned. He empties the
kettle, refills it, and replaces it on the gas ring. As though putting on the water is
a kind of sympathetic magic that will bring her home to the coffee.

It doesn't work.

He sits in his armchair and looks across the deserted park, drab in the winter
overcast. Perhaps she's left for good. Why shouldn't she? She owes him nothing.
Maybe she has met somebody . . . a young man who knows how to dance. That
would be best, really. After all, she can't go on living with him indefinitely. In
fact, he doesn't want her to. Not really. She'd be a pain in the neck. Then too,
someday soon . . .

Without thinking, he slips his hand up to his chest, as he has come to do by
habit each time he thinks of his aneurism . . . that stretched balloon. He feels

the regular heartbeat. Normal. Nothing odd in it. Yes, he decides. It would be best if she's found somebody else to live with. It would be ghastly for her to wake up some morning and find him beside her, dead. Maybe cold to the touch.

Or what if he were to have an attack while they were making love?

Good, then. That's just fine. She has found a young man on the street. Somebody kind. It's better that way.

He grunts out of the chair and goes into the kitchen to take off the kettle before the water boils away. He will enjoy a quiet, peaceful night. He will take off his shoes, put on his robe, and sit by the window, listening to the hiss of the gas fire and reading one of his Zola novels for the third or fourth time. He never tires of reading around and around his battered set of Zola. Years ago, he bought the imitation-leather books from an old man who ran a secondhand bookstore, a narrow slot of a shop created by roofing over an alley between two buildings on the Main. The old man never did much business, and buying the books was a way of helping him out without embarrassing him.

For several years the books sat unread on the top of his bedroom chest. Then one evening, for lack of something to do, he opened one and scanned it over. Within a year he had read them all. It wasn't until the first time through that he realized there was a sort of order to some of them: heroines of one book were the daughters of heroines of another, and so on. Thereafter he always read them in order. His favorite novel is *L'Assommoir,* in which he was able to predict, in his first reading, the inevitable descent of the characters from hope to alcoholism to death. The books feel good in his hand, and have a friendly smell. It is the 1906 *Edition Populaire Illustrée des Oeuvres Complètes de Émile Zola,* with drawings of substantial heroines, their round arms uplifted in supplication and round eyes raised to heaven, the line of dialogue beneath never lacking in exclamation points. Such men as appear in the plates stand back, amongst the dripping shadows, and look mercilessly down on the fallen heroines. The men are not individuals; they are part of the environment of poverty, despair, and exploitation to which futile hope gives edge.

The novels are populated by people who, if they spoke in Joual dialect and knew about modern things, could be living on the Main. It seems to LaPointe that you have to know the street, to have known the parents of the young chippies back when they were young lovers, in order to enjoy or even understand Zola.

Yes, he'll put on his robe and read for a while. Then he'll go to bed. He is looking for his robe when he notices in the corner of the bedroom Marie-Louise's shopping bag with its burden of odds and ends.

She will be back after all. The shopping bag is a hostage. He returns to the living room feeling less tired. She will surely be back within half an hour.

She is not. Evening imperceptibly deepens the sky to dusty slate as details down in the park retire into gloom. The novel is still on his lap, but it is too dark to read. The gas fire hisses, its orange-nippled ceramic elements an insubstantial glow, the room's only light. Twice, when cars stop outside, he rises to look down from the window. And once he starts up with the realization that the kettle must be burning. Then he remembers that he took it off long ago.

The air becomes hot and thick with the oxygen-robbing gas heater, which he knows he should turn down, but he is too tired and heavy to feel like moving.

As always, his daydreams stray to his wife . . . and his girls. It is late evening in their home in Laval. Lucille is doing dishes in the kitchen fixed up with modern appliances he has seen in store windows on the Main. Logs are burning in the fireplace, and he is fussing with them more than they need, because he enjoys poking at wood fires. He goes up to the girls' room—they are young again, and they are disobeying orders to get right to sleep. He finds them jumping on the bed, their long flannel nightgowns billowing out and entangling them when they land in a heap. He kisses them good night and teases them by scrubbing his whiskery cheek against their powdery ones. They complain and struggle and laugh. Lucille calls up that it is late and the girls need their sleep. He answers that they are already asleep, and the girls put their hands over their mouths to suppress giggles. He tucks them in with a final kiss, and they want a story and he says no, and they want the light left on and he says no, and they want a glass of water and he says no, and he turns out the light and leaves them and goes back down the stairs—he must get around to fixing the one that squeaks. He knows every detail of the house, the layout of the rooms, the wallpaper, the pencil marks on the kitchen doorframe that record the growth of the girls. But he never pictures a bedroom for Lucille and him. After all, Lucille is dead. No . . . gone. To the house in Laval.

He wakes with a sweaty throat and a wet mouth, and with a confused feeling that something is going on. Then he hears the sound of a key in the lock. The door opens with a slant of pale yellow light from the naked hall bulb, and Marie-Louise enters.

"My God, it's hot in here! What are you doing, sitting in the dark?"

As he gropes out of sleepiness, she finds the switch and turns on the lights. She is loaded down with parcels, which she dumps on the sofa, then holds her hands out to the gas fire. "Boy, it's cold tonight. Well? What do you think of it? Cute, eh?" She turns around to model an ankle-length cloth coat of burnt orange. "It was on sale. Well?"

She walks a couple of steps and does a comic little turn, parodying the models she has seen on television. She doesn't bother to conceal her limp, and LaPointe notices it as though for the first time. The detail had dropped from his mind. "It's . . . ah . . . fine," he says dopily. "Very nice." He wonders what time it is.

She hugs herself and rubs her upper arms vigorously. "Boy, it's the kind of cold that goes right through you. I was hoping you might have some hot coffee ready."

"I'm sorry," he says. "It didn't occur to me."

He is uneasy about the babbling quality of her speech. She's trying to say everything at once, as though she has something to hide and doesn't want to leave him space to question her. She says it's too hot in the room, yet she warms herself at the heater. Something's wrong.

"What have you been doing with yourself?" she asks lightly.

"Taking a nap." He looks at the mantel clock. Eight-thirty. "You've been shopping all this time?"

"Yes," she says with the inhaled Joual affirmative that means either yes or no. "Take a cab home?"

She pauses for a second, her back to him. "No. I walked." Her hollow tone tells him there is something in the way of a confession coming. He wishes he hadn't asked.

"No cabs?" he asks, affording her a facile excuse.

She sits on the sofa and looks directly at him for the first time. She might as well get it over with. "No money," she says. "I'm sorry, but I spent all you gave me. I got other things besides the coat and dress."

That is the confession? He smiles at himself, aware that he has been acting and thinking like a kid. "It doesn't matter," he says.

She turns her head slightly to the side and looks at him uncertainly out of the sides of her eyes. "Really?"

He laughs. "Really."

"Hey! Look at what I got!" Instantly she is up from the sofa, tearing open bags. "And I shopped around for bargains, too. I didn't waste money. Oh, did you see these?" She parts her long cloth coat and shows him thick-soled boots that go to the knee. They are a wet red plastic that clashes with the burnt orange of the coat. She rips open a bag and draws out a long dress that looks as though it were made of patchwork. She holds it up to herself by the shoulders and kicks out at the hem. "What do you think?"

"Nice. It looks . . . warm."

"Warm? Oh, I suppose so. The girl told me it's the in thing. Oh, and I got a skirt." She opens her coat again to show him the mini she is wearing. "And I got this blouse. There was another one I really liked. You know, one of those frilled collars like you see on old-time movies on TV? You know the kind I mean?"

"Yes," he lies.

"But they didn't have my size. And I got . . . let's see . . . oh, a sweater! And . . . I guess that's about it. No! I got some panties and things . . . there must have been something else. Oh, the coat! That's what cost the most. And I guess that's it!" She plunks down on the sofa amongst the clothes and ravished bags, her hands pressed between her knees, her elation suddenly evaporated. "You don't like them, do you?" she says.

"What? No, sure. I mean . . . they're fine."

"It's all the money, isn't it?"

"Don't worry about it."

"You know, we don't *have* to go out to dinner tonight like you promised. We could just stay home. That would save money."

There is a quality of pimpish insinuation in the way the proprietor of the Greek restaurant finds them a secluded table, in the way he keeps refilling her glass with raisin wine, in the way he grins and nods to the Lieutenant from behind her chair. LaPointe resents this, but Marie-Louise seems to be enjoying the special attention, so he lets it go.

Greek food is alien to her, but she eats with relish, unfolding the cooked grape leaves to get at the rice and lamb within. She doesn't eat the leaves, considering them to be only wrappings.

A candle set in red glass lights her face from a low angle that would be unkind to an older woman, but it only accents her animation as she recounts her shopping trip, or comments on the other patrons of the restaurant. He has chosen to sit with his back to the room so she can have the amusement of looking at the people and the pleasure of having the people look at her. It is a deliberate and uncommon gesture on the part of a man who normally keeps his back to walls and rooms open before him.

She doesn't really like the Greek wine, but she drinks too much of it. By the time the meal is over, she is laughing a little too loudly.

He enjoys watching the uncensored play of expression over her face. She has not yet developed a mask. She is perfectly capable of lying, but not yet of dissimulating. She is capable of wheedling, but not yet of treachery. She is vulgar, but not yet hardened. She is still young and vulnerable. He, on the other hand, is old and . . . tough.

As they finish their coffee—that Turkish coffee with thick dregs that Greeks think is Greek—she hums along with jukebox music coming from the floor above the restaurant.

"What's up there?" she asks, looking toward the stairs.

"A bar of sorts."

"With dancing?"

He shrugs. "Oh, there's a dance floor. . . ." He really feels like going home.

"Could we dance there?"

"I don't dance."

"Didn't you ever? Even when you were young?"

He smiles. "No. Not even then."

"How old are you anyway?"

"Fifty-three. I told you before."

"No, you didn't."

"I did. You forgot."

"You're older than my father. Do you realize that? You are older than my father." She seems to think that is remarkable.

It is so obvious a tactic that it would be unkind not to let it work. So they climb the stairs and enter a large dark room with a bar lit by colored bulbs behind ripple glass and a jukebox that glows with lights of ever-changing hues. They take one of the booths along the wall. The only other people there are the barmaid and a group of four young Greek boys at the next booth but one, sharing a bottle of ouzo that has been iced until it leaves wet rings on the tabletop. One of the boys leaves the booth and goes to the bar, where he lightheartedly sings the apple to the barmaid. She is wearing a short dress, and her thighs are so thick that her black hose squeaks with friction when she walks to serve the tables.

"What would you like?" LaPointe asks.

"What are they having?" She indicates the group of young men.

"Ouzo."

"Would I like that?"

"Probably."

"Do you like it?"

"No."

She feels there is a mild dig in that, so she orders ouzo defiantly. He has an Armagnac.

While the barmaid squeaks away to fetch the drinks, Marie-Louise rises and goes to the jukebox to examine its selections, slightly bending the knee of her good leg to make her limp imperceptible. LaPointe knows she doesn't care if he notices it, so the caution must be for the young Greek boys. As she leans over the jukebox, its colored light is caught in the frizzy mop of her hair, and she looks very attractive. Her bottom is round and tight under the new mini-skirt. He is proud of her. And the Greek boys do not fail to notice her and exchange appreciative looks.

She is the same age as his imaginary daughters sometimes are. She is the same age as his real wife always is. He feels two things simultaneously: he is proud of his attractive daughter, jealous of his attractive wife. Stupid.

There is some playful nudging among the Greek boys, and one of them—the boldest, or the clown—gets up and joins her, leaning close to study the record offerings. He puts a coin into the slot and gestures to her to make a selection. She smiles thanks and pushes two buttons. When he asks her to dance, she accepts without even looking at LaPointe. The music is modern and loud, and they dance without touching. Despite the jerky, primitive movements of the dance, she seems strong and controlled and graceful, and the dancing completely camouflages her limp. It is easy to see why she enjoys it so much.

The record stops without ending, like all modern music, a fade-out concealing its inability to resolve, and the dance is over. The young man says something to her, and she shakes her head, but she smiles. They return, each to his own table. As he passes, the Greek boy salutes LaPointe with a sassy little wave.

Marie-Louise slides into the booth a little out of breath and exuberant. "He's a good dancer."

"How can you tell?" LaPointe asks.

"Oh, the drinks are here. Well, 'bottoms up,'" She speaks the toast in English so accented that the second word sounds like "zeup." "Hey, this is good. Like licorice candy. But hot." She finishes it off. "May I have another one?"

"Sure. But it might make you sick."

She thrusts out her lower lip and shrugs.

He signals the waitress.

A party of older men clatters up the stairs, half drunk from celebrating a wedding. They drag out the tables from two booths and put them together, collecting chairs from everywhere. One man slaps his hand on the table and clamors for ouzo, and they are served two ice-cold bottles and a tray of glasses. One rises and proposes a toast to the father of the bride, who is the drunkest and happiest of the lot. The toaster is long-winded and somewhat incoherent; the others complain that they will never get a chance to drink, and finally they shout him down.

One of the young men has put money into the jukebox. As the music starts he saunters toward LaPointe's booth.

"You don't mind, do you?" Marie-Louise asks.

He shakes his head.

The proprietor comes up from the restaurant to check on things. When he notices the boy dancing with Marie-Louise, he frowns and crosses to the booth with the three young men. There is a short conversation during which one of the boys stretches his neck to take a look at LaPointe. As he passes the booth to offer insincere congratulations to the father of the bride, the proprietor nods and winks conspiratorially at the Lieutenant. He has taken care of everything. The young men won't be horning in on his girl again.

Marie-Louise finishes her ouzo and wants a third. For some minutes she sits, swaying her shoulders in tempo to a melody she is humming. She doesn't understand why the boys don't play more records and ask her to dance.

LaPointe is about to suggest that they go home, when one of the wedding party rises and navigates an arcing course to the jukebox. He pushes in a coin with operatic thoroughness, then presses first one button, then another. In a moment there comes the first twanging note of a stately traditional song. The old man lifts his arms slowly; his head is turned to one side and his eyes are closed; his fingers snap crisply to every second beat of the music.

The boys in the booth groan over the old-fashioned selection.

The old man looks directly at them, his eyes smiling and clever, and he slowly shuffles toward them, snapping his fingers and dipping gracefully with every third step.

"No way!" says one of the boys. "Forget it!"

But the old man advances confidently. These kids may be modern and may speak English, but their blood is Greek, and he will win.

Three other members of the wedding party are now on the dance floor, their arms around one another's shoulders, the outside two snapping their fingers to the compelling tempo, and dipping with each third step. Too drunk to walk perfectly, they dance with balance, grace, and authority.

There is a friendly scuffle in the young men's booth and one of them is pushed out onto the floor. With peevish reservation, he begins to snap his fingers mechanically, making it perfectly clear that this old-country shit is not for him. But the old man dances directly in front of him, looking him steadily in the eye and insisting silently on their common heritage. And when he puts his arm around the boy's shoulders, the peevishness evaporates and he falls into step. After all, he is a man.

The tempo of the music increases relentlessly. The five link up. Two other old men join the end of the line, one of them brandishing an ouzo bottle in his free hand. It is two steps to the side, then a strong dip forward. Marie-Louise watches with fascination. She is surprised when she notices that LaPointe is clapping his hands in time with the music, then she sees that the men at the double table are clapping also. When she starts to rise to join the dancing, LaPointe shakes his head.

"It's a men's dance."

"Oh, they won't mind."

He shrugs. Perhaps they won't. After all, she is not a Greek girl. In fact, they part to make a place for her in the line, and from the first step she is native to the simple, inevitable dance. She adds to it a flair of her own, dipping very low and bowing her head almost to the floor, then whipping it back as she snaps up again.

With this the other three young men run out to join the dance.

When the music ends, there are yelps of joy and everyone applauds his own performance. Instantly another coin is in the machine. LaPointe is recognized, and an envoy of two old men come to invite him to join the larger table. He signals for a bottle of ouzo as his contribution and brings his glass along. The instant he sits down, the glass is filled to overflowing with ouzo. He had not finished the Armagnac, and the mixture is ugly, so he downs it quickly to be rid of it. And his glass is instantly filled again.

Because she is Greek, the barmaid does not join the dancing, but she sits at the common table between two old men, one of whom complains drunkenly that nobody let him finish the toast he had rehearsed all day long. The other occasionally slips his hand between her legs where the thick thighs touch. She laughs and rolls her eyes, sometimes slapping the hand away and sometimes giving it a hard squeeze with her thighs that makes the old man whoop with naughty pleasure.

After the fourth or fifth dance, Marie-Louise is exhausted, and she sits one out, pulling up a chair across from LaPointe, between one of the boys and an old man. The old man is very drunk and insists on telling her a very important story that he cannot quite remember. She listens and laughs, despite the fact that he speaks only Greek. LaPointe knows that the boy has his hand in her lap under the table. His extravagant nonchalance gives him away.

An hour and a half later, Marie-Louise is dancing with one of the boys, while one of the old men clings to LaPointe, his hand gripping the nape of his neck, and explains that all cops are bastards, except of course LaPointe, who is a good man . . . so good that he is almost Greek. Not quite, but almost.

By the end of the night, the table is awash with water that has condensed from the icy bottles, and with spilled ouzo.

When he finds the problem of getting his key into the lock both fascinating and amusing, LaPointe realizes that he is drunk for the first time in years. Drunk on ouzo. A sick drunk. Stupid.

It is hot in the room because he forgot to turn the fire off when they left. He does it now, while she slips through to the bathroom, humming one of the Greek songs and occasionally snapping her fingers.

"Did you have a good time?" she calls when he comes into the bedroom and sits heavily on the bed. She is on the toilet, with the door wide open, talking to him without embarrassment while she pisses.

She doesn't wait for his answer. "I had a great time!" she says. "Best time of my life. I wish you could dance. Can we go there again?" As he tugs off his shoes, she wipes herself and stands up, shaking down her skirt as the toilet flushes.

LaPointe, drunk, is touched by the marital intimacy of it. It is as if they had been together for years. She must like me, he thinks. She must feel safe with me, if she doesn't mind pissing in my presence.

Now he *knows* he is drunk. He laughs at himself. Come on, LaPointe! Is that an act of love? A gesture of confidence? Pissing in your presence? With sodden seriousness, he confirms that, yes, it is. How long was it after your marriage before Lucille lost her embarrassment with you? She didn't even like to brush her teeth in your presence at first.

But . . . it could be something other than confidence, this pissing while chatting. It could be indifference.

Who cares?

Stupid, stupid. Drunk on ouzo. And you shouldn't drink with that aneur . . . anor . . . whateverthehell it is!

She undresses quickly, leaving things where they fall, and slips under the covers. The sheets are cold and she shudders as her naked legs touch them. "Hurry up. Get into bed. Make me warm."

He turns off the light before taking off his pants, then he gets in beside her. She clings to him, putting her leg over his for warmth. Soon their body heat warms the bed enough that one dares to move a leg to virgin parts of the sheet. She slips her knee between his legs and turns over, half upon him. The streetlight beneath the window makes her face visible in the dark. "What's wrong?" she asks, running her hand over his chest. She laughs at him. "Hey, I'm not your daughter, after all."

What? What put that into her head? What's wrong with her?

They make love.

Nine

HE WAKES TO dazzling sunlight streaming through the bedroom window, and to a heavy block of pain lodged behind his eyes. Ouzo.

The sunlight is unexpected after three weeks of leaden skies. It might mark the end of the pig weather, or it might be nothing more than one of those occasional wind shifts that bring diamond-hard winter cold for a few hours, like the night that Italian kid was found in the alley.

He puffs out a little breath and is not surprised to see it make a shallow cone of vapor. It will be sparkling and frigid out in the park. He slips out of bed, trying not to let cold air in to disturb Marie-Louise. When he bends forward to fish around for his slippers, he discovers the clot of ouzo pain behind his eyes is loose and jagged-edged. One eye closes involuntarily with the ache of it.

He pads into the living room muttering to himself: an ouzo hangover. Stupid, stupid, stupid. Giddiness overwhelms him briefly as he stoops down to light the gas fire. The last time he had a hangover like this was from drinking caribou, that most lethal of all liquids, with an old friend from Trois Rivières. But that was years and years ago.

As the bathtub fills, he cups his hands and drinks tap water from the sink. So desiccated is he that the water seems never to reach his stomach, being absorbed by parched tissue on its way down. He almost gags trying to swallow several aspirin with water from cupped hands. In the tub, his eyes closed, he sits a long time with steam rising all about him. The water and the heat and the aspirin combine to melt some of the ouzo out of his system; the nausea retreats, but the headache persists. Why did he drink so much? Why did he want to get drunk? He thinks about the love he and Marie-Louise made last night. It was good, and very gentle, particularly that long time he held her, between lovemakings. He believes it was good for her too. She wouldn't have faked all that. Why should she?

He did not shave last night before bed, as is his custom, but he doesn't dare try just now. He would probably cut his throat with the straight razor, shaky as he is.

While he makes coffee, he suddenly feels guilty about Marie-Louise. My God. If he feels this bad, what will *she* feel like? Poor kid.

The poor kid chatters with animation as she sits on the sofa, curled up in Lucille's pink robe. He answers in monosyllables, turning his head to look at her; it hurts when he moves his eyes.

"What was that licorice stuff we drank?" she asks. "It was good."

"Ouzo," he mutters.

"What?"

"Ouzo!"

"Hey, what's wrong? Are you mad about something?"

"No."

"You're sure you're not mad? I mean, you seem . . ."

"I'm fine."

"Say . . . you're not sick, are you."

"Sick? Me?" He manages a chuckle.

"I just thought . . . I mean, you told me to watch out for that . . . what's it called again?"

"Ou-zo. Look, I'm fine. Just a little tired."

She looks at him sideways with a childish leer. "I don't blame you. You have a right to feel tired."

He smiles wanly. He cannot quite forgive her for being so healthy and buoyant, but she does look pretty with the sunlight in her hair like that.

She goes into the bedroom to find her hairbrush. When she returns, she is humming one of the Greek songs, doing a little sliding step and dipping down, then snapping her head up on the rise. One of his eyes closes involuntarily with the snap of her head. She plunks down on the sofa and begins to brush her hair. "Hey, we'll have to go out for breakfast. I told you that I didn't buy any groceries. I spent all the money on clothes. Where will we go?"

"I'm not particularly hungry; are you?"

"Hm-m! I could eat a horse! And look what a beautiful day it is!"

The glitter of the park stings his eyes. But yes, it is a beautiful day. Perhaps a walk in the cold air would help.

With few places open on a Sunday morning, they take breakfast in one of the *variété* shops common to this *quartier,* although slowly disappearing with the invasion of large cut-rate establishments. Such shops sell oddments and orts: candy, bagels, teddy bears, Chap Stick, ginger ale, jigsaw puzzles, aspirin, newspapers, cigarettes, contraceptives, kites, everything but what you need at any given moment. Its window is piled with dusty, flyspecked articles that are never sold and never rearranged. In the jumble, knitted snow caps and suntan lotion rest side by side, one or the other always out of season, except in spring, when they both are.

The proprietor moves a stack of newspapers to the floor to make room for them at the short, cracked marble counter. He has a reputation in the district for being a "type," and he works at maintaining it. Although his counter service is usually limited to stale, thick coffee in the winter and soft drinks in summer, he can accommodate light orders, if he happens to have cheese or eggs in the refrigerator of his living space behind the shop. They ask for eggs, toast, and coffee, which the proprietor fixes up on his stove in the back room, all the while singing to himself and maintaining an animated conversation in English, his voice raised, from the other room.

"Is it sunny enough for you, Lieutenant? But I'd bet you a million bucks it

won't last. If it don't snow tonight, then tomorrow will be the same as yesterday–shitbrindle clouds and no sun." He sticks his head out through the curtain.
"Sorry, lady." He disappears back and calls, "Hey, do you want these sunny
side up?

> *Keep your sunny side up, up . . .*

Hey, you remember that one, Lieutenant? Oh-oh! I broke one. How about
having them scrambled? They're better for you that way, anyway. Egg whites
ain't good for your heart. I read that somewhere.

> *My heart is a hobo,*
> *Loves to go out berry picking,*
> *Hates to hear alarm clocks ticking.*

You've *got* to remember that one, Lieutenant. Bing Crosby." He comes from the
back room, carefully balancing two plates, which he sets down on the cracked
counter. "There you go! Two orders of scrambled. Enjoy. Yeah, Bing Crosby
sang that in one of his films. I think he was a priest. Say, do you remember
Bobby Breen, Lieutenant?

> *There's a rainbow on the river . . .*

That was a great movie. He sang that sitting on a hay wagon. You know, that
ain't easy, singing while you're on a hay wagon. Yeah, Bobby Breen and Shirley
Temple. Wonder whatever became of Shirley Temple. They don't make movies
like that any more. All this violence shit. Sorry, lady. Hey! You don't have any
forks! No wonder you ain't eating. Here! Geez! I'd forget my ass if it wasn't tied
on. Sorry, lady. Here's your coffee. Hey, did you read this morning about that
guy getting stabbed in an alley just off the Main? How about that? It's getting so
you can't take a walk around the block anymore without getting stabbed by
some son of a bitch. Sorry, lady. Things ain't what they used to be. Right,
Lieutenant? And the prices these days!

> *The moon belongs to everyone*
> *The best things in life are free . . .*

Don't you believe it! What can you get free these days? Advice. Cancer maybe.
It's a miracle a man can stay in business with the prices. Everybody out to fuck
his neighbor . . . oh, lady, I *am* sorry! Geez, I'm really sorry."
   As they walk slowly along a gravel path through the park, her hand in the
crook of his arm, she asks, "What was that *mec* jabbering about?"
   "Oh, nothing. It never occurred to him that you don't speak English."
   The crisp air has cleared LaPointe's headache away, and the little food has
settled his stomach. The thin wintery sunshine warms the back of his coat
pleasantly, but he can feel a sudden ten- or fifteen-degree drop in temperature
when he steps into a shadow. The touch of this sun, dazzling but insubstantial,
reminds him of winter mornings on his grandparents' farm, the soil of which
was so rocky and poor that the family joke said the only things that grew there
were potholes, which one could split into quarters and sell to the big farmers to
be driven into the ground as post holes. All the LaPointes, aunts, cousins, in-
laws, came to the farm for Christmas. And there were a lot of LaPointes,
because they were Catholic and part Indian, and you can't lock the door of a
teepee. The children slept three or four to a bed, and sometimes the smaller
ones were put across the bottom to fit more in. Claude LaPointe and his cousins

fought and played games and pinched under the covers, but if anyone cried out with joy or pain, then the parents would stop their pinochle games downstairs and shout up that someone was going to get his ass smacked if he didn't cut it out and go to sleep! And all the kids held their breath and tried not to laugh, and they all sputtered out at once. One of the cousins thought it was funny to spit into the air through a gap in his teeth, and when the others hid under the blankets, he would fart.

On Christmas morning they were allowed into the parlor, musty-smelling but very clean because it was kept closed, except for Sundays, or when the priest visited, or when someone had died and was laid out in a casket supported on two saw horses hidden under a big white silk sheet rented from the undertaker.

The parlor was open, too, for Christmas. Kids opening presents on the floor. Christmas tree weeping needles onto a sheet. A pallid winter sun coming in the window, its beam capturing floating motes of dust.

The smell of mustiness in the parlor . . . and the heavy, sickening smell of flowers. And Grandpapa. Grandpapa . . .

Whenever a random image or sound on the Main triggers his memory in such a way as to carry him back to his grandfather, he always pulls himself back from the brink, away from dangerous memories. Of all the family, he had loved Grandpapa most . . . needed him most. But he had not been able to kiss him goodbye. He had not even been able to cry.

". . . still mad?"

"What?" LaPointe asks, surfacing from reverie. They have rounded the park and are approaching the gate across from his apartment.

"Are you still mad?" Marie-Louise asks again. "You haven't said a word."

"No," he laughs. "I'm not mad. Just thinking."

"About what?"

"Nothing. About being a kid. About my grandfather."

"Your grandfather! *Tabernouche!*"

That is a coincidence. He hasn't heard anyone but himself use that old-fashioned expletive since the death of his mother. "You think I'm too old to have grandparents?"

"Everyone has grandparents. But, my God, they must have been dead for ages."

"Yes. For ages. You know something? I wasn't mad at you this morning. I was sick."

"*You?*"

"Yes."

She considers this for a while. "That's funny."

"I suppose so."

"Hey, what do you want to do? Let's go somewhere, do something. Okay?"

"I don't really feel like going anywhere."

"Oh? What do you usually do on Sundays?"

"When I'm not working, I sit around in the apartment. Read. Listen to music on the radio. Cook supper for myself. Does that sound dull?"

She shrugs and hums a descending note that means: yes, sort of. Then she squeezes his arm. "I know why you're leading me back to the apartment. You didn't get enough last night, did you?"

He frowns. He wishes she wouldn't talk like a bar slut. He can hardly direct her to the apartment after she has said something like that, so they leave the park and stroll through back streets between Esplanade and the Main. This day of sunshine after weeks of pig weather has brought out the old people and the babies, making it seen almost like summer. In winter, the population of the Main seems to contract at its extremities; the old and the very young stay indoors. But in summer, there are babies in prams, or toddlers in harnesses, their leashes tied to stoop railings, while old, frail-chested men in panama hats walk carefully from porch to porch. And on the Main merchants stand in their open doorways, occasionally stepping out onto the sidewalk and looking up and down the street wistfully, wondering where all the shoppers could be on such a fine day. If one stops and looks in the window, the owner will silently appear beside him, seeming to examine the merchandise with admiration, then he will drift toward the door, as though the magnetism of his body can draw the customer after him.

The weight of her arm through his is pleasant, and whenever they cross a street, he presses it against his side, as though to conduct her safely across. They walk slowly down the Main, window-shopping, and sometimes he exchanges a word or two with people on the street. He notices that she automatically bends her knee to disguise her limp when a youngish man approaches, though she doesn't bother when they are alone.

Around noon they take lunch at a small café, then they go back to the apartment.

For the past hour, Marie-Louise has puttered about, taking a bath, washing her hair, rinsing out some underclothes, trying on various combinations of the clothes she bought yesterday. She does not do domestic chores; the coffee cups go unwashed, the bed unmade. She has tuned the radio to a rock station which serves an unending stream of clatter and grunting, each bit introduced by a disc jockey who babbles with obvious delight in his own sound.

LaPointe finds the music abrasive, but he takes general pleasure in her busy presence. For a time he sits in his chair, reading the Sunday paper, but skipping the do-it-yourself column, which he finds less interesting than it used to be. Later, the paper slides from his lap as he dozes in the afternoon sunlight.

The burr of the doorbell wakes him with a snap. Who in hell? He looks out the window, but cannot see the caller standing under the entranceway. The only cars parked in the street are recognizable as those of neighbors. The doorbell burrs again.

"Yes?" he calls loudly into the old speaking tube. He has used it so seldom that he doubts its functioning.

"Claude?" the tinny membrane asks.

"Moishe?"

"Yes, Moishe."

LaPointe is confused. Moishe has never visited him before. None of the cardplayers has ever been here. How will he explain Marie-Louise?

"Claude?"

"Yes, come in. Come up. I'm on the second floor."

LaPointe turns away from the speaking tube to look over the room, then turns back and says, "Moishe? I'll come down . . ." But it is too late. Moishe has already started up the stairs.

Marie-Louise enters from the bedroom, wearing Lucille's quilted robe. "What is it?"

"Nothing," he says grumpily. "Just a friend."

"Do you want me to stay in the bedroom?"

"Ah, no." He might have suggested it if she hadn't, but when he hears it on her lips, he realizes how childish the idea is. "Turn the radio off, will you?"

There is a knock at the door, and at the same time the rock music roars as Marie-Louise turns the knob the wrong way.

"Sorry!"

"Forget it." He opens the door.

Moishe stands in the doorway, smiling uneasily. "What happened? You dropped something?"

"No, just the radio. Come in."

"Thank you." He takes off his hat as he enters. "Mademoiselle?"

Marie-Louise is standing by the radio, a towel turbaned around her newly washed hair.

La Pointe introduces them, telling Moishe that she is from Trois Rivières also, as if that explained something.

Moishe shakes hands with her, smiling and making a slight European bow.

"Well," LaPointe says with too much energy. "Ah . . . come sit down." He gestures Moishe to the sofa. "Would you like a cup of coffee?"

"No, no, thank you. I can only stay a moment. I was on my way to the shop, and I thought I would drop by. I telephoned earlier, but you didn't answer."

"We took a walk."

"Ah, I don't blame you. A beautiful day, eh, mademoiselle? Particularly after all this pig weather we appreciate it. The feast and famine principle."

She nods without understanding.

"Why did you phone?" LaPointe realizes this sounds unfriendly. He is off balance because of the girl.

"Oh, yes! About the game tomorrow night. The good priest called and said he wouldn't be able to make it. He's down with a cold, maybe a flu. And I thought maybe you wouldn't want to play three-handed cutthroat."

On the rare occasions when one of them cannot make the game, the others play cutthroat, but it isn't nearly so much fun. LaPointe is usually the absent one, working on a case, or dead tired after a series of late nights.

"What about David?" LaPointe asks. "Does he want to play?"

"Ah, you know David. He always wants to play. He says that without the burden of Martin he will show us how the game is really played!"

"All right, then let's play. Teach him a lesson."

"Good." Moishe smiles at Marie-Louise. "All this talk about pinochle must be dull for you, mademoiselle."

She shrugs. She really hasn't been paying any attention. She has been engrossed in gnawing at a broken bit of thumbnail. For the first time, LaPointe notices that she bites her fingernails. And that her toenails are painted a garish red. He wishes she had gone into the bedroom after all.

"You realize, Claude, this is the first time I have ever visited you?"

"Yes, I know," he answers too quickly.

There is a short silence.

"I'm not surprised that Martin is ill," Moishe says. "He looked a little pallid the other night."

"I didn't notice it." LaPointe cannot think of anything to say to his friend. There is no reason why he should have to explain Marie-Louise to him. It's none of his business. Still . . . "You're sure you won't have some coffee?"

Moishe protects his chest with the backs of his hands. "No, no. Thank you. I must get back to the shop." He rises. "I'm a little behind in work. David is better at finding work than I am at doing it. See you tomorrow night then, Claude. Delighted to make your acquaintance, mademoiselle." He shakes hands at the door and starts down the staircase.

Even before Moishe has reached the front door, Marie-Louise says, "He's funny."

"In what way funny?"

"I don't know. He's polite and nice. That little bow of his. And calling me mademoiselle. And he has a funny accent. Is he a friend of yours?"

LaPointe is looking out the window at Moishe descending the front stoop. "Yes, he's a friend."

"Too bad he has to work on Sundays."

"He's Jewish. Sunday is not his Sabbath. He never works on Saturdays."

Marie-Louise comes to the window and looks down at Moishe, who is walking down the street. "He's Jewish? Gee, he seemed very nice."

LaPointe laughs. "What's that supposed to mean?"

"I don't know. From what the nuns used to say about Jews . . . You know, I don't think I ever met a Jew in person before. Unless some of the men . . ." She shrugs and goes back to the gas fire, where she kneels and scrubs her hair with her fingers to dry it. The side closest to the fire dries quickly and springs back into its frizzy mop. "Let's go somewhere," she says, still scrubbing her hair.

"You bored?"

"Sure. Aren't you?"

"No."

"You ought to get a TV."

"I don't need one."

"Look, I think I'll go out, if you don't want to." She turns her head to dry the other side. "You want to screw before I go?" She continues scrubbing her hair.

She doesn't notice that he is silent for several seconds before he says a definite "No."

"Okay. I don't blame you. You worked hard last night. You know, it was real good for me. I was . . ." She decides not to finish that.

"You were surprised?" he pursues.

"No, not exactly. Older men can be real good. They don't usually blow off too quickly, you know what I mean?"

"Jesus Christ!"

She looks up at him, startled and bewildered. "What the hell's wrong with you?"

"Nothing! Forget it."

But her eyes are angry. "You know, I get sick and tired of it, the way you always get mad when I talk about . . . *making love.*" Her tone mocks the euphemism. "You know what's wrong with you? You're just pissed because someone else *a fait sauter ma cerise* before you could get at it! That's what's wrong with you!" She rises and limps strongly into the bedroom, where he can hear her getting dressed.

Twice she speaks to him from the other room. Once repeating what she thought was wrong with him, and once grumbling about anybody who didn't even have a goddamned TV in his pad . . .

He answers neither time. He sits looking out over the park, where the sun is already paling as the skies become milky again with overcast.

When she comes back into the living room, she is wearing the long patchwork dress she bought yesterday. As she puts on her new coat, she asks coldly, "Well? Coming with me?"

"Do you have your key?" He is still looking out the window.

"What?"

"You'll need your key to get back in. Do you have it?"

"Yes! I've got it!" She slams the door.

He watches her from the window, feeling angry with himself. What's wrong with him? Why is he fooling around with a kid like this anyway, like a silly old *fringalet?* There's only one thing to do; he's got to find her a job and get her the hell out of his apartment.

Marie-Louise walks huffily down the street, not bothering to flex her knee to conceal the limp, because she knows he's probably looking down at her and will feel sorry for her. She is angry about not getting her own way, but at the same time she is worried about spoiling a good thing. It's dull and boring, that frumpy apartment, but it's shelter. He lets her have money. He doesn't ask much of her. Shouldn't ruin a good thing until you've got something better. She recalls how the young Greek boy played the *tripoteux* with her under the table last night. Perhaps the old man noticed. Maybe that's why he's so irritable.

Anyway, she'll let him stew about it for a while, then she'll come back to the apartment. He'll be glad to see her. They don't get all the young stuff they want, these old guys.

Maybe she'll walk over to the Greek restaurant. See if anyone's around.

Beyond the window, evening has set in, fringing the layers of yeasty cloud. The morning's sunlight was a trick after all, a joke.

The gas fire hisses, and he dozes. He remembers the watery sunlight in the park. It reminded him of Sunday mornings in the parlor of his grandparents' farmhouse. Floating motes of dust trapped in slanting rays of sun. The smell of mustiness . . . and the heavy, sickening smell of flowers.

Grandpapa . . .

A bright winter day with sun streaming in the parlor window, and Grandpapa, thin and insubstantial in the box. All the children had to walk in a line past the coffin. The smell of flowers was thick, sweet. Claude LaPointe's shirt was borrowed, and too small; the tight collar gagged him. The children had been told to take turns looking down into dead Grandpapa's face. The little ones had to stand tiptoe to see over the edge of the coffin, but they did not dare to touch it for balance. You were supposed to kiss Grandpapa goodbye.

Claude didn't want to. He couldn't. He was afraid. But the grownups were in no mood for argument. There were already tensions and angers about who should get what from the farm, and everyone seemed to think that one uncle was grabbing more than his share. And who would take care of Grandmama?

Grandmama didn't cry. She sat in the kitchen on a wooden chair and rocked back and forth. She wrapped her long thin arms around herself and rocked and rocked.

Claude told his mother in confidence that he was afraid he would be sick if he kissed dead Grandpapa.

"Go on now! What's wrong with you? Don't you love your Grandpapa?"

Love him? More than anybody. Claude used to daydream about Grandpapa taking him away from the streets to the farm. Grandpapa never knew the daydreams; Claude was only one of the press of cousins who used to line up to mutter "Joyous Christmas, Grandpapa."

"Stop it! Stop it right now!" Mother's whisper was tense and angry. "Go kiss your grandfather."

The smooth dusty face was almost white on the side touched by a beam of winter sun. And his cheeks had never been so rosy when he was alive. He smelled like Mother's make-up. He used to smell like tobacco and leather and sweat. Claude closed his eyes tight and leaned over. He made a peck. He missed, but he pretended he had kissed Grandpapa. To avoid hearing the grownups' tight, muttered arguments about furniture and photographs and Grandmama, he went into the summer kitchen with the other kids, who by turns were making shuddering faces and scrubbing their lips with the backs of their hands. Claude scrubbed his lips, too, so everyone would think he had really kissed Grandpapa, but as he did it he knew he was being a traitor to the living Grandpapa, whom he had never kissed because they were both physically reticent types.

The fat cousin who used to fart under the covers whispered a joke about the make-up, and the girl cousins giggled. His face blank, Claude turned from the window and hit his cousin in the mouth with his fist. Although the cousin was two years older and bigger, he had no chance; Claude was bashing him with all the force of his rage, and fear, and shame, and loss.

Some grownups pulled Claude off the bleeding and howling cousin, and he was shaken around and sent upstairs to be dealt with later, after the priest left.

He sat on the edge of the bed in the grandparents' room. He had never been there before, and it seemed foreign and unfriendly, but he was glad to be alone so he could cry without the others seeing. No tears came. He waited. He opened his mouth and panted out sharp little breaths, hoping to start the crying he needed so badly. No tears would come. A hot ball of something sour in his stomach, but no tears. Others who loved Grandpapa less than Claude could cry. They could afford to let Grandpapa be dead, because they had other people. But Claude . . .

When they came up to punish him, Claude was lost in a daydream about Grandpapa coming to Trois Rivières and taking him away to live on the farm. That was how he handled it.

It is after midnight. LaPointe has been in bed for over an hour, slipping in and out of sleep, when he hears the lock turn in the front door. It closes softly, and Marie-Louise tries to tiptoe into the bedroom, but she bumps into something. She suppresses a giggle. There is movement and the rustle of clothes being taken off. She slips in beside him, and cold air comes in with her. He does not move, does not open his eyes. Soon her breathing becomes regular and shallow. She sleepily presses against his back for warmth, her knees cold against the backs of his legs.

He can smell the licorice of ouzo on her breath, and the smell of man's sweat on her.

. . . he can't breathe . . .
                                    . . . he wakes with a start. His face is wet.
He can't understand it. Why are his eyes wet?
He falls back to sleep, and next morning he does not remember the dream.

Ten

GUTTMANN HAS ARRANGED the overdue reports in stacks on the little table serving as a desk, leaving just enough room for his typewriter. He has finally made some order and sense out of the mess LaPointe dumped on him; there is a stack for this week's reports, one for last week's, one for the week before, and so on. But largest of all is the pile he mentally calls the Whatever-the-Hell-*This*-Is bunch.

The hissing roar of sandblasting across the street vibrates the cheap ripply glass of the window, causing Guttmann to look up. His eyes meet LaPointe's, which are fixed on him with a frown. Guttmann smiles and nods automatically and returns to his work. But a couple of minutes later he can still feel the Lieutenant's eyes on him, so he looks up again.

"Sir?"

"Is that all you know of that song?"

"What song, sir?"

"The song you keep humming over and over! You keep humming the same little bit!"

"I didn't realize I was humming."

"Well, *I* realize it. And it's sending me up the goddamned wall!"

"Sorry, sir."

LaPointe's grunt suggests that "Sorry" isn't enough. Ever since he came in this morning, he has been emitting dark vibrations and making little murmurs and growls of short temper each time he loses his place in the routine work on his desk. He stands up abruptly, pushing back his swivel chair with the backs of his knees. There is an indented line of white in the plaster from years of the chair banging against it. His thumbs hooked in the back of his belt, he looks out over the Hôtel de Ville, its façade latticed with scaffolding. This morning the noise of the stone-cleaning grates directly upon his nerve ends, like cold air on a bad tooth. And those monotonous zinc clouds!

Guttmann's typewriter clacks on in the rapid, one-word bursts of the experienced bad typist. His memory touches the two nights and a day he has just spent with the girl who lives in his apartment building. He passed Saturday evening in her flat, helping her doctor a head cold. She wore a thick terry-cloth robe that did nothing good for her appearance, and she had bouts of sneezing that left her limp and miserable, her face pale and her eyes brimming with tears. But her sense of humor held up, and she found this to be a ridiculous way for them to pass their first date. She got a little high on the hot toddies he made for her, and so did he, because he insisted on keeping her company by drinking one for each of hers. When he looked over her books and records, he discovered that their tastes were absolutely opposite, but their levels of appreciation about the same.

Around midnight, she kicked him out, telling him that she wanted to get a good night's sleep to fight off the cold. He suggested some light exercise might do her a world of good. She laughed and told him she didn't want him to catch her cold. He said he was willing to pay that price, but she said no.

Next morning, he telephoned her from bed. Her cold had broken and she felt well enough to go out. They passed the day visiting galleries and making jokes about the modern junk-art on display. He spent more than he could afford on dinner, and later, in his apartment, they talked about all sorts of things. They seldom agreed on details, but they found similar things funny and the same things important. After they had made love, they lay on their right sides, she coiled in against him, her bottom in his lap. She slept, breathing softly, while he lay awake for a time, sensing the subtle thrill of waves of gentleness emitting from him and enveloping her. A remarkable girl. Not only fun to talk with and great in bed, but really . . . remarkable. . . .

LaPointe turns from the window and looks flatly at Guttmann, who catches the movement and glances up with his habitual smile, which fades as he realizes he has been humming again.

"Sorry."

LaPointe nods curtly.

"By the way, sir, I ran the name Antonio Verdini and the alias Tony Green through ID. They haven't called back yet."

"They won't have anything."

"Maybe not, but I thought I should run it through anyway."

LaPointe sits again before his paper work. "Just like it says in the book," he mutters.

"Yes, sir," Guttmann says, more than a little tired of LaPointe's *cafard* this morning, "just like it says in the book." The book also says that reports of investigations must be turned in within forty-eight hours, and some of this crap on Guttmann's desk is weeks late, and almost all of it is incomplete, a couple of scribbled notes that are almost indecipherable. But Guttman decides against mentioning that.

LaPointe makes a gutteral sound and pushes aside a departmental form packet: green copy, yellow copy, blue copy, pink fucking copy . . .

"I'm going down to Bouvier's shop for a cup of coffee, if anyone wants me. You keep up the good work." He dumps all his unfinished work into Guttmann's in-box.

"Thank you, sir."

The telephone rings, catching LaPointe at the door. Guttmann answers, rather hoping it is something that will annoy the Lieutenant. He listens awhile, then puts his palm over the mouthpiece. "It's the desk. There's a guy down there asking to speak to you. It's about the Green stabbing."

"What's his name?"

Guttmann his takes hand away and repeats the question. "It's someone who knows you. A Mr. W———." He mentions the name of the wealthiest of the old Anglo families in Montreal. "Is that *the* Mr. W———?"

LaPointe nods.

Guttmann raises his eyebrows in mock surprise. "I didn't know you had Connections in Important Places, sir."

"Yes, well . . . Tell you what. While I'm down with Bouvier, you interview Mr. W———. Tell him you're my assistant and I have every confidence in you. He won't know you're lying."

"But, sir . . ."

"You're here to get experience, aren't you? No better way to learn to swim than by jumping off the dock."

LaPointe leaves, closing the door behind him.

Guttmann clears his throat before saying into the phone, "Send Mr. W——— up, will you?"

"Another cup, Claude?" Dr. Bouvier asks, catching a folder that is slipping from the tip of his high-heaped desk, holding it close to his clear lens to read the title, then tucking it back in toward the bottom.

"No, I don't think I could handle another."

Bouvier laughs ritually and pushes his glasses back up to the bridge of his stubby nose. But they slip down immediately because the dirty adhesive tape with which they are repaired is loose again. He must get them fixed someday. "Did you see the report I sent up on your stabbing? We ran his clothes through the lab and the result was zero."

"I didn't see the report. But I'm not surprised."

"If you didn't come down here to talk about the report, then what? You just come down to improve your mind? Or is the weather getting you down? One of my young men was complaining about the weather this morning, grousing about the way it keeps threatening snow without delivering. He said he wished it would either shit or get off the pot. Now, there's a daunting image for the bareheaded pedestrian. I warned the lad about the dangers of indiscriminate personification, but I doubt that he took it to heart. All right, let's talk then. I suppose you're pissed about that stabbing of yours getting into the papers so soon. I'm sorry about that; but the leak didn't come from this office. Someone up in the Commisioner's shop released it."

"Those assholes."

"Penetrating evaluation, if something of an anatomic synecdoche. But come on, it's not so grave. Just a couple of column inches. No photograph. No details. You still have the advantage of surprise as you walk your way through the case. By the way, how's that stroll coming along?"

LaPointe shrugs. "Nothing much. The victim's turning out to be a real turd, the kind anyone might have wanted to kill."

"I see. You have assholes for bosses and a turd for a victim. There's a certain consistency in that. I hear your Joan ran a name and an alias through ID this morning. Your victim?" Bouvier points his face toward LaPointe, one eye hidden behind the nicotine lens, the other huge and distorted. He is showing off a bit, proving he knows everything that goes on.

"Yes, that's the victim."

"Hm-m. An Italian kid with an Anglo alias. No record of fingerprints. Not a legal immigrant. What does that give us? A sailor who jumped ship?"

"I doubt it."

"Yes. The hands were wrong. No calluses. Any leads to a skill or a craft?"

"No." LaPointe's head rises just as Bouvier's eye is opening wide. They have the same thought at the same moment.

It is Bouvier who expresses it. "Do you think your victim was being laundered?"

"Possible."

There are a couple of small-timers up on the Italian Main who make their money by "laundering" men for the American organized-crime market. A young man who gets into trouble in Calabria or Sicily can be smuggled into Canada, usually on a Greek ship, and brought into Montreal, where he blends into the polyglot population of the Main while he learns a little English, and while the laundryman makes sure the Italian authorities are not on his tail. These "clean" men are slipped across the border to the States, where they are valuable as enforcers and hit men. Like a clean gun that the police cannot trace through registration, these laundered men have no records, no acquaintances, no fingerprints. And should they become awkward or dangerous to their employers, there is no one to avenge, even to question, their deaths.

It is possible that the good-looking kid who called himself Tony Green was in the process of being laundered when he met his death in that alley.

Dr. Bouvier takes off his glasses, turning his back so that LaPointe doesn't see the eye normally covered by the nicotine lens. He flexes the broken bridge and slips them back on, pinching the skin of his nose to make them stay up better. "All right. Who's active in the laundry business up on your patch?"

Old man Rovelli died six months ago. That leaves Canducci—Alfred (Candy Al) Canducci.

"Chocolate," LaPointe says to himself.

"What?"

"Chocolate. As in candy. As in Candy Al."

"I assume that makes some subtle sense?"

"The kid had a 'cousin' who rented his room for him. The concierge thought the name had something to do with chocolate."

"And you make that Candy Al Canducci. Interesting. And possible. I'll tell you what—I'll put in a little time on the case. Maybe your friendly family pathologist can come up with one of his 'interesting little insights.' Not that my genius is always appreciated by you street men. I remember once dropping a fresh possibility onto your colleague, Gaspard, when he was satisfied that he had already wrapped up a case. He described my assistance as being as welcome as a fart in a bathysphere. You want some more coffee?"

"No."

Guttmann has made slight rearrangements to receive Mr. Matthew St. John W——. He has moved his chair over to LaPointe's desk, and has seated himself in the Lieutenant's swivel chair. He rises to greet Mr. W——, who looks around the room with some uncertainty.

"Lieutenant LaPointe isn't here?"

"I'm sorry, sir. He's not available just now. I'm his assistant. Perhaps I could help?"

Mr. W—— looks exactly like his photographs in the society section of the Sunday papers—a slim face with fragile bones and veins close to the surface, full head of white hair combed severely back, revealing a high forehead over pale eyes. His dark blue suit is meticulously tailored, and there is not a smudge on the high shine of his narrow, pointed black shoes.

"I had hoped to see Lieutenant LaPointe." His voice is thin and slightly nasal, and its tone is chilly. He surveys the young policeman thoughtfully. He hesitates.

Not wanting to lose him, Guttmann waves a hand at the chair opposite him and says in as offhanded a voice as possible, "I believe you had some assistance to offer in the Green case, sir?"

Mr. W——— frowns, the wrinkles very shallow in his pallid forehead. "The Green case?" he asks.

Guttmann's jaw tightens. He is glad LaPointe isn't there. The victim's name was not mentioned in the newspaper. But the only thing to do is brave it out. "Yes, sir. The young man found in the alley was named Green."

Mr. W——— looks toward the corner of the room, his eyes hooded with thought. "Green," he says, testing the sound. He sighs as he sits on the straight-backed chair, lifting his trousers an inch by the creases. "You know," he says distantly, "I never knew that his name was Green. Green."

Instantly, Guttmann wishes he had somebody with him, a witness or a stenographer.

Mr. W——— has anticipated his thoughts. "Don't worry, young man. I will repeat anything I say to you. What happens to me is not important. What does matter is that everything be handled as quietly as possible. My family . . . I know I could rely on Lieutenant LaPointe to be discreet. But . . ." Mr. W——— smiles politely, indicating that he is sorry, but he has no reason to trust a young man he does not know.

"I wouldn't do anything without consulting the Lieutenant."

"Good. Good." And Mr. W——— seems willing to let the conversation rest there. A thin, polite smile on his lips, he looks past Guttmann's head to the damp, metallic skies beyond the window.

"You . . . ah . . . you say you didn't know his name was Green?" Guttmann prompts, making every effort to keep the excitement he feels from leaking into his voice.

Mr. W——— shakes his head slightly. "No, I didn't. That must seem odd to you." He laughs a little sniff of self-ridicule. "In fact, it seems odd to me . . . now. But you know how these things are. The social moment when you should have exchanged names somehow passes with the thing undone, and later it seems foolish, even impolite, to ask the other person his name. Has that ever happened to you?"

"Sir?" Guttmann is surprised to find the conversational ball suddenly in his court. "Ah, yes, I know exactly what you mean."

Mr. W——— investigates Guttmann's face carefully. "Yes. You have the look of someone who's capable of understanding."

Guttmann clears his throat. "Did you know this Green well?"

"Well enough. Well enough. He was . . . that is to say, he died before we . . ." Mr. W——— sighs, closes his eyes, and presses his fingers into the shallow sockets. "Explanations always seem so bizarre, so inadequate. You see, Green knew about the White Plot and the Ring of Seven."

"Sir?"

"I'd better begin at the beginning. Do you remember the nursery rhyme 'As I was going to St. Ives, I met a man with seven wives'? Of course, you probably never considered the significance of the repeated sevens—the warning passed to the Christian world about the Ring of the Seven and the Jewish White Plot. Not many people have troubled to study the rhyme, to unravel its implications."

"I see."

"That poor young Mr. Green stumbled upon the meaning. And now he's dead. Stabbed in an alley. Tell me, was there a bakery near where he was found?"

Guttmann glances toward the door, trying to think up something he has to go do. "Ah . . . yes, I suppose so. The district has lots of bakeries."

Mr. W——— smiles and nods with self-satisfaction. "I knew it. It's all tied up with the White Plague."

Guttmann nods. "Tied up with the White Plague, is it?"

"Ah! So Lieutenant LaPointe has told you about that, has he? Yes, the White Plague is *their* name for the steady poisoning of the gentile with white foods—flour, bread, sugar, Cream of Wheat . . ."

"Cream of Wheat?"

"That surprises you, doesn't it? I can't blame you. There was a time when we hoped against hope that Cream of Wheat wasn't in on it. But certain evidence has come into our hands. I mustn't tell you more than you need to know. There's no point in endangering you needlessly."

Guttmann leans back in the swivel chair, links his fingers, and puts his palms on the top of his head. His eyes droop, as though with fatigue.

Mr. W——— glances quickly toward the door to make sure no one is listening, then he leans forward and speaks with a confidential rush of words. "You see, the Ring of Seven is directed from Ottawa by the Zionist lobby there. I began to collect evidence against them seven years ago—note the significance of that figure—but only recently has the scope of their plot become . . ."

Guttmann is silent as he drives LaPointe up the Main in his yellow sports car. It is eleven in the morning and the street is congested with off-loading grocery and goods trucks, and with pedestrians who flow out into the street to bypass blocked sidewalks. It is necessary to crawl along and stop frequently. From time to time Guttmann glances at the Lieutenant, and he is sure there are crinkles of amusement around his eyes. But Guttmann is damned if he will give him the satisfaction of bringing it up first.

So it is LaPointe who has to ask, "Did you get a confession out of Mr. W———?"

"Very nearly, sir. Yes."

"Did you learn about Cream of Wheat?"

"What, sir? In what connection would he mention Cream of Wheat?"

"Well, he usually . . ." LaPointe laughs and nods. "You almost got me, son. You heard about Cream of Wheat, all right!" He laughs again.

"You might have warned me, sir."

"Nobody warned me the first time. I was sure I had a walk-in confession."

Guttmann pictures LaPointe being sucked in, leaning forward to catch each word, just as he had done. He has to laugh too. "I suppose this Mr. W——— is harmless enough."

"Look out for that kind!"

"I saw him! Jesus Christ, sir."

"Sorry. Yes, he's harmless enough, I suppose. There was a delicate case some years ago. Your Mr. W——— and a young man were picked up in a public bathroom. The kid was Jewish. Because of W———'s family, the thing was hushed up, and they were both back out on the street before morning. But the fear of scandal did something to the old man."

"And ever since then he comes in each time there's a murder in the papers?"

"Not every murder. Only when the victim is a young male. And only if it's a stabbing."

"Christ, talk about sophomore psychology."

"That truck's backing out!"

"I see him, sir. Are you sure you're comfortable?"

"What do you mean?"

"It must be hard to drive from over there."

"Come on, come on! Let's get going!"

Guttmann waits for the truck to clear, then eases forward. "Yes, that's real sophomore psychology stuff. The need to confess; the stabbing image."

"What are you talking about?"

"Oh, nothing, sir." It seems odd to Guttmann that LaPointe should know so much about human reactions and the human condition, but at the same time be so uneducated. He doubts that the Lieutenant could define words like "id" and "fugue." He probably recognizes the functioning of these forces and devices without having any names for them.

The worst of the traffic tangle behind them, they continue north on St. Laurent, cresting the hill at the barren little park of Carré Vallières, squeezed in between the Main and St. Dominique. It is a meager little triangle of sooty dirt, no grass, six or seven stunted trees. There are three benches of weathered wood once painted green, where old men play draughts in the summer, and in autumn huddle in their overcoats and stare ahead, or vacantly watch passers-by. For no reason he knows, LaPointe has always associated his retirement with this little square. He pictures himself sitting on one of those benches for an hour or two—always in winter, always with snow on the ground and bright sunshine. The roar of traffic up the Main passes close to the bench he has picked out for himself, and the smell of diesel fumes never leaves the air. From the top of the little rise he will be able to keep an eye on his street, even in retirement.

Once past the park and St. Joseph Street, they are on the Italian Main, where the street loses its cosmopolitan character. Unlike the lower Main, LaPointe's real patch, the quality of the Italian Main is not porous and ever-changing, with languages and people slowly permutating through the arrival and absorption of new tides of immigrants. The upper Main has been Italian for as long as anyone can remember, and its people do not move away to blend into the amorphous Canadian mass. The street and the people remain Italian.

At a signal from LaPointe, Guttmann pulls over and parks before a dingy little restaurant bearing the sign:

REPAS PASTO

They get out and cross the street, turning down Rue Dante, past a barbershop, empty save for the owner who is enthroned in one of his leather chairs, reading the paper with the air of a man completely at his ease, a man who knows he will not be interrupted by customers. Stuck in the window are sun-faded pictures of vapid young men advertising passé hairstyles. One grins from beneath a flattop, and another sports that long-sided fashion that used to be called a "duck's ass." In fact, as LaPointe knows, the only customers are the barber's relatives, who get their hair cut for free. The place is a numbers drop.

At the intersection of a narrow street, LaPointe turns down toward a small bar halfway between Rue Dante and St. Zotique. It occurs to Guttmann that in this Franco-Italian district there is something particularly appropriate about a bar being situated halfway between streets named Dante and St. Zotique. He mentions this to LaPointe, and asks if the Lieutenant ever thought of it as a kind of cultural metaphor.

"*What?*"

"Nothing, sir. Just a thought."

The interior of the bar is overwarm from a large oil heater, its orange flame dimly billowing behind a mica window. The woman behind the bar is over-blown, her chubby arms clattering with plastic bracelets, her high-piled hairdo an unnatural blue-black, her eye make-up and lipstick florid, and the deep V of her spangled blouse revealing the slopes of flaccid breasts that get most of their shape from the encasing fabric. She completes a languid yawn before asking the men what they will have.

LaPointe orders a glass of red, and Guttmann, tugging off his overcoat in the excessive heat, asks for the same thing, although he does not particularly care for wine outside meals.

From the back room, beyond a gaudy floral curtain, comes the click of pool balls followed by a curse in Italian and laughter from the other players.

"Who's your friend, Lieutenant?" the barmaid asks as she pours the wine and bestows upon Guttmann a carnivorous leer.

"Is Candy Al back there?" LaPoint asks.

"Where else would he be this time of day?"

"Tell him I want to talk to him."

"That won't be the best news he's had all week." Brushing close to Guttmann, the barmaid goes into the back room, walking with her knees slightly bent to make her broad ass swing invitingly.

"It looks like you've scored," LaPointe says as he sets his empty glass back on the bar. He always drinks off a *coup de rouge* at one go, like the workers of his home city.

"That's wonderful," Guttmann says. "Do you think I'm her first love?"

"One of the first this morning."

LaPointe knows this bar well. It serves two very different kinds of clients. Old Italian men in cloth caps often sit in pairs at the oilcloth-covered tables, talking quietly and drinking the harsh red. When they order, they hold the barmaid by her hip. It is an automatic gesture meaning nothing specific, and the right to hold the barmaid's hip goes, by immutable tradition, to the one who is paying for the drinks.

In summer, the back door is always open, and old men play at bowls on the tarmac alley where there is a thick covering of sand for this purpose. Every twenty minutes or so, a girl brings out a tray of glasses filled with wine. She collects the cork beer coasters from under empty glasses and stacks them at the end of the bar as a count of the wine drunk. The games are played for wine, and very seriously, with slow dignity and with much criticism and praise. Sometimes tipsy old men steal one or two of the coasters and put them into their pockets, not to avoid paying for the wine, but so that the barmaid will have to come looking for them, and when she does, they get a grab of her ass.

In contrast to these good people, the ones who hang out in the poolroom with its jukebox are the young toughs of the neighborhood, who squander their days gambling borrowed money and lying to one another about their sexual conquests and their knife fights. Candy Al Canducci reigns over these wise-cracking punks, who admire his flashy expensive clothes and flashy cheap women. Someday, they too . . .

He occasionally lends them money, or buys rounds of drinks. In return they serve him as flunkies, doing little errands, or standing around looking tough when he makes a personal visit to one of the bars dominated by another boss.

The whole thing is a cut-rate imitation of heavier Family action in north and east Montreal, but it has its share of violence. Occasionally there are border disputes over numbers territories, and there will be a week or two of conflicts, single members of one gang beaten up by five or six men from another, with faces and testicles the special targets of pointy-toed shoes. Sometimes there is a nighttime scuffle in a back alley, silent except for panting and the scrape of shoes, and a nasal grunt when the knife goes in.

LaPointe always knows what is happening, but he lets it go so long as no one is involved but themselves. The two things he does not permit are murder and drugs, the one because it gets into the papers and makes his patch look bad, the other just because he does not permit it. If there is a murder, he has a little chat with the bosses, and in the end some informer gives him the killer. It's a tacit understanding they have. Every once in a while, one of the bosses will feel he can stand up to LaPointe. Then things start to go badly for him. His boys begin to get picked up for every minor charge in the book; the police start to hit his numbers drops one after the other; small amounts of narcotics turn up every time LaPointe searches an apartment. The coterie of young toughs around the recalcitrant boss begins to thin out, and each of the bosses knows that with the first sign of weakness his brothers will turn on him and devour his territory. Even the proudest ends with having a little chat with LaPointe, and with turning over the killer he has been sheltering, or pulling back from his little *tentative* into drugs. Of course, there is the usual tough talk about LaPointe waking up some morning dead, but this is just face-saving. The bosses don't really want him gone. The next cop might not let them settle things among themselves, and they might not be able to trust his word, as they can always trust LaPointe's.

While there are these unspoken agreements, there is no protection. From time to time, one of the bosses makes a mistake. And when he does, LaPointe puts him away. They expect nothing else; LaPointe is like Fate—always there, always waiting. The bosses are all Catholics, and this sense of hovering punishment satisfies their need for retribution. The older ones take an odd pride in their cop and in his dogged honesty. You can't buy LaPointe. You can come to an understanding with him, but you can't buy him.

For his part, LaPointe has no delusions about his control on the Italian Main. This is not the Mafia he faces. The Mafia, with its American connections and trade union base, operates in north and east Montreal, where it occasionally becomes visible through sordid shootouts in the Naugahyde-and-chrome bars they infest. It isn't so much LaPointe's presence that prevents the organization from moving onto the Main as it is the district's own character. The Main is too poor to be worth the pain the old cop would give them.

At forty, Candy Al Canducci is the youngest of the local petty bosses; he is flashy in a "B" movie way, wise-mouthed, self-conscious, pushy; he lacks the Old-World dignity of the older bosses, most of whom are good family men who care about their children and take care of the unemployed and aged on their blocks. They're all thieves; but Candy Al is also a punk.

The barmaid's plastic bracelets clatter as she bats the gaudy curtain aside and comes back into the bar. "He doesn't want to see you, Lieutenant. Says he's busy. In conference."

There has been a silence in the back room for the past minute or two, and now there is suppressed laughter with this phrase "in conference."

The barmaid leans against the counter and plants a fist on her hip. She looks steadily at Guttmann as she toys with the crucifix around her neck, tickling her breasts by dragging the cross in and out of the cleavage.

"In conference, eh?" LaPointe asks. "Oh, I see. Well, at least give me another red."

There is a snicker from the back room, and the click of pool balls begins again.

As the barmaid takes her time going around to pour the wine, LaPointe tugs off his overcoat and drops it over a chair. Without waiting for the drink, he slaps the floral curtain aside and enters the poolroom. Guttmann takes a breath and follows him.

The hanging lamp over the pool table makes a high wainscoting of light that decapitates the half-dozen young men standing around the table. They draw back to the walls as LaPointe enters. One of them puts his hand in his pocket. A knife, probably, but mostly a sassy gesture. And one young tough pats the back of his hair into place, as though preparing for a photograph. Guttmann sets his broad body in the doorway as he notices that there is no other exit from the room. He feels a trickle of sweat under his shoulder holster. Seven against two; not much room for movement.

Candy Al Canducci continues playing, pretending not to have noticed the policemen enter. The coat of his closely cut suit hangs open, and his broad paisley tie brushes the green felt as he lines up a shot with taunting care. His pants are so tight that the outlines of his girdle-underwear can be seen.

LaPointe notices that he has changed from looking over a rather difficult shot that would have left him with good position to taking a dogmeat ball hanging on the rim of the pocket. He smiles to himself. Candy Al's cheap sense of theatrics will not permit him to punctuate some bit of lip with a missed shot.

"Let's have a talk, Canducci," LaPointe says, ignoring the ring of young men.

Candy Al brushes the chalk from his fingers, before lifting the sharp crease of one trouser leg to squat and line up the straight-in shot. "You want to talk, Canuck? All right, talk. Me, I'm playing pool." He doesn't look up to say this, but continues to examine his shot.

LaPointe shakes his head gravely. "That's too bad."

"What's too bad?"

"The way you're putting yourself in a hard place, Canducci. You're showing off for these asshole punks. First thing you know, you'll be forced to say something stupid. And then I'll have to spank you."

"Spank me? Ho-ho. You?" He rolls an in-cupped hand and looks around his coterie as if to say, Listen to this crap, will you? He draws back the cue to make his shot.

LaPointe reaches out and sweeps the object ball into its pocket. "Game's over."

For the first time, Canducci looks up into LaPointe's eyes. He detests the crinkling smile in them. He walks slowly around the end of the table to face the cop. There is an inward pressure from the ring of punks, and Guttmann glances around to pick out the first two he'd have to drop to keep them off his arms. Canducci's heart is thumping under his yellow silk shirt, as much from anger as from fear. LaPointe was right; if it hadn't been for the audience, he would never have taken this tone; now he has no choice but to play it out.

He stops before LaPointe, tapping the shaft of his cue into his palm. "You know what, Canuck? You take a lot of risks, for an old man."

LaPointe speaks over his shoulder to Guttmann. "There's something for you to learn here, son. This Canducci here and his punks are dangerous men." His eyes do not leave Candy Al's and they are still crinkled in a smile.

"Better believe it, cop."

"Oh, you're dangerous, all right. Because you're cowards, and cowards are always dangerous when they're in a pack."

Canducci pushes his face toward LaPointe's. "You got a wise mouth, you know that?"

LaPointe closes his eyes and shakes his head sadly. "Canducci, Canducci . . . what can I tell you?" He lifts his palms in a fatalistic shrug.

The next happens so quickly that Guttmann remembers only blurred fragments of motion and the sound of scuffling feet. LaPointe suddenly reaches out with one of the lifted hands, grabbing the dandy by the face and driving him back against the wall in two quick steps. Canducci's head cracks against a pinup of a nude. LaPointe's broad hand masks the face, the palm against the mouth and the fingers splayed across the eyes.

"Freeze!" he barks. "One move, and he loses his eyes!"

To make his point, he presses slightly with his fingertips, and Canducci produces a terrified squeal that is half-muffled by the heel of LaPointe's hand. LaPointe can feel saliva from the twisted mouth against his palm.

"Everyone sit on the floor," LaPointe commands. "Out away from the wall! Sit on your hands, palms up! I want the legs out in front of you! Do as I say, or this asshole will be selling pencils on the street!" Again a slight pressure on the eyes; again a squeal.

The punks exchange glances, no one wanting to be the first to obey. Then Guttmann, with a gesture that surprises LaPointe, grabs one by the arm and slams him up against the wall. The tough sits down with almost comic celerity, and the others follow.

"Sit up straight!" LaPointe orders. "And keep those hands under your asses! I want to hear knuckles crunch!"

This is a trick he learned from an old cop, now dead. When men are sitting on their hands, not only is any quick movement impossible, but they are embarrassed and humbled almost instantly, producing a sense of defeat and the desirable passivity of the prisoner mentality. It is a particularly useful device when you are badly outnumbered.

No one speaks, and for a full minute LaPointe continues to press Canducci's head against the wall, his fingers splayed over the face and eyes. Guttmann doesn't understand the delay. He looks over at the Lieutenant, whose head is hanging down and whose body appears oddly limp. "Sir?" he says uneasily.

LaPointe takes two deep breaths and swallows. The worst of it is over. The vertigo has passed. He straightens up, grabs Canducci's broad paisley tie, and snatches him away from the wall, propelling him ahead toward the gaudy curtain. One more push on the shoulder and Candy Al stumbles into the barroom. LaPointe turns back to the six young men on the floor. "You watch them," he tells Guttmann. "If one of them moves a muscle, slap his face until his ears ring." LaPointe knows exactly what threat would most sting cocky Italian boys.

When he pushes aside the curtain and enters the bar, he finds Candy Al sitting at a table, dabbing at his eyes with a handkerchief. "The Commisioner's going to hear about this," he says without much assurance. "It's a free country! You cops ain't the bosses of everything!"

LaPointe picks up his glass of red from the bar and sips it slowly, not setting down the glass until he feels recovered from the swimming dizziness and the constriction in his chest and upper arms that caught him unawares a minute ago. When the last of the effervescence has fizzed out of his blood, he leans back against the bar and looks down at Canducci, who is carefully touching the edge of his handkerchief to the corner of his eye, then examining the damp spot with tender concern.

"You got your finger in my eye! I wear contacts! That could be dangerous for a guy that wears contacts! Fucking cops." Alone out here without his gang, he reverts to the whining petty thief, alternating between playing it as the movie tough and simpering piteously.

"We're going to talk about a friend of yours," LaPointe says, sitting in the chair opposite Canducci.

"I don't have any friends!"

"That's truer than you know, shithead. The name is Antonio Verdini, alias Tony Green."

"Never heard of him."

"You rented a room for him. The concierge has given evidence."

"Well, this concierge has her head up her ass! I tell you I never met . . . whatever you said his name is."

"Was."

"What?"

"Was. Not is. He's dead. Stabbed in an alley."

The handkerchief is up to Canducci's eyes, so LaPointe misses the effect of the drop. After a short silence, the Italian says, "So, what's that to me?"

"Maybe twenty years. Stabbing is the kind of action your people go in for. The Commissioner is on my ass for an arrest. With your record, you're dogmeat. And I don't really care if you did it or not. I'll be satisfied just to get you off the street."

"I didn't kill the son of a bitch! I didn't even know he was dead until you told me. Anyway, I got an alibi."

"Oh? For what time?"

"You name it, cop! You name it, and I got an alibi for it." Candy Al dabs at his eyes again. "I think I got a busted blood vessel or something. You're gonna pay for that. Like they say in the lotteries, *un jour ce sera ton tour.*"

LaPointe reaches across the table and pats Canducci's cheek three times, the last tap not gentle. "Are you threatening me?"

Candy Al jerks his head away petulantly. "Where you get off slapping people around? You never heard of police brutality?"

"You'll have twenty years to make your complaint."

"I told you, all my time is covered."

"By them?" LaPointe tips his head toward the poolroom.

"Yeah. That's right. By them."

LaPointe dismisses them with a sharp puff of air. "How long do you think one of those kids, sitting back there with his ass in his hands, could stand up to interrogation by me?"

Canducci's eyes flicker; LaPointe's point is made. "I'm telling you I didn't kill this guy!"

"You mean you *had* him killed?"

"Shit, I don't even know this Verdini!"

"But at least you remember his name now."

There is a pause. Canducci considers his situation.

"I don't talk to cops. I think you're holding an empty bag. You got a witness? You got fingerprints? You got the knife? If you had any lever on me, we wouldn't be sitting here. We'd be downtown. You're empty, cop!" Canducci says this last loudly, to be overheard by the boys in back. He wants them to see how he treats cops.

Candy Al's reasoning is correct, so LaPointe has to take another tack. He shifts in his chair and looks out the window past Canducci's head. For a moment he seems to be absorbed in watching two kids playing in the street, coatless despite the cold. "I hear you've got something going with your boys back there," he says absently.

"What do you mean? What you talking?"

"I'm talking about the rumor that you keep your boys around for pleasure. That you pay them to use you like a woman." LaPointe shrugs. "Your flashy clothes, your silks, you wear a girdle . . . it's easy to see how a rumor like that could spread."

Canducci's face bloats with outrage. "Who's saying this? Give me a name! I'll sink my fingernails into his forehead and snatch his fucking face off!"

LaPointe lifts a hand. "Take it easy. The rumor hasn't started yet."

Canducci is confused. "What the hell you talking about?"

"But by tomorrow night, everyone on the street will be saying that you take it like a woman. I only have to drop a hint here, a wink there."

"Bullshit! Nobody would believe you! I got a doll on my arm every night."

"A smart cover-up. But always a different girl. They never hang around. Maybe because you can't satisfy them."

"Agh, I get tired of them. I need a little variety."

"That's your story. The other bosses would grab up a rumor like that in a second. They'd have big laughs over it. So Candy Al is a *fif!* Some punk would paint words on your car. Pretty soon your boys would drift away, because they don't want people saying they're queers. You'd be alone. People would talk behind their hands when you walked by. They'd whistle at you from across the street." Every touch is calculated to make the proud Italian wince.

His mind racing, Canducci glares at LaPointe for a full minute. Yes. A rumor like that would spread like clap in a nunnery. They'd love it, those shitheads over on Marconi Street. His jaw tightens and he looks down at the floor. "You'd do that? You'd spread a rumor like that about a man?"

LaPointe smaps his fingers softly. "Like that."

Candy Al glances toward the poolroom and lowers his voice. He speaks quickly to get it over with. "All right. This Verdini? A friend asked me to find a room for him because his English ain't too good. I found the room. And that's it. That's all I know. If he got himself killed, that's tough shit. I got nothing to do with it."

"What's this friend's name?"

"I don't remember. I got lots of friends."

"Just a minute ago you told me you didn't have any friends."

"Agh!"

LaPointe lets the silence sit on Canducci.

"Look! I'm giving it to you straight, Lieutenant!"

"Lieutenant? What happened to Canuck?"

Canducci shrugs, lifting his hands and dipping his head. "Agh, I was just pissed. People say things when they're pissed."

"I see. I want you to say the word 'wop' for me."

"Ah, come on!"

"Say it."

Canducci turns his head and stares at the wall. "Wop," he says softly.

"Good. Now keep talking about this kid."

"I already told you everything I know!"

After a moment of silence, LaPointe sighs and rises. "Have it your way, Canducci. But tell me one thing. Those boys back there? Which one's best?"

"That ain't funny!"

"Your friends will think so." LaPointe slaps his hand on the bar to summon the barmaid, who disappeared when she heard how things were going on in the poolroom. She has been around enough to know that it is not wise to witness Candy Al's defeats. She comes from the back room, tugging down her skirt, which is so tight across the hips that it continually rides up.

"What do I owe you?" LaPointe asks.

"Just a minute," Canducci says, raising his hand. "What's your rush? Sit down, why don't you?"

The barmaid looks from one to the other, then returns to the back room.

LaPointe sits down. "That's better. But let's cut the bullshit. I don't have the time. I'll start the story for you. This Green was brought into the country illegally. You were laundering him. You found him a room on the lower Main, away from this district where the immigration authorities might look for him if the Italian officials had sent out a want bulletin. You kept him in walking-around money. You probably arranged for him to learn a little English, because that's part of the laundering process. Now you take it from there."

Canducci looks at LaPointe for a moment. "I'm not admitting any of that, you know."

"Of course not. But let's pretend it's true."

"Okay. Just pretending what you say is true . . . This kid was a sort of distant cousin to me. The same village in Calabria. He was supposed to be a smart kid, and tough. But he gets into a little trouble back in the old country. So next thing you know he's here, and I've promised to find some kind of work for him. As a favor."

LaPointe smiles at the obliquity.

"Okay. So I get him a room, and I get him started learning some English. But I don't see him often. That wouldn't be smart, you dig? But all the time this bastard's needing money. I give him a lot, but he always needs more. He blows it on the holes. I never seen such a crotch hound. I warn him that he's beginning to get a reputation about all the squack he's stabbing, and what the super don't need right now is a reputation. He goes after all kinds. Even old women. He's sort of weird that way, you know? So the only time I visit him is to tell him he shouldn't draw attention to himself. I tell him to take it easy with the holes. But he don't listen, and he asks me for more money. Five will get nine it was a woman that put the knife into him."

"Go on."

"Go on to what? That's all! I warn him, but he don't listen. And you walk in here this morning and tell me he's got himself reamed. He should of listened."

"You don't sound too sorry for your cousin."

"I should be sorry for myself! I'm out a lot of scratch! And for what?"

"Call it a business risk. Okay, give me the names of some of his women."

"Who knows names? Shit, he was on the make day and night. Drag a net down the Main and you'll come up with half a dozen he's rammed. But I can tell you this. He went for weird action. Two at a time. Old women. Gimps. Kids. That sort of thing."

"You said something about his taking English lessons? Who was he taking them from?"

"No idea. I give him a list of ads from the papers. I let him pick for himself. The less I know about what these guys are doing, the better for me."

"What else do you want to tell me?"

"There's nothing else to tell. And listen—" Canducci points a chubby white finger at LaPointe—"there ain't no witnesses here. Anything I might have said, I would deny in court. Right?"

LaPointe nods, his eyes never leaving Candy Al's as he weighs and evaluates the story he just heard. "It could be the way you say. It could also be that the kid got too dangerous for you, drawing attention to himself and always asking you for money. It could be you decided to cut your losses."

"My word of honor!"

LaPointe's lower eyelids droop. "Well, if I have your word of honor . . . what else could I want?" He rises and begins to tug on his overcoat. "If I decide I need more from you, I'll be by. And if you try to leave town, I'll take that as a confession."

Canducci dabs at his eyes once more, then folds his mauve handkerchief carefully into his breast pocket and pats it into place. "It's a crying goddamned shame, you know that?"

"What is?"

"That way this kid gets me into trouble. That's what you get for trying to help a relative."

After LaPointe and Guttmann leave the bar, Canducci sits for a time, thinking about how he will play it. He takes several bills from his wallet. As he saunters into the poolroom where his boys are standing around sheepishly, working their hands to restore circulation, he tucks the money back into the wallet with a flourish. "Sorry about that, boys. My fault. I got a little behind in my payments. These penny-and-nickel cops don't like it when they don't get their payoff on time. Okay, rack 'em up."

They are the only customers in the A-One Café. After serving them the one-plate lunch, the old Chinese has returned to his station by the window where, his eyes empty, he looks out on the sooty brick warehouses across the street.

"Well?" LaPointe asks. "How do you like it?"

Guttmann pushes his plate aside and shakes his head. "What was it called?"

"I don't think it has a name."

"I'm not surprised."

There is a certain pride in the Lieutenant's voice when he says, "It's the worst food in Montreal, maybe in all of Canada. That's why you can always come here to talk. There's never anyone else here to disturb you."

"Hm-m!" Guttmann notices that his grunt sounded just like the Lieutenant's grumpy responses.

During the meal, LaPointe has filled him in on what he learned from Candy Al, together with a description of the operation known as laundering.

"And you think this Canducci might have killed Green, or had him killed?"

"It's possible."

Guttmann shakes his head. "With every lead, we turn another suspect. It's worse than not having any suspects. We've got that tramp, the Vet. Then we've got that guy Arnaud, the concierge's friend. Now Canducci, or one of his punks. And it seems that it might have been almost any woman on the Main who isn't under ten or over ninety. And what about the woman you talked to alone? The lesbian who runs a café. Is she a viable?"

Is she a viable? Precisely the kind of space-age jargon that LaPointe detests. But he answers. "I suppose. She had reason, and opportunity. And she's capable of it."

"What does that give us now? Four possibles?"

"Don't forget your Mr. W———. You came close to wringing a confession out of him."

Guttmann feels a flush at the nape of his neck. "Yes, sir. That's right."

LaPointe chuckles. "I'm not ragging you, kid."

"Oh? Is that so, sir?"

"No, you're thinking all right. You're thinking like a good cop. But don't forget that this Green was a turd. Just about everybody he touched would have some reason for wanting him dead. It's not all that surprising that we find a suspect behind every door. But pretty soon it will be over."

"Over? In what way over?"

"The leads are starting to thin out. The talk with Canducci didn't turn another name or address."

"The leads could be thinning out because we've already touched the killer. And passed him by."

"I haven't passed anybody by yet. And there's still the possibility that Carrot will come up with a name or two, maybe a bar he used to go to."

"Carrot?"

"The lesbian."

"But she's a suspect herself."

"All the more reason for her to help us . . . if she's innocent, that is. But I wouldn't bet on closing this case. I have a feeling that pretty soon we're going to open the last door, and find the blank wall."

"And you don't particularly care?"

"Not particularly. Not now that we know the sort of kid the victim was."

Guttmann shakes his head. "I can't buy that."

"I know you can't. But I've got other things to do besides chase around after shadows. I've got the whole neighborhood to look after."

"Tell me something, Lieutenant. If this Green were a nice kid, say a kid who grew up on the Main, wouldn't you try harder?"

"Probably. But a case like this is hard to sort out. When you're tracking a kid like this Green, you meet nothing but dirty types. Almost everyone you meet is guilty. The question is, *what* are they guilty of?"

"Guilty until proven innocent?"

"Lawyers being what they are, probably guilty even then."

"I hope I never think like that."

"Stay on the street for a few years. You will. By the way, you didn't do too badly back in Canducci's bar. We walked in without a warrant, slapped people around, and you handled yourself like a cop. What happened to all this business about civil rights and going by the book?"

Guttmann lifts his hands and lets them drop back onto the table. You can't discuss things with LaPointe. He always cuts both ways. But Guttmann realizes that he has a point. When he handled that tight moment when the boys were resisting the order to sit on their hands, he had felt . . . competent. There is a danger in being around LaPointe too long. Things get less clear; right and wrong start to blend in at the edges.

When he looks up, Guttmann sees a crinkling around LaPointe's eyes. "What is it?"

"I was just thinking about your Mr. W———."

"Honest to God, I'd give a lot if you'd get off that, sir."

"No, I wasn't going to rag you. It just occurred to me that if Mr. W——— ever did kill somebody, all he'd have to do would be to wait until it got into the papers, then come to us with a confession involving Jewish plots and Cream of Wheat. We'd toss him right out."

"That's a comforting thought."

"Oh. By the way, didn't you say something the other night about playing pinochle?"

"Sir?"

"Didn't you tell me you used to play pinochle with your grandfather?"

"Ah . . . yes, sir."

"Want to play tonight?"

"Pinochle?"

"That's what we're talking about."

"Wait a minute. I'm sorry, but this just came out of nowhere, sir. You're asking me to play pinochle with you tonight?"

"With me and a couple of friends. The man who usually plays with us is sick. And cuttthroat isn't much fun."

Guttmann senses that this offer is a gesture of acceptance. He can't remember anyone in the department having bragged about spending off time with the Lieutenant. And he is free tonight. The girl in his building takes classes on Monday nights and doesn't get back until eleven.

"Yes, sir. I'd like to play. But it's been a while, you know."

"Don't worry about it. Nothing but three old farts. But just in case you're a little rusty, I'll arrange for you to be partners with a very gentle and understanding man. A man named David Mogolevski."

Eleven

THE EVENING OF pinochle has gone well—for David.

As usual he dominated play, and as usual he overbid his hand, but the luck of the cards followed Guttmann to bail him out more times than not, and as partners they won devastatingly.

After a particularly good—and lucky—hand, David asked the young man, "Tell me, have you ever thought of becoming a priest?"

Guttmann admitted that the idea seldom crossed his mind.

"That's good. It would ruin your game."

On one occasion, when not even luck was enough to save David from his wild overbidding, he treated Guttmann to one of his grousing tirades about how difficult it was, even for a pinochle *maven* like himself, to schlep a partner who couldn't pull his own weight. Unlike Father Martin, Guttmann did not permit himself to be martyred to David's peculiar and personal view of sportsmanship. He countered with broad sarcasm, mentioning that the Lieutenant had rightly described David as a gentle and understanding partner.

But David's thick skin is impervious to such attacks. He thrust out his lower lip and nodded absently, accepting that as an accurate enough description of his character.

For his part, Moishe was slow in warming to the young intruder into their game, despite Guttmann's genuine interest in the fabric Moishe had on the loom at that moment. He had been looking forward to one of his rambling philosophic chats with Martin.

Still, so it shouldn't be a total loss, he made a venture toward drawing Guttmann out during their break for sandwiches and wine. "You went to university, right? What did you major in?"

It occurs to LaPointe that he never asked that question. He wasn't all that interested.

"Well, nothing really for the first two years. I changed my major three or four times. I was more looking for professors than for fields."

"That sounds intelligent," Moishe says.

"Finally, I settled down and took the sequence in criminology and penology."

"And what sorts of things does one study under those headings?"

David butts in. "How to steal, naturally. Theft for fun and profit. Theft and the Polish Question."

"Why don't you shut up for a while?" Moishe suggests. "Your mouth could use the rest."

David spreads his face in offended innocence and draws back, then he winks at LaPointe. He has been riding Moishe all night, piquing him here and there, ridiculing his play, when he knew perfectly well that all the cards were against him. But he is a little surprised when his gentle partner snaps back like this.

"So?" Moishe asks Guttmann. "What did you study?"

Guttmann shrugs off the value of his studies, a little embarrassed about them in the presence of LaPointe. "Oh, a little sociology, some psychology as related to the criminal and criminal motives—that sort of thing."

"No literature? No theology?"

"Some literature, sure. No theology. Would you pass the mustard, please?"

"Here you are. You know, it's interesting you should have studied criminal motives and all this. Just lately I have been thinking about crime and sin . . . the relationships, the differences."

"Oh boy," David puts in. "Here we go again! Listen! About crime it's all right to think. It's a citizen's duty. But about sin? Moishe, my old friend, AK's like us shouldn't think about sin. It's too late. Our chances have passed us by."

Guttmann laughs. "No, I'm afraid I never think about things like that, Mr. Rappaport."

"You don't?" Moishe asks gloomily, his hopes for a good talk crumbling. "That's strange. When I was a young man thinking was a popular pastime."

"Things change," David says.

"Does that mean they improve?" Moishe asks.

Guttmann glances at his watch. "Hey, I'm sorry, but I've got to be going. I have a date, and I'm already late."

"A date?" David asks. "It's after eleven. What can you do so late?"

"We'll think of something." As soon as he makes this adolescent single-entendre remark, Guttmann feels he has been disloyal to his girl.

Moishe rises. "I'll walk you to your car."

"That's isn't necessary, sir."

"You're already late for your date. And you're not familiar with the streets around here. So don't argue. Get your coat."

As they leave, Moishe has already begun with ". . . when you stop to think about it, the differences between sin and crime are greater than the similarities. Take, for instance, the matter of guilt . . ."

As the door closes behind them, David looks at LaPointe and shakes his head. "Oh, that Moishe. Sin, crime, love, duty, the law, the good, the bad . . . he's interested in everything that's so big it doesn't really matter. A scholar! But in practical things . . ." His lips flap with a puff of air. "That reminds me of something I wanted to talk to you about, Claude. A matter of law."

"I'm not a lawyer."

"I know, I know. But you know something about the law. This may come as a surprise to you, but I am not immortal. I could die. At my age, you have to think about such things. So tell me. What do I have to do to make sure the business goes to Moishe if he should, *cholilleh,* outlive me?"

LaPointe shrugs. "I don't know. Isn't all that handled in your partnership agreement?"

"Well . . . that's the problem. Actually, Moishe and I aren't partners. In the legal sense, I mean. And I have a nephew. I'd hate to see him come along and screw Moishe out of the business. And, believe me, he's capable of it. Of working for a living, he's not capable. But of screwing someone out of something? Of that he is capable."

"I don't understand. What do you mean, you and Moishe aren't partners? I thought he started the business, then later took you on as a partner."

"That's right. But you know Moishe. He's not interested in the business end of business. A beautiful person, but in business a *luftmensh.* So over the years, he sold out to me so that he wouldn't have to be bothered with taxes and records and all that."

"And you're afraid that if you die—"
                    "—*cholilleh*"—
                                                    "—he might
not get the business? Well, David, I told you I'm no lawyer. But it seems to me
that all you have to do is make out a will."

David sighs deeply. "Yes, I was afraid of that. I hoped it wouldn't be
necessary. I'm not a superstitious man, don't get me wrong. But in my opinion a
man is just asking for it, if he makes out his will while he's still alive. It's like
saying to God, Okay. I'm ready whenever you are. And speaking personally for
myself, I'm not ready. If a truck should run over me—okay, that's that. But I'm
not going to stand in the middle of the street shouting, Hey! Truckdrivers! I'm
ready!"

As LaPointe steps out onto the blustery street, turning up the collar of his
overcoat, he meets Moishe, returning from seeing Guttmann to his car. They fall
into step and walk along together, as they usually do after games.

"That's a nice young man, Claude."

"He's all right, I suppose. What did you talk about?"

"You."

LaPointe laughs. "Me as a crime? Or me as a sin?"

"Neither one, exactly. We talked about his university studies; how much the
things he learned turned out to reflect the real world."

"How did I fit into that?"

"You were the classic example of how the things he learned were *not* like it is
in the real world. The things you do and believe are the opposite of everything
he wants to do with his life, of everything he believes in. But, oddly enough, he
admires you."

"Hm-m! I didn't think he liked me all that much."

"I didn't say he likes you. He admires you. He thinks you're the best of your
kind."

"But he can live without the kind."

"That's about it."

They have reached the corner where they usually part with a handshake. But
tonight Moishe asks, "Are you in a hurry to go home, Claude?"

LaPointe realizes that Moishe is still hungry for talk; the short walk with
Guttmann couldn't have made up for his usual ramblings with Father Martin.
For himself, LaPointe has no desire to get to his apartment. He has known all
day what he will find there.

"How about a glass of tea?" Moishe suggests.

"Sure."

They go across the street to a Russian café where tea is served in glasses set in
metal holders. Their table is by the window, and they watch late passers-by in
the comfortable silence of old friends who no longer have to talk to impress one
another, or to define themselves.

"You know," Moishe says idly, "I'm afraid I frightened him off, your young
colleague. With a young girl on his mind, the last thing in the world he needed
was a long-winded talk about sin and crime." He smiles and shakes his head at
himself. "Being a bore is bad enough. Knowing you're boring but going ahead
anyway, that's worse."

"Hm-m. I could see you had something stored up."

Moishe fixes his friend with a sidelong look. "What do you mean, I had
something stored up?"

"Oh, you know. All through the game you were sending out little feelers; but
Father Martin wasn't there to take you up. You know, I sometimes think you

work out what you're going to say during the day, while you're cutting away on your fabric. Then you drop these ideas during the pinochle game, like they just popped into your head. And poor Martin is fishing around for his first thoughts, while you have everything carefully thought out."

"Guilty! And being guilty I don't mind so much as being transparent!" He laughs. "What chance does the criminal have against you, tell me that."

LaPointe shrugs. "Oh, they manage to muddle along all right."

Moishe nods. "Muddle along. System M: the big Muddle. The major organization principle of all governments. She seemed like a nice girl."

LaPointe frowns. "What?"

"That girl I met in your apartment yesterday. She seemed nice."

LaPointe looks at his friend. "Why do you say that? You know perfectly well she didn't seem nice. She seemed like a street girl, which is all she is."

"Yes, but . . ." Moishe shrugs and turns his attention to the street. After a silence, he says. "Yes, you're right. She did seem like a street girl. But all girls of her age seem nice to me. I know better, but . . . My sister was just her age when we went into the camp. She was very lovely, my sister. Very shy. She never . . . she didn't survive the camp." He stares out the window for a while. Then he says quietly, "I'm not even sure I did. Entirely. You know what I mean?"

LaPointe cannot know what he means; he doesn't answer.

"I guess that's why I imagine that all girls of her age are nice . . . are vulnerable. That's funny. Girls of her age! If she had lived, my sister would be in her fifties now. I can't picture that. I get older, but she remains twenty in my mind. You know what I mean?"

LaPointe knows exactly what he means; he doesn't answer.

Moishe closes his eyes and shakes his head. "Ach, I don't think I'm up to stumbling around in these parts of my memory. Better to let these things rest. They have been well grieved."

"Well grieved? That's a funny thing to say."

"Why funny, Claude? You think grief is shameful?"

LaPointe shrugs. "I don't think about it at all."

"That's odd. Of course grief is good! The greatest proof that God is not just playing cruel games with us is that He gave us the ability to grieve, and to forget. When one is wounded—I don't mean physically—forgetfulness cauterizes and heals it over, but there would be rancor and hate and bitterness trapped under the scar. Grief is how you drain the wound, so it doesn't poison you. You understand what I mean?"

LaPointe lifts his palms. "No, Moishe. I don't. I'm sorry . . . but I'm not Father Martin. This kind of talk . . ."

"But Claude, this isn't philosophy! Okay, maybe I say things too fancy, too preciously, but what I'm talking about isn't abstract. It's everyday life. It's . . . obvious!"

"Not to me. I don't know what you're talking about when you say grief is good. It has nothing to do with me." LaPointe realizes that his tone is unfriendly, that he is closing the door to the chat Moishe seems to need. But this talk about grief makes him uncomfortable.

Behind his round glasses, Moishe's eyes read LaPointe's face. "I see. Well . . . at least allow me to pay for the tea. That way, I won't regret having bored you. Regret! There's a little trio often confused: Grief, Remorse, Regret! Grief is the gift of the gods; Remorse is the whip of the gods; and Regret . . . ? Regret is nothing. It's what you say in a letter when you can't fill an order in time."

LaPointe looks out the window. He hopes Father Martin will get well soon.

They shake hands on the sidewalk in front of the Russian café, and LaPointe decides to take one last walk down the Main before turning in. He has to put his street to bed.

Even before switching on the green-and-red lamp, he senses in the temperature of the room, in the smell of the still air, the emptiness.

Of course, he knew she would be gone when he came back tonight. He knew it as he lay in bed beside her, smelling the ouzo she had drunk. He knew it as he tried to get back to sleep after that dream . . . what was it? Something about water?

He makes coffee and brings the cup to his armchair. The streetlamps down in the park spill damp yellow light onto the gravel paths. Sometimes it seems the snow will never come.

The silence in the room is dense, irritating. LaPointe tells himself that it's just as well Marie-Louise is gone. She was becoming a nuisance, with that silly, brief laugh of hers. He sniffs derision at himself and reaches for one of his Zolas, not caring which one. He opens the volume at random and begins to read. He has read them through and through, and it no longer matters where he begins or ends. Before long, he is looking through the page, his eyes no longer moving.

Images, some faded, some crisp, project themselves onto his memory in a sequence of their own. A thread of the past comes unraveled, and he tugs at it with gentle attention, pulling out people and moments woven so deep into the fabric of the past that they seemed forgotten. The mood of his daydream is not sadness or regret; it is curiosity. Once he has recalled and dealt with a moment or a face, it does not return to his memory. He examines the fragment, then lets it fall from him. He seldom remembers the same thing twice. There isn't time.

Some of the images come from his real life: Trois Rivières, playing in the street as a kid, his grandfather, St. Joseph's Home, Lucille, the yellow alley cat with the crooked tail, one paw lifted tentatively from the ground.

Other memories, no less vivid, come from his elaborate fantasy of living in the house in Laval with Lucille and the girls. These images are richest in detail: his workshop in the garage with nails up to hold the tools and black-painted outlines to show which tool goes where. The girls' First Holy Communions, all in white with gifts of silver rosaries and photographs posed for reluctantly and stiffly. He sees the youngest girl—the tomboy, the imp—with her scuffed knee just visible under the thin white communion stocking. . . .

He sniffs and rises. His rinsed-out cup is placed on the drainboard, where it always goes. He cleans the pressure maker and puts it where he always puts it. Then he goes into the bathroom to shave, as he always does, before going to bed. As he swishes down the black whiskers, he notices several long hairs in the bowl. She must have washed her hair before leaving. And she didn't rinse it out carefully. Sloppy twit.

He is sitting on the edge of his bed, pulling off his shoes, when something occurs to him. He pads into the living room and opens the drawer in which he keeps his house money, uncounted and wadded up. There are a bunch of twenties there, some tens. He does not know how much there was in the first place. Perhaps she took some. But that doesn't matter. What matters is that she left some.

He lies on his back in the middle of the bed, looking up at the ceiling glowing from the streetlamp outside the window.

He never realized before how big this bed is.

Guttman is tapping away on the portable typewriter when LaPointe enters with a grunt of greeting as he hangs his overcoat on the wooden rack.

"I'm beginning to see daylight at the end of the tunnel, sir."

"What are you talking about?"

"These reports."

"Ah. Good boy. You've got a future in the department. That's the important thing—the paper work." LaPointe picks up a yellow telphone memo from his desk. "What's this?"

"You got a call. I took the message."

"Hm-m." The call was from Carrot. She questioned her clients who went bar crawling with Tony Green; there seemed to be only one place he frequented regularly, the Happy Hour Whisky à Go-Go on Rachel Street. LaPointe knows the place, just one block off the Main. He decides to drop in on his way home that evening. The leads are thinning out; this is the last live one.

"Anything else?" he asks.

"You got a call from upstairs. The Commissioner wants to see you."

"That's wonderful." He sits at his desk and glances over the Morning Report: several car thefts, two muggings, somebody shot in a bar in east Montreal, another mugging, a runaway teen-ager . . . all routine. Nothing interesting, nothing from the Main.

He starts to make out his duty sheet for yesterday. What did he do yesterday? What can you write down? Drank coffee with Bouvier? Talked to Candy Al Canducci? Walked around the streets. Played pinochle? Took a glass of tea with Moishe? Went home to find the bed bigger than I remembered? He turns the green form over and looks at the three-quarters of a page left blank for "Remarks and Suggestions." He suppresses an urge to write: Why don't you shove this form up your ass?

LaPointe is feeling uncertain this morning, and diminished. He had a major *crise* while brushing his teeth. First the fizzing blood, then tight bands of jagged pain gripped his chest and upper arms. He felt himself falling forward into a gray mist in which lights exploded. When it passed, he was on his knees, his forehead on the toilet seat. As he continued brushing his teeth, he joked with himself: I guess you better get a lighter toothbrush, LaPointe.

"Tomorrow's my last day," Guttmann says.

"What?"

"Wednesday I go back to working with Sergeant Gaspard."

"Oh?" It is a noncommittal sound. He has enjoyed showing off his patch and his people to the kid; he has even enjoyed Guttmann's way of braving out his scorn for the shiny new college ideas. But it wouldn't do to seem to miss the boy.

"How did it go last night?" he asks, making conversation to avoid the goddamned paper work.

"Go, sir? Oh, with Jeanne?"

"If that's her name."

Guttmann smiles in memory. "Well, I got there late, of course. And at first she didn't believe me when I told her I was playing pinochle with three men in the back room of an upholstery shop. It sounded phony to me even while I was saying it."

"Does it matter what she thinks?"

Guttmann considers this for a second. "Yes, it does. She's a nice person."

"Ah, I see. Not just a girl. Not just a lay."

"That's the way it started, of course. And God knows I'm not knocking that part of it. But there's more. We sort of fit together. It's hard to explain, because I didn't mean that we always agree. Matter of fact, we almost never agree. It's kind of like a mold and a coin, if you know what I mean. They're exact opposites, and they fit together perfectly." There is a slight shift in his tone, and he is now thinking out the relationship aloud, rather than talking to LaPointe. "She's the only person I've ever known who . . . I mean, I don't have to be set up and ready when I talk to her. I just say what I feel like saying, and it doesn't bother me if it comes out wrong, or stupid-sounding. You know what I mean, sir?"

"How did you meet her?"

Guttmann doesn't understand why LaPointe is interested, but he enjoys the uncommon friendly tone of the chat. He has no way of knowing that his leaving tomorrow is what allows the Lieutenant to relax with him, because he won't have to deal with him further. "Well, I told you she lives in my apartment building. We met in the basement."

"Sounds romantic."

Guttmann laughs. "Yeah. There's a bunch of coin-operated washing machines down there. It was late at night, and we were alone, waiting for our washing to get done, so we started talking."

"About what?"

"I don't remember. Soap, maybe. Hell, I don't know.

"Is she pretty?"

"Pretty? Well, yes, I guess so. I mean, obviously *I* find her attractive. That first night in the basement, I wasn't thinking of much other than getting her into bed. But pretty isn't what she is mostly. If I had to pick one thing about her, it would be her nutty sense of humor."

LaPointe sniffs and shakes his head. "That sounds dangerous. I remember when I was a kid on the force, I went on a couple of blind dates set up by friends. And whenever they described my girls as 'a good talker' or 'a kid with a great sense of humor,' that always meant she was a dog. What I usually wanted at the time was a pig, not a dog."

For a second, Guttmann tries to picture the Lieutenant as a young cop going on blind dates. The image won't come into focus.

"I know what you mean," he says. "But you know what's even worse than that?"

"What?"

"When the guy who's set you up can't think of anything to say but that your girl has nice hands. That's when you're really in trouble!"

LaPointe is laughing in agreement when the phone rings. It is the Commissioner's office, and the young lady demanding that LaPointe come up immediately has a snotty, impatient tone.

After announcing on the intercom that Lieutenant LaPointe is in the outer office, the secretary with the impeding miniskirt sets busily to work, occasionally glancing accusingly at the Lieutenant. When she arrived at the office at eight that morning, the Commissioner was already at work.

The man who isn't a step AHEAD is a step BEHIND.

Resnais' mood was angry and tense, and everyone in the office was made to feel its sting. The secretary blames LaPointe for her boss's mood.

For the first time, Resnais doesn't come out of his office to greet LaPointe with his bogus handshake and smile. Three clipped words over the intercom request that he be sent in.

When LaPointe enters, Resnais is standing with his back to the window, rocking up on his toes. The gray light of the overcast day glints off the purplish suntan on his head, and there is a lighter tone to his sunlamped bronze around the ears, indicating that his haircut is fresh.

"I sent for you at eight this morning, LaPointe." His tone is crisp.

"Yes. I saw the memo."

"And?"

"I just got in."

"In this shop, we start at eight in the morning."

"I get off the street at one or two in the morning. What time do you usually get home, Commissioner?"

"That's none of your goddamned onions." Even angry, Resnais does not forget to use idioms common to the social level of his French Canadian men. "But I didn't call you up here to chew your ass about coming in late." He has decided to use vulgar expressions to get through to LaPointe.

"Do you mind if I sit down?"

"What? Oh, yes. Go ahead." Resnais sits in his high-backed chair, designed by osteopaths to reduce fatigue. He takes a deep breath and blows it out. Might as well get right to it.

The surgeon who cuts slowly does no kindness to his patient.

He glances at his note pad, open on the immaculate desk beside two sharpened pencils and a stack of blue memo cards. "I assume you know a certain Scheer, Anton P."

"Scheer? Yes, I know him. He's a pimp and a *pissou.*"

"He's also a citizen!"

"You're not telling me that Scheer had the balls to complain about me."

"No official complaint has been lodged—and won't be, if I can help it. I warned you about your methods just a couple of days ago. Did you think I was just talking out of my ass?"

LaPointe shrugs.

Resnais looks at his notes. "You ordered him off the street. You denied him the use of a public thoroughfare. Who in hell do you think you are, LaPointe?"

"It was a punishment."

"The police don't punish! The courts punish. But it wasn't enough that you ordered him off the streets, you publicly degraded him, making take off his clothes and climb into a basement well, with the possible risk of injury. Furthermore, you did this before witnesses—a crowd of witnesses including young women who laughed at him. Public degradation."

"Only his shoelaces."

"What?"

"I only ordered him to take off his shoelaces."

"My report says clothes."

"Your report is wrong."

Resnais takes one of the pencils and makes the correction. He has no doubt at all of LaPointe's honesty. But that is not the point. "It says here that there was another policeman involved. I want his name."

"He just happened to be walking with me. He had no part in it."

LaPointe's matter-of-fact tone irritates Resnais. He slaps the top of his desk. "I won't fucking well have it! I've worked too goddamned hard to build a good community image for this shop! And I don't care if you're the hero of every wet-nosed kid on the force, LaPointe. I won't have that image ruined!"

Anger is a bad weapon, but a great tool.

LaPointe looks at Resnais with the expression of bored patience he assumes when questioning suspects. When the Commissioner has calmed down, he says, "If Scheer didn't lodge a complaint, how do you know about this?"

"That's not your affair."

"Some of his friends got to you, right? Ward bosses?"

It is Resnais' habit to play it straight with his men. "All right. That's correct. A man in municipal politics brought it to my attention. He knows how I've worked to maintain good press for the force. And he didn't want to make this public if he didn't have to."

"Bullshit."

"I don't need insubordination from you."

"Tell me something. Why do you imagine your friend interfered on this pimp's behalf?"

"The man is not my friend. I know him only at the athletic club. But he's a politically potent man who can help the force . . . or hurt it." Resnais smiles bitterly. "I suppose that sounds like ass-kissing to you."

LaPointe shrugs.

Resnais stares at him for a long moment. "What are you trying to tell me?"

"Put it together. Scheer is not the run-of-the-mill pimp. He specializes in very young girls. Either your . . . friend . . . is a client, or he's open to blackmail. Why else would he help a turd like Scheer?"

Resnais considers this for a moment. Then he makes some notes on his pad. Above all, he is a good cop. "You might be right. I'll have that looked into. But nothing alters the fact that you have exposed the department to bad public opinion with your gangster methods. Have you ever thought of them that way? As gangster methods?"

LaPointe has not. But he doesn't care about that. "So you intend to tell your political friend that you gave me a sound ass-chewing and everything will be fine from now on?"

"I will tell him that I privately reprimanded you."

"And he'll pass the word on to Scheer?"

"I suppose so."

"And Scheer will come back out onto the street, sassy-assed and ready to start business again." LaPointe shakes his head slowly. "No that's not the way it's going to happen, Commissioner. Not on my patch."

"Your patch! LaPointe of the Main! I'm sick up to here of hearing about it. You may think of yourself as *the* cop of *the* street, but you're not the whole force, LaPointe. And that rundown warren of slums is not Montreal!"

LaPointe stares at Resnais. Run-down warren!

For a second, Resnais has the feeling the LaPointe is going to hit him. He knows he went too far, talking about the Main like that. But he has no intention of backing down. "You were telling me that this Scheer wouldn't be allowed to start up business again. What do you think you're going to do, Claude?" It's "Claude" now. Resnais is shifting his forensic line.

LaPointe rises and goes to Resnais' window. He never noticed that the Commissioner looks out on the Hôtel de Ville too, on the scaffolding and sandblasting. It doesn't seem right that they should share the same view. "Well, Commissioner. You can go ahead and tell your friend that you gave me a 'private reprimand.' But you'd better also tell him that if his pimp sets foot on my patch, I'll hurt him."

"I am giving you a direct order to stop your harassment of this citizen."

There is a long silence, during which LaPointe continues to look out the window as though he has not heard.

Resnais pushed his pencils back and forth with his forefinger. Finally, he speaks with a quiet, flat tone. "Well. This is the attitude I expected from you. You don't leave me any alternative. Discharging you will make a real *gibelotte* for me. I won't bullshit you by pretending it's going to be easy. The men will put up a hell of a stink. I won't come out of it smelling like a rose, and the force won't come out of it without bruises. So I'm going to rely on your loyalty to the force to make it easier. Because, you see, Claude, I've come to a decision. One way or another, you're out."

LaPointe leans slightly forward as though to see something down in the street that interests him more than the Commissioner's talk.

"Look at it this way, Claude. You came on the force when you were twenty-one. You've got thirty-two years of service. You can retire on full pay. Now, I'm not asking you to retire right now, this morning. I'd be content if you'd send in a letter of resignation effective, say, in six months. That way no one would relate your leaving to any trouble between us. You would save face, and I wouldn't have the mess of petitions and letters to the papers from the kids. Make up an excuse. Say it's for reasons of health—whatever you want. For my part, I'll see to it you're promoted to captain just before you go. That'll mean you retire on captain's pay."

Resnais swivels in his posture chair to face LaPointe, who is still looking out the window, unmoving. "One way or another, Claude, you're going. If I have to, I'll retire you under the 'good of the department' clause. I warned you to sort yourself out, but you wouldn't listen. You just don't seem to be able to change with the changing times." Resnais turns back to his desk. "I'm not denying that it would go easier on me if you would turn in your resignation voluntarily, but I don't expect you to do it for me. There's never been any love lost between us. You've always resented my drive and success. But there's no point going into that now. I'm asking you to resign quietly for the good of the department, and I honestly believe that you care about the force, in your own way." There is just the right balance between regret and firmness in his voice. Resnais evaluates the effect of the sound as he speaks, and he is pleased with it.

LaPointe takes a deep breath, like a man coming out of a daydream. "Is that all, Commissioner?"

"Yes. I expect your resignation on my desk within the week."

LaPointe sniffs and smiles to himself. He would lose nothing by turning in a resignation effective in six months. He doesn't have six months left.

By the time LaPointe has his hand on the doorknob, Resnais is already looking over his appointment calendar. He is a little behind.

The man who enslaves his minutes liberates his hours.

"Phillipe?" LaPointe says quietly.

Resnais looks up in surprise. This is the first time in the thirty years they have been on the force together that LaPointe has called him by his first name.

LaPointe's right fist is in the air. Slowly, he extends the middle finger.

When he gets back to his office, LaPointe finds Detective Sergeant Gaspard sitting on the edge of his desk, a half-empty paper cup of coffee in his hand.

"What's going on?" LaPointe asks, dropping into his swivel chair and turning it so he can look out the window.

"Nothing much. I was just trying to pump the kid here; see if he is learning the *gamique* under you."

"And?"

"Well, he's at least learned enough to keep his mouth shut. When I asked him how you were coming on the Green case, he said you'd tell me what you wanted me to know."

"Good boy," LaPointe says.

Guttmann doesn't look up from his typing for fear of losing his place, but he nods in agreement with the compliment.

"Well?" Gaspard asks. "I don't want to seem nosy, but it is technically my case, and I haven't had a word from you for a couple of days. And I want to be ready, if this case is what Resnais le Grand wanted to see you about."

Already the rumor has been around the department that Resnais was in a furious mood when he called in LaPointe.

"No, it wasn't about that," LaPointe says.

Gaspard's raised eyebrows indicate that he is more than willing to hear what it *was* all about, but instead LaPointe turns back from the window and gives him a quick rundown of progress so far.

"So you figure the kid was being laundered, eh?"

"I'm sure of it."

"And if he was such a big time *sauteux de clôtures* as you say, almost anyone might have put that knife into him—some jealous squack, somebody's lover, somebody's brother—almost anyone."

"That it?"

"You on to anything?"

"We've got suspects falling out of the trees. But most of the leads have healed up now. I've got something I'm looking into tonight; a bar the kid used to go to."

"You expect to turn something there?"

"Not much. Probably twenty more suspects."

"Hungh! Well, keep up the good work. And do your best to bring this one in, will you? I could use another letter of merit. So how's our Joan getting on? Is he as much a pain in the ass to you as he was to me?"

LaPointe shrugs. He has no intention of complimenting the kid in his presence. "Why do you ask? You want him back today?"

"No, not if you can stand to have him a while longer. He cramps my romantic form, hanging around all the time." Gaspard drains the cup, wads it up in his hand, and misses the wastebasket. "Okay, if that's all you've got to tell me about our case, I'll get back to keeping the city safe for the tourists. Just look at that kid type, will you? Now that's what I call style!"

Guttmann growls as Gaspard leaves with a laugh.

LaPointe feels a slight nausea from the ebb of angry adrenalin after his session with the Commissioner. The air in his office is warm and has an already-breathed taste. He wants to get out of here, go where he feels comfortable and alive. "Look, I'm going up on the Main. See what's going on."

"You want me to go with you?"

"No. I lose you tomorrow, and I want this paper work caught up."

"Oh." Guttmann does not try to conceal his deflation.

LaPointe tugs on his overcoat. "I'm just going to make the rounds. Talk to people. This Green thing has taken up too much of my time. I'm getting out of touch." He looks down at the young man behind the stacks of reports. "What do you have on for this evening around seven? A date to wash clothes?"

"No, sir."

"All right. Meet me at the Happy Hour Whisky à Go-Go on Rachel Street. It's our last lead. You might as well see this thing through."

Before it lost its cabaret license, the Happy Hour Whisky à Go-Go was a popular dance hall where girls from the garment shops and men from the loading docks could pick one another up, dance a little, ogle, drink, make arrangements for later on. It was a huge, noisy barn with a turning ball of mirrored surfaces depending from the ceiling, sliding globs of colored light around the walls, over the dancers, and into the orchestra, the amplified instruments of which made the floor vibrate. But once too often, the owner had been careless about letting underage girls in and about making sure his bouncers stopped fights before they got to the bottle-throwing stage, so now dancing is not permitted, and the patronage has shrunk to a handful of people sitting around the U-shaped bar, a glowing island in a vastness of dark, unused space.

At the prow of the bar is a drum stage four feet in diameter on which a go-go dancer slowly grinds her ass, her tempo in no way associated with the beat of the whining, repetitive rock music provided by a turntable behind the bar. The dancer is not young, and she is fat. Bored and dull-eyed, she undulates mechanically, her great bare breasts sloshing about as she slips her thumbs in and out of the pouch of her G-string, tugging it away from her *écu* and letting it snap back in a routine ritual of provocation.

Blue and orange lights glow dimly through the bottles of the back bar, producing most of the illumination, save for a strong narrow beam at the cash register. Ultraviolet lamps around the dancing drum cause the dancer's G-string to glow bright green. She has also applied phosphorescent paint to her nipples, and they glow green too. Standing just inside the door, far from the bar, LaPointe looks over the customers until he picks out Guttmann. From that distance, the back-lit figure of the dancer is almost invisible, save for the phosphorescent triangle of her crotch and the circles of her nipples. As she grinds away, she looks like a man with a goatee, chewing and rolling his eyes.

LaPointe climbs up on a stool beside Guttmann and orders an Armagnac. "What are you drinking?" he asks Guttmann.

"Ouzo."

"Why ouzo?"

Guttmann shrugs. "Because it's a Greek bar, I guess."

"Good thing it isn't an Arab bar. You'd be drinking camel piss." LaPointe looks along the curve of customers. A couple of young men with nothing to do; a virile-looking woman in a cloth coat sitting directly in front of the dancer, staring up with cold fascination and tickling her upper lip with her finger; two soldiers already a little drunk; an old Greek staring disconsolately into his glass; a neatly dressed man in his fifties, suit and tie, a briefcase up on the bar, watching the play of the thumbs in and out of the G-string, his starched collar picking up the ultraviolet light and glowing greenish. All in all, the typical flotsam of outsiders and losers one finds in this kind of bar in the early evenings, or in rundown movie houses in the afternoons.

The fat dancer turns her head as she jiggles from foot to foot and nods once to LaPointe. He does not nod back.

Sitting behind the bar, at the base of the drum, is a girl who attends to the jury-rigged turntable and amplifier. She is fearful of not doing her job right, so she stares at the turning disc, holding her breath, poised to lift the needle and move it to the next selection when the song runs out. She counts the bands to the one she must hit next, mouthing the numbers to herself. Occasionally she lifts her face to look up at the fat dancer. Her eyes brim with admiration and wonder. The lights, the color, and everyone watching. Show business! She appears to be fifteen or sixteen, but her face has no age. It is the bland oval of a seriously retarded child, and its permanent expression is a calm void over which, from time to time, comes a ripple of confusion and doubt.

The tune is nearing its end, and the girl is straining her concentration in preparation for changing the needle without making that horrible rasping noise. The dancer looks down at her and shakes her head. The girl doesn't know what this signal means! She is confused and frightened. She freezes! After an undulating hiss, the record goes on to the next band—the wrong band! The girl snatches her hands away from the machine, recoiling from all responsibility. But the dancer is already coming down from the drum, her great breasts flopping with the last awkward step. She growls at the girl and lifts the needle from the record herself. Then she walks along behind the bar to a back room. In a minute she emerges, wearing clacking bedroom slippers and a gossamer tent of a dressing gown through which the brown, pimpled cymbals of her nipples are visible.

She slides onto the stool next to Guttmann, her sweaty cheek squeaking on the plastic. She smells of sweat and cologne.

"Want to buy me a drink, gunner?" she asks Guttmann.

LaPointe leans forward and speaks across the young man. "He's not a mark. He's with me."

"Sorry, Lieutenant. I mean, how was I to know? You didn't come in together."

With a tip of his head, LaPointe orders her to follow as he takes up his Armagnac and walks away from the bar to a table with bentwood chairs inverted on it. He has three chairs down by the time the woman and Guttmann arrive. The table is small, and Guttmann cannot easily move his knee away from hers. She presses her leg against his to let him know she knows.

"What's the trouble now, Lieutenant?" The tone indicates that she has had run-ins with LaPointe before. She can't imagine why, but the Lieutenant has never liked her. Not even in the old days, when she was working the streets.

LaPointe wastes no time with her. "There's a kid who comes in here. Young, Italian, doesn't have much English. Good-looking. Probably calls himself Tony Green."

"He's in trouble?"

LaPointe stares at her dully. He asks questions; he doesn't answer them.

"Okay, I know the kid you mean," she says quickly, sensing his no-nonsense mood.

"Well?" he says. He has no specific questions, so he makes her do the talking.

"What can I tell you? I don't know much about him. He started coming in here a couple of months ago, sort of regular, you know. At first he can't say diddly shit in English, but now he can talk pretty good. Sometimes he comes alone, sometimes with a couple of pals. . . ." Willing though she is, she runs out of things to say.

"Go on."

"What can I say? Ah . . . he usually drinks Strega, if that's any use. Just another cock hanging out. He ain't been in for the last few nights."

"He's dead."

"No shit?" she asks, only mildly interested. "Well, that explains it, then."

"Explains what?"

"Well . . . we had a little appointment set up for last Thursday night. And he didn't show."

"That was the night he was killed."

"Just my luck. Now I'm out the fifty bucks."

"He was going to pay you fifty bucks?" LaPointe asks incredulously. "What for? Six months' worth?"

"No, he didn't want me. He had me the first night or so he was here. He's big on back-door stuff. But he didn't seem interested in a second helping."

"If not you, who then?"

She lifts her chin towards the bar. "He wanted to screw the kid that helps me with the music."

Guttmann glances at LaPointe. "Christ," he says. "A moronic kid?"

"Now wait a minute!" the dancer protests quickly. "You can't hang anything on me. The kid's nineteen. She's got consent. Ask the Lieutenant. She's nineteen, ain't she?"

"Yes, she's nineteen. With the mind of a seven-year-old."

"There you are! And anyway, she seems to like it. She never complains. Just stares off into space all the time it's going on. Look, I got to get back to my public. That butch in the front will pull her goddamned lip off if I'm late. Look, I'd tell you if I knew anything about the Italian kid. You know that, Lieutenant. Shit, the last thing I need is more trouble. But like I said, he was just another cock hanging out for a little *fonne*. Hey, did you notice that civilian in the suit? Now, there's a weirdo for you. You know what he's doing under the bar?"

"*Sacre le camp,*" LaPointe orders.

The dancer tucks down the corners of her mouth and shrugs, making a little farting noise of indifference with her mouth. Then she leaves for the back room, from which she soon appears without the slippers and dressing robe to clamber up onto the drum and stand, bored and impatient, while the retarded girl tries to set the needle down silently. She fails, and there is a screech before the whining music begins. The dancer darts a punitive glance at her, then begins to jiggle from foot to foot, running her thumbs around the belt of her G-string and in and out of the pouch.

The sting of the reprimand slides quickly from the girl's smooth mind, and soon she is lost in rapt fascination, looking up at the woman dancing in the blue and orange light, all eyes on her. Show business.

Guttmann finishes his ouzo at a gulp. "I hate to admit it, but I'm beginning to agree with you."

"You'd better watch that."

"This Green was a real shit."

"Yes. Come on. Let's go."

At the door, LaPointe looks back at the dimly lit bar, small in the cavern of the unused dance floor. The man with the goatee is chewing and rolling his eyes.

They walk side by side down Rachel toward the Main, toward the luminous cross that advertises Christianity from the crest of Mount Royal.

"It's still early," Guttmann says. "You want a cup of coffee?"

That's a switch, and LaPointe senses that the young man wants to talk, but he feels too fed up, too tired of it all. "No, thanks. I'll just go home. I'm tired."

They walk on in silence.

"That Green . . ." Guttmann mutters.

"What?"

"I mean, come on. That's *too* sick."

"No sicker than that dancer."

"Sir?"

"The girl is her daughter."

Guttmann walks on mechanically, staring ahead, his fists clenched in his overcoat pockets. They cross over St. Laurent, where LaPointe stops to say goodbye. "You have a date with your girl tonight?" he asks.

"Yes, sir. Nothing big. We're just going to sit around and talk about things."

"Like the future?"

"That sort of thing. Will you tell me something, Lieutenant? Does anyone survive a career as a cop and still feel anything but disgust for people?"

"A few do."

"You?"

LaPointe examines the boy's earnest, pained face. "See you in the morning."

"Sure."

Twelve

TWO DAYS PASS; Guttmann has returned to Detective Sergeant Gaspard to finish out his tour as a Joan. When no new leads open on the Green case, there is talk down in homicide of closing down the investigation.

Pig weather continues to depress spirits and abrade tempers, and a popular rumor circulates on the Main to the effect that Russian and American atomic testing has done irremediable damage to the polar icecap, and the weather will never return to normal.

LaPointe's time and attention is soaked up by typical problems of the Main. Mr. Rothmann's butcher shop is broken into; the newspaper vendor on the corner of Rue Roy is held up for eight dollars and thirty-five cents; and the construction force demolishing a block of row houses to make way for a high-rise parking facility arrives on the site one morning to find that extensive vandalism has ruined work and tools. On a scabby brick wall, the posse of vandals has painted:

182 PEOPLE USED TO LIVE HERE

On the Rothmann break-in, nothing was stolen and the only damage was to the doorframe and lock. Probably some street tramp or shelterless American draft avoider trying to get out of the damp cold of night. Once again, LaPointe advises Mr. Rothmann to install special police locks, and once again Mr. Rothmann argues that the police ought to pay for them. After all, he's a taxpayer, isn't he?

The holdup of the newspaper vendor is a different matter. LaPointe presses it to a quick finish because he realizes that someone might have been killed. Not the victim; the holdup man.

The paper seller could only give a description of the thief's shoes and legs, and of the gun. Tennis shoes, bell-bottom jeans. A kid. And a black gun with a tiny hole in the barrel. The tiny hole meant the weapon was one of those exact-replica waterguns the Montreal police have made repeated complaints about, to no avail. After all, the people who sell them to kids are taxpayers, aren't they? It's a free country, isn't it?

LaPointe makes two telephone calls and talks with four people on the street. The word is out: the Lieutenant wants this kid, and he wants him right now. If he doesn't have him by noon, the street is going to become a hard place to live on.

Two and a half hours later, LaPointe is sitting in the cramped kitchen of a basement flat with the thief and his parents. The father admits he doesn't know what the hell is wrong with these goddamned kids these days. The mother says she works her fingers to the bone, never sees anything but these four walls, and what thanks does it get you? You carry them under your heart for nine months, you feed them, you send them to Mass, and what does it get you?

The kid sits at the kitchen table, picking at the oilcloth. His eyes lowered, he answers LaPointe's questions in a reluctant monotone. Once he makes the mistake of sassing.

In two steps, LaPointe crosses the room and snatches the kid up by the collar of his imitation-leather jacket. "What do you think happens if a cop chases you and you flash that goddamned water pistol? Hein? You could be killed for eight lousy bucks!"

There is fear in the kid's eyes; defiance too.

LaPointe drops him back into his chair. What's the use?

It's a first offense. The Lieutenant can make arrangements, can find a job for the kid swabbing out some restaurant on the Main. The boy will pay the newspaper vendor back. He will have no record. But next time . . .

As he leaves, he hears the mother whining about carrying a child under her heart for nine months, and what thanks does she get? Heartache! Nothing but heartache!

There will be a next time.

About the vandalism at the building site, LaPointe does nothing, although this is not the first time it has happened. He goes through the motions, but he does nothing. His sympathy is with the people who are losing their homes and being shipped out to glass-and-cement suburban slums high-rising from muddy "green zones" dotted with emaciated twigs of one-year-old trees tied by rags to supporting sticks.

Corners, whole blocks of row houses are being torn down to make room for commercial buildings. Narrow streets of three-story Victorian brick with lead-sheeted mansard roofs are falling prey to the need to centralize small industry and commerce without threatening land values and the quality of life in the better neighborhoods. The residents of the Main are too poor, too ignorant, too weak politically to protect themselves from the paternal tyranny of city planning committees. The Main is a slum, anyway. Bad plumbing; rats and roaches; inadequate playgrounds. Relocating the immigrants is really for their own good; it helps to break up the language and culture nodes that delay their assimilation into New Montreal: Chicago on the St. Lawrence.

Although LaPointe knows that this blind striking out at the construction sites will change nothing, that the little people of the Main must lose their battle and ultimately their identity, he understands their need to protest, to break something.

More subtle than these dramatic attacks on the Main are the constant erosions from all points on its perimeter. Individuals and organizations have discovered that protecting what is left of old Montreal can be a profitable activity. Under the pretext of preservation, rows of homes are bought up and gutted, leaving only "quaint" shells. Good plumbing and central heating are installed, rooms enlarged, and residences are created for affluent and swinging young lawyers, pairs of career girls, braces of interior decorators. It is fashionable to surprise friends by saying you live on the Main. But these people don't live on the Main; they play house on the Main.

LaPointe sees it all happening. In his bitterest moods he feels that this bubble in his chest is consonant with the rest of it; there wouldn't be much point in surviving the Main.

When he arrives at the office Thursday morning, his temper is ragged. He has picked up word that Scheer is bragging about being back on the street before long. Obviously, the Commissioner has reported to his political acquaintance.

After scanning the Morning Report, he paws about in the three days' worth of back paper work that has accumulated since Guttmann's departure. Then he comes across a memo from Dr. Bouvier asking him to drop down to Forensic Medicine when he has a free moment.

As always, the smells of wax, chemicals, heat, and dust in the basement hall trigger memories of St. Joseph's: *moue, tranches,* the Glory Hole, Our Lady of the Chipped Cheek . . .

When LaPointe enters his office, Bouvier is just drawing a cup of coffee from his urn, his finger crooked into the cup to tell when it is nearly full.

"That you, Claude? Come in and be impressed by one of my flashes of insight, this particular one focused on the case of one Antonio Verdini—alias Green—discovered one night in an alley, his body having acquired a biologically superfluous, and even detrimental, orifice."

LaPointe grunts, in no mood for Bouvier's florid style.

"My ingenious filing system"—Bouvier waves toward his high-heaped desk—"has produced the interesting fact that our Mr. Green's uncommon appetite for ventilation was shared by"—he cocks his head in LaPointe's direction and pauses for effect—"the victims of two other unsolved murder cases."

"Oh?"

"Somehow I had expected more than 'oh.' "

"Which cases, then?"

"Men known to the department, and therefore to God, as H-49854 and H-50567, but to their intimates as MacHenry, John Albert, and Pearson, Michael X. This X indicates that his parents gave him no middle name, doubtless in a spirit of orthographic economy." Bouvier holds the two files out to LaPointe and stares proudly at him with one huge eye and one nicotine-colored blank. The Lieutenant scans rapidly, then reads more closely. These are Bouvier's personal files, fuller than the official records because they include clippings from newspapers, relevant additional information, and certain scribbled notes in his large, tangled hand.

One file is six years old, the other two and a half. Both stabbings; both males; both without signs of robbery; both at night on deserted streets.

"Well?" Bouvier gloats.

"Could be coincidences."

"There's a limit to antichance. Notice that both happened on the edges of what you call your patch—although I hear there is some difference of opinion between you and the Risen Cream as to the extent of that realm, and of its monarch's authority."

"What's all this business here?" LaPointe puts one report on Bouvier's desk, keeping his finger on a passage scribbled in the doctor's hand.

Pressing the bridge of his broken glasses to hold them in place, Bouvier leans over, his face close to the page. "Ah! Technical description of the wound. Angle of entry of the weapon."

"Identical in all three cases?"

"No. Not quite."

"Well, then?"

"That's where you discern the touch of genius in me! The angles of entry are not identical. They vary. They vary in direct proportion to the heights of the three men. If you insist on playing the game of coincidence, you have to accept that there were three killers of identical height, and who held a knife in the identical way, and all three of whom were most gifted in the use of a knife. And if you want to stack up coincidences with the abandon of a Victorian novelist, how's this? Pearson, Michael X., made love shortly before his death. Once again, that nasty habit of failing to wash up. A professor at McGill, too! You'd think he'd know better. The other fellow, MacHenry, John Albert, was an American up here on business. There is every reason to believe that he also made love shortly before contributing his personal dust to the Universal Dust. He washed up within an hour of his death. Not a full bath; just the crotch area. There's the American businessman for you! Time is money."

"Can I take these with me?" LaPointe asks rhetorically, already on his way out with the reports.

"But make sure you bring them back. I can't stand having my files in disorder!" Bouvier calls after him.

Read and reread, Bouvier's dossiers rest on LaPointe's desk, covering the unfinished paper work. He links his fingers over his head and leans back in his swivel chair to look at the large-scale city plan of Montreal tacked up on his wall, finger-smudged only in the area of the Main. His eye picks up the places where the three men were found—stabbed, but not robbed. The Green kid . . . there. In the alley almost in the center of the Main district. The American businessman . . . there. On a narrow street off Chateaubriand between Rue Roy and Rue Bousquet, on what LaPointe would call the outer edge of his patch. And that professor from McGill . . . there. Well outside the Main, on Milton Street between Lorne and Shuter, normally a busy area, but probably deserted at . . . what was it? . . . estimated time of death: between 0200 and 0400 hours.

Probably the same killer. Probably the same woman. Jealousy? Over a period of six years? Hardly what you would call a flash of jealous anger. One woman. One killer. Perhaps the woman *was* the killer. And . . . what kind of woman could unite a Canadian professor, an American businessman, and an illegal Italian alien with sperm on his brain?

The freshest of these old cases is thirty months old. All traces would be healed over by now.

He sighs and puts the files into a thick interdepartmental envelope to send them over to Gaspard in homicide. LaPointe can picture Gaspard's anger when he discovers he has inherited a set of killings with a sex link. Just the kind of thing the newspapers salivate over. Unknown Knife Slayer Stalks . . . Police Baffled . . .

All the while he is eating in a cheap café, unaware of what is on his plate, all the while he walks slowly through the Main, putting the street to bed, LaPointe carries the details of the two files in the back of his mind, turning over the sparse references to personal life, looking for bits that match up with what he knows about Tony Green. But nothing. No links. He is standing outside his apartment on Esplanade, looking up at the dark windows of his second-story flat, when he decides to return to the Quartier Général and muck around with late paper work, rather than face a night alone with his coffee and his Zola.

"What in hell are you doing here?"

"Jesus Christ! You startled me, sir."

"You leave something behind?"

Guttmann has been sitting at LaPointe's desk, his mind floating in a debris of problems and daydreams. "No. I just remembered that you have a map of the city on your wall, and I still had my key, so . . ."

"So?"

"It's about that packet of files you left for Sergeant Gaspard."

With a jerk of his thumb, LaPointe evicts Guttmann from his swivel chair and occupies it himself. "I'll bet he was happy to find three closed cases suddenly reopened."

"Oh, yes, sir. He could hardly contain his delight. He was particularly colorful on the subject of Dr. Bouvier. He said he needed that kind of help about as much as starving Pakistanis need Red Cross packages filled with menus."

"Hm-m. But that still doesn't explain what you're doing in my office."

Guttmann goes to the wall map and points out light pencil lines he has drawn on it. "I got this weird idea in the middle of the night."

LaPointe is puddling about in his paper work. "Joans aren't supposed to have ideas. It ruins their typing," he says without looking up.

"As it turned out, it wasn't much of an idea."

"No kidding? Let's hear it."

Guttmann shrugs his shoulders, not eager to share his foolishness. "Oh, it was just grade-school geometry. It occurred to me that we know where each of the three men was killed, and we know where each was going at the time. So, if we extended the lines back on the map . . ."

LaPointe laughs. "The lines would meet on the doorstep of the killer?"

"Something like that. Or if not at the doorstep of the killer, at least on the doorstep of the woman they all made love with. I assume it was one woman, don't you."

"Either that or a whorehouse?"

"Well, either way, it would be one dwelling."

LaPointe looks up at the map on which Guttmann's three lines enclose a vast triangle including the east half of the Main district and a corner of Parc Fontaine. "Well, you've narrowed it down to eastern Canada."

Guttmann realizes how stupid his idea sounds when said aloud. "It was just a wild shot. I knew that any two lines would have to meet somewhere. And I hoped that the third would zap right in there."

"I see." LaPointe moves aside the files Guttmann brought along with him and picks up a splay of unfinished reports. He wants the kid to see he came here to do some work. Not because he was lonely. Not because his bed was too big.

"Can I get you a cup of coffee, sir?"

"If you're getting one for yourself."

While Guttmann is at the machine down the hall, LaPointe's eyes wander back to the wall map. He makes a nasal puff of derision at the idea that things get solved by geometry and deduction. What you need is an informer, a lot of pressure, a fist.

With a brimming paper cup in each hand, Guttmann has some trouble with the door; he slops some and burns his fingers. "Goddamn it!" He gives the door a kick.

LaPointe glances up. This kid is usually so controlled, so polite. As Guttmann sits in his old chair against the wall, his long legs stretched out in front of him, LaPointe sips his coffee.

"What's your problem?"

"Sir?"

"Trouble with this girl of yours?"

"No, that isn't it. That's turning out to be a really fine thing."

"Oh? How long have you known her? A week?"

"How long does it take?"

LaPointe nods. That is true. He had been sure he wanted to spend his life with Lucille after knowing her for two hours. Of course, it was a year before they had the money to get married.

"No, it isn't the girl," Guttmann continues, looking into his coffee. "It's the force. I'm thinking pretty seriously about quitting." He had wanted to talk to LaPointe about this that evening after they'd been at the go-go joint, but there hadn't been an opportunity. He looks up to see how the Lieutenant is taking the news.

There is no response at all from LaPointe. Perhaps a slight shrug. He never gives advice in this kind of situation; he doesn't want the responsibility.

There is an uncomfortable, interrogative quality to the silence, so LaPointe looks up at the wall map for something to fill it. "What's that northwest-southeast line supposed to be?"

Guttmann understands. The Lieutenant doesn't want to talk about it. Well . . . "Ah, let me see. Well, that X is the alley where we found Green."

"I know that."

"And the circle is his apartment—the rooming house with the concierge with the broken lip? So I just drew a line between them and continued it on southeast to see where it would lead. Just an approximation. It cuts through the middles of blocks and such, but it must have been the general direction he came from."

"Yes, but he wasn't going back to his rooming house."

"Sir?"

"He was going to the Happy Hour Whisky à Go-Go, remember? He had a date with that dancer's retarded kid."

Guttmann looks at the map more closely and frowns. "Yeah. That's right!" He takes out his pencil and crosses to the map. Freehand, he sketches in the revised line, and the vast triangle is reduced by a considerable wedge. "That narrows it down a lot."

"Sure. To maybe thirty square blocks and six or eight thousand people. Just for the hell of it, let's take a look at the other lines. What's that one running roughly east-west?"

"That's the McGill professor. The X is where his body was found; the circle is his office on the campus."

"How do you know he was going to his office?"

"Assumption. His apartment was up north. Why would he walk west unless he was going to the campus? Maybe to do some late work. Grade papers, something like that."

"All right. Assume it. Now, what about the other line? The north-south one?"

"That's the American. His body was found right . . . here. And his hotel was downtown, right . . . ah . . . here. So I just extended the line back."

"But he wouldn't have walked south."

"Sure he would. That was the direction to his hotel, and also the best direction to go to find taxis."

"What about his car?"

"Sir?"

"Look in the report. There was something about a rented car. It was found three days later, after the rental agency placed a complaint. Don't you remember? The car was ticketed for overparking. Bouvier made some wiseassed note about the bad luck of getting a parking ticket the same night you get killed."

Guttmann taps his forehead with his knuckle. "Yes! I forgot about that."

"Don't worry about it. One line out of three isn't bad. For a Joan."

"Where was the car parked?"

"It's in the report. Somewhere a few blocks from where they found the body."

Guttmann takes up the folder on MacHenry, John Albert, and leafs quickly through it. He misses what he's looking for and has to flip back. The major reason Dr. Bouvier is able to come up with his little "insights" from time to time is his cross-indexing of information. In the standard departmental files, the murder of MacHenry, the report of the car rental agency, and the traffic report of the ticketed car would be in separate places; in fact in separate departments. But in Dr. Bouvier's files, they are together. "Here it is!" Guttmann says. "Let's see . . . the rental car . . . recovered by the agency from police garage . . . ah! It was parked near the corner of Rue Mentana and Rue Napoléon. Let's see what that gives us." He goes to the map again and sketches the new line. Then he turns back to LaPointe. "Now, how about that, Lieutenant?"

The three lines fail to intersect by a triangle half the size of a fingernail. And the center of that triangle is Carré St. Louis, a rundown little park on the edge of the Main.

LaPointe rises and approaches the map. "Could be coincidence."

"Yes, sir."

"We would be looking for a woman somewhere around Carré St. Louis who has made love three times in the past six years. It's just possible that more than one would fit that description."

"Yes, sir."

"Murders aren't solved by drawing lines on maps, you know."

"Yes, sir."

"Hm-m."

Guttmann lets the silence extend awhile before offering, "I'll bet Sergeant Gaspard would let me go with you. I've just about finished his paper work too."

LaPointe taps the pale green rectangle of the square with his thick forefinger. It has been about a week since he wandered through there on his rounds. The night of the Green killing, come to think of it. He pictures the statue of the dying Cremazie.

Pour Mon Drapeau
Je Viens Ici Mourir

The empty pond, its bottom littered. The peace symbol dripping rivulets of paint, like a bleeding swastika. The word LOVE, but the spray can ran out while they were adding FUCK YO . . .

LaPointe nods. "All right. Tomorrow morning we'll take a walk around there." He returns to his desk and finishes his cooling coffee, crushing the cup and tossing it toward the wastebasket. "What does she think about it?"

"Sir?"

"Your girl. What does she think about your decision to leave the department?"

Taken off balance, Guttmann shrugs and wanders back to his chair. "Oh, she wants me to do what I want to do. Maybe . . . maybe I shouldn't have joined up in the first place. I came out of school with the idea that I could do something . . . useful. Social work, maybe. I don't know. I knew how people felt about the police, particularly the young, and I thought . . . Anyway, I realize now I wasn't cut out to be a cop. Maybe I've always known it. Being with you these few days has sort of pushed me over the edge, you know what I mean? I just don't have the stomach for it. I don't want everyone I meet to hate me, or fear me. I don't want to live in a world populated by tramps and losers and whores and punks and junkies. It's just . . . not for me. I'd never be good at it. And nobdoy likes to be a failure. I've talked it all over with Jeanne; she understands."

"Jeanne?"

"The girl in my building."

"She's *canadienne,* this girl of yours?"

"Didn't I mention that?"

"No."

"Well, she is."

"Hm-m. You've got better taste than I thought. Are you going to drink that coffee?"

"No. Here. You know, this idea about the map was really sort of an excuse to come down here and think things over."

"And now you've decided?"

"Pretty much."

Guttmann sits in silence. LaPointe drinks the coffee as he looks at the wall map with half-closed eyes, then he scrubs his hair with his hand. "Well, I'd better call it a day."

"Can I drop you off, sir?"

"In that toy car of yours?"

"It's the only car I've got."

LaPointe seems to consider this for a moment. "All right. You can drop me off."

Guttmann feels like saying, Thank you very much, sir.

But he does not.

Thirteen

A CLAMMY MIST settles over Carré St. Louis, sweating the statue of Cremazie, sogging litter in the pond, varnishing the gnarled roots that convulse over a surface too cindery and hard-packed to penetrate. Between stunted, leafless trees, there are weathered park benches, all bearing carved sgraffiti in which vulgar, romantic, and eponymous impulses overlay and defeat one another.

Once a square of town houses around a pleasant park, Carré St. Louis has run to ruin and has been invaded by jangling, alien styles. To the west is a great Victorian pile, its capricious projections and niches bound together by a broad sign all along the front: YOUNG CHINESE MEN'S CHRISTIAN ASSOCIATION. Even the lack of repainting for many years and the hanging mist that broods over the park does not mute its garish, three-foot-high Chinese characters of red and gold. The top of the square is dominated by a grotesquerie, a crenelated castle in old gray stone and new green paint, the home of the Millwright's Union.

What in hell is a millwright, LaPointe wonders. A man who makes mills? No, that can't be right. He glances at his watch: quarter after eleven; Guttmann is late.

Only to the east of the park is the integrity of the row houses preserved; and even there it is bogus. Behind the façades, the fashionable and artsy have gutted and renovated. Soon this bit of the Main will be undermined and pried loose from the cultural mosaic. The new inhabitants will have the political leverage to get the trees trimmed, the fountain running, the spraypaint peace symbol cleaned off the side of the pool. There will be grass and shrubs and new benches, and there will be an ironwork fence around the park to which residents will have keys.

LaPointe grunts his disgust and looks around to see Guttmann crossing the park with long strides, anxious about being late.

"I couldn't find a parking place," he explains as he approaches. When La-Pointe doesn't respond, he continues with, "I'm sorry. Have you been waiting long?"

The Lieutenant blocks the small talk. "You know this square?"

"No, sir." Guttmann looks around. "God, there are a lot of houses. Where do we begin?"

"Let's take a little stroll around."

Guttmann walks beside LaPointe, their slow steps crunching the gravel of the central spine path, as they scan the buildings on both sides.

Guttmann continues along in silence, until it occurs to him to ask, "Sir? What is a millwright?"

LaPointe glances at him sideways with a fatigued expression that says, Don't you know *anything?*

They cross over from the park and walk down the east side of the square, down the row of renovated buildings. LaPointe walks with the long slow steps of the beat-pounder, his fists deep in his overcoat pockets, looking up at each doorway in turn.

"What are we looking for, sir?"

"No idea."

"It's sort of a needle in a haystack, isn't it? It occurred to me on the way over that if one of those lines on the map was just a few degrees off, the woman could live blocks away from here."

"Hm-m. If she still lives here. If it's *one* woman. If . . ."

LaPointe's pace slows slightly as he looks up at the next door. Then he walks on a little more quickly.

"If what, sir?"

"Come on. I'll buy you a cup of coffee."

They take coffee in a little place two blocks east of the square, in one of those self-conscious bohemian cafés frequented by the young. At this time of day it is empty, save for an intense couple in the far corner, a bearded boy who appears to be staggering under the impulse to communicate, a skinny girl in round glasses who is straining to understand. They work very hard at avoiding artifice.

The waitress is a young slattern who tugs a snarl out of her hair with her fingers as she repeats Guttmann's order for two cappuccini. Back at the coffee machine, she stares indifferently out a front window hung with glass beads as she lets steam hiss into the coffee. For once they are in an atmosphere in which Guttmann is more at home than LaPointe, who looks across the table and shakes his head at the young policeman. "You talk about God being on the side of drunks, fools, and kids. I didn't expect anything to come of your silly game of drawing lines on a map. Not one chance in a thousand."

"*Has* something come of it?"

"I'm afraid so. Chances are our woman works, or did work, at that school."

"School, sir?"

"Seventh building from the end of the renovated row. There was a placard on the door—brass. It's a school of sorts. One of those places that teaches French and English to foreigners in a hurry."

Guttmann's expression widens. "And Green was learning English!"

LaPointe nods.

"But wait a minute. What about the American?"

"Could have been learning French. Maybe he wanted to set up a business in Québec."

"And the McGill professor?"

"I don't know. We'll have to see how he fits in. If he does."

"But wait a minute, sir. Even if the school is the contact point, maybe it isn't a teacher. Could be one of the students."

"Over a period of six years?"

"All right. A teacher, then. So what do we do now?"

"We go talk to somebody. See if we can find out which teacher is ours." LaPointe rises.

"Aren't you going to finish your coffee, sir?"

"This swill? Just tip the greasy kid and let's get out of here."

Considering the slop and dregs he has had to drink with the Lieutenant in Chinese, Greek, and Portuguese cafés, Guttmann doubts that it is the quality of the coffee LaPointe is rejecting.

". . . so, out of a total faculty of thirteen, that would make a full-time equivalency of nine or nine and a half, considering that some of my teachers are only part-time, and some are university students training in our techniques of one-to-one intensive language assimilation." Mlle. Montjean lights her cigarette from a marble-and-gold lighter, takes a deep drag, and tilts her head back to jet the uninhaled smoke upward, away from her guests. Then she lightly touches the tip of her tongue between thumb and forefinger, as though to pluck off a bit of tobacco, a residual gesture from some earlier time when she smoked unfiltered cigarettes.

Many things about her put Guttmann in mind of a fashion model: the meticulous, underrolled coiffure, that bounces with her quick, energetic gestures; the assured, almost rehearsed moves and turns; the long slim arms and legs; the perfectly tailored suit that is both functional and feminine. And, like a model, she appears to be aware of herself at every moment, as though she were seeing herself from the outside. Guttmann finds her voice particularly pleasing in its combining of great precision of pronunciation with a low, warm note just above husky. She laughs in exactly the same key as that in which she speaks.

"I suppose that seems quite a large faculty for a little school like ours, Lieutenant, but we specialize in intensive training with a low student-to-teacher ratio. We *submerge* the student in a linguistic culture. The student who is learning French, for instance, doesn't hear a word of English for six hours a day, and he even takes lunch with instructors and other students in a French restaurant. And at night, if he wishes, the student will be taken to French nightclubs, cinema, theatre—all in the company of an instructor. We concentrate on the *music* of the language, you might say. The student learns to *hum* in French, even before he learns the words to the song. Our methods were pioneered at McGill, and indeed some of our student teachers are graduate students from there."

Mlle. Montjean suddenly stops and laughs. "I must be sounding like our promotional material."

"A little," LaPointe says. "You have a connection with McGill then?"

"No formal connection. Some of their students get experience and credit by working with us. Oh!" She butts her cigarette hurriedly. "Excuse me just a moment, won't you." She leaves the "conversation island," consisting of deeply padded white leather "comfort forms" around a kidney-shaped, glass-topped coffee table, the whole sunken two steps below the floor level. She goes quickly to her desk overlooking Carré St. Louis, and there she presses the button of a concealed tape recorder and speaks conversationally: "Maggie, remind me tomorrow to get in touch with Dr. Moreland. Subject: Evaluation Procedures for Part-time Students." She releases the button and smiles across at the policemen. "I would have forgotten that completely if I hadn't happened to mention it to you. I've got a brain like a sieve."

This is a social lie and an obvious one. Mlle. Montjean runs her specialized and very expensive school with such great efficiency that she appears to have free time for people who drop in unexpectedly. Even policemen.

The school occupies a double building: the façades of two former homes have been gutted and renovated to contain "conversation foyers," "learning environments," and audio-visual support systems on the first two floors, while the mansard-roofed third story houses Mlle. Montjean's living and working quarters. Guttmann is impressed by the way she has folded into her large living room the equipment necessary for running her business. Files are concealed within Victorian court cupboards; her hi-fi system is tied in with her dictation instruments; her business telephones are ceramic French "coffee-grinder" models; her desk is an inlaid feminine escritoire; the "conversation island" would serve equally well for staff meetings or a romantic tête-à-tête. The walls and ceiling are white stucco with attic beams revealed and varnished, and this neutral background helps to blend the improbable, but not offensive, mélange of modern, Victorian, and antique furniture.

In theory it ought not to work, this mixture of furniture styles, the stucco walls and dark beams, the Persian carpets, the modern and classical prints on the walls. But any feeling of discord and jumble is avoided by the sense that everything has been selected by one person of firm personality and taste. All the elements are aligned by one coign of vantage, one articulation of preference.

LaPointe doesn't like the place.

"I haven't offered you a drink, have I?" she says, shaking her head as though to imply she would forget it if it weren't attached. "What do you take before lunch? Dubonnet?"

Guttmann says Dubonnet would be fine.

"Lieutenant?" she asks.

"Nothing, thank you." After being shown up to the office apartment by a fussy man of uncertain function, LaPointe presented his identification card and introduced a question about the faculty of the school. Graciously, indeed overwhelmingly, Mlle. Montjean took up the cue, describing her business with a glibness that had a quality of rote. Even the asides and pauses to light a cigarette seemed considered, rehearsed. She said more than he wanted to know, as though attempting to drown questions with answers.

LaPointe sits back and lets Guttmann be the focus for her talk. This kind of woman—educated, capable, confident of her attraction and gifts—is alien to LaPointe's experience.

Of one thing he is sure; she is hiding something.

"Are you sure I can't tempt you, Lieutenant? I have everything." She gestures toward a bar at the end of the room, near a wide marble fireplace.

"Say, that's a *real* bar," Guttmann says in surprise. "That's fantastic." He rises and goes with her as she crosses to pour out the drinks. It is indeed a real bar, complete with back bar and beveled mirrors, a brass rail, copper fittings, and even a spittoon.

"I like to believe my guests will treat that as a mere decoration," she says, indicating the spittoon.

"Where did you get a turn-of-the-century bar like this?" Guttmann asks.

"Oh, they were tearing down one of those little places up on the Main, and I just bought it." She grins mischievously. "The workmen had a hell of a time getting it up here. The walnut top is one piece. They had to bring it in through the window."

Guttmann tries the bar on for size, putting his stomach against the polished wood and his foot up on the rail. "Fits just fine. I'll bet the neighbors wondered what you were up to here. I mean, a whole bar. Come on!"

"That never occurred to me. I should have had my bed brought in through the window, too. That would really have given them something to gossip about. It's one of those big circular waterbeds." She laughs lightly. Guttmann realizes she is a very attractive woman.

LaPointe's patience with this social nonsense is thin. He rises from the deep cushions of the "conversation island" and joins them at the bar. "I would like a little Armagnac after all, Mlle. Montjean. And I would like to know something about Antonio Verdini, alias Tony Green."

She does not pause in pouring out the Dubonnet, but her voice is unmodulated when she responds, "And *I* would like to know what you're doing here. Why you're interested in my school. And why you're asking these questions." She looks up and smiles at LaPointe. "Armagnac, did you say?"

"Please. Do you mind the questions?"

"I'm not sure." She takes down the Armagnac bottle and looks at it thoughtfully. "Tell me, Lieutenant LaPointe. Would my lawyer be unhappy with me, if I were to answer your questions without his being here?"

"Possibly. How did you know my name?"

"You showed me your identification when you came in."

"You barely glanced at it." There is another thing he does not mention. By habit he holds out his identification card with his thumb over his name. He's been a cop for a long time.

She sets the bottle down and looks directly at him, her eyes shifting from one of his to the other. Then she slowly raises both arms until her palms are level with her ears. In a deep, graveled voice she says, "You got me, Lieutenant. I give up. But don't tell Rocky and the rest of the mob that I ratted."

Both she and Guttman laugh. A glance from LaPointe, and she is laughing alone as she pours out the Armagnac. "Say when."

"That's fine. Now, how do you know my name?"

"Don't be so modest. Everyone on the Main knows Lieutenant LaPointe."

"You know the Main?"

"I grew up there. Don't worry about it, Lieutenant. There's no way in the world you could remember me. I left when I was just a kid. Thirteen years old. But I remember you. Of course that was twenty years ago, and you weren't a Lieutenant, and you hair was all black, and you were slimmer. But I remember you." There is something harder than amusement in the glitter of her eyes. Then she turns to Guttmann. "What do you think of that? What do you think of a woman giving away her age like that? Here I go admitting that I'm thirty-three, when I know perfectly that I could pass for thirty-two any day . . . if the light wasn't too strong."

"So you come from the street?" LaPointe says, unconvinced.

"Oh, yes, sir. From the deepest depths of the street. My mother was a hooker." She has learned to say that with the same offhandedness as one might

use to mention that her mother was a blonde, or a liberal. She evidently likes to drop bombs. But she laughs almost immediately. "Hey, what do you say, gang. Shall we drink at the bar, or go sit in a booth?"

When they have returned to the "conversation island," Mlle. Montjean assumes her most businesslike voice. She tells LaPointe that she wants to know exactly why he is here, asking questions. When she knows that, she will decide whether or not to answer without the advice of counsel.

"Have you any reason to think you might be in trouble?" he asks.

But she is not taking sucker bait like that. She smiles as she sips her aperitif.

LaPointe is not comfortable with her elusive blend of caution and practiced charm. She is so unlike the girls on his patch, though she claims to be one of them. He dislikes being kept off balance by her constant changes of verbal personality. She was the urbane vamp at first, completely castrating the policeman in Guttmann. Then there was that clowning "gun moll" routine under the guise of which she had admitted to being caught off base . . . but to nothing more. LaPointe fears that when he hits her with the fact that Green is dead, her control will be so high that it will mask any surprise she might feel. In that way, she could seem guilty without being so. She might even confuse him by being frank and honest. She is the type for whom honesty is also a ploy.

"So," LaPointe says, looking around at the costly things decorating the apartment, "you're from the Main, are you?"

"*From* is the active word, Lieutenant. I've spent my whole life being *from* the Main."

"Montjean? You say your mother was a hooker named Montjean?"

"No, I didn't say that, Lieutenant. Naturally, I have changed my name."

"From?"

Mlle. Montjean smiles. "Can I offer you another Armagnac? I'm afraid it will have to be a quick one; I have a working lunch coming up. We're involved in something that might interest you, Lieutenant. We're developing an intensive course in Joual. You'd be surprised at the number of people who want to learn the Canadian usages and accents. Salesmen, mostly, and politicians. The kinds of people who make their living by being trusted. Like policemen."

LaPointe finishes his drink and sets the tulip glass carefully on the glass tabletop. "This Antonio Verdini I mentioned . . . ?"

"Yes?" She lifts her eyebrows lazily.

"He's dead. Stabbed in an alley up on the Main."

She looks levelly at LaPointe, not a flutter in her eyelids. After a moment, her gaze falls to the marble-and-gold cigarette lighter, and she stares at it, motionless. Then she takes a cigarette from a carved teak box, lights it, tilts back her head with a bounce of her hair, and jets the uninhaled smoke over the heads of her guests. She delicately plucks an imaginary bit of tobacco from the tip of her tongue.

"Oh?" she asks.

"Presumably you were lovers," LaPointe says matter-of-factly, ignoring Guttmann's quick glance.

Mlle. Montjean shrugs. "We screwed, if that's what you mean." More of that precious bomb-dropping, a kind of counterattack against LaPointe's ballistic use of Green's death. Her control had been excellent throughout her long pause . . . but there *was* the pause.

"Our information says that he was learning English here," LaPointe continues. "I assume that's right?"

"Yes. One of our Italian-speaking instructors was guiding him through an intensive course in English."

"And that's how you met him?"

"That's how I met him, Lieutenant. Tell me, do I need a lawyer now?"

"Did you kill him?"

"No."

"Then you probably don't need a lawyer. Unless you intend to withhold information, or refuse to assist us in our inquiry."

She taps the ash from her cigarette unnecessarily, gaining time to think. Her control is still good, but for the first time she is troubled.

"You're thinking about the others, of course," LaPointe says.

"What others?"

LaPointe bends on her that melancholy patience he assumes during examination when he lacks the information necessary to lead the conversation.

"All right, Lieutenant. I'll cooperate. But let me ask you something first. Does this have to get into the papers?"

"Not necessarily."

"You see, my school is rather special—expensive, elite. Scandal would ruin it. And it's everything I've worked for. It represents ten years of work. What's more, it represents the ten thousand miles I've managed to walk away from the Main. You understand what I'm saying?"

"I understand. Tell me about the others."

"Well, it couldn't be a coincidence. Mike was killed the same way: stabbed in the street."

"Mike?"

"Michael Pearson. Dr. Michael Pearson. He used to run the Language Learning Center at McGill."

"And you were lovers?"

She smiles thinly. "You *do* run to circumlocution, don't you?"

"And what about the other one. The American?"

Her eyes open with confusion. "What other one?"

"The American. Ah . . ." He looks to Guttmann.

"John Albert MacHenry," Guttmann fills in quickly.

Mlle. Montjean glances from one to the other. "I have no idea what you're talking about. I don't think I ever met anyone by that name. I can assure you that I never . . . screwed . . . your Mr. MacHenry." She reaches over and squeezes LaPointe's arm. "That's just my homey way of saying we were not lovers, Lieutenant."

"You seem sure of that, Mlle. Montjean. Do you keep a list?"

Her smile is fixed and her eyes perfectly cold. "As a matter of fact, I do. At least, I keep a diary. And it's a fairly long list, if you will forgive my bragging. I enjoy keeping count. My analyst tells me that it's rather typical behavior in cases like mine. He tells me the reason I use so many men is because I detest them, and by scoring them one after the other I deny them any individuality. He talks like that, my analyst. Like a textbook. And can you guess when he told me all this crap? In bed. After I had scored him too. Later, he sat right there where you're sitting and told me he understood my need to screw even him. A typical gesture of rejection, he told me. And when I mentioned that he wasn't much of a lay, he tried to laugh it off. But I know I got to him." She grins. "The phony bastard."

"The point of all that being that you don't know this American, this MacHenry?"

"Precisely. Oh, I've had my share of Americans, of course. One should have an American at least once a quarter. It makes Canadians look so good by comparison. And at least once a year, one should have an Englishman. Partially to make even the Americans look good, and partially as penance. Did you know that making love with a Brit shortens one's time in purgatory?" The intercom on her desk buzzes; Mlle. Montjean butts out her cigarette and rises, flattening her skirt with her palms. "That will be my luncheon appointment. I assume I'm free to go to it?"

LaPointe rises. "Yes. But we have more to talk about."

She has crossed to her desk and is taking up a folder of material pertaining to her working lunch. She glances at her calendar. "I'm tied up all afternoon. Are you free tonight, Lieutenant?"

"Yes."

"Say nine o'clock? Here?"

"All right."

She shakes hands with Guttmann, then offers her hand to LaPointe. "You really don't remember me, do you Lieutenant?"

"I'm afraid not. Should I?"

Still holding his hand, she smiles a montage of amusement and sadness. "We'll talk about it tonight. Armagnac, isn't it?"

She shows them to the door.

By nine o'clock it is dark in the little park of Carré St. Louis. For the first time in weeks, the wind is from the north and steady. If it remains in that quarter, it will bring the cleansing snow. But its immediate effect is to hone the edge of the damp cold. LaPointe has to fold in the flap of his collar against his throat as he cuts across the deserted park, picking his way carefully over the root-veined path because the dappled light from distant streetlights serves more to confuse than to illuminate.

Suddenly he stops. Save for the hiss of wind through gnarled branches, there is no sound. But he has a tingling in the back of his neck, as though someone were watching him. He looks around through the zebra dapple of black trees and shadows interlaced with the silver of streetlights bordering the park. There is nothing to be seen.

He continues across toward Mlle. Montjean's school, where there are lights behind drawn shades on the first and third floors; probably late students learning French or English in a hurry. His knock is answered by the fussy man he met earlier. Mlle. Montjean is not in, but she is due any minute; she has left instructions that the Lieutenant is to be shown up to her apartment. The nervous man looks LaPointe over, his lips pursed critically. It isn't *his* business who Mlle. Montjean's friends are. *He* doesn't care what his employer does on her own time. But there *are* limits. A policeman, *really*. Oh, well, he'll show him up anyway.

Three lamps light the apartment, pooling three distinct areas. There is a porcelain lamp on the escritoire by the windows overlooking the square; a dim hanging lamp picks out the sunken "conversation island"; and beyond that, over the bar, is a glass ball confected of bits of colored glass and lit from within. The room is centrally heated, the dwindling fire in the fireplace largely decorative. LaPointe takes off his overcoat and makes himself at home to the extent of putting two kiln-dried, steam-cleaned logs on the fire and poking at the embers. He enjoys fiddling with open fires, and he often pictures himself in his daydream home in Laval, turning logs or pushing in burnt-off ends. The bark has begun to crackle and flutter with blue flame when Mlle. Montjean enters, her coat already off, her fur hat in her hand.

"Sorry, Lieutenant. But you know how these things are." She does not mention what things. "Oh, good. I'm glad you've tended the fire. I was afraid it would die out; and I set it especially for you." She ducks under the bar flap and begins to pour out two Armagnacs, light from the ball of glass shining in her carefully done hair. When LaPointe sits on a bar stool across from her, he realizes that she has been drinking fairly heavily, not beyond control, but perhaps a little beyond caring.

"I hope you didn't have anything big on tonight," she says.

"Nothing very big. A pinochle game I had to postpone, that's all."

"Hey, wow, Lieutenant." She makes two clicking sounds at the side of her cheek. "Pinochle! You really know how to get it on." She lifts her glass. "Salut?"

"Salut."

She finishes half her drink and sets it down on the bar. "That word 'salut' reminds me of a proof we recently had that our aural-oral system of language learning is not without its flaws. We had an Arab student here—a nephew of one of those oil pirates—and he was being preened to take over the world, or learn to surrender in six languages, or whatever the fuck they do. Dumb as a stick! But they were giving him all sorts of special tutoring at McGill—I think his uncle bribed them by buying an atomic laboratory for them, or half of South America, or something like that . . . I mean, he was *really* stupid. He was so dumb he'd have difficulty making the faculty of a polytechnic in Britain, or getting his Ph.D. in journalism in the States. . . . That line would get a laugh in an academic crowd."

"Would it?"

"You're not much of an audience, LaPointe. And now I don't even remember what that story was supposed to illustrate."

"Maybe nothing. Maybe you're just playing for time."

"Yes, maybe. How about another drink?"

"I still have this one."

"I think I'll have another." She brings it around the bar and sits beside him. "I had the weirdest experience just now. I was crossing the park, and there was someone there, in the shadows."

"Someone you know?"

"That's just it. I had the feeling I knew him, but . . . I can't explain it. I didn't see him, really. Just sort of a shadow. But I had this eerie feeling that he wanted to talk to me."

"But he didn't?"

"No."

"Then what frightened you?"

She laughed. "Nothing. I was just scared. I warned you it was a weird experience. Am I babbling, or is it my imagination?"

"It's not your imagination. This afternoon you said you knew me. Tell me about that."

As she speaks, she deals with her glass, not with him. "Oh, I was just a kid. You never really noticed me. But for years, you've been . . . important in my life." She puffs out a little laugh of self-derision. "Now *that* sounds heavy, doesn't it? I don't mean you've been important in the sense that I think of you often, because I don't. But I think of you at . . . serious times. It must be embarrassing to have a stranger tell you that she has a rather special vision of you. Is it?"

He lifts his glass and tips his head. "Yes."

"You think I'm drunk?"

He balances his thumb against his little finger. "A little."

"Drunk and disorderly," she says a distant tone. "I charge you, young woman, with being drunk, and with having a disorderly life—a disorderly mind."

"I doubt that. I think you have a very orderly mind. A very clever one."

"Clever? Yes. Neatly arranged? Yes. But disorderly nevertheless. The front shelves of my mind are all neatly stacked and efficiently arranged. But back in the stacks there is a stew of disorder, chaos, and do you know what else?"

"No. What?"

"Just a pinch of self-pity."

They both laugh.

"*Now* how about another drink?" She goes around the bar to refill her glass.

"No, thanks . . . all right. Yes. And tell me, with that self-pity you talk about, is there some hate?"

"Tons and tons, Lieutenant. But . . ." She points at him quickly, as though she just caught him slipping a card from his sleeve. "But not enough to kill." She laughs drily. "You know something, sir? I have a feeling we may spend a lot of this night talking about two different things."

"Not all of it."

"A threat?"

He shrugs. "So, tons and tons of hate. Do you hate me for not remembering you?"

"N-n-no. No, I don't blame or hate you. You were a central figure, a star actor on the Main. I had an aisle seat near the back. I spent my time staring at the one actor, so naturally I remember him. You—if you ever bothered to look out at the audience—wouldn't see them as individuals. No, not hate. Take two parts disappointment, mix in one part resentment, one part dented vanity, dilute with years of indifference, and that's what I feel. Not hate."

"You said your mother was a hooker on the street. What was her name?"

She laughs without anything being funny. "Her name was Dery."

LaPointe's memory rolls and brings up an image of twenty years ago. Yo-Yo Dery, a kind of whore you don't see around anymore. Loud, life-embracing, fun to be with, she would sometimes go with factory workers who didn't have much money, and for free, if they were good *mecs* and she liked them. Carefree and mischievous, she earned a reputation as a clown and a hellcat when, right in the middle of the dance floor of a crowded cabaret (the place where the Happy Hour Whisky à Go-Go now is), she settled a dispute with another hooker who claimed that Yo-Yo's red hair was dyed. She lifted her skirt, dropped her drawers, and proved that her red hair was natural.

"You remember her, don't you," Mlle. Montjean says, seeing his eye read the past.

"Yes. I remember her."

"But not me?"

Yes, come to think of it. Yo-Yo had a daughter. He talked to her once or twice in Yo-Yo's flat. After Lucille's death, when the need to make love got annoying, he went with street girls occasionally, always paying his way, although as a cop he could have got it free. Yo-Yo and he made love three or four times over the years. Yes, that's right. Yo-Yo had a little girl. A shy little girl.

Then he recalls how Yo-Yo died. She killed herself. She sent the kid to stay with a neighbor, and she killed herself. It astonished everybody on the Main. Yo-Yo Dery? The one who's always laughing? No! The one who proved she was a redhead? Suicide? But why?

LaPointe made the break-in. Rags stuffed in the crack under the door. He had to shatter a window with a beer bottle. Yo-Yo had slipped sideways onto the kitchen floor, her cheek resting on the bristles of a broom. There were cards laid out on the table. She had turned on the gas, and started playing solitaire.

Funny how details come back. There was a black queen on a black king. She had been cheating.

But what became of the kid? Vaguely, he recalls something about a neighbor keeping the girl until the social workers came around.

"Do you remember why they called her Yo-Yo?" Mlle. Montjean asks, almost dreamily.

He remembers. Like a Yo-Yo, up and down, up and down.

Mlle. Montjean turns the stem of her tulip glass, revolving it between her thumb and finger. "She was good to me, you know that? Presents. Clothes. We went to the park every Sunday when it wasn't too cold. She really tried to be good to me."

"That would be like her."

"Oh, sure. The good-hearted whore. A real Robert Service type. In a way, I always knew what she did for a living, even when I was four or five. That is . . .

there were always men around the flat, and they left money. What I didn't know at that age was that it wasn't the same in everyone else's house. But when I was old enough to go to school, the other kids straightened me out soon enough. They used to chant at me: 'Redhead, Redhead'—I can still hear those two singsong notes, like a French ambulance. I didn't understand why they chanted that, and why they giggled. My hair has always been brown. You see, I didn't know about Yo-Yo's epic proof in the dance hall. But all the other kids did."

This is not what LaPointe came here to listen to, and he doesn't want the burden of problems he did not cause and cannot help. "Oh, well," he says, making a gesture toward the expensive apartment, "you've come a long way from all that."

She looks at him sideways through her shoulder-length, rolled-under hair. "You sound like my analyst," she accuses.

"The one you take to bed?"

"The one I screw," she corrects. "What is it? Why are you shaking your head?"

"It must be the fashion to use the ugliest words for making love. I met a girl just recently who found the nicer words funny, and couldn't help laughing at them."

"I say screw because I mean screw. It's the *mot juste*. When I'm with a man, we don't 'go to bed', and we certainly don't 'make love'. We screw. And what's more, they don't screw me. *I screw them.*"

"As in, Screw you, mister!"

Mlle. Montjean laughs. "Now you *really* sound like my analyst. How about another Armagnac?"

"No, thanks."

She carries her glass to the divan before the fireplace, where she sits staring silently for a short time before beginning to speak, more to herself than to him. "It's funny, but I never despised the men Yo-Yo brought home—mostly good *mecs,* laughing, a little drunk, clumsy. Yo-Yo used to come in to tuck me in and kiss me good night. Then she'd close the door slowly because the hinges creaked. She had a way of waving to me with her fingertips, just before the door closed. I remember the light on the wall, a big trapezoid of yellow getting narrower until the door clicked shut, and there was only a thin line of light from the crack. Her bedroom was next to mine. I could hear her laughing. And I could hear the men. The squeak of the bedsprings. And the men grunting. They always seemed to grunt when they came." She looks over at LaPointe out of the corner of her eye and she half smiles. "You never grunted, Lieutenant. I'll say that much for you."

He lifts his empty glass in acceptance of the compliment, and immediately feels the stupidity of the gesture. "And you didn't resent me?"

"Because you screwed Yo-Yo? Hey, notice the difference? Men screwed Yo-Yo; I screw men. Deep significance there. Or maybe shallow. Or maybe none at all. No, I didn't resent you, Lieutenant! Goodness gracious, no! I could hardly have resented you."

"Why not?"

"Because you were my father," she says atonally. Then, "Hey, want another drink?"

LaPointe takes the shot in silence and doesn't speak until she has crossed to the bar and is refilling her glass. "That was cute. That 'want another drink?' part was particularly cute."

"Yeah, but kind of hokey."

"Of course you know that I was not . . ."

"Don't panic, Lieutenant. I know perfectly well that I don't owe the Gift of Life to any squirt from you—grunted or ungrunted. My father was Anonymous."

She has a bit of trouble saying the word; the drink is beginning to close down on her. "You know the famous poet, Anonymous. He's in all the collections— mostly toward the front. Hey? Aren't you just dying to know how come you're my father?"

She stands behind the bar, leaning over her glass, the ball of colored light tinting her hair, her face in the shadow. LaPointe is unable to see the expression in her unlit eyes. At a certain point, he turns away and watches the fire dwindle.

She uses a clowning, melodramatic style behind which she can hide, and occasionally her voice broadly italicizes words to prove she isn't taken in by the sentimentality that hurts.

"You see, children, it all began when I was very, very young and suffering from a case of innocence. I overheard Yo-Yo talking to some hooker she had up to the apartment for drinks. The subject was one Officer LaPointe, our beat cop, blue of uniform and blue of eye. Some yahoo had given Yo-Yo trouble, and the brave LaPointe had duly bashed him. You remember the incident?"

He shakes his head. In those days, that was not so uncommon an event that he would be likely to remember it.

"Well, bash you did, sir. *You Protected My Mother.* And the next Sunday, when she was taking me for a walk in the park, she pointed your apartment out to me. *This Was the House of the Man Who Protected My Mother.* And there were other times when she had good things to say about you. I didn't know then that she was praising you for paying for your nookie when, as a cop, you didn't have to.

"Well, sir, it was about that time that I went off to school and discovered that other kids had daddies. Before that, I had never thought about it. Living alone with Yo-Yo was simply how one lived. I neither had a daddy nor lacked one. Then the teasing about being a redhead began. And little boys wanted me to go behind the bushes and pull down my pants to show them my red hair. I couldn't understand. You see, I didn't have *any* hair, let alone red.

"So life went along, and went along, and went along. Then when I was about ten or eleven, the *Great Myth* began. One day after school, I was crying with anger and frustration and there was a ring of kids around me, chanting 'Red-head, wet to bed . . . Redhead, wet to bed!' And I screamed at them to cut it out, or else! Or else what, one of them asked, logically enough. And another asked why I didn't run home and tell my father on them. And everyone laughed—we have to save the children, Lieutenant; they're our hope for the future—so I suddenly blurted out that I would tell my father, if they didn't leave me alone! And they said I didn't have a father. And I said that I did too! Sergeant LaPointe was my father! And he would bash any son of a bitch who gave me trouble!"

There is a thud and a tinkle of glass, then silence.

"Oops. I have knocked over my glass in my efforts to decorate my fable with . . . whatever. How graceless of me."

LaPointe keeps his eyes on the fire. It would be unfair to look at her just then. He hears her walking behind the bar, the crisp crunch of glass under her shoes. He hears the squeak of the cork in the Armagnac bottle. When she speaks again, she has assumed a gruff, comic tone.

"Well, sir, that was the winter when I had a father . . . or, to be more exact, a *dad-dy.* You screwed Yo-Yo two times that winter, and both times I was awake when you came to the flat, and you chatted nonsense with me before she put me to bed. Your uniform smelled like wool, which wasn't so strange, considering the fact that it was made of wool. But it smelled good to me . . . like my blanket. Like the blanket I pressed against my nose when I sucked my thumb. At ten, I still sucked my thumb. But I've given that up in favor of cigarettes. Thumb-sucking causes lung cancer.

"And every day that winter, on my way home from school, I made a big loop out of my way so I could pass your apartment on Esplanade. I used to stand there, sometimes in the snow—grab the image of a little girl standing in the snow! Doesn't it just rip you up?—and I would look up at the windows of your apartment on the third floor. By the way, your apartment *is* on the third floor, isn't it?"

"Yes," he lies.

"I knew it. Infallible instinct. I knew you would live on the top floor, looking out over the world. Hey, wouldn't it be funny if all those afternoons I had been looking up at the wrong apartment? Wouldn't that be an ironic blast?"

He nods.

After a silence, she puffs out a sigh. "Thank God that's out of me! Pal, you have no idea what a zonker it was when you walked in here this afternoon. Talk about ghosts! I didn't really have an appointment tonight. I was walking up on the Main—the first time in years. I dropped in at a bar or two and had Armagnac, because that was your drink. And I walked around the old streets, over past your apartment, trying to decide if I should unload all this crap on you. And finally I decided that I wouldn't. I decided to keep it to myself. *Sic transit* all claims to being mistress of my fate."

LaPointe has nothing to say.

"Well!" She brings him an Armagnac he doesn't want and sits on the divan beside him. "Presumably you didn't come here to hear all this psychological vomit. What can I do for you, Lieutenant?"

It isn't an easy change to make, and LaPointe sips his drink slowly before he begins. "There have been three men killed . . . probably by the same person."

"And a neurotic man-hater seems a likely suspect?"

He ignores this. "Two of them trace to you. When was the last time you saw Antonio Verdini?"

"I checked that little fact in my diary. I thought you might ask. By the way, I'll let you read my diary if you want. I suppose you'll want the names of the men I've screwed. In case the killer was one of them. Maybe jealousy, or something like that. Although I can't imagine why any of them would be jealous. After all, my door's been open to just about anyone who knocked. I view my body as something of a public convenience."

LaPointe doesn't want to get mired again in her self-pity; he holds to the line of questioning. "When was the last time you and Verdini made love?"

"A week ago tonight. He didn't leave until about midnight. It was a longish number. He was showing off his endurance, which, by the way, was something—"

"All right." LaPointe cuts her off. He doesn't care about that. "That checks. He was killed that night, shortly after he left here."

"Hey . . . maybe I can put you on to something. He might have been just boasting, but he said he had to leave early because he was going to screw some dancer . . . no. No, a dancer's kid. That was it."

"I know about that. He never got there."

"Too bad for the kid. He was a good plumber."

LaPointe regards her flatly. "Why don't we just stick to the questions and answers, Mlle. Montjean?"

"My hearty attitude toward sex doesn't impress you, Lieutenant?"

"It impresses me. But it doesn't convince me."

"Hey! Wow! The wisdom of the streets! Mind if I take a note on that?"

"Do you want your ass spanked?"

"Whatever turns you on, Daddy!" she snaps back. She's an experienced emotional in-fighter.

He settles his patient, fatigued eyes on her for a moment before continuing. "All right. Now, this professor at McGill. Tell me about him."

She chuckles. "You hold your cool pretty well, LaPointe. Of course, you've got the advantage of being sober. And you've got another edge. Indifference is a mighty weapon."

"Let's just hear about the McGill professor."

"Mike Pearson? He was in charge of the Language Learning Center. That's where I got my idea of setting up this school. The high-saturation methods we use here were developed by Pearson. I took my M.A. under him . . . literally."

"Meaning that you and he—"

"Whenever we got a chance. Even while I was a student. The first time was on his desk. He got semen on papers he was grading. Do you know the root of the word 'seminar'? He was my first *conquest*. Think of it, Lieutenant! I was a virgin until I was twenty-four. A technical virgin, that is. Before that, I was what you might call manually self-sufficient. My analyst has given me some textbook crap about protracted virginity being common in cases of sexually traumatic events in childhood. He went on to say that it was typical that the first man should be a teacher—a father figure, an authority figure. Like a cop, I guess. That anus of an analyst always plays doctor after we've screwed. It's his way of taking an ethical shower. Think of it! A virgin at twenty-four! But I've make up for it since."

"Would your diary tell me the last time you and this Pearson were together?"

"I can tell you that myself. Mike's stabbing was in the papers. He was killed not twenty minutes after leaving here."

"Why didn't you inform the police?"

"Well, what was the point of getting involved? Mike was married. Why did the wife have to know where he spent his last night? I didn't dream his getting killed had anything to do with me. I thought he was mugged, or something like that."

"And that's why you didn't inform the police? Consideration for the wife?"

"All right, there was the reputation of the school too. It would have been messy PR. Say! Wait a minute! Why wasn't there anything in the papers about Tony's death?"

"There was."

"I didn't see it."

"His name wasn't mentioned. We didn't know it at the time. But I wonder if you would have called us, if you had known about the Verdini stabbing."

She has emptied her glass, and now she reaches automatically for his untouched one. He frowns, afraid she will get too drunk before the questioning is over. "Yes, I think I would have. Not out of civic duty, or any of that shit. But because I would have been scared, like I've been scared all afternoon, ever since you told me about it." She grins, the alcohol rising in her. "You see? That proves I didn't kill them. If I were the killer, I wouldn't be scared."

"No. But you might tell me you were."

"Ah-ha! The foxy mind of the fuzz! But you can take my word for it, Lieutenant. I don't go around stabbing men. I make *them* stab *me*." She wobbles her head in a blurred nod. "And there, Sigmund, you have a flash of revelation."

LaPointe has opened his notebook. "You say you don't know anything about the third man? The American named MacHenry?"

She shakes her head profoundly. "Nope. You see, there are *some* men in Montreal whom I have not yet screwed. But I'll get around to them. Never fear."

"I don't want you to drink anymore."

She looks at him incredulously. "What . . . did . . . you . . . say?"

"I don't want you to drink anymore until the questioning is over."

"You don't want . . . ! Well, fuck you, Lieutenant!" She glares at him, then,

in the wash of anger and drunkenness, her manner trembles and dissolves. "Or
. . . better yet . . . fuck *me*, Lieutenant. Why don't you screw me, LaPointe? I
want to be screwed, for a change."

"Come on, cut it out."

"No, really! Making it with you may be just what I need. A psychic water-
shed. The final daddy!" She slides over to him and searches his eyes. There is a
knowing leer in her expression, curiously confounded with the pleading of a
child. Her hand closes over his leg and penis. He lifts her hand away by the
wrist and stands up.

"You're drunk, Mlle. Montjean."

"And you're a coward, Lieutenant . . . Whateveryournameis! I'll admit I'm
drunk, if you'll admit you're a coward. A deal?"

LaPointe reaches into his inside coat pocket and takes out a photograph he
picked up from Dr. Bouvier that afternoon. He holds it out to her. "This man."

She waves it away with a broad, vague gesture. She is hurt, embarrassed,
drunk.

"It may not be a good likeness. It's a post-mortem shot. Would it help you to
place the man if I told you he was killed about two and a half years ago?"

Like a petulant child forced to perform a chore, she snatches the photograph
and looks at it.

The shock doesn't shatter her; it voids her. All spirit leaks out of her. She
wants to drop the photograph, but she can't let go of it. LaPointe has to reach
out and take it back.

As she puts her barriers back together, she saws her lower lip slightly between
her teeth. A very deep breath is let out slowly between pursed lips.

"But his name wasn't MacHenry. It was Davidson. Cliff Davidson."

"Perhaps that was the name he told you."

"You mean he didn't even give me his right name?"

"Evidently not."

"The son of a bitch." More soft wonder in this than anger.

"Why son of a bitch?"

She closes her eyes and shakes her head heavily. She is tired, worn out, sick of
all this.

"Why son of a bitch?" he repeats.

She rises slowly and goes to the bar—to get distance, not a drink. She leans
her elbows on the polished walnut and stares at the array of bottles in the back
bar, shining in the many colors of the glass ball light. Her back to him, she
speaks in a drone. "Clifford Davidson was the giddying and grand romance in
my life, officer. We were betrothed, each unto each. He came up to Canada to
set up some kind of manufacturing operation in Quebec City, and he came here
to learn Joual. He already spoke fair French, but he was one of your smarter
cookies. He knew it would be a tremendous in for him if he, an American, could
speak Joual French. The *canadien* workers and businessmen would eat it up."

"And you met him."

"And I met him. Yes. An exchange of glances, a brush of hands, a comparison of favorite composers, a matching up of plumbing. Love."

"Go on."

"Go on? Whither? *Quo vadis, pater?* Want to know a secret? That Latin I drop
every once in a while? That's just an affectation. It's all I got out of Ste.
Catherine's Academy: a little Latin I no longer remember, and the grooming
injunction that all proper girls keep their knees together, which advice I have
long ignored. My knees have become absolute strangers. There's always some
man coming between them. And how is *that* for an earthy little pun?"

"You and this Davidson fell in love. Go on."

"Ah, yes! Back to the interrogation. Right you go, Lieutenant! Well, let's see. Cliff and I had a glorious month together in gay, cosmopolitan Montreal. As I recall, marriage was mentioned. Then one day . . . poof! He disappeared like that fabled poofbird that flies in ever-smaller circles until it disappears up its own anus . . . poof!"

"Can you tell me the last time you saw him?"

"For that we shall need the trusty diary." She descends from the bar stool uncertainly and crosses to her desk, not unsteadily, but much too steadily "*Voilà.* My gallery of rogues." She brandishes the diary for LaPointe to see. "Ah-ha. I see you have been nipping at the Armagnac, Lieutenant. You're having a little trouble staying in focus, aren't you, you sly old dog." With large gestures she pages through the book. "No, not him. Not him either . . . although he wasn't bad. My, my, that was a night to set the waterbed a-sloshing! Come out of that book, Cliff Davidson. I know you're in there! Ah! Now let's see. The last night. Hm-m-m. I see it was a night of plans. And of love. And also . . . the night of September the eighteenth."

LaPointe glances at his notebook and closes it.

"That was the night he was stabbed?" she asks.

"Yes."

"Fancy that. Three men make love to me and end up stabbed. And to think that some guys worry about VD! I assume he was married? This MacHenry-Davidson?"

"Yes."

"A little wifey tucked away in Albany or somewhere. How quaint. You've got to hand it to these Americans. They're fantastic businessmen."

"Oh?"

"Oh, yes! Fantastic. Naturally, I never charged him for his language lessons."

LaPointe is silent for a time before asking, "May I take the diary with me?"

"Take the goddamned thing!" she screams, and she hurls it across the room at him.

It flutters open in the air and falls to the rug not halfway to him. Feckless display.

He leaves it lying on the rug. He'll get it as he goes.

When she has calmed down, she says dully, "That was a stupid thing to do."

"True."

"I'm sorry. Come on, have a nightcap with me. Proof of paternal forgiveness?"

"All right."

They sit side by side at the bar, sipping their drinks in silence, both looking ahead at the back bar. She sighs and asks, "Tell me truthfully. Aren't you a little sorry for me?"

"Yes, I am."

"Yeah. Me too. And I'm sorry for Tony. And I'm sorry for Mike. I'm even sorry for poor old Yo-Yo."

"Do you always call her that?"

"Didn't everybody?"

"I never did."

"You wouldn't," she says bitterly.

"You never call her Mother?"

She lays her hand on his shoulder and rests her cheek against her knuckles, letting him support her. "Never out loud. Never when I'm sober. You want to know something, Lieutenant? I hate you. I really hate you for not being . . . *there.*"

She feels him nod.

"Now, you're sure . . ." She yawns deeply. ". . . you're absolutely sure you don't want to screw me?"

His eyes crinkle. "Yes, I'm sure."

"That's good. Because I'm really sleepy." She takes her cheek from his shoulder and stands up. "I think I'll go to bed. If you've finished with your questions, that is."

LaPointe rises and collects his overcoat. "If I have more questions, I'll come back." He picks up the diary from the floor of the "conversation island," and she accompanies him to the door.

"This memory trip back to the Main has been heavy, Lieutenant. Heavy and rough. I sure hope I never see you again."

"For your sake, I hope it works out that way."

"You still think I might have killed those men?"

He shrugs as he tugs on his overcoat.

"LaPointe? Will you kiss me good night? You don't have to tuck me in."

He kisses her on the forehead, their only contact his hands on her shoulders.

"Very chaste indeed," she says. "And now you're off. *Quo vadis, pater?*"

"What does that mean?"

"Just some of that phony Latin I told you about."

"I see. Well, good night, Mlle. Montjean."

"Good night, Lieutenant LaPointe."

Fourteen

FROM HORIZON TO horizon the sky is streaming southward over the city. The membrane of layer-inversion has ruptured, and the pig weather is rushing through the gap, wisps and flags of torn cloud scudding beneath the higher roiling mass, all swept before a persistent north wind down off the Laurentians. Children look up at the tide of yeasty froth and have the giddying sensation that the sky is still, and the earth is rushing north.

The wind has held through the night, and by evening there will be snow. Tomorrow, taut skies of ardent blue will scintillate over snow drifts in the parks. At last it is over, this pig weather.

LaPointe stands at the window of his office, watching the sky flee south. The door opens behind him and Guttmann's head appears. "I got it, sir."

"Good. Come in. What are you carrying there?"

"Sir? Oh, just a cup of coffee."

"For me?"

"Ah . . . yes?"

"Good. Pass it over. Aren't you having any?"

"I guess not, sir. I've been drinking too much coffee lately."

"Hm-m. What did you find out?"

"I did what you told me; I checked with McGill and found that Mlle. Montjean attended on a full scholarship."

"I see." This is only part of the anwer LaPointe is looking for. As he walked through back streets of the Main toward his apartment last night, he was pestered with the question of how a girl from the streets, a chippy's daughter, managed to get the schooling that transformed her into a sophisticated, if bent and tormented, young woman. If she had been Jewish or Chinese, he would understand, but the French Canadian culture does not contain this instinctive awe for education. "How did she come by the scholarship?"

"Well, she was an intelligent student. Did well in entrance tests. Super IQ. And to a certain degree, the scholarship was a foregone conclusion."

"How come?"

"She attended Ste. Catherine's Academy. I remember the Ste. Kate girls from when I was in college. They're prepped specifically for the entrance exams. Most of them get scholarships. Not that that's any saving of money for their parents. It costs more to send a girl to Ste. Kate's than to any university in the world."

"I see."

"You want me to check out Ste. Catherine's?"

"No, I'll do it." LaPointe wads up the coffee cup and misses the wastebasket with it.

Guttmann pulls his old bentwood chair from the wall and sits on it backwards, his chin on his arms. "How did it go last night? Did it turn out to be true that she never met the American, MacHenry?"

"No. She met him." LaPointe involuntarily lays his hand over the five-year diary he has been scanning with a feeling of reluctance, invasion.

"Then why did she deny it?"

"He gave her a phony name. She probably read about his death in the papers without knowing who it was."

"How about that? She's quite a . . . quite a woman, isn't she?"

"In what way?"

"Well, you know. The way she's got it all together. Her business, her life. All under control. I admire that. And the way she talks about sex—frank, healthy, not coy, not embarrassed. She's got it all put together."

"You'd make a great social worker, son; the way you can size people up at a glance."

"We'll have a chance to find out about that." Guttmann rubs the tip of his nose with his thumb knuckle. "I've . . . ah . . . sent in my resignation, effective in two months." He glances up to see what effect this news has on the Lieutenant.

None.

"Jeanne and I talked it over last night. We've decided that I'm not cut out to be a cop."

"Does that mean you've got too much of something? Or too little?"

"Both, I guess. If I'm going to help people, me I want to do it from their side of the fence."

LaPointe smiles at the "me, I" construction. His French was better when they met . . . but more bogus. "From the way you talk it sounds like you and your Jeanne are getting married."

"You know, that's a funny thing, sir. We've never actually talked about marriage. We've talked about how children should be brought up. We've talked about how when you design a house you should put the bathroom above the kitchen to save on plumbing. But never actually about marriage. And now it's sort of too late to propose to her. We've sort of passed that moment and gone on to bigger things." Guttmann smiles comfortably and shakes his head over the way their romance is going. People in love always imagine they're interesting. He rises from his chair. "Well, sir. I've got to get going. I report this afternoon out at St. Jean de Dieu. I'll be doing my last two months on the east side."

"Be careful. It can be rough for a Roundhead out there."

Guttmann tucks down the corners of his mouth and shrugs. "After being around you, maybe I can pass." If the chair weren't in the way, he might shake hands with the Lieutenant.

But the chair is in the way.

"Well, see you around, sir."

LaPointe nods. "Yes, see you around."

A few minutes after Guttmann leaves, it occurs to LaPointe that he never learned the kid's first name.

"Lieutenant LaPointe?" Sister Marie-Thérèse enters the waiting room with a crisp rustle of her blue habit. She shakes hands firmly, realizing that uncertain pressures are vulnerable to interpretation. "You surprise me, Lieutenant. I expected an army officer." She smiles at him interrogatively, with the poise that is the signature of Ste. Catherine girls.

"I'm police, Sister."

"Ah." Meaning nothing.

As LaPointe explains that he is interested in one of their ex-students, Sister Marie-Thérèse listens politely, her face a mask of bland benevolence framed by a wide-winged wimple of perfect whiteness.

"I see," she says when he has finished. "Well, of course Ste. Catherine's is always eager to be a good citizen of Montreal, but I am afraid, Lieutenant, that our rules forbid any disclosure of our student's affairs. I am sure you understand." Her manner is gentle, her intention adamant.

"It isn't the young lady we're interested in. Not directly."

"Nevertheless . . ." She shows her palms, revealing herself to be helpless in the face of absolute rules.

"I considered getting a warrant, Sister. But since there were no criminal charges against the young lady, I thought it might be better to avoid what the newspapers might consider a nasty business."

The smile does not desert the nun's lips, but she lowers her eyes and blinks once. There are no wrinkles in her dry, almost powdery forehead. The face shows no signs of age, and none of youth.

"Still," LaPointe says, taking up his overcoat, "I understand your position. I'll come back tomorrow."

She lifts a hand toward his arm, but she does not touch him. "You say that Mlle. Montjean is not implicated in anything . . . unpleasant?"

"I said that she was not facing criminal charges."

"I see. Well, perhaps Ste. Catherine's could serve her best by cooperating with you. Will you follow me, please, Lieutenant?"

As they pass along a dark-paneled hall, he walks through air set in motion by the nun's habit, and he picks up a faint scent of soap and bread. He wonders if there is a Glory Hole here, and little girls working off punishment *tranches* by holding out their arms until their shoulders throb. He supposes not. Punishment at Ste. Catherine's would be a subtler matter, modern, kindly, and epulotic. Theirs would be a beautifully appointed little chapel, and their Virgin would not have a chip out of her cheek, would not be cross-eyed.

Two teen-aged girls dash around a corner, but arrest their run with comic abruptness when they see Sister Marie-Thérèse, and assume a sedate walk, side by side in their identical blue uniforms with SCA embroidered on bibs that bulge slightly with developing, unexplained breasts. In passing, they mutter, "Good morning, Sister." The nun nods her head, her expression neutral. But as the girls pass LaPointe they make identical tight-jawed grimaces and suck air in through their lower teeth. They'll get it later for running in the halls. Young ladies do not run. Not at Ste. Catherine's.

The Sister opens a tall oak door and stands aside to allow LaPointe to enter her office first. She does not close the door after them. As principal, she often has to meet male parents without the company of another nun, but never in rooms with closed doors.

The whole atmosphere of Ste. Catherine's Academy vibrates with sex unperformed.

With a businesslike rustle of her long skirts, she passes behind her desk and opens a middle file drawer. "You say Mlle. Montjean came to us twenty years ago?"

"About that. I don't know the exact date."

"That would be before I held my present position." She looks up from leafing through the files. "Although it certainly would not be before I came here." A careful denial that she is claiming youth. "In fact, Lieutenant, I am a Ste. Catherine girl myself."

"Oh?"

"Yes. Except for my girlhood and my years at university. I have lived all my life here. I was a teacher long before they made me principal." A slight accent on "made." An elevation to which she had not aspired, and for which she was unworthy. "It's odd that I don't remember a Mlle. Montjean."

Of course. He had forgot. "Her name was Dery when she was here."

"Dery? Claire Dery?" The tone suggests it is impossible that Claire Dery could be in trouble with the police.

"Her first name may have been Claire."

Sister Marie-Thérèse's fingers stop moving through the file folders. "You don't *know* her first name, Lieutenant?"

"No."

"I see." She does not see. She lifts out a file but does not offer it. "Now, what exactly is the information you require?"

"General background."

Her knuckles whiten as she grips the file more tightly. She has a right to know, after all. A duty to know. It's her responsibility to the school. Personally, she has no curiosity about scandal.

LaPointe settles his melancholy eyes on her face.

She compresses her lips.

He starts to rise.

"Perhaps you would like to read through the file yourself." She thrusts it toward him. "But it cannot leave the school, you understand."

The folder is bound with brown cord, and it opens automatically to the page of greatest interest to Ste. Catherine's. The information LaPointe seeks is there, in the record of fees and payments.

". . . I was sure you saw me last night in Carré St. Louis."

"No, I didn't."

"But you stopped suddenly and turned around, as though you had seen me."

"Oh, yes, I remember. I just had one of those feelings that someone was watching me."

"But *she* saw me. When she was crossing the park, I am sure she saw me."

"She mentioned that she saw someone. But she didn't recognize you."

"How could she? We have never met."

They sit diagonally opposite one another in comfortably dilapidated chairs in the bow window niche of a second-floor apartment in a brick row house on Rue de Bullion, two streets off the Main. Below them, the street is filled with a greenish gloaming, the last light of day captured and held close to the surface of the ground, causing objects in the street to be clearer than are rooftops and chimney pots. As they talk, the light leaks away; the gray clouds tumbling swiftly over the city darken and disappear; and the room behind them gradually recedes into gloom.

LaPointe has never been in the apartment before, but he has the impression that it is tidy, and characterless. They don't look at one another; their eyes wander over the scene beyond the window, where, across the street to the left, a billboard featuring a mindless smiling girl in a short tartan skirt enjoins people to smoke EXPRESS "A." Directly beneath them is a vacant lot strewn with broken bricks from houses being torn down to make way for a factory. There is a painted message of protest on the naked brick wall: 17 PEOPLE LIVED HERE. The protest will do no good; history is against the people.

In the vacant lot, half a dozen children play a game involving running and falling down, playing dead. An older girl stands against the denuded side of the next house to be demolished, watching the kids play. Her posture is grave. She is too old to run and fall down dead; she is still too young to go with men to the bars. She watches the kids, half wanting to be one of them again, half ready to be something else, to go somewhere else.

"Will you take something, Claude? A glass of schnapps maybe?"

"Please."

Moishe rises from the chair and goes into the gloom of the living room. "I've been waiting for you here all day. Once you traced your way to Claire . . ." He lifts a glass in each hand, a gesture expressive of inevitability. "I suppose you went to Ste. Catherine's Academy?"

"Yes."

"And of course you found my name in the records of payment."

"Yes."

Moishe gives a glass to LaPointe and sits down before lifting his drink. "Peace, Claude."

"Peace."

They sip their schnapps in silence. One of the kids down in the vacant lot has turned his ankle on a broken brick and is down on the hard-packed dirt. The others gather around him. The girl still stands apart.

"I'm crazy, of course," Moishe says at last.

LaPointe shrugs his shoulders.

"Oh, yes. Crazy. Crazy is not a medical term, Claude; it's a social term. I am not insane, but I *am* crazy. Society has systems and rules that it relies on for protection, for comfort . . . for camouflage. If somebody acts against the rules, society admits of only two possibilities. Either the outsider has acted for gain, or he has not acted for gain. If he has acted for gain, he is a criminal. If he has broken their rules with no thought of gain, he is crazy. The criminal they understand; his motives are their motives, even if his tactics are a little more . . . brusque. The crazy man they do not understand. Him they fear. Him they lock up, seal off. Whether they are locking him in, or locking themselves out—that's a matter of point of view." Moishe draws a long sigh, then he chuckles. "David would shake his head, eh? Even now, even at the end, Moishe the *luftmensh* looks for philosophy where there is only narrative. Poor David! What will he do without the pinochle games?"

LaPointe doesn't respond.

"I've caused you a lot of trouble, haven't I, Claude? I'm sorry. I tried to confess twice; I tried to save you the trouble. I went to your apartment Sunday for that purpose, but that young girl was there, and I could hardly . . . Then again after the game, when we were in the Russian café. I wanted to tell you; I wanted to explain; but it's so complicated. I only got as far as mentioning my sister. You remember?"

"I remember."

"She was very pretty, my sister." Moishe's voice is hushed and husky. "Delicate. Almost painfully shy. She would blush at anything. Once I asked her why she was so shy in company. She said she was embarrassed. Embarrassed at what, I asked. At my blushing, she said. Claude, *that* is shy. To be shy about being shy, *that's* shy. She . . . they put her into a special barracks in the camp. It was . . . this barracks was for the use of . . . ."

"You don't have to tell me all this, Moishe."

"I know. But some things I want to tell you. Some things I want to explain . . . to say out loud for once. In classic drama, when a man has stepped on the inevitable treadmill of fate, he has no right to escape, to avoid punishment. But he does have a right to explain, to complain. Oedipus does not have the right to make a deal with gods, but he has a right to bitch." Moishe sips his schnapps. "When the word reached me through the camp grapevine that my sister was in the special barracks, do you know what my first reaction was? It was: oh, no! Not her! She's too shy!"

LaPointe closes his eyes. He is tired to the marrow.

After a pause, Moishe continues. "She had red hair, my sister. Did you know that redheaded people blush more than others? They do. They do."

LaPointe looks over at his friend. The finger-stained round glasses are circles of bright gray reflecting the boiling sky. The eyes are invisible. "And Yo-Yo Dery had red hair too."

"Yes. Exactly. What a policeman you would have made."

"You went with Yo-Yo?"

"Only once. In all my life, that was my only experience with a woman. Think of that, Claude. I am sixty-two years old, and I have had only one physical experience with a woman. Of course, in my youth I was studious . . . very religious. Then in early manhood other things absorbed my attention. Politics. Philosophy. Oh, there were one or two girls who attracted me. And a couple of times one thing led to another and I was very close to it. But something always went wrong. A stranger happening along the path. No place to go. Once, in a field, a sudden rainstorm . . .

"Then there were the years in the camp. And after that, I was here, trying to start up my little business. Oh, I don't know. Something happens to you in the camps. First you lose your self-respect, then your appetites, eventually your mind. By clever forensics and selective forgetfulness, one can regain his self-respect. But when the appetites are gone. . . ? And the mind. . . ?

"So, with one thing and another, I end up a sixty-two-year-old man with only one experience of love. And it really *was* an experience of love, Claude. Not on her part, of course. But on mine."

"But you couldn't have been Claire Montjean's father. You weren't even in Canada—"

"No, no. By the time I met Françoise, she was experienced enough to avoid having children."

"Françoise was Yo-Yo's real name?"

Moishe nods, his light-filled glasses blinking. "I hated that nickname. Naturally."

"And you only made love once?"

"Once only. And that by accident, really. I used to see her pass the shop. With men usually. Always laughing. I knew all about her; the whole street knew. But there was the red hair . . . and something about her eyes. She reminded me of my sister. That seems funny, doesn't it? Someone like Françoise—hearty, loud, always having fun—reminding me of a girl so shy she blushed because she blushed? Sounds ridiculous. But not really. There was something very fragile in Françoise. Something inside her was broken. The noise she chose to make when it hurt was . . . laughter. But the pain was there, for those who would see it. I suppose that's why she killed herself at last.

"And the men, Claude! The men who used her like a public toilet! The men for whom she was nothing but friction and heat and a little lubrication! None of them bothered to see her pain. One after the other, they used her. They queued up. As though she were . . . in a special barracks. They sinned against love, these men. Society has no laws concerning crimes against love. Justice cries out against it, but the Law is silent on the matter."

"Are you talking about the mother now, or about the daughter?"

"What? What? Both, I guess. Yes . . . both."

"You said you made love to . . . Françoise by accident?"

"Not by intent, anyway. I used to see her walking by the shopwindow—that was back when David was only my employee, before we became partners—and she was always so pert and energetic, always a smile for everybody. You remember, don't you? You went with her yourself, I believe."

"Yes, I did. But—"

"Please. I'm not accusing. You were not like the others. There is a gentleness in you. Pain and gentleness. I'm not accusing. I'm only saying that you had a chance to know how full of life she was, how kind."

"Yes."

"So, well. One summer evening I was standing in front of the shop, taking the air. There was not so much work as there is now. We had not been 'discovered' by the interior decorators. I was standing there, and she came by. Alone for once. Somehow, I could tell she was feeling blue . . . had the *cafard*. I said, Good evening. She stopped. We talked about this and that . . . about nothing. It was one of those long, soft evenings that make you feel good, but a little melancholy, like sometimes wine does. Somehow I got the courage to ask her to take supper with me at a restaurant. I said it in a joking way, to make it easy for her to say no. But she accepted, just like that. So we had supper together. We talked, and we drank a bottle of wine. She told me about being a child on the Main. About men taking her to bed when she was only fifteen. She joked about it, of course, but she wasn't joking. And after supper, I walked her home. A warm evening, couples strolling. And all this time, I wasn't thinking about going to bed with her. I couldn't think of that. After all, she reminded me of my sister.

"When we got to her place, she invited me up. I didn't want to go home early on such an evening, to sit here alone and look out this window, so I accepted. And when we got into her apartment, she kissed her little girl good night, and she went into her bedroom and started undressing. Just like that. She undressed with the door open, and all the time she continued to chat with me about this and that. She had been sad that night, she had needed to talk; and now she was offering me what she had in return for giving her dinner and listening to her stories. How could I reject her?

"No! No!" Moishe's hands grip the arms of his chair. "This is no time for lying to myself. Maybe not wanting to reject her had something to do with it, but not much. She was undressed and I was looking at her body . . . her red hair. And I wanted her. She had told me stories about sleeping with men to get enough money for food, and now she was willing to sleep with me for giving her a dinner. I wanted to prove to her that I was not like those other men! I wanted to leave her alone! As a gesture of love. But she was nude, and it had been a gentle evening with wine, and . . . I wanted her. . . ."

"And . . . one week later . . . she committed suicide."

"But, Moishe . . ."

"Oh, I know! I know, Claude! It had nothing to do with me. I wasn't that important in her life. A coincidence; I know that. But I felt I had to do something. I had failed to show that I was not like the other men. And now I had to do something, to show that I had affection. Then I thought of the daughter."

"So you arranged to have the girl taken into Ste. Catherine's. How did you find the money?"

"That's when I began to sell out the business to David. Bit by bit, as she needed money for school, for clothes, for vacations, I arranged for a summer in Europe, and later for a loan to start her language school."

"And all this time you never talked to the girl? Never let her know what you were doing for her?"

"That wouldn't have been right. I wanted to do something. A gesture of love. If I had accepted the daughter's gratitude, even affection maybe, then it would not have been a pure gesture of love. It would have been payment for value received. It was a sort of game—staying in the background, looking after her, taking pride in her accomplishments. And she has turned out to be a wonderful woman. Hasn't she, Claude?"

LaPointe's voice has become fogged over. He clears his throat. "Yes."

"When you think of it, it's ironic that you have met her, while I have not. But I know what a wonderful woman she has become. Look what she is doing for others! A school to teach people how to communicate. What could be more important? And she is a loving person. A little too loving, I'm afraid. Men take advantage of her. Oh, I know that she has had many lovers. I know. I have kept an eye on her. In my day, or yours, to have lovers would have been the mark of a bad girl. But it's different now. Young people aren't afraid to express their love. Still . . . still . . . there are some men who take a girl's body without loving her. These people sin. They defile.

"I used to go to Carré St. Louis often at night and keep an eye on her. I came to recognize the men. When I could, I checked up on the ones who visited often. That was a game too, checking up on them. It's amazing how much you can find out by asking a little question here, a little question there. Especially if you look like me—mild, unassuming. Most of the men were all right. Not good enough for her, maybe. But that's how a father always thinks. But some of them . . . some of them were sinning against her. Taking her love. Taking advantage of her gentleness, of her need for love. The first one was that university professor. A teacher! A teacher taking advantage of an innocent student fresh from convent school! Think of that. And a married man! Would you believe it, Claude, I saw him come to her school again and again for more than a year before it occurred to me that he was taking her love . . . her body. Inexperienced as I am, I thought he was interested in her school!

"Then there was that American. He had a wife in the United States. And from the first day, he was lying to her. Did you know that he used a false name with her?"

"Yes, I learned that."

"And finally there was this Antonio Verdini. When I found out about his reputation on the Main . . ."

"He was a bad one."

"An animal! Worse! Animals don't pretend. Animals don't rape. That's what it is, you know, when a man takes the body of a woman without feeling gentleness or love for her. Rape. Those three men raped her!"

The room is quite dark now; a ghost of gloaming still haunts the vacant lot where children play at falling down dead, and the lone girl watches soberly.

On the billboard, the woman in a short tartan skirt smiles provocatively. She'll give you everything she has, if you will smoke EXPRESS "A."

While Moishe sits unmoving, calming his fury, LaPointe's mind is flooded with scraps and fragments. He recalls Moishe's wonderful skill with a knife when cutting fabric. David once said what a surgeon he would have made, and Father Martin made a weak joke about appendices being made of damask. LaPointe remembers the long discussions about sin and crime, and about sins against love. Moishe was trying to explain. Then a terribly unkind image leaks into LaPointe's mind. He wonders if, when he made love to Yo-Yo, Moishe grunted.

"Tell me about her," Moishe says quietly.

It takes LaPointe a second to find the track. "About Mlle. Montjean?"

"Yes. One of my daydreams has always been that I meet her somehow and we spend a few hours talking about this and that . . . not revealing anything to her, of course, but finding out how she thinks, what values she holds, her plans, hopes, outlook, *Weltanschauung.*" Moishe smiles wanly. "It doesn't look as though that will happen now. So why don't you tell me about her. She's an intelligent girl, eh?"

"Yes, she seems to be. She speaks Latin."

"And did you find her sensitive . . . open to people?"

"Yes."

"I knew she would be! I knew she would take that quality from her mother. And happy? Is she happy?"

LaPointe realizes what a trash it would make of all that Moishe has done, if the girl is not happy.

"Yes," LaPointe says. "She's happy. Why shouldn't she be? She has everything she could want. Education. Success. You've given her everything."

"That's good. That's good." The sky is dark and is no longer reflected in Moishe's glasses. His eyes soften. "She is happy." For a time he warms himself with that thought. Then he sighs and lifts his head, as though waking. "Don't worry about it, Claude."

"About what?"

"This business, it must be awkward for you. Painful. After all, we are friends. But you won't have to arrest me. I will handle everything. A thousand times when I was in the camp, I cursed myself for letting them take me, I regretted that I hadn't killed my body before they could degrade and soil my mind. So, after I got out, I managed to purchase some . . . medicine. You would be surprised how many people who have survived the camps have—hidden somewhere—such medicine. Not that they intend to use it. No, they hope and expect that they will never have to use it. But it is a great comfort to know it is there. To know that you will never again have to surrender yourself to indignities.

"I shall take this medicine soon. You won't have the embarrassment of having to arrest me."

After a silence, LaPointe asks, "Do you want me to stay with you?"

Moishe is tempted. It would be a comfort. But: "No, Claude. You just go do your rounds of the Main. Put the street to bed like a good beat cop. I'll sit here awhile. Maybe have another glass of schnapps. There's only a little left. Why should it go to waste?"

LaPointe sets down his empty glass and rises. He doesn't dare follow his impulse to touch Moishe. Moishe has it under control now. Sentiment might hurt him. La Pointe presses his fists deep into his overcoat pockets, grinding his knuckles against his revolver.

"What will become of her?" Moishe asks.

LaPointe follows his glance down to the adolescent girl standing alone with her back against the scabby brick wall. "What becomes of them, Claude?"

LaPointe leaves the room, softly closing the door behind him.

It is snowing on the Main, and the shops are closing; metal grids clatter down over display windows, doors are locked, one or two lights are left on in the back as deterrents to theft.

The sidewalks are thick with people, pressing, tangling, fluxing, their necks pulled into collars, their eyes squinting against the snow. At street corners and narrow places there are blockages in the pedestrian swarm, and they are pressed unwillingly against one another, threading or shouldering their way through the nuisance of these faceless and unimportant others, the wad.

Plump snowflakes the size of communion wafers slant through the garish neon of nosh bars, fish shops, saloons, cafés. People try to protect their packages from being soaked through; women put newspaper tents over their hair; those wearing glasses tilt their heads down so they can see over the top. Friends meet at bus stops and grumble; the goddamned snow; won't be able to get to work tomorrow. It was too good to last, the pig weather.

Snow crosshatches through the headlights of trucks grinding past the deserted park of Carré Vallières, at the top of the rise that separates the lower Main from the Italian Main. LaPointe sits on a bench, alone in the barren triangle of sooty dirt and stunted trees he has always associated with his retirement. Huddled in his great shapeless coat, the dark and the snow insulating and protecting him, the Lieutenant weeps.

The scar tissue over his emotions has ruptured, and his grief is pouring out. He does not sob; the tears simply flow from his eyes, and his face is wet with them.

LaPointe is grieving. For his grandfather, for Lucille, for Moishe. But principally . . . for himself. For himself.

For himself he grieves that his grandfather left him without support and comfort. For himself he grieves that Lucille died and took his ability to love with her. For himself he grieves the loss of Moishe, his last friend. At last, he pities the poor old bastard that he is, with this bubble in his chest that is going to take him away from a life he never quite got around to living. He is sorry for the poor old bastard who never had the courage to grieve his losses, and to survive them.

He slumps in the soporific pleasure of it. It feels so good to let the pressure leak away, to surrender finally. He knows, of course, that his life and force are draining out with the grief. His strength has always come from his bitterness, his reserve, his indifference. When the weeping is finished, he will be empty . . . and old.

But it feels so good to let go. Just . . . to let it all go.

At first the snow melts as it touches the sidewalk outside Chez Pete's Place, but as the slush builds up, it begins to insulate, and the large flakes remain longer before they decompose.

Inside, a dejected group of *bommes* sit around the center table, drinking their wine slowly so they won't have to buy another bottle before the proprietor makes them go out into the weather. Dirtyshirt Red glowers with disgust at two men sitting at a back table. He sneers to the ragged man sitting beside him, drinking a double red from a beer mug.

"Wouldn't ya know it? The only guy who'll drink with that potlickin' blowhard son of a bitch is a nut case!"

His mate glances over at the table and growls agreement with any slander against the Vet, that stuck-up shitlicker with his cozy kip off somewhere.

At the back table, a bottle of muscatel between them, sit the Vet and the Knife Grinder. They are together because they had enough money between them to buy the bottle. They have seen one another on the Main, of course, but they have never talked before.

"It's beginning," the Knife Grinder says, staring at the floor. "The snow. I warned everyone that it was coming, but no one would listen."

"Can you believe it?" the Vet answers. "They just caved it in! These goddamned kids come when I wasn't there, and they caved it in. Just for the hell of it."

"People fall in the snow, you know," the Knife Grinder responds. "They slip off roofs! Happens alla time, but nobody cares!"

The Vet nods. "They come and dragged off the roof. Then they caved in the sides. No reason. Just for the hell of it."

The Knife Grinder squints hard and tries to remember. "There was somebody
. . . somebody important. And he told me there wouldn't be any snow this year.
But he was lying!"

"What can you do?" the Vet asks. "I'll never find another one. They just . . .
caved it in, you know? Just for fun."

They are both staring at the same spot on the floor. A kind of sharing.

In close to buildings, where pedestrian feet have not ground it to slush, the
snow has built up to a depth of three inches. The wind is still strong, and it
blows flakes almost horizontally across the window of Le Shalom Restaurant
and Coffee Shop. Inside, where damp coats steam and puddles of melt-water
make the tiles dangerous, the Chinese waitress barks orders to the long-suffering
Greek cook, and tells customers to hold their water; has she got more than two
hands?

Two girls sit in a booth near the counter. They are giggling and excited
because a romance is beginning. One girl pushes the other with her elbow and
says, "Ask him." The other presses her hand over her mouth and shakes her
head, her eyes sparkling. "Not *me. You* ask him!" She dares a quick look at the
two grinning Hungarian boys in the next booth. "Go on!" the first girl insists,
stifling her giggle. "No, *you* ask him!"

The Chinese waitress has found time to grab a cigarette. She mutters to
herself, "For Christ's sake, *somebody* ask him!"

Four young women from the garment factory walk briskly down St. Laurent,
laughing and kidding one another about boyfriends. One tries to catch a snow-
flake on her tongue; another starts a bawdy folk song about a lute player who
will fix your spinet for you like it's never been fixed before, if you have a fresh
new *écu* to give him for the lesson. They link arms and walk four abreast with
long energetic strides as they sing at the top of their voices. They overtake an
old Chasidic Jew with *peyiss,* his *shtreimel* level on his head, his long black
overcoat collecting snowflakes. Playfully, they split, two on each side, and link
arms with the startled man who is pulled along at a pace alien to his dignified
step. "Buy us a drink, father! What do you say?" one of them shouts, and the
others laugh. The old man stops, and the girls continue on, linking up four
abreast again, their butts tweaking merrily along. He shakes his head, confused
but not displeased. Youth. Youth. He looks up to check the street sign, as he
always does before turning down toward the house he has lived in for twenty-
two years.

Snow slants against the darkened window of a fish shop in which there is a
glass tank, its sides green with algae. A lone carp glides back and forth in
narcotized despair.

The long wooden stoop of LaPointe's apartment building is blanketed with six
inches of untrodden snow. He holds the rail and half pulls himself up each step,
tired, empty. Because his head is down, he sees first her feet, then her battered
shopping bag.

"Hello," she says.

He passes her without a word and opens the front door. She follows him into
the vestibule, lit only by a fifteen-watt bulb. He leans against the banister and
looks at her, his eyes hooded.

She shrugs, her lips compressed in a flat half grin. The expression says, Well,
here I am. That's the way it goes.

LaPointe rubs his whiskered cheek. What's the use of this? He doesn't need
this. He is empty at last, and at peace. He wants to finish it off easily, cocooned

in his routine, his chair by the window, his coffee, his Zola. It's not as though she would stay. The first time she finds a handsome Greek boy to buy her ouzo and dance with her, she'll be gone again. And probably she'll come sniffing back when he gets tired of her. What is she after all? A stupid twit the age of his daughters, the age of his wife. And worst of all, he would have to tell her about this thing in his chest. It wouldn't be fair to let her wake up some morning and reach over to touch him. And find him . . .

No, it's better not to want anything, need anything. There's no point in opening yourself up to hurt. It's stupid. Stupid.

"How about a cup of coffee?" he asked.

Shibumi

Gameform of *Shibumi*

PART ONE

FUSEKI

Washington

THE SCREEN FLASHED 9, 8, 7, 6, 5, 4, 3 . . . then the projector was switched off, and lights came up in recessed sconces along the walls of the private viewing room.

The projectionist's voice was thin and metallic over the intercom. "Ready when you are, Mr. Starr."

T. Darryl Starr, sole audience member, pressed the talk button of the communication console before him. "Hey, buddy? Tell me something. What are all those numbers in front of a movie for anyway?"

"It's called academy leader, sir," the projectionist answered. "I just spliced it onto the film as a sort of joke."

"Joke?"

"Yes, sir. I mean . . . considering the nature of the film . . . it's sort of funny to have a commercial leader, don't you think?"

"Why funny?"

"Well, I mean . . . what with all the complaints about violence in movies and all that."

T. Darryl Starr grunted and scrubbed his nose with the back of his fist, then he slipped down the pilot-style sunglasses he had pushed up into his cropped hair when the lights first went off.

Joke? It damn well better *not* be a joke. I shit thee not! If anything has gone wrong, my ass will be grass. And if the slightest little thing is wrong, you can bet your danglees that Mr. Diamond and his crew will spot it. Nit-picking bastards! Ever since they took control over Middle East operations of CIA, they seemed to get their cookies by pointing out every little boo-boo.

Starr bit off the end of his cigar, spat it onto the carpeted floor, pumped it in and out of his pursed lips, then lit it from a wooden match he struck with his thumbnail. As Most Senior Field Operative, he had access to Cuban cigars. After all, RHIP.

He scooted down and hooked his legs over the back of the seat before him, like he used to do when he watched movies at the Lone Star Theater as a boy. And if the boy in front objected, Starr would offer to kick his ass up amongst his shoulder blades. The other kid always backed off, because everybody in Flat Rock knew that T. Darryl Starr was some kind of fierce and could stomp a mud puddle in any kid's chest.

That was many years and knocks ago, but Starr was still some kind of fierce. That's what it took to become CIA's Most Senior Field Operative. That, and experience. And boo-coo smarts.

And patriotism, of course.

Starr checked his watch: two minutes to four. Mr. Diamond had called for a screening at four, and he would arrive at four—exactly. If Starr's watch did not

499

read four straight up when Diamond walked into the theater, he would assume the watch was in need of repair.

He pressed his talk button again. "How does the film look?"

"Not bad, considering the conditions under which we shot it," the projectionist answered. "The light in Rome International is tricky . . . a mixture of natural light and fluorescent overheads. I had to use a combination of CC filters that brought my f-stop way down and made focus a real problem. And as for color quality—"

"I don't want to hear your piddly-assed problems!"

"Sorry, sir. I was just answering your question."

"Well, don't!"

"Sir?"

The door at the back of the private theater opened with a slap. Starr glanced at his watch; the sweep second hand was five seconds off four o'clock. Three men walked quickly down the aisle. In the lead was Mr. Diamond, a wiry man in his late forties whose movements were quick and adroit, and whose impeccably tailored clothes reflected his trim habits of mind. Following closely was Mr. Diamond's First Assistant, a tall, loosely jointed man with a vague academic air. Not a man to waste time, it was Diamond's practice to dictate memos, even while en route between meetings. The First Assistant carried a belt recorder at his hip, the pinhead microphone of which was attached to his metal-rimmed glasses. He always walked close beside Mr. Diamond, or sat near him, his head bowed to pick up the flow of clipped monotonic directives.

Considering the heraldic stiffness of CIA mentality, it was inevitable that their version of wit would suggest a homosexual relationship between Diamond and his ever-hovering assistant. Most of the jokes had to do with what would happen to the assistant's nose, should Mr. Diamond ever stop suddenly.

The third man, trailing behind and somewhat confused by the brisk pace of action and thought surrounding him, was an Arab whose Western clothes were dark, expensive, and ill-fitting. The shabby look was not his tailor's fault; the Arab's body was not designed for clothes requiring posture and discipline.

Diamond slipped into an aisle seat across the auditorium from Starr; the First Assistant sat directly behind him, and the Palestinian, frustrated in his expectation that someone would tell him where to sit, finally shambled into a seat near the back.

Turning his head so the pinhead microphone could pick up the last of his rapid, atonic dictation, Diamond closed off the thoughts he had been pursuing. "Introduce the following topics to me within the next three hours: One—North Sea oil rig accident: the media suppression thereof. Two—This professor type who is investigating the ecological damage along the Alaska pipeline: the termination thereof by apparent accident."

Both these tasks were in their final phases, and Mr. Diamond was looking forward to getting in a little tennis over the weekend. Provided, of course, these CIA fools had not screwed up this Rome International action. It was a straightforward spoiling raid that should not have presented any difficulties, but in the six months since the Mother Company had assigned him to manage CIA activities involving the Middle East, he had learned that no action is so simple as to be beyond CIA's capacity for error.

Diamond understood why the Mother Company chose to maintain its low profile by working behind the cover of CIA and NSA, but that did not make his job any easier. Not had he been particularly amused by the Chairman's light-hearted suggestion that he think of the Mother Company's use of CIA operatives as Her contribution to the hiring of the mentally handicapped.

Diamond had not yet read Starr's action report, so he reached back for it now. The First Assistant anticipated him and had the report ready to press into his hand.

As he glanced over the first page, Diamond spoke without raising his voice. "Put the cigar out, Starr." Then he lifted his hand in a minimal gesture, and the wall lights began to dim down.

Darryl Starr pushed his sunglasses up into his hair as the theater went dark and the projector beam cut through slack threads of blue smoke. On the screen appeared a jerky pan over the interior of a large, busy airport.

"This here's Rome International," Starr drawled. "Time reference: thirteen thirty-four GMT. Flight 414 from Tel Aviv has just arrived. It's going to be a piece before the action starts. Those I-talian customs jokers ain't no speed balls."

"Starr?" said Diamond, wearily.

"Sir?"

"Why haven't you put that cigar out?"

"Well, to tell you God's own truth, sir, I never heard you ask me to."

"I didn't *ask* you."

Embarrassed at being ordered around in the presence of a foreigner, Starr unhooked his leg from the seat in front and ground out the almost fresh cigar on the carpet. To save face, he continued narrating as though nothing had happened. "I expect our A-rab friend here is going to be some impressed at how we handled this one. It went off slick as catshit on linoleum."

Wide shot: customs and immigration portal. A queue of passengers await the formalities with varying degrees of impatience. In the face of official incompetence and indifference, the only passengers who are smiling and friendly are those who anticipate trouble with their passports or luggage. An old man with a snow-white goatee leans over the counter, explaining something for the third time to the customs officer. Behind him in line are two young men in their twenties, deeply tanned, wearing khaki shorts and shirts open at the throat. As they move forward, pushing their rucksacks along with their feet, camera zooms in to isolate them in mid-close-up.

"Those are our targets," Starr explained needlessly.

"Just so," the Arab said in a brittle falsetto. "I recognize one of them, one known within their organization as Avrim."

With a comically exaggerated bow of gallantry, the first young man offers to let a pretty red-headed girl precede them to the counter. She smiles thanks, but shakes her head. The Italian official in his too-small peaked cap takes the first young man's passport with a bored gesture and flicks it open, his eyes straying again and again to the girl's breasts, obviously unfettered beneath a denim shirt. He glances from the photograph to the young man's face and back again, frowning.

Starr explained. "The mark's passport picture was taken before he grew that silly-assed beard."

The immigration official shrugs and stamps the passport. The second young man is treated with the same combination of mistrust and incompetence. His passport is stamped twice, because the Italian officer was so engrossed in the red-headed girl's shirtfront that he forgot to use the ink pad the first time. The young men pick up their rucksacks, slinging them over their shoulders by one strap. Murmuring apologies and twisting sideways, they slip through a tangle of excited Italians, a large family pressing and standing on tiptoe to greet an arriving relative.

"Okay! Slow 'er down!" Starr ordered over the intercom. "Here's where it hits the fan."

The projector slowed to one-quarter speed.

From frame to flickering frame the young men move as though the air were gelatin. The leader turns back to smile at someone in the queue, the motion having the quality of a ballet in moon gravity. The second one looks out over the crowd. His nonchalant smile freezes. He opens his mouth and shouts silently, as the front of his khaki shirt bursts open and spouts blood. Before he can fall to his knees, a second bullet strikes his cheek and tears it off. The camera waves around dizzily before locating the other young man, who has dropped his rucksack and is running in nightmare slow motion toward the coin lockers. He pirouettes in the air as a slug takes him in the shoulder. He slams gracefully against the lockers and bounces back. His hip blossoms with gore, and he slips sideward to the polished granite floor. A third bullet blows off the back of his head.

The camera swishes over the terminal, seeking, losing, then finding again two men—out of focus—running toward the glass doors of the entrance. The focus is corrected, revealing them to be Orientals. One of them carries an automatic weapon. He suddenly arches his back, throws up his arms, and slides forward on his toes for a second before pitching onto his face. The gun clatters silently beside him. The second man has reached the glass doors, the smeared light of which haloes his dark outline. He ducks as a bullet shatters the glass beside his head; he veers and runs for an open elevator out of which a group of schoolchildren are oozing. A little girl slumps down, her hair billowing as though she were under water. A stray has caught her in the stomach. The next slug takes the Oriental between the shoulder blades and drives him gently into the wall beside the elevator. A grin of anguish on his face, he twists his arm up behind him, as though to pluck out the bullet. The next slug pierces his palm and enters his spine. He slides down the wall and falls with his head in the elevator car. The door closes, but reopens as the pressure pads meet the obstructing head. It closes again upon the head, then reopens. Closes. Opens.

Slow pan back over the terminal. High angle.

. . . A cluster of shocked and bewildered children around the fallen girl. One boy screams in silence . . .

. . . Two airport guards, their little Italian automatics drawn, run toward the fallen Orientals. One of them is still firing . . .

. . . The old man with the snow-white goatee sits stunned in a puddle of his own blood, his legs straight out before him, like a child playing in a sandbox. His expression is one of overwhelming disbelief. He was sure he had explained everything to the customs official . . .

. . . One of the young Israeli boys lies face down on his missing cheek, his rucksack improbably still over his shoulder . . .

. . . There is a largo minuet of stylized confusion among the gaggle of Italians who were awaiting a relative. Three of them have fallen. Others are wailing, or kneeling, and one teenaged boy is turning around and around on his heel, seeking a direction in which to run for help—or safety . . .

. . . The red-headed girl stands stiff, her eyes round with horror as she stares at the fallen boy who just seconds ago offered to let her pass ahead . . .

. . . The camera comes to rest on the young man sprawled beside the coin lockers, the back of his head missing . . .

"That-a—that-a—that-a—that's all folks!" said Starr. The beam from the projector flickered out, and the wall lights dimmed up to full.

Starr turned in his seat to field questions from Mr. Diamond or the Arab. "Well?"

Diamond was still looking toward the white screen, three fingers pressed lightly against his lips, the action report on his lap. He let the fingers slip to beside his chin. "How many?" he asked quietly.

"Sir?"

"How many killed in the action?"

"I know what you mean, sir. Things got a little wetter than we expected. We'd arranged for the I-talian police to stay clear of the area, but they got their instructions all balled up—not that *that's* anything new. I even had some trouble myself. I had to use a Beretta so the slugs would match up for I-talian. And as a handgun, a Beretta isn't worth a fart in a hurricane, as my old daddy would have said. With an S&W, I could of dropped those Japs with two shots, and I wouldn't of hit that poor little girl that stepped out into my line of fire. Of course, in the first part of the action, our Nisei boys had been instructed to make it a little messy—make it look like a Black September number. But it was those panicked I-talian cops that started spattering slugs around like a cow pissing on a flat rock, as my old—"

"Starr?" Diamond's voice was heavy with disgust. "What was the question I asked you?"

"You asked how many were dead." Starr's tone was suddenly crisp, as he discarded the good ol' boy facade behind which he habitually took cover, to lull the target with the assumption that it was dealing with a bucolic fool. "Nine dead in total." A sudden grin, and the down-home twang was back. "Let's see now. There was the two Jew targets, of course. Then our two Nisei agents I had to maximally demote. And that poor little girl that bumped into one of my slugs. And that old fella who collected a stray. And three of that family of locals that were loitering around when that second Jew ran past them. Loitering's dangerous. It ought to be against the law."

"Nine? Nine killed to get two?"

"Well, sir, you gotta remember that we were instructed to make this look like a Black September-type action. And those boys have this tendency to be some extravagant. It's their style to open eggs with sledge hammers—no offense intended to Mr. Haman here."

Diamond looked up from the report he was speed-reading. Haman? Then he remembered that the Arab observer seated behind him had been given Haman as a cover name by the imaginative CIA.

"I take no offense, Mr. Starr," said the Arab. "We are here to learn. That is why some of our own trainees are working with your men at the Riding Academy, under a Title Seventeen grant for cultural exchange. To tell truths, I am impressed that a man of your seniority took the time to deal with this matter personally."

Starr waved that aside with pleased modesty. "Think nothing of it. If you want a job done right, give it to a busy man."

"Is that something else your old daddy used to say?" Diamond asked, his eyes not leaving the report as they raced vertically down the center of the page, speed-reading.

"Matter of fact, it is, now you mention it."

"He was quite the folksy philosopher."

"I think of him more as a rotten son-of-a-bitch, sir. But he did have a way with words."

Diamond sighed nasally and returned his attention to the action report. During the months since the Mother Company had assigned him to control all CIA activities touching the interests of the oil-producing powers, he had learned that, despite their institutionalized ineptitude, men like Starr were not stupid. They were, in fact, surprisingly intelligent, in the mechanical, problem-solving sense of that word. None of the chitlin grammar, none of the scatalogical paucity of language ever appeared in Starr's written reports of wet-work assignments. Instead, one found concise, arid prose calculated to callus the imagination.

From going over his biographic printout, Diamond had learned that Starr was something of a hero figure among the younger CIA operatives—the last of the old breed from the precomputer era, from the days when Company operations had more to do with swapping shots across the Berlin Wall than with controlling the votes of congressmen by amassing evidence of their fiscal and sexual irregularities.

T. Darryl Starr was of the same stripe as his over-the-hill contemporary who left the Company to write inarticulate spy novels and dabble over his head in political crimes. When his gross ineptitude led to his being caught, he clung to truculent silence, while his cohorts sang mighty choruses of mea culpa and published at great profit. After serving a bit of soft time in federal prison, he sought to ennoble his panicked silence by falling back on The Unwritten Code, which declares, "Thou shalt not squeal—out of print." The world groaned as at an old joke, but Starr admired this bungling fool. They shared that blend of boy scout and mugger that characterizes old-timers in the CIA.

Diamond glanced up from the report. "According to this, Mr. . . . Haman, you went along on the spoiling raid as an observer."

"Yes. That is correct. As a trainee/observer."

"In that case, why did you want to see this confirmation film before reporting to your superiors?"

"Ah . . . yes. Well . . . in point of most absolute fact . . ."

"It wouldn't be possible for him to report his eyeball reactions, sir," Starr explained. "He was with us up on the mezzanine when it all started, but ten seconds later we couldn't find hide nor hair of him. A man we left behind to sweep up finally located him in the back stall of the public benjo."

The Arab laughed briefly and mirthlessly. "This is true. The calls of nature are as inopportune as they are empirical."

The First Assistant frowned and blinked. Empirical? Did he mean imperative? Imperious?

"I see," Diamond said, and he returned to his scan-reading of the seventy-five-page report.

Uncomfortable with the silence, the Arab quickly filled in with: "I do not wish to be an inquisitor, Mr. Starr, but there is something I do not understand."

"Shoot, pal."

"Exactly why did we use Orientals to make the slap?"

"What? Oh! Well, you remember that we agreed to make it look as though your own men did the *hit*. But we don't have no A-rabs in the shop, and the boys we're training out to the Academy ain't up to this kind of number." Starr did not consider it tactful to add that, with their genetic disabilities, they probably never would be. "But your Black September boys have been members of the Japanese Red Army on their operations . . . and Japs we got."

The Arab frowned in confusion. "You are saying that the Japanese were your *own* men?"

"You got it. A couple of Nisei boys with the Agency in Hawaii. Good ol' boys too. It's a real pity we had to lose 'em, but their deaths put what you call your stamp of verisimilitude on your otherwise bald and unconvincing narrative. The slugs they dig out of them will be from a Beretta, and the local cops will get credit for pinching them off. They carried documents identifying them as Red Army members helping their A-rab brothers in what you call your unending struggle against the capitalist whatevers."

"Your *own* men?" the Arab repeated in awe.

"Don't sweat it. Their papers, their clothes, even the food that'll be found in their stomachs . . . it all makes them out to be from Japan. Matter of fact, they flew in from Tokyo just a couple of hours before the hit—or slap, as we sometimes call it."

The Arab's eyes shone with admiration. This was precisely the kind of organization his uncle—and president—had sent him to the United States to study, to the end of creating a similar one, and ending their dependence on their new-found allies. "But surely your Japanese agents did not *know* they were going to be . . . what is your term for it?"

"Maximally demoted? No, they didn't know. There's a rule of thumb in the shop that actives shouldn't know more than they need to do the job. They were good men, but even so, if they'da known they were gonna do a Nathan Hale, they might'a lost some of their enthusiasm, if you catch my drift there."

Diamond continued to read, his vertical sweep of eye always well ahead of the mixing and analyzing operations of his mind, which sorted and reviewed the data in a way best described as intellectual peripheral vision. When some bit failed to fall into place, or rang false, he would pause and go back, scanning for the offending fragment.

He was on the last page when the internal alarms went off. He paused, turned back to the preceding page, and read carefully—this time horizontally. His jaw muscles rippled. He lifted his eyes and produced a characteristically understated exclamation: for a moment he did not breathe.

The First Assistant's eyes flickered. He knew the signs. There was trouble.

Diamond drew a long-suffering sigh as he handed the report back over his shoulder. Until he had evaluated the problem, he would not alert the Arab observer. His experience told him that it is unwise and wasteful to equip Arabs with unnecessary information. It is not a burden they carry gracefully.

"Well?" he asked, turning his head slightly. "Are you satisfied, Mr. Haman?"

For an instant the Arab failed to recognize his code name, then he started and giggled. "Oh, yes. Well, let us say that I am impressed by the evidence of the films."

"Does that mean impressed, but *not* satisfied?"

The Arab pulled in his neck, tilted his head, and lifted his palms, smiling in the oblique way of the rug merchant. "My good friends, it is not for me to be satisfied or unsatisfied. *Dis*satisfied? I am merely a messenger, a point of contact, what you might call . . . a . . ."

"Flunkey?" Diamond offered.

"Perhaps. I do not know that word. A short time ago, our intelligence agents learned of a plot to assassinate the last two remaining heroes of the Munich Olympics Retaliation. My uncle—and president—expressed his desire to have this plot staunched . . . is that the word?"

"It's *a* word," Diamond admitted, his voice bored. He was out of patience with this fool, who was more a broad ethnic joke than a human being.

"As you recall, the staunching of this evil plot was a condition for continued amicable relations with the Mother Company in matters relating to oil supply. In its wisdom, the Mother Company decided to have CIA handle the matter—under your close personal supervisory, Mr. Diamond. I mean no offense to my brave friend, Mr. Starr, but it must be admitted that since certain bunglings of CIA-trained men led to the downfall of a most friendly and cooperative President, our confidence in that organization has not been without limits." The Arab tipped his head onto his shoulder and grinned apologetically at Starr, who examined his cuticles with deep interest.

The Arab continued. "Our intelligence organ was able to supply CIA with the names of the two Zionist gangsters assigned to this criminal attack, and with the approximate date of their departure from Tel Aviv. To this, Mr. Starr doubtless added his own sources of information, and he decided to avert the tragedy by technique of what you call a 'spoiling raid,' arranging that the criminals be executed before they committed their crime—a most economical judicial process. Now, you have shown me certain audiovisual medias proving that this raid was successful. I shall report this to my superiors. It is for them to be satisfied or nonsatisfied; not me."

Diamond, whose mind had been elsewhere through most of the Arab's singsong monologue, now rose. "That's it, then." Without further word, he strode up
the aisle, followed immediately by his First Assistant.

Starr hooked his leg over the seat before him and drew out a cigar. "You
want to see it again?" he asked the Arab over his shoulder.

"That would be pleasant."

Starr pressed the talk button of his console. "Hey, buddy? Let's have it
again." He slipped his sunglasses up into his cropped hair as the lights dimmed
down. "Here we go. A rerun. And on prime time." Pronounced: prahm tahm.

As he walked quickly down the white-walled corridor of the Center, Diamond's fury was manifest only in the sharp click of his leather heels over the
tiles. He had trained himself to restrict his emotions to a very narrow band of
expression, but the slight tension around his mouth and his half-defocused stare
were sufficient to alert the First Assistant that anger was writhing within him.

They stepped into the elevator, and the First Assistant inserted a magnetic
card into the slot that replaced the button for Floor 16. The car dropped rapidly
from the main lobby to the subbasement suite coded as Floor 16. The first thing
Diamond had done when he took over CIA activities on behalf of the Mother
Company was to create a work area for himself in the bowels of the Center. No
CIA personnel had access to Floor 16; the office suite was enclosed in lead
sheeting with antibugging alarms designed to keep that organization in its
traditional state of ignorance. As further security against governmental curiosity,
Diamond's office was served by a direct computer link with the Mother Company through cables that were armored against the parallel-line/incidental ca-
pacitance method of eavesdropping by means of which NSA monitors telephone
and telegraph communications in the United States.

In constant touch with the research and communications facilities of Mother
Company, Diamond needed only a staff of two: his First Assistant, who was a
gifted artist at computer search; and his secretary, Miss Swivven.

They stepped out into a large open work space, the walls and carpets all in
matte white. In the center was a discussion area consisting of five lightly padded
chairs around a table, with an etched glass top that served as a screen upon
which television images generated by the computer complex could be projected.
Of the five chairs, only one could swivel: Diamond's. The others were set rigidly
into the floor and were designed to provide minimal comfort. The area was for
quick, alert discussion—not for small-talk and social fencing.

Into the wall across from the discussion area was built a console that linked
their computer with the Mother Company's master system: Fat Boy. The bank
also contained television, telephoto and teletype connections back to Fat Boy for
printout of verbal and visual data, together with local storage banks for short-
term hold and cross-reference. The First Assistant's place was always before this
console, upon which instrument he played with unique abstract artistry, and
with great affection.

Raised slightly on a dais, Diamond's own desk was conspicuously modest,
with its white plastic surface only fifty centimeters by sixty-five. It had no
drawers or shelves, nowhere to lose or overlook material, no way to delay one
matter by pushing it aside on the excuse of attending to something else. A
priority system, ordered by a complicated set of strict criteria, brought each
problem to his desk only when there was sufficient research available for decisions, which were made quickly, and matters disposed of. Diamond despised
both physical and emotional clutter.

He crossed to his desk chair (constructed by an orthopedic specialist to reduce
fatigue without providing narcotizing comfort) and sat with his back to the wide,
floor-to-ceiling window beyond which could be seen a neat patch of park and

the stele of the Washington Monument in the middle distance. He sat for a moment with his palms pressed together in a prayerlike attitude, forefingers lightly touching his lips. The First Assistant automatically took his place before the data console and awaited instructions.

Alerted by their entrance, Miss Swivven entered the work area from her anteoffice and sat in her chair beside and below Diamond's dais, her note pad ready. She was in her late twenties, lush of body, with thick honey-colored hair done up in an efficient bun. Her most salient feature was an extreme fairness of skin beneath which her veins traced faint bluish patterns.

Without raising his eyes, Diamond tilted his praying hands from his lips and directed the fingertips toward the First Assistant. "Those two Israeli boys. They belonged to some organization. Name?"

"The Munich Five, sir."

"Function?"

"To avenge the killing of Jewish athletes at the Munich Olympics. Specifically, to hunt down and kill the Palestinian terrorists involved. Not official. Nothing to do with the Israeli government."

"I see." Diamond turned his fingers toward Miss Swivven. "I'll dine here tonight. Something quick and light, but I'll need a protein shock. Make it brewer's yeast, liquid vitamins, egg yolks, and eight ounces of raw calf's liver. Do it up in a blender."

Miss Swivven nodded. It was going to be a long night.

Diamond turned in his desk chair and stared sightlessly out toward the Washington Monument. Walking across the lawn near the base was the same group of schoolchildren that passed every day at exactly this time. Without turning from the window, he said over his shoulder, "Give me a data pull on this Munich Five."

"What indices, sir?" the First Assistant asked.

"It's a small organization. And recent. Let's begin with history and membership."

"At what depth do I scan?"

"You work that out. It's what you do well."

The First Assistant turned in his chair and began instructing Fat Boy. His face was immobile, but his eyes behind the round glasses sparkled with delight. Fat Boy contained a medley of information from all the computers in the Western World, together with a certain amount of satellite-stolen data from Eastern Bloc powers. It was a blend of top-secret military information and telephone-billing records; of CIA blackmail material and drivers' permits from France, of names behind numbered Swiss bank accounts and mailing lists from direct advertising companies in Australia. It contained the most delicate information, and the most mundane. If you lived in the industrialized West, Fat Boy had you. He had your credit rating, your blood type, your political history, your sexual inclinations, your medical records, your school and university performance, random samplings of your personal telephone conversations, a copy of every telegram you ever sent or received, all purchases made on credit, full military or prison records, all magazines subscribed to, all income tax records, driving licenses, fingerprints, birth certificates—all this, if you were a private citizen in whom the Mother Company had no special interest. If, however, the Mother Company or any of her input subsidiaries, like CIA, NSA, and their counterparts in the other democratic nations, took particular notice of you, then Fat Boy knew much, much more than this about you.

Programming facts into Fat Boy was the constant work of an army of mechanics and technicians, but getting useful information out of Him was a task for an artist, a person with training, touch, and inspiration. The problem lay in the fact that Fat Boy knew too much. If one scanned a given subject too shallowly, he might not discover what he wanted to know. If he scanned too deeply, he would be overwhelmed with an unreadable mass of minutiae: results of former urine tests, boy scout merit badges won, predictions in high school annuals, preference in brand of toilet paper. The First Assistant's unique gift was his delicate touch in asking just the right questions of Fat Boy, and of demanding response at just the right depth of scan. Experience and instinct combined to send him after the right indices, the right permutations, the right rubrics, the right depths. He played the instrument of the computer masterfully, and he loved it. Working at his console was to him what sex was to other men—that is to say, what he assumed sex was to other men.

Diamond spoke over his shoulder to Miss Swivven. "When I'm ready, I'll want to talk to this Starr person, and to the Arab they call Mr. Haman. Have them kept on tap."

Under the First Assistant's manipulation, the console was warming and humming. The first responses were coming in; fragments were being stored in the local memory bank; the dialogue had begun. No two conversations with Fat Boy were alike; each took on its own patois, and the delights of the problem were beginning to stroke the First Assistant's considerable, if exclusively frontal, intellect.

It would be twenty minutes before a full picture was available. Diamond decided not to waste this time. He would take a little exercise and sun, tune up his body and clear his mind for the long haul to come. He gestured with a fingertip for Miss Swivven to follow him into the small exercise room off the principal work area.

As he stripped down to his abbreviated shorts, Miss Swivven put on a pair of round, dark eyecups, handed him a similar pair, and turned on the bank of sunlamps installed along the walls. Diamond began doing sit-ups on an inclined platform, his ankles held by a loop of velvet-covered rope, while Miss Swivven pressed against the wall, keeping her vulnerably pale skin as far away from the intense glare of ultraviolet as possible. Diamond did his sit-ups slowly, getting the most work out of the fewest repetitions. He was in excellent shape for a man of his age, but the stomach required constant attention. "Listen," he said, his voice tight with a withheld grunt as he rose and touched his right knee with his left elbow, "I'll have to bring some CIA clout in on this. Alert whoever is left at the top after that last round of cosmetic administrative shakeups."

The highest-ranking administrator below the political shills that came and went as sacrificial lambs to outraged public opinion was the Deputy International Liaison Duty Officer, who was typically referred to by his acronym. Miss Swivven informed her superior that he was still in the building.

"He'll do. Order him to keep himself on tap. Oh—and cancel my tennis date for this weekend."

Miss Swivven's eyebrows lifted above her dark eyecups. This must be something very serious indeed.

Diamond began to work with the weights. "I'll also want a Q-jump priority on Fat Boy for the rest of the afternoon, maybe longer."

"Yes, sir."

"Okay. What do you have on your pad?"

"High protein input in liquid form. Alert and freeze Mr. Starr and Mr. Haman. Alert and freeze the Deputy. Request Q-jump priority on Fat Boy."

"Good. Precede all that with a message to the Chairman." Diamond was breathing heavily with the effort of exercise. "Message: Possible that Rome International spoiling raid was imperfect. Will seek, sort, and report alternatives."

When Miss Swivven returned seven minutes later, she was carrying a large glass of thick, foamy, purplish liquid, the color lent by the pulverized raw liver. Diamond was in the last phase of his exercise routine, working isometrically against a fixed steel pipe. He stopped and accepted his dinner, as she pressed close to the wall, avoiding the sunlamps as best she could, but knowing perfectly well that she had already had enough exposure to burn her delicate skin. Although there were many advantages of her job with the Mother Company—overtime, good retirement plan, medical benefits, company vacation resort in the Canadian Rockies, Christmas parties—Miss Swivven regretted two aspects of her career: this getting sunburnt every week or so, and the occasional impersonal use Mr. Diamond made of her to relieve his tensions. Still, she was philosophic. No job is perfect.

"Note pad cleared?" Diamond asked, shuddering slightly as he finished his drink.

"Yes, sir."

Disregarding her presence, Diamond stepped out of his shorts and into a glass-fronted shower stall, where he turned on a full spray of bracing cold water, over the noise of which he asked, "Did the Chairman respond to my message?"

"Yes, sir."

After a short silence, Diamond said, "Please feel free to tell me what the response was, Miss Swivven."

"Pardon me, sir?"

Diamond turned off the shower, stepped out, and began to dry off on the rough towels designed to heighten circulation.

"Do you want me to read the Chairman's message to you, sir?"

Diamond sighed deeply. If this twit had not been the only attractive one in the over-100 wpm pool . . . "That would be nice, Miss Swivven."

She referred to her note pad, squinting against the glare of the sunlamps. "Response: Chairman to Diamond, J.O.: 'Failure in this matter not acceptable.' "

Diamond nodded as he dried his crotch meditatively. It was as he had expected.

When he returned to the work area, he was crisp-minded and prepared for decision-making, having changed into his working clothes, a jumpsuit of pale yellow that was loose and comfortable, and set his rotisserie tan off to advantage.

The First Assistant was working at the console with narrow concentration and physical exhilaration, as he tickled a cogent printout of data on the Munich Five out of Fat Boy.

Diamond sat in his swivel chair above the milky etched glass tabletop. "Punch up the RP," he instructed. "Give me a roll-down rate of five hundred WPM." He could not absorb information faster than this because the data came from half a dozen international sources, and Fat Boy's mechanical translations into English were as stilted and unrefined of idiom as a Clint Eastwood film.

MUNICH FIVE, THE . . .
ORGANIZATION . . . UNOFFICIAL . . . SPLINTER . . . GOAL
EQUALS TERMINATION OF BLACK SEPTEMBRISTS INVOLVED IN
KILLING ISRAELI ATHLETES IN MUNICH OLYMPICS . . .
LEADER AND KEYMAN EQUALS STERN, ASA . . .
MEMBERS AND SATELLITES EQUAL LEVITSON, YOEL . . .
YARIV, CHAIM . . . ZARMI, NEHEMIAH . . . STERN, HANNAH . . .

"Hold it," Diamond said. "Let's take a look at them one at a time. Just give me sketches."

STERN, ASA

BORN APRIL 13, 1909 . . . BROOKLYN, NEW YORK, USA . . .
1352 CLINTON AVENUE . . . APARTMENT 3B . . .

The First Assistant clenched his teeth. "Sorry, sir." He was probing just a shade too deeply. No one wanted to know the number of the apartment in which Asa Stern was born. Not yet, anyway. He shallowed the probe a micron.

STERN EMIGRATES TO PALESTINE PROTECTORATE . . . 1931 . . .
PROFESSION AND/OR COVER . . . FARMER, JOURNALIST,
POET, HISTORIAN . . .
INVOLVED IN STRUGGLE FOR INDEPENDENCE . . . 1945-1947
(details available) . . .
IMPRISONED BY BRITISH OCCUPATION FORCES (details
available) . . .
UPON RELEASE BECOMES CONTACT POINT FOR STERN
ORGANIZATION AND OUTSIDE SYMPATHETIC GROUPS (details
available) . . .
RETIRES TO FARM . . . 1956 . . .
REACTIVATES WITH MUNICH OLYMPICS AFFAIR (details
available) . . .
CURRENT IRRITANT POTENTIAL TO MOTHER COMPANY
EQUALS COEFFICIENT .001 . . .
REASON FOR LOW COEFFICIENT EQUALS:
    THISMAN NOW DEAD, sub CANCER, sub THROAT

"That's a surface scratch, sir." the First Assistant said. "Shall I probe a little deeper? He's obviously the pivot man."
"Obviously. But dead. No, just store the rest of his stuff in the memory bank. I'll come back to him later. Let's have a look at the other members of his group."
"It's rolling up on your screen now, sir."

LEVITSON, YOEL
BORN DECEMBER 25, 1954 . . . NEGEV, ISRAEL . . .
FATHER KILLED . . . COMBAT . . . 6-DAY WAR . . . 1967 . . .
JOINS MUNICH FIVE . . . OCTOBER 1972 . . .
KILLED . . . DECEMBER 25, 1976 . . . (IDENTITY BETWEEN
BIRTH AND DEATH DATES NOTED AND CONSIDERED
COINCIDENTAL)

"Hold that!" Diamond ordered. "Give me a little depth on this boy's death."
"Yes, sir."

KILLED . . . DECEMBER 25, 1976 . . .
VICTIM (PROBABLY PRIMARY TARGET) OF TERRORIST
BOMB . . .
SITE EQUALS CAFE IN JERUSALEM . . . BOMB ALSO KILLED
SIX ARAB BYSTANDERS. TWO CHILDREN BLINDED . . .

"Okay, forget it. It's unimportant. Return to the light scan."

CURRENT IRRITANT POTENTIAL TO MOTHER COMPANY
EQUALS COEFFICIENT .001 . . .

REASON FOR LOW COEFFICIENT EQUALS:
    THISMAN NOW DEAD, sub MULTIPLE FRACTURES, sub
COLLAPSED LUNGS . . .
****
YARIV, CHAIM
  BORN OCTOBER 11, 1952 . . . ELATH, ISRAEL . . .
  ORPHAN/KIBBUTZ BACKGROUND (details available) . . .
  JOINS MUNICH FIVE . . . SEPTEMBER 7, 1972 . . .
  CURRENT IRRITANT POTENTIAL TO MOTHER COMPANY
EQUALS COEFFICIENT .64± . . .
  REASON FOR MEZZO-COEFFICIENT EQUALS:
    THISMAN CAUSE-DEVOTED, BUT NOT LEADERTYPE . . .
****
ZARMI, NEHEMIAH
  BORN JUNE 11, 1948 . . . ASHDOD, ISRAEL . . .
  KIBBUTZ/UNIVERSITY/ARMY BACKGROUND
(details available) . . .
  ACTIVE GUERRILLA, sub NONSPONSORED (details of known/
probable/possible actions available) . . .
  JOINS MUNICH FIVE . . . SEPTEMBER 7, 1972 . . .
  CURRENT IRRITANT POTENTIAL TO MOTHER COMPANY
EQUALS COEFFICIENT .96±
  REASON FOR HIGH COEFFICIENT EQUALS:
    THISMAN CAUSE-DEVOTED AND LEADERTYPE . . .

SEE THIS! SEE THIS! SEE THIS! SEE THIS! THISMAN MAY BE
TERMINATED ON SIGHT.
****
STERN, HANNAH
  BORN APRIL 1, 1952 . . . SKOKIE, ILLINOIS, USA . . .
  UNIVERSITY/SOCIOLOGY AND ROMANCE LANGUAGES/
ACTIVE CAMPUS RADICAL (NSA/CIA DOSSIERS AVAILABLE) . . .
SAYAGAIN!SAYAGAIN!SAYAGAIN!SAYAGAIN!

Diamond looked up from the conference table screen. "What's the matter?"
"Something's in error, sir. Fat Boy is correcting himself."
"Well?"
"We'll know in a minute, sir. Fat Boy's cooking."
Miss Swivven entered from the machine room. "Sir? I have requested tele-photos of the members of the Munich Five."
"Bring them as soon as they print out."
"Yes, sir."
The First Assistant lifted his hand for attention. "Here it comes. Fat Boy is correcting himself in terms of Starr's report on the spoiling raid in Rome. He just digested the information."
Diamond read the rear-projected roll-down.

NEGATE PRIOR, RE: YARIV, CHAIM sub CURRENT IRRITANT
POTENTIAL TO MOTHER COMPANY . . .
  CORRECTED COEFFICIENT EQUALS .001 . . .
  REASON FOR LOW COEFFICIENT EQUALS:
    THISPERSON TERMINATED . . .
  NEGATE PRIOR, RE: ZARMI, NEHEMIAH sub CURRENT
IRRITANT POTENTIAL TO MOTHER COMPANY . . .
  CORRECTED COEFFICIENT EQUALS .001 . . .

REASON FOR LOW COEFFICIENT EQUALS:
    THISPERSON TERMINATED . . .
****

Diamond leaned back and shook his head. "An eight-hour lag. That could hurt us someday."

"It's not Fat Boy's fault, sir. It's an effect of rising world population and our own information explosion. Sometimes I think we know *too* much about people!" The First Assistant chuckled at the very idea. "By the way, sir, did you notice the rephrase?"

"Which rephrase?"

"THISMAN is now expressed as THISPERSON. Fat Boy must have digested the Mother Company's becoming an equal-opportunity employer." The First Assistant could not keep the pride from his voice.

"That's wonderful," Diamond said without energy.

Miss Swivven entered from the machine room and placed five telephotos on Diamond's desk, then she took her position below his dais, her note pad at the ready.

Diamond shuffled through the photographs for that of the only member of the Munich Five not known to be dead: Hannah Stern. He scanned the face, nodded to himself, and sighed fatalistically. These CIA imbeciles!

The First Assistant turned from his console and adjusted his glasses nervously. "What's wrong, sir?"

His eyes half closed as he looked through the floor-to-ceiling window at the Washington Monument threatening to violate that same chubby cloud that always hung in the evening sky at this time, Diamond tapped his upper lip with his knuckle. "Did you read Starr's action report?"

"I scanned it, sir. Mostly checking for spelling."

"What was the ostensible destination of those Israeli youngsters?"

The First Assistant always felt uncomfortable with Mr. Diamond's rhetorical style of thinking aloud. He did not like answering questions without the aid of Fat Boy. "As I recall, their destination was London."

"Right. Presumably intending to intercept certain Palestinian terrorists at Heathrow Airport before they could hijack a plane to Montreal. All right. If the Munich Five team were going to London, why did they disembark at Rome? Flight 414 from Tel Aviv is a through flight to London with stops at Rome and Paris."

"Well, sir, there could be several—"

"And why were they going to England six days before their Black September targets were due to fly out to Montreal? Why sit in the open in London for all that time, when they could have stayed securely at home?"

"Well, perhaps they—"

"And why were they carrying tickets to Pau?"

"Pau, sir?"

"Starr's action report. Bottom of page thirty-two through middle of page thirty-four. Description of contents of victims' knapsacks and clothing. List prepared by Italian police. It includes two plane tickets for Pau."

The First Assistant did not mention that he had no idea where Pau was. He made a mental note to ask Fat Boy first chance he got. "What does all this mean, sir?"

"It means that once again CIA has lived up to the traditions of Bay of Pigs and Watergate. Once again, they have screwed up." Diamond's jaw tightened. "The mindless voters of this country are wrong to worry about the dangers of CIA's internal corruption. When they bring this nation to disaster, it won't be through their villainy; it will be because of their bungling." He returned to his pristine desk and picked up the telephoto of Hannah Stern. "Fat Boy interrupted himself with that correction while it was backgrounding this Hannah Stern. Start me up on that again. And give me a little more depth."

Evaluating both the data and the gaps, Diamond analyzed Miss Stern to be a fairly common sort found on the fringes of terrorist action. Young, intelligent mid-American, cause-oriented. He knew the type. She would have been a Liberal, back when that was still fashionable. She was the kind who sought "relevance" in everything; who expressed her lack of critical judgement as freedom from prejudice; who worried about Third World hunger, but shambled about a university campus with a huge protein-gobbling dog—symbol of her love for all living things.

She first came to Israel on a summer tour at a kibbutz, her purpose being to visit her uncle and—in her own words quoted in a NSA lift from a letter home— "to discover my Jewishness."

Diamond could not repress a sigh when he read that phrase. Miss Stern obviously suffered from the democratic delusion that all people are created interesting.

Fat Boy ascribed a low coefficient of irritant potential to Miss Stern, regarding her as a typical young American intellectual woman seeking a cause to justify her existence, until marriage, career, or artsy hobbies defused her. Her personality analysis turned up none of those psychotic warps that produce the urban guerrilla who finds sexual expression in violence. Nor was she flawed by that desperate hunger for notoriety that causes actors and entertainers who, unable to remain in the public eye by virtue of their talents, suddenly discover hitherto unnoticed social convictions.

No, there was nothing in Hannah Stern's printout that would nominate her for particular attention—save for two facts: She was Asa Stern's niece. And she was the only surviving member of the Munich Five.

Diamond spoke to Miss Swivven. "Have Starr and that Arab . . . Mr. Haman . . . in the screening room in ten minutes."

"Yes, sir."

"And have the Deputy there too." He turned to the First Assistant. "You keep working on Fat Boy. I want a deep rescan of the leader, this Asa Stern. He's the one who will bleed through. Give me a list of his first-generation contacts: family, friends, accomplices, associates, acquaintances, affairs, and so on."

"Just a second, sir." The First Assistant introduced two questions into the computer, then one modifier. "Ah . . . sir? The first-generation list will have . . . ah . . . three hundred twenty-seven names, together with thumbnail sketches. And we'll cube as we move to second-generation lists—friends of friends, etc. That'll give us almost thirty-five million names. Obviously, sir, we have to have some kind of priority criterion."

The First Assistant was right; a critical decision; there are literally thousands of ways in which a list can be ordered.

Diamond thought back over the sketch on Asa Stern. His intuition was tickled by one line: Profession and/or cover . . . Farmer, Journalist, Poet, Historian. Not, then, a typical terrorist. Something worse—a romantic patriot.

"Order the list emotionally. Go for indices indicating love, friendship, trust—this sort of thing. Go from closest to most distant."

The First Assistant's eyes shone as he took a deep breath and lightly rubbed his fingertips together. This was a fine challenge demanding console virtuosity. Love, friendship, trust—these impressions and shadows could not be located through approaches resembling the Schliemann Back-bit and Nonbit Theory. No computer, not even Fat Boy, can respond to such rubrics directly. Questions have to be phrased in terms of nonfrequency counts and non sequitur exchange relationships. In its simplest forms, actions performed for no measurable reason, or contrary to linear logic, *might* indicate such underlying motives as love or friendship or trust. But great care had to be exercised, because identical actions could derive from hate, insanity, or blackmail. Moreover, in the case of love, the nature of the action seldom helps to identify its motivational impulse. Particularly difficult is separating love from blackmail.

It was a delicious assignment, infinitely complicated. As he began to insert the first probes into Fat Boy, the First Assistant's shoulders twisted back and forth, as though he were guiding a pinball with body-english.

Miss Swivven returned to the work room. "They're waiting for you in the theater, sir."

"Good. Bring those telephotos along. What on earth is wrong with you, Miss Swivven?"

"Nothing, sir. My back itches, that's all."

"For Christ's sake."

Darryl Starr sensed trouble in the air when he and the Arab received curt orders to report to the viewing room at once. His fears were confirmed when he found his direct superior sitting gloomily in the auditorium. The Deputy International Liaison Duty Officer nodded a curt greeting to Starr and grunted once toward the Arab. He blamed the oil-rich Arabian sheikdoms for many of his current problems, not the least of which was the interfering presence of Mr. Diamond in the bowels of the CIA, with his snide attitude toward every little operational peccadillo.

When first the oil-producing Arabs had run a petroleum boycott against the industrialized West to blackmail them into withdrawing their moral and legal commitments to Israel, the Deputy and other leaders of CIA proposed putting on line Contingency Plan NE385/8 (Operation Six Second War). In terms of this plan, CIA-sponsored troops of the Orthodox Islamic Maoist Falange would rescue the Arab states from the temptations of greed by occupying more than 80 percent of their oil facilities in an action calculated to require less than one minute of actual combat, although it was universally admitted that an additional three months would be required to round up such Arab and Egyptian troops as had fled in panic as far as Rhodesia and Scandinavia.

It was agreed that Operation Six Second War would be undertaken without burdening the President or Congress with those decision-making responsibilities so onerous in an election year. Phase One was instituted, and political leaders in both Black and Muslim Africa experienced an epidemic of assassinations, one or two at the hands of members of the victim's own family. Phase Two was in countdown, when suddenly everything froze up. Evidence concerning CIA operations was leaked to congressional investigating committees; lists of CIA agents were released to Leftist newspapers in France, Italy, and the Near East; internal CIA communications began to be jammed; massive tape erasures occurred in CIA memory banks, denying them the "biographic leverage" with which they normally controlled American elected officials.

Then one afternoon, Mr. Diamond and his modest staff walked into the Center carrying orders and directives that gave the Mother Company total control over all operations touching, either directly or tangentially, the oil-producing nations. Neither the Deputy nor his colleagues had ever heard of this "Mother Company," so a quick briefing was in order. They learned that the Mother Company was a consortium of major international petroleum, communications, and transportation corporations that effectively controlled the Western World's energy and information. After some consideration, the Mother Company had decided that she could not permit CIA to continue meddling in affairs that might harm or irritate those oil-producing friends in consort with whom she had been able to triple profits in two years.

No one at CIA seriously considered opposing Mr. Diamond and the Mother Company, which controlled the careers of most major governmental figures, not only through direct support, but also by the technique of using their public media subsidiaries to blacken and demoralize potential candidates, and to shape what the American masses took to be the Truth.

What chance had the scandal-ridden CIA to resist a force with enough power to build pipelines through tundra that had been demonstrated to be ecologically fragile? Who could stand against the organization that had reduced government research spending on solar, wind, tidal, and geothermal energy to a placating trickle, so as to avoid competition with their own atomic and fossil-fuel consortia? How could CIA effectively oppose a group with such overwhelming dominance that She was able, in conjunction with its Pentagon flunkies, to make the American public accept the storage of atomic wastes with lethal half-lives so long that failure and disaster were absolutely assured by the laws of anti-chance?

In Her takeover of CIA, the Mother Company had no interference from the executive branch of the government, as it was nearing election time, and all public business is arrested during this year of flesh-bartering. Nor did She really worry about the post-election pause of three years before the next democratic convulsion, for the American version of representative government assures that such qualities of intellect and ethics as might equip a man to lead a powerful nation responsibly are precisely the qualities that would prevent him from subjecting himself to the debasing performances of vote begging and delegate swapping. It is a truism of American politics that no man who can win an election deserves to.

There was one awkward moment for the Mother Company when a group of naïve young Senators decided to inquire into Arab millions in short-term paper that allowed them to manipulate American banks and hold the nation's economy hostage against the possibility—however remote—that the United States might attempt to fulfill its moral commitments to Israel. But these probes were cut short by Kuwait's threat to withdraw its money and crumble the banks, should the Senate pursue. With exceptional rhetorical adroitness, the committee reported that they could not say with certainty that the nation was vulnerable to blackmail, because they had not been permitted to continue their investigations.

This was the background to the Deputy's feelings of petulance over loss of control of his organization as he heard the doors of the auditorium bang open. He rose to his feet as Diamond entered at a brisk pace, followed by Miss Swivven who carried several rip-sheets from the Fat Boy printout and the stack of photographs of members of the Munich Five.

In minimal recognition of Diamond's arrival, Starr lifted most of the weight off his butt, then settled back with a grunt. The Arab's response to Miss Swivven's arrival was to jump to his feet, grin, and bow in jerky imitation of European suavity. Very nice looking woman, he told himself. Very lush. Skin like snow. And most gifted in what, in English, is referred to as the knockers.

"Is the projectionist in the booth?" Diamond asked, sitting apart from the others.

"Yes, sir," Starr drawled. "You fixin' to see the film again?"

"I want you fools to see it again."

The Deputy was not pleased to be grouped with a mere agent, and even less with an Arab, but he had learned to suffer in silence. It was his senior administrative skill.

"You never told us you wanted to see the film," Starr said. "I don't think the projectionist has rewound it yet."

"Have him run it backward. It doesn't matter."

Starr gave instructions through the intercom, and the wall lights dimmed.

"Starr?"

"Sir?"

"Put out the cigar."

. . . the elevator door opens and closes on the dead Japanese gunman's head. The man returns to life and slides up the wall. The hole in his palm disappears, and he tugs the bullet out of his back. He runs backward through a gaggle of school-children, one of whom floats up from the floor as a red stain on her dress is sucked back into her stomach. When he reaches the light-blurred main entrance, the Japanese ducks as fragments of broken glass rush together to form a window pane. The second gunman jumps up from the floor and catches a flying automatic weapon, and the two of them run backward, until a swish pan leaves them and discovers an Israeli boy on the tiled floor. A vacuum snaps the top of his skull back into place; the stream of gore recoils back into his hip. He leaps up and runs backward, snatching up his rucksack as he passes it. The camera waves around, then finds the second Israeli just in time to see his cheek pop on. He rises from his knees, and blood implodes into his chest as the khaki shirt instantly mends itself. The two boys walk backward. One turns and smiles. They saunter back through a group of Italians pushing and standing tiptoe to greet some arriving relative. They back down the lane to the immigration counter, and the Italian official uses his rubber stamp to suck the entrance permissions off their passports. A red-headed girl shakes her head, then smiles thanks . . .

"Stop!" called Mr. Diamond, startling Miss Swivven, who had never heard him raise his voice before.

The girl on the screen froze, a blow-back douser dimming the image to prevent the frame from burning.

"See that girl, Starr?"

"Sure."

"Can you tell me anything about her?"

Starr was confused by this seemingly arbitrary demand. He knew he was in trouble of some sort, and he fell back on his habit of taking cover behind his dumb, good-ol'-boy facade.

"Well . . . let's see. She's got a fair set of boobs, that's for sure. Taut little ass. A little skinny in the arms and waist for my taste but, like my ol' daddy used to say: the closer the bone, the sweeter the meat!" He forced a husky laugh in which he was joined by the Arab, who was anxious to prove he understood.

"Starr?" Diamond's voice was monotonic and dense. "I want you to do something for me. For the next few hours, I want you to try very hard to stop being an ass. I don't want you to entertain me, and I don't want you to supplement your answers with folksy asides. There is nothing funny about what is going on here. True to the traditions of the CIA, you have screwed up, Starr. Do you understand that?"

There was silence as the Deputy considered objecting to this defamation, but thought better of it.

"Starr? Do you understand that?"

A sigh, then quietly, "Yes, sir."

The Deputy cleared his throat and spoke in his most authoritative voice. "If there's anything the Agency can—"

"Starr? Do you recognize this girl?" Diamond asked.

Miss Swivven took the photograph from its folder and sidled down the aisle to Starr and the Arab.

Starr tilted the print to see it better in the dim light. "Yes, sir."

"Who is it?"

"It's the girl up there on the screen."

"That's right. Her name is Hannah Stern. Her uncle was Asa Stern, organizer of the Munich Five. She was the third member of the commando team."

"Third?" Starr asked. "But . . . we were told there were only two of them on the plane."

"Who told you that?"

"It was in the intelligence report we got from this fella here."

"That is correct, Mr. Diamond," the Arab put in. "Our intelligence men . . ."

But Diamond had closed his eyes and was shaking his head slowly. "Starr? Are you telling me that you based an operation on information provided by *Arab* sources?"

"Well, we . . . Yes, sir." Starr's voice was deflated. Put that way, it did seem a stupid thing to do. It was like having Italians do your political organization, or the British handle your industrial relations.

"It seems to me," the Deputy injected, "that if we have made an error based on faulty input from your Arab friends, they have to accept a goodly part of the responsibility."

"You're wrong," Diamond said. "But I suppose you're used to that. They don't have to accept anything. They own the oil."

The Arab representative smiled and nodded. "You reflect exactly the thinking of my president and uncle, who has often said that—"

"All right." Diamond rose. "The three of you remain on tap. In less than an hour, I'll call for you. I have background data coming in now. It's still possible that I may be able to make up for your bungling." He walked up the aisle, followed closely by Miss Swivven.

The Deputy cleared his throat to say something, then decided that the greater show of strength lay in silence. He fixed a long stare on Starr, glanced away from the Arab in dismissal, then left the theater.

"Well, buddy," Starr said as he pushed himself out of the theater seat, "we better get a bite to eat while the gettin's good. Looks like the shit has hit the fan."

The Arab chuckled and nodded, as he tried to envision an ardent supporter of sports fouled with camel dung.

For a time, the empty theater was dominated by the frozen image of Hannah Stern, smiling down from the screen. When the projectionist started to run the film out, it jammed. An amoeba of brown, bubbly scab spread rapidly over the young lady and consumed her.

Etchebar

HANNAH STERN SAT at a café table under the arcade surrounding the central place of Tardets. She stared numbly into the lees of her coffee, thick and granular. Sunlight was dazzling on the white buildings of the square; the shadows under the arcade were black and chill. From within the café behind her came the voices of four old Basque men playing *mousse,* to the accompaniment of a litany of *bai . . . passo . . . passo . . . alla Jainkoa! . . . passo . . . alla Jainkoa . . .* this last phrase passing through all conceivable permutations of stress and accent as the players bluffed, signaled, lied, and called upon God to witness this shit they had been dealt, or to punish this fool of a partner with whom God had punished them.

For the last seven hours, Hannah Stern had alternated between clawing through nightmare reality and floating upon escapist fantasy, between confusion and vertigo. She was stunned by emotional shock, spiritually evacuated. And now, teetering on the verge of nervous disintegration, she felt infinitely calm . . . even a little sleepy.

The real, the unreal; the important, the insignificant; the Now, the Then; the cool of her arcade, the rippling heat of the empty public square; these voices chanting in Europe's most ancient language . . . it was all indifferently tangled. It was all happening to someone else, someone for whom she felt great pity and sympathy, but whom she could not help. Someone past help.

After the massacre in Rome International, she had somehow got all the way from Italy to this café in a Basque market town. Dazed and mentally staggering, she had traveled fifteen hundred kilometers in nine hours. But now, with only another four or five kilometers to go, she had used up the last of her nervous energy. Her adrenaline well was empty, and it appeared that she was going to be defeated at the last moment by the caprice of a bumbling café owner.

First there had been terror and confusion at seeing her comrades shot down, neurasthenic incredulity during which she stood frozen as people rushed past her, knocking against her. More gunshots. Loud wailing from the family of Italians who had been awaiting a relative. Then panic clutched her; she walked blindly ahead, toward the main entrance of the terminal, toward the sunlight. She was breathing orally, shallow pants. Policemen rushed past her. She told herself to keep walking. Then she realized that the muscles in the small of her back were knotted painfully in anticipation of the bullet that never came. She passed an old man with a white goatee, sitting on the floor with his legs straight out before him, like a child at play. She could see no wound, but the pool of dark blood in which he sat was growing slowly wider. He did not seem to be in pain. He looked up at her interrogatively. She couldn't make herself stop. Their eyes locked together as she walked by. She muttered stupidly, "I'm sorry. I'm really sorry."

A fat woman in the group of waiting relatives was hysterical, wailing and choking. More attention was being paid to her than to the fallen members of the family. She was, after all, Mama.

Over the confusion, the running and shouting, a calm, singsong voice announced the first call for passengers on Air France flight 470 for Toulouse, Tarbes, and Pau. The recorded voice was ignorant of the chaos beneath its loudspeakers. When the announcement was repeated in French, the last fragment stuck to Hannah's consciousness. Gate Eleven. Gate Eleven.

The stewardess reminded Hannah to put up her seat back. "Yes. Yes. I'm sorry." A minute later, on her return down the aisle, the hostess reminded her to buckle her seat belt. "What? Oh, yes. I'm sorry."

The plane rose into thin cloud, then into crisp infinite blue. The drone of engines; the vibration of the fuselage. Hannah shivered with vulnerability and aloneness. There was a middle-aged man seated beside her, reading a magazine. From time to time his eyes slipped over the top of the page and glanced quickly at her suntanned legs below the khaki shorts. She could feel his eyes on her, and she buttoned one of the top two buttons of her shirt. The man smiled and cleared his throat. He was going to speak to her! The stupid son of a bitch was going to try to pick her up! My God!

And suddenly she was sick.

She made it to the toilet, where she knelt in the cramped space and vomited into the bowl. When she emerged, pale and fragile, the imprint of floor tile on her knees, the stewardess was solicitous but slightly superior, imagining that a short flight like this had made her airsick.

The plane banked on its approach to Pau, and Hannah looked out the window at the panorama of the Pyrenees, snow-tipped and sharp in the crystalline air, like a sea of whitecaps frozen in midstorm. Beautiful and awful.

Somewhere there, at the Basque end of the range, Nicholai Hel lived. If she could only get to Mr. Hel . . .

It was not until she was out of the terminal and standing in the chill sunlight of the Pyrenees that it occurred to her that she had no money. Avrim had carried all their money. She would have to hitchhike, and she didn't know the route. Well, she could ask the drivers. She knew that she would have no trouble getting rides. When you're pretty and young . . . and big-busted . . .

Her first ride took her into Pau, and the driver offered to find her a place to stay for the night. Instead, she talked him into taking her to the outskirts and directing her to Tardets. It must have been a hard car to shift, because his hand twice slipped off the lever and brushed her leg.

She got her next ride almost immediately. No, he wasn't going to Tardets. Only as far as Oléron. But he could find her a place to stay for the night . . .

One more car, one more suggestive driver, and Hannah reached the little village of Tardets, where she sought further directions at the café. The first barrier she met was the local accent, *langue d'oc* with heavy overlays of Soultine Basque in which *une petite cuillère* had eight syllables.

"What are you looking for?" the café owner asked, his eyes leaving her breasts only to stray to her legs.

"I'm trying to find the Château of Etchebar. The house of M. Nicholai Hel."

The proprietor frowned, squinted at the arches overhead, and scratched with one finger under the beret that Basque men take off only in bed, in coffin, or when adjudicating the game of *rebot*. No, he did not believe he had ever heard the name. Hel, you say? (He could pronounce the *h* because it is a Basque sound.) Perhaps his wife knew. He would ask. Would the Mademoiselle take something while she waited? She ordered coffee which came, thick, bitter, and often reheated, in a tin pot half the weight of which was tinker's solder, but which leaked nevertheless. The proprietor seemed to regret the leak, but to accept it with heavy fatalism. He hoped the coffee that dripped on her leg had not burned her. It was not hot enough to burn? Good. Good. He disappeared into the back of the café, ostensibly to inquire after M. Hel.

And that had been fifteen minutes ago.

Hannah's eyes dilated painfully as she looked out toward the bright square, deserted save for a litter of cars, mostly *Deu'ches* bearing '64 plates, parked at random angles, wherever their peasant drivers had managed to stop them.

With deafening roar of motor, grinding of gears, and outspewing of filthy exhaust, a German juggernaut lorry painfully navigated the corner with not ten centimeters to spare between vehicle and the *crepi* facades of the buildings. Sweating, cranking the wheel, and hiss-popping his air brakes, the German driver managed to introduce the monster into the ancient square, only to be met by the most formidable of barriers. Waddling side by side down the middle of the street, two Basque women with blank, coarse faces exchanged gossip out of the corners of their mouths. Middle-aged, dour, and vast, they plodded along on great barrel legs, indifferent to the frustration and fury of the truck driver, who crawled behind them muttering earnest imprecations and beating his fist against the steering wheel.

Hannah Stern had no way to appreciate this scene's iconographic representation of Franco-German relations in the Common Market, and at this moment the café owner reappeared, his triangular Basque face abeam with sudden comprehension.

"You are seeking M. Hel!" he told her.

"That's what I said."

"Ah, if I had known it was M. *Hel* you were seeking . . ." He shrugged from the waist, lifting his palms in a gesture implying that a little more clarity on her part would have saved them both a lot of trouble.

He then gave her directions to the Château d'Etchebar: first cross the *gave* from Tardets (the *r* rolled, both the *t* and the *s* pronounced), then pass through the village of Abense-de-Haut (five syllables, the *h* and *t* both pronounced) and on up through Lichans (no nasal, *s* pronounced), then take the right forking up into the hills of Etchebar; but not the left forking, which would carry you to Licq.

"Is it far?"

"No, not all that far. But you don't want to go to Licq, anyway."

"I mean to Etchebar! Is it far to Etchebar!" In her fatigue and nervous tension, the formidable task of getting simple information out of a Basque was becoming too much for Hannah.

"No, not far. Maybe two kilometers after Lichans."

"And how far is it to Lichans?"

He shrugged. "Oh, it could be two kilometers after Abense-de-Haut. You can't miss it. Unless you turn left at the forking. *Then* you'll miss it all right! You'll miss it because you'll be in Licq, don't you see."

The old *mousse* players had forsaken their game and were gathered behind the café owner, intrigued by all the confusion this foreign tourist was causing. They held a brief discussion in Basque, agreeing at last that if the girl took the left forking she would indeed end up in Licq. But then, Licq was not such a bad village. Was there not the famous story of the bridge at Licq built with the help of the Little People from the mountains who then . . .

"Listen!" Hannah pled. "Is there someone who could drive me to the Château of Etchebar?"

A quick conference was held between the café owner and the *mousse* players. There was some argument and a considerable amount of clarification and restatement of positions. Then the proprietor delivered the consensus opinion.

"No."

It had been decided that this foreign girl wearing walking shorts and who had a rucksack was one of the young athletic tourists who were notorious for being friendly, but for tipping very little. Therefore, there was no one who would drive her to Etchebar, except for the oldest of the *mousse* players, who was willing to gamble on her generosity, but sadly he had no car. And anyway, he did not know how to drive.

With a sigh, Hannah took up her rucksack. But when the café owner reminded her of the cup of coffee, she remembered she had no French money. She explained this with expressions of light-hearted contrition, trying to laugh off the ludicrousness of the situation. But he steadfastly stared at the cup of unpaid-for coffee, and remained dolefully silent. The *mousse* players discussed this new turn of events with animation. What? The tourist took coffee without the money to pay for it? It was not impossible that this was a matter for the law.

Finally, the proprietor sighed a rippling sigh and looked up at her, tragedy in his moist eyes. Was she really telling him that she didn't have two francs for the coffee—forget the tip—just two francs for the coffee? There was a matter of principle involved here. After all, *he* paid for his coffee; *he* paid for the gas to heat the water; and every couple of years *he* paid the tinker to mend the pot. He was a man who paid his debts. Unlike some others he could mention.

Hannah was between anger and laughter. She could not believe that all these heavy theatrics were being produced for two francs. (She did not know that the price of a cup of coffee was, in fact, *one* franc.) She had never before met that especially French version of avarice in which money—the coin itself—is the center of all consideration, more important than goods, comfort, dignity. Indeed, more important than real wealth. She had no way to know that, although they bore Basque names, these village people had become thoroughly French under the corrosive cultural pressures of radio, television, and state-controlled education, in which modern history is creatively interpreted to confect that national analgesic, *la vérité à la Cinquième République.*

Dominated by the mentality of the *petit commerçant,* these village Basques shared the Gallic view of gain in which the pleasure of earning a hundred francs is nothing beside the intense suffering caused by the loss of a centime.

Finally realizing that his dumb show of pain and disappointment was not going to extract the two francs from this young girl, the proprietor excused himself with sardonic politeness, telling her he would be right back.

When he returned twenty minutes later, after a tense conference with his wife in the back room, he asked, "You are a friend of M. Hel?"

"Yes," Hannah lied, not wanting to go into all that.

"I see. Well then, I shall assume that Mr. Hel will pay, should you fail to." He tore a sheet from the note pad provided by the Byrrh distributors and wrote something on it before folding it two times, sharpening the creases with his thumbnail. "Please give this to M. Hel," he said coldly.

His eyes no longer flicked to her breast and legs. Some things are more important than romance.

Hannah had been walking for more than an hour, over the Pont d'Abense and the glittering Gave de Saison, then slowly up into the Basque hills along a narrow tar road softened by the sun and confined by ancient stone walls over which lizards scurried at her approach. In the fields sheep grazed, lambs teetering beside the ewes, and russet *vaches de pyrénées* loitered in the shade of unkempt apple trees, watching her pass, their eyes infinitely gentle, infinitely stupid. Round hills lush with fern contained and comforted the narrow valley, and beyond the saddles of the hills rose the snow-tipped mountains, their jagged arêtes sharply traced on the taut blue sky. High above, a hawk balanced on the rim of an updraft, its wing feathers splayed like fingers constantly feeling the wind as it scanned the ground for prey.

The heat stewed a heady medley of aroma: the soprano of wildflower, the mezzotones of cut grass and fresh sheep droppings, the insistent basso profundo of softened tar.

Insulated by fatigue from the sights and smells around her, Hannah plodded along, her head down and her concentration absorbed in watching the toes of her hiking boots. Her mind, recoiling from the sensory overload of the last ten hours, was finding haven in a tunnel-vision of the consciousness. She did not dare to think, to imagine, to remember; because looming out there, just beyond the edges of here-and-now, were visions that would damage her, if she let them in. Don't think. Just walk, and watch the toes of your boots. It is all about getting to the Château d'Etchebar. It is all about contacting Nicholai Hel. There is nothing before or beyond that.

She came to a forking in the road and stopped. To the right, the way rose steeply toward the hilltop village of Etchebar, and beyond the huddle of stone and *crepi* houses she could see the wide mansard facade of what must be the château peeking between tall pine trees and surrounded by a high stone wall.

She sighed deeply and trudged on, her fatigue blending with protective emotional neurasthenia. If she could just make the château . . . Just get to Nicholai Hel . . .

Two peasant women in black dresses paused in their gossip over a low stone wall and watched the outlander girl with open curiosity and mistrust. Where was she going, this hussy showing her legs? Toward the château? Ah well, that explained it. All sorts of strange people go to the château ever since that foreigner bought it! Not that M. Hel was a bad man. Indeed, their husbands had told them he was much admired by the Basque freedom movement. But still . . . he was a newcomer. No use denying it. He had lived in the château only fourteen years, while everyone else in the village (ninety-three souls) could find his name on dozens of gravestones around the church, sometimes newly cut into pyrenean granite, sometimes barely legible on ancient stone scrubbed smooth by five centuries of rain and wind. Look! The hussy has not even bound her breasts! She wants men to look at her, that's what it is! She will have a nameless child if she is not careful! Who would marry her then? She will end up cutting vegetables and scrubbing floors in the household of her sister. And her sister's husband will pester her when he is drunk! And one day, when the sister is too far along with child to be able to do it, this one will succumb to the husband! Probably in the barn. It always happens so. And the sister will find out, and she will drive this one from the house! Where will she go then? She will become a whore in Bayonne, that's what!

A third woman joined the two. Who is that girl showing her legs? We know nothing about her—except that she is a whore from Bayonne. And not even Basque! Do you think she might be a Protestant? Oh no, I wouldn't go that far. Just a poor *putain* who has slept with the husband of her sister. It is what always happens, if you go about with your breasts unbound.

True, true.

As she passed, Hannah looked up and noticed the three women. *"Bonjour, mesdames,"* she said.

"Bonjour, mademoiselle," they chanted together, smiling in the open Basque way. "You are giving yourself a walk?" one asked.

"Yes, Madame."

"That's nice. You are lucky to have the leisure."

An elbow nudged, and was nudged back. It was daring and clever to come so close to saying it.

"You are looking for the château, Mademoiselle?"

"Yes, I am."

"Just keep going as you are, and you will find what you're looking for."

A nudge; another nudge. It was dangerous, but deliciously witty, to come so close to saying it.

Hannah stood before the heavy iron gates. There was no one in sight, and there did not seem to be any way of ringing or knocking. The château was set back a hundred meters, up a long curving allée of trees. Uncertain, she decided to try one of the smaller gates down the road, when a voice behind her asked in a singsong, "Mademoiselle?"

She returned to the gate where an old gardener in blue working apron was peering out from the other side of the barrier. "I am looking for M. Hel," she explained.

"Yes," the gardener said, with that inhaled *"oui"* that can mean almost anything, except yes. He told her to wait there, and he disappeared into the curving row of trees. A minute later she heard the hinges creak on one of the side gates, and he beckoned her with a rolling arm and a deep bow that almost cost him his balance. As she passed him, she realized that he was half-drunk. In fact, Pierre was never drunk. Also, he was never sober. The regular spacing of his daily twelve glasses of red protected him from either of those excesses.

Pierre pointed the way, but did not accompany her to the house; he returned to trimming the box hedges that formed a labyrinth. He never worked in haste, and he never avoided work, his day punctuated, refreshed, and blurred by his glass of red every half hour or so.

Hannah could hear the clip-clip-clip of his shears, the sound receding as she walked up the allée between tall blue-green cedars, the drooping branches of which wept and undulated, brushing the shadows with long kelplike sweeps. A susurrant wind hissed high in the trees like tide over sand, and the dense shade was chill. She shivered. She was dizzy after the long hot walk, having taken nothing but coffee all day long. Her emotions had been frozen by fear, then melted by despair. Frozen, then melted. Her hold on reality was slipping.

When she reached the foot of a double rank of marble steps ascending to the terraces, she stopped, uncertain which way to go.

"May I help you?" a woman's voice asked from above.

Hannah shaded her eyes and looked up toward the sunny terrace. "Hello. I am Hannah Stern."

"Well, come up, Hannah Stern." With the sunlight behind the woman, Hannah could not see her features, but from her dress and manner she seemed to be Oriental, although her voice, soft and modulated, belied the twittering stereotype of feminine Oriental speech. "We have one of those coincidences that are supposed to bring luck. My name is Hana—almost the same as yours. In Japanese, *hana* means flower. What does your Hannah mean? Perhaps, like so many Western names, it means nothing. How delightful of you to come just in time for tea."

They shook hands in the French fashion, and Hannah was struck by the calm beauty of this woman, whose eyes seemed to regard her with a mixture of kindness and humor, and whose manner made Hannah feel oddly protected and at ease. As they walked together across the broad flagstone terrace toward the house with its classic facade of four porte-fenêtres flanking the main entrance, the woman selected the best bloom from the flowers she had been cutting and offered it to Hannah with a gesture as natural as it was pleasant. "I must put these in water," she said. "Then we shall take our tea. You are a friend of Nicholai?"

"No, not really. My uncle was a friend of his."

"And you are looking him up in passing. How thoughtful of you." She opened the glass doors to a sunny reception room in the middle of which tea things were laid out on a low table before a marble fireplace with a brass screen. A door on the other side of the room clicked closed just as they entered. During the few days she was to spend at the Château d'Etchebar, all Hannah would ever see or hear of staff and servants would be doors that closed as she entered, or soft tiptoeing at the end of the hall, or the appearance of coffee or flowers on a bedside table. Meals were prepared in such a way that the mistress of the house could do the serving herself. It was an opportunity for her to show kindness and concern.

"Just leave your rucksack there in the corner, Hannah," the woman said. "And would you be so good as to pour, while I arrange these flowers?"

With sunlight flooding in through the French windows, walls of light blue, moldings of gold leaf, furniture blending Louis XV and oriental inlays, threads of gray vapor twisting up from the teapot through a shaft of sunlight, mirrors everywhere lightening, reflecting, doubling and tripling everything; this room was not in the same world as that in which young men are shot down in airports. As she poured from a silver teapot into Limoges with a vaguely Chinese feeling, Hannah was overwhelmed by reality vertigo. Too much had happened in these last hours. She was afraid she was going to faint.

For no reason, she remembered feelings of dislocation like this when she was a child in school . . . it was summer, and she was bored, and there was the drone of study all around her. She had stared until objects became big/little. And she had asked herself, "Am I me? Am I here? Is this really me thinking these thoughts? Me? Me?"

And now, as she watched the graceful, economical movements of this slender Oriental woman stepping back to criticize the flower arrangement, then making a slight correction, Hannah tried desperately to find anchorage against the tide of confusion and fatigue that was tugging her away.

That's odd, she thought. Of all that had happened that day: the horrible things in the airport, the dreamlike flight to Pau, the babbling suggestive talk of the drivers she had gotten rides from, that fool of a café owner in Tardets, the long walk up the shimmering road to Etchebar . . . of all of it, the most profound image was her walk up the cedar-lined allée in subaqueous shadow . . . shivering in the dense shadow as the wind made sea sounds in the trees. It was another world. And odd.

Was it possible that she was sitting here, pouring tea into Limoges, probably looking quite the buffoon with her tight hiking shorts and clumsy, Vibram-cleated boots?

Was it just a few hours ago she had walked dazedly past the old man sitting on the floor of Rome International? "I'm sorry," she had muttered to him stupidly.

"I'm sorry," she said now, aloud. The beautiful woman had said something which had not penetrated the layers of thought and retreat.

The woman smiled as she sat beside her. "I was just saying it is a pity that Nicholai is not here. He's been up in the mountains for several days, crawling about in those caves of his. Appalling hobby. But I expect him back this evening or tomorrow morning. And that will give you a chance to bathe and perhaps sleep a little. That would be nice, wouldn't it."

The thought of a hot bath and cool sheets was almost swooningly seductive to Hannah.

The woman smiled and drew her chair closer to the marble tea table. "How do you take your tea?" Her eyes were calm and frank. In shape, they were Oriental, but their color was hazel, semé of gold flecks. Hannah could not have guessed her race. Surely her movements were Eastern, fine and controlled; but her skin tone was café au lait, and the body within its high-collared Chinese dress of green silk had a distinctly African development of breast and buttocks. Her mouth and nose, however, were Caucasian. And her voice was cultured, low and modulated, as was her laugh when she said, "Yes, I know. It is confusing."

"Pardon me?" Hannah said, embarrassed at having her thoughts read so transparently.

"I am what the kindly disposed call a 'cosmopolitan,' and others might term a mongrel. My mother was Japanese, and it would appear that my father was a mulatto American soldier. I never had the good fortune to meet him. Do you take milk?"

"What?"

"In your tea." Hana smiled. "Are you more comfortable in English?" she asked in that language.

"Yes, in fact I am," Hannah admitted also in English, but with an American tonality.

"I assumed as much from your accent. Good then. We shall speak in English. Nicholai seldom speaks English in the house, and I fear I am getting rusty." She had, in fact, a just-perceptible accent; not a mispronunciation, but a slightly mechanical over-enunciation of her British English. It was possible that her French also bore traces of accent, but Hannah, with her alien ear, could not know that.

But something else did occur to her. "There are two cups set out. Were you expecting me, Mrs. Hel?"

"Do call me Hana. Oh, yes, I was expecting you. The man from the café in Tardets telephoned for permission to give you directions. And I received another call when you passed through Abense-de-Haut, and another when you reached Lichans." Hana laughed lightly. "Nicholai is very well protected here. You see, he has no great affection for surprises."

"Oh, that reminds me. I have a note for you." Hannah took from her pocket the folded note the café proprietor had given her.

Hana opened and glanced at it, then she laughed in her low, minor-key voice. "It is a bill. And very neatly itemized, too. Ah, these French. One franc for the telephone call. One franc for your coffee. And an additional one franc fifty—an estimate of the tip you would have left. My goodness, we have made a good bargain! We have the pleasure of your company for only three francs fifty." She laughed and set the bill aside. Then she reached across and placed her warm, dry hand upon Hannah's arm. "Young lady? I don't think you realize that you are crying."

"What?" Hannah put her hand to her cheek. It was wet with tears. My God, how long had she been crying? "I'm sorry. It's just . . . This morning my friends were . . . I *must* see Mr. Hel!"

"I know, dear. I know. Now finish your tea. There is something in it to make you rest. Then I will show you up to your room, where you can bathe and sleep. And you will be fresh and beautiful when you meet Nicholai. Just leave your rucksack here. One of the girls will see to it."

"I should explain—"

But Hana raised her hand. "You explain things to Nicholai when he comes. And he will tell me what he wants me to know."

Hannah was still sniffling and feeling like a child as she followed Hana up the wide marble staircase that dominated the entrance hall. But she could feel a delicious peace spreading within her. Whatever was in the tea was softening the crust of her memories and floating them off to a distance. "You're being very kind to me, Mrs. Hel," she said sincerely.

Hana laughed softly. "Do call me Hana. After all, I am not Nicholai's wife. I am his concubine."

Washington

THE ELEVATOR DOOR opened silently, and Diamond preceded Miss Swivven into the white workspace of the Sixteenth Floor.

". . . and I'll want them available within ten minutes after call: Starr, the Deputy, and that Arab. Do you have that?"

"Yes, sir." Miss Swivven went immediately to her cubicle to make the necessary arrangements, while the First Assistant rose from his console.

"I have the scan of Asa Stern's first-generation contacts, sir. It's coming in now." He felt a justifiable pride. There were not ten men alive who had the skill to pull a list based upon amorphous emotional relationships out of Fat Boy.

"Give me a desk RP on it," Diamond ordered as he sat in his swivel chair at the head of the conference table.

"Coming up. Oops! Just a second, sir. The list is one-hundred-eighty percent inverted. It will only take a moment to flip it."

It was typical of the computer's systemic inability to distinguish between love and hate, affection and blackmail, friendship and parasitism, that any list organized in terms of such emotional rubrics stood a 50/50 chance of coming in inverted. The First Assistant had foreseen this danger and had seeded the raw list with the names of Maurice Herzog and Heinrich Himmler (both H's). When the printout showed Himmler to be greatly admired by Asa Stern, and Herzog to be detested, the First Assistant dared the assumption that Fat Boy had done a 180.

"It's not just a naked list, is it?" Diamond asked.

"No, sir. I've requested pinhole data. Just the most salient facts attached to each name, so we can make useful identification."

"You're a goddamned genius, Llewellyn."

The First Assistant nodded in absentminded agreement as he watched the list crawl up his screen in sans-serif IBM lettering.

STERN, DAVID
    RELATIONSHIP EQUALS SON . . . WHITE CARD . . . STUDENT, AMATEUR ATHLETE . . . KILLED, 1972 sub MUNICH OLYMPICS . . .
STERN, JUDITH
    RELATIONSHIP EQUALS WIFE . . . PINK CARD . . . SCHOLAR, RESEARCHER . . .
    DEAD, 1956 sub NATURAL CAUSES . . .
ROTHMANN, MOISHE
    RELATIONSHIP EQUALS FRIEND . . . WHITE CARD . . .
PHILOSOPHER, POET . . . DEAD, 1958 sub NATURAL CAUSES . . .
KAUFMANN, S.L.
    RELATIONSHIP EQUALS FRIEND . . . RED CARD . . . POLITICAL ACTIVIST . . . RETIRED . . .
    HEL, NICHOLAI ALEXANDROVITCH
    RELATIONSHIP EQUALS FRIEND . . .

"Stop!" Diamond ordered. "Freeze that!"

The First Assistant scanned the next fragments of information. "Oh, my goodness!"

Diamond leaned back in his chair and closed his eyes. When CIA screws up, they certainly do it in style! "Nicholai Hel," Diamond pronounced, his voice a monotone.

"Sir?" the First Assistant said softly, recalling the ancient practice of executing the messenger who brings bad news. "This Nicholai Hel is identified with a *mauve* card."

"I know . . . I know."

"Ah . . . I suppose you'll want a complete pull and printout on Hel, Nicholai Alexandrovitch?" the First Assistant asked, almost apologetically.

"Yes." Diamond rose and walked to the big window beyond which the illuminated Washington Monument stood out against the night sky, while double rows of automobile headlights crawled down the long avenue toward the Center—the same automobiles that were always at the same place at this time every evening. "You'll find the pull surprisingly thin."

"Thin, sir? On a mauve card?"

"On *this* mauve card, yes."

Within the color-coding system, mauve punch cards indicated the most elusive and dangerous of men, from the Mother Company's point of view: Those who operated without reference to nationalistic or ideological prejudices, free-lance agents and assassins who could not be controlled through pressure upon governments; those who killed for either side.

Originally, color-coding of punch cards was introduced into Fat Boy for the purpose of making immediately evident certain bold characteristics of a subject's life and work. But from the very first, Fat Boy's systemic inability to deal with abstractions and shadings reduced the value of the system. The problem lay in the fact that Fat Boy was permitted to color-code himself, in terms of certain input principles.

The first of these principles was that only such people as constituted real or potential threats to the Mother Company and the governments She controlled would be represented by color-coded cards, all others being identified by standard white cards. Another principle was that there be a symbolic relationship between the color of the card and the nature of the subject's affiliations. This worked well enough in its simplest forms: Leftist agitators and terrorists were represented by red cards; Rightist politicians and activists received blue cards; sympathizers of the Left had pink cards; abettors of ultra-conservatives had powder blue. (For a brief time, devoted Liberals were assigned yellow cards, in concurrence with British political symbolism, but when the potential for effective action by Liberals was assessed by Fat Boy, they were reassigned white cards indicating political impotence.)

The value of color-coding came under criticism when the system was applied to more intricate problems. For instance, active supporters of the Provisional IRA and of the various Ulster defense organizations were randomly assigned green or orange cards, because Fat Boy's review of the tactics, philosophy, and effectiveness of the two groups made them indistinguishable from one another.

Another major problem arose from Fat Boy's mindless pursuit of logic in assigning colors. To differentiate between Chinese and European communist agents, the Chinese were assigned yellow cards; and the Europeans under their domination received a mixture of red and yellow, which produced for them orange cards, identical with those of the North Irish. Such random practices led to some troublesome errors, not the least of which was Fat Boy's longstanding assumption that Ian Paisley was an Albanian.

The most dramatic error concerned African nationalists and American Black Power actives. With a certain racial logic, these subjects were assigned black cards. For several months these men were able to operate without observation or interference from the Mother Company and her governmental subsidiaries, for the simple reason that black print on black cards is rather difficult to read.

With considerable regret, it was decided to end the color-code method, despite the millions of dollars of American taxpayers' money that had been devoted to the project.

But it is easier to introduce a system into Fat Boy than to cleanse it out, since His memory is eternal and His insistence on linear logic implacable. Therefore, color-coding remained in its vestigial form. Agents of the left were still identified with red and pink; while crypto-fascists, such as KKK members, were identified with blue, and American Legionnaires with powder blue. Logically enough, subjects who worked indifferently for both sides were identified with purple, but Fat Boy remembered His problem with Black Power actives, and so he gray'd the purple down to mauve.

Further, Fat Boy reserved the mauve card for men who dealt specifically in assassination.

The First Assistant looked up quizzically from his console. "Ah . . . I don't know what's wrong, sir. Fat Boy is running statement/correction/statement/correction patterns. On even the most basic information, his various input sources disagree. We have ages for this Nicholai Hel ranging from forty-seven to fifty-two. And look at this! Under nationality we have a choice among Russian, German, Chinese, Japanese, French, and Costa Rican. Costa Rican, sir?"

"Those last two have to do with his passports; he holds passports from France and Costa Rica. Right now he lives in France—or he did recently. The other nationalities have to do with his genetic background, his place of birth, and his major cultural inputs."

"So what is his real nationality?"

Mr. Diamond continued to look out the window, staring at nothing. "None."

"You seem to know something about this person, sir." The First Assistant's tone was interrogative but tentative. He was curious, but he knew better than to be inquisitive.

For several moments, Diamond did not answer. Then: "Yes. I know something about him." He turned away from the window and sat heavily at his desk. "Get on with the search. Turn up everything you can. Most of it will be contradictory, vague, or inaccurate, but we need to know everything we can discover."

"Then you feel that this Nicholai Hel is involved in this business?"

"With our luck? Probably."

"In what way, sir?"

"I don't know! Just get on with the search!"

"Yes, sir." The First Assistant scanned the next fragments of data. "Ah . . . sir? We have three possible birthplaces for him."

"Shanghai."

"You're sure of that, sir?"

"Yes!" Then, after a moment's pause, "Reasonably sure, that is."

Shanghai: 193?

As ALWAYS AT this season, cool evening breezes are drawn over the city from the sea, toward the warm land mass of China; and the draperies billow out from the glass doors to the veranda of the large house on Avenue Joffre in the French Concession.

General Kishikawa Takashi withdraws a stone from his lacquered *Gō ke* and holds it lightly between the tip of his middle finger and the nail of his index. Some minutes pass in silence, but his concentration is not on the game, which is in its 176th gesture and has begun to concrete toward the inevitable. The General's eyes rest on his opponent who, for his part, is completely absorbed in the patterns of black and white stones on the pale yellow board. Kishikawa-san has decided that the young boy must be sent away to Japan, and tonight he would have to be told. But not just now. It would spoil the flavor of the game; and that would be unkind because, for the first time, the young man is winning.

The sun has set behind the French Concession, over mainland China. Lanterns have been lighted in the old walled city, and the smell of thousands of cooking suppers fills the narrow, tangled streets. Along the Whangpoo and up Soochow Creek, the sampan homes of the floating city are alive with dim lights, as old women with trousers tied at the ankle arrange stones to level cooking fires on the canted decks, for the river is at low tide and the sampans have heeled over, their wooden bellies stuck in the yellow mud. People late for their suppers trot over Stealing Hen Bridge. A professional letter writer flourishes his brush carelessly, eager to finish his day's work, and knowing that his calligraphic insouciance will not be discovered by the illiterate young girl for whom he is composing a love letter on the model of one of his Sixteen Never-Fail Formulas. The Bund, that street of imposing commercial houses and hotels, gaudy statement of imperial might and confidence, is silent and dark; for the British taipans have fled; the *North China Daily News* no longer prints its gossip, its pious reprimands, its complaisant affirmations of the world situation. Even Sasson House, the most elegant facade on the Bund, built on profits from the opium trade, has been demoted to the mundane task of housing the Headquarters of the Occupation Forces. The greedy French, the swaggering British, the pompous

Germans, the opportunistic Americans are all gone. Shanghai is under the control of the Japanese.

General Kishikawa reflects on the uncanny resemblance between this young man across the Gō board and his mother: almost as though Alexandra Ivanovna had produced her son parthenogenetically—a feat those who had experienced her overwhelming social presence would consider well within her capacity. The young man has the same angular line of jaw, the same broad forehead and high cheekbones, the fine nose that is spared the Slavic curse of causing interlocutors to feel they are staring into the barrels of a shotgun. But most intriguing to Kishikawa-san are comparisons between the boy's eyes and the mother's. Comparisons and contrasts. Physically, their eyes are identical: large, deep-set, and of that startling bottle-green color unique to the Countess's family. But the polar differences in personality between mother and son are manifest in the articulation and intensity of gaze, in the dimming and crystallizing of those sinople eyes. While the mother's glance was bewitching, the son's is cool. Where the mother used her eyes to fascinate, the boy uses his to dismiss. What in her look was coquetry, in his is arrogance. The light that shone from her eyes is still and internal in his. Her eyes expressed humor; his express wit. She charmed; he disturbs.

Alexandra Ivanovna was an egotist; Nicholai is an egoist.

Although the General's Oriental frame of reference does not remark it, by Western criteria Nicholai looks very young for his fifteen years. Only the frigidity of his too-green eyes and a certain firm set of mouth keep his face from being too delicate, too finely formed for a male. A vague discomfort over his physical beauty prompted Nicholai from an early age to engage in the most vigorous and combative of sports. He trained in classic, rather old-fashioned jiujitsu, and he played rugby with the international side against the sons of the British taipans with an effectiveness that bordered on brutality. Although Nicholai understood the stiff charade of fair play and sportsmanship with which the British protect themselves from real defeat, he preferred the responsibilities of victory to the comforts of losing with grace. But he did not really like team sports, preferring to win or lose by virtue of his own skill and toughness. And his emotional toughness was such that he almost always won, as a matter of will.

Alexandra Ivanovna almost always won too, not as a matter of will, but as a matter of right. When she appeared in Shanghai in the autumn of 1922 with an astonishing amount of baggage and no visible means of support, she relied upon her previous social position in St. Petersburg to grant her leadership in the growing community of displaced White Russians—so called by the ruling British, not because they came from Belorosskiya, but because they were obviously not "red." She immediately created about her an admiring court that included the most interesting men of the colony. To be interesting to Alexandra Ivanovna, one had to be rich, handsome, or witty; and it was the major annoyance of her life that she seldom found two of these qualities in one man, and never all three.

There were no other women near the core of her society; the Countess found women dull and, in her opinion, superfluous, as she could fully occupy the minds and attentions of a dozen men at one time, keeping a soirée atmosphere witty, brisk, and just naughty enough.

In retaliation, the unwanted ladies of the International Settlement declared that nothing in this world could tempt them to be seen in public with the Countess, and they fervently wished their husbands and fiancées shared their fine sense of propriety. By shrugs and hums and pursings of lips, these peripheral ladies made it known that they suspected a causal relationship between two social paradoxes: the first being that the Countess maintained a lavish household although she had arrived penniless; and the second being that she was constantly surrounded by the most desirable men of the international community, despite the fact that she lacked all those sterner virtues the ladies had been assured by their mothers were more important and durable than mere charm and beauty. These women would have been glad to include the Countess within that body of White Russian women who trickled into China from Manchuria, sold what pitiful goods and jewelry they had managed to escape with, and finally were driven to sustain themselves by vending the comfort of their laps. But these arid, righteous women were denied that facile dismissal by the knowledge that the Countess was one of those not uncommon anomalies of the Tzarist court, a Russian noblewoman without a drop of Slavic blood in her all-too-visible (and possibly available) body. Alexandra Ivanovna (whose father's given name had been Johann) was a Hapsburg with connections to a minor German royal family that had immigrated to England with nothing but their Protestantism to recommend them, and which had recently changed its name to one of less Hunnish sound as a gesture of patriotism. Still, the proper ladies of the settlement averred that even such deep quarterings were not proof of moral rectitude in those Flapper days; nor, despite the Countess's apparent assumption, an adequate substitute for it.

During the third season of her reign, Alexandra Ivanovna appeared to settle her attentions upon a vain young Prussian who possessed that pellucid, superficial intelligence untrammelled by sensitivity that is common to his race. Count Helmut von Keitel zum Hel became her companion of record—her pet and toy. Ten years younger than she, the Count possessed great physical beauty and athletic prowess. He was an expert horseman and a fencer of note. She thought of him as a decorative setting for her, and the only public statement she ever made concerning their relationship was to speak of him as "adequate breeding stock."

It was her practice to pass the heavy, humid months of summer in a villa in the uplands. One autumn she returned later than usual to Shanghai, and thenceforward there was a baby boy in the household. As a matter of form, young von Keitel zum Hel proposed marriage. She laughed lightly and told him that, while it had been her intention all along to create a child as a living argument against mongrel egalitarianism, she did not feel the slightest impulse to have *two* children about the house. He bowed with the rigid petulance that serves Prussians as a substitute for dignity, and made arrangements to return to Germany within the month.

Far from concealing the boy or the circumstances of his birth, she made him the ornament of her salon. When official requirements made it necessary that she name him, she called him Nicholai Hel, taking the last name from a little river bordering the Keitel estate. Alexandra Ivanovna's view of her own role in the production of the lad was manifest in the fact that his full name was Nicholai Alexandrovitch Hel.

A series of English nannies followed one another through the household, so English joined French, Russian, and German as the languages of the crib, with no particular preference shown, save for Alexandra Ivanovna's conviction that certain languages were best for expressing certain classes of thought. One spoke of love and other trivia in French; one discussed tragedy and disaster in Russian; one did business in German; and one addressed servants in English.

Because the children of the servants were his only companions, Chinese was also a cradle language for Nicholai, and he developed the habit of thinking in that language because his greatest childhood dread was that his mother could read his thoughts—and she had no Chinese.

Alexandra Ivanovna considered schools appropriate only for merchants' children, so Nicholai's education was confided to a succession of tutors, all decorative young men, all devoted to the mother. When it developed that Nicholai displayed an interest in, and a considerable capacity for, pure mathematics, his mother was not at all pleased. But when she was assured by the tutor of the moment that pure mathematics was a study without practical or commercial application, she decided it was appropriate to his breeding.

The more practical aspects of Nicholai's social education—and all of his fun—came from his practice of sneaking away from the house and wandering with street urchins through the narrow alleys and hidden courtyards of the seething, noisome, noisy city. Dressed in the universal loose-fitting blue, his close-cropped hair under a round cap, he would roam alone or with friends of the hour and return home to admonitions or punishments, both of which he accepted with great calm and an infuriating elsewhere gaze in his bottle-green eyes.

In the streets, Nicholai learned the melody of this city the Westerners had confected for themselves. He saw supercilious young British "griffins" being pulled about by cadaverous rickshaw "boys" cachectic with tuberculosis, sweating with effort and malnutrition, wearing gauze masks to avoid offending the European masters. He saw the compradores, fat and buttery middlemen who profited from the Europeans' exploitation of their own people, and who aped Western ways and ethics. After making profit and gorging on exotic foods, the greatest pleasure of these compradores was to arrange to deflower twelve- or thirteen-year-old girls who had been bought in Hangchow or Soochow and who were ready to enter the brothels licensed by the French. Their tactics of defloration were . . . irregular. The only revenge the girl might have was, if she had a gift for theatrics, the profitable ploy of being deflowered rather often. Nicholai learned that all of the beggars who threatened passers-by with contact with their rotting limbs, or stuck pins into babies to make them cry pitifully, or mobbed and frightened tourists with their demands for *kumshah*—all of them, from the old men who prayed for you or cursed you, to the half-starved children who offered to perform unnatural acts with one another for your entertainment, were under the control of His Heinous Majesty, the King of Beggars, who ran a peculiar combination of guild and protection racket. Anything lost in the city, anyone hiding in the city, any service wanted in the city, could be found through a modest contribution to His Majesty's treasury.

Down at the docks, Nicholai watched sweating stevedores dogtrot up and down the gangplanks of metal ships and wooden junks with strabismic eyes painted on their prows. In the evening, after they had already worked eleven hours, chanting their constant, narcotizing *hai-yo, hai-yo* the stevedores would begin to weaken, and sometimes one would stumble under his load. Then the Gurkhas would wade in with their blackjacks and iron bars, and the lazy would find new strength . . . or lasting rest.

Nicholai watched the police openly accept "squeeze money" from withered amahs who pimped for teenaged prostitutes. He learned to recognize the secret signs of the "Greens" and the "Reds," who constituted the world's largest secret societies, and whose protection and assassination rackets extended from beggars to politicians. Chiang Kai-shek himself was a "Green," sworn to obedience to the gang. And it was the "Greens" who murdered and mutilated young university students who attempted to organize the Chinese proletariat. Nicholai could tell a "Red" from a "Green" by the way he held his cigarette, by the way he spat.

During the days, Nicholai learned from tutors: Mathematics, Classical Literature, and Philosophy. In the evenings, he learned from the streets: Commerce, Politics, Enlightened Imperialism, and the Humanities.

And at night he would sit beside his mother as she entertained the cleverest of the men who controlled Shanghai and wrung it dry from their clubs and commercial houses of the Bund. What the majority of these men thought was shyness in Nicholai, and what the brightest of them thought was aloofness, was in fact cold hatred for merchants and the merchant mentality.

Time passed; Alexandra Ivanovna's carefully placed and expertly guided investments flourished, while the rhythms of her social life slowed. She became more comfortable of body, more languid, more lush; but her vivacity and beauty ripened, rather than waned, for she had inherited that family trait that had kept her mother and aunts looking vaguely thirtyish long after they passed the half-century mark. Former lovers became old friends, and life on Avenue Joffre mellowed.

Alexandra Ivanovna began to have little fainting spells, but she did not concern herself over them, beyond accepting the well-timed swoon as essential to the amorous arsenal of any lady of blood. When a doctor of her circle who had for years been eager to examine her ascribed the spells to a weak heart, she made a nominal accommodation to what she conceived to be a physical nuisance by reducing her at-homes to one a week, but beyond that she gave her body no quarter.

". . . and they tell me, young man, that I have a weak heart. It's an essentially romantic failing, and you must promise not to take advantage of it too frequently. You must also promise to seek out a responsible tailor. That suit, my boy!"

On the seventh of July, 1937, the *North China Daily News* reported that shots had been exchanged between Japanese and Chinese at the Marco Polo bridge near Peking. Down at number Three, the Bund, British taipans lounging about in the Shanghai Club agreed that this latest development in the pointless struggle between Orientals might get out of hand, if not dealt with briskly. They made it known to Generalissimo Chiang Kai-shek that they would prefer him to rush north and engage the Japanese along a front that would shield their commercial houses from the damned nuisance of war.

The Generalissimo decided, however, to await the Japanese at Shanghai in the hope that putting the International Settlement in jeopardy would attract foreign intervention on his behalf.

When that did not work, he began a systematic harassment of Japanese companies and civilians in the international community that culminated when, at six-thirty in the evening of August 9, Sub-Lieutenant Isao Oyama and his driver, first-class seaman Yozo Saito, who were driving to inspect Japanese cotton mills outside the city, were stopped by Chinese soldiers.

They were found beside Monument Road, riddled with bullets and sexually mutilated.

In response, Japanese warships moved up the Whangpoo. A thousand Japanese sailors were landed to protect their commercial colony at Chapei, across Soochow creek. They were faced by 10,000 elite Chinese soldiers dug in behind barricades.

The outcry of the comfortable British taipans was reinforced by messages sent by European and American ambassadors to Nanking and Tokyo demanding that Shanghai be excluded from the zone of hostilities. The Japanese agreed to this request, provided that Chinese forces also withdraw from the demilitarized zone.

But on August 12, the Chinese cut all telephone lines to the Japanese Consulate and to Japanese commercial firms. The next day, Friday 13, the Chinese 88th Division arrived at North Station and blocked all roads leading out of the settlement. It was their intention to bottle up as large a buffer of civilians as possible between themselves and the vastly outnumbered Japanese.

On August 14, Chinese pilots in American-built Northrops flew over Shanghai. One high explosive bomb crashed through the roof of the Palace Hotel; another exploded in the street outside the Café Hotel. Seven hundred twenty-nine people dead; eight hundred sixty-one wounded. Thirty-one minutes later another Chinese plane bombed The Great World Amusement Park which had been converted into a refugee camp for women and children. One thousand twelve dead; one thousand seven wounded.

For the trapped Chinese there was no escape from Shanghai; the Generalissimo's troops had closed all the roads. For the foreign taipans, however, there was always escape. Sweating coolies grunted and chanted *hai-yo, hai-yo* as they struggled up gangplanks, carrying the loot of China under the supervision of white-suited young griffins with their checklists, and Gurkhas with their blackjacks. The British on the *Raj Putana,* Germans on the *Oldenburg,* Americans on the *President McKinley,* Dutchmen on the *Tasman* said goodbye to one another, the women daubing at eyes with tiny handkerchiefs, the men exchanging diatribes against the unreliable and ungrateful Orientals, as in the background ships' bands played a gallimaufry of national anthems.

That night, from behind its barricades of sandbags and trapped Chinese civilians, Chiang Kai-shek's artillery opened up on the Japanese ships at anchor in the river. The Japanese returned fire, destroying barricades of both kinds.

Through all of this, Alexandra Ivanovna refused to leave her home on Avenue Joffre, now a deserted street, its shattered windows open to evening breezes and looters. As she was of no nationality, neither Soviet nor Chinese nor British, she was outside formal systems of protection. At any event, she had no intention at her age of leaving her home and carefully collected furnishings to reestablish herself God knows where. After all, she reasoned, the Japanese whom she knew were no duller than the rest, and they could hardly be less efficient administrators than the English had been.

The Chinese made their firmest stand of the war at Shanghai; it was three months before the outnumbered Japanese could drive them out. In their attempts to attract foreign intervention, the Chinese permitted a number of bombing "mistakes" to add to the toll in human lives and physical destruction caused by Japanese shelling.

And they maintained their barricades across the roads, keeping in place the protective buffer of tens of thousands of civilians . . . their own countrymen.

Throughout those terrible months, the resilient Chinese of Shanghai continued to go about their daily lives as best they could, despite the shelling from the Japanese and the bombings from American-made Chinese planes. Medicine, then food, then shelter, and finally water became scarce; but life went on in the teeming, frightened city; and the bands of boys clad in blue cotton with whom Nicholai roamed the streets found new, if grim, games involving the toppling ruins of buildings, desperate scrambles for make-shift air raid shelters, and playing in geysers from broken water mains.

Only once did Nicholai have a brush with death. He was with other street urchins in the district of the great department stores, the Wing On and The Sincere, when one of the common "mistakes" brought Chinese dive-bombers over densely packed Nanking Road. It was the lunch hour, and the crowds were thick when The Sincere received a direct hit, and one side of the Wing On was sheared away. Ornate ceilings caved in upon the faces of people staring up in horror. The occupants of a crowded elevator screamed in one voice as the cable was cut, and it plunged to the basement. An old woman who had been facing an exploding window was stripped of flesh in front, while from behind she seemed untouched. The old, the lame, and children were crushed under foot by those who stampeded in panic. The boy who had been standing next to Nicholai grunted and sat down heavily in the middle of the street. He was dead; a chip of stone had gone through his chest. As the thunder of bombs and the war of collapsing masonry ebbed, there emerged through it the high-pitched scream from thousands of voices. A stunned shopper whimpered as she searched through shards of glass that had been a display counter. She was an exquisite young woman clothed in the Western "Shanghai" mode, an ankle-length dress of green silk slit to above the knee, and a stiff little collar standing around her curved, porcelain neck. Her extreme pallor might have come from the pale rice powders fashionable with the daughters of rich Chinese merchants, but it did not. She was searching for the ivory figurine she had been examining at the moment of the bombing, and for the hand in which she had been holding it.

Nicholai ran away.

A quarter of an hour later, he was sitting on a rubble heap in a quiet district where weeks of bombing had left blocks of empty and toppling shells. Dry sobs racked his body and seared his lungs, but he did not cry; no tears streaked the plaster dust that coated his face. In his mind, he repeated again and again: "Northrop bombers. American bombers."

When at last the Chinese soldiers were driven out, and their barricades broken, thousands of civilians fled the nightmare city of bombed-out buildings on the interior walls of which could be seen the checkerboard patterns of gutted apartments. In the rubble: a torn calendar with a date encircled, a charred photograph of a young woman, a suicide note and a lottery ticket in the same envelope.

By a cruel perversity of fate, the Bund, monument to foreign imperialism, was relatively unscathed. Its empty windows stared out over the desolation of the city the taipans had created, drained, then deserted.

Nicholai was among the small gaggle of blue-clad Chinese children who lined the streets to watch the first parade of Japanese occupation troops. Army news photographers had passed out pieces of sticky candy and small *hinomaru* rising-sun flags, which the children were ordered to wave as the motion picture cameras recorded their bewildered enthusiasm. An officious young officer conducted the event, adding greatly to the confusion with his barked instructions in heavily accented Chinese. Uncertain of what to make of an urchin with blond hair and green eyes, he ordered Nicholai to the back of the crowd.

Nicholai had never seen soldiers like these, rough and efficient, but certainly no parade-ground models. They did not march with the robot synchronization of the German or the British; they passed in clean but rumpled ranks, marching jerkily behind serious young officers with moustaches and comically long swords.

Despite the fact that rather few dwellings were intact in the residential areas when the Japanese entered the city, Alexandra Ivanovna was surprised and annoyed when a staff car, little flags fluttering from its fenders, arrived in her driveway and a junior officer announced in a metallic French that General Kishikawa Takashi, governor of Shanghai, was to be billeted upon her. But her vivid instinct for self-preservation persuaded her that there might be some advantage to cultivating friendly relations with the General, particularly as so many of the good things of life were in short supply. Not for an instant did she doubt that this General would automatically enlist himself among her admirers.

She was mistaken. The General took time from a busy schedule to explain to her in a curiously accented but grammatically flawless French that he regretted any inconvenience the necessities of war might bring to her household. But he made it clear that she was a guest in his house, not he in hers. Always correct in his attitude toward her, the General was too occupied with his work to waste time on flirtations. At first Alexandra Ivanovna was puzzled, later annoyed, and finally intrigued by this man's polite indifference, a response she had never inspired from a heterosexual man. For his part, he found her interesting, but unnecessary. And he was not particularly impressed by the heritage that had made even the haughty women of Shanghai stand in reluctant awe. From the point of view of his thousand years of samurai breeding, her lineage appeared to be only a couple of centuries of Hunnish chieftainship.

Nevertheless, as a matter of politeness, he arranged weekly suppers, taken in the Western style, during the light conversation of which he learned a great deal about the Countess and her withdrawn, self-contained son; while they learned very little about the General. He was in his late fifties—young for a Japanese general—and a widower with one daughter living in Tokyo. Although an intensely patriotic man in the sense that he loved the physical things of his country—the lakes, mountains, misted valleys—he had never viewed his army career as the natural fulfillment of his personality. As a young man, he had dreamed of being a writer, although in his heart he had always known that the traditions of his family would ultimately conduct him into a military career. Pride in self and devotion to duty made him a hard-working and conscientious administrative officer but, although he had passed more than half his life in the army, his habits of mind caused him to think of the military as an avocation. His mind, not his heart; his time, not his passions, were given to his work.

In result of unstinting effort that often kept the General in his office on the Bund from early morning until midnight, the city began to recover. Public services were restored, the factories were repaired, and Chinese peasants began to trickle back into the city. Life and noise slowly returned to the streets, and occasionally one heard laughter. While not good by any civilized standards, living conditions for the Chinese worker were certainly superior to those he had experienced under the Europeans. There was work, clean water, basic sanitary services, rudimentary health facilities. The profession of begging was banned, but prostitution of course throve, and there were many acts of petty brutality, for Shanghai was an occupied city, and soldiers are men at their most beastly.

When General Kishikawa's health began to suffer from his self-imposed work load, he began a more salubrious routine that brought him to his home on Avenue Joffre in time for dinner each evening.

One evening after dinner, the General mentioned in passing that he was devoted to the game of Gō. Nicholai, who seldom spoke save in brief answer to direct questions, admitted that he also played the game. The General was amused and impressed by the fact that the boy said this in flawless Japanese. He laughed when Nicholai explained that he had been learning Japanese from textbooks and with the assistance of the General's own batman.

"You speak it well, for only six months' study," the General said.

"It is my fifth language, sir. All languages are mathematically similar. Each new one is easier to learn than the last. Then too"—the lad shrugged—"I have a gift for languages."

Kishikawa-san was pleased with the way Nicholai said this last, without braggadocio and without British coyness, as he might have said he was left-handed, or green-eyed. At the same time, the General had to smile to himself when he realized that the boy had obviously rehearsed his first sentence, for while that had been quite correct, his subsequent statements had revealed errors of idiom and pronunciation. The General kept his amusement to himself, recognizing that Nicholai was of an age to take himself very seriously and to be deeply stung by embarrassment.

"I shall help you with your Japanese, if you wish," Kishikawa-san said. "But first, let us see if you are an interesting opponent at Gō."

Nicholai was given a four-stone handicap, and they played a quick, time-limit game, as the General had a full day of work tomorrow. Soon they were absorbed, and Alexandra Ivanovna, who could never see much point in social events of which she was not the center, complained of feeling a bit faint and retired.

The General won, but not as easily as he should have. As he was a gifted amateur capable of giving professionals close combat with minimum handicaps, he was greatly impressed by Nicholai's peculiar style of play.

"How long have you been playing Gō?" he asked, speaking in French to relieve Nicholai of the task of alien expression.

"Oh, four or five years, I suppose, sir."

The General frowned. "Five years? But . . . how old are you?"

"Thirteen, sir. I know I look younger than I am. It's a family trait."

Kishikawa-san nodded and smiled to himself as he thought of Alexandra Ivanovna who, when she had filled out her identity papers for the Occupation Authority, had taken advantage of this "family trait" by blatantly setting down a birth date that suggested she had been the mistress of a White Army general at the age of eleven and had given birth to Nicholai while still in her teens. The General's intelligence service had long ago apprised him of the facts concerning the Countess, but he allowed her this trivial gesture of coquetry, particularly considering what he knew of her unfortunate medical history.

"Still, even for a man of thirteen, you play a remarkable game, Nikko." During the course of the game, the General had manufactured this nickname that allowed him to avoid the troublesome "l." It remained forever his name for Nicholai. "I suppose you have not had any formal training?"

"No, sir. I have never had any instruction at all. I learned from reading books."

"Really? That is unheard of."

"Perhaps so, sir. But I am very intelligent."

For a moment, the General examined the lad's impassive face, its absinthe eyes frankly returning the officer's gaze. "Tell me, Nikko. Why did you choose to study Gō? It is almost exclusively a Japanese game. Certainly none of your friends played the game. They probably never even heard of it."

"That is precisely why I chose Gō, sir."

"I see." What a strange boy. At once both vulnerably honest and arrogant. "And has your reading given you to understand what qualities are necessary to be a fine player?"

Nicholai considered for a moment before answering. "Well, of course one must have concentration. Courage. Self-control. That goes without saying. But more important than these, one must have . . . I don't know how to say it. One must be both a mathematician and a poet. As though poetry were a science; or mathematics an art. One must have an affection for proportion to play Gō at all well. I am not expressing myself well, sir. I'm sorry."

"On the contrary. You are doing very well in your attempt to express the inexpressible. Of these qualities you have named, Nikko, where do you believe your own strengths lie?"

"In the mathematics, sir. In concentration and self-control."

"And your weaknesses?"

"In what I called poetry."

The General frowned and glanced away from the boy. It was strange that he should recognize this. At his age, he should not be able to stand outside himself and report with such detachment. One might expect Nikko to realize the need for certain Western qualities to play Gō well, qualities like concentration, self-control, courage. But to recognize the need for the receptive, sensitive qualities he called poetry was outside that linear logic that is the Western mind's strength . . . and limitation. But then—considering that Nicholai was born of the best blood of Europe but raised in the crucible of China—was he really Western? Certainly he was not Oriental either. He was of no racial culture. Or was it better to think of him as the sole member of a racial culture of his own?

"You and I share that weakness, sir." Nicholai's green eyes crinkled with humor. "We both have weaknesses in the area I called poetry."

The General looked up in surprise. "Ah?"

"Yes, sir. My play lacks much of this quality. Yours has too much of it. Three times during the game you relented in your attack. You chose to make the graceful play, rather than the conclusive one."

Kishikawa-san laughed softly. "How do you know I was not considering your age and relative inexperience?"

"That would have been condescending and unkind, and I don't believe you are those things." Nicholai's eyes smiled again. "I am sorry, sir, that there are no honorifics in French. It must make my speech sound abrupt and insubordinate."

"Yes, it does a little. I was just thinking that, in fact."

"I am sorry, sir."

The General nodded. "I assume you have played Western chess?"

Nicholai shrugged. "A little. It doesn't interest me."

"How would you compare it with Gō?"

Nicholai thought for a second. "Ah . . . what Gō is to the philosophers and warriors, chess is to accountants and merchants."

"Ah! The bigotry of youth. It would be more kind, Nikko, to say that Gō apeals to the philosopher in any man, and chess to the merchant in him."

But Nicholai did not recant. "Yes, sir, that would be more kind. But less true."

The General rose from his cushion, leaving Nicholai to replace the stones. "It is late, and I need my sleep. We'll play again soon, if you wish."

"Sir?" said Nicholai, as the General reached the door.

"Yes?"

Nicholai kept his eyes down, shielding himself from the hurt of possible rejection. "Are we to be friends, sir?"

The General gave the question the consideration its serious tone requested. "That could be, Nikko. Let us wait and see."

It was that very night that Alexandra Ivanovna, deciding at last that General Kishikawa was not of the fabric of the men she had known in the past, came to tap at his bedroom door.

For the next year and a half, they lived as a family. Alexandra Ivanovna became more subdued, more contented, perhaps a little plumper. What she lost in effervescence she gained in an attractive calm that caused Nicholai, for the first time in his life, to like her. Without haste, Nicholai and the General constructed a relationship that was as profound as it was undemonstrative. The one had never had a father; the other, a son. Kishikawa-san was of a temperament to enjoy guiding and shaping a clever, quick-minded young man, even one who was occasionally too bold in his opinions, too confident of his attributes.

Alexandra Ivanovna found emotional shelter in the lee of the General's strong, gentle personality. He found spice and amusement in her flashes of temperament and wit. Between the General and the woman—politeness, generosity, gentleness, physical pleasure. Between the General and the boy—confidence, honesty, ease, affecttion, respect.

Then one evening after dinner, Alexandra Ivanovna joked as usual about the nuisance of her swooning fits and retired early to bed . . . where she died.

Now the sky is black to the east, purple over China. Out in the floating city the orange and yellow lanterns are winking out, as people make up beds on the canted decks of sampans heeled over in the mud. The air has cooled on the dark plains of inland China, and breezes are no longer drawn in from the sea. The curtains no longer billow inward as the General balances his stone on the nail of his index finger, his mind ranging far from the game before him.

It is two months since Alexandra Ivanovna died, and the General has received orders transferring him. He cannot take Nicholai with him, and he does not want to leave him in Shanghai where he has no friends and where his lack of formal citizenship denies him even the most rudimentary diplomatic protection. He has decided to send the boy to Japan.

The General examines the mother's refined face, expressed more economically, more angularly in the boy. Where will he find friends, this young man? Where will he find soil appropriate to his roots, this boy who speaks six languages and thinks in five, but who lacks the smallest fragment of useful training? Can there be a place in the world for him?

"Sir?"

"Yes? Oh . . . ah . . . Have you played, Nikko?"

"Some time ago, sir."

"Ah, yes. Excuse me. And do you mind telling me where you played?"

Nicholai pointed out his stone, and Kishikawa-san frowned because the unlikely placement had the taste of a *tenuki*. He marshaled his fragmented attention and examined the board carefully, mentally reviewing the outcome of each placement available to him. When he looked up, Nicholai's bottle-green eyes were on him, smiling with relish. The game could be played on for several hours, and the outcome would be close. But it was inevitable that Nicholai would win. This was the first time.

The General regarded Nicholai appraisingly for some seconds, then he laughed. "You are a demon, Nikko!"

"That is true, sir," Nicholai admitted, enormously pleased with himself. "Your attention was wandering."

"And you took advantage of that?"

"Of course."

The General began to collect his stones and return them to the *Gō ke*. "Yes," he said to himself. "Of course." Then he laughed again. "What do you say to a cup of tea, Nikko?" Kishikawa-san's major vice was his habit of drinking strong, bitter tea at all hours of day and night. In the heraldry of their affectionate but reserved relationship, the offer of a cup of tea was the signal for a chat. While the General's batman prepared the tea, they walked out into the cool night air of the veranda, both wearing *yukatas*.

After a silence during which the General's eye wandered over the city, where the occasional light in the ancient walled town indicated that someone was celebrating, or studying, or dying, or selling herself, he asked Nicholai, seemingly apropos of nothing, "Do you ever think about the war?"

"No, sir. It has nothing to do with me."

The egoism of youth. The confident egoism of a young man brought up in the knowledge that he was the last and most rarefied of a line of selective breeding that had its sources long before tinkers became Henry Fords, before coin-changers became Rothschilds, before merchants became Medici.

"I am afraid, Nikko, that our little war is going to touch you after all." And with this entree, the General told the young man of the orders transferring him to combat, and of his plans to send Nicholai to Japan where he would live in the home of a famous player and teacher of Gō.

". . . my oldest and closest friend, Otake-san—whom you know by reputation as Otake of the Seventh *Dan*."

Nicholai did indeed recognize the name. He had read Otake-san's lucid commentaries on the middle game.

"I have arranged for you to live with Otake-san and his family, among the other disciples of his school. It is a very great honor, Nikko."

"I realize that, sir. And I am excited about learning from Otake-san. But won't he scorn wasting his instruction on an amateur?"

The General chuckled. "Scorn is not a style of mind that my old friend would employ. Ah! Our tea is ready."

The batman had taken away the *Gō ban* of *kaya*, and in its place was a low table set for tea. The General and Nicholai returned to their cushions. After the first cup, the General sat back slightly and spoke in a businesslike tone. "Your mother had very little money as it turns out. Her investments were scattered in small local companies, most of which collapsed upon the eve of our occupation. The men who owned the companies simply returned to Britain with the capital in their pockets. It appears that, for the Westerner, the great moral crisis of war obscures minor ethical considerations. There is this house . . . and very little more. I have arranged to sell the house for you. The proceeds will go for your maintenance and instruction in Japan."

"As you think best, sir."

"Good. Tell me, Nikko. Will you miss Shanghai?"

Nicholai considered for a second. "No."

"Will you feel lonely in Japan?"

Nicholai considered for a second. "Yes."

"I shall write to you."

"Often?"

"No, not often. Once a month. But you must write to me as often as you feel the need to. Perhaps you will be less lonely than you fear. There are other young people studying with Otake-san. And when you have doubts, ideas, questions, you will find Otake-san a valuable person to discuss them with. He will listen with interest, but will not burden you with advice." The General smiled. "Although I think you may find one of my friend's habits of speech a little disconcerting at times. He speaks of everything in terms of Gō. All of life, for him, is a simplified paradigm of Gō."

"He sounds as though I shall like him, sir."

"I am sure you will. He is a man who has all my respect. He possesses a quality of . . . how to express it? . . . of *shibumi.*"

"*Shibumi,* sir?" Nicholai knew the word, but only as it applied to gardens or architecture, where it connoted an understated beauty. "How are you using the term, sir?"

"Oh, vaguely. And incorrectly, I suspect. A blundering attempt to describe an ineffable quality. As you know, *shibumi* has to do with great refinement underlying commonplace appearances. It is a statement so correct that it does not have to be bold, so poignant it does not have to be pretty, so true it does not have to be real. *Shibumi* is understanding, rather than knowledge. Eloquent silence. In demeanor, it is modesty without pudency. In art, where the spirit of *shibumi* takes the form of *sabi,* it is elegant simplicity, articulate brevity. In philosophy, where *shibumi* emerges as *wabi,* it is spiritual tranquility that is not passive; it is being without the angst of becoming. And in the personality of a man, it is . . . how does one say it? Authority without domination? Something like that."

Nicholai's imagination was galvanized by the concept of *shibumi.* No other ideal had ever touched him so. "How does one achieve this *shibumi,* sir?"

"One does not achieve it, one . . . discovers it. And only a few men of infinite refinement ever do that. Men like my friend Otake-san."

"Meaning that one must learn a great deal to arrive at *shibumi?*"

"Meaning, rather, that one must pass through knowledge and arrive at simplicity."

From that moment, Nicholai's primary goal in life was to become a man of *shibumi;* a personality of overwhelming calm. It was a vocation open to him while, for reasons of breeding, education, and temperament, most vocations were closed. In pursuit of *shibumi* he could excel invisibly, without attracting the attention and vengeance of the tyrannical masses.

Kishikawa-san took from beneath the tea table a small sandalwood box wrapped in plain cloth and put it into Nicholai's hands. "It is a farewell gift. Nikko. A trifle."

Nicholai bowed his head in acceptance and held the package with great tenderness; he did not express his gratitude in inadequate words. This was his first conscious act of *shibumi.*

Although they spoke late into their last night together about what *shibumi* meant and might mean, in the deepest essential they did not understand one another. To the General, *shibumi* was a kind of submission; to Nicholai, it was a kind of power.

Both were captives of their generations.

Nicholai sailed for Japan on a ship carrying wounded soldiers back for family leave, awards, hospitalization, a life under the burden of mutilation. The yellow mud of the Yangtze followed the ship for miles out to sea, and it was not until the water began to blend from khaki to slate blue that Nicholai unfolded the simple cloth that wrapped Kishikawa-san's farewell gift. Within a fragile sandalwood box, swathed in rich paper to prevent damage, were two *gō ke* of black lacquer worked with silver in the Heidatsu process. On the lids of the bowls, lakeside tea houses wreathed in mist were implied, nestling against the shores of unstated lakes. Within one bowl were black Nichi stones from Kishiu. Within the other, white stones of Miyazaki clam shell . . . lustrous, curiously cool to the touch in any weather.

No one observing the delicate young man standing at the rail of the rusty freighter, his hooded green eyes watching the wallow and plunge of the sea as he contemplated the two gifts the General had given him—these *Gō ke,* and the lifelong goal of *shibumi*—would have surmised that he was destined to become the world's most highly paid assassin.

Washington

THE FIRST ASSISTANT sat back from his control console and puffed out a long sigh as he pushed his glasses up and lightly rubbed the tender red spots on the bridge of his nose. "It's going to be difficult getting reliable information out of Fat Boy, sir. Each input source offers conflicting and contradictory data. You're sure he was born in Shanghai?"

"Reasonably, yes."

"Well, there's nothing on that. In a chronological sort, the first I come up with has him living in Japan."

"Very well. Start there, then!"

The First Assistant felt he had to defend himself from the irritation in Mr. Diamond's voice. "It's not as easy as you might think, sir. Here's an example of the kind of garble I'm getting. Under the rubric of 'languages spoken,' I get Russian, French, Chinese, German, English, Japanese, and Basque. *Basque?* That can't be right, can it?"

"It *is* right."

"Basque? Why would anyone learn to speak Basque?"

"I don't know. He studied it while he was in prison."

"Prison, sir?"

"You'll come to it later. He did three years in solitary confinement."

"You . . . you seem to be uniquely familiar with the data, sir."

"I've kept an eye on him for years."

The First Assistant considered asking why this Nicholai Hel had received such special attention, but he thought better of it. "All right, sir. Basque it is. Now how about this? Our first firm data come from immediately after the war, when it seems he worked for the Occupation Forces as a cryptographer and translator. Now, assuming he left Shanghai when we believe he did, we have six years unaccounted for. The only window Fat Boy gives me on that doesn't seem to make any sense. It suggests that he spent those six years studying some kind of game. A game called Gō—whatever that is."

"I believe that's correct."

"Can that be? Throughout the entire Second World War, he spent his time studying a board game?" The First Assistant shook his head. Neither he nor Fat Boy was comfortable with conclusions that did not proceed from solid linear logic. And it was not logical that a mauve-card international assassin would have passed five or six years (Christ! They didn't even know exactly how many!) learning to play some silly game!

Japan

FOR NEARLY FIVE years Nicholai lived within the household of Otake-san; a student, and a member of the family. Otake of the Seventh *Dan* was a man of two contradictory personalities; in competition he was cunning, cold-minded, noted for his relentless exploitation of flaws in the opponent's play or mental toughness. But at home in his sprawling, rather disorganized household amid his sprawling extended family that included, besides his wife, father, and three children, never fewer than six apprenticed pupils, Otake-san was paternal, generous, even willing to play the clown for the amusement of his children and pupils. Money was never plentiful, but they lived in a small mountain village with few expensive distractions, so it was never a problem. When they had less, they lived on less; when they had more, they spent it freely.

None of Otake-san's children had more than average gifts in the art of Gō. And of his pupils, only Nicholai possessed that ineffable constellation of talents that makes the player of rank: a gift for conceiving abstract schematic possibilities; a sense of mathematical poetry in the light of which the infinite chaos of probability and permutation is crystallized under the pressure of intense concentration into geometric blossoms; the ruthless focus of force on the subtlest weakness of an opponent.

In time, Otake-san discovered an additional quality in Nicholai that made his play formidable: In the midst of play, Nicholai was able to rest in profound tranquility for a brief period, then return to his game fresh-minded.

It was Otake-san who first happened upon the fact that Nicholai was a mystic.

Like most mystics, Nicholai was unaware of his gift, and at first he could not believe that others did not have similar experiences. He could not imagine life without mystic transport, and he did not so much pity those who lived without such moments as he regarded them as creatures of an entirely different order.

Nicholai's mysticism came to light late one afternoon when he was playing an exercise game with Otake-san, a very tight and classic game in which only vaguest nuances of development separated their play from textbook models. Partway through the third hour, Nicholai felt the gateway open to him for rest and oneness, and he allowed himself to expand into it. After a time, the feeling dissolved, and Nicholai sat, motionless and rested, wondering vaguely why the teacher was delaying in making an obvious placement. When he looked up, he was surprised to find Otake-san's eyes on his face and not on the *Gō ban.*

"What is wrong, Teacher? Have I made an error?"

Otake-san examined Nicholai's face closely. "No, Nikko. There was no particular brilliance in your last two plays, but also no fault. But . . . how can you play while you daydream?"

"Daydream? I was not daydreaming, Teacher."

"Were you not? Your eyes were defocused and your expression empty. In fact, you did not even look at the board while making your plays. You placed the stones while gazing out into the garden."

Nicholai smiled and nodded. Now he understood. "Oh, I see. In fact, I just returned from resting. So, of course, I didn't have to look at the board."

"Explain to me, please, why you did not have to look at the board, Nikko."

"I . . . ah . . . well, I was resting." Nicholai could see that Otake-san did not understand, and this confused him, assuming as he did that mystic experience was common.

Otake-san sat back and took another of the mint drops that he habitually sucked to relieve pains in his stomach resulting from years of tight control under the pressures of professional play. "Now tell me what you mean when you say that you were resting."

"I suppose 'resting' isn't the correct word for it, Teacher. I don't know what the word is. I have never heard anyone give a name to it. But you must know the sensation I mean. The departing without leaving. The . . . you know . . . the flowing into all things, and . . . ah . . . understanding all things." Nicholai was embarrassed. The experience was too simple and basic to explain. It was as though the Teacher had asked him to explain breathing, or the scent of flowers. Nicholai was sure that Otake-san knew exactly what he meant; after all, he had only to recall his own rest times. Why did he ask these questions?

Otake-san reached out and touched Nicholai's arm. "I know, Nikko, that this is difficult for you to explain. And I believe I understand a little of what you experience—not because I also have experienced it, but because I have read of it, for it has always attracted my curiosity. It is called mysticism."

Nicholai laughed. "Mysticism! But surely, Teacher—"

"Have you ever talked to anyone about this . . . how did you phrase it? . . . 'departing without leaving'?"

"Well . . . no. Why would anyone talk about it?"

"Not even our good friend Kishikawa-san?"

"No, Teacher. It never came up. I don't understand why you are asking me these questions. I am confused. And I am beginning to feel shame."

Otake-san pressed his arm. "No, no. Don't feel shame. Don't be frightened. You see, Nikko, what you experience . . . what you call 'resting' . . . is not very common. Few people experience these things, except in a light and partial way when they are very young. This experience is what saintly men strive to achieve through discipline and meditation, and foolish men seek through drugs. Throughout all ages and in all cultures, a certain fortunate few have been able to gain this state of calm and oneness with nature (I use these words to describe it because they are the words I have read) without years of rigid discipline. Evidently, it comes to them quite naturally, quite simply. Such people are called mystics. It is an unfortunate label because it carries connotations of religion and magic about it. In fact, all the words used to describe this experience are rather theatrical. What you call 'a rest,' others call ecstasy."

Nicholai grinned uncomfortably at this word. How could the most real thing in the world be called mysticism? How could the quietest emotion imaginable be called ecstasy?

"You smile at the word, Nikko. But surely the experience is pleasurable, is it not?"

"Pleasurable? I never thought of it that way. It is . . . necessary."

"Necessary?"

"Well, how would one live day in and day out without times of rest?"

Otake-san smiled. "Some of us are required to struggle along without such rest."

"Excuse me, Teacher. But I can't imagine a life like that. What would be the point of living a life like that?"

Otake-san nodded. He had found in his reading that mystics regularly reported an inability to understand people who lack the mystic gift. He felt a bit uneasy when he recalled that when mystics lose their gift—and most of them do at some time or other—they experience panic and deep depression. Some retreat into religion to rediscover the experience through the mechanics of meditation. Some even commit suicide, so pointless does life without mystic transport seem.

"Nikko? I have always been intensely curious about mysticism, so please permit me to ask you questions about this 'rest' of yours. In my readings, mystics who report their transports always use such gossamer terms, so many seeming contradictions, so many poetic paradoxes. It is as though they were attempting to describe something too complicated to be expressed in words."

"Or too simple, sir."

"Yes. Perhaps that is it. Too simple." Otake-san pressed his fist against his chest to relieve the pressure and took another mint drop. "Tell me. How long have you had these experiences?"

"Always."

"Since you were a baby?"

"Always."

"I see. And how long do these experiences last?"

"It doesn't matter, Teacher. There is not time there."

"It is timeless?"

"No. There is neither time nor timelessness."

Otake-san smiled and shook his head. "Am I to have the gossamer terms and the poetic paradoxes from you as well?"

Nicholai realized that these bracketing oxymorons made that which was infinitely simple seem chaotic, but he didn't know how to express himself with the clumsy tool of words.

Otake-san came to his aid. "So you are saying that you have no sense of time during these experiences. You do not know how long they last?"

"I know exactly how long they last, sir. When I depart, I don't leave. I am where my body is, as well as everywhere else. I am not daydreaming. Sometimes the rest lasts a minute or two. Sometimes it lasts hours. It lasts for as long as it is needed."

"And do they come often, these . . . rests?"

"This varies. Twice or three times a day at most. But sometimes I go a month without a rest. When this happens, I miss them very much. I become frightened that they may never come back."

"Can you bring one of these rest periods on at will?"

"No. But I can block them. And I must be careful not to block them away, if I need one."

"How can you block them away?"

"By being angry. Or by hating."

"You can't have this experience if you hate?"

"How could I? The rest is the very opposite of hate."

"Is it love, then?"

"Love is what it might be, if it concerned people. But it doesn't concern people."

"What does it concern?"

"Everything. Me. Those two are the same. When I am resting, everything and I are . . . I don't know how to explain."

"You become one with everything?"

"Yes. No, not exactly. I don't *become* one with everything. I *return* to being one with everything. Do you know what I mean?"

"I am trying to. Please take this 'rest' you experienced a short time ago, while we were playing. Describe to me what happened."

Nicholai lifted his palms helplessly. "How can I do that?"

"Try. Begin with: we were playing and you had just placed stone fifty-six . . . and . . . Go on."

"It was stone fifty-eight, Teacher."

"Well, fifty-eight then. And what happened?"

"Well . . . the flow of the play was just right, and it began to bring me to the meadow. It always begins with some kind of flowing motion . . . a stream or river, maybe the wind making waves in a field of ripe rice, the glitter of leaves moving in a breeze, clouds flowing by. And for me, if the structure of the Gō stones is flowing classically, that too can bring me to the meadow."

"The meadow?"

"Yes. That's the place I expand into. It's how I recognize that I am resting."

"Is it a real meadow?"

"Yes, of course."

"A meadow you visited at one time? A place in your memory?"

"It's not in my memory. I've never been there when I was diminished."

"Diminished?"

"You know . . . when I'm in my body and not resting."

"You consider normal life to be a diminished state, then?"

"I consider time spent at rest to be normal. Time like this . . . temporary, and . . . yes, diminished."

"Tell me about the meadow, Nikko."

"It is triangular. And it slopes uphill, away from me. The grass is tall. There are no animals. Nothing has ever walked on the grass or eaten it. There are flowers, a breeze . . . warm. Pale sky. I'm always glad to be the grass again."

"You *are* the grass?"

"We are one another. Like the breeze, and the yellow sunlight. We're all . . . mixed in together."

"I see. I see. Your description of the mystic experience resembles others I have read. And this meadow is what the writers call your 'gateway' or 'path.' Do you ever think of it in those terms?"

"No."

"So. What happens then?"

"Nothing. I am at rest. I am everywhere at once. And everything is unimportant and delightful. And then . . . I begin to diminish. I separate from the sunlight and the meadow, and I contract again back into my bodyself. And the rest is over." Nicholai smiled uncertainly. "I suppose I am not describing it very well, Teacher. It's not . . . the kind of thing one describes."

"No, you describe it very well, Nikko. You have evoked a memory in me that I had almost lost. Once or twice when I was a child . . . in summer, I think . . . I experienced brief transports such as you describe. I read once that most people have occasional mystic experiences when they are children, but soon outgrow them. And forget them. Will you tell me something else? How is it you are able to play Gō while you are transported . . . while you are in your meadow?"

"Well, I am here as well as there. I depart, but I don't leave. I am part of this room and that garden."

"And me, Nikko? Are you part of me too?"

Nicholai shook his head. "There are no animals in my rest place. I am the only thing that sees. I see for us all, for the sunlight, for the grass."

"I see. And how can you play your stones without looking at the board? How do you know where the lines cross? How do you know where I placed my last stone?"

Nicholai shrugged. It was too obvious to explain. "I am part of everything, Teacher. I share . . . no . . . I flow with everything. The *Gō ban,* the stones. The board and I are amongst one another. How could I not know the patterns of play?"

"You see from within the board then?"

"Within and without are the same thing. But 'see' isn't exactly right either. If one is everyplace, he doesn't have to 'see.' " Nicholai shook his head. "I can't explain."

Otake-san pressed Nikko's arm lightly, then withdrew his hand. "I won't question you further. I confess that I envy the mystic peace you find. I envy most of all your gift for finding it so naturally—without the concentration and exercise that even holy men must apply in search of it. But while I envy it, I also feel some fear on your behalf. If the mystic ecstasy has become—as I suspect it has—a natural and necessary part of your inner life, then what will become of you, should this gift fade, should these experiences be denied you?"

"I cannot imagine that happening, Teacher."

"I know. But my reading has revealed to me that these gifts can fade; the paths to inner peace can be lost. Something can happen that fills you with constant and unrelenting hate or fear, and then it would be gone."

The thought of losing the most natural and most important psychic activity of his life disturbed Nicholai. With a brief rush of panic, he realized that fear of losing it might be fear enough to cause him to lose it. He wanted to be away from this conversation, from these new and incredible doubts. His eyes lowered to the *Gō ban,* he considered his reaction to such a loss.

"What would you do, Nikko?" Otake-san repeated after a moment of silence.

Nicholai looked up from the board, his green eyes calm and expressionless. "If someone took my rest times from me, I would kill him."

This was said with a fatalistic calm that made Otake-san know it was not anger, only a simple truth. It was the quiet assurance of the statement that disturbed Otake-san most.

"But, Nikko. Let us say it was not a man who took this gift from you. Let us say it was a situation, an event, a condition of life. What would you do then?"

"I would seek to destroy it, whatever it was. I would punish it."

"Would that bring the path to rest back?"

"I don't know, Teacher. But it would be the least vengeance I could exact for so great a loss."

Otake-san sighed, part in regret for Nikko's particular vulnerability, part in sympathy for whoever might happen to be the agent of the loss of his gift. He had no doubt at all that the young man would do what he said. Nowhere is a man's personality so clearly revealed as in his Gō game, if his play be read by one with the experience and intelligence to interpret it. And Nicholai's play, brilliant and audacious as it was, bore the aesthetic blemishes of frigidity and almost inhuman concentration of purpose. From his reading of Nicholai's game, Otake-san knew that his star pupil might achieve greatness, might become the first non-Japanese to rise to the higher *dans;* but he knew also that the boy would never know peace or happiness in the smaller game of life. It was a blessed compensation that Nikko possessed the gift of retirement into mystic transport. But a gift with a poisoned core.

Otake-san sighed again and considered the pattern of stones. The game was about a third played out. "Do you mind, Nikko, if we do not finish? My nagging old stomach is bothering me. And the development is sufficiently classic that the seeds of the outcome have already taken root. I don't anticipate either of us making a serious error, do you?"

"No, sir." Nicholai was glad to leave the board, and to leave this small room where he had learned for the first time that his mystic retreats were vulnerable . . . that something could happen to deny him an essential part of his life. "At all events, Teacher, I think you would have won by seven or eight stones."

Otake-san glanced at the board again. "So many? I would have thought only five or six." He smiled at Nikko. It was their kind of joke.

In fact, Otake-san would have won by at least a dozen stones, and they both knew it.

The years passed, and the seasons turned easily in the Otake household where traditional roles, fealties, hard work, and study were balanced against play, devilment, and affection, this last no less sincere for being largely tacit.

Even in their small mountain village, where the dominant chords of life vibrated in sympathy with the cycle of the crops, the war was a constant tone in the background. Young men whom everybody knew left to join the army, some never to return. Austerity and harder work became their lot. There was great excitement when news came of the attack at Pearl Harbor on the eighth of December 1941; knowledgeable men agreed that the war would not last more than a year. Victory after victory was announced by enthusiastic voices over the radio as the army swept European imperialism from the Pacific.

But still, some farmers grumbled privately as almost impossible production quotas were placed on them, and they felt the pressures of decreasing consumer goods. Otake-san turned more to writing commentaries, as the number of Gō tournaments was restricted as a patriotic gesture in the general austerity. Occasionally the war touched the Otake household more directly. One winter evening, the middle son of the Otake family came home from school crushed and ashamed because he had been ridiculed by his classmates as a *yowamushi,* a weak worm, because he wore mittens on his sensitive hands during the bruising afternoon calisthenics when all the boys exercised on the snow-covered courtyard, stripped to the waist to demonstrate physical toughness and "samurai spirit."

And from time to time Nicholai overheard himself described as a foreigner, a *gaijin,* a "redhead," in tones of mistrust that reflected the xenophobia preached by jingoistic schoolteachers. But he did not really suffer from his status as an outsider. General Kishikawa had been careful that his identity papers designated his mother as a Russian (a neutral) and his father as a German (an ally). Too, Nicholai was protected by the great respect in which the village held Otake-san, the famed player of Gō who brought honor to their village by choosing to live there.

When Nicholai's game had improved sufficiently that he was allowed to play preliminary matches and accompany Otake-san as a disciple to the great championship games held in out-of-the-way resorts where the players could be "sealed in" away from the distractions of the world, he had opportunities to see at first hand the spirit with which Japan went to war. At railroad stations there were noisy send-offs for recruits, and large banners reading:

* * *

FELICITATIONS ON YOUR CALL TO COLORS AND WE PRAY FOR YOUR LASTING MILITARY FORTUNE.

He heard of a boy from the neighboring village who, failing his physical examination, begged to be accepted in any role, rather than face the unspeakable *haji* of being unworthy to serve. His pleas were ignored, and he was sent home by train. He stood staring out the window, muttering again and again to himself, *"Haji desu, haji desu."* Two days later, his body was found along the tracks. He had chosen not to face the disgrace of returning to the relatives and friends who had sent him off with such joy and celebration.

For the people of Japan, as for the people of its enemies, this was a just war into which they had been forced. There was a certain desperate pride in the knowledge that tiny Japan, with almost no natural resources other than the spirit of the people, stood alone against the hordes of the Chinese, and the vast industrial might of America, Britain, Australia, and all the European nations but four. And every thinking person knew that, once Japan was weakened by the overwhelming odds against it, the crushing mass of the Soviet Union would descend upon them.

But at first there were only victories. When the village learned that Tokyo had been bombed by Doolittle, the news was received with bewilderment and outrage. Bewilderment, because they had been assured that Japan was invulnerable. Outrage, because although the effect of the bombing was slight, the American bombers had scattered their incendiaries randomly, destroying homes and schools and not touching—by ironic accident—a single factory or military establishment. When he heard of the American bombers, Nicholai remembered the Northrop planes that had bombed The Sincere department store in Shanghai. He could still see the doll-like Chinese girl in her green silk dress, a stiff little collar standing around her porcelain neck, her face pale beneath its rice powder as she searched for her hand.

Although the war tinted every aspect of life, it was not the dominant theme of Nicholai's formative years. Three things were more important to him: the regular improvement of his game; his rich and resuscitative returns to states of mystic calm whenever his psychic vigor flagged; and, during his seventeenth year, his first love.

Mariko was one of Otake-san's disciples, a shy and delicate girl only a year older than Nikko, who lacked the mental toughness to become a great player, but whose game was intricate and refined. She and Nicholai played many practice bouts together, drilling opening and middle games particularly. Her shyness and his aloofness suited one another comfortably, and frequently they would sit together in the little garden at evening, talking a little, sharing longish silences.

Occasionally they walked together into the village on some errand or other, and arms accidentally brushed, thrilling the conversation into an awkward silence. Eventually, with a boldness that belied the half hour of self-struggle that had preceded the gesture, Nicholai reached across the practice board and took her hand. Swallowing, and concentrating on the board with desperate attention, Mariko returned the pressure of his fingers without looking up at him, and for the rest of the morning they played a very ragged and disorganized game while they held hands, her palm moist with fear of discovery, his trembling with fatigue at the awkward position of his arm, but he could not lighten the strength of his grip, much less relinquish her hand, for fear that this might signal rejection.

They were both relieved to be freed by the call to the noon meal, but the tingle of sin and love was effervescent in their blood all that day. And the next day they exchanged a brushing kiss.

One spring night when Nicholai was almost eighteen, he dared to visit Mariko in her small sleeping room. In a household containing so many people and so little space, meeting at night was an adventure of stealthy movements, soft whispers, and breaths caught in the throat while hearts pounded against one another's chest at the slightest real or imagined sound.

Their lovemaking was bungling, tentative, infinitely gentle.

Although Nicholai exchanged letters with General Kishikawa monthly, only twice during the five years of his apprenticeship could the General free himself from administrative duties for brief leaves of absence in Japan.

The first of these lasted only one day, for the General spent most of his leave in Tokyo with his daughter, recently widowed when her naval officer husband went down with his ship during the victory of the Coral Sea, leaving her pregnant with her first child. After sharing in her bereavement and arranging for her welfare, the General stopped over in the village to visit the Otakes and to bring Nicholai a present of two boxes of books selected from confiscated libraries, and given with the injunction that the boy must not allow his gift of languages to atrophy. The books were in Russian, English, German, French and Chinese. These last were useless to Nicholai because, although he had picked up a fluid knowledge of rough-and-ready Chinese from the streets of Shanghai, he never learned to read the language. The General's own limitation to French was demonstrated by the fact that the boxes included four copies of *Les Misérables* in four different languages—and perhaps a fifth in Chinese, for all Nicholai knew.

That evening the General took dinner with Otake, both avoiding any talk about the war. When Otake-san praised the work and progress of Nicholai, the General assumed the role of Japanese father, making light of his ward's gifts and asserting that it was a great kindness on Otake's part to burden himself with so lazy and inept a pupil. But he could not mask the pride that shone in his eyes.

The General's visit coincided with *jusanya,* the Autumn Moon-Viewing Festival, and offerings of flowers and autumn grasses were placed on an altar in the garden where the moon's rays would fall on them. In normal times, there would have been fruit and food among the offerings, but with war shortages Otake-san tempered his traditionalism with common sense. He might, like his neighbors, have offered the food, then returned it to the family table the next day, but such a thing was unthinkable to him.

After dinner, Nicholai and the General sat in the garden, watching the rising moon disentangle itself from the branches of a tree.

"So, Nikko? Tell me. Have you attained the goal of *shibumi* as you once told me you would?" There was a teasing tone to his voice.

Nicholai glanced down. "I was rash, sir. I was young."

"Younger, yes. I assume you are finding flesh and youth considerable obstacles in your quest. Perhaps you will be able, in time, to acquire the laudable refinement of behavior and facade that might be called *shibusa.* Whether you will ever achieve the profound simplicity of spirit that is *shibumi* is moot. Seek it, to be sure. But be prepared to accept less with grace. Most of us have to."

"Thank you for your guidance, sir. But I would rather fail at becoming a man of *shibumi* than succeed at any other goal."

The General nodded and smiled to himself. "Yes, of course you would. I had forgotten certain facets of your personality. We have been apart too long." They shared the garden in silence for a time. "Tell me, Nikko, are you keeping your languages fresh?"

Nicholai had to confess that, when he had glanced at a few of the books the General had brought, he discovered that his German and English were rusting.

"You must not let that happen. Particularly your English. I shall not be in a position to help you much when this war is over, and you have nothing to rely upon but your gift for language."

"You speak as though the war will be lost, sir."

Kishikawa-san was silent for a long time, and Nicholai could read sadness and fatigue in his face, dim and pale in the moonlight. "All wars are lost ultimately. By both sides, Nikko. The day of battles between professional warriors is gone. Now we have wars between opposing industrial capacities, opposing populations. The Russians, with their sea of faceless people, will defeat the Germans. The Americans, with their anonymous factories, will defeat us. Ultimately."

"What will you do when this happens, sir?"

The General shook his head slowly. "That doesn't matter. Until the end, I shall do my duty. I shall continue to work sixteen hours a day on petty administrative problems. I shall continue to perform as a patriot."

Nicholai looked at him quizzically. He had never heard Kishikawa-san speak of patriotism.

The General smiled faintly. "Oh, yes, Nikko. I am a patriot after all. Not a patriot of politics, or ideology, or military bands, or the *hinomaru*. But a patriot all the same. A patriot of gardens like this, of moon festivals, of the subtleties of Gō, of the chants of women planting rice, of cherry blossoms in brief bloom—of things Japanese. The fact that I know we cannot win this war has nothing to do with the fact that I must continue to do my duty. Do you understand that, Nikko?"

"Only the words, sir."

The General chuckled softly. "Perhaps that is all there is. Go to your bed now, Nikko. Let me sit alone for a while. I shall leave before you arise in the morning, but it pleased me to have this little time with you."

Nicholai bowed his head and rose. Long after he had gone, the General was still sitting, regarding the moonlit garden calmly.

Much later, Nicholas learned that General Kishikawa had attempted to provide money for his ward's maintenance and training, but Otake-san had refused it, saying that if Nicholai were so unworthy a pupil as the General claimed, it would be unethical of him to accept payment for his training. The General smiled at his old friend and shook his head. He was trapped into accepting a kindness.

The tide of war turned against the Japanese, who had staked all their limited production capabilities on a short all-out struggle resulting in a favorable peace. Evidence of incipient defeat was everywhere: in the hysterical fanaticism of government morale broadcasts, in reports by refugees of devastating "carpet bombing" by American planes concentrating on residential areas, in ever-increasing shortages of the most basic consumer goods.

Even in their agricultural village, food was in short supply after farmers met their production quotas; and many times the Otake family subsisted on *zosui*, a gruel of chopped carrots and turnip tops boiled with rice, rendered palatable only by Otake-san's burlesque sense of humor. He would eat with many gestures and sounds of delight, rolling his eyes and patting his stomach in such a way as to make his children and students laugh and forget the bland, loamy taste of the food in their mouths. At first, refugees from the cities were cared for with compassion; but as time passed, these additional mouths to feed became a burden; the refugees were referred to by the mildly pejorative term *sokaijin;* and there was grumbling amongst the peasants about these urban drones who were rich or important enough to be able to escape the horrors of the city, but not capable of working to maintain themselves.

Otake-san had permitted himself one luxury, his small formal garden. Late in the war he dug it up and converted it to the planting of food. But, typical of him, he arranged the turnips and radishes and carrots in mixed beds so their growing tops were attractive to the eye. "They are more difficult to weed and care for, I confess. But if we forsake beauty in our desperate struggle to live, then the barbarian has already won."

Eventually, the official broadcasts were forced to admit the occasional loss of a battle or an island, because to fail to do so in the face of the contradictions of returning wounded soldiers would have cost them the last semblance of credibility. Each time such a defeat was announced (always with an explanation of tactical withdrawal, or reorganization of defense lines, or intentional shortening of supply lines) the broadcast was ended by the playing of the old, beloved song, "Umi Yukaba," the sweet autumnal strains of which became identified with this era of darkness and loss.

Otake-san now traveled to play in Gō tournaments very seldom, because transportation was given over to military and industrial needs. But the playing of the national game and reports of important contests in the newspapers were never given up entirely, because it was realized that this was one of the traditional refinements of culture for which they were fighting.

In the course of accompanying his teacher to these infrequent tournaments, Nicholai witnessed the effects of the war. Cities flattened; people homeless. But the bombers had not broken the spirit of the people. It is an ironic fiction that strategic (i.e., anti-civilian) bombing can break a nation's will to fight. In Germany, Britain, and Japan, the effect of strategic bombing was to give the people a common cause, to harden their will to resist in the crucible of shared difficulties.

Once, when their train was stopped for hours at a station because of damage to the railroad lines, Nicholai walked slowly back and forth on the platform. All along the facade of the station were rows of litters on which lay wounded soldiers on their way to hospitals. Some were ashen with pain and rigid with the effort to contain it, but none cried out; there was not a single moan. Old people and children passed from stretcher to stretcher, tears of compassion in their eyes, bowing low to each wounded soldier and muttering, "Thank you. Thank you. *Gokuro sama. Gokuro sama.*"

One bent old woman approached Nicholai and stared into his Western face with its uncommon glass-green eyes. There was no hate in her expression, only a mixture of bewilderment and disappointment. She shook her head sadly and turned away.

Nicholai found a quiet end of the platform where he sat looking at a billowing cloud. He relaxed and concentrated on the slow churning within it, and in a few minutes he found escape into a brief mystic transport, in which state he was invulnerable to the scene about him, and to his racial guilt.

The General's second visit was late in the war. He arrived unannounced one spring afternoon and, after a private conversation with Otake-san, invited Nicholai to take a trip with him to view the cherry blossoms along the Kajikawa river near Niigata. Before turning inland over the mountains, their train brought them north through the industrialized strip between Yokohama and Tokyo, where it crawled haltingly over a roadbed weakened by bombing and overuse, past mile after mile of rubble and destruction caused by indiscriminate carpet bombing that had leveled homes and factories, schools and temples, shops, theaters, hospitals. Nothing stood higher than the chest of a man, save for the occasional jagged stump of a truncated smokestack.

The train was shunted around Tokyo, through sprawling suburbs. All around them was evidence of the great air raid of March 9 during which more than three hundred B-29's spread a blanket of incendiaries over residential Tokyo. Sixteen square miles of the city became an inferno, with temperatures in excess of 1800 degrees Fahrenheit melting roof tiles and buckling pavements. Walls of flame leapt from house to house, over canals and rivers, encircling throngs of panicked civilians who ran back and forth across ever-shrinking islands of safety, hopelessly seeking a break in the tightening ring of fire. Trees in the parks hissed and steamed as they approached their kindling points, then with a loud crack burst into flame from trunk to tip in one instant. Hordes waded out into the canals to avoid the terrible heat; but they were pushed farther out, over their heads, by screaming throngs pressing in from the shores. Drowning women lost their grip on babies held high until the last moment.

The vortex of flames sucked air in at its base, creating a firestorm of hurricane force that roared inward to feed the conflagration. So great were the blast-furnace winds that American planes circling overhead to take publicity photographs were buffeted thousands of feet upward.

Many of those who died that night were suffocated. The voracious fires literally snatched the breath from their lungs.

With no effective fighter cover left, the Japanese had no defense against the wave after wave of bombers that spread their jellied fire over the city. Firemen wept with frustration and shame as they dragged useless hoses toward the walls of flame. The burst and steaming water mains provided only limp trickles of water.

When dawn came, the city still smoldered, and in every pile of rubble little tongues of flame licked about in search of combustible morsels. The dead were everywhere. One hundred thirty thousand of them. The cooked bodies of children were stacked like cordwood in schoolyards. Elderly couples died in one another's arms, their bodies welded together in final embrace. The canals were littered with the dead, bobbing in the still-tepid water.

Silent groups of survivors moved from pile to pile of charred bodies in search of relatives. At the bottom of each pile were found a number of coins that had been heated to a white heat and had burned their way down through the dead. One fleshless young woman was discovered wearing a kimono that appeared unharmed by the flames, but when the fabric was touched, it crumbled into ashy dust.

In later years, Western conscience was to be shamed by what happened at Hamburg and Dresden, where the victims were Caucasians. But after the March 9 bombing of Tokyo, *Time* magazine described the event as "a dream come true," an experiment that proved that "properly kindled, Japanese cities will burn like autumn leaves."

And Hiroshima was still to come.

Throughout the journey, General Kishikawa sat stiff and silent, his breathing so shallow that one could see no movement beneath the rumpled civilian suit he wore. Even after the horror of residential Tokyo was behind them, and the train was rising into the incomparable beauty of mountains and high plateaus, Kishikawa-san did not speak. To relieve the silence, Nicholai asked politely about the General's daughter and baby grandson in Tokyo. Even as he spoke the last word, he realized what must have happened. Why else would the General have received leave during these last months of the war?

When he spoke, Kishikawa-san's eyes were kind, but wounded and void. "I looked for them, Nikko. But the district where they lived was . . . it no longer exists. I have decided to say good-bye to them among the blossoms of Kajikawa, where once I brought my daughter when she was a little girl, and where I always planned to bring my . . . grandson. Will you help me say good-bye to them, Nikko?"

Nicholai cleared his throat. "How can I do that, sir?"

"By walking among the cherry trees with me. By allowing me to speak to you when I can no longer support the silence. You are almost my son, and you . . ." The General swallowed several times in succession and lowered his eyes.

Half an hour later, the General pressed his eye sockets with his fingers and sniffed. Then he looked across at Nicholai. "Well! Tell me about your life, Nikko. Is your game developing well? Is *shibumi* still a goal? How are the Otakes managing to get along?"

Nicholai attacked the silence with a torrent of trivia that shielded the General from the cold stillness in his heart.

For three days they stayed in an old-fashioned hotel in Niigata, and each morning they went to the banks of the Kajikawa and walked slowly between rows of cherry trees in full bloom. Viewed from a distance, the trees were clouds of vapor tinted pink. The path and road were covered with a layer of blossoms that were everywhere fluttering down, dying at their moment of greatest beauty. Kishikawa-san found solace in the insulating symbolism.

They talked seldom and in quiet tones as they walked. Their communication consisted of fragments of running thought concreted in single words or broken phrases, but perfectly understood. Sometimes they sat on the high embankments of the river and watched the water flow by until it seemed that the water was still, and they were flowing upstream. The General wore kimonos of browns and rusts, and Nicholai dressed in the dark-blue uniform of the student with its stiff collar and peaked cap covering his light hair. So much did they look like the typical father and son that passers-by were surprised to notice the striking color of the young man's eyes.

On their last day, they remained among the cherry trees later than usual, walking slowly along the broad avenue until evening. As light drained from the sky, an eerie gloaming seemed to rise from the ground, illuminating the trees from beneath and accenting the pink snowfall of petals. The General spoke quietly, as much to himself as to Nicholai. "We have been fortunate. We have enjoyed the three best days of the cherry blossoms. The day of promise, when they are not yet perfect. The perfect day of enchantment. And today they are already past their prime. So this is the day of memory. The saddest day of the three . . . but the richest. There is a kind of—solace? . . . no . . . perhaps comfort—in all that. And once again I am struck by what a tawdry magician's trick Time is after all. I am sixty-six years old, Nikko. Viewed from your coign of vantage—facing toward the future—sixty-six years is a great deal of time. It is all of the experience of your life more than three times over. But, viewed from my coign of vantage—facing toward the past—this sixty-six years was the fluttering down of a cherry petal. I feel that my life was a picture hastily sketched but never filled in . . . for lack of time. Time. Only yesterday—but more than fifty years ago—I walked along this river with my father. There were no embankments then, no cherry trees. It was only yesterday . . . but another century. Our victory over the Russian navy was still ten years in the future. Our fighting on the side of the allies in the Great War was still twenty and more years away. I can see my father's face. (And in my memory, I am always looking up at it.) I can remember how big and strong his hand felt to my small fingers. I can still feel in my chest . . . as though nerves themselves have independent memories . . . the melancholy tug I felt then over my inability to tell my father that I loved him. We did not have the habit of communicating in such bold and earthy terms. I can see each line in my father's stern but delicate profile. Fifty years. But all the insignificant, busy things—the terribly important, now forgotten things that cluttered the intervening time collapse and fall away from my memory. I used to think I felt sorry for my father because I could never tell him

I loved him. It was for myself that I felt sorry. I needed the saying more than he needed the hearing."

The light from the earth was dimming, and the sky was growing purple, save to the west where the bellies of storm clouds were mauve and salmon.

"And I remember another yesterday when my daughter was a little girl. We walked along here. At this very moment, the nerves in my hand remember the feeling of her chubby fingers clinging to one of mine. These mature trees were newly planted saplings then—poor skinny things tied to supporting poles with strips of white cloth. Who would have thought such awkward, adolescent twigs could grow old and wise enough to console without presuming to advise? I wonder . . . I wonder if the Americans will have all these cut down because they do not bear obvious fruit. Probably. And probably with the best of intentions."

Nicholai was a little uneasy. Kishikawa-san had never opened himself in this way. Their relationship had always been characterized by understanding reticence.

"When last I visited, Nikko, I asked you to keep your gift of languages fresh. Have you done so?"

"Yes, sir. I have no chance to speak anything but Japanese, but I read all the books you brought, and sometimes I talk to myself in the various languages."

"Particularly in English, I hope."

Nicholai stared into the water. "Least often English."

Kishikawa-san nodded to himself. "Because it is the language of the Americans?"

"Yes."

"Have you ever met an American?"

"No, sir."

"But you hate them all the same?"

"It is not difficult to hate barbarian mongrels. I don't have to know them as individuals to hate them as a race."

"Ah, but you see, Nikko, the Americans are not a race. That, in fact, is their central flaw. They are, as you say, mongrels."

Nicholai looked up in surprise. Was the General defending the Americans? Just three days ago they had ridden past Tokyo and seen the effects of the greatest firebombing of the war, one directed specifically against residential areas and civilians. Kishikawa-san's own daughter . . . his baby grandson . . .

"I have met Americans, Nikko. I served briefly with the military attaché in Washington. Did I ever tell you about that?"

"No, sir."

"Well, I was not a very successful diplomat. One must develop a certain obliquity of conscience, an elastic attitude toward the truth, to be effective in diplomacy. I lacked these gifts. But I came to know Americans and to appreciate their virtues and flaws. They are very skillful merchants, and they have a great respect for fiscal achievement. These may seem thin and tawdry virtues to you, but they are consonant with the patterns of the industrial world. You call the Americans barbarians, and you are right, of course. I know this better than you. I know they have tortured and sexually mutilated prisoners. I know they have set men afire with their flamethrowers to see how far they could run before they collapsed. Yes, barbarians. But, Nikko, our own soldiers have done similar things, things ghastly and cruel beyond description. War and hatred and fear have made beasts of our own countrymen. And we are not barbarians; our morality should have been stiffened by a thousand years of civilization and culture. In a way of speaking, the very barbarianism of the Americans is their excuse—no, such things cannot be excused. Their explanation. How can we condemn the brutality of the Americans, whose culture is a thin paste and patchwork thrown together in a handful of decades, when we ourselves are snarling beasts without compassion and humanity, despite our thousand years of pure breeding and tradition? America, after all, was populated by the lees and failures of Europe. Recognizing this, we must see them as innocent. As innocent as the adder, as innocent as the jackal. Dangerous and treacherous but not sinful. You spoke of them as a despicable race. They are not a race. They are not even a culture. They are a cultural stew of the orts and leavings of the European feast. At best, they are a mannered technology. In place of ethics, they have rules. Size functions for them as quality functions for us. What for us is honor and dishonor, for them is winning and losing. Indeed, you must not think in terms of race; race is nothing, culture is everything. By race, you are Caucasian; but culturally you are not, and therefore you are not. Each culture has its strengths and weaknesses; they cannot be evaluated against one another. The only sure criticism that can be made is that a mixture of cultures always results in a blend of the worst of both. That which is evil in a man or a culture is the strong, vicious animal within. That which is good in a man or a culture is the fragile, artificial accretion of restraining civilization. And when cultures cross-breed, the dominant and base elements inevitably prevail. So, you see, when you accuse the Americans of being barbarians, you have really defended them against responsibility for their insensitivity and shallowness. It is only in pointing out their mongrelism that you touch their real flaw. And is flaw the right word? After all, in the world of the future, a world of merchants and mechanics, the base impulses of the mongrel are those that will dominate. The Westerner is the future, Nikko. A grim and impersonal future of technology and automation, it is true—but the future nevertheless. You will have to live in this future, my son. It will do you no good to dismiss the American with disgust. You must seek to understand him, if only to avoid being harmed by him.''

Kishikawa-san had been speaking very softly, almost to himself, as they walked slowly along the wide path in the fading gloaming. The monologue had the quality of a lesson from loving teacher to wayward pupil; and Nicholai had listened with total attention, his head bowed. After a minute or two of silence, Kishikawa-san laughed lightly and clapped his hands together. "Enough of this! Advice helps only him who gives it, and that only insofar as it lightens the burdens of conscience. In the final event, you will do what fate and your breeding dictate, and my advice will affect your future as much as a cherry blossom falling into the river alters its course. There is really something else I wanted to talk to you about, and I have been avoiding it by technique of rambling on about cultures and civilizations and the future—subjects deep and vague enough to hide myself within."

They strolled on in silence as night came and with it an evening breeze that brought the petals down in a dense pink snow that brushed their cheeks and covered their hair and shoulders. At the end of the wide path they came to a bridge, and they paused on the rise to look down at the faintly phosphorescent foam where the river swirled around rocks. The General took a deep breath and let it out in a long stream through pursed lips as he steeled himself to tell Nicholai what was on his mind.

"This is our last chat, Nikko. I have been transferred to Manchukuo. We expect the Russians to attack as soon as we are so weak that they can participate in the war—and therefore in the peace—without risk. It is not likely that staff officers will survive being captured by the communists. Many intend to perform *seppuku*, rather than face the ignominy of surrender. I have decided to follow this course, not because I seek to avoid dishonor. My participation in this bestial war has dirtied me beyond the capacity of *seppuku* to cleanse—as it has every soldier, I fear. But, even if there is no sanctification in the act, there is at least ... dignity. I have made this decision during these past three days, as we walked among the cherry trees. A week ago, I did not feel free to release myself from indignity, so long as my daughter and grandson were hostages held by fate. But now . . . circumstances have released me. I regret leaving you to the storms of chance, Nikko, as you are a son to me. But . . ." Kishikawa-san sighed deeply. "But . . . I can think of no way to protect you from what is coming. A discredited, defeated old soldier would be no shield for you. You are neither Japanese nor European. I doubt if anyone can protect you. And, because I cannot help you by staying, I feel free to depart. Do I have your understanding, Nikko? And your permission to leave you?"

Nicholai stared into the rapids for some time before he found a way to express himself. "Your guidance, your affection will always be with me. In that way, you can never leave me."

His elbows on the railing looking down at the ghost glow of the foam, the General nodded his head.

The last few weeks in the Otake household were sad ones. Not because of the rumors of setbacks and defeats from all sides. Not because food shortages and bad weather combined to make hunger a constant companion. But because Otake of the Seventh *Dan* was dying.

For years, the tensions of top-level professional play had manifested themselves in almost continuous stomach cramps, which he kept at bay through his habit of taking mint drops; but the pain became ever more intense, and was finally diagnosed as stomach cancer.

When they learned that Otake-san was dying, Nicholai and Mariko discontinued their romantic liaison, without discussion and most naturally. That universal burden of illogical shame that marks the adolescent Japanese prevented them from engaging in so life-embracing an activity as lovemaking while their teacher and friend was dying.

In result of one of those ironies of life that continue to surprise us, although experience insists that irony is Fate's most common figure of speech, it was not until they ended their physical relationship that the household began to suspect them. While they had been engaged in their dangerous and exciting romance, fear of discovery had made them most circumspect in their public behavior toward one another. Once they were no longer guilty of shameful actions, they began to spend more time together, openly walking along the road or sitting in the garden; and it was only then that sly, if affectionate, rumors about them began to be signaled around the family through sidelong glances and lifted eyebrows.

Often, after practice games had been allowed to trail off inconclusively, they talked about what the future would hold, when the war was lost and their beloved teacher was gone. What would life be like when they were no longer members of the Otake household, when American soldiers occupied the nation? Was it true, as they had heard, that the Emperor would call upon them to die on the beaches in a last effort to repulse the invader? Would not such a death be preferable, after all, to life under the barbarians?

They were discussing such things when Nicholai was called by Otake-san's youngest son and told that the teacher would speak with him. Otake-san was waiting in his private six-mat study, the sliding doors of which gave onto the little garden with its decoratively arranged vegetables. This evening its green and brown tones were muted by an unhealthy mist that had descended from the mountains. The air in the room was humid and cool, and the sweet smell of rotting leaves was balanced by the delicious acrid aroma of burning wood. And there was also the faint tone of mint in the air, for Otake-san still took the mint drops that had failed to control the cancer that was draining away his life.

"It is good of you to receive me, Teacher," Nicholai said after several moments of silence. He did not like the formal sound of that, but he could find no balance between the affection and compassion he felt, and the native solemnity of the occasion. During the past three days, Otake-san had arranged long conversations with each of his children and students in turn; and Nicholai, his most promising apprentice, was the last.

Otake-san gestured to the mat beside him, where Nicholai knelt at right angles to the teacher in the polite position that permitted his own face to be read while it protected the privacy of the older man. Uncomfortable with the silence that endured several minutes, Nicholai felt impelled to fill with trivia. "Mist from the mountains is not common at this time of year, Teacher. Some say it is unhealthy. But it brings a new beauty to the garden and to . . ."

Otake-san lifted his hand and shook his head slightly. No time for this. "I shall speak in broad game plan, Nikko, recognizing that my generalizations will be tempered by small exigencies of localized play and conditions."

Nicholai nodded and remained silent. It was the teacher's practice to speak in terms of Gō whenever he dealt with anything of importance. As General Kishikawa had once said, for Otake-san life was a simplistic metaphor for Gō.

"Is this a lesson, Teacher?"

"Not exactly."

"A chastisement, then?"

"It may appear to you to be so. It is really a criticism. But not only of you. A criticism . . . an analysis . . . of what I perceive to be a volatile and dangerous mixture—you and your future life. Let us begin with the recognition that you are a brilliant player." Otake-san lifted his hand. "No. Do not bother with formulas of polite denial. I have seen brilliance of play equal to yours, but never in a man of your age, and not in any player now living. But there are other qualities than brilliance in the successful person, so I shall not burden you with unqualified compliments. There is something distressing in your play, Nikko. Something abstract and unkind. Your play is somehow inorganic . . . unliving. It has the beauty of a crystal, but lacks the beauty of a blossom."

Nicholai's ears were warming, but he gave no outward sign of embarrassment or anger. To chastise and correct is the right, the duty of a teacher.

"I am not saying that your play is mechanical and predictable, for it is seldom that. What prevents it from being so is your astonishing . . ."

Otake-san drew a sudden breath and held it, his eyes staring unseeing toward the garden. Nicholai kept his gaze down, not wishing to embarrass his teacher by observing his struggle with pain. Long seconds passed, and still Otake-san did not breathe. Then, with a little gasp, he unhitched his breath from the notch at which he had held it and slowly let it out, testing for pain all along the exhalation. The crisis passed, and he took two long, thankful breaths through his open mouth. He blinked several times and . . .

". . . what prevents your play from being mechanical and predictable is your astonishing audacity, but even that flair is tainted with the unhuman. You play only against the situation on the board; you deny the importance—the existence even—of your opponent. Have you not yourself told me that when you are in one of your mystic transports, from which you garner rest and strength, you play without reference to your adversary? There is something devilish in this. Something cruelly superior. Arrogant, even. And at odds with your goal of *shibumi*. I do not bring this to your attention for your correction and improvement, Nikko. These qualities are in your bones and unchangeable. And I am not even sure I would have you change if you could; for these that are your flaws are also your strengths."

"Do we speak of Gō only, Teacher?"

"We speak in terms of Gō." Otake-san slipped his hand into his kimono and pressed the palm against his stomach while he took another mint drop. "For all your brilliance, dear student, you have vulnerabilities. There is your lack of experience, for instance. You waste concentration thinking your way through problems that a more experienced player reacts to by habit and memory. But this is not a significant weakness. You can gain experience, if you are careful to avoid empty redundancy. Do not fall into the error of the artisan who boasts of twenty years experience in his craft while in fact he has had only one year of experience—twenty times. And never resent the advantage of experience your elders have. Recall that they have paid for this experience in the coin of life and have emptied a purse that cannot be refilled." Otake-san smiled faintly. "Recall also that the old must make much of their experience. It is all they have left."

For a time, Otake-san's eyes were dull with inner focus as he gazed upon the drab garden, its features disintegrating in the mist. With an effort he pulled his mind from eternal things to continue his last lesson. "No, it is not your lack of experience that is your greatest flaw. It is your disdain. Your defeats will not come from those more brilliant than you. They will come from the patient, the plodding, the mediocre."

Nicholai frowned. This was consonant with what Kishikawa-san had told him as they walked along the cherry trees of the Kajikawa.

"Your scorn for mediocrity blinds you to its vast primitive power. You stand in the glare of your own brilliance, unable to see into the dim corners of the room, to dilate your eyes and see the potential dangers of the mass, the wad of humanity. Even as I tell you this, dear student, you cannot quite believe that lesser men, in whatever numbers, can really defeat you. But we are in the age of the mediocre man. He is dull, colorless, boring—but inevitably victorious. The amoeba outlives the tiger because it divides and continues in its immortal monotony. The masses are the final tyrants. See how, in the arts, *Kabuki* wanes and *Nō* withers while popular novels of violence and mindless action swamp the mind of the mass reader. And even in that timid genre, no author dares to produce a genuinely superior man as his hero, for in his rage of shame the mass man will send his *yojimbo,* the critic, to defend him. The roar of the plodders is inarticulate, but deafening. They have no brain, but they have a thousand arms to grasp and clutch at you, drag you down."

"Do we still speak of Gō, Teacher?"

"Yes. And of its shadow: life."

"What do you advise me to do then?"

"Avoid contact with them. Camouflage yourself with politeness. Appear dull and distant. Live apart and study *shibumi.* Above all, do not let him bait you into anger and aggression. Hide, Nikko."

"General Kishikawa told me almost the same thing."

"I do not doubt it. We discussed you at length his last night here. Neither of us could guess what the Westerner's attitude toward you will be, when he comes. And more than that, we fear your attitude toward him. You are a convert to our culture, and you have the fanaticism of the convert. It is a flaw in your character. And tragic flaws lead to . . ." Otake-san shrugged.

Nicholai nodded and lowered his eyes, waiting patiently for the teacher to dismiss him.

After a time of silence, Otake-san took another mint drop and said, "Shall I share a great secret with you, Nikko? All these years I have told people I take mint drops to ease my stomach. The fact is, I *like* them. But there is no dignity in an adult who munches candy in public."

"No *shibumi,* sir."

"Just so." Otake-san seemed to daydream for a moment. "Yes. Perhaps you are right. Perhaps the mountain mist is unhealthy. But it lends a melancholy beauty to the garden, and so we must be grateful to it."

After the cremation, Otake-san's plans for family and students were carried out. The family collected its belongings to go live with Otake's brother. The students were dispersed to their various homes. Nicholai, now over twenty, although he looked no more than fifteen, was given the money General Kishikawa had left for him and permitted to do what he chose, to go where he wanted. He experienced that thrilling social vertigo that accompanies total freedom in a context of pointlessness.

On the third day of August 1945, all the Otake household were gathered with their cases and packages on the train platform. There was neither the time nor the privacy for Nicholai to say to Mariko what he felt. But he managed to put special emphasis and gentleness into his promise to visit her as soon as possible, once he had established himself in Tokyo. He looked forward to his visit, because Mariko always spoke so glowingly of her family and friends in her home city, Hiroshima.

Washington

THE FIRST ASSISTANT pushed back from his console and shook his head. "There's just not much to work with, sir. Fat Boy doesn't have anything firm on this Hel before he arrives in Tokyo." There was irritation in the First Assistant's tone; he was exasperated by people whose lives were so crepuscular or uneventful as to deny Fat Boy a chance to demonstrate his capacity for knowing and revealing.

"Hm-m," Mr. Diamond grunted absently, as he continued to sketch notes of his own. "Don't worry, the data will thicken up from this point on. Hel went to work for the Occupation Forces shortly after the war, and from then on he remained more or less within our scope of observation."

"Are you sure you really need this probe, sir? You seem to know all about him already."

"I can use the review. Look, something just occurred to me. All we have tying Nicholai Hel to the Munich Five and this Hannah Stern is a first-generation relationship between Hel and the uncle. Let's make sure we're not flying with the wild geese. Ask Fat Boy where Hel is living now." He pressed a buzzer at the side of his desk.

"Yes, sir," the First Assistant said, turning back to his console.

Miss Swivven entered the work area in response to Diamond's buzzer. "Sir?"

"Two things. First: get me all available photographs of Hel, Nicholai Alexandrovitch. Llewellyn will give you the mauve card ID code. Second: contact Mr. Able of the OPEC Interest Group and ask him to come here as soon as possible. When he arrives, bring him down here, together with the Deputy and those two idiots who screwed up. You'll have to escort them down; they don't have access to the Sixteenth Floor."

"Yes, sir." Upon leaving, Miss Swivven closed the door to the wirephoto room just a bit too firmly, and Diamond looked up, wondering what on earth had gotten into her.

Fat Boy was responding to interrogation, His answer clattering up on the First Assistant's machine. "Ah . . . it seems this Nicholai Hel has several residences. There's an apartment in Paris, a place on the Dalmatian coast, a summer villa in Morocco, an apartment in New York, another in London—ah! Here we are. Last known residence equals a château in the bleeding village of Etchebar. This appears to be his principal residence, considering the amount of time he has spent there during the last fifteen years."

"And where is this Etchebar?"

"Ah . . . it's in the Basque Pyrenees, sir."

"Why is it called a 'bleeding' village?"

"I was wondering that myself, sir." The First Assistant queried the computer, and when the answer came he chuckled to himself. "Amazing! Poor Fat Boy had a little trouble translating from French to English. The word *bled* is evidently French for 'a small hamlet.' Fat Boy mistranslated it to 'bleeding.' Too much input from British sources just of late, I suspect."

Mr. Diamond glared across at the First Assistant's back. "Let's pretend that's interesting. So. Hannah Stern took a plane from Rome to the city of Pau. Ask Fat Boy what's the nearest airport to this Etchebar. If it's Pau, then we know we have trouble."

The question was passed on to the computer. The RP screen went blank, then flashed a list of airports arranged in order of their distance from Etchebar. The first on the list was Pau.

Diamond nodded fatalistically.

The First Assistant sighed and slipped his forefinger under his metal glasses, lightly rubbing the red dents. "So there it is. We have every reason to assume that Hannah Stern is now in contact with a mauve-card man. Only three mauve-card holders left alive in the world, and our girl has found one of them. Rotten luck!"

"That it is. Very well, now we know for sure that Nicholai Hel is in the middle of this business. Get back to your machine and root out all we know about him so we can fill Mr. Able in when he gets here. Begin with his arrival in Tokyo."

Japan

THE OCCUPATION WAS in full vigor; the evangelists of democracy were dictating their creed from the Dai Ichi Building across the moat from—but significantly out of sight of—the Imperial Palace. Japan was a physical, economic, and emotional shambles, but the Occupation put their idealistic crusade before mundane concerns for the well-being of the conquered people; a mind won was worth more than a life lost.

With millions of others, Nicholai Hel was flotsam on the chaos of the postwar struggle for survival. Rocketing inflation soon reduced his small store of money to a valueless wad of paper. He sought manual work with the crews of Japanese laborers clearing debris from the bombings; but the foremen mistrusted his motives and doubted his need, considering his race. Nor had he recourse to assistance from any of the occupying powers, as he was a citizen of none of their countries. He joined the flood of the homeless, the jobless, the hungry who wandered the city, sleeping in parks, under bridges, in railway stations. There was a surfeit of workers and a paucity of work, and only young women possessed services valuable to the gruff, overfed soldiers who were the new masters.

When his money ran out, he went two days without food, returning each night from his search for work to sleep in Shimbashi Station together with hundreds of others who were hungry and adrift. Finding places for themselves on or under the benches and in tight rows filling the open spaces, they dozed fitfully, or jolted up from nightmares, hag-ridden with hunger. Each morning the police cleared them out, so traffic could flow freely. And each morning there were eight or ten who did not respond to the prodding of the police. Hunger, sickness, old age, and loss of the will to live had come during the night to remove the burden of life.

Nicholai wandered the rainy streets with thousands of others, looking for any kind of work; looking, at last, for anything to steal. But there was no work, and nothing worth stealing. His high-collared student's uniform was muddy in patches and always damp, and his shoes leaked. He had ripped off the sole of one because it was loose, and the indignity of its flap-flap was unacceptable. He later wished he had bound it on with a rag.

The night of his second day without food, he returned late through the rain to Shimbashi Station. Crowded together under the vast metal vault, frail old men and desperate women with children, their meager belongings rolled up in scraps of cloth, arranged little spaces for themselves with a silent dignity that filled Nicholai with pride. Never before had he appreciated the beauty of the Japanese spirit. Jammed together, frightened, hungry, cold, they dealt with one another under these circumstances of emotional friction with the social lubrication of muttered forms of politeness. Once during the night, a man attempted to steal something from a young woman, and in a brief, almost silent scuffle in a dark corner of the vast waiting room, justice was dealt out quickly and terminally.

Nicholai had the good fortune to find a place under one of the benches where he would not be trod upon by people seeking to relieve themselves during the night. On the bench above him was a woman with two children, one a baby. She talked softly to them until they fell asleep after reminding her, without insistence, that they were hungry. She told them that grandfather was not really dead after all, and was coming to take them away soon. Later, she confected word pictures of her little village on the coast. After they fell asleep, she wept silently.

The old man on the floor beside Nicholai took great pains to set out his valuables on a folded bit of cloth close to his face before nestling down. They consisted of a cup, a photograph, and a letter that had been folded and refolded until the creases were thin and furry. It was a form letter of regret from the army. Before closing his eyes, the old man said good night to the young foreigner beside him, and Nicholai smiled and said good night.

Before a fitful sleep overtook him, Nicholai composed his mind and escaped from the acid gnaw of hunger into mystic transport. When he returned from his little meadow with its waving grasses and yellow sunlight, he was full although hungry, peaceful although desperate. But he knew that tomorrow he must find work or money, or soon he would die.

When the police rousted them shortly before dawn, the old man was dead. Nicholai wrapped the cup, photograph, and letter into his own bundle because it seemed a terrible thing to let all the old man had treasured be swept up and thrown away.

By noon Nicholai had drifted down to Hibiya Park in search of work or something to steal. Hunger was no longer a matter of unsatisfied appetite. It was a jagged cramp and a spreading weakness that made his legs heavy and his head light. As he drifted on the tide of desperate people, waves of unreality washed over him; people and things alternated between being indiscriminate forms and objects of surprising fascination. Sometimes he would find himself flowing within a stream of faceless people, allowing their energy and direction to be his, permitting his thoughts to spiral and short-circuit in a dreamy carousel without meaning. His hunger brought mystic transport close to the surface of his consciousness, and wisps of escape ended with sudden jolts of reality. He would find himself standing, staring at a wall or the face of a person, sensing that this was a remarkable event. No one had ever examined that particular brick with

care and affection before. He was the very first! No one had ever looked at that man's ear in such sharp focus. That must mean something. Mustn't it?

The lightheaded hunger, the shattered spectrum of reality, the aimless drifting were all seductively pleasant, but something within him warned that this was dangerous. He must break out of it or he would die. Die? Die? Did that sound have any meaning?

A dense rivulet of humanity carried him out of the park through an entrance where two broad avenues intersected with a congestion of military vehicles, charcoal automobiles, clanging tramcars, and wobbling bicycles pulling two-wheeled carts loaded down with incredibly heavy and bulky cargoes. There had been a minor accident, and traffic was snarled for a block in every direction while a helpless Japanese traffic policeman in huge white gloves was trying to settle things between a Russian driving an American jeep and an Australian driving an American jeep.

Nicholai was pushed forward unwillingly by the curious crowd that seeped into the spaces around the congealed traffic, intensifying the confusion. The Russians spoke only Russian, the Australians only English, the policeman only Japanese; and all three were engaged in a vigorous discussion of blame and responsibility. Nicholai was pressed against the side of the Australian jeep, whose officer occupant was sitting, staring ahead with stoic discomfort, while his driver was shouting that he would gladly settle this thing man-to-man with the Russian driver, the Russian officer, both at once, or the whole fucking Red Army, if it came to that!

"Are you in a hurry, sir?"

"What?" The Australian officer was surprised to be addressed in English by this ragged lad in a tarnished Japanese student's uniform. It was a couple of seconds before he realized from the green eyes in the gaunt young face that the boy was not Oriental. "Of course I'm in a hurry! I have a meeting—" He snapped his wrist over and looked at his watch. "—twelve minutes ago!"

"I'll help you," Nicholai said. "For money."

"I beg your pardon?" The accent was comic-opera British raj, as is often the case with colonials who feel called upon to play it for more English than the English.

"Give me some money, and I'll help you."

The officer gave his watch another petulant glance. "Oh, very well. Get on with it."

The Australians did not understand what Nicholai said, first in Japanese to the policeman, then in Russian to the Red officer, but they made out the name "MacArthur" several times. The effect of evoking the Emperor's emperor was immediate. Within five minutes a swath had been forced through the tangle of vehicles, and the Australian jeep was conducted onto the grass of the park, whence it was able to cross overland to a wide gravel path and make its way through astonished strollers, finally bouncing down over a curb into a side street that was beyond the jam of traffic, leaving behind a clotted chaos of vehicles sounding horns and bells angrily. Nicholai had jumped into the jeep beside the driver. Once they were free from their problem, the officer ordered the driver to pull over.

"Very well, now what do I owe you?"

Nicholai had no idea of the value of foreign money now. He clutched at a figure. "A hundred dollars."

"*A hundred dollars? Are you mad?*"

"Ten dollars," Nicholai amended quickly.

"Out for whatever you can get, is that it?" the officer sneered. But he tugged out his wallet. "Oh, God! I haven't any scrip at all. Driver?"

"Sorry, sir. Stony."

"Hm! Look. Tell you what. That's my building across the way." He indicated the San Shin Building, center of communications for Allied Occupation Forces. "Come along, and I'll have you taken care of."

Once within the San Shin Building, the officer turned Nicholai over to the office of Pay and Accounts with instructions to make out a voucher for ten dollars in scrip, then he left to make what remained of his appointment, but not before fixing Nicholai with a quick stare. "See here. You're not British, are you?" At that period, Nicholai's English had the accent of his British tutors, but the officer could not align the lad's public school accent with his clothes and physical appearance.

"No," Nicholai answered.

"Ah!" the officer said with obvious relief. "Thought not." And he strode off toward the elevators.

For half an hour, Nicholai sat on a wooden bench outside the office, awaiting his turn; while in the corridor around him people chatted in English, Russian, French, and Chinese. The San Shin Building was one of the few anodes on which the various occupying powers collected, and one could feel the reserve and mistrust underlying their superficial camaraderie. More than half the people working here were civilian civil servants, and Americans outnumbered the others by the same ratio as their soldiers outnumbered the others combined. It was the first time Nicholai heard the growled *r*'s and metallic vowels of American speech.

He was becoming ill and sleepy by the time an American secretary opened the door and called his name. Once in the anteroom, he was given a form to fill in while the young secretary returned to her typing, occasionally stealing glances at this improbable person in dirty clothes. But she was only casually curious; her real attention was on a date she had for that night with a major who was, the other girls all said, real nice and always brought you to a real fine restaurant and gave you a real good time before.

When he handed over his form, the secretary glanced at it, lifted her eyebrows and sniffed, but brought it in to the woman in charge of Pay and Accounts. In a few minutes, Nicholai was called into the inner office.

The woman in charge was in her forties, plumpish and pleasant. She introduced herself as Miss Goodbody. Nicholai did not smile.

Miss Goodbody gestured toward Nicholai's voucher form. "You really have to fill this out, you know."

"I can't. I mean, I can't fill in all the spaces."

"Can't?" Years of civil service recoiled at the thought. "What do you mean . . ." She glanced at the top line of the form. ". . . Nicholai?"

"I can't give you an address. I don't have one. And I don't have an identification card number. Or a—what was it?—sponsoring agency."

"Sponsoring agency, yes. The unit or organization for which you work, or for which your parents work."

"I don't have a sponsoring agency. Does it matter?"

"Well, we can't pay you without a voucher form filled out correctly. You understand that, don't you?"

"I'm hungry."

For a moment, Miss Goodbody was nonplussed. She leaned forward. "Are your parents with the Occupation Forces, Nicholai?" She had come to the assumption that he was an army brat who had run away from home.

"No."

"Are you here alone?" she asked with disbelief.

"Yes."

"Well . . ." She frowned and made a little shrug of futility. "Nicholai, how old are you?"

"I'm twenty-one years old."

"Oh, my. Excuse me. I assumed—I mean, you look no more than fourteen or ..fteen. Oh, well, that's a different matter. Now, let's see. What shall we do?" There was a strong maternal urge in Miss Goodbody, the sublimation of a life of untested sexuality. She was oddly attracted to this young man who had the appearance of a motherless child, but the age of a potential mate. Miss Goodbody identified this mélange of contradictory feelings as Christian concern for a fellow being.

"Couldn't you just give me my ten dollars? Maybe five dollars?"

"Things don't work like that, Nicholai. Even assuming we find a way to fill out this form, it will be ten days before it clears AP&R."

Nicholai felt hope drain away. He lacked the experience to know that the gossamer barriers of organizational dysfunction were as impenetrable as the pavements he trod all day. "I can't have any money then?" he asked atonally.

Miss Goodbody half-shrugged and rose. "I'm sorry, but . . . Listen. It's after my lunch hour. Come with me to the employees' cafeteria. We'll have a bite to eat, and we'll see if we can work something out." She smiled at Nicholai and laid her hand on his shoulder. "Is that all right?"

Nicholai nodded.

The next three months before Miss Goodbody was transferred back to the United States remained forever thrilling and shimmering in her memory. Nicholai was the closest thing to a child she would ever have, and he was her only prolonged affair. She never dared to talk out, or even to analyze for herself, the complex of feelings that tingled through her mind and body during those months. Certainly she enjoyed being needed by someone, enjoyed the security of dependency. Also, she was a genuinely good person who liked giving help to someone who needed it. And in their sexual relations there was a tang of delicious shame, the spice of being at one time mother and lover, a heady brew of affection and sin.

Nicholai never did get his ten dollars; the task of sending through a voucher without an identification card number proved too much even for Miss Goodbody's twenty-odd years of bureaucratic experience. But she did manage to introduce him to the director of translation services, and within a week he was working eight hours a day, translating documents, or sitting in interminable conferences, repeating in two or three languages such overworded and cautious statements as a given representative dared to make in public. He learned that, in diplomacy, the principal function of communication is to mask meaning.

His relations with Miss Goodbody were friendly and polite. As soon as possible he repaid, over her protests, her outlay for clothes and toilet articles, and he insisted on assuming his share of their living expenses. He did not like her enough to be willing to owe her anything. This is not to say he disliked her—she was not the kind one could dislike; she did not arouse feelings of that intensity. At times her mindless babble was annoying; and her hovering attention could be burdensome; but she tried so hard, if clumsily, to be considerate, and she was so dewily grateful for her sexual experiences that he tolerated her with some real affection, affection of the kind one has for a maladroit pet.

Nicholai suffered only one significant problem in living with Miss Goodbody. Because of the high concentration of animal fat in their diets, Westerners have a faintly unpleasant smell that offends the Japanese olfactory sense and dampens ardor notably. Before he became acclimated to this, Nicholai had some difficulty giving himself over to physical transports, and it took him rather a long time to achieve climax. To be sure, Miss Goodbody benefited experientially from her unconscious taint; but as she had minimal grounds for comparison, she assumed that Nicholai's sexual endurance was common. Emboldened by her experience with him, after she returned to the United States she launched into several short-lived affairs, but they were all relative disappointments. She ended with becoming the "grand old woman" of the Feminist Movement.

It was not totally without relief that Nicholai saw Miss Goodbody off on her homeward-bound ship and returned to move out of her government-alloted quarters to a house he had rented in the Asakusa district of northwest Tokyo where, in this rather old-fashioned quarter, he could live with invisible elegance—nearly *shibumi*—and deal with Westerners only during the forty hours a week that produced his living, a luxurious level of living by Japanese standards because of his relatively high pay and, even more important, his access to goods at American post exchanges and commissaries. For Nicholai was now in possession of that most important of human endowments: identification papers. These had been obtained by means of a little winking collusion between Miss Goodbody and friends in the civil service. Nicholai had one ID card that identified him as an American civilian employee, and another that identified him as Russian. On the unlikely event that he might be questioned by American military police, he could produce his Russian identity; and for all other curious nationals, his American papers. Relations between the Russians and Americans were founded in mistrust and mutual fear, and they avoided interfering with one another's nationals over petty events, much as a man crossing the street to rob a bank might avoid jaywalking.

During the next year, Nicholai's life and work expanded. So far as work went, he was sometimes called upon to serve in the cryptography section of Sphinx/FE, before that intelligence organization was consumed by the insatiable new bureaucratic infragovernment of the CIA. Upon one occasion it was not possible to translate the decoded message into English because the Russian into which it had been reduced was almost gibberish. Nicholai asked to see the original cryptograph. Combining his childhood penchant for pure mathematics, his ability to conceive in abstract permutations as developed and displayed in his Gō training, and his native facility in six languages, he was able to locate the errors in decoding fairly easily. He discovered that the original message had been wrongly encoded by someone who wrote a stilted Russian that was organized, quaintly enough, in the Chinese word order, producing by chance a message that baffled the complicated decoding machines of Sphinx/FE. Nicholai had known Chinese who spoke their imperfectly learned Russian in this stilted way, so once he stumbled on the key, the content of the communication fell into place easily. But the clerk/accountant mentalities of the Cryptology Section were impressed, and Nicholai was heralded a "boy wonder"—for most of them assumed he was still a boy. One thoroughly "hep" young code clerk fanned his fingers at Nicholai, calling him a real "quiz kid" and describing the decoding job as "reet, neat, and com-plete!"

So Nicholai was transferred to Sphinx/FE on a permanent basis, given a raise in rank and salary, and allowed to pass his days in a small secluded office, amusing himself with the game of untangling and translating messages in which he had not the slightest interest.

In time, and somewhat to his surprise, Nicholai arrived at a kind of emotional truce with the Americans among whom he worked. This is not to say that he came to like them, or to trust them; but he came to realize that they were not the amoral, depraved people their political and military behavior suggested they were. True, they were culturally immature, brash and clumsy, materialistic and historically myopic, loud, bold, and endlessly tiresome in social encounters; but at bottom they were good-hearted and hospitable; willing to share—indeed insistent upon sharing—their wealth and ideology with all the world.

Above all, he came to recognize that all Americans were merchants, that the core of the American Genius, of the Yankee Spirit, was buying and selling. They vended their democratic ideology like hucksters, supported by the great protection racket of armaments deals and economic pressures. Their wars were monumental exercises in production and supply. Their government was a series of social contracts. Their education was sold as so much per unit hour. Their marriages were emotional deals, the contracts easily broken if one party failed in his debt-servicing. Honor for them consisted in fair trading. And they were not, as they thought, a classless society; they were a one-class society—the mercantile. Their elite were the rich; their workers and farmers were best viewed as flawed and failed scramblers up the middle-class monetary ladder. The peasants and proletariat of America had values identical to those of the insurance salesmen and business executives, the only difference being that these values were expressed in more modest fiscal terms: the motor boat rather than the yacht; the bowling league rather than the country club; Atlantic City rather than Monaco.

Training and inclination had combined to make Nicholai respect and feel affection for all members of the real classes: farmers, artisans, artists, warriors, scholars, priests. But he could feel nothing but disdain for the artificial class of the merchant, who sucks up his living through buying and selling things he does not create, who collects power and wealth out of proportion to his discrimination, and who is responsible for all that is kitsch, for all that is change without progress, for all that is consumption without use.

Following the advice of his mentors to maintain a diffident facade of distant *shibumi,* Nicholai was careful to mask his attitudes from his fellow workers. He avoided their envy by occasionally asking advice on some simple decoding problem, or phrasing his questions so as to guide them to the correct answers. For their parts, they treated him as a kind of freak, an intellectual phenomenon, a boy wonder who had dropped from another planet. To this degree, they were numbly aware of the genetic and cultural gulf separating him from them, but as they saw it, it was they who were within, and he who was without.

And that suited him perfectly, for his real life was centered on his house, built around a courtyard, off a narrow side street in the Asakusa district. Americanization was slow to penetrate this old-fashioned quarter in the northwest section of the city. To be sure, there were little shops engaged in producing imitations of Zippo lighters and cigarette cases bearing the image of the one-dollar bill, and from some bars came the music of Japanese orchestras imitating the "big band" sound, and peppy girl singers squeaking their way through "Don't Sit Under the Apple Tree With Anyone Else But Me," and one saw the occasional young man dressed like a movie gangster in the thought that he looked modern and American, and there were radio advertisements in English promising that Akadama wine would make you bery-bery happy. But the veneer was thin, and still in late May the district celebrated the Festival of Sanja Matsuri, the streets blocked by sweating young men staggering under the weight of black-lacquered, lavishly gilted palanquins, their eyes shining with saki-reinforced trance as they reeled under the weight of their burdens and chanted *washoi, washoi, washoi,* under the direction of magnificently tattooed men wearing only *fundoshi* breechcloths that revealed the complicated "suits of ink" covering their shoulders, backs, arms, and thighs.

Nicholai was returning home through the rain, somewhat fogged with saki after participating in the Festival, when he met Mr. Watanabe, a retired printmaker who was selling matches on the street because his pride would not allow him to beg, although he was seventy-two and all his family was gone. Nicholai declared himself to be in desperate need of matches and offered to buy the entire stock. Mr. Watanabe was delighted to be of service, as the sale would forestall hunger for another day. But when he discovered that the rain had made the matches useless, his sense of honor would not allow him to sell them, despite the fact that Nicholai declared he was particularly seeking soggy matches for an experiment he had in mind.

The next morning, Nicholai woke up with a heavy saki hangover behind his eyes, and no very clear recollection of his conversation with Mr. Watanabe as they had taken a supper of *soba* eaten standing beside the booth, hunched over to keep the rain out of the noodle soup; but he soon learned that he had a permanent house guest. Within a week, Mr. Watanabe came to feel that he was essential to Nicholai and the daily routine of the Asakusa house, and that it would be unkind of him to abandon the friendless young man.

It was a month later that the Tanaka sisters became part of the household. Nicholai was taking a lunchtime stroll in Hibiya Park when he encountered the sisters, robust country girls of eighteen and twenty-one who had fled the starvation that followed floods in the north, and who were reduced to offering themselves to passers-by. Nicholai was their first prospective client, and they approached him so awkwardly and shyly that his compassion was mixed with laughter, for more experienced hookers had equipped them with a scant vocabulary of English consisting solely of the most graphic and vulgar names for items of anatomy and sexual variants. Once installed in the Asakusa house, they reverted to their hard-working, merry, giggling peasant selves, and were the constant concern—and objects of harried affection—for Mr. Watanabe, who had very strict views of proper behavior for young girls. In the natural course of things, the Tanaka sisters came to share Nicholai's bed, where their natural rural vigor was expressed in playful explorations of uncommon and often ballistically improbable combinations. They satisfied the young man's need for sexual expression, unencumbered by emotional involvement beyond affection and gentleness.

Nicholai was never sure just how Mrs. Shimura, the last addition to the family, first entered the household. She simply was there when he returned one evening, and she stayed on. Mrs. Shimura was in her mid-sixties, dour, crabby, constantly grumbling, infinitely kind, and a wonderful cook. There was a brief struggle for territorial domination between Mr. Watanabe and Mrs. Shimura, which was fought out on the grounds of daily marketing, for Mr. Watanabe was in charge of household funds, while Mrs. Shimura was responsible for their daily menus. They came finally to doing the food shopping together, she in charge of quality, he in charge of price; and hard was the lot of the poor greengrocer caught in the crossfire of their bickering.

Nicholai never thought of his guests as a staff of servants because they never thought of themselves in that way. Indeed, it was Nicholai who seemed to lack any precise role with concomitant rights, save that he procured the money on which they all lived.

During these months of freedom and new experience, Nicholai's mind and sensations were exercised in many directions. He maintained body tone through the study and practice of an occult branch of martial arts that accented the use of common household articles as lethal weapons. He was attracted by the mathematical clarity and calculating precision of this rarefied system of combat, the name of which was, by tradition, never spoken aloud, but was formed by a superimposition of the symbols *hoda* (naked) and *korosu* (kill). Throughout his future life, although he was seldom armed, he was never unarmed; for in his hands a comb, a matchbox, a rolled magazine, a coin, even a folded piece of writing paper could be put to deadly use.

For his mind, there was the fascination and intellectual cushion of Gō. He no longer played, because for him the game was intimately tied to his life with Otake-san, to rich and gentle things now gone; and it was safer to close the gates of regret. But he still read commentaries of games and worked out problems for himself on the board. The work at the San Shin Building was mechanical and had no more intellectual challenge than solving crossword puzzles; so, to sop up some of his mental energy, Nicholai began work on a book called *Blossoms and Thorns on the Path Toward Gō,* which was eventually published privately under a pseudonym and enjoyed a certain popularity among the most advanced aficionados of the game. The book was an elaborate joke in the form of a report and commentary on a fictional master's game played at the turn of the century. While the play of the "masters" seemed classic and even brilliant to the average player, there were little blunders and irrelevant placements that brought frowns to the more experienced of the readers. The delight of the book lay in the commentary by a well-informed fool who found a way to make each of the blunders seem a touch of audacious brilliance, and who stretched the limits of imagination by attaching to the moves metaphors for life, beauty, and art, all stated with great refinement and demonstrations of scholarship, but all empty of significance. The book was, in fact, a subtle and eloquent parody of the intellectual parasitism of the critic, and much of the delight lay in the knowledge that both the errors of play and the articulate nonsense of the commentary were so arcane that most readers would nod along in grave agreement.

The first of every month, Nicholai wrote to Otake-san's widow and received in reply fragments of family news concerning ex-pupils and the Otake children. It was by this means that Mariko's death in Hiroshima was confirmed.

When he had learned of the atomic bombing, he had feared that Mariko might be among the victims. He wrote several times to the address she had given him. The first letters simply disappeared into the vortex of disorder left by the bombing, but the last one was returned with the note that this address no longer existed. For a time he played avoidance games in his mind, imagining that Mariko might have been visiting a relative when the bomb was dropped, or she might have been fetching something from a deep cellar, or she might . . . he constructed dozens of improbable narratives accounting for her survival. But she had promised to write him through Mrs. Otake, and no letter ever came.

He was emotionally prepared to receive the final news when it came from Otake-san's widow. Still, for a time, he was diminished and voided, and he felt acid hate for the Americans among whom he worked. But he struggled to cleanse himself of this hate, because such black thoughts blocked the path to mystic transport wherein lay his salvation from the draining effects of depression and sadness. So, for all of one day, he wandered alone and sightless through the streets of his district, remembering Mariko, turning images of her over with the fingers of his mind, recalling the delight and fear and shame of their sexual unions, smiling to himself over private jokes and nonsense. Then, late in the evening, he said good-bye to her and set her aside with gentle affection. There remained autumnal emptiness, but no searing pain and hate, so he was able to cross into his triangular meadow and become one with the sunlight and the waving grass, and he found strength and rest there.

He had also come to peace with the loss of General Kishikawa. After their last long chat among the snowing cherry trees of the Kajikawa, Nicholai received no further word. He knew that the General had been transferred to Manchuria; he learned that the Russians had attacked across the border during the last days of the war when the action involved no military risk and great political gain; and he knew from talking to survivors that some ranking officers had escaped into *seppuku,* and none of those captured by the communists survived the rigors of the "reeducation" camps.

Nicholai consoled himself with the thought that Kishikawa-san had at least escaped the indignity of facing the brutal machinery of the Japanese War Crimes Commission, where justice was perverted by deeply imbedded racism of the kind that had sent Japanese-Americans into concentration camps, while German- and Italian-Americans (formidable voting blocs) were free to profit from the defense industry; this despite the fact that Nisei soldiers in the American army proved their patriotism by being the most decorated and casualty-ridden of all units, although insulted by restriction to the European theater for fear of their loyalty if faced by Japanese troops. The Japanese War Crimes Trials were infected by the same racist assumptions of subhumanity as had condoned the dropping of a uranium bomb on a defeated nation already suing for peace, and the subsequent dropping of a larger plutonium bomb for reasons of scientific curiosity.

What troubled Nicholai most was that the mass of the Japanese condoned the punishment of their military leaders, not for the Japanese reason that many of them had placed their personal glorification and power lust before the interests of their nation and people, but for the Western reason that these men had somehow sinned against retroactive rules of human behavior based on a foreign notion of morality. Many Japanese seemed not to realize that the propaganda of the victor becomes the history of the vanquished.

Young and emotionally alone, surviving precariously in the shadow of the Occupying Forces, whose values and methods he did not care to learn, Nicholai needed an outlet for his energies and frustrations. He found one during his second year in Tokyo, a sport that would take him out of the crowded, sordid city to the unoccupied, un-American mountains: caving.

It was his practice to take lunch with the young Japanese who worked in the San Shin motor pool, because he felt more comfortable with them than with the wisecracking, metal-voiced Americans of the Crypto Center. Since knowing some English was a prerequisite for even the most menial job, most of the men in the motor pool had attended the university, and some of those who washed jeeps and chauffeured officers were graduate mechanical engineers unable to sustain themselves in a jobless, ruined economy.

At first the young Japanese were stiff and uncomfortable in Nicholai's company, but it was not long before, in the open and free way of youth, they accepted him as a green-eyed Japanese who had had the misfortune to misplace his epicanthic fold. He was admitted to their circle and even joined in their hoarse, bawdy laughter concerning the sexual misadventures of the American officers they chauffeured. All these jokes had the same central figure of ridicule: the stereotypic American who was constantly and blindly randy, but tactically incompetent.

The subject of caving came up during one of these lunch breaks when they were all squatting under the corrugated metal roof of a rain shelter, eating from metal boxes the rice and fish that were the rations for Japanese workers. Three of the ex-university men were caving enthusiasts, or had been, before the last desperate year of the war and the chaos of the Occupation. They talked about the fun and difficulty of their expeditions into the mountains and lamented their lack of money and basic supplies to return. By this time, Nicholai had been long in the city, and its noise and congestion were eroding his village-life sensibilities. He drew the young men out on the subject of exploring caves and asked what supplies and equipment were needed. It turned out that their requirements were minimal, although inaccessible on the pittance they were paid by the Occupation Forces. Nicholai suggested that he collect whatever was needed, if they would take him along and introduce him to the sport. The offer was snatched up eagerly, and two weeks later four of them passed a weekend in the mountains, cave-bashing by day and spending their nights at cheap mountain inns where they drank too much saki and talked late into the night in the way of bright young men the world over, the conversation drifting from the Nature of Art, to bawdy double entendre, to plans for the future, to strained puns, to improvised haiku, to horseplay, to politics, to sex, to memories, to silence.

After his first hour underground, Nicholai knew this was the sport for him. His body, lithe and wiry, seemed designed for slithering through tight spots. The rapid and narrow calculations of method and risk were consonant with the mental training Gō had given him. And the fascination of danger was seductive to him. He could never have climbed mountains, because the public bravado of it offended his sense of *shibumi* and dignified reserve. But the moments of risk and daring in the caves were personal, silent, and unobserved; and they had the special spice of involving primitive animal fears. In vertical work down a shaft, there was the thrill and fear of falling, native to all animals and honed keener by the knowledge that the fall would be into a black void below, rather than into the decorative landscape beneath the mountain climber. In the caves, there was the constant presence of cold and damp, primordial fears for man, and real ones for the caver, as most grave accidents and deaths result from hypothermia. There was also the animal dread of the dark, of endless blackness and the ever-present thought of getting lost in mazes of slits and belly crawls so tight that retreat was impossible because of the jointing of the human body. Flash flooding could fill the narrow caves with water with only minutes of warning, or none. And there was the constant mental pressure of knowing that just above him, often scraping against his back as he wriggled through a tight cave, were thousands of tons of rock that must inevitably one day obey gravity and fill in the passage.

It was the perfect sport for Nicholai.

He found the subjective dangers particularly attractive and exhilarating. He enjoyed pitting mental control and physical skill against the deepest and most primitive dreads of the animal within him, the dark, fear of falling, fear of drowning, the cold, solitude, the risk of being lost down there forever, the constant mental erosion of those tons of rock above. The senior ally of the caver is logic and lucid planning. The senior foes are imagination and the hounds of panic. It is easy for the caver to be a coward and difficult to be brave, for he works alone, unseen, uncriticized, unpraised. Nicholai enjoyed the foes he met and the private arena in which he met them. He delighted in the idea that most of the foes were within himself, and the victories unobserved.

Too, there were the unique delights of emerging. Dull, quotidian things took on color and value after hours inside the earth, particularly if there had been danger and physical victory. The sweet air was drunk in with greedy breaths. A cup of bitter tea was something to warm stiff hands, something to delight the eye with its rich color, something to smell gorgeously, a rush of heat down the throat, a banquet of subtly varying flavors. The sky was significantly blue, the grass importantly green. It was good to be slapped on the back by a comrade, touched by a human hand. It was good to hear voices and make sounds that revealed feelings, that shared ideas, that amused friends. Everything was novel and there to be tasted.

For Nicholai, the first hour after emerging from a cave had almost the quality of the life he knew during mystic transport. For that brief hour before objects and experiences retreated again into the commonplace he was almost united with the yellow sunlight and the fragrant grasses.

The four young men went into the mountains every free weekend, and although their amateur class and jury-rigged equipment limited them to bashing about in cave networks that were modest by international caving standards, it was always a thorough test of their will, endurance, and skill, followed by nights of fellowship, talk, saki, and bad jokes richly appreciated. Although in later life Nicholai was to gain a wide reputation for his participation in significant underground expeditions, these apprentice outings were never surpassed for pure fun and adventure.

By the time he was twenty-three, Nicholas had a lifestyle that satisfied most of his needs and compensated for most of his losses, save that of General Kishikawa. To replace the household of Otake-san, he had filled his home in Asakusa with people who took roughly the territorial roles of family members. He had lost his boyhood, and largely boyish, love; but he satisfied his body needs with the irrepressible and inventive Tanaka sisters. His once consuming involvement with the mental disciplines and delights of Gō had been replaced by the emotional and physical ones of caving. In a peculiar and not altogether healthy way, his training in Naked/Kill combat gave vent to the most corrosive aspects of his hatred for those who had destroyed his nation and youth; for during his practice periods he fantasized round-eyed opponents, and felt better for it.

Most of what he had lost was personal and organic, most of his substitutes were mechanical and external; but the gap in quality was bridged in large part by his occasional retreats into the soul-rest of mystic experience.

The most onerous part of his life was the forty hours a week he passed in the basement of the San Shin Building in remunerative drudgery. Breeding and training had given him the inner resources to satisfy his needs without the energy sponge of gainful employment so vital to the men of the egalitarian WAD who have difficulty filling their time and justifying their existence without work. Pleasure, study, and comfort were adequate to him; he did not need the crutch of recognition, the reassurance of power, the narcotic of fun. Unfortunately, circumstance had made it necessary to earn a living, and yet more ironic, to earn it amongst the Americans. (Although Nicholai's co-workers were a mixture of Americans, Britons, and Australians, American methods, values, and objectives were dominant, so he soon came to think of Britons as incompetent Americans and Australians as Americans-in-training.)

English was the language of the Crypto Center, but Nicholai's sense of euphony recoiled at the swallowed mushiness or effete whine of upper class British speech, and the metallic clatter and bow-string twang of American, so he developed an accent of his own, one that took a middle course between the American and the British noises. The effect of this artifice was to cause his Anglophonic associates, throughout his life, to assume he was a native English speaker, but from "somewhere else."

Occasionally, his co-workers would seek to include Nicholai in their plans for parties or outings, never dreaming that what they intended as benevolent condescension toward the foreigner was regarded by Nicholai as presumptuous egalitarianism.

It was not their irritating assumption of equality that annoyed Nicholai so much as their cultural confusions. The Americans seemed to confuse standard of living with quality of life, equal opportunity with institutionalized mediocrity, bravery with courage, machismo with manhood, liberty with freedom, wordiness with articulation, fun with pleasure—in short, all of the misconceptions common to those who assume that justice implies equality for all, rather than equality for equals.

In his most benevolent moods, he thought of Americans as children—energetic, curious, naïve, good-hearted, badly brought up children—in which respect he could detect very little difference between Americans and Russians. Both were hale, vigorous, physical peoples, both excelling in things material, both baffled by beauty, both swaggeringly confident that theirs was the ultimate ideology, both infantile and contentious, and both terribly dangerous. Dangerous because their toys were cosmic weapons that threatened the existence of civilization. The danger lay less in their malice than in their blundering. It was ironic to realize that the destruction of the world would not be the work of Machiavelli, but of Sancho Panza.

He never felt comfortable, having his source of survival dependent on these people, but there was no alternative, and he lived with his discomfort by ignoring it. It was not until the damp and blustery March of his second year that he was forced to learn that, when one dines with wolves, it is moot if one is guest or entrée.

Despite the melancholy weather, the eternal resilience of the Japanese spirit was expressed by the light, optimistic song "Ringo no Uta," which was sweeping the nation and could be heard sung at half voice or hummed under the breath by thousands of people rebuilding from the physical and emotional rubble of the war. The cruel winters of famine were past; the springs of flood and poor harvest were behind; and there was a feeling abroad that the world was on the mend. Even beneath the damp winds of March, trees had begun to collect the faint greenish haze of early spring, the ghost of plenty.

When he arrived at his office that morning, his mood was so benevolent that he even found comic charm in the precious military obscurantism of the sign on his door: SCAP/COMCEN/SPHINX-FE (N-CODE/D-CODE).

His mind ranging elsewhere, he set himself to cleaning up a machine breakout of intercepted messages from the Soviet Occupation Forces of Manchuria, routine communications framed in low-grade code. As he had no interest in the military and political games of the Russians and Americans, he normally worked messages without attending to their content, much as a good stenographer types without reading. It was for this reason that he had already begun on another problem when the import of what he had just read blossomed in his mind. He pulled the sheet from his out box and read it again.

General Kishikawa Takashi was being flown to Tokyo by the Russians to face trial as a Class A War Criminal.

Washington

CONDUCTED BY MISS SWIVVEN, the four men entered the elevator and stood in silence as she slipped her magnetically coded card into the slot marked "Floor 16." The Arab trainee-in-terror whose code name was Mr. Haman lost his balance when, contrary to expectation, the elevator dropped rapidly into the bowels of the building. He bumped into Miss Swivven, who made a slight squeak as his shoulder brushed hers.

"I am so sorry, Madame. I had the assumption that the direction from the first floor to the sixteenth was upward. It should be so, mathematically speaking, but—"

A frown from his OPEC superior stemmed the falsetto babble, so he turned his attention to the taut nape of Miss Swivven's neck.

The OPEC troubleshooter (codetermed Mr. Able, because he was top man in an able-baker-charlie-dog sequence) was embarrassed by his fellow Arab's twittering voice and blundering ways. A third-generation Oxford man whose family had long enjoyed the cultural advantages of participating with the British in the exploitation of their people, Mr. Able scorned this parvenu son of a goatherd who had probably struck oil while overzealously driving a tent peg.

He was further annoyed at being called away from an intimate social affair to deal with some unexplained problem resulting, no doubt, from the incompetence of his compatriot and these CIA ruffians. Indeed, had the summons not borne the authority of the Chairman of the Mother Company, he would have ignored it, for at the moment of interruption he had been enjoying a most charming and titillating chat with a lovely young man whose father was an American senator.

Reacting to the OPEC man's frigid disdain, the Deputy stood well back in the elevator, attempting to appear occupied with more important worries than this little matter.

Darryl Starr, for his part, sought to maintain an image of cool indifference by jingling the coins in his pocket while he whistled between his teeth.

With palpable G-press, the elevator stopped, and Miss Swivven inserted a second magnetic card into the slot to open the doors. The goatherd took this opportunity to pat her ass. She flinched and drew away.

Ah, he thought. A woman of modesty. Probably a virgin. So much the better. Virginity is important to Arabs, who dread comparison, and with good reason.

Daryl Starr quite openly, and the Deputy more guardedly, examined their surroundings, for neither had ever before been admitted to the "Sixteenth Floor" of their building. But Mr. Able shook hands with Diamond curtly and demanded. "What is this all about? I am not pleased to be called here summarily, particularly on an evening when I had something else in hand."

"You'll be even less pleased when I explain," Diamond said. He turned to Starr. "Sit down. I want you to learn the magnitude of your screw-up in Rome."

Starr shrugged with pretended indifference and slid into a white plastic molded chair at the conference table with its etched glass surface for rear projection of computer data. The goatherd was lost in admiring the view beyond the picture window.

"Mr. Haman?" Diamond said.

The Arab's nose touched the glass as he watched with delight the patterns of headlights making slow progress past the Washington Monument—the same cars that always crawled down that avenue at precisely this time of night.

"Mr. Haman?" Diamond repeated.

"What? Oh, yes! I always forget this code name I have been assigned. How humorous of me!"

"Sit," Diamond said dully.

"Pardon me?"

"Sit!"

Grinning awkwardly, the Arab joined Starr at the table as Diamond gestured the OPEC representative to the head of the table, and he himself occupied his orthopedically designed swivel chair on its raised dais. "Tell me, Mr. Able, what do you know about the spoiling raid at Rome International this morning?"

"Almost nothing. I do not burden myself with tactical details. Economic strategy is my concern." He flicked an imaginary speck of dust from the sharp crease of his trousers.

Diamond nodded curtly. "Neither of us should have to deal with this sort of business, but the stupidity of your people and the incompetence of mine makes it necessary—"

"Now, just a minute—" the Deputy began.

"—makes it necessary that we take a hand in the affair. I want to sketch you in on the background, so you'll know what we've got here. Miss Swivven, take notes please." Diamond looked up sharply at the CIA Deputy. "Why are you hovering around like that?"

Lips tight and nostrils flared, the Deputy said, "Perhaps I was waiting for you to order me to sit, as you have the others."

"Very well." Diamond's gaze was flat and fatigued. "Sit."

With an air of having won a diplomatic victory, the Deputy took his place beside Starr.

At no time during the conference was Diamond's snide and bullying tone applied to Mr. Able, for they had worked together on many projects and problems, and they had a certain mutual respect based, not upon friendship to be sure, but upon shared qualities of administrative skill, lucid problem analysis, and capacity to make decisions untrammeled by romantic notions of ethics. It was their role to represent the powers behind them in all paralegal and extra-diplomatic relationships between the Arab oil-producing nations and the Mother Company, whose interests were intimately linked, although neither trusted the other further than the limits of their mutual gain. The nations represented by Mr. Able were potent in the international arena beyond the limited gifts and capacities of their peoples. The industrialized world had recklessly permitted itself to become dependent on Arab oil for survival, although they knew the supply was finite and, indeed, sharply limited. It was the goal of primitive nations, who knew they were the darlings of the technological world only because the needed oil happened to be under their rock and sand, to convert that oil and concomitant political power into more enduring sources of wealth before the earth was drained of the noxious ooze, to which end they were energetically purchasing land all over the world, buying out companies, infiltrating banking systems, and exercising financial control over political figures throughout the industrialized West. They had certain advantages in effecting these designs. First, they could maneuver quickly because they were not burdened by the viscous political systems of democracy. Second the politicians of the West are corrupt and available. Third, the mass of Westerners are greedy, lazy, and lacking any sense of history, having been conditioned by the atomic era to live on the rim of doomsday, and therefore only concerned with ease and prosperity in their own lifetimes.

The cluster of energy corporations that constitute the Mother Company could have broken the blackmail stranglehold of the Arab nations at any time. Raw oil is worthless until it is converted into a profitable pollutant, and they alone controlled the hoarding and distribution facilities. But the Mother Company's long-range objective was to use the bludgeon of contrived oil shortages to bring into their control all sources of energy: coal, atomic, solar, geothermic. As one aspect of their symbiotic affair, OPEC served the Mother Company by creating shortages when She wanted to build pipelines over fragile tundra, or block major governmental investment in research into solar and wind energy, or create natural gas shortfalls when pressing for removal of price controls. In return, the Mother Company serviced the OPEC nations in many ways, not the least of which was applying political pressure during the oil embargo to prevent the Western nations from taking the obvious step of occupying the land and liberating the oil for the common good. Doing this required more rhetorical suppleness than the Arabs realized, because the Mother Company was, at the same time, mounting vast propaganda programs to make the masses believe She was working to make America independent from foreign oil imports, using major stockholders who were also beloved figures from the entertainment world to gain popular support for their exploration of fossil fuel, their endangering of mankind with atomic wastes, their contaminating of the seas with off-shore drilling and reckless mishandling of oil freighters.

Both the Mother Company and the OPEC powers were passing through a delicate period of transition; the one attempting to convert Her oil monopoly into a hegemony over all other energy sources, so Her power and profit would not wane with the depletion of the world's oil supply; the other striving to transform its oil wealth into industrial and territorial possessions throughout the

Western world. And it was to ease their way through this difficult and vulnerable period that they granted unlimited authority to Mr. Diamond and Mr. Able to deal with the three most dangerous obstacles to their success: the vicious efforts of the PLO to use their nuisance value to gain a share of the Arab spoils; the mindless and bungling interference of the CIA and its sensory organ the NSA; and Israel's tenacious and selfish insistence upon survival.

In bold, it was Mr. Diamond's role to control the CIA and, through the international power of the Mother Company, the actions of the Western states; while Mr. Able was assigned the task of keeping the individual Arab states in line. This last was particularly difficult as those powers are an uneasy blend of medieval dictatorships and chaotic military socialisms.

Keeping the PLO in line was their major problem. Both OPEC and the Mother Company agreed that the Palestinians were a pest out of all proportion to their significance, but the vagaries of history had made them and their petty cause a rallying point for the divergent Arab nations. Everyone would gladly have been rid of their stupidity and viciousness, but unfortunately these diseases, although communicable, are not fatal. Still, Mr. Able did what he could to keep them defused and impotent, and had recently drained much of the potency from them by creating the Lebanon disaster.

But he had not been able to prevent Palestinian terrorists from making the Munich Olympics blunder, which wasted years of anti-Jewish propaganda that had been thriving on the basis of latent anti-Semitism throughout the West. Mr. Able had done what he could; he had alerted Mr. Diamond of the event beforehand. And Diamond sent the information on to the West German government, assuming they would handle the matter. Instead, they lay back and let it happen, not that protection of Jews has ever been a dominant theme in the German conscience.

Although there was a long history of cooperation between Diamond and Able, and a certain mutual admiration, there was no friendship. Diamond was uncomfortable with Mr. Able's sexual ambiguity. Beyond that, he detested the Arab's cultural advantages and social ease, for Diamond had been raised on the streets of New York's West Side, and like many risen plebes was driven by that reverse snobbism that assumes breeding to be a personality flaw.

For his part, Mr. Able viewed Diamond with disdain he never bothered to disguise. He saw his own role as a patriotic and noble one, laboring to create a power base for his people when their oil was gone. But Diamond was a whore, willing to submerge the interests of his own people in return for wealth and an opportunity to play at the game of power. He dismissed Diamond as a prototypic American, one whose view of honor and dignity was circumscribed by lust for gain. He thought of Americans as a decadent people whose idea of refinement is fluffy toilet paper. Affluent children who race about their highways, playing with their CB radios, pretending to be World War II pilots. Where is the fiber in a people whose best-selling poet is Rod McKuen, the Howard Cosell of verse?

Mr. Able's mind was running to thoughts like these, as he sat at the head of the conference table, his face impassive, a slight smile of polite distance on his lips. He never permitted his disgust to show, knowing that his people must continue to cooperate with the Americans—until they had finished the task of buying their nation out from under them.

Mr. Diamond was sitting back in his chair, examining the ceiling while he thought of a way to introduce this problem so that it would not seem to be entirely his fault. "All right," he said, "a little background. After the Munich Olympics screw-up, we had your commitment that you would control the PLO and avoid that kind of bad press in the future."

Mr. Able sighed. Well, at least Diamond had not begun his story with the escape of the Israelites across the Red Sea.

"As a sop to them," Diamond continued, "we arranged that whatshisname would be permitted to appear on the UN floor and unleash his slobbering fulminations against the Jews. But despite your assurances, we recently discovered that a cell of Black Septembrists—including two who had participated in the Munich raid—had your permission to run a stupid skyjacking out of Heathrow."

Mr. Able shrugged. "Circumstances alter intentions. I do not owe you an explanation for everything we do. Suffice it to say that this last exercise in blood lust was their price for biding their time until American pressure saps Israel's ability to defend itself."

"And we went along with you on that. As passive assistance, I ordered CIA to avoid any counteraction against the Septembrists. These orders were probably redundant, as the traditions of incompetence within the organization would have effectively neutralized them anyway."

The Deputy cleared his throat to object, but Diamond hushed him with a lift of the hand and continued. "We went a step beyond passive assistance. When we learned that a small, informal group of Israelis was on the track of those responsible for the Munich massacre, we decided to interdict them with a spoiling raid. The leader of this group was one Asa Stern, an ex-political whose son was among the athletes killed in Munich. Because we knew that Stern was suffering from terminal cancer—he died two weeks ago—and his little group consisted only of a handful of idealistic young amateurs, we assumed the combined forces of your Arab intelligence organization and our CIA would be adequate to blow them away."

"And it was not?"

"And it was not. These two men at the table were responsible for the operation, although the Arab was really no more than an agent-in-training. In a very wet and public action they managed to terminate two of the three members of Stern's group . . . along with seven bystanders. But one member, a girl named Hannah Stern, niece of the late leader, slipped through them."

Mr. Able sighed and closed his eyes. Did nothing ever work correctly in this country with its cumbersome form of government? When would they discover that the world is in a post-democratic era? "You say that *one* young woman escaped this spoiling raid? Surely this is not very serious. I cannot believe that one woman is going to London alone and manage singlehandedly to kill six highly trained and experienced Palestinian terrorists who have not only the protection of your organization and mine but, through your good offices, that of British MI-5 and MI-6! It is ridiculous."

"It would be ridiculous. But Miss Stern is not going to London. We are quite sure she went to France. We are also sure that she is now, or soon will be, in contact with one Nicholai Hel—a mauve-card man who is perfectly capable of penetrating your people and mine and all the British, of terminating the Black Septembrists, and of being back in France in time for a luncheon engagement."

Mr. Able looked at Diamond quizzically. "Is that admiration I detect in your voice?"

"No! I would not call it admiration. But Hel is a man we must not ignore. I am going to fill you in on his background so you can appreciate the special lengths to which we may have to go to remedy this screw-up." Diamond turned to the First Assistant, who sat unobtrusively at his console. "Roll up the printout on Hel."

As Fat Boy's lean, prosaic data appeared, rear-projected on the tabletop before them, Diamond quickly sketched out biographic details leading to Nicholai Hel's learning that General Kishikawa was a prisoner of the Russians and scheduled for trial before the War Crimes Commission.

Japan

NICHOLAI REQUESTED AND received a leave of absence, to free his time and energy for the task of locating the General. The next week was nightmarish, a desperate struggle in slow motion against the spongy but impenetrable barricades of red tape, autonomic secrecy, international mistrust, bureaucratic inertia, and individual indifference. His efforts through the Japanese civil government were fruitless. Its systems were static and mired because grafted upon the Japanese propensity toward overorganization and shared authority designed to lessen the burden of individual responsibility for error were elements of alien democracy that brought with them the busy inaction characteristic of that wasteful form of government.

Nicholai then turned to the military governments and, through perseverance, managed to piece together a partial mosaic of events leading to the General's arrest. But in doing so, he had to make himself dangerously visible, although he realized that for one living on forged identity papers and lacking the protection of formal nationality, it was perilous to irritate bureaucrats who thrive on the dysfunctional status quo.

The results of this week of probing and pestering were meager. Nicholai learned that Kishikawa-san had been delivered to the War Crimes Commission by the Soviets, who would be in charge of prosecuting his case, and that he was currently being held in Sugamo Prison. He discovered that an American legal officer was responsible for the defense, but it was not until he had deluged that man with letters and telephone calls that he was granted an interview, and the best he could get was a half hour squeezed into the early morning.

Nicholai rose before dawn and took a crowded tram to the Yotsuya district. A damp, slate-gray morning was smudging the eastern sky as he walked across the Akebonobashi, Bridge of Dawn, beyond which crouched the forbidding bulk of the Ichigaya Barracks which had become symbolic of the inhuman machinery of Western justice.

For three-quarters of an hour, he sat on a wooden bench outside the counsel's office in the basement. Eventually a short-tempered overworked secretary showed him into Captain Thomas's cluttered work room. The Captain waved him to a chair without looking up from a deposition he was scanning. Only after finishing it and scribbling a marginal note did Captain Thomas raise his eyes.

"Yes?" There was more fatigue than curtness in his tone. He was personally responsible for the defense of six accused war criminals, and he had to work with limited personnel and resources, compared to the vast machinery of research and organization at the disposal of the prosecution in their offices above. Unfortunately for his peace of mind, Captain Thomas was idealistic about the fairness of Anglo-Saxon law, and he drove himself so hard that weariness, frustration, and bitter fatalism tainted his every word and gesture. He wanted nothing more than to see all this mess over and return to civilian life and to his small-town legal practice in Vermont.

Nicholai explained that he was seeking information about General Kishikawa.

"Why?"

"He is a friend."

"A friend?" The Captain was dubious.

"Yes, sir. He . . . helped me when I was in Shanghai."

Captain Thomas tugged the Kishikawa brief from under a stack of similar folders. "But you were just a child then."

"I am twenty-three, sir."

The Captain's eyebrows went up. Like everyone else, he was fooled by Nicholai's genetic disposition toward youthful appearance. "I'm sorry. I assumed you were much younger. What do you mean when you say that Kishikawa helped you?"

"He cared for me when my mother died."

"I see. You're British, are you?"

"No."

"Irish?" Again the accent that was always identified as being from "someplace else."

"No, Captain. I work for SCAP as a translator." It was best to sidestep the irrelevant tangle of his nationality—or rather, his lack thereof.

"And you're offering yourself as a character witness, is that it?"

"I want to help you in any way I can."

Captain Thomas nodded and fumbled about for a cigarette. "To be perfectly frank, I don't believe you can help all that much. We're understaffed here, and overworked. I've had to decide to concentrate my energy on cases where there is some chance of success. And I wouldn't put Kishikawa's in that category. That probably sounds cold-blooded to you, but I might as well be honest."

"But . . . I can't believe General Kishikawa was guilty of anything! What is he being accused of?"

"He's in the Class A grab bag: crimes against humanity—whatever the hell that means."

"But who's testifying against him? What do they say he did?"

"I don't know. The Russians are handling the prosecution, and they're not permitting me to examine their documents and sources until the day before the trial. I assume the charges will center around his actions as military governor of Shanghai. Their propaganda people have several times used the label: 'The Tiger of Shanghai.' "

" 'The Tiger of'—! That is insane! He was an administrator. He got the water supply working again—the hospitals. How can they . . . ?"

"During his governorship, four men were sentenced and executed. Did you know that?"

"No, but—"

"For all I know, those four men might have been murderers or looters or rapists. I *do* know that the average number of executions for capital crimes during the ten years of British control was fourteen point six. You would think that comparison would be in your general's favor. But the men executed under him are being described as 'heroes of the people.' And you can't go around executing heroes of the people and get away with it. Particularly if you are known as 'The Tiger of Shanghai.' "

"He was never called that!"

"That's what they're calling him now." Captain Thomas sat back and pressed his forefingers into his sunken eye sockets. Then he tugged at his sandy hair in an effort to revive himself." "And you can bet your Aunt Tilly's twat that that title will be used a hundred times during the trial. I'm sorry if I sound defeatist, but I happen to know that winning this one is very important to the Soviets. They're making a big propaganda number out of it. As you probably know, they've picked up a lot of flack for failing to repatriate their war prisoners. They've been keeping them in 'reeducation camps' in Siberia until they can be returned fully indoctrinated. And they have not delivered a single war criminal, other than Kishikawa. So this is a set piece for them, a chance to let the people of the world know they're doing their job, vigorously purging Japanese Capitalist Imperialists, making the world safe for socialism. Now, you seem to think this Kishikawa is innocent. Okay, maybe so. But I assure you that he qualifies as a war criminal. You see, the primary qualification for that honor is to be on the losing side—and that he was." Captain Thomas lighted one cigarette from another and stubbed out the punk in an overflowing ashtray. He puffed out a breath in a mirthless chuckle. "Can you imagine what would have happened to FDR or General Patton if the other side had won? Assuming they had been so self-righteous as to set up war-crimes trials. Shit, the only people who would have escaped being labeled 'warmongers' would have been those isolationist hicks who kept us out of the League of Nations. And chances are they would have been set up as puppet rulers, just as we have set up their opposite numbers in the Diet. That's the way it is, son. Now, I've got to get back to work. I go to trial tomorrow representing an old man who's dying of cancer and who claims he never did anything but obey the commands of his Emperor. But he'll probably be called the 'Leopard of Luzon' or the 'Puma of Pago-Pago.' And you know what, kid? For all I know, he might really have been the Leopard of Luzon. It won't matter much one way or the other."

"Can I at least see him? Visit him?"

Captain Thomas's head was down; he was already scanning the folder on the forthcoming trial. "What?"

"I want to visit General Kishikawa. May I?"

"I can't do anything about that. He's a Russian prisoner. You'll have to get permission from them."

"Well, how do *you* get to see him?"

"I haven't yet."

"You haven't even talked to him?"

Captain Thomas looked up blearily. "I've got six weeks before he goes to trial. The Leopard of Luzon goes up tomorrow. Go see the Russians. Maybe they can help you."

"Whom do I see?"

"Shit, boy, I don't know!"

Nicholai rose. "I see. Thank you."

He had reached the door when Captain Thomas said, "I'm sorry, son. Really."

Nicholai nodded and left.

In months to come, Nicholai was to reflect on the differences between Captain Thomas and his Russian opposite number, Colonel Gorbatov. They were symbolic variances in the superpowers' ways of thinking and dealing with men and problems. The American had been genuinely concerned, compassionate, harried, ill-organized . . . ultimately useless. The Russian was mistrustful, indifferent, well prepared and informed, and ultimately of some value to Nicholai, who sat in a large, overstuffed chair as the Colonel stirred his glass of tea thoughtfully until two large lumps of sugar disintegrated and swirled at the bottom, but never completely dissolved.

"You are sure you will not take tea?" the Colonel asked.

"Thank you, no." Nicholai preferred to avoid wasting time on social niceties.

"For myself, I am addicted to tea. When I die, the fellow who does my autopsy will find my insides tanned like boot leather." Gorbatov smiled automatically at the old joke, then set down the glass in its metal holder. He unthreaded his round metal-rimmed glasses from his ears and cleaned them, or rather distributed the smudge evenly, using his thumb and finger. As he did so, he settled his hooded eyes on the young man sitting across from him. Gorbatov waas farsighted and could see Nicholai's boyish face and startling green eyes better with his glasses off. "So you are a friend of General Kishikawa? A friend concerned with his welfare. Is that it?"

"Yes, Colonel. And I want to help him, if I can."

"That's understandable. After all, what are friends for?"

"At very least, I would like permission to visit him in prison."

"Yes, of course you would. That's understandable." The Colonel replaced his glasses and sipped his tea. "You speak Russian very well, Mr. Hel. With quite a refined accent. You have been trained very carefully."

"It's not a matter of being trained. My mother was Russian."

"Yes, of course."

"I never learned Russian formally. It was a cradle language."

"I see. I see." It was Gorbatov's style to place the burden of communication on the other person, to draw him out by contributing little beyond constant indications that he was unconvinced. Nicholai allowed the transparent tactic to work because he was tired of fencing, frustrated with short leads and blind alleys, and eager to learn about Kishikawa-san. He offered more information than necessary, but even as he spoke, he realized that his story did not have the sound of truth. That realization made him explain even more carefully, and the meticulous explanations made it sound more and more as though he were lying.

"In my home, Colonel, Russian, French, German, and Chinese were all cradle languages."

"It must have been uncomfortable, sleeping in so crowded a cradle."

Nicholai tried to laugh, but the sound was thin and unconvincing.

"But of course," Gorbatov went on, "you speak English as well?" The question was posed in English with a slight British accent.

"Yes," Nicholai answered in Russian. "And Japanese. But these were learned languages."

"Meaning: not cradle?"

"Meaning just that." Nicholai instantly regretted the brittle sound his voice had assumed.

"I see." The Colonel leaned back in his desk chair and regarded Nicholai with a squint of humor in his Mongol-shaped eyes. "Yes," he said at last, "very well trained. And disarmingly young. But for all your cradle and post-cradle languages, Mr. Hel, you are an American, are you not?"

"I *work* for the Americans. As a translator."

"But you showed an American identification card to the men downstairs."

"I was issued the card because of my work."

"Oh, of course. I see. But as I recall, my question was not *whom* you worked for—we already knew that—but what your nationality is. You are an American, are you not?"

"No, Colonel, I am not."

"What then?"

"Well . . . I suppose I am more Japanese than anything."

"Oh? You will excuse me if I mention that you do not look particularly Japanese?"

"My mother was Russian, as I told you. My father was German."

"Ah! That clarifies everything. A typical Japanese ancestry."

"I cannot see what difference it makes what my nationality is!"

"It's not important that you be able to see it. Please answer my question."

The sudden frigidity of tone caused Nicholai to calm his growing anger and frustration. He drew a long breath. "I was born in Shanghai. I came here during the war—under the protection of General Kishikawa—a family friend."

"Then of what nation are you a citizen?"

"None."

"How awkward that must be for you."

"It is, yes. It made it very difficult to find work to support myself."

"Oh, I am sure it did, Mr. Hel. And in your difficulties, I understand how you might be willing to do almost anything to secure employment and money."

"Colonel Gorbatov, I am not an agent of the Americans. I am in their employ, but I am not their agent."

"You make distinctions in shading which, I confess, are lost upon me."

"But why would the Americans want to interview General Kishikawa? What reason would they have to go through an elaborate charade just to contact an officer with a largely administrative career?"

"Precisely what I hoped you would clarify for me, Mr. Hel." The Colonel smiled.

Nicholai rose. "It is evident to me, Colonel, that you are enjoying our conversation more than I. I must not squander your valuable time. Surely there are flies waiting to have their wings pulled off."

Gorbatov laughed aloud. "I haven't heard that tone for years! Not only the cultivated sound of court Russian, but even the snide disdain! That's wonderful! Sit down, young man. Sit down. And tell me why you must see General Kishikawa."

Nicholai dropped into the overstuffed chair, voided, weary. "It is more simple than you are willing to believe. Kishikawa-san is a friend. Almost a father. Now he is alone, without family, and in prison. I must help him, if I can. At very least, I must see him . . . talk to him."

"A simple gesture of filial piety. Perfectly understandable. Are you sure you won't have a glass of tea?"

"Quite sure, thank you."

As he refilled his glass, the Colonel opened a manila folder and glanced at the contents. Nicholai assumed that the preparation of this file was the cause of his three-hour wait in the outer offices of the headquarters of Soviet Occupation Forces. "I see that you also carry papers identifying you as a citizen of the USSR. Surely that is sufficiently uncommon as to merit an explanation?"

"Your sources of information within SCAP are good."

The Colonel shrugged. "They are adequate."

"I had a friend—a woman—who helped me get employment with the Americans. It was she who got my American identification card for me—"

"Excuse me, Mr. Hel. I seem to be expressing myself poorly this afternoon. I did not ask you about your American papers. It was your Russian identity card that interested me. Will you forgive my vagueness?"

"I was trying to explain that."

"Oh, do excuse me."

"I was going to tell you that this woman realized I might get into some trouble if the Americans discovered I was not a citizen. To avoid this, she also had papers made up indicating a Russian nationality, so I could show them to curious American MP's and avoid questioning."

"And how often have you been driven to this baroque expedient?"

"Never."

"Hardly a frequency that justifies the effort. And why Russian? Why was not some other nationality selected from that crowded cradle of yours?"

"As you have pointed out, I do not look convincingly Oriental. And the attitude of the Americans toward German nationals is hardly friendly."

"While their attitude toward Russians, on the other hand, is fraternal and compassionate? Is that it?"

"Of course not. But they mistrust and fear you, and for that reason, they do not treat Soviet citizens high-handedly."

"This woman friend of yours was very astute. Tell me why she went to such efforts on your behalf. Why did she take such risks?"

Nicholai did not answer, which was sufficient answer.

"Ah, I see," Colonel Gorbatov said. "Of course. Then too, Miss Goodbody was a woman no longer burdened with her first youth."

Nicholai flushed with anger. "You know all about this!"

Gorbatov tugged off his glasses and redistributed the smear. "I know certain things. About Miss Goodbody, for instance. And about your household in the Asakusa district. My, my my. *Two* young ladies to share your bed? Profligate youth! And I know that your mother was the Countess Alexandra Ivanovna. Yes, I know certain things about you."

"And you have believed me all the while, haven't you."

Gorbatov shrugged. "It would be more accurate to say that I have believed the details with which your story is garnished. I know that you visited Captain Thomas of the War Crimes Tribunal Staff last . . ." He glanced at the folder. ". . . last Tuesday morning at seven-thirty. I presume he told you there was nothing he could do for you in the matter of General Kishikawa who, apart from being a major war criminal guilty of sins against humanity, is also the only high-ranking officer of the Japanese Imperial Army to survive the rigors of reeducation camp, and is therefore a figure of value to us from the point of view of prestige and propaganda." The Colonel threaded his glasses from ear to ear. "I am afraid there is nothing you can do for the General, young man. And if you pursue this, you will expose yourself to investigation by American Intelligence—a title more indicative of what they seek than of what they possess. And if there was nothing my ally and brother-in-arms, Captain Thomas, could do for you, then certainly there is nothing I can do. He, after all, represents the defense. I represent the prosecution. You are quite sure you will not take a glas of tea?"

Nicholai grasped for whatever he could get. "Captain Thomas told me I would need your permission to visit the General."

"That is true."

"Well?"

The Colonel turned in his desk chair toward the window and tapped his front teeth with his forefinger as he looked out on the blustery day. "Are you sure he would want a visit from you, Mr. Hel? I have talked to the General. He is a man of pride. It might not be pleasant for him to appear before you in his present state. He has twice attempted to commit suicide, and now he is watched over very strictly. His present condition is degrading."

"I must try to see him. I owe him . . . very much."

The Colonel nodded without looking back from the window. He seemed lost in thoughts of his own.

"Well?" Nicholai asked after a time.

Gorbatov did not answer.

"May I visit the General?"

His voice distant and atonic, the Colonel said, "Yes, of course." He turned to Nicholai and smiled. "I shall arrange it immediately."

Although so crowded into the swaying elevated car of the Yamate loop line that he could feel the warmth of pressing bodies seep through the damp of their clothing and his, Nicholai was isolated within his confusion and doubts.

Through gaps between people, he watched the city passing beneath, dreary in the chill wet day, sucked empty of color by the leaden skies.

There had been subtle threat in Colonel Gorbatov's atonic permission to visit Kishikawa-san, and all morning Nicholai had felt diminished and impotent against the foreboding he felt. Perhaps Gorbatov had been right when he suggested that this visit might not, after all, be an act of kindness. But how could he allow the General to face his forthcoming trial and disgrace alone? It would be an act of indifference for which he could never forgive himself. Was it for his own peace of mind, then, that he was going to Sugamo Prison? Were his motives at base selfish?

At the Komagome Station, one stop before Sugamo Prison, Nicholai had a sudden impulse to get off the train—to return home, or at least wander about for a while and consider what he was doing. But this survival warning came too late. Before he could push his way to the doors, they clattered shut, and the tram jerked away. He was certain he should have gotten off. He was equally certain that now he would go through with it.

Colonel Gorbatov had been generous; he had arranged that Nicholai would have an hour with Kishikawa-san. But now as Nicholai sat in the chilly visiting room, staring at the flaking green paint on the walls, he wondered if there would be anything to say that could fill a whole hour. A Japanese guard and an Americn MP stood by the door, ignoring one another, the Japanese staring at the floor before him, while the American devoted his attention to the task of snatching hairs from his nostrils. Nicholai had been searched with embarrassing thoroughness in an anteroom before being admitted to the visiting area. The rice cakes he had brought along wrapped in paper had been taken from him by the American MP, who took Nicholai for an American on the strength of his identification card and explained, "Sorry, pal. But you can't bring chow with you. This—ah—whatshisname, the gook general—he's tried to bump himself off. We can't run the risk of poison or whatever. You dig?"

Nicholai said that he dug. And he joked with the MP, realizing that he must put himself on the good side of the authorities, if he was to help Kishikawa-san in any way. "Yeah, I know what you mean, sergeant. I sometimes wonder how any Japanese officers survived the war, what with their inclination toward suicide."

"Right. And if anything happened to this guy, my ass would be in a sling. Hey. What in hell's this?" The sergeant held up a small magnetic Gō board Nicholai had thought to bring along at the last minute, in case there was nothing to say and the embarrassment should hang too heavily.

Nicholai shrugged. "Oh, a game. Sort of a Japanese chess."

"Oh yeah?"

The Japanese guard, who stood about awkwardly in the knowledge of his redundancy in this situation, was glad to be able to tell his American opposite number in broken English that it was indeed a Japanese game.

"Well, I don't know, pal. I don't know if you can bring this in with you."

Nicholai shrugged again. "It's up to you, sergeant. I thought it might be something to pass the time if the General didn't feel like talking."

"Oh? You talk gook?"

Nicholai had often wondered how that word, a corruption of the Korean name for its people, had become the standard term of derogation in the American military vocabulary for all Orientals.

"Yes, I speak Japanese." Nicholai recognized the need for duplicity where sensibility meets stony ignorance. "You probably noticed from my ID card that I work for Sphinx?" He looked steadily at the sergeant and tipped his head slightly toward the Japanese guard, indicating that he didn't want to go into this too deeply with alien ears around.

The MP frowned in his effort to think, then he nodded conspiratorily. "I see. Yeah, I sort of wondered how come an American was visiting this guy."

"A job's a job."

"Right. Well, I guess it's okay. What harm can a game do?" He returned the miniature Gō board and conducted Nicholai to the visiting room.

Five minutes later the door opened, and General Kishikawa entered, followed by two more guards, another Japanese, and a thick-set Russian with the immobile, meaty face of the Slavic peasant. Nicholai rose in greeting, as the two new protectors took up their positions against the wall.

As Kishikawa-san approached. Nicholai automatically made a slight head bow of filial obeisance. The gesture was not lost upon the Japanese guards, who exchanged brief glances, but remained silent.

The General shuffled forward and took the chair opposite Nicholai, across the rough wooden table. When at last he lifted his eyes, the young man was struck by the General's appearance. He had expected an alteration in Kishikawa-san's features, an erosion of his gentle virile manner, but not this much.

The man sitting opposite him was old, frail, diminished. There was an oddly priestly look to his transparent skin and slow, uncertain movements. When finally he spoke, his voice was soft and monotonic, as if communication was a pointless burden.

""Why have you come, Nikko?"

"To be with you, sir."

"I see."

There followed a silence during which Nicholai could think of nothing to say, and the General had nothing to say. Finally, with a long, fluttering sigh, Kishikawa-san assumed the responsibility for the conversation because he did not want Nicholai to feel uncomfortable with the silence. "You look well, Nikko. Are you?

"Yes, sir."

"Good. Good. You grow more like your mother each day. I can see her eyes in yours." He smiled faintly. "Someone should have advised your family that this particular color of green was meant for jade or ancient glass, not for human eyes. It is disconcerting."

Nicholai forced a smile. "I shall speak to an ophthalmologist, sir, to see if there is a remedy for our blunder."

"Yes. Do that."

"I shall."

"Do." The General gazed away and seemed for a second to forget Nicholai's presence. Then: "So? How are you getting on?"

"Well enough. I work for the Americans. A translator."

"So? And do they accept you?"

"They ignore me, which is just as well."

"Better, really."

There was another brief silence, which Nicholai was going to break with small talk when Kishikawa-san raised his hand.

"Of course you have questions. I will tell you things quickly and simply, then we shall discuss them no further."

Nicholai bowed his head in compliance.

"I was in Manchuria, as you know. I became sick—pneumonia. I was in fever and coma when the Russians attacked the hospital unit where I was. When I became myself again, I was in a reeducation camp, under constant surveillance and unable to use the portal through which so many of my brother officers had escaped the indignity of surrender and the humiliations of . . . reeducation. Only a few other officers were captured. They were taken away somewhere and not heard of again. Our captors assumed that officers were either incapable or unworthy of . . . reeducation. I assumed this would be my fate also, and I awaited it with such calm as I could manage. But no. Evidently, the Russians thought that one thoroughly reeducated officer of general rank would be a useful thing to introduce into Japan, to aid them with their plans for the future of our country. Many . . . many . . . many methods of reeducation were employed. The physical ones were easiest to bear—hunger, sleeplessness, beatings. But I am a stubborn old man, and I do not reeducate easily. As I had no family left alive in Japan, as hostages, they were denied the emotional whip with which they had reeducated others. A long time passed. A year and a half, I think. It is difficult to tell the seasons when you never see the light of day, and when endurance is measured in five more minutes . . . five more minutes . . . I can stand this for five more minutes." The General was lost for a time in memories of specific torments. Then, with a faint start, he returned to his story. "Sometimes they lost patience with me and made the error of giving me periods of rest in unconsciousness. A long time passed in this way. Months measured in minutes. Then suddenly they stopped all efforts toward my reeducation. I assumed, of course, that I would be killed. But they had something more degrading in mind for me. I was cleaned and deloused. A plane trip. A long ride on a railroad. Another plane trip. And I was here. For a month, I was kept here with no idea of their intentions. Then, two weeks ago, a Colonel Gorbatov visited me. He was quite frank with me. Each occupying nation has offered up its share of war criminals. The Soviets have had none to offer, no direct participation in the machinery of international justice. Before me, that is."

"But, sir—"

Kishikawa-san lifted his hand for silence. "I decided I would not face this final humiliation. But I had no way to release myself. I have no belt. My clothes, as you see, are of stout canvas that I have not the strength to tear. I eat with a wooden spoon and bowl. I am permitted to shave only with an electric razor, and only under close surveillance." The General smiled a gray smile. "The Soviets prize me, it would appear. They are concerned not to lose me. Ten days ago, I stopped eating. It was easier than you might imagine. They threatened me, but when a man decides to live no longer, he removes the power of others to make potent threats. So . . . they held me down on a table and forced a rubber tube down my throat. And they fed me liquids. It was ghastly . . . humiliating . . . eating and vomiting all at once. It was without dignity. So I promised to start eating again. And here I am."

Throughout this minimal explanation, Kishikawa-san had riveted his eyes on the rough surface of the table, intense and defocused.

Nicholai's eyes stung with brimming tears. He stared ahead, not daring to blink and send tears down his cheeks that would embarrass his father—his friend, that is.

Kishikawa-san drew a long breath and looked up. "No, no. There's no point in that, Nikko. The guards are looking on. Don't give them this satisfaction." He reached across and patted Nicholai's cheek with a firmness that was almost an admonitory slap.

At this point, the American sergeant straightened up, ready to protect his Sphinx compatriot from this gook general.

But Nicholai scrubbed his face with his hands, as though in fatigue, and with this gesture he rid himself of the tears.

"So!" Kishikawa-san said with new energy. "It is nearly time for the blossoms of Kajikawa. Do you intend to visit them?"

Nicholai swallowed. "Yes."

"That's good. The Occupation Forces have not chopped them down, then?"

"Not physically."

The General nodded. "And have you friends in your life, Nikko?"

"I . . . I have people living with me."

"As I recall from a letter from our friend Otake shortly before his death, there was a girl in his household, a student—I am sorry, but I don't remember her name. Evidently you were not totally indifferent to her charms. Do you still see her?"

Nicholai considered before answering. "No, sir, I don't."

"Not a quarrel, I hope."

"No. Not a quarrel."

"Ah, well, at your age affections ebb and flow. When you get older, you will discover that you cling to some with desperation." The effort to make Nicholai comfortable with social talk seemed to exhaust Kishikawa-san. There was really nothing he wanted to say, and after his experiences of the past two years, nothing he wanted to know. He bowed his head and stared at the table, slipping into the tight cycle of abbreviated thoughts and selected memories from his childhood with which he had learned to narcotize his imagination.

At first, Nicholai found comfort in the silence too. Then he realized that they were not together in it, but alone and apart. He drew the miniature Gō board and packet of metal stones from his pocket and set it on the table.

"They have given us an hour together, sir."

Kishikawa-san tugged his mind to the present. "What? Ah, yes. Oh, a game. Good, yes. It is something we can do together painlessly. But I have not played for a long time, and I shall not be an interesting opponent for you, Nikko."

"I haven't played since the death of Otake-san myself, sir."

"Oh? Is that so?"

"Yes. I am afraid I have made a waste of the years of training."

"No. It is one of the things one cannot waste. You have learned to concentrate deeply, to think subtly, to have affection for abstractions, to live at a distance from quotidian things. Not a waste. Yes, let's play."

Automatically returning to their first days together, and forgetting that Nicholai was now a far superior player, General Kishikawa offered a two stone advantage, which Nicholai of course accepted. For a time they played a vague and undistinguished game, concentrating only deeply enough to absorb mental energy that would otherwise have tormented them with memories, and with anticipations of things to come. Eventually the General looked up and sighed with a smile. "This is no good. I have played poorly and driven all *aji* out of the game."

"So have I."

Kishikawa-san nodded. "Yes. So have you."

"We'll play again, if you wish, sir. During my next visit. Perhaps we'll play better."

"Oh? Have you permission to visit me again?"

"Yes. Colonel Gorbatov has arranged that I may come tomorrow. After that . . . I'll apply to him again and see."

The General shook his head. "He is a very shrewd man, this Gorbatov."

"In what way, sir?"

"He has managed to remove my 'stone of refuge' from the board."

"Sir?"

"Why do you think he let you come here, Nikko? Compassion? You see, once they had removed from me all means of escape into an honorable death, I decided that I would face the trial in silence, in a silence as dignified as possible. I would not, as others have done, struggle to save myself by implicating friends and superiors. I would refuse to speak at all, and accept their sentence. This did not please Colonel Gorbatov and his compatriots. They would be cheated out of the propaganda value of their only war criminal. But there was nothing they could do. I was beyond the sanctions of punishment and the attractions of leniency. And they lacked the emotional hostages of my family, because, so far as they knew, my family had died in the carpet bombing of Tokyo. Then . . . then fate offered them you."

"Me, sir?"

"Gorbatov was perceptive enough to realize that you would not expose your delicate position with the Occupation Forces by making efforts to visit me unless you honored and loved me. And he reasoned—not inaccurately—that I reciprocate these feelings. So now he has his emotional hostage. He allowed you to come here to show me that he had you. And he does have you, Nikko. You are uniquely vulnerable. You have no nationality, no consulate to protect you, no friends who care about you, and you live on forged identity papers. He told me all of this. I am afraid he has 'confined the cranes to their nest,' my son."

The impact of what Kishikawa-san was saying grew in Nicholai. All the time and effort he had spent trying to contact the General, all this desperate combat against institutional indifference, had had the final effect of stripping the General of his armor of silence. He was not a consolation to Kishikawa-san; he was a weapon against him. Nicholai felt a medley of anger, shame, outrage, self-pity, and sorrow for Kishikawa-san.

The General's eyes crinkled into a listless smile. "This is not your fault, Nikko. Nor is it mine. It is fate only. Bad luck. We will not talk about it again. We will play when you come back, and I promise to offer you a better game."

The General rose and walked to the door, where he waited to be escorted out by the Japanese and Russian guards, who left him standing there until Nicholai nodded to the American MP, who in turn nodded to his opposite numbers.

For a time, Nicholai sat numbly, picking the metal stones off the magnetic board with his fingernail.

The American sergeant approached and asked in a low, conspiratorial voice, "Well? You find out what you were looking to?"

"No," Nicholai said absently. Then more firmly: "No, but we'll talk again."

"You going to soften him up with that silly-assed gook game again?"

Nicholai stared at the sergeant, his green eyes arctic.

Uncomfortable under the gaze, the MP explained, "I mean . . . well, it's only a sort of chess or checkers or something, isn't it?"

Intending to scour this prole with his disdain for things Western, Nicholai said, "Gō is to Western chess what philosophy is to double-entry accounting."

But obtuseness is its own protection against both improvement and punishment. The sergeant's response was frank and naïve: "No shit?"

A needle-fine rain stung Nicholai's cheek as he stared across from the Bridge of Dawn to the gray bulk of the Ichigaya Barracks, blurred but not softened by the mist, its rows of windows smeared with wan yellow light, indicating that the Japanese War Crimes Trials were in progress.

He leaned against the parapet, his eyes defocused, rain running from his hair, down his face and neck. His first thought after leaving Sugamo Prison had been to appeal to Captain Thomas for help against the Russians, against this emotional blackmail of Colonel Gorbatov. But even as he formed the idea, he realized the pointlessness of appealing to the Americans, whose basic attitudes and objectives regarding the disposition of Japanese leaders were identical with the Soviets'.

After descending from the tramcar and wandering without destination in the rain, he had stopped at the rise of the bridge to look down for a few seconds and collect his thoughts. That was half an hour ago, and still he was stunned to inaction by a combination of churning fury and draining helplessness.

Although his fury had its roots in love of a friend and filial obligation, it was not without base self-pity. It was anguishing that *he* should be the means by which Gorbatov would deny Kishikawa-san the dignity of silence. The ironic unfairness of it was overwhelming. Nicholai was still young, and still assumed that equity was the basic impulse of Fate; that karma was a system, rather than a device.

As he stood on the bridge in the rain, his thoughts descending into bittersweet self-pity, it was natural that he should entertain the idea of suicide. The thought of denying Gorbatov his principal weapon was comforting, until he realized that the gesture would be empty. Surely, Kishikawa-san would not be informed of his death; he would be told that Nicholai had been taken into custody as hostage against the General's cooperation. And probably, after Kishikawa had disgraced himself with confessions that implicated associates, they would deliver the final punishment: they would tell him that Nicholai had been dead all the time, and that he had shamed himself and involved innocent friends in vain.

The wind gusted and drilled the needle rain into his cheek. Nicholai swayed and gripped the edge of the parapet as he felt waves of helplessness drain him. Then, with an involuntary shudder, he remembered a terrible thought that had strayed into his mind during his conversation with the General. Kishikawa had spoken of his attempt to starve himself to death, and of the disgusting humiliation of being force-fed through a tube shoved down his gagging throat. At that moment, the thought flashed through Nicholai's mind that, had he been with the General during this humiliation, he would have reached out and given him escape into death. The plastic identity card in Nicholai's pocket would have been weapon enough, used in the styles of Naked/Kill. The thing would have been over in an instant.*

The image of releasing Kishikawa-san from the trap of life had scarcely sketched itself in Nicholai's mind before he rejected it as too ghastly to consider. But now, in the rain, within sight of that machine for racial vengeance, the War Crimes Trials, the idea returned again, and this time it lingered. It was particularly bitter that fate was demanding that he kill the only person close to him. But honorable death was the only gift he could offer. And he recalled the ancient adage: Who must do the harsh things? He who can.

The act would, of course, be Nicholai's last. He would attract to himself all their fury and disappointment, and they would punish him. Obviously, suicide would be easier for Nicholai than releasing the General with his own hands. But it would be pointless . . . and selfish.

As he walked in the rain toward the underground station, Nicholai felt a chill in the pit of his stomach, but he was calm. Finally he had a path.

There was no sleep that night, nor could Nicholai abide the company of the vigorous, life-embracing Tanaka sisters, whose peasant energy seemed part of

---

* In the course of this book, Nicholai Hel will avail himself of the tactics of Naked/Kill, but these will never be described in detail. In an early book, the author portrayed a dangerous ascent of a mountain. In the process of converting this novel into a vapid film, a fine young climber was killed. In a later book, the author detailed a method for stealing paintings from any well-guarded museum. Shortly after the Italian version of this book appeared, three paintings were stolen in Milan by the exact method described, and two of these were irreparably mutilated.

Simple social responsibility now dictates that he avoid exact descriptions of tactics and events which, although they might be of interest to a handful of readers, might contribute to the harm done to (and by) the uninitiated.

In a similar vein, the author shall keep certain advanced sexual techniques in partial shadow, as they might be dangerous, and would certainly be painful, to the neophyte.

some alien world of light and hope, and for that reason both banal and irritating.

Alone in the dark of a room that gave out onto the small garden, the panels slid back so he could hear the rain pattering on broadleafed plants and hissing softly in the gravel, protected from the cold by a padded kimono, he knelt beside a charcoal brazier that had long ago gone out and was barely warm to the touch. Twice he sought retreat into mystic transport, but his mind was too charged with fear and hate to allow him to cross over the lower path. Although he could not know it at this time, Nicholai would not again be able to find his way to the small mountain meadow where he enriched himself by being one with the grass and yellow sunlight. Events were to leave him with an impenetrable barrier of hate that would block him from ecstasy.

In the early morning, Mr. Watanabe found Nicholai still kneeling in the garden room, unaware that the rain had stopped and had been succeeded by a raw cold. Mr. Watanabe closed the panels fussily and lighted the brazier, all the while muttering about negligent young people who would ultimately have to pay the price in poor health for their foolishness.

"I should like to have a talk with you and Mrs. Shimura," Nicholai said in a quiet tone that staunched the flow of Mr. Watanabe's avuncular grumpiness.

An hour later, having had a light breakfast, the three of them knelt around a low table on which were the rolled-up deed to the house and a rather informally worded paper Nicholai had drawn up giving his possessions and furnishings to the two of them equally. He informed them that he would leave later that afternoon, probably never to return. There would be difficulty; there would be strangers asking questions and making life complicated for a few days; but after that it was not likely that the foreigners would concern themselves with the little household. Nicholai did not have much money, as he spent most of what he earned as it came in. What little he had was wrapped in cloth on the table. If Mr. Watanabe and Mrs. Shimura could not earn enough to support the house, he gave them permission to sell it and use the income as they would. It was Mrs. Shimura who insisted that they set aside a portion as dowry for the Tanaka sisters.

When this was settled, they took tea together and talked of business details. Nicholai had hoped to avoid the burden of silence, but soon their modest affairs were exhausted, and there was nothing more to say.

A cultural blemish of the Japanese is their discomfort with genuine expression of emotions. Some tend to mask feelings with stoic silence or behind the barricade of polite good form. Others hide in emotional hyperbole, in extravagances of gratitude or sorrow.

It was Mrs. Shimura who anchored herself in silence, while Mr. Watanabe wept uncontrollably.

With the same excessive consideration of security as yesterday, the four guards stood along the wall on the door side of the small visitors' room. The two Japanese looked tense and uncomfortable; the American MP yawned in boredom; and the stocky Russian seemed to daydream, which certainly he was not doing. Early in his conversation with Kishikawa-san, Nicholai had tested the guards, speaking first in Japanese. It was clear that the American did not understand, but he was less sure of the Russian, so he made up a nonsense statement and read a slight frown on the broad brow. When Nicholai shifted to French, losing the Japanese guards, but not the Russian, he was sure this man was no common soldier, despite his appearance of Slavic intellectual viscosity. It was necessary, therefore, to find another code in which to speak, and he chose the cryptography of Gō, reminding the General, as he took out the small magnetic board, that Otake-san had always used the idioticon of his beloved game when discussing important things.

"Do you want to continue the game, sir?" Nicholai asked. "The fragrance has gone bad: *Aji ga warui.*"

Kishikawa-san looked up in mild confusion. They were only four or five plays into the game; this was a most peculiar thing to say.

Three plays passed in silence before the General began to glimpse what Nicholai might have meant. He tested this out by saying, "It seems to me that the game is in *korigatachi,* that I am frozen into position without freedom of development."

"Not quite, sir. I see the possibility of a *sabaki,* but of course you would join the *hama.*"

"Isn't that dangerous for you? Isn't it in fact a *ko* situation?"

"More a *uttegae,* in truth. And I see nothing else for your honor—and mine."

"No, Nikko. You are too kind. I cannot accept the gesture. For you such a play would be a most dangerous aggression, a suicidal *de.*"

"I am not asking your permission. I could not put you in that impossible position. Having decided how I shall play it, I am explaining the configuration to you. They believe they have *tsuru no sugomori.* In fact they face a *seki.* They intended to drive you to the wall with a *shicho,* but I have the privilege of being your *shicho atari.*"

Out of the corner of his eye, Nicholai saw one of the Japanese guards frown. Obviously he played a bit, and he realized this conversation was nonsense.

Nicholai reached across the rough wooden table and placed his hand on the General's arm. "Foster-father, the game will end in two minutes. Permit me to guide you."

Tears of gratitude stood in Kishikawa-san's eyes. He seemed more frail than before, both very old and rather childlike. "But I cannot permit . . ."

"I act without permission, sir. I have decided to perform a loving disobedience. I do not even seek your forgiveness."

After a moment of consideration, Kishikawa-san nodded. A slight smile squeezed the tears from his eyes and sent one down each side of his nose. "Guide me, then."

"Turn your head and look out the window, sir. It is all overcast and damp, but soon the season of the cherry will be with us."

Kishikawa-san turned his head and looked calmly out into the rectangle of moist gray sky. Nicholai took a lead pencil from his pocket and held it lightly between his fingers. As he spoke, he concentrated on the General's temple where a slight pulse throbbed under the transparent skin.

"Do you recall when we walked beneath the blossoms of Kajikawa, sir? Think of that. Remember walking there years before with your daughter, her hand small in yours. Remember walking with your father along the same bank, your hand small in his. Concentrate on these things."

Kishikawa-san lowered his eyes and reposed his mind, as Nicholai continued speaking quietly, the lulling drone of his voice more important than the content. After a few moments, the General looked at Nicholai, the hint of a smile creasing the corners of his eyes. He nodded. Then he turned again to the gray, dripping scene beyond the window.

As Nicholai continued to talk softly, the American MP was engrossed in dislodging a bit of something from between his teeth with his fingernail; but Nicholai could feel tension in the attitude of the brighter of the Japanese guards, who was bewildered and uncomfortable with the tone of this conversation. Suddenly, with a shout, the Russian "guard" leapt forward.

He was too late.

For six hours Nicholai sat in the windowless interrogation room after surrendering himself without struggle or explanation to the stunned, confused, and therefore violent guards. In his first fury the American MP sergeant had hit him twice with his truncheon, once on the point of the shoulder, once across the face, splitting his eyebrow against the sharp bone behind it. There was little pain, but the eyebrow bled profusely, and Nicholai suffered from the messy indignity of it.

Frightened by anticipation of repercussions for allowing their prisoner to be killed under their eyes, the guards screamed threats at Nicholai as they raised the alarm and summoned the prison doctor. When he arrived, there was nothing the fussy, uncertain Japanese doctor could do for the General, who had been nerve-dead seconds after Nicholai's strike, and body-dead within a minute. Shaking his head and sucking breaths between his teeth, as though admonishing a mischievous child, the doctor attended to Nicholai's split eyebrow, relieved to have something to do within the scope of his competence.

While two fresh Japanese guards watched over Nicholai, the others reported to their superiors, giving versions of the event that showed them to be blameless, while their opposite numbers were revealed to be something between incompetent and perfidious.

When the MP sergeant returned, he was accompanied by three others of his nationality; no Russians, no Japanese. Dealing with Nicholai was to be an American show.

In grim silence, Nicholai was searched and stripped, dressed in the same coarse "suicide-proof" uniform the General had worn, and brought down the hall to be left, barefoot and with his wrists handcuffed behind his back, in the stark interrogation room, where he sat in silence on a metal chair bolted to the floor.

To subdue his imagination, Nicholai focused his mind on the middle stages of a famous contest between Gō masters of the major schools, a game he had memorized as a part of his training under Otake-san. He reviewed the placements, switching by turns from one point of view to the other, examining the implications of each. The considerable effort of memory and concentration was sufficient to close out the alien and chaotic world around him.

There were voices beyond the door, then the sound of keys and bolts, and three men entered. One was the MP sergeant who had been industriously picking his teeth when Kishikawa-san died. The second was a burly man in civilian dress whose porcine eyes had that nervous look of superficial intelligence thinned by materialistic insensitivity one sees in politicians, film producers, and automobile salesmen. The third, the leaves of a major on his shoulders, was a taut, intense man with large bloodless lips and drooping lower eyelids. It was this third who occupied the chair opposite Nicholai, while the burly civilian stood behind Nicholai's chair, and the sergeant stationed himself near the door.

"I am Major Diamond." The officer smiled, but there was a flat tone to his accent, that metallic mandibular sound that blends the energies of the garment district with overlays of acquired refinement—the kind of voice one associates with female newscasters in the United States.

At the moment of their arrival, Nicholai had been puzzling over a move in the recalled master game that had the fragrance of a *tenuki*, but which was in fact a subtle reaction to the opponent's preceding play. Before looking up, he concentrated on the board, freezing its patterns in his memory so he could return to it later. Only then did he lift his expressionless bottle-green eyes to the Major's face.

"What did you say?"

"I am Major Diamond, CID."

"Oh?" Nicholai's indifference was not feigned.

The Major opened his attaché case and drew out three typed sheets stapled together. "If you will just sign this confession, we can get on with it."

Nicholai glanced at the paper. "I don't think I want to sign anything."

Diamond's lips tightened with irritation. "You're denying murdering General Kishikawa?"

"I am not denying anything. I helped my friend to his escape from . . ." Nicholai broke off. What was the point of explaining to this man something his mercantile culture could not possible comprehend? "Major, I don't see any value in continuing this conversation."

Major Diamond glanced toward the burly civilian behind Nicholai, who leaned over and said, "Listen. You might as well sign the confession. We know all about your activities on behalf of the Reds!"

Nicholai did not bother to look toward the man.

"You're not going to tell us you haven't been in contact with a certain Colonel Gorbatov?" the civilian persisted.

Nicholai took a long breath and did not answer. It was too complicated to explain; and it didn't matter if they understood or not.

The civilian gripped Nicholai's shoulder. "You're in maximum trouble, boy! Now, you'd better sign this paper, or—"

Major Diamond frowned and shook his head curtly, and the civilian released his grip. The Major put his hands on his knees and leaned forward, looking into Nicholai's eyes with worried compassion. "Let me try to explain all this to you. You're confused right now, and tht's perfectly understandable. We know the Russians are behind this murder of General Kishikawa. I'll admit to you that we don't know why. That's one of the things we want you to help us with. Let me be open and frank with you. We know you've been working for the Russians for some time. We know you infiltrated a most sensitive area in Sphinx/FE with forged papers. A Russian identity card was found on you, together with an American one. We also know that your mother was a communist and your father a Nazi; that you were in Japan during the war; and that your contacts included militarist elements of the Japanese government. One of these contacts was with this Kishikawa." Major Diamond shook his head and sat back. "So you see, we know rather a lot about you. And I'm afraid it's all pretty damning. That's what my associate means when he says that you're in great trouble. It's possible that I may be able to help you . . . if you are willing to cooperate with us. What do you say?"

Nicholai was overwhelmed by the irrelevance of all this. Kishikawa-san was dead; he had done what a son must do; he was ready to face punishment; the rest didn't matter.

"Are you denying what I have said?" the Major asked.

"You have a handful of facts, Major, and from them you have made ridiculous conclusions."

Diamond's lips tightened. "Our information came from Colonel Gorbatov himself."

"I see." So Gorbatov was going to punish him for snatching away his propaganda prey by giving the Americans certain half-truths and allowing them to do his dirty work. How Slavic in its duplicity, in its involute obliquity.

"Of course," Diamond continued, "we don't take everything the Russians tell us at face value. That's why we want to give you a chance to tell us your side of the story."

"There is no story."

The civilian touched his shoulder again. "You deny that you knew General Kishikawa during the war?"

"No."

"You deny that he was a part of the Japanese military/industrial machine?"

"He was a soldier." The more accurate response would have been that he was a warrior, but that distinction would have meant nothing to these Americans with their mercantile mentalities.

"Do you deny being close to him?" the civilian pursed.

"No."

Major Diamond took up the questioning, his tone and expression indicating that he was honestly uncertain and sought to understand. "Your papers *were* forged, weren't they, Nicholai?"

"Yes."

"Who helped you obtain forged papers?"

Nicholai was silent.

The Major nodded and smiled. "I understand. You don't want to implicate a friend. I understand that. Your mother was Russian, wasn't she?"

"Her nationality was Russian. There was no Slavic blood in her."

The civilian cut in. "So you admit that your mother was a communist?"

Nicholai found a bitter humor in the thought of Alexandra Ivanovna being a communist. "Major, to the degree my mother took any interest in politics—a very modest degree indeed—she was to the political right of Attila." He repeated "Attila" again, mispronouncing it with an accent on the second syllable, so the Americans would understand.

"Sure," the civilian said. "And I suppose you're going to deny that your father was a Nazi?"

"He might have been. From what I understand, he was stupid enough. I never met him."

Diamond nodded. "So what you're really saying, Nicholai, is that the bulk of our accusations are true."

Nicholai sighed and shook his head. He had worked with the American military mentality for two years, but he could not pretend to understand its rigid penchant for forcing facts to fit convenient preconceptions. "If I understand you, Major—and frankly I don't much care if I do—you are accusing me of being both a communist and a Nazi, of being both a close friend of General Kishikawa's and his hired assassin, of being both a Japanese militarist and a Soviet spy. And you seem to believe that the Russians would arrange the killing of a man they intended to subject to the indignities of a War Crimes Trial to the end of garnering their bit of the propaganda glory. None of this offends your sense of rational probability?"

"We don't pretend to understand every twist and turn of it," Major Diamond admitted.

"Don't you really? What becoming humility."

The civilian's grip tightened painfully on his shoulder. "We don't need wise-assed talk from you! You're in heavy trouble! This country is under military occupation, and you're not a citizen of anywhere, boy! We can do anything we want with you, with no interference from consulates and embassies!"

The Major shook his head, and the civilian released his grip and stepped back. "I don't think that tone is going to do us any good. It's obvious that Nicholai isn't easily frightened." He smiled half shyly, then said, "But still, what my associate says is true. You have committed a capital crime, the penalty for which is death. But there are ways in which you can help us in our fight against international communism. A little cooperation from you, and something might be arranged to your advantage."

Nicholai recognized the haggling tone of the marketplace. Like all Americans, this Major was a merchant at heart; everything had a price, and the good man was he who bargained well.

"Are you listening to me?" Diamond asked.

"I can hear you," Nicholai modified.

"And? Will you cooperate?"

"Meaning sign your confession?"

"That and more. The confession implicates the Russians in the assassination. We'll also want to know about the people who helped you infiltrate Sphinx/FE. And about the Russian intelligence community here, and their contacts with unpurged Japanese militarists."

"Major. The Russians had nothing to do with my actions. Believe me that I don't care one way or the other about their politics, just as I don't care about yours. You and the Russians are only two slightly different forms of the same thing: the tyranny of the mediocre. I have no reason to protect the Russians."

"Then you will sign the confession?"

"No."

"But you just said—"

"I said that I would not protect or assist the Russians. I also have no intention of assisting your people. If it is your intention to execute me—with or without the mockery of a military trial—then please get to it."

"Nicholai, we *will* get your signature on the confession. Please believe me."

Nicholai's green eyes settled calmly on the Major's. "I am no longer a part of this conversation." He lowered his eyes and returned his concentration to the patterns of stones in the Gō game he had temporarily frozen in his memory. He began again considering the alternative responses to that clever seeming *tenuki*.

There was an exchange of nods between the Major and the burly civilian, and the latter took a black leather case from his pocket. Nicholai did not break his concentration as the MP sergeant pushed up his sleeve and the civilian cleared the syringe of air by squirting an arcing jet into the air.

When, much later, he tried to remember the events of the subsequent seventy-two hours, Nicholai could only recall shattered tesserae of experience, the binding grout of chronological sequence dissolved by the drugs they pumped into him. The only useful analogy he could devise for the experience was that of a motion picture in which he was both actor and audience member—a film with both slow and fast motion, with freeze frames and superimpositions, with the sound track from one sequence playing over the images of another, with single-frame subliminal flashes that were more felt than perceived, with long stretches of underexposed, out-of-focus pictures, and dialogue played under speed, mushy and basso.

At this period, the American intelligence community had just begun experimenting with the use of drugs in interrogation, and they often made errors, some mind-destroying. The burly civilian "doctor" tried many chemicals and combinations on Nicholai, sometimes accidentally losing his victim to hysteria or to comatose indifference, sometimes creating mutually cancelling effects that left Nicholai perfectly calm and lucid, but so displaced in reality that while he responded willingly to interrogation, his answers were in no way related to the questions.

Throughout the three days, during those moments when Nicholai drifted into contact with himself, he experienced intense panic. They were attacking, probably damaging, his mind; and Nicholai's genetic superiority was as much intellectual as sensual. He dreaded that they might crush his mind, and hundreds of years of selective breeding would be reduced to their level of humanoid rubble.

Often he was outside himself, and Nicholai the audience member felt pity for Nicholai the actor, but could do nothing to help him. During those brief periods when he could reason, he tried to flow with the nightmare distortions, to accept and cooperate with the insanity of his perceptions. He knew intuitively that if he struggled against the pulsing warps of unreality, something inside might snap with the effort, and he would never find his way back again.

Three times during the seventy-two hours, his interrogators' patience broke, and they allowed the MP sergeant to pursue the questioning in more conventional third-degree ways. He did this with the aid of a nine-inch tube of canvas filled with iron filings. The impact of this weapon was terrible. It seldom broke the surface of the skin, but it crushed bone and tissue beneath.

A civilized man who could not really condone this sort of thing, Major Diamond left the interrogation during each of the beatings, unwilling to witness the torture he had ordered. The "doctor" remained, curious to see the effects of pain inflicted under heavily drugged conditions.

The three periods of physical torture registered differently upon Nicholai's perception. Of the first, he remembered nothing. Had it not been for his right eye swollen closed and a loose tooth oozing the saline taste of blood, the thing might never have happened. The second beating was excruciatingly painful. The combined and residual effects of the drugs at this moment were such that he was intensely aware of sensation. His skin was so sensitive that the brush of his clothes against it was painful, and the air he breathed stung his nostrils. In this hypertactile condition, the torture was indescribable. He yearned for unconsciousness, but the sergeant's talents were such that he could deny blissful emptiness forever.

The third session was not painful at all, but it was by far the most frightening. With perfect, but insane, lucidity, Nicholai both received and observed the punishment. Again, he was both audience and actor, and he watched it happen with only mild interest. He felt nothing; the drugs had short-circuited his nerves. The terror lay in the fact that he could *hear* the beating as though the sound were amplified by powerful microphones within his flesh. He heard the liquid crunch of tissue; he heard the crisp splitting of skin; he heard the granular grating of fragmented bone; he heard the lush pulsing of his blood. In the mirror of the mirror of his consciousness, he was calmly terrified. He realized that to be able to hear all this while feeling nothing was insane, and to experience anesthetized indifference to the event was beyond the verge of madness.

At one moment, his mind swam to the surface of reality and he spoke to the Major, telling that he was the son of General Kishikawa and that they would be making a terminal error not to kill him, because if he lived, there was no escaping him. He spoke mushily; his tongue was thick with the drugs and his lips were split with the beating; but his tormentors would not have understood him anyway. He had unknowingly spoken in French.

Several times during the three days of interrogation the handcuffs that bound his wrists behind him were removed. The "doctor" noticed that his fingers were white and cold with lack of circulation, so the cuffs were taken off for a few minutes while his wrists were massaged, then they were replaced. Throughout the rest of his life, Nicholai carried shiny tan bracelets of scar from the handcuffs.

During the seventy-third hour, neither knowing what he was doing nor caring, Nicholai signed the confession implicating the Russians. So lost to reality was he that he signed it in Japanese script and in the middle of the typewritten page, though they had tried to direct his trembling hand to the bottom. So useless was this confession that the Americans were finally reduced to forging his signature, which of course they might have done at the outset.

The final fate of this "confession" is worth noting as a metaphor of intelligence-community bungling. Some months later, when American Sphinx people thought an opportune time had come to make a threatening shot across the bow of their Russian counterparts, the document was brought to Colonel Gorbatov by Major Diamond, who sat in silence on the other side of the Colonel's desk and awaited his reaction to this damning proof of active espionage.

The Colonel glanced over the pages with operatic indifference, then he unhooked his round metal-rimmed glasses from each ear and polished them between thumb and finger with excruciating care before threading the temples on again. With the bottom of his spoon, he crushed the undissolved lump of sugar in his teacup, drank off the tea in one long sip, then replaced the cup exactly in the center of the saucer.

"So?" he said lazily.

And that was all there was to that. The threatening gesture had been made and ignored, and it had not the slightest effect on the covert operation of the two powers in Japan.

For Nicholai the last hours of the interrogation dissolved into confusing but not unpleasant dreams. His nervous system was so shattered by the various drugs that it functioned only minimally, and his mind had recoiled into itself. He dozed from level of unreality to level of unreality, and soon he found himself walking along the banks of the Kajikawa beneath a snowfall of blossoms. Beside him, but far enough away so that General Kishikawa might have walked between them, had he been there, was a young girl. Though he had never met her, he knew she was the General's daughter. The girl was talking to him about how she would marry one day and have a son. And quite conversationally, the girl mentioned that both she and the son would die, incinerated in the firebombing of Tokyo. Once she had mentioned this, it was logical that she should become Mariko, who had died at Hiroshima. Nicholai was delighted to see her again, and so they played a practice game of Gō, she using black cherry petals for stones, he using white. Nicholai then became one of the stones, and from his microscopic position on the board, he looked around at the enemy stone forming thicker and thicker walls of containment. He tried to form defensive "eyes," but all of them turned out to be false, so he fled, rushing along the yellow surface of the board, the black lines blurring past him as he gathered momentum, until he shot off the edge of the board into thick darkness that dissolved into his cell . . .

. . . Where he opened his eyes.

It was freshly painted gray, and there were no windows. The overhead light was so painfully bright that he squinted to keep his vision from smearing.

Nicholai lived in solitary confinement in that cell for three years.

The transition from the nightmare of interrogation to the years of solitary existence under the burden of "silent treatment" was not abrupt. Daily at first, then less often, Nicholai was visited by the same fussy, distracted Japanese prison doctor who had confirmed the General's death. The treatments consisted only of prophylactic dressings with no cosmetic efforts to close cuts or remove crushed bone and cartilage. Throughout each session the doctor repeatedly shook his head and sucked his teeth and muttered to himself, as though he disapproved of him for participating in this senseless violence.

The Japanese guards had been ordered to deal with the prisoner in absolute silence, but during the first days it was necessary that they instruct him in the rudiments of routine and behavior. When they spoke to him they used the brusque verb forms and a harsh staccato tone that implied no personal antipathy, only recognition of the social gulf between prisoner and master. Once routine was established, they stopped speaking to him, and for the greater part of three years he heard no other human voice than his own, save for one half hour each three months when he was visited by a minor prison official who was responsible for the social and psychological welfare of the inmates.

Almost a month passed before the last effects of the drugs leached from his mind and nerves, and only then could he dare to relax his guard against those unexpected plunges into waking nightmares of space/time distortion that would grip him suddenly and rush him toward madness, leaving him panting and sweating in the corner of his cell, drained of energy and frightened lest the damage to his mind be permanent.

There were no inquiries into the disappearance of Hel, Nicholai Alexandrovitch (TA/737804). There were no efforts to free him, or to hasten his trial. He was a citizen of no nation; he had no papers; no consulate official came forward to defend his civil rights.

The only faint ripple on the surface of routine caused by Nicholai Hel's disappearance was a brief visit to the San Shin Building some weeks later by Mrs. Shimura and Mr. Watanabe, who had spent nights of whispered conversation, screwing up their courage to make this hopeless gesture on behalf of their benefactor. Fobbed off on a minor official, they made their inquiries in hushed, rapid words and with every manifestation of diffident humility. Mrs. Shimura did all of the talking, Mr. Watanabe only bowing and keeping his eyes down in the face of the incalculable power of the Occupation Forces and their inscrutable ways. They knew that by coming to the den of the Americans they were exposing themselves to the danger of losing their home and the little security Nicholai had provided, but their sense of honor and fairness dictated that they run this risk.

The only effect of this tentative and frightened inquiry was a visit to the Asakusa house by a team of military police searching for evidence of Nicholai's wrongdoing. In the course of this search, the officer in charge appropriated as material to the investigation Nicholai's small collection of prints by Kiyonobu and Sharaku, which he had purchased when he could afford them, feeling distressed that the owners were forced by the economic and moral anarchy of the Occupation to relinquish these national treasures, and eager to do what little he could to keep them out of the hands of the barbarians.

As it turned out, these prints had a minor influence on the downward path of egalitarian American art. They were sent home by the confiscating officer, whose twilight child promptly filled in the open spaces with Crayola, so ingeniously managing to stay within the lines that the doting mother was convinced anew of her boy's creative potential and directed its education toward art. This gifted youngster eventually became a leader in the Pop Art movement because of the mechanical precision of his reproductions of tinned foods.

Throughout the three years of confinement, Nicholai was technically awaiting trial for espionage and murder, but no legal proceedings were ever instigated; he was never tried or sentenced, and for this reason he lacked access to even the spartan privileges enjoyed by the ordinary prisoner. The Japanese administrators of Sugamo Prison were under the thrall of the Occupation, and they held Nicholai in close confinement because they were ordered to, despite the fact that he was an embarrassing exception to their rigid organizational pattern. He was the only inmate who was not a Japanese citizen, the only one who had never been sentenced, and the only one being held in solitary confinement with no record of misbehavior in prison. He would have been a troublesome administrative anomaly, had not those in charge treated him as institutional people treat all manifestations of disturbing individuality: they ignored him.

Once he was no longer tormented by unexpected returns of drug panic, Nicholai began to accommodate himself to the routines and chronological articulations of solitary life. His cell was a windowless six-foot cube of gray cement with one overhead light recessed into the ceiling and covered by thick shatterproof glass. The light was on twenty-four hours a day. At first Nicholai hated the constant glare that denied him retreat into the privacy of darkness and made sleeping fitful and thin. But when, three times in the course of his confinement, the light burned out and he had to live in total dark until the guard noticed it, he realized that he had become so accustomed to constant light that he was frightened by the weight of absolute dark closing in around him. These three visits by a trustee prisoner to replace the light bulb under the close surveillance of a guard were the only events outside the established and predictable routine of Nicholai's life, save for one brief power failure that occurred in the middle of the night during his second year. The sudden darkness woke Nicholai from his sleep, and he sat on the edge of his metal bunk, staring into the black, until the light came back on, and he could return to sleep.

Other than the light, only three features characterized the freshly painted gray cube in which Nicholai lived: the bed, the door, the toilet. The bed was a narrow tray of steel secured to the wall, its two front legs sunken into the cement of the floor. For reasons of hygiene, the bunk was off the floor in the Western style, but only by eight inches. For reasons of security, and to deny materials that might be used to commit suicide, the bed had neither boards nor wire mesh, only the flat shelf of metal on which there were two quilted pads for warmth and comfort. This bed was opposite the door, which was the most intricate feature of the cell. It was of heavy steel and opened out on silent, well-greased hinges, and it fit into its sill so exactly that the air in the cell was compressed when the door was closed and the prisoner felt some temporary discomfort in his eardrums. Let into the door was an observation window of thick wire-reinforced glass through which guards routinely monitored the actions of the prisoner. At the base of the door was a riveted steel panel that hinged from the bottom for passing in food. The third feature of the cell was a tiled depression that was the squat toilet. With Japanese nicety of concern for dignity, this was in the corner on the same wall as the door, so the inmate could attend to his physical needs out of range of observation. Directly above this convenience was a ventilation pipe three inches in diameter set flush into the cement ceiling.

Within the strict context of solitary confinement, Nicholai's life was crowded with events that punctuated and measured his time. Twice a day, morning and evening, he received food through the hinged inner door, and in the mornings there was also a pail of water and a small bar of gritty soap that made a thin, greasy lather. Every day, he bathed from head to foot, splashing up water with cupped hands to rinse himself, drying himself off with his rough padded shirt, then using what was left of the water to rinse down the toilet.

His diet was minimal but healthy: unpolished rice, a stew of vegetables and fish, and thin tepid tea. The vegetables varied slightly with the seasons and were always crisp enough not to have had the value cooked out of them. His food was served on a compartmented metal tray with one set of throwaway wooden chopsticks joined at the base. When the small door opened, the trustee always waited until the prisoner had passed out his soiled tray together with the used chopsticks and paper wrapper (even this had to be accounted for) before he would pass in the new meal.

Twice a week, at midday, the cell door was opened, and a guard beckoned him out. Since the guards were prohibited from speaking to him, all communications were carried out in uneconomical and sometimes comic mime. He followed the guard to the end of the corridor, where a steel door was opened (it always groaned on its hinges), and he was permitted to step out into the exercise area, a narrow alley between two featureless buildings, both ends of which were blocked off by high brick walls, where he could walk alone for twenty minutes with a rectangle of open sky above him and fresh air to breathe. He knew that he was under the constant surveillance of guards in the tower at the end of the lane, but their glass windows always reflected the sky, and he could not see them, so the illusion of being alone and almost free was maintained. Except for two times when he was sick with fever, he never declined to take his twenty minutes in the open air, even during rain or snow; and after the first month, he always used this time to run as hard as he could, up and down the short alley, stretching his muscles and burning off as much as he could of the energy that seethed within him.

By the end of the first month, when the lingering effects of the drugs had worn off, Nicholai made a decision for survival, part of the impulse for which came from bone-deep stubbornness and part from sustaining thoughts of vengeance. He always ate every morsel of food, and twice a day, after each meal, he exercised vigorously in his cell, developing routines that kept every muscle in his wiry body taut and quick. After each exercise period, he would sit in lotus in the corner of his cell and concentrate on the pulse of blood in his temples until he achieved the peace of middle-density meditation which, although it was a pallid substitute for the lost soul-rest of mystic transportation, was sufficient to keep his mind calm and dry, unspoiled by despair and self-pity. He trained himself never to think of the future, but to assume there would be one, because the alternative would lead to destructive despair.

After several weeks, he decided to keep mental track of the days as a gesture of confidence that someday he would get out and rejoin his life. He arbitrarily decided to call the next day Monday and to assume it was the first day of April. He was wrong by eight days, but he did not discover this for three years.

His solitary life was busy. Two meals, one bath, two exercise periods, and two terms of meditation each day. Twice a week, the pleasure of running up and down the narrow exercise lane. And there were two other bold demarcations of time. Once a month, he was visited by a barber/trustee who shaved him and went over his head with hand-operated clippers that left a half-inch of stubbly hair. This old prisoner obeyed the injunction against speaking, but he winked and grinned constantly to express brotherhood. Also once a month, always two days after the visit of the barber, he would return from his exercise run to find his bedding changed, and the walls and floor of his cell dripping with water laced with disinfectant, the stench of which lasted three and sometimes four days.

One morning, after he had passed six months in silence in that cell, he was startled out of his meditation by the sound of the door being unlocked. His first reaction was to be annoyed, and a little fearful, at this rupture in reliable routine. Later he learned that this visit was not a break in routine, but only the final element in the cycles that measured his life out. Once every six months he was to be visited by an elderly, overworked civil servant whose duty it was to attend to the social and psychological needs of the inmates of this enlightened prison. The old man introduced himself as Mr. Hirata and told Nicholai that they had permission to speak. He sat on the edge of Nicholai's low bed-shelf, placed his overstuffed briefcase beside him, opened it, fumbled within for a fresh questionnaire, and inserted it into the spring clamp of the clipboard on his lap. In an atonic, bored voice, he asked questions about Nicholai's health and well-being, and with every nod of Nicholai's head, he made a check mark beside the appropriate question.

After scanning with the tip of his pen to make sure he had checked off all the required questions, Mr. Hirata looked up with moist, fatigued eyes and asked if Mr. Hel (Heru) had any formal requests or complaints to make.

Nicholai automatically shook his head . . . then he changed his mind. "Yes," he tried to say. But his throat was thick and only a creaking sound came out. It occurred to him suddenly that he had fallen out of the habit of speaking. He cleared his throat and tried again. "Yes, sir. I would like books, paper, brushes, ink."

Mr. Hirata's thick, hooked eyebrows arched, and he cast his eyes to the side as he sucked in a great breath between his teeth. Clearly, the request was extravagant. It would be very difficult. It would make trouble. But he dutifully registered the request in the space provided for that purpose.

Nicholai was surprised to realize how desperately he wanted the books and paper, although he knew that he was making the error of hoping for something and risking disappointment, thus damaging the fine balance of his twilight existence in which desire had been submerged and hope diminished to the size of expectation. He plunged ahead recklessly. "It is my only chance, sir."

"So? Only chance?"

"Yes, sir. I have nothing . . ." Nicholai growled and cleared his throat again. Speaking was so difficult! "I have nothing to occupy my mind. And I believe I am going mad."

"So?"

"I have found myself thinking often of suicide."

"Ah." Mr. Hirata frowned deeply and sucked in his breath. Why must there always be problems such as these? Problems for which there are no clear instructions in the manual of regulations? "I shall report your request, Mr. Heru."

From the tone, Nicholai knew that the report would be made without energy, and his request would fall into the bureaucratic abyss. He had noticed that Mr. Hirata's glance fell often upon his battered face, where the scars and swellings of the beatings he had taken were still purplish, and each time the glance had flicked away with discomfort and embarrassment.

Nicholai touched his fingers to his broken eyebrow. "It was not your guards, sir. Most of these wounds came from my interrogation at the hands of the Americans."

"*Most* of them? And the rest?"

Nicholai looked down at the floor and cleared his throat. His voice was raspy and weak, and he needed to be glib and persuasive just now. He promised himself that he would not let his voice fall into disuse again through lack of exercise. "Yes, most. The rest . . . I must confess that I have done some harm to myself. In despair I have run my head against the wall. It was a stupid and shameful thing to do, but with nothing to occupy my mind . . ." He allowed his voice to trail off, and he kept his eyes on the floor.

Mr. Hirata was disturbed as he considered the ramifications of madness and suicide on his career, particularly now when he was only a few years from retirement. He promised he would do what he could, and he left the cell troubled by that most harrowing of torments for civil servants: the need to make an independent decision.

Two days later, upon returning from his twenty minutes of fresh air, Nicholai found a paper-wrapped package at the foot of his iron bed. It contained three old books that smelled of mildew, a fifty-sheet pad of paper, a bottle of Western-style ink, and a cheap but brand-new fountain pen.

When he examined the books, Nicholai was crestfallen. They were useless. Mr. Hirata had gone to a secondhand bookstore and had purchased (out of his own money, to avoid the administrative complexity of a formal requisition for articles that might turn out to be prohibited) the three cheapest books he could find. Having no language but Japanese, and knowing from Hel's record that he read French, Mr. Hirata bought what he assumed were French books from a stack that had once been part of the library of a missionary priest, confiscated by the government during the war. The priest had been Basque, and so were the books. All printed before 1920, one was a description of Basque life written for children and including stiff, touched-up photographs and etchings of rural scenes. Although the book was in French, it had no apparent value to Nicholai. The second book was a slim volume of Basque *dictons*, parables, and folktales written in Basque on the left-hand page, and in French on the right. The third was a French/Basque dictionary compiled in 1898 by a priest from Haute Soule, who attempted, in a turgid and lengthy introduction, to identify scholarship in the Basque language with the virtues of piety and humility.

Nicholai tossed the books aside and squatted in the corner of the cell he reserved for meditation. Having made the error of hoping for something, he paid the penalty of disappointment. He found himself weeping bitterly, and soon chest-racking sobs were escaping from him involuntarily. He moved over to the toilet corner, so that the guards might not see him break down like this. He was surprised and frightened to discover how close to the surface was this terrible despair, despite the fact that he had trained himself to live by taut routine and avoid all thoughts of the past and the future. Worn out at last and empty of tears, he brought himself to middle-density meditation, and when he was calmed, he faced his problem.

Question: Why had he hoped for the books so desperately that he made himself vulnerable to the pains of disappointment? Answer: Without admitting it to himself, he had realized that his intellect, honed through Gō training, had something of the properties of a series-wound motor which, if it bore no load, would run ever faster and faster until it burned itself out. This is why he had diminished his life through rigid routine, and why he passed more time than was necessary in the pleasant vacuum of meditation. He had no one to speak to, and he even avoided thought. To be sure, impressions passed unsummoned through his mind, but they were, for the greater part, surd images lacking the linear logic of worded thought. He had not been conscious of avoiding the use of his mind for fear it would run toward panic and despair in this solitary and silent cell, but that was why he had leapt at the chance to have books and paper, why he had yearned terribly for the company and mental occupation of the books.

And *these* were the books? A children's travelogue; a thin volume of folk wisdom; and a dictionary compiled by a preciously pious priest!

And most of it in Basque, a language Nicholai had barely heard of, the most ancient language of Europe and no more related to any other language in the world than the Basque people, with their peculiar blood-type distribution and cranial formation, are related to any other race.

Nicholai squatted in silence and confronted his problem. There was only one answer: he must somehow use these books. With them, he would teach himself Basque. After all, he had much more than the Rosetta stone here; he had page-by-page translation, and a dictionary. His mind was trained to the abstract crystalline geometry of Gō. He had worked in cryptography. He would construct a Basque grammar. And he would keep his other languages alive too. He would translate the Basque folktales into Russian, English, Japanese, German. In his mind, he could translate them also into his ragged street Chinese, but he could go no further, for he had never learned to write the language.

He stripped the bedding off and made a desk of the iron shelf beside which he knelt as he arranged his books and pen and paper. At first he attempted to hold rein on his excitement, lest they decide to take his treasures back, plunging him into what Saint-Exupéry had called the torture of hope. Indeed, his next exercise period in the narrow lane was a torment, and he returned having steeled himself to find that they had confiscated his books. But when they were still there, he abandoned himself to the joys of mental work.

After his discovery that he had all but lost the use of his voice, he initiated the practice of talking to himself for several hours each day, inventing social situations or recounting aloud the political or intellectual histories of each of the nations whose language he spoke. At first, he was self-conscious about talking to himself, not wanting the guards to think his mind was going. But soon thinking aloud became a habit, and he would mutter to himself throughout the day.

From his years in prison came Hel's lifelong characteristic of speaking in a voice so soft it was nearly a whisper and was rendered understandable only by his great precision of pronunciation.

In later years, this precise, half-whispered voice was to have a daunting and chilling effect on the people with whom his bizarre profession brought him in contact. And for those who made the fatal error of acting treacherously against him, the stuff of nightmare was hearing his soft, exact voice speak to them out of the shadows.

The first *dicton* in the book of adages was *"Zahar hitzak, zuhur hitzak,"* which was translated as "Old sayings are wise sayings." His inadequate dictionary provided him only with the word *zahar* meaning old. And the first notes of his amateur little grammar were:

Zuhur = wise.
Basque plural either "ak" or "zak."
Radical for "adages/sayings" is either "hit" or "hitz."
Note: verb "to say/to speak" probably built on this radical.
Note: is possible that parallel structures do not require verb of simple being.

And from this meager beginning Nicholai constructed a grammar of the Basque language word by word, concept by concept, structure by structure. From the first, he forced himself to pronounce the language he was learning, to keep it alive and vital in his mind. Without guidance, he made several errors that were to haunt his spoken Basque forever, much to the amusement of his Basque friends. For instance, he decided that the *h* would be mute, as in French. Also, he had to choose how he would pronounce the Basque *x* from a range of possibilities. It might have been a *z*, or a *sh*, or a *tch*, or a guttural Germanic *ch*. He arbitrarily chose the latter. Wrongly, to his subsequent embarrassment.

His life was now full, even crowded, with events he had to leave before he tired of them. His day began with breakfast and a bath of cold water. After burning off excess physical energy with isometric exercise, he would allow himself a half hour of middle-density meditation. Then the study of Basque occupied him until supper, after which he exercised again until his body was worn and tired. Then another half hour of meditation. Then sleep.

His biweekly runs in the narrow exercise lane were taken out of time for Basque study. And each day, as he ate or exercised, he talked to himself in one of his languages to keep them fresh and available. As he had seven languages, he assigned one day of the week to each, and his personal weekly calendar read: Monday, втоРник, lai-bai-sam, jeudi, Freitag, Larunbat, and Nitiyoo-bi.

The most significant event of Nicholai Hel's years in solitary imprisonment was the flowering of his proximity sense. This happened quite without his will and, in its incipient stages, without his conscious recognition. It is assumed by those who study paraperceptual phenomena that the proximity sense was, early in the development of man, as vigorous and common as the five other perceptual tools, but it withered through disuse as man developed away from his prey/hunter existence. Too, the extraphysical nature of this "sixth sense" derived from central cortex energies that are in diametric contradiction to rational reasoning, which style of understanding and arranging experience was ultimately to characterize the man animal. To be sure, certain primitive cultures still maintain rudimentary proximity skills, and even thoroughly acculturated people occasionally receive impulses from the vestigial remnants of their proximity system and find themselves tingling with the awareness that somebody is staring at them from behind, or somebody is thinking of them, or they experience vague, generalized senses of well-being or doom; but these are passing and gossamer sensations that are shrugged away because they are not and cannot be understood within the framework of pedestrian logical comprehension, and because acceptance of them would undermine the comfortable conviction that all phenomena are within the rational spectrum.

Occasionally, and under circumstances only partly understood, the proximity sense will emerge fully developed in a modern man. In many ways, Nicholai Hel was characteristic of those few who have flourishing proximity systems. All of his life had been intensely mental and internal. He had been a mystic and had experienced ecstatic transportation, and therefore was not uncomfortable wtith the extralogical. Gō had trained his intellect to conceive in terms of liquid permutations, rather than the simple problem/solution grid of Western cultures. Then a shocking event in his life had left him isolated within himself for a protracted period of time. All of these factors are consonant with those characterizing that one person in several million who exist in our time with the additional gift (or burden) of proximity sense.

This primordial perception system developed so slowly and regularly in Nicholai that he was unaware of it for fully a year. His prison existence was measured off in so many short, redundant bits that he had no sense of the passage of time outside the prison walls. He never dwelt upon himself, and he was never bored. In seeming contradiction of physical laws, time is heavy only when it is empty.

His conscious recognition of his gift was occasioned by a visit by Mr. Hirata. Nicholai was working over his books when he lifted his head and said aloud to himself (in German, for it was Friday), "That's odd. Why is Mr. Hirata coming to visit me?" Then he looked at his improvised calendar and realized that, indeed, six months had passed since Mr. Hirata's last visit.

Several minutes later, he broke off from his study again to wonder who this stranger with Mr. Hirata was, because the person whose approach he sensed was not one of the regular guards, each of whom had a characteristic forepresence that Nicholai recognized.

Shortly later, the cell door was unlocked, and Mr. Hirata entered, accompanied by a young man who was in training for social work within the prison system, and who diffidently stood apart while the older man ran routinely through his list of questions and meticulously checked off each response on his clipboard sheet.

In response to the final catch-all question, Nicholai requested more paper and ink, and Mr. Hirata pulled in his neck and sucked air between his teeth to indicate the overwhelming difficulty of such a request. But there was something in his attitude that left Nicholai confident that his request would be fulfilled.

When Mr. Hirata was preparing to leave, Nicholai asked him, "Excuse me, sir. Did you pass near my cell about ten minutes ago?"

"Ten minutes ago? No. Why do you ask?"

"You didn't pass near my cell? Well then, did you think about me?"

The two prison officials exchanged glances. Mr. Hirata had informed his apprentice of this prisoner's precarious mental condition bordering on the suicidal. "No," the senior man began, "I don't believe I—ah, a moment! Why yes! Just before entering this wing, I spoke to the young man here about you."

"Ah," Nicholai said. "That explains it, then."

Uneasy glances were exchanged. "Explains what?"

Nicholai realized that it would be both difficult and unkind to introduce something so abstract and ethereal as the proximity sense to a civil service mentality, so he shook his head and said, "Nothing. It's not important."

Mr. Hirata shrugged and departed.

For the rest of that day and all of the next, Nicholai contemplated this ability he had discovered in himself to intercept parasensually the physical proximity and directed concentration of people. During his twenty minutes of exercise in the narrow court beneath a rectangle of stormy sky, he closed his eyes as he walked and tested if he could concentrate on some feature of the walls and know when he had approached it. He discovered that he could and, in fact, that he could spin around with his eyes closed to disorient himself and still concentrate on a crack in the wall or an oddly shaped stone and walk directly to it, then reach out and touch within several inches of it. So this proximity sense worked to some degree with inanimate objects as well. While doing this, he felt a flow of human concentration directed at him, and he knew, although he could not see past the sky-reflecting glass of the guard tower, that his antics were being observed and commented on by the men there. He could distinguish between the qualities of their intercepted concentration and tell that they were two in number, a strong-willed man and a man with weaker will—or who was, perhaps, relatively indifferent to the carryings-on of a crazed inmate.

Back in his cell, he pondered this gift further. How long had he had it? Where did it come from? What were its potential uses? So far as he remembered at first, it had developed during this last year in prison. And so slowly had it formed that he couldn't recall its coming. For some time now he had known, without thinking anything of it, when the guards were approaching his cell, and whether it was the short one with the wall eyes, or the Polynesian-looking one who probably had Ainu blood. And he had known which of the trustees was bringing his breakfast almost immediately upon waking.

But had there been traces of it before prison? Yes. Yes, he realized with dawning memory. There had always been modest, vestigial signals from his proximity system. Even as a child, he had always known immediately upon entering if a house was empty or occupied. Even in silence, he had always known whether his mother had remembered or forgotten some duty or chore for him. He could feel the lingering charge in the air of a recent argument or lovemaking in any room he entered. But he had considered these to be common experiences shared by everyone. To a degree, he was right. Many children, and a few adults, occasionally sense such vibrant impalpables through the remnants of their proximity systems, although they explain them away with such terms as "mood," or "edgyness," or "intuition." The only uncommon thing about Nicholai's contact with his proximity system was its consistency. He had always been sensitive to its messages.

It was during his experiences of caving with his Japanese friends that his paraperceptive gift first manifested itself boldly, although at the time he gave it neither consideration nor name. Under the special conditions of total dark, of concentrated background fear, of extreme physical effort, Nicholai's primitive central cortex powers cut into his sensory circuit. Deep in an unknown labyrinth with his companions, wriggling along a fault with millions of tons of rock inches above his spine, exertion throbbing in his temples, he had only to close his eyes (in order to be rid of the overriding impulse of the sensory system to pour energy out through the eyes, even in total darkness) and he could reach out with his proximity sense and tell, with unverifiable assurance, in which direction lay empty space, and in which heavy rock. His friends at first joked about his "hunches." One night as they sat in bivouac at the entrance of a cave system they had been exploring that day, the sleepy conversation drifted around to Nicholai's uncanny ability to orient himself. One young man put forth the conjecture that, without knowing it, Nicholai was reading subtle echoes from his breathing and scuffling and perhaps smelling differences in the subterranean air, air, and from these slight but certainly not mystical signals he could make his famous "hunches." Nicholai was willing to accept this explanation; he didn't really care much.

One of the team who was learning English to the end of getting a better job with the Occupation Forces slapped Nicholai on the shoulder and growled, "Clever, these Occidentals, at *orienting* themselves."

And another, a wry boy with a monkey face who was the clown of the group, said that it was not a bit odd that Nicholai should be able to see in the dark. He was, after all, a man of the twilight!

The tone of this statement signaled that it was meant to be a joke, but there was silence around the campfire for some seconds, as they tried to unravel the tortuous and oblique pun that was the common stock of the monkey-faced one's humor. And as it dawned on each in turn, there were groans and supplications to spare them, and one lad threw his cap at the offending wit.*

During the day and a half in his cell devoted to an examination of this proximity sense, Nicholai discovered several things about its nature. In the first place, it was not a simple sense, like hearing or sight. A better analogy might be the sense of touch, that complicated constellation of reactions that includes sensitivity to heat and pressure, headache and nausea, the elevator feelings of rising or falling, and balance controls through the liquid of the middle ear—all of which are lumped up rather inadequately under the label of "touch." In the case of the proximity sense, there are two bold classes of sensory reaction, the qualitative and the quantitative; and there are two broad divisions of control, the active and the passive. The quantitative aspect deals largely with simple proximity, the distance and direction of animate and inanimate objects. Nicholai soon learned that the range of his intercepts was quite limited in the case of the inanimate, passive object—a book, a stone, or a man who was daydreaming. The presence of such an object could be passively sensed at no more than four or five meters, after which the signals were too weak to be felt. If, however, Nicholai concentrated on the object and built a bridge of force, the effective distance could be roughly doubled. And if the object was a man (or in some cases, an animal) who was thinking about Nicholai and sending out his own force bridge, the distance could be doubled again. The second aspect of the proximity sense was qualitative, and this was perceptible only in the cases of a human object. Not only could Nicholai read the distance and direction of an emitting source, but he could feel, through the sympathetic vibrations of his own emotions, the quality of emissions: friendly, antagonistic, threatening, loving, puzzled, angry, lustful. As the entire system was generated by the central cortex, the more primitive emotions were transmitted with greatest distinction: fear, hate, lust.

Having discovered these sketchy facts about his gifts, Nicholai turned his mind away from them and applied himself again to his studies and to the task of keeping his languages fresh. He recognized that, so long as he was in prison, the gifts could serve little purpose beyond that of a kind of parlor game. He had no way to foresee that, in later years, his highly developed proximity sense would not only assist him in earning worldwide reputation as a foremost cave explorer, but would serve him as both weapon and armor in his vocation as professional exterminator of international terrorists.

---

* The pun was almost Shakespearean in its sophomoric obliquity. It was formed on the fact that Japanese friends called Nicholai "Nikko" to avoid the awkward *l*. And the most convenient Japanese pronunciation of Hel is *heru*.

PART TWO

SABAKI

Washington

Mr. Diamond glanced up from the rear-projected roll down and spoke to the First Assistant. "Okay, break off here and jump ahead on the time line. Give us a light scan of his counterterrorist activities from the time he left prison to the present."

"Yes, sir. It will take just a minute to reset."

With the help of Fat Boy and the sensitive manipulations of the First Assistant, Diamond had introduced his guests to the broad facts of Nicholai Hel's life up to the middle of his term of imprisonment, occasionally providing a bit of amplification or background detail from his own memory. It had taken only twenty-two minutes to share this information with them because Fat Boy was limited to recorded incidents and facts; motives, passions, and ideals being alien to its vernacular.

Throughout the twenty-two minutes, Darryl Starr had slouched in his white plastic chair, yearning for a cigar, but not daring to light up. He assumed glumly that the details of this gook-lover's life were being inflicted on him as a kind of punishment for screwing up the Rome hit by letting the girl get away. In an effort to save face, he had assumed an attitude of bored resignation, sucking at his teeth and occasionally relieving himself of a fluttering sigh. But something disturbed him more than being punished like a recalcitrant schoolboy. He sensed that Diamond's interest in Nicholai Hel went beyond professionalism. There was something personal in it, and Starr's years of experience in the trenches of CIA operations made him wary of contaminating the job at hand with personal feelings.

As became the nephew of an important man and a CIA trainee-in-terror, the PLO goatherd at first adopted an expression of strictest attention to the information rear-projected on the glass conference table, but soon his concentration strayed to the taut pink skin of Miss Swivven's calves, at which he grinned occasionally in his version of seductive gallantry.

The Deputy had responded to each bit of information with a curt nod of his head meant to create the impression that the CIA was current with all this information, and that he was merely ticking it off mentally. In fact, CIA did not have access to Fat Boy, although the Mother Company's biographic computer system had long ago consumed and digested everything in the tape banks of CIA and NSA.

For his part, Mr. Able had maintained a facade of thin boredom and marginal politeness, although he had been intrigued by certain episodes in Hel's biography, particularly those that revealed mysticism and the rare gift of proximity sense, for this refined man's tastes ran to the occult and exotic, which appetites were manifest in his sexual ambiguities.

A muted bell rang in the adjoining machine room, and Miss Swivven rose to collect the telephotos of Nicholai Hel that Mr. Diamond had requested. There was silence in the conference room for a minute, save for the hum and click of the First Assistant's console, where he was probing Fat Boy's international memory banks and recording certain fragments in his own short-term storage unit. Mr. Diamond lighted a cigarette (he permitted himself four a day) and turned his chair to look out on the spotlighted Washington Monument beyond the window, as he tapped his lips meditatively with his knuckle.

Mr. Able sighed aloud, straightened the crease of one trouser leg elegantly, and glanced at his watch. "I do hope this isn't going to take much longer. I have plans for this evening." Visions of that senator's Ganymede son had been in and out of his mind all evening.

"Ah," Diamond said, "here we are." He held out his hand for the photographs Miss Swivven was bringing from the machine room and leafed through them quickly. "They're in chronological order. This first is a blowup of his identification picture taken when he started working for Sphinx/FE Cryptography."

He passed it on to Mr. Able, who examined the photograph, grainy with excessive enlargement. "Interesting face. Haughty. Fine. Stern."

He pushed the picture across to the Deputy, who glanced at it briefly as though he were already familiar with it, then gave it to Darryl Starr.

"Shee-it," Starr exclaimed. "He looks like a kid! Fifteen-sixteen years old!"

"His appearance is misleading," Diamond said. "At the time this picture was taken he could have been as old as twenty-three. The youthfulness is a family trait. At this moment, Hel is somewhere between fifty and fifty-three, but I have been told that he looks like a man in his midthirties."

The Palestinian goatherd reached for the photograph, but it was passed back to Mr. Able, who looked at it again and said, "What's wrong with the eyes? They look odd. Artificial."

Even in black and white, the eyes had an unnatural transparency, as though they were underexposed.

"Yes," Diamond said, "his eyes are strange. They're a peculiar bright green, like the color of antique bottles. It's his most salient recognition feature."

Mr. Able looked obliquely at Diamond. "Have you met this man personally?"

"I . . . I have been interested in him for years," Diamond said evasively, as he passed along the second photograph.

Mr. Able winced as he looked at the picture. It would have been impossible to recognize this as the same man. The nose had been broken and was pushed to the left. There was a high ridge of scar tissue along the right cheek, and another diagonally across the forehead, bisecting the eyebrow. The lower lip had been thickened and split, and there was a puffy knob below the left cheekbone. The eyes were closed, and the face at rest.

Mr. Able pushed it over to the Deputy gingerly, as though he did not want to touch it.

The Palestinian held out his hand, but the picture was passed on to Starr. "Shit-o-dear! Looks like he went to Fistcity against a freight train!"

"What you see there," Diamond explained, "is the effect of a vigorous interrogation by Army Intelligence. The picture was taken some three years after the beating, while the subject was anesthetized in preparation for plastic surgery. And here he is a week after the operation." Diamond slid the next picture along the conference table.

The face was still a little puffy in result of recent surgery, but all signs of the disfigurement were erased, and a general tightening-up had even removed the faint lines and marks of age.

"And how old was he at this time?" Mr. Able asked.

"Between twenty-four and twenty-eight."

"Amazing. He looks younger than in the first photograph."

The Palestinian tried to turn his head upside down to see the picture as it passed by him.

"These are blowups of passport photos. The Costa Rican one dates from shortly after his plastic surgery, and the French one the year after that. We also believe he has an Albanian passport, but we have no copy of it."

Mr. Able quickly shuffled through the passport photos which, true to their kind, were overlit and of poor quality. One feature caught his attention, and he turned back to the French picture. "Are you sure this is the same man?"

Diamond took the picture back and glanced at it. "Yes, this is Hel."

"But the eyes—"

"I know what you mean. Because the peculiar color of his eyes would blow any disguise, he has several pairs of noncorrective contact lenses that are clear in the center but colored in the iris."

"So he can have whatever color eyes he wants to have. Interesting."

"Oh yes. Hel runs to the ingenious."

The OPEC man smiled. "That's the second time I have detected a hint of admiration in your voice."

Diamond looked at him coldly. "You're mistaken."

"Am I? I see. Are these the most recent pictures you have of the ingenious—but not admired—Mr. Hel?"

Diamond took up the remaining sheaf of photographs and tossed them onto the conference table. "Sure. We have plenty. And they're typical examples of CIA efficiency."

The Deputy's eyebrows arched in martyred resignation.

Mr. Able leafed through the pictures with a puzzled frown, then pushed them toward Starr.

The Palestinian leapt up and slapped his hand down on the stack, then grinned sheepishly as everyone glared at his surprisingly rude gesture. He pulled the photographs over to him and examined them carefully.

"I don't understand," he admitted. "What is this?"

In each of the pictures, the central figure was blurred. They had been taken in a variety of settings—cafés, city streets, the seashore, the bleachers of a jai-alai match, an airport terminal—and all had the image compression characteristic of a telephoto lens; but in not one of them was it possible to recognize the man being photographed, for he had suddenly moved at the instant of the shutter click.

"This really is something I do not understand," the goatherd confessed, as though that were remarkable. "It is something that my comprehension does not . . . comprehend."

"It appears," Diamond explained, "that Hel cannot be photographed unless he wants to be, although there's reason to believe he's indifferent about CIA's efforts to keep track of him and record his actions."

"Then why does he spoil each photograph?" Mr. Able asked.

"By accident. It has to do with this proximity sense of his. He can feel concentration being focused on him. Evidently the feeling of being tracked by a camera lens is identical with that of being sighted through the scope of a rifle, and the moment of releasing the shutter feels just like that of squeezing a trigger."

"So he ducks at the instant the picture is being taken," Mr. Able realized. "Amazing. Truly amazing."

"Is that admiration I detect?" Diamond asked archly.

Mr. Able smiled and tipped his head, granting the touch. "One thing I must ask. The Major who figured in the rather brutal interrogation of Hel was named Diamond. I am aware, of course, of the penchant of your people for identifying themselves with precious stones and metals—the mercantile world is richly ornamented with Pearls and Rubys and Golds—but nevertheless the coincidence of names here makes me uncomfortable. Coincidence, after all, is Fate's major weapon."

Diamond tapped the edges of the photographs on his desk to align them and set them aside, saying offhandedly, "The Major Diamond in question was my brother."

"I see," Mr. Abel said.

Darryl Starr glanced uneasily toward Diamond, his worries about personal involvement confirmed.

"Sir?" the First Assistant said. "I'm ready with the printout of Hel's counterterrorist activities."

"All right. Bring it up on the table. Just surface stuff. No details. I only want to give these gentlemen a feeling for what we're facing."

Although Diamond had requested a shallow probe of Hel's known counterterrorist activities, the first outline to appear on the conference table was so brief that Diamond felt called upon to fill in. "Hel's first operation was not, strictly speaking, counterterrorist. As you see, it was a hit on the leader of a Soviet Trade Commission to Peking, not long after the Chinese communists had firmed up their control over that country. The operation was so inside and covert that most of the tapes were degaussed by CIA before the Mother Company began requiring them to give dupes of everything to Fat Boy. In bold, it went like this: the American intelligence community was worried about a Soviet/Chinese coalition, despite the fact that there were many grounds for dispute between them— matters of boundaries, ideology, unequal industrial development, racial mistrust. The Think Tank boys came up with a plan to exploit their underlying differences and break up any developing union. They proposed to send an agent into Peking to kill the head of the Soviet commission and plant incriminating directives from Moscow. The Chinese would think the Russians had sacrificed one of their own to create an incident as an excuse for breaking off the negotiations. The Soviets, knowing better, would think the Chinese had made the hit for the same reason. And when the Chinese brought out the incriminating directives as evidence of Russian duplicity, the Soviets would claim that Peking had manufactured the documents to justify their cowardly attack. The Chinese, knowing perfectly well that this was not the case, would be confirmed in their belief that the whole thing was a Russian plot.

"That the plan worked is proved by the fact that Sino-Soviet relations never did take firm root and are today characterized by mistrust and hostility, and Western bloc powers are able to play one of them off against the other and prevent what would be an overwhelming alliance.

"The little stumbling block to the ingenious plot of the Think Tank boys was finding an agent who knew enough Chinese to move through that country under cover, who could pass for a Russian when the necessity arose, and who was willing to take on a job that had slight chance of success, and almost no chance for escape after the hit was made. The operative had to be brilliant, multilingual, a trained killer, and desperate enough to accept an assignment that offered not one chance in a hundred of survival.

"CIA ran a key-way sort, and they found only one person among those under their control who fit the description . . ."

Japan

It WAS EARLY autumn, the fourth autumn Hel had passed in his cell in Sugamo Prison. He knelt on the floor before his desk/bed, lost in an elusive problem of Basque grammar, when he felt a tingling at the roots of the hair on the nape of his neck. He lifted his head and concentrated on the projections he was intercepting. This person's approaching aura was alien to him. There were sounds at the door, and it swung open. A smiling guard with a triangular scar on his forehead entered, one Nicholai had never seen or felt before.

The guard cleared his throat. "Come with me, please."

Hel frowned. The *O . . . nasai* form? Respect language from a guard to a prisoner? He carefully arranged his notes and closed the book before rising. He instructed himself to be calm and careful. There could be hope in this unprecedented rupture of routine . . . or danger. He rose and preceded the guard out of the cell.

"Mr. Hel? Delighted to make your acquaintance." The polished young man rose to shake Hel's hand as he entered the visitors' room. The contrast between his close-fitting Ivy League suit and narrow tie and Hel's crumpled gray prison uniform was no greater than that between their physiques and temperaments. The hearty CIA agent was robust and athletic, capable of the first-naming and knee-jerk congeniality that marks the American salesman. Hel, slim and wiry, was reserved and distant. The agent, who was noted for winning immediate confidences, was a creature of words and reason. Hel was a creature of meaning and undertone. It was the battering ram and the rapier.

The agent nodded permission for the guard to leave. Hel sat on the edge of his chair, having had nothing but his steel cot to sit on for three years, and having lost the facility for sitting back and relaxing. After all that time of not hearing himself addressed in social speech, he found the urbane chat of the agent not so much disturbing as irrelevant.

"I've asked them to bring up a little tea," the agent said, smiling with a gruff shagginess of personality that he had always found so effective in public relations. "One thing you've got to hand to these Japanese, they make a good cup of tea—what my limey friends call a 'nice cuppa.'" He laughed at his failure to produce a recognizable cockney accent.

Hel watched him without speaking, taking some pleasure in the fact that the American was caught off balance by the battered appearance of his face, at first glancing away uneasily, and subsequently forcing himself to look at it without any show of disgust.

"You're looking pretty fit, Mr. Hel. I had expected that you would show the effects of physical inactivity. Of course, you have one advantage. You don't overeat. Most people overeat, if you want my opinion. The old human body would do better with a lot less food than we give it. We sort of clog up the tubes with chow, don't you agree? Ah, here we are! Here's the tea."

The guard entered with a tray on which there was a thick pot and two handleless Japanese cups. The agent poured clumsily, like a friendly bear, as though gracelessness were proof of virility. Hel accepted the cup, but he did not drink.

"Cheers," the agent said, taking his first sip. He shook his head and laughed. "I guess you don't say 'cheers' when you're drinking tea. What do you say?"

Hel set his cup on the table beside him. "What do you want with me?"

Trained in courses on one-to-one persuasion and small-group management, the agent believed he could sense a cool tone in Hel's attitude, so he followed the rules of his training and flowed with the ambience of the feedback. "I guess you're right. It would be best to get right to the point. Look, Mr. Hel, I've been reviewing your case, and if you ask me, you got a raw deal. That's my opinion anyway."

Hel let his eyes settle on the young man's open, frank face. Controlling impulses to reach out and break it, he lowered his eyes and said, "That is your opinion, is it?"

The agent folded up his grin and put it away. He wouldn't beat around the bush any longer. He would tell the truth. There was an adage he had memorized during his persuasion courses: Don't overlook the truth; properly handled, it can be an effective weapon. But bear in mind that weapons get blunted with overuse.

He leaned forward and spoke in a frank, concerned tone. "I think I can get you out of here, Mr. Hel."

"At what cost to me?"

"Does that matter?"

Hel considered this for a moment. "Yes."

"Okay. We need a job done. You're capable of doing it. We'll pay you with your freedom."

"I have my freedom. You mean you'll pay me with my liberty."

"Whatever."

"What kind of liberty are you offering?"

"What?"

"Liberty to do what?"

"I don't think I follow you there. Liberty, man. Freedom. You can do what you want, go where you want."

"Oh, I see. You are offering me citizenship and a considerable amount of money as well."

"Well . . . no. What I mean is . . . Look, I'm authorized to offer you your freedom, but no one said anything about money or citizenship."

"Let me be sure I understand you. You are offering me a chance to wander around Japan, vulnerable to arrest at any moment, a citizen of no country, and free to go anywhere and do anything that doesn't cost money. Is that it?"

The agent's discomfort pleased Hel. "Ah . . . I'm only saying that the matter of money and citizenship hadn't been discussed."

"I see." Hel rose. "Why don't you return when you have worked out the details of your proposal."

"Aren't you going to ask about the task we want you to perform?"

"No. I assume it to be maximally difficult. Very dangerous. Probably involving murder. Otherwise, you wouldn't be here."

"Oh, I don't think I'd call it murder, Mr. Hel. I wouldn't use that word. It's more like . . . like a soldier fighting for his country and killing one of the enemy."

"That's what I said: murder."

"Have it your own way then."

"I shall. Good afternoon."

The agent began to have the impression that he was being handled, while all of his persuasion training had insisted that he do the handling. He fell back upon his natural defense of playing it for the hale good fellow. "Okay, Mr. Hel. I'll have a talk with my superiors and see what I can get for you. I'm on your side in this, you know. Hey, know what? I haven't even introduced myself. Sorry about that."

"Don't bother. I am not interested in who you are."

"All right. But take my advice, Mr. Hel. Don't let this chance get away. Opportunity doesn't knock twice, you know."

"Penetrating observation. Did you make up the epigram?"

"I'll see you tomorrow."

"Very well. And ask the guard to knock on my cell door twice. I wouldn't want to confuse him with opportunity."

Back in CIA Far East Headquarters in the basement of the Dai Ichi Building, Hel's demands were discussed. Citizenship was easy enough. Not American citizenship, of course. That high privilege was reserved for defecting Soviet dancers. But they could arrange citizenship of Panama or Nicaragua or Costa Rica—any of the CIA control areas. It would cost a bit in local baksheesh, but it could be done.

About payment they were more reluctant, not because they had any need to economize within their elastic budget, but a Protestant respect for lucre as a sign of God's grace made them regret seeing it wasted. And wasted it would probably be, as the mathematical likelihood of Hel's returning alive was slim. Another fiscal consideration was the expense they would be put to in transporting Hel to the United States for cosmetic surgery, as he had no chance of getting to Peking with a memorable face like that. Still, they decided at last, they really had no choice. Their key-way sort had delivered only one punch card for a man qualified to do the job.

Okay. Make it Costa Rican citizenship and 100 K.

Next problem . . .

But when they met the next morning in the visitor's room, the American agent discovered that Hel had yet another request to make. He would take the assignment on only if CIA gave him the current addresses of the three men who had interrogated him: the "doctor," the MP sergeant, and Major Diamond.

"Now, wait a minute, Mr. Hel. We can't agree to that sort of thing. CIA takes care of its own. We can't offer them to you on a platter like that. Be reasonable. Let bygones be bygones. What do you say?"

Hel rose and asked that the guard conduct him back to his cell.

The frank-faced young American sighed and shook his head. "All right. Let me call the office for an okay. Okay?"

Washington

". . . AND I ASSUME Mr. Hel was successful in his enterprise," Mr. Able said. "For, if he were not, we wouldn't be sitting about here concerning ourselves with him."

"That's correct," Diamond said. "We have no details, but about four months after he was introduced into China through Hong Kong, we got word that he had been picked up by a bush patrol of the Foreign Legion in French Indo-China. He was in pretty bad shape . . . spent a couple of months in a hospital in Saigon . . . then he disappeared from our observation, for a period before emerging as a free-lance counterterrorist. We have him associated with a long list of hits against terrorist groups and individuals, usually in the pay of governments through their intelligence agencies." He spoke to the First Assistant. "Let's run through them at a high scan rate."

Superficial details of one extermination action after another flashed up on the surface of the conference table as Nicholai Hel's career from the early fifties to the mid-seventies was laid out by Fat Boy. Occasionally one or another of the men would ask for a freeze, as he questioned Diamond about some detail.

"Jesus H. Christ!" Darryl Starr said at one point. "This guy really works both sides of the street! In the States he's hit both Weathermen and tri-K's; in Belfast he's moved against both parts of the Irish stew; he seems to have worked for just about everybody except the A-rabs, Junta Greeks, the Spanish, and the Argentines. And did you eyeball the weapons used in the hits? Along with the conventional stuff of handguns and nerve-gas pipes, there were such weirdo weapons as a pocket comb, a drinking straw, a folded sheet of paper, a door key, a light bulb . . . This guy'd strangle you with your own skivvies, if you wasn't careful!"

"Yes," Diamond said. "That has to do with his Naked/Kill training. It has been estimated that, for Nicholai Hel, the average Western room contains just under two hundred lethal weapons."

Starr shook his head and sucked his teeth aloud. "Gettin' rid of a fella like that would be hardern' snapping snot off a fingernail."

Mr. Able paled at the earthy image.

The PLO goatherd shook his head and tished. "I cannot understand these sums so extravagant he receives for his servicing. In my country a man's life can be purchased for what, in dollars, would be two bucks thirty-five cents."

Diamond glanced at him tiredly. "That's a fair price for one of your countrymen. The basic reason governments are willing to pay Hel so much for exterminating terrorists is that terrorism is the most economical means of warfare. Consider the cost of mounting a force capable of protecting every individual in a nation from attack in the street, in his home, in his car. It costs millions of dollars just to search for the victim of a terrorist kidnapping. It's quite a bargain if the government can have the terrorist exterminated for a few hundred thousand, and avoid the antigovernment propaganda of a trial at the same time." Diamond turned to the First Assistant. "What is the average fee Hel gets for a hit?"

The First Assistant posed the simple question to Fat Boy. "Just over quarter of a million, sir. That's in dollars. But it seems he has refused to accept American dollars since 1963."

Mr. Able chuckled. "An astute man. Even if one runs all the way to the bank to change dollars for real money, their plunging value will cost him some fiscal erosion."

"Of course," the First Assistant continued, "that average fee is skewed. You'd get a better idea of his pay if you used the mean."

"Why is that?" the Deputy asked, pleased to have something to say.

"It seems that he occasionally takes on assignments without pay."

"Oh?" Mr. Able said. "That's surprising. Considering his experiences at the hands of the Occupation Forces and his desire to live in a style appropriate to his tastes and breeding, I would have assumed he worked for the highest bidder."

"Not quite," Diamond corrected. "Since 1967 he has taken on assignments for various Jewish militant groups without pay—some kind of twisted admiration for their struggle against larger forces."

Mr. Able smiled thinly.

"Take another case," Diamond continued. "He has done services without pay for ETA-6, the Basque Nationalist organization. In return, they protect him and his château in the mountains. That protection, by the way, is very effective. We have three known incidents of men going into the mountains to effect retribution for some action of Hel's, and in each case the men have simply disappeared. And every once in a while Hel takes on a job for no other reason than his disgust at the actions of some terrorist group. He did one like that not too long ago for the West German government. Flash that one up, Llewellyn."

The men around the conference table scanned the details of Hel's penetration into a notorious group of German urban terrorists that led to the imprisonment of the man after whom the group was named and the death of the woman.

"He was involved in that?" Mr. Able asked with a slight tone of awe.

"That was one heavy number," Starr admitted. "I shit thee not!"

"Yes, but his highest pay for a single action was in the United States," Diamond said. "And interestingly enough, it was a private individual who footed the bill. Let's have that one, Llewellyn."

"Which one is that, sir?"

"Los Angeles—May of seventy-four."

As the rear-projection came up, Diamond explained, "You'll remember this. Five members of a gang of urban vandals and thieves calling themselves the Symbiotic Maoist Falange were put away in an hour-long firefight in which three hundred fifty police SWAT forces, FBI men, and CIA advisers poured thousands of rounds into the house in which they were holed up."

"What did Hel have to do with that?" Starr asked.

"He had been hired by a certain person to locate the guerrillas and put them away. A plan was worked out in which the police and FBI were to be tipped off, the whole thing timed so they would arrive after the wet work was done, so they could collect the glory . . . and responsibility. Unfortunately for Hel, they arrived half an hour too early, and he was in the house when they surrounded it and opened fire, along with gas- and firebombing. He had to break through the floor and hide in the crawl space while the place burned down around him. In the confusion of the last minute, he was able to get out and join the mob of officers. Evidently he was dressed as a SWAT man—flack vest, baseball cap, and all."

"But as I recall," Mr. Able said, "there were reports of firing from within the house during the action."

"That was the released story. Fortunately, no one ever stopped to consider that, although two submachine guns and an arsenal of handguns and shotguns were found in the charred wreckage, not one of the three hundred fifty police (and God knows how many onlookers) was so much as scratched after an hour of firing."

"But it seems to me that I remember seeing a photograph of a brick wall with chips out of it from bullets."

"Sure. When you surround a building with over three hundred gunhappy heavies and open fire, a fair number of slugs are going to pass in one window and out another."

Mr. Able laughed. "You're saying the police and FBI and CIA were firing on themselves?"

Diamond shrugged. "You don't buy geniuses for twenty thousand a year."

The Deputy felt he had to come to the defense of his organization. "I should remind you that CIA was there purely in an advisory capacity. We are prohibited by law from doing domestic wet work."

Everyone looked at him in silence, until Mr. Able broke it with a question for Diamond: "Why did this individual go to the expense of having Mr. Hel do the hit, when the police were only too willing?"

"The police might have taken a prisoner. And that prisoner might have testified in a subsequent trial."

"Ah, yes. I see."

Diamond turned to the First Assistant. "Pick up the scan rate and just skim the rest of Hel's known operations."

In rapid chronological order, sketches of action after action flashed up on the tabletop. San Sebastian, sponsor ETA-6; Berlin, sponsor German government; Cairo, sponsor unknown; Belfast, sponsor IRA; Belfast, sponsor UDA; Belfast, sponsor British government—and on and on. Then the record suddenly stopped.

"He retired two years ago." Diamond explained.

"Well, if he is retired . . ." Mr. Able lifted his palms in a gesture that asked what they were so worried about.

"Unfortunately, Hel has an overdeveloped sense of duty to friends. And Asa Stern was a friend."

"Tell me. Several times this word 'stunt' came up on the printout. I don't understand that."

"It has to do with Hel's system for pricing his services. He calls his actions 'stunts'; and he prices them the same way movie stunt men do, on the basis of two factors: the difficulty of the job, and the danger of failure. For instance, if a hit is hard to accomplish for reasons of narrow access to the mark or difficult penetration into the organization, the price will be higher. But if the consequences of the act are not too heavy because of the incompetence of the organization against which the action is performed, the price is lower (as in the case of the IRA, for instance, or CIA). Or take a reverse case of that: Hel's last stunt before retirement. There was a man in Hong Kong who wanted to get his brother out of Communist China. For someone like Hel, this wasn't too difficult, so you might imagine the fee would be relatively modest. But the price of capture would have been death, so that adjusted the fee upward. See how it goes?"

"How much did he receive for that particular . . . stunt?"

"Oddly enough, nothing—in money. The man who hired him operates a training academy for the most expensive concubines in the world. He buys baby girls from all over the Orient and educates them in tact and social graces. Only about one in fifty develop into beautiful and skillful enough products to enter his exclusive trade. The rest he simply equips with useful occupations and releases at the age of eighteen. In fact, all the girls are free to leave whenever they want, but because they get fifty percent of their yearly fee—between one and two hundred thousand dollars—they usually continue to work for him for ten or so years, then they retire in the prime of life with five hundred thousand or so in the bank. This man had a particularly stellar pupil, a woman of about thirty who went on the market for quarter-of-a-mil per year. In return for getting the brother out, Hel took two years of her service. She lives with him now at his château. Her name is Hana—part Japanese, part Negro, part Cauc. As an interesting sidelight, this training academy passes for a Christian orphanage. The girls wear dark-blue uniforms, and the women who train them wear nuns' habits. The place is called the Orphanage of the Passion."

Starr produced a low whistle. "You're telling me that this squack of Hel's gets a quarter of a million a year? What's that come to per screw, I wonder?"

"In your case," Diamond said, "about a hundred twenty-five thousand."

The PLO goatherd shook his head. "This Nicholai Hel must be very rich from the point of view of money, eh?"

"Not so rich as you might imagine. In the first place, his 'stunts' are expensive to set up. This is particularly true when he has to neutralize the government of the country in which the stunt takes place. He does this through the information brokerage of a man we have never been able to locate—a man known only as the Gnome. The Gnome collects damaging facts about governments and political figures. Hel buys this information and uses it as blackmail against any effort on the part of the government to hamper his actions. And this information is very expensive. He also spends a lot of money mounting caving expeditions in Belgium, the Alps, and his own mountains. It's a hobby of his and an expensive one. Finally, there's the matter of his château. In the fifteen years since he bought it, he has spent a little over two million in restoring it to its original condition, importing the last of the world's master stonemasons, wood carvers, tile makers, and what not. And the furniture in the place is worth a couple of million more."

"So," Mr. Able said, "he lives in great splendor, this Hel of yours."

"Splendor, I guess. But primitive. The château is completely restored. No electricity, no central heating, nothing modern except an underground telephone line that keeps him informed of the arrival and approach of any strangers."

Mr. Able nodded to himself. "So a man of eighteenth-century breeding has created an eighteenth-century world for himself in splendid isolation in the mountains. How interesting. But I am surprised he did not return to Japan and live in the style he was bred to."

"From what I understand, when he got out of prison and discovered to what degree the traditional ways of life and ethical codes of Japan had been 'perverted' by Americanism, he decided to leave. He has never been back."

"How wise. For him, the Japan of his memory will always remain what it was in gentler, more noble times. Pity he's an enemy. I would like your Mr. Hel."

"Why do you call him *my* Mr. Hel?"

Mr. Able smiled. "Does that irritate you?"

"Any stupidity irritates me. But let's get back to our problem. No, Hel is not as rich as you might imagine. He probably needs money, and that might give us an angle on him. He owns a few thousand acres in Wyoming, apartments in half a dozen world capitals, a mountain lodge in the Pyrenees, but there's less than half a million in his Swiss bank. He still has the expenses of his château and his caving expeditions. Even assuming he sells off the apartments and the Wyoming land, life in his château would be, by his standards, a modest existence."

"A life of . . . what was the word?" Mr. Able asked, smiling faintly to himself at the knowledge he was annoying Diamond.

"I don't know what you mean."

"That Japanese word for things reserved and understated?"

"*Shibumi!*"

"Ah, yes. So even without taking any more 'stunts,' your—I mean, *our* Mr. Hel would be able to live out a life of *shibumi.*"

"I wouldn't be so sure," Starr interposed. "Not with nookie at a hundred K a throw!"

"Will you shut up, Starr," Diamond said.

Not quite able to follow what was going on here, the PLO goatherd had risen from the conference table and strayed to the window, where he looked down and watched an ambulance with a flashing dome light thread its way through the partially congealed traffic—as that ambulance did every night at precisely this time. Starr's colorful language had attracted his attention, and he was thumbing through his pocket English/Arabic dictionary, muttering, "Nookie . . . nookie . . . ." when suddenly the Washington Monument and the wide avenue of cars vanished, and the window was filled with a blinding light.

The goatherd screamed and threw himself to the floor, covering his head in anticipation of the explosion.

Everyone in the room reacted characteristically. Starr leapt up and whipped out his Magnum. Miss Swivven slumped into a chair. The Deputy covered his face with a sheet of typing paper. Diamond closed his eyes and shook his head at these asses with which he was surrounded. Mr. Able examined his cuticles. And the First Assistant, absorbed in his technological intercourse with Fat Boy, failed to notice that anything had happened.

"Get off the floor, for chrissake," Diamond said. "It's nothing. The street-scene film has broken, that's all."

"Yes, but . . ." the goatherd babbled.

"You came down in the elevator. You must have known you were in the basement."

"Yes, but . . ."

"Did you think you were looking down from the Sixteenth Floor?"

"No, but . . ."

"Miss Swivven, shut the rear projector off and make a note to have it repaired." Diamond turned to Mr. Able. "I had it installed to create a better working environment, to keep the office from feeling shut up in the bowels of the earth."

"And you have been capable of fooling yourself?"

Starr snapped his gun back into its holster and glared at the window, as though to say it had been lucky . . . *this* time.

With ruminantial ambiguity, the goatherd grinned sheepishly as he got to his feet. "Boy-o-boy, that was a good one! I guess the joke was on me!"

Out in the machine room, Miss Swivven threw a switch, and the glaring light in the window went out, leaving a matte white rectangle that had the effect of sealing the room up and reducing its size.

"All right," Diamond said, "now you have some insight into the man we're dealing with. I want to talk a little strategy, and for that I would as soon have you two out of here." He pointed Starr and the PLO goatherd toward the exercise and sun room. "Wait in there until you're called."

Appearing indifferent to his dismissal, Starr ambled toward the sun room, followed by the Arab who insisted on explaining again that he guessed the joke had been on him.

When the door closed behind them, Diamond addressed the two men at the conference table, speaking as though the First Assistant were not present, as indeed in many ways he was not.

"Let me lay out what I think we ought to do. First—"

"Just a moment, Mr. Diamond," Mr. Able interrupted. "I am concerned about one thing. Just what is your relationship to Nicholai Hel?"

"How do you mean?"

"Oh, come now! It is evident that you have taken a particular interest in this person. You are familiar with so many details that do not appear in the computer printout."

Diamond shrugged. "After all, he's a mauve-card man; and it's my job to keep current with—"

"Excuse me for interrupting you again, but I am not interested in evasions. You have admitted that the officer in charge of the interrogation of Nicholai Hel was your brother."

Diamond stared at the OPEC troubleshooter for a second. "That's right. Major Diamond was my brother. My older brother."

"You were close to your brother?"

"When our parents died, my brother took care of me. He supported me while he was working his way through college. Even while he was working his way up through the OSS—a notoriously WASP organization—and later with CIA, he continued to—"

"Do spare us the domestic details. I would be correct to say that you were very close to him?"

Diamond's voice was tight. "Very close."

"All right. Now there is something you passed over rather quickly in your biographic sketch of Nicholai Hel. You mentioned that he required, as a part of his pay for doing the Peking assignment that got him out of prison, the current addresses of the three men involved in beating and torturing him during his interrogation. May I presume he did not want the addresses for the purpose of sending Christmas cards . . . or Hanukkah greetings?"

Diamond's jaw muscles rippled.

"My dear friend, if this affair is as serious as you seem to believe it is, and if you are seeking my assistance in clearing it up, then I insist upon understanding everything that might bear upon the matter."

Diamond pressed his palms together and hooked the thumbs under his chin. He spoke from behind the fingers, his voice mechanical and atonic. "Approximately one year after Hel showed up in Indo-China, the 'doctor' who had been in charge of administering drugs during the interrogation was found dead in his abortion clinic in Manhattan. The coroner's report described the death as accidental, a freak fall which had resulted in one of the test tubes he was carrying shattering and going through his throat. Two months later, the MP sergeant who had administered the physical aspects of the interrogation and who had been transferred back to the United States died in an automobile accident. He had evidently fallen asleep at the wheel and driven his car off the road and over a cliff. Exactly three months later, Major Diamond—then Lieutenant Colonel Diamond—was on assignment in Bavaria. He had a skiing accident." Diamond paused and tapped his lips with his forefingers.

"Another freak accident, I suppose?" Mr. Able prompted.

"That's right. As best they could tell, he had taken a bad jump. He was found with a ski pole through his chest."

"Hm-m-m," Mr. Able said after a pause. "So this is the way CIA protects its own? It must be quite a satisfaction for you to have under your control the organization that gave away your brother's life as part of a fee."

Diamond looked across at the Deputy. "Yes. It has been a satisfaction."

The Deputy cleared his throat. "Actually, I didn't enter the Company until the spring of—"

"Tell me something," Mr. Able said. "Why haven't you taken retributive action against Hel before now?"

"I did once. And I will again. I have time."

"You did once? When was— Ah! Of course! Those policemen who surrounded that house in Los Angeles and opened fire half an hour before schedule! That was your doing?"

Diamond's nod had the quality of a bow to applause.

"So there is some revenge motive in all of this for you, it would seem."

"I am acting in the best interest of the Mother Company. I have a message from the Chairman telling me that failure in this would be unacceptable. If Hel has to be terminated to assure the success of the Septembrists skyjacking then, yes, I shall take some personal satisfaction in that. It will be a life for a life, not, as in his case, three murders for one beating!"

"I doubt that he considered them murders. More likely he thought of them as executions. And if my guess is right, it was not the pain of the beatings that he was avenging."

"What, then?"

"The *indignity* of them. That's something you would have no way to understand."

Diamond puffed out a short laugh. "You really imagine you know Hel better than I do?"

"In some ways, yes—despite your years of studying him and his actions. You see, he and I—accepting our cultural differences—are of the same caste. You will never see this Hel clearly, squinting as you do across the indefinite but impassable barrier of breeding—a great gulf fixed, as the Qoran or one of those books terms it. But let us not descend to personalities. Presumably you sent those two plebes from the room for some other reason than a desire to improve the quality of the company."

Diamond was stiffly silent for a moment, then he drew a short breath and said, "I have decided to pay a visit to Hel's place in the Basque country."

"This will be the first time you have met him face to face?"

"Yes."

"And you have considered the possibility that it may be more difficult to get out of those mountains than to get in?"

"Yes. But I believe I shall be able to convince Mr. Hel of the foolishness of attempting to assist Miss Stern. In the first place, there is no logical reason why he should take on this assignment for a misguided middle-class girl he doesn't even know. Hel has nothing but disgust for amateurs of all kinds, including amateurs in terror. Miss Stern may see herself as a noble soldier in the service of all that is right in the world, but I assure you that Hel will view her as a pain in the ass."

Mr. Able tilted his head in doubt. "Even assuming that Mr. Hel does look upon Miss Stern as a proctological nuisance (whether or not he reflects on the happy pun), there remains the fact that Hel was a friend of the late Asa Stern, and you have yourself said that he has strong impulses toward loyalty to friends."

"True. But there are fiscal pressures we can bring to bear. We know that he retired as soon as he had accumulated enough money to live out his life in comfort. Mounting a 'stunt' against our PLO friends would be a costly matter. It's probable that Hel is relying on the eventual sale of his Wyoming land for financial security. Within two hours, that land will no longer be his. All records of his having bought it will disappear and be replaced by proof that the land is held by the Mother Company." Diamond smiled. "By way of fringe benefit, there happens to be a little coal on that land that can be profitably stripped off. To complete his financial discomfort, two simple cables to Switzerland from the Chairman will cause Hel's money held in a Swiss bank to vanish."

"And I imagine the money will turn up in Mother Company assets?"

"Part of it. The rest will be held by the banks as transactional costs. The Swiss are nothing if not frugal. It's a Calvinist principle that there is an entrance fee to heaven, to keep the riff-raff out. It is my intention to perform these fiscally punitive actions, regardless of Hel's decision to take or reject Miss Stern's job."

"A gesture in memory of your brother?"

"You may think of it that way, if you like. But it will also serve as a financial interdiction to Hel's being a nuisance to the Mother Company and to the nations whose interest you represent."

"What if money pressures alone are not sufficient to persuade him?"

"Naturally, I have a secondary line of action to address that contingency. The Mother Company will bring pressure upon the British government to spare no effort in protecting the Black Septembrists involved in the Munich Olympics debacle. It will be their task to make sure they are unmolested in their skyjacking of the Montreal plane. This will not require as much pressure as you might imagine because, now that the North Sea oil fields are producing, England's economic interests are more closely allied to those of OPEC than to those of the West."

Mr. Able smiled. "Frankly, I cannot imagine the MI-5 and MI-6 lads being an effective deterrent to Mr. Hel. The greater part of their energies are applied to writing imaginative memoirs of their daring exploits during the Second World War."

"True. But they will have a certain nuisance value. Also, we shall have the services of the French internal police to help us contain Hel within that country. And we are moving on another front. It is inconceivable that Hel would try to enter England to put the Septembrists away without first neutralizing the British police. I told you that he does this by buying blackmail material from an information broker known as the Gnome. For years the Gnome has evaded international efforts to locate and render him dysfunctional. Through the good services of Her communications subsidiaries, the Mother Company is beginning to close in on this man. We know that he lives somewhere near the city of Bayonne, and we're actively involved in tightening down on him. If we get to him before Hel does, we can interdict the use of blackmail leverage against the British police."

Mr. Able smiled. "You have a fertile mind, Mr. Diamond—when personal revenge is involved." Mr. Able turned suddenly to the Deputy. "Do you have something to contribute?"

Startled, the Deputy said, "Pardon me? What?"

"Never mind." Mr. Able glanced again at his watch. "Let's do get on with it. I assume you didn't ask me here so you could parade before me your array of tactics and interdictions. Obviously, you need my help in the unlikely event that all the machines you have set into motion fail, and Hel manages to put the Septembrists away."

"Exactly. And it is because this is a bit delicate that I wanted those two buffoons out of the room while we talked about it. I accept the fact that the nations you represent are committed to protecting the PLO, and therefore the Mother Company is, and therefore CIA is. But let's be frank among ourselves. We would all be happier if the Palestinian issue (and the Palestinians with it) would simply disappear. They're a nasty, ill-disciplined, vicious lot whom history happened to put in the position of a symbol of Arab unity. All right so far?"

Mr. Able waved away the obvious with his hand.

"Very well. Let's consider our posture, should everything fail and Hel manage to exterminate the Septembrists. All that would really concern us would be assuring the PLO that we had acted vigorously on its behalf. Considering their barbaric nature, I think they would be mollified if we took vengeance on their behalf by destroying Nicholai Hel and everything he possesses."

"Sowing the land with salt?" Mr. Able mused.

"Just so."

Mr. Able was silent for a time, his eyes lowered as he tickled his upper lip with his forefinger. "Yes, I believe we can rely on the PLO's sophomoric mentality to that degree. They would accept a major act of revenge—provided it was lurid enough—as proof that we are devoted to their interests." He smiled to himself. "And do not imagine that it has escaped my notice that such an eventuality would allow you to slay two birds with one stone. You would solve the tactical problem at hand, and avenge your brother at one stroke. Is it possible that you would rather see all your devices fail and Nicholai Hel somehow break through and hit the Septembrists, freeing you to devise and execute a maximal punishment for him?"

"I shall do everything in my power to prevent the hit in the first instance. That would be best for the Mother Company, and Her interests take priority over my personal feelings." Diamond glanced toward the First Assistant. It was most likely that he reported directly to the Chairman on Diamond's devotion to the Company.

"That's it then," Mr. Able said, rising from the conference table. "If there is not further need for me, I shall return to the social event this business interrupted."

Diamond rang for Miss Swivven to escort Mr. Able out of the building.

The Deputy rose and cleared his throat. "I don't assume you'll be needing me?"

"Have I ever? But I'll expect you to keep yourself available to execute instructions. You may go."

Diamond directed the First Assistant to roll back the information on Nicholai Hel and be prepared to project it at a slow enough rate to accommodate the literacy of Starr and the PLO goatherd, who were returning from the exercise room, the Arab rubbing his inflamed eyes as he put his English/Arabic dictionary back into his pocket. "Goodness my gracious, Mr. Diamond! It is most difficult to read in that room. The lights along the walls are so bright!"

"I want you two to sit here and learn everything you're capable of about Nicholai Hel. I don't care if it takes all night. I've decided to bring you along when I visit this man—not because you'll be of any use, but because you're responsible for this screw-up, and I'm going to make you see it out to the end."

"That's mighty white of you," Starr muttered.

Diamond spoke to Miss Swivven as she reentered from the elevator. "Note the following. One: Hel's Wyoming land, terminate. Two: Swiss money, terminate. Three: The Gnome, intensify search for. Four: MI-5 and MI-6, alert and instruct. All right, Llewellyn, start the roll-down for our blundering friends here. And you two had better pray that Nicholai Hel has not already gone underground."

Gouffre Port-de-Larrau

AT THAT MOMENT, Nicholai Hel was 393 meters underground, revolving slowly on the end of a cable half a centimeter thick. Seventy-five meters below him, invisible in the velvet black of the cave, was the tip of a vast rubble cone, a collection of thousands of years of debris from the natural shaft. And at the base of the rubble cone his caving partner was waiting for him to finish his eleventh descent down the twisting shaft that wound above him like a mammoth wood screw turned inside out.

The two Basque lads operating the winch at the edge of the *gouffre* almost four hundred meters above had set double friction clamps to hold the cable fast while they replaced a spent cable drum with a fresh one. This was the most unnerving moment of the descent—and the most uncomfortable. Unnerving, because Hel was now totally dependent on the cable, after ninety minutes of negotiating the narrow, twisting shaft with its bottlenecks, narrow ledges, tricky dihedrons, and tight passages down which he had to ease himself gingerly, never surrendering to gravity because the cable was slack to give him maneuvering freedom. Throughout the descent there was the constant irritation of keeping the cable from fouling or from becoming entangled with the telephone line that dangled beside it. But through all the problems of the shaft, some challenging and some only irritating, there was the constant comfort of the rock walls, close and visible in the beam of his helmet light, theoretically available for clinging to, should something go wrong with the cable or the winch.

But now he was out of the shaft and dangling just below the roof of the first great cave, the walls of which had receded beyond the throw of his helmet light, and he hung there in the infinite void; the combined weight of his body, of four hundred meters of cable, and of the watertight container of food and equipment depending from two friction clamps four hundred meters above. Hel had full faith in the clamp-and-winch system; he had designed it himself and built it in his workshop. It was a simple affair, pedal-driven by the powerful legs of the Basque mountain lads above, and geared so low that descent was very slow. Sliding safety clamps were designed to bite into the cable and arrest it if it exceeded a certain rate of descent. The fulcrum was a tripod of aluminum tubes formed in an open tepee directly over the narrow entrance hole at the bottom of the *gouffre.* Hel trusted the mechanical system that prevented him from plummeting down through the dark onto the tip of that pile of rubble and boulders that filled about half of the first great cave, but all the same he muttered imprecations at the boys above to get on with it. He had to breathe orally, his mouth wide open, because he was hanging in the middle of a waterfall produced by the outflow of an underground stream into the shaft at meter point 370, making the last ninety-five meters a free descent through an icy spray that seeped up his arms, despite the tight rings of rubber at his wrists, and trickled up to shock his hot armpits. His helmet lamp was useless in the waterfall, so he turned it off and hung limp in the roar and echoing hiss of the water, his harness beginning to chafe his ribs and crotch. There was a certain advantage to his blindness. Inevitably, in the twisting, scrambling descent, the cable always got wound up, and when he gave his weight to the line and began the free descent through the roof of the first cave, he started to spin, slowly at first, then faster, then slowing down and pausing, then beginning to spin in the opposite direction. Had he been able to see the slant of the spray swirling around him, he would have felt the pangs of vertigo, but in the total dark there was only a sensation of "ballooning" as the speed of his spin tended to spread out his arms and legs.

Hel felt himself being drawn upward a short distance to loosen the safety clamps, then there was a stomach-clutching drop of several centimeters as his weight was transferred to the new cable drum, and he began a twisting descent through the waterfall, which soon broke up into thick mist. Eventually, he could make out a smear of light below where his caving partner awaited him, standing well aside from the line of fall of rock and water and, God forbid, possibly Hel.

The scrape of his dangling equipment container told Hel he had reached the tip of the rubble cone, and he pulled up his legs so as to make his first contact with the rock a sitting one, because the lads above would lock up with the first sign of slack, and it could be comically difficult to unharness oneself while standing tiptoe on the rim of a boulder.

Le Cagot scrambled over and helped with the unharnessing and unstrapping of equipment because Hel's legs and arms were numb with loss of circulation in the wet cold, and his fingers felt fat and insensitive as they fumbled with straps and buckles.

"So, Niko!" Le Cagot boomed, his basso voice reverberating in the cave. "You finally decided to drop in for a visit! Where have you been? By the Two Balls of Christ, I thought you had decided to give it over and go home! Come on. I have made some tea."

Le Cagot hoisted the container on his shoulder and started down the unstable rubble cone, picking his way quickly through familiarity, and avoiding loose stones that would precipitate an avalanche. Opening and closing his hands to restore circulation, Hel followed his partner's steps exactly because Le Cagot knew the treacherous and unstable rubble cone better than he. The gruff old Basque poet had been down here for two days, making base camp at the foot of the cone and taking little Theseus sorties into the small caves and galleries that gave out from the principal chamber. Most of these had run out into blocks and blank walls, or pinched out into cracks too narrow for penetration.

Le Cagot pawed around in the equipment container Hel had descended with. "What is this? You promised to bring a bottle of Izarra! Don't tell me you drank it on your way down! If you did this to me, Niko, then by the Epistolary

Balls of Paul I shall have to do you hurt, though that would cause me some sadness, for you are a good man, despite your misfortune of birth." It was Le Cagot's conviction that any man so unlucky as not to be born Basque suffered from a tragic genetic flaw.

"It's in there somewhere," Hel said as he lay back on a flat rock and sighed with painful pleasure as his knotted muscles began to stretch and relax.

During the past forty hours, while Le Cagot had been making base camp and doing light peripheral explorations, Hel had made eleven trips up and down through the *gouffre* shaft, bringing down food, equipment, nylon rope, and flares. What he needed most of all now was a few hours of sleep, which he could take at any time in the constant blackness of a cave, despite the fact that, by outside time, it was shortly before dawn.

Nicholai Hel and Beñat Le Cagot had been a caving team for sixteen years, during which they had done most of the major systems in Europe, occasionally making news in the limited world of the speleologue with discoveries and new records of depth and distance. Over the years their division of duties had become automatic. Le Cagot, a bull of strength and endurance despite his fifty years, always went down first, sweeping up as he made his slow descent, clearing ledges and dihedrons of loose rock and rubble that could be knocked off by the cable and kill a man in the shaft. He always brought the battery telephone down with him and established some kind of base camp, well out of the line of fall for rock and water. Because Hel was more lithe and tactically more skillful, he made all the equipment trips when, as in the case of this new hole, the access shaft was sinuous and twisting, and gear could not be lowered without the guidance of an accompanying man. Usually this only entailed two or three trips. But this time they had discovered all the signs of a great network of caverns and galleries, the exploration of which would require a great deal of equipment, so Hel had had to make eleven chafing, grueling trips. And now that the job was over and his body was no longer sustained by the nervous energy of danger, fatigue was overtaking him, and his knotted muscles were slackening painfully.

"Do you know what, Niko? I have been giving a great problem the benefit of my penetrating and illuminating mind." Le Cagot poured himself a large portion of Izzara into the metal cap of a flask. After two days alone in the dark cave, Le Cagot's gregarious personality was hungry for conversation which, for him, consisted of monologues delivered to an appreciative audience. "And here's what I have been thinking, Niko. I have decided that all cavers are mad, save of course for Basque cavers, in whom what is madness for others is a manifestation of bravery and thirst for adventure. Do you agree?"

Hel hum-grunted as he descended into a coma/sleep that seemed to soften the slab of stone beneath him.

"But, you protest, is it fair to say the caver is more crazy than the mountain climber? It is! And why? Because the caver faces the more dangerous friction. The climber confronts only the frictions of his body and strength. But the caver faces erosions of nerve and primordial fears. The primitive beast that lingers within man has certain deep dreads, beyond logic, beyond intelligence. He dreads the dark. He fears being underground, which place he has always called the home of evil forces. He fears being alone. He dreads being trapped. He fears the water from which, in ancient times, he emerged to become Man. His most primitive nightmares involve falling through the dark, or wandering lost through mazes of alien chaos. And the caver—crazy being that he is—volitionally chooses to face these nightmare conditions. That is why he is more insane than the climber, because the thing he risks at every moment is his sanity. This is what I have been thinking about, Niko . . . Niko? Niko? What, do you sleep while I am talking to you? Lazy bastard! I swear by the Perfidious Balls of Judas that not one man in a thousand would sleep while I am talking! You insult the poet in me! It is like closing your eyes to a sunset, or stopping your ears to a Basque melody. You know that, Niko? Niko? Are you dead? Answer yes or no. Very well, for your punishment, I shall drink your portion of the Izzara."

The shaft to the cave system they were preparing to explore had been discovered by accident the year before, but it had been kept secret because a part of the conical *gouffre* above it was in Spain, and there was a risk that the Spanish authorities might seal off the entrance as they had at Gouffre Pierre-Saint-Martin after the tragic fall and death of Marcel Loubens in 1952. During the winter, a team of young Basque lads had slowly shifted the boundary stones to put the *gouffre* well within France, moving twenty markers a little at a time so as to fool the Spanish border guards who checked the area routinely. This adjustment in borders seemed perfectly legitimate to them; after all, it was all Basque land, and they were not particularly interested in an arbitrary boundary established by the two occupying nations.

There was another reason for shifting the border. Since Le Cagot and the two Basque boys operating the winch were known activists in ETA, an arrival of Spanish border police while they were working the cave might end with their passing their lives in a Spanish prison.

Although the Gouffre Port-de-Larrau was rather distant from the vast field of funnel-shaped depressions that characterize the area around Pic d'Anie and earn it the name "the Gruyère of France," it had been visited occasionally by curious teams of cavers, each of which had been disappointed to find it "dry," its shaft clogged with boulders and rubble after a few meters down. In time the word spread amongst the tight community of deep cavers that there was no point in making the long climb up to Gouffre Port-de-Larrau, when there was so much better caving to be had in the vast *gouffre* field above Ste. Engrace, where the mountainsides and high plateaus were strewn with the conical depressions of *gouffres* formed by infalls of surface rock and earth into cave systems in the calciate rock below.

But a year ago, two shepherds tending flocks in the high grazing lands were sitting at the edge of Gouffre Port-de-Larrau, taking a lunch of fresh cheese, hard bread, and *xoritzo,* that strong red sausage, one bit of which will flavor a mouthful of bread. One of the lads thoughtlessly tossed a stone down toward the mouth of the *gouffre* and was surprised at the startled flight of two crows. It is well-known that crows make nests only over shafts of considerable depth, so it was puzzling that these birds had nested over the little dimple of Gouffre Larrau. In curiosity, they scrambled down the side of the funnel and dropped stones down the shaft. With the echoing and reechoing of the stones and the rubble they knocked off on their way down, it was impossible to tell how deep the shaft was, but one thing was sure: it was no longer a little dimple. Evidently the great earthquake of 1962 that had almost destroyed the village of Arrete had also cleared out some of the choke stones and rubble blocking the shaft.

When, two months later, the second transhumance brought the lads down to the valley, they informed Beñat Le Cagot of their discovery, knowing that the blustery poet of Basque separatism was also an avid caver. He swore them to secrecy and carried the news of the find to Nicholai Hel, with whom he lived in safety, whenever recent actions made remaining in Spain particularly unwise.

Neither Hel nor Le Cagot allowed himself to become too excited over the find. They realized that chances were against finding any great cave system at the bottom of the shaft—assuming they got to the bottom. In all probability, the earthquake had cleared only the upper portions of the shaft. Or, as is often the case, they might find that centuries of infall down the *gouffre* had built up the rubble cone below until it rose to the roof of the cave and its tip actually entered the shaft, choking it off forever.

Despite all these protective doubts, they decided to make a preliminary light exploration immediately—just clearing their way down and taking a look—nothing major.

With autumn, bad weather came to the mountains, and that was an advantage, for it would diminish any inclinations toward energetic border patrolling on the part of the Spanish (the French being congenitally disinclined to such rigors). The heavy weather would, however, make hard work of bringing into those desolate mountains the winch, the cable drums, the battery phones, the fulcrum tripod, and all the equipment and food they would need for the survey.

Le Cagot sniffed and made light of these tasks, reminding Hel that smuggling contraband over those mountains was the traditional occupation of the Soultain Basque.

"Did you know that we once brought a piano over from Spain?"

"I heard something about that. How did you do it?"

"Ah-ha! Wouldn't the flat hats like to know! Actually, it was fairly simple. Another insurmountable problem that crumbled in the face of Basque ingenuity."

Hel nodded fatalistically. There was no way to avoid the story now, as various manifestations of Basque racial superiority constituted the principal theme of Le Cagot's conversation.

"Because, Niko, you are something of an honorary Basque—despite your ludicrous accent—I shall tell you how we got the piano over. But you must promise to guard the secret to the death. Do you promise?"

"Pardon me?" Hel had been attending to something else.

"I accept your promise. Here's how we did it. We brought the piano over note by note. It took eighty-eight trips. The fellow stumbled while carrying the middle C and dented it, and to this day that piano has two B-flats side by side. That is the truth! I swear it on the Hopeless Balls of Saint Jude! Why would I lie?"

Two and a half days spent bringing the gear up to the *gouffre,* a day taken to set it up and test it, and the work of exploration began. Hel and Le Cagot took turns down in the shaft, clearing rubble from the narrow ledges, chipping off sharp outcroppings that threatened to abrade the cable, breaking down the triangular wedges of boulders that blocked off the shaft. And any one of those wedges might have proved too firmly lodged to be broken down; any one of them might turn out to be the tip of the clogging rubble cone; and their exploration would come to an inglorious end.

The shaft turned out not to be a dead fall, but rather an inside-out screw which so twisted the cable that each time they came to a short free drop their first task was to put their body weight on the line and accept the dizzying spin and counterspin necessary to unwind the cable. In addition to breaking up clogs and sweeping rubble from ledges, they often had to chip away at the mother rock, particularly in "jugs" and bottlenecks, to make a relatively straight line of fall for the cable, so it would pay out without rubbing against edges of stone, which friction would sooner or later scar and weaken the cable, the thickness of which was already minimal: a hundred percent safety limit when carrying Le Cagot's eighty-two kilos plus a gear container. In designing the pedal winch, Hel had chosen the lightest cable possible for two reasons: flexibility through corkscrew passages and weight. It was not so much the weight of the cable drums that concerned him; his real concern was the weight of the paid-out line. When a man is down three or four hundred meters, the weight of the cable in the shaft triples the work of the men working the winch.

As it was always black in the shaft, they soon lost any sense of diurnal time, and sometimes came up surprised to find it was night. Each man worked as long as his body strength would allow, to reduce the time wasted bringing one man back up and lowering the other. There were exciting times when a clog would break through, revealing ten meters of open shaft; and spirits, both at the end of the cable and above at the telephone headset, would soar. At other times, a jam of choke stone would be loosened only to collapse into the next obstruction a meter or two down, thickening the clog.

The young men working the winch were new to the task, and on one occasion they failed to set the friction safety clamps. Hel was working down below, pecking away at a four-stone pyramid clog with a short-handled pick. Suddenly the clog gave away under his feet. The cable above him was slack. He fell . . .

About thirty centimeters to the next clog.

For a fraction of a second, he was a dead man. And for a few moments he huddled in silence as the adrenaline spurt made his stomach flutter. Then he put on his headset and in his soft prison voice gave slow, clear instructions on the use of the clamps. And he returned to work.

When both Hel and Le Cagot were too worn of body, too scuffed of knuckle and knee, too stiff of forearm to make a fist around the pick handle, they would sleep, taking shelter in a shepherd's *artzain chola* shelter used during the summer pasturage on the flank pf Pic d'Orhy, this highest of the Basque mountains. Too knotted and tense to find sleep quickly, they would chat while the wind moaned around the south flank of Pic d'Orhy. It was there that Hel first heard the adage that the Basque, wherever they roam in the world, always yearn with a low-grade romantic fever to return to the Eskual-herri.

Orhiko choria Orhin laket: "the birds of Orhy are happy only at Orhy."

The meanest and most desperate time was spent at a thick jam at meter point 365, where they had to work in a constant rain of icy seep water. They could hear the roar and hiss of an underground river that entered the shaft close below. From the sound, it was evident that the river fell a long way after entering the shaft, and the chances were that the water had kept the rest of the hole clear of rock jams.

When Hel came up after three hours of picking away at the heavy clog, he was pale and shivering with bone-deep cold, his lips purple with incipient hypothermia, the skin of his hands and face bleached and wrinkled from hours in the water. Le Cagot had a great laugh at his expense and told him to stand aside and see how the rock would tremble and retreat before the force of a Basque. But he wasn't long down in the hole before his voice came gasping and spitting over the headphones, damning the clog, the cold rain, the stupid shaft, the mountain, the hobby of caving, and all of creation by the Vaporous Balls of the Holy Ghost! Then suddenly there was silence. His voice came up the line, breathless and hushed. "It's going to slip. Make sure the goddamned clamps are set. If I fall and destroy my magnificent body, I'll come back up and kick many asses!"

"Wait!" Hel shouted over the telephone. The line above was still slack to give Le Cagot work room.

There was a grunt as he delivered the last blow, then the cable tensed. For a time there was silence, then his voice came, strained and metallic: "That is it, my friends and admirers! We are through. And I am hanging in a goddamned waterfall." There was a pause. "By the way, my arm is broken."

Hel took a long breath and pictured the schematic of the shaft in his mind. Then he spoke into the mouthpiece in his calm, soft voice. "Can you make it up through the corkscrew one-handed?"

There was no answer from below.

"Beñat? Can you make it up?"

"Considering the alternative, I think I had better give it a try."

"We'll take it slow and easy."

"That would be nice."

On instructions from Hel, the lad began to pedal. The system was so low-geared that it was easy to maintain a slow pace, and for the first twenty meters there was no difficulty. Then Le Cagot entered the corkscrew that twisted up for almost eighty meters. He couldn't be pulled up through this; the niches and slits they had cut into the rock for the free passage of the pay line were only centimeters wide. Le Cagot would have to climb, sometimes locking himself in a wedging stance while he called for slack in the cable so that he could reach up and flick it out of a narrow slit. All this one-handed.

At first, Le Cagot's voice came over the line regularly, joking and humming, the predictable manifestations of his ebullient braggadocio. It was his habit to talk and sing constantly when underground. He claimed, as poet and egotist, to delight in the sound of his voice enriched with reverberation and echo. Hel had always known that the chatter served the additional purpose of filling the silence and pressing back the dark and loneliness, but he never mentioned this. Before long, the joking, singing, and swearing with which he showed off for those above and numbed his sense of danger began to be replaced by the heavy rasp of labored breathing. Occasionally there were tight dental grunts as a movement shocked waves of pain up his broken arm.

Up and down the cable went. A few meters up, then slack had to be given so Le Cagot could work out some cable jam. If he had both hands free, he could hold the line clear above him and come up fairly steadily.

The first lad at the pedal winch wore out, and they locked the pay line in the double clamps while the second boy took his place. The pedaling was easier now that more than half the weight of the cable was up in the drums, but still Le Cagot's progress was slow and irregular. Two meters up; three meters of slack for clearing a foul; take up the slack; a meter up; two meters down; two and a half meters up.

Hel did not talk to Le Cagot over the phones. They were old friends, and Hel would not insult him by seeming to think he needed the psychological support of being "talked up." Feeling useless and worn with tension and with silly but unavoidable attempts to help Le Cagot up by means of sympathetic kinesodics and "body English," Hel stood beside the take-up drum, listening to Le Cagot's rasping breath over the line. The cable had been painted with red stripes every ten meters, so by watching them come slowly into the pulley blocks Hel could tell where Le Cagot was in the shaft. In his mind, he could see the features around Beñat; that little ledge where he could get a toehold; that snarled dihedron where the cable was sure to foul; that bottleneck in which his broken arm must take some punishment.

Le Cagot's breathing was coming in gulps and gasps. Hel marked the cable with his eye; Le Cagot would now be at the most difficult feature of the ascent, a double dihedron at meter point 44. Just below the double dihedron was a narrow ledge where one could get purchase for the first jackknife squeeze, a maneuver hard enough for a man with two good arms, consisting of chimney climbing so narrow in places that all one could get was a heel-and-knee wedge, so wide in others that the wedge came from the flats of the feet to the back of the neck. And all the time the climber had to keep the slack cable from cross-threading between the overhanging knobs above.

"Stop," said Le Cagot's abraded voice. He would be at the ledge, tilting back his head and looking up at the lower of the two dihedrons in the beam of his helmet lamp. "I think I'll rest here a moment."

Rest? Hel said to himself. On a ledge six centimeters wide?

Obviously that was the end. Le Cagot was spent. Effort and pain had drained him, and the toughest bit was still above him. Once past the double dihedron, his weight could be taken on the cable and he could be dragged up like a sack of millet. But he had to make that reflex dihedron on his own.

The boy working the pedals looked toward Hel, his black Basque eyes round with fear. Papa Cagot was a folk hero to these lads. Had he not brought to the world an appreciation of Basque poetry in his tours of universities throughout England and the United States, where involved young people applauded his revolutionary spirit and listened with hushed attention to verse they could never understand? Was it not Papa Cagot who had gone into Spain with this outlander, Hel, to rescue thirteen who were in prison without trial?

Le Cagot's voice came over the wire. "I think I'll stay here for a while." He was no longer panting and rasping, but there was a calm of resignation alien to his boisterous personality. "This place suits me."

Not sure exactly what he was going to do, Nicholai began to speak in his soft voice. "Neanderthals. Yes, they're probably Neanderthals."

"What are you talking about?" Le Cagot wanted to know.

"The Basque."

"That in itself is good. But what is this about Neanderthals?"

"I've been giving some study to the origin of the Basque race. You know the facts as well as I. Their language is the only pre-Aryan tongue to survive. And there is certain evidence that they are a race apart from the rest of Europe. Type O blood is found in only forty percent of Europeans, while it appears in nearly sixty percent of the Basque. And among the Eskualdun, Type B blood is almost unknown. All this suggests that we have a totally separate race, a race descended from some different primate ancestor."

"Let me warn you right now, Niko. This talk is taking a path I do not like!"

". . . then too there is the matter of skull shape. The round skull of the Basque is more closely related to Neanderthal man than the higher Cro-Magnon, from which the superior peoples of the world descent."

"Niko? By the Two Damp Balls of John the Baptist, you will end by making me angry!"

"I'm not saying that it's a matter of intelligence that separates the Basque from the human. After all, they have learned a great deal at the feet of their Spanish masters—"

"Argh!"

"—no, it's more a physical thing. While they have a kind of flashy strength and courage—good for a quick screw or a bandit raid—the Basque are shown up when it comes to sticking power, to endurance—"

"Give me some slack!"

"Not that I blame them. A man is what he is. A trick of nature, a wrinkle in time has preserved this inferior race in their mountainous corner of the world where they have managed to survive because, let's face it, who else would want this barren wasteland of Eskual-Herri?"

"I'm coming up, Niko! Enjoy the sunlight! It's your last day!"

"Bullshit, Beñat. Even *I* would have trouble with that double dihedron. And I have two good arms and don't suffer the blemish of being a Neanderthal."

Le Cagot did not answer. His heavy breathing alone came over the wire, and sometimes a tight nasal snort as his broken arm took a shock.

Twenty centimeters now, thirty then, the boy at the winch took up the slack, his attention riveted to the cable markings as they passed through the tripod blocks, swallowing in sympathetic pain with the inhuman gasping that filled his earphones. The second lad held the taut take-up cable in his hand, a useless gesture of assistance.

Hel took off his headphones and sat on the rim of the *gouffre*. There was nothing more he could do, and he did not want to hear Beñat go, if he went. He lowered his eyes and brought himself into middle-density meditation, narcotizing his emotions. He did not emerge until he heard a shout from the lad at the winch. Mark 40 meters was in the blocks. They could take him on the line!

Hel stood at the narrow crevice of the *gouffre* mouth. He could hear Le Cagot down there, his limp body scraping against the shaft walls. Notch by notch, the lads brought him out with infinite slowness so as not to hurt him. The sunlight penetrated only a meter or two into the dark hole, so it was only a few seconds between the appearance of Le Cagot's harness straps and the time he was dangling free, unconscious and ashen-faced, from the pulley above.

When he regained consciousness, Le Cagot found himself lying on a board bed in the shepherd's *artzain xola,* his arm in an improvised sling. While the lads made a brushwood fire, Hel sat on the edge of the bed looking down into his comrade's weatherbeaten face with its sunken eyes and its sun-wrinkled skin still gray with shock under the full rust-and-gray beard.

"Could you use some wine?" Hel asked.

"Is the pope a virgin?" Le Cagot's voice was weak and raspy. "You squeeze it for me, Niko. There are two things a one-armed man cannot do. And one of them is to drink from a *xahako.*"

Because drinking from a goatskin *xahako* is a matter of automatic coordination between hand and mouth, Nicholai was clumsy and squirted some wine into Beñat's beard.

Le Cagot coughed and gagged on the inexpertly offered wine. "You are the worst nurse in the world, Niko. I swear it by the Swallowed Balls of Jonah!"

Hel smiled. "What's the other thing a one-handed man can't do?" he asked quietly.

"I can't tell you, Niko. It is bawdy, and you are too young."

In fact, Nicholai Hel was older than Le Cagot, although he looked fifteen years younger.

"It's night, Beñat. We'll bring you down into the valley in the morning. I'll find a veterinarian to set that arm. Doctors work only on Homo sapiens."

Then Le Cagot remembered. "I hope I didn't hurt you too much when I got to the surface. But you had it coming. As the saying is: *Nola neurtcen baituçu; Hala neurtuco çare çu.*"

"I'll survive the beating you gave me."

"Good." Le Cagot grinned. "You really are simpleminded, my friend. Do you think I couldn't see through your childish ploy? You thought to enrage me to give me strength to make it up. But it didn't work, did it?"

"No, it didn't work. The Basque mind is too subtle for me."

"It is too subtle for everybody but Saint Peter—who, by the way, was a Basque himself, although not many people know it. So, tell me! What does our cave look like?"

"I haven't been down."

"Haven't been down? *Alla Jainkoa!* But I didn't get to the bottom! We haven't properly claimed it for ourselves. What if some ass of a Spaniard should stumble into the hole and claim it?"

"All right. I'll go down at dawn."

"Good. Now give me some more wine. And hold it steady this time! Not like some boy trying to piss his name into a snowbank!"

The next morning Hel went down on the line. It was clear all the way. He passed through the waterfall and down to the place where the shaft opened into the great cave. As he hung, spinning on the cable while the lads above held him in clamps as they replaced drums, he knew they had made a real find. The cavern was so vast that his helmet light could not penetrate to the walls.

Soon he was on the tip of the rubble heap, where he tied off his harness to a boulder so he could find it again. After carefully negotiating the rubble heap, where stones were held in delicate balance and counterbalance, he found himself on the cave floor, some two hundred meters below the tip of the cone. He struck off a magnesium flare and held it away behind him so he would not be blinded by its light. The cave was vast—larger than the interior of a cathedral—and myriad arms and branches led off in every direction. But the flow of the underground river was toward France, so that would be the route of major exploration when they returned. Filled though he was with the natural curiosity of a veteran caver, Hel could not allow himself to investigate further without Le Cagot. That would be unfair. He picked his way up the rubble cone and found the tied-off cable.

Forty minutes later he emerged into the misty morning sunlight of the *gouffre*. After a rest, he helped the lads dismount the aluminum-tube triangle and the anchoring cables for the winch. They rolled several heavy boulders over the opening, partly to hide it from anyone who might wander that way, but also to block the entrance to protect next spring's sheep from falling in.

They scattered stone and pebbles to efface the marks of the winch frame and cable tie-offs, but they knew that most of the work of concealment would be done by the onset of winter.

Back in the *artzain xola*, Hel made his report to Le Cagot, who was enthusiastic despite his swollen arm throbbing with pain.

"Good, Niko. We shall come back next summer. Listen. I've been pondering something while you were down in the hole. We must give our cave a name, no? And I want to be fair about naming it. After all, you were the first man in, although we must not forget that my courage and skill opened the last of the chokes. So, taking all this into consideration, I have come up with the perfect name for the cave."

"And that is?"

"Le Cagot's Cave! How does that sound?"

Hel smiled. "God knows it's fair."

All that was a year ago. When the snow cleared from the mountain, they came up and began descents of exploration and mapping. And now they were ready to make their major penetration along the course of the underground river.

For more than an hour, Hel had slept on the rock slab, fully clothed and booted, while Le Cagot had passed the time talking to himself and the unconscious Hel, all the while sipping at the bottle of Izarra, taking turns. One drink for himself. The next on Niko's behalf.

When at last Hel began to stir, the hardness of the rock penetrating even the comatose sleep of his fatigue, La Cagot interrupted his monologue to nudge his companion with his boot. "Hey! Niko? Going to sleep your life away? Wake up and see what you have done! You've drunk up half a bottle of Izarra, greedy bastard!"

Hel sat up and stretched his cramped muscles. His inactivity had permitted the cave's damp cold to soak in to the bone. He reached out for the Izarra bottle, and found it empty.

"I drank the other half," Le Cagot admitted. "But I'll make you some tea." While Beñat fiddled with the portable solid-fuel cooker, Hel got out of his harness and paratrooper jumpsuit specially modified with bands of elastic at the neck and wrists to keep water out. He peeled off his four thin sweaters that kept his body warmth in and replaced the innermost with a dry jersey made of loosely knitted fabric, then he put three of the damp sweaters on again. They were made of good Basque wool and were warm even when wet. All this was done by the light of a device of his own design, a simple connection of a ten-watt bulb to a wax-sealed automobile battery which, for all its primitive nature, had the effect of keeping at bay the nerve-eroding dark that pressed in from all sides. A fresh battery could drive the little bulb day and night for four days and, if necessary, could be sent up, now that they had widened the bottleneck and double dihedron, to be recharged from the pedal-driven magneto that kept their telephone battery fresh.

Hel tugged off his gaiters and boots. "What time is it?"

Le Cagot was carrying over a tin cup of tea. "I can't tell you."

"Why not?"

"Because if I turn over my wrist, I will pour out your tea, ass! Here. Take the cup!" Le Cagot snapped his fingers to shake off the burn. *"Now* I will look at my watch. The time at the bottom of Le Cagot's Cave—and perhaps elsewhere in the world—is exactly six thirty-seven, give or take a little."

"Good." Hel shuddered at the taste of the thin tisane Le Cagot always brewed as tea. "That gives us five or six hours to eat and rest before we follow the stream into that big sloping tunnel. Is everything laid out?"

"Does the devil hate the wafer?"

"Have you tested the Brunton compass?"

"Do babies shit yellow?"

"And you're sure there's no iron in the rock?"

"Did Moses start forest fires?"

"And the fluorescein is packed up?"

"Is Franco an asshole?"

"Fine then. I'm going to get into a bag and get some sleep."

"How can you sleep! This is the big day! Four times we have been down in this hole, measuring, map-making, marking. And each time we have resisted our desire to follow the river course, saving the greatest adventure for last. And now the time has come! Surely you cannot sleep! Niko? Niko? I'll be damned." Le Cagot shrugged and sighed. "There is no understanding these Orientals."

Between them, they would be carrying twenty pounds of fluorescein dye to dump into the underground river when at last they could follow it no longer, either because their way was blocked by infall, or the river disappeared down a siphon. They had estimated that the outfall of the river had to be into the Torrent of Holçarté, and during the winter, while Le Cagot was up to patriotic mischief in Spain, Hel had investigated the length of that magnificent gorge where the torrent had cut a channel two hundred meters deep into the rock. He found several outfalls of underground streams, but only one seemed to have the flow velocity and position to make it a likely candidate. In a couple of hours, two young Basque caving enthusiasts would make camp by the outfall, taking turns watching the stream. With the first trace of dye color in the water, they would mark the time with their watch, synchronized with Le Cagot's. From this timing, and from their dead-reckoning navigation through the cave system, Hel and Le Cagot would estimate if it was feasible to follow the stream underwater in scuba gear and accomplish that finale of any thorough exploration of a cave, a trip from the vertical shaft to the light and air of the outfall.

After five hours of deep sleep, Hel awoke as he always did, instantly and thoroughly, without moving a muscle or opening his eyes. His highly developed proximity sense reported to him immediately. There was only one person within aura range, and that person's vibrations were defuse, defocused, vulnerable. The person was daydreaming or meditating or asleep. Then he heard Le Cagot's baritone snoring.

Le Cagot was in his sleeping bag, fully dressed, only his long, tousled hair and rust-gray beard visible in the dim light of the ten-watt battery lamp. Hel got up and set the solid-fuel stove going with a popping blue flame. While the water was coming to a boil, he searched about in the food containers for his tea, a strong tannic *cha* which he brewed so long it had twice the caffeine of coffee.

A man who committed himself totally to all physical activities, Le Cagot was a deep sleeper. He did not even stir when Hel tugged his arm out of the bag to check the time. They should be moving out. Hel kicked the side of Beñat's sleeping bag, but he got no more response than a groan and a muttered curse. He kicked again, and Le Cagot turned over on his side and coiled up, hoping this tormentor would evaporate. When the water was starting to form pinpoint bubbles along the sides of the pan, Hel gave his comrade a third and more vigorous kick. The aura changed wavelengths. He was awake.

Without turning over, Le Cagot growled thickly. "There is an ancient Basque proverb saying that those who kick sleeping men inevitably die."

"Everybody dies."

"You see? Another proof of the truth of our folk wisdom."

"Come on, get up!"

"Wait a minute! Give me a moment to arrange the world in my head, for the love of Christ!"

"I'm going to finish this tea, then I'm setting off. I'll tell you about the cave when I get back."

"All right!" Le Cagot kicked his way angrily out of the sleeping bag and sat on the stone slab beside Hel, hunching moodily over his tea. "Jesus, Mary, Joseph and the Donkey! What kind of tea is this?"

"Mountain *cha.*"

"Tastes like horse piss."

"I'll have to take your word for that. I lack your culinary experience."

Hel drank off the rest of his tea, then he hefted the two packs and selected the lighter one. He took up his coil of Edelrid rope and a fat carabiner on which were threaded a ring of smaller carabiners. Then he made a quick check of the side pocket of his pack to make sure he had the standard assortment of pitons for various kinds of fissures. The last thing he did before setting off was to replace the batteries for his helmet lamp with fresh ones. This device was another of his own design, based on the use of the experimental Gerard/Simon battery, a small and powerful cylinder, eight of which could be fitted into the helmet between the crown and webbing. It was one of Hel's hobbies to design and make caving equipment in his workshop. Although he would never consider patenting or manufacturing these devices, he often gave prototypes to old caving friends as presents.

Hel looked down at Le Cagot, still hunched petulantly over his tea. "You'll find me at the end of the cave system. I'll be easy to recognize; I'll be the one with the victorious look on his face." And he started down the long corridor that was the river's channel.

"By the Rocky Balls of St. Peter, you have the soul of a slavedriver! You know that?" Le Cagot shouted after Hel, as he rapidly donned his gear, grumbling to himself, "I swear there's a trace of Falange blood in his veins!"

Shortly after entering the gallery, Hel paused and waited for Le Cagot to catch up. The entire performance of exhortation and grousing was part of the established heraldry of their relationship. Hel was the leader by virtue of personality, of route-finding skills granted him by his proximity sense, and of the physical dexterity of his lithe body. Le Cagot's bullish strength and endurance made him the best backup man in caving. From the first, they had fallen into patterns that allowed Le Cagot to save face and maintain his self-respect. It was Le Cagot who told the stories when they emerged from the caves. It was Le Cagot who constantly swore, bullied, and complained, like an ill-mannered child. The poet in Le Cagot had confected for himself the role of the *miles gloriosus,* the Falstaffian clown—but with a unique difference: his braggadocio was founded on a record of reckless, laughing courage in numberless guerrilla actions against the fascist who oppressed his people in Spain.

When Le Cagot caught up with Hel, they moved together down the slanting, rapidly narrowing cut, its floor and walls scrubbed clean by the action of the underground stream, revealing the formational structure of the cave system. The rock above was limestone, but the floor along which the stream ran was ancient foliate schist. For eons, soak water had penetrated the porous limestone to the depth of the impermeable schist, along which bed it flowed, seeking depth and ultimate outfall. Slowly the slightly acid seep water had dissolved the limestone immediately above the schist, making a water pipe for itself. And slowly it had eaten at the edges of the water pipe until it had undermined its structure and caused infalls, which rubble it patiently eroded by absorptions and scrubbing; and the rubble itself acted as an abrasive carried along in the current, aiding in the work of undermining, causing greater infalls and multiplying the effect: and so, by geometric progression in which effects were also causes, through hundreds of thousands of years the great cave system was developed. The bulk of the work was accomplished by the silent, minute, relentless work of scrubbing and dissolution, and only occasionally was this patient action punctuated by the high geological drama of major collapses, most of them triggered by the earthquakes common to this underground system of faults and fissures which found surface expression in a landscape of karst, the abrupt outcroppings and frequent funnel pits and *gouffres* that earned this region its caving reputation.

For more than an hour they inched along the corridor, descending gently, while the sides and roof of their tunnel slowly closed in on them until they were easing along a narrow ledge beside the rushing current, the bed of which was a deep vertical cut not more than two meters wide, but some ten meters deep. The roof continued to close down on them, and soon they were moving with difficulty, bent over double, their packs scraping the rock overhead. Le Cagot swore at the pain in his trembling knees as they pushed along the narrow ledge walking in a half-squat that tormented the muscles of their legs.

As the shaft continued to narrow, the same unspoken thought harried them both. Wouldn't it be a stupid irony if, after their work of preparation and building up supplies, this was all there was? If this sloping shaft came to an end at a swallow down which the river disappeared?

The tunnel began to curve slowly to the left. Then suddenly their narrow ledge was blocked by a knob of rock that protruded out over the gushing stream. It was not possible for Hel to see around the knob, and he could not wade through the riverbed; it was too deep in this narrow cut, and even if it had not been, the possibility of a vertical swallow ahead in the dark was enough to deter him. There were stories of cavers who had stepped into swallows while wading through underground rivers. It was said that they were sucked straight down, one hundred, two hundred meters through a roaring column of water at the bottom of which their bodies were churned in some great "giant's caldron" of boiling foam and rock until they were broken up enough to be washed away. And months afterward bits of equipment and clothing were found in streams and torrents along the narrow valleys of the outfall rivers. These, of course, were campfire tales and mostly lies and exaggerations. But like all folk narratives, they reflected real dreads, and for most cavers in these mountains the nightmare of the sudden swallow is more eroding to the nerves than thoughts of falling while scaling walls, or avalanches, or even being underground during an earthquake. And it is not the thought of drowning that makes the swallow awful, it is the image of being churned to fragments in that boiling giant's caldron.

"Well?" Le Cagot asked from behind, his voice reverberating in the narrow tunnel. "What do you see?"

"Nothing."

"That's reassuring. Are you just going to stand there? I can't squat here forever like a Béarnais shepherd with the runs!"

"Help me get my pack off."

In their tight, stooped postures, getting Hel's pack off was not easy, but once he was free of it he could straighten up a bit. The cut was narrow enough that he could face the stream, set his feet, and let himself fall forward to the wall on the other side. This done, he turned carefully onto his back, his shoulders against one side of the cut, his Vibram boot cleats giving him purchase against the ledge. Wriggling sideward in this pressure stance, using shoulders and palms and the flats of his feet in a traverse chimney climb, he inched along under the projecting knob of rock, the stream roaring only a foot below his buttocks. It was a demanding and chafing move, and he lost some skin from his palms, but he made slow progress.

Le Cagot's laughter echoed, filling the cave. "Ola! What if it suddenly gets wider, Niko? Maybe you had better lock up there and let me use you like a bridge. That way at least one of us would make it!" And he laughed again.

Mercifully, it didn't get wider. Once past the knob, the cut narrowed, and the roof rose overhead to a height beyond the beam of Hel's lamp. He was able to push himself back to the interrupted ledge. He continued to inch along it, still curving to the left. His heart sank when his lamp revealed ahead that the diaclase through which they had been moving came to an abrupt end at an infall of boulders, under which the river gurgled and disappeared.

When he got to the base of the infall *raillère* and looked around, he could see that he was at the bottom of a great wedge only a couple of meters wide where he stood, but extending up beyond the throw of his light. He rested for a moment, then began a corner climb at the angle of the diaclase and the blocking wall of rubble. Foot- and handholds were many and easy, but the rock was rotten and friable, and each stance had to be tested carefully, each hold tugged to make sure it would not come away in his hand. When he climbed a slow, patient thirty meters, he wriggled into a gap between two giant boulders wedged against one another. Then he was on a flat ledge from which he could see nothing in front or to the sides. He clapped his hands once and listened. The echo was late, hollow, and repeated. He was at the mouth of a big cave.

His return to the knob was rapid; he rappelled down the infall clog on a doubled line which he left in place for their ascent. From his side of the knob he called to Le Cagot, who had retreated a distance back up the tunnel to a narrow place where he could lock himself into a butt-and-heels stance and find some relief from the quivering fatigue of his half-squatting posture.

Le Cagot came back to the knob. "So? Is it a go?"

"There's a big hole."

"Fantastic!"

The packs were negotiated on a line around the knob, then Le Cagot repeated Hel's chimney traverse around that tight bit, complaining bitterly all the while and cursing the knob by the Trumpeting Balls of Joshua and the Two Inhospitable Balls of the Innkeeper.

Because Hel had left a line in place and had cleared out much of the rotten rock, the climb back up the scree clog was not difficult. When they were together on the flat slab just after the crawl between two counterbalanced boulders that was later to be known as the Keyhole, Le Cagot struck off a magnesium flare, and the stygian chaos of that great cavern was seen for the first time in the numberless millennia of its existence.

"By the Burning Balls of the Bush," Le Cagot said in an awed hush. "A climbing cave!"

It was an ugly sight, but sublime. The raw crucible of creation that was this "climbing" cave muted the egos of these two humanoid insects not quite two meters tall standing on their little flake of stone suspended between the floor of the cave a hundred meters below and the cracked and rotten dome more than a hundred meters above. Most caves feel serene and eternal, but climbing caves are terrible in their organic chaos. Everything here was jagged and fresh; the floor was lost far below in layers of house-size boulders and rubble; and the roof was scarred with fresh infalls. This was a cavern in the throes of creation, an adolescent cave, awkward and unreliable, still in the process of "climbing," its floor rising from infall and rubble as its roof regularly collapsed. It might soon (twenty thousand years, fifty thousand years) stabilize and become an ordinary cave. Or it might continue to climb up the path of its fractures and faults until it reached the surface, forming in its final infall the funnel-shaped indentation of the classic "dry" *gouffre*. Of course, the youth and instability of the cave was relative and had to be considered in geological time. The "fresh" scars on the roof could be as young as three years old, or as old as a hundred.

The flare fizzled out, and it was some time before they got their cave eyes back sufficiently to see by the dim light of their helmet lamps. In the spot-dancing black, Hel heard Le Cagot say, "I baptize this cave and christen it. It shall be called Le Cagot Cave!"

From the splattering sound, Hel knew Le Cagot was not wasting water on the baptism. "Won't that be confusing?" he asked.

"What do you mean?"

"The first cave has the same name."

"Hm-m-m. That's true. Well, then, I christen this place Le Cagot's Chaos! How's that?"

"Fine."

"But I haven't forgotten your contribution to this find, Niko. I have decided to name that nasty outcropping back there—the one we had to traverse—Hel's Knob. How's that?"

"I couldn't ask for more."

"True. Shall we go on?"

"As soon as I catch up." Hel knelt over his notebook and compass, and in the light of his helmet lamp scratched down estimates of distance and direction, as he had every hundred or so meters since they left base camp at the rubble heap. After replacing everything in its waterproof packet, he said, "All right. Let's go."

Moving cautiously from boulder to boulder, squeezing between cracks and joints, picking their way around the shoulders of massive, toppling rocks the size of barns, they began to cross the Chaos. The Ariadne's String of the underground river was lost to them beneath layers upon layers of boulders, seeping, winding, bifurcating and rejoining, weaving its thousand threads along the schist floor far below. The recentness of the infalls and the absence of weather erosion that so quickly tames features on the surface combined to produce an insane jumble of precariously balanced slabs and boulders, the crazy canting of which seemed to refute gravity and create a carnival fun house effect in which water appears to run up hill, and what looks level is dangerously slanted. Balance had to be maintained by feel, not by eye, and they had to move by compass because their sense of direction had been mutilated by their twisting path through the vertigo madness of the Chaos. The problems of pathfinding were quite the opposite of those posed by wandering over a featureless moonscape. It was the confusing abundance of salient features that overloaded and cloyed the memory. And the vast black void overhead pressed down on their subconsciouses, oppressed by that scarred, unseen dome pregnant with infall, one-ten-thousandth part of which could crush them like ants.

Some two hours and five hundred meters later they had crossed enough of the Chaos to be able to see the far end of the cave where the roof sloped down to join the tangle of jagged young fall stone. During the past half-hour, a sound had grown around them, emerging so slowly out of the background ambience of gurgle and hiss far below that they didn't notice it until they stopped to rest and chart their progress. The thousand strands of the stream below were weaving tighter and tighter together, and the noise that filled the cavern was compounded of a full range of notes from thin cymbal hiss to basso tympany. It was a waterfall, a big waterfall somewhere behind that meeting of roof and rubble that seemed to block off the cave.

For more than an hour, they picked back and forth along the rubble wall, squeezing into crevices and triangular tents formed of slabs weighing tons, but they could find no way through the tangle. There were no boulders at this newer end of the Chaos, only raw young slabs, many of which were the size of village *frontons*, some standing on end, some flat, some tilted at unlikely angles, some jetting out over voids for three-fourths of their length, held up by the cantilevering weight of another slab. And all the while, the rich roar of the waterfall beyond this infall lured them to find a way through.

"Let's rest and collect ourselves!" Le Cagot shouted over the noise, as he sat on a small fragment of slab, tugged off his pack, and pawed around inside for a meal of hardtack, cheese, and *xoritzo*. "Aren't you hungry?"

Hel shook his head. He was scratching away at his notebook, making bold estimates of direction and even vaguer guesses of slope, as the clinometer of his Brunton compass had been useless in the wilderness of the Chaos.

"Could that be the outfall behind the wall?" Le Cagot asked.

"I don't think so. We're not much more than halfway to the Torrent of Holçarté, and we must still be a couple of hundred meters too high."

"And we can't even get down to the water to dump the dye in. What a nuisance this wall is! What's worse, we just ran out of cheese. Where are you going?"

Hel had dropped off his pack and was beginning a free climb of the wall. "I'm going to take a look at the tip of the heap."

"Try a little to your left!"

"Why? Do you see something there?"

"No. But I'm sitting right in the line of your fall, and I'm too comfortable to move."

They had not given much thought to trying the top of the slab heap because, even if there was a way to squeeze through, it would bring them out directly above the waterfall, and it would probably be impossible to pass through that roaring cascade. But the base and flanks of the clog had produced no way through, so the tip was all that was left.

Half an hour later, Le Cagot heard a sound above him. He tilted back his head to direct the beam of his lamp toward it. Hel was climbing back down in the dark. When he reached the slab, he slumped down to a sitting position, then lay back on his pack, one arm over his face. He was worn out and panting with effort, and the lens of his helmet lamp was cracked from a fall.

"You're sure you won't have anything to eat?" Le Cagot asked.

His eyes closed, his chest heaving with great gulps of air, sweat running down his face and chest despite the damp cold of the cave, Hel responded to his companion's grim sense of humor by making the Basque version of the universal hand language of animosity: he tucked his thumb into his fist and offered it to Le Cagot. Then he let the fist fall and lay there panting. His attempts to swallow were painful; the dryness in his throat was sharp-edged. Le Cagot passed his *xahako* over, and Hel drank greedily, beginning with the tip touching his teeth, because he had no light, then pulling it farther away and directing the thin jet of wine to the back of his throat by feel. He kept pressure on the sac, swallowing each time the back of his throat filled, drinking for so long that Le Cagot began to worry about his wine.

"Well?" Le Cagot asked grudgingly. "Did you find a way through?"

Hel grinned and nodded.

"Where did you come out?"

"Dead center above the waterfall."

"Shit!"

"No, I think there's a way around to the right, down through the spray."

"Did you try it?"

Hel shrugged and pointed to the broken helmet lens. "But I couldn't make it alone. I'll need you to protect me from above. There's a good belaying stance."

"You shouldn't have risked trying, Niko. One of these days you'll kill yourself, then you'll be sorry."

When he had wriggled through the mad network of cracks that brought him out beside Hel on a narrow ledge directly above the roaring waterfall, Le Cagot was exuberant with wonder. It was a long drop, and the mist rose through the windless air, back up the column of water, boiling all about them like a steam bath with a temperature of 40°. All they could see through the mist was the head of the falls below and a few meters of slimy rock to the sides of their ledge. Hel led the way to the right, where the ledge narrowed to a few centimeters, but continued around the shoulder of the cave opening. It was a worn, rounded ledge, obviously a former lip of the waterfall. The cacophonous crash of the falls made sign language their only means of communication as Hel indicated to Le Cagot the "good" belaying stance he had found, an outcrop of rock into which Le Cagot had to squeeze himself with difficulty and pay out the defending line around Hel's waist as he worked his way down the edge of the falls. The natural line of descent would bring him through the mist, through the column of water, and—it was to be hoped—behind it. Le Cagot grumbled about this "good" stance as he fixed his body into the wedge and drove a covering piton into the limestone above him, complaining that a piton in limestone is largely a psychological decoration.

Hel began his descent, stopping each time he found the coincidence of a foothold for himself and a crack in the rock to drive in a piton and thread his line through the carabiner. Fortunately, the rock was still well-toothed and offered finger- and toeholds; the change in the falls course had been fairly recent, and it had not had time to wear all the ledge smooth. The greatest problem was with the line overhead. By the time he had descended twenty meters and had laced the line through eight carabiners, it took dangerous effort to tug slack against the heavy friction of the soaked rope through so many snap links; the effort of pulling on the line lifted his body partially out of his footholds. And this weakening of his stance occurred, of course, just when Le Cagot was paying out line from above and was, therefore, least able to hold him, should he slip.

He inched down through the sheath of mist until the oily black-and-silver sheet of the waterfall was only a foot from his helmet lamp, and there he paused and collected himself for the diciest moment of the descent.

First he would have to establish a cluster of pitons, so that he could work independently of Le Cagot, who might blindly resist on the line and arrest Hel while he was under the falls, blinded by the shaft of water, feeling for holds he could not see. And he would be taking the weight of the falling water on his back and shoulders. He had to give himself enough line to move all the way through the cascade, because he would not be able to breathe until he was behind it. On the other hand, the more line he gave himself, the greater his drop would be if the water knocked him off. He decided to give himself about three meters of slack. He would have liked more to avoid the possibility of coming to the end of his slack while still under the column of water, but his judgment told him that three meters was the maximum length that would swing him back out of the line of the falls, should he fall and knock himself out for long enough to drown, if he was hanging in the falls.

Hel edged to the face of the metallic, glittering sheet of water until it was only inches away from his face, and soon he began to have the vertigo sensation that the water was standing still, and his body rising through the roar and the mist. He reached into the face of the falls, which split in a heavy, throbbing bracelet around his wrist, and felt around for the deepest handhold he could find. His fingers wriggled their way into a sharp little crack, unseen behind the water. The hold was lower than he would have wished, because he knew the weight of the water on his back would force him down, and the best handhold would have been high, so the weight would have jammed his fingers in even tighter. But it was the only crack he could find, and his shoulder was beginning to tire from the pounding of the water on his outstretched arm. He took several deep breaths, fully exhaling each one because he knew that it is more the buildup of carbon dioxide in the lungs than the lack of oxygen that forces a man to gasp for air. The last breath he took deeply, stretching his diaphragm to its full. Then he let a third of it out, and he swung into the falls.

It was almost comic, and surely anticlimactic.

The sheet of falling water was less than twenty centimeters thick, and the same movement that swung him into it sent him through and behind the cascade, where he found himself on a good ledge below which was a book corner piled with rubble so easy that a healthy child could make the climb down.

It was so obvious a go that there was no point in testing it, so Hel broke back through the sheet of water and scrambled up to Le Cagot's perch where, shouting over the din of the falls into Beñat's ear, their helmets clicking together occasionally, he explained the happy situation. They decided to leave the line in place to facilitate the return, and down they went one after the other, until they were at the base of the rubble-packed book corner.

It was a peculiar phenomenon that, once they were behind the silver-black sheet of the falls, they could speak in almost normal volume, as the curtain of water seemed to block out sound, and it was quieter behind the falls than without. As they descended, the falls slowly broke up as a great quantity of its water spun off in the mist, and the weight of the cascade at the bottom was considerably less than it was above. Its mass was diffused, and passing through it was more like going through a torrential rainfall than a waterfall. They advanced cautiously through the blinding, frigid steam, over a slick rock floor scrubbed clean of rubble. As they pressed on, the mists thinned until they found themselves in the clear dark air, the noise of the falls receding behind them. They paused and looked around. It was beautiful, a diamond cave of more human dimensions than the awful Le Cagot's Chaos; a tourist cave, far beyond the access capacities of any tourist.

Although it was wasteful, their curiosity impelled them to scratch off another magnesium flare.

Breathtakingly beautiful. Behind them, billowing clouds of mist churning lazily in the suction of the falling water. All around and above them, wet and dripping, the walls were encrusted with aragonite crystals that glittered as Le Cagot moved the flare back and forth. Along the north wall, a frozen waterfall of flowstone oozed down the side and puddled like ossified taffy. To the east, receding and overlapping curtains of calcite drapery, delicate and razor sharp, seemed to ripple in an unfelt spelean wind. Close to the walls, thickets of slender crystal stalactites pointed down toward stumpy stalagmites, and here and there the forest was dominated by a thick column formed by the union of these patient speleothems.

They did not speak until the glare sputtered orange and went out, and the glitter of the walls was replaced by dancing dots of light in their eyes as they dilated to accommodate the relatively feeble helmet lamps. Le Cagot's voice was uncharacteristically hushed when he said, "We shall call this Zazpiak Bat Cove."

Hel nodded. *Zazpiak bat:* "Out of seven, let there be one," the motto of those who sought to unite the seven Basque provinces into a Trans-Pyrenean republic. An impractical dream, neither likely nor desirable, but a useful focus for the activities of men who choose romantic danger over safe boredom, men who are capable of being cruel and stupid, but never small or cowardly. And it was right that the cuckoo-land dream of a Basque nation be represented by a fairyland cave that was all but inaccessible.

He squatted down and made a rough measurement back to the top of the waterfall with his clinometer, then he did a bit of mental arithmetic. "We're down almost to the level of the Torrent of Holçarté. The outfall can't be far ahead."

"Yes," Le Cagot said, "but where is the river? What have you done with it?"

It was true that the river had disappeared. Broken up by the falls, it had evidently sounded through cracks and fissures and must be running below them somewhere. There were two possibilities. Either it would emerge again within the cave somewhere before them, or the cracks around the base of the waterfall constituted its final swallow before its outfall into the gorge. This latter would be unfortunate, because it would deny them any hope of final conquest by swimming through to the open air and sky. It would also make the long vigil of the Basque lads camped at the outfall pointless.

Le Cagot took the lead as they advanced through Zazpiak Bat Cavern, as he always did when the going was reasonably easy. They both knew that Nicholai was the better rock tactician; it was not necessary for Le Cagot to admit it, or for Hel to accent it. The lead simply changed automatically with the nature of a cave's features. Hel led through shafts, down faces, around cornices; while Le Cagot led as they entered caves and dramatic features, which he therefore "discovered" and named.

As he led, Le Cagot was testing his voice in the cave, singing one of those whining, atonic Basque songs that demonstrate the race's ability to withstand aesthetic pain. The song contained that uniquely Basque onomatopoeia that goes beyond imitations of sounds, to imitations of emotional states. In the refrain of Le Cagot's song, work was being done sloppily *(kirri-marra)* by a man in confused haste *(tarrapatakan)*.

He stopped singing when he approached the end of the diamond cave and stood before a broad, low-roofed gallery that opened out like a black, toothless grin. Indeed, it held a joke.

Le Cagot directed his lamp down the passage. The slope increased slightly, but it was no more than 15°, and there was enough overhead space for a man to stand erect. It was an avenue, a veritable boulevard! And yet more interesting, it was probably the last feature of the cave system. He stepped forward . . . and fell with a clatter of gear.

The floor of the passage was thickly coated with clay marl, as slick and filthy as axle grease and flat on his back, Le Cagot was slipping down the incline, not moving very fast at first, but absolutely helpless to arrest his slide. He cursed and pawed around for a hold, but everything was coated with the slimy mess, and there were no boulders or outcroppings to cling to. His struggling did no more than turn him around so that he was going down backward, half-sitting, helpless, furious, and risible. His slide began to pick up speed. From back on the edge of the marl shaft, Hel watched the helmet light grow smaller as it receded, turning slowly like the beam of a lighthouse. There was nothing he could do. The situation was basically comic, but if there was a cliff at the end of the passage . . .

There was no cliff at the end of the passage. Hel had never known a marl chute at this depth. At a good distance away, perhaps sixty meters, the light stopped moving. There was no sound, no call for help. Hel feared that Le Cagot had been bashed against the side of the passage and was lying there broken up.

Then came a sound up through the passage, Le Cagot's voice roaring with fury and outrage, the words indistinct because of the covering reverberations, but carrying the tonalities of wounded dignity. One phrase in the echoing outpour was decipherable: ". . . by the Perforated Balls of Saint Sebastian!"

So Le Cagot was unhurt. The situation might even be funny, were it not that their only coil of rope had gone down with him, and not even that ox of Urt could throw a coil of line sixty meters uphill.

Hel blew out a deep sigh. He would have to go back through Zazpiak Bat Cavern, through the base of the waterfall, up the rubble corner, back out through the falls, and up that dicey climb through icy mists to retrieve the line they had left in place to ease their retreat. The thought of it made him weary.

But . . . He tugged off his pack. No point carrying it with him. He called down the marl passage, spacing his words out so they would be understood through the muffling reverberations.

"I'm . . . going . . . after . . . line!"

The dot of light below moved. Le Cagot was standing up. "Why . . . don't . . . you . . . do . . . that!" came the call back. Suddenly the light disappeared, and there was the echoing sound of a splash, followed by a medley of angry roaring, scrambling, sputtering, and swearing. Then the light reappeared.

Hel's laughter filled both the passage and the cave. Le Cagot had evidently fallen into the river which must have come back to the surface down there. What a beginner's stunt!

Le Cagot's voice echoed back up the marl chute: "I . . . may . . . kill . . . you . . . when . . . you . . . get . . . down . . . here!"

Hel laughed again and set off back to the lip of the falls.

Three-quarters of an hour later, he was back at the head of the marl chute, fixing the line into a healthy crack by means of a choke nut.

Hel tried at first to take a rope-controlled glissade on his feet, but that was not on. The marl was too slimy. Almost at once he found himself on his butt, slipping down feet first, a gooey prow bone of black marl building up at his crotch and oozing back over his hip. It was nasty stuff, an ignoble obstacle, formidable enough but lacking the clean dignity of a cave's good challenges: cliffs and rotten rock, vertical shafts and dicey siphons. It was a mosquito of a problem, stupid and irritating, the overcoming of which brought no glory. Marl chutes are despised by all cavers who have mucked about in them.

When Hel glissed silently to his side, Le Cagot was sitting on a smooth slab, finishing off a hardtack biscuit and a cut of *xoritzo*. He ignored Hel's approach, still sulky over his own undignified descent, and dripping wet from his dunking.

Hel looked around. No doubt of it, this was the end of the cave system, The chamber was the size of a small house, or of one of the reception rooms of his château at Etchebar. Evidently, it was sometimes filled with water—the walls were smooth, and the flocr was free of rubble. The slab on which Le Cagot was taking his lunch covered two-thirds of the floor, and in the distant corner there was a neat cubic depression about five meters on each edge—a regular "wine cellar" of a sump constituting the lowest point of the entire cave system. Hel went to the edge of the Wine Cellar and directed his beam down. The sides were smooth, but it looked to be a fairly easy corner climb, and he wondered why Le Cagot hadn't climbed down to be the first man to the end of the cave.

"I was saving it for you," Le Cagot explained.

"An impulse toward fair play?"

"Exactly."

There was something very wrong here. Basque to the bone though he was, Le Cagot had been educated in France, and the concept of fair play is totally alien to the mentality of the French, a people who have produced generations of aristocrats, but not a single gentleman; a culture in which the legal substitutes for the fair; a language in which the only word for fair play is borrowed English.

Still, there was no point in standing there and letting the floor of that final Wine Cellar go virgin. Hel looked down, scanning for the best holds.

. . . Wait a minute! That splash. Le Cagot had fallen into water. Where was it?

Hel carefully lowered his boot into the Wine Cellar. A few centimeters down, it broke the surface of a pool so clear it appeared to be air. The features of the rock below were so sharp that no one would suspect they were under water.

"You bastard," Hel whispered. Then he laughed. "And you climbed right down into it, didn't you?"

The instant he pulled up his boot, the ripples disappeared from the surface, sucked flat by a strong siphon action below. Hel knelt at the side of the sump and examined it with fascination. The surface was not still at all; it was drawn tight and smooth by the powerful current below. Indeed, it bowed slightly, and when he put in his finger, there was a strong tug and a wake of eddy patterns behind it. He could make out a triangular opening down at the bottom of the sump which must be the outflow of the river. He had met trick pools like these before in caves, pools into which the water entered without bubbles to mark its current, the water so purified of those minerals and microorganisms that give it its tint of color.

Hel examined the walls of their small chamber for signs of water line. Obviously, the outflow through that triangular pope down there had to be fairly constant, while the volume of the underground river varied with rainfall and seep water. This whole chamber, and that marl chute behind them acted as a kind of cistern that accepted the difference between inflow and outflow. That would account for marl appearing this far underground. There were doubtless times when this chamber in which they sat was full of water which backed up through the long chute. Indeed, upon rare occasions of heavy rain, the waterfall back there probably dropped into a shallow lake that filled the floor of Zazpiak Cavern. That would explain the stubbiness of the stalagmites in that diamond cave. If they had arrived at some other time, say a week after heavy rains had seeped down, they might have found their journey ending in Zazpiak Cavern. They had planned all along to consider a scuba exploration to the outfall in some future run, should the timing on the dye test prove practicable. But if they had been stopped by a shallow lake in the cavern above, it would have been unlikely that Hel would ever find that marl chute under water, swim all the way down it, locate this Wine Cellar sump, pass out through the triangular opening, and make it through that powerful current to the outfall. They were lucky to have made their descent after a long dry spell.

"Well?" Le Cagot said, looking at his watch. "Shall we drop the dye in?"

"What time is it?"

"A little before eleven."

"Let's wait for straight up. It'll make calculation easier." Hel looked down through the invisible pane of water. It was difficult to believe that there at the bottom, among those clear features of the floor, a current of great force was rushing, sucking. "I wish I knew two things," he said.

"Only two?"

"I wish I knew how fast that water was moving. And I wish I knew if that triangular pipe was clear."

"Let's say we get a good timing—say ten minutes—are you going to try swimming it next time we come down?"

"Of course. Even with fifteen minutes."

Le Cagot shook his head. "That's a lot of line, Niko. Fifteen minutes through a pipe like that is a lot of line for me to haul you back against the current if you run into trouble. No, I don't think so. Ten minutes is maximum. If it's longer than that, we should let it go. It's not so bad to leave a few of Nature's mysteries virgin."

Le Cagot was right, of course.

"You have any bread in your pack?" Hel asked.

"What are you going to do?"

"Cast it upon the waters."

Le Cagot tossed over a cut of his flute baguette; Hel set it gently on the surface of the sump water and watched its motion. It sank slowly, seeming to fall in slow motion through clear air, as it pulsed and vibrated with unseen eddies. It was an unreal and eerie sight, and the two men watched it fascinated. Then suddenly, like magic, it was gone. It had touched the current down there and had been snatched into the pipe faster than the eye could follow.

Le Cagot whistled under his breath. "I don't know, Niko. That looks like a bad thing."

But already Hel was making preliminary decisions. He would have to enter the pipe feet first with no fins because it would be suicidal to rush head first through that triangular pipe, in case he met a choking boulder inside there. That could be a nasty knock. Then too, he would want to be head first coming out if it was not a go, so he could help Le Cagot's weight on the safety line by pushing with his feet.

"I don't like it, Niko. That little hole there could kill your ass and, what is worse, reduce the number of my admirers by one. And remember, dying is a serious business. If a man dies with a sin on his soul, he goes to Spain."

"We have a couple of weeks to think it over. After we get out, we'll talk about it and see if it's worth dragging scuba gear down here. For all we know, the dye test will tell us the pipe's too long for a try. What time is it?"

"Coming up to the hour."

"Let's drop off the dye then."

The fluorescein dye they had carried down was in two-kilo bags. Hel tugged them out of their packs, and Le Cagot cut off the corners and lined them along the edge of the Wine Cellar sump. When the second hand swept to twelve, they pushed them all in. Bright green smoke seeped from the cuts as the bags dropped through the crystal water. Two of them disappeared instantly through the triangular pipe, but the other two lay on the bottom, their smoking streams of color rushing horizontally toward the pipe until the nearly empty bags were snatched away by the current. Three seconds later, the water was clear and still again.

"Niko? I have decided to christen this little pool Le Cagot's Soul."

"Oh?"

"Yes. Because it is clear and pure and lucid."

"And treacherous and dangerous?"

"You know, Niko, I begin to suspect that you are a man of prose. It is a blemish in you."

"No one's perfect."

"Speak for yourself."

The return to the base of the rubble cone was relatively quick. Their newly discovered cave system was, after all, a clean and easy one with no long crawls through tight passages and around breakdowns, and no pits to contend with, because the underground river ran along the surface of a hard schist bed.

The Basque boys dozing up at the winch were surprised to hear their voices over the headsets of the field telephones hours before they had expected them.

"We have a surprise for you," one lad said over the line.

"What's that?" Le Cagot asked.

"Wait till you get up and see for yourself."

The long haul up from the tip of the rubble cone to the first corkscrew shaft was draining for each of the men. The strain on the diaphragm and chest from hanging in a parachute harness is very great, and men have been known to suffocate from it. It was such a constriction of the diaphragm that caused Christ's death on the cross—a fact the aptness of which did not escape Le Cagot's notice and comment.

To shorten the torture of hanging in the straps and struggling to breathe, the lads at the low-geared winch pedaled heroically until the man below could take a purchase within the corkscrew and rest for a while, getting some oxygen back into his blood.

Hel came up last, leaving the bulk of their gear below for future explorations. After he negotiated the double dihedron with a slack cable, it was a short straight haul up to the cone point of the *gouffre*, and he emerged from blinding blackness . . . into blinding white.

While they had been below, an uncommon atmospheric inversion had seeped into the mountains, creating that most dangerous of weather phenomena: a whiteout.

For several days, Hel and his mountaineer companions had known that conditions were developing toward a whiteout because, like all Basques from Haute Soule, they were constantly if subliminally attuned to the weather patterns that could be read in the eloquent Basque sky as the dominant winds circled in their ancient and regular boxing of the compass. First *Ipharra*, the north wind, sweeps the sky clear of clouds and brings a cold, greenish-blue light to the Basque sky, tinting and hazing the distant mountains. *Ipharra* weather is brief, for soon the wind swings to the east and becomes the cool *Iduzki-haizea*, "the sunny wind," which rises each morning and falls at sunset, producing the paradox of cool afternoons with warm evenings. The atmosphere is both moist and clear, making the contours of the countryside sharp, particularly when the sun is low and its oblique light picks out the textures of bush and tree; but the moisture blues and blurs details on the distant mountains, softening their outlines, smudging the border between mountain and sky. Then one morning one looks out to find that the atmosphere has become crystalline, and distant mountains have lost their blue haze, have closed in around the valley, their razor outlines acid-etched into the ardent blue of the sky. This is the time of *Hego-churia*, "the white southeast wind." In autumn, *Hego-churia* often dominates the weather for weeks on end, bringing the Pays Basque's grandest season. With a kind of karma justice, the glory of *Hego-churia* is followed by the fury of *Haize-hegoa*, the bone-dry south wind that roars around the flanks of the mountains, crashing shutters in the villages, ripping roof tiles off, cracking weak trees, scudding blinding swirls of dust along the ground. In true Basque fashion, paradox being the normal way of things, this dangerous south wind is warm velvet to the touch. Even while it roars down valleys and clutches at houses all through the night, the stars remain sharp and close overhead. It is a capricious wind, suddenly relenting into silences that ring like the silence after a gunshot, then returning with full fury, destroying the things that man makes, testing and shaping the things that God makes, shortening tempers and fraying nerve ends with its constant screaming around corners and reedy moaning down chimneys. Because the *Haize-hegoa* is capricious and dangerous, beautiful and pitiless, nerve-racking and sensual, it is often used in Basque sayings as a symbol of Woman. Finally spent, the south wind veers around to the west, bringing rain and heavy clouds that billow gray in their bellies but glisten silver around the edges. There is—as there always is in Basqueland—an old saying to cover the phenomenon: *Hegoak hegala urean du*, "The south wind flies with one wing in the water." The rain of the southwest wind falls plump and vertically and is good for the land. But it veers again and brings the *Haize-belza*, "the black

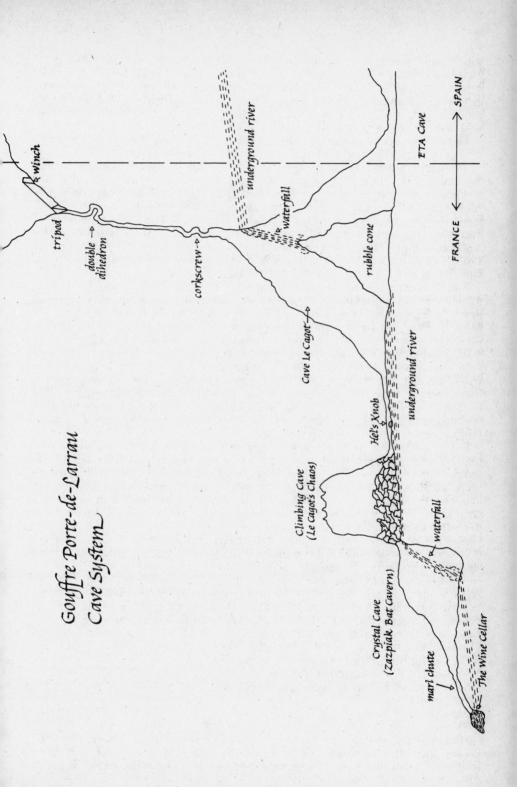

Gouffre Porte-de-Larrau
Cave System

winch

tripod

double
dihedron

corkscrew

underground river

waterfall

rubble cone

Cave Le Cagot

Hel's Knob

Climbing Cave
(Le Cagot's Chaos)

underground river

waterfall

Crystal Cave
(Zazpiak Bat Cavern)

marl chute

The Wine Cellar

ETA Cave

FRANCE ← → SPAIN

wind," with its streaming squalls that drive rain horizontally, making umbrellas useless, indeed, comically treacherous. Then one evening, unexpectedly, the sky lightens and the surface wind falls off, although high altitude streams continue to rush cloud layers overhead, tugging them apart into wisps. As the sun sets, chimerical archipelagos of fleece are scudded southward where they pile up in gold and russet against the flanks of the high mountains.

This beauty lasts only one evening. The next morning brings the greenish light of *Ipharra*. The north wind has returned. The cycle begins again.

Although the winds regularly cycle around the compass, each with its distinctive personality, it is not possible to say that Basque weather is predictable; for in some years there are three or four such cycles, and in other years only one. Also, within the context of each prevailing wind there are vagaries of force and longevity. Indeed, sometimes the wind turns through a complete personality during a night, and the next morning it seems that one of the dominant phases has been skipped. Too, there are the balance times between the dominance of two winds, when neither is strong enough to dictate. At such times, the mountain Basque say, "There is no weather today."

And when there is no weather, no motion of wind in the mountains, then sometimes comes the beautiful killer: the whiteout. Thick blankets of mist develop, dazzling white because they are lighted by the brilliant sun above the layer. Eye-stinging, impenetrable, so dense and bright that the extended hand is a faint ghost and the feet are lost in milky glare, a major whiteout produces conditions more dangerous than simple blindness; it produces vertigo and sensory inversion. A man experienced in the ways of the Basque mountains can move through the darkest night. His blindness triggers off a compensating heightening of other senses; the movement of wind on his cheek tells him that he is approaching an obstacle; small sounds of rolling pebbles give him the slant of the ground and the distance below. And the black is never complete; there is always some skyglow picked up by widely dilated eyes.

But in a whiteout, none of these compensating sensory reactions obtains. The dumb nerves of the eyes, flooded and stung with light, persist in telling the central nervous system that they can see, and the hearing and tactile systems relax, slumber. There is no wind to offer subtle indications of distance, for wind and whiteout cannot coexist. And all sound is perfidious, for it carries far and crisp through the moisture-laden air, but seems to come from all directions at once, like sound under water.

And it was into a blinding whiteout that Hel emerged from the black of the cave shaft. As he unbuckled his parachute harness, Le Cagot's voice came from somewhere up on the rim of the *gouffre*.

"This is the surprise they told us about."

"How nice." When Hel scrambled up the *gouffre* side, he could dimly make out five forms hovering around the winch. He had to approach within a meter before he recognized the other two as the lads who had been camping down in Holçarté Gorge, waiting for the outfall of dye from the underground stream. "You climbed up through this?" Nicholai asked.

"It was forming as we came. We just made it."

"What is it like lower down?"

They were all mountain men here; they knew what he meant.

"It's grayer."

"Much?"

"Much."

If the sheet of mist was grayer below, passing down through it would be folly in this Swiss-cheese mountainside dotted with treacherous cracks and steep *gouffres*. They would have to climb upward and hope to break out of the mist before they ran out of mountain. It is always wisest to do so in a whiteout: it is difficult to fall *up* a mountain.

Alone, Hel could have made it down the mountain, despite the blinding mist with its sensory trickery. He could have relied on a combination of his proximity sense and intimate knowledge of the features of the mountain to move cautiously down over terrain hidden in the blinding haze. But he could not be responsible for Le Cagot and the four Basque lads.

Because it was impossible to see clearly farther than a meter and to see at all farther than three, they roped up, and Hel led a slow and careful ascent, picking the long and easy way around outcroppings of rock, across slides of scree, past the rims of deep *gouffres*. The blanket of mist did not thicken, but it grew ever more blindingly bright as they rose toward the sun. After three-quarters of an hour, Hel suddenly broke through into sunlight and taut blue skies, and the scene that greeted him was beautiful, and awful. In the absolute stillness of the mist layer, the motion of his body up through it created languorous swirls and billows that churned lazily behind him and down into which his rope passed to the next man only ten meters below, but hidden behind the milky wall. He was almost at eye level with a platform of dense white mist that stretched flat and stable for hundreds of kilometers, filling all the valleys below as though with a great snow. Through this blanket of mist, the tops of the Basque Pyrenees stuck up, clear and sharp-edged in the ardent sunlight, like bits of mosaic tesserae set in a fleecy plaster. And above was the taut dark-blue sky peculiar to the Basque country. The stillness was so absolute that he could hear the squeak and surge of blood through his temples.

Then he heard another sound, Le Cagot's voice from below demanding, "Are we to stand here forever? By the Complaining Balls of Jeremiah, you should have relieved yourself before we started!" And when he broke through the layer of mist, he said, "Oh, I see. You were admiring the Basque spectacle all by yourself, while we dangled down there like bait on a line! You're a selfish man, Niko."

The sun was beginning to sink, so they moved around the flank of the mountain with some haste, to arrive at the highest of the *artzain xola* shelters before dark. When they got there, they found it already occupied by two old shepherds driven up from the other side of the mountain by the whiteout. Their heavy packs revealed them to be smugglers in a minor way. The Basque temperament is more comfortable with smuggling than with commerce; with poaching than with hunting. Socially condoned activities lack spice.

There was an exchange of greetings and wine, and the eight of the "fist" to the intruder, declaring that, if his will had power, that plane would fall from the sky like a wounded bird, littering Spain with the bodies of two hundred stupid vacationers on their way to Lisbon, and relieving the world of the burden of surplus population, for anyone who would fly through so perfect a moment was, by definition, an expendable being.

Le Cagot's gall up, he went on to extend his malediction to all those outlanders who defiled the mountains: the tourists, the backpackers, the hunters, and especially the skiers who bring vile machines into the mountains because they are too soft to walk up the hill, and who build ugly lodges and noisy après-ski amusements. The filthy shits! It was for dealing with loud-mouthed skiers and their giggling bunnies that God said, on the eighth day, let there also be handguns!

One of the old shepherds nodded sagely and agreed that outlanders were universally evil. *"Atzerri; otzerri."*

Following the ritual of conversation among strangers, Hel matched this ancient *dicton* with "But I suppose *chori bakhoitzari eder bere ohantzea.*"

"True," Le Cagot said, *"Zahar hitzak, zuhur hitzak."*

Hel smiled. These were the first words of Basque he had learned, years ago in his cell in Sugamo Prison. "With the possible exception," he said, "of that one."

The old smugglers considered this response for a moment, then both laughed aloud and slapped their knees. *"Hori phensatu zuenak, ongi afaldu zuen!"* (An Englishman with a clever story "dines out on it." Within the Basque culture, it is the listener who enjoys the feast.)

They sat in silence, drinking and eating slowly as the sun fell, drawing after it the gold and russet of the cloud layer. One of the young cavers stretched his legs out with a satisfied grunt and declared that this was the life. Hel smiled to himself, knowing that this would probably not be the life for this young man, touched as he was by television and radio. Like most of the Basque young, he would probably end up lured to the factories of the big cities, where his wife could have a refrigerator, and he could drink Coca-Cola in a café with plastic tables—the good life that was a product of the French Economic Miracle.

"It is the good life," Le Cagot said lazily. "I have traveled, and I have turned the world over in my hand, like a stone with attractive veining, and this I have discovered: a man is happiest when there is a balance between his needs and his possessions. Now the question is: how to achieve this balance. One could seek to do this by increasing his goods to the level of his appetites, but that would be stupid. It would involve doing unnatural things—bargaining, haggling, scrimping, working. Ergo? Ergo, the wise man achieves the balance by reducing his needs to the level of his possessions. And this is best done by learning to value the free things of life: the mountains, laughter, poetry, wine offered by a friend, older and fatter women. Now, me? I am perfectly capable of being happy with what I have. The problem is getting enough of it in the first place!"

"Le Cagot?" one of the old smugglers asked, as he made himself comfortable in a corner of the *artzain xola.* "Give us a story to sleep on."

"Yes," said his companion. "Let it be of old things."

A true folk poet, who would rather tell a story than write one, Le Cagot began to weave fables in his rich basso voice, while the others listened or dozed. Everyone knew the tales, but the pleasure lay in the art of telling them. And Basque is a language more suited to storytelling than to exchanging information. No one can learn to speak Basque beautifully; like eye color or blood type, it is something one has to be born to. The language is subtle and loosely regulated, with its circumlocutory word orders, its vague declensions, its doubled conjugations, both synthetic and periphrastic, with its old "story" forms mixed with formal verb patterns. Basque is a song, and while outlanders may learn the words, they can never master the music.

Le Cagot told of the *Basa-andere,* the Wildlady who kills men in the most wonderful way. It is widely known that the *Basa-andere* is beautiful and perfectly formed for love, and that the soft golden hair that covers all her body is strangely appealing. Should a man have the misfortune to come upon her in the forest (she is always to be found kneeling beside a stream, combing the hair of her stomach with a golden comb), she will turn to him and fix him with a smile, then lie back and lift her knees, offering her body. Now, everyone knows that the pleasure from her is so intense that a man dies of it during climax, but still many and many have willingly died, their backs arched in the agony of unimaginable pleasure.

One of the old smugglers declared that he once found a man in the mountains who had died so, and in his dim staring eyes there was an awful mixture of fright and pleasure.

And the quietest of the young lads prayed that God would give him the strength to resist, should he ever come upon the *Basa-andere* with her golden comb. "You say she is all covered with golden hair, Le Cagot? I cannot imagine breasts covered with hair. Are the nipples visible then?"

Le Cagot sniffed and stretched out on the ground. "In truth, I cannot say from personal experience, child. These eyes have never seen the *Basa-andere*. And I am glad of that, for had we met, that poor lady would at this moment be dead from pleasure."

The old man laughed and ripped up a turf of grass, which he threw at the poet. "Truly, Le Cagot, you are as full of shit as God is of mercy!"

"True," Le Cagot admitted. "So true. Have you ever heard me tell the story of . . ."

When dawn came the whiteout was gone, churned away by the night winds. Before they broke up, Hel paid the lads for their assistance and asked them to take apart the winch and tripod and bring them down to a barn in Larrau for storage, as they were already beginning to plan the next exploration into the cave, this time with wet suits and scuba gear, for the boys camping down by the fallout in the Gorge of Holçarté had marked the appearance of dye in the water at eight minutes after the hour. Although eight minutes is not a long time, it would indicate considerable distance, considering the speed of the water through that triangular pipe at the bottom of the Wine Cellar. But if the water pipe was not filled with obstructions or too narrow for a man, they might have the pleasure of exploring their cave from entrance shaft to outfall before they shared the secret of its existence with the caving fraternity.

Hel and Le Cagot trotted and glissaded down the side of the mountain to the narrow track on which they had parked Hel's Volvo. He delivered the door a mighty kick with his boot, as was his habit, and after examining the satisfying dent, they got in and drove down to the village of Larrau, where they stopped off to have a breakfast of bread, cheese, and coffee, after having splashed and scrubbed away most of the dried mud with which they were caked.

Their hostess was a vigorous widow with a strong ample body and a bawdy laugh who used two rooms of her house as a café/restaurant/tobacco shop. She and Le Cagot had a relationship of many years, for when things got too hot for him in Spain, he often crossed into France through the Forest of Irraty that abutted this village. Since time beyond memory, the Forest of Irraty had been both a sanctuary and an avenue for smugglers and bandits crossing from the Basque provinces under Spanish occupation to those under French. By ancient tradition, it is considered impolite—and dangerous—to seem to recognize anyone met in this forest.

When they entered the café, still wet from the pump in back, they were questioned by the half-dozen old men taking their morning wine. How had it gone up at the *gouffre?* Was there a cave under the hole?

Le Cagot was ordering breakfast, his hand resting proprietarily on the hip of the hostess. He did not have to think twice about guarding the secret of the new cave, for he automatically fell into the Basque trait of responding to direct questions with misleading vagueness that is not quite lying.

"Not all holes lead to caves, my friends."

The hostess's eyes glittered at what she took to be double entendre. She pushed his hand away with pleased coquetry.

"And did you meet Spanish border patrols?" an old man asked.

"No, I was not required to burden hell with more Fascist souls. Does that please you, Father?" Le Cagot addressed this last to the gaunt revolutionary priest sitting in the darkest corner of the café, who had turned his face away upon the entrance of Le Cagot and Hel. Father Xavier nurtured a smoldering hate for Le Cagot and a flaming one for Hel. Though he never faced danger personally, he wandered from village to village along the border, preaching the revolution and attempting to bind the goals of Basque independence to those of the Church—the Basque manifestation of that general effort on the part of God-merchants to diversify into social and political issues, now that the world was no longer a good market for hell-scare and soul-saving.

The priest's hatred (which he termed "righteous wrath") for Le Cagot was based on the fact that praise and hero worship that properly belonged to the ordained leaders of the revolution was being siphoned away by this blaspheming and scandalous man who had spent a part of his life in the Land of the Wolves, out of the Pays Basque. But at least Le Cagot was a native son. This Hel was a different matter. He was an outlander who never went to Mass and who lived with an Oriental woman. And it was galling to the priest that young Basque cavers, boys who should have chosen their idols from the ranks of the priesthood, told stories of his spelunking exploits and of the time he had crossed with Le Cagot into Spain and broken into a military prison in Bilbao to release ETA prisoners. This was the kind of man who could contaminate the revolution and divert its energies from the establishment of a Basque Theocracy, a last fortress of fundamentalist Catholicism in a land where Christian practices were primitive and deep, and where the key to the gates of heaven was a profound weapon of control.

Shortly after he bought his home in Etchebar, Hel began to receive unsigned threats and hate notes. Upon two occasions there were "spontaneous" midnight charivaris outside the château, and live cats bound in burning straw were thrown at the walls of the house, where they screamed in their death throes. Although Hel's experience had taught him to despise these fanatical Third World priests who incite children to their deaths for the purpose of linking the cause of social reform to the church to save that institution from natural atrophy in the face of knowledge and enlightenment, he would nevertheless have ignored this kind of harassment. But he intended to make the Basque country his permanent home, now that the Japanese culture was infected with Western values, and he had to put an end to these insults because the Basque mentality ridicules those who are ridiculed. Anonymous letters and the mob frenzy of the charivari are manifestations of cowardice, and Hel had an intelligent fear of cowards, who are always more dangerous than brave men, when they outnumber you or get a chance to strike from behind, because they are forced to do maximal damage, dreading as they do the consequences of retaliation, should you survive.

Through Le Cagot's contacts, Hel discovered the author of these craven acts, and a couple of months later he came across the priest in the back room of a café in Ste. Engrace, where he was eating a free meal in silence, occasionally glaring at Nicholai, who was taking a glass of red with several men of the village—men who had previously been sitting at the priest's table, listening to his wisdom and cant.

When the men went off to work, Hel joined the priest at his table. Father Xavier started to rise, but Hel gripped his forearm and returned him to his chair. "You are a good man, Father," he said in his prison whisper. "A saintly man. In fact, at this moment you are closer to heaven than you know. Finish your food and listen well. There will be no more anonymous letters, no more charivaris. Do you understand?"

"I'm afraid I don't—"

"Eat."

"What?"

"Eat!"

Father Xavier pushed another forkful of piperade into his mouth and chewed sullenly.

"Eat faster, Father. Fill your mouth with food you have not earned."

The priest's eyes were damp with fury and fear, but he shoveled forkful after forkful into his mouth and swallowed as rapidly as he could.

"If you choose to stay in this corner of the world, Father, and if you do not feel prepared to join your God, then this is what you will do. Each time we meet in a village, you will leave that village immediately. Each time we meet on the trails, you will step off the track and turn your back as I pass. You can eat faster than that!"

The priest choked on his food, and Hel left him gasping and gagging. That evening, he told the story to Le Cagot with instructions to make sure it got around. Hel considered public humiliation of this coward to be necessary.

"Hey, why don't you answer me, Father Esteka?" Le Cagot asked.*

The priest rose and left the café, as Le Cagot called after him, "Hola! Aren't you going to finish your piperade?"

Because they were Catholic, the old men in the café could not laugh; but they grinned, because they were Basque.

Le Cagot patted the hostess's bottom and sent her after their food. "I don't think we have made a great friend there, Niko. And he is a man to be feared." Le Cagot laughed, "After all, his father was French and very active in the Resistance."

Hel smiled. "Have you ever met one who was not?"

"True. It is astonishing that the Germans managed to hold France with so few divisions, considering that everyone who wasn't draining German resources by the clever maneuver of surrendering en masse and making the Nazi's feed them was vigorously and bravely engaged in the Resistance. Is there a village without its Place de la Resistance? But one has to be fair; one has to understand the Gallic notion of resistance. Any hotelier who overcharged a German was in the Resistance. Each whore who gave a German soldier the clap was a freedom fighter. All those who obeyed while viciously withholding their cheerful morning *bonjours* were heroes of liberty!"

Hel laughed. "You're being a little hard on the French."

"It is history that is hard on them. I mean real history, not the *verité à la cinquième République* that they teach in their schools. The truth be known, I admire the French more than any other foreigners. In the centuries they have lived beside the Basque, they have absorbed certain virtues—understanding, philosophic insight, a sense of humor—and these have made them the best of the 'others.' But even I am forced to admit that they are a ridiculous people, just as one must confess that the British are bungling, the Italians incompetent, the Americans neurotic, the Germans romantically savage, the Arabs vicious, the Russians barbaric, and the Dutch make cheese. Take the particular manifestation of French ridiculousness that makes them attempt to combine their myopic devotion to money with the pursuit of phantom *gloire*. The same people who dilute their burgundy for modest profit willingly spend millions of francs on the atomic contamination of the Pacific Ocean in the hope that they will be thought to be the technological equals of the Americans. They see themselves as the feisty David against the grasping Goliath. Sadly for their image abroad, the rest of the world views their actions as the ludicrous egotism of the amorous ant climbing a cow's leg and assuring her that he will be gentle."

Le Cagot looked down at the tabletop thoughtfully. "I cannot think of anything further to say about the French just now."

The widow had joined them at table, sitting close to Le Cagot and pressing her knee against his. "Hey, you have a visitor down at Etchehelia," she told Hel,

---

* *Esteka* is Basque for "sexual deficiency."

using the Basque name for his château. "It is a girl. An outsider. Arrived yesterday evening."

Hel was not surprised that this news was already in Larrau, three mountains and fifteen kilometers from his home. It had doubtless been common knowledge in all the local villages within four hours of the visitor's arrival.

"What do you know about her?" Hel asked.

The widow shrugged and tucked down the corners of her mouth, indicating that she knew only the barest facts. "She took coffee *chez* Jaureguiberry and did not have money to pay. She walked all the way from Tardets to Etchebar and was seen from the hills several times. She is young, but not too young to bear. She wore short pants that showed her legs, and it is said that she has a plump chest. She was received by your woman, who paid her bill with Jaureguiberry. She has an English accent. And the old gossips in your village say that she is a whore from Bayonne who was turned out from her farm for sleeping with the husband of her sister. As you see, very little is known of her."

"You say she is young with a plump chest?" Le Cagot asked. "No doubt she is seeking me, the final experience."

The widow pinched his thigh.

Hel rose from the table. "I think I'll go home and take a bath and a little sleep. You coming?"

Le Cagot looked at the widow sideways. "What do you think? Should I go?"

"I don't care what you do, old man."

But as he started to rise, she tugged him back by his belt.

"Maybe I'll stay a while, Niko. I'll come back this evening and take a look at your girl with the naked legs and the big boobs. If she pleases me, I may bless you with an extension of my visit. Ouch!"

Hel paid and went out to his Volvo, which he kicked in the rear fender, then drove away toward his home.

Château d'Etchebar

AFTER PARKING IN the square of Etchebar (he did not permit automobiles on his property) and giving the roof a parting bash with his fist, Hel walked down the private road to his château feeling, as he always did upon returning home, a paternal affection for this perfect seventeenth-century house into which he had put years of devotion and millions of Swiss francs. It was the thing he loved most in the world, a physical and emotional fortress against the twentieth century. He paused along the path up from the heavy gates to pat the earth in around a newly planted shrub, and as he was doing this he felt the approach of that vague and scattered aura that could only be Pierre, his gardener.

"Bonjour, M'sieur," Pierre greeted in his singsong way, as he recognized Hel through the haze of his regularly spaced glasses of red that began with his rising at dawn.

Hel nodded. "I hear we have a guest, Pierre."

"It is so. A girl. She still sleeps. The women have told me that she is a whore from—"

"I know. Is Madame awake?"

"To be sure. She was informed of your approach twenty minutes ago." Pierre looked up into the sky and nodded sagely. "Ah, ah, ah," he said, shaking his head. Hel realized that he was preparing to make a weather prediction, as he did every time they met on the grounds. All the Basque of Haute Soule believe they have special genetic gifts for meteorological prognostication based upon their mountain heritage and the many folk adages devoted to reading weather signs. Pierre's own predictions, delivered with a quiet assurance that was never diminished by his unvarying inaccuracy, had constituted the principal topic of his conversation with M'sieur Hel for fifteen years, even since the village drunk had been elevated to the rank of the outlander's gardener and his official defender from village gossip.

"Ah, M'sieur, there will be rain before this day is out," Pierre chanted, nodding to himself with resigned conviction. "So there is no point in my setting out these flowers today."

"Is that so, Pierre?" How many hundreds of times had they had this conversation?

"Yes, it is so. Last night at sunset there was red and gold in the little clouds near the mountains. It is a sure sign."

"Oh? But doesn't the saying go the other way? Isn't it *arrats gorriak eguraldi?*"

"That is how the saying goes, M'sieur. However . . ." Pierre's eyes glittered with conspiratorial slyness as he tapped the side of his long nose. ". . . everything depends on the phase of the moon."

"Oh?"

Pierre closed his eyes and nodded slowly, smiling benevolently on the ignorance of all outlanders, even such basically good men as M'sieur Hel. "When the moon is ascending, the rule is as you have said; but when the moon is descending, it is the other way."

"I see. Then when the moon is descending it is: *Goiz gorriak dakarke uri?*"

Pierre frowned, uncomfortable about being forced to a firm prediction. He considered for a moment before answering. "That varies, M'sieur."

"I'm sure it does."

"And . . . there is an additional complication."

"You're going to tell me about it."

Pierre glanced about uneasily and shifted to French, to avoid the risk of offending the earth spirits who, of course, understand only Basque. "*Vous voyez, M'sieur, de temps en temps, la lune se trompe!*"

Hel drew a long breath and shook his head. "Good morning, Pierre."

"Good morning, M'sieur." Pierre tottered down the path to see if there was something else requiring his attention.

His eyes closed and his mind afloat, Hel sat neck-deep in the Japanese wooden tub filled with water so hot that lowering himself into it had been an experience on the limen between pain and pleasure. The servants had fired up the wood-stoked water boiler as soon as they heard that M. Hel was approaching from Larrau, and by the time he had scrubbed himself thoroughly and taken a shock shower in icy water, his Japanese tub was full, and the small bathing room was billowing with dense steam.

Hana dozed across from him, sitting on a higher bench that allowed her to sit neck-deep too. As always when they bathed together, their feet were in casual embrace.

"Do you want to know about the visitor, Nicholai?"

Hel shook his head slowly, not willing to interrupt his comatose relaxation. "Later," he muttered.

After a quarter of an hour, the water cooled enough that it was possible to make a movement in the tub without discomfort. He opened his eyes and smiled sleepily at Hana. "One grows old, my friend. After a couple of days in the mountains, the bath becomes more a medical necessity than a pleasure."

Hana smiled back and squeezed his foot between hers. "Was it a good cave?"

He nodded. "An easy one, really. A walk-in cave with no long crawls, no siphons. Still, it was just about all the work my body could handle."

He climbed the steps on the side of the tub and slid back the padded panel that closed the bathing room off from the small Japanese garden he had been perfecting for the past fifteen years, and which he assumed would be acceptable in another fifteen. Steam billowed past him into the cool air, which felt bracing on his skin, still tight and tingling from the heat. He had learned that a hot tub, twenty minutes of light meditation, an hour of lovemaking, and a quick shower replenished his body and spirit better than a night's sleep; and this routine was habitual with him upon returning from a caving bash or, in the old days, from a counterterrorist stunt.

Hana left the tub and put a lightly padded kimono over her still-wet body. She helped him into his bathing kimono, and they walked across the garden, where he stopped for a moment to adjust a sounding stone in the stream leading from the small pond because the water was low and the sound of it was too treble to please him. The bathing room with its thick plank walls was half hidden in a stand of bamboo that bordered the garden on three sides. Across from it was a low structure of dark wood and sliding paper panels that contained his Japanese room, where he studied and meditated, and his "gun room," where he kept the implements of the trade from which he had recently retired. The fourth side of the garden was closed off by the back of his château, and both of the Japanese buildings were freestanding, so as to avoid breaking the mansard perfection of its marble facade. He had worked through all of one summer, building the Japanese structures with two craftsmen he brought from Kyushu for the purpose, men old enough to remember how to work in wood-and-wedge.

Kneeling at a low lacquered table, facing out toward the Japanese garden, they took a light meal of melon balls (warm, to accent the musky flavor), tart plums (glaucous, icy, and full of juice), unflavored rice cakes, and a half glass of chilled Irouléguy.

The meal done, Hana rose from the table. "Shall I close the panels?"

"Leave one ajar, so we can see the garden."

Hana smiled. Nicholai and his garden . . . like a father with a delicate but willful child. The garden was the most important of his possessions, and often, after a trip, he would return home unannounced, change clothes, and work in the garden for hours before anyone knew he was home. To him, the garden with its subtle articulations was a concrete statement of *shibumi,* and there was an autumnal correctness to the fact that he would probably not live to see its full statement.

She let her kimono fall away. "Shall we have a wager?"

He laughed. "All right. The winner receives . . . let's see. How about one half-hour of the Delight of the Razor?"

"Fine. I am sure I shall enjoy it very much."

"That sure of yourself?"

"My good friend, you have been off in the mountains for three days. Your body has been manufacturing love, but there has been no outlet. You are at a great disadvantage in the wager."

"We shall see."

With Hana and Nicholai, the foreplay was as much mental as physical. They were both Stage IV lovemakers, she by virtue of her excellent training, he because of the mental control he had learned as a youth, and his gift of proximity sense, which allowed him to eavesdrop on his partner's sensations and know precisely where she was in relation to climax contractions. The game was to cause the other to climax first, and it was played with no holds or techniques barred. To the winner went the Delight of the Razor, a deeply relaxing thrill massage in which the skin of the arms, legs, chest, back, stomach, and pubes is lightly brushed with a keenly honed razor. The tingling delight, and the background fear of a slip, combine to require the person receiving the massage to relax completely as the only alternative to unbearable tension and pleasure. Typically, the Delight of the Razor begins with the extremities, sweeping waves of thrill inward as the razor approaches the erogenous areas, which become ardent with pleasure and the shadow of fear. There are subtleties of technique when the razor comes to these zones that are dangerous to describe.

The Delight of the Razor culminates in quick oral lovemaking.

Whichever of them won the wager by making the other climax first would receive the Delight of the Razor, and there was a special cachet to their way of playing the game. They knew one another well enough to bring both of them to the threshold of climax quickly, and the game was played out there, on the teetering edge of pleasure and control.

It was not until after he got away from Sugamo Prison and began his life in the West that Hel's sexual experience took on form and articulation. Before that there had been only amateur play. His relationship with Mariko had not been physical in essence; it had been youthful affection, and their bungling sexual experiences had been nothing more than a physical footnote to their gentle and uncertain affection.

With the Tanaka sisters, Hel entered Stage I lovemaking, that healthy and simplistic stage of sexual curiosity during which strong young animals brimming with the impulse to continue their species exercise themselves on one another's bodies. Although plebeian and monotonic, Stage I is wholesome and honest, and Hel enjoyed his time spent in that rank, regretting only that so many people are sensationally crippled by their cultures and can accept the strong, sweaty lovemaking of Stage I only when disguised as romance, love, affection, or even self-expression. In their confusion, they build relationships upon the sand of passion. Hel considered it a great pity that mass man had come into contact with romantic literature, which created expectations beyond the likelihood of fulfillment and contributed to that marital delinquency characteristic of Western sexual adolescents.

During his brief sojourn in Stage II—the use of sex as psychological aspirin, as social narcosis, a kind of bloodletting to reduce fevers and pressures—Hel began to have glimpses of the fourth level of sexual experience. Because he realized that sexual activity would be a significant part of his life, and because he detested amateurism in all its forms, he undertook to prepare himself. He received professional tactical training in Ceylon and in the exclusive bordellos of Madagascar, where he lived for four months, learning from women of every race and culture.

Stage III, sexual gourmandizing, is the highest stage ever reached by Westerners and, indeed, by most Orientals. Hel moved through this stage leisurely and with high appetite because he was young, his body strong and taut, and his imagination fertile. He was in no danger of getting bogged down in the sexual black masses of artificial stimulation with which the nastier-than-thou jetsetters and the soft intellectuals of the literary and filmmaking worlds seek to compensate for callused nerve ends and imaginations by roiling among one another's tepid flesh and lubricating fluids.

Even while in the sexual smorgasbord of Stage III, Hel began to experiment with such refined tactics as climax hovering and mental intercourse. He found it amusing to associate sexual techniques with Gō nomenclature. Such terms as *aji keshi, ko, furikawari,* and *hane* lent themselves easily as illuminating images; while others, such as *kaketsugi, nozoki,* and *yosu-miru,* could be applied to lovemaking only with a liberal and procrustean view of metaphor.

By the age of thirty, Hel's sexual interests and capacities led him naturally to

Stage IV, the final "game phase," in which excitation and climax are relatively trivial terminal gestures in an activity that demands all the mental vigor and reserve of championship Gō, the training of a Ceylonese whore, and the endurance and agility of a gifted grade VI rock climber. The game of his preference was an invention of his own which he called *"kikashi* sex." This could only be played with another Stage IV lovemaker, and only when both were feeling particularly strong. The game was played in a small room, about six *tatami*. Both players dressed in formal kimonos and knelt facing one another, their backs against opposite walls. Each, through concentration alone, was required to come to the verge of climax and to hover there. No contact was permitted, only concentration and such gestures as could be made with one hand.

The object of the game was to cause climax before climaxing yourself, and it was best played while it was raining.

In time, he abandoned *kikashi* sex as being somewhat too demanding, and also because it was a lonely and selfish experience, lacking the affection and caressing of afterplay that decorates the best of lovemaking.

Hana's eyes were squeezed shut with effort, and her lips were stretched over her teeth. She tried to escape from the involute position in which he held her, but he would not release her.

"I thought we agreed that you weren't permitted to do that!" she pled.

"I didn't agree to anything."

"Oh, Nikko . . . I can't! . . . I can't hold on! Damn you!"

She arched her back and emitted a squeak of final effort to avoid climaxing. Her delight infected Hel, who relinquished his control to allow himself to climax just after she did. Then suddenly his proximity sense sounded the alarm. She was faking! Her aura was not dancing, as it would at climax. He tried to void his mind and arrest his climax, but it was too late. He had broken over the rim of control.

"You devil!" he shouted as he came.

She was laughing as she climaxed a few seconds later.

She lay on her stomach, humming sleepily in appreciation as he slowly inched the razor over her buttock, a perfect object blending the fineness of her Japanese blood with the useful shape of her Black. He kissed it gently and continued the Delight.

"In two months your tenure with me is over, Hana."

"Hmm-hmm." She did not want to break her languor by speaking.

"Have you considered my suggestion that you stay on with me?"

"Hmm-hmm."

"And?"

"Unh-nh-nh-nh-nh." The prolonged sound through slack lips meant, "Don't make me talk."

He chuckled and turned her over onto her back, continuing the thrill massage with close attention to technique and detail. Hana was in a perfect state. She was in her midthirties, the youngest a woman can be and still possess the training and experience of a grand lover. Because of the excellent care she took of her body and because of the time-annihilating effects of her ideal blend of Oriental, Black, and Caucasian strains, she would be in her prime for another fifteen years. She was a delight to look at, and to work on. Her greatest quality lay in her ability to receive pleasure completely and graciously.

When the Delight of the Razor had closed to her centers and had rendered her moist and passive, he concluded the event with its classic quick finish. And for a time they lay together in that comfortable lover's twine that knows how to deal with the extra arm.

"I *have* thought about staying on, Nikko," she said, her voice buzzing against his chest. "There are many reasons that might prompt me to do so. This is the most beautiful spot in the world. I shall always be grateful to you for showing me this corner of the Basque country. And certainly you have constructed a life of *shibumi* luxury here that is attractive. And there is you, so quiet and stern when you deal with the outside world, so boyish in lovemaking. You are not without a certain charm."

"Thank you."

"And I must also confess that it is much rarer to find a well-trained man than an accomplished woman. But . . . it is lonely here. I know that I am free to go to Bayonne or Paris whenever I wish—and I have a good time when I do go—but day to day, despite your attention and the delights of your conversation, and despite the bawdy energy of our friend Le Cagot, it is lonely for a woman whose interests and appetites have been so closely honed as mine have been."

"I understand that."

"It is different for you, Nikko. You are a recluse by nature. You despise the outside world, and you don't need it. I too find that most of the people out there either bore or annoy me. But I am not a recluse by nature, and I have a vivid curiosity. Then too . . . there is another problem."

"Yes?"

"Well, how shall I put this? Personalities such as yours and mine are meant to dominate. Each of us should function in a large society, giving flavor and texture to the mass. The two of us together in one place is like a wasteful concentration of spice in one course of an otherwise bland meal. Do you see what I mean?"

"Does that mean that you have decided to leave when your tenure is up?"

She blew a jet of breath over the hairs of his chest. "It means that I have not yet made up my mind." She was silent for a time, then she said, "I suppose I would really prefer to have the best of both worlds, spending half of every year here, resting and learning with you, and half of each year out there, stunning my audience."

"I see nothing wrong with that."

She laughed. "It would mean that you would have to make do for six months each year with the bronzed, long-legged, mindless nymphs of the Côte Basque. Actresses and models and that sort. Could you do that?"

"As easily as you could make do with round-armed lads possessing excellent muscle tone and honest, empty eyes. For both of us, it would be like subsisting on hors d'oeuvres. But why not? There is some amusement in hors d'oeuvres, though they cloy without nourishing."

"Let me think about it, Nikko. It is an attractive idea." She raised herself onto one elbow and looked down into his half-closed, amused eyes. "Then too, freedom is also attractive. Maybe I won't make any decision at all."

"That's a kind of decision."

They dressed and went to shower beneath the perforated copper cask designed for that purpose by the first enlightened owner of the château nearly three hundred years before.

It was not until they were taking tea in the cream-and-gold east salon that Hel asked about the visitor.

"She is still asleep. When she arrived yesterday evening, she was desperate. She had walked from the village after flying in to Pau from Rome and hitchhiking to Tardets. Although she tried to chat and follow the forms of politeness, I could tell from the first that she was very distraught. She began weeping while she was taking tea. Weeping without knowing she was doing it. I gave her something to calm her and put her to bed. But she awoke during the night with nightmares, and I sat on the edge of her bed, stroking her hair and humming to her, until she was calm and dropped off again."

"What is her problem?"

"She talked about it while I stroked her hair. There was a nasty business at the airport in Rome. Two of her friends were shot and killed."

"Shot by whom?"

"She didn't say. Perhaps she didn't know."

"Why were they shot?"

"I have no idea."

"Did she tell you why she came to our home?"

"Evidently all three of them were on their way here. She had no money, only her plane ticket."

"Did she give you her name?"

"Yes. Hannah Stern. She said her uncle was a friend of yours."

Hel set his cup down, closed his eyes, and pushed out a long nasal sigh. "Asa Stern was a friend. He's dead. I am indebted to him. There was a moment when, without his help, I would have died."

"And this indebtedness, does it extend to the girl as well?"

"We'll see. Did you say the blow-away in Rome International happened yesterday afternoon?"

"Or morning. I am not sure which."

"Then it should be on the news at noon. When the girl wakes up, please have her come and see me. I'll be in the garden, Oh, and I think Le Cagot will take dinner with us—if he finishes his business in Larrau in time."

Hel worked in the garden for an hour and a half, trimming, controlling, striving for modest and subtle effects. He was not an artist, but he was sensitive; so while his garden, the major statement of his impulse to create, lacked *sabi*, it had the *shibui* features that separate Japanese art from the mechanical dynamics of Western art and the florid hyperbole of Chinese. There was that sweet melancholy, that forgiving sadness that characterizes the beautiful in the Japanese mind. There was intentional imperfection and organic simplicity that created, then satisfied, aesthetic tensions, functioning rather as balance and imbalance function in Western art.

Just before noon, a servant brought out a battery radio, and Hel listened in his gun room for the twelve o'clock broadcast of BBC World Service. The news reader was a woman whose distinctive voice has been a source of amusement for the international Anglophone community for years. To that peculiar pronunciation that is BBC's own, she adds a clipped, half-strangled sound which the world audience has long taken to be the effect of an uncomfortable suppository, although there is lively dispute and extensive wagering between those who maintain that the suppository is made of sandpaper and those who promote the ice-cube theory.

Buried among the trivia of collapsing governments, the falling dollar, and Belfast bombings was a description of the atrocity at Rome International. Two Japanese men, subsequently identified from papers on their persons as Red Army members working in behalf of the Black Septembrists, opened fire with automatic weapons, killing two young Israeli men, whose identities are being withheld. The Red Army assassins were themselves killed in an exchange of gunfire with Italian police and special agents, as were several civilian bystanders. And now for news of a lighter note . . .

"Mr. Hel?"

He switched off the radio and beckoned to the young woman standing in the doorway of the gun room. She was wearing fresh khaki walking shorts and a short-sleeved shirt with three top buttons open. As hors d'oeuvres go, she was a promising morsel: long strong legs, slim waist, aggressive bosom, reddish hair fluffy from recent washing. More soubrette than heroine, she was in that brief desirable moment between coltishness and *zaftig*. But her face was soft and without lines of experience, giving the strain she was under the look of petulance.

"Mr. Hel?" she said again, her tone uncertain.

"Come in and sit down, Miss Stern."

She took a chair beneath a rack of metal devices she did not recognize to be weapons and smiled faintly. "I don't know why, but I thought of you as an older man. Uncle Asa spoke of you as a friend, a man of his own age."

"We were of an age; we shared an era. Not that that's pertinent to anything." He looked at her flatly, evaluating her. And finding her wanting.

Uncomfortable under the expressionless gaze of his bottle-green eyes, she sought the haven of small talk. "Your wife—Hana, that is—has been very kind to me. She sat up with me last night and—"

He cut her off with a gesture. "Begin by telling me about your uncle. Why he sent you here. After that, give me the details of the events at Rome International. Then tell me what your plans are and what they have to do with me."

Surprised by his businesslike tone, she took a deep breath, gathered her thoughts, and began her story, characteristically enough, with herself. She told him that she had been raised in Skokie, had attended Northwestern University, had taken an active interest in political and social issues, and had decided upon graduation to visit her uncle in Israel—to find her roots, discover her Jewishness.

Hel's eyelids drooped at this last, and he breathed a short sigh. With a rolling motion of his hand he gestured her to get on with it.

"You knew, of course, that Uncle Asa was committed to punishing those who committed the Munich murders."

"That was on the grapevine. We never spoke of such things in our letters. When I first heard of it, I thought your uncle was foolish to come out of retirement and attempt something like that with his old friends and contacts either gone or decayed into politics. I could only assume it was the desperate act of a man who knew he was in his final illness."

"But he first organized our cell a year and a half ago, and he didn't become sick until a few months ago."

"That is not true. Your uncle has been ill for several years. There were two brief remissions. At the time you say he organized your cell, he was combating pain with drugs. That might account for his crepuscular thinking."

Hannah Stern frowned and looked away. "You don't sound as though you held my uncle in much esteem."

"On the contrary, I liked him very much. He was a brilliant thinker and a man of generous spirit—a man of *shibumi.*"

"A man of . . . what?"

"Never mind. Your uncle never belonged in the business of terror. He was emotionally unequipped for it—which of course says a good deal in his favor as a human being. In happier times, he would have lived the gentle life of a teacher and scholar. But he was passionate in his sense of justice, and not only for his own people. The way things were twenty-five years ago, in what is now Israel, passionate and generous men who were not cowards had few options open to them."

Hannah was not used to Hel's soft, almost whispered prison voice, and she found herself leaning close to hear his words.

"You are wrong to imagine that I did not esteem your uncle. There was a moment in Cairo sixteen years ago when he risked his safety, possibly his life, to help me. What is more significant, he also risked the success of a project he was devoted to. I had been shot in the side. The situation was such that I could not seek medical assistance. When I met him, I had gone two days with a wad of blood-soaked cloth under my shirt, wandering in the back streets because I didn't dare try a hotel. I was dazed with fever. No, I esteem him a great deal. And I am in his debt." Hel had said this in a soft monotone, without the histrionics she would have associated with sincerity. He told her these things because he thought that, in fairness to the uncle, she had a right to know the extent of his debt of honor. "Your uncle and I never met again after that business in Cairo. Our friendship grew through years of exchanging letters that both of us used as outlets for testing ideas, for sharing our attitudes toward books we were reading, for complaining about fate and life. We enjoyed that freedom from embarrassment one only finds in talking to a stranger. We were very close strangers." Hel wondered if this young woman could understand such a relationship. Deciding she could not, he focused in on the business at hand. "All right, after his son was killed in Munich, your uncle formed a cell to aid him in his mission of punishment. How many people, and where are they now?"

"I am the only one left."

"*You* were within the cell?"

"Yes. Why? Does that seem—"

"Never mind." Hel was convinced now that Asa Stern had been acting in dazed desperation, to introduce this soft college liberal into an action cell. "How large was the cell?"

"We were five. We called ourselves the Munich Five."

His eyelids drooped again. "How theatrical. Nothing like telegraphing the stunt."

"I beg your pardon?"

"Five in the cell? Your uncle, you, the two hit in Rome—who was the fifth member? David O. Selznick?"

"I don't understand what you mean. The fifth man was killed in a café bombing in Jerusalem. He and I were . . . we were . . ." Her eyes began to shine with tears.

"I'm sure you were. It's a variation of the summer vacation romance: one of the fringe benefits of being a committed young revolutionary with all humanity as your personal flock. All right, tell me how far you had got before Asa died."

Hannah was confused and hurt. This was nothing like the man her uncle had described, the honest professional who was also a gentle man of culture, who paid his debts and refused to work for the uglier of the national and commercial powers. How could her uncle have been fond of a man who showed so little human sympathy? Who was so lacking in understanding?

Hel, of course, understood only too well. He had several times had to clean up after these devoted amateurs. He knew that when the storm broke, they either ran or, from equally cowardly impulses, shot up everything in sight.

Hannah was surprised to find that no tears came, their flow cauterized by Hel's cold adherence to fact and information. She sniffed and said, "Uncle Asa had sources of information in England. He learned that the last remaining two of the Munich murderers were with a group of Black Septembrists planning to hijack a plane departing from Heathrow."

"How large a group?"

"Five or six. We were never sure."

"Had you identified which of them were involved in Munich?"

"No."

"So you were going to put all five of them under?"

She nodded.

"I see. And your contacts in England? What is their character and what are they going to do for you?"

"They are urban guerrillas working for the freedom of Northern Ireland from English domination."

"Oh, God."

"There is a kind of brotherhood among all freedom fighters, you know. Our tactics may be different, but our ultimate goals are the same. We all look forward to a day when—"

"Please," he interrupted. "Now, what were these IRA's going to do for you?"

"Well . . . they were keeping watch on the Septembrists. They were going to house us when we arrived in London. And they were going to furnish us with arms."

" 'Us' being you and the two who got hit in Rome?"

"Yes."

"I see. All right, now tell me what happened in Rome. BBC identifies the stuntmen as Japanese Red Army types acting for the PLO. Is that correct?"

"I don't know."

"Weren't you there?"

"Yes! I was there!" She controlled herself. "But in the confusion . . . people dying . . . gunfire all around me . . ." In her distress, she rose and turned her back on this man she felt was intentionally tormenting her, testing her. She told herself that she mustn't cry, but tears came nonetheless. "I'm sorry. I was terrified. Stunned. I don't remember everything." Nervous and lacking something to do with her hands, she reached out to take a simple metal tube from the rack on the wall before her.

"Don't touch that!"

She jerked her hand away, startled to hear him raise his voice for the first time. A shot of righteous anger surged through her. "I wasn't going to hurt your toys!"

"They might hurt you." His voice was quiet and modulated again. "That is a nerve gas tube. If you had turned the bottom half, you would be dead now. And what is more important, so would I."

She grimaced and retreated from the weapons rack, crossing to the open sliding door leading to the garden, where she leaned against the sill to regain something of her composure.

"Young woman, I intend to help you, if that is possible. I must confess that it may not be possible. Your little amateur organization has made every conceivable mistake, not the least of which was aligning yourselves with IRA dummies. Still, I owe it to your uncle to hear you out. Perhaps I can protect you and get you back to the bourgeois comfort of your home, where you can express your social passions by campaigning against litter in national parks. But if I am to help you at all, I have to know how the stones lie on the board. So I want you to save your passion and theatrics for your memoirs and answer my questions as fully and as succinctly as you can. If you're not prepared to do that just now, we can chat again later. But it is possible that I may have to move quickly. Typically in patterns like this, after a spoiling raid (and that's probably what the Rome International number was) time favors the other fellows. Shall we talk now, or shall we go take luncheon?"

Hannah slid down to the *tatami* floor, her back against the sill, her profile cameoed against the sunlit garden. After a moment, she said, "I'm sorry. I've been through a lot."

"I don't doubt that. Now tell me about the Rome hit. Facts and impressions, not emotions."

She looked down and drew little circles on her tanned thigh with her fingernail, then she pulled up her knees and hugged them to her breast. "All right. Avrim and Chaim went through passport check ahead of me. I was slowed down by the Italian officer, who was sort of flirting and ogling my breasts. I suppose I should have kept my shirt buttoned all the way up. Finally, he stamped my passport, and I started out into the terminal. Then the gunshots broke out. I saw Avrim run . . . and fall . . . the side of his head all . . . all. Wait a minute." She sniffed and drew several deep, controlling breaths. "I started to run too . . . everyone was running and screaming . . . an old man with a white beard was hit . . . a child . . . a fat old woman. Then there were gunshots coming from the other side of the terminal and from the overhanging mezzanine, and the Oriental gunmen were hit. Then suddenly there was no more gunfire, only screams, and people all around, bleeding and hurt. I saw Chaim lying against the lockers, his legs all wrong and crooked. He had been shot in the face. So I . . . I just walked away. I just walked away. I didn't know what I was doing, where I was going. Then I heard the announcement on the loudspeaker for the plane for Pau. And I just kept walking straight ahead until I came to the departure gate. And . . . and that's all."

"All right. That's fine. Now tell me this. Were you a target?"

"What?"

"Was anyone shooting specifically at you?"

"I don't know! How *could* I know?"

"Were the Japanese using automatic weapons?"

"What?"

"Did they go rat-a-tat, or bang! bang! bang!"

She looked up at him sharply. "I know what an automatic weapon is! We used to practice with them out in the mountains!"

"Rat-a-tat or bang bang?"

"They were machine guns."

"And did anyone standing close to you go down?"

She thought hard, squeezing her knees to her lips. "No. No one standing close to me."

"If professionals using automatic weapons didn't drop anyone near you, then you were not a target. It is possible they didn't identify you as being with your two friends. Particularly as you left the check-through line some time after them. All right, please turn your mind to the shots that came from the mezzanine and blew away the Japanese hitmen. What can you tell me about them?"

She shook her head. "Nothing. I don't remember anything. The guns were not automatics." She looked at Hel obliquely. "They went bang bang."

He smiled. "That's the way. Humor and anger are more useful just now than the wetter emotions. Now, the radio report said something about 'special agents' being with the Italian police. Can you tell me anything about them?"

"No. I never saw the people firing from the mezzanine."

Hel nodded and bowed his head, his palms pressed together and the forefingers lightly touching his lips. "Give me a moment to put this together." He fixed his eyes on the weave pattern of the *tatami*, then defocused as he reviewed the information in hand.

Hannah sat on the floor, framed in the doorway, and gazed out on the Japanese garden where sunlight reflected from the small stream glittered through bamboo leaves. Typical of her class and culture, she lacked the inner resources necessary to deal with the delights of silence, and soon she was uncomfortable. "Why aren't there any flowers in your . . ."

He lifted his hand to silence her without looking up.

Four minutes later he raised his head. "What?"

"Pardon me?"

"Something about flowers."

"Oh, nothing important. I just wondered why you didn't have any flowers in your garden."

"There are three flowers."

"Three varieties?"

"No. Three flowers. One to signal each of the seasons of bloom. We are between seasons now. All right, let's see what we know or can assume. It's pretty obvious that the raid in Rome was organized either by PLO or by the Septembrists, and that they had learned of your intentions—probably through your London-based IRA comrades, who would sell their mothers into Turkish seraglios if the price was right (and if any self-respecting Turk would use them).

The appearance of Japanese Red Army fanatics would seem to point to Septembrists, who often use others to do their dangerous work, having little appetite for personal risk. But things get a little complicated at this point. The stunt men were disposed of within seconds, and by men stationed in the mezzanine. Probably not Italian police, because the thing was done efficiently. The best bet is that the tip-off was tipped off. Why? The only reason that comes quickly to mind is that no one wanted the Japanese stunt men taken alive. And why? Possibly because they were not Red Army dum-dums at all. And that, of course, would bring us to CIA. Or to the Mother Company, which controls CIA, and everything else in American government, for that matter."

"What is the Mother Company? I've never heard of them."

"Few Americans have. It is a control organization of the principal international oil and energy companies. They've been in bed with the Arabs forever, using those poor benighted bastards as pawns in their schemes of induced shortages and profiteering. The Mother Company is a wiry opponent; they can't be got at through nationalistic pressures. Although they put up a huge media front of being loyal American (or British or German or Dutch) companies, they are in fact international infragoverments whose only patriotism is profit. Chances are that your father owns stock in them, as do half the gray-haired ladies of your country."

Hannah shook her head. "I can't feature CIA taking sides with the Black Septembrists. The United States supports Israel; they're allies."

"You underestimate the elastic nature of your country's conscience. They have made a palpable shift since the oil embargo. American devotion to honor varies inversely with its concern for central heating. It is a property of the American that he can be brave and self-sacrificing only in short bursts. That is why they are better at war than at responsible peace. They can face danger, but not inconvenience. They toxify their air to kill mosquitoes. They drain their energy sources to provide themselves with electric carving knives. We must never forget that there was always Coca-Cola for the soldiers in Viet Nam."

Hannah felt a chauvinistic sting. "Do you think it's fair to generalize like that about a people?"

"Yes. Generalization is flawed thinking only when applied to individuals. It is the most accurate way to describe the mass, the Wad. And yours is a democracy, a dictatorship of the Wad."

"I refuse to believe that Americans were involved in the blood and horror of what went on in that airport. Innocent children and old men . . ."

"Does the sixth of August mean anything to you?"

"Sixth of August? No. Why?" She gripped her legs closer to her chest.

"Never mind." Hel rose. "I have to think this out a bit. We'll talk again this afternoon."

"Do you intend to help me?"

"Probably. But probably not in any style you have in mind. By the way, can you stand a bit of avuncular advice?"

"What would that be?"

"It is a sartorial indiscretion for a young lady so lavishly endowed with pubic hair as you to wear shorts that brief, and to sit in so revealing a posture. Unless, of course, it is your intention to prove that your red hair is natural. Shall we take lunch?"

Lunch was set at a small round table in the west reception room giving out onto the rolling green and allée that descended to the principal gates. The *porte fenêtres* were open, and the long curtains billowed lazily with cedar-scented breezes. Hana had changed to a long dress of plum-colored silk, and when Hel and Hannah entered, she smiled at them as she put the finishing touches to a centerpiece of delicate bell-shaped flowers. "What perfect timing. Lunch was just this minute set." In fact, she had been awaiting them for ten minutes, but one of her charms was making others feel socially graceful. A glance at Hannah's face told her that things had gone distressingly for her during the chat with Hel, so Hana took the burden of civilized conversation upon herself.

As Hannah opened her starched linen napkin, she noticed that she had not been served the same things as Hana and Hel. She had a bit of lamb, chilled asparagus in mayonnaise, and rice pilaf, while they had fresh or lightly sauteed vegetables with plain brown rice.

Hana smiled and explained. "Our age and past indiscretions require that we eat a little cautiously, my dear. But we do not inflict our spartan regimen on our guests. In fact, when I am away from home, in Paris for instance, I go on a spree of depraved eating. Eating for me is what you might call a managed vice. A vice particularly difficult to control when one is living in France where, depending on your point of view, the food is either the world's second best or the world's very worst."

"What do you mean?" Hannah asked.

"From a sybaritic point of view, French food is second only to classic Chinese cuisine. But it is so handled, and sauced, and prodded, and chopped, and stuffed, and seasoned as to be a nutritive disaster. That is why no people in the West have so much delight with eating as the French, or so much trouble with their livers."

"And what do you think about American food?" Hannah asked, a wry expression on her face, because she was of that common kind of American abroad who seeks to imply sophistication by degrading everything American.

"I couldn't really say; I have never been in America. But Nicholai lived there for a time, and he tells me that there are certain areas in which American cooking excels."

"Oh?" Hannah said, looking archly at Hel. "I'm surprised to hear that Mr. Hel has anything good to say about American or Americans."

"It's not Americans I find annoying; it's Americanism: a social disease of the postindustrial world that must inevitably infect each of the mercantile nations in turn, and is called 'American' only because your nation is the most advanced case of the malady, much as one speaks of Spanish flu, or Japanese Type-B encephalitis. Its symptoms are a loss of work ethic, a shrinking of inner resources, and a constant need for external stimulation, followed by spiritual decay and moral narcosis. You can recognize the victim by his constant efforts to get in touch with himself, to believe his spiritual feebleness is an interesting psychological warp, to construe his fleeing from responsibility as evidence that he and his life are uniquely open to new experience. In the latter stages, the sufferer is reduced to seeking that most trivial of human activities: fun. As for your food, no one denies that the Americans excel in one narrow rubric: the snack. And I suspect there's something symbolic in that."

Hana disapproved of Hel's ingracious tone, so she took control of the dinner talk as she brought Hannah's plate to the sideboard to replenish it. "My English is imperfect. There is more than one asparagus here, but the word 'asparaguses' sounds awkward. Is it one of those odd Latin plurals, Nicholai? Does one say asperagae, or something like that?"

"One would say that only if he were that overinformed/undereducated type who attends concerti for celli and afterward orders cups of capuccini. Or, if he is American, dishes of raspberry Jell-I."

"*Arrêtes un peu et sois sage,*" Hana said with a slight shake of her head. She smiled at Hannah. "Isn't he a bore on the subject of Americans? It's a flaw in his personality. His sole flaw, he assures me. I've been wanting to ask you, Hannah, what did you read at university?"

"What did I read?"

"What did you major in," Hel clarified.

"Oh. Sociology."

He might have guessed it. Sociology, that descriptive pseudo-science that disguises its uncertainties in statistical mists as it battens on the narrow gap of information between psychology and anthropology. The kind of nonmajor that so many Americans use to justify their four-year intellectual vacations designed to prolong adolescence.

"What did you study in school?" Hannah asked her hostess thoughtlessly.

Hana smiled to herself. "Oh . . . informal psychology, anatomy, aesthetics—that sort of thing."

Hannah applied herself to the asparagus, asking casually, "You two aren't married, are you? I mean . . . you joked the other night about being Mr. Hel's concubine."

Hana's eyes widened in rare astonishment. She was not accustomed to that inquisitive social gaucherie that Anglo-Saxon cultures mistake for admirable frankness. Hel opened his palm toward Hana, gesturing her to answer, his eyes wide with mischievous innocence.

"Well . . ." Hana said, ". . . in fact, Mr. Hel and I are not married. And in fact I am his concubine. Will you take dessert now? We have just received our first shipment of the magnificent cherries of Itxassou, of which the Basque are justly proud."

Hel knew Hana was not going to get off that easily, and he grinned at her as Miss Stern pursued, "I don't think you mean concubine. In English, concubine means someone who is hired for . . . well, for her sexual services. I think you mean 'mistress.' And even mistress is sort of old-fashioned. Nowadays people just say they are living together."

Hana looked at Hel for help. He laughed and interceded for her. "Hana's English is really quite good. She was only joking about the asparagus. She knows the difference among a mistress, a concubine, and a wife. A mistress is unsure of her wage, a wife has none; and they are both amateurs. Now, do try the cherries."

Hel sat on a stone bench in the middle of the cutting gardens, his eyes closed and his face lifted to the sky. Although the mountain breeze was cool, the thin sunlight penetrated his *yukata* and made him warm and drowsy. He hovered on the delicious verge of napping until he intercepted the approaching aura of someone who was troubled and tense.

"Sit down, Miss Stern," he said, without opening his eyes. "I must compliment you on the way you conducted yourself at lunch. Not once did you refer to your problems, seeming to sense that in this house we don't bring the world to our table. To be truthful, I hadn't expected such good form from you. Most people of your age and class are so wrapped up in themselves—so concerned with what they're 'into'—that they fail to realize that style and form are everything, and substance a passing myth." He opened his eyes and smiled as he made a pallid effort to imitate the American accent: "It ain't what you do, it's how you do it."

Hannah perched on the marble balustrade before him, her thighs flattened by her weight. She was barefoot, and she had not heeded his advice about changing into less revealing clothes. "You said we should talk some more?"

"Hm-m-m. Yes. But first let me apologize for my uncivil tone, both during our little chat and at lunch. I was angry and annoyed. I have been retired for almost two years now, Miss Stern. I am no longer in the profession of exterminating terrorists; I now devote myself to gardening, to caving, to listening to the grass grow, and to seeking a kind of deep peace I lost many years ago—lost because circumstances filled me with hate and fury. And then you come along with a legitimate claim to my assistance because of my debt to your uncle, and you threaten me with being pressed back into my profession of violence and fear. And fear is a good part of why I was annoyed with you. There is a certain amount of antichance in my work. No matter how well-trained one is, how careful, how coolheaded, the odds regularly build up over the years; and there comes a time when luck and antichance weigh heavily against you. It's not that I've been lucky in my work—I mistrust luck—but I have never been greatly hampered by bad luck. So there's a lot of bad luck out there waiting for its turn. I've tossed up the coin many times, and it has come down heads. There are more than twenty years' worth of tails waiting their turn. So! What I wanted to explain was the reason I have been impolite to you. It's fear mostly. And some annoyance. I've had time to consider now. I think I know what I should do. Fortunately, the proper action is also the safest."

"Does that mean you don't intend to help me?"

"On the contrary. I am going to help you by sending you home. My debt to your uncle extends to you, since he sent you to me; but it does not extend to any abstract notion of revenge or to any organization with which you are allied."

She frowned and looked away, out toward the mountains. "Your view of the debt to my uncle is a convenient one for you."

"So it turns out, yes."

"But . . . my uncle gave the last years of his life to hunting down those killers, and it would make that all pretty pointless if I didn't try to do something."

"There's nothing you can do. You lack the training, the skill, the organization. You didn't even have a plan worthy of the name."

"Yes, we did."

He smiled. "All right. Let's take a look at your plan. You said that the Black Septembrists were intending to hijack a plane from Heathrow. Presumably your group was going to hit them at that time. Were you going to take them on the plane, or before they boarded?"

"I don't know."

"You don't know?"

"Avrim was the leader after Uncle Asa died. He told us no more than he thought we had to know, in case one of us was captured or something like that. But I don't believe we were going to meet them on the plane. I think we were going to execute them in the terminal."

"And when was this to take place?"

"The morning of the seventeenth."

"That's six days away. Why were you going to London so soon? Why expose yourself for six days?"

"We weren't going to London. We were coming here. Uncle Asa knew we didn't have much chance of success without him. He had hoped he would be strong enough to accompany us and lead us. The end came too fast for him."

"So he sent you here? I don't believe that."

"He didn't exactly send us here. He had mentioned you several times. He said that if we got into trouble we could come to you and you would help."

"I'm sure he meant that I would help you get away after the event."

She shrugged.

He sighed. "So you three youngsters were going to pick up your arms from your IRA contacts in London, loiter around town for six days, take a taxi out to Heathrow, stroll into the terminal, locate the targets in the waiting area, and blow them away. Was that your plan?"

Her jaw tightened, and she looked away. It did sound silly, put like that.

"So, Miss Stern, notwithstanding your disgust and horror over the incident at Rome International, it turns out that you were planning to be responsible for the same kind of messy business—a stand-up blow-away in a crowded waiting room. Children, old women, and bits thereof flying hither and yon as the dedicated young revolutionaries, eyes flashing and hair floating, shoot their way into history. Is that what you had in mind?"

"If you're trying to say we are no different from those killers who murdered young athletes in Munich or who shot my comrades in Rome—!"

"The differences are obvious! *They* were well organized and professional!" He cut himself off short. "I'm sorry. Tell me this: what are your resources?"

"Resources?"

"Yes. Forgetting your IRA contacts—and I think we can safely forget them— what kind of resources were you relying on? Were the boys killed in Rome well trained?"

"Avrim was. I don't think Chaim had ever been involved in this sort of thing before."

"And money?"

"Money? Well, we were hoping to get some from you. We didn't need all that much. We had hoped to stay here for a few days—talk to you and get your advice and instructions. Then fly directly to London, arriving the day before the operation. All we needed was air fare and a little more."

Hel closed his eyes. "My dear, dumb, lethal girl. If I were to undertake something like you people had in mind, it would cost between a hundred and a hundred-fifty-thousand dollars. And I am not speaking of my fee. That would be only the setup money. It costs a lot to get in, and often even more to get out. Your uncle knew that." He looked out over the horizon line of mountain and sky. "I'm coming to realize that what he had put together was a suicide raid."

"I don't believe that! He would never lead us into suicide without telling us!"

"He probably didn't intend to have you up front. Chances are he was going to use you three children as backups, hoping he could do the number himself, and you three would be able to walk away in the confusion. Then too . . ."

"Then too, what?"

"Well, we have to realize that he had been on drugs for a long time to manage his pain. Who knows what he was thinking; who knows how much he had left to think with toward the end?"

She drew up one knee and hugged it to her chest, revealing again her erubescence. She pressed her lips against her knee and stared over the top of it across the garden. "I don't know what to do."

Hel looked at her through half-closed eyes. Poor befuddled twit, seeking purpose and excitement in life, when her culture and background condemned her to mating with merchants and giving birth to advertising executives. She was frightened and confused, and not quite ready to give up her affair with danger and significance and return to a life of plans and possessions. "You really don't have much choice. You'll have to go home. I shall be delighted to pay your way."

"I can't do that."

"You can't do anything else."

For a moment, she sucked lightly on her knee. "Mr. Hel—may I call you Nicholai?"

"Certainly not."

"Mr. Hel. You're telling me that you don't intend to help me, is that it?"

"I am helping you when I tell you to go home."

"And if I refuse to? What if I go ahead with this on my own?"

"You would fail—almost surely die."

"I know that. The question is, could you let me try to do it alone? Would your sense of debt to my uncle allow you to do that?"

"You're bluffing."

"And if I'm not?"

Hel glanced away. It was just possible that this bourgeois muffin was dumb enough to drag him into it, or at least to make him decide how far loyalty and honor went. He was preparing to test her, and himself, when he felt an approaching presence he recognized as Pierre's, and he turned to see the gardener shuffling toward them from the château.

"Good afternoon, 'sieur, m'selle. It must be pleasant to have the leisure to sun oneself." He drew a folded sheet of paper from the pocket of his blue worker's smock and handed it to Hel with great solemnity, then he explained that he could not stay for there were a thousand things to be done, and he went on toward the garden and his gatehouse, for it was time to soften his day with another glass.

Hel read the note.

He folded it and tapped it against his lips. "It appears, Miss Stern, that we may not have all the freedom of option we thought. Three strangers have arrived in Tardets and are asking questions about me and, more significantly, about you. They are described as Englishmen or *Amérlos*—the village people wouldn't be able to distinguish those accents. They were accompanied by French Special Police, who are being most cooperative."

"But how could they know I am here?"

"A thousand ways. Your friends, the ones who were killed in Rome, did they have plane tickets on them?"

"I suppose so. In fact, yes. We each carried our own tickets. But they were not to here; they were to Pau."

"That's close enough. I am not completely unknown." Hel shook his head at this additional evidence of amateurism. Professionals always buy tickets to points well past their real destinations, because reservations go into computers and are therefore available to government organizations and to the Mother Company.

"Who do you think the men are?" she asked.

"I don't know."

"What are you going to do?"

He shrugged. "Invite them to dinner."

After leaving Hannah, Hel sat for half an hour in his garden, watching the accumulation of heavy-bellied storm clouds around the shoulders of the mountains and considering the lie of the stones on the board. He came to two conclusions at about the same time. It would rain that night, and his wisest course would be to rush the enemy.

From the gun room he telephoned the Hôtel Dabadie where the Americans were staying. A certain amount of negotiation was required. The Dabadies would send the three *Amérlos* up to the château for dinner that evening, but there was the problem of the dinners they had prepared for their guests. After all, a hotel makes its money on its meals, not its rooms. Hel assured them that the only fair and proper course would be to include the uneaten dinners in their bill. It was, God knows, not the fault of the Dabadies that the strangers decided at the last moment to dine with M. Hel. Business is business. And considering that waste of food is abhorrent to God, perhaps it would be best if the Dabadies ate the dinners themselves, inviting the abbé to join them.

He found Hana reading in the library, wearing the quaint little rectangular glasses she needed for close work. She looked over the top of them as he entered. "Guests for dinner?" she asked.

He caressed her cheek with his palm. "Yes, three. Americans."

"How nice. With Hannah and Le Cagot, that will make quite a dinner party."

"It will that."

She slipped in a bookmark and closed the volume. "Is this trouble, Nikko?"

"Yes."

"It has something to do with Hannah and her problems?"

He nodded.

She laughed lightly. "And just this morning you invited me to stay on with you for half of each year, trying to entice me with the great peace and solitude of your home."

"It will be peaceful soon. I have retired, after all."

"Can one? Can one completely retire from such a trade as yours? Ah well, if we are to have guests, I must send down to the village. Hannah will need some clothes. She cannot take dinner in those shorts of hers, particularly considering her somewhat cavalier attitude toward modest posture."

"Oh? I hadn't noticed."

A greeting bellow from the allée, a slamming of the salon *porte fenêtre* that rattled the glass, a noisy search to find Hana in the library, a vigorous hug with a loud smacking kiss on her cheek, a cry for a little hospitality in the form of a glass of wine, and all the household knew that Le Cagot had returned from his duties in Larrau. "Now, where is this young girl with the plump breasts that all the valley is talking about? Bring her on. Let her meet her destiny!"

Hana told him that the young woman was napping, but that Nicholai was working in the Japanese garden.

"I don't want to see him. I've had enough of his company for the last three days. Did he tell you about my cave? I practically had to drag your man through it. Sad to confess, he's getting old, Hana. It's time for you to consider your future and to look around for an ageless man—perhaps a robust Basque poet?"

Hana laughed and told him that his bath would be ready in half an hour. "And after that you might choose to dress up a bit; we're having guests for dinner."

"Ah, an audience. Good. Very well, I'll go get some wine in the kitchen. Do you still have that young Portuguese girl working for you?"

"There are several."

"I'll go sample around a bit. And wait until you see me dressed up! I bought some fancy clothes a couple of months ago, and I haven't had a chance to show them off yet. One look at me in my new clothes, and you'll melt, by the Balls . . ."

Hana cast a sidelong glance at him, and he instantly refined his language.

". . . by the Ecstasy of Ste. Therese. All right, I'm off to the kitchen." And he marched through the house, slamming doors and shouting for wine.

Hana smiled after Le Cagot. From the first he had taken to her, and his gruff way of showing his approval was to maintain a steady barrage of hyperbolic gallantry. For her part, she liked his honest, rough ways, and she was pleased that Nicholai had a friend so loyal and entertaining as this mythical Basque. She thought of him as a mythic figure, a poet who had constructed an outlandish romantic character, and who spent the rest of his life playing the role he had created. She once asked Hel what had happened to make the poet protect himself within this opéra-bouffe, picaresque façade of his. Hel could not give her the details; to do so would betray a confidence, one Le Cagot was unaware he had invested, because the conversation had taken place one night when the poet was crushed by sadness and nostalgia, and very drunk. Many years ago, the sensitive young poet who ultimately assumed the persona of Le Cagot had been a scholar of Basque literature, and had taken a university post in Bilbao. He married a beautiful and gentle Spanish Basque girl, and they had a baby. One night, for vague motives, he joined a student demonstration against the repression of Basque culture. His wife was with him, although she had no personal interest in politics. The federal police broke up the demonstration with gunfire. The wife was killed. Le Cagot was arrested and spent the next three years in prison. When he escaped, he learned that the baby had died while he was in jail. The young poet drank a great deal and participated in pointless and terribly violent antigovernment actions. He was arrested again; and when he again escaped, the young poet no longer existed. In his place was Le Cagot, the invulnerable caricature who became a folk legend for his patriotic verse, his participation in Basque Separatist causes, and his bigger-than-life personality, which brought him invitations to lecture and read his poetry in universities throughout the Western world. The name he gave to his persona was borrowed from the Cagots, an ancient pariah race of untouchables who had practiced a variant of Christianity which brought down upon them the rancor and hatred of their Basque neighbors. The Cagots sought relief from persecution through a request to Pope Leo X in 1514, which was granted in principle, but the restrictions and indignities continued to the end of the nineteenth century, when they ceased to exist as a distinct race. Their persecution took many forms. They were required to wear on their clothing the distinctive sign of the Cagot in the shape of a goose footprint. They could not walk barefooted. They could not carry arms. They could not frequent public places, and even in entering church they had to use a low side door constructed especially for the purpose, which door is still to be seen in many village churches. They could not sit near others at Mass, or kiss the cross. They could rent land and grow food, but they could not sell their produce. Under pain of death, they could not marry or have sexual relations outside their race.

All that remained for the Cagots were the artisan trades. For many centuries, both by restriction and privilege, they were the land's only woodcutters, carpenters, and joiners. Later, they also became the Basque masons and weavers. Because their misshapen bodies were considered funny, they became the strolling musicians and entertainers of their time, and most of what is now called Basque folk art and folklore was created by the despised Cagots.

Although it was long assumed that the Cagots were a race apart, propagated in Eastern Europe and driven along before the advancing Visigoths until they were deposited, like moraine rubble before a glacier, in the undesirable land of the Pyrenees, modern evidence suggests they were isolated pockets of Basque lepers, ostracized at first for prophylactic reasons, physically diminished in result of their disease, eventually taking on distinguishable characteristics because of enforced intermarriage. This theory goes a long way toward explaining the various limitations placed upon their freedom of action.

Popular tradition has it that the Cagots and their descendents had no earlobes. To this day, in the more traditional Basque villages, girls of five and six years of age have their ears pierced and wear earrings. Without knowing the source of the tradition, the mothers respond to the ancient practice of demonstrating that their girls have lobes in which to wear earrings.

Today the Cagots have disappeared, having either withered and grown extinct, or slowly merged with the Basque population (although this last suggestion is a risky one to advance in a Basque bar), and their name has all but fallen from use, save as a pejorative term for bent old women.

The young poet whose sensitivity had been cauterized by events chose Le Cagot as his pen name to bring attention to the precarious situation of contemporary Basque culture, which is in danger of disappearing, like the suppressed bards and minstrels of former times.

A little before six, Pierre tottered down to the square of Etchebar, the cumulative effect of his day's regularly spaced glasses of wine having freed him from the tyranny of gravity to such a degree that he navigated toward the Volvo by means of tacking. He had been sent to pick up two ensembles which Hana had ordered by telephone after asking Hannah for her sizes and translating them into European standards. After the dresses, Pierre was to collect three dinner guests from the Hôtel Dabadie. Having twice missed the door handle, Pierre pulled down the brim of his beret and focused all of his attention on the not-inconsiderable task of getting into the car, which he eventually accomplished, only to slap his forehead as he remembered an omission. He struggled out again and delivered a glancing kick to the rear fender in imitation of M'sieur Hel's ritual, then he found his way to the driver's seat again. With his native Basque mistrust for things mechanical, Pierre limited his gear options to reverse and low, in which he drove with the throttle wide open, using all the road and both verges. Such sheep, cows, men, and wobbly Solex mopeds as suddenly appeared before his bumper he managed to avoid by twisting the wheel sharply, then seeking the road again by feel. He abjured the effete practice of using the foot brake, and even the emergency brake he viewed as a device only for parking. As he always stopped without depressing the clutch, he avoided the nuisance of having to turn off the engine, which always bucked and died as he reached his destination and hauled back on the brake lever. Fortunately for the peasants and villagers between the château and Tardets, the sound of the Volvo's loosened body clattering and clanking and the roar of its engine at full speed in low gear preceded Pierre by half a kilometer, and there was usually time to scurry behind trees or jump over stone walls. Pierre felt a justified pride in his driving skills, for he had never been involved in an accident. And this was all the more notable considering the wild and careless drivers all around him, whom he frequently observed swerving into ditches and up on sidewalks, or crashing into one another as he roared through stop signs or up one-way streets. It was not so much the maladroit recklessness of these other drivers that disturbed Pierre as their blatant rudeness, for often they had shouted vulgar things at him, and he could not count the number of times he had seen through his rearview mirror a finger, a fist, or even a whole forearm, throwing an angry *figue* at him.

Pierre brought the Volvo to a bucking and coughing stop in the center of the Place of Tardets and clawed his way out. After bruising his toe against the battered door, he set about his commissions, the first of which was to share a hospitable glass with old friends.

No one thought it odd that Pierre always delivered a kick to the car upon entering or leaving, as Volvo-bashing was a general practice in southwestern France, and could even be encountered as far away as Paris. Indeed, carried to cosmopolitan centers around the world by tourists, Volvo-bashing was slowly becoming a cult activity throughout the world, and this pleased Nicholai Hel, since he had begun it all.

Some years before, seeking a car-of-all-work for the château, Hel had followed the advice of a friend and purchased a Volvo on the assumption that a car so expensive, lacking in beauty, comfort, speed, and fuel economy must have something else to recommend it. And he was assured that this something else was durability and service. His battle with rust began on the third day; and little errors of construction and design and set-up (misaligned wheels that wore out his tires within five thousand kilometers, a windshield wiper that daintily avoided contact with the glass, a rear hatch catch so designed as to require two hands to close it, so that loading and unloading was a burlesque of inefficient motion) required that he return the automobile frequently to the dealer some 150 kilometers away. It was the dealer's view that these problems were the manufacturer's and the manufacturer's view that the responsibility lay with the dealer; and after months of receiving polite but vague letters of disinterested condolence from the company, Hel decided to bite the bullet and set the car to the brutish tasks of transporting sheep and bringing equipment up rough mountain roads, hoping that it would soon fall apart and justify his purchase of a vehicle with a more reliable service infrastructure. Sadly, while he had found no truth in the company's reputation for service, there was some basis for the car's claim to durability and, while it always ran poorly, it always ran. Under other circumstances, Hel would have viewed durability as a virtue in a machine, but he could find little consolation in the threat that his problems would go on for years.

Having observed Pierre's skills as a chauffeur, Hel thought to shorten his torment by allowing Pierre to drive the car whenever he chose. But this plot was foiled because ironic fate shielded Pierre from accidents. So Hel came to accept his Volvo as one of the comic burdens of life, but he allowed himself to vent his frustration by kicking or bashing the car each time he got in or out.

It was not long before his caving associates fell into the practice of bashing his Volvo whenever they passed it, at first as a joke and later by habit. Soon they and the young men they traveled with began to bash any Volvo they passed. And in the illogical way of fads, Volvo-bashing began to spread, here taking on an anti-Establishment tone, there a quality of youthful exuberance; here as an expression of antimaterialism, there as a manifestation of in-cult with-itness.

Even owners of Volvos began to accept the bashing craze, for it proved that they traveled in circles of the internationally aware. And there were cases of owners secretly bashing their own Volvos, to gain unearned reputations as cosmopolites. There were persistent, though probably apocryphal, rumors that Volvo was planning to introduce a prebashed model in its efforts to attract the smart set to an automobile that had sacrificed everything to passenger safety (despite their use of Firestone 500 tires on many models) and primarily appealed to affluent egotists who assumed that the continuance of their lives was important to the destiny of Man.

After his shower, Hel found laid out in the dressing room his black broadcloth Edwardian suit, which had been designed to protect either guests in simple business suits or those in evening wear from feeling under- or overdressed. When he met Hana at the top of the principal staircase, she was in a long dress of Cantonese style that had the same social ambiguity as his suit.

"Where's Le Cagot?" he asked as they went down to a small salon to await their guests. "I've felt his presence several times today, but I haven't heard or seen him."

"I assume he is dressing in his room." Hana laughed lightly. "He told me that I would be so taken by his new clothes that I would swoon amorously into his arms."

"Oh, God." Le Cagot's taste in clothes, as in most things, ran to operatic overstatement. "And Miss Stern?"

"She has been in her room most of the afternoon. You evidently gave her rather a bad time during your chat."

"Hm-m-m."

"She'll be down shortly after Pierre returns with clothes for her. Do you want to hear the menu?"

"No, I'm sure it's perfect."

"Not that, but adequate. These guests give us a chance to be rid of the roebuck old M. Ibar gave us. It's been hanging just over a week, so it should be ready. Is there something special I should know about our guests?"

"They are strangers to me. Enemies, I believe."

"How should I treat them?"

"Like any guest in our house. With that particular charm of yours that makes all men feel interesting and important. I want these people to be off balance and unsure of themselves. They are Americans. Just as you or I would be uncomfortable at a barbecue, they suffer from social vertigo at a proper dinner. Even their *gratin*, the jetset, are culturally as bogus as airlines cuisine."

"What on earth is a 'barbecue'?"

"A primitive tribal ritual featuring paper plates, elbows, flying insects, encrusted meat, hush puppies, and beer."

"I daren't ask what a 'hush puppy' is."

"Don't."

They sat together in the darkening salon, their fingers touching. The sun was down behind the mountains, and through the open *porte fenêtres* they could see a silver gloaming that seemed to rise from the ground of the park, its dim light filling the space beneath the black-green pines, the effect rendered mutable and dear by the threat of an incoming storm.

"How long did you live in America, Nikko?"

"About three years, just after I left Japan. In fact, I still have an apartment in New York."

"I've always wanted to visit New York."

"You'd be disappointed. It's a frightened city in which everyone is in hot and narrow pursuit of money: the bankers, the muggers, the businessmen, the whores. If you walk the streets and watch their eyes, you see two things: fear and fury. They are diminished people hovering behind triple-locked doors. They fight with men they don't hate, and make love to women they don't like. Asea in a mongrel society, they borrow orts and leavings from the world's cultures. Kir is a popular drink among those desperate to be 'with it,' and they affect Perrier, although they have one of the world's great waters in the local village of Saratoga. Their best French restaurants offer what we would think of as thirty-franc meals for ten times that much, and the service is characterized by insufferable snottiness on the part of the waiter, usually an incompetent peasant who happens to be able to read the menu. But then, Americans enjoy being abused by waiters. It's their only way of judging the quality of the food. On the other hand, if one must live in urban America—a cruel and unusual punishment at best—one might as well live in the real New York, rather than in the artificial ones farther inland. And there are some good things. Harlem has real tone. The municipal library is adequate. There is a man named Jimmy Fox who is the best barman in North America. And twice I even found myself in conversation about the nature of *shibui*—not *shibumi*, of course. It's more within the range of the mercantile mind to talk of the characteristics of the beautiful than to discuss the nature of Beauty."

She struck a long match and lighted a lamp on the table before them. "But I remember you mentioning once that you enjoyed your home in America."

"Oh, that was not New York. I own a couple of thousand hectares in the state of Wyoming, in the mountains."

"Wy-om-ing. Romantic-sounding name. Is it beautiful?"

"More sublime, I would say. It's too ragged and harsh to be beautiful. It is to this Pyrenees country what an ink sketch is to a finished painting. Much of the open land of America is attractive. Sadly, it is populated by Americans. But then, one could say a similar thing of Greece or Ireland."

"Yes, I know what you mean. I've been to Greece. I worked there for a year, employed by a shipping magnate."

"Oh? You never mentioned that."

"There was nothing really to mention. He was very rich and very vulgar, and he sought to purchase class and status, usually in the form of spectacular wives. While in his employ, I surrounded him with quiet comfort. He made no other demands of me. By that time, there were no other demands he could make."

"I see. Ah—here comes Le Cagot."

Hana had heard nothing, because Le Cagot was sneaking down the stairs to surprise them with his sartorial splendor. Hel smiled to himself because Le Cagot's preceding aura carried qualities of boyish mischief and ultra-sly delight.

He appeared at the door, his bulk half-filling the frame, his arms in cruciform to display his fine new clothes. "Regard! Regard, Niko, and burn with envy!"

Obviously, the evening clothes had come from a theatrical costumer. They were an eclectic congregation, although the *fin-de-siècle* impulse dominated, with a throat wrapping of white silk in place of a cravat, and a richly brocaded waistcoat with double rows of rhinestone buttons. The black swallowtail coat was long, and its lapels were turned in gray silk. With his still-wet hair parted in the middle and his bushy beard covering most of the cravat, he had something of the appearance of a middle-aged Tolstoi dressed up as a Mississippi riverboat gambler. The large yellow rose he had pinned to his lapel was oddly correct, consonant with this amalgam of robust bad taste. He strode back and forth, brandishing his long *makila* like a walking stick. The *makila* had been in his family for generations, and there were nicks and dents on the polished ash shaft and a small bit missing from the marble knob, evidences of use as a defensive weapon by grandfathers and great-grandfathers. The handle of a *makila* unscrews, revealing a twenty-centimeter blade designed for foining, while the butt in the left hand is used for crossed parries, and its heavy marble knob is an effective clubbing weapon. Although now largely decorative and ceremonial, the *makila* once figured importantly in the personal safety of the Basque man alone on the road at night or roving in the high mountains.

"That is a wonderful suit," Hana said with excessive sincerity.

"Is it not? Is it not?"

"How did you come by this . . . suit?" Hel asked.

"It was given to me."

"In result of your losing a bet?"

"Not at all. It was given to me by a woman in appreciation for . . . ah, but to mention the details would be ungallant. So, when do we eat? Where are these guests of yours?"

"They are approaching up the allée right now," Hel said, rising and crossing toward the central hall.

Le Cagot peered out through the *porte fenêtre*, but he could see nothing because evening and the storm had pressed the last of the gloaming into the earth. Still, he had become used to Hel's proximity sensitivity, so he assumed there was someone out there.

Just as Pierre was reaching for the handle of the pull bell, Hel opened the door. The chandeliers of the hall were behind him, so he could read the faces of his three guests, while his own was in shadow. One of them was obviously the leader; the second was a gunny CIA type, Class of '53; and the third was an Arab of vague personality. All three showed signs of recent emotional drain resulting from their ride up the mountain road without headlights, and with Pierre showing off his remarkable driving skills.

"Do come in," Hel said, stepping from the doorway and allowing them to pass before him into the reception hall, where they were met by Hana who smiled as she approached.

"It was good of you to accept our invitation on such short notice. I am Hana. This is Nicholai Hel. And here is our friend, M. Le Cagot." She offered her hand.

The leader found his aplomb. "Good evening. This is Mr. Starr. Mr. . . . Haman. And I am Mr. Diamond." The first crack of thunder punctuated his last word.

Hel laughed aloud. "That must have been embarrassing. Nature seems to be in a melodramatic mood."

PART THREE

SEKI

Château d'Etchebar

FROM THE MOMENT they had the heart-squeezing experience of driving with Pierre in the battered Volvo, the three guests never quite got their feet on firm social ground. Diamond had expected to get down to cases immediately with Hel, but that clearly was not on. While Hana was conducting the party to the blue-and-gold salon for a glass of Lillet before dinner, Diamond held back and said to Hel, "I suppose you're wondering why—"

"After dinner."

Diamond stiffened just perceptibly, then smiled and half-bowed in a gesture he instantly regretted as theatrical. That damned clap of thunder!

Hana refilled glasses and handed around canapés as she guided the conversation in such a way that Darryl Starr was soon addressing her as "Ma'am" and feeling that her interest in Texas and things Texan was a veiled fascination with him; and the PLO trainee called Haman grinned and nodded with each display of concern for his comfort and well being. Even Diamond soon found himself recounting impressions of the Basque country and feeling both lucid and insightful. All five men rose when Hana excused herself, saying that she had to attend to the young lady who would be dining with them.

There was a palpable silence after she left, and Hel allowed the slight discomfort to lie there, as he watched his guests with distant amusement.

It was Darryl Starr who found a relevant remark to fill the void. "Nice place you got here."

"Would you like to see the house?" Hel asked.

"Well . . . no, don't trouble yourself on my account."

Hel said a few words aside to Le Cagot, who then crossed to Starr and with gruff bonhomie pulled him from his chair by his arm and offered to show him the garden and the gun room. Starr explained that he was comfortable where he was, thank you, but Le Cagot's grin was accompanied by painful pressure around the American's upper arm.

"Indulge my whim in this, my good friend," he said.

Starr shrugged—as best he could—and went along.

Diamond was disturbed, torn between a desire to control the situation and an impulse, which he recognized to be childish, to demonstrate that his social graces were as sophisticated as Hel's. He realized that both he and this event were being managed, and he resented it. For something to say, he mentioned, "I see you're not having anything to drink before dinner, Mr. Hel."

"That's true."

Hel did not intend to give Diamond the comfort of rebounding conversational overtures; he would simply absorb each gesture and leave the chore of initiation constantly with Diamond, who chuckled and said, "I feel I should tell you that your driver is a strange one."

"Oh?"

"Yes. He parked the car out in the village square and we had to walk the rest of the way. I was sure the storm would catch us."

"I don't permit automobiles on my grounds."

"Yes, but after he parked the car, he gave the front door a kick that I'm sure must have dented it."

Hel frowned and said, "How odd. I'll have to talk to him about that."

At this point, Hana and Miss Stern joined the men, the young woman looking refined and desirable in a summer tea dress she had chosen from those Hana had bought for her. Hel watched Hannah closely as she was introduced to the two men, grudgingly admiring her control and ease while confronting the people who had engineered the killing of her comrades in Rome. Hana beckoned her to sit beside her and managed immediately to focus the social attention on her youth and beauty, guiding her in such a way that only Hel could sense traces of the reality vertigo the girl was feeling. At one moment, he caught her eyes and nodded slightly in approval of aplomb. There was some bottom to this girl after all. Perhaps if she were in the company of a woman like Hana for four or five years . . . who knows?

There was a gruff laugh from the hall and Le Cagot reentered, his arm around Starr's shoulders. The Texan looked a bit shaken and his hair was tousled, but Le Cagot's mission was accomplished; the shoulder holster under Starr's left armpit was now empty.

"I don't know about you, my friends," Le Cagot said in his accented English with the overgrowled *r* of the Francophone who has finally conquered that difficult consonant, "but I am ravenous! *Bouffons!* I could eat for four!"

The dinner, served by the light of two candelabra on the table and lamps in wall sconces, was not sumptuous, but it was good: trout from the local *gave,* roebuck with cherry sauce, garden vegetables cooked in the Japanese style, the courses separated by conversation and appropriate ices, finally a salad of greens before dessert of fruit and cheeses. Compatible wines accompanied each entrée and *relevé,* and the particular problem of game in a fruit sauce was solved by a fine pink wine which, while it could not support the flavors, did not contradict them either. Diamond noted with slight discomfort that Hel and Hana were served only rice and vegetables during the early part of the meal, though they joined the others in salad. Further, although their hostess drank wine with the rest of them, Hel's glass was little more than moistened with each bottle, so that in total he drank less than a full glass.

"You don't drink, Mr. Hel?" he asked.

"But I do, as you see. It is only that I don't find two sips of wine more delicious than one."

Fadding with wines and waxing pseudopoetic in their failure to describe tastes lucidly is an affectation of socially mobile Americans, and Diamond fancied himself something of an authority. He sipped, swilled and examined the pink that accompanied the roebuck, then said, "Ah, there are Tavels, and there are Tavels."

Hel frowned slightly. "Ah . . . . that's true, I suppose."

"But this *is* a Tavel, isn't it?"

When Hel shrugged and changed the subject diplomatically, the nape of Diamond's neck horripilated with embarrassment. He had been so sure it was Tavel.

Throughout dinner, Hel maintained a distant silence, his eyes seldom leaving Diamond, though they appeared to focus slightly behind him. Effortlessly, Hana evoked jokes and stories from each of the guests in turn and her delight and amusement was such that each felt he had outdone himself in cleverness and charm. Even Starr, who had been withdrawn and petulant after his rough treatment at Le Cagot's hands, was soon telling Hana of his boyhood in Flatrock, Texas, and of his adventures fighting against the gooks in Korea.

At first Le Cagot attended to the task of filling himself with food. Soon the ends of his wrapped cravat were dangling, and the long swallowtailed coat was cast aside, so by the time he was ready to dominate the party and hold forth at his usual length with vigorous and sometimes bawdy tales, he was down to his spectacular waistcoat with its rhinestone buttons. He was seated next to Hannah, and out of the blue he reached over, placed his big warm hand on her thigh, and gave it a friendly squeeze. "Tell me something in all frankness, beautiful girl. Are you struggling against your desire for me? Or have you given up the struggle? I ask you this only that I may know how best to proceed. In the meantime, eat, eat! You will need your strength. So! You men are from America, eh? Me, I was in America three times. That's why my English is so good. I could probably pass for an American, eh? From the point of view of accent, I mean."

"Oh, no doubt of it," Diamond said. He was beginning to realize how important to such men as Hel and Le Cagot was the heraldry of sheer style, even when faced by enemies, and he wanted to show that he could play any game they could.

"But of course once people saw the clear truth shining in my eyes, and heard the music of my thoughts, the game would be up! They would know I was not an American."

Hel concealed a slight smile behind a finger.

"You're hard on Americans," Diamond said.

"Maybe so," Le Cagot admitted. "And maybe I am being unjust. We get to see only the dregs of them here: merchants on vacation with their brassy wives, military men with their papier-mâché, gum-chewing women, young people seeking to 'find themselves,' and worst of all, academic drudges who manage to convince granting agencies that the world would be improved if they were beshat upon Europe. I sometimes think that America's major export product is bewildered professors on sabbaticals. Is it true that everyone in the United States over twenty-five years of age has a Ph.D?" Le Cagot had the bit well between his teeth, and he began one of his tales of adventure, based as usual on a real event, but decorated with such improvements upon dull truth as occurred to him as he went along. Secure in the knowledge that Le Cagot would dominate things for many minutes, Hel let his face freeze in a politely amused expression while his mind sorted out and organized the moves that would begin after dinner.

Le Cagot had turned to Diamond. "I am going to shed some light upon history for you, American guest of my friend. Everyone knows that the Basque and the Fascists have been enemies since before the birth of history. But few know the real source of this ancient antipathy. It was our fault, really. I confess it at last. Many years ago, the Basque people gave up the practice of shitting by the roadside, and in doing this we deprived the Falange of its principal source of nourishment. And that is the truth, I swear it by Methuselah's Wrinkled B—"

"Beñat?" Hana interrupted, indicating the young girl with a nod of her head.

"—by Methuselah's Wrinkled *Brow*. What's wrong with you?" he asked Hana, his eyes moist with hurt. "Do you think I have forgotten my manners?"

Hel pushed back his chair and rose. "Mr. Diamond and I have a bit of business to attend to. I suggest you take your cognac on the terrace. You might just have time before the rain comes."

As they stepped down from the principal hall to the Japanese garden, Hel took Diamond by the arm. "Allow me to guide you; I didn't think to bring a lantern."

"Oh? I know about your mystic proximity sense, but I didn't know you could see in the dark as well."

"I can't. But we are on my ground. Perhaps you would be well advised to remember that."

Hel lighted two spirit lamps in the gun room and gestured Diamond toward a low table on which there was a bottle and glasses. "Serve yourself. I'll be with you in a moment." He carried one of the lamps to a bookcase filled with pull drawers of file cards, some two hundred thousand cards in all. "May I assume that Diamond is your real name?"

"It is."

Hel searched for the proper key card containing all cross references to Diamond. "And your initials are?"

"Jack O." Diamond smiled to himself as he compared Hel's crude card file with his own sophisticated information system, Fat Boy. "I didn't see any reason to use an alias, assuming that you would see a family resemblance between me and my brother."

"Your brother?"

"Don't you remember my brother?"

"Not offhand." Hel muttered to himself as he fingered through a drawer of cards. As the information on Hel's cards was in six languages, the headings were arranged phonetically. "D. D-A, D-AI diphthong, D-AI-M . . . ah, here we are. Diamond, Jack O. Do have a drink, Mr. Diamond. My filing system is a bit cumbersome, and I haven't been called on to use it since my retirement."

Diamond was surprised that Hel did not even remember his brother. To cover his temporary confusion, he picked up the bottle and examined the label. "Armagnac?"

"Hm-m-m." Hel made a mental note of the cross-reference indices and sought those cards. "We're close to the Armagnac country here. You'll find that very old and very good. So you are a servant of the Mother Company, are you? I can therefore assume that you already have a good deal of information about me from your computer. You'll have to give me a moment to catch up with you."

Diamond carried his glass with him and wandered about the gun room, looking at the uncommon weapons in cases and racks along the walls. Some of these he recognized: the nerve-gas tube, air-driven glass sliver projectors, dry-ice guns, and the like. But others were foreign to him: simple metal disks, a device that seemed to be two short rods of hickory connected by a metal link, a thimblelike cone that slipped over the finger and came to a sharp point. On the table beside the Armagnac bottle he found a small, French-made automatic. "A pretty common sort of weapon among all this exotica," he said.

Hel glanced up from the card he was reading. "Oh yes, I noticed that when we came in. It's not mine, actually. It belongs to your man, the bucolic tough from Texas. I thought he might feel more relaxed without it."

"The thoughtful host."

"Thank you." Hel set aside the card he was reading and pulled open another drawer in search of the next. "That gun tells us rather a lot. Obviously, you decided not to travel armed because of the nuisance of boarding inspections. So your lad was given the gun after he got here. Its make tells us he received the gun from French police authorities. That means you have them in your pocket."

Diamond shrugged. "France needs oil too, just like every other industrial country."

"Yes. *Ici on n'a pas d'huile, mais on a des idées.*"

"Meaning?"

"Nothing really. Just a slogan from French internal propaganda. So I see here that the Major Diamond from Tokyo was your brother. That's interesting—mildly interesting, anyway." Now that he considered it, Hel found a certain resemblance between the two, the narrow face, the intense black eyes set rather close together, the falciform nose, the thin upper lip and heavy, bloodless lower, a certain intensity of manner.

"I thought you would have guessed that when you first heard my name."

"Actually, I had pretty much forgotten him. After all, our account was settled. So you began working for the Mother Company in the Early Retirement Program, did you? That is certainly consonant with your brother's career."

Some years before, the Mother Company had discovered that its executives after the age of fifty began to be notably less productive, just at the time the Company was paying them the most. The problem was presented to Fat Boy, who offered the solution of organizing an Early Retirement Divsion that would arrange for the accidental demise of a small percentage of such men, usually while on vacation, and usually of apparent stroke or heart attack. The savings to the Company were considerable. Diamond had risen to the head of this division before being promoted to conducting Mother Company's control over CIA and NSA.

". . . so it appears that both you and your brother found a way to combine native sadism with the comforting fringe benefits of working for big business, he for the army and CIA, you for the oil combines. Both products of the American Dream, the mercantile mumpsimus. Just bright young men trying to get ahead."

"But at least neither of us ended up as hired killers."

"Rubbish. Any man is a killer who works for a company that pollutes, strip-mines, and contaminates the air and water. The fact that you and your unlamented brother killed from institutional and patriotic ambush doesn't mean you're not killers—it only means you're cowards."

"You think a coward would walk into your lair as I have done?"

"A certain kind of coward would. A coward who was afraid of his cowardice."

Diamond laughed thinly. "You really hate me, don't you."

"Not at all. You're not a person, you're an organization man. One couldn't hate you as an individual; one could only hate the phylum. At all events, you're not the sort to evoke such intense emotions as hate. Disgust might be closer to the mark."

"Still, for all the disdain of your breeding and private education, it is people like me—what you sneeringly call the merchant class—who hire you and send you out to do their dirty work."

Hel shrugged. "It has always been so. Throughout all history, the merchants have cowered behind the walls of their towns, while the paladins did battle to protect them, in return for which the merchants have always fawned and bowed and played the lickspittle. One cannot really blame them. They are not bred to courage. And, more significantly, you can't put bravery in the bank." Hel read the last information card quickly and tossed it on the stack to be refiled later. "All right, Diamond. Now I know who you are and what you are. At least, I know as much about you as I need to, or choose to."

"I assume your information came from the Gnome?"

"Much of it came from the person you call the Gnome."

"We would give a great deal to know how that man came by his intelligence."

"I don't doubt it. Of course, I wouldn't tell you if I knew. But the fact is, I haven't the slightest idea."

"But you do know the identity and location of the Gnome."

Hel laughed. "Of course I do. But the gentleman and I are old friends."

"He's nothing more or less than a blackmailer."

"Nonsense. He is an artisan in the craft of information. He has never taken money from a man in return for concealing the facts he collects from all over the world."

"No, but he provides men like you with the information that protects you from punishment by governments, and for that he makes a lot of money."

"The protection is worth a great deal. But if it will set your mind at rest, the man you call the Gnome is very ill. It is doubtful that he will live out the year."

"So you will soon be without protection?"

"I shall miss him as a man of wit and charm. But the loss of protection is a matter of little importance to me. I am, as Fat Boy must have informed you, fully retired. Now what do you say we get on with our little business."

"Before we start, I have a question I want to ask you."

"I have a question for you as well, but let's leave that for later. So that we don't waste time with exposition, allow me to give you the picture in a couple of sentences, and you may correct me if I stray." Hel leaned against the wall, his face in the shadows and his soft prison voice unmodulated. "We begin with Black Septembrists murdering Israeli athletes in Munich. Among the slain was Asa Stern's son. Asa Stern vows to have vengeance. He organizes a pitiful little amateur cell to this end—don't think badly of Mr. Stern for the paucity of this effort; he was a good man, but he was sick and partially drugged. Arab intelligence gets wind of this effort. The Arabs, probably through an OPEC representative, ask the Mother Company to erase this irritant. The Mother Company turns the task over to you, expecting you to use your CIA bully boys to do the job. You learn that the revenge cell—I believe they called themselves the Munich Five—was on its way to London to put the last surviving members of the Munich murder away. CIA arranges a spoiling action in Rome International. By the way, I assume those two fools back in the house were involved in the raid?"

"Yes."

"And you're punishing them by making them clean up after themselves?"

"That's about it."

"You're taking the risks, Mr. Diamond. A foolish associate is more dangerous than a clever opponent."

"That's my concern."

"To be sure. All right, your people do a messy and incomplete job in Rome. Actually, you should be grateful they did as well as they did. With a combination of Arab Intelligence and the CIA competence, you're lucky they didn't go to the wrong airport. But that, as you have said, is your concern. Somehow, probably when the raid was evaluated in Washington, you discovered that the Israeli boys were not going to London. They carried airline tickets for Pau. You also discovered that one of the cell members, the Miss Stern with whom you just took dinner, had been overlooked by your killers. Your computer was able to relate me to Asa Stern, and the Pau destination nailed it down. Is that it?"

"That roughly is it."

"All right. So much for catching up. The ball, I believe, is in your court."

Diamond had not yet decided how he would present his case, what combination of threat and promise would serve to neutralize Nicholai Hel. To gain time, he pointed to a pair of odd-looking pistols with curved handles like old-fashioned dueling weapons and double nine-inch barrels that were slightly flared at the ends. "What are these?"

"Shotguns, in a way of speaking."

"Shotguns?"

"Yes. A Dutch industrialist had them made for me. A gift in return for a rather narrow action involving his son who was held captive on a train by Moluccan terrorists. Each gun, as you see, has two hammers which drop simultaneously on special shotgun shells with powerful charges that scatter loads of half-centimeter ball bearings. All the weapons in this room are designed for a particular situation. These are for close work in the dark, or for putting away a roomful of men on the instant of break-in. At two meters from the barrel, they lay down a spread pattern a meter in diameter." Hel's bottle-green eyes settled on Diamond. "Do you intend to spend the evening talking about guns?"

"No. I assume that Miss Stern has asked you to help her kill the Septembrists now in London?"

Hel nodded.

"And she took it for granted that you would help, because of your friendship for her uncle?"

"She made that assumption."

"And what do you intend to do?"

"I intend to listen to your proposal."

"My proposal?"

"Isn't that what merchants do? Make proposals?"

"I wouldn't exactly call it a proposal."

"What would you call it?"

"I would call it a display of deterrent action, partially already on line, partially ready to be brought on line, should you be so foolish as to interfere."

Hel's eyes crinkled in a smile that did not include his lips. He made a rolling gesture with his hand, inviting Diamond to get on with it.

"I'll confess to you that, under different conditions, neither the Mother Company nor the Arab interests we are allied with would care much one way or another what happened to the homicidal maniacs of the PLO. But these are difficult times within the Arab community, and the PLO has become something of a rallying banner, an issue more of public relations than of private taste. For this reason, the Mother Company is committed to their protection. This means that you will not be allowed to interfere with those who intend to hijack that plane in London."

"How will I be prevented?"

"Do you recall that you used to own several thousand acres of land in Wyoming?"

"I assume the tense is not a matter of grammatical carelessness."

"That's right. Part of that land was in Boyle County, the rest in Custer County. If you contact the county clerk offices, you will discover that there exists no record of your having purchased that land. Indeed, the records show that the land in question is now, and has been for many years, in the hands of one of Mother Company's affiliates. There is some coal under the land, and it is scheduled for strip-mining."

"Do I understand that if I cooperate with you, the land will be returned to me?"

"Not at all. That land, representing as it does most of what you have saved for your retirement, has been taken from you as a punishment for daring to involve yourself in the affairs of the Mother Company."

"May I assume you suggested this punishment?"

Diamond tipped his head to the side. "I had that pleasure."

"You are a vicious little bastard, aren't you. You're telling me that if I pull out of this affair, the land will be spared from strip-mining?"

Diamond pushed out his lower lip. "Oh, I'm afraid I couldn't make an arrangement like that. America needs all its natural energy to make it independent from foreign sources." He smiled at this repetition of the worn party line. "Then too, you can't put beauty in the bank." He was enjoying himself.

"I don't understand what you're doing, Diamond. If you intend to take the land and destroy it, no matter what I do, then what leverage does that give you over my actions?"

"As I said, taking your land was in the nature of a warning shot across your bow. And a punishment."

"Ah, I see. A personal punishment. From you. For your brother?"

"That's right."

"He deserved death, you know. I was tortured for three days. This face of mine is not completely mobile even now, after all the operations."

"He was my brother! Now, let's pass on to the sanctions and penalties you will incur, should you fail to cooperate. Under the key group KL443, Code Number 45-389-75, you had approximately one-and-a-half million dollars in gold bullion in the Federal Bank of Zurich. That represented nearly all the rest of what you intended to retire on. Please note the past tense again."

Hel was silent for a moment. "The Swiss too need oil."

"The Swiss need oil too," Diamond echoed. "That money will reappear in your account seven days after the successful accomplishment of the hijacking by the Septembrists. So you see, far from interrupting their plans and killing some of their number, it would benefit you to do everything in your power to make sure they succeed."

"And presumably that money serves also as your personal protection."

"Precisely. Should anything happen to me or my friends while we are your guests, that money disappears, victim of an accounting error."

Hel was attracted to the sliding doors giving out on his Japanese garden. The rain had come, hissing in the gravel and vibrating the tips of black and silver foliage. "And that is it?"

"Not quite. We are aware that you probably have a couple of hundred thousand here and there as emergency funds. A psychological profile of you from Fat Boy tells us that it is just possible that you may put such things as loyalty to a dead friend and his niece ahead of all considerations of personal benefit. All part of being selectively bred and tutored in Japanese concepts of honor, don't you know. We are prepared for that foolish eventuality as well. In the first place, the British MI-5 and MI-6 are alerted to keep tabs on you and to arrest you the moment you set foot on their soil. To assist them in this task, the French Internal Security forces are committed to making sure you do not leave this immediate district. Descriptions of you have been distributed. If you are discovered in any village other than your own, you will be shot on sight. Now, I am familiar with your history of accomplishments in the face of improbable odds, and I realize that, for you, these forces we have put on line are more in the nature of nuisances than deterrents. But we are going through the motions nonetheless. The Mother Company must be *seen* to be doing everything in Her power to protect the London Septembrists. Should that protection fail—and I almost hope it does—then the Mother Company must be seen to mete out punishment—punishment of an intensity that will satisfy our Arab friends. And you know what those people are like. To satisfy their taste for revenge, we would be forced to do something very thorough and very . . . imaginative."

Hel was silent for a moment. "I told you at the outset of our chat that I had a question for you, merchant. Here it is. Why did you come here?"

"That should be obvious."

"Perhaps I didn't accent my question properly. Why did *you* come here? Why didn't you send a messenger? Why bring your face into my presence and run the risk of my remembering you?"

Diamond stared at Hel for a moment. "I'll be honest with you . . ."

"Don't break any habits on my account."

"I wanted to tell you about the loss of your land in Wyoming personally. I wanted to display in person the mass of punishment I have designed, if you are rash enough to disobey the Mother Company. It's something I owe my brother."

Hel's emotionless gaze settled on Diamond, who stood rigid with defiance, his eyes shining with a tear glaze that revealed the body fright within him. He had taken a dangerous plunge, this merchant. He had left the cover of laws and systems behind which corporate men hide and from which their power derives, and he had run the risk of showing his face to Nicholai Alexandrovitch Hel. Diamond was subconsciously aware of his dependent anonymity, of his role as a social insect clawing about in the frantic nests of profit and success. Like others of his caste, he found spiritual solace in the cowboy myth. At this moment,

Diamond saw himself as a virile individualist striding bravely down the dusty street of a Hollywood back lot, his hand hovering an inch above the computer in his holster. It is revealing of the American culture that its prototypic hero is the cowboy: an uneducated, boorish, Victorian migrant agricultural worker. At base, Diamond's role was ludicrous: the Tom Mix of big business facing a *yojimbo* with a garden. Diamond possessed the most extensive computer system in the world; Hel had some file cards. Diamond had all the governments of the industrialized West in his pocket; Hel had some Basque friends. Diamond represented atomic energy, the earth's oil supply, the military/industrial symbiosis, the corrupt and corrupting governments established by the Wad to shield itself from responsibility; Hel represented *shibumi*, a faded concept of reluctant beauty. And yet, it was obvious that Hel had a considerable advantage in any battle that might be joined.

Hel turned his face away and shook his head slightly. "This must be embarrassing to be you."

During the silence, Diamond's fingernails had dug into his palms. He cleared his throat. "Whatever you think of me, I cannot believe that you will sacrifice the years remaining to you for one gesture that would be appreciated by no one but that middle-class dumpling I met at dinner. I think I know what you are going to do, Mr. Hel. You are going to consider this matter at length and realize at last that a handful of sadistic Arabs is not worth this home and life you have made for yourself here; you will realize that you are not honor-bound to the desperate hopes of a sick and drug-befuddled man; and finally you will decide to back off. One of the reasons you will do this is because you would consider it demeaning to make an empty gesture of courage to impress me, a man you despise. Now, I don't expect you to tell me that you're backing off right now. That would be too humiliating, too damaging to your precious sense of dignity. But that is what you will do at last. To be truthful, I almost wish you would persist in this matter. It would be a pity to see the punishments I have devised for you go unused. But, fortunately for you, the Chairman of the Mother Company is adamant that the Septembrists go unmolested. We are arranging what will be called the Camp David Peace Talks in the course of which Israel will be pressured into leaving her southern and eastern borders naked. As a by-product of these talks, the PLO will be dealt out of the Middle Eastern game. They have served their irritant purpose. But the Chairman wants to keep the Palestinians mollified until this coup comes off. You see, Mr. Hel, you're swimming in deep currents, involved with forces just a little beyond shotgun pistols and cute gardens."

Hel regarded Diamond in silence for a moment. Then he turned toward his garden. "This conversation is over," he said quietly.

"I see." Diamond took a card from his pocket. "I can be contacted at this number. I shall be back at my office within ten hours. When you tell me that you have decided not to interfere in this business, I shall initiate the release of your Swiss funds."

As Hel no longer seemed to be aware of his presence, Diamond put the card on the table. "There's nothing more for us to discuss at this time, so I'll be on my way."

"What? Oh, yes. I am sure you can find your way out, Diamond. Hana will serve you coffee before sending you and your lackeys back to the village. No doubt Pierre has been fortifying himself with wine for the past few hours and will be in good form to give you a memorable ride."

"Very well. But first . . . there was that question I had for you."

"Well?"

"That rosé I had with dinner. What was it?"

"Tavel, of course."

"I knew it!"

"No, you didn't. You almost knew it."

The arm of the garden extending toward the Japanese building had been designed for listening to rain. Hel worked for weeks each rainy season, barefoot and wearing only sodden shorts, as he tuned the garden. The gutters and downspouts had been drilled and shaped, plants moved and removed, gravel distributed, sounding stones arranged in the stream, until the blend of soprano hissing of rain through gravel, the basso drip onto broad-leaved plants, the reedy resonances of quivering bamboo leaves, the counterpoint of the gurgling stream, all were balanced in volume in such a way that, if one sat precisely in the middle of the *tatami*'d room, no single sound dominated. The concentrating listener could draw one timbre out of the background, or let it merge again, as he shifted the focus of his attention, much as the insomniac can tune in or out the ticking of a clock. The effort required to control the instrument of a well-tuned garden is sufficient to repress quotidian worries and anxieties, but this anodyne property is not the principal goal of the gardener, who must be more devoted to creating a garden than to using it.

Hel sat in the gun room, hearing the rain, but lacking the peace of spirit to listen to it. There was bad *aji* in this affair. It wasn't of a piece, and it was treacherously . . . personal. It was Hel's way to play against the patterns on the board, not against fleshy, inconsistent living opponents. In this business, moves would be made for illogical reasons; there would be human filters between cause and effect. The whole thing stank of passion and sweat.

He released a long sigh in a thin jet of breath. "Well?" he asked. "And what do you make of all this?"

There was no answer. Hel felt her aura take on a leporine palpitation between the urge to flee and fear of movement. He slid back the door panel to the tea room and beckoned with his finger.

Hannah Stern stood in the doorway, her hair wet with rain, and her sodden dress clinging to her body and legs. She was embarrassed at being caught eavesdropping, but defiantly unwilling to apologize. In her view, the importance of the matters at hand outweighed any consideration of good form and rules of polite behavior. Hel might have told her that, in the long run, the "minor" virtues are the only ones that matter. Politeness is more reliable than the moist virtues of compassion, charity, and sincerity; just as fair play is more important than the abstraction of justice. The major virtues tend to disintegrate under the pressures of convenient rationalization. But good form is good form, and it stands immutable in the storm of circumstance.

Hel might have told her this, but he was not interested in her spiritual education, and he had no wish to decorate the unperfectible. At all events, she would probably have understood only the words, and if she were to penetrate to meanings, what use would be the barriers and foundations of good form to a woman whose life would be lived out in some Scarsdale or other?

"Well?" he asked again. "What did you make of all that?"

She shook her head. "I had no idea they were so . . . organized; so . . . cold-blooded. I've caused you a lot of trouble, haven't I."

"I don't hold you responsible for anything that has happened so far. I have long known that I have a karma debt. Considering the fact that my work has cut across the grain of social organization, a certain amount of bad luck would be expected. I've not had that bad luck, and so I've built up a karma debt; a weight of antichance against me. You were the vehicle for karma balance, but I don't consider you the cause. Do you understand any of that?"

She shrugged. "What are you going to do?"

The storm was passing, and the winds behind it blew in from the garden and made Hannah shudder in her wet dress.

"There are padded kimonos in that chest. Get out of those clothes."

"I'm all right."

"Do as I tell you. The tragic heroine with the sniffles is too ludicrous an image."

It was consonant with the too-brief shorts, the unbuttoned shirt front, and the surprise Hannah affected (believed she genuinely felt) when men responded to her as an object that she unzipped and stepped out of the wet dress before she sought out the dry kimono. She had never confessed to herself that she took social advantage of having a desirable body that appeared to be available. If she had thought of it, she would have labeled her automatic exhibitionism a healthy acceptance of her body—an absence of "hang-ups."

"What are you going to do?" she asked again, as she wrapped the warm kimono about her.

"The real question is what are you going to do. Do you still intend to press on with this business? To throw yourself off the pier in the hopes that I will have to jump in after you?"

"Would you? Jump in after me?"

"I don't know."

Hannah stared out into the dark of the garden and hugged the comforting kimono to herself. "I don't know . . . I don't know. It all seemed so clear just yesterday. I knew what I had to do, what was the only just and right thing to do."

"And now. . . ?"

She shrugged and shook her head. "You'd rather I went home and forgot all about it, wouldn't you?"

"Yes. And that might not be as easy as you think, either. Diamond knows about you. Getting you safely home will take a little doing."

"And what happens to the Septembrists who murdered our athletes in Munich?"

"Oh, they'll die. Everyone dies, eventually."

"But . . . if I just go home, then Avrim's death and Chaim's would be pointless!"

"That's true. They were pointless deaths, and nothing you might do would change that."

Hannah stepped close to Hel and looked up at him, her face full of confusion and doubt. She wanted to be held, comforted, told that everything would be just fine.

"You'll have to decide what you intend to do fairly quickly. Let's go back to the house. You can think things out tonight."

They found Hana and Le Cagot sitting in the cool of the wet terrace. The gusting wind had followed the storm, and the air was fresh and washed. Hana rose as they approached and took Hannah's hand in an unconscious gesture of kindness.

Le Cagot was sprawled on a stone bench, his eyes closed, his brandy glass loose in his fingers, and his heavy breathing occasionally rippling in a light snore.

"He dropped off right in the middle of a story," Hana explained.

"Hana," Hel said. "Miss Stern won't be staying with us after tonight. Would you see to having her things packed by morning? I'm going to take her up to the lodge." He turned to Hannah. "I have a mountain place. You can stay there, out of harm's way, while I consider how to get you back to your parents safely."

"I haven't decided that I *want* to go home."

Instead of responding, Hel kicked the sole of Le Cagot's boot. The burly Basque started and smacked his lips several times. "Where was I? Ah . . . I was telling you of those three nuns in Bayonne. Well, I met them—"

"No, you decided not to tell that one, considering the presence of ladies."

"Oh? Well, good! You see, little girl, a story like that would inflame your passions. And when you come to me, I want you to do so of your own will, and not driven by blinding lust. What happened to our guests?"

"They've gone. Probably back to the United States."

"I am going to tell you something in all frankness, Niko. I do not like those men. There is cowardice in their eyes; and that makes them dangerous. You must either invite a better class of guests, or risk losing my patronage. Hana, wonderful and desirable woman, do you want to go to bed with me?"

She smiled. "No, thank you, Beñat."

"I admire your self control. What about you, little girl?"

"She's tired," Hana said.

"Ah well, perhaps it's just as good. It would be a little crowded in my bed, what with the plump Portuguese kitchen maid. So! I hate to leave you without the color and charm of my presence, but the magnificent machine that is my body needs draining, then sleep. Good night, my friends." He grunted to his feet and started to leave, then he noticed Hannah's kimono. "What's this? What happened to your clothes? Oh, Niko, Niko. Greed is a vice. Ah well . . . good night."

Hana had gently stroked the tension from his back and shoulders as he lay on his stomach, and now she tugged his hair until he was half asleep. She placed her body over his, fitting her lap to his buttocks, her legs and arms over his, her warm weight protecting him, comforting, forcing him to relax. "This is trouble, isn't it?" she whispered.

He hummed in affirmation.

"What are you going to do?"

"I don't know," he breathed. "Get the girl away from here first. They may think that her death would cancel my debt to the uncle."

"You are sure they won't find her? There's no such thing as a secret in these valleys."

"Only the mountain men will know where she is. They're my people; and they don't talk to police, by habit and tradition."

"And what then?"

"I don't know. I'll think about it."

"Shall I bring you pleasure?"

"No. I'm too tense. Let me be selfish. Let me bring you pleasure."

Larun

HEL WAS AWAKE at dawn and put in two hours of work on the garden before he took breakfast with Hana in the *tatami*'d room overlooking the newly raked sea gravel that flowed down to the edge of the stream. "In time, Hana, this will be an acceptable garden. I hope you are here to enjoy it with me."

"I have been giving that matter consideration, Nikko. The idea is not without its attractions. You were very thorough last night."

"I was working out some stresses. That's an advantage."

"If I were selfish, I would hope for such stresses always."

He chuckled. "Oh, will you telephone down to the village and arrange for the next flight back to the United States for Miss Stern? It will be Pau to Paris, Paris to New York, New York to Chicago."

"She is leaving us then?"

"Not just yet. I don't want her in the open. But the reservations will be stored in the airline's computer bank, and will be immediately available to Fat Boy. It will throw them off the track."

"And who is 'Fat Boy'?"

"A computer. The final enemy. It arms stupid men with information."

"You sound bitter this morning."

"I am. Even self-pitying."

"I had avoided that phrase, but it is the right one. And it's not becoming in a man like you."

"I know." He smiled. "No one in the world would dare correct me like that, Hana. You're a treasure."

"It's my role to be a treasure."

"True. By the way, where is Le Cagot? I haven't heard him thundering about."

"He went off an hour ago with Miss Stern. He's going to show her some of the deserted villages. I must say she seemed to be in good spirits."

"The shallow recover quickly. You can't bruise a pillow. When will they be back?"

"By lunch surely. I promised Beñat a roast of *gigot*. You said you were taking Hannah to the lodge. When will you be leaving?"

"After twilight. I'm being watched."

"You intend to spend the night there with her?"

"Hm-m. I suppose so. I wouldn't want to come back down those roads in the dark."

"I know you don't like Hannah, but—"

"I don't like her type, thrill-seeking middle-class muffins tickling themselves with the thrill of terror and revolution. Her existence has already cost me a great deal."

"Do you intend to punish her while you're up there?"

"I hadn't thought about it."

"Don't be harsh. She's a good child."

"She is twenty-four years old. She has no right to be a child at that age. And she is not good. At best, she is 'cute.'"

Hel knew what Hana meant by "punishing" the girl. He had occasionally avenged himself on young women who had annoyed him by making love to them, using his tactical skills and exotic training to create an experience the woman could never approach again and would seek in vain through affairs and marriages for the rest of her life.

Hana felt no jealousy concerning Hannah; that would have been ridiculous. During the two years they had lived together, both she and Hel had been free to go off on little trips and seek sexual diversion, exercises of physical curiosity that kept their appetites in tone and made more precious, by comparison, what they had. Hana once chided him lightheartedly, complaining that he had the better of the arrangement, for a trained man can accomplish decent levels of exercise with a willing amateur; while even the most gifted and experienced woman has difficulty, with the gauche instrument of a bumbling man, achieving much beyond lust-scratching. Still, she enjoyed the occasional well-muscled young man of Paris or the Côte d'Azure, primarily as objects of physical beauty: toys to cuddle.

They drove along the twisting valley road, already dark with descending evening. The mountains rising sharply to their left were featureless geometric shapes, while those to their right were pink and amber in the horizontal rays of the setting sun. When they started from Etchebar, Hannah had been full of chatter about the robust good time she had had that afternoon with Le Cagot, wandering through deserted villages in the uplands, where she had noticed that each church clock had had its hands removed by the departing peasants. Le Cagot had explained that removing the hands of the clocks was considered necessary, because there would be no one in the churches to keep the clock weights screwed up, and one could not allow God's clock to be inaccurate. The dour tone of primitive Basque Catholicism was expressed in a *memento mori* inscription on the tower of one deserted church: "Each hour wounds, the last kills."

She was silent now, awed by the desolate beauty of the mountains rising so abruptly from the narrow valley that they seemed to overhang. Twice, Hel frowned and glanced over at her to find her eyes soft and a calm smile on her lips. He had been attracted and surprised by the alpha saturation in her aura, uncommon and unexpected in a person he had dismissed as a peppy twit. It was the timbre of calm and inner peace. He was going to question her about her decision concerning the Septembrists, when his attention was arrested by the approach of a car from behind driving with only wing lights. It flashed through his mind that Diamond or his French police lackeys might have learned that he was moving her to a safer place, and his hands gripped the wheel as he recalled the features of the road, deciding where he would force the car to pass him, then knock it into the ravine that raced along to their left. He had taken an exhaustive course in offensive driving, in result of which he always drove heavy cars, like his damned Volvo, for just such emergencies as this.

The road was never straight, constantly curving and twisting as it followed the course of the river ravine. There was no place a safe pass could be made, but that, of course, would not deter a French driver, whose adolescent impulse to pass is legendary. The car behind continued to close the distance until it was only a meter from his back bumper. It flashed its headlights and sounded its horn, then whipped around while they were in a tight blind curve.

Hel relaxed and slowed to let the car pass. The horn and the lights told him that this was not an assassination attempt. No professional would telegraph his move like that. It was just another childish French driver.

He shook his head paternally as the underpowered Peugeot strained its motor in its laboring effort to pass, the young driver's knuckles white on the steering wheel, his eyes bulging from their sockets in his effort to hold the road.

In his experience, Hel had found that only older North American drivers, with the long distances they habitually travel on good roads with competent machines, have become inured to the automobile as toy and as manhood metaphor. The French driver's infantile recklessness often annoyed him, but not so much as did the typical Italian driver's use of the automobile as an extension of his penis, or the British driver's use of it as a substitute.

For half an hour after leaving the valley road, they pulled up toward the mountains of Larun, over an unimproved road that writhed like a snake in its final agony. Some of the cutbacks were inside the turning radius of the Volvo, and negotiating them required two cuts and a bit of skidding close to the edge of loose gravel verges. They were never out of low gear, and they rose so steeply that they climbed out of the night that had pooled in the valley and into the zebra twilight of the high mountains: a blinding glare on the windshield when they turned toward the west, then blackness when outcroppings of rock blocked the setting sun.

Even this primitive road petered out, and they continued to ascend along faint ruts pressed into stubbly alpine meadows. The setting sun was now red and huge, its base flattened as it melted into the shimmering horizon. There were snow fields on the peaks above them glowing pink, then soon mauve, then purple against a black sky. The first stars glittered in the darkening east while the sky to the west was still hazy blue around the blood-red rim of the sinking sun.

Hel stopped the car by an outcropping of granite and set the hand brake. "We have to pack in from here. It's another two and a half kilometers."

"Up?" Hannah asked.

"Mostly up."

"God, this lodge of yours is certainly out of the way."

"That's its role." They got out and unloaded her pack from the car, experiencing the characteristic frustration of the Volvo's diabolic rear latch. They had walked twenty meters before it occurred to him to perform his satisfying ritual. Rather than go back, he picked up a jagged rock and hurled it, a lucky shot that hit a rear window and made a large cobweb of crackled safety glass.

"What was that all about?" Hannah asked.

"Just a gesture. Man against the system. Let's go. Stay close. I know the trail by feel."

"How long will I be up here all alone?"

"Until I decide what to do with you."

"Will you be staying tonight?"

"Yes."

They walked on for a minute before she said, "I'm glad."

He maintained a brisk pace because the light was draining fast. She was strong and young, and could stay with him, walking in silence, captured by the rapid but subtle color shifts of a mountain twilight. Again, as before down in the valley, he intercepted a surprising alpha tone in her aura—that rapid, mid-volume signal that he associated with meditation and soul peace, and not at all with the characteristic signature timbres of young Westerners.

She stopped suddenly as they were crossing the last alpine meadow before the narrow ravine leading to the lodge.

"What is it?"

"Look. These flowers. I've never seen anything like them before." She bent close to the wiry-stalked bells of dusty gold, just visible in the groundglow.

He nodded. "They're unique to this meadow and to one other over there." He gestured westward, toward the Table of the Three Kings, no longer visible in the gloom. "We're just above twelve hundred here. Both here and over there, they grow only at twelve hundred. Locally they are called the Eye of Autumn, and most people have never seen them, because they bloom for only three or four days."

"Beautiful. But it's almost dark, and they're still open."

"They never close. Tradition has it that they live so short a time they dare not close."

"That's sad."

He shrugged.

They sat opposite one another at a small table, finishing supper as they looked out through the plate-glass wall that gave onto the steep, narrow gully that was the only access to the lodge. Normally, Hel would be uneasy sitting in front of a glass wall, his form lighted by an oil lamp, while all was dark beyond. But he knew that the double plate glass was bulletproof.

The lodge was built of local stone and was simple of design: one large room with a cantilevered sleeping balcony. When first they arrived, he had acquainted Hannah with its features. The stream that flowed from a permanent snowfield above passed directly under the lodge, so one could get water through a trap door without going outside. The four-hundred-liter oil tank that fueled the stove and space heater was encased in the same stone as the lodge, so that incoming gunfire could not rupture it. There was a boiler-plate shutter that closed over the only door. The larder was cut into the face of granite that constituted one wall of the lodge, and contained thirty days' supply of food. Set into the bulletproof plate-glass wall was one small pane that could be broken out to permit firing down into the tight ravine up which anyone approaching the lodge would have to pass. The walls of the ravine were smooth, and all covering boulders had been dislodged and rolled to the bottom.

"Lord, you could hold an army off forever!" she exclaimed.

"Not an army, and not forever; but it would be a costly position to take." He took a semiautomatic rifle with telescopic sights from its rack and gave it to her. "Can you use this weapon?"

"Well . . . I suppose so."

"I see. Well, the important thing is that you shoot if you see anyone approaching up the gully who is not carrying a *xahako*. It doesn't matter if you hit him or not. The sound of your fire will carry in these mountains, and within half an hour help will be here."

"What's a . . . ah . . ."

"A *xahako* is a wine skin like this one. The shepherds and smugglers in these hills all know you are here. They're my friends. And they all carry *xahakos*. An outlander wouldn't."

"Am I really in all that much danger   "

"I don't know."

"But why would they want to kill me?"

"I'm not sure they do. But it's a possibility. They might reason that my involvement would be over if you were dead, and there was nothing more I could do to repay my debt to your uncle. That would be stupid thinking, because if they killed you while you were in my protection, I would be forced to make a countergesture. But we are dealing here with merchant and military mentalities, and stupidity is their intellectual idiom. Now let's see if you can manage everything."

He rehearsed her in lighting the stove and space heater, in drawing water from the trap door over the stream, and in loading clips into the rifle. "By the way, remember to take one of these mineral tablets each day. The water running under the floor is snowmelt. It has no minerals, and in time it will leach the minerals out of your system."

"God, how long will I be here?"

"I'm not sure. A week. Maybe two. Once those Septembrists have accomplished their hijack, the pressure will be off you."

While he made supper from tinned foods in the larder, she had wandered about the lodge, touching things, thinking her own thoughts.

And now they sat across the round table by the glass wall, the candlelight reversing the shadows on her soft young face on which lines of character and experience had not yet developed. She had been silent throughout the meal, and she had drunk more wine than was her habit, and now her eyes were moist and vague. "I should tell you that you don't have to worry about me anymore. I know what I'm going to do now. Early this morning, I decided to go home and try my best to forget all this anger and . . . ugliness. It's not my kind of thing. More than that, I realize now that it's all—I don't know—all sort of unimportant." She played absently with the candle flame, passing her finger through it just quickly enough to avoid being burned. "A strange thing happened to me last night. Weird. But wonderful. I've been feeling the effects of it all day long."

Hel thought of the alpha timbres he had been intercepting.

"I couldn't sleep. I got up and wandered around your house in the dark. Then I went to the garden. The air was cool and there was no breeze at all. I sat by the stream, and I could see the dark flicker of the water. I was staring at it, not thinking of anything in particular, then all at once I . . . it was a feeling I almost remember having when I was a child. All at once, all the pressures and confusions and fears were gone. They dissolved away, and I felt light. I felt like I was transported somewhere else, someplace I've never been to, but I know very well. It was sunny and still, and there was grass all around me; and I seemed to understand everything. Almost as though I was . . . I don't know. Almost as though I was—ouch!" She snapped her hand back and sucked the singed finger.

He laughed and shook his head, and she laughed too. "That was a stupid thing to do," she said.

"True. I think you were going to say that it was almost as though you and the grass and the sun were all one being, parts of the same thing."

She stared at him, her finger still to her lips. "How did you know that?"

"It's an experience others have had. You said you remembered similar feelings when you were a child?"

"Well, not exactly remember. No, not remember at all. It's just that when I was there. I had the feeling that this wasn't new and strange. It was something I had done before—but I don't actually remember doing it before. You know what I mean?"

"I think I do. You might have been participating in the atavistic—"

"I'll tell you what! I'm sorry, I don't mean to interrupt you. But I'll tell you what it's like. It's like the very best high on pot or something, when you're in a perfect mood and everything's going just right. It's not exactly like that, because you never get there with hooch, but it's where you think you're going. You know what I mean?"

"No."

"You never use pot or anything?"

"No. I've never had to. My inner resources are intact."

"Well. It was something like that."

"I see. How's your finger?"

"Oh, it's fine. The point is that, after the feeling had passed last night, I found myself sitting there in your garden, rested and clear-minded. And I wasn't confused any more. I knew there was no point in trying to punish the Septembrists. Violence doesn't get you anywhere. It's irrelevant. Now I think I just want to go home. Spend a little time getting in touch with myself. Then maybe—I don't know. See what's happening around me, maybe. Deal with that." She poured herself out another glass of wine and drank it down, then she put her hand on Hel's arm. "I guess I've been a lot of trouble to you."

"I believe the American idiom is 'a pain in the ass.' "

"I wish there were some way I could make it up to you."

He smiled at her obliquity.

She poured another glass of wine and said, "Do you think Hana minds your being here?"

"Why should she?"

"Well, I mean . . . do you think she minds our spending the night together?"

"What does that phrase signify to you?"

"What? Well . . . we'll be sleeping together."

"Sleeping together?"

"In the same place, I mean. You know what I mean."

He regarded her without speaking. Her experience of mystic transport, even if it was a unique event prompted by an overload of tension and desperation, rather than the function of a spirit in balance and peace, gave her a worthiness in his eyes. But this new acceptance was not free from a certain envy, that this vague-minded muffin should be able to achieve the state that he had lost years ago, probably forever. He recognized the envy to be adolescent and small on his part, but this recognition was not sufficient to banish the feeling.

She had been frowning into the candle flame, trying to sort out her emotions. "I should tell you something."

"Should you?"

"I want to be honest with you."

"Don't bother."

"No, I want to be. Even before I met you, I used to think about you . . . daydream, sort of. All the stories my uncle used to tell about you. I was really surprised at how young you are—how young you appear, that is. And I suppose if I analyzed my feelings, there's a sort of father projection. Here you are, the great myth in the flesh. I was scared and confused, and you protected me. I can see all the psychological impulses that would draw me toward you, can't you?"

"Have you considered the possibility that you're a randy young woman with a healthy and uncomplicated desire to climax? Or do you find that psychologically unsubtle?"

She looked at him and nodded. "You certainly know how to put a person down, don't you. You don't leave a person much to cover herself with."

"That's true. And perhaps it's uncivil of me. I'm sorry. Here is what I think is going on with you. You're alone, lonely, confused. You want to be cuddled and comforted. You don't know how to ask for that, because you're a product of the Western culture; so you negotiate for it, bartering sex for cuddling. It's not an uncommon negotiation for the Western woman to engage in. After all, she's limited to negotiating with the Western male, whose concept of social exchange is brittle and limited, and who demands earnest money in the form of sex, because that's the only part of the bargain he is comfortable with. Miss Stern, you may sleep with me tonight if you wish. I'll hold you and comfort you, if that's what you want."

Both gratitude and too much wine moistened her eyes. "I would like that, yes."

But the animal lurking within is seldom tethered by good intentions. When he awoke to her attentions and felt emanating from her the alpha/theta syncopation that attends sexual excitation, his response was not solely dictated by a desire to shield her from rejection.

She was exceptionally ripe and easy, all of her nerves close to the surface and desperately sensitive. Because she was still young, there was a bit of difficulty keeping her lubricated, but beyond that mechanical nuisance he could hold her in climax without much effort.

Her eyes rolled back again and she pleaded, "No . . . please . . . I can't again! I'll die if I do again!" But her involuntary contractions rushed closer and closer together, and she was gasping in her fourth orgasm, which he prolonged until her fingernails were clawing frantically at the nap of the rug.

He recalled Hana's injunction against dimming Hannah's future experience by comparison, and he had no particular impulse to climax himself, so he brought her back down slowly, stroking and cooling her as the muscles of her buttocks, stomach, and thighs quivered with the fatigue of repeated orgasm, and she lay still on the pile of pillows, half-unconscious and feeling that her flesh was melting.

He washed in frigid meltwater, then went up to the overhanging balcony to sleep.

Some time later, he felt her approach silently. He made space for her and a nest in his arms and lap. As she dipped toward sleep, she said dreamily, "Nicholai?"

"Please don't call me by my first name," he murmured.

She was silent for a time. "Mr. Hel? Don't be scared by this, because it's just a passing thing. But at this moment, I am in love with you."

"Don't be foolish."

"Do you know what I wish?"

He did not answer.

"I wish it were morning and I could go out and pick you a bunch of flowers . . . those Eyes of Autumn we saw."

He chuckled and folded her in. "Good night, Miss Stern."

Etchebar

IT WAS MIDMORNING before Hana heard the splash of a slab of rock into the stream and came from the château to find Hel rearranging the sounding stones, his trouser legs rolled up, and his forearms dripping with water.

"Will I ever get this right, Hana?"

She shook her head. "Only you will ever know, Nikko. Is Hannah safely set up at the lodge?"

"Yes. I think the girls have heated the water by now. Do you feel like taking a bath with me?"

"Certainly."

They sat opposite one another, their feet in their habitual caress, their eyes closed and their bodies weightless.

"I hope you were kind to her," Hana murmured sleepily.

"I was."

"And you? How was it for you?"

"For me?" He opened his eyes. "Madame, do you have anything pressing on your schedule just now?"

"I'll have to consult my *carnet de bal*, but it is possible that I can accommodate you."

Shortly after noon, when he had reason to hope the local PTT would be functioning at least marginally, Hel placed a transatlantic call to the number Diamond had left with him. He had decided to tell the Mother Company that Hannah Stern had decided to return home, leaving the Septembrists unmolested. He assumed Diamond would take personal satisfaction in the thought that he had frightened Nicholai Hel off, but just as praise from such a source would not have pleased him, so scorn could not embarrass him.

It would be more than an hour before the viscous and senile French telephone system could place his call, and he chose to pass the interval inspecting the grounds. He felt lighthearted, well-disposed toward everything, enjoying that generalized euphoria that follows a close call with danger. For a whole constellation of impalpable reasons, he had dreaded getting involved in a business that was trammeled with personalities and passions.

He was wandering through the privet maze on the east lawns when he came across Pierre, who was in his usual vinous fog of contentment. The gardener looked up into the sky and pontificated. "Ah, M'sieur. Soon there will be a storm. The signs all insist on it."

"Oh?"

"Oh yes, there is no doubt. The little clouds of the morning have been herded against the flank of *ahuñe-mendi*. The first of the *ursoa* flew up the valley this afternoon. The *sagarra* turned its leaves over in the wind. These are sure signs. A storm is inevitable."

"That's too bad. We could have used a little rain."

"True, M'sieur. But look! Here comes M'sieur Le Cagot. How finely he dresses!"

Le Cagot was approaching across the lawn, still wearing the rumpled theatrical evening dress of two nights ago. As he neared, Pierre tottered away, explaining that there were many thousands of things that demanded his immediate attention.

Hel greeted Le Cagot. "I haven't seen you in a while, Beñat. Where have you been?"

"Bof. I've been up in Larrau with the widow, helping her put out the fire in her belly." Le Cagot was uneasy, his badinage mechanical and flat.

"One day, Beñat, that widow will have you in the trap, and you'll be . . . What is it? What's wrong?"

Le Cagot put his hands on Hel's shoulders. "I have hard news for you, friend. A terrible thing has happened. That girl with the plump breasts? Your guest? . . ."

Hel closed his eyes and turned his head to the side. After a silence he said quietly, "Dead?"

"I'm afraid so. A *contrabandier* heard the shots. By the time he got to your lodge, she was dead. They had shot her . . . many, many times."

Hel took a long, slow breath and held it for a moment, then he let it out completely, as he absorbed the first shock and avoided the flash of mind-fogging fury. Keeping his mind empty, he walked back toward the château, while Le Cagot followed, respecting his friend's armor of silence.

Hel had sat for ten minutes at the threshold of the *tatami*'d room, staring out over the garden, while Le Cagot slumped beside him. He refocused his eyes and said in a monotone, "All right. How did they get into the lodge?"

"They didn't have to. She was found in the meadow below the ravine. Evidently she was picking wildflowers. There was a large bunch found in her hand."

"Silly twit," Hel said in a tone that might have been affectionate. "Do we know who shot her?"

"Yes. Early this morning, down in the village of Lescun, two outlanders were seen. Their descriptions are those of the *Amérlo* from Texas I met here and that little Arab snot."

"But how did they know where she was? Only our people knew that."

"There is only one way. Someone must have informed."

"One of *our* people?"

"I know. I know!" Le Cagot spoke between his teeth. "I have asked around. Sooner or later, I shall find out who it was. And when I do, by the Prophetic Balls of Joseph in Egypt, I swear that the blade of my *makila* will puncture his black heart!" Le Cagot was ashamed and furious that one of his own, a mountain Basque, had disgraced the race in this way. "What do you say, Niko? Shall we go get them, the *Amérlo* and the Arab?"

Hel shook his head. "By now they are on a plane bound for the United States. Their time will come."

Le Cagot smashed his fists together, breaking the skin over a knuckle. "But *why*, Niko! Why kill such a morsel? What harm could she do, the poor muffin?"

"They wanted to prevent me from doing something. They thought they could erase my debt to the uncle by killing the niece."

"They are mistaken, of course."

"Of course." Hel sat up straight as his mind began to function in a different timbre. "Will you help me, Beñat?"

"Will I help you? Does asparagus make your piss stink?"

"They have French Internal Security forces all over this part of the country with orders to put me away if I attempt to leave the area."

"Bof! The only charm of the Security Force is its epic incompetence."

"Still, they will be a nuisance. And they might get lucky. We'll have to neutralize them. Do you remember Maurice de Lhandes?"

"The man they call the Gnome? Yes, of course."

"I have to get in touch with him. I'll need his help to get safely into Britain. We'll go through the mountains tonight, into Spain to San Sabastian. I need a fishing boat to take me along the coast to St. Jean de Luz. Would you arrange that?"

"Would a cow lick Lot's wife?"

"Day after tomorrow, I'll be flying out from Biarritz to London. They'll be watching the airports. But they're spread thin, and that's to our advantage. Starting about noon that day, I want reports leaked to the authorities that I have appeared in Oloron, Pau, Bayonne, Bilbao, Mauléon, St. Jean Pied de Port, Bordeaux, Ste. Engrace, and Dax—all at the same time. I want their cross-communications confused, so that the report from Biarritz will be just one drop in a torrent of information. Can that be arranged?"

"Can it be arranged? Do . . . I can't think of an old saying for it just now. Yes, it can be arranged. This is like the old days, eh?"

"I'm afraid so."

"You're taking me with you, of course."

"No. It's not your kind of thing."

"Hola! Don't let the gray in my beard fool you. A boy lives inside this body! A very mean boy!"

"It's not that. If this were breaking into a prison or blowing away a guardpost, there is no one I'd rather have with me. But this won't be a matter of courage. It must be done by craft."

As was his custom when in the open air, Le Cagot had turned aside and unbuttoned his trousers to relieve himself as he talked. "You don't think I am capable of craft? I am subtlety itself! Like the chameleon, I blend with all backgrounds!"

Hel could not help smiling. This self-created folk myth standing before him, resplendent in rumpled *fin-de-siècle* evening clothes, the rhinestone buttons of his brocade waistcoat sparkling in the sun, his beret tugged low over his sunglasses, his rust-and-steel beard covering a silk cravat, the battered old *makila* under his arm as he held his penis in one hand and sprayed urine back and forth like a schoolboy—this man was laying claim to being subtle and inconspicuous.

"No, I don't want you to come with me, Beñat. You can help most by making the arrangements I asked for."

"And after that? What do I do while you are off amusing yourself? Pray and twiddle my thumbs?"

"I'll tell you what. While I'm gone, you can press on with preparations for the exploration of your cave. Get the rest of the gear we need down into the hole. Wet suits. Air tanks. When I get back, we'll take a shot at exploring it from light to light. How's that?"

"It's better than nothing. But not much."

A serving girl came from the house to tell Hel that he was wanted in the château.

He found Hana standing with the telephone in the butler's pantry, blocking the mouthpiece with her palm. "It is Mr. Diamond returning your call to the United States."

Hel looked at the phone, then glanced down to the floor. "Tell him I'll get back to him soon."

They had finished supper in the *tatami*'d room, and now they were watching the evening permutations of shifting shadow through the garden. He had told her that he would be away for about a week.

"Does this have to do with Hannah?"

"Yes." He saw no reason to tell her the girl was dead.

After a silence, she said, "When you get back, it will be close to the end of my stay with you."

"I know. By then you'll have to decide if you're interested in continuing our life together."

"I know." She lowered her eyes and, for the first time he could remember, her cheeks colored with the hint of a blush. "Nikko? Would it be too silly for us to consider becoming married?"

"Married?"

"Never mind. Just a silly thought that wandered through my mind. I don't believe I would want it anyway." She had touched on the idea gingerly and had fled instantly from his first reaction.

For several minutes, he was deep in thought. "No, it's not all that silly. If you decide to give me years of your life, then of course we should do something to assure your economic future. Let's talk about it when I return."

"I could never mention it again."

"I realize that, Hana. But I could."

PART FOUR

UTTEGAE

St. Jean de Luz/Biarritz

THE OPEN FISHING boat plowed the ripple path of the setting moon, quicksilver on the sea, like an effect from the brush of a kitsch watercolorist. The diesel motor chugged bronchially and gasped as it was turned off. The bow skewed when the boat crunched up on the pebble beach. Hel slipped over the side and stood knee-deep in the surging tide, his duffel bag on his shoulder. A wave of his hand was answered by a blurred motion from the boat, and he waded toward the deserted shore, his canvas pants heavy with water, his rope-soled espadrilles digging into the sand. The motor coughed and began its rhythmic thunking, as the boat made its way out to sea, along the matte-black shore toward Spain.

From the brow of a dune, he could see the lights of cafés and bars around the small harbor of St. Jean de Luz, where fishing boats heaved sleepily on the oily water of the docking slips. He shifted the weight of the duffel and made for the Café of the Whale, to confirm a telegraph order he had made for dinner. The owner of the café had been a master chef in Paris, before retiring back to his home village. He enjoyed displaying his prowess occasionally, particularly when M. Hel granted him carte blanche as regards menu and expense. The dinner was to be prepared and served in the home of Monsieur de Lhandes, the "fine little gentleman" who lived in an old mansion down the shore, and who was never to be seen in the streets of St. Jean de Luz because his physiognomy would cause comment, and perhaps ridicule, from ill-brought-up children. M. de Lhandes was a midget, little more than a meter tall, though he was over sixty years old.

Hel's tap at the back door brought Mademoiselle Pinard to peer cautiously through the curtain, then a broad smile cracked her face, and she opened the door wide. "Ah, Monsieur Hel! Welcome. It has been too long since last we saw you! Come in, come in! Ah, you are wet! Monsieur de Lhandes is so looking forward to your dinner."

"I don't want to drip on your floor, Mademoiselle Pinard. May I take off my pants?"

Mademoiselle Pinard blushed and slapped at his shoulder with delight. "Oh, Monsieur Hel! Is this any way to speak? Oh, men!" In obedience to their established routine of chaste flirtation, she was both flustered and delighted. Mademoiselle Pinard was somewhat older than fifty—she had always been somewhat older than fifty. Tall and sere, with dry nervous hands and an unlubricated walk, she had a face too long for her tiny eyes and thin mouth, so rather a lot of it was devoted to forehead and chin. If there had been more character in her face, she would have been ugly; as it was, she was only plain. Mademoiselle Pinard was the mold from which virgins are made, and her redoubtable virtue was in no way lessened by the fact that she had been Bernard de Lhandes's companion, nurse, and mistress for thirty years. She was the kind of woman who said *"Zut!"* or *"Ma foi!"* when exasperated beyond the control of good taste.

As she showed him to the room that was always his when he visited, she said in a low voice, "Monsieur de Lhandes is not well, you know. I am delighted that he will have your company this evening, but you must be very careful. He is close to God. Weeks, months only, the doctor tells me."

"I'll be careful, darling. Here we are. Do you want to come in while I change my clothes?"

"Oh, Monsieur!"

Hel shrugged. "Ah well. But one day, your barriers will fall, Mademoiselle Pinard. And then . . . Ah, then . . ."

"Monster! And Monsieur de Lhandes your good friend! Men!"

"We are victims of our appetites, Mademoiselle. Helpless victims. Tell me, is dinner ready?"

"The chef and his assistants have been cluttering up the kitchen all day. Everything is in readiness."

"Then I'll see you at dinner, and we'll satisfy our appetites together."

"Oh, Monsieur!"

They took dinner in the largest room of the house, one lined with shelves on which books were stacked and piled in a disarray that was evidence of de Lhandes's passion for learning. Since he considered it outrageous to read and eat at the same time—diluting one of his passions with the other—de Lhandes had struck on the idea of combining library and dining room, the long refectory table serving both functions. They sat at one end of this table, Bernard de Lhandes at the head, Hel to his right, Mademoiselle Pinard to his left. Like most of the furniture, the table and chairs had been cut down and were somewhat too big for de Lhandes and somewhat too small for his rare guests. Such, de Lhandes had once told Hel, was the nature of compromise: a condition that satisfied no one, but left each with the comforting feeling that others had been done in too.

Dinner was nearly over, and they were resting and chatting between courses. There had been Neva caviar with blinis, still hot on their napkins, St. Germain Royal (de Lhandes found a hint too much mint), suprême de sole au Château Yquem, quail under the ashes (de Lhandes mentioned that walnut would have been a better wood for the log fire, but he could accept the flavor imparted by oak cinders), rack of baby lamb Edward VII (de Lhandes regretted that it was not cold enough, but he realized that Hel's arrangements were spur of the moment), riz à la grècque (the bit too much red pepper de Lhandes attributed to the chef's place of birth), morels (the bit too little lemon juice de Lhandes attributed to the chef's personality), Florentine artichoke bottoms (the gross imbalance between gruyère and parmesan in the mornay sauce de Lhandes attributed to the chef's perversity, for the error had been mentioned before), and Danicheff salad (which de Lhandes found perfect, to his slight annoyance).

From each of these dishes, de Lhandes took the smallest morsel that would still allow him to have all the flavors in his mouth at once. His heart, liver, and digestive system were such a ruin that his doctor restricted him to the blandest of foods. Hel, from dietary habit, ate very little. Mademoiselle Pinard's appetite was good, though her concept of exquisite table manners involved taking minute bites and chewing them protractedly with circular, leporine motions confined to the very front of her mouth, where her napkin often and daintily went to brush thin lips. One of the reasons the chef of the Café of the Whale enjoyed doing these occasional suppers for Hel was the great feast his family and friends always enjoyed later that same night.

"It's appalling how little we eat, Nicholai," de Lhandes said in his surprisingly deep voice. "You with your monk's attitude toward food, and I with my ravished constitution! Picking about like this, I feel like a rich ten-year-old in a luxurious bordello!"

Mademoiselle Pinard went behind her napkin for a moment.

"And these thimblesful of wine!" de Lhandes complained. "Ah, that I have descended to this! A man who, through knowledge and money, converted gluttony into a major art! Fate is either ironic or just, I don't know which. But look at me! Eating as though I were a bloodless nun doing penance for her daydreams about the young curé!"

The napkin concealed Mademoiselle Pinard's blush.

"How sick are you, old friend?" Hel asked. Honesty was common currency between them.

"I am finally sick. This heart of mine is more a sponge than a pump. I have been in retirement for—what? Five years now? And for four of them I have been of no use to dear Mademoiselle Pinard—save as an observer, of course."

The napkin.

The meal ended with a bombe, fruit, *glacés variées*—no brandies or *digestifs*—and Mademoiselle Pinard retired to allow the men to chat.

De Lhandes slid down from his chair and made his way to the fireside, stopping for breath twice, where he occupied a low chair that nevertheless left his feet straight out before him.

"All chairs are *chaises longues* for me, my friend" He laughed. "All right, what can I do for you?"

"I need help."

"Of course. Good comrades though we are, you would not come by boat in the dead of night for the sole purpose of disgracing a supper by picking at it. You know that I have been out of the information business for several years, but I have orts and bits left from the old days, and I shall help you if I can."

"I should tell you that they have got my money. I won't be able to pay you immediately."

De Lhandes waved a dismissing hand. "I'll send you a bill from hell. You'll recognize it by the singed edges. Is it a person, or a government?"

"Government. I have to get into England. They'll be waiting for me. The affair is very heavy, so my leverage will have to be strong."

De Lhandes sighed. "Ah, my. If only it were America. I have something on America that would make the Statue of Liberty lie back and spread her knees. But England? No one thing. Fragments and scraps. Some nasty enough, to be sure, but no one big thing."

"What sort of things have you?"

"Oh, the usual. Homosexuality in the foreign office . . ."

"That's not news."

"At this level, it's interesting. And I have photographs. There are few things so ludicrous as the postures a man assumes while making love. Particularly if he is no longer young. And what else have I? Ah . . . a bit of rambunctiousness in the royal family? The usual political peccadillos and payoffs? A blocked inquiry into that flying accident that cost the life of . . . you remember." De Lhandes looked to the ceiling to recall what was in his files. "Oh, there's evidence that the embrace between the Arab oil interests and the City is more intimate than is generally known. And there's a lot of individual stuff on government people—fiscal and sexual irregularities mostly. You're absolutely sure you don't want something on the United States? I have a real bell ringer there. It's an unsalable item. Too big for almost any use. It would be like opening an egg with a sledge hammer."

"No, it has to be English. I haven't time to set up indirect pressure from Washington to London."

"Hm-m-m. Tell you what. Why don't you take the whole lot? Arrange to have it published, one shot right after the other. Scandal after scandal eroding the edifice of confidence—you know the sort of thing. No single arrow strong enough alone, but in fascine . . . who knows? It's the best I can offer."

"Then it will have to do. Set it up the usual way? I bring photocopies with me? We arrange a 'button-down' trigger system with the German magazines as primary receivers?"

"It's not failed yet. You're sure you don't want the Statue of Liberty's brazen hymen?"

"Can't think of what I'd do with it."

"Ah well, painful image at best. Well . . . can you spend the night with us?"

"If I may. I fly out of Biarritz tomorrow at noon, and I have to lie low. The locals have a bounty on me."

"Pity. They ought to protect you as the last surviving member of your species. You know, I've been thinking about you lately, Nicholai Alexandrovitch. Not often, to be sure, but with some intensity. Not often, because when you get to the bang or whimper moment of life, you don't spend much time contemplating the minor characters of your personal farce. And one of the difficult things for egocentric Man to face is that he is a minor character in every biography but his own. I am a bit player in your life; you in mine. We have known one another for more than twenty years but, discounting business (and one must always discount business), we have shared perhaps a total of twelve hours of intimate conversation, of honest inquiry into one another's minds and emotions. I have known you, Nicholai, for half a day. Actually, that's not bad. Most good friends and married couples (those are seldom the same thing) could not boast twelve hours of honest interest after a lifetime of shared space and irritations, of territorial assertions and squabbles. So . . . I've known you for half a day, my friend, and I have come to love you. I think very highly of myself for having accomplished that, as you are not an easy man to love. Admire? Yes, of course. Respect? If fear is a part of respect, then of course. But love? Ah, that's a different business. Because there is in love an urge to forgive, and you're a hard man to forgive. Half saintly ascetic, half Vandal marauder, you don't make yourself available for forgiveness. In one persona, you are above forgiveness; in another, beneath it. And always resentful of it. One has the feeling that you would never forgive a man for forgiving you. (That probably doesn't mean much, but it rolls well off the tongue, and a song must have music as well as words.) And after my twelve hours of knowing you, I would capsulize you—reduce you to a definition—by calling you a medieval antihero."

Hel smiled. "Medieval antihero? What on earth does that mean?"

"Who has the floor now, you or I? Let's have a little silent respect for the dying. It's part of your being Japanese—culturally Japanese, that is. Only in Japan was the classical moment simultaneous with the medieval. In the West, philosophy, art, political and social ideal, all are identified with periods before or after the medieval moment, the single exception being that glorious stone bridge to God, the cathedral. Only in Japan was the feudal moment also the philosophic moment. We of the West are comfortable with the image of the warrior priest, or the warrior scientist, even the warrior industrialist. But the warrior philosopher? No, that concept irritates our sense of propriety. We speak of 'death and violence' as though they were two manifestations of the same impulse. In fact, death is the very opposite of violence, which is always concerned with the struggle for life. Our philosophy is focused on managing life;

yours on managing death. We seek comprehension; you seek dignity. We learn how to grasp; you learn how to let go. Even the label 'philosopher' is misleading, as our philosophers hve always been animated by the urge to share (indeed, inflict) their insights; while your lot are content (perhaps selfishly) to make your separate and private peace. To the Westerner, there is something disturbingly feminine (in the sense of yang-ish, if that coinage doesn't offend your ear) in your view of manhood. Fresh from the battlefield, you don soft robes and stroll through your gardens with admiring compassion for the falling cherry petal; and you view both the gentleness and the courage as manifestations of manhood. To us, that seems capricious at least, if not two-faced. By the way, how *does* your garden grow?"

"It's becoming."

"Meaning?"

"Each year it is simpler."

"There! You see? That goddamned Japanese penchant for paradoxes that turn out to be syllogisms! Look at yourself. A warrior gardener! You are indeed a medieval Japanese, as I said. And you are also an antihero—not in the sense in which critics and scholars lusting for letters to dangle after their names use (misuse) the term. What they call antiheroes are really unlikely heroes, or attractive villains—the fat cop or Richard III. The true antihero is a version of the hero—not a clown with a principal role, not an audience member permitted to work out his violent fantasies. Like the classic hero, the antihero leads the mass toward salvation. There was a time in the comedy of human development when salvation seemed to lie in the direction of order and organization, and all the great Western heroes organized and directed their followers against the enemy: chaos. Now we are learning that the final enemy is not chaos, but organization; not divergence, but similarity; not primitivism, but progress. And the new hero—the antihero—is one who makes a virtue of attacking the organization, of destroying the systems. We realize now that salvation of the race lies in that nihilist direction, but we still don't know how far." De Lhandes paused to catch his breath, then seemed to be ready to continue. But his glance suddenly crossed Hel's, and he laughed. "Oh, well. Let that be enough. I wasn't really speaking to you anyway."

"I've been aware of that for some time."

"It is a convention in Western tragedy that a man is permitted one long speech before he dies. Once he has stepped on the inevitable machinery of fate that will carry him to his bathetic denouement, nothing he can say or do will alter his lot. But he is permitted to make his case, to bitch at length against the gods—even in iambic pentameter."

"Even if doing so interrupts the flow of the narrative?"

"To hell with it! For two hours of narcosis against reality, of safe, vicarious participation in the world of action and death, one should be willing to pay the price of a couple minutes worth of insight. Structurally sound or not. But have it your way. All right. Tell me, do the governments still remember 'the Gnome'? And do they still scratch the earth trying to find his lair, and gnash their teeth in frustrated fury?"

"They do indeed, Maurice. Just the other day there was an *Amérlo* scab at home asking about you. He would have given his genitals to know how you came by your information."

"Would he indeed? Being an *Amérlo,* he probably wasn't risking much. And what did you tell him?"

"I told him everything I knew."

"Meaning nothing at all. Good. Candor is a virtue. You know, I really don't have any very subtle or complicated sources of information. In fact, the Mother Company and I are nourished by the same data. I have access to Fat Boy through the purchased services of one of their senior computer slaves, a man named Llewellyn. My skill lies in being able to put two and two together better than they can. Or, to be more precise, I am able to add one and a half plus one and two thirds in such a way as to make ten. I am not better informed than they; I am simply smarter."

Hel laughed. "They would give almost anything to locate and silence you. You've been bamboo under their fingernails for a long time."

"Ha, that knowledge brightens my last days, Nicholai. Being a nuisance to the government lackeys has made my life worth living. And a precarious living it has been. When you trade in information, you carry stock that has very short shelf life. Unlike brandy, information cheapens with age. Nothing is duller than yesterday's sins. And sometimes I used to acquire expensive pieces, only to have them ruined by leakage. I remember buying a very hot item from the United States: what in time became known as the Watergate Cover-up. And while I was holding the merchandise on my shelf, waiting for you or some other international to purchase it as leverage against the American government, a pair of ambitious reporters sniffed the story out and saw in it a chance to make their fortunes—and *voilà!* The material was overnight useless to me. In time, each of the criminals wrote a book or did a television program describing his part in the rape of American civil rights, and each was paid lavishly by the stupid American public, which seems to have a peculiar impulse toward having their noses rubbed in their own shit. Doesn't it seem unjust to you that I should end up losing several hundred thousand worth of spoiled stock on my shelves, while even the master villain himself makes a fortune doing television shows with that British leech who has shown that he would sniff up to anybody for money, even Idi Amin? It's a peculiar one, this trade I'm in."

"Have you been an information broker all your life, Maurice?"

"Except for a short stint as a professional basketball player."

"Old fool!"

"Listen, let us be serious for a moment. You described this thing you're doing as hard. I wouldn't presume to advise you, but have you considered the fact that you've been in retirement for a time? Is your mental conditioning still taut?"

"Reasonably. I do a lot of caving, so fear doesn't clog my mind too much. And, fortunately, I'll be up against the British."

"That's an advantage, to be sure. The MI-5 and -6 boys have a tradition of being so subtle that their fakes go unnoticed. And yet . . . There is something wrong with this affair, Nicholai Alexandrovitch. There's something in your tone that disturbs me. Not quite doubt, but a certain dangerous fatalism. Have you decided that you are going to fail?"

Hel was silent for a time. "You're very perceptive, Maurice."

"C'est mon métier."

"I know. There is something wrong—something untidy—about all this. I recognize that to come back out of retirement I am challenging karma. I think that, ultimately, this business will put me away. Not the task at hand. I imagine that I can relieve these Septembrists of the burden of their lives easily enough. The complications and the dangers will be ones I have dealt with before. But after that, the business gets tacky. There will be an effort to punish me. I may accept the punishment, or I may not. If I do not, then I shall have to go into the field again. I sense a certain—" He shrugged. "—a certain emotional fatigue. Not exactly fatalistic resignation, but a kind of dangerous indifference. It is possible, if the indignities pile up, that I shall see no particular reason to cling to life."

De Lhandes nodded. It was this kind of attitude that he had sensed. "I see. Permit me to suggest something, old friend. You say that the governments do me the honor of still being hungry for my death. They would give a lot to know who and where I am. If you get into a tight spot, you have my permission to bargain with that information."

"Maurice!—"

"No, no! I am not suffering from a bout of quixotic courage. I'm too old to contract such a childhood disease. It would be our final joke on them. You see, you would be giving them an empty bag. By the time they get here, I shall have departed."

"Thank you, but I couldn't do it. Not on your account, but on mine." Hel rose. "Well, I have to get some sleep. The next twenty-four hours will be trying. Mostly mind play, without the refreshment of physical danger. I'll be leaving before first light."

"Very well. For myself, I think I shall sit up for a few more hours and review the delights of an evil life."

"All right. *Au revoir,* old friend."

"Not *au revoir,* Nicholai."

"It is that close?"

De Lhandes nodded.

Hel leaned over and kissed his comrade on both cheeks. "*Adieu,* Maurice."

"*Adieu,* Nicholai."

Hel was caught at the door by, "Oh, Nicholai, would you do something for me?"

"Anything."

"Estelle has been wonderful to me these last years. Did you know her name was Estelle?"

"No, I didn't."

"Well, I want to do something special for her—a kind of going-away present. Would you drop by her room? Second at the head of the stairs. And afterward, tell her it was a gift from me."

Hel nodded. "It will be my pleasure, Maurice."

De Lhandes was looking into the fading fire. "Hers too, let us hope," he muttered.

Hel timed his arrival at the Biarritz airport to minimize the period he would have to stand out in the open. He had always disliked Biarritz, which is Basque only in geography; the Germans, the English, and the international smart set have perverted it into a kind of Brighton on Biscay.

He was not five minutes in the terminal before his proximity sense intercepted the direct and intense observation he had expected, knowing they would be looking for him at all points of departure. He lounged against the counter of the bar where he was taking a *jus d'ananas* and lightly scanned the crowd. Immediately, he picked up the young French Special Services officer in civilian clothes and sunglasses. Pushing himself off the bar, he walked directly toward the man, feeling as he approached the lad's tension and confusion.

"Excuse me, sir," Hel said in a French larded with German accent. "I have just arrived, and I cannot discover how to make my connection to Lourdes. Could you assist me?"

The young policeman scanned Hel's face uncertainly. This man filled the general description, save for the eyes, which were dark brown. (Hel was wearing noncorrective brown contact lenses.) But there was nothing in the description about his being German. And he was supposed to be leaving the country, not entering it. In a few brusque words, the police agent directed Hel to the information office.

As he walked away, Hel felt the agent's gaze fixed on him, but the quality of the concentration was muffled by confusion. He would, of course, report the spotting, but without much certainty. And the central offices would at this moment be receiving reports of Hel's appearance in half a dozen cities at the same time. Le Cagot was seeing to that.

As Hel crossed the waiting room, a towheaded boy ran into his legs. He caught up the child to keep him from falling.

"Rodney! Oh, I *am* sorry, sir." The good-looking woman in her late twenties was on the scene in an instant, apologizing to Hel and admonishing the child all at the same time. She was British and dressed in a light summer frock designed to reveal not only her suntan, but the places she had not suntanned. In a babble of that brutally mispronounced French resulting from the Britisher's assumption that if foreigners had anything worth saying they would say it in a real language, the young woman managed to mention that the boy was her nephew, that she was returning with him from a short vacation, and that she was taking the next flight for England, that she herself was unmarried, and that her name was Alison Browne, with an *e*.

"My name is Nicholai Helm."

"Delighted to meet you, Mr. Hel."

That was it. She had not heard the *m* because she was prepared not to. She would be a British agent, covering the action of the French.

Hel said he hoped they would be sitting together on the plane, and she smiled seductively and said that she would be willing to speak to the ticket agent about that. He offered to purchase a fruit juice for her and little Rodney, and she accepted, not failing to mention that she did not usually accept such offers from strange men, but this was an exception. They had, after all, quite literally run into one another. (Giggle.)

While she was busy dabbing her handkerchief at Rodney's juice-stained collar, leaning forward and squeezing in her shoulders to advertise her lack of a bra, Hel excused himself for a moment.

At the sundries shop he purchased a cheap memento of Biarritz, a box to contain it, a pair of scissors, and some wrapping paper—a sheet of white tissue and one of an expensive metal foil. He carried these items to the men's room, and worked rapidly wrapping the present, which he brought back to the bar and gave to Rodney, who was by now whining as he dangled and twisted from Miss Browne's hand.

"Just a little nothing to remind him of Biarritz. I hope you don't mind?"

"Well, I shouldn't. But as it's for the boy. They've called twice for our flight. Shouldn't we be boarding?"

Hel explained that these French, with their anal compulsion for order, always called early for the planes; there was no rush. He turned the talk to the possibility of their getting together in London. Dinner, or something?

At the last moment they went to the boarding counter, Hel taking his place in the queue in front of Miss Browne and little Rodney. His small duffel bag passed the X-ray scanner without trouble. As he walked rapidly toward the plane, which was revving up for departure, he could hear the protests of Miss Browne and the angry demands of the security guards behind him. When the plane took off, Hel did not have the pleasure of the seductive Miss Browne and little Rodney.

Heathrow

PASSENGERS PASSING THROUGH customs were directed to enter queues in relation to their status: "British Subjects," "Commonwealth Subjects," "Common Market Citizens," and "Others." Having traveled on his Costa Rican passport, Hel was clearly an "Other," but he never had the opportunity to enter the designated line, for he was immediately approached by two smiling young men, their husky bodies distorting rather extreme Carnaby Street suits, their meaty faces expressionless behind their moustaches and sunglasses. As he always did when he met modern young men, Hel mentally shaved and crewcut them to see whom he was really dealing with.

"You will accompany us, Mr. Hel," one said, as the other took the duffel from his hand. They pressed close to him on either side and escorted him toward a door without a doorknob at the end of the debarcation area.

Two knocks, and the door was opened from the other side by a uniformed officer, who stood aside as they passed through. They walked without a word to the end of a long windowless corridor of institutional green, where they knocked. The door was opened by a young man struck from the same mold as the guards, and from within came a familiar voice.

"Do come in, Nicholai. We've just time for a glass of something and a little chat before you catch your plane back to France. Leave the luggage, there's a good fellow. And you three may wait outside."

Hel took a chair beside the low coffee table and waved away the brandy bottle lifted in offer. "I thought you had finally been cashiered out, Fred."

Sir Wilfred Pyles squirted a splash of soda into his brandy. "I had more or less the same idea about you. But here we are, two of yesterday's bravos, sitting on opposite sides, just like the old days. You're sure you won't have one? No? Well, I imagine the sun's over the yardarm somewhere around the world, so—cheers."

"How's your wife?"

"More pleasant than ever."

"Give her my love when next you see her."

"Let's hope that's not too soon. She died last year."

"Sorry to hear that."

"Don't be. Is that enough of the small talk?"

"I should think so."

"Good. Well, they dragged me out of the mothballs to deal with you, when they got word from our petroleum masters that you might be on your way. I assume they thought I might be better able to handle you, seeing that we've played this game many times, you and I. I was directed to intercept you here, find out what I could about your business in our misty isle, then see you safely back on a plane to the place from whence you came."

"They thought it would be as easy as that, did they?"

Sir Wilfred waved his glass. "Well, you know how these new lads are. All by the book and no complexities."

"And what do you assume, Fred?"

"Oh, I assume it won't be quite that easy. I assume you came with some sort of nasty leverage gained from your friend, the Gnome. Photocopies of it in your luggage, I shouldn't wonder."

"Right on top. You'd better take a look."

"I shall, if you don't mind," Sir Wilfred said, unzipping the bag and taking out a manila folder. "Nothing else in here I should know about, I trust? Drugs? Subversive or pornographic literature?"

Hel smiled.

"No? I feared as much." He opened the folder and began to scan the information, sheet by sheet, his matted white eyebrows working up and down with each uncomfortable bit of information. "By the way," he asked between pages, "what on earth did you do to Miss Browne?"

"Miss Browne? I don't believe I know a—"

"Oh, come now. No coyness between old enemies. We got word that she is this moment sitting in a French detention center while those gentlemen of Froggish inclination comb and recomb her luggage. The report we received was quite thorough, including the amusing detail that the little boy who was her cover promptly soiled himself, and the consulate is out the cost of fresh garments."

Hel couldn't help laughing.

"Come. Between us. What on earth did you do?"

"Well, she came on with all the subtlety of a fart in a bathosphere, so I neutralized her. You don't train them as you did in the old days. The stupid twit accepted a gift."

"What sort of a gift?"

"Oh, just a cheap memento of Biarritz. It was wrapped up in tissue paper. But I had cut out a gun shape from metal foil paper and slipped it between the sheets of tissue."

Sir Wilfred sputtered with laughter. "So, the X-ray scanner picked up a gun each time the package passed through, and the poor officials could find nothing! How delicious: I think I must drink to that." He measured out the other half, then returned to the task of familiarizing himself with the leverage information, occasionally allowing himself such interjections as: "Is that so? Wouldn't have thought it of him." "Ah, we've known this for some time. Still, wouldn't do to broadcast it around." "Oh, my. That *is* a nasty bit. How on earth did he find that out?"

When he finished reading the material, Sir Wilfred carefully tapped the pages together to make the ends even, then replaced them in the folder. "No single thing here sufficient to force us very far."

"I'm aware of that, Fred. But the mass? One piece released to the German press each day?"

"Hm-m. Quite. It would have a disastrous effect on confidence in the government just now, with elections on the horizon. I suppose the information is in 'button-down' mode?"

"Of course."

"Feared as much."

Holding the information in "button-down" mode involved arrangements to have it released to the press immediately, if a certain message was not received by noon of each day. Hel carried with him a list of thirteen addresses to which he was to send cables each morning. Twelve of these were dummies; one was an associate of Maurice de Lhandes who would, upon receipt of the message, telephone to another intermediary, who would telephone de Lhandes. The code between Hel and de Lhandes was a simple one based upon an obscure poem by Barro, but it would take much longer than twenty-four hours for the intelligence boys to locate the one letter in the one word of the message that was the active signal. The term "button-down" came from a kind of human bomb, rigged so that the device would not go off, so long as the man held a button down. But any attempt to struggle with him or to shoot him would result in his releasing the button.

Sir Wilfred considered his position for a moment. "It is true that this information of yours can be quite damaging. But we are under tight orders from the Mother Company to protect these Black September vermin, and we are no more eager to bring down upon our heads the ire of the Company than is any other industrial country. It appears that we shall have to choose between misfortunes."

"So it appears."

Sir Wilfred pushed out his lower lip and squinted at Hel in evaluation. "This is a very wide-open and dangerous thing you're doing, Nicholai—walking right into our arms like this. It must have taken a great deal of money to draw you out of retirement."

"Point of fact, I am not being paid for this."

"Hm-m-m. That, of course, would have been my second guess." He drew a long sigh. "Sentiment is a killer, Nicholai. But of course you know that. All right, tell you what. I shall carry your message to my masters. We'll see what they have to say, Meanwhile, I suppose I shall have to hide you away somewhere. How would you like to spend a day or two in the country? I'll make a telephone call or two to get the government lads thinking, then I'll run you out in my banger."

Middle Bumley

SIR WILFRED'S IMMACULATE 1931 Rolls crunched over the gravel of a long private drive and came to a stop under the porte cochère of a rambling house, most of the charm of which derived from the aesthetic disorder of its having grown without plan through many architectural impulses.

Crossing the lawn to greet them were a sinewy woman of uncertain years and two girls in their mid-twenties.

"I think you'll find it amusing here, Nicholai," Sir Wilfred said. "Our host is an ass, but he won't be about. The wife is a bit dotty, but the daughters are uniquely obliging. Indeed, they have gained something of a reputation for that quality. What do you think of the house?"

"Considering your British penchant for braggadocio through meiosis—the kind of thing that makes you call your Rolls a banger—I'm surprised you didn't describe the house as thirty-seven up, sixteen down."

"Ah, Lady Jessica!" Sir Wilfred said to the older woman as she approached wearing a frilly summer frock of a vague color she would have called "ashes of roses." "Here's the guest I telephoned about. Nicholai Hel."

She pressed a damp hand into his. "So pleased to have you. To meet you, that is. This is my daughter, Broderick."

Hel shook hands with an overly slim girl whose eyes were huge in her emaciated face.

"I know it's an uncommon name for a girl," Lady Jessica continued, "but my husband had quite settled on having a boy—I mean he wanted to have a boy in the sense of fathering a son—not in the other sense—my goodness, what must you think of him? But he had Broderick instead—or rather, we did."

"In the sense that you were her parents?" Hel sought to release the skinny girl's hand.

"Broderick is a model," the mother explained.

Hel had guessed as much. There was a vacuousness of expression, a certain limpness of posture and curvature of spine that marked the fashionable model of that moment.

"Nothing much really," Broderick said, trying to blush under her troweled-on makeup. "Just the odd job for the occasional international magazine."

The mother tapped the daughter's arm. "Don't say you do 'odd jobs'! What will Mr. Hel think?"

A clearing of the throat by the second daughter impelled Lady Jessica to say, "Oh, yes. And here is Melpomene. It is conceivable she might act one day."

Melpomene was a substantial girl, thick of bosom, ankle, and forearm, rosy of cheek, and clear of eye. She seemed somehow imcomplete without her hockey stick. Her handshake was firm and brisk. "Just call me Pom. Everyone does."

"Ah . . . if we could just freshen up?" Sir Wilfred suggested.

"Oh, of course! I'll have the girls show you everything—I mean, of course, where your rooms are and all. What must you think?"

As Hel was laying out his things from the duffel bag, Sir Wilfred tapped on the door and came in. "Well, what do you think of the place? We should be cozy here for a couple of days, while the masters ponder the inevitable, eh? I've been on the line to them, and they say they'll come up with a decision by morning."

"Tell me, Fred. Have your lads been keeping a watch on the Septembrists?"

"On your targets? Of course."

"Assuming that your government goes along with my proposal, I'll want all the background material you have."

"I expected no less. By the bye, I assured the masters that you could pull this off—should their decision go that way—with no hint of collusion or responsibility on our part. It is that way, isn't it?"

"Not quite. But I can work it so that, whatever their suspicions, the Mother Company will not be able to *prove* collusion."

"The next best thing, I suppose."

"Fortunately, you picked me up before I went through passport check, so my arrival won't be in your computers and therefore not in theirs."

"Wouldn't rely on that overly much. Mother Company has a million eyes and ears."

"True. You're absolutely sure this is a safe house?"

"Oh, yes! The ladies are not what you would call subtle, but they have another quality quite as good—they're totally ignorant. They haven't the slightest idea of what we're doing here. Don't even know what I do for a living. And the man of the house, if you can call him that, is no trouble at all. We seldom let him into the country, you see."

Sir Wilfred went on to explain that Lord Biffen lived in the Dordogne, the social leader of a gaggle of geriatric tax avoiders who infested that section of France, to the disgust and discomfort of the local peasants. The Biffens were typical of their sort: Irish peerage that every other generation stiffened its sagging finances by introducing a shot of American hog-butcher blood. The gentleman had overstepped himself in his lust to avoid taxes and had got into a shady thing or two in free ports in the Bahamas. That had given the government a hold on him and on his British funds, so he was most cooperative, remaining in France when he was ordered to, where he exercised his version of the shrewd businessman by cheating local women out of antique furniture or automobiles, always being careful to intercept his wife's mail to avoid her discovering his petty villainies. "Silly old fart, really. You know the type. Outlandish ties; walking shorts with street shoes and ankle stockings? But the wife and daughters, together with the establishment here, are of some occasional use to us. What do you think of the old girl?"

"A little obsessed."

"Hm-m. Know what you mean. But if you'd gone twenty-five years getting only what the old fellow had to offer, I fancy you'd be a little sperm mad yourself. Well, shall we join them?"

After breakfast the next morning, Sir Wilfred sent the ladies away and sat back with his last cup of coffee. "I was on the line with the masters this morning. They've decided to go along with you—with a couple of provisos, of course."

"They had better be minor."

"First, they want assurance that this information will never be used against them again."

"You should have been able to give them that assurance. You know that the man you call the Gnome always destroys the originals as soon as the deal is made. His reputation rests on that."

"Yes, quite so. And I shall undertake to assure them on that account. Their second proviso is that I report to them, telling them that I have considered your plan carefully and believe it to be airtight and absolutely sure not to involve the government directly."

"Nothing in this business is airtight."

"All right. Airtight-ish, then. So I'm afraid that you will have to take me into your confidence—familarize me with details of dastardly machinations, and all that."

"Certain details I cannot give you until I have gone over your observation reports on the Septembrists. But I can sketch the bold outlines for you."

Within an hour, they had agreed on Hel's proposal, although Sir Wilfred had some reservations about the loss of the plane, as it was a Concorde, ". . . and we've had trouble enough trying to ram the damned thing down the world's throat as it is."

"It's not my fault that the plane in question is that uneconomical, polluting monster."

"Quite so. Quite so."

"So there it is, Fred. If your people do your part well, the stunt should go off without the Mother Company's having any proof of your complicity. It's the best plan I could work up, considering that I've had only a couple of days to think about it. What do you say?"

"I don't dare give my masters the details. They're political men—the least reliable of all. But I shall report that I consider the plan worth cooperating with."

"Good. When do I get the observation reports on the Septembrists?"

"They'll be here by courier this afternoon. You know, something occurs to me, Nicholai. Considering the character of your plan, you really don't have to involve yourself at all. We could dispose of the Arabs ourselves, and you could return to France immediately."

Hel looked at Sir Wilfred flatly for fully ten seconds. Then they both laughed at once.

"Ah well," Sir Wilfred said, waving a hand, "you can't blame me for trying. Let's take a little lunch. And perhaps there's time for a nap before the reports come in."

"I hardly dare go to my room."

"Oh? Did they also visit you last night?"

"Oh, yes, and I chucked them out."

"Waste not, want not, I always say."

Sir Wilfred dozed in his chair, warmed by the setting sun beyond the terrace. On the other side of the white metal table, Hel was scanning the observation reports on the PLO actives.

"There it is," he said finally.

"What? Hm-m? There what is?"

"I was looking for something in the list of contacts and acquaintances the Septembrists have made since their arrival."

"And?"

"On two occasions, they spent time with this man you have identified as 'Pilgrim Y'. He works in a food-preparation service for the airlines."

"Is that so? I really don't know the file. I was only dragged into this—unwillingly, I might mention—when you got involved. What's all this about food preparation?"

"Well, obviously the Septembrists are not going to try to smuggle their guns through your detection devices. They don't know that they have the passive cooperation of your government. So I had to know how they were going to get their weapons aboard. They've gone to a well-worn method. The weapons will come aboard with the prepared dinners. The food trucks are never searched more than desultorily. You can run anything through them."

"So now you know where their weapons will be. So what?"

"I know where they will have to come to collect them. And that's where I'll be."

"And what about you? How are you going to get arms aboard for yourself, without leaving trace of our complicity in this?"

"I'll carry my weapons right through the checkpoint."

"Oh, yes. I'd forgotten about that for a moment. Naked/Kill and all that. Stab a man with a drinking straw. What a nuisance that's been to us over the years."

Hel closed the report. "We have two days until the plane departs. How shall we fill our time?"

"Loll about here, I suppose. Keep you out of sight."

"Are you going up to dress for dinner?"

"No, I think I'll not take dinner tonight. I should have followed your example and forsaken my midday lie by. Had to contend with both of them. Probably walk with a limp the rest of my life."

Heathrow

THE PLANE WAS almost full of passengers, all adults, most of them the sort who could afford the surcharge for flying Concorde. Couples chatted; stewards and stewardesses leaned over seats making the cooing noises of experienced nannies; businessmen asked one another what they sold; unacquainted pairs said those inane things calculated to lead to assignations in Montreal; the conspicuously busy kept their noses in documents and reports or fiddled ostentatiously with pocket recorders; the frightened babbled about how much they loved flying, and tried to appear casual as they scanned the information card designating procedures and exits in case of emergency.

A muscular young Arab and a well-dressed Arab woman sat together near the back, a curtain separating them from the service area, where food and drinks were stored. Beside the curtain stood a flight attendant who smiled down at the Arab couple, his bottle-green eyes vacant.

Two young Arabs, looking like rich students, entered the plane and sat together about halfway down. Just before the doors were closed, a fifth Arab, dressed as a businessman, rushed down the mobile access truck and aboard the plane, babbling to the receiving steward something about just making it and being delayed by business until the last moment. He came to the back of the plane and took a seat opposite the Arab couple, to whom he nodded in a friendly way.

With an incredible roar, the engines tugged the plane from the loading ramp, and soon the bent-nosed pterodactyl was airborne.

When the seat-belt sign flashed off, the pretty Arab woman undid her belt and rose. "It is this way to the ladies' room?" she asked the green-eyed attendant, smiling shyly.

He had one hand behind the curtain. As he smiled back at her, he pressed the button on which his finger rested, and two soft gongs echoed through the passenger area. At this sound, each of the 136 passengers, except the PLO Arabs, lowered his head and stared at the back of the seat before him.

"Any one of these, Madam," Hel said, holding the curtain aside for her to pass through.

At that instant, the Arab businessman addressed a muffled question to Hel, meaning to attract his attention while the girl got the weapons from the food container.

"Certainly, sir," Hel said, seeming not to understand the question. "I'll get you one."

He slipped a comb from his pocket as he turned and followed the girl, snapping the curtain behind him.

"But wait!" the Arab businessman said—but Hel was gone.

Three seconds later he returned, a magazine in his hand. "I'm sorry, sir, we don't seem to have a copy of *Paris Match*. Will this do?"

"Stupid fool!" muttered the businessman, staring at the drawn curtain in confusion. Had this grinning idiot not seen the girl? Had she stepped into the rest room upon his approach? Where *was* she?

Fully a minute passed. The four Arabs aboard were so concerned with the girl's failure to emerge through the curtain, an automatic weapon in her hands, they failed to notice that everyone else on the plane was sitting with his head down, staring at the seat back before him.

Unable to control themselves longer, the two Arab students who had sat together in the waist of the plane rose and started back down the aisle. As they approached the smiling, daydreaming steward with the green eyes, they exchanged worried glances with the older businessman and the muscular lad who was the woman's companion. The older man gestured with his head for the two to pass on behind the curtain.

"May I help you?" Hel asked, rolling up the magazine into a tight cylinder.

"Bathroom," one of them muttered, as the other said, "Drink of water."

"I'll bring it to you, sir," Hel said. "Not the bathroom, of course," he joked with the taller one.

They passed him, and he followed them behind the curtain.

Four seconds later, he emerged, a harried expression on his face. "Sir," he said confidentially to the older businessman, "You're not a doctor by any chance?"

"Doctor? No. Why?"

"Oh, it's nothing. Not to worry. The gentleman's had a little accident."

"Accident?"

"Don't worry. I'll get help from a member of the cabin crew. Nothing serious, I'm sure." Hel had in his hand a plastic drinking cup, which he had crushed and creased down the center.

The businessman rose and stepped into the aisle.

"If you would just stay with him, sir, while I fetch someone," Hel said, following the businessman into the service area.

Two seconds later, he was standing again at his station, looking over the passengers with that expression of vague compassion airline stewards affect. When his gaze fell on the worried muscular young man beside him, he winked and said, "It was nothing at all. Dizzy spell, I guess. First time in a supersonic plane, perhaps. The other gentleman is assisting him. I don't speak Arabic, unfortunately."

A minute passed. Another. The muscular young man's tension grew, while this mindless steward standing before him hummed a popular tune and gazed vacantly around, fiddling with the small plastic name tag pinned to his lapel.

Another minute passed.

The muscular lad could not contain himself. He leaped up and snatched the curtain aside. On the floor, in the puppet-limbed sprawl of the dead, were his four companions. He never felt the edge of the card; he was nerve dead before his body reached the floor.

Other than the hissing roar of the plane's motors, there was silence in the plane. All the passengers stared rigidly ahead. The flight crew stood facing the front of the plane, their eyes riveted on the decorated plastic panel before them.

Hel lifted the intercom phone from its cradle. His soft voice sounded metallic through the address system. "Relax. Don't look back. We will land within fifteen minutes." He replaced the phone and dialed the pilot's cabin. "Send the message exactly as you have been instructed to. That done, open the envelope in your pocket and follow the landing instructions given."

Its pterodactyl nose bent down again, the Concorde roared in for a landing at a temporarily evacuated military airfield in northern Scotland. When it stopped and its engines had whined down to silence, the secondary entrance portal opened, and Hel descended on mobile stairs that had been rolled up to the door. He stepped into the vintage 1931 Rolls that had chased the plane across the runway, and they drove away.

Just before turning off to a control building, Hel looked back and saw the passengers descending and lining themselves up in four-deep ranks beside the plane under the direction of a man who had posed as senior steward. Five military buses were already crossing the airstrip to pick them up.

Sir Wilfred sat at the scarred wooden desk of the control office, sipping a whiskey, while Hel was changing from the flight attendant's uniform to his own clothes.

"Did the message sound all right?" Hel asked.

"Most dramatic. Most effective. The pilot radio'd back that the plane was being skyjacked, and right in the middle of the message, he broke off, leaving nothing but dead air and the hiss of static."

"And he was on clear channel, so there will be independent corroborations of your report?"

"He must have been heard by half a dozen radio operators all across the North Atlantic."

"Good. Now, tomorrow your search planes will come back with reports of having found floating wreckage, right?"

"As rain."

"The wreckage will be reported to have been picked up, and the news will be released over BBC World Service that there was evidence of an explosion, and that the current theory is that an explosive device in the possession of Arab skyjackers was detonated accidentally, destroying the plane."

"Just so."

"What are your plans for the plane, Fred? Surely the insurance companies will be curious."

"Leave that to us. If nothing else remains of the Empire, we retain at least that penchant for duplicity that earned us the title Perfidious Albion."

Hel laughed. "All right. It must have been quite a job to gather that many operatives from all over Europe and have them pose as passengers."

"It was indeed. And the pilots and crew were RAF fellows who had really very little check-out time on a Concorde."

"Now you tell me."

"Wouldn't have done to make you edgy, old man."

"I regret your problem of having a hundred-fifty people in on the secret. It was the only way I could do it and still keep your government to the lee of the Mother Company's revenge. And, after all, they are all your own people."

"True enough. But that is no assurance of long-term reliability. But I've arranged to manage the problem."

"Oh? How so?"

"Where do you imagine those buses are going?"

Hel adjusted his tie and zipped up his duffle. "All hundred-fifty of them?"

"No other airtight way, old boy. And within two days, we'll have to attend to the extermination crew as well. But there's a bright side to everything, if you look hard enough. We're having a bit of an unemployment problem in the country just now, and this will produce scads of openings for bright young men and women in the secret service."

Hel shook his head. "You're really a tough old fossil, aren't you, Fred."

"In time, even the soul gets callused. Sure you won't have a little farewell drink?"

PART FIVE

SHICHO

Château d'Etchebar

HIS MUSCLES MELTING in the scalding water, his body weightless, Hel dozed as his feet enclosed Hana's in slack embrace. It was a cool day for the season, and dense steam billowed, filling the small bathing house.

"You were very tired when you came home last night," Hana said after a sleepy silence.

"Is that a criticism?" he muttered without moving his lips.

She laughed lightly. "On the contrary. Fatigue is an advantage in our games."

"True."

"Was your trip . . . successful?"

He nodded.

She was never inquisitive about his affairs; her training prohibited it, but her training also taught her to create opportunities for him to speak about his work if he wanted to. "Your business? It was the same sort of thing you did in China when we met?"

"Same genre, different phylum."

"And those unpleasant men who visited us, were they involved?"

"They weren't on the ground, but they were the enemy." His tone changed. "Listen, Hana. I want you to take a little vacation. Go to Paris or the Mediterranean for a few weeks."

"Back only ten hours and you are already trying to be rid of me?"

"There may be some trouble from those 'unpleasant men.' And I want you safely out of the way. Anyway"—he smiled,—"you could probably use the spice of a strong young lad or two."

"And what of you?"

"Oh, I'll be out of the enemy's range. I'm going into the mountains and work that cave Beñat and I discovered. They're not likely to find me there."

"When do you want me to leave, Nikko?"

"Today. As soon as you can."

"You don't think I would be safe here with our friends in the mountains protecting me?"

"That chain's broken. Something happened to Miss Stern. Somebody informed."

"I see." She squeezed his foot between hers. "Be careful, Nikko."

The water had cooled enough to make slow movements possible, and Hel flicked his fingers, sending currents of hotter water toward his stomach. "Hana? You told me that you could not bring up the subject of marriage again, but I said that I could and would. I'm doing that now."

She smiled and shook her head. "I've been thinking about that for the past few days, Nikko. No, not marriage. That would be too silly for such as you and I."

"Do you want to go away from here?"

"No."

"What then?"

"Let's not make plans. Let's remain together for a month at a time. Perhaps forever—but only a month at a time. Is that all right with you?"

He smiled and nestled his feet into hers. "I have great affection for you, Hana."

"I have great affection for you, Nicholai."

"By the Skeptical Balls of Thomas! What's going on in here?" Le Cagot had snatched open the door of the bathing room and entered, bringing unwelcomed cool air with him. "Are you two making your own private whiteout? Good to see you back, Niko! You must have been lonely without me." He leaned against the wooden tub, his chin hooked over the rim. "And good to see you too, Hana! You know, this is the first time I've seen all of you. I shall tell you the truth— you are a desirable woman. And that is praise from the world's most desirable man, so wear it in health."

"Get out of here!" Hel growled, not because he was uncomfortable with nudity, but because Le Cagot's tease would go flat if he didn't seem to rise to the bait.

"He shouts to hide his delight at seeing me again, Hana. It's an old trick, Mother of Heaven, you have fine nipples! Are you sure there isn't a bit of Basque in that genetic stew of yours? Hey, Niko, when do we see if there is light and air at the other end of Le Cagot's Cave? Everything is in readiness. The air tank is down, the wet suit. Everything."

"I'm ready to go up today."

"When today?"

"In a couple of hours. Get out."

"Good. That gives me time to visit your Portuguese maid. All right, I'm off. You two will have to resign yourselves to getting on without my company." He slammed the door behind him, swirling the scant steam that remained in the room.

After they had made love and taken breakfast, Hana began her packing. She had decided to go to Paris because in late August that city would be relatively empty of vacationing bourgeois Parisians.

Hel puttered for a time in his garden, which had roughened somewhat in his absence. It was there Pierre found him.

"Oh, M'sieur, the weather signs are all confused."

"Is that so?"

"It is so. It has rained for two days, and now neither the Eastwind nor the Northwind have dominance, and you know what that means."

"I'm confident you will tell me."

"It will be dangerous in the mountains, M'sieur. This is the season of the whiteout."

"You're sure of that?"

Pierre tapped the tip of his rubicund drunkard's nose with his forefinger, signifying that there were things only the Basque knew for certain, and weather was but one of them.

Hel took some consolation in Pierre's assurance. At least they would not have to contend with a whiteout.

The Volvo rolled into the village square of Larrau, where they would pick up the Basque lads who operated the pedal winch. They parked near the widow's bar, and one of the children playing *pala* against the church wall ran over and did Hel the service of bashing the hood of the car with a stick, as he had seen the man do so often. Hel thanked him, and followed Le Cagot to the bar.

"Why are you bringing your *makila* along, Beñat?" He hadn't noticed before that Le Cagot was carrying his ancient Basque sword/cane under his arm.

"I promised myself that I would carry it until I discover which of my people informed on that poor little girl. Then, by the Baby-Killing Balls of Herod, I shall ventilate his chest with it. Come, let's take a little glass with the widow. I shall give her the pleasure of laying my palm upon her ass."

The Basque lads who had been awaiting them since morning now joined them over a glass, talking eagerly about the chances of M'sieur Hel being able to swim the underground river to the daylight. Once that air-to-air exploration had been made, the cave system would be officially discovered, and they would be free to go down into the hole themselves and, what is more, to talk about it later.

The widow twice pushed Le Cagot's hand away; then, her virtue clearly demonstrated, she allowed it to remain on her ample bottom as she stood beside the table, keeping his glass full.

The door to the W.C. in back opened, and Father Xavier entered the low-ceilinged bar, his eyes bright with fortifying wine and the ecstasy of fanaticism. "So?" he said to the young Basque lads. "Now you sit with this outlander and his lecherous friend? Drinking their wine and listening to their lies?"

"You must have drunk deep of His blood this morning, Father Esteka!" Le Cagot said. "You've swallowed a bit of courage."

Father Xavier snarled something under his breath and slumped down in a chair at the most distant table.

"Holà," Le Cagot pursued. "If your courage is so great, why don't you come up the mountain with us, eh? We are going to descend into a bottomless pit from which there is no exit. It will be a foretaste of hell for you—get you used to it!"

"Let him be," Hel muttered. "Let's go and leave the silly bastard to pickle in his own hate."

"God's eyes are everywhere!" the priest snarled, glaring at Hel. "His wrath is inescapable!"

"Shut your mouth, convent girl," Le Cagot said, "or I shall put this *makila* where it will inconvenience the Bishop!"

Hel put a restraining hand on Le Cagot's arm; they finished off their wine and left.

Gouffre Porte-de-Larrau

HEL SQUATTED ON the flat slab that edged their base camp beside the rubble cone, his helmet light turned off to save the batteries, listening over the field telephone to Le Cagot's stream of babble, invective, and song as he descended on the cable, constantly bullying and amusing the Basque lads operating the pedal winch above. Le Cagot was taking a breather, braced up in the bottom of the corkscrew before allowing himself to be lowered into the void of Le Cagot's Cave, down into the waterfall, where he would have to hang, twisting on the line, while the lads locked up and replaced the cable drum.

After ordering them to be quick about the job and not leave him hanging there, dangling like Christ on the tree, or he would come back up and do them exquisite bodily damage, he said, "All right, Niko. I'm coming down!"

"That's the only way gravity works," Hel commented, as he looked up for the first glimpse of Le Cagot's helmet light emerging through the mist of the waterfall.

A few meters below the opening into the principal cave, the descent stopped, and the Basque boy on the phones announced that they were changing drums.

"Get on with it!" Le Cagot ordered. "This cold shower is abusing my manhood!"

Hel was considering the task of carrying the heavy air tank all the way to the Wine Cellar at the end of the system, glad that he could rely on Le Cagot's bull strength, when a muffled shout came over the earphones. Then a sharp report. His first reaction was that something had snapped. A cable? The tripod? His body instinctively tightened in kinesthetic sympathy for Le Cagot. There were two more crisp reports. Gunfire!

Then silence.

Hel could see Le Cagot's helmet lamp, blurred through the mist of the waterfall, winking on and off as he turned slowly on the end of the cable.

"What in hell is going on?" Le Cagot asked over the phones.

"I don't know."

A voice came over the telephone, thin and distant. "I warned you to stay out of this, Mr. Hel."

"Diamond?" Hel asked, unnecessarily.

"That is correct. The merchant. The one who would not dare meet you face to face."

"You call this face to face?"

"It's close enough."

Le Cagot's voice was tight with the strain on his chest and diaphragm from hanging in the harness. "What is going on?"

"Diamond?" Hel was forcing himself to remain calm. "What happened to the boys at the winch?"

"They're dead."

"I see. Listen. It's me you want, and I'm at the bottom of the shaft. I'm not the one hanging from the cable. It is my friend. I can instruct you how to lower him."

"Why on earth should I do that?"

From the background, Hel heard Darryl Starr's voice. "That's the son of a bitch that took my piece. Let him hang there, turning slowly in the wind, the mammy-jammer!"

There was the sound of a childish giggle—the PLO scab they called Haman.

"What makes you think I involved myself in your business?" Hel asked, his voice conversational, although he was frantically playing for time to think.

"The Mother Company keeps sources close to our friends in England—just to confirm their allegiance. I believe you met our Miss Biffen, the young model?"

"If I get out of here, Diamond . . ."

"Save your breath, Hel. I happen to know that is a 'bottomless pit from which there is no exit.' "

Hel took a slow breath. Those were Le Cagot's words in the widow's bar that afternoon.

"I warned you," Diamond continued, "that we would have to take counteraction of a kind that would satisfy the vicious tastes of our Arab friends. You will be a while dying, and that will please them. And I have arranged a more visible monument to your punishment. That château of yours? It ceased to exist an hour and a half ago."

"Diamond . . ." Hel had nothing to say, but he wanted to keep Diamond on the other end of the line. "Le Cagot is nothing to you. Why let him hang there?"

"It's a detail sure to amuse our Arab friends."

"Listen, Diamond—there are men coming to relieve those lads. They'll find us and get us out."

"That isn't true. In fact, it's a disappointingly pallid lie. But to forestall the possibility of someone stumbling upon this place accidentally, I intend to send men up to bury your Basque friends here, dismantle all this bric-a-brac, and roll boulders into the pit to conceal the entrance. I tell you this as an act of kindness—so you won't waste yourself on fruitless hope."

Hel did not respond.

"Do you remember what my brother looked like, Hel?"

"Vaguely."

"Good. Keep him in mind."

There was a rattling over the headphones, as they were taken off and tossed aside.

"Diamond? Diamond?" Hel squeezed the phone line in his fingers. The only sound over the phone was Le Cagot's labored breathing.

Hel turned on his helmet light and the ten-watt bulb connected to battery, so Le Cagot could see something below him and not feel deserted.

"Well, what about that, old friend?" Le Cagot's half-strangled voice came over the line. "Not exactly the denouement I would have chosen for this colorful character I have created for myself."

For a desperate moment, Hel considered attempting to scale the walls of the cave, maybe get above Le Cagot and let a line down to him.

Impossible. It would take hours of work with drill and expansion bolts to move up that featureless, overhanging face; and long before that, Le Cagot would be dead, strangled in the harness webbing that was even now crushing the breath out of him.

Could Le Cagot get out of this harness and up the cable to the mouth of the corkscrew? From there it was barely conceivable that he might work his way up to the surface by free climbing.

He suggested this to Beñat over the phone.

Le Cagot's voice was a weak rasp. "Can't . . . ribs . . . weight of . . . water . . ."

"Beñat!"

"What, for the love of God?"

A last slim possibility had occurred to Hel. The telephone line. It wasn't tied off firmly, and the chances that it would take a man's weight were slight; but it was just possible that it had fouled somewhere above, perhaps tangled with the descent cable.

"Beñat? Can you get onto the phone line? Can you cut yourself out of your harness?"

Le Cagot hadn't breath enough left to answer, but from the vibration in the phone line, Hel knew he was trying to follow instructions. A minute passed. Two. The mist-blurred helmet lamp was dancing jerkily up near the roof of the cave. Le Cagot was clinging to the phone line, using his last strength before unconsciousness to hack away at the web straps of his harness with his knife.

He gripped the wet phone line with all his force and sawed through the last strap. His weight jerked onto the phone line . . . snatching it loose.

"Christ!" he cried.

His helmet light rushed down toward Hel. For a fraction of a second, the coiling phone line puddled at Hel's feet. With a fleshy slap, Le Cagot's body hit the tip of the rubble cone, bounced, tumbled in a clatter of rock and debris, then lodged head-downward not ten meters from Hel.

"Beñat!"

Hel rushed to him. He wasn't dead. The chest was crushed; it convulsed in heaving gasps that spewed bloody foam from the mouth. The helmet had taken the initial impact but had come off during the bouncing down the rubble. He was bleeding from his nose and ears. Hanging head down, he was choking on his own blood.

As gently as possible, Hel lifted Le Cagot's torso in his arms and settled it more comfortably. The damage he might do by moving him did not matter; the man was dying. Indeed, Hel resented the powerful Basque constitution that denied his friend immediate release into death.

Le Cagot's breath was rapid and shallow; his open eyes were slowly dilating. He coughed, and the motion brought him racking pain.

Hel caressed the bearded cheek, slick with blood.

"How . . ." Le Cagot choked on the word.

"Rest, Beñat. Don't talk."

"How . . . do I look?"

"You look fine."

"They didn't get my face?"

"Handsome as a god."

"Good." Le Cagot's teeth clenched against a surge of pain. The bottom ones had been broken off in the fall. "The priest . . ."

"Rest, my friend. Don't fight it. Let it take you."

"The priest!" The blood froth at the corner of his mouth was already sticky.

"I know." Diamond had quoted Le Cagot's description of the cave as a bottomless pit. The only person he could have heard it from was the fanatic, Father Xavier. And it must have been the priest who gave away Hannah's place of refuge as well. The confessional was his source of information, his Fat Boy.

For an endless three minutes, Le Cagot's gurgling rasps were the only sound. The blood pulsing from his ears began to thicken.

"Niko?"

"Rest. Sleep."

"How do I look?"

"Magnificent, Beñat."

Suddenly Le Cagot's body stiffened and a thin whine came from the back of his throat. "Christ!"

"Pain?" Hel asked stupidly, not knowing what to say.

The crisis of agony passed, and Le Cagot's body seemed to slump into itself. He swallowed blood and asked, "What did you say?"

"Pain?" Hel repeated.

"No . . . thanks . . . I have all I need."

"Fool," Hel said softly.

"Not a bad exit line, though."

"No, not bad."

"I bet that you won't make so fine a one when you go."

Hel closed his eyes tightly, squeezing the tears out, as he caressed his friend's cheek.

Le Cagot's breath snagged and stopped. His legs began to jerk in spasms. The breath came back, rapid gasps rattling in the back of his throat. His broken body contorted in final agony and he cried, "Argh! By the Four Balls of Jesus, Mary, and Joseph . . ."

Pink lung blood gushed from his mouth, and he was dead.

Hel grunted with relief from pain as he slipped off the straps of the air cylinder and wedged it into an angle between two slabs of raw rock that had fallen in from the roof of the Climbing Cave. He sat heavily, his chin hanging to his chest, as he sucked in great gulps of air with quivering inhalations, and exhalations that scoured his lungs and made him cough. Sweat ran from his hair, despite the damp cold of the cave. He crossed his arms over his chest and gingerly fingered the raw bands on his shoulders where the air tank straps had rubbed away the skin, even through three sweaters under his parachutist's overalls. An air tank is an awkward pack through rough squeezes and hard climbs. If drawn up tight, it constricts movement and numbs the arms and fingers; if slackened, it chafes the skin and swings, dangerously threatening balance.

When his breathing calmed, he took a long drink of water-wine from his *xahako*, then lay back on a slab of rock, not even bothering to take off his helmet. He was carrying as little as possible: the tank, all the rope he could handle, minimal hardware, two flares, his *xahako*, the diving mask in a rubberized pouch which also contained a watertight flashlight, and a pocketful of glucose cubes for rapid energy. Even stripped down to necessities, it was too much for his body weight. He was used to moving through caves freely, leading and carrying minimal weight, while the powerful Le Cagot bore the brunt of their gear. He missed his friend's strength; he missed the emotional support of his constant flow of wit and invective and song.

But he was alone now. His reserves of strength were sapped; his hands were torn and stiff. The thought of sleep was delicious, seductive . . . deadly. He knew that if he slept, the cold would seep in, the attractive, narcotic cold. Mustn't sleep. Sleep is death. Rest, but don't close your eyes. Close your eyes, but don't sleep. No. Mustn't close your eyes! His eyebrows arched with the effort to keep the lids open over the upward-rolling eyes. Mustn't sleep. Just rest for a moment. Not sleep. Just close your eyes for a moment. Just close . . . eyes.

He had left Le Cagot on the side of the rubble heap where he died. There was no way to bury him; the cave itself would be a vast mausoleum, now that they had rolled stones in over the opening. Le Cagot would lie forever in the heart of his Basque mountains.

When at last the blood had stopped oozing, Hel had gently wiped the face clean before covering the body with a sleeping bag.

After covering the body, Hel had squatted beside it, seeking middle-density meditation to clear his mind and tame his emotions. He had achieved only fleeting wisps of peace, but when he tugged his mind back to the present, he was able to consider his situation. Decision was simple; all alternatives were closed off. His chance of making it, alone and overloaded, all the way down that long shaft and around Hel's Knob, through the gargantuan chaos of the Climbing Cave, through the waterfall into the Crystal Cavern, then down that foul marl chute to the Wine Cellar sump—his chances of negotiating all these obstacles without belaying and help from Le Cagot were slim. But it was a kind of Pascal's Bet. Slim or not, his only hope lay in making the effort. He would not think about the task of swimming out through the pipe at the bottom of the Wine Cellar, that pipe through which water rushed with such volume that it pulled the surface of the pool tight and bowed. He would face one problem at a time.

Negotiating Hel's Knob had come close to ending his problems. He had tied a line to the air tank and balanced it on the narrow ledge beside the stream rushing through that wedge-shaped cut, then he undertook the knob with a strenuous heel-and-shoulder scramble, lying back at almost full length, his knees quivering with the strain and the extra weight of rope cross-coiled bandolier style over his chest. Once past the obstacle, he faced the task of getting the tank around. There was no Le Cagot to feed the line out to him. There was nothing for it but to tug the tank into the water and take up slack rapidly as it bounced along the bottom of the stream. He was not able to take line in quickly enough; the tank passed his stance underwater and continued on, the line jerking and bobbing. He had no point of belay; when the slack snapped out, he was pulled from his thin ledge. He couldn't let go. To lose the tank was to lose everything. He straddled the narrow shaft, one boot on the ledge, the cleats of the other flat against the smooth opposite wall where there was no purchase. All the strength of his legs pressed into the stance, the cords of his crotch stood out, stretched and vulnerable. The line ran rapidly through his hands. He clenched his jaw and squeezed his fists closed over the rope. The pain seared as his palms took the friction of the wet line that cut into them. Water ran behind his fists, blood before. To handle the pain, he roared, his scream echoing unheard through the narrow diaclose.

The tank was stopped.

He hauled it back against the current, hand over hand, the rope molten iron in his raw palms, the cords of his crotch knotting and throbbing. When his hand touched the web strap of the tank, he pulled it up and hooked it behind his neck. With that weight dangling at his chest, the move back to the ledge was dicey. Twice he pushed off the smooth wall, and twice he tottered and fell back, catching himself again with the flat of his sole, his crotch feeling like it would tear with the stretch. On the third try he made it over and stood panting against the wall, only his heels on the ledge, his toes over the roaring stream.

He moved the last short distance to the scree wall that blocked the way to the Climbing Cave, and he slumped down in the book corner, exhausted, the tank against his chest, his palms pulsing with pain.

He couldn't stay there long. His hands would stiffen up and become useless.

He rerigged the tank to his back and checked the fittings and faceplate of the mask. If they were damaged, that was it. The mask had somehow survived banging against the tank. Now he began the slow climb up the corner between the side of the shaft and the boulder wall under which the river had disappeared. As before, there were many foot- and handholds, but it was all friable rottenrock, chunks of which came off in his hands, and grains of stone worked their way into his skinless palms. His heart thumped convulsively in his chest, squirting throbs of blood into his temples. When at last he made the flat ledge between two counterbalanced boulders that was the keyhole to the Climbing Cave, he lay out flat on his stomach and rested, his cheek against the rock and saliva dripping from the corner of his mouth.

He cursed himself for resting there too long. His palms were growing sticky with scab fluid, and they hinged awkwardly, like lobster claws. He got to his feet and stood there, opening and closing his hands, breaking through the crusts of pain, until they articulated smoothly again.

For an unmeasurable time, he stumbled forward through the Climbing Cave, feeling his way around the house-sized boulders that dwarfed him, squeezing between counterbalanced slabs of recent infall from the scarred roof far above the throw of his helmet light, edging his way along precariously perched rocks that would long ago have surrendered to gravity, had they been subjected to the weather erosion of the outside. The river was no guide, lost far below the jumble of infall, ravelled into thousands of threads as it found its way along the schist floor of the cavern. Three times, in his fatigue and stress, he lost his way, and the terror of it was that he was wasting precious energy stumbling around blindly. Each time, he forced himself to stop and calm himself, until his proximity sense suggested the path toward open space.

At last, there was sound to guide him. As he approached the end of the Climbing Cave, the threads of water far below wove themselves together, and slowly he became aware of the roar and tympani of the great waterfall that led down to the Crystal Cave. Ahead, the roof of the cave sloped down and was joined by a blocking wall of jagged, fresh infall. Making it up that wall, through the insane network of cracks and chimneys, then down the other side through the roaring waterfall without the safety of a belay from Le Cagot would be the most dangerous and difficult part of the cave. He would have to rest before that.

It was then that Hel had slipped off the straps of his air tank and sat down heavily on a rock, his chin hanging to his chest as he gasped for air and sweat ran from his hair into his eyes.

He had taken a long drink from his *xahako,* then had lain back on the slab of rock, not bothering to take off his helmet.

His body whimpered for rest. But he mustn't sleep. Sleep is death. Just rest for a moment. Not sleep. Just close your eyes for a moment. Just close . . . eyes . . .

"Ahgh!" He started awake, driven from his shallow, tormented sleep by the image of Le Cagot's helmet light rushing down toward him from the roof of the cave! He sat up, shivering and sweating. The thin sleep had not rested him; fatigue wastes in his body were thickening up; his hands were a pair of stiff paddles; his shoulders were knotted; the nausea of repeated adrenaline shock was clogging his throat.

He sat there, slumped over, not caring if he went on or not. Then, for the first time, the staggering implications of what Diamond had said over the phones burst upon his consciousness. His château no longer existed? What had they done? Had Hana escaped?

Concern for her, and the need to avenge Le Cagot, did for his body what food and rest might have done. He clawed his remaining glucose cubes from the pouch and chewed them, washing them down with the last of his water-wine. It would take the sugar several minutes to work its way into his bloodstream. Meanwhile, he set his jaw and began the task of limbering up his hands, breaking up the fresh scabbing, accepting the gritty sting of movement.

When he could handle it, he slung the air tank on and began the hard climb up the jumble of infall that blocked off the mouth of the Crystal Cave. He recalled Le Cagot telling him to try a bit to the left, because he was sitting in the line of fall and was too comfortable to move.

Twice, he had to struggle out of the tank harness while clinging to scant points of purchase because the crack he had to wriggle through was too tight for a man and tank at once without risking damage to the mask slung from his chest. Each time, he took care to tie the tank securely, because a fall might knock off its fitting, exploding the cylinder and leaving him with no air to make the final cave swim and making all this work and torture futile.

When he achieved the thin ledge directly above the roaring waterfall, he directed his lamp down the long drop, up which mist rose and billowed in the windless air. He paused only long enough to catch his breath and slow his heartbeat. There could be no long rests from now on, no chances for his body and hands to stiffen up, or for his imagination to cripple his determination.

The deafening roar of the falls and the roiling 40° mist insulated his mind from any thoughts of wider scope than the immediate task. He edged along the slimy, worn ledge that had once been the lip of the waterfall until he found the outcrop of rock from which Le Cagot had belayed him during his first descent along the glistening sheet of falling water. There would be no protecting belay this time. As he inched down, he came upon the first of the pitons he had driven in before, snapped a carabiner into the first and tied off a doubled line, threading and snapping in another at each piton, to shorten his fall, should be come off the face. Again, as before, it was not long before the combined friction of the line passing through these snap links made pulling it through difficult and dangerous, as the effort tended to lift him from the scant boot jams and fingerholds the face provided.

The water and the rope tortured his palms, and he clutched at his holds ever harder and harder, as though to punish the pain with excess. When he reached the point at which he would have to break through the sheet of water and pass behind the falls, he discovered that he could no longer drag down slack. The weight of water on the line, the number of carabiners through which it was strung, and his growing weakness combined to make this impossible. He would have to abandon the rope and climb free from here on. As before, he reached through the silver-and-black surface of the falls, which split in a heavy, throbbing bracelet around his wrist. He felt for and located the sharp little crack, invisible behind the face of the falls, into which he had wedged his fingers before. Ducking through the falls would be harder this time. The tank presented additional surface to the falls; his fingers were raw and numb; and his reserves of strength were gone. One smooth move. Just swing through it. There is a good ledge behind the cascade, and a book corner piled with rubble that made an easy climb down. He took three deep breaths and swung under the face of the falls.

Recent rains had made the falls twice as thick as before and more than twice as heavy. Its weight battered his helmet and shoulders and tried to tear the tank from his back. His numbed fingers were pried from the sharp crack; and he fell.

The first thing he became aware of was the relative quiet. The second thing was the water. He was behind the falls, at the base of the scree pile, sitting hip-deep in water. He may have been unconscious for a time, but he had no sense of it. The events were strung together in his mind: the battering of the water on his back and tank; the pain as his skinless fingers were wrenched from their hold; clatter, noise, pain, shock as he fell to the rubble pile and tumbled down it—then this relative silence, and waist-deep water where, before, there had been wet rock. The silence was no problem; he was not stunned. He had noticed last time how the falls seemed to muffle the roar once he was behind it. But the water? Did that mean recent rains had seeped down, making a lake of the floor of the Crystal Cave?

Was he injured? He moved his legs; they were all right. So were his arms. His right shoulder was hurt. He could lift it, but there was gritty pain at the top of its arc. A bone bruise, maybe. Painful, but not debilitating. He had decided that he had come through the fall miraculously unhurt, when he became aware of a peculiar sensation. The set of his teeth wasn't right. They were touching cusp to cusp. The smallest attempt to open his mouth shocked him with such agony that he felt himself slipping toward unconsciousness. His jaw was broken.

The face mask. Had it taken the fall? He tugged it from its pouch and examined it in the light of his lamp, which was yellowing because the batteries were fading. The faceplate was cracked.

It was a hairline crack. It might hold, so long as there was no wrench or torque on the rubber fittings. And what was the chance of that, down in the ripping current at the bottom of the Wine Cellar? Not much.

When he stood, the water came only to midshin. He waded out through the largely dissipated waterfall into the Crystal Cavern, and the water got deeper as the mist of frigid water thinned behind him.

One of the two magnesium flares had broken in his fall; its greasy powder had coated the other flare, which had to be wiped off carefully before it could be lighted, lest the flame rush down the sides burning his hand. He struck off the flare on its cap; it sputtered and blossomed into brilliant white light, illuminating the distant walls, encrusted with glittering crystals, and picking out the beauty of calcite drapery and slender stalactites. But these last did not point down to stumpy stalagmites, as they had done before. The floor of the cave was a shallow lake that covered the low speleothems. His first fears were supported: recent rains had filled this nether end of the cave system; the whole long marl chute at the far end of the cave was underwater.

Hel's impulse was to give in, to wade out to the edge of the cave and find a shelf to sit on where he could rest and lose himself in meditation. It seemed too hard now; the mathematics of probability too steep. At the outset, he had thought that this last, improbable task, the swim through the Wine Cellar toward light and air, would be the easiest from a psychological point of view. Denied alternatives, the weight and expanse of the entire cave system behind him, the final swim would have the strength of desperation. Indeed, he had thought his chances of making it through might be greater than they would have been if he had Le Cagot to belay him, for in that case he would have worked to only half the limit of his endurance, needing the rest to return, should the way be blocked, or too long. As it was, he had hoped his chances would be almost doubled, as there was no coming back through that force of water.

But now . . . the Crystal Cave had flooded, and his swim was doubled in length. The advantage of despair was gone.

Wouldn't it be better to sit out death in dignity, rather than struggle against fate like a panicked animal? What chance did he have? The slightest movement of his jaw shocked him with agony; his shoulder was stiff and it ground painfully in its socket; his palms were flayed; even the goddamned faceplate of his mask was unlikely to withstand the currents of that underground pipe. This thing wasn't even a gamble. It was like flipping coins against Fate, with Fate having both heads and tails. Hel won only if the coin landed on edge.

He waded heavily toward the side wall of the cavern, where flowstone oozed down like frozen taffy. He would sit there and wait it out.

His flare sputtered out, and the eternal spelaean darkness closed in on his mind with a crushing weight. Spots of light like minute crystal organisms under a microscope sketched across the darkness with each movement of his eyes. They faded, and the dark was total.

Nothing in the world would be easier than to accept death with dignity, with *shibumi*.

And Hana? And that insane Third World priest who had contributed to the death of Le Cagot and Hannah Stern? And Diamond?

All right. All right, damn it! He wedged the rubberized flashlight between two outcroppings of aragonite, and in its beam attached the mask to the air tank, grunting with pain as he tightened the connections with his flayed fingers. After carefully threading the straps over his bruised shoulder, he opened the inflow valve, then dipped up a little spit water to clear the faceplate of breath mist. The pressure of the mask against his broken jaw was painful, but he could manage it.

His legs were still unhurt; he would swim with legs only, holding the flashlight in his good hand. As soon as it was deep enough, he laid out on the water and swam—swimming was easier than wading.

In the pellucid water of the cave, unclouded by organisms, the flashlight picked up underwater features as though through air. It was not until he had entered the marl chute that he felt the influence of the current—more a suction downward than a push from behind.

The pressure of the water plugged his ears, making his breathing loud in the cavities of his head.

The suction increased as he neared the bottom of the marl chute, and the force of the water torqued his body toward the sunken sump of the Wine Cellar. From here on, he would not swim; the current would carry him, would drag him through; all his effort must be bent to slowing his speed and to controlling his direction. The pull of the current was an invisible force; there was no air in the water, no particles, no evidence of the tons of force that gripped him.

It was not until he attempted to grasp a ledge, to stop for a moment and collect himself before entering the sump, that he knew the power of the current. The ledge was ripped from his hold, and he was turned over on his back and drawn down into the sump. He struggled to reverse himself, tucking up and rolling, because he must enter the outflow pipe below feet first if he was to have any chance at all. If he were carried head first into an obstruction, that would be it.

Inexplicably, the suction seemed to lessen once he was in the sump, and he settled slowly toward the bottom, his feet toward the triangular pipe below. He took a deep breath and braced his nerves, remembering how that current had snatched away the dye packets so quickly that the eye could not follow them.

Almost leisurely, his body floated toward the bottom of the sump pit. That was his last clear image.

The current gripped him, and he shot into the pipe. His foot hit something; the leg crumpled, the knee striking his chest; he was spinning; the flashlight was gone; he took a blow on the spine, another on the hip.

And suddenly he was lodged behind a choke stone, and the water was roaring past him, tearing at him. The mask twisted, and the faceplate blew out, the broken pieces cutting his leg as they flashed past. He had been holding his breath from fear for several seconds, and the need for air was pounding in his temples. Water rushed over his face and eddied up his nostrils. It was the goddamned tank! He was wedged in there because the space was too narrow for both his body and the tank! He gripped his knife with all the force of his body focused on his right hand, as the water sought to twist the knife from his grasp. Had to cut away the tank! The weight of the current against the cylinder pressed the straps against his shoulders. No way to slip the knife under. He must saw through the webbing directly against his chest.

White pain.

His pulse throbbed, expanding in his head. His throat convulsed for air. Cut harder! Cut, damn it!

The tank went, smashing his foot as it rushed out under him. He was moving again, twisting. The knife was gone. With a terrible crunching sound, something hit the back of his head. His diaphragm heaved within him, sucking for breath. His heartbeat hammered in his head as he tumbled and twisted in the chaos of foam and bubbles.

Bubbles . . . Foam! He could see! Swim up! Swim!

PART SIX

TSURU
NO
SUGOMORI

Etchebar

HEL PARKED THE Volvo in the deserted square of Etchebar and got out heavily, forgetting to close the door behind him, neglecting to give the car its ritual bash. He drew a long breath and pushed it out slowly, then he walked up the curving road toward his château.

From behind half-closed shutters women of the village watched him and admonished their children not to play in the square until M. Hel was gone. It had been eight days since M. Hel had gone into the mountains with Le Cagot, and those terrible men in uniform had descended on the village and done dreadful things to the château. No one had seen M. Hel since then; it had been rumored that he was dead. Now he was returning to his demolished home, but no one dared to greet him. In this ancient high mountain village, primitive instincts prevailed; everyone knew it was unwise to associate with the unfortunate, lest the misfortune be contagious. After all, was it not God's will that this terrible thing happen? Was not the outlander being punished for living with an Oriental woman, possibly without the sanction of marriage. And who could know what other things God was punishing him for? Oh yes, one could feel pity—one was required by the church to feel pity—but it would be unwise to consort with those whom God punishes. One must be compassionate, but not to the extent of personal risk.

As he walked up the long allée, Hel could not see what they had done to his home; the sweeping pines screened it from view. But from the bottom of the terrace, the extent of the damage was clear. The central block and the east wing were gone, the walls blown away and rubble thrown in all directions, blocks of granite and marble lying partially buried in the scarred lawn as much as fifty meters away; a low jagged wall rimmed the gaping cellars, deep in shadow and dank with seep water from underground springs. Most of the west wing still stood, the rooms open to the weather where the connecting walls had been ripped away. It had been burned out; floors had caved in, and charred beams dangled, broken, into the spaces below. The glass had been blown from every window and *porte-fenêtre,* and above them were wide daggers of soot where flames had roared out. The smell of burned oak was carried on a soft wind that fluttered shreds of drapery.

There was no sound other than the sibilance of the wind through the pines as he picked his way through the rubble to investigate the standing walls of the west wing. At three places he found holes drilled into the granite blocks. The charges they had placed had failed to go off; and they had contented themselves with the destruction of the fire.

It was the Japanese garden that pained him most. Obviously, the raiders had been instructed to take special pains with the garden. They had used flame throwers. The sounding stream wound through charred stubble and, even after a week, its surface carried an oily residue. The bathing house and its surrounding bamboo grove were gone, but already a few shoots of bamboo, that most tenacious grass, were pushing through the blackened ground.

The *tatami*'d dependency and its attached gun room had been spared, save that the rice-paper doors were blown in by the concusion. These fragile structures had bent before the storm and had survived.

As he walked across the ravished garden, his shoes kicked up puffs of fine black ash. He sat heavily on the sill of the *tatami*'d room, his legs dangling over the edge. It was odd and somehow touching that tea utensils were still set out on the low lacquered table.

He was sitting, his head bent in deep fatigue, when he felt the approach of Pierre.

The old man's voice was moist with regret. "Oh, M'sieur! Oh! M'sieur! See what they have done to us! Poor Madame. You have seen her? She is well?"

For the past four days, Hel had been at the hospital in Oloron, leaving Hana's side only when ordered to by the doctors.

Pierre's rheumy eyes drooped with compassion as he realized his patron's physical state. "But look at you, M'sieur!" A bandage was wrapped under Hel's chin and over his head, to hold the jaw in place while it mended; bruises on his face were still plum colored; inside his shirt, his upper arm was wrapped tightly to his chest to prevent movement of the shoulder, and both his hands were bandaged from the wrists to the second knuckle.

"You don't look so good yourself, Pierre," he said, his voice muffled and dental.

Pierre shrugged. "Oh, I shall be all right. But see, our hands are the same!" He lifted his hands, revealing wraps of gauze covering the gel on his burned palms. He had a bruise over one eyebrow.

Hel noticed a dark stain down the front of Pierre's unbuttoned shirt. Obviously, a glass of wine had slipped from between the awkward paddles at the ends of his wrists. "How did you hurt your head?"

"It was the bandits, M'sieur. One of them struck me with a rifle butt when I was trying to stop them."

"Tell me what happened."

"Oh, M'sieur! It was too terrible!"

"Just tell me about it. Be calm, and tell me."

"Perhaps we could go to the gate house? I shall offer you a little glass, and maybe I will have one myself. Then I shall tell you."

"All right."

As they walked to Pierre's gate house, the old gardener suggested that M. Hel stay with him, for the bandits had spared his little home.

Hel sat in a deep chair with broken springs from which litter had been thrown by Pierre to make a space for his guest. The old man had drunk from the bottle, an easier thing to hold, and was now staring out over the valley from the small window of his second-floor living quarters.

"I was working, M'sieur. Attending to a thousand things. Madame had called down to Tardets for a car to take her to where the airplanes land, and I was waiting for it to arrive. I heard a buzzing from far out over the mountains. The sound grew louder. They came like huge flying insects, skimming over the hills, close to the earth."

"What came?"

"The bandits! In autogiros!"

"In helicopters?"

"Yes. Two of them. With a great noise, they landed in the park, and the ugly machines vomited men out. The men all had guns. They were dressed in mottled green clothes, with orange berets. They shouted to one another as they ran toward the château. I called after them, telling them to go away. The women of the kitchen screamed and fled toward the village. I ran after the bandits, threatening to tell M'sieur Hel on them if they did not go at once. One of them hit me with his gun, and I fell down. Great noise! Explosions! And all the time the two great autogiros sat on the lawn, their wings turning around and around. When I could stand, I ran toward the château. I was willing to fight them, M'sieur. I was willing to fight them!"

"I know."

"Yes, but they were by then running back toward their machines. I was knocked down again! When I got to the château . . . Oh, M'sieur! All gone! Smoke and flame everywhere! Everything! Everything! Then, M'sieur . . . Oh, God in mercy! I saw Madame at the window of the burning part. All around her, flame. I rushed in. Fiery things were falling all about me. When I got to her, she was just standing there. She could not find her way out! The windows had burst in upon her, and the glass . . . Oh, M'sieur, the glass!" Pierre had been struggling to contain his tears. He snatched off his beret and covered his face with it. There was a diagonal line across his forehead separating white skin from his deeply weatherbeaten face. Not for forty years had his beret been off while he was outdoors. He scrubbed his eyes with his beret, snorted loudly, and put it on again. "I took Madame and brought her out. The way was blocked by burning things. I had to pull them away with my hands. But I got out! I got her out! But the glass! . . ." Pierre broke down; he gulped as tears flowed from his nostrils.

Hel rose and took the old man in his arms. "You were brave, Pierre."

"But I am the *patron* when you are not here! And I failed to stop them!"

"You did all a man could do."

"I tried to fight them!"

"I know."

"And Madame? She will be well?"

"She will live."

"And her eyes?"

Hel looked away from Pierre as he drew a slow breath and let it out in a long jet. For a time he did not speak. Then, clearing his throat, he said, "We have work to do, Pierre."

"But, M'sieur. What work? The château is gone!"

"We shall clean up and repair what is left. I'll need your help to hire the men and to guide them in their work."

Pierre shook his head. He had failed to protect the château. He was not to be trusted.

"I want you to find men. Clear the rubble. Seal the west wing from the weather. Repair what must be repaired to get us through the winter. And next spring, we shall start to build again."

"But, M'sieur! It will take forever to rebuild the château!"

"I didn't say we would ever finish, Pierre."

Pierre considered this. "All right," he said, "all right. Oh, you have mail, M'sieur. A letter and a package. They are here somewhere." He rummaged about the chaos of bottomless chairs, empty boxes, and refuse of no description with which he had furnished his home. "Ah! Here they are. Just where I put them for safekeeping."

Both the package and letter were from Maurice de Lhandes. While Pierre fortified himself with another draw at the bottle, Hel read Maurice's note:

My Dear Friend:
      I wadded up and threw away my first epistolary effort because it began with a phrase so melodramatic as to bring laughter to me and,

I feared, embarrassment to you. And yet, I can find no other way to say what I want to say. So here is that sophomoric first phrase:

When you read this, Nicholai, I shall be dead.

(Pause here for my ghostly laughter and your compassionate embarrassment.)

There are many reasons I might cite for my close feelings for you, but these three will do. First: Like me, you have always given the governments and the companies reason for fear and concern. Second: You were the last person, other than Estelle, to whom I spoke during my life. And third: Not only did you never make a point of my physical peculiarity, you also never overlooked it, or brutalized my sensibilities by talking about it man to man.

I am sending you a gift (which you have probably already opened, greedy pig). It is something that may one day be of benefit to you. Do you remember my telling you that I had something on the United States of America? Something so dramatic that it would make the Statue of Liberty fall back and offer you whatever orifice you choose to use? Well, here it is.

I have sent you only the photocopy; I have destroyed the originals. But the enemy will not know that I have destroyed them, and the enemy does not know that I am dead. (Remarkable how peculiar it is to write that in the present tense!)

They will have no way to know that the originals are not in my possession in the button-down mode; so, with a little histrionic skill on your part, you should be able to manipulate them as you will.

As you know, native intelligence has always saved me from the foolishness of believing in life after death. But there can be nuisance value after death—and that thought pleases me.

Please visit Estelle from time to time, and make her feel desirable. And give my love to your magnificent Oriental.

With all amicable sentiments,

PS. Did I mention the other night during dinner that the morels did not have enough lemon juice? I should have.

Hel broke the string on the package and scanned the contents. Affidavits, photographs, records, all revealing the persons and governmental organizations involved in the assassination of John F. Kennedy and with the cover-up of certain aspects of that assassination. Particularly interesting were statements from a person identified as the Umbrella Man, from another called the Man on the Fire Escape, and a third, the Knoll Commando.

Hel nodded. Very strong leverage indeed.

After a simple meal of sausage, bread, and onion washed down with raw red wine in Pierre's littered room, they took a walk together over the grounds, staying well away from the painful scar of the château. Evening was falling, wisps of salmon and mauve clouds piling up against the mountains.

Hel mentioned that he would be gone for several days, and they could begin the work of repair when he returned.

"You would trust me to do it, M'sieur? After how I have failed you?" Pierre was feeling self-pitying. He had decided that he might have protected the Madame better if he had been totally sober.

Hel changed the subject. "What can we expect for weather tomorrow, Pierre?"

The old man glanced listlessly at the sky, and he shrugged. "I don't know,

M'sieur. To tell you the truth, I cannot really read the weather. I only pretend, to make myself seem important."

"But, Pierre, your predictions are unfailing. I rely on them, and they have served me well."

Pierre frowned, trying to remember. "Is this so, M'sieur?"

"I wouldn't dare go into the mountains without your advice."

"Is this so?"

"I am convinced that it is a matter of wisdom, and age, and Basque blood. I may achieve the age in time, even the wisdom. But the Basque blood . . ." Hel sighed and struck at a shrub they were passing.

Pierre was silent for a time as he pondered this. Finally he said, "You know? I think that what you say is true, M'sieur. It is a gift, probably. Even I believe it is the signs in the sky, but in reality it is a gift—a skill that only my people enjoy. For instance, you see how the sheep of the sky have russet fleeces? Now, it is important to know that the moon is in a descending phase, and that birds were swooping low this morning. From this, I can tell with certainty that . . ."

The Church at Alos

FATHER XAVIER'S HEAD was bent, his fingers pressed against his temple, his hand partially masking the dim features of the old woman on the other side of the confessional's wicker screen. It was an attitude of compassionate understanding that permitted him to think his own thoughts while the penitent droned on, recalling and admitting every little lapse, hoping to convince God, by the tiresome pettiness of her sins, that she was innocent of any significant wrongdoing. She had reached the point of confessing the sins of others—of asking forgiveness for not having been strong enough to prevent her husband from drinking, for having listened to the damning gossip of Madame Ibar, her neighbor, for permitting her son to miss Mass and join the hunt for boar instead.

Automatically humming an ascending interrogative note at each pause, Father Xavier's mind was dealing with the problem of superstition. At Mass that morning, the itinerate priest had made use of an ancient superstition to gain their attention and to underline his message of faith and revolution. He himself was too well educated to believe in the primitive fears that characterize the faith of the mountain Basque; but as a soldier of Christ, he felt it his duty to grasp each weapon that came to hand and to strike a blow for the Church Militant. He knew the superstition that a clock striking during the *Sagara* (the elevation of the Host) was an infallible sign of imminent death. Setting a clock low beside the altar where he could see it, he had timed the *Sagara* to coincide with its striking of the hour. There had been an audible gasp in the congregation, followed by a profound silence. And taking his theme from the omen of impending death, he had told them it meant the death of repression against the Basque people, and the death of ungodly influences within the revolutionary movement. He had been satisfied with the effect, manifest in part by several invitations to take supper and to pass the night in the homes of local peasants, and in part by an uncommonly large turnout for evening confession—even several men, although only old men, to be sure.

Would this last woman never end her catalogue of trivial omissions? Evening was setting in, deepening the gloom of the ancient church, and he was feeling the pangs of hunger. Just before this self-pitying chatterbox had squeezed her bulk into the confessional, he had peeked out and discovered that she was the last of the penitents. He breathed a sigh and cut into her stream of petty flaws, calling her his daughter and telling her that Christ understood and forgave, and giving her a penance of many prayers, so she would feel important.

When she left the box, he sat back to give her time to leave the church. Undue haste in getting to a free dinner with wine would be unseemly. He was preparing to rise, when the curtain hissed and another penitent slipped into the shadows of the confessional.

Father Xavier sighed with impatience.

A very soft voice said, "You have only seconds to pray, Father."

The priest strained to see through the screen into the shadows of the confessional, then he gasped. It was a figure with a bandage around its head, like the cloth tied under the chins of the dead to keep their mouths from gaping! A ghost?

Father Xavier, too well educated for superstition, pressed back away from the screen and held his crucifix before him. "Begone! *I! Abi!*"

The soft voice said, "Remember Beñat Le Cagot."

"Who are you? What—"

The wicker screen split, and the point of Le Cagot's *makila* plunged between the priest's ribs, piercing his heart and pinning him to the wall of the confessional.

Never again would it be possible to shake the villager's faith in the superstition of the *Sagara*, for it had proved itself. And in the months that followed, a new and colorful thread was woven into the folk myth of Le Cagot—he who had mysteriously vanished into the mountains, but who was rumored to appear suddenly whenever Basque freedom fighters needed him most. With a vengeful will of its own, Le Cagot's *makila* had flown to the village of Alos and punished the perfidious priest who had informed on him.

New York

As HE STOOD in the plush private elevator, mercifully without Musak, Hel moved his jaw gingerly from side to side. In the eight days he had been setting up this meeting, his body had mended well. The jaw was still stiff, but did not require the undignified gauze sling; his hands were tender, but the bandages were gone, as were the last yellowish traces of bruise on his forehead.

The elevator stopped and the door opened directly into an outer office, where a secretary rose and greeted him with an empty smile. "Mr. Hel? The Chairman will be with you soon. The other gentleman is waiting inside. Would you care to join him?" The secretary was a handsome young man with a silk shirt open to the middle of his chest and tight trousers of a soft fabric that revealed the bulge of his penis. He conducted Hel to an inner reception room decorated like the parlor of a comfortable rural home: overstuffed chairs in floral prints, lace curtains, a low tea table, two Lincoln rockers, bric-a-brac in a glass-front étagère, framed photographs of three generations of family on an upright piano.

The gentleman who rose from the plump sofa had Semitic features, but an Oxford accent. "Mr. Hel? I've been looking forward to meeting you. I am Mr.

Able, and I represent OPEC interests in such matters as these." There was an extra pressure to his handshake that hinted at his sexual orientation. "Do sit down, Mr. Hel. The Chairman will be with us soon. Something came up at the last moment, and she was called away briefly."

Hel selected the least distasteful chair. "She?"

Mr. Able laughed musically. "Ah, you did not know that the Chairman was a woman?"

"No, I didn't. Why isn't she called the Chairwoman, or one of those ugly locutions with which Americans salve their social consciences at the sacrifice of euphony: chairperson, mailperson, freshperson—that sort of thing?"

"Ah, you will find the Chairman unbound by conventions. Having become one of the most powerful people in the world, she does not have to seek recognition; and achieving equality would, for her, be a great step down." Mr. Able smiled and tilted his head coquettishly. "You know, Mr. Hel, I learned a great deal about you before Ma summoned me to this meeting."

"Ma?"

"Everyone close to the Chairman calls her Ma. Sort of a family joke. Head of the Mother Company, don't you see?"

"I do see, yes."

The door to the outer office opened, and a muscular young man with a magnificent suntan and curly golden hair entered carrying a tray.

"Just set it down here," Mr. Able told him. Then to Hel he said, "Ma will doubtless ask me to pour."

The handsome beachboy left after setting out the tea things, thick, cheap china in a blue-willow pattern.

Mr. Able noticed Hel's glance at the china. "I know what you're thinking. Ma prefers things to be what she calls 'homey.' I learned about your colorful background, Mr. Hel, at a briefing session a while ago. Of course I never expected to meet you—not after Mr. Diamond's report of your death. Please believe that I regret what the Mother Company special police did to your home. I consider it unpardonable barbarism."

"Do you?" Hel was impatient with the delay, and he had no desire to pass the time chatting with this Arab. He rose and crossed to the piano with its row of family photographs.

At this moment, the door to the inner office opened, and the Chairman entered.

Mr. Able rose quickly to his feet. "Mrs. Perkins, may I introduce Nicholai Hel?"

She took Hel's hand and pressed it warmly between her plump, stubby fingers. "Land sakes, Mr. Hel, you just couldn't know how I have looked forward to meeting you." Mrs. Perkins was a chubby woman in her mid-fifties. Clear maternal eyes, neck concealed beneath layers of chin, gray hair done up in a bun, with wisps that had escaped the net chignon, pigeon-breasted, plump forearms with deeply dimpled elbows, wearing a silk dress of purple paisley. "I see that you're looking at my family. My pride and joy, I always call them. That's my grandson there. Rascally little fella. And this is Mr. Perkins. Wonderful man. Cordon-bleu cook and just a magician with flowers." She smiled at her photographs and shook her head with proprietary affection. "Well, maybe we should turn to our business. Do you like tea, Mr. Hel?" She lowered herself into a Lincoln rocker with a puff of sigh. "I don't know what I'd do without my tea."

"Have you looked at the information I forwarded to you, Mrs. Perkins?" He lifted his hand to Mr. Able, indicating that he would forego a cup of tea made from tea bags.

The Chairman leaned forward and placed her hand on Hel's arm. "Why don't you just call me Ma? Everyone does."

"Have you looked at the information, Mrs. Perkins?"

The warm smile disappeared from her face and her voice became almost metallic. "I have."

"You will recall that I made a precondition to our talk your promise that Mr. Diamond be kept ignorant of the fact that I am alive."

"I accepted that precondition." She glanced quickly at Mr. Able. "The contents of Mr. Hel's communication are eyes-only for me. You'll have to follow my lead in this."

"Certainly, Ma."

"And?" Hel asked.

"I won't pretend that you do not have us in a tight spot, Mr. Hel. For a variety of reasons, we would not care to have things upset just now, when our Congress is dismantling that Cracker's energy bill. If I understand the situation correctly, we would be ill-advised to take counteraction against you, as that would precipitate the information into the European press. It is currently in the hands of an individual whom Fat Boy identifies as the Gnome. Is that correct?"

"Yes."

"So it's all a matter of price, Mr. Hel. What *is* your price?"

"Several things. First, you have taken some land in Wyoming from me. I want it back."

The Chairman waved a pudgy hand at so trivial a matter.

"And I shall require that your subsidiaries stop all strip-mining in a radius of three hundred miles from my land."

Mrs. Perkins's jaw worked with controlled anger, her cold eyes fixed on Hel. Then she blinked twice and said, "All right."

"Second, there is money of mine taken from my Swiss account."

"Of course. Of course. Is that all?"

"No. I recognize that you could undo any of these actions at will. So I shall have to leave this leverage information on line for an indefinite period. If you offend me in any way, the button will be released."

"I see. Fat Boy informs me that this Gnome person is in poor health."

"I have heard the rumor."

"You realize that if he should die, your protection is gone?"

"Not exactly, Mrs. Perkins. Not only would he have to die, but your people would have to be sure he was dead. And I happen to know that you have never located him and don't have even an idea of his physical appearance. I suspect that you will intensify your search for the Gnome, but I'm gambling that he is hidden away where you will never find him."

"We shall see. You have no further demands upon us?"

"I have further demands. Your people destroyed my home. It may not be possible to repair it, as there no longer are craftsmen of the quality that built it. But I intend to try."

"How much?"

"Four million."

"No house is worth four million dollars!"

"It's now five million."

"My dear boy, I started my professional career with less than a quarter of that, and if you think—"

"Six million."

Mrs. Perkins's mouth snapped shut. There was absolute silence, as Mr. Able nervously directed his glance away from the pair looking at one another across the tea table, one with a cold fixed stare, the other with lids half-lowered over smiling green eyes.

Mrs. Perkins drew a slow, calming breath. "Very well. But that, I suggest, had better be the last of your demands."

"In point of fact, it is not."

"Your price has reached its market maximum. There is a limit to the degree to which what is good for the Mother Company is good for America."

"I believe, Mrs. Perkins, that you'll be pleased by my last demand. If your Mr. Diamond had done his work competently, if he had not allowed personal enmity for me to interfere with his judgment, you would not now be facing this predicament. My last demand is this: I want Diamond. And I want the CIA gunny named Starr, and that PLO goatherd you call Mr. Haman. Don't think of it as additional payment. I am rendering you a service—meting out punishment for incompetence."

"And that is your last demand?"

"That is my last demand."

The Chairman turned to Mr. Able. "How have your people taken the death of the Septembrists in that plane accident?"

"Thus far, they believe it was just that, an accident. We have not informed them that it was an assassination. We were awaiting your instructions, Ma."

"I see. This Mr. Haman . . . he is related to the leader of the PLO movement, I believe."

"That is true, Ma."

"How will his death go down?"

Mr. Able considered this for a moment. "We may have to make concessions again. But I believe it can be handled."

Mrs. Perkins turned again to Hel. She stared at him for several seconds. "Done."

He nodded. "Here is how it will be set up. You will show Diamond the information now in your hands concerning the Kennedy assassination. You will tell him you have a line on the Gnome, and you can trust no one but him to kill the Gnome and secure the originals. He will realize how dangerous it would be to have other eyes than his see this material. You will instruct Diamond to go to the Spanish Basque village of Oñate. He will be contacted by a guide who will take them into the mountains, where they will find the Gnome. I shall take it from there. One other thing . . . and this is most important. I want all three of them to be well armed when they go into the mountains."

"Did you get that?" she asked Mr. Able, her eyes never leaving Hel's face.

"Yes, Ma."

She nodded. Then her stern expression dissolved and she smiled, wagging a finger at Hel. "You're quite a fellow, young man. A real horse trader. You would have gone a long way in the commercial world. You've got the makings of a real fine businessman."

"I'll overlook that insult."

Mrs. Perkins laughed, her wattles jiggling. "I'd love to have a good long gabfest with you, son, but there are folks waiting for me in another office. We've got a problem with some kids demonstrating against one of our atomic-power plants. Young people just aren't what they used to be, but I love them all the same, the little devils." She pushed herself out of the rocker. "Lord, isn't it true what they say: woman's work is never done."

Gouffre Field/
Col. Pierre St. Martin

IN ADDITION TO being exasperated and physically worn, Diamond was stung with the feeling that he looked foolish, stumbling through this blinding fog, clinging obediently to a length of rope tied to the waist of his guide whose ghostly figure he could only occasionally make out, not ten feet ahead. A rope around Diamond's waist strung back into the brilliant mist, where its knotted end was grasped by Starr; and the Texan in turn was linked to the PLO trainee Haman, who complained each time they rested for a moment, sitting on the damp boulders of the high col. The Arab was not used to hours of heavy exercise; his new climbing boots were chafing his ankles, and the muscles of his forearm were throbbing with the strain of his white-knuckled grip on the line that linked him to the others, terrified of losing contact and being alone and blind in this barren terrain. This was not at all what he had had in mind when he had postured before the mirror of his room in Oñate two days earlier, cutting a romantic figure with his mountain clothes and boots, a heavy Magnum in the holster at his side. He had even practiced drawing the weapon as quickly as he could, admiring the hard-eyed professional in the mirror. He recalled how excited he had been in that mountain meadow a month before, emptying his gun into the jerking body of that Jewess after Starr had killed her.

As annoying as any physical discomfort to Diamond was the wiry old guide's constant humming and singing as he led them slowly along, skirting the rims of countless deep pits filled with dense vapor, the danger of which the guide had made evident through extravagant mime not untouched with gallows humor as he opened his mouth and eyes wide and flailed his arms about in imitation of a man falling to his death, then pressed his palms together in prayer and rolled his impish eyes upward. Not only did the nasal whine of the Basque songs erode Diamond's patience, but the voice seemed to come from everywhere at once, because of the peculiar underwater effect of a whiteout.

Diamond had tried to ask the guide how much longer they would be groping through this soup, how much farther it was to where the Gnome was hiding out. But the only response was a grin and a nod. When they were turned over to the guide in the mountains by a Spanish Basque who had contacted them in the village, Diamond had asked if he could speak English, and the little old man had grinned and said, "A lee-tle bit." When, some time later, Diamond had asked how long it would be before they arrived at their destination, the guide had answered, "A lee-tle bit." That was an odd-enough response to cause Diamond to ask the guide his name. "A lee-tle bit."

Oh, fine! Just wonderful!

Diamond understood why the Chairman had sent him to deal with this matter personally. Trusting him with information so inflamable as this was a mark of special confidence, and particularly welcome after a certain coolness in Ma's communications after those Septembrists had died in that midair explosion. But they had been two days in the mountains now, linked up like children playing blind man's bluff, bungling forward through this blinding whiteout that filled their eyes with stinging light. They had passed a cold and uncomfortable night sleeping on the stony ground after a supper of hard bread, a greasy sausage that burned the mouth, and harsh wine from some kind of squirt bag that Diamond could not manage. How much longer could it be before they got to the Gnome's hiding place? If only this stupid peasant would stop his chanting!

At that moment, he did. Diamond almost bumped into the grinning guide, who had stopped in the middle of a rock-strewn little plateau through which they had been picking their way, avoiding the dangerous *gouffres* on all sides.

When Starr and Haman joined them, the guide mimed that they must stay there, while he went ahead for some purpose or other.

"How long will you be gone?" Diamond asked, accenting each word slowly, as though that would help.

"A lee-tle bit," the guide answered, and he disappeared into the thick cloud. A moment later, the guide's voice seemed to come from all directions at once. "Just make yourselves comfortable, my friends."

"That shithead speaks American after all," Starr said. "What the hell's going on?"

Diamond shook his head, uneasy with the total silence around them.

Minutes passed, and the sense of abandonment and danger was strong enough to hush even the complaining Arab. Starr took out his revolver and cocked it.

Seeming to come from both near and far, Nicholai Hel's voice was characteristically soft. "Have you figured it out yet, Diamond?"

They strained to peer through the dazzling light. Nothing.

"Jesus H. Christ!" Starr whispered.

Haman began to whimper.

Not ten meters from them, Hel stood invisible in the brilliant whiteout. His head was cocked to the side as he concentrated to distinguish the three quite different energy patterns emanating from them. His proximity sense read panic in all three, but of varying qualities. The Arab was falling apart. Starr was on the verge of firing wildly into the blinding vapor. Diamond was struggling for self-control.

"Spread out," Starr whispered. He was the professional.

Hel felt Starr moving around to the left, as the Arab went to his hands and knees and crawled toward the right, feeling before him for the rim of a deep *gouffre* he could not see. Diamond stood riveted.

Hel cocked back the double hammers of each of the shotgun pistols the Dutch industrialist had given him years before. Starr's projecting aura was closing in from the left. Hel gripped the handle as tightly as he could, aimed for the center of the Texan's aura, and squeezed the trigger.

The roar of two shotgun shells firing at once was deafening. The blast pattern of eighteen ball bearings blew a puffing hole through the mist, and for an instant Hel saw Starr flying backward, his arms wide, his feet off the ground, his chest and face splattered. Immediately, the whiteout closed in and healed the hole in the mist.

Hel let the pistol drop from his stunned hand. The pain of the wrenching kick throbbed to his elbow.

His ears ringing with the blast, the Arab began to whimper. Every fiber of him yearned to flee, but in which direction? He knelt, frozen on his hands and knees as a dark-brown stain grew at the crotch of his khaki trousers. Keeping as low to the ground as he could, he inched forward, straining to see through the dazzling fog. A boulder took form before him, its gray ghost shape becoming solid only a foot before he touched it. He hugged the rock for comfort, sobbing silently.

Hel's voice was soft and close. "Run, goatherd."

The Arab gasped and leaped away. His last scream was a prolonged, fading one, as he stumbled into the mouth of a deep *gouffre* and landed with a liquid crunch far below.

As the echoing rattle of dislodged stones faded away, Hel leaned back against the boulder and drew a slow deep breath, the second shotgun pistol dangling from his hand. He directed his concentration toward Diamond, still crouching motionless out there in the mist, ahead of him and slightly to the left.

After the Arab's sudden scream, silence ran in Diamond's ears. He breathed shallowly through his mouth, so as to make no sound, his eyes darting back and forth over the curtain of blinding cloud, his skin tingling with anticipation of pain.

A ten-second eternity passed, then he heard Hel's prison-hushed voice. "Well? Isn't this what you have in mind, Diamond? You're living out the machismo fantasies of the corporation man. The cowboy face to face with the *yojimbo*. Is it fun?"

Diamond turned his head from side to side, trying desperately to identify the direction from which the voice came. No good! All directions seemed right.

"Let me help you, Diamond. You are now approximately eight meters from me."

Which direction? Which direction?

"You might as well get a shot off, Diamond. You might be lucky."

Mustn't speak! He'll fire at my voice!

Diamond held his heavy Magnum in both fists and fired into the fog. Again to the left, then to the right, then farther to the left. "You son of a bitch!" he cried, still firing. "You son of a bitch!"

Twice the hammer clicked on spent brass.

"Son of a bitch." With effort, Diamond lowered his pistol while his whole upper body shook with emotion and desperation.

Hel touched his earlobe with the tip of his finger. It was sticky and it stung. A chip of rock from a near stray had nicked it. He raised his second shotgun pistol and leveled it at the place in the whiteout from which the rapid pulses of panicked aura emanated.

Then he paused and lowered the gun. Why bother?

This unexpected whiteout had converted the catharsis of revenge he had planned into a mechanical slaughter of stymied beasts. There was no satisfaction in this, no measurement in terms of skill and courage. Knowing they would be three, and well armed, Hel had brought only the two pistols with him, limiting himself to only two shots. He had hoped this might make a contest of it.

But this? And that emotionally shattered merchant out there in the fog? He was too loathsome for even punishment.

Hel started to move away from his boulder noiselessly, leaving Diamond to shudder, alone and frightened in the whiteout, expecting death to roar through him at any instant.

Then Hel stopped. He remembered that Diamond was a servant of the Mother Company, a corporate lackey. Hel thought of offshore oil rigs contaminating the sea, of strip-mining over virgin land, of oil pipelines through tundra, of atomic-energy plants built over the protests of those who would ultimately suffer contamination. He recalled the adage: Who must do the hard things? He who can. With a deep sigh, and with disgust souring the back of his throat, he turned and raised his arm.

Diamond's maniac scream was sandwiched between the gun's roar and its echo. Through a billowing hole in the fog, Hel glimpsed the spattered body twisting in the air as it was blown back into the wall of vapor.

Château d'Etchebar

HANA'S POSTURE WAS maximally submissive; her only weapons in the game were voluptuous sounds and the rippling vaginal contractions at which she was so expert. Hel had the advantage of distraction, his endurance aided by the task of controlling movement very strictly, as their position was complicated and arcane, and a slight error could do them physical hurt. Despite the advantage, it was he who was driven to muttering, "You devil!" between clenched teeth.

Instantly she was sure he had broken, she pressed outward and joined him in climax, her joy expressed aloud and enthusiastically.

After some minutes of grateful nestling, he smiled and shook his head. "It would appear I lose again."

"So it would appear." She laughed impishly.

Hana sat at the doorway oof the *tatami*'d room, facing the charred ruin of the garden, her kimono puddled about her hips, bare above the waist to receive the kneading and stroking that had been set as the prize in this game. Hel knelt behind her, dragging his fingertips up her spine and scurrying waves of tingle up the nape of her neck, into the roots of her hair.

His eyes defocused, all muscles of his face relaxed, he permitted his mind to wander in melancholy joy and autumnal peace. He had made a final decision the night before, and he had been rewarded for it.

He had passed hours kneeling alone in the gun room, reviewing the lay of the stones on the board. It was inevitable that, sooner or later, the Mother Company would rupture his gossamer armor. Either their relentless investigations would reveal de Lhandes to be dead, or the facts concerning Kennedy's death would eventually come out. And then they would come after him.

He could struggle, cut off many arms of the faceless corporate hydra, but ultimately they would get him. And probably with something as impersonal as a bomb, or as ironic as a stray slug. Where was the dignity in that? The *shibumi?*

At last, the cranes were confined to their nest. He would live in peace and affection with Hana until they came after him. Then he would withdraw from the game. Voluntarily. By his own hand.

Almost immediately after coming to this understanding of the state of the game and the sole path to dignity, Hel felt years of accumulated disgust and hate melt from him. Once severed from the future, the past becomes an insignificant parade of trivial events, no longer organic, no longer potent or painful.

He had an impulse to account for his life, to examine the fragments he had carried along with him. Late into the night, with the warm Southwind moaning in the eaves, he knelt before the lacquered table on which were two things: the Gō bowls Kishikawa-san had given him, and the yellowed letter of official regret, its creases furry with opening and folding, that he had carried away from

Shimbashi Station because it was all that was left of the dignified old man who had died in the night.

Through all the years he had wandered adrift in the West, he had carried with him three spiritual sea anchors: the Gō bowls that symbolized his affection for his foster father, the faded letter that symbolized the Japanese spirit, and his garden—not the garden they had destroyed, but the idea of garden in Hel's mind of which that plot had been an imperfect statement. With these three things, he felt fortunate and very rich.

His newly liberated mind drifted from wisp of idea to wisp of memory, and soon—quite naturally—he found himself in the triangular meadow, one with the yellow sunlight and the grass.

Home . . . after so many years of wandering.

"Nikko?"

"Hm-m-m?"

She snuggled her back against his bare chest. He pressed her to him and kissed her hair. "Nikko, are you sure you didn't let me win?"

"Why would I do that?"

"Because you're a very strange person. And rather nice."

"I did not let you win. And to prove it to you, next time we'll wager the maximum penalty."

She laughed softly. "I thought of a pun—a pun in English."

"Oh?"

"I should have said: You're on."

"Oh, that is terrible." He hugged her from behind, cupping her breasts in his hands.

"The one good thing about all of this is your garden, Nikko. I am glad they spared it. After the years of love and work you invested, it would have broken my heart if they had harmed your garden."

"I know."

There was no point in telling her the garden was gone.

It was time now to take the tea he had prepared for them.